William Shakespeare, John Heminge, Henry Condell

Shakespeare a reprint of his collected works

as put forth in 1632, part III

William Shakespeare, John Heminge, Henry Condell

Shakespeare a reprint of his collected works
as put forth in 1632, part III

ISBN/EAN: 9783742858665

Manufactured in Europe, USA, Canada, Australia, Japa

Cover: Foto ©Andreas Hilbeck / pixelio.de

Manufactured and distributed by brebook publishing software
(www.brebook.com)

William Shakespeare, John Heminge, Henry Condell

Shakespeare a reprint of his collected works

SHAKESPEARE

A REPRINT

of his

COLLECTED WORKS

As put forth in 1623

PART III CONTAINING

THE TRAGEDIES

LONDON

Printed for Lionel Booth 307 Regent Street 1864

SHAKESPEARE;

A REPRINT OF THE "FAMOUS FOLIO OF 1623."

ADVERTISEMENT.

THE taſk undertaken by the Publiſher more than four years ago, of reproducing in a portable form the Firſt Folio Edition of the Plays of Shakeſpeare, without the ſlighteſt alteration or attempt at correction, is now accompliſhed, and the ſtudents of the works of our "gentle Shakeſpeare" are enabled, at a moderate coſt, to obtain a volume identical with that iſſued by the poet's friends Heminge and Condell, in 1623—a work held now ſo highly in repute by collectors that a copy ſold lately for the large ſum of 716*l.*

The Firſt Folio Edition, publiſhed ſeven years after the poet's death, contained nineteen plays never before printed. The ſmall quarto editions of the ſeventeen various plays printed anterior to the Folio were not iſſued by authority, nor are they anywhere aſſerted to have had the ineſtimable benefit of the poet's reviſion or corrections; but, on the contrary, they are ſtated by Heminge and Condell to have been "diuerſe ſtolne, and ſurreptitious copies, maimed and deformed by the frauds and ſtealthes of iniurious impoſtors." The Firſt Folio is therefore, it has been well obſerved, "the moſt important edition extant." Its reproduction in the exact words and letters of the original will, it is confidently hoped, prove acceptable to all ſtudents of his writings, and ſhould find a place in every Engliſhman's library.

The favour with which Parts I. (containing the Comedies) and II. (containing the Hiſtories) have been received will, it is truſted, be ſtill accorded to the completed work. No pains have been ſpared to render this third Part, containing the Tragedies, worthy of its predeceſſors.

It is no ſmall matter for congratulation that, neither in Part I., which was publiſhed December 1861, nor in Part II., which followed in November 1863, have any errors been pointed out that have not, on examination, proved to have been errors or misſconceptions on the part of the critics. The book hitherto has paſſed the ordeal of adverſe intereſts unſcathed, and the learned editors of the Cambridge edition, now in progreſs of publication, have pronounced it "the moſt correct reprint ever iſſued."

Neverthelefs, as ſtated in the introduction to Part I., it has always been borne in mind that the chances of error in paſſing an elaborate work through the preſs, are ſo varied and unaccountable, that any pretence to infallibility would be more than preſumptuous; the communication, therefore, of any—the moſt trifling—departure from the original, which may be diſcovered, will be moſt thankfully acknowledged, and the required correction effected by a cancel.

The Firſt Folio contained all the known plays excepting "Pericles, Prince of Tyre," which was firſt publiſhed in folio in the third impreſſion, 1664 (previouſly in quarto, 1609, 1611, and 1619). It is propoſed to print this play ſeparately, to be bound up with this edition, bringing together in one volume the whole acknowledged plays of Shakeſpeare in the exact language of the originals.

The Verſes oppoſite the Title to Part III. are reprinted from the ſecond edition of Shakeſpeare (1632), *and are ſaid by Warton, and by Godwin, in his life of Edward and John Philips, nephews and pupils of Milton, to have been the firſt lines of poetry ever printed of our immortal Milton; they are iſſued as an appropriate completion of the various panegyrics publiſhed in the firſt and ſecond folios.*

Regent Street,
November 1864.

SHAKESPEARE.

Collation of the Edition of 1623.

(Continued.)

THE TRAGEDIES.

*** *The Collation is given with each Part, to prevent the chance of the errors and peculiarities of the Original Edition, herein faithfully reproduced, being miſtaken as errors of this Reprint.*

The Prologue, and firſt page of Troylus and Creſſida (unpaged)—then pages 79 and 80, then twenty-five pages without pagination, and the laſt page blank.
Coriolanus—pages 1 to 30.
Titus Andronicus—pages 31 to 52 (page 51 copies vary).
Romeo and Juliet—pages 53 to 79 (pages 77 and 78 wanting).
Tymon of Athens—pages 80, 81, 82, then again commencing pages 81 to 98.
The Actors' Names—one page, the next page blank.
Julius Cæſar—pages 109 to 130.
Macbeth—pages 131 to 151.
Hamlet—pages 152 to 156, then one hundred pages omitted, and continuing pages 257 to 282 (pages 279 and 282 are miſprinted 259 and 280), page 278 copies vary.
King Lear—pages 283 to 309 (page 308 miſprinted 38).
Othello—pages 310 to 339.
Anthonie and Cleopatra—pages 340 to 368.
Cymbeline—pages 369 to 399 (pages 379 and 399 miſprinted 389 and 993).

The

The SIGNATURES in the ORIGINAL VOLUME are as follows :—

A, containing title, verſes, and introductory matter, 9 leaves.

The Tempeſt to the Winter's Tale—A to C c 2, in ſixes (V is miſprinted V v).

King John to Troylus and Creſſida—a to g, in ſixes (a 3 is miſprinted A a 3); gg, 8 leaves; h to x, and ¶, and ¶ ¶, in ſixes; ¶ ¶ ¶ one leaf (m 3 is miſprinted l 3; x 3 is not marked).

Coriolanus to Cymbeline—a a to f f, in ſixes (b b 2 is miſprinted B b 2); g g has 8 leaves (five of which are marked g g, g g 2, G g, g g 2, g g 3); h h, k k to v v, x, y y to b b b, in ſixes (n n and n n 2 are miſprinted N n and N n 2; o o is miſprinted O o; o o 2 has no ſignature; t t 2 is miſprinted t t 3; x x, x x 2, x x 3, are miſprinted x, x 2, and x 3; y y 2 and y y 3 are miſprinted y 2 and y 3). The volume ends thus:—

Printed at the Charges of W. Jaggard, Ed. Blount, I. Smithweeke, and W. Aſpley, 1623.

The ſignatures in the *reprint* are from A to 5 U (1 leaf), in fours, commencing with the Tempeſt; the preliminary leaves being the ſame as in the original.

A diſtinct and conſecutive pagination throughout the volume, at the bottom of each page, has alſo been added, to facilitate reference, from the Tempeſt to Cymbeline, pages 1 to 889.

WHat neede my Shakeſpeare *for his honor'd bones,*
The labour of an Age,in piled ſtones
Or that his hallow'd Reliques ſhould be hid
Vnder a ſtarre-ypointing Pyramid?
Deare Sonne of Memory,great Heire of Fame,
What needſt thou ſuch dull witneſſe of thy Name?
Thou in our wonder and aſtoniſhment
Haſt built thy ſelfe a laſting Monument:
For whil'ſt to th' ſhame of ſlow-endeavouring Art
Thy eaſie numbers flow,and that each part,
Hath from the leaves of thy unvalued Booke,
Thoſe Delphicke Lines with deepe impreſſion tooke
Then thou our fancy of her ſelfe bereaving,
Doſt make us Marble with too much conceiving,
And ſo Sepulcher'd in ſuch pompe doſt lie
That Kings for ſuch a Tombe would wiſh to die.

Mr. WILLIAM

SHAKESPEARES

TRAGEDIES.

Publiſhed according to the True Originall Copies.

LONDON

Printed by Isaac Iaggard, and Ed. Blount, 1623; and Re-Printed for Lionel Booth, 307 Regent Street, 1864.

The Prologue.

IN Troy there lyes the Scene: From Iles of Greece
The Princes Orgillous, their high blood chaf'd
Haue to the Port of Athens sent their shippes
Fraught with the ministers and instruments
Of cruell Warre: Sixty and nine that wore
Their Crownets Regall, from th' Athenian bay
Put forth toward Phrygia, and their vow is made
To ransacke Troy, within whose strong emures
The rauish'd Helen, Menelaus Queene,
With wanton Paris sleepes, and that's the Quarrell.
To Tenedos they come,
And the deepe-drawing Barke do there disgorge
Their warlike frautage: now on Dardan Plaines
The fresh and yet vnbruised Greekes do pitch
Their braue Pauillions. Priams six-gated City,
Dardan and Timbria, Helias, Chetas, Troien,
And Antenonidus with massie Staples
And corresponsiue and fulfilling Bolts
Stirre vp the Sonnes of Troy.
Now Expectation tickling skittish spirits,
On one and other side, Troian and Greeke,
Sets all on hazard. And hither am I come,
A Prologue arm'd, but not in confidence
Of Authors pen, or Actors voyce; but suited
In like conditions, as our Argument;
To tell you (faire Beholders) that our Play
Leapes ore the vaunt and firstlings of those broyles,
Beginning in the middle: starting thence away,
To what may be digested in a Play:
Like, or finde fault, do as your pleasures are,
Now good, or bad, 'tis but the chance of Warre.

THE TRAGEDIE OF
Troylus and Creſsida.

Actus Primus. Scœna Prima.

Enter Pandarus and Troylus.

Troylus.
CAll here my Varlet, Ile vnarme againe.
Why ſhould I warre without the wals of Troy
That finde ſuch cruell battell here within?
Each Troian that is maſter of his heart,
Let him to field, *Troylus* alas hath none.
Pan. Will this geere nere be mended?
Troy. The Greeks are ſtrong, & skilful to their ſtrength,
Fierce to their skill, and to their fierceneſſe Valiant:
But I am weaker then a womans teare;
Tamer then ſleepe, fonder then ignorance;
Leſſe valiant then the Virgin in the night,
And skilleſſe as vnpractis'd Infancie.
Pan. Well, I haue told you enough of this: For my part, Ile not meddle nor make no farther. Hee that will haue a Cake out of the Wheate, muſt needes tarry the grinding.
Troy. Haue I not tarried?
Pan. I the grinding; but you muſt tarry the bolting.
Troy. Haue I not tarried?
Pan. I the boulting; but you muſt tarry the leau'ing.
Troy. Still haue I tarried.
Pan. I, to the leauening: but heeres yet in the word hereafter, the Kneading, the making of the Cake, the heating of the Ouen, and the Baking; nay, you muſt ſtay the cooling too, or you may chance to burne your lips.
Troy. Patience her ſelfe, what Goddeſſe ere ſhe be,
Doth leſſer blench at ſufferance, then I doe:
At *Priams* Royall Table doe I ſit;
And when faire *Creſſid* comes into my thoughts,
So (Traitor) then ſhe comes, when ſhe is thence.
Pan. Well:
She look'd yeſternight fairer, then euer I ſaw her looke,
Or any woman elſe.
Troy. I was about to tell thee, when my heart,
As wedged with a ſigh, would riue in twaine,
Leaſt *Hector*, or my Father ſhould perceiue me:
I haue (as when the Sunne doth light a-ſcorne)
Buried this ſigh, in wrinkle of a ſmile:
But ſorrow, that is couch'd in ſeeming gladneſſe,
Is like that mirth, Fate turnes to ſudden ſadneſſe.
Pan. And her haire were not ſomewhat darker then *Helens*, well go too, there were no more compariſon betweene the Women. But for my part ſhe is my Kinſwoman, I would not (as they tearme it) praiſe it, but I wold ſome-body had heard her talke yeſterday as I did: I will not diſpraiſe your ſiſter *Caſſandra's* wit, but ———
Troy. Oh *Pandarus*! I tell thee *Pandarus*;
When I doe tell thee, there my hopes lye drown'd:
Reply not in how many Fadomes deepe
They lye indrench'd. I tell thee, I am mad
In *Creſſids* loue. Thou anſwer'ſt ſhe is Faire,
Powr'ſt in the open Vlcer of my heart,
Her Eyes, her Haire, her Cheeke, her Gate, her Voice,
Handleſt in thy diſcourſe. O that her Hand
(In whoſe compariſon, all whites are Inke)
Writing their owne reproach; to whoſe ſoft ſeizure,
The Cignets Downe is harſh, and ſpirit of Senſe
Hard as the palme of Plough-man. This thou tel'ſt me;
As true thou tel'ſt me, when I ſay I loue her:
But ſaying thus, inſtead of Oyle and Balme,
Thou lai'ſt in euery gaſh that loue hath giuen me,
The Knife that made it.
Pan. I ſpeake no more then truth.
Troy. Thou do'ſt not ſpeake ſo much.
Pan. Faith, Ile not meddle in't: Let her be as ſhee is, if ſhe be faire, 'tis the better for her: and ſhe be not, ſhe ha's the mends in her owne hands.
Troy. Good *Pandarus*: How now *Pandarus*?
Pan. I haue had my Labour for my trauell, ill thought on of her, and ill thought on of you: Gone betweene and betweene, but ſmall thankes for my labour.
Troy. What art thou angry *Pandarus*? what with me?
Pan. Becauſe ſhe's Kinne to me, therefore ſhee's not ſo faire as *Helen*, and ſhe were not kin to me, ſhe would be as faire on Friday, as *Helen* is on Sunday. But what care I? I care not and ſhe were a Black-a-Moore, 'tis all one to me.
Troy. Say I ſhe is not faire?
Troy. I doe not care whether you doe or no. Shee's a Foole to ſtay behinde her Father: Let her to the Greeks, and ſo Ile tell her the next time I ſee her: for my part, Ile meddle nor make no more i'th'matter.
Troy. *Pandarus?* *Pan.* Not I.
Troy. Sweete *Pandarus.*
Pan. Pray you ſpeake no more to me, I will leaue all as I found it, and there an end. *Exit Pand.*
Sound Alarum.
Tro. Peace you vngracious Clamors, peace rude ſounds,
Fooles on both ſides, *Helen* muſt needs be faire,
When with your bloud you daily paint her thus.
I cannot fight vpon this Argument:
It

It is too ſtaru'd a ſubiect for my Sword,
But *Pandarus* : O Gods ! How do you plague me?
I cannot come to *Creſſid* but by *Pandar*,
And he's as teachy to be woo'd to woe,
As ſhe is ſtubborne, chaſt, againſt all ſuite.
Tell me *Apollo* for thy *Daphnes* Loue
What *Creſſid* is, what *Pandar*, and what we :
Her bed is *India*, there ſhe lies, a Pearle,
Between our Ilium, and where ſhee recides
Let it be cald the wild and wandring flood,
Our ſelfe the Merchant, and this ſayling *Pandar*,
Our doubtfull hope, our conuoy and our Barke.

Alarum. Enter Æneas.

Æne. How now Prince *Troylus*?
Wherefore not a field?

Troy. Becauſe not there; this womans anſwer ſorts.
For womaniſh it is to be from thence:
What newes *Æneas* from the field to day?

Æne. That *Paris* is returned home, and hurt.

Troy. By whom *Æneas*?

Æne. *Troylus* by *Menelaus*.

Troy. Let *Paris* bleed, 'tis but a ſcar to ſcorne,
Paris is gor'd with *Menelaus* horne. *Alarum.*

Æne. Harke what good ſport is out of Towne to day.

Troy. Better at home, if would I might were may:
But to the ſport abroad, are you bound thither?

Æne. In all ſwift haſt.

Troy. Come goe wee then togither. *Exeunt.*

Enter Creſſid and her man.

Cre. Who were thoſe went by?

Man. Queene *Hecuba*, and *Hellen*.

Cre. And whether go they?

Man. Vp to the Eaſterne Tower,
Whoſe height commands as ſubiect all the vaile,
To ſee the battell: *Hector* whoſe pacience,
Is as a Vertue fixt, to day was mou'd:
He chides *Andromache* and ſtrooke his Armorer,
And like as there were husbandry in Warre
Before the Sunne roſe, hee was harneſt lyte,
And to the field goe's he; where euery flower
Did as a Prophet weepe what it forſaw,
In *Hectors* wrath.

Cre. What was his cauſe of anger?

Man. The noiſe goe's this;
There is among the Greekes,
A Lord of Troian blood, Nephew to *Hector*,
They call him *Aiax*.

Cre. Good; and what of him?

Man. They ſay he is a very man *per ſe* and ſtands alone.

Cre. So do all men, vnleſſe they are drunke, ſicke, or haue no legges.

Man. This man Lady, hath rob'd many beaſts of their particular additions, he is as valiant as the Lyon, churliſh as the Beare, ſlow as the Elephant: a man into whom nature hath ſo crowded humors, that his valour is cruſht into folly, his folly ſauced with diſcretion : there is no man hath a vertue, that he hath not a glimpſe of, nor any man an attaint, but he carries ſome ſtaine of it. He is melancholy without cauſe, and merry againſt the haire, hee hath the ioynts of euery thing, but euery thing ſo out of ioynt, that hee is a gowtie *Briareus*, many hands and no vſe; or purblinded *Argus*, all eyes and no ſight.

Cre. But how ſhould this man that makes me ſmile, make *Hector* angry?

Man. They ſay he yeſterday cop'd *Hector* in the battell and ſtroke him downe, the diſdaind & ſhame whereof, hath euer ſince kept *Hector* faſting and waking.

Enter Pandarus.

Cre. Who comes here?

Man. Madam your Vncle *Pandarus*.

Cre. *Hectors* a gallant man.

Man. As may be in the world Lady.

Pan. What's that? what's that?

Cre. Good morrow Vncle *Pandarus*.

Pan. Good morrow Cozen *Creſſid*: what do you talke of? good morrow *Alexander*: how do you Cozen? when were you at Illium?

Cre. This morning Vncle.

Pan. What were you talking of when I came? Was *Hector* arm'd and gon ere yea came to Illium? *Hellen* was not vp? was ſhe?

Cre. *Hector* was gone but *Hellen* was not vp?

Pan. E'ene ſo; *Hector* was ſtirring early.

Cre. That were we talking of, and of his anger.

Pan. Was he angry?

Cre. So he ſaies here.

Pan. True he was ſo; I know the cauſe too, heele lay about him to day I can tell them that, and there's *Troylus* will not come farre behind him, let them take heede of *Troylus*; I can tell them that too.

Cre. What is he angry too?

Pan. Who *Troylus*?
Troylus is the better man of the two.

Cre. Oh *Iupiter*; there's no compariſon.

Pan. What not betweene *Troylus* and *Hector*? do you know a man if you ſee him?

Cre. I, if I euer ſaw him before and knew him.

Pan. Well I ſay *Troylus* is *Troylus*.

Cre. Then you ſay as I ſay,
For I am ſure he is not *Hector*.

Pan. No not *Hector* is not *Troylus* in ſome degrees.

Cre. 'Tis iuſt, to each of them he is himſelfe.

Pan. Himſelfe? alas poore *Troylus* I would he were.

Cre. So he is.

Pan. Condition I had gone bare-foote to India.

Cre. He is not *Hector*.

Pan. Himſelfe? no? hee's not himſelfe, would a were himſelfe: well, the Gods are aboue, time muſt friend or end: well *Troylus* well, I would my heart were in her body; no, *Hector* is not a better man then *Troylus*.

Cre. Excuſe me.

Pan. He is elder.

Cre. Pardon me, pardon me.

Pan. Th'others not come too't, you ſhall tell me another tale when th'others come too't: *Hector* ſhall not haue his will this yeare.

Cre. He ſhall not neede it if he haue his owne.

Pan. Nor his qualities.

Cre. No matter.

Pan. Nor his beautie.

Cre. 'Twould not become him, his own's better.

Pan. You haue no iudgement Neece; *Hellen* her ſelfe ſwore th'other day that *Troylus* for a browne fauour (for ſo 'tis I muſt confeſſe) not browne neither.

Cre. No, but browne.

Pan. Faith to ſay truth, browne and not browne.

Cre. To ſay the truth, true and not true.

Pan. She prais'd his complexion aboue *Paris*.

Cre. Why *Paris* hath colour inough.

Pan. So, he has.

Cre. Then *Troylus* ſhould haue too much, if ſhe prasi'd him aboue, his complexion is higher then his, he hauing colour

colour enough, and the other higher, is too flaming a praise for a good complexion, I had as lieue *Hellens* golden tongue had commended *Troylus* for a copper nose.

Pan. I sweare to you,
I thinke *Hellen* loues him better then *Paris*.

Cre. Then shee's a merry Greeke indeed.

Pan. Nay I am sure she does, she came to him th'other day into the compast window, and you know he has not past three or foure haires on his chinne.

Cres. Indeed a Tapsters Arithmetique may soone bring his particulars therein, to a totall.

Pand. Why he is very yong, and yet will he within three pound lift as much as his brother *Hector*.

Cres. Is he is so young a man, and so old a lifter?

Pan. But to prooue to you that *Hellen* loues him, she came and puts me her white hand to his clouen chin.

Cres. *Iuno* haue mercy, how came it clouen?

Pan. Why, you know 'tis dimpled,
I thinke his smyling becomes him better then any man in all Phrigia.

Cre. Oh he smiles valiantly.

Pan. Dooes hee not?

Cre. Oh yes, and 'twere a clow'd in *Autumne*.

Pan. Why go to then, but to proue to you that *Hellen* loues *Troylus*.

Cre. *Troylus* wil stand to thee
Proofe, if youle prooue it so.

Pan. *Troylus*? why he esteemes her no more then I esteeme an addle egge.

Cre. If you loue an addle egge as well as you loue an idle head, you would eate chickens i'th'shell.

Pan. I cannot chuse but laugh to thinke how she tickled his chin, indeed shee has a maruel's white hand I must needs confesse.

Cre. Without the racke.

Pan. And shee takes vpon her to spie a white haire on his chinne.

Cre. Alas poore chin? many a wart is richer.

Pand. But there was such laughing, Queene *Hecuba* laught that her eyes ran ore.

Cre. With Milstones.

Pan. And *Cassandra* laught.

Cre. But there was more temperate fire vnder the pot of her eyes: did her eyes run ore too?

Pan. And *Hector* laught.

Cre. At what was all this laughing?

Pand. Marry at the white haire that *Hellen* spied on *Troylus* chin.

Cres. And t'had beene a greene haire, I should haue laught too.

Pand. They laught not so much at the haire, as at his pretty answere.

Cre. What was his answere?

Pan. Quoth shee, heere's but two and fifty haires on your chinne; and one of them is white.

Cre. This is her question.

Pand That's true, make no question of that, two and fiftie haires quoth hee, and one white, that white haire is my Father, and all the rest are his Sonnes. *Iupiter* quoth she, which of these haires is *Paris* my husband? The forked one quoth he, pluckt out and giue it him: but there was such laughing, and *Hellen* so blusht, and *Paris* so chaft, and all the rest so laught, that it past.

Cre. So let it now,
For is has beene a great while going by.

Pan. Well Cozen,
I told you a thing yesterday, think on't.

Cre. So I does.

Pand. Ile be sworne 'tis true, he will weepe you an'twere a man borne in Aprill. *Sound a retreate.*

Cres. And Ile spring vp in his teares, an'twere a nettle against May.

Pan. Harke they are comming from the field, shal we stand vp here and see them, as they passe toward Ilium, good Neece do, sweet Neece *Cressida*.

Cre. At your pleasure.

Pan. Heere, heere, here's an excellent place, heere we may see most brauely, Ile tel you them all by their names, as they passe by, but marke *Troylus* aboue the rest.

Enter Æneas.

Cre. Speake not so low'd.

Pan. That's *Æneas*, is not that a braue man, hee's one of the flowers of Troy I can you, but marke *Troylus*, you shal see anon.

Cre. Who's that?

Enter Antenor.

Pan. That's *Antenor*, he has a shrow'd wit I can tell you, and hee's a man good inough, hee's one o'th soundest iudgement in Troy whosoeuer, and a proper man of person: when comes *Troylus*? Ile shew you *Troylus* anon, if hee see me, you shall see him him nod at me.

Cre. Will he giue you the nod?

Pan. You shall see.

Cre. If he do, the rich shall haue, more.

Enter Hector.

Pan. That's *Hector*, that, that, looke you, that there's a fellow. Goe thy way *Hector*, there's a braue man Neece, O braue *Hector*! Looke how hee lookes? there's a countenance; ist not a braue man?

Cre. O braue man!

Pan. Is a not? It dooes a mans heart good, looke you what hacks are on his Helmet, looke you yonder, do you see? Looke you there? There's no iesting, laying on, tak't off, who ill as they say, there be hacks.

Cre. Be those with Swords?

Enter Paris.

Pan. Swords, any thing he cares not, and the diuell come to him, it's all one, by Gods lid it dooes ones heart good. Yonder comes *Paris*, yonder comes *Paris*: looke yee yonder Neece, ist not a gallant man to, ist not? Why this is braue now: who said he came hurt home to day? Hee's not hurt, why this will do *Hellens* heart good now, ha? Would I could see *Troylus* now, you shall *Troylus* anon.

Cre. Whose that?

Enter Hellenus.

Pan. That's *Hellenus*, I maruell where *Troylus* is, that's *Helenus*, I thinke he went not forth to day: that's *Hellenus*.

Cre. Can *Hellenus* fight Vncle?

Pan. *Hellenus* no: yes heele fight indifferent, well, I maruell where *Troylus* is; harke, do you not haere the people crie *Troylus*? *Hellenus* is a Priest.

Cre. What sneaking fellow comes yonder?

Enter Trylus.

Pan. Where? Yonder? That's *Dæphobus*. 'Tis *Troylus*! Ther's a man Neece, hem? Braue *Troylus*, the Prince of Chiualrie.

Cre. Peace, for shame peace.

Pand. Marke him, not him: O braue *Troylus*: looke well vpon him Neece, looke you how his Sword is bloudied, and his Helme more hackt then *Hectors*, and how he lookes,

lookes, and how he goes. O admirable youth! he ne're saw three and twenty. Go thy way *Troylus*, go thy way, had I a sister were a *Grace*, or a daughter a Goddesse, hee should take his choice. O admirable man! *Paris*? *Paris* is durt to him, and I warrant, *Helen* to change, would giue money to boot.

Enter common Souldiers.

Cres. Heere come more.

Pan. Asses, fooles, dolts, chaffe and bran, chaffe and bran; porredge after meat. I could liue and dye i'th'eyes of *Troylus*. Ne're looke, ne're looke; the Eagles are gon, Crowes and Dawes, Crowes and Dawes: I had rather be such a man as *Troylus*, then *Agamemnon*, and all Greece.

Cres. There is among the Greekes *Achilles*, a better man then *Troylus*.

Pan. *Achilles*? a Dray-man, a Porter, a very Camell.

Cres. Well, well.

Pan. Well, well? Why haue you any discretion? haue you any eyes? Do you know what a man is? Is not birth, beauty, good shape, discourse, manhood, learning, gentlenesse, vertue, youth, liberality, and so forth: the Spice, and salt that seasons a man?

Cres. I, a minc'd man, and then to be bak'd with no Date in the pye, for then the mans dates out.

Pan. You are such another woman, one knowes not at what ward you lye.

Cres. Vpon my backe, to defend my belly; vpon my wit, to defend my wiles; vppon my secrecy, to defend mine honesty; my Maske, to defend my beauty, and you to defend all these: and at all these wardes I lye at, at a thousand watches.

Pan. Say one of your watches.

Cres. Nay Ile watch you for that, and that's one of the cheefest of them too: If I cannot ward what I would not haue hit, I can watch you for telling how I took the blow, vnlesse it swell past hiding, and then it's past watching.

Enter Boy.

Pan. You are such another.

Boy. Sir, my Lord would instantly speake with you.

Pan. Where?

Boy. At your owne house.

Pan. Good Boy tell him I come, I doubt he bee hurt. Fare ye well good Neece.

Cres. Adieu Vnkle.

Pan. Ile be with you Neece by and by.

Cres. To bring Vnkle.

Pan. I, a token from *Troylus*.

Cres. By the same token, you are a Bawd. *Exit Pand.*

Words, vowes, gifts, teares, & loues full sacrifice,
He offers in anothers enterprise:
But more in *Troylus* thousand fold I see,
Then in the glasse of *Pandar*'s praise may be;
Yet hold I off. Women are Angels wooing,
Things won are done, ioyes soule lyes in the dooing:
That she belou'd, knowes nought, that knowes not this;
Men prize the thing vngain'd, more then it is.
That she was neuer yet, that euer knew
Loue got so sweet, as when desire did sue:
Therefore this maxime out of loue I teach;
"*Atchieuement, is command*; *vngain'd, beseech.*
That though my hearts Contents firme loue doth beare,
Nothing of that shall from mine eyes appeare. *Exit.*

Senet. Enter Agamemnon, Nestor, Vlysses, Diomedes, Menelaus, with others.

Agam. Princes:
What greefe hath set the Iaundies on your cheekes?
The ample proposition that hope makes
In all designes, begun on earth below
Fayles in the promist largenesse: checkes and disasters
Grow in the veines of actions highest rear'd.
As knots by the conflux of meeting sap,
Infect the sound Pine, and diuerts his Graine
Tortiue and erant from his course of growth.
Nor Princes, is it matter new to vs,
That we come short of our suppose so farre,
That after seuen yeares siege, yet Troy walles stand,
Sith euery action that hath gone before,
Whereof we haue Record, Triall did draw
Bias and thwart, not answering the ayme:
And that vnbodied figure of the thought
That gaue't surmised shape. Why then (you Princes)
Do you with cheekes abash'd, behold our workes,
And thinke them shame, which are (indeed) nought else
But the protractiue trials of great Ioue,
To finde persistiue constancie in men?
The finenesse of which Mettall is not found
In Fortunes loue: for then, the Bold and Coward,
The Wise and Foole, the Artist and vn-read,
The hard and soft, seeme all affin'd, and kin.
But in the Winde and Tempest of her frowne,
Distinction with a lowd and powrefull fan,
Puffing at all, winnowes the light away;
And what hath masse, or matter by it selfe,
Lies rich in Vertue, and vnmingled.

Nestor. With due Obseruance of thy godly seat,
Great *Agamemnon*, *Nestor* shall apply
Thy latest words.
In the reproofe of Chance,
Lies the true proofe of men: The Sea being smooth,
How many shallow bauble Boates dare saile
Vpon her patient brest, making their way
With those of Nobler bulke?
But let the Ruffian *Boreas* once enrage
The gentle *Thetis*, and anon behold
The strong ribb'd Barke through liquid Mountaines cut,
Bounding betweene the two moyst Elements
Like *Perseus* Horse. Where's then the sawcy Boate,
Whose weake vntimber'd sides but euen now
Co-riual'd Greatnesse? Either to harbour fled,
Or made a Toste for Neptune. Euen so,
Doth valours shew, and valours worth diuide
In stormes of Fortune.
For, in her ray and brightnesse,
The Heard hath more annoyance by the Brieze
Then by the Tyger: But, when the splitting winde
Makes flexible the knees of knotted Oakes,
And Flies fled vnder shade, why then
The thing of Courage,
As rowz'd with rage, with rage doth sympathize,
And with an accent tun'd in selfe-same key,
Retyres to chiding Fortune.

Vlys. *Agamemnon*:
Thou great Commander, Nerue, and Bone of Greece,
Heart of our Numbers, soule, and onely spirit,
In whom the tempers, and the mindes of all
Should be shut vp: Heare what *Vlysses* speakes,
Besides the applause and approbation
The which most mighty for thy place and sway,

¶ And

And thou most reuerend for thy stretcht-out life,
I giue to both your speeches : which were such,
As *Agamemnon* and the hand of Greece
Should hold vp high in Brasse : and such againe
As venerable *Nestor* (hatch'd in Siluer)
Should with a bond of ayre, strong as the Axletree
In which the Heauens ride, knit all Greekes eares
To his experienc'd tongue : yet let it please both
(Thou Great, and Wise) to heare *Vlysses* speake.
Aga. Speak Prince of *Ithaca*, and be't of lesse expect :
That matter needlesse of importlesse burthen
Diuide thy lips ; then we are confident
When ranke *Thersites* opes his Masticke iawes,
We shall heare Musicke, Wit, and Oracle.
Vlys. Troy yet vpon his basis had bene downe,
And the great *Hectors* sword had lack'd a Master
But for these instances.
The specialty of Rule hath beene neglected ;
And looke how many Grecian Tents do stand
Hollow vpon this Plaine, so many hollow Factions.
When that the Generall is not like the Hiue,
To whom the Forragers shall all repaire,
What Hony is expected? Degree being vizarded,
Th'vnworthiest shewes as fairely in the Maske.
The Heauens themselues, the Planets, and this Center,
Obserue degree, priority, and place,
Insisture, course, proportion, season, forme,
Office, and custome, in all line of Order :
And therefore is the glorious Planet Sol
In noble eminence, enthron'd and sphear'd
Amid'st the other, whose med'cinable eye
Corrects the ill Aspects of Planets euill,
And postes like the Command'ment of a King,
Sans checke, to good and bad. But when the Planets
In euill mixture to disorder wander,
What Plagues, and what portents, what mutiny ?
What raging of the Sea? shaking of Earth ?
Commotion in the Windes? Frights, changes, horrors,
Diuert, and cracke, rend and deracinate
The vnity, and married calme of States
Quite from their fixure ? O, when Degree is shak'd,
(Which is the Ladder to all high designes)
The enterprize is sicke. How could Communities,
Degrees in Schooles, and Brother-hoods in Cities,
Peacefull Commerce from diuidable shores,
The primogenitiue, and due of Byrth,
Prerogatiue of Age, Crownes, Scepters, Lawrels,
(But by Degree) stand in Authentique place?
Take but Degree away, vn-tune that string,
And hearke what Discord followes : each thing meetes
In meere oppugnancie. The bounded Waters,
Should lift their bosomes higher then the Shores,
And make a soppe of all this solid Globe :
Strength should be Lord of imbecility,
And the rude Sonne should strike his Father dead :
Force should be right, or rather, right and wrong,
(Betweene whose endlesse iarre, Iustice recides)
Should loose her names, and so should Iustice too.
Then euery thing includes it selfe in Power,
Power into Will, Will into Appetite,
And Appetite (an vniuersall Wolfe,
So doubly seconded with Will, and Power)
Must make perforce an vniuersall prey,
And last, eate vp himselfe.
Great *Agamemnon* :
This Chaos, when Degree is suffocate,
Followes the choaking :
And this neglection of Degree, is it
That by a pace goes backward in a purpose
It hath to climbe. The Generall's disdain'd
By him one step below ; he, by the next,
That next, by him beneath : so euery step
Exampled by the first pace that is sicke
Of his Superiour, growes to an enuious Feauer
Of pale, and bloodlesse Emulation.
And 'tis this Feauer that keepes Troy on foote,
Not her owne sinewes. To end a tale of length,
Troy in our weaknesse liues, not in her strength.
Nest. Most wisely hath *Vlysses* heere discouer'd
The Feauer, whereof all our power is sicke.
Aga. The Nature of the sicknesse found (*Vlysses*)
What is the remedie?
Vlys. The great *Achilles*, whom Opinion crownes,
The sinew, and the fore-hand of our Hoste,
Hauing his eare full of his ayery Fame,
Growes dainty of his worth, and in his Tent
Lyes mocking our designes. With him, *Patroclus*,
Vpon a lazie Bed, the liue-long day
Breakes scurrill Iests,
And with ridiculous and aukward action,
(Which Slanderer, he imitation call's)
He Pageants vs. Sometime great *Agamemnon*,
Thy toplesse deputation he puts on ;
And like a strutting Player, whose conceit
Lies in his Ham-string, and doth thinke it rich
To heare the woodden Dialogue and sound
'Twixt his stretcht footing, and the Scaffolage,
Such to be pittied, and ore-rested seeming
He acts thy Greatnesse in : and when he speakes,
'Tis like a Chime a mending. With tearmes vnsquar'd,
Which from the tongue of roaring *Typhon* dropt,
Would seemes Hyperboles. At this fusty stuffe,
The large *Achilles* (on his prest-bed lolling)
From his deepe Chest, laughes out a lowd applause,
Cries excellent, 'tis *Agamemnon* iust.
Now play me *Nestor* ; hum, and stroke thy Beard
As he, being drest to some Oration :
That's done, as neere as the extreamest ends
Of paralels ; as like, as *Vulcan* and his wife,
Yet god *Achilles* still cries excellent,
'Tis *Nestor* right. Now play him (me) *Patroclus*,
Arming to answer in a night-Alarme,
And then (forsooth) the faint defects of Age
Must be the Scene of myrth, to cough, and spit,
And with a palsie fumbling on his Gorget,
Shake in and out the Riuet : and at this sport
Sir Valour dies ; cries, O enough *Patroclus*,
Or, giue me ribs of Steele, I shall split all
In pleasure of my Spleene. And in this fashion,
All our abilities, gifts, natures, shapes,
Seuerals and generals of grace exact,
Atchieuments, plots, orders, preuentions,
Excitements to the field, or speech for truce,
Successe or losse, what is, or is not, serues
As stuffe for these two, to make paradoxes.
Nest. And in the imitation of these twaine,
Who (as *Vlysses* sayes) Opinion crownes
With an Imperiall voyce, many are infect :
Aiax is growne selfe-will'd, and beares his head
In such a reyne, in full as proud a place
As broad *Achilles*, and keepes his Tent like him ;
Makes factious Feasts, railes on our state of Warre
Bold

Bold as an Oracle, and sets *Thersites*
A slaue, whose Gall coines slanders like a Mint,
To match vs in comparisons with durt,
To weaken and discredit our exposure,
How ranke soeuer rounded in with danger.
Vlys. They taxe our policy, and call it Cowardice,
Count Wisedome as no member of the Warre,
Fore-stall prescience, and esteeme no acte
But that of hand: The still and mentall parts,
That do contriue how many hands shall strike
When fitnesse call them on, and know by measure
Of their obseruant toyle, the Enemies waight,
Why this hath not a fingers dignity:
They call this Bed-worke, Mapp'ry, Closset-Warre:
So that the Ramme that batters downe the wall,
For the great swing and rudenesse of his poize,
They place before his hand that made the Engine,
Or those that with the finenesse of their soules,
By Reason guide his execution.
Nest. Let this be granted, and *Achilles* horse
Makes many *Thetis* sonnes. *Tucket*
Aga. What Trumpet? Looke *Menelaus.*
Men. From Troy. *Enter Æneas.*
Aga. What would you 'fore our Tent?
Æne. Is this great *Agamemnons* Tent, I pray you?
Aga. Euen this.
Æne. May one that is a Herald, and a Prince,
Do a faire message to his Kingly eares?
Aga. With surety stronger then *Achilles* arme,
'Fore all the Greekish heads, which with one voyce
Call *Agamemnon* Head and Generall.
Æne. Faire leaue, and large security. How may
A stranger to those most Imperial lookes,
Know them from eyes of other Mortals?
Aga. How?
Æne. I: I aske, that I might waken reuerence,
And on the cheeke be ready with a blush
Modest as morning, when she coldly eyes
The youthfull Phœbus:
Which is that God in office guiding men?
Which is the high and mighty *Agamemnon*?
Aga. This Troyan scornes vs, or the men of Troy
Are ceremonious Courtiers.
Æne. Courtiers as free, as debonnaire; vnarm'd,
As bending Angels: that's their Fame, in peace:
But when they would seeme Souldiers, they haue galles,
Good armes, strong ioynts, true swords, & *Ioues* accord,
Nothing so full of heart. But peace *Æneas*,
Peace Troyan, lay thy finger on thy lips,
The worthinesse of praise distaines his worth:
If that he prais'd himselfe, bring the praise forth.
But what the repining enemy commends,
That breath Fame blowes, that praise sole pure transcẽds.
Aga. Sir, you of Troy, call you your selfe *Æneas*?
Æne. I Greeke, that is my name.
Aga. What's your affayre I pray you?
Æne. Sir pardon, 'tis for *Agamemnons* eares.
Aga. He heares nought priuatly
That comes from Troy.
Æne. Nor I from Troy come not to whisper him,
I bring a Trumpet to awake his eare,
To set his sence on the attentiue bent,
And then to speake.
Aga. Speake frankely as the winde,
It is not *Agamemnons* sleeping houre;
That thou shalt know Troyan he is awake,
He tels thee so himselfe.
Æne. Trumpet blow loud,
Send thy Brasse voyce through all these lazie Tents,
And euery Greeke of mettle, let him know,
What Troy meanes fairely, shall be spoke alowd.
The Trumpets sound.
We haue great *Agamemnon* heere in Troy,
A Prince calld *Hector*, *Priam* is his Father:
Who in this dull and long-continew'd Truce
Is rusty growne. He bad me take a Trumpet,
And to this purpose speake: Kings, Princes, Lords,
If there be one among'st the fayr'st of Greece,
That holds his Honor higher then his ease,
That seekes his praise, more then he feares his perill,
That knowes his Valour, and knowes not his feare,
That loues his Mistris more then in confession,
(With truant vowes to her owne lips he loues)
And dare avow her Beauty, and her Worth,
In other armes then hers: to him this Challenge.
Hector, in view of Troyans, and of Greekes,
Shall make it good, or do his best to do it.
He hath a Lady, wiser, fairer, truer,
Then euer Greeke did compasse in his armes,
And will to morrow with his Trumpet call,
Midway betweene your Tents, and walles of Troy,
To rowze a Grecian that is true in loue.
If any come, *Hector* shal honour him:
If none, hee'l say in Troy when he retyres,
The Grecian Dames are sun-burnt, and not worth
The splinter of a Lance: Euen so much.
Aga. This shall be told our Louers Lord *Æneas*,
If none of them haue soule in such a kinde,
We left them all at home: But we are Souldiers,
And may that Souldier a meere recreant proue,
That meanes not, hath not, or is not in loue:
If then one is, or hath, or meanes to be,
That one meets *Hector*; if none else, Ile be he.
Nest. Tell him of *Nestor*, one that was a man
When *Hectors* Grandsire suckt: he is old now,
But if there be not in our Grecian mould,
One Noble man, that hath one spark of fire
To answer for his Loue; tell him from me,
Ile hide my Siluer beard in a Gold Beauer,
And in my Vantbrace put this wither'd brawne,
And meeting him, wil tell him, that my Lady
Was fayrer then his Grandame, and as chaste
As may be in the world: his youth in flood,
Ile pawne this truth with my three drops of blood.
Æne. Now heauens forbid such scarsitie of youth.
Vlys. Amen.
Aga. Faire Lord *Æneas*,
Let me touch your hand:
To our Pauillion shal I leade you first:
Achilles shall haue word of this intent,
So shall each Lord of Greece from Tent to Tent:
Your selfe shall Feast with vs before you goe,
And finde the welcome of a Noble Foe. *Exeunt.*
Manet Vlysses, and Nestor.
Vlys. *Nestor.*
Nest. What sayes *Vlysses*?
Vlys. I haue a young conception in my braine,
Be you my time to bring it to some shape.
Nest. What is't?
Vlysses. This 'tis:
Blunt wedges riue hard knots: the seeded Pride
That hath to this maturity blowne vp

In ranke *Achilles*, muſt or now be cropt,
Or ſhedding breed a Nurſery of like euil
To ouer-bulke vs all.
Neſt. Wel, and how?
Vlyſ. This challenge that the gallant *Hector* ſends,
How euer it is ſpred in general name,
Relates in purpoſe onely to *Achilles.*
Neſt. The purpoſe is perſpicuous euen as ſubſtance,
Whoſe groſſeneſſe little charracters ſumme vp,
And in the publication make no ſtraine,
But that *Achilles*, were his braine as barren
As bankes of Lybia, though (*Apollo* knowes)
'Tis dry enough, wil with great ſpeede of iudgement,
I, with celerity, finde *Hectors* purpoſe
Pointing on him.
Vlyſ. And wake him to the anſwer, thinke you?
Neſt. Yes, 'tis moſt meet; who may you elſe oppoſe
That can from *Hector* bring his Honor off,
If not *Achilles*; though't be a ſportfull Combate,
Yet in this triall, much opinion dwels.
For heere the Troyans taſte our deer'ſt repute
With their fin'ſt Pallate: and truſt to me *Vlyſſes*,
Our imputation ſhall be oddely poiz'd
In this wilde action. For the ſucceſſe
(Although particular) ſhall giue a ſcantling
Of good or bad, vnto the Generall:
And in ſuch Indexes, although ſmall prickes
To their ſubſequent Volumes, there is ſeene
The baby figure of the Gyant-maſſe
Of things to come at large. It is ſuppos'd,
He that meets *Hector*, iſſues from our choyſe;
And choiſe being mutuall acte of all our ſoules,
Makes Merit her election, and doth boyle
As 'twere, from forth vs all: a man diſtill'd
Out of our Vertues; who miſcarrying,
What heart from hence receyues the conqu'ring part
To ſteele a ſtrong opinion to themſelues,
Which entertain'd, Limbes are in his inſtruments,
In no leſſe working, then are Swords and Bowes
Directiue by the Limbes.
Vlyſ. Giue pardon to my ſpeech:
Therefore 'tis meet, *Achilles* meet not *Hector*:
Let vs (like Merchants) ſhew our fowleſt Wares,
And thinke perchance they'l ſell: If not,
The luſter of the better yet to ſhew,
Shall ſhew the better. Do not conſent,
That euer *Hector* and *Achilles* meete:
For both our Honour, and our Shame in this,
Are dogg'd with two ſtrange Followers.
Neſt. I ſee them not with my old eies: what are they?
Vlyſ. What glory our *Achilles* ſhares from *Hector*,
(Were he not proud) we all ſhould weare with him:
But he already is too inſolent,
And we were better parch in Affricke Sunne,
Then in the pride and ſalt ſcorne of his eyes
Should he ſcape *Hector* faire. If he were foyld,
Why then we did our maine opinion cruſh
In taint of our beſt man. No, make a Lott'ry,
And by deuice let blockiſh *Aiax* draw
The ſort to fight with *Hector*: Among our ſelues,
Giue him allowance as the worthier man,
For that will phyſicke the great Myrmidon
Who broyles in lowd applauſe, and make him fall
His Creſt, that prouder then blew Iris bends.
If the dull brainleſſe *Aiax* come ſafe off,
Wee'l dreſſe him vp in voyces: if he faile,
Yet go we vnder our opinion ſtill,
That we haue better men. But hit or miſſe,
Our proiects life this ſhape of ſence aſſumes,
Aiax imploy'd, pluckes downe *Achilles* Plumes.
Neſt. Now *Vlyſſes*, I begin to relliſh thy aduice,
And I wil giue a taſte of it forthwith
To *Agamemnon*, go we to him ſtraight:
Two Curres ſhal tame each other, Pride alone
Muſt tarre the Maſtiffes on, as 'twere their bone. *Exeunt*

Enter Aiax, and Therſites.

Aia. *Therſites*?
Ther. *Agamemnon*, how if he had Biles (ful) all ouer generally.
Aia. *Therſites*?
Ther. And thoſe Byles did runne, ſay ſo; did not the General run, were not that a botchy core?
Aia. Dogge.
Ther. Then there would come ſome matter from him: I ſee none now.
Aia. Thou Bitch-Wolfes-Sonne, canſt ẏͧ not heare? Feele then. *Strikes him.*
Ther. The plague of Greece vpon thee thou Mungrel beefe-witted Lord.
Aia. Speake then you whinid'ſt leauen ſpeake, I will beate thee into handſomneſſe.
Ther. I ſhal ſooner rayle thee into wit and holineſſe: but I thinke thy Horſe wil ſooner con an Oration, then ẏͧ learn a prayer without booke: Thou canſt ſtrike, canſt thou? A red Murren o'th thy Iades trickes.
Aia. Toads ſtoole, learne me the Proclamation.
Ther. Doeſt thou thinke I haue no ſence thou ſtrik'ſt (me thus?
Aia. The Proclamation.
Ther. Thou art proclaim'd a foole, I thinke.
Aia. Do not Porpentine, do not; my fingers itch.
Ther. I would thou didſt itch from head to foot, and I had the ſcratching of thee, I would make thee the loth-ſom'ſt ſcab in Greece.
Aia. I ſay the Proclamation.
Ther. Thou grumbleſt & raileſt euery houre on *Achilles*, and thou art as ful of enuy at his greatnes, as *Cerberus* is at *Proſerpina's* beauty. I, that thou barkſt at him.
Aia. Miſtreſſe *Therſites.*
Ther. Thou ſhould'ſt ſtrike him.
Aia. Coblofe.
Ther. He would pun thee into ſhiuers with his fiſt, as a Sailor breakes a bisket.
Aia. You horſon Curre. *Ther.* Do, do.
Aia. Thou ſtoole for a Witch.
Ther. I, do, do, thou ſodden-witted Lord: thou haſt no more braine then I haue in mine elbows: An Aſinico may tutor thee. Thou ſcuruy valiant Aſſe, thou art heere but to threſh Troyans, and thou art bought and ſolde among thoſe of any wit, like a Barbarian ſlaue. If thou vſe to beat me, I wil begin at thy heele, and tel what thou art by inches, thou thing of no bowels thou.
Aia. You dogge.
Ther. You ſcuruy Lord.
Aia. You Curre.
Ther. *Mars* his Ideot: do rudenes, do Camell, do, do.

Enter Achilles, and Patroclus.

Achil. Why how now *Aiax*? wherefore do you this?
How now *Therſites*? what's the matter man?
Ther. You ſee him there, do you?
Achil. I, what's the matter.
Ther. Nay looke vpon him.
Achil. So I do: what's the matter?

Ther.

Ther. Nay but regard him well.
Achil. Well, why I do ſo.
Ther. But yet you looke not well vpon him: for who ſome euer you take him to be, he is *Aiax*.
Achil. I know that foole.
Ther. I, but that foole knowes not himſelfe.
Aiax. Therefore I beate thee.
Ther. Lo, lo, lo, lo, what *modicums* of wit he vtters: his euaſions haue eares thus long. I haue bobb'd his Braine more then he has beate my bones: I will buy nine Sparrowes for a peny, and his *Piamater* is not worth the ninth part of a Sparrow. This Lord (*Achilles*) *Aiax* who wears his wit in his belly, and his guttes in his head, Ile tell you what I ſay of him.
Achil. What?
Ther. I ſay this *Aiax* ———
Achil. Nay good *Aiax*.
Ther. Has not ſo much wit.
Achil: Nay, I muſt hold you.
Ther. As will ſtop the eye of *Helens* Needle, for whom hecomes to fight.
Achil. Peace foole.
Ther. I would haue peace and quietnes, but the foole will not: he there, that he, looke you there.
Aiax. O thou damn'd Curre, I ſhall ———
Achil. Will you ſet your wit to a Fooles.
Ther. No I warrant you, for a fooles will ſhame it.
Pat. Good words *Therſites*.
Achil. What's the quarrell?
Aiax. I bad thee vile Owle, goe learne me the tenure of the Proclamation, and he rayles vpon me.
Ther. I ſerue thee not.
Aiax. Well, go too, go too.
Ther. I ſerue heere voluntary.
Achil. Your laſt ſeruice was ſufferance, 'twas not voluntary, no man is beaten voluntary: *Aiax* was heere the voluntary, and you as vnder an Impreſſe.
Ther. E'ne ſo, a great deale of your wit too lies in your ſinnewes, or elſe there be Liars. *Hector* ſhall haue a great catch, if he knocke out either of your braines, he were as good cracke a fuſtie nut with no kernell.
Achil. What with me to *Therſites*?
Ther. There's *Vlyſſes*, and old *Neſtor*, whoſe Wit was mouldy ere their Grandſires had nails on their toes, yoke you like draft-Oxen, and make you plough vp the warre.
Achil. What? what?
Ther. Yes good ſooth, to *Achilles*, to *Aiax*, to ———
Aiax. I ſhall cut out your tongue.
Ther. 'Tis no matter, I ſhall ſpeake as much as thou afterwards.
Pat. No more words *Therſites*.
Ther. I will hold my peace when *Achilles* Brooch bids me, ſhall I?
Achil. There's for you *Patroclus*.
Ther. I wi'l ſee you hang'd like Clotpoles ere I come any more to your Tents; I will keepe where there is wit ſtirring, and leaue the faction of fooles. *Exit.*
Pat. A good riddance.
Achil. Marry this Sir is proclaim'd through al our hoſt,
That *Hector* by the fift houre of the Sunne,
Will with a Trumpet, 'twixt our Tents and Troy
To morrow morning call ſome Knight to Armes,
That hath a ſtomacke, and ſuch a one that dare
Maintaine I know not what: 'tis traſh. Farewell.
Aiax. Farewell? who ſhall anſwer him?
Achil. I know not, 'tis put to Lottry: otherwiſe
He knew his man.
Aiax. O meaning you, I wil go learne more of it. *Exit.*

Enter Priam, Hector, Troylus, Paris and Helenus.

Pri. After ſo many houres, liues, ſpeeches ſpent,
Thus once againe ſayes *Neſtor* from the Greekes,
Deliuer *Helen*, and all damage elſe
(As honour, loſſe of time, trauaile, expence,
Wounds, friends, and what els deere that is conſum'd
In hot digeſtion of this comorant Warre)
Shall be ſtroke off. *Hector*, what ſay you too't.
Hect. Though no man leſſer feares the Greeks then I,
As farre as touches my particular: yet dread *Priam*,
There is no Lady of more ſofter bowels,
More ſpungie, to ſucke in the ſenſe of feare,
More ready to cry out, who knowes what followes
Then *Hector* is: the wound of peace is ſurety,
Surety ſecure: but modeſt Doubt is cal'd
The Beacon of the wiſe: the tent that ſearches
To'th'bottome of the worſt. Let *Helen* go,
Since the firſt ſword was drawne about this queſtion,
Euery tythe ſoule 'mongſt many thouſand diſmes,
Hath bin as deere as *Helen*: I meane of ours:
If we haue loſt ſo many tenths of ours
To guard a thing not ours, nor worth to vs
(Had it our name) the valew of one ten;
What merit's in that reaſon which denies
The yeelding of her vp.
Troy. Fie, fie, my Brother;
Weigh you the worth and honour of a King
(So great as our dread Father) in a Scale
Of common Ounces? Wil you with Counters ſumme
The paſt proportion of his infinite,
And buckle in a waſte moſt fathomleſſe,
With ſpannes and inches ſo diminutiue,
As feares and reaſons? Fie for godly ſhame?
Hel. No maruel though you bite ſo ſharp at reaſons,
You are ſo empty of them, ſhould not our Father
Beare the great ſway of his affayres with reaſons,
Becauſe your ſpeech hath none that tels him ſo.
Troy. You are for dreames & ſlumbers brother Prieſt
You furre your gloues with reaſon: here are your reaſons
You know an enemy intends you harme,
You know, a ſword imploy'd is perillous,
And reaſon flyes the obiect of all harme.
Who maruels then when *Helenus* beholds
A Grecian and his ſword, if he do ſet
The very wings of reaſon to his heeles:
Or like a Starre diſorb'd. Nay, if we talke of Reaſon,
And flye like chidden Mercurie from Ioue,
Let's ſhut our gates and ſleepe: Manhood and Honor
Should haue hard hearts, wold they but fat their thoghts
With this cramm'd reaſon: reaſon and reſpect,
Makes Liuers pale, and luſtyhood deiect.
Hect. Brother, ſhe is not worth
What ſhe doth coſt the holding.
Troy. What's aught, but as 'tis valew'd?
Hect. But value dwels not in particular will,
It holds his eſtimate and dignitie
As well, wherein 'tis precious of it ſelfe,
As in the prizer: 'Tis made Idolatrie,
To make the ſeruice greater then the God,
And the will dotes that is inclineable
To what infectiouſly it ſelfe affects,
Without ſome image of th'affected merit.
Troy. I take to day a Wife, and my election
Is led on in the conduct of my Will;

¶ 3 My

My Will enkindled by mine eyes and eares,
Two traded Pylots 'twixt the dangerous ſhores
Of Will, and Iudgement. How may I auoyde
(Although my will diſtaſte what it elected)
The Wife I choſe, there can be no euaſion
To blench from this, and to ſtand firme by honour.
We turne not backe the Silkes vpon the Merchant
When we haue ſpoyl'd them; nor the remainder Viands
We do not throw in vnreſpectiue ſame,
Becauſe we now are full. It was thought meete
Paris ſhould do ſome vengeance on the Greekes;
Your breath of full conſent bellied his Sailes,
The Seas and Windes (old Wranglers) tooke a Truce,
And did him ſeruice; he touch'd the Ports deſir'd,
And for an old Aunt whom the Greekes held Captiue,
He brought a Grecian Queen, whoſe youth & freſhneſſe
Wrinkles *Apolloes*, and makes ſtale the morning.
Why keepe we her? the Grecians keepe our Aunt:
Is ſhe worth keeping? Why ſhe is a Pearle,
Whoſe price hath launch'd aboue a thouſand Ships,
And turn'd Crown'd Kings to Merchants.
If you'l auouch, 'twas wiſedome *Paris* went,
(As you muſt needs, for you all cride, Go, go:)
If you'l confeſſe, he brought home Noble prize,
(As you muſt needs) for you all clapt your hands,
And cride ineſtimable; why do you now
The iſſue of your proper Wiſedomes rate,
And do a deed that Fortune neuer did?
Begger the eſtimation which you priz'd,
Richer then Sea and Land? O Theft moſt baſe!
That we haue ſtolne what we do feare to keepe.
But Theeues vnworthy of a thing ſo ſtolne,
That in their Country did them that diſgrace,
We feare to warrant in our Natiue place.

Enter Caſſandra with her haire about her eares.

Caſ. Cry *Troyans*, cry.
Priam. What noyſe? what ſhreeke is this?
Troy. 'Tis our mad ſiſter, I do know her voyce.
Caſ. Cry Troyans.
Hect. It is *Caſſandra.*
Caſ. Cry Troyans cry; lend me ten thouſand eyes,
And I will fill them with Propheticke teares.
Hect. Peace ſiſter, peace.
Caſ. Virgins, and Boyes; mid-age & wrinkled old,
Soft infancie, that nothing can but cry,
Adde to my clamour: let vs pay betimes
A moity of that maſſe of moane to come.
Cry Troyans cry, practiſe your eyes with teares,
Troy muſt not be, nor goodly Illion ſtand,
Our fire-brand Brother *Paris* burnes vs all.
Cry Troyans cry, a *Helen* and a woe;
Cry, cry, Troy burnes, or elſe let *Helen* goe. *Exit.*
Hect. Now youthfull *Troylus*, do not theſe hie ſtrains
Of diuination in our Siſter, worke
Some touches of remorſe? Or is your bloud
So madly hot, that no diſcourſe of reaſon,
Nor feare of bad ſucceſſe in a bad cauſe,
Can qualifie the ſame?
Troy. Why Brother *Hector*,
We may not thinke the iuſtneſſe of each acte
Such, and no other then euent doth forme it,
Nor once deiect the courage of our mindes;
Becauſe *Caſſandra's* mad, her brainſicke raptures
Cannot diſtaſte the goodneſſe of a quarrell,
Which hath our ſeuerall Honours all engag'd
To make it gracious. For my priuate part,
I am no more touch'd, then all *Priams* ſonnes,
And Ioue forbid there ſhould be done among'ſt vs
Such things as might offend the weakeſt ſpleene,
To fight for, and maintaine.
Par. Elſe might the world conuince of leuitie,
As well my vnder-takings as your counſels:
But I atteſt the gods, your full conſent
Gaue wings to my propenſion, and cut off
All feares attending on ſo dire a proiect.
For what (alas) can theſe my ſingle armes?
What propugnation is in one mans valour
To ſtand the puſh and enmity of thoſe
This quarrell would excite? Yet I proteſt,
Were I alone to paſſe the difficulties,
And had as ample power, as I haue will,
Paris ſhould ne're retract what he hath done,
Nor faint in the purſuite.
Pri. *Paris*, you ſpeake
Like one be-ſotted on your ſweet delights;
You haue the Hony ſtill, but theſe the Gall,
So to be valiant, is no praiſe at all.
Par. Sir, I propoſe not meerely to my ſelfe,
The pleaſures ſuch a beauty brings with it:
But I would haue the ſoyle of her faire Rape
Wip'd off in honourable keeping her.
What Treaſon were it to the ranſack'd Queene,
Diſgrace to your great worths, and ſhame to me,
Now to deliuer her poſſeſsion vp
On termes of baſe compulſion? Can it be,
That ſo degenerate a ſtraine as this,
Should once ſet footing in your generous boſomes?
There's not the meaneſt ſpirit on our partie,
Without a heart to dare, or ſword to draw,
When *Helen* is defended: nor none ſo Noble,
Whoſe life were ill beſtow'd, or death vnfam'd,
Where *Helen* is the ſubiect. Then (I ſay)
Well may we fight for her, whom we know well,
The worlds large ſpaces cannot paralell.
Hect. *Paris* and *Troylus*, you haue both ſaid well:
And on the cauſe and queſtion now in hand,
Haue gloz'd, but ſuperficially; not much
Vnlike young men, whom *Ariſtotle* thought
Vnfit to heare Morall Philoſophie.
The Reaſons you alledge, do more conduce
To the hot paſſion of diſtemp'red blood,
Then to make vp a free determination
'Twixt right and wrong: For pleaſure, and reuenge,
Haue eares more deafe then Adders, to the voyce
Of any true deciſion. Nature craues
All dues be rendred to their Owners: now
What neerer debt in all humanity,
Then Wife is to the Husband? If this law
Of Nature be corrupted through affection,
And that great mindes of partiall indulgence,
To their benummed wills reſiſt the ſame,
There is a Law in each well-ordred Nation,
To curbe thoſe raging appetites that are
Moſt diſobedient and refracturie.
If *Helen* then be wife to Sparta's King
(As it is knowne ſhe is) theſe Morall Lawes
Of Nature, and of Nation, ſpeake alowd
To haue her backe return'd. Thus to perſiſt
In doing wrong, extenuates not wrong,
But makes it much more heauie. *Hectors* opinion

Is this in way of truth: yet nere the lesse,
My spritely brethren, I propend to you
In resolution to keepe *Helen* still;
For 'tis a cause that hath no meane dependance,
Vpon our ioynt and seuerall dignities.

Tro. Why? there you toucht the life of our designe:
Were it not glory that we more affected,
Then the performance of our heauing spleenes,
I would not wish a drop of *Troian* blood,
Spent more in her defence. But worthy *Hector*,
She is a theame of honour and renowne,
A spurre to valiant and magnanimous deeds,
Whose present courage may beate downe our foes,
And fame in time to come canonize vs.
For I presume braue *Hector* would not loose
So rich aduantage of a promis'd glory,
As smiles vpon the fore-head of this action,
For the wide worlds reuenew.

Hect. I am yours,
You valiant off-spring of great *Priamus*,
I haue a roisting challenge sent among'st
The dull and factious nobles of the Greekes,
Will strike amazement to their drowsie spirits,
I was aduertiz'd, their Great generall slept,
Whil'st emulation in the armie crept:
This I presume will wake him. *Exeunt.*

Enter Thersites *solus.*

How now *Thersites*? what lost in the Labyrinth of thy furie? shall the Elephant *Aiax* carry it thus? he beates me, and I raile at him: O worthy satisfaction, would it were otherwise: that I could beate him, whil'st he rail'd at me: Sfoote, Ile learne to coniure and raise Diuels, but Ile see some issue of my spitefull execrations. Then ther's *Achilles*, a rare Enginer. If *Troy* be not taken till these two vndermine it, the wals will stand till they fall of themselues. O thou great thunder-darter of Olympus, forget that thou art *Ioue* the King of gods: and *Mercury*, loose all the Serpentine craft of thy Caduceus, if thou take not that little little lesse then little wit from them that they haue, which short-arm'd ignorance it selfe knowes, is so abundant scarse, it will not in circumuention deliuer a Flye from a Spider, without drawing the massie Irons and cutting the web: after this, the vengeance on the whole Camp, or rather the bone-ach, for that me thinkes is the curse dependant on those that warre for a placket. I haue said my prayers and diuell, enuie, say Amen: What ho? my Lord *Achilles*?

Enter Patroclus.

Patr. Who's there? *Thersites.* Good *Thersites* come in and raile.

Ther. If I could haue remembred a guilt counterfeit, thou would'st not haue slipt out of my contemplation, but it is no matter, thy selfe vpon thy selfe. The common curse of mankinde, follie and ignorance be thine in great reuenew; heauen blesse thee from a Tutor, and Discipline come not neere thee. Let thy bloud be thy direction till thy death, then if she that laies thee out sayes thou art a faire coarse, Ile be sworne and sworne vpon't she neuer shrowded any but Lazars, Amen. Wher's *Achilles*?

Patr. What art thou deuout? wast thou in a prayer?

Ther. I, the heauens heare me.

Enter Achilles.

Achil. Who's there?

Patr. *Thersites*, my Lord.

Achil. Where, where, art thou come? why my cheese, my digestion, why hast thou not seru'd thy selfe into my Table, so many meales? Come, what's *Agamemnon*?

Ther. Thy Commander *Achilles*, then tell me *Patroclus*, what's *Achilles*?

Patr. Thy Lord *Thersites*: then tell me I pray thee, what's thy selfe?

Ther. Thy knower *Patroclus*: then tell me *Patroclus*, what art thou?

Patr. Thou maist tell that know'st.

Achil. O tell, tell.

Ther. Ile declin the whole question: *Agamemnon* commands *Achilles*, *Achilles* is my Lord, I am *Patroclus* knower, and *Patroclus* is a foole.

Patro. You rascall.

Ter. Peace foole, I haue not done.

Achil. He is a priuiledg'd man, proceede *Thersites*.

Ther. *Agamemnon* is a foole, *Achilles* is a foole, *Thersites* is a foole, and as aforesaid, *Patroclus* is a foole.

Achil. Deriue this? come?

Ther. *Agamemnon* is a foole to offer to command *Achilles*, *Achilles* is a foole to be commanded of *Agamemon*, *Thersites* is a foole to serue such a foole: and *Patroclus* is a foole positiue.

Patr. Why am I a foole?

Enter Agamemnon, Vlisses, Nestor, Diomedes, Aiax, and Chalcas.

Ther. Make that demand to the Creator, it suffises me thou art. Looke you, who comes here?

Achil. *Patroclus*, Ile speake with no body: come in with me *Thersites*. *Exit.*

Ther. Here is such patcherie, such iugling, and such knauerie: all the argument is a Cuckold and a Whore, a good quarrel to draw emulations, factions, and bleede to death vpon: Now the dry Suppeago on the Subiect, and Warre and Lecherie confound all.

Agam. Where is *Achilles*?

Patr. Within his Tent, but ill dispos'd my Lord.

Agam. Let it be knowne to him that we are here:
He sent our Messengers, and we lay by
Our appertainments, visiting of him:
Let him be told of, so perchance he thinke
We dare not moue the question of our place,
Or know not what we are.

Pat. I shall so say to him.

Vlis. We saw him at the opening of his Tent,
He is not sicke.

Aia. Yes, Lyon sicke, sicke of proud heart; you may call it Melancholly if will fauour the man, but by my head, it's pride; but why, why, let him show vs the cause? A word my Lord.

Nes. What moues *Aiax* thus to bay at him?

Vlis. *Achilles* hath inueigled his Foole from him.

Nes. Who, *Thersites*?

Vlis. He.

Nes. Then will *Aiax* lacke matter, if he haue lost his Argument.

Vlis. No, you see he is his argument that has his argument *Achilles*.

Nes. All the better, their fraction is more our wish then their faction; but it was a strong counsell that a Foole could disunite.

Vlis. The amitie that wisedome knits, not folly may easily vntie. *Enter Patroclus.*

Here

Here comes *Patroclus.*
Nes. No *Achilles* with him?
Vlis. The Elephant hath ioynts, but none for curtesie:
His legge are legs for necessitie, not for flight.
Patro. *Achilles* bids me say he is much sorry:
If any thing more then your sport and pleasure,
Did moue your greatnesse, and this noble State,
To call vpon him; he hopes it is no other,
But for your health, and your digestion sake;
An after Dinners breath.
Aga. Heare you *Patroclus*:
We are too well acquainted with these answers:
But his euasion winged thus swift with scorne,
Cannot outflye our apprehensions.
Much attribute he hath, and much the reason,
Why we ascribe it to him, yet all his vertues,
Not vertuously of his owne part beheld,
Doe in our eyes, begin to loose their glosse;
Yea, and like faire Fruit in an vnholdsome dish,
Are like to rot vntasted: goe and tell him,
We came to speake with him; and you shall not sinne,
If you doe say, we thinke him ouer proud,
And vnder honest; in selfe-assumption greater
Then in the note of iudgement: & worthier then himselfe
Here tends the sauage strangenesse he puts on,
Disguise the holy strength of their command:
And vnder write in an obseruing kinde
His humorous predominance, yea watch
His pettish lines, his ebs, his flowes, as if
The passage and whole carriage of this action
Rode on his tyde. Goe tell him this, and adde,
That if he ouerhold his price so much,
Weele none of him; but let him, like an Engin
Not portable, lye vnder this report.
Bring action hither, this cannot goe to warre:
A stirring Dwarfe, we doe allowance giue,
Before a sleeping Gyant: tell him so.
Pat. I shall, and bring his answere presently.
Aga. In second voyce weele not be satisfied,
We come to speake with him, *Vliss.s* enter you.
Exit Vlisses.
Aiax. What is he more then another?
Aga. No more then what he thinkes he is.
Aia. Is he so much, doe you not thinke, he thinkes himselfe a better man then I am?
Ag. No question.
Aiax. Will you subscribe his thought, and say he is?
Ag. No, Noble *Aiax*, you are as strong, as valiant, as wise, no lesse noble, much more gentle, and altogether more tractable.
Aiax. Why should a man be proud? How doth pride grow? I know not what it is.
Aga. Your minde is the cleerer *Aiax*, and your vertues the fairer; he that is proud, eates vp himselfe; Pride is his owne Glasse, his owne trumpet, his owne Chronicle, and what euer praises it selfe but in the deede, deuoures the deede in the praise.
Enter Vlysses.
Aiax. I do hate a proud man, as I hate the ingendring of Toades.
Nest. Yet he loues himselfe: is't not strange?
Vlis. *Achilles* will not to the field to morrow.
Ag. What's his excuse?
Vlis. He doth relye on none,
But carries on the streame of his dispose,
Without obseruance or respect of any,
In will peculiar, and in selfe admission.
Aga. Why, will he not vpon our faire request,
Vntent his person, and share the ayre with vs?
Vlis. Things small as nothing, for requests sake onely
He makes important; possest he is with greatnesse,
And speakes not to himselfe, but with a pride
That quarrels at selfe-breath. Imagin'd wroth
Holds in his bloud such swolne and hot discourse,
That twixt his mentall and his actiue parts,
Kingdom'd *Achilles* in commotion rages,
And batters gainst it selfe; what should I say?
He is so plaguy proud, that the death tokens of it,
Cry no recouery.
Ag. Let *Aiax* goe to him.
Deare Lord, goe you and greete him in his Tent;
'Tis said he holds you well, and will be led
At your request a little from himselfe.
Vlis. O *Agamemnon*, let it not be so.
Weele consecrate the steps that *Aiax* makes,
When they goe from *Achilles*; shall the proud Lord,
That bastes his arrogance with his owne seame,
And neuer suffers matter of the world,
Enter his thoughts: saue such as doe reuolue
Aud ruminate himselfe. Shall he be worshipt,
Of that we hold an Idoll, more then hee?
No, this thrice worthy and right valiant Lord,
Must not so staule his Palme, nobly acquir'd,
Nor by my will assubiugate his merit,
As amply titled as *Achilles* is: by going to *Achilles*,
That were to enlard his fat already, pride,
And adde more Coles to Cancer, when he burnes
With entertaining great *Hiperion.*
This L. goe to him? *Iupiter* forbid,
And say in thunder, *Achilles* goe to him.
Nest. O this is well, he rubs the veine of him.
Dio. And how his silence drinkes vp this applause.
Aia. If I goe to him, with my armed fist, Ile pash him ore the face.
Ag. O no, you shall not goe.
Aia. And a be proud with me, ile phese his pride: let me goe to him.
Vlis. Not for the worth that hangs vpon our quarrel.
Aia. A paultry insolent fellow.
Nest. How he describes himselfe.
Aia. Can he not be sociable?
Vlis. The Rauen chides blacknesse.
Aia. Ile let his humours bloud.
Ag. He will be the Physitian that should be the patient.
Aia. And all men were a my minde.
Vlis. Wit would be out of fashion.
Aia. A should not beare it so, a should eate Swords first: shall pride carry it?
Nest. And 'twould, you'ld carry halfe.
Vlis. A would haue ten shares.
Aia. I will knede him, Ile make him supple, hee's not yet through warme.
Nest. Force him with praises, poure in, poure in: his ambition is dry.
Vlis. My L. you feede too much on this dislike.
Nest Our noble Generall, doe not doe so.
Diom. You must prepare to fight without *Achilles.*
Vlis. Why, 'tis this naming of him doth him harme.
Here is a man, but 'tis before his face,
I will be silent.
Nest. Wherefore should you so?

He

He is not emulous, as *Achilles* is.

Vlis. 'Know the whole world, he is as valiant.

Aia. A horson dog, that shal palter thus with vs, would he were a *Troian.*

Nest. What a vice were it in *Aiax* now———

Vlis. If he were proud.

Dio. Or couetous of praise.

Vlis. I, or surley borne.

Dio. Or strange, or selfe affected.

Vl. Thank the heauens L. thou art of sweet composure;
Praise him that got thee, she that gaue thee sucke:
Fame be thy Tutor, and thy parts of nature
Thrice fam'd beyond, beyond all erudition;
But he that disciplin'd thy armes to fight,
Let *Mars* deuide Eternity in twaine,
And giue him halfe, and for thy vigour,
Bull-bearing *Milo*: his addition yeelde
To sinnowie *Aiax*: I will not praise thy wisdome,
Which like a bourne, a pale, a shore confines
Thy spacious and dilated parts; here's *Nestor*
Instructed by the Antiquary times:
He must, he is, he cannot but be wise.
But pardon Father *Nestor*, were your dayes
As greene as *Aiax*, and your braine so temper'd,
You should not haue the eminence of him,
But be as *Aiax*.

Aia. Shall I call you Father?

Vlis. I my good Sonne.

Dio. Be rul'd by him Lord *Aiax*.

Vlis. There is no tarrying here, the Hart *Achilles*
Keepes thicket: please it our Generall,
To call together all his state of warre,
Fresh Kings are come to *Troy*; to morrow
We must with all our maine of power stand fast:
And here's a Lord, come Knights from East to West,
And cull their flowre, *Aiax* shall cope the best.

Ag. Goe we to Counsaile, let *Achilles* sleepe;
Light Botes may saile swift, though greater bulkes draw deepe. *Exeunt.* *Musicke sounds within.*

Enter Pandarus and a Seruant.

Pan. Friend, you, pray you a word: Doe not you follow the yong Lord *Paris*?

Ser. I sir, when he goes before me.

Pan. You depend vpon him I meane?

Ser. Sir, I doe depend vpon the Lord.

Pan. You depend vpon a noble Gentleman: I must needes praise him.

Ser. The Lord be praised.

Pa. You know me, doe you not?

Ser. Faith sir, superficially.

Pa. Friend know me better, I am the Lord *Pandarus*.

Ser. I hope I shall know your honour better.

Pa. I doe desire it.

Ser. You are in the state of Grace?

Pa. Grace, not so friend, honor and Lordship are my title: What Musique is this?

Ser. I doe but partly know sir: it is Musicke in parts.

Pa. Know you the Musitians.

Ser. Wholly sir.

Pa. Who play they to?

Ser. To the hearers sir.

Pa. At whose pleasure friend?

Ser. At mine sir, and theirs that loue Musicke.

Pa. Command, I meane friend.

Ser. Who shall I command sir?

Pa. Friend, we vnderstand not one another: I am too courtly, and thou art too cunning. At whose request doe these men play?

Ser. That's too't indeede sir: marry sir, at the request of *Paris* my L. who's there in person; with him the mortall *Venus*, the heart bloud of beauty, loues inuisible soule.

Pa. Who? my Cosin *Cressida*.

Ser. No sir, *Helen*, could you not finde out that by her attributes?

Pa. It should seeme fellow, that thou hast not seen the Lady *Cressida*. I come to speake with *Paris* from the Prince *Troylus*: I will make a complementall assault vpon him, for my businesse seethes.

Ser. Sodden businesse, there's a stewed phrase indeede.

Enter Paris and Helena.

Pan. Faire be to you my Lord, and to all this faire company: faire desires in all faire measure fairely guide them, especially to you faire Queene, faire thoughts be your faire pillow.

Hel. Deere L. you are full of faire words.

Pan. You speake your faire pleasure sweete Queene: faire Prince, here is good broken Musicke.

Par. You haue broke it cozen: and by my life you shall make it whole againe, you shall peece it out with a peece of your performance. *Nel*, he is full of harmony.

Pan. Truely Lady no.

Hel. O sir.

Pan. Rude in sooth, in good sooth very rude.

Paris. Well said my Lord: well, you say so in fits.

Pan. I haue businesse to my Lord, deere Queene: my Lord will you vouchsafe me a word.

Hel. Nay, this shall not hedge vs out, weele heare you sing certainely.

Pan. Well sweete Queene you are pleasant with me, but, marry thus my Lord, my deere Lord, and most esteemed friend your brother *Troylus*.

Hel. My Lord *Pandarus*, hony sweete Lord.

Pan. Go too sweete Queene, goe to.
Commends himselfe most affectionately to you.

Hel. You shall not bob vs out of our melody:
If you doe, our melancholly vpon your head.

Pan. Sweete Queene, sweete Queene, that's a sweete Queene I faith———

Hel. And to make a sweet Lady sad, is a sower offence.

Pan. Nay, that shall not serue your turne, that shall it not in truth la. Nay, I care not for such words, no, no. And my Lord he desires you, that if the King call for him at Supper, you will make his excuse.

Hel. My Lord *Pandarus*?

Pan. What saies my sweete Queene, my very, very sweete Queene?

Par. What exploit's in hand, where sups he to night?

Hel. Nay but my Lord?

Pan. What saies my sweete Queene? my cozen will fall out with you.

Hel. You must not know where he sups.

Par. With my disposer *Cressida*.

Pan. No, no; no such matter, you are wide, come your disposer is sicke.

Par. Well, Ile make excuse.

Pan. I good my Lord: why should you say *Cressida*? no, your poore disposer's sicke.

Par. I spie.

Pan. You

Pan. You ſpie, what doe you ſpie : come, giue me an Inſtrument now ſweete Queene.

Hel. Why this is kindely done ?

Pan. My Neece is horrible in loue with a thing you haue ſweete Queene.

Hel. She ſhall haue it my Lord, if it be not my Lord *Paris.*

Pand. Hee? no, ſheele none of him, they two are twaine.

Hel. Falling in after falling out, may make them three.

Pan. Come, come, Ile heare no more of this, Ile ſing you a ſong now.

Hel. I, I, prethee now: by my troth ſweet Lord thou haſt a fine fore-head.

Pan. I you may, you may.

Hel. Let thy ſong be loue : this loue will vndoe vs al. Oh *Cupid, Cupid, Cupid.*

Pan. Loue? I that it ſhall yfaith.

Par. I, good now loue, loue, no thing but loue.

Pan. In good troth it begins ſo.

Loue, loue, nothing but loue, ſtill more :
For O loues Bow,
Shootes Bucke and Doe :
The Shaft confounds not that it wounds,
But tickles ſtill the ſore :
Theſe Louers cry, oh ho they dye ;
Yet that which ſeemes the wound to kill,
Doth turne oh ho, to ha ha he :
So dying loue liues ſtill,
O ho a while, but ha ha ha ;
O ho grones out for ha ha ha---hey ho.

Hel. In loue yfaith to the very tip of the noſe.

Par. He eates nothing but doues loue, and that breeds hot bloud, and hot bloud begets hot thoughts, and hot thoughts beget hot deedes, and hot deedes is loue.

Pan. Is this the generation of loue? Hot bloud, hot thoughts, and hot deedes, why they are Vipers, is Loue a generation of Vipers?
Sweete Lord whoſe a field to day?

Par. Hector, Deiphœbus, Helenus, Anthenor, and all the gallantry of *Troy.* I would faine haue arm'd to day, but my *Nell* would not haue it ſo.
How chance my brother *Troylus* went not?

Hel. He hangs the lippe at ſomething; you know all Lord *Pandarus?*

Pan. Not I hony ſweete Queene : I long to heare how they ſped to day :
Youle remember your brothers excuſe?

Par. To a hayre.

Pan. Farewell ſweete Queene.

Hel. Commend me to your Neece.

Pan. I will ſweete Queene. *Sound a retreat.*

Par. They're come from fielde : let vs to *Priams* Hall
To greete the Warriers. Sweet *Hellen,* I muſt woe you,
To helpe vnarme our *Hector* : his ſtubborne Buckles,
With theſe your white enchanting fingers toucht,
Shall more obey then to the edge of Steele,
Or force of Greekiſh ſinewes : you ſhall doe more
Then all the Iland Kings, diſarme great *Hector.*

Hel. 'Twill make vs proud to be his ſeruant *Paris* :
Yea what he ſhall receiue of vs in duetie,
Giues vs more palme in beautie then we haue :
Yea ouerſhines our ſelfe.
Sweete aboue thought I loue thee. *Exeunt.*

Enter Pandarus and Troylus Man.

Pan. How now, where's thy Maiſter, at my Couzen *Creſsidas?*

Man. No ſir, he ſtayes for you to conduct him thither.

Enter Troylus.

Pan. O here he comes: How now, how now?

Troy. Sirra walke off.

Pan. Haue you ſeene my Couſin?

Troy. No *Pandarus* : I ſtalke about her doore
Like a ſtrange ſoule vpon the Stigian bankes
Staying for waftage. O be thou my *Charon,*
And giue me ſwift tranſportance to thoſe fields,
Where I may wallow in the Lilly beds
Propos'd for the deſeruer. O gentle *Pandarus,*
From *Cupids* ſhoulder plucke his painted wings,
And flye with me to *Creſsid.*

Pan. Walke here ith' Orchard, Ile bring her ſtraight. *Exit Pandarus.*

Troy. I am giddy; expectation whirles me round,
Th'imaginary reliſh is ſo ſweete,
That it inchants my ſence : what will it be
When that the watry pallats taſte indeede
Loues thrice reputed Nectar? Death I feare me
Sounding diſtruction, or ſome ioy too fine,
Too ſubtile, potent, and too ſharpe in ſweetneſſe,
For the capacitie of my ruder powers;
I feare it much, and I doe feare beſides,
That I ſhall looſe diſtinction in my ioyes,
As doth a battaile, when they charge on heapes
The enemy flying. *Enter Pandarus.*

Pan. Shee's making her ready, ſheele come ſtraight; you muſt be witty now, ſhe does ſo bluſh, & fetches her winde ſo ſhort, as if ſhe were fraid with a ſprite : Ile fetch her; it is the prettieſt villaine, ſhe fetches her breath ſo ſhort as a newtane Sparrow. *Exit Pand.*

Troy. Euen ſuch a paſſion doth imbrace my boſome:
My heart beates thicker then a feauorous pulſe,
And all my powers doe their beſtowing looſe,
Like vaſſalage at vnawares encountring
The eye of Maieſtie.

Enter Pandarus and Creſsida.

Pan. Come, come, what neede you bluſh?
Shames a babie; here ſhe is now, ſweare the oathes now to her, that you haue ſworne to me. What are you gone againe, you muſt be watcht ere you be made tame, muſt you? come your wayes, come your wayes, and you draw backward weele put you i'th fils : why doe you not ſpeak to her? Come draw this curtaine, & let's ſee your picture. Alaſſe the day, how loath you are to offend day light? and 'twere darke you'ld cloſe ſooner : So, ſo, rub on, and kiſſe the miſtreſſe; how now, a kiſſe in fee-farme? build there Carpenter, the ayre is ſweete. Nay, you ſhall fight your hearts out ere I part you. The Faulcon, as the Tercell, for all the Ducks ith Riuer : go too, go too.

Troy. You haue bereft me of all words Lady.

Pan. Words pay no debts; giue her deedes : but ſheele bereaue you 'oth' deeds too, if ſhee call your actiuity in queſtion : what billing againe? here's in witneſſe whereof the Parties interchangeably. Come in, come in, Ile go get a fire?

Creſ. Will you walke in my Lord?

Troy. O *Creſsida,* how often haue I wiſht me thus?

Creſ. Wiſht my Lord? the gods grant? O my Lord.

Troy. What ſhould they grant? what makes this pretty abruption: what too curious dreg eſpies my ſweete Lady in the fountaine of our loue?

Creſ. More

Cres. More dregs then water, if my teares haue eyes.

Troy. Feares make diuels of Cherubins, they neuer see truely.

Cres. Blinde feare, that seeing reason leads, findes safe footing, then blinde reason, stumbling without feare : to feare the worst, oft cures the worse.

Troy. Oh let my Lady apprehend no feare,
In all *Cupids* Pageant there is presented no monster.

Cres. Not nothing monstrons neither?

Troy. Nothing but our vndertakings, when we vowe to weepe seas, liue in fire, eate rockes, tame Tygers; thinking it harder for our Mistresse to deuise imposition inough, then for vs to vndergoe any difficultie imposed. This is the monstruositie in loue Lady, that the will is infinite, and the execution confin'd; that the desire is boundlesse, and the act a slaue to limit.

Cres. They say all Louers sweare more performance then they are able, and yet reserue an ability that they neuer performe: vowing more then the perfection of ten; and discharging lesse then the tenth part of one. They that haue the voyce of Lyons, and the act of Hares : are they not Monsters?

Troy. Are there such? such are not we : Praise vs as we are tasted, allow vs as we proue : our head shall goe bare till merit crowne it: no perfection in reuersion shall haue a praise in present: wee will not name desert before his birth, and being borne his addition shall be humble : few words to faire faith. *Troylus* shall be such to *Cressid*, as what enuie can say worst, shall be a mocke for his truth; and what truth can speake truest, not truer then *Troylus*.

Cres. Will you walke in my Lord?

Enter Pandarus.

Pan. What blushing still? haue you not done talking yet?

Cres. Well Vnckle, what folly I commit, I dedicate to you.

Pan. I thanke you for that : if my Lord get a Boy of you, youle giue him me: be true to my Lord, if he flinch, chide me for it.

Tro. You know now your hostages: your Vnckles word and my firme faith.

Pan. Nay, Ile giue my word for her too : our kindred though they be long ere they are wooed, they are constant being wonne : they are Burres I can tell you, they'le sticke where they are throwne.

Cres. Boldnesse comes to mee now, and brings mee heart : Prince *Troylus*, I haue lou'd you night and day, for many weary moneths.

Troy. Why was my *Cressid* then so hard to win?

Cres. Hard to seeme won : but I was won my Lord
With the first glance; that euer pardon me,
If I confesse much you will play the tyrant;
I loue you now, but not till now so much
But I might maister it; infaith I lye :
My thoughts were like vnbrideled children grow
Too head-strong for their mother : see we fooles,
Why haue I blab'd : who shall be true to vs
When we are so vnsecret to our selues?
But though I lou'd you well, I woed you not,
And yet good faith I wisht my selfe a man;
Or that we women had mens priuiledge
Of speaking first. Sweet, bid me hold my tongue,
For in this rapture I shall surely speake
The thing I shall repent : see, see, your silence
Comming in dumbnesse, from my weakenesse drawes
My soule of counsell from me. Stop my mouth.

Troy. And shall, albeit sweete Musicke issues thence.

Pan. Pretty yfaith.

Cres. My Lord, I doe beseech you pardon me,
'Twas not my purpose thus to beg a kisse :
I am asham'd; O Heauens, what haue I done!
For this time will I take my leaue my Lord.

Troy. Your leaue sweete *Cressid*?

Pan. Leaue : and you take leaue till to morrow morning.

Cres. Pray you content you.

Troy. What offends you Lady?

Cres. Sir, mine owne company.

Troy. You cannot shun your selfe.

Cres. Let me goe and try :
I, haue a kinde of selfe recides with you :
But an vnkinde selfe, that it selfe will leaue,
To be anothers foole. Where is my wit?
I would be gone : I speake I know not what.

Troy. Well know they what they speake, that speakes so wisely.

Cre. Perchance my Lord, I shew more craft then loue,
And fell so roundly to a large confession,
To Angle for your thoughts: but you are wise,
Or else you loue not : for to be wise and loue,
Exceedes mans might, that dwels with gods aboue.

Troy. O that I thought it could be in a woman :
As if it can, I will presume in you,
To feede for aye her lampe and flames of loue.
To keepe her constancie in plight and youth,
Out-liuing beauties outward, with a minde
That doth renew swifter then blood decaies :
Or that perswasion could but thus conuince me,
That my integritie and truth to you,
Might be affronted with the match and waight
Of such a winnowed puriritie in loue :
How were I then vp-lifted! but alas,
I am as true, as truths simplicitie,
And simpler then the infancie of truth.

Cr s. In that Ile warre with you.

Troy. O vertuous fight,
When right with right wars who shall be most right :
True swaines in loue, shall in the world to come
Approue their truths by *Troylus*, when their rimes,
Full of protest, of oath and big compare;
Wants similes, truth tir'd with iteration,
As true as steele, as plantage to the Moone :
As Sunne to day : as Turtle to her mate :
As Iron to Adamant : as Earth to th'Center :
Yet after all comparisons of truth,
(As truths authenticke author to be cited)
As true as *Troylus*, shall crowne vp the Verse,
And sanctifie the numbers.

Cres. Prophet may you be :
If I be false, or swerue a haire from truth,
When time is old and hath forgot it selfe :
When water drops haue worne the Stones of *Troy*;
And blinde obliuion swallow'd Cities vp;
And mightie States characterlesse are grated
To dustie nothing; yet let memory,
From false to false, among false Maids in loue, I
Vpbrald my falsehood, when they'aue said as false,
As Aire, as Water, as Winde, as sandie earth;
As Foxe to Lambe; as Wolfe to Heifers Calfe;
Pard to the Hinde, or Stepdame to her Sonne;
Yea, let them say, to sticke the heart of falsehood,

As

As falſe as *Creſſid.*

Pand. Go too, a bargaine made: ſeale it, ſeale it, Ile be the witneſſe here I hold your hand: here my Couſins, if euer you proue falſe one to another, ſince I haue taken ſuch paines to bring you together, let all pittifull goers betweene be cal'd to the worlds end after my name: call them all Panders; let all conſtant men be *Troyluſſes*, all falſe women *Creſſids*, and all brokers betweene, Panders: ſay, Amen.

Troy. Amen.

Creſ. Amen.

Pan. Amen.

Whereupon I will ſhew you a Chamber, which bed, becauſe it ſhall not ſpeake of your prettie encounters, preſſe it to death: away.

And *Cupid* grant all tong-tide Maidens heere,
Bed, Chamber, and Pander, to prouide this geere. *Exeunt.*

Enter Vlyſſes, Diomedes, Neſtor, Agamemnon, Menelaus and Chalcas. Flouriſh.

Cal. Now Princes for the ſeruice I haue done you,
Th'aduantage of the time promps me aloud,
To call for recompence: appeare it to your minde,
That through the ſight I beare in things to loue,
I haue abandon'd Troy, left my poſſeſſion,
Incur'd a Traitors name, expoſ'd my ſelfe,
From certaine and poſſeſt conueniences,
To doubtfull fortunes, ſequeſtring from me all
That time, acquaintance, cuſtome and condition,
Made tame, and moſt familiar to my nature:
And here to doe you ſeruice am become,
As new into the world, ſtrange, vnacquainted.
I doe beſeech you, as in way of taſte,
To giue me now a little benefit:
Out of thoſe many regiſtred in promiſe,
Which you ſay, liue to come in my behalfe.

Agam. What would'ſt thou of vs Troian? make demand?

Cal. You haue a Troian priſoner, cal'd *Anthenor*,
Yeſterday tooke: Troy holds him very deere.
Oft haue you (often haue you, thankes therefore)
Deſir'd my *Creſſid* in right great exchange.
Whom Troy hath ſtill deni'd: but this *Anthenor*,
I know is ſuch a wreſt in their affaires;
That their negotiations all muſt ſlacke,
Wanting his mannage: and they will almoſt,
Giue vs a Prince of blood, a Sonne of *Priam*,
In change of him. Let him be ſent great Princes,
And he ſhall buy my Daughter: and her preſence,
Shall quite ſtrike off all ſeruice I haue done,
In moſt accepted paine.

Aga. Let *Diomedes* beare him,
And bring vs *Creſſid* hither: *Calcas* ſhall haue
What he requeſts of vs: good *Diomed*
Furniſh you fairely for this enterchange;
Withall bring word, if *Hector* will to morrow
Be anſwer'd in his challenge. *Aiax* is ready.

Dio. This ſhall I vndertake, and 'tis a burthen
Which I am proud to beare. *Exit.*

Enter Achilles *and* Patroclus *in their Tent.*

Vliſ. *Achilles* ſtands i'th entrance of his Tent;
Pleaſe it our Generall to paſſe ſtrangely by him,
As if he were forgot: and Princes all,
Lay negligent and looſe regard vpon him;
I will come laſt, 'tis like heele queſtion me,
Why ſuch vnplauſiue eyes are bent? why turn'd on him?
If ſo, I haue deriſion medicinable,
To vſe betweene your ſtrangeneſſe and his pride,
Which his owne will ſhall haue deſire to drinke;
It may doe good, pride hath no other glaſſe
To ſhow it ſelfe, but pride: for ſupple knees,
Feede arrogance, and are the proud mans fees.

Agam. Weele execute your purpoſe, and put on
A forme of ſtrangeneſſe as we paſſe along,
So doe each Lord, and either greete him not,
Or elſe diſdainfully, which ſhall ſhake him more,
Then if not lookt on. I will lead the way.

Achil. What comes the Generall to ſpeake with me?
You know my minde, Ile fight no more 'gainſt Troy.

Aga. What ſaies *Achilles*, would he ought with vs?

Neſ. Would you my Lord ought with the Generall?

Achil. No.

Neſ. Nothing my Lord.

Aga. The better.

Achil. Good day, good day.

Men. How doe you? how doe you?

Achi. What, do's the Cuckold ſcorne me?

Aiax. How now *Patroclus*?

Achil. Good morrow *Aiax*?

Aiax. Ha.

Achil. Good morrow.

Aiax. I, and good next day too. *Exeunt.*

Achil. What meane theſe fellowes? know they not *Achilles*?

Patr. They paſſe by ſtrangely: they were vſ'd to bend
To ſend their ſmiles before them to *Achilles*:
To come as humbly as they vs'd to creepe to holy Altars.

Achil. What am I poore of late?
'Tis certaine, greatneſſe once falne out with fortune,
Muſt fall out with men too: what the declin'd is,
He ſhall as ſoone reade in the eyes of others,
As feele in his owne fall: for men like butter-flies,
Shew not their mealie wings, but to the Summer:
And not a man for being ſimply man,
Hath any honour; but honour'd for thoſe honours
That are without him; as place, riches, and fauour,
Prizes of accident, as oft as merit:
Which when they fall, as being ſlippery ſtanders;
The loue that leand on them as ſlippery too,
Doth one plucke downe another, and together
Dye in the fall. But 'tis not ſo with me;
Fortune and I are friends, I doe enioy
At ample point, all that I did poſſeſſe,
Saue theſe mens lookes: who do me thinkes finde out
Something not worth in me ſuch rich beholding,
As they haue often giuen. Here is *Vliſſes*,
Ile interrupt his reading: how now *Vliſſes*?

Vliſ. Now great *Thetis* Sonne.

Achil. What are you reading?

Vliſ. A ſtrange fellow here
Writes me, that man, how dearely euer parted,
How much in hauing, or without, or in,
Cannot make boaſt to haue that which he hath;
Nor feeles not what he owes, but by reflection:
As when his vertues ſhining vpon others,
Heate them, and they retort that heate againe
To the firſt giuer.

Achil. This is not ſtrange *Vliſſes*:
The beautie that is borne here in the face,
The bearer knowes not, but commends it ſelfe,
Not going from it ſelfe: but eye to eye oppos'd,

Salutes

Salutes each other with each others forme.
For speculation turnes not to it selfe,
Till it hath trauail'd, and is married there
Where it may see it selfe: this is not strange at all.
Vlis. I doe not straine it at the position,
It is familiar; but at the Authors drift,
Who in his circumstance, expresly proues
That no may is the Lord of any thing,
(Though in and of him there is much consisting,)
Till he communicate his parts to others:
Nor doth he of himselfe know them for ought,
Till he behold them formed in th'applause,
Where they are extended: who like an arch reuerb'rate
The voyce againe; or like a gate of steele,
Fronting the Sunne, receiues and renders backe
His figure, and his heate. I was much rapt in this,
And apprehended here immediately:
The vnknowne *Aiax*;
Heauens what a man is there? a very Horse, (are
That has he knowes not what. Nature, what things there
Most abiect in regard, and deare in vse.
What things againe most deere in the esteeme,
And poore in worth: now shall we see to morrow,
An act that very chance doth throw vpon him?
Aiax renown'd? O heauens, what some men doe,
While some men leaue to doe!
How some men creepe in skittish fortunes hall,
Whiles others play the Ideots in her eyes:
How one man eates into anothers pride,
While pride is feasting in his wantonnesse
To see these Grecian Lords; why, euen already,
They clap the lubber *Aiax* on the shoulder,
As if his foote were on braue *Hectors* brest,
And great *Troy* shrinking.
Achil. I doe beleeue it:
For they past by me, as mysers doe by beggars,
Neither gaue to me good word, nor looke:
What are my deedes forgot?
Vlis. Time hath (my Lord) a wallet at his backe,
Wherein he puts almes for obliuion:
A great siz'd monster of ingratitudes:
Those scraps are good deedes past,
Which are deuour'd as fast as they are made,
Forgot as soone as done: perseuerance, deere my Lord,
Keepes honor bright, to haue done, is to hang
Quite out of fashion, like a rustie male,
In monumentall mockrie: take the instant way,
For honour trauels in a straight so narrow,
Where one but goes a breast, keepe then the path:
For emulation hath a thousand Sonnes,
That one by one pursue; if you giue way,
Or hedge aside from the direct forth right;
Like to an entred Tyde, they all rush by,
And leaue you hindmost:
Or like a gallant Horse falne in first ranke,
Lye there for pauement to the abiect, neere
Ore-run and trampled on: then what they doe in present,
Though lesse then yours in past, must ore-top yours:
For time is like a fashionable Hoste,
That slightly shakes his parting Guest by th'hand;
And with his armes out-stretcht, as he would flye,
Graspes in the commer: the welcome euer smiles,
And farewels goes out sighing: O let not vertue seeke
Remuneration for the thing it was: for beautie, wit,
High birth, vigor of bone, desert in seruice,
Loue, friendship, charity, are subiects all
To enuious and calumniating time:
One touch of nature makes the whole world kin:
That all with one consent praise new borne gaudes,
Though they are made and moulded of things past,
And goe to dust, that is a little guilt,
More laud then guilt oredusted.
The present eye praises the pres nt obiect:
Then maruell not thou great and compleat man,
That all the Greekes begin to worship *Aiax*;
Since things in motion begin to catch the eye,
Then what not stirs: the cry went out on thee,
And still it might, and yet it may againe,
If thou would'st not entombe thy selfe aliue,
And case thy reputation in thy Tent;
Whose glorious deedes, but in these fields of late,
Made emulous missions 'mongst the gods themselues,
And draue great *Mars* to faction.
Achil. Of this my priuacie,
I haue strong reasons.
Vlis. But 'gainst your priuacie
The reasons are more potent and heroycall:
'Tis knowne *Achilles*, that you are in loue
With one of *Priams* daughters.
Achil. Ha? knowne?
Vlis. Is that a wonder?
The prouidence that's in a watchfull State,
Knowes almost euery graine of Plutoes gold;
Findes bottome in th'vncomprehensiue deepes;
Keepes place with thought; and almost like the gods,
Doe thoughts vnuaile in their dumbe cradles:
There is a mysterie (with whom relation
Durst neuer meddle) in the soule of State;
Which hath an operation more diuine,
Then breath or pen can giue expressure to:
All the commerse that you haue had with Troy,
As perfectly is ours, as yours, my Lord.
And better would it fit *Achilles* much,
To throw downe *Hector* then *Polixena*.
But it must grieue yong *Pirhus* now at home,
When fame shall in her Iland sound her trumpe;
And all the Greekish Girles shall tripping sing,
Great *Hectors* sister did *Achilles* winne;
But our great *Aiax* brauely beate downe him.
Farewell my Lord: I as your louer speake;
The foole slides ore the Ice that you should breake.
Patr. To this effect *Achilles* haue I mou'd you;
A woman impudent and mannish growne,
Is not more loth'd, then an effeminate man,
In time of action: I stand condemn'd for this;
They thinke my little stomacke to the warre,
And your great loue to me, restraines you thus:
Sweete, rouse your selfe; and the weake wanton *Cupid*
Shall from your necke vnloose his amorous fould,
And like a dew drop from the Lyons mane,
Be shooke to ayrie ayre.
Achil. Shall *Aiax* fight with *Hector*?
Patr. I, and perhaps receiue much honor by him.
Achil. I see my reputation is at stake,
My fame is shrowdly gored.
Patr. O then beware:
Those wounds heale ill, that men doe giue themselues:
Omission to doe what is necessary,
Seales a commission to a blanke of danger,
And danger like an ague subtly taints
Euen then when we sit idely in the sunne.
Achil. Goe call *Thersites* hither sweet *Patroclus*,

¶ ¶ Ile

Ile send the foole to *Aiax*, and desire him
T'inuite the Troian Lords after the Combat
To see vs here vnarm'd: I haue a womans longing,
An appetite that I am sicke withall,
To see great *Hector* in his weedes of peace; *Enter Thersi.*
To talke with him, and to behold his visage,
Euen to my full of view. A labour sau'd.

Ther. A wonder.

Achil. What?

Ther. *Aiax* goes vp and downe the field, asking for himselfe.

Achil. How so?

Ther. Hee must fight singly to morrow with *Hector*, and is so prophetically proud of an heroicall cudgelling, that he raues in saying nothing.

Achil. How can that be?

Ther. Why he stalkes vp and downe like a Peacock, a stride and a stand: ruminates like an hostesse, that hath no Arithmatique but her braine to set downe her reckoning: bites his lip with a politique regard, as who should say, there were wit in his head and twoo'd out; and so there is: but it lyes as coldly in him, as fire in a flint, which will not shew without knocking. The mans vndone for euer; for if *Hector* breake not his necke i'th'combat, heele break't himselfe in vaine-glory. He knowes not mee: I said, good morrow *Aiax*; And he replyes, thankes *Agamemnon*. What thinke you of this man, that takes me for the Generall? Hee's growne a very land-fish, languagelesse, a monster: a plague of opinion, a man may weare it on both sides like a leather Ierkin.

Achil. Thou must be my Ambassador to him *Thersites*.

Ther. Who, I: why, heele answer no body: he professes notanswering; speaking is for beggers: he weares his tongue in's armes: I will put on his presence; let *Patroclus* make his demands to me, you shall see the Pageant of *Aiax*.

Achil. To him *Patroclus*; tell him, I humbly desire the valiant *Aiax*, to inuite the most valorous *Hector*, to come vnarm'd to my Tent, and to procure safe conduct for his person, of the magnanimious and most illustrious, sixe or seauen times honour'd Captaine, Generall of the Grecian Armie *Agamemnon*, &c. doe this.

Patro. *Ioue* blesse great *Aiax*.

Ther. Hum.

Patr. I come from the worthy *Achilles*.

Ther. Ha?

Patr. Who most humbly desires you to inuite *Hector* to his Tent.

Ther. Hum.

Patr. And to procure safe conduct from *Agamemnon*.

Ther. *Agamemnon*?

Patr. I my Lord.

Ther. Ha?

Patr. What say you too't.

Ther. God buy you with all my heart.

Patr. Your answer sir.

Ther. If to morrow be a faire day, by eleuen a clocke it will goe one way or other; howsoeuer, he shall pay for me ere he has me.

Patr. Your answer sir.

Ther. Fare you well withall my heart.

Achil. Why, but he is not in this tune, is he?

Ther. No, but he's out a tune thus: what musicke will be in him when *Hector* has knockt out his braines, I know not: but I am sure none, vnlesse the Fidler *Apollo* get his sinewes to make catlings on.

Achil. Come, thou shalt beare a Letter to him straight.

Ther. Let me carry another to his Horse; for that's the more capable creature.

Achil. My minde is troubled like a Fountaine stir'd,
And I my selfe see not the bottome of it.

Ther. Would the Fountaine of your minde were cleere againe, that I might water an Asse at it: I had rather be a Ticke in a Sheepe, then such a valiant ignorance.

Enter at one doore Æneas with a Torch, at another Paris, Diephœbus, Anthenor, Diomed the Grecian, with Torches.

Par. See hoa, who is that there?

Dieph. It is the Lord *Æneas*.

Æne. Is the Prince there in person?
Had I so good occasion to lye long
As you Prince *Paris*, nothing but heauenly businesse,
Should rob my bed-mate of my company.

Diom. That's my minde too: good morrow Lord *Æneas*.

Par. A valiant Greeke *Æneas*, take his hand,
Witnesse the processe of your speech within;
You told how *Diomed* in a whole weeke by dayes
Did haunt you in the Field.

Æne. Health to you valiant sir,
During all question of the gentle truce:
But when I meete you arm'd, as blacke defiance,
As heart can thinke, or courage execute.

Diom. The one and other *Diomed* embraces,
Our bloods are now in calme; and so long health:
But when contention, and occasion meetes,
By *Ioue*, Ile play the hunter for thy life,
With all my force, pursuite and pollicy.

Æne. And thou shalt hunt a Lyon that will flye
With his face backward, in humaine gentlenesse:
Welcome to Troy; now by *Anchises* life,
Welcome indeede: by *Venus* hand I sweare,
No man aliue can loue in such a sort,
The thing he meanes to kill, more excellently.

Diom. We simpathize. *Ioue* let *Æneas* liue
(If to my sword his fate be not the glory)
A thousand compleate courses of the Sunne,
But in mine emulous honor let him dye:
With euery ioynt a wound, and that to morrow.

Æne. We know each other well.

Dio. We doe, and long to know each other worse.

Par. This is the most, despightful'st gentle greeting;
The noblest hatefull loue, that ere I heard of.
What businesse Lord so early?

Æne. I was sent for to the King; but why, I know not.

Par. His purpose meets you; it was to bring this Greek
To *Calcha's* house; and there to render him,
For the enfreed *Anthenor*, the faire *Cressid*:
Lers haue your company; or if you please,
Haste there before vs. I constantly doe thinke
(Or rather call my thought a certaine knowledge)
My brother *Troylus* lodges there to night.
Rouse him, and giue him note of our approach,
With the whole quality whereof, I feare
We shall be much vnwelcome.

Æne. That I assure you:
Troylus had rather Troy were borne to Greece,
Then *Cressid* borne from Troy.

Par. There

Par. There is no helpe:
The bitter disposition of the time will haue it so.
On Lord, weele follow you.
Æne. Good morrow all. *Exit Æneas*
Par. And tell me noble *Diomed*; faith tell me true,
Euen in the soule of sound good fellow ship,
Who in your thoughts merits faire *Helen* most?
My selfe, or *Menelaus*?
Diom. Both alike.
He merits well to haue her, that doth seeke her,
Not making any scruple of her soylure,
With such a hell of paine, and world of charge.
And you as well to keepe her, that defend her,
Not pallating the taste of her dishonour,
With such a costly losse of wealth and friends:
He like a puling Cuckold, would drinke vp
The lees and dregs of a flat tamed peece:
You like a letcher, out of whorish loynes,
Are pleas'd to breede out your inheritors:
Both merits poyz'd, each weighs no lesse nor more,
But he as he, which heauier for a whore.
Par. You are too bitter to your country-woman.
Dio. Shee's bitter to her countrey: heare me *Paris*,
For euery false drop in her baudy veines,
A Grecians life hath sunke: for euery scruple
Of her contaminated carrion weight,
A Troian hath beene slaine. Since she could speake,
She hath not giuen so many good words breath,
As for her, Greekes and Troians suffred death.
Par. Faire *Diomed*, you doe as chapmen doe,
Dispraise the thing that you desire to buy:
But we in silence hold this vertue well;
Weele not commend, what we intend to sell.
Here lyes our way. *Exeunt.*

Enter Troylus and Cressida.

Troy. Deere trouble not your selfe: the morne is cold.
Cres. Then sweet my Lord, Ile call mine Vnckle down;
He shall vnbolt the Gates.
Troy. Trouble him not:
To bed, to bed: sleepe kill those pritty eyes,
And giue as soft attachment to thy sences,
As Infants empty of all thought.
Cres. Good morrow then.
Troy. I prithee now to bed.
Cres. Are you a weary of me?
Troy. O *Cressida*! but that the busie day
Wak't by the Larke, hath rouz'd the ribauld Crowes,
And dreaming night will hide our eyes no longer:
I would not from thee.
Cres. Night hath beene too briefe.
Troy. Beshrew the witch! with venemous wights she (stayes,
As hidiously as hell; but flies the graspes of loue,
With wings more momentary, swift then thought:
You will catch cold, and curse me.
Cres. Prithee tarry, you men will neuer tarry;
O foolish *Cressid*, I might haue still held off,
And then you would haue tarried. Harke, ther's one vp?
Pand. within. What's all the doores open here?
Troy. It is your Vnckle. *Enter Pandarus.*
Cres. A pestilence on him: now will he be mocking:
I shall haue such a life.
Pan. How now, how now? how goe maiden-heads?
Heare you Maide: wher's my cozin *Cressid*?
Cres. Go hang your self, you naughty mocking Vnckle:
You bring me to doo----and then you floute me too.
Pan. To do what? to do what? let her say what:
What haue I brought you to doe?
Cres. Come, come, beshrew your heart: youle nere be good, nor suffer others.
Pan. Ha, ha: alas poore wretch: a poore *Chipochia*, hast not slept to night? would he not (a naughty man) let it sleepe: a bug-beare take him. *One knocks.*
Cres. Did not I tell you? would he were knockt ith' head. Who's that at doore? good Vnckle goe and see.
My Lord, come you againe into my Chamber:
You smile and mocke me, as if I meant naughtily.
Troy. Ha, ha.
Cre. Come you are deceiu'd, I thinke of no such thing.
How earnestly they knocke: pray you come in. *Knocke.*
I would not for halfe *Troy* haue you seene here. *Exeunt*
Pan. Who's there? what's the matter? will you beate downe the doore? How now, what's the matter?
Æne. Good morrow Lord, good morrow.
Pan. Who's there my Lord *Æneas*? by my troth I knew you not: what newes with you so early?
Æne. Is not Prince *Troylus* here?
Pan. Here? what should he doe here?
Æne. Come he is here, my Lord, doe not deny him: It doth import him much to speake with me.
Pan. Is he here say you? 'tis more then I know, Ile be sworne: For my owne part I came in late: what should he doe here?
Æne. Who, nay then: Come, come, youle doe him wrong, ere y'are ware: youle be so true to him, to be false to him: Doe not you know of him, but yet goe fetch him hither, goe.

Enter Troylus.

Troy. How now, what's the matter?
Æne. My Lord, I scarce haue leisure to salute you,
My matter is so rash: there is at hand,
Paris your brother, and *Deiphoebus*,
The Grecian *Diomed*, and our *Anthenor*
Deliuer'd to vs, and for him forth-with,
Ere the first sacrifice, within this houre,
We must giue vp to *Diomeds* hand
The Lady *Cressida*.
Troy. Is it concluded so?
Æne. By *Priam*, and the generall state of *Troy*,
They are at hand, and ready to effect it.
Troy. How my atchieuements mocke me;
I will goe meete them: and my Lord *Æneas*,
We met by chance; you did not finde me here.
Æn. Good, good, my Lord, the secrets of nature
Haue not more gift in taciturnitie. *Exennt.*

Enter Pandarus and Cressid.

Pan. Is't possible? no sooner got but lost: the diuell take *Anthenor*; the yong Prince will goe mad: a plague vpon *Anthenor*; I would they had brok's necke.
Cres. How now? what's the matter? who was here?
Pan. Ah, ha!
Cres. Why sigh you so profoundly? wher's my Lord? gone? tell me sweet Vnckle, what's the matter?
Pan. Would I were as deepe vnder the earth as I am aboue.
Cres. O the gods! what's the matter?
Pan. Prythee get thee in: would thou had'st nere been borne; I knew thou would'st be his death. O poore Gentleman: a plague vpon *Anthenor*.

¶ ¶ 2 *Cres.* Good

Creſ. Good Vnckle I beſeech you, on my knees, I beſeech you what's the matter?

Pan. Thou muſt be gone wench, thou muſt be gone; thou art chang'd for *Anthenor*: thou muſt to thy Father, and be gone from *Troylus*: 'twill be his death: 'twill be his baine, he cannot beare it..

Creſ. O you immortall gods! I will not goe.

Pan. Thou muſt.

Creſ. I will not Vnckle: I haue forgot my Father:
I know no touch of conſanguinitie:
No kin, no loue, no bloud, no ſoule, ſo neere me,
As the ſweet *Troylus*: O you gods diuine!
Make *Creſſids* name the very crowne of falſhood!
If euer ſhe leaue *Troylus*: time, orce and death,
Do to this body what extremitie you can;
But the ſtrong baſe and building of my loue,
Is as the very Center of the earth,
Drawing all things to it. I will goe in and weepe.

Pan. Doe, doe.

Creſ. Teare my bright heire, and ſcratch my praiſed cheekes,
Cracke my cleere voyce with ſobs, and breake my heart
With ſounding *Troylus*. I will not goe from *Troy*. *Exeunt.*

Enter Paris, Troylus, Æneas, Deiphebus, Anthenor and Diomedes.

Par. It is great morning, and the houre prefixt
Of her deliuerie to this valiant Greeke
Comes faſt vpon: good my brother *Troylus*,
Tell you the Lady what ſhe is to doe,
And haſt her to the purpoſe.

Troy. Walke into her houſe:
Ile bring her to the Grecian preſently;
And to his hand, when I deliuer her,
Thinke it an Altar, and thy brother *Troylus*
A Prieſt, there offring to it his heart.

Par. I know what 'tis to loue,
And would, as I ſhall pittie, I could helpe.
Pleaſe you walke in, my Lords. *Exeunt.*

Enter Pandarus and Creſſid.

Pan. Be moderate, be moderate.

Creſ. Why tell you me of moderation?
The griefe is fine, full perfect that I taſte,
And no leſſe in a ſenſe as ſtrong
As that which cauſeth it. How can I moderate it?
If I could temporiſe with my affection,
Or brew it to a weake and colder pallat,
The like alaiment could I giue my griefe:
My loue admits no qualifying croſſe; *Enter Troylus.*
No more my griefe, in ſuch a precious loſſe.

Pan. Here, here, here, he comes, a ſweet ducke.

Creſ. O *Troylus*, *Troylus*!

Pan. What a paire of ſpectacles is here? let me embrace too: oh hart, as the goodly ſaying is; O heart, heauie heart, why ſigheſt thou without breaking? where he anſwers againe; becauſe thou canſt not eaſe thy ſmart by friendſhip, nor by ſpeaking: there was neuer a truer rime; let vs caſt away nothing, for we may liue to haue neede of ſuch a Verſe: we ſee it, we ſee it: how now Lambs?

Troy. *Creſſid*: I loue thee in ſo ſtrange a puritie;
That the bleſt gods, as angry with my fancie,
More bright in zeale, then the deuotion which
Cold lips blow to their Deities: take thee from me.

Creſ. Haue the gods enuie?

Pan. I, I, I, I, 'tis too plaine a caſe.

Creſ. And is it true, that I muſt goe from Troy?

Troy. A hatefull truth.

Creſ. What, and from *Troylus* too?

Troy. From Troy, and *Troylus*.

Creſ. Iſt poſſible?

Troy. And ſodainely, where iniurie of chance
Puts backe leaue-taking, iuſtles roughly by
All time of pauſe; rudely beguiles our lips
Of all reioyndure: forcibly preuents
Our lockt embraſures; ſtrangles our deare vowes,
Euen in the birth of our owne laboring breath.
We two, that with ſo many thouſand ſighes
Did buy each other, muſt poorely ſell our ſelues,
With the rude breuitie and diſcharge of our
Iniurious time; now with a robbers haſte
Crams his rich theeuerie vp, he knowes not how.
As many farwels as be ſtars in heauen,
With diſtinct breath, and conſign'd kiſſes to them,
He fumbles vp into a looſe adiew;
And ſcants vs with a ſingle famiſht kiſſe,
Diſtaſting with the ſalt of broken teares. *Enter Æneus.*

Æneas within. My Lord, is the Lady ready?

Troy. Harke, you are call'd: ſome ſay the genius ſo
Cries, come to him that inſtantly muſt dye.
Bid them haue patience: ſhe ſhall come anon.

Pan. Where are my teares? raine, to lay this winde, or my heart will be blowne vp by the root.

Creſ. I muſt then to the Grecians?

Troy. No remedy.

Creſ. A wofull *Creſſid* 'mong'ſt the merry Greekes.

Troy. When ſhall we ſee againe?

Troy. Here me my loue: be thou but true of heart.

Creſ. I true? how now? what wicked deeme is this?

Troy. Nay, we muſt vſe expoſtulation kindely,
For it is parting from vs:
I ſpeake not, be thou true, as fearing thee:
For I will throw my Gloue to death himſelfe,
That there's no maculation in thy heart:
But be thou true, ſay I, to faſhion in
My ſequent proteſtation: be thou true,
And I will ſee thee.

Creſ. O you ſhall be expos'd, my Lord to dangers
As infinite, as imminent: but Ile be true.

Troy. And Ile grow friend with danger;
Weare this Sleeue.

Creſ. And you this Gloue.
When ſhall I ſee you?

Troy. I will corrupt the Grecian Centinels,
To giue thee nightly viſitation.
But yet be true.

Creſ. O heauens: be true againe?

Troy. Heare why I ſpeake it; Loue:
The Grecian youths are full of qualitie,
Their louing well compos'd, with guift of nature,
Flawing and ſwelling ore with Arts and exerciſe:
How nouelties may moue, and parts with perſon.
Alas, a kinde of godly iealouſie;
Which I beſeech you call a vertuous ſinne:
Makes me affraid.

Creſ. O heauens, you loue me not!

Troy. Dye I a villaine then:
In this I doe not call your faith in queſtion
So mainely as my merit: I cannot ſing,
Nor heele the high Lauolt; nor ſweeten talke;
Nor play at ſubtill games; faire vertues all;

To

To which the Grecians are moſt prompt and pregnant:
But I can tell that in each grace of theſe,
There lurkes a ſtill and dumb-diſcourſiue diuell,
That tempts moſt cunningly: but be not tempted.
Creſ. Doe you thinke I will:
Troy. No, but ſomething may be done that we wil not:
And ſometimes we are diuels to our ſelues,
When we will tempt the frailtie of our powers,
Preſuming on their changefull potencie.
Æneas within. Nay, good my Lord?
Troy. Come kiſſe, and let vs part.
Paris within. Brother *Troylus*?
Troy. Good brother come you hither,
And bring *Æneas* and the Grecian with you.
Creſ. My Lord, will you be true? *Exit.*
Troy. Who I? alas it is my vice, my fault:
Whiles others fiſh with craft for great opinion,
I, with great truth, catch meere ſimplicitie;
Whil'ſt ſome with cunning guild their copper crownes,
With truth and plainneſſe I doe weare mine bare:

Enter the Greekes.

Feare not my truth; the morrall of my wit
Is plaine and true, ther's all the reach of it.
Welcome ſir *Diomed*, here is the Lady
Which for *Antenor*, we deliuer you.
At the port (Lord) Ile giue her to thy hand,
And by the way poſſeſſe thee what ſhe is.
Entreate her faire; and by my ſoule, faire Greeke,
If ere thou ſtand at mercy of my Sword,
Name *Creſſid*, and thy life ſhall be as ſafe
As *Priam* is in Illion?
Diom. Faire Lady *Creſsid*,
So pleaſe you ſaue the thankes this Prince expects:
The luſtre in your eye, heauen in your cheeke,
Pleades your faire viſage, and to *Diomed*
You ſhall be miſtreſſe, and command him wholly.
Troy. Grecian, thou do'ſt not vſe me curteouſly,
To ſhame the ſeale of my petition towards,
I praiſing her. I tell thee Lord of Greece:
Shee is as farre high ſoaring o're thy praiſes,
As thou vnworthy to be cal'd her ſeruant:
I charge thee vſe her well, euen for my charge:
For by the dreadfull *Pluto*, if thou do'ſt not,
(Though the great bulke *Achilles* be thy guard)
Ile cut thy throate.
Diom. Oh be not mou'd Prince *Troylus*;
Let me be priuiledg'd by my place and meſſage,
To be a ſpeaker free? when I am hence,
Ile anſwer to my luſt: and know my Lord;
Ile nothing doe on charge: to her owne worth
She ſhall be priz'd: but that you ſay, be't ſo;
Ile ſpeake it in my ſpirit and honor, no.
Troy. Come to the Port. Ile tell thee *Diomed*,
This braue, ſhall oft make thee to hide thy head:
Lady, giue me your hand, and as we walke,
To our owne ſelues bend we our needefull talke.

Sound Trumpet.

Par. Harke, *Hectors* Trumpet.
Æne. How haue we ſpent this morning
The Prince muſt thinke me tardy and remiſſe,
That ſwore to ride before him in the field.
Par. 'Tis *Troylus* fault: come, come, to field with him. *Exeunt.*

Dio. Let vs make ready ſtraight.
Æne. Yea, with a Bridegroomes freſh alacritie
Let vs addreſſe to tend on *Hectors* heeles:
The glory of our *Troy* doth this day lye
On his faire worth, and ſingle Chiualrie.

Enter Aiax armed, Achilles, Patroclus, Agamemnon, Menelaus, Vliſſes, Neſter, Calcas, &c.

Aga. Here art thou in appointment freſh and faire,
Anticipating time. With ſtarting courage,
Giue with thy Trumpet a loud note to Troy
Thou dreadfull *Aiax*, that the appauled aire
May pierce the head of the great Combatant,
And hale him hither.
Aia. Thou, Trumpet, ther's my purſe;
Now cracke thy lungs, and ſplit thy braſen pipe:
Blow villaine, till thy ſphered Bias cheeke
Out-ſwell the collicke of puft *Aquilon*:
Come, ſtretch thy cheſt, and let thy eyes ſpout bloud:
Thou bloweſt for *Hector.*
Vliſ. No Trumpet anſwers.
Achil. 'Tis but early dayes.
Aga. Is not yong *Diomed* with *Calcas* daughter?
Vliſ. 'Tis he, I ken the manner of his gate,
He riſes on the toe: that ſpirit of his
In aſpiration lifts him from the earth.
Aga. Is this the Lady *Creſſid*?
Dio. Euen ſhe.
Aga. Moſt deerely welcome to the Greekes, ſweete Lady.
Neſt. Our Generall doth ſalute you with a kiſſe.
Vliſ. Yet is the kindeneſſe but particular; 'twere better ſhe were kiſt in generall.
Neſt. And very courtly counſell: Ile begin. So much for *Neſtor.*
Achil. Ile take that winter from your lips faire Lady *Achilles* bids you welcome.
Mene. I had good argument for kiſſing once.
Patro. But that's no argument for kiſſing now;
For thus pop't *Paris* in his hardiment.
Vliſ. Oh deadly gall, and theame of all our ſcornes,
For which we looſe our heads, to gild his hornes.
Patro. The firſt was *Menelaus* kiſſe, this mine:
Patroclus kiſſes you.
Mene. Oh this is trim.
Patr. *Paris* and I kiſſe euermore for him.
Mene. Ile haue my kiſſe ſir: Lady by your leaue.
Creſ. In kiſſing doe you render, or receiue.
Patr. Both take and giue.
Creſ. Ile make my match to liue,
The kiſſe you take is better then you giue: therefore no kiſſe.
Mene. Ile giue you boote, Ile giue you three for one.
Creſ. You are an odde man, giue euen, or giue none.
Mene. An odde man Lady, euery man is odde.
Creſ. No, *Paris* is not; for you know 'tis true,
That you are odde, and he is euen with you.
Mene. You fillip me a'th' head.
Creſ. No, Ile be ſworne.
Vliſ. It were no match, your naile againſt his horne:
May I ſweete Lady beg a kiſſe of you?
Creſ. You may.
Vliſ. I doe deſire it.
Creſ. Why begge then?
Vliſ. Why then for *Venus* ſake, giue me a kiſſe:
When *Hellen* is a maide againe, and his ———
Creſ. I am your debtor, claime it when 'tis due.

Vliſ. Neuer's my day, and then a kiſſe of you.
Diom. Lady a word, Ile bring you to your Father.
Neſt. A woman of quicke ſence.
Vliſ. Fie, fie, vpon her:
Ther's a language in her eye, her cheeke, her lip;
Nay, her foote ſpeakes, her wanton ſpirites looke out
At euery ioynt, and motiue of her body:
Oh theſe encounterers ſo glib of tongue,
That giue a coaſting welcome ere it comes;
And wide vnclaſpe the tables of their thoughts,
To euery tickling reader: ſet them downe,
For ſluttiſh ſpoyles of opportunitie;
And daughters of the game. *Exennt.*

Enter all of Troy, Hector, Paris, Æneas, Helenus and Attendants. Floriſh.

All. The Troians Trumpet.
Aga. Yonder comes the troope.
Æne. Haile all you ſtate of Greece: what ſhalbe done
To him that victory commands? or doe you purpoſe,
A victor ſhall be knowne: will you the Knights
Shall to the edge of all extremitie
Purſue each other; or ſhall be diuided
By any voyce, or order of the field: *Hector* bad aske?
Aga. Which way would *Hector* haue it?
Æne. He cares not, heele obey conditions.
Aga. 'Tis done like *Hector*, but ſecurely done,
A little proudly, and great deale diſpriſing
The Knight oppos'd.
Æne. If not *Achilles* ſir, what is your name?
Achil. If not *Achilles*, nothing.
Æne. Therefore *Achilles*: but what ere, know this,
In the extremity of great and little:
Valour and pride excell themſelues in *Hector*;
The one almoſt as infinite as all;
The other blanke as nothing: weigh him well:
And that which lookes like pride, is curteſie:
This *Aiax* is halfe made of *Hectors* bloud;
In loue whereof, halfe *Hector* ſtaies at home:
Halfe heart, halfe hand, halfe *Hector*, comes to ſeeke
This blended Knight, halfe Troian, and halfe Greeke.
Achil. A maiden battaile then? O I perceiue you.
Aga. Here is ſir, *Diomed*: goe gentle Knight,
Stand by our *Aiax*: as you and Lord *Æneas*
Conſent vpon the order of their fight,
So be it: either to the vttermoſt,
Or elſe a breach: the Combatants being kin,
Halfe ſtints their ſtrife, before their ſtrokes begin.
Vliſ. They are oppos'd already.
Aga. What Troian is that ſame that lookes ſo heauy?
Vliſ. The yongeſt Sonne of *Priam*;
A true Knight; they call him *Troylus*;
Not yet mature, yet matchleſſe, firme of word,
Speaking in deedes, and deedeleſſe in his tongue;
Not ſoone prouok't, nor being prouok't, ſoone calm'd;
His heart and hand both open, and both free:
For what he has, he giues; what thinkes, he ſhewes;
Yet giues he not till iudgement guide his bounty,
Nor dignifies an impaire thought with breath:
Manly as *Hector*, but more dangerous;
For *Hector* in his blaze of wrath ſubſcribes
To tender obiects; but he, in heate of action,
Is more vindecatiue then iealous loue.
They call him *Troylus*; and on him erect,
A ſecond hope, as fairely built as *Hector*.
Thus ſaies *Æneas*, one that knowes the youth,
Euen to his inches: and with priuate ſoule,
Did in great Illion thus tranſlate him to me. *Alarum.*
Aga. They are in action.
Neſt. Now *Aiax* hold thine owne.
Troy. *Hector*, thou ſleep'ſt, awake thee.
Aga. His blowes are wel diſpos'd there *Aiax*. *trũpets*
Diom. You muſt no more. *ceaſe.*
Æne. Princes enough, ſo pleaſe you.
Aia. I am not warme yet, let vs fight againe.
Diom. As *Hector* pleaſes.
Hect. Why then will I no more:
Thou art great Lord, my Fathers ſiſters Sonne;
A couſen german to great *Priams* ſeede:
The obligation of our bloud forbids
A gorie emulation 'twixt vs twaine:
Were thy commixion, Greeke and Troian ſo,
That thou could'ſt ſay, this hand is Grecian all,
And this is Troian: the ſinewes of this Legge,
All Greeke, and this all Troy: my Mothers bloud
Runs on the dexter cheeke, and this ſiniſter
Bounds in my fathers: by *Ioue* multipotent,
Thou ſhould'ſt not beare from me a Greekiſh member
Wherein my ſword had not impreſſure made
Of our ranke feud: but the iuſt gods gainſay,
That any drop thou borrwd'ſt from thy mother,
My ſacred Aunt, ſhould by my mortall Sword
Be drained. Let me embrace thee *Aiax*:
By him that thunders, thou haſt luſtie Armes;
Hector would haue them fall vpon him thus.
Cozen, all honor to thee.
Aia. I thanke thee *Hector*:
Thou art too gentle, and too free a man:
I came to kill thee Cozen, and beare hence
A great addition, earned in thy death.
Hect. Not *Neoptolymus* ſo mirable,
On whoſe bright creſt, fame with her lowd'ſt (O yes)
Cries, This is he; could'ſt promiſe to himſelfe,
A thought of added honor, torne from *Hector*.
Æne. There is expectance here from both the ſides,
What further you will doe?
Hect. Weele anſwere it:
The iſſue is embracement: *Aiax*, farewell.
Aia. If I might in entreaties finde ſucceſſe,
As ſeld I haue the chance; I would deſire
My famous Couſin to our Grecian Tents.
Diom. 'Tis *Agamemnons* wiſh, and great *Achilles*
Doth long to ſee vnarm'd the valiant *Hector*.
Hect. *Æneas*, call my brother *Troylus* to me:
And ſignifie this louing enterview
To the expecters of our Troian part:
Deſire them home. Giue me thy hand, my Couſin:
I will goe eate with thee, and ſee your Knights.

Enter Agamemnon and the reſt.

Aia. Great *Agamemnon* comes to meete vs here.
Hect. The worthieſt of them, tell me name by name:
But for *Achilles*, mine owne ſerching eyes
Shall finde him by his large and portly ſize.
Aga. Worthy of Armes: as welcome as to one
That would be rid of ſuch an enemie.
But that's no welcome: vnderſtand more cleere
What's paſt, and what's to come, is ſtrew'd with huskes
And formeleſſe ruine of obliuion:
But in this extant moment, faith and troth,
Strain'd purely from all hollow bias drawing:
Bids thee with moſt diuine integritie,
From heart of very heart, great *Hector* welcome.
Hect. I thanke thee moſt imperious *Agamemnon*.

Aga. My well-fam'd Lord of Troy, no lesse to you.
Men. Let me confirme my Princely brothers greeting,
You brace of warlike Brothers, welcome hither.
Hect. Who must we answer?
Æne. The Noble *Menelaus*.
Hect. O, you my Lord, by *Mars* his gauntlet thanks,
Mocke not, that I affect th'vntraded Oath,
Your *quondam* wife sweares still by *Venus* Gloue
Shee's well, but bad me not commend her to you.
Men. Name her not now sir, she's a deadly Theame.
Hect. O pardon, I offend.
Nest. I haue (thou gallant Troyan) seene thee oft
Labouring for destiny, make cruell way
Through rankes of Greekish youth: and I haue seen thee
As hot as *Perseus*, spurre thy Phrygian Steed,
And seene thee scorning forfeits and subduments,
When thou hast hung thy aduanced sword i'th'ayre,
Not letting it decline, on the declined:
That I haue said vnto my standers by,
Loe Iupiter is yonder, dealing life.
And I haue seene thee pause, and take thy breath,
When that a ring of Greekes haue hem'd thee in,
Like an Olympian wrestling. This haue I seene,
But this thy countenance (still lockt in steele)
I neuer saw till now. I knew thy Grandsire,
And once fought with him; he was a Souldier good,
But by great Mars, the Captaine of vs all,
Neuer like thee. Let an oldman embrace thee,
And (worthy Warriour) welcome to our Tents.
Æne. 'Tis the old *Nestor*.
Hect. Let me embrace thee good old Chronicle,
That hast so long walk'd hand in hand with time:
Most reuerend *Nestor*, I am glad to claspe thee.
Ne. I would my armes could match thee in contention
As they contend with thee in courtesie.
Hect. I would they could.
Nest. Ha? by this white beard I'ld fight with thee to morrow. Well, welcom, welcome: I haue seen the time.
Vlys. I wonder now, how yonder City stands,
When we haue heere her Base and pillar by vs.
Hect. I know your fauour Lord *Vlysses* well.
Ah sir, there's many a Greeke and Troyan dead,
Since first I saw your selfe, and *Diomed*
In Illion, on your Greekish Embassie.
Vlys. Sir, I foretold you then what would ensue,
My prophesie is but halfe his iourney yet;
For yonder wals that pertly front your Towne,
Yond Towers, whose wanton tops do busse the clouds,
Must kisse their owne feet.
Hect. I must not beleeue you:
There they stand yet: and modestly I thinke,
The fall of euery Phrygian stone will cost
A drop of Grecian blood: the end crownes all,
And that old common Arbitrator, Time,
Will one day end it.
Vlys. So to him we leaue it.
Most gentle, and most valiant *Hector*, welcome;
After the Generall, I beseech you next
To Feast with me, and see me at my Tent.
Achil. I shall forestall thee Lord *Vlysses*, thou:
Now *Hector* I haue fed mine eyes on thee,
I haue with exact view perus'd thee *Hector*,
And quoted ioynt by ioynt.
Hect. Is this *Achilles*?
Achil. I am *Achilles*.
Hect. Stand faire I prythee, let me looke on thee.
Achil. Behold thy fill.
Hect. Nay, I haue done already.
Achil. Thou art to breefe, I will the second time,
As I would buy thee, view thee, limbe by limbe.
Hect. O like a Booke of sport thou'lt reade me ore:
But there's more in me then thou vnderstand'st.
Why doest thou so oppresse me with thine eye?
Achil. Tell me you Heauens, in which part of his body
Shall I destroy him? Whether there, or there, or there,
That I may giue the locall wound a name,
And make distinct the very breach, where-out
Hectors great spirit flew. Answer me heauens.
Hect. It would discredit the blest Gods, proud man,
To answer such a question: Stand againe;
Think'st thou to catch my life so pleasantly,
As to prenominate in nice coniecture
Where thou wilt hit me dead?
Achil. I tell thee yea.
Hect. Wert thou the Oracle to tell me so,
I'ld not beleeue thee: henceforth guard thee well,
For Ile not kill thee there, nor there, nor there,
But by the forge that stythied Mars his helme,
Ile kill thee euery where, yea, ore and ore.
You wisest Grecians, pardon me this bragge,
His insolence drawes folly from my lips,
But Ile endeuour deeds to match these words,
Or may I neuer———
Aiax. Do not chafe thee Cosin:
And you *Achilles*, let these threats alone
Till accident, or purpose bring you too't.
You may euery day enough of *Hector*
If you haue stomacke. The generall state I feare,
Can scarse intreat you to be odde with him.
Hect. I pray you let vs see you in the field,
We haue had pelting Warres since you refus'd
The Grecians cause.
Achil. Dost thou intreat me *Hector*?
To morrow do I meete thee fell as death,
To night, all Friends.
Hect. Thy hand vpon that match.
Aga. First, all you Peeres of Greece go to my Tent,
There in the full conuiue you: Afterwards,
As *Hectors* leysure, and your bounties shall
Concurre together, seuerally intreat him.
Beate lowd the Taborins, let the Trumpets blow,
That this great Souldier may his welcome know. *Exeunt*
Troy. My Lord *Vlysses*, tell me I beseech you,
In what place of the Field doth *Calchas* keepe?
Vlys. At *Menelaus* Tent, most Princely *Troylus*,
There *Diomed* doth feast with him to night,
Who neither lookes on heauen, nor on earth,
But giues all gaze and bent of amorous view
On the faire *Cressid*.
Troy. Shall I (sweet Lord) be bound to thee so much,
After we part from *Agamemnons* Tent,
To bring me thither?
Vlys. You shall command me sir:
As gentle tell me, of what Honour was
This *Cressida* in Troy, had she no Louer there
That wailes her absence?
Troy. O sir, to such as boasting shew their scarres,
A mocke is due; will you walke on my Lord?
She was belou'd, she lou'd; she is, and dooth;
But still sweet Loue is food for Fortunes tooth. *Exeunt*

Enter Achilles, and Patroclus.

Achil. Ile heat his blood with Greekish wine to night,
Which

Which with my Cemitar Ile coole to morrow:
Patroclus, let vs Feast him to the hight.

Pat. Heere comes *Thersites.* *Enter Thersites.*

Achil. How now, thou core of Enuy?
Thou crusty batch of Nature, what's the newes?

Ther. Why thou picture of what thou seem'st, & Idoll of Ideot-worshippers, here's a Letter for thee.

Achil. From whence, Fragment?

Ther. Why thou full dish of Foole, from Troy.

Pat. Who keepes the Tent now?

Ther. The Surgeons box, or the Patients wound.

Patr. Well said aduersity, and what need these tricks?

Ther. Prythee be silent boy, I profit not by thy talke, thou art thought to be *Achilles* male Varlot.

Patro. Male Varlot you Rogue? What's that?

Ther. Why his masculine Whore. Now the rotten diseases of the South, guts-griping Ruptures, Catarres, Loades a grauell i'th'backe, Lethargies, cold Palsies, and the like, take and take againe, such prepostrous discoueries.

Pat. Why thou damnable box of enuy thou, what mean'st thou to curse thus?

Ther. Do I curse thee?

Patr. Why no, you ruinous But, you whorson indistinguishable Curre.

Ther. No? why art thou then exasperate, thou idle, immateriall skiene of Sleyd silke; thou greene Sarcenet flap for a sore eye, thou tassell of a Prodigals purse thou: Ah how the poore world is pestred with such water-flies, diminutiues of Nature.

Pat. Out gall.

Ther. Finch Egge.

Ach. My sweet *Patroclus*, I am thwarted quite
From my great purpose in to morrowes battell:
Heere is a Letter from Queene *Hecuba*,
A token from her daughter, my faire Loue,
Both taxing me, and gaging me to keepe
An Oath that I haue sworne. I will not breake it,
Fall Greekes, faile Fame, Honor or go, or stay,
My maior vow lyes heere; this Ile obay:
Come, come *Thersites*, helpe to trim my Tent,
This night in banquetting must all be spent.
Away *Patroclus*. *Exit.*

Ther. With too much bloud, and too little Brain, these two may run mad: but if with too much braine, and too little blood, they do, Ile be a curer of madmen. Heere's *Agamemnon*, an honest fellow enough, and one that loues Quailes, but he has not so much Braine as eare-wax; and the goodly transformation of Iupiter there his Brother, the Bull, the primatiue Statue, and oblique memoriall of Cuckolds, a thrifty shooing-horne in a chaine, hanging at his Brothers legge, to what forme but that he is, shold wit larded with malice, and malice forced with wit, turne him too: to an Asse were nothing; hee is both Asse and Oxe; to an Oxe were nothing, hee is both Oxe and Asse: to be a Dogge, a Mule, a Cat, a Fitchew, a Toade, a Lizard, an Owle, a Puttocke, or a Herring without a Roe, I would not care: but to be *Menelaus*, I would conspire against Destiny. Aske me not what I would be, if I were not *Thersites*: for I care not to bee the lowse of a Lazar, so I were not *Menelaus*. Hoy-day, spirits and fires.

Enter Hector, Aiax, Agamemnon, Vlysses, Nestor, Diomed, with Lights.

Aga. We go wrong, we go wrong.

Aiax. No yonder 'tis, there where we see the light.

Hect. I trouble you.

Aiax. No, not a whit.

Enter Achilles.

Vlys. Heere comes himselfe to guide you?

Achil. Welcome braue *Hector*, welcome Princes all.

Agam. So now faire Prince of Troy, I bid goodnight, *Aiax* commands the guard to tend on you.

Hect. Thanks, and goodnight to the Greeks general.

Men. Goodnight my Lord.

Hect. Goodnight sweet Lord *Menelaus*.

Ther. Sweet draught: sweet quoth-a? sweet sinke, sweet sure.

Achil. Goodnight and welcom, both at once, to those that go, or tarry.

Aga. Goodnight.

Achil. Old *Nestor* tarries, and you too *Diomed*,
Keepe *Hector* company an houre, or two.

Dio. I cannot Lord, I haue important businesse,
The tide whereof is now, goodnight great *Hector*.

Hect. Giue me your hand.

Vlys. Follow his Torch, he goes to *Chalcas* Tent,
Ile keepe you company.

Troy. Sweet sir, you honour me.

Hect. And so good night.

Achil. Come, come, enter my Tent. *Exeunt.*

Ther. That same *Diomed*'s a false-hearted Rogue, a most vniust Knaue; I will no more trust him when hee leeres, then I will a Serpent when he hisses: he will spend his mouth & promise, like Brabler the Hound; but when he performes, Astronomers foretell it, that it is prodigious, there will come some change: the Sunne borrowes of the Moone when *Diomed* keepes his word. I will rather leaue to see *Hector*, then not to dogge him: they say, he keepes a Troyan Drab, and vses the Traitour *Chalcas* his Tent. Ile after——Nothing but Letcherie? All incontinent Varlets. *Exeunt*

Enter Diomed.

Dio. What are you vp here ho? speake?

Chal. Who cals?

Dio. *Diomed*, *Chalcas* (I thinke) wher's you Daughter?

Chal. She comes to you.

Enter Troylus and Vlisses.

Vlis. Stand where the Torch may not discouer vs.

Enter Cressid.

Troy. *Cressid* comes forth to him.

Dio. How now my charge?

Cres. Now my sweet gardian: harke a word with you.

Troy. Yea, so familiar?

Vlis. She will sing any man at first sight.

Ther. And any man may finde her, if he can take her life: she's noted.

Dio. Will you remember?

Cal. Remember? yes.

Dio. Nay, but doe then; and let your minde be coupled with your words.

Troy. What should she remember?

Vlis. List?

Cres. Sweete hony Greek, tempt me no more to folly.

Ther. Roguery.

Dio. Nay then.

Cres. Ile tell you what.

Dio. Fo, fo, come tell a pin, you are a forsworne.----

Cres. In faith I cannot: what would you haue me do?

Ther. A iugling tricke, to be secretly open.

Dio. What did you sweare you would bestow on me?

Cres. I prethee do not hold me to mine oath,
Bid me doe not any thing but that sweete Greeke.

Dio. Good

Dio. Good night.
Troy. Hold, patience.
Vlis. How now Troian ?
Cres. *Diomed.*
Dio. No, no, good night: Ile be your foole no more.
Troy. Thy better must.
Cres. Harke one word in your eare.
Troy. O plague and madnesse !
Vlis. You are moued Prince, let vs depart I pray you,
Lest your displeasure should enlarge it selfe
To wrathfull tearmes: this place is dangerous;
The time right deadly: I beseech you goe.
Troy. Behold, I pray you.
Vlis. Nay, good my Lord goe off:
You flow to great distraction: come my Lord ?
Troy. I pray thee stay?
Vlis. You haue not patience, come.
Troy. I pray you stay? by hell and hell torments,
I will not speake a word.
Dio. And so good night.
Cres. Nay, but you part in anger.
Troy. Doth that grieue thee? O withered truth !
Vlis. Why, how now Lord?
Troy. By *Ioue* I will be patient.
Cres. Gardian? why Greeke?
Dio. Fo, fo, adew, you palter.
Cres. In faith I doe not: come hither once againe.
Vlis. You shake my Lord at something; will you goe?
you will breake out.
Troy. She stroakes his cheeke.
Vlis. Come, come.
Troy. Nay stay, by *Ioue* I will not speake a word.
There is betweene my will, and all offences,
A guard of patience; stay a little while.
Ther. How the diuell Luxury with his fat rumpe and potato finger, tickles these together: frye lechery, frye.
Dio. But will you then?
Cres. In faith I will lo; neuer trust me else.
Dio. Giue me some token for the surety of it.
Cres. Ile fetch you one. *Exit.*
Vlis. You haue sworne patience.
Troy. Feare me not sweete Lord.
I will not be my selfe, nor haue cognition
Of what I feele: I am all patience. *Enter Cressid.*
Ther. Now the pledge, now, now, now.
Cres. Here *Diomed*, keepe this Sleeue.
Troy. O beautie! where is thy Faith?
Vlis. My Lord.
Troy. I will be patient, outwardly I will.
Cres. You looke vpon that Sleeue? behold it well:
He lou'd me: O false wench: giue't me againe.
Dio. Whose was't?
Cres. It is no matter now I haue't againe.
I will not meete with you to morrow night:
I prythee *Diomed* visite me no more.
Ther. Now she sharpens: well said Whetstone.
Dio. I shall haue it.
Cres. What, this?
Dio. I that.
Cres. O all you gods! O prettie, prettie pledge;
Thy Maister now lies thinking in his bed
Of thee and me, and sighes, and takes my Gloue,
And giues memoriall daintie kisses to it;
As I kisse thee.
Dio. Nay, doe not snatch it from me.
Cres. He that takes that, rakes my heart withall.
Dio. I had your heart before, this followes it.
Troy. I did sweare patience.
Cres. You shall not haue it *Diomed*; faith you shall not:
Ile giue you something else.
Dio. I will haue this: whose was it?
Cres. It is no matter.
Dio. Come tell me whose it was?
Cres. 'Twas one that lou'd me better then you will.
But now you haue it, take it.
Dio. Whose was it?
Cres. By all *Dianas* waiting women yond:
And by her selfe, I will not tell you whose.
Dio. To morrow will I weare it on my Helme,
And grieue his spirit that dares not challenge it.
Troy. Wert thou the diuell, and wor'st it on thy horne,
It should be challeng'd.
Cres. Well, well, 'tis done, 'tis past; and yet it is not:
I will not keepe my word.
Dio. Why then farewell,
Thou neuer shalt mocke *Diomed* againe.
Cres. You shall not goe: one cannot speake a word,
But it strait starts you.
Dio. I doe not like this fooling.
Ther. Nor I by *Pluto*: but that that likes not me, pleases me best.
Dio. What shall I come? the houre.
Cres. I, come: O *Ioue!* doe, come: I shall be plagu'd.
Dio. Farewell till then. *Exit.*
Cres. Good night: I prythee come:
Troylus farewell; one eye yet lookes on thee;
But with my heart, the other eye, doth see.
Ah poore our sexe; this fault in vs I finde:
The errour of our eye, directs our minde.
What errour leads, must erre: O then conclude,
Mindes swai'd by eyes, are full of turpitude. *Exit.*
Ther. A proofe of strength she could not publish more;
Vnlesse she say, my minde is now turn'd whore.
Vlis. Al's done my Lord.
Troy. It is.
Vlis. Why stay we then?
Troy. To make a recordation to my soule
Of euery syllable that here was spoke:
But if I tell how these two did coact;
Shall I not lye, in publishing a truth?
Sith yet there is a credence in my heart:
An esperance so obstinately strong,
That doth inuert that test of eyes and eares;
As if those organs had deceptious functions,
Created onely to calumniate.
Was *Cressed* here?
Vlis. I cannot coniure Troian.
Troy. She was not sure.
Vlis. Most sure she was.
Troy. Why my negation hath no taste of madnesse?
Vlis. Nor mine my Lord: *Cressid* was here but now.
Troy. Let it not be beleeu'd for womanhood:
Thinke we had mothers; doe not giue aduantage
To stubborne Criticks, apt without a theame
For deprauation, to square the generall sex
By *Cressids* rule. Rather thinke this not *Cressid*.
Vlis. What hath she done Prince, that can soyle our mothers?
Troy. Nothing at all, vnlesse that this were she.
Ther. Will he swagger himselfe out on's owne eyes?
Troy. This she? no, this is *Diomids Cressida*:
If beautie haue a soule, this is not she:
If

If ſoules guide vowes; if vowes are ſanctimonie;
If ſanctimonie be the gods delight:
If there be rule in vnitie it ſelfe,
This is not ſhe: O madneſſe of diſcourſe!
That cauſe ſets vp, with, and againſt thy ſelfe
By foule authoritie: where reaſon can reuolt
Without perdition, and loſſe aſſume all reaſon,
Without reuolt. This is, and is not *Creſſid*:
Within my ſoule, there doth conduce a fight
Of this ſtrange nature, that a thing inſeperate,
Diuides more wider then the skie and earth:
And yet the ſpacious bredth of this diuiſion,
Admits no Orifex for a point as ſubtle,
As *Ariachnes* broken woofe to enter:
Inſtance, O inſtance! ſtrong as *Plutoes* gates:
Creſſid is mine, tied with the bonds of heauen;
Inſtance, O inſtance, ſtrong as heauen it ſelfe:
The bonds of heauen are ſlipt, diſſolu'd, and loos'd,
And with another knot fiue finger tied,
The fractions of her faith, orts of her loue:
The fragments, ſcraps, the bits, and greazie reliques,
Of her ore-eaten faith, are bound to *Diomed*

Vliſ. May worthy *Troylus* be halfe attached
With that which here his paſſion doth expreſſe?

Troy. I Greeke: and that ſhall be divulged well
In Characters, as red as *Mars* his heart
Inflam'd with *Venus*: neuer did yong man fancy
With ſo eternall, and ſo fixt a ſoule.
Harke Greek: as much I doe *Creſſida* loue;
So much by weight, hate I her *Diomed*,
That Sleeue is mine, that heele beare in his Helme:
Were it a Caske compos'd by *Vulcans* skill,
My Sword ſhould bite it: Not the dreadfull ſpout,
Which Shipmen doe the Hurricano call,
Conſtring'd in maſſe by the almighty Fenne,
Shall dizzie with more clamour Neptunes eare
In his diſcent; then ſhall my prompted ſword,
Falling on *Diomed.*

Ther. Heele tickle it for his concupie.

Troy. O *Creſſid*! O falſe *Creſſid!* falſe, falſe, falſe:
Let all vntruths ſtand by thy ſtained name,
And theyle ſeeme glorious.

Vliſ. O containe your ſelfe:
Your paſſion drawes eares hither.

Enter Æneas.

Æne. I haue beene ſeeking you this houre my Lord:
Hector by this is arming him in Troy.
Aiax your Guard, ſtaies to conduct you home.

Troy. Haue with you Prince: my curteous Lord adew:
Farewell reuolted faire: and *Diomed*,
Stand faſt, and weare a Caſtle on thy head.

Vli. Ile bring you to the Gates.

Troy. Accept diſtracted thankes.

Exeunt Troylus, Æneas, and Vliſſes.

Ther. Would I could meete that roague *Diomed*, I would croke like a Rauen: I would bode, I would bode: *Patroclus* will giue me any thing for the intelligence of this whore: the Parrot will not doe more for an Almond, then he for a commodious drab: Lechery, lechery, ſtill warres and lechery, nothing elſe holds faſhion. A burning diuell take them.

Enter Hector and Andromache.

And. When was my Lord ſo much vngently temper'd,
To ſtop his eares againſt admoniſhment?
Vnarme, vnarme, and doe not fight to day.

Hect. You traine me to offend you: get you gone.
By the euerlaſting gods, Ile goe.

And. My dreames will ſure proue ominous to the day.

Hect. No more I ſay. *Enter Caſſandra.*

Caſſa. Where is my brother *Hector*?

And. Here ſiſter, arm'd, and bloudy in intent:
Conſort with me in loud and deere petition:
Purſue we him on knees: for I haue dreampt
Of bloudy turbulence; and this whole night
Hath nothing beene but ſhapes, and formes of ſlaughter.

Caſſ. O, 'tis true.

Hect. Ho? bid my Trumpet ſound.

Caſſ. No notes of ſallie, for the heauens, ſweet brother.

Hect. Begon I ſay: the gods haue heard me ſweare.

Caſſ. The gods are deafe to hot and peeuiſh vowes;
They are polluted offrings, more abhord
Then ſpotted Liuers in the ſacrifice.

And. O be perſwaded, doe not count it holy,
To hurt by being iuſt; it is as lawfull:
For we would count giue much to as violent thefts,
And rob in the behalfe of charitie.

Caſſ. It is the purpoſe that makes ſtrong the vowe;
But vowes to euery purpoſe muſt not hold:
Vnatme ſweete *Hector*.

Hect. Hold you ſtill I ſay;
Mine honour keepes the weather of my fate:
Life euery man holds deere, but the deere man
Holds honor farre more precious, deere, then life.

Enter Troylus.

How now yong man? mean'ſt thou to fight to day?

And. *Caſſandra*, call my father to perſwade.

Exit Caſſandra.

Hect. No faith yong *Troylus*; doffe thy harneſſe youth:
I am to day ith'vaine of Chiualrie:
Let grow thy Sinews till their knots be ſtrong;
And tempt not yet the bruſhes of the warre.
Vnarme thee, goe; and doubt thou not braue boy,
Ile ſtand to day, for thee, and me, and Troy.

Troy. Brother, you haue a vice of mercy in you;
Which better fits a Lyon, then a man.

Hect. What vice is that? good *Troylus* chide me for it.

Troy. When many times the captiue Grecian fals,
Euen in the fanne and winde of your faire Sword:
You bid them riſe, and liue.

Hect. O 'tis faire play.

Troy. Fooles play, by heauen *Hector*.

Hect. How now? how now?

Troy. For th'loue of all the gods
Let's leaue the Hermit Pitty with our Mothers;
And when we haue our Armors buckled on,
The venom'd vengeance ride vpon our ſwords,
Spur them to ruthfull worke, reine them from ruth.

Hect., Fie ſauage, fie.

Troy. *Hector*, then 'tis warres.

Hect. *Troylus*, I would not haue you fight to day.

Troy. Who ſhould with-hold me?
Not fate, obedience, nor the hand of *Mars*,
Beckning with fierie trunchion my retire;
Not *Priamus*, and *Hecuba* on knees;
Their eyes ore-galled with recourſe of teares;
Nor you my brother, with your true ſword drawne
Oppos'd to hinder me, ſhould ſtop my way:
But by my ruine.

Enter Priam and Caſſandra.

Caſſ. Lay hold vpon him *Priam*, hold him faſt:
He is thy crutch; now if thou looſe thy ſtay,
Thou on him leaning, and all Troy on thee,

Fall

Fall all together.
Priam. Come *Hector*, come, goe backe:
Thy wife hath dreampt: thy mother hath had visions;
Cassandra doth foresee; and I my selfe,
Am like a Prophet suddenly enrapt,
to tell thee that this day is ominous:
Therefore come backe.
Hect. *Æneas* is a field,
And I do stand engag'd to many Greekes,
Euen in the faith of valour, to appeare
This morning to them.
Priam. I, but thou shalt not goe,
Hect. I must not breake my faith:
You know me dutifull, therefore deare sir,
Let me not shame respect; but giue me leaue
To take that course by your consent and voice,
Which you doe here forbid me, Royall *Priam.*
Cass. O *Priam*, yeelde not to him.
And. Doe not deere father.
Hect. *Andromache* I am offended with you:
Vpon the loue you beare me, get you in.
Exit Andromache.
Troy. This foolish, dreaming, superstitious girle,
Makes all these bodements.
Cass. O farewell, deere *Hector*:
Looke how thou diest; looke how thy eye turnes pale:
Looke how thy wounds doth bleede at many vents:
Harke how Troy roares; how *Hecuba* cries out;
How poore *Andromache* shrils her dolour forth;
Behold distraction, frenzie, and amazement,
Like witlesse Antickes one another meete,
And all cry *Hector*, *Hectors* dead: O *Hector*!
Troy. Away, away.
Cas. Farewell: yes, soft: *Hector* I take my leaue;
Thou do'st thy selfe, and all our Troy deceiue. *Exit.*
Hect. You are amaz'd, my Liege, at her exclaime:
Goe in and cheere the Towne, weele forth and fight:
Doe deedes of praise, and tell you them at night.
Priam. Farewell: the gods with safetie stand about thee. *Alarum.*
Troy. They are at it, harke: proud *Diomed*, beleeue I come to loose my arme, or winne my sleeue.

Enter Pandar.

Pand. Doe you heare my Lord? do you heare?
Troy. What now?
Pand. Here's a Letter come from yond poore girle.
Troy. Let me reade.
Pand. A whorson tisicke, a whorson rascally tisicke, so troubles me; and the foolish fortune of this girle, and what one thing, what another, that I shall leaue you one o'th's dayes: and I haue a rheume in mine eyes too; and such an ache in my bones; that vnlesse a man were curst, I cannot tell what to thinke on't. What sayes shee there?
Troy. Words, words, meere words, no matter from the heart;
Th'effect doth operate another way.
Goe winde to winde, there turne and change together:
My loue with words and errors still she feedes;
But edifies another with her deedes.
Pand. Why, but heare you?
Troy. Hence brother lackie; ignomie and shame
Pursue thy life, and liue aye with thy name.
A Larum. *Exeunt.*

Enter Thersites in excursion.

Ther. Now they are clapper-clawing one another, Ile goe looke on: that dissembling abhominable varlet *Diomede*, has got that same scuruie, doting, foolish yong knaues Sleeue of Troy, there in his Helme: I would faine see them meet; that, that same yong Troian asse, that loues the whore there, might send that Greekish whore-maisterly villaine, with the Sleeue, backe to the dissembling luxurious drabbe, of a sleeuelesse errant. O'th' tother side, the pollicie of those craftie swearing rascals; that stole old Mouse-eaten dry cheese, *Nestor*: and that same dog-foxe *Vlisses* is not prou'd worth a Black-berry. They set me vp in pollicy, that mungrill curre *Aiax*, against that dogge of as bad a kinde, *Achilles*. And now is the curre *Aiax* prouder then the curre *Achilles*, and will not arme to day. Whereupon, the Grecians began to proclaime barbarisme; and pollicie growes into an ill opinion.
Enter Diomed and Troylus.
Soft, here comes Sleeue, and th'other.
Troy. Flye not: for should'st thou take the Riuer Stix, I would swim after.
Diom. Thou do'st miscall retire:
I doe not flye; but aduantagious care
Withdrew me from the oddes of multitude:
Haue at thee?
Ther. Hold thy whore Grecian: now for thy whore Troian: Now the Sleeue, now the Sleeue.
Euter Hector.
Hect. What art thou Greek? art thou for *Hectors* match?
Art thou of bloud, and honour?
Ther. No, no: I am a rascall: a scuruie railing knaue: a very filthy roague.
Hect. I doe beleeue thee, liue.
Ther. God a mercy, that thou wilt beleeue me; but a plague breake thy necke——for frighting me: what's become of the wenching rogues? I thinke they haue swallowed one another. I would laugh at that miracle----yet in a sort, lecherie eates it selfe: Ile seeke them. *Exit.*

Enter Diomed and Seruants.
Dio. Goe, goe, my seruant, take thou *Troylus* Horse;
Present the faire Steede to my Lady *Cressid*:
Fellow, commend my seruice to her beauty;
Tell her, I haue chastis'd the amorous Troyan.
And am her Knight by proofe.
Ser. I goe my Lord. *Enter Agamemnon.*
Aga. Renew, renew, the fierce *Polidamus*
Hath beate downe *Menon*: bastard *Margarelon*
Hath *Doreus* prisoner.
And stands Calossus-wise wauing his beame,
Vpon the pashed courses of the Kings:
Epistropus and *Cedus*, *Polixines* is slaine;
Amphimacus, and *Thous* deadly hurt;
Patroclus tane or slaine, and *Palamedes*
Sore hurt and bruised; the dreadfull Sagittary
Appauls our numbers, haste we *Diomed*
To re-enforcement, or we perish all.
Enter Nestor.
Nest. Coe beare *Patroclus* body to *Achilles*,
And bid the snaile-pac'd *Aiax* arme for shame;
There is a thousand *Hectors* in the field:
Now here he fights on *Galathe* his Horse,
And there lacks worke: anon he's there a foote,
And there they flye or dye, like scaled sculs,
Before

Before the belching Whale; then is he yonder,
And there the straying Greekes, ripe for his edge,
Fall downe before him, like the mowers swath;
Here, there, and euery where, he leaues and takes;
Dexteritie so obaying appetite,
That what he will, he does, and does so much,
That proofe is call'd impossibility.

Enter Vlisses.

Vlis. Oh, courage, courage Princes: great *Achilles*
Is arming, weeping, cursing, vowing vengeance;
Patroclus wounds haue rouz'd his drowzie bloud,
Together with his mangled *Myrmidons*,
That noselesse, handlesse, hackt and chipt, come to him;
Crying on *Hector*. *Aiax* hath lost a friend,
And foames at mouth, and he is arm'd, and at it:
Roaring for *Troylus*; who hath done to day,
Mad and fantasticke execution;
Engaging and redeeming of himselfe,
With such a carelesse force, and forcelesse care,
As if that luck in very spight of cunning, bad him win all.

Enter Aiax.

Aia. *Troylus*, thou coward *Troylus*. *Exit.*
Dio. I, there, there.
Nest. So, so, we draw together. *Exit.*

Enter Achilles.

Achil. Where is this *Hector*?
Come, come, thou boy-queller, shew thy face:
Know what it is to meete *Achilles* angry.
Hector, wher's *Hector*? I will none but *Hector*. *Exit.*

Enter Aiax.

Aia. *Troylus*, thou coward *Troylus*, shew thy head.

Enter Diomed.

Diom. *Troylus*, I say, wher's *Troylus*?
Aia. What would'st thou?
Diom. I would correct him.
Aia. Were I the Generall,
Thou should'st haue my office,
Ere that correction: *Troylus* I say, what *Troylus*?

Enter Troylus.

Troy. Oh traitour *Diomed*!
Turne thy false face thou traytor,
And pay thy life thou owest me for my horse.
Dio. Ha, art thou there?
Aia. Ile fight with him alone, stand *Diomed*.
Dio. He is my prize, I will not looke vpon.
Troy. Come both you coging Greekes, haue at you both. *Exit Troylus.*

Enter Hector.

Hect. Yea *Troylus*? O well fought my yongest Brother.

Euter Achilles.

Achil. Now doe I see thee; haue at thee *Hector*.
Hect. Pause if thou wilt.
Achil. I doe disdaine thy curtesie, proud Troian;
Be happy that my armes are out of vse:
My rest and negligence befriends thee now,
But thou anon shalt heare of me againe:
Till when, goe seeke thy fortune. *Exit.*
Hect. Fare thee well:
I would haue beene much more a fresher man,
Had I expected thee: how now my Brother?

Enter Troylus.

Troy. *Aiax* hath tane *Æneas*; shall it be?
No, by the flame of yonder glorious heauen,
He shall not carry him: Ile be tane too,
Or bring him off: Fate heare me what I say;
I wreake not, though thou end my life to day. *Exit.*

Enter one in Armour.

Hect. Stand, stand, thou Greeke,
Thou art a goodly marke:
No? wilt thou not? I like thy armour well,
Ile frush it, and vnlocke the riuets all,
But Ile be maister of it: wilt thou not beast abide?
Why then flye on, Ile hunt thee for thy hide. *Exit.*

Enter Achilles with Myrmidons.

Achil. Come here about me you my *Myrmidons*:
Marke what I say; attend me where I wheele:
Strike not a stroake, but keepe your selues in breath;
And when I haue the bloudy *Hector* found,
Empale him with your weapons round about:
In fellest manner execute your arme.
Follow me sirs, and my proceedings eye;
It is decreed, *Hector* the great must dye. *Exit.*

Enter Thersites, Menelaus, and Paris.

Ther. The Cuckold and the Cuckold maker are at it: now bull, now dogge, lowe; *Paris* lowe; now my double hen'd sparrow; lowe *Paris*, lowe; the bull has the game: ware hornes ho?

Exit Paris and Menelaus.

Enter Bastard.

Bast. Turne slaue and fight.
Ther. What art thou?
Bast. A Bastard Sonne of *Priams*.
Ther. I am a Bastnrd too, I loue Bastards, I am a Bastard begot, Bastard instructed, Bastard in minde, Bastard in valour, in euery thing illegitimate: one Beare will not bite another, and wherefore should one Bastard? take heede, the quarrel's most ominous to vs: if the Sonne of a whore fight for a whore, he tempts iudgement: farewell Bastard.
Bast. The diuell take thee coward. *Exeunt.*

Enter Hector.

Hect. Most putrified core so faire without:
Thy goodly armour thus hath cost thy life.
Now is my daies worke done; Ile take good breath:
Rest Sword, thou hast thy fill of bloud and death.

Enter Achilles and his Myrmidons.

Achil. Looke *Hector* how the Sunne begins to set;
How vgly night comes breathing at his heeles,
Euen with the vaile and darking of the Sunne.
To close the day vp, *Hectors* life is done.
Hect. I am vnarm'd, forgoe this vantage Greeke.
Achil. Strike fellowes, strike, this is the man I seeke.
So Illion fall thou: now Troy sinke downe;
Here lyes thy heart, thy sinewes, and thy bone.
On *Myrmidons*, cry you all a maine,
Achilles hath the mighty *Hector* slaine. *Retreat.*
Harke, a retreat vpon our Grecian part.
Gree. The Troian Trumpets sounds the like my Lord.
Achi. The dragon wing of night ore-spreds the earth
And stickler-like the Armies seperates
My halfe supt Sword, that frankly would haue fed,
Pleas'd with this dainty bed; thus goes to bed.
Come, tye his body to my horses tayle;
Along the field, I will the Troian traile. *Exeunt.*

Sound Retreat. *Shout.*

Enter Agamemnon, Aiax, Menelaus, Nestor, Diomed, and the rest marching.

Aga. Harke, harke, what shout is that?
Nest. Peace Drums.

Sol. Achill

Sold. *Achilles*, *Achilles*, *Hector*'s ſlaine, *Achilles*.
Dio. The bruite is, *Hector*'s ſlaine, and by *Achilles*.
Aia. If it be ſo, yet bragleſſe let it be:
Great *Hector* was a man as good as he.
Agam. March patiently along; let one be ſent
To pray *Achilles* ſee vs at our Tent.
If in his death the gods haue vs befrended,
Great Troy is ours, and our ſharpe wars are ended.
Exeunt.

Enter Æneas, Paris, Anthenor and Deiphœbus.

Æne. Stand hoe, yet are we maiſters of the field,
Neuer goe home; here ſtarue we out the night.

Enter Troylus.

Troy. *Hector* is ſlaine.
All. *Hector*? the gods forbid.
Troy. Hee's dead: and at the murtherers Horſes taile,
In beaſtly ſort, drag'd through the ſhamefull Field.!
Frowne on you heauens, effect your rage with ſpeede:
Sit gods vpon your throanes, and ſmile at Troy.
I ſay at once, let your briefe plagues be mercy,
And linger not our ſure deſtructions on.
Æne. My Lord, you doe diſcomfort all the Hoſte.
Troy. You vnderſtand me not, that tell me ſo:
I doe not ſpeake of flight, of feare, of death,
But dare all imminence that gods and men,
Addreſſe their dangers in. *Hector* is gone:
Who ſhall tell *Priam* ſo? or *Hecuba*?
Let him that will a ſcreechoule aye be call'd,
Goe in to Troy, and ſay there, *Hector*'s dead:
There is a word will *Priam* turne to ſtone;
Make wels, and *Niobes* of the maides and wiues;
Coole ſtatues of the youth: and in a word,
Scarre Troy out of it ſelfe. But march away,
Hector is dead: there is no more to ſay.
Stay yet: you vile abhominable Tents,
Thus proudly pight vpon our Phrygian plaines:
Let Titan riſe as early as he dare,
Ile through, and through you; & thou great ſiz'd coward:
No ſpace of Earth ſhall ſunder our two hates,
Ile haunt thee, like a wicked conſcience ſtill,
That mouldeth goblins ſwift as frenſies thoughts.
Strike a free march to Troy, with comfort goe:
Hope of reuenge, ſhall hide our inward woe.

Enter Pandarus.

Pand. But heare you? heare you?
Troy. Hence broker, lackie, ignomy, and ſhame
Purſue thy life, and liue aye with thy name. *Exeunt.*

Pan. A goodly medcine for mine akingbones: oh world, world, world! thus is the poore agent diſpiſde: Oh traitours and bawdes; how earneſtly are you ſet aworke, and how ill requited? why ſhould our indeuour be ſo deſir'd, and the performance ſo loath'd? What Verſe for it? what inſtance for it? let me ſee.
Full merrily the humble Bee doth ſing,
Till he hath loſt his hony, and his ſting.
And being once ſubdu'd in armed taile,
Sweete hony, and ſweete notes together faile.
Good traders in the fleſh, ſet this in your painted cloathes;
As many as be here of Panders hall,
Your eyes halfe out, weepe out at *Pandar*'s fall:
Or if you cannot weepe, yet giue ſome grones;
Though not for me, yet for your akingbones:
Brethren and ſiſters of the hold-dore trade,
Some two months hence, my will ſhall here be made:
It ſhould be now, but that my feare is this:
Some galled Gooſe of Wincheſter would hiſſe:
Till then, Ile ſweate, and ſeeke about for eaſes;
And at that time bequeath you my diſeaſes. *Exeunt.*

¶ ¶ ¶

FINIS.

The Tragedy of Coriolanus:

Actus Primus. Scœna Prima.

Enter a Company of Mutinous Citizens, with Staues, Clubs, and other weapons.

1. *Citizen.*

Before we proceed any further, heare me speake.

All. Speake, speake.

1. *Cit.* You are all resolu'd rather to dy then to famish?

All. Resolu'd, resolu'd.

1. *Cit.* First you know, *Caius Martius* is chiefe enemy to the people.

All. We know't, we know't.

1. *Cit.* Let vs kill him, and wee'l haue Corne at our own price. Is't a Verdict?

All. No more talking on't; Let it be done, away, away

2. *Cit.* One word, good Citizens.

1. *Cit.* We are accounted poore Citizens, the Patricians good: what Authority surfets one, would releeue vs. If they would yeelde vs but the superfluitie while it were wholsome, wee might guesse they releeued vs humanely: But they thinke we are too deere, the leannesse that afflicts vs, the obiect of our misery, is as an inuentory to particularize their abundance, our sufferance is a gaine to them. Let vs reuenge this with our Pikes, ere we become Rakes. For the Gods know, I speake this in hunger for Bread, not in thirst for Reuenge.

2. *Cit.* Would you proceede especially against *Caius Martius.*

All. Against him first: He's a very dog to the Commonalty.

2. *Cit.* Consider you what Seruices he ha's done for his Country?

1. *Cit.* Very well, and could bee content to giue him good report for't, but that hee payes himselfe with beeing proud.

All. Nay, but speak not maliciously.

1. *Cit.* I say vnto you, what he hath done Famouslie, he did it to that end: though soft conscienc'd men can be content to say it was for his Countrey, he did it to please his Mother, and to be partly proud, which he is, euen to the altitude of his vertue.

2. *Cit.* What he cannot helpe in his Nature, you account a Vice in him: You must in no way say he is couetous.

1. *Cit.* If I must not, I neede not be barren of Accusations he hath faults (with surplus) to tyre in repetition.

Showts within.

What showts are these? The other side a'th City is risen: why stay we prating heere? To th'Capitoll.

All. Come, come.

1 *Cit.* Soft, who comes heere?

Enter Menenius Agrippa.

2 *Cit.* Worthy *Menenius Agrippa*, one that hath alwayes lou'd the people.

1 *Cit.* He's one honest enough, wold al the rest wer so.

Men. What work's my Countrimen in hand?
Where go you with Bats and Clubs? The matter
Speake I pray you.

2 *Cit.* Our busines is not vnknowne to th'Senat, they haue had inkling this fortnight what we intend to do, w^t now wee'l shew em in deeds: they say poore Suters haue strong breaths, they shal know we haue strong arms too.

Menen. Why Masters, my good Friends, mine honest Neighbours, will you vndo your selues?

2 *Cit.* We cannot Sir, we are vndone already.

Men. I tell you Friends, most charitable care
Haue the Patricians of you for your wants.
Your suffering in this dearth, you may as well
Strike at the Heauen with your staues, as lift them
Against the Roman State, whose course will on
The way it takes: cracking ten thousand Curbes
Of more strong linke assunder, then can euer
Appeare in your impediment. For the Dearth,
The Gods, not the Patricians make it, and
Your knees to them (not armes) must helpe. Alacke,
You are transported by Calamity
Thether, where more attends you, and you slander
The Helmes o'th State; who care for you like Fathers,
When you curse them, as Enemies.

2 *Cit.* Care for vs? True indeed, they nere car'd for vs yet. Suffer vs to famish, and their Store-houses cramm'd with Graine: Make Edicts for Vsurie, to support Vsurers; repeale daily any wholsome Act established against the rich, and prouide more piercing Statutes daily, to chaine vp and restraine the poore. If the Warres eate vs not vppe, they will; and there's allthe loue they beare vs.

Menen. Either you must
Confesse your selues wondrous Malicious,
Or be accus'd of Folly. I shall tell you
A pretty Tale, it may be you haue heard it,
But since it serues my purpose, I will venture
To scale't a little more.

2 *Citizen.* Well,
Ile heare it Sir: yet you must not thinke
To fobbe off our disgrace with a tale:
But and't please you deliuer.

Men. There was a time, when all the bodies members
Rebell'd against the Belly; thus accus'd it:
That onely like a Gulfe it did remaine

a a I'th

I'th midd'st a th'body, idle and vnactiue,
Still cubbording the Viand, neuer bearing
Like labour with the rest, where th'other Instruments
Did see, and heare, deuise, instruct, walke, feele,
And mutually participate, did minister
Vnto the appetite; and affection common
Of the whole body, the Belly answer'd.

2.Cit. Well sir, what answer made the Belly.

Men. Sir, I shall tell you with a kinde of Smile,
Which ne're came from the Lungs, but euen thus:
For looke you I may make the belly Smile,
As well as speake, it taintingly replyed
To'th'discontented Members, the mutinous parts
That enuied his receite: euen so most fitly,
As you maligne our Senators, for that
They are not such as you.

2.Cit. Your Bellies answer: What
The Kingly crown'd head, the vigilant eye,
The Counsailor Heart, the Arme our Souldier,
Our Steed the Legge, the Tongue our Trumpeter,
With other Muniments and petty helpes
In this our Fabricke, if that they———

Men. What then? Foreme, this Fellow speakes.
What then? What then?

2 Cit. Should by the Cormorant belly be restrain'd,
Who is the sinke a th'body.

Men. Well, what then?

2.Cit. The former Agents, if they did complaine,
What could the Belly answer?

Men. I will tell you,
If you'l bestow a small (of what you haue little)
Patience awhile; you'st heare the Bellies answer.

2.Cit. Y'are long about it.

Men. Note me this good Friend;
Your most graue Belly was deliberate,
Not rash like his Accusers, and thus answered.
True is it my Incorporate Friends (quoth he)
That I receiue the generall Food at first
Which you do liue vpon: and fit it is,
Because I am the Store-house, and the Shop
Of the whole Body. But, if you do remember,
I send it through the Riuers of your blood
Euen to the Court, the Heart, to th'seate o'th'Braine,
And through the Crankes and Offices of man,
The strongest Nerues, and small inferiour Veines
From me receiue that naturall competencie
Whereby they liue. And though that all at once
(You my good Friends, this sayes the Belly) marke me.

2.Cit. I sir, well, well.

Men. Though all at once, cannot
See what I do deliuer out to each,
Yet I can make my Awdit vp, that all
From me do backe receiue the Flowre of all,
And leaue me but the Bran. What say you too't?

2.Cit. It was an answer, how apply you this?

Men. The Senators of Rome, are this good Belly,
And you the mutinous Members: For examine
Their Counsailes, and their Cares; disgest things rightly,
Touching the Weale a'th Common, you shall finde
No publique benefit which you receiue
But it proceeds, or comes from them to you,
And no way from your selues. What do you thinke?
You, the great Toe of this Assembly?

2.Cit. I the great Toe? Why the great Toe?

Men. For that being one o'th lowest, basest, poorest
Of this most wise Rebellion, thou goest formost:
Thou Rascall, that art worst in blood to run,
Lead'st first to win some vantage.
But make you ready your stiffe bats and clubs,
Rome, and her Rats, are at the point of battell,
The one side must haue baile.

Enter Caius Martius.

Hayle, Noble *Martius*.

Mar. Thanks. What's the matter you dissentious rogues
That rubbing the poore Itch of your Opinion,
Make your selues Scabs.

2.Cit. We haue euer your good word.

Mar. He that will giue good words to thee, wil flatter
Beneath abhorring. What would you haue, you Curres,
That like nor Peace, nor Warre? The one affrights you,
The other makes you proud. He that trusts to you,
Where he should finde you Lyons, findes you Hares:
Where Foxes, Geese you are: No surer, no,
Then is the coale of fire vpon the Ice,
Or Hailstone in the Sun. Your Vertue is,
To make him worthy, whose offence subdues him,
And curse that Iustice did it. Who deserues Greatnes,
Deserues your Hate: and your Affections are
A sickmans Appetite; who desires most that
Which would encrease his euill. He that depends
Vpon your fauours, swimmes with finnes of Leade,
And hewes downe Oakes, with rushes. Hang ye: trust ye?
With euery Minute you do change a Minde,
And call him Noble, that was now your Hate:
Him vilde, that was your Garland. What's the matter,
That in these seuerall places of the Citie,
You cry against the Noble Senate, who
(Vnder the Gods) keepe you in awe, which else
Would feede on one another? What's their seeking?

Men. For Corne at their owne rates, wherof they say
The Citie is well stor'd.

Mar. Hang 'em: They say?
They'l sit by th'fire, and presume to know
What's done i'th Capitoll: Who's like to rise,
Who thriues, & who declines: Side factions, & giue out
Coniecturall Marriages, making parties strong,
And feebling such as stand not in their liking,
Below their cobled Shooes. They say ther's grain enough?
Would the Nobility lay aside their ruth,
And let me vse my Sword, I'de make a Quarrie
With thousands of these quarter'd slaues, as high
As I could picke my Lance.

Menen. Nay these are almost thoroughly perswaded:
For though abundantly they lacke discretion
Yet are they passing Cowardly. But I beseech you,
What sayes the other Troope?

Mar. They are dissolu'd: Hang em;
They said they were an hungry, sigh'd forth Prouerbes
That Hunger-broke stone wals: that dogges must eate
That meate was made for mouths. That the gods sent not
Corne for the Richmen onely: With these shreds
They vented their Complainings, which being answer'd
And a petition granted them, a strange one,
To breake the heart of generosity,
And make bold power looke pale, they threw their caps
As they would hang them on the hornes a'th Moone,
Shooting their Emulation.

Menen. What is graunted them?

Mar. Fiue Tribunes to defend their vulgar wisdoms
Of their owne choice. One's *Iunius Brutus*,
Sicinius Velutus, and I know not. Sdeath,

The

The rabble should haue first vnroo'st the City
Ere so preuayl'd with me; it will in time
Win vpon power, and throw forth greater Theames
For Insurrections arguing.
Menen. This is strange.
Mar. Go get you home you Fragments.
Enter a Messenger hastily.
Mess. Where's *Caius Martius*?
Mar. Heere: what's the matter?
Mes. The newes is sir, the Volcies are in Armes.
Mar. I am glad on't, then we shall ha meanes to vent
Our mustie superfluity. See our best Elders.

Enter Sicinius Velutus, Annius Brutus Cominius, Titus Lartius, with other Senatours.

1.*Sen.* *Martius* 'tis true, that you haue lately told vs,
The Volces are in Armes.
Mar. They haue a Leader,
Tullus Auffidius that will put you too't:
I sinne in enuying his Nobility:
And were I any thing but what I am,
I would wish me onely he.
Com. You haue fought together?
Mar. Were halfe to halfe the world by th'eares, & he vpon my partie, I'de reuolt to make
Onely my warres with him. He is a Lion
That I am proud to hunt.
1.*Sen.* Then worthy *Martius*,
Attend vpon *Cominius* to these Warres.
Com. It is your former promise.
Mar. Sir it is,
And I am constant: *Titus Lucius*, thou
Shalt see me once more strike at *Tullus* face.
What art thou stiffe? Stand'st out?
Tit. No *Caius Martius*,
Ile leane vpon one Crutch, and fight with tother,
Ere stay behinde this Businesse.
Men. Oh true-bred.
Sen. Your Company to'th'Capitoll, where I know
Our greatest Friends attend vs.
Tit. Lead you on: Follow *Cominius*, we must followe you, right worthy you Priority.
Com. Noble *Martius*.
Sen. Hence to your homes, be gone.
Mar. Nay let them follow,
The Volces haue much Corne: take these Rats thither,
To gnaw their Garners. Worshipfull Mutiners,
Your valour puts well forth: Pray follow. *Exeunt.*
Citizens steale away. Manet Sicin. & Brutus.
Sicin. Was euer man so proud as is this *Martius*?
Bru. He has no equall.
Sicin. When we were chosen Tribunes for the people.
Bru. Mark'd you his lip and eyes.
Sicin. Nay, but his taunts.
Bru. Being mou'd, he will not spare to gird the Gods.
Sicin. Bemocke the modest Moone.
Bru. The present Warres deuoure him, he is growne
Too proud to be so valiant.
Sicin. Such a Nature, tickled with good successe, disdaines the shadow which he treads on at noone, but I do wonder, his insolence can brooke to be commanded vnder *Cominius*?
Bru. Fame, at the which he aymes,
In whom already he's well grac'd, cannot
Better be held, nor more attain'd then by
A place below the first: for what miscarries
Shall be the Generals fault, though he performe
To th'vtmost of a man, and giddy censure
Will then cry out of *Martius*: Oh, if he
Had borne the businesse.
Sicin. Besides, if things go well,
Opinion that so stickes on *Martius*, shall
Of his demerits rob *Cominius*.
Bru. Come: halfe all *Cominius* Honors are to *Martius*
Though *Martius* earn'd them not: and all his faults
To *Martius* shall be Honors, though indeed
In ought he merit not.
Sicin. Let's hence, and heare
How the dispatch is made, and in what fashion
More then his singularity, he goes
Vpon this present Action.
Bru. Let's along. *Exeunt*

Enter Tullus Auffidius with Senators of Coriolus.

1.*Sen.* So, your opinion is *Auffidius*,
That they of Rome are entred in our Counsailes,
And know how we proceede,
Auf. Is it not yours?
What euer haue bin thought one in this State
That could be brought to bodily act, ere Rome
Had circumuention: 'tis not foure dayes gone
Since I heard thence, these are the words, I thinke
I haue the Letter heere: yes, heere it is;
They haue prest a Power, but it is not knowne
Whether for East or West: the Dearth is great,
The people Mutinous: And it is rumour'd,
Cominius, Martius your old Enemy
(Who is of Rome worse hated then of you)
And *Titus Lartius*, a most valiant Roman,
These three leade on this Preparation
Whether 'tis bent: most likely, 'tis for you:
Consider of it.
1.*Sen.* Our Armie's in the Field:
We neuer yet made doubt but Rome was ready
To answer vs.
Auf. Nor did you thinke it folly,
To keepe your great pretences vayl'd, till when
They needs must shew themselues, which in the hatching
It seem'd appear'd to Rome. By the discouery,
We shalbe shortned in our ayme, which was
To take in many Townes, ere (almost) Rome
Should know we were a-foot.
2.*Sen.* Noble *Auffidius*,
Take your Commission, hye you to your Bands,
Let vs alone to guard *Corioles*
If they set downe before's: for the remoue
Bring vp your Army: but (I thinke) you'l finde
Th'haue not prepar'd for vs.
Auf. O doubt not that,
I speake from Certainties. Nay more,
Some parcels of their Power are forth already,
And onely hitherward. I leaue your Honors.
If we, and *Caius Martius* chance to meete,
'Tis sworne betweene vs, we shall euer strike
Till one can do no more.
All. The Gods assist you.
Auf. And keepe your Honors safe.
1.*Sen.* Farewell.
2.*Sen.* Farewell.
All. Farewell. *Exeunt omnes.*

aa2 *Enter*

Enter Volumnia and Virgilia, mother and wife to Martius: They ſet them downe on two lowe ſtooles and ſowe.

Volum. I pray you daughter ſing, or expreſſe your ſelfe in a more comfortable ſort: If my Sonne were my Huſband, I ſhould freelier reioyce in that abſence wherein he wonne Honor, then in the embracements of his Bed, where he would ſhew moſt loue. When yet hee was but tender-bodied, and the onely Sonne of my womb; when youth with comelineſſe pluck'd all gaze his way; when for a day of Kings entreaties, a Mother ſhould not ſel him an houre from her beholding; I conſidering how Honour would become ſuch a perſon, that it was no better then Picture-like to hang by th'wall, if renowne made it not ſtirre, was pleas'd to let him ſeeke danger, where he was like to finde fame: To a cruell Warre I ſent him, from whence he return'd, his browes bound with Oake. I tell thee Daughter, I ſprang not more in ioy at firſt hearing he was a Man-child, then now in firſt ſeeing he had proued himſelfe a man.

Virg. But had he died in the Buſineſſe Madame, how then?

Volum. Then his good report ſhould haue beene my Sonne, I therein would haue found iſſue. Heare me profeſſe ſincerely, had I a dozen ſons each in my loue alike, and none leſſe deere then thine, and my good *Martius*, I had rather had eleuen dye Nobly for their Countrey, then one voluptuouſly ſurfet out of Action.

Enter a Gentlewoman.

Gent. Madam, the Lady *Valeria* is come to viſit you.

Virg. Beſeech you giue me leaue to retire my ſelfe.

Volum. Indeed you ſhall not:
Me thinkes, I heare hither your Husbands Drumme:
See him plucke *Auffidius* downe by th'haire:
(As children from a Beare) the *Volces* ſhunning him:
Me thinkes I ſee him ſtampe thus, and call thus,
Come on you Cowards, you were got in feare
Though you were borne in Rome; his bloody brow
With his mail'd hand, then wiping, forth he goes
Like to a Harueſt man, that task'd to mowe
Or all, or looſe his hyre.

Virg. His bloody Brow? Oh Iupiter, no blood.

Volum. Away you Foole; it more becomes a man
Then gilt his Trophe. The breſts of *Hecuba*
When ſhe did ſuckle *Hector*, look'd not louelier
Then *Hectors* forhead, when it ſpit forth blood
At Grecian ſword. *Contenning*, tell *Valeria*
We are fit to bid her welcome. *Exit Gent.*

Vir. Heauens bleſſe my Lord from fell *Auffidius.*

Vol, Hee'l beat *Auffidius* head below his knee,
And treade vpon his necke.

Enter Valeria with an Vſher, and a Gentlewoman.

Val. My Ladies both good day to you.

Vol. Sweet Madam.

Vir. I am glad to ſee your Ladyſhip.

Val. How do you both? You are manifeſt houſe-keepers. What are you ſowing heere? A fine ſpotte in good faith. How does your little Sonne?

Vir. I thanke your Lady-ſhip: Well good Madam.

Vol. He had rather ſee the ſwords, and heare a Drum, then looke vpon his Schoolmaſter.

Val. A my word the Fathers Sonne: Ile ſweare 'tis a very pretty boy. A my troth, I look'd vpon him a Wenſday halfe an houre together: ha's ſuch a confirm'd countenance. I ſaw him run after a gilded Butterfly, & when he caught it, he let it go againe, and after it againe, and o-uer and ouer he comes, and vp againe: catcht it again: or whether his fall enrag'd him, or how 'twas, hee did ſo ſet his teeth, and teare it. Oh, I warrant how he mammockt it.

Vol. One on's Fathers moods.

Val. Indeed la, tis a Noble childe.

Virg. A Cracke Madam.

Val. Come, lay aſide your ſtitchery, I muſt haue you play the idle Huſwife with me this afternoone.

Virg. No (good Madam)
I will not out of doores.

Val. Not out of doores?

Volum. She ſhall, ſhe ſhall.

Virg. Indeed no, by your patience; Ile not ouer the threſhold, till my Lord returne from the Warres.

Val. Fye, you confine your ſelfe moſt vnreaſonably: Come, you muſt go viſit the good Lady that lies in.

Virg. I will wiſh her ſpeedy ſtrength, and viſite her with my prayers: but I cannot go thither.

Volum. Why I pray you.

Vlug. 'Tis not to ſaue labour, nor that I want loue.

Val. You would be another *Penelope*: yet they ſay, all the yearne ſhe ſpun in *Vliſſes* abſence, did but fill *Atbica* full of Mothes. Come, I would your Cambrick were ſenſible as your finger, that you might leaue pricking it for pitie. Come you ſhall go with vs.

Vir. No good Madam, pardon me, indeed I will not foorth.

Val. In truth la go with me, and Ile tell you excellent newes of your Husband.

Virg. Oh good Madam, there can be none yet.

Val. Verily I do not ieſt with you: there came newes from him laſt night.

Vir. Indeed Madam.

Val. In earneſt it's true; I heard a Senatour ſpeake it. Thus it is: the Volcies haue an Army forth, againſt whõ *Cominius* the Generall is gone, with one part of our Romane power. Your Lord, and *Titus Lartius*, are ſet down before their Citie *Carioles*, they nothing doubt preuailing, and to make it breefe Warres. This is true on mine Honor, and ſo I pray go with vs.

Virg. Giue me excuſe good Madame, I will obey you in euery thing heereafter.

Vol. Let her alone Ladie, as ſhe is now:
She will but diſeaſe our better mirth.

Valeria. In troth I thinke ſhe would:
Fare you well then. Come good ſweet Ladie.
Prythee *Virgilia* turne thy ſolemneſſe out a doore,
And go along with vs.

Virgil. No
At a word Madam; Indeed I muſt not,
I wiſh you much mirth.

Val. Well, then farewell. *Exeunt Ladies*

Enter Martius, Titus Lartius, with Drumme and Colours, with Captaines and Souldiers, as before the City Corialus: to them a Meſſenger.

Martius. Yonder comes Newes:
A Wager they haue met.

Lar. My horſe to yours, no.

Mar. Tis done.

Lart. Agreed.

Mar.

Mar. Say, ha's our Generall met the Enemy?
Mess. They lye in view, but haue not spoke as yet.
Lart. So, the good Horse is mine.
Mart. Ile buy him of you.
Lart. No, Ile nor sel, nor giue him: Lend you him I will
For halfe a hundred yeares: Summon the Towne.
Mar. How farre off lie these Armies?
Mess. Within this mile and halfe.
Mar. Then shall we heare their Larum, & they Ours.
Now Mars, I prythee make vs quicke in worke,
That we with smoaking swords may march from hence
To helpe our fielded Friends. Come, blow thy blast.

They Sound a Parley: Enter two Senators with others on the Walles of Corialus.

Tullus Auffidious, is he within your Walles?
1.Senat. No, nor a man that feares you lesse then he,
That's lesser then a little: *Drum a farre off.*
Hearke, our Drummes
Are bringing forth our youth: Wee'l breake our Walles
Rather then they shall pound vs vp our Gates,
Which yet seeme shut, we haue but pin'd with Rushes,
They'le open of themselues. Harke you, farre off
Alarum farre off.
There is *Auffidious.* List what worke he makes
Among'st your clouen Army.
Mart. Oh they are at it.
Lart. Their noise be our instruction. Ladders hoa.

Enter the Army of the Volces.

Mar. They feare vs not, but issue forth their Citie.
Now put your Shields before your hearts, and fight
With hearts more proofe then Shields.
Aduance braue *Titus*,
They do disdaine vs much beyond our Thoughts,
which makes me sweat with wrath. Come on my fellows
He that retires, Ile take him for a *Volce*,
And he shall feele mine edge.
Alarum, the Romans are beat back to their Trenches Enter Martius Cursing.
Mar. All the contagion of the South, light on you,
You Shames of Rome: you Heard of Byles and Plagues
Plaister you o're, that you may be abhorr'd
Farther then seene, and one infect another
Against the Winde a mile: you soules of Geese,
That beare the shapes of men, how haue you run
From Slaues, that Apes would beate; *Pluto* and Hell,
All hurt behinde, backes red, and faces pale
With flight and agued feare, mend and charge home,
Or by the fires of heauen, Ile leaue the Foe,
And make my Warres on you: Looke too't: Come on,
If you'l stand fast, wee'l beate them to their Wiues,
As they vs to our Trenches followes.
Another Alarum, and Martius followes them to gates, and is shut in.
So, now the gates are ope: now proue good Seconds,
'Tis for the followers Fortune, widens them,
Not for the flyers: Marke me, and do the like.
Enter the Gati.
1.Sol. Foole-hardinesse, not I.
2.Sol. Nor I.
1.Sol. See they haue shut him in. *Alarum continues*
All. To th'pot I warrant him. *Enter Titus Lartius*
Tit. What is become of *Martius*?
All. Slaine (Sir) doubtlesse.
1.Sol. Following the Flyers at the very heeles,
With them he enters: who vpon the sodaine
Clapt to their Gates, he is himselfe alone,
To answer all the City.
Lar. Oh Noble Fellow!
Who sensibly out-dares his sencelesse Sword,
And when it bowes, stand'st vp: Thou art left *Martius*,
A Carbuncle intire: as big as thou art
Weare not so rich a Iewell. Thou was't a Souldier
Euen to *Calues* wish, not fierce and terrible
Onely in strokes, but with thy grim lookes, and
The Thunder-like percussion of thy sounds
Thou mad'st thine enemies shake, as if the World
Were Feauorous, and did tremble.

Enter Martius bleeding, assaulted by the Enemy.

1.Sol. Looke Sir.
Lar. O 'tis *Martius*.
Let's fetch him off, or make remaine alike.
They fight, and all enter the City.
Enter certaine Romanes with spoiles.
1.Rom. This will I carry to *Rome*.
2.Rom. And I this.
3.Rom. A Murrain on't, I tooke this for Siluer. *exeunt.*
Alarum continues still a-farre off.
Enter Martius, and Titus with a Trumpet.
Mar. See heere these mouers, that do prize their hours
At a crack'd Drachme: Cushions, Leaden Spoones,
Irons of a Doit, Dublets that Hangmen would
Bury with those that wore them. These base slaues,
Ere yet the fight be done, packe vp, downe with them.
And harke, what noyse the Generall makes: To him
There is the man of my soules hate, *Auffidious*,
Piercing our Romanes: Then Valiant *Titus* take
Conuenient Numbers to make good the City,
Whil'st I with those that haue the spirit, wil haste
To helpe *Cominius*.
Lar. Worthy Sir, thou bleed'st,
Thy exercise hath bin too violent,
For a second course of Fight.
Mar. Sir, praise me not:
My worke hath yet not warm'd me. Fare you well:
The blood I drop, is rather Physicall
Then dangerous to me: To *Auffidious* thus, I will appear (and fight.
Lar. Now the faire Goddesse Fortune,
Fall deepe in loue with thee, and her great charmes
Misguide thy Opposers swords, Bold Gentleman:
Prosperity be thy Page.
Mar. Thy Friend no lesse,
Then those she placeth highest: So farewell.
Lar. Thou worthiest *Martius*,
Go sound thy Trumpet in the Market place,
Call thither all the Officers a'th'Towne,
Where they shall know our minde. Away. *Exeunt*
Enter Cominius as it were in retire, with soldiers.
Com. Breath you my friends, wel fought, we are come (off,
Like Romans, neither foolish in our stands,
Nor Cowardly in retyre: Beleeue me Sirs,
We shall be charg'd againe. Whiles we haue strooke
By Interims and conueying gusts, we haue heard
The Charges of our Friends. The Roman Gods,
Leade their successes, as we wish our owne,
That both our powers, with smiling Fronts encountring,
May giue you thankfull Sacrifice. Thy Newes?
Enter a Messenger.
Mess. The Cittizens of *Corioles* haue yssued,
And giuen to *Lartius* and to *Martius* Battaile:
aa 3 I saw

I ſaw our party to their Trenches driuen,
And then I came away.
Com. Though thou ſpeakeſt truth,
Me thinkes thou ſpeak'ſt not well. How long is't ſince?
Meſ. Aboue an houre, my Lord.
Com.'Tis not a mile: briefely we heard their drummes.
How could'ſt thou in a mile confound an houre,
And bring thy Newes ſo late?
Meſ. Spies of the *Volces*
Held me in chace, that I was forc'd to wheele
Three or foure miles about, elſe had I ſir
Halfe an houre ſince brought my report.

Enter Martius.

Com. Whoſe yonder,
That doe's appeare as he were Flead? O Gods,
He has the ſtampe of *Martius*, and I haue
Before time ſeene him thus.
Mar. Come I too late?
Com. The Shepherd knowes not Thunder frō a Taber,
More then I know the ſound of *Martius* Tongue
From euery meaner man.
Martius. Come I too late?
Com. I, if you come not in the blood of others,
But mantled in your owne.
Mart. Oh! let me clip ye
In Armes as ſound, as when I woo'd in heart;
As merry, as when our Nuptiall day was done,
And Tapers burnt to Bedward.
Com. Flower of Warriors, how is't with *Titus Lartius*?
Mar. As with a man buſied about Decrees:
Condemning ſome to death, and ſome to exile,
Ranſoming him, or pittying, threatning th'other;
Holding *Corioles* in the name of Rome,
Euen like a fawning Grey-hound in the Leaſh,
To let him ſlip at will.
Com. Where is that Slaue
Which told me they had beate you to your Trenches?
Where is he? Call him hither.
Mar. Let him alone,
He did informe the truth: but for our Gentlemen,
The common file, (a plague-Tribunes for them)
The Mouſe ne're ſhunn'd the Cat, as they did budge
From Raſcals worſe then they.
Com. But how preuail'd you?
Mar. Will the time ſerue to tell, I do not thinke:
Where is the enemy? Are you Lords a'th Field?
If not, why ceaſe you till you are ſo?
Com. *Martius*, we haue at diſaduantage fought,
And did retyre to win our purpoſe.
Mar. How lies their Battell? Know you on wͨ ſide
They haue plac'd their men of truſt?
Com. As I gueſſe *Martius*,
Their Bands i'th Vaward are the Antients
Of their beſt truſt: O're them *Auffidious*,
Their very heart of Hope.
Mar. I do beſeech you,
By all the Battailes wherein we haue fought,
By th'Blood we haue ſhed together,
By th'Vowes we haue made
To endure Friends, that you directly ſet me
Againſt *Affidious*, and his *Antiats*,
And that you not delay the preſent (but
Filling the aire with Swords aduanc'd) and Darts,
We proue this very houre.
Com. Though I could wiſh,
You were conducted to a gentle Bath,
And Balmes applyed to you, yet dare I neuer
Deny your asking, take your choice of thoſe
That beſt can ayde your action.
Mar. Thoſe are they
That moſt are willing; if any ſuch be heere,
(As it were ſinne to doubt) that loue this painting
Wherein you ſee me ſmear'd, if any feare
Leſſen his perſon, then an ill report:
If any thinke, braue death out-weighes bad life,
And that his Countries deerer then himſelfe,
Let him alone: Or ſo many ſo minded,
Waue thus to expreſſe his diſpoſition,
And follow *Martius*.

They all ſhout and waue their ſwords, take him vp in their Armes, and caſt vp their Caps.

Oh me alone, make you a ſword of me:
If theſe ſhewes be not outward, which of you
But is foure *Volces*? None of you, but is
Able to beare againſt the great *Auffidious*
A Shield, as hard as his. A certaine number
(Though thankes to all) muſt I ſelect from all:
The reſt ſhall beare the buſineſſe in ſome other fight
(As cauſe will be obey'd:) pleaſe you to March,
And foure ſhall quickly draw out my Command,
Which men are beſt inclin'd.
Com. March on my Fellowes:
Make good this oſtentation, and you ſhall
Diuide in all, with vs. *Exeunt*

Titus Lartius, hauing ſet a guard vpon Carioles, going with Drum and Trumpet toward Cominius, and Caius Martius, Enters with a Lieutenant, other Souldiours, and a Scout.

Lar. So, let the Ports be guarded; keepe your Duties
As I haue ſet them downe. If I do ſend, diſpatch
Thoſe Centuries to our ayd, the reſt will ſerue
For a ſhort holding, if we looſe the Field,
We cannot keepe the Towne.
Lieu. Feare not our care Sir.
Lart. Hence; and ſhut your gates vpon's:
Our Guider come, to th'Roman Campe conduct vs. *Exit*

Alarum, as in Battaile.

Enter Martius and Auffidius at ſeueral doores.

Mar. Ile fight with none but thee, for I do hate thee
Worſe then a Promiſe-breaker.
Auffid. We hate alike:
Not Affricke ownes a Serpent I abhorre
More then thy Fame and Enuy: Fix thy foot.
Mar. Let the firſt Budger dye the others Slaue,
And the Gods doome him after.
Auf. If I flye *Martius*, hollow me like a Hare.
Mar. Within theſe three houres *Tullus*
Alone I fought in your *Corioles* walles,
And made what worke I pleas'd: 'Tis not my blood,
Wherein thou ſeeſt me maskt, for thy Reuenge
Wrench vp thy power to th'higheſt.
Auf. Wer't thou the *Hector*,
That was the whip of your bragg'd Progeny,
Thou ſhould'ſt not ſcape me heere.

Heere they fight, and certaine Volces come in the ayde of Auffi. Martius fights til they be driuen in breathles.

Officious and not valiant, you haue ſham'd me
In your condemned Seconds.

Flouriſh.

Flourish. Alarum. A Retreat is founded. Enter at one Doore Cominius, with the Romanes: At another Doore Martius, with his Arme in a Scarfe.

Com. If I ſhould tell thee o're this thy dayes Worke,
Thou't not beleeue thy deeds: but Ile report it,
Where Senators ſhall mingle teares with ſmiles,
Where great Patricians ſhall attend, and ſhrug,
I'th'end admire: where Ladies ſhall be frighted,
And gladly quak'd, heare more: where the dull Tribunes,
That with the fuſtie Plebeans, hate thine Honors,
Shall ſay againſt their hearts, We thanke the Gods
Our Rome hath ſuch a Souldier.
Yet cam'ſt thou to a Morſell of this Feaſt,
Hauing fully din'd before.

Enter Titus with his Power, from the Purſuit.

Titus Lartius. Oh Generall:
Here is the Steed, wee the Capariſon:
Hadſt thou beheld——
Martius. Pray now, no more:
My Mother, who ha's a Charter to extoll her Bloud,
When ſhe do's prayſe me, grieues me:
I haue done as you haue done, that's what I can,
Induc'd as you haue beene, that's for my Countrey:
He that ha's but effected his good will,
Hath ouerta'ne mine Act.
Com. You ſhall not be the Graue of your deſeruing,
Rome muſt know the value of her owne:
'Twere a Concealement worſe then a Theft,
No leſſe then a Traducement,
To hide your doings, and to ſilence that,
Which to the ſpire, and top of prayſes vouch'd,
Would ſeeme but modeſt: therefore I beſeech you,
In ſigne of what you are, not to reward
What you haue done, before our Armie heare me.
Martius. I haue ſome Wounds vpon me, and they ſmart
To heare themſelues remembred.
Com. Should they not:
Well might they feſter 'gainſt Ingratitude,
And tent themſelues with death: of all the Horſes,
Whereof we haue ta'ne good, and good ſtore of all,
The Treaſure in this field atchieued, and Citie,
We render you the Tenth, to be ta'ne forth,
Before the common diſtribution,
At your onely choyſe.
Martius. I thanke you Generall:
But cannot make my heart conſent to take
A Bribe, to pay my Sword: I doe refuſe it,
And ſtand vpon my common part with thoſe,
That haue beheld the doing.

A long flouriſh. They all cry, Martius, Martius, caſt vp their Caps and Launces: Cominius and Lartius ſtand bare.

Mar. May theſe ſame Inſtruments, which you prophane,
Neuer ſound more: when Drums and Trumpets ſhall
I'th'field proue flatterers, let Courts and Cities be
Made all of falſe-fac'd ſoothing:
When Steele growes ſoft, as the Paraſites Silke,
Let him be made an Ouerture for th'Warres:
No more I ſay, for that I haue not waſh'd
My Noſe that bled, or foyl'd ſome debile Wretch,
Which without note, here's many elſe haue done,
You ſhoot me forth in acclamations hyperbolicall,
As if I lou'd my little ſhould be dieted
In prayſes, ſawc'ſt with Lyes.
Com. Too modeſt are you:
More cruell to your good report, then gratefull
To vs, that giue you truly: by your patience,
If 'gainſt your ſelfe you be incens'd, wee'le put you
(Like one that meanes his proper harme) in Manacles,
Then reaſon ſafely with you: Therefore be it knowne,
As to vs, to all the World, That *Caius Martius*
Weares this Warres Garland: in token of the which,
My Noble Steed, knowne to the Campe, I giue him,
With all his trim belonging; and from this time,
For what he did before *Corioles*, call him,
With all th'applauſe and Clamor of the Hoaſt,
Marcus Caius Coriolanus. Beare th'addition Nobly euer?
Flouriſh. Trumpets ſound, and Drums.
Omnes. Marcus Caius Coriolanus.
Martius. I will goe waſh:
And when my Face is faire, you ſhall perceiue
Whether I bluſh, or no: howbeit, I thanke you,
I meane to ſtride your Steed, and at all times
To vnder-creſt your good Addition,
To th'faireneſſe of my power.
Com. So, to our Tent:
Where ere we doe repoſe vs, we will write
To Rome of our ſucceſſe: you *Titus Lartius*
Muſt to *Corioles* backe, ſend vs to Rome
The beſt, with whom we may articulate,
For their owne good, and ours.
Lartius. I ſhall, my Lord.
Martius. The Gods begin to mocke me:
I that now refus'd moſt Princely gifts,
Am bound to begge of my Lord Generall.
Com. Tak't, 'tis yours: what is't?
Martius. I ſometime lay here in *Corioles*,
At a poore mans houſe: he vs'd me kindly,
He cry'd to me: I ſaw him Priſoner:
But then *Auffidius* was within my view,
And Wrath o're-whelm'd my pittie: I requeſt you
To giue my poore Hoſt freedome.
Com. Oh well begg'd:
Were he the Butcher of my Sonne, he ſhould
Be free, as is the Winde: deliuer him, *Titus.*
Lartius. Martius, his Name.
Martius. By *Iupiter* forgot:
I am wearie, yea, my memorie is tyr'd:
Haue we no Wine here?
Com. Goe we to our Tent:
The bloud vpon your Viſage dryes, 'tis time
It ſhould be lookt too: come. *Exeunt.*

A flouriſh. Cornets. Enter Tullus Auffidius bloudie, with two or three Souldiors.

Auffi. The Towne is ta'ne.
Sould. 'Twill be deliuer'd backe on good Condition.
Auffid. Condition?
I would I were a Roman, for I cannot,
Being a *Volce*, be that I am. Condition?
What good Condition can a Treatie finde
I'th'part that is at mercy? fiue times, *Martius*,
I haue fought with thee; ſo often haſt thou beat me:
And would'ſt doe ſo, I thinke, ſhould we encounter
As

As often as we eate. By th'Elements,
If ere againe I meet him beard to beard,
He's mine, or I am his: Mine Emulation
Hath not that Honor in't it had: For where
I thought to cruſh him in an equall Force,
True Sword to Sword: Ile potche at him ſome way,
Or Wrath, or Craft may get him.

Sol. He's the diuell.

Auf. Bolder, though not ſo ſubtle: my valors poiſon'd,
With onely ſuff'ring ſtaine by him: for him
Shall flye out of it ſelfe, nor ſleepe, nor ſanctuary,
Being naked, ſicke; nor Phane, nor Capitoll,
The Prayers of Prieſts, nor times of Sacrifice:
Embarquements all of Fury, ſhall lift vp
Their rotten Priuiledge, and Cuſtome 'gainſt
My hate to *Martius.* Where I finde him, were it
At home, vpon my Brothers Guard, euen there
Againſt the hoſpitable Canon, would I
Waſh my fierce hand in's heart. Go you to th'Citie,
Learne how 'tis held, and what they are that muſt
Be Hoſtages for Rome.

Soul. Will not you go?

Auf. I am attended at the Cyprus groue. I pray you
('Tis South the City Mils) bring me word thither
How the world goes: that to the pace of it
I may ſpurre on my iourney.

Soul. I ſhall ſir.

Actus Secundus.

Enter Menenius with the two Tribunes of the people, Sicinius & Brutus.

Men. The Agurer tels me, wee ſhall haue Newes to night.

Bru. Good or bad?

Men. Not according to the prayer of the people, for they loue not *Martius.*

Sicin. Nature teaches Beaſts to know their Friends.

Men. Pray you, who does the Wolfe loue?

Sicin. The Lambe.

Men. I, to deuour him, as the hungry Plebeians would the Noble *Martius.*

Bru. He's a Lambe indeed, that baes like a Beare.

Men. Hee's a Beare indeede, that liues like a Lambe. You two are old men, tell me one thing that I ſhall aske you.

Both. Well ſir.

Men. In what enormity is *Martius* poore in, that you two haue not in abundance?

Bru. He's poore in no one fault, but ſtor'd withall.

Sicin. Eſpecially in Pride.

Bru. And topping all others in boaſting.

Men. This is ſtrange now: Do you two know, how you are cenſured heere in the City, I mean of vs a'th'right hand File, do you?

Both. Why? ho ware we cenſur'd?

Men. Becauſe you talke of Pride now, will you not be angry.

Both. Well, well ſir, well.

Men. Why 'tis no great matter: for a very little theefe of Occaſion, will rob you of a great deale of Patience: Giue your diſpoſitions the reines, and bee angry at your pleaſures (at the leaſt) if you take it as a pleaſure to you, in being ſo: you blame *Martius* for being proud.

Brut. We do it not alone, ſir.

Men. I know you can doe very little alone, for your helpes are many, or elſe your actions would growe wondrous ſingle: your abilities are to Infant-like, for dooing much alone. You talke of Pride: Oh, that you could turn your eyes toward the Napes of your neckes, and make but an Interiour ſuruey of your good ſelues. Oh that you could.

Both. What then ſir?

Men. Why then you ſhould diſcouer a brace of vnmeriting, proud, violent, teſtie Magiſtrates (alias Fooles) as any in Rome.

Sicin. *Menenius*, you are knowne well enough too.

Men. I am knowne to be a humorous *Patritian*, and one that loues a cup of hot Wine, with not a drop of alaying Tiber in't: Said, to be ſomething imperfect in fauouring the firſt complaint, haſty and Tinder-like vppon, to triuiall motion: One, that conuerſes more with the Buttocke of the night, then with the forhead of the morning. What I think, I vtter, and ſpend my malice in my breath. Meeting two ſuch Weales men as you are (I cannot call you *Licurguſſes*,) if the drinke you giue me, touch my Palat aduerſly, I make a crooked face at it, I can ſay, your Worſhippes haue deliuer'd the matter well, when I finde the Aſſe in compound, with the Maior part of your ſyllables. And though I muſt be content to beare with thoſe, that ſay you are reuerend graue men, yet they lye deadly, that tell you haue good faces, if you ſee this in the Map of my Microcoſme, followes it that I am knowne well enough too? What harme can your beeſome Conſpectuities gleane out of this Charracter, if I be knowne well enough too.

Bru. Come ſir come, we know you well enough.

Menen. You know neither mee, your ſelues, nor any thing: you are ambitious, for poore knaues cappes and legges: you weare out a good wholeſome Forenoone, in hearing a cauſe betweene an Orendge wife, and a Forſetſeller, and then reiourne the Controuerſie of three-pence to a ſecond day of Audience. When you are hearing a matter betweene party and party, if you chaunce to bee pinch'd with the Collicke, you make faces like Mummers, ſet vp the bloodie Flagge againſt all Patience, and in roaring for a Chamber-pot, diſmiſſe the Controuerſie bleeding, the more intangled by your hearing: All the peace you make in their Cauſe, is calling both the parties Knaues. You are a payre of ſtrange ones.

Bru. Come, come, you are well vnderſtood to bee a perfecter gyber for the Table, then a neceſſary Bencher in the Capitoll.

Men. Our very Prieſts muſt become Mockers, if they ſhall encounter ſuch ridiculous Subiects as you are, when you ſpeake beſt vnto the purpoſe. It is not woorth the wagging of your Beards, and your Beards deſerue not ſo honourable a graue, as to ſtuffe a Botchers Cuſhion, or to be intomb'd in an Aſſes Packe-ſaddle; yet you muſt bee ſaying, *Martius* is proud: who in a cheape eſtimation, is worth all your predeceſſors, ſince *Deucalion*, though peraduenture ſome of the beſt of 'em were hereditarie hangmen. Godden to your Worſhips, more of your conuerſation would infect my Braine, being the Heardſmen of the Beaſtly Plebeans. I will be bold to take my leaue of you.

Bru. and Scic. *Aside.*

Enter

Enter Volumina, Virgilia, and Valeria.

How now (my as faire as Noble) Ladyes, and the Moone were shee Earthly, no Nobler; whither doe you follow your Eyes so fast?

Volum. Honorable *Menenius*, my Boy *Martius* approches: for the loue of *Iuno* let's goe.

Menen. Ha? *Martius* comming home?

Volum. I, worthy *Menenius*, and with most prosperous approbation.

Menen. Take my Cappe *Iupiter*, and I thanke thee: hoo, *Martius* comming home?

2. Ladies. Nay, 'tis true.

Volum. Looke, here's a Letter from him, the State hath another, his Wife another, and (I thinke) there's one at home for you.

Menen. I will make my very house reele to night:
A Letter for me?

Virgil. Yes certaine, there's a Letter for you, I saw't.

Menen. A Letter for me? it giues me an Estate of seuen yeeres health; in which time, I will make a Lippe at the Physician: The most soueraigne Prescription in *Galen*, is but Emperickqutique; and to this Preseruatiue, of no better report then a Horse-drench. Is he not wounded? he was wont to come home wounded?

Virgil. Oh no, no, no.

Volum. Oh, he is wounded, I thanke the Gods for't.

Menen. So doe I too, if it be not too much: brings a Victorie in his Pocket? the wounds become him.

Volum. On's Browes: *Menenius*, hee comes the third time home with the Oaken Garland.

Menen. Ha's he disciplin'd *Auffidius* soundly?

Volum. *Titus Lartius* writes, they fought together, but *Auffidius* got off.

Menen. And 'twas time for him too, Ile warrant him that: and he had stay'd by him, I would not haue been so fiddious'd, for all the Chests in Carioles, and the Gold that's in them. Is the Senate possest of this?

Volum. Good Ladies let's goe. Yes, yes, yes: The Senate ha's Letters from the Generall, wherein hee giues my Sonne the whole Name of the Warre: he hath in this action out-done his former deeds doubly.

Valer. In troth, there's wondrous things spoke of him.

Menen. Wondrous: I, I warrant you, and not without his true purchasing.

Virgil. The Gods graunt them true.

Volum. True? pow waw.

Mene. True? Ile be sworne they are true: where is hee wounded, God saue your good Worships? *Martius* is comming home: hee ha's more cause to be prowd: where is he wounded?

Volum. Ith' Shoulder, and ith' left Arme: there will be large Cicatrices to shew the People, when hee shall stand for his place: he receiued in the repulse of *Tarquin* seuen hurts ith' Body.

Mene. One ith' Neck, and two ith' Thigh, there's nine that I know.

Volum. Hee had, before this last Expedition, twentie fiue Wounds vpon him.

Mene. Now it's twentie seuen; euery gash was an Enemies Graue. Hearke, the Trumpets.

A showt, and flourish.

Volum. These are the Vshers of *Martius*:
Before him, hee carryes Noyse;
And behinde him, hee leaues Teares:
Death, that darke Spirit, in's neruie Arme doth lye,
Which being aduanc'd, declines, and then men dye.

A Sennet. Trumpets sound.
Enter Cominius the Generall, and Titus Latius: betweene them Coriolanus, crown'd with an Oaken Garland, with Captaines and Souldiers, and a Herauld.

Herauld. Know Rome, that all alone *Martius* did fight
Within Corioles Gates: where he hath wonne,
With Fame, a Name to *Martius Caius*:
These in honor followes *Martius Caius Coriolanus*.
Welcome to Rome, renowned *Coriolanus*.

Sound. Flourish.

All. Welcome to Rome, renowned *Coriolanus*.

Coriol. No more of this, it does offend my heart: pray now no more.

Com. Looke, Sir, your Mother.

Coriol. Oh! you haue, I know, petition'd all the Gods for my prosperitie. *Kneeles.*

Volum. Nay, my good Souldier, vp:
My gentle *Martius*, worthy *Caius*,
And by deed-atchieuing Honor newly nam'd,
What is it (*Coriolanus*) must I call thee?
But oh, thy Wife.

Corio. My gracious silence, hayle:
Would'st thou haue laugh'd, had I come Coffin'd home,
That weep'st to see me triumph? Ah my deare,
Such eyes the Widowes in Carioles were,
And Mothers that lacke Sonnes.

Mene. Now the Gods Crowne thee.

Com. And liue you yet? Oh my sweet Lady, pardon.

Volum. I know not where to turne.
Oh welcome home: and welcome Generall,
And y'are welcome all.

Mene. A hundred thousand Welcomes:
I could weepe, and I could laugh,
I am light, and heauie; welcome:
A Curse begin at very root on's heart,
That is not glad to see thee.
Yon are three, that Rome should dote on:
Yet by the faith of men, we haue
Some old Crab-trees here at home,
That will not be grafted to your Rallish.
Yet welcome Warriors:
Wee call a Nettle, but a Nettle;
And the faults of fooles, but folly.

Com. Euer right.

Cor. *Menenius*, euer, euer.

Herauld. Giue way there, and goe on.

Cor. Your Hand, and yours?
Ere in our owne house I doe shade my Head,
The good Patricians must be visited,
From whom I haue receiu'd not onely greetings,
But with them, change of Honors.

Volum. I haue liued,
To see inherited my very Wishes,
And the Buildings of my Fancie:
Onely there's one thing wanting,
Which (I doubt not) but our Rome
Will cast vpon thee.

Cor. Know, good Mother,
I had rather be their seruant in my way,
Then sway with them in theirs.

Com. On, to the Capitall. *Flourish. Cornets.*

Exeunt in State, as before.

Enter

Enter Brutus and Scicinius.

Bru. All tongues ſpeake of him, and the bleared ſights
Are ſpectacled to ſee him. Your pratling Nurſe
Into a rapture lets her Baby crie,
While ſhe chats him: the Kitchin *Malkin* pinnes
Her richeſt Lockram 'bout her reechie necke,
Clambring the Walls to eye him:
Stalls, Bulkes, Windowes, are ſmother'd vp,
Leades fill'd, and Ridges hors'd
With variable Complexions; all agreeing
In earneſtneſſe to ſee him: ſeld-ſhowne Flamins
Doe preſſe among the popular Throngs, and puffe
To winne a vulgar ſtation: our veyl'd Dames
Commit the Warre of White and Damaske
In their nicely gawded Cheekes, toth' wanton ſpoyle
Of *Phœbus* burning Kiſſes: ſuch a poother,
As if that whatſoeuer God, who leades him,
Were ſlyly crept into his humane powers,
And gaue him gracefull poſture.

Scicin. On the ſuddaine, I warrant him Conſull.

Brutus. Then our Office may, during his power, goe ſleepe.

Scicin. He cannot temp'rately tranſport his Honors,
From where he ſhould begin, and end, but will
Loſe thoſe he hath wonne.

Brutus. In that there's comfort.

Scici. Doubt not,
The Commoners, for whom we ſtand, but they
Vpon their ancient mallice, will forget
With the leaſt cauſe, theſe his new Honors,
Which that he will giue them, make I as little queſtion,
As he is prowd to doo't.

Brutus. I heard him ſweare,
Were he to ſtand for Conſull, neuer would he
Appeare i'th'Market place, nor on him put
The Naples Veſture of Humilitie,
Nor ſhewing (as the manner is) his Wounds
Toth' People, begge their ſtinking Breaths.

Scicin. 'Tis right.

Brutus. It was his word:
Oh he would miſſe it, rather then carry it,
But by the ſuite of the Gentry to him,
And the deſire of the Nobles.

Scicin. I wiſh no better, then haue him hold that purpoſe, and to put it in execution.

Brutus. 'Tis moſt like he will.

Scicin. It ſhall be to him then, as our good wills; a ſure deſtruction.

Brutus. So it muſt fall out
To him, or our Authorities, for an end.
We muſt ſuggeſt the People, in what hatred
He ſtill hath held them: that to's power he would
Haue made them Mules, ſilenc'd their Pleaders,
And diſpropertied their Freedomes; holding them,
In humane Action, and Capacitie,
Of no more Soule, nor fitneſſe for the World,
Then Cammels in their Warre, who haue their Prouand
Onely for bearing Burthens, and ſore blowes
For ſinking vnder them.

Scicin. This (as you ſay) ſuggeſted,
At ſome time, when his ſoaring Inſolence
Shall teach the People, which time ſhall not want,
If he be put vpon't, and that's as eaſie,
As to ſet Dogges on Sheepe, will be his fire
To kindle their dry Stubble: and their Blaze
Shall darken him for euer.

Enter a Meſſenger.

Brutus. What's the matter?

Meſſ. You are ſent for to the Capitoll:
'Tis thought, that *Martius* ſhall be Conſull:
I haue ſeene the dumbe men throng to ſee him,
And the blind to heare him ſpeak: Matrons flong Gloues,
Ladies and Maids their Scarffes, and Handkerchers,
Vpon him as he paſs'd: the Nobles bended
As to *Ioues* Statue, and the Commons made
A Shower, and Thunder, with their Caps, and Showts:
I neuer ſaw the like.

Brutus. Let's to the Capitoll,
And carry with vs Eares and Eyes for th' time,
But Hearts for the euent.

Scicin. Haue with you. *Exeunt.*

Enter two Officers, to lay Cuſhions, as it were, in the Capitoll.

1. *Off.* Come, come, they are almoſt here: how many ſtand for Conſulſhips?

2. *Off.* Three, they ſay: but 'tis thought of euery one, *Coriolanus* will carry it.

1. *Off.* That's a braue fellow: but hee's vengeance prowd, and loues not the common people.

2. *Off.* 'Faith, there hath beene many great men that haue flatter'd the people, who ne're loued them; and there be many that they haue loued, they know not wherefore: ſo that if they loue they know not why, they hate vpon no better a ground. Therefore, for *Coriolanus* neyther to care whether they loue, or hate him, manifeſts the true knowledge he ha's in their diſpoſition, and out of his Noble careleſneſſe lets them plainely ſee't.

1. *Off.* If he did not care whether he had their loue, or no, hee waued indifferently, 'twixt doing them neyther good, nor harme: but hee ſeekes their hate with greater deuotion, then they can render it him; and leaues nothing vndone, that may fully diſcouer him their oppoſite. Now to ſeeme to affect the mallice and diſpleaſure of the People, is as bad, as that which he diſlikes, to flatter them for their loue.

2. *Off.* Hee hath deſerued worthily of his Countrey, and his aſſent is not by ſuch eaſie degrees as thoſe, who hauing beene ſupple and courteous to the People, Bonnetted, without any further deed, to haue them at all into their eſtimation, and report: but hee hath ſo planted his Honors in their Eyes, and his actions in their Hearts, that for their Tongues to be ſilent, and not confeſſe ſo much, were a kinde of ingratefull Iniurie: to report otherwiſe, were a Mallice, that giuing it ſelfe the Lye, would plucke reproofe and rebuke from euery Eare that heard it.

1. *Off.* No more of him, hee's a worthy man: make way, they are comming.

A Sennet. Enter the Patricians, and the Tribunes of the People, Lictors before them: Coriolanus, Menenius, Cominius the Conſul: Scicinius and Brutus take their places by themſelues: Coriolanus ſtands.

Menen. Hauing determin'd of the Volces,
And to ſend for *Titus Lartius*: it remaines,
As the maine Point of this our after-meeting,

To

To gratifie his Noble seruice, that hath
Thus stood for his Countrey. Therefore please you,
Most reuerend and graue Elders, to desire
The present Consull, and last Generall,
In our well-found Successes, to report
A little of that worthy Worke, perform'd
By *Martius Caius Coriolanus:* whom
We met here, both to thanke, and to remember,
With Honors like himselfe.

1.*Sen.* Speake, good *Cominius:*
Leaue nothing out for length, and make vs thinke
Rather our states defectiue for requitall,
Then we to stretch it out. Masters a'th' People,
We doe request your kindest eares: and after
Your louing motion toward the common Body,
To yeeld what passes here.

Scicin. We are conuented vpon a pleasing Treatie, and haue hearts inclinable to honor and aduance the Theame of our Assembly.

Brutus. Which the rather wee shall be blest to doe, if he remember a kinder value of the People, then he hath hereto priz'd them at.

Menen. That's off, that's off: I would you rather had been silent: Please you to heare *Cominius* speake?

Brutus. Most willingly: but yet my Caution was more pertinent then the rebuke you giue it.

Menen. He loues your People, but tye him not to be their Bed-fellow: Worthie *Cominius* speake.

Coriolanus rises, and offers to goe away.

Nay, keepe your place.

Senat. Sit *Coriolanus:* neuer shame to heare
What you haue Nobly done.

Coriol. Your Honors pardon:
I had rather haue my Wounds to heale againe,
Then heare say how I got them.

Brutus. Sir, I hope my words dis-bench'd you not?

Coriol. No Sir: yet oft,
When blowes haue made me stay, I fled from words.
You sooth'd not, therefore hurt not: but your People,
I loue them as they weigh—

Menen. Pray now sit downe.

Corio. I had rather haue one scratch my Head i'th'Sun,
When the Alarum were strucke, then idly sit
To heare my Nothings monster'd. *Exit Coriolanus*

Menen. Masters of the People,
Your multiplying Spawne, how can he flatter?
That's thousand to one good one, when you now see
He had rather venture all his Limbes for Honor,
Then on ones Eares to heare it. Proceed *Cominius.*

Com. I shall lacke voyce: the deeds of *Coriolanus*
Should not be vtter'd feebly: it is held,
That Valour is the chiefest Vertue,
And most dignifies the hauer: if it be,
The man I speake of, cannot in the World
Be singly counter-poys'd. At sixteene yeeres,
When *Tarquin* made a Head for Rome, he fought
Beyond the marke of others: our then Dictator,
Whom with all prayse I point at, saw him fight,
When with his Amazonian Shinne he droue
The brizled Lippes before him: he bestrid
An o're-prest Roman, and i'th' Consuls view
Slew three Opposers: *Tarquins* selfe he met,
And strucke him on his Knee: in that dayes feates,
When he might act the Woman in the Scene,
He prou'd best man i'th' field, and for his meed
Was Brow-bound with the Oake. His Pupill age
Man-entred thus, he waxed like a Sea,
And in the brunt of seuenteene Battailes since,
He lurcht all Swords of the Garland: for this last,
Before, and in Corioles, let me say
I cannot speake him home: he stopt the flyers,
And by his rare example made the Coward
Turne terror into sport: as Weeds before
A Vessell vnder sayle, so men obey'd,
And fell below his Stem: his Sword, Deaths stampe,
Where it did marke, it tooke from face to foot:
He was a thing of Blood, whose euery motion
Was tim'd with dying Cryes: alone he entred
The mortall Gate of th'Citie, which he painted
With shunlesse destinie: aydelesse came off,
And with a sudden re-inforcement strucke
Carioles like a Planet: now all's his,
When by and by the dinne of Warre gan pierce
His readie sence: then straight his doubled spirit
Requickned what in flesh was fatigate,
And to the Battaile came he, where he did
Runne reeking o're the liues of men, as if 'twere
A perpetuall spoyle: and till we call'd
Both Field and Citie ours, he neuer stood
To ease his Brest with panting.

Menen. Worthy man.

Senat. He cannot but with measure fit the Honors which we deuise him.

Com. Our spoyles he kickt at,
And look'd vpon things precious, as they were
The common Muck of the World: he couets lesse
Then Miserie it selfe would giue, rewards his deeds
With doing them, and is content
To spend the time, to end it.

Menen. Hee's right Noble, let him be call'd for.

Senat. Call *Coriolanus.*

Off. He doth appeare.

Enter Coriolanus.

Menen. The Senate, *Coriolanus*, are well pleas'd to make thee Consull.

Corio. I doe owe them still my Life, and Seruices.

Menen. It then remaines, that you doe speake to the People.

Corio. I doe beseech you,
Let me o're-leape that custome: for I cannot
Put on the Gowne, stand naked, and entreat them
For my Wounds sake, to giue their sufferage:
Please you that I may passe this doing.

Scicin. Sir, the People must haue their Voyces,
Neyther will they bate one iot of Ceremonie.

Menen. Put them not too't:
Pray you goe fit you to the Custome,
And take to you, as your Predecessors haue,
Your Honor with your forme.

Corio. It is a part that I shall blush in acting,
And might well be taken from the People.

Brutus. Marke you that.

Corio. To brag vnto them, thus I did, and thus
Shew them th'vnaking Skarres, which I should hide,
As if I had receiu'd them for the hyre
Of their breath onely.

Menen. Doe not stand vpon't:
We recommend to you Tribunes of the People
Our purpose to them, and to our Noble Consull
Wish we all Ioy, and Honor.

Senat. To

Senat. To *Coriolanus* come all ioy and Honor.

Flourish Cornets.

Then Exeunt. Manet Sicinius and Brutus.

Bru. You see how he intends to vse the people.

Scicin. May they perceiue's intent: he wil require them
As if he did contemne what he requested,
Should be in them to giue.

Bru. Come, wee'l informe them
Of our proceedings heere on th'Market place,
I know they do attend vs.

Enter seuen or eight Citizens.

1.Cit. Once if he do require our voyces, wee ought not to deny him.

2.Cit. We may Sir if we will.

3.Cit. We haue power in our selues to do it, but it is a power that we haue no power to do: For, if hee shew vs his wounds, and tell vs his deeds, we are to put our tongues into those wounds, and speake for them: So if he tel vs his Noble deeds, we must also tell him our Noble acceptance of them. Ingratitude is monstrous, and for the multitude to be ingratefull, were to make a Monster of the multitude; of the which, we being members, should bring our selues to be monstrous members.

1.Cit. And to make vs no better thought of a little helpe will serue: for once we stood vp about the Corne, he himselfe stucke not to call vs the many-headed Multitude.

3.Cit. We haue beene call'd so of many, not that our heads are some browne, some blacke, some Abram, some bald; but that our wits are so diuersly Coulord; and truely I thinke, if all our wittes were to issue out of one Scull, they would flye East, West, North, South, and their consent of one direct way, should be at once to all the points a'th Compasse.

2.Cit. Thinke you so? Which way do you iudge my wit would flye.

3.Cit. Nay your wit will not so soone out as another mans will, 'tis strongly wadg'd vp in a blocke-head: but if it were at liberty, 'twould sure Southward.

2 Cit. Why that way?

3 Cit. To loose it selfe in a Fogge, where being three parts melted away with rotten Dewes, the fourth would returne for Conscience sake, to helpe to get thee a Wife.

2 Cit. You are neuer without your trickes, you may, you may.

3 Cit. Are you all resolu'd to giue your voyces? But that's no matter, the greater part carries it, I say. If hee would incline to the people, there was neuer a worthier man.

Enter Coriolanus in a gowne of Humility, with Menenius.

Heere he comes, and in the Gowne of humility, marke his behauiour: we are not to stay altogether, but to come by him where he stands, by ones, by twoes, & by threes. He's to make his requests by particulars, wherein euerie one of vs ha's a single Honor, in giuing him our own voices with our owne tongues, therefore follow me, and Ile direct you how you shall go by him.

All. Content, content.

Men. Oh Sir, you are not right: haue you not knowne The worthiest men haue done't?

Corio. What must I say, I pray Sir?
Plague vpon't, I cannot bring
My tougne to such a pace. Looke Sir, my wounds,
I got them in my Countries Seruice, when
Some certaine of your Brethren roar'd, and ranne
From th'noise of our owne Drummes.

Menen. Oh me the Gods, you must not speak of that,
You must desire them to thinke vpon you.

Coriol. Thinke vpon me? Hang 'em,
I would they would forget me, like the Vertues
Which our Diuines lose by em.

Men. You'l marre all,
Ile leaue you: Pray you speake to em, I pray you
In wholsome manner. *Exit*

Enter three of the Citizens.

Corio. Bid them wash their Faces,
And keepe their teeth cleane: So, heere comes a brace,
You know the cause (Sir) of my standing heere.

3 Cit. We do Sir, tell vs what hath brought you too't.

Corio. Mine owne desert.

2 Cit. Your owne desert.

Corio. I, but mine owne desire.

3 Cit. How not your owne desire?

Corio. No Sir, 'twas neuer my desire yet to trouble the poore with begging.

3 Cit. You must thinke if we giue you any thing, we hope to gaine by you.

Corio. Well then I pray, your price a'th'Consulship.

1 Cit. The price is, to aske it kindly.

Corio. Kindly sir, I pray let me ha't: I haue wounds to shew you, which shall bee yours in priuate: your good voice Sir, what say you?

2 Cit. You shall ha't worthy Sir.

Corio. A match Sir, there's in all two worthie voyces begg'd: I haue your Almes, Adieu.

3 Cit. But this is something odde.

2 Cit. And 'twere to giue againe: but 'tis no matter.

Exeunt. Enter two other Citizens.

Coriol. Pray you now, if it may stand with the tune of your voices, that I may bee Consull, I haue heere the Customarie Gowne.

1. You haue deserued Nobly of your Countrey, and you haue not deserued Nobly.

Coriol. Your Ænigma.

1. You haue bin a scourge to her enemies, you haue bin a Rod to her Friends, you haue not indeede loued the Common people.

Coriol. You should account mee the more Vertuous, that I haue not bin common in my Loue, I will sir flatter my sworne Brother the people to earne a deerer estimation of them, 'tis a condition they account gentle: & since the wisedome of their choice, is rather to haue my Hat, then my Heart, I will practice the insinuating nod, and be off to them most counterfetly, that is sir, I will counterfet the bewitchment of some popular man, and giue it bountifull to the desirers: Therefore beseech you, I may be Consull.

2. Wee hope to finde you our friend: and therefore giue you our voices heartily.

1. You haue receyued many wounds for your Countrey.

Coriol. I wil not Seale your knowledge with shewing them. I will make much of your voyces, and so trouble you no farther.

Both. The Gods giue you ioy Sir heartily.

Coriol. Most sweet Voyces:
Better it is to dye, better to sterue,
Then craue the higher, which first we do deserue.
Why in this Wooluish tongue should I stand heere,
To begge of Hob and Dicke, that does appeere
Their

Their needlesse Vouches: Custome calls me too't.
What Custome wills in all things, should we doo't?
The Dust on antique Time would lye vnswept,
And mountainous Error be too highly heapt,
For Truth to o're-peere. Rather then foole it so,
Let the high Office and the Honor go
To one that would doe thus. I am halfe through,
The one part suffered, the other will I doe.

Enter three Citizens more.

Here come moe Voyces.
Your Voyces? for your Voyces I haue fought,
Watcht for your Voyces: for your Voyces, beare
Of Wounds, two dozen odde: Battailes thrice six
I haue seene, and heard of: for your Voyces,
Haue done many things, some lesse, some more:
Your Voyces? Indeed I would be Consull.

1.Cit. Hee ha's done Nobly, and cannot goe without any honest mans Voyce.

2.Cit. Therefore let him be Consull: the Gods giue him ioy, and make him good friend to the People.

All. Amen, Amen. God saue thee, Noble Consull.

Corio. Worthy Voyces.

Enter Menenius, with Brutus and Scicinius.

Mene. You haue stood your Limitation:
And the Tribunes endue you with the Peoples Voyce,
Remaines, that in th'Officiall Markes inuested,
You anon doe meet the Senate.

Corio. Is this done?

Scicin. The Custome of Request you haue discharg'd:
The People doe admit you, and are summon'd
To meet anon, vpon your approbation.

Corio. Where? at the Senate-house?

Scicin. There, *Coriolanus.*

Corio. May I change these Garments?

Scicin. You may, Sir.

Cori. That Ile straight do: and knowing my selfe again,
Repayre toth'Senate-house.

Mene. Ile keepe you company. Will you along?

Brut. We stay here for the People.

Scicin. Fare you well. *Exeunt Coriol. and Mene.*
He ha's it now: and by his Lookes, me thinkes,
'Tis warme at's heart.

Brut. With a prowd heart he wore his humble Weeds:
Will you dismisse the People?

Enter the Plebeians.

Scici. How now, my Masters, haue you chose this man?

1.Cit. He ha's our Voyces, Sir.

Brut. We pray the Gods, he may deserue your loues.

2.Cit. Amen, Sir: to my poore vnworthy notice,
He mock'd vs, when he begg'd our Voyces.

3.Cit. Certainely, he flowted vs downe-right.

1.Cit. No, 'tis his kind of speech, he did not mock vs.

2.Cit. Not one amongst vs, saue your selfe, but sayes
He vs'd vs scornefully: he should haue shew'd vs
His Marks of Merit, Wounds receiu'd for's Countrey.

Scicin. Why so he did, I am sure.

All. No, no: no man saw 'em.

3.Cit. Hee said hee had Wounds,
Which he could shew in priuate:
And with his Hat, thus wauing it in scorne,
I would be Consull, sayes he: aged Custome,
But by your Voyces, will not so permit me.
Your Voyces therefore: when we graunted that,
Here was, I thanke you for your Voyces, thanke you
Your most sweet Voyces: now you haue left your Voyces,
I haue no further with you. Was not this mockerie?

Scicin. Why eyther were you ignorant to see't?
Or seeing it, of such Childish friendlinesse,
To yeeld your Voyces?

Brut. Could you not haue told him,
As you were lesson'd: When he had no Power,
But was a pettie seruant to the State,
He was your Enemie, euer spake against
Your Liberties, and the Charters that you beare
I'th' Body of the Weale: and now arriuing
A place of Potencie, and sway o'th' State,
If he should still malignantly remaine
Fast Foe toth'*Plebeij*, your Voyces might
Be Curses to your selues. You should haue said,
That as his worthy deeds did clayme no lesse
Then what he stood for: so his gracious nature
Would thinke vpon you, for your Voyces,
And translate his Mallice towards you, into Loue,
Standing your friendly Lord.

Scicin. Thus to haue said,
As you were fore-aduis'd, had toucht his Spirit,
And try'd his Inclination: from him pluckt
Eyther his gracious Promise, which you might
As cause had call'd you vp, haue held him to;
Or else it would haue gall'd his surly nature,
Which easily endures not Article,
Tying him to ought, so putting him to Rage,
You should haue ta'ne th'aduantage of his Choller,
And pass'd him vnelected.

Brut. Did you perceiue,
He did sollicite you in free Contempt,
When he did need your Loues: and doe you thinke,
That his Contempt shall not be brusing to you,
When he hath power to crush? Why, had your Bodyes
No Heart among you? Or had you Tongues, to cry
Against the Rectorship of Iudgement?

Scicin. Haue you, ere now, deny'd the asker:
And now againe, of him that did not aske, but mock,
Bestow your su'd-for Tongues?

3.Cit. Hee's not confirm'd, we may deny him yet.

2.Cit. And will deny him:
Ile haue fiue hundred Voyces of that sound.

1.Cit. I twice fiue hundred, & their friends, to piece 'em.

Brut. Get you hence instantly, and tell those friends,
They haue chose a Consull, that will from them take
Their Liberties, make them of no more Voyce
Then Dogges, that are as often beat for barking,
As therefore kept to doe so.

Scici. Let them assemble: and on a safer Iudgement,
All reuoke your ignorant election: Enforce his Pride,
And his old Hate vnto you: besides, forget not
With what Contempt he wore the humble Weed,
How in his Suit he scorn'd you: but your Loues,
Thinking vpon his Seruices, tooke from you
Th'apprehension of his present portance,
Which most gibingly, vngrauely, he did fashion
After the inueterate Hate he beares you.

Brut. Lay a fault on vs, your Tribunes,
That we labour'd (no impediment betweene)
But that you must cast your Election on him.

Scici. Say you chose him, more after our commandment,
Then as guided by your owne true affections, and that
Your Minds pre-occupy'd with what you rather must do,
Then what you should, made you against the graine
To Voyce him Consull. Lay the fault on vs.

b b *Brut.* I,

Brut. I, ſpare vs not : Say, we read Lectures to you,
How youngly he began to ſerue his Countrey,
How long continued, and what ſtock he ſprings of,
The Noble Houſe, o'th' *Martians* : from whence came
That *Ancus Martius, Numaes* Daughters Sonne:
Who after great *Hoſtilius* here was King,
Of the ſame Houſe *Publius* and *Quintus* were,
That our beſt Water, brought by Conduits hither,
And Nobly nam'd, ſo twice being Cenſor,
Was his great Anceſtor.

Scicin. One thus deſcended,
That hath beſide well in his perſon wrought,
To be ſet high in place, we did commend
To your remembrances : but you haue found,
Skaling his preſent bearing with his paſt,
That hee's your fixed enemie ; and reuoke
Your ſuddaine approbation.

Brut. Say you ne're had don't,
(Harpe on that ſtill) but by our putting on :
And preſently, when you haue drawne your number,
Repaire toth' Capitoll.

All. We will ſo : almoſt all repent in their election.
Exeunt Plebeians.

Brut. Let them goe on :
This Mutinie were better put in hazard,
Then ſtay paſt doubt, for greater :
If, as his nature is, he fall in rage
With their refuſall, both obſerue and anſwer
The vantage of his anger.

Scicin. Toth' Capitoll, come :
We will be there before the ſtreame o'th' People :
And this ſhall ſeeme, as partly 'tis, their owne,
Which we haue goaded on-ward. *Exeunt.*

Actus Tertius.

Cornets. Enter Coriolanus, Menenius, all the Gentry, Cominius, Titus Latius, and other Senators.

Corio. *Tullus Auffidius* then had made new head.

Latius. He had, my Lord, and that it was which caus'd
Our ſwifter Compoſition.

Corio. So then the Volces ſtand but as at firſt,
Readie when time ſhall prompt them, to make roade
Vpon's againe.

Com. They are worne (Lord Conſull) ſo,
That we ſhall hardly in our ages ſee
Their Banners waue againe.

Corio. Saw you *Auffidius*?

Latius. On ſafegard he came to me, and did curſe
Againſt the Volces, for they had ſo vildly
Yeelded the Towne : he is retyred to Antium.

Corio. Spoke he of me?

Latius. He did, my Lord.

Corio. How? what?

Latius. How often he had met you Sword to Sword :
That of all things vpon the Earth, he hated
Your perſon moſt : That he would pawne his fortunes
To hopeleſſe reſtitution, ſo he might
Be call'd your Vanquiſher.

Corio. At Antium liues he?

Latius. At Antium.

Corio. I wiſh I had a cauſe to ſeeke him there,
To oppoſe his hatred fully. Welcome home.
Enter Scicinius and Brutus.
Behold, theſe are the Tribunes of the People,
The Tongues o'th' Common Mouth. I do deſpiſe them :
For they doe pranke them in Authoritie,
Againſt all Noble ſufferance.

Scicin. Paſſe no further.

Cor. Hah? what is that?

Brut. It will be dangerous to goe on--No further.

Corio. What makes this change?

Mene. The matter?

Com. Hath he not paſs'd the Noble, and the Common?

Brut. *Cominius*, no.

Corio. Haue I had Childrens Voyces?

Senat. Tribunes giue way, he ſhall toth' Market place.

Brut. The People are incens'd againſt him.

Scicin. Stop, or all will fall in broyle.

Corio. Are theſe your Heard?
Muſt theſe haue Voyces, that can yeeld them now,
And ſtraight diſclaim their toungs? what are your Offices?
You being their Mouthes, why rule you not their Teeth?
Haue you not ſet them on?

Mene. Be calme, be calme.

Corio. It is a purpos'd thing, and growes by Plot,
To curbe the will of the Nobilitie :
Suffer't, and liue with ſuch as cannot rule,
Nor euer will be ruled.

Brut. Call't not a Plot :
The People cry you mockt them : and of late,
When Corne was giuen them *gratis*, you repin'd,
Scandal'd the Suppliants : for the People, call'd them
Time-pleaſers, flatterers, foes to Nobleneſſe.

Corio. Why this was knowne before.

Brut. Not to them all.

Corio. Haue you inform'd them ſithence?

Brut. How? I informe them?

Com. You are like to doe ſuch buſineſſe.

Brut. Not vnlike each way to better yours.

Corio. Why then ſhould I be Conſull? by yond Clouds
Let me deſerue ſo ill as you, and make me
Your fellow Tribune.

Scicin. You ſhew too much of that,
For which the People ſtirre : if you will paſſe
To where you are bound, you muſt enquire your way,
Which you are out of, with a gentler ſpirit,
Or neuer be ſo Noble as a Conſull,
Nor yoake with him for Tribune.

Mene. Let's be calme.

Com. The People are abus'd : ſet on, this paltring
Becomes not Rome : nor ha's *Coriolanus*
Deſeru'd this ſo diſhonor'd Rub, layd falſely
I'th' plaine Way of his Merit.

Corio. Tell me of Corne : this was my ſpeech,
And I will ſpeak't againe.

Mene. Not now, not now.

Senat. Not in this heat, Sir, now.

Corio. Now as I liue, I will.
My Nobler friends, I craue their pardons :
For the mutable ranke-ſented Meynie,
Let them regard me, as I doe not flatter,
And therein behold themſelues : I ſay againe,
In ſoothing them, we nouriſh 'gainſt our Senate
The Cockle of Rebellion, Inſolence, Sedition,
Which we our ſelues haue plowed for, ſow'd, & ſcatter'd,
By mingling them with vs, the honor'd Number,
Who lack not Vertue, no, nor Power, but that
Which they haue giuen to Beggers.

Mene. Well, no more.

Senat. No more words, we beſeech you.

Corio. How? no more?

As

As for my Country, I haue ſhed my blood,
Not fearing outward force: So ſhall my Lungs
Coine words till their decay, againſt thoſe Meazels
Which we diſdaine ſhould Tetter vs, yet ſought
The very way to catch them.
Bru. You ſpeake a'th'people, as if you were a God,
To puniſh; Not a man, of their Infirmity.
Sicin. 'Twere well we let the people know't.
Mene. What, what? His Choller?
Cor. Choller? Were I as patient as the midnight ſleep,
By Ioue, 'twould be my minde.
Sicin. It is a minde that ſhall remain a poiſon
Where it is: not poyſon any further.
Corio. Shall remaine?
Heare you this Triton of the *Minnoues*? Marke you
His abſolute Shall?
Com. 'Twas from the Cannon.
Cor. Shall? O God! but moſt vnwiſe Patricians: why
You graue, but wreakleſſe Senators, haue you thus
Giuen Hidra heere to chooſe an Officer,
That with his peremptory Shall, being but
The horne, and noiſe o'th'Monſters, wants not ſpirit
To ſay, hee'l turne your Current in a ditch,
And make your Channell his? If he haue power,
Then vale your Ignorance: If none, awake
Your dangerous Lenity: If you are Learn'd,
Be not as common Fooles; if you are not,
Let them haue Cuſhions by you. You are Plebeians,
If they be Senators: and they are no leſſe,
When both your voices blended, the great'ſt taſte
Moſt pallates theirs. They chooſe their Magiſtrate,
And ſuch a one as he, who puts his Shall,
His popular Shall, againſt a grauer Bench
Then euer frown'd in Greece. By Ioue himſelfe,
It makes the Conſuls baſe; and my Soule akes
To know, when two Authorities are vp,
Neither Supreame; How ſoone Confuſion
May enter 'twixt the gap of Both, and take
The one by th'other.
Com. Well, on to'th'Market place.
Corio. Who euer gaue that Counſell, to giue forth
The Corne a'th'Store-houſe gratis, as 'twas vs'd
Sometime in Greece.
Mene. Well, well, no more of that.
Cor. Thogh there the people had more abſolute powre
I ſay they noriſht diſobedience: fed, the ruin of the State.
Bru. Why ſhall the people giue
One that ſpeakes thus, their voyce?
Corio. Ile giue my Reaſons,
More worthier then their Voyces. They know the Corne
Was not our recompence, reſting well aſſur'd
They ne're did ſeruice for't; being preſt to'th'Warre,
Euen when the Nauell of the State was touch'd,
They would not thred the Gates: This kinde of Seruice
Did not deſerue Corne gratis. Being i'th'Warre,
There Mutinies and Reuolts, wherein they ſhew'd
Moſt Valour, ſpoke not for them. Th'Accuſation
Which they haue often made againſt the Senate,
All cauſe vnborne, could neuer be the Natiue
Of our ſo franke Donation. Well, what then?
How ſhall this Boſome-multiplied, digeſt
The Senates Courteſie? Let deeds expreſſe
What's like to be their words, We did requeſt it,
We are the greater pole, and in true feare
They gaue vs our demands. Thus we debaſe
The Nature of our Seats, and make the Rabble
Call our Cares, Feares; which will in time
Breake ope the Lockes a'th'Senate, and bring in
The Crowes to pecke the Eagles.
Mene. Come enough.
Bru. Enough, with ouer meaſure.
Corio. No, take more.
What may be ſworne by, both Diuine and Humane,
Seale what I end withall. This double worſhip,
Whereon part do's diſdaine with cauſe, the other
Inſult without all reaſon: where Gentry, Title, wiſedom
Cannot conclude, but by the yea and no
Of generall Ignorance, it muſt omit
Reall Neceſſities, and giue way the while
To vnſtable Slightneſſe. Purpoſe ſo barr'd, it followes,
Nothing is done to purpoſe. Therefore beſeech you,
You that will be leſſe fearefull, then diſcreet,
That loue the Fundamentall part of State
More then you doubt the change on't: That preferre
A Noble life, before a Long, and Wiſh,
To iumpe a Body with a dangerous Phyſicke,
That's ſure of death without it: at once plucke out
The Multitudinous Tongue, let them not licke
The ſweet which is their poyſon. Your diſhonor
Mangles true iudgement, and bereaues the State
Of that Integrity which ſhould becom't:
Not hauing the power to do the good it would
For th'ill which doth controul't.
Bru. Has ſaid enough.
Sicin. Ha's ſpoken like a Traitor, and ſhall anſwer
As Traitors do.
Corio. Thou wretch, deſpight ore-whelme thee:
What ſhould the people do with theſe bald Tribunes?
On whom depending, their obedience failes
To'th'greater Bench, in a Rebellion:
When what's not meet, but what muſt be, was Law,
Then were they choſen: in a better houre,
Let what is meet, be ſaide it muſt be meet,
And throw their power i'th'duſt.
Bru. Manifeſt Treaſon.
Sicin. This a Conſull? No.

Enter an Ædile.

Bru. The Ediles hoe: Let him be apprehended:
Sicin. Go call the people, in whoſe name my Selfe
Attach thee as a Traitorous Innouator:
A Foe to'th'publike Weale. Obey I charge thee,
And follow to thine anſwer.
Corio. Hence old Goat.
All. Wee'l Surety him.
Com. Ag'd ſir, hands off.
Corio. Hence rotten thing, or I ſhall ſhake thy bones
Out of thy Garments.
Sicin. Helpe ye Citizens.

Enter a rabble of Plebeians with the Ædiles.

Mene. On both ſides more reſpect.
Sicin. Heere's hee, that would take from you all your power.
Bru. Seize him Ædiles.
All. Downe with him, downe with him.
2 Sen. Weapons, weapons, weapons:

They all buſtle about Coriolanus.

Tribunes, Patricians, Citizens: what ho:
Sicinius, Brutus, Coriolanus, Citizens.
All. Peace, peace, peace, ſtay, hold, peace.
Mene. What is about to be? I am out of Breath,
Confuſions neere, I cannot ſpeake. You, Tribunes
To'th'people: *Coriolanus*, patience: Speak good *Sicinius*.

Bb 2 *Sicin.*

Scici. Heare me, People peace.
All. Let's here our Tribune : peace, ſpeake, ſpeake, ſpeake.
Scici. You are at point to loſe your Liberties :
Martius would haue all from you; *Martius*,
Whom late you haue nam'd for Conſull.
Mene. Fie, fie, fie, this is the way to kindle, not to quench.
Sena. To vnbuild the Citie,and to lay all flat.
Scici. What is the Citie,but the People?
All. True,the People are the Citie.
Brut. By the conſent of all, we were eſtabliſh'd the Peoples Magiſtrates.
All. You ſo remaine.
Mene. And ſo are like to doe.
Com. That is the way to lay the Citie flat,
To bring the Roofe to the Foundation,
And burie all, which yet diſtinctly raunges
In heapes, and piles of Ruine.
Scici. This deſerues Death.
Brut. Or let vs ſtand to our Authoritie,
Or let vs loſe it : we doe here pronounce,
Vpon the part o'th'People, in whoſe power
We were elected theirs, *Martius* is worthy
Of preſent Death.
Scici. Therefore lay hold of him:
Beare him toth' Rock Tarpeian, and from thence
Into deſtruction caſt him.
Brut. Ædiles ſeize him.
All Ple. Yeeld *Martius*, yeeld.
Mene. Heare me one word, 'beſeech you Tribunes, heare me but a word.
Ædiles. Peace,peace.
Mene. Be that you ſeeme,truly your Countries friend,
And temp'rately proceed to what you would
Thus violently redreſſe.
Brut. Sir,thoſe cold wayes,
That ſeeme like prudent helpes, are very poyſonous,
Where the Diſeaſe is violent. Lay hands vpon him,
And beare him to the Rock. *Corio. drawes his Sword.*
Corio. No,Ile die here:
There's ſome among you haue beheld me fighting,
Come trie vpon your ſelues, what you haue ſeene me.
Mene. Downe with that Sword, Tribunes withdraw a while.
Brut. Lay hands vpon him.
Mene. Helpe *Martius*,helpe : you that be noble,helpe him young and old.
All. Downe with him,downe with him. *Exeunt.*
In this Mutinie, the Tribunes, the Ædiles, and the People are beat in.
Mene. Goe,get you to our Houſe: be gone,away,
All will be naught elſe.
2. Sena. Get you gone.
Com. Stand faſt, we haue as many friends as enemies.
Mene. Shall it be put to that?
Sena. The Gods forbid:
I prythee noble friend,home to thy Houſe,
Leaue vs to cure this Cauſe.
Mene. For 'tis a Sore vpon vs,
You cannot Tent your ſelfe: be gone,'beſeech you.
Corio. Come Sir,along with vs.
Mene. I would they were Barbarians,as they are,
Though in Rome litter'd: not Romans,as they are not,
Though calued i'th'Porch o'th' Capitoll :
Be gone, put not your worthy Rage into your Tongue,
One time will owe another.
Corio. On faire ground,I could beat fortie of them.
Mene. I could my ſelfe take vp a Brace o'th' beſt of them, yea,the two Tribunes.
Com. But now 'tis oddes beyond Arithmetick,
And Manhood is call'd Foolerie, when it ſtands
Againſt a falling Fabrick. Will you hence,
Before the Tagge returne? whoſe Rage doth rend
Like interrupted Waters,and o're-beare
What they are vs'd to beare.
Mene. Pray you be gone:
Ile trie whether my old Wit be in requeſt
With thoſe that haue but little: this muſt be patcht
With Cloth of any Colour.
Com. Nay, come away. *Exeunt Coriolanus and Cominius.*
Patri. This man ha's marr'd his fortune.
Mene. His nature is too noble for the World:
He would not flatter *Neptune* for his Trident,
Or *Ioue*, for's power to Thunder: his Heart's his Mouth:
What his Breſt forges,that his Tongue muſt vent,
And being angry, does forget that euer
He heard the Name of Death. *A Noiſe within.*
Here's goodly worke.
Patri. I would they were a bed.
Mene. I would they were in Tyber.
What the vengeance, could he not ſpeake 'em faire?
Enter Brutus and Sicinius with the rabble againe.
Sicin. Where is this Viper,
That would depopulate the city,& be euery man himſelf
Mene. You worthy Tribunes.
Sicin. He ſhall be throwne downe the Tarpeian rock
With rigorous hands: he hath reſiſted Law,
And therefore Law ſhall ſcorne him further Triall
Then the ſeueritie of the publike Power,
Which he ſo ſets at naught.
1 Cit. He ſhall well know the Noble Tribunes are
The peoples mouths,and we their hands.
All. He ſhall ſure ont.
Mene. Sir,ſir. *Sicin.* Peace.
Me. Do not cry hauocke, where you ſhold but hunt
With modeſt warrant.
Sicin. Sir,how com'ſt that you haue holpe
To make this reſcue?
Mene. Heere me ſpeake? As I do know
The Conſuls worthineſſe, ſo can I name his Faults.
Sicin. Conſull? what Conſull?
Mene. The Conſull *Coriolanus*.
Bru. He Conſull.
All. No,no,no,no,no.
Mene. If by the Tribunes leaue,
And yours good people,
I may be heard, I would craue a word or two,
The which ſhall turne you to no further harme,
Then ſo much loſſe of time.
Sic. Speake breefely then,
For we are peremptory to diſpatch
This Viporous Traitor: to eiect him hence
Were but one danger,and to keepe him heere
Our certaine death: therefore it is decreed,
He dyes to night.
Menen. Now the good Gods forbid,
That our renowned Rome, whoſe gratitude
Towards her deſerued Children, is enroll'd
In Ioues owne Booke,like an vnnaturall Dam
Should now eate vp her owne.

Sicin.

Sicin. He's a Disease that must be cut away.

Mene. Oh he's a Limbe, that ha's but a Disease
Mortall, to cut it off: to cure it, easie.
What ha's he done to Rome, that's worthy death?
Killing our Enemies, the blood he hath lost
(Which I dare vouch, is more then that he hath
By many an Ounce) he dropp'd it for his Country:
And what is left, to loose it by his Countrey,
Were to vs all that doo't, and suffer it
A brand to th'end a'th World.

Sicin. This is cleane kamme.

Brut. Meerely awry:
When he did loue his Country, it honour'd him.

Menen. The seruice of the foote
Being once gangren'd, is not then respected
For what before it was.

Bru. Wee'l heare no more:
Pursue him to his house, and plucke him thence,
Least his infection being of catching nature,
Spred further.

Menen. One word more, one word:
This Tiger-footed-rage, when it shall find
The harme of vnskan'd swiftnesse, will (too late)
Tye Leaden pounds too's heeles. Proceed by Processe,
Least parties (as he is belou'd) breake out,
And sacke great Rome with Romanes.

Brut. If it were so?

Sicin. What do ye talke?
Haue we not had a taste of his Obedience?
Our Ediles smot: our selues resisted: come.

Mene. Consider this: He ha's bin bred i'th'Warres
Since a could draw a Sword, and is ill-school'd
In boulted Language: Meale and Bran together
He throwes without distinction. Giue me leaue,
Ile go to him, and vndertake to bring him in peace,
Where he shall answer by a lawfull Forme
(In peace) to his vtmost perill.

1.Sen. Noble Tribunes,
It is the humane way: the other course
Will proue to bloody: and the end of it,
Vnknowne to the Beginning.

Sic. Noble *Menenius*, be you then as the peoples officer:
Masters, lay downe your Weapons.

Bru. Go not home.

Sic. Meet on the Market place: wee'l attend you there:
Where if you bring not *Martius*, wee'l proceede
In our first way.

Menen. Ile bring him to you.
Let me desire your company: he must come,
Or what is worst will follow.

Sena. Pray you let's to him. *Exeunt Omnes.*

Enter Coriolanus with Nobles.

Corio. Let them pull all about mine eares, present me
Death on the Wheele, or at wilde Horses heeles,
Or pile ten hilles on the Tarpeian Rocke,
That the precipitation might downe stretch
Below the beame of sight; yet will I still
Be thus to them.

Enter Volumnia.

Noble. You do the Nobler.

Corio. I muse my Mother
Do's not approue me further, who was wont
To call them Wollen Vassailes, things created
To buy and sell with Groats, to shew bare heads
In Congregations, to yawne, be still, and wonder,
When one but of my ordinance stood vp
To speake of Peace, or Warre. I talke of you,
Why did you wish me milder? Would you haue me
False to my Nature? Rather say, I play
The man I am.

Volum. Oh sir, sir, sir,
I would haue had you put your power well on
Before you had worne it out.

Corio. Let go.

Vol. You might haue beene enough the man you are,
With striuing lesse to be so: Lesser had bin
The things of your dispositions, if
You had not shew'd them how ye were dispos'd
Ere they lack'd power to crosse you.

Corio. Let them hang.

Volum. I, and burne too.

Enter Menenius with the Senators.

Men. Come, come, you haue bin too rough, somthing too rough: you must returne, and mend it.

Sen. There's no remedy,
Vnlesse by not so doing, our good Citie
Cleaue in the midd'st, and perish.

Volum. Pray be counsail'd;
I haue a heart as little apt as yours,
But yet a braine, that leades my vse of Anger
To better vantage.

Mene. Well said, Noble woman:
Before he should thus stoope to'th'heart, but that
The violent fit a'th'time craues it as Physicke
For the whole State; I would put mine Armour on,
Which I can scarsely beare.

Corio. What must I do?

Mene. Returne to th'Tribunes.

Corio. Well, what then? what then?

Mene. Repent, what you haue spoke.

Corio. For them, I cannot do it to the Gods,
Must I then doo't to them?

Volum. You are too absolute,
Though therein you can neuer be too Noble,
But when extremities speake. I haue heard you say,
Honor and Policy, like vnseuer'd Friends,
I'th'Warre do grow together: Grant that, and tell me
In Peace, what each of them by th'other loose,
That they combine not there?

Corio. Tush, tush.

Mene. A good demand.

Volum. If it be Honor in your Warres, to seeme
The same you are not, which for your best ends
You adopt your policy: How is it lesse or worse
That it shall hold Companionship in Peace
With Honour, as in Warre; since that to both
It stands in like request.

Corio. Why force you this?

Volum. Because, that
Now it lyes you on to speake to th'people:
Not by your owne instruction, nor by'th'matter
Which your heart prompts you, but with such words
That are but roated in your Tongue;
Though but Bastards, and Syllables
Of no allowance, to your bosomes truth.
Now, this no more dishonors you at all,
Then to take in a Towne with gentle words,
Which else would put you to your fortune, and
The hazard of much blood.
I would dissemble with my Nature, where
My Fortunes and my Friends at stake, requir'd
I should do so in Honor. I am in this

bb 3 Your

Your Wife, your Sonne: These Senators, the Nobles,
And you, will rather shew our generall Lowts,
How you can frowne, then spend a fawne vpon 'em,
For the inheritance of their loues, and safegard
Of what that want might ruine.
Menen. Noble Lady,
Come goe with vs, speake faire: you may salue so,
Not what is dangerous present, but the losse
Of what is past.
Volum. I pry thee now, my Sonne,
Goe to them, with this Bonnet in thy hand,
And thus farre hauing stretcht it (here be with them)
Thy Knee bussing the stones: for in such businesse
Action is eloquence, and the eyes of th'ignorant
More learned then the eares, wauing thy head,
Which often thus correcting thy stout heart,
Now humble as the ripest Mulberry,
That will not hold the handling: or say to them,
Thou art their Souldier, and being bred in broyles,
Hast not the soft way, which thou do'st confesse
Were fit for thee to vse, as they to clayme,
In asking their good loues, but thou wilt frame
Thy selfe (forsooth) hereafter theirs so farre,
As thou hast power and person.
Menen. This but done,
Euen as she speakes, why their hearts were yours:
For they haue Pardons, being ask'd, as free,
As words to little purpose.
Volum. Prythee now,
Goe, and be rul'd: although I know thou hadst rather
Follow thine Enemie in a fierie Gulfe,
Then flatter him in a Bower. *Enter Cominius.*
Here is *Cominius.*
Com. I haue beene i'th' Market place: and Sir 'tis fit
You make strong partie, or defend your selfe
By calmenesse, or by absence: all's in anger.
Menen. Onely faire speech.
Com. I thinke 'twill serue, if he can thereto frame his spirit.
Volum. He must, and will:
Prythee now say you will, and goe about it.
Corio. Must I goe shew them my vnbarb'd Sconce?
Must I with my base Tongue giue to my Noble Heart
A Lye, that it must beare well? I will doo't:
Yet were there but this single Plot, to loose
This Mould of *Martius*, they to dust should grinde it,
And throw't against the Winde. Toth' Market place:
You haue put me now to such a part, which neuer
I shall discharge toth' Life.
Com. Come, come, wee'le prompt you.
Volum. I prythee now sweet Son, as thou hast said
My praises made thee first a Souldier; so
To haue my praise for this, performe a part
Thou hast not done before.
Corio. Well, I must doo't:
Away my disposition, and possesse me
Some Harlots spirit: My throat of Warre be turn'd,
Which quier'd with my Drumme into a Pipe,
Small as an Eunuch, or the Virgin voyce
That Babies lull a-sleepe: The smiles of Knaues
Tent in my cheekes, and Schoole-boyes Teares take vp
The Glasses of my sight: A Beggars Tongue
Make motion through my Lips, and my Arm'd knees
Who bow'd but in my Stirrop, bend like his
That hath receiu'd an Almes. I will not doo't,
Least I surcease to honor mine owne truth,
And by my Bodies action, teach my Minde
A most inherent Basenesse.
Volum. At thy choice then:
To begge of thee, it is my more dis-honor,
Then thou of them. Come all to ruine, let
Thy Mother rather feele thy Pride, then feare
Thy dangerous Stoutnesse: for I mocke at death
With as bigge heart as thou. Do as thou list,
Thy Valiantnesse was mine, thou suck'st it from me:
But owe thy Pride thy selfe.
Corio. Pray be content:
Mother, I am going to the Market place:
Chide me no more. Ile Mountebanke their Loues,
Cogge their Hearts from them, and come home belou'd
Of all the Trades in Rome. Looke, I am going:
Commend me to my Wife, Ile returne Consull,
Or neuer trust to what my Tongue can do
I'th way of Flattery further.
Volum. Do your will. *Exit Volumnia*
Com. Away, the Tribunes do attend you: arm your self
To answer mildely: for they are prepar'd
With Accusations, as I heare more strong
Then are vpon you yet.
Corio. The word is, Mildely. Pray you let vs go,
Let them accuse me by inuention: I
Will answer in mine Honor.
Menen. I, but mildely.
Corio. Well mildely be it then, Mildely. *Exeunt*

Enter Sicinius and Brutus.

Bru. In this point charge him home, that he affects
Tyrannicall power: If he euade vs there,
Inforce him with his enuy to the people,
And that the Spoile got on the *Antiats*
Was ne're distributed. What, will he come?

Enter an Edile.

Edile. Hee's comming.
Bru. How accompanied?
Edile. With old *Menenius*, and those Senators
That alwayes fauour'd him.
Sicin. Haue you a Catalogue
Of all the Voices that we haue procur'd, set downe by'th (Pole?
Edile. I haue: 'tis ready.
Sicin. Haue you collected them by Tribes?
Edile. I haue.
Sicin. Assemble presently the people hither:
And when they heare me say, it shall be so,
I'th'right and strength a'th'Commons: be it either
For death, for fine, or Banishment, then let them
If I say Fine, cry Fine; if Death, cry Death,
Insisting on the olde prerogatiue
And power i'th Truth a'th Cause.
Edile. I shall informe them.
Bru. And when such time they haue begun to cry,
Let them not cease, but with a dinne confus'd
Inforce the present Execution
Of what we chance to Sentence.
Edi. Very well.
Sicin. Make them be strong, and ready for this hint
When we shall hap to giu't them.
Bru. Go about it,
Put him to Choller straite, he hath bene vs'd
Euer to conquer, and to haue his worth
Of contradiction. Being once chaft, he cannot
Be rein'd againe to Temperance, then he speakes
What's

What's in his heart, and that is there which lookes
With vs to breake his necke.

Enter Coriolanus, Menenius, and Cominius, with others.

Sicin. Well, heere he comes.
Mene. Calmely, I do beseech you.
Corio. I, as an Hostler, that fourth poorest peece
Will beare the Knaue by'th Volume:
Th'honor'd Goddes
Keepe Rome in safety, and the Chaires of Iustice
Supplied with worthy men, plant loue amongs
Through our large Temples with ẏ shewes of peace
And not our streets with Warre.
1 Sen. Amen, Amen.
Mene. A Noble wish.

Enter the Edile with the Plebeians.

Sicin. Draw neere ye people.
Edile. List to your Tribunes. Audience:
Peace I say.
Corio. First heare me speake.
Both Tri. Well, say: Peace hoe.
Corio. Shall I be charg'd no further then this present?
Must all determine heere?
Sicin. I do demand,
If you submit you to the peoples voices,
Allow their Officers, and are content
To suffer lawfull Censure for such faults
As shall be prou'd vpon you.
Corio. I am Content.
Mene. Lo Citizens, he sayes he is Content.
The warlike Seruice he ha's done, consider: Thinke
Vpon the wounds his body beares, which shew
Like Graues i'th holy Church-yard.
Corio. Scratches with Briars, scarres to moue
Laughter onely.
Mene. Consider further:
That when he speakes not like a Citizen,
You finde him like a Soldier: do not take
His rougher Actions for malicious sounds:
But as I say, such as become a Soldier,
Rather then enuy you.
Com. Well, well, no more.
Corio. What is the matter,
That being past for Consull with full voyce:
I am so dishonour'd, that the very houre
You take it off againe.
Sicin. Answer to vs.
Corio. Say then: 'tis true, I ought so
Sicin. We charge you, that you haue contriu'd to take
From Rome all season'd Office, and to winde
Your selfe into a power tyrannicall,
For which you are a Traitor to the people.
Corio. How? Traytor?
Mene. Nay temperately: your promise.
Corio. The fires i'th'lowest hell. Fould in the people:
Call me their Traitor, thou iniurious Tribune.
Within thine eyes sate twenty thousand deaths
In thy hands clutcht: as many Millions in
Thy lying tongue, both numbers. I would say
Thou lyest vnto thee, with a voice as free,
As I do pray the Gods.
Sicin. Marke you this people?
All. To'th'Rocke, to'th'Rocke with him.
Sicin. Peace:
We neede not put new matter to his charge:
What you haue seene him do, and heard him speake:
Beating your Officers, cursing your selues,
Opposing Lawes with stroakes, and heere defying
Those whose great power must try him.
Euen this so criminall, and in such capitall kinde
Deserues th'extreamest death.
Bru. But since he hath seru'd well for Rome.
Corio. What do you prate of Seruice.
Brut. I talke of that, that know it.
Corio. You?
Mene. Is this the promise that you made your mother.
Com. Know, I pray you.
Corio. Ile know no further:
Let them pronounce the steepe Tarpeian death,
Vagabond exile, Fleaing, pent to linger
But with a graine a day, I would not buy
Their mercie, at the price of one faire word,
Nor checke my Courage for what they can giue,
To haue't with saying, Good morrow.
Sicin. For that he ha's
(As much as in him lies) from time to time
Enui'd against the people; seeking meanes
To plucke away their power: as now at last,
Giuen Hostile stroakes, and that not in the presence
Of dreaded Iustice, but on the Ministers
That doth distribute it. In the name a'th'people,
And in the power of vs the Tribunes, wee
(Eu'n from this instant) banish him our Citie
In perill of precipitation
From off the Rocke Tarpeian, neuer more
To enter our Rome gates. I'th'Peoples name,
I say it shall bee so.
All. It shall be so, it shall be so: let him away:
Hee's banish'd, and it shall be so.
Com. Heare me my Masters, and my common friends.
Sicin. He's sentenc'd: No more hearing.
Com. Let me speake:
I haue bene Consull, and can shew from Rome
Her Enemies markes vpon me. I do loue
My Countries good, with a respect more tender,
More holy, and profound, then mine owne life,
My deere Wiues estimate, her wombes encrease,
And treasure of my Loynes: then if I would
Speake that.
Sicin. We know your drift. Speake what?
Bru. There's no more to be said, but he is banish'd
As Enemy to the people, and his Countrey.
It shall bee so.
All. It shall be so, it shall be so.
Corio. You common cry of Curs, whose breath I hate,
As reeke a'th'rotten Fennes: whose Loues I prize,
As the dead Carkasses of vnburied men,
That do corrupt my Ayre: I banish you,
And heere remaine with your vncertaintie.
Let euery feeble Rumor shake your hearts:
Your Enemies, with nodding of their Plumes
Fan you into dispaire: Haue the power still
To banish your Defenders, till at length
Your ignorance (which findes not till it feeles,
Making but reseruation of your selues,
Still your owne Foes) deliuer you
As most abated Captiues, to some Nation
That wonne you without blowes, despising
For you the City. Thus I turne my backe;
There is a world elsewhere.

Exeunt Coriolanus, Cominius, with Cumalys.

They all shout, and throw vp their Caps.

Edile.

Edile. The peoples Enemy is gone, is gone.
All. Our enemy is banish'd, he is gone: Hoo, oo.
Sicin. Go see him out at Gates, and follow him
As he hath follow'd you, with all despight
Giue him deseru'd vexation. Let a guard
Attend vs through the City.
All. Come, come, lets see him out at gates, come:
The Gods preserue our Noble Tribunes, come. *Exeunt.*

Actus Quartus.

Enter Coriolanus, Volumnia, Virgilia, Menenius, Cominius, with the yong Nobility of Rome.

Corio. Come leaue your teares: a brief farwel: the beast
With many heads butts me away. Nay Mother,
Where is your ancient Courage? You were vs'd
To say, Extreamities was the trier of spirits,
That common chances. Common men could beare,
That when the Sea was calme, all Boats alike
Shew'd Mastership in floating. Fortunes blowes,
When most strooke home, being gentle wounded, craues
A Noble cunning. You were vs'd to load me
With Precepts that would make inuincible
The heart that conn'd them.
Virg. Oh heauens! O heauens!
Corio. Nay, I prythee woman.
Vol. Now the Red Pestilence strike al Trades in Rome,
And Occupations perish.
Corio. What, what, what:
I shall be lou'd when I am lack'd. Nay Mother,
Resume that Spirit, when you were wont to say,
If you had beene the Wife of *Hercules*,
Six of his Labours youl'd haue done, and sau'd
Your Husband so much swet. *Cominius*,
Droope not, Adieu: Farewell my Wife, my Mother,
Ile do well yet. Thou old and true *Menenius*,
Thy teares are salter then a yonger mans,
And venomous to thine eyes. My (sometime) Generall,
I haue seene the Sterne, and thou hast oft beheld
Heart-hardning spectacles. Tell these sad women,
'Tis fond to waile ineuitable strokes,
As 'tis to laugh at 'em. My Mother, you wot well
My hazards still haue beene your solace, and
Beleeu't not lightly, though I go alone
Like to a lonely Dragon, that his Fenne
Makes fear'd, and talk'd of more then seene: your Sonne
Will or exceed the Common, or be caught
With cautelous baits and practice.
Volum. My first sonne,
Whether will thou go? Take good *Cominius*
With thee awhile: Determine on some course
More then a wilde exposture, to each chance
That start's i'th'way before thee.
Corio. O the Gods!
Com. Ile follow thee a Moneth, deuise with thee
Where thou shalt rest, that thou may'st heare of vs,
And we of thee. So if the time thrust forth
A cause for thy Repeale, we shall not send
O're the vast world, to seeke a single man,
And loose aduantage, which doth euer coole
Ith'absence of the needer.
Corio. Fare ye well:
Thou hast yeares vpon thee, and thou art too full
Of the warres surfets, to go roue with one
That's yet vnbruis'd: bring me but out at gate.
Come my sweet wife, my deerest Mother, and
My Friends of Noble touch: when I am forth,
Bid me farewell, and smile. I pray you come:
While I remaine aboue the ground, you shall
Heare from me still, and neuer of me ought
But what is like me formerly.
Menen. That's worthily
As any eare can heare. Come, let's not weepe,
If I could shake off but one seuen yeeres
From these old armes and legges, by the good Gods
I'ld with thee, euery foot.
Corio. Giue me thy hand, come. *Exeunt*

Enter the two Tribunes, Sicinius, and Brutus, with the Edile.

Sicin. Bid them all home, he's gone: & wee'l no further,
The Nobility are vexed, whom we see haue sided
In his behalfe.
Brut. Now we haue shewne our power,
Let vs seeme humbler after it is done,
Then when it was a dooing.
Sicin. Bid them home: say their great enemy is gone,
And they, stand in their ancient strength.
Brut. Dismisse them home. Here comes his Mother.

Enter Volumnia, Virgilia, and Menenius.

Sicin. Let's not meet her.
Brut. Why?
Sicin. They say she's mad.
Brut. They haue tane note of vs: keepe on your way.
Volum. Oh y'are well met:
Th'hoorded plague a'th'Gods requit your loue.
Menen. Peace, peace, be not so loud.
Volum. If that I could for weeping, you should heare,
Nay, and you shall heare some. Will you be gone?
Virg. You shall stay too: I would I had the power
To say so to my Husband.
Sicin. Are you mankinde?
Volum. I foole, is that a shame. Note but this Foole,
Was not a man my Father? Had'st thou Foxship
To banish him that strooke more blowes for Rome
Then thou hast spoken words.
Sicin. Oh blessed Heauens!
Volum. Moe Noble blowes, then euer ỹ wise words.
And for Romes good, Ile tell thee what: yet goe:
Nay but thou shalt stay too: I would my Sonne
Were in Arabia, and thy Tribe before him,
His good Sword in his hand.
Sicin. What then?
Virg. What then? Hee'ld make an end of thy posterity
Volum. Bastards, and all.
Good man, the Wounds that he does beare for Rome!
Menen. Come, come, peace.
Sicin. I would he had continued to his Country
As he began, and not vnknit himselfe
The Noble knot he made.
Bru. I would he had.
Volum. I would he had? 'Twas you incenst the rable.
Cats, that can iudge as fitly of his worth,
As I can of those Mysteries which heauen
Will not haue earth to know.
Brut. Pray let's go.
Volum. Now pray sir get you gone.
You haue done a braue deede: Ere you go, heare this:
As farre as doth the Capitoll exceede
The meanest house in Rome; so farre my Sonne

This

This Ladies Husband heere; this (do you see)
Whom you haue banish'd, does exceed you all.
Bru. Well, well, wee'l leaue you.
Sicin. Why stay we to be baited
With one that wants her Wits. *Exit Tribunes.*
Volum. Take my Prayers with you.
I would the Gods had nothing else to do,
But to confirme my Cursses. Could I meete 'em
But once a day, it would vnclogge my heart
Of what lyes heauy too't.
Mene. You haue told them home,
And by my troth you haue cause: you'l Sup with me.
Volum. Angers my Meate: I suppe vpon my selfe,
And so shall sterue with Feeding: Come, let's go,
Leaue this faint-puling, and lament as I do,
In Anger, *Iuno*-like: Come, come, come. *Exeunt*
Mene. Fie, fie, fie. *Exit.*

Enter a Roman, and a Volce.

Rom. I know you well sir, and you know mee: your name I thinke is *Adrian.*

Volce. It is so sir, truly I haue forgot you.

Rom. I am a Roman, and my Seruices are as you are, against 'em. Know you me yet.

Volce. Nicanor: no.

Rom. The same sir.

Volce. You had more Beard when I last saw you, but your Fauour is well appear'd by your Tongue. What's the Newes in Rome: I haue a Note from the Volcean state to finde you out there. You haue well saued mee a dayes iourney.

Rom. There hath beene in Rome straunge Insurrections: The people, against the Senatours, Patricians, and Nobles.

Vol. Hath bin; is it ended then? Our State thinks not so, they are in a most warlike preparation, & hope to com vpon them, in the heate of their diuision

Rom. The maine blaze of it is past, but a small thing would make it flame againe. For the Nobles receyue so to heart, the Banishment of that worthy *Coriolanus*, that they are in a ripe aptnesse, to take al power from the people, and to plucke from them their Tribunes for euer. This lyes glowing I can tell you, and is almost mature for the violent breaking out.

Vol. Coriolanus Banisht?

Rom. Banish'd sir.

Vol. You will be welcome with this intelligence *Nicanor.*

Rom. The day serues well for them now. I haue heard it saide, the fittest time to corrupt a mans Wife, is when shee's falne out with her Husband. Your Noble *Tullus Auffidius* well appeare well in these Warres, his great Opposer *Coriolanus* being now in no request of his countrey.

Volce. He cannot choose: I am most fortunate, thus accidentally to encounter you. You haue ended my Businesse, and I will merrily accompany you home.

Rom. I shall betweene this and Supper, tell you most strange things from Rome: all tending to the good of their Aduersaries. Haue you an Army ready say you?

Vol. A most Royall one: The Centurions, and their charges distinctly billetted already in th'entertainment, and to be on foot at an houres warning.

Rom. I am ioyfull to heare of their readinesse, and am the man I thinke, that shall set them in present Action. So sir, heartily well met, and most glad of your Company.

Volce. You take my part from me sir, I haue the most cause to be glad of yours.

Rom. Well, let vs go together. *Exeunt.*

Enter Coriolanus in meane Apparrell, Disguisd, and muffled.

Corio. A goodly City is this *Antium.* Citty,
'Tis I that made thy Widdowes: Many an heyre
Of these faire Edifices fore my Warres
Haue I heard groane, and drop: Then know me not,
Least that thy Wiues with Spits, and Boyes with stones
In puny Battell slay me. Saue you sir.

Enter a Citizen.

Cit. And you.

Corio. Direct me, if it be your will, where great *Auffidius* lies: Is he in *Antium?*

Cit. He is, and Feasts the Nobles of the State, at his house this night.

Corio. Which is his house, beseech you?

Cit. This heere before you.

Corio. Thanke you sir, farewell. *Exit Citizen*
Oh World, thy slippery turnes! Friends now fast sworn,
Whose double bosomes seemes to weare one heart,
Whose Houres, whose Bed, whose Meale and Exercise
Are still together: who Twin (as 'twere) in Loue,
Vnseparable, shall within this houre,
On a dissention of a Doit, breake out
To bitterest Enmity: So fellest Foes,
Whose Passions, and whose Plots haue broke their sleep
To take the one the other, by some chance,
Some tricke not worth an Egge, shall grow deere friends
And inter-ioyne their yssues. So with me,
My Birth-place haue I, and my loues vpon
This Enemie Towne: Ile enter, if he slay me
He does faire Iustice: if he giue me way,
Ile do his Country Seruice. *Exit.*

Musicke playes. Enter a Seruingman.

1 *Ser.* Wine, Wine, Wine: What seruice is heere? I thinke our Fellowes are asleepe.

Enter another Seruingman.

2 *Ser.* Where's *Cotus:* my M.cals for him: *Cotus. Exit*

Enter Coriolanus.

Corio. A goodly House:
The Feast smels well: but I appeare not like a Guest.

Enter the first Seruingman.

1 *Ser.* What would you haue Friend? whence are you? Here's no place for you: Pray go to the doore? *Exit*

Corio. I haue deseru'd no better entertainment, in being *Coriolanus.* *Enter second Seruant.*

2 *Ser.* Whence are you sir? Ha's the Porter his eyes in his head, that he giues entrance to such Companions? Pray get you out.

Corio. Away.

2 *Ser.* Away? Get you away.

Corio. Now th'art troublesome.

2 *Ser.* Are you so braue: Ile haue you talkt with anon

Enter 3 Seruingman, the 1 meets him.

3 What Fellowes this?

1 A strange one as euer I look'd on: I cannot get him out o'th'house: Prythee call my Master to him.

3 What haue you to do here fellow? Pray you auoid the house.

Corio. Let me but stand, I will not hurt your Harth.

3 What are you?

Corio. A Gentleman.

3 A maru'llous poore one.

Corio. True, so I am.

3 Pray you poore Gentleman, take vp some other station,

tion : Heere's no place for you, pray you auoid : Come.
Corio. Follow your Function, go, and batten on colde bits. *Pushes him away from him.*
3 What you will not? Prythee tell my Maister what a strange Guest he ha's heere.
2 And I shall. *Exit second Seruingman.*
3 Where dwel'st thou?
Corio. Vnder the Canopy.
3 Vnder the Canopy?
Corio. I.
3 Where's that?
Corio. I'th City of Kites and Crowes.
3 I'th City of Kites and Crowes? What an Asse it is, then thou dwel'st with Dawes too?
Corio. No, I serue not thy Master.
3 How sir? Do you meddle with my Master?
Corio. I, tis an honester seruice, then to meddle with thy Mistris : Thou prat'st, and prat'st, serue with thy trencher : Hence. *Beats him away*

Enter Auffidius with the Seruingman.

Auf. Where is this Fellow?
2 Here sir, I'de haue beaten him like a dogge, but for disturbing the Lords within.
Auf. Whence com'st thou? What woldst y͂? Thy name? Why speak'st not? Speake man : What's thy name?
Corio. If *Tullus* not yet thou know'st me, and seeing me, dost not thinke me for the man I am, necessitie commands me name my selfe.
Auf. What is thy name?
Corio. A name vnmusicall to the Volcians eares,
And harsh in sound to thine.
Auf. Say, what's thy name?
Thou hast a Grim apparance, and thy Face
Beares a Command in't : Though thy Tackles torne,
Thou shew'st a Noble Vessell : What's thy name?
Corio. Prepare thy brow to frowne : knowst y͂ me yet?
Auf. I know thee not? Thy Name?
Corio. My name is *Caius Martius*, who hath done
To thee particularly, and to all the Volces
Great hurt and Mischiefe : thereto witnesse may
My Surname *Coriolanus*. The painfull Seruice,
The extreme Dangers, and the droppes of Blood
Shed for my thanklesse Country, are requitted :
But with that Surname, a good memorie
And witnesse of the Malice and Displeasure
Which thou should'st beare me, only that name remains.
The Cruelty and Enuy of the people,
Permitted by our dastard Nobles, who
Haue all forsooke me, hath deuour'd the rest :
And suffer'd me by th'voyce of Slaues to be
Hoop'd out of Rome. Now this extremity,
Hath brought me to thy Harth, not out of Hope
(Mistake me not) to saue my life : for if
I had fear'd death, of all the Men i'th'World
I would haue voided thee. But in meere spight
To be full quit of those my Banishers,
Stand I before thee heere : Then if thou hast
A heart of wreake in thee, that wilt reuenge
Thine owne particular wrongs, and stop those maimes
Of shame seene through thy Country, speed thee straight
And make my misery serue thy turne : So vse it,
That my reuengefull Seruices may proue
As Benefits to thee. For I will fight
Against my Cankred Countrey, with the Spleene
Of all the vnder Fiends. But if so be,
Thou dar'st not this, and that to proue more Fortunes
Th'art tyr'd, then in a word, I also am
Longer to liue most wearie : and present
My throat to thee, and to thy Ancient Malice :
Which not to cut, would shew thee but a Foole,
Since I haue euer followed thee with hate,
Drawne Tunnes of Blood out of thy Countries brest,
And cannot liue but to thy shame, vnlesse
It be to do thee seruice.
Auf. Oh *Martius*, *Martius*;
Each word thou hast spoke, hath weeded from my heart
A roote of Ancient Enuy. If Iupiter
Should from yond clowd speake diuine things,
And say 'tis true; I'de not beleeue them more
Then thee all-Noble *Martius*. Let me twine
Mine armes about that body, where against
My grained Ash an hundred times hath broke,
And scarr'd the Moone with splinters : heere I cleep
The Anuile of my Sword, and do contest
As hotly, and as Nobly with thy Loue,
As euer in Ambitious strength, I did
Contend against thy Valour. Know thou first,
I lou'd the Maid I married : neuer man
Sigh'd truer breath. But that I see thee heere
Thou Noble thing, more dances my rapt heart,
Then when I first my wedded Mistris saw
Bestride my Threshold. Why, thou Mars I tell thee,
We haue a Power on foote : and I had purpose
Once more to hew thy Target from thy Brawne,
Or loose mine Arme for't : Thou hast beate mee out
Twelue seuerall times, and I haue nightly since
Dreamt of encounters 'twixt thy selfe and me :
We haue beene downe together in my sleepe,
Vnbuckling Helmes, fisting each others Throat,
And wak'd halfe dead with nothing. Worthy *Martius*,
Had we no other quarrell else to Rome, but that
Thou art thence Banish'd, we would muster all
From twelue, to seuentie : and powring Warre
Into the bowels of vngratefull Rome,
Like a bold Flood o're-beate. Oh come, go in,
And take our Friendly Senators by'th'hands
Who now are heere, taking their leaues of mee,
Who am prepar'd against your Territories,
Though not for Rome it selfe.
Corio. You blesse me Gods.
Auf. Therefore most absolute Sir, if thou wilt haue
The leading of thine owne Reuenges, take
Th'one halfe of my Commission, and set downe
As best thou art experienc'd, since thou know'st
Thy Countries strength and weaknesse, thine own waies
Whether to knocke against the Gates of Rome,
Or rudely visit them in parts remote,
To fright them, ere destroy. But come in,
Let me commend thee first, to those that shall
Say yea to thy desires. A thousand welcomes,
And more a Friend, then ere an Enemie,
Yet *Martius* that was much. Your hand : most welcome. *Exeunt*

Enter two of the Seruingmen.

1 Heere's a strange alteration?
2 By my hand, I had thoght to haue stroken him with a Cudgell, and yet my minde gaue me, his cloathes made a false report of him.
1 What an Arme he has, he turn'd me about with his finger and his thumbe, as one would set vp a Top.
2 Nay, I knew by his face that there was some-thing in him. He had sir, a kinde of face me thought, I cannot tell

tell how to tearme it.

1 He had so, looking as it were, would I were hang'd but I thought there was more in him, then I could think.

2 So did I, Ile be sworne: He, is simply the rarest man i'th'world.

1 I thinke he is: but a greater soldier then he, You wot one.

2 Who my Master?

1 Nay, it's no matter for that.

2 Worth six on him.

1 Nay not so neither: but I take him to be the greater Souldiour.

2 Faith looke you, one cannot tell how to say that: for the Defence of a Towne, our Generall is excellent.

1 I, and for an assault too.

Enter the third Seruingman.

3 Oh Slaues, I can tell you Newes, News you Rascals

Both. What, what, what? Let's partake.

3 I would not be a Roman of all Nations; I had as liue be a condemn'd man.

Both. Wherefore? Wherefore?

3 Why here's he that was wont to thwacke our Generall, *Caius Martius.*

1 Why do you say, thwacke our Generall?

3 I do not say thwacke our Generall, but he was alwayes good enough for him

2 Come we are fellowes and friends: he was euer too hard for him, I haue heard him say so himselfe.

1 He was too hard for him directly, to say the Troth on't before *Corioles*, he scotcht him, and notcht him like a Carbinado.

2 And hee had bin Cannibally giuen, hee might haue boyld and eaten him too.

1 But more of thy Newes.

3 Why he is so made on heere within, as if hee were Son and Heire to Mars, set at vpper end o'th'Table: No question askt him by any of the Senators, but they stand bald before him. Our Generall himselfe makes a Mistris of him, Sanctifies himselfe with's hand, and turnes vp the white o'th'eye to his Discourse. But the bottome of the Newes is, our Generall is cut i'th'middle, & but one halfe of what he was yesterdav. For the other ha's halfe, by the intreaty and graunt of the whole Table. Hee'l go he sayes, and sole the Porter of Rome Gates by th'eares. He will mowe all downe before him, and leaue his passage poul'd.

2 And he's as like to do't, as any man I can imagine.

3 Doo't? he will doo't: for look you sir, he has as many Friends as Enemies: which Friends sir as it were, durst not (looke you sir) shew themselues (as we terme it) his Friends, whilest he's in Directitude.

1 Directitude? What's that?

3 But when they shall see sir, his Crest vp againe, and the man in blood, they will out of their Burroughes (like Conies after Raine) and reuell all with him.

1 But when goes this forward.:

3 To morrow, to day, presently, you shall haue the Drum strooke vp this afternoone: 'Tis as it were a parcel of their Feast, and to be executed ere they wipe their lips.

2 Why then wee shall haue a stirring World againe: This peace is nothing, but to rust Iron, encrease Taylors, and breed Ballad-makers.

1 Let me haue Warre say I, it exceeds peace as farre as day do's night: It's sprightly walking, audible, and full of Vent. Peace, is a very Apoplexy, Lethargie, mull'd, deafe, sleepe, insensible, a getter of more bastard Children, then warres a destroyer of men.

2 'Tis so, and as warres in some sort may be saide to be a Rauisher, so it cannot be denied, but peace is a great maker of Cuckolds.

1 I, and it makes men hate one another.

3 Reason, because they then lesse neede one another: The Warres for my money. I hope to see Romanes as cheape as Volcians. They are rising, they are rising.

Both. In, in, in, in. *Exeunt*

Enter the two Tribunes, Sicinius, and Brutus.

Sicin. We heare not of him, neither need we fear him,
His remedies are tame, the present peace,
And quietnesse of the people, which before
Were in wilde hurry. Heere do we make his Friends
Blush, that the world goes well: who rather had,
Though they themselues did suffer by't, behold
Dissentious numbers pestring streets, then see
Our Tradesmen singing in their shops, and going
About their Functions friendly.

Enter Menenius.

Bru. We stood too't in good time. Is this *Menenius*?

Sicin. 'Tis he, 'tis he: O he is grown most kind of late:
Haile Sir. *Mene.* Haile to you both.

Sicin. Your *Coriolanus* is not much mist, but with his Friends: the Commonwealth doth stand, and so would do, were he more angry at it.

Mene. All's well, and might haue bene much better, if he could haue temporiz'd.

Sicin. Where is he, heare you?

Mene. Nay I heare nothing:
His Mother and his wife, heare nothing from him.

Enter three or foure Citizens.

All. The Gods preserue you both.

Sicin. Gooden our Neighbours.

Bru. Gooden to you all, gooden to you all.

1 Our selues, our wiues, and children, on our knees,
Are bound to pray for you both.

Sicin. Liue, and thriue.

Bru. Farewell kinde Neighbours:
We wisht *Coriolanus* had lou'd you as we did.

All. Now the Gods keepe you.

Both Tri. Farewell, farewell. *Exeunt Citizens*

Sicin. This is a happier and more comely time,
Then when these Fellowes ran about the streets,
Crying Confusion.

Bru. *Caius Martius* was
A worthy Officer i'th'Warre, but Insolent,
O'recome with Pride, Ambitious, past all thinking
Selfe-louing.

Sicin. And affecting one sole Throne, without assistãce

Mene. I thinke not so.

Sicin. We should by this, to all our Lamention,
If he had gone forth Consull, found it so.

Bru. The Gods haue well preuented it, and Rome
Sits safe and still, without him.

Enter an Ædile.

Ædile. Worthy Tribunes,
There is a Slaue whom we haue put in prison,
Reports the Volces with two seuerall Powers
Are entred in the Roman Territories,
And with the deepest malice of the Warre,
Destroy, what lies before 'em.

Mene. 'Tis *Auffidius*,
Who hearing of our *Martius* Banishment,
Thrusts forth his hornes againe into the world
Which were In-shell'd, when *Martius* stood for Rome,

And

And durst not once peepe out.
Sicin. Come, what talke you of *Martius.*
Bru. Go see this Rumorer whipt, it cannot be,
The Voices dare breake with vs.
Mene. Cannot be?
We haue Record, that very well it can,
And three examples of the like, hath beene
Within my Age. But reason with the fellow
Before you punish him, where he heard this,
Least you shall chance to whip your Information,
And beate the Messenger, who bids beware
Of what is to be dreaded.
Sicin. Tell not me: I know this cannot be.
Bru. Not possible.
Enter a Messenger.
Mes. The Nobles in great earnestnesse are going
All to the Senate-house: some newes is comming
That turnes their Countenances.
Sicin. 'Tis this Slaue:
Go whip him fore the peoples eyes: His raising,
Nothing but his report.
Mes. Yes worthy Sir,
The Slaues report is seconded, and more
More fearfull is deliuer'd.
Sicin. What more fearefull?
Mes. It is spoke freely out of many mouths,
How probable I do not know, that *Martius*
Joyn'd with *Auffidius*, leads a power 'gainst Rome,
And vowes Reuenge as spacious, as betweene
The yong'st and oldest thing.
Sicin. This is most likely.
Bru. Rais'd onely, that the weaker sort may wish
Good *Martius* home againe.
Sicin. The very tricke on't.
Mene. This is vnlikely,
He, and *Auffidius* can no more attone
Then violent'st Contrariety.
Enter Messenger.
Mes. You are sent for to the Senate:
A fearefull Army, led by *Caius Martius*,
Associated with *Auffidius*, Rages
Vpon our Territories, and haue already
O're-borne their way, consum'd with fire, and tooke
What lay before them.
Enter Cominius.
Com. Oh you haue made good worke.
Mene. What newes? What newes?
Com. You haue holp to rauish your owne daughters, &
To melt the Citty Leades vpon your pates,
To see your Wiues dishonour'd to your Noses.
Mene. What's the newes? What's the newes?
Com. Your Temples burned in their Ciment, and
Your Franchises, whereon you stood, confin'd
Into an Augors boare.
Mene. Pray now, your Newes:
You haue made faire worke I feare me: pray your newes,
If *Martius* should be ioyn'd with Volceans.
Com. If? He is their God, he leads them like a thing
Made by some other Deity then Nature,
That shapes man Better: and they follow him
Against vs Brats, with no lesse Confidence,
Then Boyes pursuing Summer Butter-flies,
Or Butchers killing Flyes.
Mene. You haue made good worke,
You and your Apron men: you, that stood so much
Vpon the voyce of occupation, and
The breath of Garlicke-eaters.
Com. Hee'l shake your Rome about your eares.
Mene. As *Hercules* did shake downe Mellow Fruite:
You haue made faire worke.
Brut. But is this true sir?
Com. I, and you'l looke pale
Before you finde it other. All the Regions
Do smilingly Reuolt, and who resists
Are mock'd for valiant Ignorance,
And perish constant Fooles: who is't can blame him?
Your Enemies and his, finde something in him.
Mene. We are all vndone, vnlesse
The Noble man haue mercy.
Com. Who shall aske it?
The Tribunes cannot doo't for shame; the people
Deserue such pitty of him, as the Wolfe
Doe's of the Shepheards: For his best Friends, if they
Should say be good to Rome, they charg'd him, euen
As those should do that had deseru'd his hate,
And therein shew'd like Enemies.
Me. 'Tis true, if he were putting to my house, the brand
That should consume it, I haue not the face
To say, beseech you cease. You haue made faire hands,
You and your Crafts, you haue crafted faire.
Com. You haue brought
A Trembling vpon Rome, such as was neuer
S'incapeable of helpe.
Tri. Say not, we brought it.
Mene. How? Was't we? We lou'd him,
But like Beasts, and Cowardly Nobles,
Gaue way vnto your Clusters, who did hoote
Him out o'th'Citty.
Com. But I feare
They'l roare him in againe. *Tullus Auffidius*,
The second name of men, obeyes his points
As if he were his Officer: Desperation,
Is all the Policy, Strength, and Defence
That Rome can make against them.
Enter a Troope of Citizens.
Mene. Heere come the Clusters.
And is *Auffidius* with him? You are they
That made the Ayre vnwholsome, when you cast
Your stinking, greasie Caps, in hooting
At *Coriolanus* Exile. Now he's comming,
And not a haire vpon a Souldiers head
Which will not proue a whip: As many Coxcombes
As you threw Caps vp, will he tumble downe,
And pay you for your voyces. 'Tis no matter,
If he could burne vs all into one coale,
We haue deseru'd it.
Omnes. Faith, we heare fearfull Newes.
1 *Cit.* For mine owne part,
When I said banish him, I said 'twas pitty.
2 And so did I.
3 And so did I: and to say the truth, so did very many of vs, that we did we did for the best, and though wee willingly consented to his Banishment, yet it was against our will.
Com. Y'are goodly things, you Voyces.
Mene. You haue made good worke
You and your cry. Shal's to the Capitoll?
Com. Oh I, what else? *Exeunt both.*
Sicin. Go Masters get you home, be not dismaid,
These are a Side, that would be glad to haue
This true, which they so seeme to feare. Go home,
And shew no signe of Feare.

1. *Cit.*

1 *Cit.* The Gods bee good to vs: Come Masters let's home, I euer said we were i'th wrong, when we banish'd him.

2 *Cit.* So did we all. But come, let's home. *Exit Cit.*

Bru. I do not like this Newes.

Sicin. Nor I.

Bru. Let's to the Capitoll: would halfe my wealth
Would buy this for a lye.

Sicin. Pray let's go. *Exeunt Tribunes.*

Enter Auffidius with his Lieutenant.

Auf. Do they still flye to'th'Roman?

Lieu. I do not know what Witchcraft's in him: but
Your Soldiers vse him as the Grace 'fore meate,
Their talke at Table, and their Thankes at end,
And you are darkned in this action Sir,
Euen by your owne.

Auf. I cannot helpe it now,
Vnlesse by vsing meanes I lame the foote
Of our designe. He beares himselfe more proudlier,
Euen to my person, then I thought he would
When first I did embrace him. Yet his Nature
In that's no Changeling, and I must excuse
What cannot be amended.

Lieu. Yet I wish Sir,
(I meane for your particular) you had not
Ioyn'd in Commission with him: but either haue borne
The action of your selfe, or else to him, had left it soly.

Auf. I vnderstand thee well, and be thou sure
When he shall come to his account, he knowes not
What I can vrge against him, although it seemes
And so he thinkes, and is no lesse apparant
To th'vulgar eye, that he beares all things fairely:
And shewes good Husbandry for the Volcian State,
Fights Dragon-like, and does atcheeue as soone
As draw his Sword: yet he hath left vndone
That which shall breake his necke, or hazard mine,
When ere we come to our account.

Lieu. Sir, I beseech you, think you he'l carry Rome?

Auf. All places yeelds to him ere he sits downe,
And the Nobility of Rome are his:
The Senators and Patricians loue him too:
The Tribunes are no Soldiers: and their people
Will be as rash in the repeale, as hasty
To expell him thence. I thinke hee'l be to Rome
As is the Aspray to the Fish, who takes it
By Soueraignty of Nature. First, he was
A Noble seruant to them, but he could not
Carry his Honors eeuen: whether 'was Pride
Which out of dayly Fortune euer taints
The happy man; whether detect of iudgement,
To faile in the disposing of those chances
Which he was Lord of: or whether Nature,
Not to be other then one thing, not moouing
From th'Caske to th'Cushion: but commanding peace
Euen with the same austerity and garbe,
As he controll'd the warre. But one of these
(As he hath spices of them all) not all,
For I dare so farre free him, made him fear'd,
So hated, and so banish'd: but he ha's a Merit
To choake it in the vtt'rance: So our Vertue,
Lie in th'interpretation of the time,
And power vnto it selfe most commendable,
Hath not a Tombe so euident as a Chaire
T'extoll what it hath done.
One fire driues out one fire; one Naile, one Naile;
Rights by rights fouler, strengths by strengths do faile.
Come let's away: when *Caius* Rome is thine,
Thou art poor'st of all; then shortly art thou mine. *exeunt*

Actus Quintus.

Enter Menenius, Cominius, Sicinius, Brutus, the two Tribunes, with others.

Menen. No, Ile not go: you heare what he hath said
Which was sometime his Generall: who loued him
In a most deere particular. He call'd me Father:
But what o'that? Go you that banish'd him
A Mile before his Tent, fall downe, and knee
The way into his mercy: Nay, if he coy'd
To heare *Cominius* speake, Ile keepe at home.

Com. He would not seeme to know me.

Menen. Do you heare?

Com. Yet one time he did call me by my name:
I vrg'd our old acquaintance, and the drops
That we haue bled together. *Coriolanus*
He would not answer too: Forbad all Names,
He was a kinde of Nothing, Titlelesse,
Till he had forg'd himselfe a name a'th'fire
Of burning Rome.

Menen. Why so: you haue made good worke:
A paire of Tribunes, that haue wrack'd for Rome,
To make Coales cheape: A Noble memory.

Com. I minded him, how Royall 'twas to pardon
When it was lesse expected. He replyed
It was a bare petition of a State
To one whom they had punish'd.

Menen. Very well, could he say lesse.

Com. I offered to awaken his regard
For's priuate Friends. His answer to me was
He could not stay to picke them, in a pile
Of noysome musty Chaffe. He said, 'twas folly
For one poore graine or two, to leaue vnburnt
And still to nose th'offence.

Menen. For one poore graine or two?
I am one of those: his Mother, Wife, his Childe,
And this braue Fellow too: we are the Graines,
You are the musty Chaffe, and you are smelt
Aboue the Moone. We must be burnt for you.

Sicin. Nay, pray be patient: If you refuse your ayde
In this so neuer-needed helpe, yet do not
Vpbraid's with our distresse. But sure if you
Would be your Countries Pleader, your good tongue
More then the instant Armie we can make
Might stop our Countryman.

Mene. No: Ile not meddle.

Sicin. Pray you go to him.

Mene. What should I do?

Bru. Onely make triall what your Loue can do,
For Rome, towards *Martius.*

Mene. Well, and say that *Martius* returne mee,
As *Cominius* is return'd, vnheard: what then?
But as a discontented Friend, greefe-shot
With his vnkindnesse. Say't be so?

Sicin. Yet your good will
Must haue that thankes from Rome, after the measure
As you intended well.

Mene. Ile vndertak't:
I thinke hee'l heare me. Yet to bite his lip,
And humme at good *Cominius*, much vnhearts mee.

He was not taken well, he had not din'd,
The Veines vnfill'd, our blood is cold, and then
We powt vpon the Morning, are vnapt
To giue or to forgiue; but when we haue stufft
These Pipes, and these Conueyances of our blood
With Wine and Feeding, we haue suppler Soules
Then in our Priest-like Fasts: therefore Ile watch him
Till he be dieted to my request,
And then Ile set vpon him.

Bru. You know the very rode into his kindnesse,
And cannot lose your way.

Mene. Good faith Ile proue him,
Speed how it will. I shall ere long, haue knowledge
Of my successe. *Exit.*

Com. Hee'l neuer heare him.

Sicin. Not.

Com. I tell you, he doe's sit in Gold, his eye
Red as 'twould burne Rome: and his Iniury
The Gaoler to his pitty. I kneel'd before him,
'Twas very faintly he said Rise: dismist me
Thus with his speechlesse hand. What he would do
He sent in writing after me: what he would not,
Bound with an Oath to yeeld to his conditions:
So that all hope is vaine, vnlesse his Noble Mother,
And his Wife, who (as I heare) meane to solicite him
For mercy to his Countrey: therefore let's hence,
And with our faire intreaties hast them on. *Exeunt*

Enter Menenius to the Watch or Guard.

1.*Wat.* Stay: whence are you.

2.*Wat.* Stand, and go backe.

Me. You guard like men, 'tis well. But by your leaue, I am an Officer of State, & come to speak with *Coriolanus*

1 From whence? *Mene.* From Rome.

1 You may not passe, you must returne: our Generall will no more heare from thence.

2 You'l see your Rome embrac'd with fire, before You'l speake with *Coriolanus.*

Mene. Good my Friends,
If you haue heard your Generall talke of Rome,
And of his Friends there, it is Lots to Blankes,
My name hath touch't your eares: it is *Menenius.*

1 Be it so, go back: the vertue of your name,
Is not heere passable.

Mene. I tell thee Fellow,
Thy Generall is my Louer: I haue beene
The booke of his good Acts, whence men haue read
His Fame vnparalell'd, happely amplified:
For I haue euer verified my Friends,
(Of whom hee's cheefe) with all the size that verity
Would without lapsing suffer: Nay, sometimes,
Like to a Bowle vpon a subtle ground
I haue tumbled past the throw: and in his praise
Haue (almost) stampt the Leasing. Therefore Fellow,
I must haue leaue to passe.

1 Faith Sir, if you had told as many lies in his behalfe, as you haue vttered words in your owne, you should not passe heere: no, though it were as vertuous to lye, as to liue chastly. Therefore go backe.

Men. Prythee fellow, remember my name is *Menenius*, alwayes factionary on the party of your Generall.

2 Howsoeuer you haue bin his Lier, as you say you haue, I am one that telling true vnder him, must say you cannot passe. Therefore go backe.

Mene. Ha's he din'd can'st thou tell? For I would not speake with him, till after dinner.

1 You are a Roman, are you?

Mene. I am as thy Generall is.

1 Then you should hate Rome, as he do's. Can you, when you haue pusht out your gates, the very Defender of them, and in a violent popular ignorance, giuen your enemy your shield, thinke to front his reuenges with the easie groanes of old women, the Virginall Palms of your daughters, or with the palsied intercession of such a decay'd Dotant as you seeme to be? Can you think to blow out the intended fire, your City is ready to flame in, with such weake breath as this? No, you are deceiu'd, therfore backe to Rome, and prepare for your execution: you are condemn'd, our Generall has sworne you out of repreeue and pardon.

Mene. Sirra, if thy Captaine knew I were heere,
He would vse me with estimation.

1 Come, my Captaine knowes you not.

Mene. I meane thy Generall.

1 My Generall cares not for you. Back I say, go: least I let forth your halfe pinte of blood. Backe, that's the vtmost of your hauing, backe.

Mene. Nay but Fellow, Fellow.

Enter Coriolanus with Auffidius.

Corio. What's the matter?

Mene. Now you Companion: Ile say an arrant for you: you shall know now that I am in estimation: you shall perceiue, that a Iacke gardant cannot office me from my Son *Coriolanus*, guesse but my entertainment with him: if thou stand'st not i'th state of hanging, or of some death more long in Spectatorship, and crueller in suffering, behold now presently, and swoond for what's to come vpon thee. The glorious Gods sit in hourely Synod about thy particular prosperity, and loue thee no worse then thy old Father *Menenius* do's. O my Son, my Son! thou art preparing fire for vs: looke thee, heere's water to quench it. I was hardly moued to come to thee: but beeing assured none but my selfe could moue thee, I haue bene blowne out of your Gates with sighes: and coniure thee to pardon Rome, and thy petitionary Countrimen. The good Gods asswage thy wrath, and turne the dregs of it, vpon this Varlet heere: This, who like a blocke hath denyed my accesse to thee.

Corio. Away.

Mene. How? Away?

Corio. Wife, Mother, Child, I know not. My affaires
Are Seruanted to others: Though I owe
My Reuenge properly, my remission lies
In Volcean brests. That we haue beene familiar,
Ingrate forgetfulnesse shall poison rather
Then pitty: Note how much, therefore be gone.
Mine eares against your suites, are stronger then
Your gates against my force. Yet for I loued thee,
Take this along, I writ it for thy sake,
And would haue sent it. Another word *Menenius*,
I will not heare thee speake. This man *Auffidius*
Was my belou'd in Rome: yet thou behold'st.

Auffid. You keepe a constant temper. *Exeunt*

Manet the Guard and Menenius.

1 Now sir, is your name *Menenius*?

2 'Tis a spell you see of much power:
You know the way home againe.

1 Do you heare how wee are shent for keeping your greatnesse backe?

2 What cause do you thinke I haue to swoond?

Menen. I neither care for th'world, nor your General: for such things as you, I can scarse thinke ther's any, y'are so slight. He that hath a will to die by himselfe, feares it not

not from another : Let your Generall do his worst. For you, bee that you are, long; and your misery encreafe with your age. I say to you, as I was said to, Away. *Exit*

1 A Noble Fellow I warrant him.

2 The worthy Fellow is our General. He's the Rock, The Oake not to be winde-shaken. *Exit Watch.*

Enter Coriolanus and Auffidius.

Corio. We will before the walls of Rome to morrow
Set downe our Hoast. My partner in this Action,
You must report to th'Volcian Lords, how plainly
I haue borne this Businesse.

Auf. Onely their ends you haue respected,
Stopt your eares against the generall suite of Rome :
Neuer admitted a priuat whisper, no not with such frends
That thought them sure of you.

Corio. This last old man,
Whom with a crack'd heart I haue sent to Rome,
Lou'd me, aboue the measure of a Father,
Nay godded me indeed. Their latest refuge
Was to send him : for whose old Loue I haue
(Though I shew'd sowrely to him) once more offer'd
The first Conditions which they did refuse,
And cannot now accept, to grace him onely,
That thought he could do more : A very little
I haue yeelded too. Fresh Embasses, and Suites,
Nor from the State, nor priuate friends heereafter
Will I lend eare to. Ha? what shout is this? *Shout within*
Shall I be tempted to infringe my vow
In the same time 'tis made? I will not.

Enter Virgilia, Volumnia, Valeria, yong Martius, with Attendants.

My wife comes formost, then the honour'd mould
Wherein this Trunke was fram'd, and in her hand
The Grandchilde to her blood. But out affection,
All bond and priuiledge of Nature breake;
Let it be Vertuous to be Obstinate.
What is that Curt'sie worth? Or those Doues eyes,
Which can make Gods forsworne? I melt, and am not
Of stronger earth then others: my Mother bowes,
As if Olympus to a Mole-hill should
In supplication Nod : and my yong Boy
Hath an Aspect of intercession, which
Great Nature cries, Deny not. Let the Volces
Plough Rome, and harrow Italy, Ile neuer
Be such a Gosling to obey instinct; but stand
As if a man were Author of himself, & knew no other kin

Virgil. My Lord and Husband.

Corio. These eyes are not the same I wore in Rome.

Virg. The sorrow that deliuers vs thus chang'd,
Makes you thinke so.

Corio. Like a dull Actor now, I haue forgot my part,
And I am out, euen to a full Disgrace. Best of my Flesh,
Forgiue my Tyranny : but do not say,
For that forgiue our Romanes. O a kisse
Long as my Exile, sweet as my Reuenge!
Now by the iealous Queene of Heauen, that kisse
I carried from thee deare; and my true Lippe
Hath Virgin'd it ere since. You Gods, I pray,
And the most noble Mother of the world
Leaue vnsaluted : Sinke my knee i'th'earth, *Kneeles*
Of thy deepe duty, more impression shew
Then that of common Sonnes.

Volum. Oh stand vp blest!
Whil'st with no softer Cushion then the Flint
I kneele before thee, and vnproperly
Shew duty as mistaken, all this while,
Betweene the Childe, and Parent.

Corio. What's this? your knees to me?
To your Corrected Sonne?
Then let the Pibbles on the hungry beach
Fillop the Starres : Then, let the mutinous windes
Strike the proud Cedars 'gainst the fiery Sun :
Murd'ring Impossibility, to make
What cannot be, slight worke.

Volum. Thou art my Warriour, I hope to frame thee
Do you know this Lady?

Corio. The Noble Sister of *Publicola*;
The Moone of Rome : Chaste as the Isicle
That's curdied by the Frost, from purest Snow,
And hangs on *Dians* Temple : Deere *Valeria.*

Volum. This is a poore Epitome of yours,
Which by th'interpretation of full time,
May shew like all your selfe.

Corio. The God of Souldiers :
With the consent of supreame Ioue, informe
Thy thoughts with Noblenesse, that thou mayst proue
To shame vnvulnerable, and sticke i'th Warres
Like a great Sea-marke standing euery flaw,
And sauing those that eye thee.

Volum. Your knee, Sirrah.

Corio. That's my braue Boy.

Volum. Euen he, your wife, this Ladie, and my selfe,
Are Sutors to you.

Corio. I beseech you peace:
Or if you'ld aske, remember this before;
The thing I haue forsworne to graunt, may neuer
Be held by you denials. Do not bid me
Dismisse my Soldiers, or capitulate
Againe, with Romes Mechanickes. Tell me not
Wherein I seeme vnnaturall : Desire not t'allay
My Rages and Reuenges, with your colder reasons.

Volum. Oh no more, no more:
You haue said you will not grant vs any thing :
For we haue nothing else to aske, but that
Which you deny already : yet we will aske,
That if you faile in our request, the blame
May hang vpon your hardnesse, therefore heare vs.

Corio. *Auffidius*, and you Volces marke, for wee'l
Heare nought from Rome in priuate. Your request?

Volum. Should we be silent & not speak, our Raiment
And state of Bodies would bewray what life
We haue led since thy Exile. Thinke with thy selfe,
How more vnfortunate then all liuing women
Are we come hither; since that thy sight, which should
Make our eies flow with ioy, harts dance with comforts,
Constraines them weepe, and shake with feare & sorow,
Making the Mother, wife, and Childe to see,
The Sonne, the Husband, and the Father tearing
His Countries Bowels out; and to poore we
Thine enmities most capitall : Thou barr'st vs
Our prayers to the Gods, which is a comfort
That all but we enioy. For how can we?
Alas! how can we, for our Country pray?
Whereto we are bound, together with thy victory :
Whereto we are bound : Alacke, or we must loose
The Countrie our deere Nurse, or else thy person
Our comfort in the Country. We must finde
An euident Calamity, though we had
Our wish, which side should win. For either thou
Must as a Forraine Recreant be led
With Manacles through our streets, or else
Triumphantly treade on thy Countries ruine,

And beare the Palme, for hauing brauely ſhed
Thy Wife and Childrens blood: For my ſelfe, Sonne,
I purpoſe not to waite on Fortune, till
Theſe warres determine: If I cannot perſwade thee,
Rather to ſhew a Noble grace to both parts,
Then ſeeke the end of one; thou ſhalt no ſooner
March to aſſault thy Country, then to treade
(Truſt too't, thou ſhalt not) on thy Mothers wombe
That brought thee to this world.

Virg. I, and mine, that brought you forth this boy,
To keepe your name liuing to time.

Boy. A ſhall not tread on me: Ile run away
Till I am bigger, but then Ile fight.

Corio. Not of a womans tenderneſſe to be,
Requires nor Childe, nor womans face to ſee:
I haue ſate too long.

Volum. Nay, go not from vs thus:
If it were ſo, that our requeſt did tend
To ſaue the Romanes, thereby to deſtroy
The Volces whom you ſerue, you might condemne vs
As poyſonous of your Honour. No, our ſuite
Is that you reconcile them: While the Volces
May ſay, this mercy we haue ſhew'd: the Romanes,
This we receiu'd, and each in either ſide
Giue the All-haile to thee, and cry be Bleſt
For making vp this peace. Thou know'ſt (great Sonne)
The end of Warres vncertaine: but this certaine,
That if thou conquer Rome, the benefit
Which thou ſhalt thereby reape, is ſuch a name
Whoſe repetition will be dogg'd with Curſes:
Whoſe Chronicle thus writ, The man was Noble,
But with his laſt Attempt, he wip'd it out:
Deſtroy'd his Country, and his name remaines
To th'inſuing Age, abhorr'd. Speake to me Son:
Thou haſt affected the fiue ſtraines of Honor,
To imitate the graces of the Gods.
To teare with Thunder the wide Cheekes a'th'Ayre,
And yet to change thy Sulphure with a Boult
That ſhould but riue an Oake. Why do'ſt not ſpeake?
Think'ſt thou it Honourable for a Nobleman
Still to remember wrongs? Daughter, ſpeake you:
He cares not for your weeping. Speake thou Boy,
Perhaps thy childiſhneſſe will moue him more
Then can our Reaſons. There's no man in the world
More bound to's Mother, yet heere he let's me prate
Like one i'th'Stockes. Thou haſt neuer in thy life,
Shew'd thy deere Mother any curteſie,
When ſhe (poore Hen) fond of no ſecond brood,
Ha's clock'd thee to the Warres: and ſafelie home
Loden with Honor. Say my Requeſt's vniuſt,
And ſpurne me backe: But, if it be not ſo
Thou art not honeſt, and the Gods will plague thee
That thou reſtrain'ſt from me the Duty, which
To a Mothers part belongs. He turnes away:
Down Ladies: let vs ſhame him with him with our knees
To his ſur-name *Coriolanus* longs more pride
Then pitty to our Prayers. Downe: an end,
This is the laſt. So, we will home to Rome,
And dye among our Neighbours: Nay, behold's,
This Boy that cannot tell what he would haue,
But kneeles, and holds vp hands for fellowſhip,
Doe's reaſon our Petition with more ſtrength
Then thou haſt to deny't. Come, let vs go:
This Fellow had a Volcean to his Mother:
His Wife is in *Corioles*, and his Childe
Like him by chance: yet giue vs our diſpatch:
I am huſht vntill our City be afire, & then Ile ſpeak a litle

Holds her by the hand ſilent.

Corio. O Mother, Mother!
What haue you done? Behold, the Heauens do ope,
The Gods looke downe, and this vnnaturall Scene
They laugh at. Oh my Mother, Mother: Oh!
You haue wonne a happy Victory to Rome.
But for your Sonne, beleeue it: Oh beleeue it,
Moſt dangerouſly you haue with him preuail'd,
If not moſt mortall to him. But let it come:
Auffidius, though I cannot make true Warres,
Ile frame conuenient peace. Now good *Auffidius*,
Were you in my ſteed, would you haue heard
A Mother leſſe? or granted leſſe *Auffidius*?

Auf. I was mou'd withall.

Corio. I dare be ſworne you were:
And ſir, it is no little thing to make
Mine eyes to ſweat compaſſion. But (good ſir)
What peace you'l make, aduiſe me: For my part,
Ile not to Rome, Ile backe with you, and pray you
Stand to me in this cauſe. Oh Mother! Wife!

Auf. I am glad thou haſt ſet thy mercy, & thy Honor
At difference in thee: Out of that Ile worke
My ſelfe a former Fortune.

Corio. I by and by; But we will drinke together:
And you ſhall beare
A better witneſſe backe then words, which we
On like conditions, will haue Counter-ſeal'd.
Come enter with vs: Ladies you deſerue
To haue a Temple built you: All the Swords
In Italy, and her Confederate Armes
Could not haue made this peace. *Exeunt.*

Enter Menenius and Sicinius.

Mene. See you yon'd Coin a'th Capitol, yon'd corner (ſtone?

Sicin. Why what of that?

Mene. If it be poſſible for you to diſplace it with your little finger, there is ſome hope the Ladies of Rome, eſpecially his Mother, may preuaile with him. But I ſay, there is no hope in't, our throats are ſentenc'd, and ſtay vppon execution.

Sicin. Is't poſsible, that ſo ſhort a time can alter the condition of a man.

Mene. There is differency between a Grub & a Butterfly, yet your Butterfly was a Grub: this *Martius*, is growne from Man to Dragon: He has wings, hee's more then a creeping thing.

Sicin. He lou'd his Mother deerely.

Mene. So did he mee: and he no more remembers his Mother now, then an eight yeare old horſe. The tartneſſe of his face, ſowres ripe Grapes. When he walks, he moues like an Engine, and the ground ſhrinkes before his Treading. He is able to pierce a Corſlet with his eye: Talkes like a knell, and his hum is a Battery. He ſits in his State, as a thing made for *Alexander*. What he bids bee done, is finiſht with his bidding. He wants nothing of a God but Eternity, and a Heauen to Throne in.

Sicin. Yes, mercy, if you report him truly.

Mene. I paint him in the Character. Mark what mercy his Mother ſhall bring from him: There is no more mercy in him, then there is milke in a male-Tyger, that ſhall our poore City finde: and all this is long of you.

Sicin. The Gods be good vnto vs.

Mene. No, in ſuch a caſe the Gods will not bee good vnto vs. When we baniſh'd him, we reſpected not them: and he returning to breake our necks, they reſpect not vs.

Enter a Meſſenger.

Meſſ.

Mes. Sir, if you'ld saue your life, flye to your House,
The Plebeians haue got your Fellow Tribune,
And hale him vp and downe; all swearing, if
The Romane Ladies bring not comfort home,
They'l giue him death by Inches.

Enter another Messenger.

Sicin. What's the Newes?
Mess. Good Newes, good newes, the Ladies haue (preuayl'd,
The Volcians are dislodg'd, and *Martius* gone:
A merrier day did neuer yet greet Rome,
No, not th'expulsion of the *Tarquins*.
Sicin. Friend, art thou certaine this is true?
Is't most certaine.
Mes. As certaine as I know the Sun is fire:
Where haue you lurk'd that you make doubt of it:
Ne're through an Arch so hurried the blowne Tide,
As the recomforted through th'gates. Why harke you:

Trumpets, Hoboyes, Drums beate, altogether.

The Trumpets, Sack-buts, Psalteries, and Fifes,
Tabors, and Symboles, and the showting Romans;
Make the Sunne dance. Hearke you. *A shout within*
Mene. This is good Newes:
I will go meete the Ladies. This *Volumnia*,
Is worth of Consuls, Senators, Patricians,
A City full: Of Tribunes such as you,
A Sea and Land full: you haue pray'd well to day:
This Morning, for ten thousand of your throates,
I'de not haue giuen a doit. Harke, how they ioy.

Sound still with the Shouts.

Sicin. First, the Gods blesse you for your tydings:
Next, accept my thankefulnesse.
Mess. Sir, we haue all great cause to giue great thanks.
Sicin. They are neere the City.
Mes. Almost at point to enter.
Sicin. Wee'l meet them, and helpe the ioy. *Exeunt.*

Enter two Senators, with Ladies, passing ouer the Stage, with other Lords.

Sena. Behold our Patronnesse, the life of Rome:
Call all your Tribes together, praise the Gods,
And make triumphant fires, strew Flowers before them:
Vnshoot the noise that Banish'd *Martius*;
Repeale him, with the welcome of his Mother:
Cry welcome Ladies, welcome.
All. Welcome Ladies, welcome.

A Flourish with Drummes & Trumpets.

Enter Tullus Auffidius, with Attendants.

Auf. Go tell the Lords a'th'City, I am heere:
Deliuer them this Paper: hauing read it,
Bid them repayre to th'Market place, where I
Euen in theirs, and in the Commons eares
Will vouch the truth of it. Him I accuse:
The City Ports by this hath enter'd, and
Intends t'appeare before the People, hoping
To purge himselfe with words. Dispatch.

Enter 3 or 4 Conspirators of Auffidius Faction.

Most Welcome.
1.*Con.* How is it with our Generall?
Auf. Euen so, as with a man by his owne Almes impoyson'd, and with his Charity slaine.
2.*Con.* Most Noble Sir, If you do hold the same intent
Wherein you wisht vs parties: Wee'l deliuer you
Of your great danger.
Auf. Sir, I cannot tell,
We must proceed as we do finde the People.
3.*Con.* The People will remaine vncertaine, whil'st
'Twixt you there's difference: but the fall of either
Makes the Suruiuor heyre of all.
Auf. I know it:
And my pretext to strike at him, admits
A good construction. I rais'd him, and I pawn'd
Mine Honor for his truth: who being so heighten'd,
He watered his new Plants with dewes of Flattery,
Seducing so my Friends: and to this end,
He bow'd his Nature, neuer knowne before,
But to be rough, vnswayable, and free.
3.*Consp.* Sir, his stoutnesse
When he did stand for Consull, which he lost
By lacke of stooping.
Auf. That I would haue spoke of:
Being banish'd for't, he came vnto my Harth,
Presented to my knife his Throat: I tooke him,
Made him ioynt-seruant with me: Gaue him way
In all his owne desires: Nay, let him choose
Out of my Files, his proiects, to accomplish
My best and freshest men, seru'd his designements
In mine owne person: holpe to reape the Fame
Which he did end all his; and tooke some pride
To do my selfe this wrong: Till at the last
I seem'd his Follower, not Partner; and
He wadg'd me with his Countenance, as if
I had bin Mercenary.
1.*Con.* So he did my Lord:
The Army marueyl'd at it, and in the last,
When he had carried Rome, and that we look'd
For no lesse Spoile, then Glory.
Auf. There was it:
For which my sinewes shall be stretcht vpon him,
At a few drops of Womens rhewme, which are
As cheape as Lies; he sold the Blood and Labour
Of our great Action; therefore shall he dye,
And Ile renew me in his fall. But hearke.

Drummes and Trumpets sounds, with great showts of the people.

1.*Con.* Your Natiue Towne you enter'd like a Poste,
And had no welcomes home, but he returnes
Splitting the Ayre with noyse.
2.*Con.* And patient Fooles,
Whose children he hath slaine, their base throats teare
With giuing him glory.
3.*Con.* Therefore at your vantage,
Ere he expresse himselfe, or moue the people
With what he would say, let him feele your Sword:
Which we will second, when he lies along
After your way. His Tale pronounc'd, shall bury
His Reasons, with his Body.
Auf. Say no more. Heere come the Lords,

Enter the Lords of the City.

All Lords. You are most welcome home.
Auff. I haue not deseru'd it.
But worthy Lords, haue you with heede perused
What I haue written to you?
All. We haue.
1.*Lord.* And greeue to heare't:
What faults he made before the last, I thinke
Might haue found easie Fines: But there to end
Where he was to begin, and giue away
The benefit of our Leuies, answering vs
With our owne charge: making a Treatie, where
There was a yeelding; this admits no excuse.

Auf. He approaches, you ſhall heare him.

Enter Coriolanus marching with Drumme, and Colours. The Commoners being with him.

Corio. Haile Lords, I am return'd your Souldier:
No more infected with my Countries loue
Then when I parted hence: but ſtill ſubſiſting
Vnder your great Command. You are to know,
That proſperouſly I haue attempted, and
With bloody paſſage led your Warres, euen to
The gates of Rome: Our ſpoiles we haue brought home
Doth more then counterpoize a full third part
The charges of the Action. We haue made peace
With no leſſe Honor to the *Antiates*
Then ſhame to th'Romaines. And we heere deliuer
Subſcrib'd by'th'Conſuls, and Patricians,
Together with the Seale a'th Senat, what
We haue compounded on.

Auf. Read it not Noble Lords,
But tell the Traitor in the higheſt degree
He hath abus'd your Powers.

Corio. Traitor? How now?

Auf. I Traitor, *Martius*.

Corio. *Martius*?

Auf. I *Martius*, *Caius Martius*: Do'ſt thou thinke
Ile grace thee with that Robbery, thy ſtolne name
Coriolanus in *Corioles*?
You Lords and Heads a'th'State, perfidiouſly
He ha's betray'd your buſineſſe, and giuen vp
For certaine drops of Salt, your City Rome:
I ſay your City to his Wife and Mother,
Breaking his Oath and Reſolution, like
A twiſt of rotten Silke, neuer admitting
Counſaile a'th'warre: But at his Nurſes teares
He whin'd and roar'd away your Victory,
That Pages bluſh'd at him, and men of heart
Look'd wond'ring each at others.

Corio. Hear'ſt thou Mars?

Auf. Name not the God, thou boy of Teares.

Corio. Ha?

Aufid. No more.

Corio. Meaſureleſſe Lyar, thou haſt made my heart
Too great for what containes it. Boy? Oh Slaue,
Pardon me Lords, 'tis the firſt time that euer
I was forc'd to ſcoul'd. Your iudgments my graue Lords
Muſt giue this Curre the Lye: and his owne Notion,
Who weares my ſtripes impreſt vpon him, that
Muſt beare my beating to his Graue, ſhall ioyne
To thruſt the Lye vnto him.

1 *Lord.* Peace both, and heare me ſpeake.

Corio. Cut me to peeces Volces men and Lads,
Staine all your edges on me. Boy, falſe Hound:
If you haue writ your Annales true, 'tis there,
That like an Eagle in a Doue-coat, I
Flatter'd your Volcians in *Corioles*.
Alone I did it, Boy.

Auf. Why Noble Lords,
Will you be put in minde of his blinde Fortune,
Which was your ſhame, by this vnholy Braggart?
'Fore your owne eyes, and eares?

All Conſp. Let him dye for't.

All People. Teare him to peeces, do it preſently:
He kill'd my Sonne, my daughter, he kill'd my Coſine
Marcus, he kill'd my Father.

2 *Lord.* Peace hoe: no outrage, peace:
The man is Noble, and his Fame folds in
This Orbe o'th'earth: His laſt offences to vs
Shall haue Iudicious hearing. Stand *Auffidius*,
And trouble not the peace.

Corio. O that I had him, with ſix *Auffidiuſſes*, or more:
His Tribe, to vſe my lawfull Sword.

Auf. Inſolent Villaine.

All Conſp. Kill, kill, kill, kill, kill him.

Draw both the Conſpirators, and kils Martius, who falles, Auffidius ſtands on him.

Lords. Hold, hold, hold, hold.

Auf. My Noble Maſters, heare me ſpeake.

1. *Lord.* O *Tullus*.

2. *Lord.* Thou haſt done a deed, whereat
Valour will weepe.

3. *Lord.* Tread not vpon him Maſters, all be quiet,
Put vp your Swords.

Auf. My Lords,
When you ſhall know (as in this Rage
Prouok'd by him, you cannot) the great danger
Which this mans life did owe you, you'l reioyce
That he is thus cut off. Pleaſe it your Honours
To call me to your Senate, Ile deliuer
My ſelfe your loyall Seruant, or endure
Your heavieſt Cenſure.

1. *Lord.* Beare from hence his body,
And mourne you for him. Let him be regarded
As the moſt Noble Coarſe, that euer Herald
Did follow to his Vrne.

2. *Lord.* His owne impatience,
Takes from *Auffidius* a great part of blame:
Let's make the Beſt of it.

Auf. My Rage is gone,
And I am ſtrucke with ſorrow. Take him vp:
Helpe three a'th'cheefeſt Souldiers, Ile be one.
Beate thou the Drumme that it ſpeake mournfully:
Traile your ſteele Pikes. Though in this City hee
Hath widdowed and vnchilded many a one,
Which to this houre bewaile the Iniury,
Yet he ſhall haue a Noble Memory. Aſſiſt.

Exeunt bearing the Body of Martius. A dead March Sounded.

FINIS.

The Lamentable Tragedy of Titus Andronicus.

Actus Primus. Scœna Prima.

Flourish. Enter the Tribunes and Senators aloft And then enter Saturninus and his Followers at one doore, and Bassianus and his Followers at the other, with Drum & Colours.

Saturninus.

NOble Patricians, Patrons of my right,
Defend the iustice of my Cause with Armes.
And Countrey-men, my louing Followers,
Pleade my Successiue Title with your Swords.
I was the first borne Sonne, that was the last
That wore the Imperiall Diadem of Rome:
Then let my Fathers Honours liue in me,
Nor wrong mine Age with this indignitie.

Bassianus. Romaines, Friends, Followers,
Fauourers of my Right:
If euer *Bassianus*, *Cæsars* Sonne,
Were gracious in the eyes of Royall Rome,
Keepe then this passage to the Capitoll:
And suffer not Dishonour to approach
Th'Imperiall Seate to Vertue: consecrate
To Iustice, Continence, and Nobility:
But let Desert in pure Election shine;
And Romanes, fight for Freedome in your Choice.

Enter Marcus Andronicus aloft with the Crowne.

Princes, that striue by Factions, and by Friends,
Ambitiously for Rule and Empery:
Know, that the people of Rome for whom we stand
A speciall Party, haue by Common voyce
In Election for the Romane Emperie,
Chosen *Andronicus*, Sur-named *Pious*,
For many good and great deserts to Rome.
A Nobler man, a brauer Warriour,
Liues not this day within the City Walles.
He by the Senate is accited home,
From weary Warres against the barbarous Gothes,
That with his Sonnes (a terror to our Foes)
Hath yoak'd a Nation strong, train'd vp in Armes.
Ten yeares are spent, since first he vndertooke
This Cause of Rome, and chasticed with Armes
Our Enemies pride. Fiue times he hath return'd
Bleeding to Rome, bearing his Valiant Sonnes
In Coffins from the Field.
And now at last, laden with Honours Spoyles,
Returnes the good *Andronicus* to Rome,
Renowned *Titus*, flourishing in Armes.
Let vs intreat, by Honour of his Name,
Whom (worthily) you would haue now succeede,
And in the Capitoll and Senates right,
Whom you pretend to Honour and Adore,
That you withdraw you, and abate your Strength,
Dismisse your Followers, and as Suters should,
Pleade your Deserts in Peace and Humblenesse.

Saturnine. How fayre the Tribune speakes,
To calme my thoughts.

Bassia. *Marcus Andronicus*, so I do affie
In thy vprightnesse and Integrity:
And so I Loue and Honor thee, and thine,
Thy Noble Brother *Titus*, and his Sonnes,
And Her (to whom my thoughts are humbled all)
Gracious *Lauinia*, Romes rich Ornament,
That I will heere dismisse my louing Friends:
And to my Fortunes, and the Peoples Fauour,
Commit my Cause in ballance to be weigh'd.
Exit Souldiours.

Saturnine. Friends, that haue beene
Thus forward in my Right,
I thanke you all, and heere Dismisse you all,
And to the Loue and Fauour of my Countrey,
Commit my Selfe, my Person, and the Cause:
Rome, be as iust and gracious vnto me,
As I am confident and kinde to thee.
Open the Gates, and let me in.

Bassia. Tribunes, and me, a poore Competitor.
Flourish. They go vp into the Senat house.

Enter a Captaine.

Cap. Romanes make way: the good *Andronicus*,
Patron of Vertue, Romes best Champion,
Successefull in the Battailes that he fights,
With Honour and with Fortune is return'd,
From whence he circumscribed with his Sword,
And brought to yoke the Enemies of Rome.

Sound Drummes and Trumpets. And then enter two of Titus Sonnes; After them, two men bearing a Coffin couered with blacke, then two other Sonnes. After them, Titus Andronicus, and then Tamora the Queene of Gothes, & her two Sonnes Chiron and Demetrius, with Aaron the Moore, and others, as many as can bee: They set downe the Coffin, and Titus speakes.

Andronicus. Haile Rome:
Victorious in thy Mourning Weedes:

Loe,

Loe as the Barke that hath discharg'd his fraught,
Returnes with precious lading to the Bay,
From whence at first she wegih'd her Anchorage:
Commeth *Andronicus* bound with Lawrell bowes,
To resalute his Country with his teares,
Teares of true ioy for his returne to Rome,
Thou great defender of this Capitoll,
Stand gracious to the Rites that we intend.
Romaines, of fiue and twenty Valiant Sonnes,
Halfe of the number that King *Priam* had,
Behold the poore remaines aliue and dead!
These that Suruiue, let Rome reward with Loue:
These that I bring vnto their latest home,
With buriall amongst their Auncestors.
Heere Gothes haue giuen me leaue to sheath my Sword:
Titus vnkinde, and carelesse of thine owne,
Why suffer'st thou thy Sonnes vnburied yet,
To houer on the dreadfull shore of Stix?
Make way to lay them by their Bretheren.

They open the Tombe.

There greete in silence as the dead are wont,
And sleepe in peace, slaine in your Countries warres:
O sacred receptacle of my ioyes,
Sweet Cell of vertue and Noblitie,
How many Sonnes of mine hast thou in store,
That thou wilt neuer render to me more?
Luc. Giue vs the proudest prisoner of the Gothes,
That we may hew his limbes, and on a pile
Ad manus fratrum, sacrifice his flesh:
Before this earthly prison of their bones,
That so the shadowes be not vnappeas'd,
Nor we disturb'd with prodigies on earth.
Tit. I giue him you, the Noblest that Suruiues,
The eldest Son of this distressed Queene.
Tam. Stay Romaine Bretheren, gracious Conqueror,
Victorious *Titus*, rue the teares I shed,
A Mothers teares in passion for her sonne:
And if thy Sonnes were euer deere to thee,
Oh thinke my sonnes to be as deere to mee.
Sufficeth not, that we are brought to Rome
To beautifie thy Triumphs, and returne
Captiue to thee, and to thy Romaine yoake,
But must my Sonnes be slaughtred in the streetes,
For Valiant doings in their Countries cause?
O! If to fight for King and Common-weale,
Were piety in thine, it is in these:
Andronicus, staine not thy Tombe with blood.
Wilt thou draw neere the nature of the Gods?
Draw neere them then in being mercifull.
Sweet mercy is Nobilities true badge,
Thrice Noble *Titus*, spare my first borne sonne.
Tit. Patient your selfe Madam, and pardon me.
These are the Brethren, whom you Gothes beheld
Aliue and dead, and for their Bretheren slaine,
Religiously they aske a sacrifice:
To this your sonne is markt, and die he must,
T'appease their groaning shadowes that are gone.
Luc. Away with him, and make a fire straight,
And with our Swords vpon a pile of wood,
Let's hew his limbes till they be cleane consum'd.

Exit Sonnes with Alarbus.

Tamo. O cruell irreligious piety.
Chi. Was euer Scythia halfe so barbarous?
Dem. Oppose me Scythia to ambitious Rome,
Alarbus goes to rest, and we suruiue,
To tremble vnder *Titus* threatning lookes,
Then Madam stand resolu'd, but hope withall,
The selfe same Gods that arm'd the Queene of Troy
With opportunitie of sharpe reuenge
Vpon the Thracian Tyrant in his Tent,
May fauour *Tamora* the Queene of Gothes,
(When Gothes were Gothes, and *Tamora* was Queene)
To quit the bloody wrongs vpon her foes.

Enter the Sonnes of Andronicus againe.

Luci. See Lord and Father, how we haue perform'd
Our Romaine rightes, *Alarbus* limbs are lopt,
And intrals feede the sacrifising fire,
Whose smoke like incense doth perfume the skie.
Remaineth nought but to interre our Brethren,
And with low'd Larums welcome them to Rome.
Tit. Let it be so, and let *Andronicus*
Make this his latest farewell to their soules.

Flourish.

Then Sound Trumpets, and lay the Coffins in the Tombe.

In peace and Honour rest you heere my Sonnes,
Romes readiest Champions, repose you heere in rest,
Secure from worldly chaunces and mishaps:
Heere lurks no Treason, heere no enuie swels,
Heere grow no damned grudges, heere are no stormes,
No noyse, but silence and Eternall sleepe,
In peace and Honour rest you heere my Sonnes.

Enter Lauinia.

Laui. In peace and Honour, liue Lord *Titus* long,
My Noble Lord and Father, liue in Fame:
Loe at this Tombe my tributarie teares,
I render for my Bretherens Obsequies:
And at thy feete I kneele, with teares of ioy
Shed on the earth for thy returne to Rome.
O blesse me heere with thy victorious hand,
Whose Fortune Romes best Citizens applau'd.
Ti. Kind Rome,
That hast thus louingly reseru'd
The Cordiall of mine age to glad my hart,
Lauinia liue, out-liue thy Fathers dayes:
And Fames eternall date for vertues praise.
Marc. Long liue Lord *Titus*, my beloued brother,
Gracious Triumpher in the eyes of Rome.
Tit. Thankes Gentle Tribune,
Noble brother *Marcus*.
Mar. And welcome Nephews from succesfull wars,
You that suruiue and you that sleepe in Fame:
Faire Lords your Fortunes are all alike in all,
That in your Countries seruice drew your Swords.
But safer Triumph is this Funerall Pompe,
That hath aspir'd to *Solons* Happines,
And Triumphs ouer chaunce in honours bed.
Titus Andronicus, the people of Rome,
Whose friend in iustice thou hast euer bene,
Send thee by me their Tribune and their trust,
This Palliament of white and spotlesse Hue,
And name thee in Election for the Empire,
With these our late deceased Emperours Sonnes:
Be *Candidatus* then, and put it on,
And helpe to set a head on headlesse Rome.
Tit. A better head her Glorious body fits,
Then his that shakes for age and feeblenesse:

What

What ſhould I d'on this Robe and trouble you,
Be choſen with proclamations to day,
To morrow yeeld vp rule, reſigne my life,
And ſet abroad new buſineſſe for you all.
Rome I haue bene thy Souldier forty yeares,
And led my Countries ſtrength ſucceſſefully,
And buried one and twenty Valiant Sonnes,
Knighted in Field, ſlaine manfully in Armes,
In right and Seruice of their Noble Countrie:
Giue me a ſtaffe of Honour for mine age,
But not a Scepter to controule the world,
Vpright he held it Lords, that held it laſt.
Mar. *Titus*, thou ſhalt obtaine and aske the Emperie.
Sat. Proud and ambitious Tribune can'ſt thou tell?
Titus. Patience Prince *Saturninus*.
Sat. Romaines do me right.
Patricians draw your Swords, andſheath them not
Till *Saturninus* be Romes Emperour:
Andronicus would thou wert ſhipt to hell,
Rather then rob me of the peoples harts.
Luc. Proud *Saturnine*, interrupter of the good
That Noble minded *Titus* meanes to thee.
Tit. Content thee Prince, I will reſtore to thee
The peoples harts, and weane them from themſelues.
Baſs. *Andronicus*, I do not flatter thee
But Honour thee, and will doe till I die:
My Faction if thou ſtrengthen with thy Friend?
I will moſt thankefull be, and thankes to men
Of Noble mindes, is Honourable Meede.
Tit, People of Rome, and Noble Tribunes heere,
I aske your voyces and your Suffrages,
Will you beſtow them friendly on *Andronicus*?
Tribunes. To gratifie the good *Andronicus*,
And Gratulate his ſafe returne to Rome,
The people will accept whom he admits.
Tit. Tribunes I thanke you, and this ſure I make,
That you Create your Emperours eldeſt ſonne,
Lord *Saturnine*, whoſe Vertues will I hope,
Reflect on Rome as Tytans Rayes on earth,
And ripen Iuſtice in this Common-weale:
Then if you will elect by my aduiſe,
Crowne him, and ſay: Long liue our Emperour.
Mar. An. With Voyces and applauſe of euery ſort,
Patricians and Plebeans we Create
Lord *Saturninus* Romes Great Emperour.
And ſay, *Long liue our Emperour Saturnine.*
A long Flouriſh till they come downe.
Satu. *Titus Andronicus*, for thy Fauours done,
To vs in our Election this day,
I giue thee thankes in part of thy Deſerts,
And will with Deeds requite thy gentleneſſe:
And for an Onſet *Titus* to aduance
Thy Name, and Honorable Familie,
Lauinia will I make my Empreſſe,
Romes Royall Miſtris, Miſtris of my hart
And in the Sacred *Pathan* her eſpouſe:
Tell me *Andronicus* doth this motion pleaſe thee?
Tit. It doth my worthy Lord, and in this match,
I hold me Highly Honoured of your Grace,
And heere in ſight of Rome, to *Saturnine*,
King and Commander of our Common-weale,
The Wide-worlds Emperour, do I Conſecrate,
My Sword, my Chariot, and my Priſonerss,
Preſents well Worthy Romes Imperiall Lord:
Receiue them then, the Tribute that I owe,
Mine Honours Enſignes humbled at my feete.
Satu. Thankes Noble *Titus*, Father of my life,
How proud I am of thee, and of thy gifts
Rome ſhall record, and when I do forget
The leaſt of theſe vnſpeakable Deſerts,
Romans forget your Fealtie to me.
Tit. Now Madam are your priſoner to an Emperour,
To him that for you Honour and your State,
Will vſe you Nobly and your followers.
Satu. A goodly Lady, truſt me of the Hue
That I would chooſe, were I to chooſe a new:
Cleere vp Faire Queene that cloudy countenance,
Though chance of warre
Hath wrought this change of cheere,
Thou com'ſt not to be made a ſcorne in Rome:
Princely ſhall be thy vſage euery way.
Reſt on my word, and let not diſcontent
Daunt all your hopes: Madam he comforts you,
Can make your Greater then the Queene of Gothes?
Lauinia you are not diſpleaſ'd with this?
Lau. Not I my Lord, ſith true Nobilitie,
Warrants theſe words in Princely curteſie.
Sat. Thankes ſweete *Lauinia*, Romans let vs goe:
Ranſomleſſe heere we ſet our Priſoners free,
Proclaime our Honors Lords with Trumpe and Drum.
Baſs. Lord *Titus* by your leaue, this Maid is mine.
Tit. How ſir? Are you in earneſt then my Lord?
Baſs. I Noble *Titus*, and reſolu'd withall,
To doe my ſelfe this reaſon, and this right.
Marc. *Suum cuiquam*, is our Romane Iuſtice,
This Prince in Iuſtice ceazeth but his owne.
Luc. And that he will and ſhall, if *Lucius* liue.
Tit. Traytors auant, where is the Emperours Guarde?
Treaſon my Lord, *Lauinia* is ſurpris'd.
Sat. Surpris'd, by whom?
Baſs. By him that iuſtly may
Beare his Betroth'd, from all the world away.
Muti. Brothers helpe to conuey her hence away,
And with my Sword Ile keepe this doore ſafe.
Tit. Follow my Lord, and Ile ſoone bring her backe.
Mut. My Lord you paſſe not heere.
Tit. What villaine Boy, bar'ſt me my way in Rome?
Mut. Helpe *Lucius* helpe. *He kils him.*
Luc. My Lord you are vniuſt, and more then ſo,
In wrongfull quarrell, you haue ſlaine your ſon.
Tit. Nor thou, nor he are any ſonnes of mine,
My ſonnes would neuer ſo diſhonour me.
Traytor reſtore *Lauinia* to the Emperour.
Luc. Dead if you will, but not to be his wife,
That is anothers lawfull promiſt Loue.

Enter aloft the Emperour with Tamora and her two ſonnes, and Aaron the Moore.

Empe. No *Titus*, no, the Emperour needs her not,
Nor her, nor thee, nor any of thy ſtocke:
Ile truſt by Leiſure him that mocks me once.
Thee neuer: nor thy Trayterous haughty ſonnes,
Confederates all, thus to diſhonour me.
Was none in Rome to make a ſtale
But *Saturnine*? Full well *Andronicus*
Agree theſe Deeds, with that proud bragge of thine,
That ſaid'ſt, I beg'd the Empire at thy hands.
Tit. O monſtrous, what reproachfull words are theſe?
Sat. But goe thy wayes, goe giue that changing peece,
To him that flouriſht for her with his Sword:
A Valliant ſonne in-law thou ſhalt enioy:
One, fit to bandy with thy lawleſſe Sonnes,
To

To ruffle in the Common-wealth of Rome.
Tit. These words are Razors to my wounded hart.
Sat. And therefore louely *Tamora* Queene of Gothes,
That like the stately *Thebe* mong'st her Nimphs
Dost ouer-shine the Gallant'st Dames of Rome,
If thou be pleas'd with this my sodaine choyse,
Behold I choose thee *Tamora* for my Bride,
And will Create thee Empresse of Rome.
Speake Queene of Goths dost thou applau'd my choyse?
And heere I sweare by all the Romaine Gods,
Sith Priest and Holy-water are so neere,
And Tapers burne so bright, and euery thing
In readines for *Hymeneus* stand,
I will not resalute the streets of Rome,
Or clime my Pallace, till from forth this place,
I leade espous'd my Bride along with me,
Tamo. And heere in sight of heauen to Rome I sweare,
If *Saturnine* aduance the Queen of Gothes,
Shee will a Hand-maid be to his desires,
A louing Nurse, a Mother to his youth.
Satur. Ascend Faire Qeene,
Panthean Lords, accompany
Your Noble Emperour and his louely Bride,
Sent by the heauens for Prince *Saturnine*,
Whose wisedome hath her Fortune Conquered,
There shall we Consummate our Spousall rites.
Exeunt omnes.
Tit. I am not bid to waite vpon this Bride:
Titus when wer't thou wont to walke alone,
Dishonoured thus and Challenged of wrongs?

Enter Marcus and Titus Sonnes.

Mar O *Titus* see! O see what thou hast done!
In a bad quarrell, slaine a Vertuous sonne.
Tit. No foolish Tribune, no: No sonne of mine,
Nor thou, nor these Confedrates in the deed,
That hath dishonoured all our Family,
Vnworthy brother, and vnworthy Sonnes.
Luci. But let vs giue him buriall as becomes:
Giue *Mutius* buriall with our Bretheren.
Tit. Traytors away, he rest's not in this Tombe:
This Monument fiue hundreth yeares hath stood,
Which I haue Sumptuously re-edified:
Heere none but Souldiers, and Romes Seruitors,
Repose in Fame: None basely slaine in braules,
Bury him where you can, he comes not heere.
Mar. My Lord this is impiety in you,
My Nephew *Mutius* deeds do plead for him,
He must be buried with his bretheren.
Titus two Sonnes speakes.
And shall, or him we will accompany.
Ti. And shall! What villaine was it spake that word?
Titus sonne speakes.
He that would vouch'd it in any place but heere.
Tit. What would you bury him in my despight?
Mar. No Noble *Titus*, but intreat of thee,
To pardon *Mutius*, and to bury him.
Tit. *Marcus*, Euen thou hast stroke vpon my Crest,
And with these Boyes mine Honour thou hast wounded,
My foes I doe repute you euery one.
So trouble me no more, but get you gone.
1.Sonne. He is not himselfe, let vs withdraw.
2.Sonne. Not I tell *Mutius* bones be buried.
The Brother and the sonnes kneele.
Mar. Brother, for in that name doth nature plea'd.
2.Sonne. Father, and in that name doth nature speake.
Tit. Speake thou no more if all the rest will speede.
Mar. Renowned *Titus* more then halfe my soule.
Luc. Deare Father, soule and substance of vs all.
Mar. Suffer thy brother *Marcus* to interre
His Noble Nephew heere in vertues nest,
That died in Honour and *Lauinia's* cause.
Thou art a Romaine, be not barbarous:
The Greekes vpon aduise did bury *Aiax*
That slew himselfe: And *Laertes* sonne,
Did graciously plead for his Funerals:
Let not young *Mutius* then that was thy ioy,
Be bar'd his entrance heere.
Tit. Rise *Marcus*, rise,
The dismall'st day is this that ere I saw,
To be dishonored by my Sonnes in Rome:
Well, bury him, and bury me the next.
They put him in the Tombe.
Luc. There lie thy bones sweet *Mutius* with thy friends
Till we with Trophees do adorne thy Tombe.
They all kneele and say.
No man shed teares for Noble *Mutius*,
He liues in Fame, that di'd in vertues cause. *Exit.*
Mar. My Lord to step out of these sudden dumps,
How comes it that the subtile Queene of Gothes,
Is of a sodaine thus aduanc'd in Rome?
Ti. I know not *Marcus*: but I know it is,
(Whether by deuise or no) the heauens can tell,
Is she not then beholding to the man,
That brought her for this high good turne so farre?
Yes, and will Nobly him remunerate.

Flourish.
Enter the Emperor, Tamora, and her two sons, with the Moore at one doore. Enter at the other doore Bassianus and Lauinia with others.

Sat. So *Bassianus*, you haue plaid your prize,
God giue you ioy sir of your Gallant Bride.
Bass. And you of yours my Lord: I say no more,
Nor wish no lesse, and so I take my leaue.
Sat. Traytor, if Rome haue law, or we haue power,
Thou and thy Faction shall repent this Rape.
Bass. Rape call you it my Lord, to cease my owne,
My true betrothed Loue, and now my wife?
But let the lawes of Rome determine all,
Meane while I am possest of that is mine.
Sat. 'Tis good sir: you are very short with vs,
But if we liue, weele be as sharpe with you.
Bass. My Lord, what I haue done as best I may,
Answere I must, and shall do with my life,
Onely thus much I giue your Grace to know,
By all the duties that I owe to Rome,
This Noble Gentleman Lord *Titus* heere,
Is in opinion and in honour wrong'd,
That in the rescue of *Lauinia*,
With his owne hand did slay his youngest Son,
In zeale to you, and highly mou'd to wrath.
To be controul'd in that he frankly gaue:
Receiue him then to fauour *Saturnine*,
That hath expre'st himselfe in all his deeds,
A Father and a friend to thee, and Rome.
Tit. Prince *Bassianus* leaue to plead my Deeds,
'Tis thou, and those, that haue dishonoured me,
Rome and the righteous heauens be my iudge,
How I haue lou'd and Honour'd *Saturnine*.
Tam. My worthy Lord if euer *Tamora*,

Were

Were gracious in thofe Princely eyes of thine,
Then heare me fpeake indifferently for all:
And at my fute (fweet) pardon what is paft.
Satu. What Madam, be difhonoured openly,
And bafely put it vp without reuenge?
Tam. Not fo my Lord,
The Gods of Rome for-fend,
I fhould be Authour to difhonouryou.
But on mine honour dare, I vndertake
For good Lord *Titus* innocence in all:
Whofe fury not diffembled fpeakes his griefes:
Then at my fute looke gracioufly on him,
Loofe not fo noble a friend on vaine fuppofe,
Nor with fowre lookes afflict his gentle heart.
My Lord, be rul'd by me, be wonne at laft,
Diffemble all your griefes and difcontents,
You are but newly planted in your Throne,
Leaft then the people, and Patricians too,
Vpon a iuft furuey take *Titus* part,
And fo fupplant vs for ingratitude,
Which Rome reputes to be a hainous finne.
Yeeld at intreats, and then let me alone:
Ile finde a day to maffacre them all,
And race their faction, and their familie,
The cruell Father, and his trayt'rous fonnes,
To whom I fued for my deare fonnes life.
And make them know what 'tis to let a Queene.
Kneele in the ftreetes, and beg for grace in vaine.
Come, come, fweet Emperour, (come *Andronicus*)
Take vp this good old man, and cheere the heart,
That dies in tempeft of thy angry frowne.
King. Rife *Titus*, rife,
My Empreffe hath preuail'd.
Titus. I thanke your Maieftie,
And her my Lord.
Thefe words, thefe lookes,
Infufe new life in me.
Tamo. *Titus*, I am incorparate in Rome,
A Roman now adopted happily.
And muft aduife the Emperour for his good,
This day all quarrels die *Andronicus*.
And let it be mine honour good my Lord,
That I haue reconcil'd your friends and you.
For you Prince *Baffianus*, I haue paft
My word and promife to the Emperour,
That you will be more milde and tractable.
And feare not Lords:
And you *Lauinia*,
By my aduife all humbled on your knees,
You fhall aske pardon of his Maieftie.
Son. We doe,
And vow to heauen, and to his Highnes,
That what we did, was mildly, as we might,
Tendring our fifters honour and our owne.
Mar. That on mine honour heere I do proteft.
King. Away and talke not, trouble vs no more.
Tamora. Nay, nay,
Sweet Emperour, we muft all be friends,
The Tribune and his Nephews kneele for grace,
I will not be denied, fweet hart looke back.
King. *Marcus*,
For thy fake and thy brothers heere,
And at my louely *Tamora's* intreats,
I doe remit thefe young mens haynous faults.
Stand vp: *Lauinia*, though you left me like a churle,
I found a friend, and fure as death I fware,
I would not part a Batchellour from the Prieft.
Come, if the Emperours Court can feaft two Brides,
You are my gueft *Lauinia*, and your friends:
This day fhall be a Loue-day *Tamora*.
Tit. To morrow and it pleafe your Maieftie,
To hunt the Panther and the Hart with me,
With horne and Hound,
Weele giue your Grace *Bon iour*.
Satur. Be it fo *Titus*, and Gramercy to. *Exeunt.*

Actus Secunda.

Flourifh. *Enter Aaron alone.*

Aron. Now climbeth *Tamora* Olympus toppe,
Safe out of Fortunes fhot, and fits aloft,
Secure of Thunders cracke or lightning flafh,
Aduanc'd about pale enuies threatning reach:
As when the golde nSunne falutes the morne,
And hauing gilt the Ocean with his beames,
Gallops the Zodiacke in his gliftering Coach,
And ouer-lookes the higheft piering hills:
So *Tamora*:
Vpon her wit doth earthly honour waite,
And vertue ftoopes and trembles at her frowne.
Then *Aaron* arme thy hart, and fit thy thoughts,
To mount aloft with thy Emperiall Miftris,
And mount her pitch, whom thou in triumph long
Haft prifoner held, fettred in amorous chaines,
And fafter bound to *Aarons* charming eyes,
Then is *Prometheus* ti'de to *Caucafus*.
Away with flauifh weedes, and idle thoughts,
I will be bright and fhine in Pearle and Gold,
To waite vpon this new made Empreffe.
To waite faid I? To wanton with this Queene,
This Goddeffe, this *Semerimis*, this Queene,
This Syren, that will charme Romes *Saturnine*,
And fee his fhipwracke, and his Common weales.
Hollo, what ftorme is this?
Enter Chiron and Demetrius brauing.
Dem. *Chiron* thy yeres wants wit, thy wit wants edge
And manners to intru'd where I am grac'd,
And may for ought thou know'ft affected be.
Chi. *Demetrius*, thou doo'ft ouer-weene in all,
And fo in this, to beare me downe with braues,
'Tis not the difference of a yeere or two
Makes me leffe gracious, or thee more fortunate:
I am as able, and as fit, as thou,
To ferue, and to deferue my Miftris grace,
And that my fword vpon thee fhall approue,
And plead my paffions for *Lauinia's* loue.
Aron. Clubs, clubs, thefe louers will not keep the peace.
Dem. Why Boy, although our mother (vnaduifed)
Gaue you a daunfing Rapier by your fide,
Are you fo defperate growne to threat your friends?
Goe too: haue your Lath glued within your fheath,
Till you know better how to handle it.
Chi. Meane while fir, with the little skill I haue,
Full well fhalt thou perceiue how much I dare.
Deme. I Boy, grow ye fo braue? *They drawe.*
Aron. Why how now Lords?
So nere the Emperours Pallace dare you draw,
And

And maintaine ſuch a quarrell openly?
Full well I wote, the ground of all this grudge.
I would not for a million of Gold,
The cauſe were knowne to them it moſt concernes.
Nor would your noble mother for much more
Be ſo diſhonored in the Court of Rome:
For ſhame put vp.
Deme. Not I, till I haue ſheath'd
My rapier in his boſome, and withall
Thruſt theſe reprochfull ſpeeches downe his throat,
That he hath breath'd in my diſhonour heere.
Chi. For that I am prepar'd, and full reſolu'd,
Foule ſpoken Coward,
That thundreſt with thy tongue,
And with thy weapon nothing dar'ſt performe.
Aron. A way I ſay.
Now by the Gods that warlike Gothes adore,
This pretty brabble will vndoo vs all:
Why Lords, and thinke you not how dangerous
It is to ſet vpon a Princes right?
What is *Lauinia* then become ſo looſe,
Or *Baſsianus* ſo degenerate,
That for her loue ſuch quarrels may be broacht,
Without controulement, Iuſtice, or reuenge?
Young Lords beware, and ſhould the Empreſſe know,
This diſcord ground, the muſicke would not pleaſe.
Chi. I care not I, knew ſhe and all the world,
I loue *Lauinia* more then all the world.
Demet. Youngling,
Learne thou to make ſome meaner choiſe,
Lauinia is thine elder brothers hope.
Aron. Why are ye mad? Or know ye not in Rome,
How furious and impatient they be,
And cannot brooke Competitors in loue?
I tell you Lords, you doe but plot your deaths,
By this deuiſe.
Chi. *Aaron*, a thouſand deaths would I propoſe,
To atchieue her whom I do loue.
Aron. To atcheiue her, how?
Deme. Why, mak'ſt thou it ſo ſtrange?
Shee is a woman, therefore may be woo'd,
Shee is a woman, therfore may be wonne,
Shee is *Lauinia* therefore muſt be lou'd.
What man, more water glideth by the Mill
Then wots the Miller of, and eaſie it is
Of a cut loafe to ſteale a ſhiue we know:
Though *Baſsianus* be the Emperours brother,
Better then he haue worne *Vulcans* badge.
Aron, I, and as good as *Saturnius* may.
Deme. Then why ſhould he diſpaire that knowes to court it
With words, faire lookes, and liberality:
What haſt not thou full often ſtrucke a Doe,
And borne her cleanly by the Keepers noſe?
Aron. Why then it ſeemes ſome certaine ſnatch or ſo
Would ſerue your turnes.
Chi. I ſo the turne were ſerued.
Deme. *Aaron* thou haſt hit it.
Aron. Would you had hit it too,
Then ſhould not we be tir'd with this adoo:
Why harke yee, harke yee, aud are you ſuch fooles,
To ſquare for this? Would it offend you then?
Chi. Faith not me.
Deme. Nor me, ſo I were one.
Aron. For ſhame be friends, & ioyne for that you iar:
'Tis pollicie, and ſtratageme muſt doe
That you affect, and ſo muſt you reſolue,
That what you cannot as you would atcheiue,
You muſt perforce accompliſh as you may:
Take this of me, *Lucrece* was not more chaſt
Then this *Lauinia, Baſsianus* loue,
A ſpeedier courſe this lingring languiſhment
Muſt we purſue, and I haue found the path:
My Lords, a ſolemne hunting is in hand.
There will the louely Roman Ladies troope:
The Forreſt walkes are wide and ſpacious,
And many vnfrequented plots there are,
Fitted by kinde for rape and villanie:
Single you thither then this dainty Doe,
And ſtrike her home by force, if not by words:
This way or not at all, ſtand you in hope.
Come, come, our Empreſſe with her ſacred wit
To villainie and vengance conſecrate,
Will we acquaint with all that we intend,
And ſhe ſhall file our engines with aduiſe,
That will not ſuffer you to ſquare your ſelues,
But to your wiſhes height aduance you both.
The Emperours Court is like the houſe of Fame,
The pallace full of tongues, of eyes, of eares:
The Woods are ruthleſſe, dreadfull, deafe, and dull:
There ſpeake, and ſtrike braue Boyes, & take your turnes.
There ſerue your luſts, ſhadow'd from heauens eye,
And reuell in *Lauinia's* Treaſurie.
Chi. Thy counſell Lad ſmells of no cowardiſe.
Deme. *Sit fas aut nefas*, till I finde the ſtreames,
To coole this heat, a Charme to calme their fits,
Per Stigia per manes Vehor. *Exeunt.*

Enter Titus Andronicus and his three ſonnes, making a noyſe with hounds and hornes, and Marcus.

Tit. The hunt is vp, the morne is bright and gray,
The fields are fragranr, and the Woods are greene,
Vncouple heere, and let vs make a bay,
And wake the Emperour, and his louely Bride,
And rouze the Prince, and ring a hunters peale,
That all the Court may eccho with the noyſe.
Sonnes let it be your charge, as it is ours,
To attend the Emperours perſon carefully:
I haue bene troubled in my ſleepe this night,
But dawning day new comfort hath inſpir'd.

Winde Hornes.
Heere a cry of houndes, and winde hornes in a peale, then Enter Saturninus, Tamora, Baſsianus, Lauinia, Chiron, Demetrius, and their Attendants.

Ti. Many good morrowes to your Maieſtie,
Madam to you as many and as good.
I promiſed your Grace, a Hunters peale.
Satur. And you haue rung it luſtily my Lords,
Somewhat to earely for new married Ladies.
Baſs. *Lauinia*, how ſay you?
Laui. I ſay no:
I haue bene awake two houres and more.
Satur. Come on then, horſe and Chariots letvs haue,
And to our ſport: Madam, now ſhall ye ſee,
Our Romaine hunting.
Mar. I haue dogges my Lord,
Will rouze the proudeſt Panther in the Chaſe,
And clime the higheſt Pomontary top.
Tit. And I haue horſe will follow where the game
Makes way, and runnes likes Swallowes ore the plaine
Deme. Chiron

Deme. *Chiron* we hunt not we, with Horſe nor Hound
But hope to plucke a dainty Doe to ground. *Exeunt*

Enter Aaron alone.

Aron. He that had wit, would thinke that I had none,
To bury ſo much Gold vnder a Tree,
And neuer after to inherit it.
Let him that thinks of me ſo abiectly,
Know that this Gold muſt coine a ſtrategeme,
Which cunningly effected, will beget
A very excellent peece of villany:
And ſo repoſe ſweet Gold for their vnreſt,
That haue their Almes out of the Empreſſe Cheſt.

Enter Tamora to the Moore.

Tamo. My louely *Aaron*,
Wherefore look'ſt thou ſad,
When euery thing doth make a Gleefull boaſt?
The Birds chaunt melody on euery buſh,
The Snake lies rolled in the cheerefull Sunne,
The greene leaues quiuer with the cooling winde,
And make a cheker'd ſhadow on the ground:
Vnder their ſweete ſhade, *Aaron* let vs ſit,
And whil'ſt the babling Eccho mock's the Hounds,
Replying ſhrilly to the well tun'd-Hornes,
As if a double hunt were heard at once,
Let vs ſit downe, and marke their yelping noyſe:
And after conflict, ſuch as was ſuppos'd.
The wandring Prince and *Dido* once enioy'd,
When with a happy ſtorme they were ſurpris'd,
And Curtain'd with a Counſaile-keeping Caue,
We may each wreathed in the others armes,
(Our paſtimes done) poſſeſſe a Golden ſlumber,
Whiles Hounds and Hornes, and ſweet Melodious Birds
Be vnto vs, as is a Nurſes Song
Of Lullabie, to bring her Babe aſleepe.

Aron. Madame,
Though *Venus* gouerne your deſires,
Saturne is Dominator ouer mine:
What ſignifies my deadly ſtanding eye,
My ſilence, and my Cloudy Melancholie,
My fleece of Woolly haire, that now vncurles,
Euen as an Adder when ſhe doth vnrowle
To do ſome fatall execution?
No Madam, theſe are no Veneriall ſignes,
Vengeance is in my heart, death in my hand,
Blood, and reuenge, are Hammering in my head.
Harke *Tamora*, the Empreſſe of my Soule,
Which neuer hopes more heauen, then reſts in thee,
This is the day of Doome for *Baſsianus*;
His *Philomel* muſt looſe her tongue to day,
Thy Sonnes make Pillage of her Chaſtity,
And waſh their hands in *Baſſianus* blood.
Seeſt thou this Letter, take it vp I pray thee,
And giue the King this fatall plotted Scrowle,
Now queſtion me no more, we are eſpied,
Heere comes a parcell of our hopefull Booty,
Which dreads not yet their liues deſtruction.

Enter Baſſianus and Lauinia.

Tamo. Ah my ſweet *Moore*:
Sweeter to me then life.

Aron. No more great Empreſſe, *Baſſianus* comes,
Be croſſe with him, and Ile goe fetch thy Sonnes
To backe thy quarrell what ſo ere they be.

Baſſi. Whom haue we heere?
Romes Royall Empreſſe,
Vnfurniſht of our well beſeeming troope?
Or is it *Dian* habited like her,
Who hath abandoned her holy Groues,
To ſee the generall Hunting in this Forreſt?

Tamo. Sawcie controuler of our priuate ſteps:
Had I the power, that ſome ſay *Dian* had,
Thy Temples ſhould be planted preſently.
With Hornes, as was *Acteons*, and the Hounds
Should driue vpon his new transformed limbes,
Vnmannerly Intruder as thou art.

Laui. Vnder your patience gentle Empreſſe,
'Tis thought you haue a goodly gift in Horning,
And to be doubted, that your *Moore* and you
Are ſingled forth to try experiments:
Ioue ſheild your husband from his Hounds to day,
'Tis pitty they ſhould take him for a Stag.

Baſſi. Beleeue me Queene, your ſwarth Cymerion,
Doth make your Honour of his bodies Hue,
Spotted, deteſted, and abhominable.
Why are you ſequeſtred from all your traine?
Diſmounted from your Snow-white goodly Steed,
And wandred hither to an obſcure plot,
Accompanied with a barbarous *Moore*,
If foule deſire had not conducted you?

Laui. And being intercepted in your ſport,
Great reaſon that my Noble Lord, be rated
For Saucineſſe, I pray you let vs hence,
And let her ioy her Rauen coloured loue,
This valley fits the purpoſe paſſing well.

Baſſi. The King my Brother ſhall haue notice of this.

Laui. I, for theſe ſlips haue made him noted long,
Good King, to be ſo mightily abuſed.

Tamora. Why I haue patience to endure all this?

Enter Chiron and Demetrius.

Dem. How now deere Soueraigne
And our gracious Mother,
Why doth your Highnes looke ſo pale and wan?

Tamo. Haue I not reaſon thinke you to looke pale.
Theſe two haue tic'd me hither to this place,
A barren, deteſted vale you ſee it is.
The Trees though Sommer, yet forlorne and leane,
Ore-come with Moſſe, and balefull Miſſelto.
Heere neuer ſhines the Sunne, heere nothing breeds,
Vnleſſe the nightly Owle, or fatall Rauen:
And when they ſhew'd me this abhorred pit,
They told me heere at dead time of the night,
A thouſand Fiends, a thouſand hiſſing Snakes,
Ten thouſand ſwelling Toades, as many Vrchins,
Would make ſuch fearefull and confuſed cries,
As any mortall body hearing it,
Should ſtraite fall mad, or elſe die ſuddenly.
No ſooner had they told this helliſh tale,
But ſtrait they told me they would binde me heere,
Vnto the body of a diſmall yew,
And leaue me to this miſerable death.
And then they call'd me foule Adultereſſe,
Laſciuious Goth, and all the bittereſt tearmes
That euer eare did heare to ſuch effect.
And had you not by wondrous fortune come,
This vengeance on me had they executed:
Reuenge it, as you loue your Mothers life,
Or be ye not henceforth cal'd my Children.

Dem. This is a witneſſe that I am thy Sonne. *ſtab him.*

Chi. And this for me,
Strook home to ſhew my ſtrength.

Laui. I come *Semeramis*, nay Barbarous *Tamora*.

d d For

For no name fits thy nature but thy owne.
Tam. Giue me thy poyniard, you shal know my boyes
Your Mothers hand shall right your Mothers wrong.
Deme. Stay Madam heere is more belongs to her,
First thrash the Corne, then after burne the straw:
This Minion stood vpon her chastity,
Vpon her Nuptiall vow, her loyaltie.
And with that painted hope, braues your Mightinesse,
And shall she carry this vnto her graue?
Chi. And if she doe,
I would I were an Eunuch,
Drag hence her husband to some secret hole,
And make his dead Trunke-Pillow to our lust.
Tamo. But when ye haue the hony we desire,
Let not this Waspe out-liue vs both to sting.
Chir. I warrant you Madam we will make that sure:
Come Mistris, now perforce we will enioy,
That nice-preserued honesty of yours.
Laui. Oh *Tamora*, thou bear'st a woman face.
Tamo. I will not heare her speake, away with her.
Laui. Sweet Lords intreat her heare me but a word.
Demet. Listen faire Madam, let it be your glory
To see her teares, but be your hart to them,
As vnrelenting flint to drops of raine.
Laui. When did the Tigers young-ones teach the dam?
O doe not learne her wrath, she taught it thee,
The milke thou suck'st from her did turne to Marble,
Euen at thy Teat thou had'st thy Tyranny,
Yet euery Mother breeds not Sonnes alike,
Do thou intreat her shew a woman pitty.
Chiro. What,
Would'st thou haue me proue my selfe a bastard?
Laui. 'Tis true,
The Rauen doth not hatch a Larke,
Yet haue I heard, Oh could I finde it now,
The Lion mou'd with pitty, did indure
To haue his Princely pawes par'd all away.
Some say, that Rauens foster forlorne children,
The whil'st their owne birds famish in their nests:
Oh be to me though thy hard hart say no,
Nothing so kind but something pittifull.
Tamo. I know not what it meanes, away with her.
Lauin. Oh let me teach thee for my Fathers sake,
That gaue thee life when well he might haue slaine thee:
Be not obdurate, open thy deafe eares.
Tamo. Had'st thou in person nere offended me.
Euen for his sake am I pittilesse:
Remember Boyes I powr'd forth teares in vaine,
To saue your brother from the sacrifice,
But fierce *Andronicus* would not relent,
Therefore away with her, and vse her as you will,
The worse to her, the better lou'd of me.
Laui. Oh *Tamora*,
Be call'd a gentle Queene,
And with thine owne hands kill me in this place,
For 'tis not life that I haue beg'd so long,
Poore I was slaine, when *Bassianus* dy'd.
Tam. What beg'st thou then? fond woman let me go?
Laui. 'Tis present death I beg, and one thing more,
That womanhood denies my tongue to tell:
Oh keepe me from their worse then killing lust,
And tumble me into some loathsome pit,
Where neuer mans eye may behold my body,
Doe this, and be a charitable murderer.
Tam. So should I rob my sweet Sonnes of their fee,
No let them satisfie their lust on thee.
Deme. Away,
For thou hast staid vs heere too long.
Lauinia. No Garace,
No womanhood? Ah beastly creature,
The blot and enemy to our generall name,
Confusion fall——
Chi. Nay then Ile stop your mouth
Bring thou her husband,'
This is the Hole where *Aaron* bid vs hide him.
Tam. Farewell my Sonnes, see that you make her sure,
Nere let my heart know merry cheere indeed,
Till all the *Andronici* be made away:
Now will I hence to seeke my louely *Moore*,
And let my spleenefull Sonnes this Trull deflour. *Exit.*

Enter Aaron with two of Titus Sonnes.

Aron. Come on my Lords, the better foote before,
Straight will I bring you to the lothsome pit.
Where I espied the Panther fast asleepe.
Quin. My sight is very dull what ere it bodes.
Marti. And mine I promise you, were it not for shame,
Well could I leaue our sport to sleepe a while.
Quin. What art thou fallen?
What subtile Hole is this,
Whose mouth is couered with Rude growing Briers,
Vpon whose leaues are drops of new-shed-blood,
As fresh as mornings dew distil'd on flowers,
A very fatall place it seemes to me:
Speake Brother hast thou hurt thee with the fall?
Martius. Oh Brother,
With the dismal'st obiect
That euer eye with sight made heart lament.
Aron. Now will I fetch the King to finde them heere,
That he thereby may haue a likely gesse,
How these were they that made away his Brother.
Exit Aaron.
Marti. Why dost not comfort me and helpe me out,
From this vnhallow'd and blood-stained Hole?
Quintus. I am surprised with an vncouth feare,
A chilling sweat ore-runs my trembling ioynts,
My heart suspects more then mine eie can see.
Marti. To proue thou hast a true diuining heart,
Aaron and thou looke downe into this den,
And see a fearefull sight of blood and death.
Quintus. *Aaron* is gone,
And my compassionate heart
Will not permit mine eyes once to behold
The thing whereat it trembles by surmise:
Oh tell me how it is, for nere till now
Was I a child, to feare I know not what.
Marti. Lord *Bassianus* lies embrewed heere,
All on a heape like to the slaughtred Lambe,
In this detested, darke, blood-drinking pit.
Quin. If it be darke, how doost thou know 'tis he?
Mart. Vpon his bloody finger he doth weare
A precious Ring, that lightens all the Hole:
Which like a Taper in some Monument,
Doth shine vpon the dead mans earthly cheekes,
And shewes the ragged intrailes of the pit:
So pale did shine the Moone on *Piramus*,
When he by night lay bath'd in Maiden blood:
O Brother helpe me with thy fainting hand.
If feare hath made thee faint, as mee it hath,
Out of this fell deuouring receptacle,
As hatefull as *Ocitus* mistie mouth.
Quint. Reach me thy hand, that I may helpe thee out,
Or

Or wanting ſtrength to doe thee ſo much good,
I may be pluckt into the ſwallowing wombe,
Of this deepe pit, poore *Baſsianus* graue:
I haue no ſtrength to plucke thee to the brinke.

Martius. Nor I no ſtrength to clime without thy help.

Quin. Thy hand once more, I will not looſe againe,
Till thou art heere aloft, or I below,
Thou can'ſt not come to me, I come to thee. *Boths fall in.*

Enter the Emperour, Aaron the Moore.

Satur. Along with me, Ile ſee what hole is heere,
And what he is that now is leapt into it.
Say, who art thou that lately did'ſt deſcend,
Into this gaping hollow of the earth?

Marti. The vnhappie ſonne of old *Andronicus*,
Brought hither in a moſt vnluckie houre,
To finde thy brother *Baſsianus* dead.

Satur. My brother dead? I know thou doſt but ieſt,
He and his Lady both are at the Lodge,
Vpon the North-ſide of this pleaſant Chaſe,
'Tis not an houre ſince I left him there.

Marti. We know not where you left him all aliue,
But out alas, heere haue we found him dead.

Enter Tamora, Andronicus, and Lucius.

Tamo. Where is my Lord the King?

King. Heere *Tamora*, though grieu'd with killing griefe.

Tam. Where is thy brother *Baſsianus*?

King Now to the bottome doſt thou ſearch my wound,
Poore *Baſsianus* heere lies murthered.

Tam. Then all too late I bring this fatall writ,
The complot of this timeleſſe Tragedie,
And wonder greatly that mans face can fold,
In pleaſing ſmiles ſuch murderous Tyrannie.
She giueth Saturnine a Letter.

Saturninus reads the Letter.

And if we miſſe to meete him hanſomely,
Sweet huntſman, Baſsianus 'tis we meane,
Doe thou ſo much as dig the graue for him,
Thou know'ſt our meaning, looke for thy reward
Among the Nettles at the Elder tree:
Which ouer-ſhades the mouth of that ſame pit:
Where we decreed to bury Baſsianus
Doe this and purchaſe vs thy laſting friends.

King. Oh *Tamora*, was euer heard the like?
This is the pit, and this the Elder tree,
Looke ſirs, if you can finde the huntſman out,
That ſhould haue murthered *Baſsianus* heere.

Aron. My gracious Lord heere is the bag of Gold.

King. Two of thy whelpes, fell Curs of bloody kind
Haue heere bereft my brother of his life:
Sirs drag them from the pit vnto the priſon,
There let them bide vntill we haue deuis'd
Some neuer heard-of tortering paine for them.

Tamo. What are they in this pit,
Oh wondrous thing!
How eaſily murder is diſcouered?

Tit. High Emperour, vpon my feeble knee,
I beg this boone, with teares, not lightly ſhed,
That this fell fault of my accurſed Sonnes,
Accurſed, if the faults be prou'd in them.

King. If it be prou'd? you ſee it is apparant,
Who found this Letter, *Tamora* was it you?

Tamora. *Andronicus* himſelfe did take it vp:

Tit. I did my Lord,
Yet let me be their baile,
For by my Fathers reuerent Tombe I vow
They ſhall be ready at your Highnes will,
To anſwere their ſuſpition with their liues.

King. Thou ſhalt not baile them, ſee thou follow me:
Some bring the murthered body, ſome the murtherers,
Let them not ſpeake a word, the guilt is plaine,
For by my ſoule, were there worſe end then death,
That end vpon them ſhould be executed.

Tamo. *Andronicus* I will entreat the King,
Feare not thy Sonnes, they ſhall do well enough.

Tit. Come *Lucius* come,
Stay not to talke with them. *Exeunt.*

Enter the Empreſſe Sonnes, with Lauinia, her hands cut off and her tongue cut out, and rauiſht.

Deme. So now goe tell and if thy tongue can ſpeake,
Who t'was that cut thy tongue and rauiſht thee.

Chi. Write downe thy mind, bewray thy meaning ſo,
And if thy ſtumpes will let thee play the Scribe.

Dem. See how with ſignes and tokens ſhe can ſcowle.

Chi. Goe home,
Call for ſweet water, waſh thy hands.

Dem. She hath no tongue to call, nor hands to waſh.
And ſo let's leaue her to her ſilent walkes.

Chi. And t'were my cauſe, I ſhould goe hang my ſelfe.

Dem. If thou had'ſt hands to helpe thee knit the cord.
Exeunt.

Winde Hornes.

Enter Marcus from hunting, to Lauinia.

Who is this, my Neece that flies away ſo faſt?
Coſen a word, where is your husband?
If I do dreame, would all my wealth would wake me;
If I doe wake, ſome Planet ſtrike me downe,
That I may ſlumber in eternall ſleepe.
Speake gentle Neece, what ſterne vngentle hands
Hath lopt, and hew'd, and made thy body bare
Of her two branches, thoſe ſweet Ornaments
Whoſe circkling ſhadowes, Kings haue ſought to ſleep in
And might not gaine ſo great a happines
As halfe thy Loue: Why dooſt not ſpeake to me?
Alas, a Crimſon riuer of warme blood,
Like to a bubling fountaine ſtir'd with winde,
Doth riſe and fall betweene thy Roſed lips,
Comming and going with thy hony breath.
But ſure ſome *Tereus* hath defloured thee,
And leaſt thou ſhould'ſt detect them, cut thy tongue.
Ah, now thou turn'ſt away thy face for ſhame:
And notwithſtanding all this loſſe of blood,
As from a Conduit with their iſſuing Spouts,
Yet doe thy cheekes looke red as *Titans* face,
Bluſhing to be encountred with a Cloud,
Shall I ſpeake for thee? ſhall I ſay 'tis ſo?
Oh that I knew thy hart, and knew the beaſt
That I might raile at him to eaſe my mind.
Sorrow concealed, like an Ouen ſtopt,
Doth burne the hart to Cinders where it is.
Faire *Philomela* ſhe but loſt her tongue,
And in a tedious Sampler ſowed her minde.
But louely Neece, that meane is cut from thee,
A craftier *Tereus* haſt thou met withall,
And he hath cut thoſe pretty fingers off,

That could haue better sowed then *Philomel.*
Oh had the monster seene those Lilly hands,
Tremble like Aspen leaues vpon a Lute,
And make the silken strings delight to kisse them,
He would not then haue toucht them for his life.
Or had he heard the heauenly Harmony,
Whic h that sweet tongue hath made:
He would haue dropt his knife and fell asleepe,
As *Cerberus* at the Thracian Poets feete.
Come, let vs goe, and make thy father blinde,
For such a sight will blinde a fathers eye.
One houres storme will drowne the fragrant meades,
What, will whole months of teares thy Fathers eyes?
Doe not draw backe, for we will mourne with thee:
Oh could our mourning ease thy misery. *Exeunt*

Actus Tertius.

Enter the Iudges and Senatours with Titus two sonnes bound, passing on the Stage to the place of execution, and Titus going before pleading.

Ti. Heare me graue fathers, noble Tribunes stay,
For pitty of mine age, whose youth was spent
In dangerous warres, whilst you securely slept:
For all my blood in Romes great quarrell shed,
For all the frosty nights that I haue watcht,
And for these bitter teares, which now you see,
Filling the aged wrinkles in my cheekes,
Be pittifull to my condemned Sonnes,
Whose soules is not corrupted as 'tis thought:
For two and twenty sonnes I neuer wept,
Because they died in honours lofty bed.
Andronicus lyeth downe, and the Iudges passe by him.
For these, Tribunes, in the dust I write
My harts deepe languor, and my soules sad teares:
Let my teares stanch the earths drie appetite.
My sonnes sweet blood, will make it shame and blush:
O earth! I will be friend thee more with raine. *Exeunt*
That shall distill from these two ancient ruines,
Then youthfull Aprill shall with all his showres
In summers drought: Ile drop vpon thee still,
In Winter with warme teares Ile melt the snow,
And keepe erernall spring time on thy face,
So thou refuse to drinke my deare sonnes blood.

Enter Lucius, with his weapon drawne.

Oh reuerent Tribunes, oh gentle aged men,
Vnbinde my sonnes, reuerse the doome of death,
And let me say (that neuer wept before)
My teares are now preualing Oratours.
Lu. Oh noble father, you lament in vaine,
The Tribunes heare not, no man is by,
And you recount your sorrowes to a stone.
Ti. Ah *Lucius* for thy brothers let me plead,
Graue Tribunes, once more I intreat of you.
Lu. My gracious Lord, no Tribune heares you speake.
Ti. Why 'tis no matter man, if they did heare.
They would not marke me: oh if they did heare
They would not pitty me.
Therefore I tell my sorrowes bootles to the stones.
Who though they cannot answere my distresse,
Yet in some sort they are better then the Tribunes,
For that they will not intercept my tale;
When I doe weepe, they humbly at my feete
Receiue my teares, and seeme to weepe with me,
And were they but attired in graue weedes,
Rome could afford no Tribune like to these.
A stone is as soft waxe,
Tribunes more hard then stones:
A stone is silent, and offendeth not,
And Tribunes with their tongues doome men to death.
But wherefore stand'st thou with thy weapon drawne?
Lu. To rescue my two brothers from their death,
For which attempt the Iudges haue pronounc'st
My euerlasting doome of banishment.
Ti. O happy man, they haue befriended thee:
Why foolish *Lucius*, dost thou not perceiue
That Rome is but a wildernes of Tigers?
Tigers must pray, and Rome affords no prey
But me and and mine: how happy art thou then,
From these deuourers to be banished?
But who comes with our brother *Marcus* heere?

Enter Marcus and Lauinia.

Mar. *Titus*, prepare thy noble eyes to weepe,
Or if not so, thy noble heart to breake:
I bring consuming sorrow to thine age.
Ti. Will it consume me? Let me see it then.
Mar. This was thy daughter.
Ti. Why *Marcus* so she is.
Luc. Aye me this obiect kils me.
Ti. Faint-harted boy, arise and looke vpon her,
Speake *Lauinia*, what accursed hand
Hath made thee handlesse in thy Fathers sight?
What foole hath added water to the Sea?
Or brought a faggot to bright burning Troy?
My griefe was at the height before thou cam'st,
And now like *Nylus* it disdaineth bounds:
Giue me a sword, Ile chop off my hands too,
For they haue fought for Rome, and all in vaine:
And they haue nur'st this woe,
In feeding life:
In bootelesse prayer haue they bene held vp,
And they haue seru'd me to effectlesse vse.
Now all the seruice I require of them,
Is that the one will helpe to cut the other:
'Tis well *Lauinia*, that thou hast no hands,
For hands to do Rome seruice, is but vaine.
Luci. Speake gentle sister, who hath martyr'd thee?
Mar. O that delightfull engine of her thoughts,
That blab'd them with such pleasing eloquence,
Is torne from forth that pretty hollow cage,
Where like a sweet mellodius bird it sung,
Sweet varied notes inchanting euery eare.
Luci. Oh say thou for her,
Who hath done this deed?
Marc. Oh thus I found her straying in the Parke,
Seeking to hide herselfe as doth the Deare
That hath receiude some vnrecuring wound.
Tit. It was my Deare,
And he that wounded her,
Hath hurt me more, then had he kild me dead:
For now I stand as one vpon a Rocke,
Inuiron'd with a wildernesse of Sea.
Who markes the waxing tide,
Grow waue by waue,

Expecting

Expecting euer when some enuious surge,
Will in his brinish bowels swallow him.
This way to death my wretched sonnes are gone:
Heere stands my other sonne, a banisht man,
And heere my brother weeping at my woes.
But that which giues my soule the greatest spurne,
Is deere *Lauinia*, deerer then my soule.
Had I but seene thy picture in this plight,
It would haue madded me. What shall I doe?
Now I behold thy liuely body so?
Thou hast no hands to wipe away thy teares,
Nor tongue to tell me who hath martyr'd thee:
Thy husband he is dead, and for his death
Thy brothers are condemn'd, and dead by this.
Looke *Marcus*, ah sonne *Lucius* looke on her:
When I did name her brothers, then fresh teares
Stood on her cheekes, as doth the hony dew,
Vpon a gathred Lillie almost withered.,
Mar. Perchance she weepes because they kil'd her husband,
Perchance because she knowes him innocent.
Ti. If they did kill thy husband then be ioyfull,
Because the law hath tane reuenge on them.
No, no, they would not doe so foule a deede,
Witnes the sorrow that their sister makes.
Gentle *Lauinia* let me kisse thy lips,
Or make some signes how I may do thee ease:
Shall thy good Vncle, and thy brother *Lucius*,
And thou and I sit round about some Fountaine,
Looking all downewards to behold our cheekes
How they are stain'd in meadowes, yet not dry
With miery slime left on them by a flood:
And in the Fountaine shall we gaze so long,
Till the fresh taste be taken from that cleerenes,
And made a brine pit with our bitter teares?
Or shall we cut away our hands like thine?
Or shall we bite our tongues, and in dumbe shewes
Passe the remainder of our hatefull dayes?
What shall we doe? Let vs that haue our tongues
Plot some deuise of further miseries
To make vs wondred at in time to come.
Lu. Sweet Father cease your teares, for at your griefe
See how my wretched sister sobs and weeps.
Mar. Patience deere Neece, good *Titus* drie thine eyes.
Ti. Ah *Marcus*, *Marcus*, Brother well I wot,
Thy napkin cannot drinke a teare of mine,
For thou poore man hast drown'd it with thine owne.
Lu. Ah my *Lauinia* I will wipe thy cheekes.
Ti Marke *Marcus* marke, I vnderstand her signes,
Had she a tongue to speake, now would she say
That to her brother which I said to thee.
His Napkin with her true teares all bewet,
Can do no seruice on her sorrowfull cheekes.
Oh what a simpathy of woe is this!
As farre from helpe as Limbo is from blisse,

Enter Aron the Moore alone.

Moore. *Titus Andronicus*, my Lord the Emperour,
Sends thee this word, that if thou loue thy sonnes,
Let *Marcus*, *Lucius*, or thy selfe old *Titus*,
Or any one of you, chop off your hand,
And send it to the King: he for the same,
Will send thee hither both thy sonnes aliue,
And that shall be the ransome for their fault.
Ti. Oh gracious Emperour, oh gentle *Aaron*.
Did euer Rauen sing so like a Larke,
That giues sweet tydings of the Sunnes vprise?
With all my heart, Ile send the Emperour my hand,
Good *Aron* wilt thou help to chop it off?
Lu. Stay Father, for that noble hand of thine,
That hath throwne downe so many enemies,
Shall not be sent: my hand will serue the turne,
My youth can better spare my blood then you,
And therfore mine shall saue my brothers liues.
Mar. Which of your hands hath not defended Rome,
And rear'd aloft the bloody Battleaxe,
Writing destruction on the enemies Castle?
Oh none of both but are of high desert:
My hand hath bin but idle, let it serue
To ransome my two nephewes from their death,
Then haue I kept it to a worthy end.
Moore. Nay come agree, whose hand shallgoe along
For feare they die before their pardon come.
Mar. My hand shall goe.
Lu. By heauen it shall not goe.
Ti. Sirs striue no more, such withered hearbs as these
Are meete for plucking vp, and therefore mine.
Lu. Sweet Father, if I shall be thought thy sonne,
Let me redeeme my brothers both from death.
Mar. And for our fathers sake, and mothers care,
Now let me shew a brothers loue to thee.
Ti. Agree betweene you, I will spare my hand.
Lu. Then Ile goe fetch an Axe.
Mar. But I will vse the Axe. *Exeunt*
Ti. Come hither *Aaron*, Ile deceiue them both,
Lend me thy hand, and I will giue thee mine,
Moore. If that be cal'd deceit, I will be honest,
And neuer whil'st I liue deceiue men so:
But Ile deceiue you in another sort,
And that you'l say ere halfe an houre passe.

He cuts off Titus hand.

Enter Lucius and Marcus againe.

Ti. Now stay you strife, what shall be, is dispatcht:
Good *Aron* giue his Maiestie me hand,
Tell him, it was a hand that warded him
From thousand dangers: bid him bury it:
More hath it merited: That let it haue.
As for for my sonnes, say I account of them,
As iewels purchast at an easie price,
And yet deere too, because I bought mine owne.
Aron. I goe *Andronicus*, and for thy hand,
Looke by and by to haue thy sonnes with thee:
Their heads I meane: Oh how this villany
Doth fat me with the very thoughts of it.
Let fooles doe good, and faire men call for grace,
Aron will haue his soule blacke like his face. *Exit.*
Ti. O heere I lift this one hand vp to heauen,
And bow this feeble ruine to the earth,
If any power pitties wretched teares,
To that I call: what wilt thou kneele with me?
Doe then deare heart, for heauen shall heare our prayers,
Or with our sighs weele breath the welkin dimme,
And staine the Sun with fogge as somtime cloudes,
When they do hug him in their melting bosomes.
Mar. Oh brother speake with possibilities,
And do not breake into these deepe extreames.
Ti. Is not my sorrow deepe, hauing no bottome?

Then be my paſſions bottomleſſe with them.
Mar. But yet let reaſon gouerne thy lament.
Titus. If there were reaſon for theſe miſeries,
Then into limits could I binde my woes:
When heauen doth weepe, doth not the earth oreflow?
If the windes rage, doth not the Sea wax mad,
Threatning the welkin with his big-ſwolne face?
And wilt thou haue a reaſon for this coile?
I am the Sea. Harke how her ſighes doe flow:
Shee is the weeping welkin, I the earth:
Then muſt my Sea be moued with her ſighes,
Then muſt my earth with her continuall teares,
Become a deluge: ouerflow'd and drown'd:
For why, my bowels cannot hide her woes,
But like a drunkard muſt I vomit them:
Then giue me leaue, for looſers will haue leaue,
To eaſe their ſtomackes with their bitter tongues,

Enter a meſſenger with two heads and a hand.

Meſſ. Worthy *Andronicus*, ill art thou repaid,
For that good hand thou ſentſt the Emperour:
Heere are the heads of thy two noble ſonnes.
And heeres thy hand in ſcorne to thee ſent backe:
Thy griefes, their ſports: Thy reſolution mockt,
That woe is me to thinke vpon thy woes,
More then remembrance of my fathers death. *Exit.*
Marc. Now let hot Ætna coole in Cicilie,
And be my heart an euer-burning hell:
Theſe miſeries are more then may be borne.
To weepe with them that weepe, doth eaſe ſome deale,
But ſorrow flouted at, is double death.
Luci. Ah that this ſight ſhould make ſo deep a wound,
And yet deteſted life not ſhrinke thereat:
That euer death ſhould let life beare his name,
Where life hath no more intereſt but to breath.
Mar. Alas poore hart that kiſſe is comfortleſſe,
As frozen water to a ſtarued ſnake.
Titus. When will this fearefull ſlumber haue an end?
Mar. Now farwell flatterie, die *Andronicus*,
Thou doſt not ſlumber, ſee thy two ſons heads,
Thy warlike hands, thy mangled daughter here:
Thy other baniſht ſonnes with this deere ſight
Strucke pale and bloodleſſe, and thy brother I,
Euen like a ſtony Image, cold and numme.
Ah now no more will I controule my griefes,
Rent off thy ſiluer haire, thy other hand
Gnawing with thy teeth, and be this diſmall ſight
The cloſing vp of our moſt wretched eyes:
Now is a time to ſtorme, why art thou ſtill?
Titus. Ha, ha, ha,
Mar. Why doſt thou laugh? it fits not with this houre.
Ti. Why I haue not another teare to ſhed:
Beſides, this ſorrow is an enemy,
And would vſurpe vpon my watry eyes,
And make them blinde with tributarie teares.
Then which way ſhall I finde Reuenges Caue?
For theſe two heads doe ſeeme to ſpeake to me,
And threat me, I ſhall neuer come to bliſſe,
Till all theſe miſchiefes be returned againe,
Euen in their throats that haue committed them.
Come let me ſee what taske I haue to doe,
You heauie people, circle me about,
That I may turne me to each one of you,
And ſweare vnto my ſoule to right your wrongs.
The vow is made, come Brother take a head,
And in this hand the other will I beare.
And *Lauinia* thou ſhalt be employd in theſe things:
Beare thou my hand ſweet wench betweene thy teeth:
As for thee boy, goe get thee from my ſight,
Thou art an Exile, and thou muſt not ſtay,
Hie to the *Gothes*, and raiſe an army there,
And if you loue me, as I thinke you doe,
Let's kiſſe and part, for we haue much to doe. *Exeunt.*

Manet Lucius.

Luci. Farewell *Andronicus* my noble Father:
The woful'ſt man that euer liu'd in Rome:
Farewell proud Rome, til *Lucius* come againe,
Heloues his pledges dearer then his life:
Farewell *Lauinia* my noble ſiſter,
O would thou wert as thou to fore haſt beene,
But now, nor *Lucius* nor *Lauinia* liues
But in obliuion and hateful griefes:
If *Lucius* liue, he will requit your wrongs,
And make proud *Saturnine* and his Empreſſe
Beg at the gates likes *Tarquin* and his Queene.
Now will I to the Gothes and raiſe a power,
To be reueng'd on Rome and *Saturnine.* *Exit Lucius*

A Bnaket.
Enter Andronicus, Marcus, Lauinia, and the Boy.

An. So, ſo, now ſit, and looke you eate no more
Then will preſerue iuſt ſo much ſtrength in vs
As will reuenge theſe bitter woes of ours.
Marcus vnknit that ſorrow-wreathen knot:
Thy Neece and I (poore Creatures) want our hands
And cannot paſſionate our tenfold griefe,
With foulded Armes. This poore right hand of mine,
Is left to tirranize vppon my breaſt.
Who when my hart all mad with miſery,
Beats in this hollow priſon of my fleſh,
Then thus I thumpe it downe.
Thou Map of woe, that thus doſt talk in ſignes,
When thy poore hart beates without ragious beating,
Thou canſt not ſtrike it thus to make it ſtill?
Wound it with ſighing girle, kil it with grones:
Or get ſome little knife betweene thy teeth,
And iuſt againſt thy hart make thou a hole,
That all the teares that thy poore eyes let fall
May run into that ſinke, and ſoaking in,
Drowne the lamenting foole, in Sea ſalt teares.
Mar. Fy brother fy, teach her not thus to lay
Such violent hands vppon her tender life.
An How now! Has ſorrow made thee doate already?
Why *Marcus*, no man ſhould be mad but I:
What violent hands can ſhe lay on her life:
Ah, wherefore doſt thou vrge the name of hands,
To bid *Æneas* tell the tale twice ore
How Troy was burnt, and he made miſerable?
O handle not the theame, to talke of hands,
Leaſt we remember ſtill that we haue none,
Fie, fie, how Frantiquely I ſquare my talke
As if we ſhould forget we had no hands:
If *Marcus* did not name the word of hands.
Come, lets fall too, and gentle girle eate this,
Heere is no drinke? Harke *Marcus* what ſhe ſaies,
I can interpret all her martir'd ſignes,
She ſaies, ſhe drinkes no other drinke but teares
Breu'd with her ſorrow: meſh'd vppon her cheekes,

Speech-

Speechlesse complaynet, I will learne thy thought:
In thy dumb action, will I be as perfect
As begging Hermits in their holy prayers.
Thou shalt not sighe nor hold thy stumps to heauen,
Nor winke, nor nod, nor kneele, nor make a signe,
But I (of these) will wrest an Alphabet,
And by still practice, learne to know thy meaning.
Boy. Good grandsire leaue these bitter deepe laments,
Make my Aunt merry, with some pleasing tale.
Mar. Alas, the tender boy in passion mou'd,
Doth weepe to see his grandsires heauinesse.
An. Peace tender Sapling, thou art made of teares,
And teares will quickly melt thy life away.
Marcus strikes the dish with a knife.
What doest thou strike at *Marcus* with knife.
Mar. At that that I haue kil'd my Lord, a Flys
An. Out on the murderour: thou kil'st my hart,
Mine eyes cloi'd with view of Tirranie:
A deed of death done on the Innocent
Becoms not *Titus* broher: get thee gone,
I see thou art not for my company.
Mar. Alas (my Lord) I haue but kild a flie.
An. But? How: if that Flie had a father and mother?
How would he hang his slender gilded wings
And buz lamenting doings in the ayer,
Poore harmelesse Fly,
That with his pretty buzing melody,
Came heere to make vs merry,
And thou hast kil'd him.
Mar. Pardon me sir,
It was a blacke illfauour'd Fly,
Like to the Empresse Moore, therefore I kild him.
An. O, o, o,
Then pardon me for reprehending thee,
For thou hast done a Charitable deed:
Giue me thy knife, I will insult on him,
Flattering my selfes, as if it were the Moore,
Come hither purposely to poyson me.
There's for thy selfe, and thats for *Tamira*: Ah sirra,
Yet I thinke we are not brought so low,
But that betweene vs, we can kill a Fly,
That comes in likenesse of a Cole-blacke Moore.
Mar. Alas poore man, griefe ha's so wrought on him,
He takes false shadowes, for true substances.
An. Come, take away: *Lauinia*, goe with me,
Ile to thy closset, and goe read with thee
Sad stories, chanced in the times of old.
Come boy, and goe with me, thy sight is young,
And thou shalt read, when mine begin to dazell. *Exeunt*

Actus Quartus.

Enter young Lucius and Lauinia running after him, and the Boy flies from her with his bookes vnder his arme. Enter Titus and Marcus.

Boy. Helpe Grandsier helpe, my Aunt *Lauinia*,
Followes me euery where I know not why.
Good Vncle *Marcus* see how swift she comes,
Alas sweet Aunt, I know not what you meane.
Mar. Stand by me *Lucius*, doe not feare thy Aunt.
Titus. She loues thee boy too well to doe thee harme
Boy. I when my father was in Rome she did.
Mar. What meanes my Neece *Lauinia* by these signes?
Ti. Feare not *Lucius*, somewhat doth she meane:
See *Lucius* see, how much she makes of thee:
Some whether would she haue thee goe with her.
Ah boy, *Cornelia* neuer with more care
Read to her sonnes, then she hath read to thee,
Sweet Poetry, and Tullies Oratour:
Canst thou not gesse wherefore she plies thee thus?
Boy. My Lord I know not I, nor can I gesse,
Vnlesse some fit or frenzie do possesse her:
For I haue heard my Grandsier say full oft,
Extremitie of griefes would make men mad.
And I haue read that *Hecubæ* of Troy,
Ran mad through sorrow, that made me to feare,
Although my Lord, I know my noble Aunt,
Loues me as deare as ere my mother did,
And would not but in fury fright my youth,
Which made me downe to throw my bookes, and flie
Causles perhaps, but pardon me sweet Aunt,
And Madam, if my Vncle *Marcus* goe,
I will most willingly attend your Ladyship.
Mar. *Lucius* I will.
Ti. How now *Lauinia*, *Marcus* what meanes this?
Some booke there is that she desires to see,
Which is it girle of these? Open them boy,
But thou art deeper read and better skild,
Come and take choyse of all my Library,
And so beguile thy sorrow, till the heauens
Reueale the damn'd contriuer of this deed.
What booke?
Why lifts she vp her armes in sequence thus?
Mar. I thinke she meanes that ther was more then one
Confederate in the fact, I more there was:
Or else to heauen she heaues them to reuenge.
Ti. *Lucius* what booke is that she tosseth so?
Boy. Grandsier 'tis Ouids Metamorphosis,
My mother gaue it me.
Mar. For loue of her that's gone,
Perhahs she culd it from among the rest.
Ti. Soft, so busily she turnes the leaues,
Helpe her, what would she finde? *Lauinia* shall I read?
This is the tragicke tale of *Philomel*?
And treates of *Tereus* treason and his rape,
And rape I feare was roote of thine annoy.
Mar. See brother see, note how she quotes the leaues
Ti. *Lauinia*, wert thou thus surpriz'd sweet girle,
Rauisht and wrong'd as *Philomela* was?
Forc'd in the ruthlesse, vast, and gloomy woods?
See, see, I such a place there is where we did hunt,
(O had we neuer, neuer hunted there)
Patern'd by that the Poet heere describes,
By nature made for murthers and for rapes.
Mar. O why should nature build so foule a den,
Vnlesse the Gods delight in tragedies?
Ti. Giue signes sweet girle, for heere are none but friends
What Romaine Lord it was durst do the deed?
Or slunke not *Saturnine*, as *Tarquin* ersts,
That left the Campe to sinne in *Lucrece* bed.
Mar. Sit downe sweet Neece, brother sit downe by me,
Appollo, *Pallas*, *Ioue*, or *Mercury*,
Inspire me that I may this treason finde.
My Lord looke heere, looke heere *Lauinia*.

He writes his Name with his staffe, and guides it with feete and mouth.

This sandie plot is plaine, guide if thou canst
This

This after me, I haue writ my name,
Without the helpe of any hand at all.
Curst be that hart that forc'st vs to that shift:
Write thou good Neece, and heere display at last,
What God will haue discouered for reuenge,
Heauen guide thy pen to print thy sorrowes plaine,
That we may know the Traytors and the truth.

She takes the staffe in her mouth, and guides it with her stumps and writes.

Ti. Oh doe ye read my Lord what she hath writs?
Stuprum, Chiron, Demetrius.
Mar. What, what, the lustfull sonnes of *Tamora*,
Performers of this hainous bloody deed?
Ti. *Magni Dominator poli,*
Tam lentus audis scelera, tam lentus vides?
Mar. Oh calme thee, gentle Lord: Although I know
There is enough written vpon this earth,
To stirre a mutinie in the mildest thoughts,
And arme the mindes of infants to exclaimes.
My Lord kneele downe with me: *Lauinia* kneele,
And kneele sweet boy, the Romaine *Hectors* hope,
And sweare with me, as with the wofull Feere
And father of that chast dishonoured Dame,
Lord *Junius Brutus* sweare for *Lucrece* rape,
That we will prosecute (by good aduise)
Mortall reuenge vpon these traytorous Gothes,
And see their blood, or die with this reproach.
Ti. Tis sure enough, and you knew how.
But if you hunt these Beare-whelpes, then beware
The Dam will wake, and if she winde you once,
Shee's with the Lyon deepely still in league.
And lulls him whilst she palyeth on her backe,
And when he sleepes will she do what she list.
You are a young huntsman *Marcus*, let it alone:
And come, I will goe get a leafe of brasse,
And with a Gad of steele will write these words,
And lay it by: the angry Northerne winde
Will blow these sands like *Sibels* leaues abroad,
And wheres your lesson then. Boy what say you?
Boy. I say my Lord, that if I were a man,
Their mothers bed-chamber should not be safe,
For these bad bond-men to the yoake of Rome.
Mar. I that's my boy, thy father hath full oft,
For his vngratefull country done the like.
Boy. And Vncle so will I, and if I liue.
Ti. Come goe with me into mine Armorie,
Lucius Ile fit thee, and withall, my boy
Shall carry from me to the Empresse sonnes,
Presents that I intend to send them both,
Come, come, thou'lt do thy message, wilt thou not?
Boy. I with my dagger in their bosomes Grandsire:
Ti. No boy not so, Ile teach thee another course,
Lauinia come, *Marcus* looke to my house,
Lucius and Ile goe braue it at the Court,
I marry will we sir, and weele be waited on. *Exeunt.*
Mar. O heauens! Can you heare a good man grone
And not relent, or not compassion him?
Marcus attend him in his extasie,
That hath more scars of sorrow in his heart,
Then foe-mens markes vpon his batter'd shield,
But yet so iust, that he will not reuenge,
Reuenge the heauens for old *Andronicus*. *Exit*

Enter Aron, Chiron and Demetrius at one dore: and at another dore young Lucius and another, with a bundle of weapons, and verses writ vpon them.

Chi. *Demetrius* heeres the sonne of *Lucius*,
He hath some message to deliuer vs.
Aron. I some mad message from his mad Grandfather.
Boy. My Lords, with all the humblenesse I may,
I greete your honours from *Andronicus*,
And pray the Romane Gods confound you both.
Deme. Gramercie louely *Lucius*, what's the newes?
For villanie's markt with rape. May it please you,
My Grandsire well aduis'd hath sent by me,
The goodliest weapons of his Armorie,
To gratifie your honourable youth,
The hope of Rome, for so he bad me say:
And so I do and with his gifts present
Your Lordships, when euer you haue need,
You may be armed and appointed well,
And so I leaue you both: like bloody villaines. *Exit*
Deme. What's heere? a scrole, & written round about?
Let's see.
Integer vitæ scelerisque purus, non egit maury iaculis nec arcus.
Chi. O 'tis a verse in *Horace*, I know it well.
I read it in the Grammer long agoe.
Moore. I iust, a verse in *Horace*: right, you haue it,
Now what a thing it is to be an Asse?
Heer's no sound iest, the old man hath found their guilt,
And sends the weapons wrapt about with lines,
That wound (beyond their feeling) to the quick:
But were our witty Empresse well a foot,
She would applaud *Andronicus* conceit:
But let her rest, in her vnrest a while.
And now young Lords, wa'st not a happy starre
Led vs to Rome strangers, and more then so;
Captiues, to be aduanced to this height?
It did me good before the Pallace gate,
To braue the Tribune in his brothers hearing.
Deme. But me more good, to see so great a Lord
Basely insinuate, and send vs gifts.
Moore. Had he not reason Lord *Demetrius*?
Did you not vse his daughter very friendly?
Deme. I would we had a thousand Romane Dames
At such a bay, by turne to serue our lust.
Chi. A charitable wish, and full of loue.
Moore. Heere lack's but you mother for to say, Amen.
Chi. And that would she for twenty thousand more.
Deme. Come, let vs go, and pray to all the Gods
For our beloued mother in her paines.
Moore. Pray to the deuils, the gods haue giuen vs ouer.
Flourish.
Dem. Why do the Emperors trumpets flourish thus?
Chi. Belike for ioy the Emperour hath a sonne.
Deme. Soft, who comes heere?
Enter Nurse with a blacke a Moore childe.
Nur. Good morrow Lords:
O tell me, did you see *Aaron* the Moore?
Aron. Well, more or lesse, or nere a whit at all,
Heere *Aaron* is, and what with *Aaron* now?
Nurse. Oh gentle *Aaron*, we are all vndone,
Now helpe, or woe betide thee euermore.
Aron. Why, what a catterwalling dost thou keepe?
What dost thou wrap and fumble in thine armes?
Nurse. O that which I would hide from heauens eye,
Our Empresse shame, and stately Romes disgrace,
She is deliuered Lords, she is deliuered.
Aron To whom?
Nurse. I meane she is brought a bed?
Aron. Wel God giue her good rest,

What

What hath he sent her?
Nurse. A deuill.
Aron. Why then she is the Deuils Dam: a ioyfull issue.
Nurse. A ioylesse, dismall, blacke &, sorrowfull issue,
Heere is the babe as loathsome as a toad,
Among'st the fairest breeders of our clime,
The Empresse sends it thee, thy stampe, thy seale,
And bids thee christen it with thy daggers point.
Aron. Out you whore, is black so base a hue?
Sweet blowse, you are a beautious blossome sure.
Deme. Villaine what hast thou done?
Aron. That which thou canst not vndoe.
Chi. Thou hast vndone our mother.
Deme. And therein hellish dog, thou hast vndone,
Woe to her chance, and damn'd her loathed choyce,
Accur'st the off-spring of so foule a fiend.
Chi. It shall not liue.
Aron. It shall not die.
Nurse. *Aaron* it must, the mother wils it so.
Aron. What, must it *Nurse*? Then let no man but I
Doe execution on my flesh and blood.
Deme. Ile broach the Tadpole on my Rapiers point:
Nurse giue it me, my sword shall soone dispatch it.
Aron. Sooner this sword shall plough thy bowels vp.
Stay murtherous villaines, will you kill your brother?
Now by the burning Tapers of the skie,
That sh'one so brightly when this Boy was got,
He dies vpon my Semitars sharpe point,
That touches this my first borne sonne and heire.
I tell you young-lings, not *Enceladus*
With all his threatning band of *Typhons* broode,
Nor great *Alcides*, nor the God of warre,
Shall ceaze this prey out of his fathers hands:
What, what, ye sanguine shallow harted Boyes,
Ye white-limb'd walls, ye Ale-house painted signes,
Cole-blacke is better then another hue,
In that it scornes to beare another hue:
For all the water in the Ocean,
Can neuer turne the Swans blacke legs to white,
Although she laue them hourely in the flood:
Tell the Empresse from me, I am of age
To keepe mine owne, excuse it how she can.
Deme. Wilt thou betray thy noble mistris thus?
Aron. My mistris is my mistris: this my selfe,
The vigour, and the picture of my youth:
This, before all the world do I preferre,
This mauger all the world will I keepe safe,
Or some of you shall smoake for it in Rome.
Deme. By this our mother is for euer sham'd.
Chi. Rome will despise her for this foule escape.
Nur. The Emperour in his rage will doome her death.
Chi. I blush to thinke vpon this ignominie.
Aron. Why ther's the priuiledge your beauty beares:
Fie trecherous hue, that will betray with blushing
The close enacts and counsels of the hart:
Heer's a young Lad fram'd of another leere,
Looke how the blacke slaue smiles vpon the father;
As who should say, old Lad I am thine owne.
He is your brother Lords, sensibly fed
Of that selfe blood that first gaue life to you,
And from that wombe where you imprisoned were
He is infranchised and come to light:
Nay he is your brother by the surer side,
Although my seale be stamped in his face.
Nurse. *Aaron* what shall I say vnto the Empresse?
Dem. Aduise thee *Aaron*, what is to be done,
And we will all subscribe to thy aduise:
Saue thou the child, so we may all be safe.
Aron. Then sit we downe and let vs all consult.
My sonne and I will haue the winde of you:
Keepe there, now talke at pleasure of your safety.
Deme. How many women saw this childe of his?
Aron. Why so braue Lords, when we ioyne in league
I am a Lambe: but if you braue the *Moore*,
The chafed Bore, the mountaine Lyonesse,
The Ocean swells not so at *Aaron* stormes:
But say againe, how many saw the childe?
Nurse. *Cornelia*, the midwife, and my selfe,
And none else but the deliuered Empresse.
Aron. The Empresse, the Midwife, and your selfe,
Two may keepe counsell, when the the third's away:
Goe to the Empresse, tell her this I said, *He kils her*
Weeke, weeke, so cries a Pigge prepared to th'spit.
Deme. What mean'st thou *Aaron*?
Wherefore did'st thou this?
Aron. O Lord sir, 'tis a deed of pollicie?
Shall she liue to betray this guilt of our's:
A long tongu'd babling Gossip? No Lords no:
And now be it knowne to you my full intent.
Not farre, one *Muliteus* my Country-man
His wife but yesternight was brought to bed,
His childe is like to her, faire as you are:
Goe packe with him, and giue the mother gold,
And tell them both the circumstance of all,
And how by this their Childe shall be aduaunc'd,
And be receiued for the Emperours heyre,
And substituted in the place of mine,
To calme this tempest whirling in the Court,
And let the Emperour dandle him for his owne.
Harke ye Lords, ye see I haue giuen her physicke,
And you must needs bestow her funerall,
The fields are neere, and you are gallant Groomes:
This done, see that you take no longer daies
But send the Midwife presently to me.
The Midwife and the Nurse well made away,
Then let the Ladies tattle what they please.
Chi. *Aaron* I see thou wilt not trust the ayre with se(crets.
Deme. For this care of *Tamora*,
Her selfe, and hers are highly bound to thee. *Exeunt.*
Aron. Now to the Gothes, as swift as Swallow flies,
There to dispose this treasure in mine armes,
And secretly to greete the Empresse friends:
Come on you thick-lipt-slaue, Ile beare you hence,
For it is you that puts vs to our shifts:
Ile make you feed on berries, and on rootes,
And feed on curds and whay, and sucke the Goate,
And cabbin in a Caue, and bring you vp
To be a warriour, and command a Campe. *Exit*

Enter Titus, old Marcus, young Lucius, and other gentlemen with bowes, and Titus beares the arrowes with Letters on the end of them.

Tit. Come *Marcus*, come, kinsmen this is the way.
Sir Boy let me see your Archerie,
Looke yee draw home enough, and 'tis there straight:
Terras Astrea reliquit, be you remembred *Marcus*.
She's gone, she's fled, sirs take you to your tooles,
You Cosens shall goe sound the Ocean:
And cast your nets, haply you may find her in the Sea,
Yet ther's as little iustice as at Land:
No *Publius* and *Sempronius*, you must doe it,
'Tis

'Tis you muſt dig with Mattocke, and with Spade,
And pierce the inmoſt Center of the earth:
Then when you come to *Plutoes* Region,
I pray you deliuer him this petition,
Tell him it is for iuſtice, and for aide,
And that it comes from old *Andronicus*,
Shaken with ſorrowes in vngratefull Rome.
Ah Rome! Well, well, I made thee miſerable,
What time I threw the peoples ſuffrages
On him that thus doth tyrannize ore me.
Goe get you gone, and pray be carefull all,
And leaue you not a man of warre vnſearcht,
This wicked Emperour may haue ſhipt her hence,
And kinſmen then we may goe pipe for iuſtice.

Marc. O *Publius* is not this a heauie caſe
To ſee thy Noble Vnckle thus diſtract?

Publ. Therefore my Lords it highly vs concernes,
By day and night t'attend him carefully:
And feede his humour kindely as we may,
Till time beget ſome carefull remedie.

Marc. Kinſmen, his ſorrowes are paſt remedie.
Ioyne with the Gothes, and with reuengefull warre,
Take wreake on Rome for this ingratitude,
And vengeance on the Traytor *Saturnine.*

Tit. *Publius* how now? how now my Maiſters?
What haue you met with her?

Publ. No my good Lord, but *Pluto* ſends you word,
If you will haue reuenge from hell you ſhall,
Marrie for iuſtice ſhe is ſo imploy'd,
He thinkes with *Ioue* in heauen, or ſome where elſe:
So that perforce you muſt needs ſtay a time.

Tit. He doth me wrong to feed me with delayes,
Ile diue into the burning Lake below,
And pull her out of *Acaron* by the heeles.
Marcus we are but ſhrubs, no Cedars we,
No big-bon'd-men, fram'd of the Cyclops ſize,
But mettall *Marcus*, ſteele to the very backe,
Yet wrung with wrongs more then our backe can beare:
And ſith there's no iuſtice in earth nor hell,
We will ſollicite heauen, and moue the Gods
To ſend downe Iuſtice for to wreake'our wongs:
Come to this geare, you are a good Archer *Marcus.*

He giues them the Arrowes.

Ad Iouem, that's for you: here *ad Appollonem*,
Ad Martem, that's for my ſelfe,
Heere Boy to *Pallas*, heere to *Mercury*,
To *Saturnine*, to *Caius*, not to *Saturnine*,
You were as good to ſhoote againſt the winde.
Too it Boy, *Marcus* looſe when I bid:
Of my word, I haue written to effect,
Ther's not a God left vnſollicited.

Marc. Kinſmen, ſhoot all your ſhafts into the Court,
We will afflict the Emperour in his pride.

Tit, Now Maiſters draw, Oh well ſaid *Lucius*:
Good Boy in *Virgoes* lap, giue it *Pallas.*

Marc. My Lord, I aime a Mile beyond the Moone,
Your letter is with *Iupiter* by this.

Tit. Ha, ha, *Publius*, *Publius*, what haſt thou done?
See, ſee, thou haſt ſhot off one of *Taurus* hornes.

Mar. This was the ſport my Lord, when *Publius* ſhot,
The Bull being gal'd, gaue *Aries* ſuch a knocke,
That downe fell both the Rams hornes in the Court,
And who ſhould finde them but the Empreſſe villaine:
She laught, and told the Moore he ſhould not chooſe
But giue them to his Maiſter for a preſent.

Tit. Why there it goes, God giue your Lordſhip ioy.

Enter the Clowne with a basket and two Pigeons in it.

Titus. Newes, newes, from heauen,
Marcus the poaſt is come.
Sirrah, what tydings? haue you any letters?
Shall I haue Iuſtice, what ſayes *Iupiter*?

Clowne. Ho the Iibbetmaker, he ſayes that he hath taken them downe againe, for the man muſt not be hang'd till the next weeke.

Tit. But what ſayes *Iupiter* I aske thee?

Clowne. Alas ſir I know not *Iupiter*:
I neuer dranke with him in all my life.

Tit. Why villaine art not thou the Carrier?

Clowne. I of my Pigions ſir, nothing elſe.

Tit. Why, did'ſt thou not come from heauen?

Clowne. From heauen? Alas ſir, I neuer came there, God forbid I ſhould be ſo bold, to preſſe to heauen in my young dayes. Why I am going with my pigeons to the Tribunall Plebs, to take vp a matter of brawle, betwixt my Vncle, and one of the Emperialls men.

Mar. Why ſir, that is as fit as can be to ſerue for your Oration, and let him deliuer the Pigions to the Emperour from you.

Tit. Tell mee, can you deliuer an Oration to the Emperour with a Grace?

Clowne. Nay truely ſir, I could neuer ſay grace in all my life.

Tit. Sirrah come hither, make no more adoe,
But giue your Pigeons to the Emperour,
By me thou ſhalt haue Iuſtice at his hands.
Hold, hold, meane while her's money for thy charges.
Giue me pen and inke.
Sirrah, can you with a Grace deliuer a Supplication?

Clowne. I ſir

Titus. Then here is a Supplication for you, and when you come to him, at the firſt approach you muſt kneele, then kiſſe his foote, then deliuer vp your Pigeons, and then looke for your reward. Ile be at hand ſir, ſee you do it brauely.

Clowne. I warrant you ſir, let me alone.

Tit. Sirrha haſt thou a knife? Come let me ſee it.
Heere *Marcus*, fold it in the Oration,
For thou haſt made it like an humble Suppliant:
And when thou haſt giuen it the Emperour,
Knocke at my dore, and tell me what he ſayes.

Clowne. God be with you ſir, I will. *Exit.*

Tit. Come *Marcus* let vs goe, *Publius* follow me. *Exeunt.*

Enter Emperour and Empreſſe, and her two ſonnes, the Emperour brings the Arrowes in his hand that Titus ſhot at him.

Satur. Why Lords,
What wrongs are theſe? was euer ſeene
An Emperour in Rome thus ouerborne,
Troubled, Confronted thus, and for the extent
Of egall iuſtice, vs'd in ſuch contempt?
My Lords, you know the mightfull Gods,
(How euer theſe diſturbers of our peace
Buz in the peoples eares) there nought hath paſt,
But euen with law againſt the willfull Sonnes
Of old *Andronicus.* And what and if
His ſorrowes haue ſo ouerwhelm'd his wits,
Shall we be thus afflicted in his wreakes,
His fits, his frenzie, and his bitterneſſe?
And now he writes to heauen for his redreſſe.
See, heeres to *Ioue*, and this to *Mercury*,

This

This to *Apollo*, this to the God of warre:
Sweet ſcrowles to flie about the ſtreets of Rome:
What's this but Libelling againſt the Senate,
And blazoning our Iniuſtice euery where?
A goodly humour, is it not my Lords?
As who would ſay, in Rome no Iuſtice were.
But if I liue, his fained extaſies
Shall be no ſhelter to theſe outrages:
But he and his ſhall know, that Iuſtice liues
In *Saturninus* health; whom if he ſleepe,
Hee'l ſo awake, as he in fury ſhall
Cut off the proud'ſt Conſpirator that liues.

Tamo. My gracious Lord, my louely *Saturnine*,
Lord of my life, Commander of my thoughts,
Calme thee, and beare the faults of *Titus* age,
Th'effects of ſorrow for his valiant Sonnes,
Whoſe loſſe hath pier'ſt him deepe, and ſcar'd his heart;
And rather comfort his diſtreſſed plight,
Then proſecute the meaneſt or the beſt
For theſe contempts. Why thus it ſhall become
High witted *Tamora* to gloſe with all: *Aſide.*
But *Titus*, I haue touch'd thee to the quicke,
Thy life blood out: If *Aaron* now be wiſe,
Then is all ſafe, the Anchor's in the Port.

Enter Clowne.

How now good fellow, would'ſt thou ſpeake with vs?

Clow. Yea forſooth, and your Miſterſhip be Emperiall.

Tam. Empreſſe I am, but yonder ſits the Emperour.

Clo. 'Tis he; God & Saint Stephen giue you good den;
I haue brought you a Letter, & a couple of Pigions heere.

He reads the Letter.

Satu. Goe take him away, and hang him preſently.

Clowne. How much money muſt I haue?

Tam. Come ſirrah you muſt be hang'd.

Clow. Hang'd? ber Lady, then I haue brought vp a neck
to a faire end. *Exit.*

Satu. Deſpightfull and intollerable wrongs,
Shall I endure this monſtrous villany?
I know from whence this ſame deuiſe proceedes:
May this be borne? As if his traytrous Sonnes,
That dy'd by law for murther of our Brother,
Haue by my meanes beene butcher'd wrongfully?
Goe dragge the villaine hither by the haire,
Nor Age, nor Honour, ſhall ſhape priuiledge:
For this proud mocke, Ile be thy ſlaughter man:
Sly franticke wretch, that holp'ſt to make me great,
In hope thy ſelfe ſhould gouerne Rome and me.

Enter Nuntius Emillius.

Satur. What newes with thee *Emillius*?

Emil. Arme my Lords, Rome neuer had more cauſe,
The Gothes haue gather'd head, and with a power
Of high reſolued men, bent to the ſpoyle
They hither march amaine, vnder conduct
Of *Lucius*, Sonne to old *Andronicus*:
Who threats in courſe of this reuenge to do
As much as euer *Coriolanus* did.

King. Is warlike *Lucius* Generall of the Gothes?
Theſe tydings nip me, and I hang the head
As flowers with froſt, or graſſe beat downe with ſtormes:
I, now begins our ſorrowes to approach,
'Tis he the common people loue ſo much,
My ſelfe hath often heard them ſay,
(When I haue walked like a priuate man)
That *Lucius* baniſhment was wrongfully,
And they haue wiſht that *Lucius* were their Emperour.

Tam. Why ſhould you feare? Is not our City ſtrong?

King. I, but the Cittizens fauour *Lucius*,
And will reuolt from me, to ſuccour him.

Tam. *King*, be thy thoughts Imperious like thy name.
Is the Sunne dim'd, that Gnats do flie in it?
The Eagle ſuffers little Birds to ſing,
And is not carefull what they meane thereby,
Knowing that with the ſhadow of his wings,
He can at pleaſure ſtint their melodie.
Euen ſo mayeſt thou, the giddy men of Rome,
Then cheare thy ſpirit, for know thou Emperour,
I will enchaunt the old *Andronicus*,
With words more ſweet, and yet more dangerous
Then baites to fiſh, or hony ſtalkes to ſheepe,
When as the one is wounded with the baite,
The other rotted with delicious foode.

King. But he will not entreat his Sonne for vs.

Tam. If *Tamora* entreat him, then he will,
For I can ſmooth and fill his aged eare,
With golden promiſes, that were his heart
Almoſt Impregnable, his old eares deafe,
Yet ſhould both eare and heart obey my tongue.
Goe thou before to our Embaſſadour,
Say, that the Emperour requeſts a parly
Of warlike *Lucius*, and appoint the meeting.

King. *Emillius* do this meſſage Honourably,
And if he ſtand in Hoſtage for his ſafety,
Bid him demaund what pledge will pleaſe him beſt.

Emill. Your bidding ſhall I do effectually. *Exit.*

Tam. Now will I to that old *Andronicus*,
And temper him with all the Art I haue,
To plucke proud *Lucius* from the warlike Gothes.
And now ſweet Emperour be blithe againe,
And bury all thy feare in my deuiſes.

Satu. Then goe ſucceſſantly and plead for him. *Exit.*

Actus Quintus.

Flouriſh. Enter Lucius with an Army of Gothes, with Drum and Souldiers.

Luci. Approued warriours, and my faithfull Friends,
I haue receiued Letters from great Rome,
Which ſignifies what hate they beare their Emperour,
And how deſirous of our ſight they are.
Therefore great Lords, be as your Titles witneſſe,
Imperious and impatient of your wrongs,
And wherein Rome hath done you any ſcathe,
Let him make treble ſatiſfaction.

Goth. Braue ſlip, ſprung from the Great *Andronicus*,
Whoſe name was once our terrour, now our comfort,
Whoſe high exploits, and honourable Deeds,
Ingratefull Rome requites with foule contempt:
Behold in vs, weele follow where thou lead'ſt,
Like ſtinging Bees in hotteſt Sommers day,
Led by their Maiſter to the flowred fields,
And be aueng'd on curſed *Tamora*:
And as he ſaith, ſo ſay we all with him.

Luci. I humbly thanke him, and I thanke you all.
But who comes heere, led by a luſty *Goth*?

Enter a Goth leading of Aaron with his child in his armes.

Goth. Renowned *Lucius*, from our troups I ſtraid,
To gaze vpon a ruinous Monaſterie,

And

And as I earneftly did fixe mine eye
Vpon the wafted building, fuddainely
I heard a childe cry vnderneath a wall:
I made vnto the noyfe, when foone I heard,
The crying babe control'd with this difcourfe:
Peace Tawny flaue, halfe me, and halfe thy Dam,
Did not thy Hue bewray whofe brat thou art?
Had nature lent thee, but thy Mothers looke,
Villaine thou might'ft haue bene an Emperour.
But where the Bull and Cow are both milk-white,
They neuer do beget a cole-blacke-Calfe:
Peace, villaine peace, euen thus he rates the babe,
For I muft beare thee to a trufty Goth,
Who when he knowes thou art the Empreffe babe,
Will hold thee dearely for thy Mothers fake.
With this, my weapon drawne I rufht vpon him,
Surpriz'd him fuddainely, and brought him hither
To vfe, as you thinke neeedefull of the man.
Luci. Oh worthy Goth, this is the incarnate deuill,
That rob'd *Andronicus* of his good hand:
This is the Pearle that pleaf'd your Empreffe eye,
And heere's the Bafe Fruit of his burning luft.
Say wall-ey'd flaue, whether would'ft thou conuay
This growing Image of thy fiend-like face?
Why doft not fpeake? what deafe? Not a word?
A halter Souldiers, hang him on this Tree,
And by his fide his Fruite of Baftardie.
Aron. Touch not the Boy, he is of Royall blood.
Luci. Too like the Syre for euer being good.
Firft hang the Child that he may fee it fprall,
A fight to vexe the Fathers foule withall.
Aron. Get me a Ladder *Lucius*, faue the Childe,
And beare it from me to the Empreffe:
If thou do this, Ile fhew thee wondrous things,
That highly may aduantage thee to heare;
If thou wilt not, befall what may befall,
Ile fpeake no more: but vengeance rot you all.
Luci. Say on, and if it pleafe me which thou fpeak'ft,
Thy child fhall liue, and I will fee it Nourifht.
Aron. And if it pleafe thee? why affure thee *Lucius*,
'Twill vexe thy foule to heare what I fhall fpeake:
For I muft talke of Murthers, Rapes, and Maffacres,
Acts of Blacke-night, abhominable Deeds,
Complots of Mifchiefe, Treafon, Villanies
Ruthfull to heare, yet pittioufly preform'd,
And this fhall all be buried by my death,
Vnleffe thou fweare to me my Childe fhall liue.
Luci. Tell on thy minde,
I fay thy Childe fhall liue.
Aron. Sweare that he fhall, and then I will begin.
Luci. Who fhould I fweare by,
Thou beleeueft no God,
That graunted, how can'ft thou beleeue an oath?
Aron. What if I do not, as indeed I do not,
Yet for I know thou art Religious,
And haft a thing within thee, called Confcience,
With twenty Popifh trickes and Ceremonies,
Which I haue feene thee carefull to obferue:
Therefore I vrge thy oath, for that I know
An Ideot holds his Bauble for a God,
And keepes the oath which by that God he fweares,
To that Ile vrge him: therefore thou fhalt vow
By that fame God, what God fo ere it be
That thou adoreft, and haft in reuerence,
To faue my Boy, to nourifh and bring him vp,
Ore elfe I will difcouer nought to thee.
Luci. Euen by my God I fweare to to thee I will.
Aron. Firft know thou,
I begot him on the Empreffe.
Luci. Oh moft Infatiate luxurious woman!
Aron. Tut *Lucius*, this was but a deed of Charitie,
To that which thou fhalt heare of me anon,
'Twas her two Sonnes that murdered *Baffianus*,
They cut thy Sifters tongue, and rauifht her,
And cut her hands off, and trim'd her as thou faw'ft.
Lucius. Oh deteftable villaine!
Call'ft thou that Trimming?
Aron. Why fhe was wafht, and cut, and trim'd,
And 'twas trim fport for them that had the doing of it.
Luci. Oh barbarous beaftly villaines like thy felfe!
Aron. Indeede, I was their Tutor to inftruct them,
That Codding fpirit had they from their Mother,
As fure a Card as euer wonne the Set:
That bloody minde I thinke they learn'd of me,
As true a Dog as euer fought at head.
Well, let my Deeds be witneffe of my worth:
I trayn'd thy Bretheren to that guilefull Hole,
Where the dead Corps of *Baffianus* lay:
I wrote the Letter, that thy Father found,
And hid the Gold within the Letter mention'd.
Confederate with the Queene, and her two Sonnes,
And what not done, that thou haft caufe to rue,
Wherein I had no ftroke of Mifcheife in it.
I play'd the Cheater for thy Fathers hand,
And when I had it, drew my felfe apart,
And almoft broke my heart with extreame laughter.
I pried me through the Creuice of a Wall,
When for his hand, he had his two Sonnes heads,
Beheld his teares, and laught fo hartily,
That both mine eyes were rainie like to his:
And when I told the Empreffe of this fport,
She founded almoft at my pleafing tale,
And for my tydings, gaue me twenty kiffes.
Goth. What canft thou fay all this, and neuer blufh?
Aron. I, like a blacke Dogge, as the faying is.
Luci. Art thou not forry for thefe hainous deedes?
Aron. I, that I had not done a thoufand more:
Euen now I curfe the day, and yet I thinke
Few come within few compaffe of my curfe,
Wherein I did not fome Notorious ill,
As kill a man, or elfe deuife his death,
Rauifh a Maid, or plot the way to do it,
Accufe fome Innocent, and forfweare my felfe,
Set deadly Enmity betweene two Friends,
Make poore mens Cattell breake their neckes,
Set fire on Barnes and Hayftackes in the night,
And bid the Owners quench them with the teares:
Oft haue I dig'd vp dead men from their graues,
And fet them vpright at their deere Friends doore,
Euen when their forrowes almoft was forgot,
And on their skinnes, as on the Barke of Trees,
Haue with my knife carued in Romaine Letters,
Let not your forrow die, though I am dead.
Tut, I haue done a thoufand dreadfull things
As willingly, as one would kill a Fly,
And nothing greeues me hartily indeede,
But that I cannot doe ten thoufand more.
Luci. Bring downe the diuell, for he muft not die
So fweet a death as hanging prefently.
Aron. If there be diuels, would I were a deuill,
To liue and burne in euerlafting fire,
So I might haue your company in hell,

But

But to torment you with my bitter tongue.
Luci. Sirs ſtop his mouth, & let him ſpeake no more.
Enter Emillius.
Goth. My Lord, there is a Meſſenger from Rome
Deſires to be admitted to your preſence.
Luc. Let him come neere.
Welcome *Emillius*, what the newes from Rome?
Emi. Lord *Lucius*, and you Princes of the Gothes,
The Romaine Emperour greetes you all by me,
And for he vnderſtands you are in Armes,
He craues a parly at your Fathers houſe
Willing you to demand your Hoſtages,
And they ſhall be immediately deliuered.
Goth. What ſaies our Generall?
Luc. *Emillius*, let the Emperour giue his pledges
Vnto my Father, and my Vncle *Marcus*, *Flouriſh.*
And we will come: march away. *Exeunt.*

Enter Tamora, and her two Sonnes diſguiſed.

Tam. Thus in this ſtrange and ſad Habilliament,
I will encounter with *Andronicus*,
And ſay, I am Reuenge ſent from below,
To ioyne with him and right his hainous wrongs:
Knocke at his ſtudy where they ſay he keepes,
To ruminate ſtrange plots of dire Reuenge,
Tell him Reuenge is come to ioyne with him,
And worke confuſion on his Enemies.
They knocke and Titus opens his ſtudy dore.
Tit. Who doth molleſt my Contemplation?
Is it your tricke to make me ope the dore,
That ſo my ſad decrees may flie away,
And all my ſtudie be to no effect?
You are deceiu'd, for what I meane to do,
See heere in bloody lines I haue ſet downe:
And what is written ſhall be executed.
Tam. *Titus*, I am come to talke with thee,
Tit. No not a word: how can I grace my talke,
Wanting a hand to giue it action,
Thou haſt the ods of me, therefore no more.
Tam. If thou did'ſt know me,
Thou would'ſt talke with me.
Tit. I am not mad, I know thee well enough,
Witneſſe this wretched ſtump,
Witneſſe theſe crimſon lines,
Witneſſe theſe Trenches made by griefe and care,
Witneſſe the tyring day, andheauie night,
Witneſſe all ſorrow, that I know thee well
For our proud Empreſſe, Mighty *Tamora*:
Is not thy comming for my other hand?
Tamo. Know thou ſad man, I am not *Tamora*,
She is thy Enemie, and I thy Friend,
I am Reuenge ſent from th'infernall Kingdome,
To eaſe the gnawing Vulture of the mind,
By working wreakefull vengeance on my Foes:
Come downe and welcome me to this worlds light,
Conferre with me of Murder and of Death,
Ther's not a hollow Caue or lurking place,
No Vaſt obſcurity, or Miſty vale,
Where bloody Murther or deteſted Rape,
Can couch for feare, but I will finde them out,
And in their eares tell them my dreadfull name,
Reuenge, which makes the foule offenders quake.
Tit. Art thou Reuenge? and art thou ſent to me,
To be a torment to mine Enemies?
Tam. I am, therefore come downe and welcome me.
Tit. Doe me ſome ſeruice ere I come to thee:
Loe bythy ſide where Rape and Murder ſtands,
Now giue ſome ſurance that thou art Reuenge,
Stab them, or teare them on thy Chariot wheeles,
And then Ile come and be thy Waggoner,
And whirle along with thee about the Globes.
Prouide thee two proper Palfries, as blacke as Iet,
To hale thy vengefull Waggon ſwift away,
And finde out Murder in their guilty cares.
And when thy Car is loaden with their heads,
I will diſmount, and by the Waggon wheele,
Trot like a Seruile footeman all day long,
Euen from *Eptons* riſing in the Eaſt,
Vntill his very downefall in the Sea.
And day by day Ile do this heauy taske,
So thou deſtroy Rapine and Murder there.
Tam. Theſe are my Miniſters, and come with me.
Tit. Are them thy Miniſters, what are they call'd?
Tam. Rape and Murder, therefore called ſo,
Cauſe they take vengeance of ſuch kind of men.
Tit. Good Lord how like the Empreſſe Sons they are,
And you the Empreſſe: But we worldly men,
Haue miſerable mad miſtaking eyes:
Oh ſweet Reuenge, now do I come to thee,
And if one armes imbracement will content thee,
I will imbrace thee in it by and by.
Tam. This cloſing with him, fits his Lunacie,
What ere I forge to feede his braine-ſicke fits,
Do you vphold, and maintaine in your ſpeeches,
For now he firmely takes me for Reuenge,
And being Credulous in this mad thought,
Ile make him ſend for *Lucius* his Sonne,
And whil'ſt I at a Banquet hold him ſure,
Ile find ſome cunning practiſe out of hand
To ſcatter and diſperſe the giddie Gothes,
Or at the leaſt make them his Enemies:
See heere he comes, and I muſt play my theame.
Tit. Long haue I bene forlorne, and all for thee,
Welcome dread Fury to my woefull houſe,
Rapine and Murther, you are welcome too,
How like the Empreſſe and her Sonnes you are.
Well are you fitted, had you but a Moore,
Could not all hell afford you ſuch a deuill?
For well I wote the Empreſſe neuer wags;
But in her company there is a Moore,
And would you repreſent our Queene aright
It were conuenient you had ſuch a deuill:
But welcome as you are, what ſhall we doe?
Tam. What would'ſt thou haue vs doe *Andronicus*?
Dem. Shew me a Murtherer, Ile deale with him.
Chi. Shew me a Villaine that hath done a Rape,
And I am ſent to be reueng'd on him.
Tam. Shew me a thouſand that haue done thee wrong,
And Ile be reuenged on them all.
Tit. Looke round about the wicked ſtreets of Rome,
And when thou find'ſt a man that's like thy ſelfe,
Good Murder ſtab him, hee's a Murtherer.
Goe thou with him, and when it is thy hap
To finde another that is like to thee,
Good Rapine ſtab him, he is a Rauiſher.
Go thou with them, and in the Emperours Court,
There is a Queene attended by a Moore,
Well maiſt thou know her by thy owne proportion,
For vp and downe ſhe doth reſemble thee.
I pray thee doe on them ſome violent death,
They haue bene violent to me and mine.
e e *Tamora.*

Tam. Well haſt thou leſſon'd vs, this ſhall we do.
But would it pleaſe thee good *Andronicus*,
To ſend for *Lucius* thy thrice Valiant Sonne,
Who leades towards Rome a Band of Warlike Gothes,
And bid him come and Banquet at thy houſe.
When he is heere, euen at thy Solemne Feaſt,
I will bring in the Empreſſe and her Sonnes,
The Emperour himſelfe, and all thy Foes,
And at thy mercy ſhall they ſtoop, and kneele,
And on them ſhalt thou eaſe, thy angry heart:
What ſaies *Andronicus* to this deuiſe?

Enter Marcus.

Tit. Marcus my Brother, 'tis ſad *Titus* calls,
Go gentle *Marcus* to thy Nephew *Lucius*,
Thou ſhalt enquire him out among the Gothes,
Bid him repaire to me, and bring with him
Some of the chiefeſt Princes of the Gothes,
Bid him encampe his Souldiers where they are,
Tell him the Emperour, and the Empreſſe too,
Feaſts at my houſe, and he ſhall Feaſt with them,
This do thou for my loue, and ſo let him,
As he regards his aged Fathers life.
Mar. This will I do, and ſoone returne againe.
Tam. Now will I hence about thy buſineſſe,
And take my Miniſters along with me.
Tit. Nay, nay, let Rape and Murder ſtay with me,
Or els Ile call my Brother backe againe,
And cleaue to no reuenge but *Lucius*.
Tam. What ſay you Boyes, will you bide with him,
Whiles I goe tell my Lord the Emperour,
How I haue gouern'd our determined ieſt?
Yeeld to his Humour, ſmooth and ſpeake him faire,
And tarry with him till I turne againe.
Tit. I know them all, though they ſuppoſe me mad,
And will ore-reach them in their owne deuiſes,
A payre of curſed hell-hounds and their Dam.
Dem. Madam depart at pleaſure, leaue vs heere.
Tam. Farewell *Andronicus*, reuenge now goes
To lay a complot to betray thy Foes.
Tit. I know thou doo'ſt, and ſweet reuenge farewell.
Chi. Tell vs old man, how ſhall we be imploy'd?
Tit. Tut, I haue worke enough for you to doe,
Publius come hither, *Caius*, and *Valentine*.
Pub. What is your will?
Tit. Know you theſe two?
Pub. The Empreſſe Sonnes
I take them, *Chiron*, *Demetrius*.
Titus. Fie *Publius*, fie, thou art too much deceau'd,
The one is Murder, Rape is the others name,
And therefore bind them gentle *Publius*,
Caius, and *Valentine*, lay hands on them,
Oft haue you heard me wiſh for ſuch an houre,
And now I find it, therefore binde them ſure,
Chi. Villaines forbeare, we are the Empreſſe Sonnes.
Pub. And therefore do we, what we are commanded.
Stop cloſe their mouthes, let them not ſpeake a word,
Is he ſure bound, looke that you binde them faſt. *Exeunt.*

Enter Titus Andronicus with a knife, and Lauinia with a Baſon.

Tit. Come, come *Lauinia*, looke, thy Foes are bound,
Sirs ſtop their mouthes, let them not ſpeake to me,
But let them heare what fearefull words I vtter.
Oh Villaines, *Chiron*, and *Demetrius*,
Here ſtands the ſpring whom you haue ſtain'd with mud,
This goodly Sommer with your Winter mixt,
You kil'd her husband, and for that vil'd fault,
Two of her Brothers were condemn'd to death,
My hand cut off, and made a merry ieſt,
Both her ſweet Hands, her Tongue, and that more deere
Then Hands or tongue, her ſpotleſſe Chaſtity,
Inhumaine Traytors, you conſtrain'd and for'ſt.
What would you ſay, if I ſhould let you ſpeake?
Villaines for ſhame you could not beg for grace.
Harke Wretches, how I meane to martyr you,
This one Hand yet is left, to cut your throats,
Whil'ſt that *Lauinia* tweene her ſtumps doth hold:
The Baſon that receiues your guilty blood.
You know your Mother meanes to feaſt with me,
And calls herſelfe Reuenge, and thinkes me mad.
Harke Villaines, I will grin'd your bones to duſt,
And with your blood and it, Ile make a Paſte,
And of the Paſte a Coffen I will reare,
And make two Paſties of your ſhamefull Heads,
And bid that ſtrumpet your vnhallowed Dam,
Like to the earth ſwallow her increaſe.
This is the Feaſt, that I haue bid her to,
And this the Banquet ſhe ſhall ſurfet on,
For worſe then *Philomel* you vſ'd my Daughter,
And worſe then *Progne*, I will be reueng'd,
And now prepare your throats: *Lauinia* come.
Receiue the blood, and when that they are dead,
Let me goe grin'd their Bones to powder ſmall,
And with this hatefull Liquor temper it,
And in that Paſte let their vil'd Heads be bakte,
Come, come, be euery one officious,
To make this Banket, which I wiſh might proue,
More ſterne and bloody then the Centaures Feaſt.
He cuts their throats.
So now bring them in, for Ile play the Cooke,
And ſee them ready, gainſt their Mother comes. *Exeunt.*

Enter Lucius, Marcus, and the Gothes.

Luc. Vnckle *Marcus*, ſince 'tis my Fathers minde
That I repair to Rome, I am content.
Goth. And ours with thine befall, what Fortune will.
Luc. Good Vnckle take you in this barbarous *Moore*,
This Rauenous Tiger, this accurſed deuill,
Let him receiue no ſuſtenance, fetter him,
Till he be brought vnto the Emperous face,
For teſtimony of her foule proceedings.
And ſee the Ambuſh of our Friends be ſtrong,
If ere the Emperour meanes no good to vs.
Aron. Some deuill whiſper curſes in my eare,
And prompt me that my tongue may vtter forth,
The Venemous Mallice of my ſwelling heart.
Luc. Away Inhumaine Dogge, Vnhallowed Slaue,
Sirs, helpe our Vnckle, to conuey him in, *Flouriſh.*
The Trumpets ſhew the Emperour is at hand.

Sound Trumpets. Enter Emperour and Empreſſe, with Tribunes and others.

Sat. What, hath the Firemament more Suns then one?
Luc. What bootes it thee to call thy ſelfe a Sunne?
Mar. Romes Emperour & Nephewe breake the parle
Theſe quarrels muſt be quietly debated,
The Feaſt is ready which the carefull *Titus*,
Hath

Hath ordained to an Honourable end,
For Peace, for Loue, for League, and good to Rome:
Please you therfore draw nie and take your places.
Satur. Marcus we will. *Hoboyes.*

A Table brought in.
Enter Titus like a Cooke, placing the meat on the Table, and Lauinia with a vale ouer her face.

Titus. Welcome my gracious Lord,
Welcome Dread Queene,
Welcome ye Warlike Gothes, welcome *Lucius*,
And welcome all: although the cheere be poore,
'Twill fill your stomacks, please you eat of it.
Sat. Why art thou thus attir'd *Andronicus*?
Tit. Because I would be sure to haue all well,
To entertaine your Highnesse, and your Empresse.
Tam. We are beholding to you good *Andronicus*?
Tit. And if your Highnesse knew my heart, you were:
My Lord the Emperour resolue me this,
Was it well done of rash *Virginius*,
To slay his daughter with his owne right hand,
Because she was enfor'st, stain'd, and deflowr'd?
Satur. It was *Andronicus*.
Tit. Your reason, Mighty Lord?
Sat. Because the Girle, should not suruine her shame,
And by her presence still renew his sorrowes.
Tit. A reason mighty, strong, and effectuall,
A patterne, president, and liuely warrant,
For me (most wretched) to performe the like:
Die, die, *Lauinia*, and thy shame with thee,
And with thy shame, thy Fathers sorrow die.
He kils her.
Sat. What hast done, vnnaturall and vnkinde?
Tit. Kil'd her for whom my teares haue made me blind.
I am as wofull as *Virginius* was,
And haue a thousand times more cause then he.
Sat. What was she rauisht? tell who did the deed,
Tit. Wilt please you eat,
Wilt please your Hignesse feed?
Tam. Why hast thou slaine thine onely Daughter?
Titus. Not I, 'twas *Chiron* and *Demetrius*,
They rauisht her, and cut away her tongue,
And they, 'twas they, that did her all this wrong.
Satu. Go fetch them hither to vs presently.
Tit. Why there they are both, baked in that Pie,
Whereof their Mother dantily hath fed,
Eating the flesh that she herselfe hath bred.
'Tis true, 'tis true, witnesse my kniues sharpe point.
He stabs the Empresse.
Satu. Die franticke wretch, for this accursed deed.
Luc. Can the Sonnes eye, behold his Father bleed?
There's meede for meede, death for a deadly deed.
Mar. You sad fac'd men, people and Sonnes of Rome,
By vprores seuer'd like a flight of Fowle,
Scattred by windes and high tempestuous gusts:
Oh let me teach you how, to knit againe
This scattred Corne, into one mutuall sheafe,
These broken limbs againe into one body.
Goth. Let Rome herselfe be bane vnto herselfe,
And shee whom mightie kingdomes cursie too,
Like a forlorne and desperate castaway,
Doe shamefull execution on her selfe.
But if my frostie signes and chaps of age,
Graue witnesses of true experience,
Cannot induce you to attend my words,
Speake Romes deere friend, as'erst our Auncestor,
When with his solemne tongue he did discourse
To loue-sicke *Didoes* sad attending eare,
The story of that balefull burning night,
When subtilGreekes surpriz'd King *Priams* Troy:
Tell vs what *Sinon* hath bewicht our eares,
Or who hath brought the fatall engine,in,
That giues our Troy, our Rome the ciuill wound.
My heart is not compact of flint nor steele,
Nor can I vtter all our bitter griefe,
But floods of teares will drowne my Oratorie,
And breake my very vttrance, euen in the time
When it should moue you to attend me most,
Lending your kind hand Commiseration.
Heere is a Captaine, let him tell the tale,
Your hearts will throb and weepe to heare him speake.
Luc. This Noble Auditory, be it knowne to you,
That cursed *Chiron* and *Demetrius*
Were they that murdred our Emperours Brother,
And they it were that rauished our Sister,
For their fell faults our Brothers were beheaded,
Our Fathers teares despis'd, and basely cousen'd,
Of that true hand that fought Romes quarrell out,
And sent her enemies vnto the graue.
Lastly, my selfe vnkindly banished,
The gates shut on me, and turn'd weeping out,
To beg reliefe among Romes Enemies,
Who drown'd their enmity in my true teares,
And op'd their armes to imbrace me as a Friend:
And I am turned forth, be it knowne to you,
That haue preseru'd her welfare in my blood,
And from her bosome tooke the Enemies point,
Sheathing the steele in my aduentrous body.
Alas you know, I am no Vaunter I,
My scars can witnesse, dumbe although they are,
That my report is iust and full of truth:
But soft, me thinkes I do digresse too much,
Cyting my worthlesse praise: Oh pardon me,
For when no Friends are by, men praise themselues,
Marc. Now is my turne to speake: Behold this Child,
Of this was *Tamora* deliuered,
The issue of an Irreligious *Moore*,
Chiefe Architect and plotter of these woes,
The Villaine is aliue in *Titus* house,
And as he is, to witnesse this is true.
Now iudge what course had *Titus* to reuenge
These wrongs, vnspeakeable past patience,
Or more then any liuing man could beare.
Now you haue heard the truth, what say you Romaines?
Haue we done ought amisse? shew vs wherein,
And from the place where you behold vs now,
The poore remainder of *Andronici*,
Will hand in hand all headlong cast vs downe,
And on the ragged stones beat forth our braines,
And make a mutuall closure of our house:
Speake Romaines speake, and if you say we shall,
Loe hand in hand, *Lucius* and I will fall.
Emilli. Come come, thou reuerent man of Rome,
And bring our Emperour gently in thy hand,
Lucius our Emperour: for well I know,
The common voyce do cry it shall be so.
Mar. *Lucius*, all haile Romes Royall Emperour,
Goe, goe into old *Titus* sorrowfull house,
And hither hale that misbelieuing *Moore*,
To be adiudg'd some direfull slaughtering death,
As punishment for his most wicked life.
Lucius all haile to Romes gracious Gouernour.

Luc. Thankes gentle Romanes, may I gouerne ſo,
To heale Romes harmes, and wipe away her woe.
But gentle people, giue me ayme a-while,
For Nature puts me to a heauy taske:
Stand all aloofe, but Vnckle draw you neere,
To ſhed obſequious teares vpon this Trunke:
Oh take this warme kiſſe on thy pale cold lips,
Theſe ſorrowfull drops vpon thy bloud-ſlaine face,
The laſt true Duties of thy Noble Sonne.

Mar. Teare for teare, and louing kiſſe for kiſſe,
Thy Brother *Marcus* tenders on thy Lips:
O were the ſumme of theſe that I ſhould pay
Countleſſe, and infinit, yet would I pay them.

Luc. Come hither Boy, come, come, and learne of vs
To melt in ſhowres: thy Grandſire lou'd thee well:
Many a time he danc'd thee on his knee:
Sung thee aſleepe, his Louing Breſt, thy Pillow:
Many a matter hath he told to thee,
Meete, and agreeing with thine Infancie:
In that reſpect then, like a louing Childe,
Shed yet ſome ſmall drops from thy tender Spring,
Becauſe kinde Nature doth require it ſo:
Friends, ſhould aſſociate Friends, in Greefe and Wo.
Bid him farwell, commit him to the Graue,
Do him that kindneſſe, and take leaue of him.

Boy. O Grandſire, Grandſire: euen with all my heart
Would I were Dead, ſo you did Liue againe.
O Lord, I cannot ſpeake to him for weeping,
My teares will choake me, if I ope my mouth.

Romans. You ſad *Andronici*, haue done with woes,
Giue ſentence on this execrable Wretch,
That hath beene breeder of theſe dire euents.

Luc. Set him breſt deepe in earth, and famiſh him:
There let him ſtand, and raue, and cry for foode:
If any one releeues, or pitties him,
For the offence, he dyes. This is our doome:
Some ſtay, to ſee him faſt'ned in the earth.

Aron. O why ſhould wrath be mute, & Fury dumbe?
I am no Baby I, that with baſe Prayers
I ſhould repent the Euils I haue done.
Ten thouſand worſe, then euer yet I did,
Would I performe if I might haue my will:
If one good Deed in all my life I did,
I do repent it from my very Soule.

Lucius. Some louing Friends conuey the Emp. hence,
And giue him buriall in his Fathers graue.
My Father, and *Lauinia*, ſhall forthwith
Be cloſed in our Houſholds Monument:
As for that heynous Tyger *Tamora*,
No Funerall Rite, nor man in mournfull Weeds:]
No mournfull Bell ſhall ring her Buriall:
But throw her foorth to Beaſts and Birds of prey:
Her life was Beaſt-like, and deuoid of pitty,
And being ſo, ſhall haue like want of pitty.
See Iuſtice done on *Aaron* that damn'd Moore,
From whom, our heauy happes had their beginning:
Then afterwards, to Order well the State,
That like Euents, may ne're it Ruinate. *Exeunt omnes.*

FINIS.

THE TRAGEDIE OF ROMEO and IVLIET.

Actus Primus. Scœna Prima.

Enter Sampſon and Gregory, with Swords and Bucklers, of the Houſe of Capulet.

Sampſon.

GRegory: A my word wee'l not carry coales.

Greg. No, for then we ſhould be Colliars.

Samp. I mean, if we be in choller, wee'l draw.

Greg. I, While you liue, draw your necke out o'th Collar.

Samp. I ſtrike quickly, being mou'd.

Greg. But thou art not quickly mou'd to ſtrike.

Samp. A dog of the houſe of *Mountague*, moues me.

Greg. To moue, is to ſtir: and to be valiant, is to ſtand: Therefore, if thou art mou'd, thou runſt away.

Samp. A dogge of that houſe ſhall moue me to ſtand. I will take the wall of any Man or Maid of *Mountagues*.

Greg. That ſhewes thee a weake ſlaue, for the weakeſt goes to the wall.

Samp. True, and therefore women being the weaker Veſſels, are euer thruſt to the wall: therefore I will puſh *Mountagues* men from the wall, and thruſt his Maides to the wall.

Greg. The Quarrell is betweene our Maſters, and vs (their men.

Samp. 'Tis all one, I will ſhew my ſelfe a tyrant: when I haue fought with the men, I will bee ciuill with the Maids, and cut off their heads.

Greg. The heads of the Maids?

Sam. I, the heads of the Maids, or their Maiden-heads, Take it in what ſence thou wilt.

Greg. They muſt take it ſence, that feele it.

Samp. Me they ſhall feele while I am able to ſtand: And 'tis knowne I am a pretty peece of fleſh.

Greg. 'Tis well thou art not Fiſh: If thou had'ſt, thou had'ſt beene poore Iohn. Draw thy Toole, here comes of the Houſe of the *Mountagues*.

Enter two other Seruingmen.

Sam. My naked weapon is out: quarrel, I wil back thee

Gre. How? Turne thy backe, and run.

Sam. Feare me not.

Gre. No marry: I feare thee.

Sam. Let vs take the Law of our ſides: let them begin.

Gr. I wil frown as I paſſe by, & let thẽ take it as they liſt

Sam. Nay, as they dare. I wil bite my Thumb at them, which is a diſgrace to them, if they beare it.

Abra. Do you bite your Thumbe at vs ſir?

Samp. I do bite my Thumbe, ſir.

Abra. Do you bite your Thumb at vs, ſir?

Sam. Is the Law of our ſide, if I ſay I? *Gre.* No.

Sam. No ſir, I do not bite my Thumbe at you ſir: but I bite my Thumbe ſir.

Greg. Do you quarrell ſir?

Abra. Quarrell ſir? no ſir.

Sam. If you do ſir, I am for you, I ſerue as good a man (as you

Abra. No better? *Samp.* Well ſir.

Enter Benuolio.

Gr. Say better: here comes one of my maſters kinſmen.

Samp. Yes, better.

Abra. You Lye.

Samp. Draw if you be men. *Gregory*, remember thy waſhing blow. *They Fight.*

Ben. Part Fooles, put vp your Swords, you know not what you do.

Enter Tibalt.

Tyb. What art thou drawne, among theſe heartleſſe Hindes? Turne thee *Benuolio*, looke vpon thy death.

Ben. I do but keepe the peace, put vp thy Sword,
Or manage it to part theſe men with me.

Tyb. What draw, and talke of peace? I hate the word
As I hate hell, all *Mountagues*, and thee:
Haue at thee Coward. *Fight.*

Enter three or foure Citizens with Clubs.

Offi. Clubs, Bils, and Partiſons, ſtrike, beat them down
Downe with the *Capulets*, downe with the *Mountagues*.

Enter old Capulet in his Gowne, and his wife.

Cap. What noiſe is this? Giue me my long Sword ho.

Wife. A crutch, a crutch: why call you for a Sword?

Cap. My Sword I ſay: Old *Mountague* is come,
And flouriſhes his Blade in ſpight of me.

Enter old Mountague, & his wife.

Moun. Thou villaine *Capulet*. Hold me not, let me go

2. Wife. Thou ſhalt not ſtir a foote to ſeeke a Foe.

Enter Prince Eskales, with his Traine.

Prince. Rebellious Subiects, Enemies to peace,
Prophaners of this Neighbor-ſtained Steele,
Will they not heare? What hoe, you Men, you Beaſts,
That quench the fire of your pernitious Rage,
With purple Fountaines iſſuing from your Veines:
On paine of Torture, from thoſe bloody hands
Throw your miſtemper'd Weapons to the ground,
And heare the Sentence of your moued Prince.
Three ciuill Broyles, bred of an Ayery word,
By thee old *Capulet* and *Mountague*,
Haue thrice diſturb'd the quiet of our ſtreets,
And made *Verona*'s ancient Citizens
Caſt by their Graue beſeeming Ornaments,
To wield old Partizans, in hands as old,

Cankred with peace, to part your Cankred hate,
If euer you disturbe our streets againe,
Your liues shall pay the forfeit of the peace.
For this time all the rest depart away:
You *Capulet* shall goe along with me,
And *Mountague* come you this afternoone,
To know our Fathers pleasure in this case:
To old Free-towne, our common iudgement place:
Once more on paine of death, all men depart. *Exeunt.*

Moun. Who set this auncient quarrell new abroach?
Speake Nephew, were you by, when it began:

Ben. Heere were the seruants of your aduersarie,
And yours close fighting ere I did approach,
I drew to part them, in the instant came
The fiery *Tibalt*, with his sword prepar'd,
Which as he breath'd defiance to my eares,
He swong about his head, and cut the windes,
Who nothing hurt withall, hist him in scorne.
While we were enterchanging thrusts and blowes,
Came more and more, and fought on part and part,
Till the Prince came, who parted either part.

Wife. O where is *Romeo*, saw you him to day?
Right glad am I, he was not at this fray.

Ben. Madam, an houre before the worshipt Sun
Peer'd forth the golden window of the East,
A troubled mind draue me to walke abroad,
Where vnderneath the groue of Sycamour,
That West-ward rooteth from this City side:
So earely walking did I see your Sonne:
Towards him I made, but he was ware of me,
And stole into the couert of the wood,
I measuring his affections by my owne,
Which then most sought, wher most might not be found:
Being one too many by my weary selfe,
Pursued my Honour, not pursuing his
And gladly shunn'd, who gladly fled from me.

Mount. Many a morning hath he there beene seene,
With teares augmenting the fresh mornings deaw,
Adding to cloudes, more cloudes with his deepe sighes,
But all so soone as the all-cheering Sunne,
Should in the farthest East begin to draw
The shadie Curtaines from *Auroras* bed,
Away from light steales home my heauy Sonne,
And priuate in his Chamber pennes himselfe,
Shuts vp his windowes, lockes faire day-light out,
And makes himselfe an artificiall night:
Blacke and portendous must this humour proue,
Vnlesse good counsell may the cause remoue.

Ben. My Noble Vncle doe you know the cause?

Moun. I neither know it, nor can learne of him.

Ben. Haue you importun'd him by any meanes?

Moun. Both by my selfe and many others Friends,
But he his owne affections counseller,
Is to himselfe (I will not say how true)
But to himselfe so secret and so close,
So farre from sounding and discouery,
As is the bud bit with an enuious worme,
Ere he can spread his sweete leaues to the ayre,
Or dedicate his beauty to the same.
Could we but learne from whence his sorrowes grow,
We would as willingly giue cure, as know.

Enter Romeo.

Be.n See where he comes, so please you step aside,
Ile know his greeuance, or be much denide.

Moun. I would thou wert so happy by thy stay,
To heare true shrift. Come Madam let's away. *Exeunt.*

Ben. Good morrow Cousin.

Rom. Is the day so young?

Ben. But new strooke nine.

Rom. Aye me, sad houres seeme long:
Was that my Father that went henec so fast?

Ben. It was: what sadnes lengthens *Romeo's* houres?

Ro. Not hauing that, which hauing, makes them short

Ben. In loue.

Romeo. Out.

Ben. Of loue.

Rom. Out of her fauour where I am in loue.

Ben. Alas that loue so gentle in his view,
Should be so tyrannous and rough in proofe.

Rom. Alas that loue, whose view is muffled still,
Should without eyes, see path-wayes to his will:
Where shall we dine? O me: what fray was heere?
Yet tell me not, for I haue heard it all:
Heere's much to do with hate, but more with loue:
Why then, O brawling loue, O louing hate,
O any thing, of nothing first created:
O heauie lightnesse, serious vanity,
Mishapen Chaos of welseeing formes,
Feather of lead, bright smoake, cold fire, sicke health,
Still waking sleepe, that is not what it is:
This loue feele I, that feele no loue in this.
Doest thou not laugh?

Ben. No Coze, I rather weepe.

Rom. Good heart, at what?

Ben. At thy good hearts oppresion.

Rom. Why such is loues transg ression.
Griefes of mine owne lie heauie in my breast,
Which thou wilt propagate to haue it preast
With more of thine, this loue that thou hast showne,
Doth adde more griefe, to too much of mine owne.
Loue, is a smoake made with the fume of sighes,
Being purg'd, a fire sparkling in Louers eyes,
Being vext, a Sea nourisht with louing teares,
What is it else? a madnesse, most discreet,
A choking gall, and a preseruing sweet:
Farewell my Coze.

Ben. Soft I will goe along.
And if you leaue me so, you do me wrong.

Rom. Tut I haue lost my selfe, I am not here,
This is not *Romeo*, hee's some other where.

Ben. Tell me in sadnesse, who is that you loue?

Rom. What shall I grone and tell thee?

Ben. Grone, why no: but sadly tell me who.

Rom. A sicke man in sadnesse makes his will:
A word ill vrg'd to one that is so ill:
In sadnesse Cozin, I do loue a woman.

Ben. I aym'd so neare, when I suppos'd you lou'd.

Rom. A right good marke man, and shee's faire I loue

Ben. A right faire marke, faire Coze, is soonest hit.

Rom. Well in that hit you misse, sheel not be hit
With Cupids arrow, she hath *Dians* wit:
And in strong proofe of chastity well arm'd:
From loues weake childish Bow, she liues vncharm'd.
Shee will not stay the siege of louing tearmes,
Nor bid th'incounter of assailing eyes.
Nor open her lap to Sainct-seducing Gold:
O she is rich in beautie, onely poore,
That when she dies, with beautie dies her store.

Ben. Then she hath sworne, that she will still liue chast?

Rom. She hath, and in that sparing make huge wast?
For beauty steru'd with her seuerity,
Cuts beauty off from all posteritie.

She

She is too faire, too wiſewi: ſely too faire,
To merit bliſſe by making me diſpaire:
She hath forſworne to loue, and in that vow
Do I liue dead, that liue to tell it now.

Ben. Be rul'd by me, forget to thinke of her.

Rom. O teach me how I ſhould forget to thinke.

Ben. By giuing liberty vnto thine eyes,
Examine other beauties,

Ro. 'Tis the way to cal hers (exquiſit) in queſtion more,
Theſe happy maskes that kiſſe faire Ladies browes,
Being blacke, puts vs in mind they hide the faire:
He that is ſtrooken blind, cannot forget
The precious treaſure of his eye-ſight loſt:
Shew me a Miſtreſſe that is paſſing faire,
What doth her beauty ſerue but as a note,
Where I may read who paſt that paſſing faire.
Farewell thou can'ſt not teach me to forget,

Ben. Ile pay that doctrine, or elſe die in debt. *Exeunt*

Enter Capulet, Countie Paris, and the Clowne.

Capu. *Mountague* is bound as well as I,
In penalty alike, and 'tis not hard I thinke,
For men ſo old as wee, to keepe the peace.

Par. Of Honourable reckoning are you both,
And pittie 'tis you liu'd at ods ſo long:
But now my Lord, what ſay you to my ſute?

Capu. But ſaying ore what I haue ſaid before,
My Child is yet a ſtranger in the world,
Shee hath not ſeene the change of fourteene yeares,
Let two more Summers wither in their pride,
Ere we may thinke her ripe to be a Bride.

Pari. Younger then ſhe, are happy mothers made.

Capu. And too ſoone mar'd are thoſe ſo early made:
Earth hath ſwallowed all my hopes but ſhe,
Shee's the hopefull Lady of my earth:
But wooe her gentle *Paris*, get her heart,
My will to her conſent, is but a part,
And ſhee agree, within her ſcope of choiſe,
Lyes my conſent, and faire according voice:
This night I hold an old accuſtom'd Feaſt,
Whereto I haue inuited many a Gueſt,
Such as I loue, and you among the ſtore,
One more, moſt welcome makes my number more:
At my poore houſe, looke to behold this night,
Earth-treading ſtarres, that make darke heauen light,
Such comfort as do luſty young men feele,
When well apparrel'd Aprill on the heele
Of limping Winter treads, euen ſuch delight
Among freſh Fennell buds ſhall you this night
Inherit at my houſe: heare all, all ſee:
And like her moſt, whoſe merit moſt ſhall be:
Which one more veiw, of many, mine being one,
May ſtand in number, though in reckning none.
Come, goe with me: goe ſirrah trudge about,
Through faire *Verona*, find thoſe perſons out,
Whoſe names are written there, and to them ſay,
My houſe and welcome, on their pleaſure ſtay. *Exit.*

Ser. Find them out whoſe names are written. Heere it is written, that the Shoo-maker ſhould meddle with his Yard, and the Tayler with his Laſt, the Fiſher with his Penſill, and the Painter with his Nets. But I am ſent to find thoſe perſons whoſe names are writ, & can neuer find what names the writing perſon hath here writ (I muſt to the learned) in good time.

Enter Benuolio, and Romeo.

Ben. Tut man, one fire burnes out anothers burning,
One paine is leſned by anothers anguiſh:
Turne giddie, and be holpe by backward turning:
One deſparate greefe, cures with anothers lauguiſh:
Take thou ſome new infection to the eye,
And the rank poyſon of the old wil die.

Rom. Your Plantan leafe is excellent for that.

Ben. For what I pray thee?

Rom. For your broken ſhin.

Ben. Why *Romeo* art thou mad?

Rom. Not mad, but bound more then a mad man is:
Shut vp in priſon, kept without my foode,
Whipt and tormented: and Godden good fellow,

Ser. Godgigoden, I pray ſir can you read?

Rom. I mine owne fortune in my miſerie.

Ser. Perhaps you haue learn'd it without booke:
But I pray can you read any thing you ſee?

Rom. I, if I know the Letters and the Language.

Ser. Ye ſay honeſtly, reſt you merry.

Rom. Stay fellow, I can read.

He reades the Letter.

Seigneur Martino, and his wife and daughter: County Anſelme and his beautious ſiſters: the Lady widdow of Vtruuio, Seigneur Placentio, and his louely Neeces: Mercutio and his brother Valentine: mine vncle Capulet his wife and daughters: my faire Neece Roſaline, Liuia, Seigneur Valentio, & his Coſen Tybalt: Lucio and the liuely Helena.

A faire aſſembly, whither ſhould they come?

Ser. Vp.

Rom. Whither? to ſupper?

Ser. To our houſe.

Rom. Whoſe houſe?

Ser. My Maiſters.

Rom. Indeed I ſhould haue askt you that before.

Ser. Now Ile tell you without asking. My maiſter is the great rich *Capulet*, and if you be not of the houſe of *Mountagues* I pray come and cruſh a cup of wine. Reſt you merry. *Exit.*

Ben. At this ſame auncient Feaſt of *Capulets*
Sups the faire *Roſaline*, whom thou ſo loues:
With all the admired Beauties of *Verona*,
Go thither and with vnattainted eye,
Compare her face with ſome that I ſhall ſhow,
And I will make thee thinke thy Swan a Crow.

Rom. When the deuout religion of mine eye
Maintaines ſuch falſhood, then turne teares to fire:
And theſe who often drown'd could neuer die,
Tranſparent Heretiques be burnt for liers.
One fairer then my loue: the all-ſeeing Sun
Nere ſaw her match, ſince firſt the world begun.

Ben. Tut, you ſaw her faire, none elſe being by,
Herſelfe poyſ'd with herſelfe in either eye:
But in that Chriſtall ſcales let there be waid,
Your Ladies loue againſt ſome other Maid
That I will ſhow you, ſhining at this Feaſt,
And ſhe ſhew ſcant ſhell, well, that now ſhewes beſt.

Rom. Ile goe along, no ſuch ſight to be ſhowne,
But to reioyce in ſplendor of mine owne.

Enter Capulets Wife and Nurſe.

Wife Nurſe wher's my daughter? call her forth to me.

Nurſe. Now by my Maidenhead, at twelue yeare old
I bad her come, what Lamb: what Ladi-bird, God forbid,
Where's this Girle? what *Iuliet*?

Enter Iuliet.

Iuliet. How now, who calls?

Nur. Your Mother.

Iuliet. Madam I am heere, what is your will?

Wife. This is the matter: Nurſe giue leaue awhile, we muſt

muſt talke in ſecret. Nurſe come backe againe, I haue remembred me, thou'ſe heare our counſell. Thou knoweſt my daughter's of a prety age.

Nurſe. Faith I can tell her age vnto an houre.

Wife. Shee's not fourteene.

Nurſe. Ile lay fourteene of my teeth,
And yet to my teene be it ſpoken,
I haue but foure, ſhee's not fourteene.
How long is it now to *Lammas* tide?

Wife. A fortnight and odde dayes.

Nurſe. Euen or odde, of all daies in the yeare come *Lammas* Eue at night ſhall ſhe be fourteene. *Suſan* & ſhe, God reſt all Chriſtian ſoules, were of an age. Well *Suſan* is with God, ſhe was too good for me. But as I ſaid, on *Lamas* Eue at night ſhall ſhe be fourteene, that ſhall ſhe marie, I remember it well. 'Tis ſince the Earth-quake now eleuen yeares, and ſhe was wean'd I neuer ſhall forget it, of all the daies of the yeare, vpon that day: for I had then laid Worme-wood to my Dug ſitting in the Sunne vnder the Douehouſe wall, my Lord and you were then at *Mantua*, nay I doe beare a braine. But as I ſaid, when it did taſt the Worme-wood on the nipple of my Dugge, and felt it bitter, pretty foole, to ſee it teachie, and fall out with the Dugge, Shake quoth the Doue-houſe, 'twas no neede I trow to bid mee trudge: and ſince that time it is a eleuen yeares, for then ſhe could ſtand alone, nay bi'th' roode ſhe could haue runne, & wadled all about: for euen the day before ſhe broke her brow, & then my Husband God be with his ſoule, a was a merrie man, tooke vp the Child, yea quoth hee, doeſt thou fall vpon thy face? thou wilt fall backeward when thou haſt more wit, wilt thou not *Iule*? And by my holy-dam, the pretty wretch lefte crying, & ſaid I: to ſee now how a Ieſt ſhall come about. I warrant, & I ſhall liue a thouſand yeares, I neuer ſhould forget it: wilt thou not *Iulet* quoth he? and pretty foole it ſtinted, and ſaid I.

Old La. Inough of this, I pray thee hold thy peace.

Nurſe. Yes Madam, yet I cannot chuſe but laugh, to thinke it ſhould leaue crying, & ſay I: and yet I warrant it had vpon it brow, a bumpe as big as a young Cockrels ſtone? A perilous knock, and it cryed bitterly. Yea quoth my husband, fall'ſt vpon thy face, thou wilt fall backward when thou commeſt to age: wilt thou not *Iule*? It ſtinted: and ſaid I.

Iule. And ſtint thou too, I pray thee *Nurſe*, ſay I.

Nur. Peace I haue done: God marke thee too his grace thou waſt the prettieſt Babe that ere I nurſt, and I might liue to ſee thee married once, I haue my wiſh.

Old La. Marry that marry is the very theame
I came to talke of, tell me daughter *Iuliet*,
How ſtands your diſpoſition to be Married?

Iuli. It is an houre that I dreame not of.

Nur. An houre, were not I thine onely Nurſe, I would ſay thou had'ſt ſuckt wiſedome from thy teat.

Old La. Well thinke of marriage now, yonger then you
Heere in *Verona*, Ladies of eſteeme,
Are made already Mothers. By my count
I was your Mother, much vpon theſe yeares
That you are now a Maide, thus then in briefe:
The valiant *Paris* ſeekes you for his loue.

Nurſe. A man young Lady, Lady, ſuch a man as all the world. Why hee's a man of waxe.

Old La. *Veronas* Summer hath not ſuch a flower.

Nurſe. Nay hee's a flower, infaith a very flower.

Old La: What ſay you, can you loue the Gentleman?
This night you ſhall behold him at our Feaſt,
Read ore the volume of young *Paris* face,
And find delight, writ there with Beauties pen:
Examine euery ſeuerall liniament,
And ſee how one another lends content:
And what obſcur'd in this faire volume lies,
Find written in the Margent of his eyes.
This precious Booke of Loue, this vnbound Louer,
To Beautifie him, onely lacks a Couer.
The fiſh liues in the Sea, and 'tis much pride
For faire without, the faire within to hide:
That Booke in manies eyes doth ſhare the glorie,
That in Gold claſpes, Lockes in the Golden ſtorie:
So ſhall you ſhare all that he doth poſſeſſe,
By hauing him, making your ſelfe no leſſe.

Nurſe. No leſſe, nay bigger: women grow by men.

Old La. Speake briefly, can you like of *Paris* loue?

Iuli. Ile looke to like, if looking liking moue.
But no more deepe will I endart mine eye,
Then your conſent giues ſtrength to make flye.

Enter a Seruing man.

Ser. Madam, the gueſts are come, ſupper ſeru'd vp, you cal'd, my young Lady askt for, the Nurſe cur'ſt in the Pantery, and euery thing in extremitie: I muſt hence to wait, I beſeech you follow ſtraight. *Exit.*

Mo. We follow thee, *Iuliet*, the Countie ſtaies.

Nurſe. Goe Gyrle, ſeeke happie nights to happy daies. *Exeunt.*

Enter Romeo, Mercutio, Benuolio, with fiue or ſixe other Maskers, Torch-bearers.

Rom. What ſhall this ſpeeh be ſpoke for our excuſe?
Or ſhall we on without Apologie?

Ben. The date is out of ſuch prolixitie,
Weele haue no *Cupid*, hood winkt with a skarfe,
Bearing a Tartars painted Bow of lath,
Skaring the Ladies like a Crow-keeper.
But let them meaſure vs by what they will.
Weele meaſure them a Meaſure, and be gone.

Rom. Giue me a Torch, I am not for this ambling.
Being but heauy I will beare the light.

Mer. Nay gentle *Romeo*, we muſt haue you dance.

Rom. Not I beleeue me, you haue dancing ſhooes
With nimble ſoles, I haue a ſoale of Lead
So ſtakes me to the ground, I cannot moue.

Mer. You are a Louer, borrow *Cupids* wings,
And ſoare with them aboue a common bound.

Rom. I am too ſore enpearced with his ſhaft,
To ſoare with his light feathers, and to bound:
I cannot bound a pitch aboue dull woe,
Vnder loues heauy burthen doe I ſinke.

Hora. And to ſinke in it ſhould you burthen loue,
Too great oppreſſion for a tender thing.

Rom. Is loue a tender thing? it is too rough,
Too rude, too boyſterous, and it pricks like thorne.

Mer. If loue be rough with you, be rough with loue,
Pricke loue for pricking, and you beat loue downe,
Giue me a Caſe to put my viſage in,
A Viſor for a Viſor, what care I
What curious eye doth quote deformities:
Here are the Beetle-browes ſhall bluſh for me.

Ben. Come knocke and enter, and no ſooner in,
But euery man betake him to his legs.

Rom. A Torch for me, let wantons light of heart
Tickle the ſenceleſſe ruſhes with their heeles:
For I am prouerb'd with a Grandſier Phraſe,
Ile be a Candle-holder and looke on,
The game was nere ſo faire, and I am done.

Mer. Tut,

Mer. Tut, duns the Mouse, the Constables owne word,
If thou art dun, weele draw thee from the mire.
Or saue your reuerence loue, wherein thou stickest
Vp to the eares, come we burne day-light ho.
Rom. Nay that's not so.
Mer. I meane sir I delay,
We wast our lights in vaine, lights, lights, by day;
Take our good meaning, for our Iudgement sits
Fiue times in that, ere once in our fine wits.
Rom. And we meane well in going to this Maske,
But 'tis no wit to go.
Mer. Why may one aske?
Rom. I dreampt a dreame to night.
Mer, And so did I.
Rom. Well what was yours?
Mer. That dreamers often lye.
Ro. In bed a sleepe while they do dreame things true.
Mer. O then I see Queene Mab hath beene with you: She is the Fairies Midwife, & she comes in shape no bigger then Agat-stone, on the fore-finger of an Alderman, drawne with a teeme of little Atomies, ouer mens noses as they lie asleepe: her Waggon Spokes made of long Spinners legs: the Couer of the wings of Grashoppers, her Traces of, the smallest Spiders web, her coullers of the Moonshines watry Beames, her Whip of Crickets bone, the Lash of Philome, her Waggoner, a small gray-coated Gnat, not halfe so bigge as a round little Worme, prickt from the Lazie-finger of a man. Her Chariot is an emptie Haselnut, made by the Ioyner Squirrel or old Grub, time out a mind, the Faries Coach-makers: & in this state she gallops night by night, through Louers braines: and then they dreame of Loue. On Courtiers knees, that dreame on Cursies strait: ore Lawyers fingers, who strait dreamt on Fees, ore Ladies lips, who strait on kisses dreame, which oft the angry Mab with blisters plagues, because their breath with Sweet meats tainted are. Sometime she gallops ore a Courtiers nose, & then dreames he of smelling out a sute: & somtime comes she with Tith pigs tale, tickling a Parsons nose as a lies asleepe, then he dreames of another Benefice. Sometime she driueth ore a Souldiers necke, & then dreames he of cutting Forraine throats, of Breaches, Ambuscados, Spanish Blades: Of Healths fiue Fadome deepe, and then anon drums in his eares, at which he startes and wakes; and being thus frighted, sweares a prayer or two & sleepes againe: this is that very Mab that plats the manes of Horses in the night: & bakes the Elklocks in foule sluttish haires, which once vntangled, much misfortune bodes,
This is the hag, when Maides lie on their backs,
That presses them, and learnes them first to beare,
Making them women of good carriage:
This is she.
Rom. Peace, peace, *Mercutio* peace,
Thou talk'st of nothing.
Mer. True, I talke of dreames:
Which are the children of an idle braine,
Begot of nothing, but vaine phantasie,
Which is as thin of substance as the ayre,
And more inconstant then the wind, who wooes
Euen now the frozen bosome of the North:
And being anger'd, puffes away from thence,
Turning his side to the dew dropping South.
Ben. This wind you talke of blowes vs from our selues,
Supper is done, and we shall come too late.
Rom. I feare too early, for my mind misgiues,
Some consequence yet hanging in the starres,
Shall bitterly begin his fearefull date
With this nights reuels, and expire the tearme
Of a despised life clos'd in my brest:
By some vile forfeit of vntimely death.
But he that hath the stirrage of my course,
Direct my sute: on lustie Gentlemen.
Ben. Strike Drum.
They march about the Stage, and Seruingmen come forth with their napkins.
Enter Seruant.
Ser. Where's *Potpan*, that he helpes not to take away? He shift a Trencher? he scrape a Trencher?
1. When good manners, shall lie in one or two mens hands, and they vnwasht too, 'tis a foule thing.
Ser. Away with the Ioynstooles, remoue the Court-cubbord, looke to the Plate: good thou, saue mee a piece of Marchpane, and as thou louest me, let the Porter let in *Susan Grindstone*, and *Nell*, *Anthonie* and *Potpan*.
2. I Boy readie.
Ser. You are lookt for, and cal'd for, askt for, & sought for, in the great Chamber.
1 We cannot be here and there too, chearly Boyes,
Be brisk awhile, and the longer liuer take all.
Exeunt.
Enter all the Guests and Gentlewomen to the Maskers.
1. *Capu.* Welcome Gentlemen,
Ladies that haue their toes
Vnplagu'd with Cornes, will walke about with you:
Ah my Mistresses, which of you all
Will now deny to dance? She that makes dainty,
She Ile sweare hath Cornes: am I come neare ye now?
Welcome Gentlemen, I haue seene the day
That I haue worne a Visor, and could tell
A whispering tale in a faire Ladies eare:
Such as would please: 'tis gone, 'tis gone, 'tis gone,
You are welcome Gentlemen, come Musitians play:
Musicke plaies: and the dance.
A Hall, Hall, giue roome, and foote it Girles,
More light you knaues, and turne the Tables vp:
And quench the fire, the Roome is growne too hot.
Ah sirrah, this vnlookt for sport comes well:
Nay sit, nay sit, good Cozin *Capulet*,
For you and I are past our dauncing daies:
How long 'ist now since last your selfe and I
Were in a Maske?
2. *Capu.* Berlady thirty yeares.
1. *Capu.* What man: 'tis not so much, 'tis not so much,
'Tis since the Nuptiall of *Lucentio*,
Come Pentycost as quickely as it will,
Some fiue and twenty yeares, and then we Maskt.
2. *Cap.* 'Tis more, 'tis more, his Sonne is elder sir:
His Sonne is thirty.
3. *Cap.* Will you tell me that?
His Sonne was but a Ward two yeares agoe.
Rom. What Ladie is that which doth inrich the hand
Of yonder Knight?
Ser. I know not sir.
Rom. O she doth teach the Torches to burne bright:
It seemes she hangs vpon the cheeke of night,
As a rich Iewel in an Æthiops eare:
Beauty too rich for vse, for earth too deare:
So shewes a Snowy Doue trooping with Crowes,
As yonder Lady ore her fellowes showes;
The measure done, Ile watch her place of stand,
And touching hers, make blessed my rude hand.
Did

Did my heart loue till now, forſweare it ſight,
For I neuer ſaw true Beauty till this night.
Tib. This by his voice, ſhould be a *Mountague.*
Fetch me my Rapier Boy, what dares the ſlaue
Come hither couer'd with an antique face,
To fleere and ſcorne at our Solemnitie?
Now by the ſtocke and Honour of my kin,
To ſtrike him dead I hold it not a ſin.
Cap. Why how now kinſman,
Wherefore ſtorme you ſo?
Tib. Vncle this is a *Mountague*, our foe:
A Villaine that is hither come in ſpight,
To ſcorne at our Solemnitie this night.
Cap. Young *Romeo* is it?
Tib. 'Tis he, that Villaine *Romeo.*
Cap. Content thee gentle Coz, let him alone,
A beares him like a portly Gentleman:
And to ſay truth, *Verona* brags of him,
To be a vertuous and well gouern'd youth:
I would not for the wealth of all the towne,
Here in my houſe do him diſparagement:
Therfore be patient, take no note of him,
It is my will, the which if thou reſpect,
Shew a faire preſence, and put off theſe frownes,
An ill beſeeming ſemblance for a Feaſt.
Tib. It fits when ſuch a Villaine is a gueſt,
Ile not endure him.
Cap. He ſhall be endu'rd.
What goodman boy, I ſay he ſhall, go too,
Am I the Maiſter here or you? go too,
Youle not endure him, God ſhall mend my ſoule,
Youle make a Mutinie among the Gueſts:
You will ſet cocke a hoope, youle be the man.
Tib. Why Vncle, 'tis a ſhame.
Cap. Go too, go too,
You are a ſawcy Boy, 'iſt ſo indeed?
This tricke may chance to ſcath you, I know what,
You muſt contrary me, marry 'tis time.
Well ſaid my hearts, you are a Princox, goe,
Be quiet, or more light, more light for ſhame,
Ile make you quiet. What, chearely my hearts.
Tib. Patience perforce, with wilfull choler meeting,
Makes my fleſh tremble in their different greeting:
I will withdraw, but this intruſion ſhall
Now ſeeming ſweet, conuert to bitter gall. *Exit.*
Rom. If I prophane wirh my vnworthieſt hand,
This holy ſhrine, the gentle ſin is this,
My lips to bluſhing Pilgrims did ready ſtand,
To ſmooth that rough touch, with a tender kiſſe.
Iul. Good Pilgrime,
You do wrong your hand too much.
Which mannerly deuotion ſhewes in this,
For Saints haue hands, that Pilgrims hands do tuch,
And palme to palme, is holy Palmers kiſſe.
Rom. Haue not Saints lips, and holy Palmers too?
Iul. I Pilgrim, lips that they muſt vſe in prayer.
Rom. O then deare Saint, let lips do what hands do,
They pray (grant thou) leaſt faith turne to diſpaire.
Iul. Saints do not moue,
Though grant for prayers ſake.
Rom. Then moue not while my prayers effect I take:
Thus from my lips, by thine my ſin is purg'd.
Iul. Then haue my lips the ſin that they haue tooke.
Rom. Sin from my lips? O treſpaſſe ſweetly vrg'd:
Giue me my ſin againe.
Iul. You kiſſe by'th'booke.
Nur. Madam your Mother craues a word with you.
Rom. What is her Mother?
Nurſ. Marrie Batcheler,
Her Mother is the Lady of the houſe,
And a good Lady, and a wiſe, and Vertuous,
I Nur'ſt her Daughter that you talkt withall:
I tell you, he that can lay hold of her,
Shall haue the chincks.
Rom. Is ſhe a *Capulet*?
O deare account! My life is my foes debt.
Ben. Away, be gone, the ſport is at the beſt.
Rom. I ſo I feare, the more is my vnreſt.
Cap. Nay Gentlemen prepare not to be gone,
We haue a trifling fooliſh Banquet towards:
Is it e'ne ſo? why then I thanke you all.
I thanke you honeſt Gentlemen, good night:
More Torches here: come on, then let's to bed.
Ah ſirrah, by my faie it waxes late,
Ile to my reſt.
Iuli. Come hither Nurſe,
What is yond Gentleman:
Nur. The Sonne and Heire of old *Tyberio.*
Iuli. What's he that now is going out of doore?
Nur. Marrie that I thinke be young *Petruchio.*
Iul. What's he that follows here that would not dance?
Nur. I know not.
Iul. Go aske his name: if he be married,
My graue is like to be my wedded bed.
Nur. His name is *Romeo*, and a *Mountague*,
The onely Sonne of your great Enemie.
Iul. My onely Loue ſprung from my onely hate,
Too early ſeene, vnknowne, and knowne too late,
Prodigious birth of Loue it is to me,
That I muſt loue a loathed Enemie.
Nur. What's this? whats this?
Iul. A rime, I learne euen now
Of one I dan'ſt withall.
One cals within, Iuliet.
Nur. Anon, anon:
Come let's away, the ſtrangers all are gone.
Exeunt.

Chorus.

Now old deſire doth in his death bed lie,
And yong affection gapes to be his Heire,
That faire, for which Loue gron'd for and would die,
With tender *Iuliet* matcht, is now not faire.
Now *Romeo* is beloued, and Loues againe,
A like bewitched by the charme of lookes:
But to his foe ſuppos'd he muſt complaine,
And ſhe ſteale Loues ſweet bait from fearefull hookes:
Being held a foe, he may not haue acceſſe
To breath ſuch vowes as Louers vſe to ſweare,
And ſhe as much in Loue, her meanes much leſſe,
To meete her new Beloued any where:
But paſſion lends them Power, time, meanes to meete,
Temp'ring extremities with extreame ſweete.

Enter Romeo alone.

Rom. Can I goe forward when my heart is here?
Turne backe dull earth, and find thy Center out.

Enter Benuolio, with Mercutio.

Ben. *Romeo*, my Cozen *Romeo*, *Romeo.*
Merc. He is wiſe,
And on my life hath ſtolne him home to bed.
Ben. He ran this way and leapt this Orchard wall.
Call good *Mercutio*:
Nay, Ile coniure too.

Mer.

Mer. *Romeo*, Humours, Madman, Paſſion, Louer,
Appeare thou in the likeneſſe of a ſigh,
Speake but one rime, and I am ſatisfied:
Cry me but ay me, Prouant, but Loue and day,
Speake to my goſhip *Venus* one faire word,
One Nickname for her purblind Sonne and her,
Young *Abraham Cupid* he that ſhot ſo true,
When King *Cophetua* lou'd the begger Maid,
He heareth not, he ſtirreth not, he mouethn ot,
The Ape is dead, I muſt coniure him,
I coniure thee by *Roſalines* bright eyes,
By her High forehead, and her Scarlet lip,
By her Fine foote, Straight leg, and Quiuering thigh,
And the Demeanes, that there Adiacent lie,
That in thy likeneſſe thou appeare to vs.
Ben. And if he heare thee thou wilt anger him.
Mer. This cannot anger him, t'would anger him
To raiſe a ſpirit in his Miſtreſſe circle,
Of ſome ſtrange nature, letting it ſtand
Till ſhe had laid it, and coniured it downe,
That were ſome ſpight.
My inuocation is faire and honeſt, & in his Miſtris name,
I coniure onely but to raiſe vp him.
Ben. Come, he hath hid himſelfe among theſe Trees
To be conſorted with the Humerous night:
Blind is his Loue, and beſt befits the darke.
Mer. If Loue be blind, Loue cannot hit the marke,
Now will he ſit vnder a Medler tree,
And wiſh his Miſtreſſe were that kind of Fruite,
As Maides call Medlers when they laugh alone,
O *Romeo* that ſhe were, O that ſhe were
An open, or thou a Poprin Peare,
Romeo goodnight, Ile to my Truckle bed,
This Field-bed is to cold for me to ſleepe,
Come ſhall we go?
Ben. Go then, for 'tis in vaine to ſeeke him here
That meanes not to be found. *Exeunt.*
Rom. He ieaſts at Scarres that neuer felt a wound,
But ſoft, what light through yonder window breaks?
It is the Eaſt, and *Iuliet* is the Sunne,
Ariſe faire Sun and kill the enuious Moone,
Who is already ſicke and pale with griefe,
That thou her Maid art far more faire then ſhe:
Be not her Maid ſince ſhe is enuious,
Her Veſtal liuery is but ſicke and greene,
And none but fooles do weare it, caſt it off:
It is my Lady, O it is my Loue, O that ſhe knew ſhe were,
She ſpeakes, yet ſhe ſayes nothing, what of that?
Her eye diſcourſes, I will anſwere it:
I am too bold 'tis not to me ſhe ſpeakes:
Two of the faireſt ſtarres in all the Heauen,
Hauing ſome buſineſſe do entreat her eyes,
To twinckle in their Spheres till they returne.
What if her eyes were there, they in her head,
The brightneſſe of her cheeke would ſhame thoſe ſtarres,
As day-light doth a Lampe, her eye in heauen,
Would through the ayrie Region ſtreame ſo bright,
That Birds would ſing, and thinke it were not night:
See how ſhe leanes her cheeke vpon her hand.
O that I were a Gloue vpon that hand,
That I might touch that cheeke.
Iul. Ay me.
Rom. She ſpeakes.
Oh ſpeake againe bright Angell, for thou art
As glorious to this night being ore my head,
As is a winged meſſenger of heauen,
Vnto the white vpturned wondring eyes
Of mortalls that fall backe to gaze on him,
When he beſtrides the lazie puffing Cloudes,
And ſailes vpon the boſome of the ayre.
Iul. O *Romeo, Romeo*, wherefore art thou *Romeo*?
Denie thy Father and refuſe thy name:
Or if thou wilt not, be but ſworne my Loue,
And Ile no longer be a *Capulet*.
Rom. Shall I heare more, or ſhall I ſpeake at this?
Iu. 'Tis but thy name that is my Enemy:
Thou art thy ſelfe, though not a *Mountague*,
What's *Mountague*? it is nor hand nor foote,
Nor arme, nor face, O be ſome other name
Belonging to a man.
What? in a names that which we call a Roſe,
By any other word would ſmell as ſweete,
So *Romeo* would, were he not *Romeo* cal'd,
Retaine that deare perfection which he owes,
Without that title *Romeo*, doffe thy name,
And for thy name which is no part of thee,
Take all my ſelfe.
Rom. I take thee at thy word:
Call me but Loue, and Ile be new baptiz'd,
Hence foorth I neuer will be *Romeo*.
Iuli. What man art thou, that thus beſcreen'd in night
So ſtumbleſt on my counſell?
Rom. By a name,
I know not how to tell thee who I am:
My name deare Saint, is hatefull to my ſelfe,
Becauſe it is an Enemy to thee,
Had I it written, I would teare the word.
Iuli. My eares haue yet not drunke a hundred words
Of thy tongues vttering, yet I know the ſound.
Art thou not *Romeo*, and a *Montague*?
Rom. Neither faire Maid, if either thee diſlike.
Iul. How cam'ſt thou hither.
Tell me, and wherefore?
The Orchard walls are high, and hard to climbe,
And the place death, conſidering who thou art,
If any of my kinſmen find thee here,
Rom. With Loues light wings
Did I ore-perch theſe Walls,
For ſtony limits cannot hold Loue out,
And what Loue can do, that dares Loue attempt:
Therefore thy kinſmen are no ſtop to me.
Iul. If they do ſee thee, they will murther thee.
Rom. Alacke there lies more perill in thine eye,
Then twenty of their Swords, looke thou but ſweete,
And I am proofe againſt their enmity.
Iul. I would not for the world they ſaw thee here.
Rom. I haue nights cloake to hide me from their eyes
And but thou loue me, let them finde me here,
My life were better ended by their hate,
Then death proroged wanting of thy Loue.
Iul. By whoſe direction found'ſt thou out this place?
Rom. By Loue that firſt did promp me to enquire,
He lent me counſell, and I lent him eyes,
I am no Pylot, yet wert thou as far
As that vaſt-ſhore-waſhet with the fartheſt Sea,
I ſhould adueuture for ſuch Marchandiſe.
Iul. Thou knoweſt the maske of night is on my face,
Elſe would a Maiden bluſh bepaint my cheeke,
For that which thou haſt heard me ſpeake to night,
Faine would I dwell on forme, faine, faine, denie
What I haue ſpoke, but farewell Complement,
Doeſt thou Loue? I know thou wilt ſay I,
And

And I will take thy word, yet if thou swear'st,
Thou maiest proue false: at Louers periuries
They say *Ioue* laught, oh gentle *Romeo*,
If thou dost Loue, pronounce it faithfully:
Or if thou thinkest I am too quickly wonne,
Ile frowne and be peruerse, and say thee nay,
So thou wilt wooe: But else not for the world.
In truth faire *Mountague* I am too fond:
And therefore thou maiest thinke my behauiour light,
But trust me Gentleman, Ile proue more true,
Then those that haue coying to be strange,
I should haue beene more strange, I must confesse,
But that thou ouer heard'st ere I was ware
My true Loues passion, therefore pardon me,
And not impute this yeelding to light Loue,
Which the darke night hath so discouered.
Rom. Lady, by yonder Moone I vow,
That tips with siluer all these Fruite tree tops.
Iul. O sweare not by the Moone, th'inconstant Moone,
That monethly changes in her circled Orbe,
Least that thy Loue proue likewise variable.
Rom. What shall I sweare by?
Iul. Do not sweare at all:
Or if thou wilt sweare by thy gratious selfe,
Which is the God of my Idolatry,
And Ile beleeue thee.
Rom. If my hearts deare loue.
Iuli. Well do not sweare, although I ioy in thee:
I haue no ioy of this contract to night,
It is too rash, too vnaduis'd, too sudden,
Too like the lightning which doth cease to be
Ere, one can say, it lightens, Sweete good night:
This bud of Loue by Summers ripening breath,
May proue a beautious Flower when next we meete:
Goodnight, goodnight, as sweete repose and rest,
Come to thy heart, as that within my brest.
Rom. O wilt thou leaue me so vnsatisfied?
Iuli. What satisfaction can'st thou haue to night?
Ro. Th'exchange of thy Loues faithfull vow for mine.
Iul. I gaue thee mine before thou did'st request it:
And yet I would it were to giue againe.
Rom. Would'st thou withdraw it,
For what purpose Loue?
Iul. But to be franke and giue it thee againe,
And yet I wish but for the thing I haue,
My bounty is as boundlesse as the Sea,
My Loue as deepe, the more I giue to thee
The more I haue, for both are Infinite:
I heare some noyse within deare Loue adue:
Cals within.
Anon good Nurse, sweet *Mountague* be true:
Stay but alittle, I will come againe.
Rom. O blessed blessed night, I am afear'd
Being in night, all this is but a dreame,
Too flattering sweet to be substantiall.
Iul. Three words deare *Romeo*,
And goodnight indeed,
If that thy bent of Loue be Honourable,
Thy purpose marriage, send me word to morrow,
By one that Ile procure to come to thee,
Where and what time thou wilt performe the right,
And all my Fortunes at thy foote Ile lay,
And follow thee my Lord throughout the world.
Within: Madam.
I come, anon: but if thou meanest not well,
I do beseech theee *Within*: Madam.
(By and by I come)
To cease thy strife, and leaue me to my griefe,
To morrow will I send.
Rom. So thriue my soule.
Iu. A thousand times goodnight. *Exit.*
Rome. A thousand times the worse to want thy light,
Loue goes toward Loue as school-boyes frō thier books
But Loue frō Loue, towards schoole with heauie lookes.

Enter Iuliet agaaine.

Iul. Hist *Romeo* hist: O for a Falkners voice,
To lure this Tassell gentle backe againe,
Bondage is hoarse, and may not speake aloud,
Else would I teare the Caue where Eccho lies,
And make her ayrie tongue more hoarse, then
With repetition of my *Romeo*.
Rom. It is my soule that calls vpon my name.
How siluer sweet, sound Louers tongues by night,
Like softest Musicke to attending eares.
Iul. *Romeo.*
Rom. My Neece.
Iul. What a clock to morrow
Shall I send to thee?
Rom. By the houre of nine.
Iul. I will not faile, 'tis twenty yeares till then,
I haue forgot why I did call thee backe.
Rom. Let me stand here till thou remember it.
Iul. I shall forget, to haue thee still stand there,
Remembring how I Loue thy company.
Rom. And Ile still stay, to haue thee still forget,
Forgetting any other home but this.
Iul. 'Tis almost morning, I would haue thee gone,
And yet no further then a wantons Bird,
That let's it hop a little from his hand,
Like a poore prisoner in his twisted Gyues,
And with a silken thred plucks it backe againe,
So louing Iealous of his liberty.
Rom. I would I were thy Bird.
Iul. Sweet so would I,
Yet I should kill thee with much cherishing:
Good night, good night.
Rom. Parting is such sweete sorrow,
That I shall say goodnight, till it be morrow.
Iul. Sleepe dwell vpon thine eyes, peace in thy brest.
Rom. Would I were sleepe and peace so sweet to rest,
The gray ey'd morne smiles on the frowning night,
Checkring the Easterne Clouds with streakes of light,
And darknesse fleckel'd like a drunkard reeles,
From forth dayes pathway, made by *Titans* wheeles.
Hence will I to my ghostly Fries close Cell,
His helpe to craue, and my deare hap to tell. *Exit.*

Enter Frier alone with a basket.

Fri. The gray ey'd morne smiles on the frowning night,
Checkring the Easterne Cloudes with streaks of light:
And fleckled darknesse like a drunkard reeles,
From forth daies path, and *Titans* burning wheeles:
Now ere the Sun aduance his burning eye,
The day to cheere, and nights danke dew to dry,
I must vpfill this Osier Cage of ours,
With balefull weedes, and precious Iuiced flowers,
The earth that's Natures mother, is her Tombe,
What is her burying graue that is her wombe:
And from her wombe children of diuers kind

We sucking on her naturall bosome find :
Many for many vertues excellent :
None but for some, and yet all different.
Omickle is the powerfull grace that lies
In Plants, Hearbs, stones, and their true qualities :
For nought so vile, that on the earth doth liue,
But to the earth some speciall good doth giue :
Nor ought so good, but strain'd from that faire vse,
Reuolts from true birth, stumbling on abuse.
Vertue it selfe turnes vice being misapplied,
And vice sometime by action dignified.

Enter Romeo.

Within the infant rin'd of this weake flower,
Poyson hath residence, and medicine power :
For this being smelt, with that part cheares each part,
Being tasted slayes all sences with the heart.
Two such opposed Kings encampe them still,
In man as well as Hearbes, grace and rude will :
And where the worser is predominant,
Full soone the Canker death eates vp that Plant.

Rom. Good morrow Father.

Fri. Benedecite.
What early tongue so sweet saluteth me ?
Young Sonne, it argues a distempered head,
So soone to bid goodmorrow to thy bed ;
Care keepes his watch in euery old mans eye,
And where Care lodges, sleepe will neuer lye :
But where vnbrused youth with vnstuft braine
Doth couch his lims, there, golden sleepe doth raigne;
Therefore thy earlinesse doth me assure,
Thou art vprous'd with some distemprature;
Or if not so, then here I hit it right.
Our Romeo hath not beene in bed to night.

Rom. That last is true, the sweeter rest was mine.

Fri. God pardon sin: wast thou with *Rosaline* ?

Rom. With *Rosaline*, my ghostly Father ? No,
I haue forgot that name, and that names woe.

Fri. That's my good Son, but wher hast thou bin then ?

Rom. Ile tell thee ere thou aske it me agen :
I haue beene feasting with mine enemie,
Where on a sudden one hath wounded me,
That's by me wounded: both our remedies
Within thy helpe and holy phisicke lies :
I beare no hatred, blessed man: for loe
My intercession likewise steads my foe.

Fri. Be plaine good Son, rest homely in thy drift,
Ridling confession, findes but ridling shrift.

Rom. Then plainly know my hearts deare Loue is set,
On the faire daughter of rich *Capulet* :
As mine on hers, so hers is set on mine;
And all combin'd, saue what thou must combine
By holy marriage: when and where, and how,
We met, we wooed, and made exchange of vow :
Ile tell thee as we passe, but this I pray,
That thou consent to marrie vs to day.

Fri. Holy S. *Francis*, what a change is heere ?
Is *Rosaline* that thou didst Loue so deare
So soone forsaken ? young mens Loue then lies
Not truely in their hearts, but in their eyes.
Iesu *Maria*, what a deale of brine
Hath washt thy sallow cheekes for *Rosaline* ?
How much salt water throwne away in wast,
To season Loue that of it doth not tast.
The Sun not yet thy sighes, from heauen cleares,
Thy old grones yet ringing in my auncient eares :
Lo here vpon thy cheeke the staine doth sit,
Of an old teare that is not washt off yet.
If ere thou wast thy selfe, and these woes thine,
Thou and these woes, were all for *Rosaline*.
And art thou chang'd? pronounce this sentence then,
Women may fall, when there's no strength in men.

Rom. Thou chid'st me oft for louing *Rosaline*.

Fri. For doting, not for louing pupill mine.

Rom. And bad'st me bury Loue.

Fri. Not in a graue,
To lay one in, another out to haue.

Rom. I pray thee chide me not, her I Loue now
Doth grace for grace, and Loue for Loue allow :
The other did not so.

Fri. O she knew well,
Thy Loue did read by rote, that could not spell :
But come young wauerer, come goe with me,
In one respect, Ile thy assistant be :
For this alliance may so happy proue,
To turne your houshould rancor to pure Loue.

Rom. O let vs hence, I stand on sudden hast.

Fri. Wisely and slow, they stumble that run fast.

Exeunt

Enter Benuolio and Mercutio.

Mer. Where the deu le should this *Romeo* be ? came he not home to night ?

Ben. Not to his Fathers, I spoke with his man.

Mer. Why that same pale hard-harted wench, that *Rosaline* torments him so, that he will sure run mad.

Ben. *Tibalt*, the kinsman to old *Capulet*, hath sent a Letter to his Fathers house.

Mer. A challenge on my life.

Ben. *Romeo* will answere it.

Mer. Any man that can write, may answere a Letter.

Ben. Nay, he will answere the Letters Maister how he dares, being dared.

Mer. Alas poore *Romeo*, he is already dead stab'd with a white wenches blacke eye, runne through the eare with a Loue song, the very pinne of his heart, cleft with the blind Bowe-boyes but-shaft, and is he a man to encounter *Tybalt* ?

Ben. Why what is *Tibalt* ?

Mer. More then Prince of Cats. Oh hee's the Couragious Captaine of Complements : he fights as you sing pricksong, keeps time, distance, and proportion, he rests his minum, one, two, and the third in your bosom: the very butcher of a silk button, a Dualist, a Dualist: a Gentleman of the very first house of the first and second cause: ah the immortall Passado, the Punto reuerso, the Hay.

Ben. The what?

Mer. The Pox of such antique lisping affecting phantacies, these new tuners of accent : Iesu a very good blade, a very tall man, a very good whore. Why is not this a lamentable thing Grandsire, that we should be thus afflicted with these strange flies : these fashion Mongers, these pardon-mee's, who stand so much on the new form, that they cannot sit at ease on the old bench. O their bones, their bones.

Enter Romeo.

Ben. Here comes *Romeo*, here comes *Romeo*.

Mer. Without his Roe, like a dryed Hering. O flesh, flesh, how art thou fishified ? Now is he for the numbers that *Petrarch* flowed in : *Laura* to his Lady, was a kitchen wench, marrie she had a better Loue to berime her : *Dido* a dowdie, *Cleopatra* a Gipsie, *Hellen* and *Hero*, hildinsgs and Harlots: *Thisbie* a gray eie or so, but not to the purpose. Signior *Romeo*, *Bon iour*, there's a French salutation to your

ff French

French flop : you gaue vs the the counterfait fairely laſt night.

Romeo. Good morrow to you both, what counterfeit did I giue you?

Mer. The ſlip ſir, the ſlip, can you not conceiue?

Rom. Pardon *Mercutio*, my buſineſſe was great, and in ſuch a caſe as mine, a man may ſtraine curteſie.

Mer. That's as much as to ſay, ſuch a caſe as yours conſtrains a man to bow in the hams.

Rom. Meaning to curſie.

Mer. Thou haſt moſt kindly hit it.

Rom. A moſt curteous expoſition.

Mer. Nay, I am the very pinck of curteſie.

Rom. Pinke for flower.

Mer. Right.

Rom. Why then is my Pump well flowr'd.

Mer. Sure wit, follow me this ieaſt, now till thou haſt worne out thy Pump, that when the ſingle ſole of it is worne, the ieaſt may remaine after the wearing, ſole-ſingular.

Rom. O ſingle ſol'd ieaſt,
Soly ſingular for the ſingleneſſe.

Mer. Come betweene vs good *Benuolio*, my wits faints.

Rom. Swits and ſpurs,
Swits and ſpurs, or Ile crie a match.

Mer. Nay, if our wits run the Wild-Gooſe chaſe, I am done : For thou haſt more of the Wild-Gooſe in one of thy wits, then I am ſure I haue in my whole fiue. Was I with you there for the Gooſe?

Rom. Thou waſt neuer with mee for any thing, when thou waſt not there for the Gooſe.

Mer. I will bite thee by the eare for that ieſt.

Rom. Nay, good Gooſe bite not.

Mer. Thy wit is a very Bitter-ſweeting,
It is a moſt ſharpe ſawce.

Rom. And is it not well ſeru'd into a Sweet-Gooſe?

Mer. Oh here's a wit of Cheuerell, that ſtretches from an ynch narrow, to an ell broad.

Rom. I ſtretch it out for that word, broad, which added to the Gooſe, proues thee farre and wide, abroad Gooſe.

Mer. Why is not this better now, then groning for Loue, now art thou ſociable, now art thou *Romeo*: now art thou what thou art, by Art as well as by Nature, for this driueling Loue is like a great Naturall, that runs lolling vp and downe to hid his bable in a hole.

Ben. Stop there, ſtop there.

Mer. Thou deſir'ſt me to ſtop in my tale againſt the haire.

Ben. Thou would'ſt elſe haue made thy tale large.

Mer. O thou art deceiu'd, I would haue made it ſhort, or I was come to the whole depth of my tale, and meant indeed to occupie the argument no longer.

Enter Nurſe and her man.

Rom. Here's goodly geare.
A ſayle, a ſayle.

Mer. Two, two: a Shirt and a Smocke.

Nur. *Peter*?

Peter. Anon.

Nur. My Fan *Peter*?

Mer. Good *Peter* to hide her face?
For her Fans the fairer face?

Nur. God ye good morrow Gentlemen.

Mer. God ye gooden faire Gentlewoman.

Nur. Is it gooden?

Mer. 'Tis no leſſe I tell you : for the bawdy hand of the Dyall is now vpon the pricke of Noone.

Nur. Out vpon you: what a man are you?

Rom. One Gentlewoman,
That God hath made, himſelfe to mar.

Nur. By my troth it is ſaid, for himſelfe to, mar qua-t ha: Gentlemen, can any of you tel me where I may find the young *Romeo*?

Romeo. I can tell you: but young *Romeo* will be older when you haue found him, then he was when you ſought him : I am the youngeſt of that name, for fault of a worſe.

Nur. You ſay well.

Mer. Yea is the worſt well,
Very well tooke : Ifaith, wiſely, wiſely.

Nur. If you be he ſir,
I deſire ſome confidence with you?

Ben. She will endite him to ſome Supper.

Mer. A baud, a baud, a baud. So ho.

Rom. What haſt thou found?

Mer. No Hare ſir, vnleſſe a Hare ſir in a Lenten pie, that is ſomething ſtale and hoare ere it be ſpent.
An old Hare hoare, and an old Hare hoare is very good meat in Lent.
But a Hare that is hoare is too much for a ſcore, when it hoares ere it be ſpent,
Romeo will you come to your Fathers? Weele to dinner thither.

Rom. I will follow you.

Mer. Farewell auncient Lady :
Farewell Lady, Lady, Lady.

Exit. Mercutio, Benuolio.

Nur. I pray you ſir, what ſawcie Merchant was this that was ſo full of his roperie?

Rom. A Gentleman Nurſe, that loues to heare himſelfe talke, and will ſpeake more in a minute, then he will ſtand to in a Moneth.

Nur. And a ſpeake any thing againſt me, Ile take him downe, & a were luſtier then he is, and twentie ſuch Iacks: and if I cannot, Ile finde thoſe that ſhall : ſcuruie knaue, I am none of his flurt-gils, I am none of his skaines mates, and thou muſt ſtand by too and ſuffer euery knaue to vſe me at his pleaſure.

Pet. I ſaw no man vſe you at his pleaſure : if I had, my weapon ſhould quickly haue beene out, I warrant you, I dare draw aſſoone as another man, if I ſee occaſion in a good quarrell, and the law on my ſide.

Nur. Now afore God, I am ſo vext, that euery part about me quiuers, skuruy knaue : pray you ſir a word : and as I told you, my young Lady bid me enquire you out, what ſhe bid me ſay, I will keepe to my ſelfe : but firſt let me tell ye, if ye ſhould leade her in a fooles paradiſe, as they ſay, it were a very groſſe kind of behauiour, as they ſay: for the Gentlewoman is yong : & therefore, if you ſhould deale double with her, truely it were an ill thing to be offered to any Gentlewoman, and very weake dealing.

Nur. Nurſe commend me to thy Lady and Miſtreſſe, I proteſt vnto thee.

Nur. Good heart, and yfaith I will tell her as much : Lord, Lord ſhe will be a ioyfull woman.

Rom. What wilt thou tell her Nurſe? thou doeſt not marke me?

Nur. I will tell her ſir, that you do proteſt, which as I take it, is a Gentleman-like offer.

Rom. Bid her deuiſe ſome meanes to come to ſhrift this afternoone,
And there ſhe ſhall at Frier *Lawrence* Cell
Beſhriu'd and married : here is for thy paines.

Nur. No truly ſir not a penny.

Rom. Go too, I ſay you ſhall.

Nurſe

Nur. This afternoone sir? well she shall be there.
Ro. And stay thou good Nurse behind the Abbey wall,
Within this houre my man shall be with thee,
And bring thee Cords made like a tackled staire,
Which to the high top gallant of my ioy,
Must be my conuoy in the secret night.
Farewell, be trustie and Ile quite thy paines:
Farewell, commend me to thy Mistresse.
Nur. Now God in heauen blesse thee: harke you sir,
Rom. What saist thou my deare Nurse?
Nurse. Is your man secret, did you nere heare say two may keepe counsell putting one away.
Ro. Warrant thee my man as true as steele.
Nur. Well sir, my Mistresse is the sweetest Lady, Lord, Lord, when 'twas a little prating thing. O there is a Noble man in Towne one *Paris*, that would faine lay knife aboard: but she good soule had as leeue a see Toade, a very Toade as see him: I anger her sometimes, and tell her that *Paris* is the properer man, but Ile warrant you, when I say so, shee lookes as pale as any clout in the versall world. Doth not Rosemarie and *Romeo* begin both with a letter?
Rom. I Nurse, what of that? Both with an *R*
Nur. A mocker that's the dogsname. *R.* is for the no, I know it begins with some other letter, and she hath the prettiest sententious of it, of you and Rosemary, that it would do you good to heare it.
Rom. Commend me to thy Lady.
Nur. I a thousand times. *Peter?*
Pet. Anon.
Nur. Before and apace. *Exit Nurse and Peter.*

Enter Iuliet.

Iul. The clocke strook nine, when I did send the Nurse,
In halfe an houre she promised to returne,
Perchance she cannot meete him: that's not so:
Oh she is lame, Loues Herauld should be thoughts,
Which ten times faster glides then the Sunnes beames,
Driuing backe shadowes ouer lowring hils.
Therefore do nimble Pinion'd Doues draw Loue,
And therefore hath the wind-swift *Cupid* wings:
Now is the Sun vpon the highmost hill
Of this daies iourney, and from nine till twelue,
I three long houres, yet she is not come.
Had she affections and warme youthfull blood,
She would be as swift in motion as a ball,
My words would bandy her to my sweete Loue,
And his to me, but old folkes,
Many faine as they were dead,
Vnwieldie, slow, heauy, and pale as lead.

Enter Nurse.

O God she comes, O hony Nurse what newes?
Hast thou met with him? send thy man away.
Nur. *Peter* stay at the gate.
Iul. Now good sweet Nurse:
O Lord, why lookest thou sad?
Though newes, be sad, yet tell them merrily.
If good thou sham'st the musicke of sweet newes,
By playing it to me, with so sower a face.
Nur. I am a weary, giue me leaue awhile,
Fie how my bones ake, what a iaunt haue I had?
Iul. I would thou had'st my bones, and I thy newes:
Nay come I pray thee speake, good good Nurse speake.
Nur. Iesu what hast? can you not stay a while?
Do you not see that I am out of breath?
Iul. How art thou out of breath, when thou hast breth
To say to me, that thou art out of breath?
The excuse that thou dost make in this delay,
Is longer then the tale thou dost excuse.
Is thy newes good or bad? answere to that,
Say either, and Ile stay the circustance:
Let me be satisfied, ist good or bad?
Nur. Well, you haue made a simple choice, you know not how to chuse a man: *Romeo*, no not he though his face be better then any mans, yet his legs excels all mens, and for a hand, and a foote, and a body, though they be not to be talkt on, yet they are past compare: he is not the flower of curtesie, but Ile warrant him as gentle a Lambe: go thy waies wench, serue God, What haue you din'd at home?
Iul. No no: but all this this did I know before
What saies he of our marriage? what of that?
Nur. Lord how my head akes, what a head haue I?
It beates as it would fall in twenty peeces.
My backe a tother side: o my backe, my backe:
Beshrew your heart for sending me about
To catch my death with iaunting vp and downe.
Iul. Ifaith: I am sorrie that that thou art so well.
Sweet sweet, sweet Nurse, tell me what saies my Loue?
Nur. Your Loue saies like an honest Gentleman,
And a courteous, and a kind, and a handsome,
And I warrant a vertuous: where is your Mother?
Iul. Where is my Mother?
Why she is within, where should she be?
How odly thou repli'st:
Your Loue saies like an honest Gentleman:
Where is your Mother?
Nur. O Gods Lady deare,
Are you so hot? marrie come vp I trow,
Is this the Poultis for my aking bones?
Henceforward do your messages your selfe.
Iul. Heere's such a coile, come what saies *Romeo*?
Nur. Haue you got leaue to go to shrift to day?
Iul. I haue.
Nur. Then high you hence to Frier *Lawrence* Cell,
There staies a Husband to make you a wife:
Now comes the wanton bloud vp in your cheekes,
Thei'le be in Scarlet straight at any newes:
Hie you to Church, I must an other way,
To fetch a Ladder by the which your Loue
Must climde a birds nest Soone when it is darke:
I am the drudge, and toile in your delight:
But you shall beare the burthen soone at night.
Go Ile to dinner, hie you to the Cell.
Iui. Hie to high Fortune, honest Nurse, farewell. *Exeunt.*

Enter Frier and Romeo.

Fri. So smile the heauens vpon this holy act,
That after houres, with sorrow chide vs not.
Rom. Amen, amen, but come what sorrow can,
It cannot counteruaile the exchange of ioy
That one short minute giues me in her sight:
Do thou but close our hands with holy words,
Then Loue-deuouring death do what he dare,
It is inough. I may but call her mine.
Fri. These violent delights haue violent endes,
And in their triumph: die like fire and powder;
Which as they kisse consume. The sweetest honey
Is loathsome in his owne deliciousnesse,
And in the taste confoundes the appetite.
Therefore Loue moderately, long Loue doth so,
Too swift arriues as tardie as too slow.

Enter Iuliet.

Here comes the Lady. Oh so light a foot
Will nere weare out the euerlasting flint,

A Louer may beſtride the Goſſamours,
That ydles in the wanton Summer ayre,
And yet not fall, ſo light is vanitie.
Iul. Good euen to my ghoſtly Confeſſor.
Fri. *Romeo* ſhall thanke thee Daughter for vs both.
Iul. As much to him, elſe in his thanks too much.
Fri. Ah *Iuliet*, if the meaſure of thy ioy
Be heapt like mine, and that thy skill be more
To blaſon it, then ſweeten with thy breath
This neighbour ayre, and let rich muſickes tongue,
Vnfold the imagin'd happineſſe that both
Receiue in either, by this deere encounter.
Iul. Conceit more rich in matter then in words,
Brags of his ſubſtance, not of Ornament:
They are but beggers that can count their worth,
But my true Loue is growne to ſuch ſuch exceſſe,
I cannot ſum vp ſome of halfe my wealth.
Fri. Come, come with me, & we will make ſhort worke,
For by your leaues, you ſhall not ſtay alone,
Till holy Church incorporate two in one.

Enter Mercutio, Benuolio, and men.

Ben. I pray thee good *Mercutio* lets retire,
The day is hot, the *Capulets* abroad:
And if we meet, we ſhal not ſcape a brawle, for now theſe
hot dayes, is the mad blood ſtirring.
Mer. Thou art like one of theſe fellowes, that when he
enters the confines of a Tauerne, claps me his Sword vpon
the Table, and ſayes, God ſend me no need of thee: and by
the operation of the ſecond cup, drawes him on the Draw-
er, when indeed there is no need.
Ben. Am I like ſuch a Fellow?
Mer. Come, come, thou art as hot a Iacke in thy mood,
as any in *Italie*: and aſſoone moued to be moodie, and aſſoone moodie to be mou'd.
Ben. And what too?
Mer. Nay, and there were two ſuch, we ſhould haue
none ſhortly, for one would kill the other: thou, why thou
wilt quarrell with a man that hath a haire more, or a haire
leſſe in his beard, then thou haſt: thou wilt quarrell with a
man for cracking Nuts, hauing no other reaſon, but becauſe thou haſt haſell eyes: what eye, but ſuch an eye,
would ſpie out ſuch a quarrell? thy head is as full of quarrels, as an egge is full of meat, and yet thy head hath bin
beaten as addle as an egge for quarreling: thou haſt quarrel'd with a man for coffing in the ſtreet, becauſe he hath
wakened thy Dog that hath laine aſleepe in the Sun. Did'ſt
thou not fall out with a Tailor for wearing his new Doublet before Eaſter? with another, for tying his new ſhooes
with old Riband, and yet thou wilt Tutor me from quarrelling?
Ben. And I were ſo apt to quarell as thou art, any man
ſhould buy the Fee-ſimple of my life, for an houre and a
quarter.
Mer. The Fee-ſimple? O ſimple.

Enter Tybalt, Petruchio, and others.

Ben. By my head here comes the *Capulets*.
Mer. By my heele I care not.
Tyb. Follow me cloſe, for I will ſpeake to them.
Gentlemen, Good den, a word with one of you.
Mer. And but one word with one of vs? couple it with
ſomething, make it a word and a blow.
Tib. You ſhall find me apt inough to that ſir, and you
will giue me occaſion.
Mercu. Could you not take ſome occaſion without
giuing?
Tib. *Mercutio* thou conſort'ſt with *Romeo*.
Mer. Conſort? what doſt thou make vs Minſtrels? &
thou make Minſtrels of vs, looke to heare nothing but diſ-
cords: heere's my fiddleſticke, heere's that ſhall make you
daunce. Come conſort.
Ben. We talke here in the publike haunt of men:
Either withdraw vnto ſome priuate place,
Or reaſon coldly of your greeuances:
Or elſe depart, here all eies gaze on vs.
Mer. Mens eyes were made to looke, and let them gaze.
I will not budge for no mans pleaſure I.

Enter Romeo.

Tib. Well peace be with you ſir, here comes my man.
Mer. But Ile be hang'd ſir if he weare your Liuery:
Marry go before to field, heele be your follower,
Your worſhip in that ſenſe, may call him man.
Tib. *Romeo*, the loue I beare thee, can affoord
No better terme then this: Thou art a Villaine.
Rom. *Tibalt*, the reaſon that I haue to loue thee,
Doth much excuſe the appertaining rage
To ſuch a greeting: Villaine am I none;
Therefore farewell, I ſee thou know'ſt me not.
Tib. Boy, this ſhall not excuſe the iniuries
That thou haſt done me, therefore turne and draw.
Rom. I do proteſt I neuer iniur'd thee,
But lou'd thee better then thou can'ſt deuiſe:
Till thou ſhalt know the reaſon of my loue,
And ſo good *Capulet*, which name I tender
As dearely as my owne, be ſatisfied.
Mer. O calme, diſhonourable, vile ſubmiſſion:
Alla ſtucatho carries it away.
Tybalt, you Rat-catcher, will you walke?
Tib. What woulds thou haue with me?
Mer. Good King of Cats, nothing but one of your nine
liues, that I meane to make bold withall, and as you ſhall
vſe me hereafter dry beate the reſt of the eight. Will you
pluck your Sword out of his Pilcher by the eares? Make
haſt, leaſt mine be about your eares ere it be out.
Tib. I am for you.
Rom. Gentle *Mercutio*, put thy Rapier vp.
Mer. Come ſir, your Paſſado.
Rom. Draw *Benuolio*, beat downe their weapons:
Gentlemen, for ſhame forbeare this outrage,
Tibalt, *Mercutio*, the Prince expreſly hath
Forbidden bandying in *Verona* ſtreetes.
Hold *Tybalt*, good *Mercutio*.

Exit Tybalt.

Mer. I am hurt.
A plague a both the Houſes, I am ſped:
Is he gone and hath nothing?
Ben. What art thou hurt?
Mer. I, I, a ſcratch, a ſcratch, marry 'tis inough,
Where is my Page? go Villaine fetch a Surgeon.
Rom. Courage man, the hurt cannot be much.
Mer. No: 'tis not ſo deepe as a well, nor ſo wide as a
Church doore, but 'tis inough, 'twill ſerue: aske for me to
morrow, and you ſhall find me a graue man. I am pepper'd
I warrant, for this world: a plague a both your houſes.
What, a Dog, a Rat, a Mouſe, a Cat to ſcratch a man to
death: a Braggart, a Rogue, a Villaine, that fights by the
booke of Arithmeticke, why the deu'le came you be-
tweene vs? I was hurt vnder your arme.
Rom. I thought all for the beſt.
Mer. Helpe me into ſome houſe *Benuolio*;
Or I ſhall faint: a plague a both your houſes.
They haue made wormes meat of me,

I

I haue it, and soundly to your Houses. *Exit.*

Rom. This Gentleman the Princes neere Alie,
My very Friend hath got his mortall hurt
In my behalfe, my reputation stain'd
With *Tibalts* slaunder, *Tybalt* that an houre
Hath beene my Cozin: O Sweet *Iuliet*,
Thy Beauty hath made me Effeminate,
And in my temper softned Valours steele.

Enter Benuolio.

Ben. O *Romeo, Romeo*, braue *Mercutio's* is dead,
That Gallant spirit hath aspir'd the Cloudes,
Which too vntimely here did scorne the earth.

Rom. This daies blacke Fate, on mo daies doth depend,
This but begins, the wo others must end.

Enter Tybalt.

Ben. Here comes the Furious *Tybalt* backe againe.

Rom. He gon in triumph, and *Mercutio* slaine?
Away to heauen respectiue Lenitie,
And fire and Fury, be my conduct now.
Now *Tybalt* take the Villaine backe againe
That late thou gau'st me, for *Mercutios* soule
Is but a little way aboue our heads,
Staying for thine to keepe him companie:
Either thou or I, or both, must goe with him.

Tib. Thou wretched Boy that didst consort him here,
Shalt with him hence.

Rom. This shall determine that.

They fight. Tybalt falles.

Ben. *Romeo*, away be gone:
The Citizens are vp, and *Tybalt* slaine,
Stand not amaz'd, the Prince will Doome thee death
If thou art taken: hence, be gone, away.

Rom. O! I am Fortunes foole.

Ben. Why dost thou stay?

Exit Romeo.

Enter Citizens.

Citi. Which way ran he that kild *Mercutio*?
Tibalt that Murtherer, which way ran he?

Ben. There lies that *Tybalt*.

Citi. Vp sir go with me:
I charge thee in the Princes names obey.

Enter Prince, old Montague, Capulet, their Wiues and all.

Prin. Where are the vile beginners of this Fray?

Ben. O Noble Prince, I can discouer all
The vnluckie Mannage of this fatall brall:
There lies the man slaine by young *Romeo*,
That slew thy kinsman braue *Mercutio*.

Cap. Wi. *Tybalt*, my Cozin? O my Brothers Child,
O Prince, O Cozin, Husband, O the blood is spild
Of my deare kinsman. Prince as thou art true,
For bloud of ours, shed bloud of *Mountague*.
O Cozin, Cozin.

Prin. *Benuolio*, who began this Fray?

Ben. *Tybalt* here slaine, whom *Romeo's* hand did slay,
Romeo that spoke him faire, bid him bethinke
How nice the Quarrell was, and vrg'd withall
Your high displeasure: all this vttered,
With gentle breath, calme looke, knees humbly bow'd
Could not take truce with the vnruly spleene
Of *Tybalts* deafe to peace, but that he Tilts
With Peircing steele at bold *Mercutio's* breast,
Who all as hot, turnes deadly point to point,
And with a Martiall scorne, with one hand beates
Cold death aside, and with the other sends
It back to *Tybalt*, whose dexterity
Retorts it: *Romeo* he cries aloud,
Hold Friends, Friends part, and swifter then his tongue,
His aged arme, beats downe their fatall points,
And twixt them rushes, vnderneath whose arme,
An enuious thrust from *Tybalt*, hit the life
Of stout *Mercutio*, and then *Tybalt* fled.
But by and by comes backe to *Romeo*,
Who had but newly entertained Reuenge,
And too't they goe like lightning, for ere I
Could draw to part them, was stout *Tybalt* slaine:
And as he fell, did *Romeo* turne and flie:
This is the truth, or let *Benuolio* die.

Cap. Wi. He is a kinsman to the *Mountague*,
Affection makes him false, he speakes not true:
Some twenty of them fought in this blacke strife,
And all those twenty could but kill one life.
I beg for Iustice, which thou Prince must giue:
Romeo slew *Tybalt*, *Romeo* must not liue.

Prin. *Romeo* slew him, he slew *Mercutio*,
Who now the price of his deare blood doth owe.

Cap. Not *Romeo* Prince, he was *Mercutios* Friend,
His fault concludes, but what the law should end,
The life of *Tybalt*.

Prin. And for that offence,
Immediately we doe exile him hence:
I haue an interest in your hearts proceeding:
My bloud for your rude brawles doth lie a bleeding.
But Ile Amerce you with so strong a fine,
That you shall all repent the losse of mine.
It will be deafe to pleading and excuses,
Nor teares, nor prayers shall purchase our abuses.
Therefore vse none, let *Romeo* hence in hast,
Else when he is found, that houre is his last.
Beare hence this body, and attend our will:
Mercy not Murders, pardoning those that kill.

Exeunt.

Enter Iuliet alone.

Iul. Gallop apace, you fiery footed steedes,
Towards *Phœbus* lodging, such a Wagoner
As *Phaeton* would whip you to the west,
And bring in Cloudie night immediately.
Spred thy close Curtaine Loue-performing night,
That run-awayes eyes may wincke, and *Romeo*
Leape to these armes, vntalkt of and vnseene,
Louers can see to doe their Amorous rights,
And by their owne Beauties: or if Loue be blind,
It best agrees with night: come ciuill night,
Thou sober suted Matron all in blacke,
And learne me how to loose a winning match,
Plaid for a paire of stainlesse Maidenhoods,
Hood my vnman'd blood bayting in my Cheekes,
With thy Blacke mantle, till strange Loue grow bold,
Thinke true Loue acted simple modestie:
Come night, come *Romeo*, come thou day in night,
For thou wilt lie vpon the wings of night
Whiter then new Snow vpon a Rauens backe:
Come gentle night, come louing blackebrow'd night.
Giue me my *Romeo*, and when I shall die,
Take him and cut him out in little starres,
And he will make the Face of heauen so fine,
That all the world will be in Loue with night,
And pay no worship to the Garish Sun.
O I haue bought the Mansion of a Loue,
But not possest it, and though I am sold,
Not yet enioy'd, so tedious is this day,
As is the night before some Festiuall,

To an impatient child that hath new robes
And may not weare them, O here comes my Nurse:
Enter Nurse with cords.
And she brings newes and euery tongue that speaks
But *Romeos*, name, speakes heauenly eloquence:
Now Nurse, what newes? what hast thou there?
The Cords that *Romeo* bid thee fetch?
Nur. I, I, the Cords.
Iuli. Ay me, what newes?
Why dost thou wring thy hands.
Nur. A welady, hee's dead, hee's dead,
We are vndone Lady, we are vndone.
Alacke the day, hee's gone, hee's kil'd, he's dead.
Iul. Can heauen be so enuious?
Nur. *Romeo* can,
Though heauen cannot. O *Romeo, Romeo*,
Who euer would haue thought it *Romeo*.
Iuli. What diuell art thou,
That dost torment me thus?
This torture should be roar'd in dismall hell,
Hath *Romeo* slaine himselfe? say thou but I,
And that bare vowell I shall poyson more
Then the death-darting eye of Cockatrice,
I am not I, if there be such an I.
Or those eyes shot, that makes thee answere I:
If he be slaine say I, or if not, no.
Briefe, sounds, determine of my weale or wo.
Nur. I saw the wound, I saw it with mine eyes,
God saue the marke, here on his manly brest,
A pitteous Coarse, a bloody piteous Coarse:
Pale, pale as ashes, all bedawb'd in blood,
All in gore blood, I sounded at the sight-
Iul. O breake my heart,
Poore Banckrout breake at once,
To prison eyes, nere looke on libertie.
Vile earth to earth resigne, end motion here,
And thou and *Romeo* presse on heauie beere.
Nur. O *Tybalt, Tybalt*, the best Friend I had:
O curteous *Tybalt* honest Gentleman,
That euer I should liue to see thee dead.
Iul. What storme is this that blowes so contrarie?
Is *Romeo* slaughtred? and is *Tybalt* dead?
My dearest Cozen, and my dearer Lord:
Then dreadfull Trumpet sound the generall doome,
For who is liuing, if those two are gone?
Nur. *Tybalt* is gone, and *Romeo* banished,
Romeo that kil'd him, he is banished.
Iul. O God!
Did *Rom'os* hand shed *Tybalts* blood
It did, it did, alas the day, it did.
Nur. O Serpent heart, hid with a flowring face.
Iul. Did euer Dragon keepe so faire a Caue?
Beautifull Tyrant, fiend Angelicall:
Rauenous Doue-feather'd Rauen,
Woluish-rauening Lambe,
Dispised substance of Diuinest show:
Iust opposite to what thou iustly seem'st,
A dimne Saint, an Honourable Villaine:
O Nature! what had'st thou to doe in hell,
When thou did'st bower the spirit of a fiend
In mortall paradise of such sweet flesh?
Was euer booke containing such vile matter
So fairely bound? O that deceit should dwell
In such a gorgeous Pallace.
Nur. There's no trust, no faith, no honestie in men,
All periur'd, all forsworne, all naught, all dissemblers,
Ah where's my man? giue me some Aqua-vitæ?
These griefes, these woes, these sorrowes make me old:
Shame come to *Romeo*.
Iul. Blister'd be thy tongue
For such a wish, he was not borne to shame:
Vpon his brow shame is asham'd to sit;
For 'tis a throane where Honour may be Crown'd
Sole Monarch of the vniuersall earth:
O what a beast was I to chide him?
Nur. Will you speake well of him,
That kil'd your Cozen?
Iul. Shall I speake ill of him that is my husband?
Ah poore my Lord, what tongue shall smooth thy name,
When I thy three houres wife haue mangled it.
But wherefore Villaine did'st thou kill my Cozin?
That Villaine Cozin would haue kil'd my husband:
Backe foolish teares, backe to your natiue spring,
Your tributarie drops belong to woe,
Which you mistaking offer vp to ioy:
My husband liues that *Tibalt* would haue slaine,
And *Tibalt* dead that would haue slaine my husband:
All this is comfort, wherefore weepe I then?
Some words there was worser then *Tybalts* death
That murdered me, I would forget it feine,
But oh, it presses to my memory,
Like damned guilty deedes to sinners minds,
Tybalt is dead and *Romeo* banished:
That banished, that one word banished,
Hath slaine ten thousand *Tibalts*: *Tibalts* death
Was woe inough if it had ended there:
Or if sower woe delights in fellowship,
And needly will be rankt with other griefes,
Why followed not when she said *Tibalts* dead,
Thy Father or thy Mother, nay or both,
Which moderne lamentation might haue mou'd.
But which a rere-ward following *Tybalts* death
Romeo is banished to speake that word,
Is Father, Mother, *Tybalt, Romeo, Iuliet*,
All slaine, all dead: *Romeo* is banished,
There is no end, no limit, measure, bound,
In that words death, no words can that woe sound.
Where is my Father and my Mother Nurse?
Nur. Weeping and wailing ouer *Tybalts* Coarse,
Will you go to them? I will bring you thither.
Iu. Wash they his wounds with tears: mine shal be spent
When theirs are drie for *Romeo's* banishment.
Take vp those Cordes, poore ropes you are beguil'd,
Both you and I for *Romeo* is exild:
He made you for a high-way to my bed,
But I a Maid, die Maiden widowed.
Come Cord, come Nurse, Ile to my wedding bed,
And death not *Romeo*, take my Maiden head.
Nur. Hie to your Chamber, Ile find *Romeo*
To comfort you, I wot well where he is:
Harke ye your *Romeo* will be heere at night,
Ile to him, he is hid at *Lawrence* Cell.
Iul. O find him, giue this Ring to my true Knight,
And bid him come, to take his last farewell.
Exit.

Enter Frier and Romeo.

Fri. *Romeo* come forth,
Come forth thou fearfull man,
Affliction is enamor'd of thy parts:
And thou art wedded to calamitie.
Rom. Father what newes?

What

What is the Princes Doome?
What sorrow craues acquaintance at my hand,
That I yet know not?
Fri. Too familiar
Is my deare Sonne with such sowre Company:
I bring thee tydings of the Princes Doome.
Rom. What lesse then Doomesday,
Is the Princes Doome?
Fri. A gentler iudgement vanisht from his lips,
Not bodies death, but bodies banishment.
Rom. Ha, banishment? be mercifull, say death:
For exile hath more terror in his looke,
Much more then death: do not say banishment.
Fri. Here from *Verona* art thou banished:
Be patient, for the world is broad and wide.
Rom. There is no world without *Verona* walles,
But Purgatorie, Torture, hell it selfe:
Hence banished, is banisht from the world,
And worlds exile is death. Then banished,
Is death, mistearm'd, calling death banished,
Thou cut'st my head off with a golden Axe,
And smilest vpon the stroke that murders me.
Fri. O deadly sin, O rude vnthankefulnesse!
Thy falt our Law calles death, but the kind Prince
Taking thy part, hath rusht aside the Law,
And turn'd that blacke word death, to banishment.
This is deare mercy, and thou seest it not.
Rom. 'Tis Torture and not mercy, heauen is here
Where *Iuliet* liues, and euery Cat and Dog,
And little Mouse, euery vnworthy thing
Liue here in Heauen and may looke on her,
But *Romeo* may not. More Validitie,
More Honourable state, more Courtship liues
In carrion Flies, then *Romeo*: they may seaze
On the white wonder of deare *Iuliets* hand,
And steale immortall blessing from her lips,
Who euen in pure and vestall modestie
Still blush, as thinking their owne kisses sin.
This may Flies doe, when I from this must flie,
And saist thou yet, that exile is not death?
But *Romeo* may not, hee is banished.
Had'st thou no poyson mixt, no sharpe ground knife,
No sudden meane of death, though nere so meane,
But banished to kill me? Banished?
O Frier, the damned vse that word in hell:
Howlings attends it, how hast thou the hart
Being a Diuine, a Ghostly Confessor,
A Sin-Absoluer, and my Friend profest:
To mangle me with that word, banished?
Fri. Then fond Mad man, heare me speake.
Rom. O thou wilt speake againe of banishment.
Fri. Ile giue thee Armour to keepe off that word,
Aduersities sweete milke, Philosophie,
To comfort thee, though thou art banished.
Rom. Yet banished? hang vp Philosophie:
Vnlesse Philosohpie can make a *Iuliet*,
Displant a Towne, reuerse a Princes Doome,
It helpes not, it preuailes not, talke no more.
Fri. O then I see, that Mad men haue no eares.
Rom. How should they,
When wisemen haue no eyes?
Fri. Let me dispaire with thee of thy estate,
Rom. Thou can'st not speake of that ye dost not feele,
Wert thou as young as *Iuliet* my Loue:
An houre but married, *Tybalt* murdered,
Doting like me, and like me banished,
Then mightest thou speake,
Then mightest thou teare thy hayre,
And fall vpon the ground as I doe now,
Taking the measure of an vnmade graue.
Enter Nurse, and knockes.
Frier. Arise one knockes,
Good *Romeo* hide thy selfe.
Rom. Not I,
Vnlesse the breath of Hartsicke groanes
Mist-like infold me from the search of eyes.
Knocke
Fri. Harke how they knocke:
(Who's there) *Romeo* arise,
Thou wilt be taken, stay a while, stand vp:
Knocke.
Run to my study: by and by, Gods will
What simplenesse is this: I come, I come.
Knocke.
Who knocks so hard?
Whence come you? what's your will?
Enter Nurse.
Nur. Let me come in,
And you shall know my errand:
I come from Lady *Iuliet*.
Fri. Welcome then.
Nur. O holy Frier, O tell me holy Frier,
Where's my Ladies Lord? where's *Romeo*?
Fri. There on the ground,
With his owne teares made drunke.
Nur. O he is euen in my Mistresse case,
Iust in her case. O wofull simpathy:
Pittious predicament, euen so lies she,
Blubbring and weeping, weeping and blubbring,
Stand vp, stand vp, stand and you be a man,
For *Iuliets* sake, for her sake rise and stand:
Why should you fall into so deepe an O.
Rom. Nurse.
Nur. Ah sir, ah sir, deaths the end of all.
Rom. Speak'st thou of *Iuliet*? how is it with her?
Doth not she thinke me an old Murtherer,
Now I haue stain'd the Childhood of our ioy,
With blood remoued, but little from her owne?
Where is she? and how doth she? and what sayes
My conceal'd Lady to our conceal'd Loue?
Nur. Oh she sayes nothing sir, but weeps and weeps,
And now fals on her bed, and then starts vp,
And *Tybalt* calls, and then on *Romeo* cries,
And then downe falls againe.
Ro. As if that name shot from the dead leuell of a Gun,
Did murder her, as that names cursed hand
Murdred her kinsman. Oh tell me Frier, tell me,
In what vile part of this Anatomie
Doth my name lodge? Tell me, that I may sacke
The hatefull Mansion.
Fri. Hold thy desperate hand:
Art thou a man? thy forme cries out thou art:
Thy teares are womanish, thy wild acts denote
The vnreasonable Furie of a beast.
Vnseemely woman, in a seeming man,
And ill beseeming beast in seeming both,
Thou hast amaz'd me. By my holy order,
I thought thy disposition better temper'd.
Hast thou slaine *Tybalt*? wilt thou slay thy selfe?
And slay thy Lady, that in thy life lies,
By doing damned hate vpon thy selfe?
Why rayl'st thou on thy birth? the heauen and earth?
Since

Since birth,and heauen and earth,all three do meete
In thee at once, which thou at once would'st loose.
Fie,fie,thou sham'st thy shape, thy loue, thy wit,
Which like a Vsurer abound'st in all :
And vsest none in that true vse indeed,
Which should bedecke thy shape, thy loue, thy wit :
Thy Noble shape, is but a forme of waxe,
Digressing from the Valour of a man,
Thy deare Loue sworne but hollow periurie,
Killing that Loue which thou hast vow'd to cherish.
Thy wit, that Ornament, to shape and Loue,
Mishapen in the conduct of them both :
Like powder in a skillesse Souldiers flaske,
Is set a fire by thine owne ignorance,
And thou dismembred with thine owne defence.
What,rowse thee man, thy *Iuliet* is aliue,
For whose deare sake thou wast but lately dead.
There art thou happy. *Tybalt* would kill thee,
But thou slew'st *Tybalt*, there art thou happie.
The law that threatned death became thy Friend,
And turn'd it to exile, there art thou happy.
A packe or blessing light vpon thy backe,
Happinesse Courts thee in her best array,
But like a mishaped and sullen wench,
Thou puttest vp thy Fortune and thy Loue:
Take heed, take heed, for such die miserable.
Goe get thee to thy Loue as was decreed,
Ascend her Chamber, hence and comfort her:
But looke thou stay not till the watch be set,
For then thou canst not passe to *Mantua*,
Where thou shalt liue till we can finde a time
To blaze your marriage, reconcile your Friends,
Beg pardon of thy Prince, and call thee backe,
With twenty hundred thousand times more ioy
Then thou went'st forth in lamentation.
Goe before Nurse, commend me to thy Lady,
And bid her hasten all the house to bed,
Which heauy sorrow makes them apt vnto.
Romeo is comming.

Nur. O Lord,I could haue staid here all night,
To heare good counsell: oh what learning is!
My Lord Ile tell my Lady you will come.

Rom. Do so, and bid my Sweete prepare to chide.

Nur. Heere sir, a Ring she bid me giue you sir:
Hie you, make hast, for it growes very late.

Rom. How well my comfort is reuiu'd by this.

Fri. Go hence,
Goodnight, and here stands all your state:
Either be gone before the watch be set,
Or by the breake of day disguis'd from hence,
Soiourne in *Mantua*, Ile find out your man,
And he shall signifie from time to time,
Euery good hap to you, that chaunces heere :
Giue me thy hand, 'tis late, farewell, goodnight.

Rom. But that a ioy past ioy, calls out on me,
It were a griefe, so briefe to part with thee :
Farewell. *Exeunt*.

Enter old Capulet, his Wife and Paris.

Cap. Things haue falne out sir so vnluckily,
That we haue had no time to moue our Daughter :
Looke you, she Lou'd her kinsman *Tybalt* dearely,
And so did I. Well, we were borne to die.
'Tis very late, she'l not come downe to night :
I promise you, but for your company,
I would haue bin a bed an houre ago.

Par. These times of wo, affoord no times to wooe:
Madam goodnight, commend me to your Daughter.

Lady. I will, and know her mind early to morrow,
To night, she is mewed vp to her heauinesse.

Cap. Sir *Paris*, I will make a desperate tender
Of my Childes loue : I thinke she will be rul'd
In all respects by me : nay more, I doubt it not.
Wife, go you to her ere you go to bed,
Acquaint her here, of my Sonne *Paris* Loue,
And bid her, marke you me, on Wendsday next,
But soft, what day is this?

Par. Monday my Lord.

Cap. Monday, ha ha: well Wendsday is too soone,
A Thursday let it be: a Thursday tell her,
She shall be married to this Noble Earle :
Will you be ready? do you like this hast?
Weele keepe no great adoe, a Friend or two,
For harke you, *Tybalt* being slaine so late,
It may be thought we held him carelesly,
Being our kinsman, if we reuell much :
Therefore weele haue some halfe a dozen Friends,
And there an end. But what say you to Thursday?

Paris. My Lord,
I would that Thursday were to morrow.

Cap. Well, get you gone, a Thursday, be it then :
Go you to *Iuliet* ere you go to bed,
Prepare her wife, against this wedding day.
Farewell my Lord, light to my Chamber hoa,
Afore me, it is so late, that we may call it early by and by,
Goodnight. *Exeunt*.

Enter Romeo and Iuliet aloft.

Iul. Wilt thou be gone? It is not yet neere day:
It was the Nightingale, and not the Larke,
That pier'st the fearefull hollow of thine eare,
Nightly she sings on yond Pomgranet tree,
Beleeue me Loue, it was the Nightingale.

Rom. It was the Larke the Herauld of the Morne:
No Nightingale: looke Loue what enuious streakes
Do lace the seuering Cloudes in yonder East :
Nights Candles are burnt out, and Iocond day
Stands tipto on the mistie Mountaines tops,
I must be gone and liue, or stay and die.

Iul. Yond light is not daylight, I know it I:
It is some Meteor that the Sun exhales,
To be to thee this night a Torch-bearer,
And light thee on thy way to *Mantua*.
Therefore stay yet, thou need'st not to be gone,

Rom. Let me be tane, let me be put to death,
I am content, so thou wilt haue it so.
Ile say yon gray is not the mornings eye,
'Tis but the pale reflexe of *Cinthias* brow.
Nor that is not Larke whose noates do beate
The vaulty heauen so high aboue our heads,
I haue more care to stay, then will to go :
Come death and welcome, *Iuliet* wills it so.
How ist my soule, lets talke, it is not day.

Iuli. It is, it is, hie hence be gone away :
It is the Larke that sings so out of tune,
Straining harsh Discords, and vnpleasing Sharpes.
Some say the Larke makes sweete Diuision;
This doth not so: for she diuideth vs.
Some say, the Larke and loathed Toad change eyes,
O now I would they had chang'd voyces too :

Since arme from arme that voyce doth vs affray,
Hunting thee hence, with Hunt s-vp to the day,
O now be gone, more light and itli ght growes.
Rom. More light & light, more darke & darke our woes.
Enter Madam and Nurse.
Nur. Madam.
Iul. Nurse.
Nur. Your Lady Mother is comming to your chamber,
The day is broke, be wary, looke about.
Iul. Then window let day in, and let life out.
Rom. Farewell, farewell, one kisse and Ile descend.
Iul. Art thou gone so? Loue, Lord, ay Husband, Friend,
I must heare from thee euery day in the houre,
For in a minute there are many dayes,
O by this count I shall be much in yeares,
Ere I againe behold my *Romeo.*
Rom. Farewell:
I will omit no oportunitie,
That may conuey my greetings Loue, to thee.
Iul. O thinkest thou we shall euer meet againe?
Rom. I doubt it not, and all these woes shall serue
For sweet discourses in our time to come.
Iuilet. O God! I haue an ill Diuining soule,
Me thinkes I see thee now, thou art so lowe,
As one dead in the bottome of a Tombe,
Either my eye-sight failes, or thou look'st pale.
Rom. And trust me Loue, in my eye so do you:
Drie sorrow drinkes our blood. Adue, adue. *Exit.*
Iul. O Fortune, Fortune, all men call thee fickle,
If thou art fickle, what dost thou with him
That is renown'd for faith? be fickle Fortune:
For then I hope thou wilt not keepe him long,
But send him backe.
Enter Mother.
Lad. Ho Daughter, are you vp?
Iul: Who ist that calls? Is it my Lady Mother.
Is she not downe so late, or vp so early?
What vnaccustom'd cause procures her hither?
Lad. Why how now *Iuliet?*
Iul. Madam I am not well.
Lad. Euermore weeping for your Cozins death?
What wilt thou wash him from his graue with teares?
And if thou could'st, thou could'st not make him liue:
Therefore haue done, some griefe shewes much of Loue,
But much of griefe, shewes still some want of wit.
Iul. Yet let me weepe, for such a feeling losse.
Lad. So shall you feele the losse, but not the Friend
Which you weepe for.
Iul. Feeling so the losse,
I cannot chuse but euer weepe the Friend.
La. Well Girle, thou weep'st not so much for his death,
As that the Villaine liues which slaughter'd him.
Iul. What Villaine, Madam?
Lad. That same Villaine *Romeo.*
Iul. Villaine and he, be many Miles assunder:
God pardon, I doe with all my heart:
And yet no man like he, doth grieue my heart.
Lad. That is because the Traitor liues.
Iul. I Madam from the reach of these my hands:
Would none but I might venge my Cozins death.
Lad. We will haue vengeance for it, feare thou not.
Then weepe no more, Ile send to one in *Mantua,*
Where that same banisht Run-agate doth liue,
Shall giue him such an vnaccustom'd dram,
That he shall soone keepe *Tybalt* company:
And then I hope thou wilt be satisfied.
Iul. Indeed I neuer shall be satisfied
With *Romeo,* till I behold him. Dead
Is my poore heart so for a kinsman vext:
Madam if you could find out but a man
To beare a poyson, I would temper it;
That *Romeo* should vpon receit thereof,
Soone sleepe in quiet. O how my heart abhors
To heare him nam'd, and cannot come to him,
To wreake the Loue I bore my Cozin,
Vpon his body that hath slaughter'd him.
Mo. Find thou the meanes, and Ile find such a man.
But now Ile tell thee ioyfull tidings Gyrle.
Iul. And ioy comes well, in such a needy time,
What are they, beseech your Ladyship?
Mo. Well, well, thou hast a carefull Father Child?
One who to put thee from thy heauinesse,
Hath sorted out a sudden day of ioy,
That thou expects not, nor I lookt not for.
Iul. Madam in happy time, what day is this?
Mo. Marry my Child, early next Thursday morne,
The gallant, young, and Noble Gentleman,
The Countie *Paris* at Saint *Peters* Church,
Shall happily make thee a ioyfull Bride.
Iul. Now by Saint *Peters* Church, and *Peter* too,
He shall not make me there a ioyfull Bride.
I wonder at this hast, that I must wed
Ere he that should be Husband comes to woe:
I pray you tell my Lord and Father Madam,
I will not marrie yet, and when I doe, I sweare
It shallbe *Romeo,* whom you know I hate
Rather then *Paris.* These are newes indeed.
Mo. Here comes your Father, tell him so your selfe,
And see how he will take it at your hands.

Enter Capulet and Nurse.

Cap. When the Sun sets, the earth doth drizzle daew
But for the Sunset of my Brothers Sonne,
It raines downright.
How now? A Conduit Gyrle, what still in teares?
Euermore showring in one little body?
Thou counterfaits a Barke, a Sea, a Wind:
For still thy eyes, which I may call the Sea,
Do ebbe and flow with teares, the Barke thy body is
Sayling in this salt floud, the windes thy sighes,
Who raging with the teares and they with them,
Without a sudden calme will ouer set
Thy tempest tossed body. How now wife?
Haue you deliuered to her our decree?
Lady. I sir;
But she will none, she giues you thankes,
I would the foole were married to her graue.
Cap. Soft, take me with you, take me with you wife,
How, will she none? doth she not giue vs thanks?
Is she not proud? doth she not count her blest,
Vnworthy as she is, that we haue wrought
So worthy a Gentleman, to be her Bridegroome
Iul. Not proud you haue,
But thankfull that you haue:
Proud can I neuer be of what I haue,
But thankfull euen for hate, that is meant Loue.
Cap. How now?
How now? Chopt Logicke? what is this?
Proud, and I thanke you: and I thanke you not.
Thanke me no thankings, nor proud me no prouds,
But fettle your fine ioints 'gainst Thursday next,
To

To go with *Paris* to Saint *Peters* Church:
Or I will drag thee, on a Hurdle thither.
Out you greene ſickneſſe carrion, out you baggage,
You tallow face.
Lady. Fie, fie, what are you mad?
Iul. Good Father, I beſeech you on my knees
Heare me with patience, but to ſpeake a word.
Fa. Hang thee young baggage, diſobedient wretch,
I tell thee what, get thee to Church a Thurſday,
Or neuer after looke me in the face.
Speake not, reply not, do not anſwere me.
My fingers itch, wife: we ſcarce thought vs bleſt,
That God had lent vs but this onely Child,
But now I ſee this one is one too much,
And that we haue a curſe in hauing her:
Out on her Hilding.
Nur. God in heauen bleſſe her,
You are too blame my Lord to rate her ſo.
Fa. And why my Lady wiſedome? hold your tongue,
Good Prudence, ſmatter with your goſſip, go.
Nur. I ſpeake no treaſon,
Father, O Godigoden,
May not one ſpeake?
Fa. Peace you mumbling foole,
Vtter your grauitie ore a Goſſips bowles
For here we need it not.
La. You are too hot.
Fa. Gods bread, it makes me mad:
Day, night, houre, ride, time, worke, play,
Alone in companie, ſtill my care hath bin
To haue her matcht, and hauing now prouided
A Gentleman of Noble Parentage,
Of faire Demeanes, Youthfull, and Nobly Allied,
Stuft as they ſay with Honourable parts,
Proportion'd as ones thought would wiſh a man,
And then to haue a wretched puling foole,
A whining mammet, in her Fortunes tender,
To anſwer, Ile not wed, I cannot Loue:
I am too young, I pray you pardon me.
But, and you will not wed, Ile pardon you.
Graze where you will, you ſhall not houſe with me:
Looke too't, thinke on't, I do not vſe to ieſt.
Thurſday is neere, lay hand on heart, aduiſe,
And you be mine, Ile giue you to my Friend:
And you be not, hang, beg, ſtraue, die in the ſtreets,
For by my ſoule, Ile nere acknowledge thee,
Nor what is mine ſhall neuer do thee good:
Truſt too't, bethinke you, Ile not be forſworne *Exit.*
Iuli. Is there no pittie ſitting in the Cloudes,
That ſees into the bottome of my griefe?
O ſweet my Mother caſt me not away,
Delay this marriage, for a month, a weeke,
Or if you do not, make the Bridall bed
In that dim Monument where *Tybalt* lies.
Mo. Talke not to me, for Ile not ſpeake a word,
Do as thou wilt, for I haue done with thee. *Exit.*
Iul. O God!
O Nurſe, how ſhall this be preuented?
My Husband is on earth, my faith in heauen,
How ſhall that faith returne againe to earth,
Vnleſſe that Husband ſend it me from heauen,
By leauing earth? Comfort me, counſaile me:
Hlacke, alacke, that heauen ſhould practiſe ſtratagems
Vpon ſo ſoft a ſubiect as my ſelfe.
What ſaiſt thou? haſt thou not a word of ioy?
Some comfort Nurſe.
Nur. Faith here it is,
Romeo is baniſhed, and all the world to nothing,
That he dares nere come backe to challenge you:
Or if he do, it needs muſt be by ſtealth.
Then ſince the caſe ſo ſtands as now it doth,
I thinke it beſt you married with the Countie,
O hee's a Louely Gentleman:
Romeos a diſh-clout to him: an Eagle Madam
Hath not ſo greene, ſo quicke, ſo faire an eye
As *Paris* hath, beſhrow my very heart,
I thinke you are happy in this ſecond match,
For it excels your firſt: or if it did not,
Your firſt is dead, or 'twere as good he were,
As liuing here and you no vſe of him.
Iul. Speakeſt thou from thy heart?
Nur. And from my ſoule too,
Or elſe beſhrew them both.
Iul. Amen.
Nur. What?
Iul. Well, thou haſt comforted me marue'lous much,
Go in, and tell my Lady I am gone,
Hauing diſpleaſ'd my Father, to *Lawrence* Cell,
To make confeſſion, and to be abſolu'd.
Nur. Marrie I will, and this is wiſely done.
Iul. Auncient damnation, O moſt wicked fiend!
It is more ſin to wiſh me thus forſworne,
Or to diſpraiſe my Lord with that ſame tongue
Which ſhe hath praiſ'd him with aboue compare,
So many thouſand times? Go Counſellor,
Thou and my boſome henchforth ſhall be twaine:
Ile to the Frier to know his remedie,
If all elſe faile, my ſelfe haue power to die. *Exeunt.*

Enter Frier and Countie Paris.

Fri. On Thurſday ſir? the time is very ſhort.
Par. My Father *Capulet* will haue it ſo,
And I am nothing ſlow to ſlack his haſt.
Fri. You ſay you do not know the Ladies mind?
Vneuen is the courſe, I like it not.
Pa. Immoderately ſhe weepes for *Tybalts* death,
And therfore haue I little talke of Loue,
For *Venus* ſmiles not in a houſe of teares.
Now ſir, her Father counts it dangerous
That ſhe doth giue her ſorrow ſo much ſway:
And in his wiſedome, haſts our marriage,
To ſtop the inundation of her teares,
Which too much minded by her ſelfe alone,
May be put from her by ſocietie.
Now doe you know the reaſon of this haſt?
Fri. I would I knew not why it ſhould be ſlow'd.
Looke ſir, here comes the Lady towards my Cell.
Enter Iuliet.
Par. Happily met, my Lady and my wife.
Iul. That may be ſir, when I may be a wife.
Par. That may be, muſt be Loue, on Thurſday next.
Iul. What muſt be ſhall be.
Fri. That's a certaine text.
Par. Come you to make confeſſion to this Father?
Iul. To anſwere that, I ſhould confeſſe to you.
Par. Do not denie to him, that you Loue me.
Iul. I will confeſſe to you that I Loue him.
Par. So will ye, I am ſure that you Loue me.
Iul. If I do ſo, it will be of more price,
Being ſpoke behind your backe, then to your face.
Par. Poore ſoule, thy face is much abuſ'd with teares.
Iuli. The

Iul. The teares haue got ſmall victorie by that:
For it was bad inough before their ſpight.
Pa. Thou wrong'ſt it more then teares with that report.
Iul. That is no ſlaunder ſir, which is a truth,
And what I ſpake, I ſpake it to thy face.
Par. Thy face is mine, and thou haſt ſlaundred it.
Iul. It may be ſo, for it is not mine owne.
Are you at leiſure, Holy Father now,
Or ſhall I come to you at euening Maſſe?
Fri. My leiſure ſerues me penſiue daughter now.
My Lord you muſt intreat the time alone.
Par. Godſheild: I ſhould diſturbe Deuotion,
Iuliet, on Thurſday early will I rowſe yee,
Till then adue, and keepe this holy kiſſe. *Exit Paris.*
Iul. O ſhut the doore, and when thou haſt done ſo,
Come weepe with me, paſt hope, paſt care, paſt helpe.
Fri. O *Iuliet*, I alreadie know thy griefe,
It ſtreames me paſt the compaſſe of my wits:
I heare thou muſt and nothing may prorogue it,
On Thurſday next be married to this Countie.
Iul. Tell me not Frier that thou heareſt of this,
Vnleſſe thou tell me how I may preuent it:
If in thy wiſedome, thou canſt giue no helpe,
Do thou but call my reſolution wiſe,
And with' his knife, Ile helpe it preſently.
God ioyn'd my heart, and *Romeos*, thou our hands,
And ere this hand by thee to *Romeo* ſeal'd:
Shall be the Labell to another Deede,
Or my true heart with trecherous reuolt,
Turne to another, this ſhall ſlay them both:
Therefore out of thy long expetien'ſt time,
Giue me ſome preſent counſell, or behold
Twixt my extreames and me, this bloody knife
Shall play the vmpeere, arbitrating that,
Which the commiſſion of thy yeares and art,
Could to no iſſue of true honour bring:
Be not ſo long to ſpeak, I long to die,
If what thou ſpeak'ſt, ſpeake not of remedy.
Fri. Hold Daughter, I doe ſpie a kind of hope,
Which craues as deſperate an execution,
As that is deſperate which we would preuent.
If, rather then to marrie Countie *Paris*
Thou haſt the ſtrength of will to ſtay thy ſelfe,
Then is it likely thou wilt vndertake
A thinglike death to chide away this ſhame,
That coap'ſt with death himſelfe, to ſcape fro it:
And if thou dar'ſt, Ile giue thee remedie.
Iul. Oh bid me leape, rather then marrie *Paris*,
From of the Battlements of any Tower,
Or walke in theeuiſh waies, or bid me lurke
Where Serpents are: chaine me with roaring Beares
Or hide me nightly in a Charnell houſe,
Orecouered quite with dead mens ratling bones,
With reekie ſhankes and yellow chappels ſculls:
Or bid me go into a new made graue,
And hide me with a dead man in his graue,
Things that to heare them told, haue made me tremble,
And I will doe it without feare or doubt,
To liue an vnſtained wife to my ſweet Loue.
Fri. Hold then: goe home, be merrie, giue conſent,
To marrie *Paris*: wenſday is to morrow,
To morrow night looke that thou lie alone,
Let not thy Nurſe lie with thee in thy Chamber:
Take thou this Violl being then in bed,
And this diſtilling liquor drinke thou off,
When preſently through all thy veines ſhall run,
A cold and drowſie humour: for no pulſe
Shall keepe his natiue progreſſe, but ſurceaſe:
No warmth, no breath ſhall teſtifie thou liueſt,
The Roſes in thy lips and cheekes ſhall fade
To many aſhes, the eyes windowes fall
Like death when he ſhut vp the day of life:
Each part depriu'd of ſupple gouernment,
Shall ſtiffe and ſtarke, and cold appeare like death,
And in this borrowed likeneſſe of ſhrunke death
Thou ſhalt continue two and forty houres,
And then awake, as from a pleaſant ſleepe.
Now when the Bridegroome in the morning comes,
To rowſe thee from thy bed, there art thou dead:
Then as the manner of our country is,
In thy beſt Robes vncouer'd on the Beere,
Be borne to buriall in thy kindreds graue:
Thou ſhalt be borne to that ſame ancient vault,
Where all the kindred of the *Capulets* lie,
In the meane time againſt thou ſhalt awake,
Shall *Romeo* by my Letters know our drift,
And hither ſhall he come, and that very night
Shall *Romeo* beare thee hence to *Mantua*.
And this ſhall free thee from this preſent ſhame,
If no inconſtant toy nor womaniſh feare,
Abate thy valour in the acting it.
Iul. Giue me, giue me, O tell not me of care.
Fri. Hold get you gone, be ſtrong and proſperous:
In this reſolue, Ile ſend a Frier with ſpeed
To *Mantua* with my Letters to thy Lord.
Iu. Loue giue me ſtrength,
And ſtrength ſhall helpe afford:
Farewell deare father. *Exit*

Enter Father Capulet, Mother, Nurſe, and Seruing men, two or three.

Cap. So many gueſts inuite as here are writ,
Sirrah, go hire me twenty cunning Cookes.
Ser. You ſhall haue none ill ſir, for Ile trie if they can licke their fingers.
Cap. How canſt thou trie them ſo?
Ser. Marrie ſir, 'tis an ill Cooke that cannot licke his owne fingers: therefore he that cannot licke his fingers goes not with me.
Cap. Go be gone, we ſhall be much vnfurniſht for this time: what is my Daughter gone to Frier *Lawrence*?
Nur. I forſooth.
Cap. Well he may chance to do ſome good on her,
A peeuiſh ſelfe-wild harlotry it is.
Enter Iuliet.
Nur. See where ſhe comes from ſhrift
With merrie looke.
Cap. How now my headſtrong,
Where haue you bin gadding?
Iul. Where I haue learnt me to repent the ſin
Of diſobedient oppoſition:
To you and your beheſts, and am enioyn'd
By holy *Lawrence*, to fall proſtrate here,
To beg your pardon: pardon I beſeech you,
Henceforward I am euer rul'd by you.
Cap. Send for the Countie, goe tell him of this,
Ile haue this knot knit vp to morrow morning.
Iul. I met the youthfull Lord at *Lawrence* Cell,
And gaue him what becomed Loue I might,
Not ſtepping ore the bounds of modeſtie.
Cap. Why I am glad on't, this is well, ſtand vp,
This

This is as't ſhould be, let me ſee the County:
I marrie go I ſay, and fetch him hither.
Now afore God, this reueren'd holy Frier,
All our whole Cittie is much bound to him.
Iul. Nurſe will you goe with me into my Cloſet,
To helpe me ſort ſuch needfull ornaments,
As you thinke fit to furniſh me to morrow?
Mo. No not till Thurſday, there's time inough.
Fa. Go Nurſe, go with her,
Weele to Church to morrow.
Exeunt Iuliet and Nurſe.
Mo. We ſhall be ſhort in our prouiſion,
'Tis now neere night.
Fa. Tuſh, I will ſtirre about,
And all things ſhall be well, I warrant thee wife:
Go thou to *Iuliet*, helpe to deckevp her,
Ile not to bed to night, let me alone:
Ile play the huſwife for this once. What ho?
They are all forth, well I will walke my ſelfe
To Countie *Paris*, to prepare him vp
Againſt to morrow, my heart is wondrous light,
Since this ſame way-ward Gyrle is ſo reclaim'd.
Exeunt Father and Mother.

Enter Iuliet and Nurſe.
Iul. I thoſe attires are beſt, but gentle Nurſe
I pray thee leaue me to my ſelfe to night:
For I haue need of many Oryſons,
To moue the heauens to ſmile vpon my ſtate,
Which well thou know'ſt, is croſſe and full of ſin.
Enter Mother.
Mo. What are you buſie ho? need you my help?
Iul. No Madam, we haue cul'd ſuch neceſſaries
As are behoouefull for our ſtate to morrow:
So pleaſe you, let me now be left alone;
And let the Nurſe this night ſit vp with you,
For I am ſure, you haue your hands full all,
In this ſo ſudden buſineſſe.
Mo. Goodnight.
Get thee to bed and reſt, for thou haſt need. *Exeunt.*
Iul. Farewell:
God knowes when we ſhall meete againe.
I haue a faint cold feare thrills through my veines,
That almoſt freezes vp the heate of fire:
Ile call them backe againe to comfort me.
Nurſe, what ſhould ſhe do here?
My diſmall Sceane, I needs muſt act alone:
Come Viall, what if this mixture do not worke at all?
Shall I be married then to morrow morning?
No, no, this ſhall forbid it. Lie thou there,
What if it be a poyſon which the Frier
Subtilly hath miniſtred to haue me dead,
Leaſt in this marriage he ſhould be diſhonour'd,
Becauſe he married me before to *Romeo*?
I feare it is, and yet me thinkes it ſhould not,
For he hath ſtill beene tried a holy man.
How, if when I am laid into the Tombe,
I wake before the time that *Romeo*
Come to redeeme me? There's a fearefull point:
Shall I not then be ſtifled in the Vault?
To whoſe foule mouth no healthſome ayre breaths in,
And there die ſtrangled ere my *Romeo* comes.
Or if I liue, is it not very like,
The horrible conceit of death and night,
Together with the terror of the place,
As in a Vaulte, an ancient receptacle,
Where for theſe many hundred yeeres the bones
Of all my buried Aunceſtors are packt,
Where bloody *Tybalt*, yet but greene in earth,
Lies feſtring in his ſhrow'd, where as they ſay,
At ſome houres in the night, Spirits reſort:
Alacke, alacke, is it not like that I
So early waking, what with loathſome ſmels,
And ſhrikes like Mandrakes torne out of the earth,
That liuing mortalls hearing them, run mad.
O if I walke, ſhall I not be diſtraught,
Inuironed with all theſe hidious feares,
And madly play with my forefathers ioynts?
And plucke the mangled *Tybalt* from his ſhrow'd?
And in this rage, with ſome great kinſmans bone,
As (with a club) daſh out my deſperate braines.
O looke, me thinks I ſee my Cozins Ghoſt,
Seeking out *Romeo* that did ſpit his body
Vpon my Rapiers point: ſtay *Tybalt*, ſtay;
Romeo, Romeo, Romeo, here's drinke: I drinke to thee.

Enter Lady of the houſe, and Nurſe.
Lady. Hold,
Take theſe keies, and fetch more ſpices Nurſe.
Nur. They call for Dates and Quinces in the Paſtrie.
Enter old Capulet.
Cap. Come, ſtir, ſtir, ſtir,
The ſecond Cocke hath Crow'd,
The Curphew Bell hath rung, 'tis three a clocke:
Looke to the bakte meates, good *Angelica*,
Spare not for coſt.
Nur. Go you Cot-queane, go,
Get you to bed, faith youle be ſicke to morrow
For this nights watching.
Cap. No not a whit: what? I haue watcht ere now
All night for leſſe cauſe, and nere beene ſicke.
La. I you haue bin a Mouſe-hunt in your time,
But I will watch you from ſuch watching now.
Exit Lady and Nurſe.
Cap. A iealous hood, a iealous hood,
Now fellow, what there?
Enter three or foure with ſpits, and logs, and baskets.
Fel. Things for the Cooke ſir, but I know not what.
Cap. Make haſt, make haſt, ſirrah, fetch drier Logs.
Call *Peter*, he will ſhew thee where they are.
Fel. I haue a head ſir, that will find out logs,
And neuer trouble *Peter* for the matter.
Cap. Maſſe and well ſaid, a merrie horſon, ha,
Thou ſhalt be loggerhead; good Father, 'tis day.
Play Muſicke
The Countie will be here with Muſicke ſtraight,
For ſo he ſaid he would, I heare him neere,
Nurſe, wife, what ho? what Nurſe I ſay?
Enter Nurſe.
Go waken *Iuliet*, go and trim her vp,
Ile go and chat with *Paris*: hie, make haſt,
Make haſt, the Bridegroome, he is come already:
Make haſt I ſay.
Nur. Miſtris, what Miſtris? *Iuliet*? Faſt I warrant her ſhe.
Why Lambe, why Lady, fie you ſluggabed,
Why Loue I ſay? Madam, ſweet heart: why Bride?
What not a word? You take your peniworths now,
Sleepe for a weeke, for the next night I warrant
The Countie *Paris* hath ſet vp his reſt,
That you ſhall reſt but little, God forgiue me:
Marrie and Amen: how ſound is ſhe a ſleepe?

I must needs wake her : Madam, Madam, Madam,
I, let the Countie take you in your bed,
Heele fright you vp yfaith. Will it not be?
What drest, and in your clothes, and downe againe?
I must needs wake you : Lady, Lady, Lady?
Alas, alas, helpe, helpe, my Ladyes dead,
Oh weladay, that euer I was borne,
Some Aqua-vitæ ho, my Lord, my Lady?

Mo. What noise is heere? *Enter Mother.*

Nur. O lamentable day.

Mo. What is the matter?

Nur. Looke, looke, oh heauie day.

Mo. O me, O me, my Child, my onely life:
Reuiue, looke vp, or I will die with thee:
Helpe, helpe, call helpe.

Enter Father.

Fa. For shame bring *Iuliet* forth, her Lord is come.

Nur. Shee's dead: deceast, shee's dead: alacke the day.

M. Alacke the day, shee's dead, shee's dead, shee's dead.

Fa. Ha? Let me see her: out alas shee's cold,
Her blood is setled and her ioynts are stiffe:
Life and these lips haue long bene sep erated:
Death lies on her like an vntimely frost
Vpon the swetest flower of all the field.

Nur. O Lamentable day!

Mo. O wofull time.

Fa. Death that hath tane her hence to make me waile,
Ties vp my tongue, and will not let me speake.

Enter Frier and the Countie.

Fri. Come, is the Bride ready to go to Church?

Fa. Ready to go, but neuer to returne.
O Sonne, the night before thy wedding day,
Hath death laine with thy wife: there she lies,
Flower as she was, deflowred by him.
Death is my Sonne in law, death is my Heire,
My Daughter he hath wedded. I will die,
And leaue him all life liuing, all is deaths.

Pa. Haue I thought long to see this mornings face,
And doth it giue me such a sight as this?

Mo. Accur'st, vnhappie, wretched hatefull day,
Most miserable houre, that ere time saw
In lasting labour of his Pilgrimage.
But one, poore one, one poore and louing Child,
But one thing to reioyce and solace in,
And cruell death hath catcht it from my sight.

Nur. O wo, O wofull, wofull, wofull day,
Most lamentable day, most wofull day,
That euer, euer, I did yet behold.
O day, O day, O day, O hatefull day,
Neuer was seene so blacke a day as this:
O wofull day, O wofull day.

Pa. Beguild, diuorced, wronged, spighted, slaine,
Most detestable death, by thee beguil'd,
By cruell, cruell thee, quite ouerthrowne:
O loue, O life; not life, but loue in death.

Fat. Despis'd, distressed, hated, martir'd, kil'd,
Vncomfortable time, why cam'st thou now
To murther, murther our solemnitie?
O Child, O Child; my soule, and not my Child,
Dead art thou, alacke my Child is dead,
And with my Child, my ioyes are buried.

Fri. Peace ho for shame, confusions: Care liues not
In these confusions, heauen and your selfe
Had part in this faire Maid, now heauen hath all,
And all the better is it for the Maid:
Your part in her, you could not keepe from death,
But heauen keepes his part in eternall life:
The most you sought was her promotion,
For 'twas your heauen, she shouldst be aduan'st,
And weepe ye now, seeing she is aduan'st
Aboue the Cloudes, as high as Heauen it selfe?
O in this loue, you loue your Child so ill,
That you run mad, seeing that she is well:
Shee's not well married, that liues married long,
But shee's best married, that dies married yong.
Drie vp your teares, and sticke your Rosemarie
On this faire Coarse, and as the custome is,
And in her best array beare her to Church:
For though some Nature bids all vs lament,
Yet Natures teares are Reasons merriment.

Fa. All things that we ordained Festiuall,
Turne from their office to blacke Funerall:
Our instruments to melancholy Bells,
Our wedding cheare, to a sad buriall Feast:
Our solemne Hymnes, to sullen Dyrges change:
Our Bri dall flowers serue for a buried Coarse:
And all things change them to the contrarie.

Fri. Sir go you in; and Madam, go with him,
And go sir *Paris*, euery one prepare
To follow this faire Coarse vnto her graue:
The heauens do lowre vpon you, for some ill:
Moue them no more, by crossing their high will. *Exeunt*

Mu. Faith we may put vp our Pipes and be gone.

Nur. Honest goodfellowes: Ah put vp, put vp,
For well you know, this is a pitifull case.

Mu. I by my troth, the case may be amended.

Enter Peter.

Pet. Musitions, oh Musitions,
Hearts ease, hearts ease,
O, and you will haue me liue, play hearts ease.

Mu. Why hearts ease;

Pet. O Musitions,
Because my heart it selfe plaies, my heart is full.

Mu. Not a dump we, 'tis no time to play now.

Pet. You will not then?

Mu. No.

Pet. I will then giue it you soundly.

Mu. What will you giue vs?

Pet. No money on my faith, but the gleeke.
I will giue you the Minstrell.

Mu. Then will I giue you the Seruing creature.

Peter. Then will I lay the seruing Creatures Dagger on your pate. I will carie no Crochets, Ile Re you, Ile Fa you, do you note me?

Mu. And you Re vs, and Fa vs, you Note vs.

2.*M.* Pray you put vp your Dagger,
And put out your wit.
Then haue at you with my wit.

Peter. I will drie-beate you with an yron wit,
And put vp my yron Dagger.
Answere me like men:
When griping griefes the heart doth wound, then Musicke with her siluer sound.
Why siluer sound? why Musicke with her siluer sound?
what say you *Simon Catling*?

Mu. Mary sir, because siluer hath a sweet sound.

Pet. Pratest, what say you *Hugh Rebicke*?

2.*M.* I say siluer sound, because Musitions sound for siluer

Pet. Pratest to, what say you *Iames Sound-Post*?

3.*Mu.* Faith I know not what to say.

Pet. O I cry you mercy, you are the Singer.
I will say for you; it is Musicke with her siluer sound,

Becauſe Muſitions haue no gold for ſounding:
Then Muſicke with her ſiluer ſound, with ſpeedy helpe doth lend redreſſe. *Exit.*

Mu. What a peſtilent knaue is this ſame?

M.2. Hang him Iacke, come weele in here, tarrie for the Mourners, and ſtay dinner. *Exit.*

Enter Romeo.

Rom. If I may truſt the flattering truth of ſleepe,
My dreames preſage ſome ioyfull newes at hand:
My boſomes L. ſits lightly in his throne:
And all thisan day an vccuſtom'd ſpirit,
Lifts me aboue the ground with cheerefull thoughts.
I dreamt my Lady came and found me dead,
(Strange dreame that giues a dead man leaue to thinke,)
And breath'd ſuch life with kiſſes in my lips,
That I reuiu'd and was an Emperour.
Ah me, how ſweet is loue it ſelfe poſſeſt,
When but loues ſhadowes are ſo rich in ioy.

Enter Romeo's man.

Newes from *Verona*, how now *Balthazer?*
Doſt thou not bring me Letters from the Frier?
How doth my Lady? Is my Father well?
How doth my Lady *Iuliet?* that I aske againe,
For nothing can be ill, if ſhe be well.

Man. Then ſhe is well, and nothing can be ill.
Her body ſleepes in *Capels* Monument,
And her immortall part with Angels liue,
I ſaw her laid low in her kindreds Vault,
And preſently tooke Poſte to tell it you:
O pardon me for bringing theſe ill newes,
Since you did leaue it for my office Sir.

Rom. Is it euen ſo?
Then I denie you Starres.
Thou knoweſt my lodging, get me inke and paper,
And hire Poſt-Horſes, I will hence to night.

Man. I do beſeech you ſir, haue patience:
Your lookes are pale and wild, and do import
Some miſaduenture.

Rom. Tuſh, thou art deceiu'd,
Leaue me, and do the thing I bid thee do.
Haſt thou no Letters to me from the Frier?

Man. No my good Lord.

Exit Man.

Rom. Mo matter: Get thee gone,
And hyre thoſe Horſes, Ile be with thee ſtraight.
Well *Iuliet*, I will lie with thee to night:
Lets ſee for meanes: O miſchiefe thou art ſwift,
To enter in the thoughts of deſperate men:
I do remember an Appothecarie,
And here abouts dwells, which late I noted
In tattred weeds, with ouerwhelming browes,
Culling of Simples, meager were his lookes,
Sharpe miſerie had worne him to the bones:
And in his needie ſhop a Tortoyrs hung,
An Allegater ſtuft, and other skins
Of ill ſhap'd fiſhes, and about his ſhelues,
A beggerly account of emptie boxes,
Greene earthen pots, Bladders, and muſtie ſeedes,
Remnants of packthred, and old cakes of Roſes
Were thinly ſcattered, to make vp a ſhew.
Noting this penury, to my ſelfe I ſaid,
An if a man did need a poyſon now,
Whoſe ſale is perſent death in *Mantua*,
Here liues a Caitiffe wretch would ſell it him.
O this ſame thought did but fore-run my need,
And this ſame needie man muſt ſell it me.
As I remember, this ſhould be the houſe,
Being holy day, the beggers ſhop is ſhut.
What ho? Appothecarie?

Enter Appothecarie.

App. Who call's ſo low'd?

Rom. Come hither man, I ſee that thou art poore,
Hold, there is fortie Duckets, let me haue
A dram of poyſon, ſuch ſoone ſpeeding geare,
As will diſperſe it ſelfe through all the veines,
That the life-wearie-taker may fall dead,
And that the Trunke may be diſcharg'd of breath,
As violently, as haſtie powder fier'd
Doth hurry from the fatall Canons wombe.

App. Such mortall drugs I haue, but *Mantuas* law
Is death to any he, that vtters them.

Rom. Art thou ſo bare and full of wretchedneſſe,
And fear'ſt to die? Famine is in thy cheekes,
Need and opreſſion ſtarueth in thy eyes,
Contempt and beggery hangs vpon thy backe:
The world is not thy friend, nor the worlds law:
The world affords no law to make thee rich.
Then be not poore, but breake it, and take this.

App. My pouerty, but not my will conſents.

Rom. I pray thy pouerty, and not thy will.

App. Put this in any liquid thing you will
And drinke it off, and if you had the ſtrength
Of twenty men, it would diſpatch you ſtraight.

Rom. There's thy Gold,
Worſe poyſon to mens ſoules,
Doing more murther in this loathſome world,
Then theſe poore compounds that thou maieſt not ſell.
I ſell thee poyſon, thou haſt ſold me none,
Farewell, buy food, and get thy ſelfe in fleſh.
Come Cordiall, and not poyſon, go with me
To *Iuliets* graue, for there muſt I vſe thee.

Exeunt.

Enter Frier Iohn to Frier Lawrence.

Iohn. Holy *Franciſcan* Frier, Brother, ho?

Enter Frier Lawrence.

Law. This ſame ſhould be the voice of Frier *Iohn*.
Welcome from *Mantua*, what ſayes *Romeo?*
Or if his mind be writ, giue me his Letter.

Iohn. Going to find a bare-foote Brother out,
One of our order to aſſociate me,
Here in this Citie viſiting the ſick,
And finding him, the Searchers of the Towne
Suſpecting that we both were in a houſe
Where the infectious peſtilence did raigne,
Seal'd vp the doores, and would not let vs forth,
So that my ſpeed to *Mantua* there was ſtaid.

Law. Who bare my Letter then to *Romeo?*

Iohn. I could not ſend it, here it is againe,
Nor get a meſſenger to bring it thee,
So fearefull were they of infection.

Law. Vnhappie Fortune: by my Brotherhood
The Letter was not nice, but full of charge,
Of deare import, and the neglecting it
May do much danger: Frier *Iohn* go hence,
Get me an Iron Crow, and bring it ſtraight
Vnto my Cell.

Iohn. Brother Ile go and bring it thee. *Exit.*

Law. Now muſt I to the Monument alone,
Within this three houres will faire *Iuliet* wake,
Shee will beſhrew me much that *Romeo*
Hath had no notice of theſe accidents:
But I will write againe to *Mantua*,

And keepe her at my Cell till *Romeo* come,
Poore liuing Coarse, clos'd in a dead mans Tombe,
Exit.

Enter Paris and his Page.

Par. Giue me thy Torch Boy, hence and stand aloft,
Yet put it out, for I would not be seene:
Vnder yond young Trees lay thee all along,
Holding thy eare close to the hollow ground,
So shall no foot vpon the Churchyard tread,
Being loose, vnfirme with digging vp of Graues,
But thou shalt heare it: whistle then to me,
As signall that thou hearest some thing approach,
Giue me those flowers. Do as I bid thee, go.
Page. I am almost afraid to stand alone
Here in the Churchyard, yet I will aduenture.
Pa. Sweet Flower with flowers thy Bridall bed I strew:
O woe, thy Canopie is dust and stones,
Which with sweet water nightly I will dewe,
Or wanting that, with teares destil'd by mones;
The obsequies that I for thee will keepe,
Nightly shall be, to strew thy graue, and weepe.
Whistle Boy.
The Boy giues warning, something doth approach,
What cursed foot wanders this wayes to night,
To crosse my obsequies, and true loues right?
What with a Torch? Muffle me night a while.

Enter Romeo, and Peter.

Rom. Giue me that Mattocke, & the wrenching Iron,
Hold take this Letter, early in the morning
See thou deliuer it to my Lord and Father,
Giue me the light; vpon thy life I charge thee,
What ere thou hear'st or seest, stand all aloofe,
And do not interrupt me in my course.
Why I descend into this bed of death,
Is partly to behold my Ladies face:
But chiefly to take thence from her dead finger,
A precious Ring: a Ring that I must vse,
In deare employment, therefore hence be gone:
But if thou iealous dost returne to prie
In what I further shall intend to do,
By heauen I will teare thee ioynt by ioynt,
And strew this hungry Churchyard with thy limbs:
The time, and my intents are sauage wilde:
More fierce and more inexorable farre,
Then emptie Tygers, or the roaring Sea.
Pet. I will be gone sir, and not troubl e you
Ro. So shalt thou shew me friendship: take thou that,
Liue and be prosperous, and farewell good fellow.
Pet. For all this same, Ile hide me here about,
His lookes I feare, and his intents I doubt.
Rom. Thou detestable mawe, thou wombe of death,
Gorg'd with the dearest morsell of the earth:
Thus I enforce thy rotten Iawes to open,
And in despight, Ile cram thee with more food.
Par. This is that banisht haughtie *Mountague*,
That murdred my Loues Cozin; with which griefe,
It is supposed the faire Creature died,
And here is come to do some villanous shame
To the dead bodies: I will apprehend him.
Stop thy vnhallowed toyle, vile *Mountague:*
Can vengeance be pursued further then death?
Condemned vallaine, I do apprehend thee.
Obey and go with me, for thou must die,
Rom. I must indeed, and therfore came I hither:
Good gentle youth, tempt not a desperate man,
Flie hence and leaue me, thinke vpon those gone,
Let them affright thee. I beseech thee Youth,
Put not an other sin vpon my head,
By vrging me to furie. O be gone,
By heauen I loue thee better then my selfe,
For I come hither arm'd against my selfe:
Stay not, be gone, liue, and hereafter say,
A mad mans mercy bid thee run away.
Par. I do defie thy commisseration,
And apprehend thee for a Fellon here.
Ro. Wilt thou prouoke me? Then haue at thee Boy.
Pet. O Lord they fight, I will go call the Watch.
Pa. O I am slaine, if thon be mercifull,
Open the Tombe, lay me with *Iuliet.*
Rom. In faith I will, let me peruse this face:
Mercutius kinsman, Noble Countie *Paris*,
What said my man, when my betossed soule
Did not attend him as we rode? I thinke
He told me *Paris* should haue married *Iuliet.*
Said he not so? Or did I dreame it so?
Or am I mad, hearing him talke of *Iuliet*,
To thinke it was so? O giue me thy hand,
One, writ with me in sowre misfortunes booke.
Ile burie thee in a triumphant graue.
A Graue; O no, a Lanthorne; slaughtred Youth:
For here lies *Iuliet*, and her beautie makes
This Vault a feasting presence full of light.
Death lie thou there, by a dead man inter'd.
How oft when men are at the point of death,
Haue they beene merrie? Which their Keepers call
A lightning before death? Oh how may I
Call this a lightning? O my Loue, my Wife,
Death that hath suckt the honey of thy breath,
Hath had no power yet vpon thy Beautie:
Thou are not conquer'd: Beauties ensigne yet
Is Crymson in thy lips, and in thy cheekes,
And Deaths pale flag is not aduanced there.
Tybalt, ly'st thou there in thy bloudy sheet?
O what more fauour can I do to thee,
Then with that hand that cut thy youth in twaine,
To sunder his that was thy enemie?
Forgiue me Cozen. Ah deare *Iuliet*:
Why art thou yet so faire? I will beleeue,
Shall I beleeue, that vnsubstantiall death is amorous?
And that the leane abhorred Monster keepes
Thee here in darke to be his Paramour?
For feare of that, I still will stay with thee,
And neuer from this Pallace of dym night
Depart againe: come lie thou in my armes,
Heere's to thy health, where eere thou tumblest in.
O true Appothecarie!
Thy drugs are quicke. Thus with a kisse I die.
Depart againe; here, here will I remaine,
With Wormes that are thy Chambermaides: O here
Will I set vp my euerlasting rest:
And shake the yoke of inauspicious starres
From this world-wearied flesh: Eyes looke your last:
Armes take your last embrace: And lips, O you
The doores of breath, seale with a righteous kisse
A datelesse bargaine to ingrossing death:
Come bitter conduct, come vnsauoury guide,
Thou desperate Pilot, now at once run on
The dashing Rocks, thy Sea-sicke wearie Barke:
Heere's to my Loue. O true Appothecary:

Thy drugs are quicke. Thus with a kiſſe I die.
Enter Frier with Lanthorne, Crow, and Spade.
Fri. St. Francis be my ſpeed, how oft to night
Haue my old feet ſtumbled at graues? Who's there?
Man. Here's one, a Friend, & one that knowes you well.
Fri. Bliſſe be vpon you. Tell me good my Friend
What Torch is yond that vainely lends his light
To grubs, and eyeleſſe Sculles? As I diſcerne,
It burneth in the *Capels* Monument.
Man. It doth ſo holy ſir,
And there's my Maſter, one that you loue.
Fri. Who is it?
Man. Romeo.
Fri. How long hath he bin there?
Man. Full halfe an houre.
Fri. Go with me to the Vault.
Man. I dare not Sir.
My Maſter knowes not but I am gone hence,
And fearefully did menace me with death,
If I did ſtay to looke on his entents.
Fri. Stay, then Ile go alone, feares comes vpon me.
O much I feare ſome ill vnluckie thing.
Man. As I did ſleepe vnder this young tree here,
I dreamt my maiſter and another fought,
And that my Maiſter ſlew him.
Fri. Romeo.
Alacke, alacke, what blood is this which ſtaines
The ſtony entrance of this Sepulcher?
What meane theſe Maſterleſſe, and goarie Swords
To lie diſcolour'd by this place of peace?
Romeo, oh pale: who elſe? what *Paris* too?
And ſteept in blood? Ah what an vnkind houre
Is guiltie of this lamentable chance?
The Lady ſtirs.
Iul. O comfortable Frier, where's my Lord?
I do remember well where I ſhould be:
And there I am, where is my *Romeo?*
Fri. I heare ſome noyſe Lady, come from that neſt
Of death, contagion, and vnnaturall ſleepe,
A greater power then we can contradict
Hath thwarted our entents, come, come away,
Thy husband in thy boſome there lies dead:
And *Paris* too: come Ile diſpoſe of thee,
Among a Siſterhood of holy Nunnes:
Stay not to queſtion, for the watch is comming.
Come, go good *Iuliet*, I dare no longer ſtay. *Exit.*
Iul. Go get thee hence, for I will not away,
What's here? A cup clos'd in my true lo: es hand?
Poyſon I ſee hath bin his timeleſſe end
O churle, drinke all? and left no friendly drop,
To helpe me after, I will kiſſe thy lips,
Happlie ſome poyſon yet doth hang on them,
To make me die wth a reſtoratiue.
Thy lips are warme.
Enter Boy and Watch.
Watch. Lead Boy, which way?
Iul. Yea noiſe?
Then ile be briefe. O happy Dagger.
'Tis in thy ſheath, there ruſt and let me die *Kils herſelfe.*
Boy. This is the place,
There where the Torch doth burne
Watch. The ground is bloody,
Search about the Churchyard.
Go ſome of you, who ere you find attach.
Pittifull ſight, here lies the Countie ſlaine,
And *Iuliett* bleeding, warme and newly dead
Who here hath laine theſe two dayes buried.
Go tell the Prince, runne to the *Capulets*,
Raiſe vp the *Mountagues*, ſome others ſearch,
We ſee the ground whereon theſe woes do lye,
But the true ground of all theſe piteous woes,
We cannot without circumſtance deſcry.
Enter Romeo's man.
Watch. Here's *Romeo's* man,
We found him in the Churchyard.
Con. Hold him in ſafety, till the Prince come hither.
Enter Frier, and another Watchman.
3. *Wat.* Here is a Frier that trembles, ſighes, and weepes
We tooke this Mattocke and this Spade from him,
As he was comming from this Church-yard ſide.
Con. A great ſuſpition, ſtay the Frier too.
Enter the Prince.
Prin. What miſaduenture is ſo earely vp,
That calls our perſon from our mornings reſt?

Enter Capulet and his Wife.
Cap. What ſhould it be that they ſo ſhrike abroad?
Wife. O the people in the ſtreete crie *Romeo.*
Some *Iuliet*, and ſome *Paris*, and all runne
With open outcry toward out Monument.
Pri. What feare is this which ſtartles in your eares?
Wat. Soueraigne, here lies the Countie *Paris* ſlaine,
And *Romeo* dead, and *Iuliet* dead before,
Warme and new kil'd.
Prin. Search,
Seeke, and know how, this foule murder comes.
Wat. Here is a Frier, and Slaughter'd *Romeos* man,
With Inſtruments vpon them fit to open
Theſe dead mens Tombes.
Cap. O heauen!
O wife looke how our Daughter bleedes!
This Dagger hath miſtaine, for loe his houſe
Is empty on the backe of *Mountague*,
And is miſheathed in my Daughters boſome.
Wife. O me, this ſight of death, is as a Bell
That warnes my old age to a Sepulcher.
Enter Mountague.
Pri. Come *Mountague*, for thou art early vp
To ſee thy Sonne and Heire, now early downe.
Moun. Alas my liege, my wife is dead to night,
Griefe of my Sonnes exile hath ſtopt her breath:
What further woe conſpires againſt my age?
Prin. Looke: and thou ſhalt ſee.
Moun. O thou vntaught, what manners in is this,
To preſſe before thy Father to a graue?
Prin. Seale vp the mouth of outra ge for a while,
Till we can cleare theſe ambiguities,
And know their ſpring, their head, their true deſcent,
And then will I be generall of your woes,
And lead you euen to death? meane time forbeare,
And let miſchance be ſlaue to patience,
Bring forth the parties of ſuſpition.
Fri. I am the greateſt, able to doe leaſt,
Yet moſt ſuſpected as the time and place
Doth make againſt me of this direfull murther:
And heere I ſtand both to impeach and purge
My ſelfe condemned, and my ſelfe excus'd.
Prin. Then ſay at once, what thou doſt know in this?
Fri. I will be briefe, for my ſhort date of breath
Is not ſo long as is a tedious tale.
Romeo there dead, was husband to that *Iuliet*,
And ſhe there dead, that's *Romeos* faithfull wife:

I

I married them; and their ſtolne marriage day
Was *Tybalts* Doomeſday: whoſe vntimely death
Baniſh'd the new-made Bridegroome from this Citie:
For whom (and not for *Tybalt*) *Iuliet* pinde.
You, to remoue that ſiege of Greefe from her,
Betroth'd, and would haue married her perforce
To Countie *Paris*. Then comes ſhe to me,
And (with wilde lookes) bid me deuiſe ſome meanes
To rid her from this ſecond Marriage,
Or in my Cell there would ſhe kill her ſelfe.
Then gaue I her (ſo Tutor'd by my Art)
A ſleeping Potion, which ſo tooke effect
As I intended, for it wrought on her
The forme of death. Meane time, I writ to *Romeo*,
That he ſhould hither come, as this dyre night,
To helpe to take her from her borrowed graue,
Being the time the Potions force ſhould ceaſe.
But he which bore my Letter, Frier *John*,
Was ſtay'd by accident; and yeſternight
Return'd my Letter backe. Then all alone,
At the prefixed houre of her waking,
Came I to take her from her Kindreds vault,
Meaning to keepe her cloſely at my Cell,
Till I conueniently could ſend to *Romeo*.
But when I came (ſome Minute ere the time
Of her awaking) heere vntimely lay
The Noble *Paris*, and true *Romeo* dead.
Shee wakes, and I intreated her come foorth,
And beare this worke of Heauen, with patience:
But then, a noyſe did ſcarre me from the Tombe,
And ſhe (too deſperate) would not go with me,
But (as it ſeemes) did violence on her ſelfe.
All this I know, and to the Marriage her Nurſe is priuy:
And if ought in this miſcarried by my fault,
Let my old life be ſacrific'd, ſome houre before the time,
Vnto the rigour of ſeuereſt Law.

Prin. We ſtill haue knowne thee for a Holy man.
Where's *Romeo's* man? What can he ſay to this?

Boy. I brought my Maſter newes of *Iuliets* death,
And then in poſte he came from *Mantua*
To this ſame place, to this ſame Monument.
This Letter he early bid me giue his Father,
And threatned me with death, going in the Vault,
If I departed not, and left him there.

Prin. Giue me the Letter, I will look on it.
Where is the Counties Page that rais'd the Watch?
Sirra, what made your Maſter in this place?

Page. He came with flowres to ſtrew his Ladies graue,
And bid me ſtand aloofe, and ſo I did:
Anon comes one with light to ope the Tombe,
And by and by my Maiſter drew on him,
And then I ran away to call the Watch.

Prin. This Letter doth make good the Friers words,
Their courſe of Loue, the tydings of her death:
And heere he writes, that he did buy a poyſon
Of a poore Pothecarie, and therewithall
Came to this Vault to dye, and lye with *Iuliet*.
Where be theſe Enemies? *Capulet*, *Mountague*,
See what a ſcourge is laide vpon your hate,
That Heauen finds meanes to kill your ioyes with Loue;
And I, for winking at your diſcords too,
Haue loſt a brace of Kinſmen: All are puniſh'd.

Cap. O Brother *Mountague*, giue me thy hand,
This is my Daughters ioynture, for no more
Can I demand.

Moun. But I can giue thee more:
For I will raiſe her Statue in pure Gold,
That whiles *Verona* by that name is knowne,
There ſhall no figure at that Rate be ſet,
As that of True and Faithfull *Iuliet*.

Cap. As rich ſhall *Romeo* by his Lady ly,
Poore ſacrifices of our enmity.

Prin. A glooming peace this morning with it brings,
The Sunne for ſorrow will not ſhew his head;
Go hence, to haue more talke of theſe ſad things,
Some ſhall be pardon'd, and ſome puniſhed.
For neuer was a Storie of more Wo,
Then this of *Iuliet*, and her *Romeo*. *Exeunt omnes*

G g

FINIS.

THE LIFE OF TYMON OF ATHENS.

Actus Primus. Scœna Prima.

Enter Poet, Painter, Ieweller, Merchant, and Mercer, at seuerall doores.

Poet.

GOod day Sir.

Pain. I am glad y'are well.

Poet. I haue not seene you long, how goes the World?

Pain. It weares sir, as it growes.

Poet. I that's well knowne:
But what particular Rarity? What strange,
Which manifold record not matches: see
Magicke of Bounty, all these spirits thy power
Hath coniur'd to attend.
I know the Merchant.

Pain. I know them both: th'others a Ieweller.

Mer. O 'tis a worthy Lord.

Iew. Nay that's most fixt.

Mer. A most incomparable man, breath'd as it were,
To an vntyreable and continuate goodnesse:
He passes.

Iew. I haue a Iewell heere.

Mer. O pray let's see't. For the Lord *Timon*, sir?

Iewel. If he will touch the estimate. But for that——

Poet. When we for recompence haue prais'd the vild,
It staines the glory in that happy Verse,
Which aptly sings the good.

Mer. 'Tis a good forme.

Iewel. And rich: heere is a Water looke ye.

Pain. You are rapt sir, in some worke, some Dedication to the great Lord.

Poet. A thing slipt idlely from me.
Our Poesie is as a Gowne, which vses
From whence 'tis nourisht: the fire i'th'Flint
Shewes not, till it be strooke: our gentle flame
Prouokes it selfe, and like the currant flyes
Each bound it chases. What haue you there?

Pain. A Picture sir: when comes your Booke forth?

Poet. Vpon the heeles of my presentment sir.
Let's see your peece.

Pain. 'Tis a good Peece.

Poet. So 'tis, this comes off well, and excellent.

Pain. Indifferent.

Poet. Admirable: How this grace
Speakes his owne standing: what a mentall power
This eye shootes forth? How bigge imagination
Moues in this Lip, to th'dumbnesse of the gesture,
One might interpret.

Pain. It is a pretty mocking of the life:
Heere is a touch: Is't good?

Poet. I will say of it,
It Tutors Nature, Artificiall strife
Liues in these toutches, liuelier then life.

Enter certaine Senators.

Pain. How this Lord is followed.

Poet. The Senators of Athens, happy men.

Pain. Looke moe.

Po. You see this confluence, this great flood of visitors,
I haue in this rough worke, shap'd out a man
Whom this beneath world doth embrace and hugge
With amplest entertainment: My free drift
Halts not particularly, but moues it selfe
In a wide Sea of wax, no leuell'd malice
Infects one comma in the course I hold,
But flies an Eagle flight, bold, and forth on,
Leauing no Tract behinde.

Pain. How shall I vnderstand you?

Poet. I will vnboult to you.
You see how all Conditions, how all Mindes,
As well of glib and slipp'ry Creatures, as
Of Graue and austere qualitie, tender downe
Their seruices to Lord *Timon*: his large Fortune,
Vpon his good and gracious Nature hanging,
Subdues and properties to his loue and tendance
All sorts of hearts; yea, from the glasse-fac'd Flatterer
To *Apemantus*, that few things loues better
Then to abhorre himselfe; euen hee drops downe
The knee before him, and returnes in peace
Most rich in *Timons* nod.

Pain. I saw them speake together.

Poet. Sir, I haue vpon a high and pleasant hill
Feign'd Fortune to be thron'd.
The Base o'th'Mount
Is rank'd with all deserts, all kinde of Natures
That labour on the bosome of this Sphere,
To propagate their states; among'st them all,
Whose eyes are on this Soueraigne Lady fixt,
One do I personate of Lord *Timons* frame,
Whom Fortune with her Iuory hand wafts to her,
Whose present grace, to present slaues and seruants
Translates his Riuals.

Pain. 'Tis conceyu'd, to scope
This Throne, this Fortune, and this Hill me thinkes

With

With one man becken'd from the rest below,
Bowing his head against the steepy Mount
To climbe his happinesse, would be well exprest
In our Condition.

Poet. Nay Sir, but heare me on:
All those which were his Fellowes but of late,
Some better then his valew; on the moment
Follow his strides, his Lobbies fill with tendance,
Raine Sacrificiall whisperings in his eare,
Make Sacred euen his styrrop, and through him
Drinke the free Ayre.

Pain. I marry, what of these?

Poet. When Fortune in her shift and change of mood
Spurnes downe her late beloued; all his Dependants
Which labour'd after him to the Mountaines top,
Euen on their knees and hand, let him sit downe,
Not one accompanying his declining foot.

Pain. Tis common:
A thousand morall Paintings I can shew,
That shall demonstrate these quicke blowes of Fortunes,
More pregnantly then words. Yet you do well,
To shew Lord *Timon*, that meane eyes haue seene
The foot aboue the head.

Trumpets sound.
Enter Lord Timon, addressing himselfe curteously to euery Sutor.

Tim. Imprison'd is he, say you?

Mes. I my good Lord, fiue Talents is his debt,
His meanes most short, his Creditors most straite:
Your Honourable Letter he desires
To those haue shut him vp, which failing,
Periods his comfort.

Tim. Noble *Ventidius* well:
I am not of that Feather, to shake off
My Friend when he must neede me. I do know him
A Gentleman, that well deserues a helpe,
Which he shall haue. Ile pay the debt, and free him.

Mes. Your Lordship euer bindes him.

Tim. Commend me to him, I will send his ransome,
And being enfranchized bid him come to me;
'Tis not enough to helpe the Feeble vp,
But to support him after. Fare you well.

Mes. All happinesse to your Honor. *Exit.*

Enter an old Athenian.

Oldm. Lord *Timon*, heare me speake.

Tim. Freely good Father.

Oldm. Thou hast a Seruant nam'd *Lucilius*.

Tim. I haue so: What of him?

Oldm. Most Noble *Timon*, call the man before thee.

Tim. Attends he heere, or no? *Lucillius.*

Luc. Heere at your Lordships seruice.

Oldm. This Fellow heere, L. *Timon*, this thy Creature,
By night frequents my house. I am a man
That from my first haue beene inclin'd to thrift,
And my estate deserues an Heyre more rais'd,
Then one which holds a Trencher.

Tim. Well: what further?

Old. One onely Daughter haue I, no Kin else,
On whom I may conferre what I haue got:
The Maid is faire, a'th'youngest for a Bride,
And I haue bred her at my deerest cost
In Qualities of the best. This man of thine
Attempts her loue: I prythee (Noble Lord)
Ioyne with me to forbid him her resort,
My selfe haue spoke in vaine.

Tim. The man is honest.

Oldm. Therefore he will be *Timon*,
His honesty rewards him in it selfe,
It must not beare my Daughter.

Tim. Does she loue him?

Oldm. She is yong and apt:
Our owne precedent passions do instruct vs
What leuities in youth.

Tim. Loue you the Maid?

Luc. I my good Lord, and she accepts of it.

Oldm. If in her Marriage my consent be missing,
I call the Gods to witnesse, I will choose
Mine heyre from forth the Beggers of the world,
And dispossesse her all.

Tim. How shall she be endowed,
If she be mated with an equall Husband?

Oldm. Three Talents on the present; in future, all.

Tim. This Gentleman of mine
Hath seru'd me long:
To build his Fortune, I will straine a little,
For 'tis a Bond in men. Giue him thy Daughter,
What you bestow, in him Ile counterpoize,
And make him weigh with her.

Oldm. Most Noble Lord,
Pawne me to this your Honour, she is his.

Tim. My hand to thee,
Mine Honour on my promise.

Luc. Humbly I thanke your Lordship, neuer may
That state or Fortune fall into my keeping,
Which is not owed to you. *Exit*

Poet. Vouchsafe my Labour,
And long liue your Lordship.

Tim. I thanke you, you shall heare from me anon:
Go not away. What haue you there, my Friend?

Pain. A peece of Painting, which I do beseech
Your Lordship to accept.

Tim. Painting is welcome.
The Painting is almost the Naturall man:
For since Dishonor Traffickes with mans Nature,
He is but out-side: These Pensil'd Figures are
Euen such as they giue out. I like your worke,
And you shall finde I like it; Waite attendance
Till you heare further from me.

Pain. The Gods preserue ye.

Tim. Well fare you Gentleman: giue me your hand.
We must needs dine together: sir your Iewell
Hath suffered vnder praise.

Iewel. What my Lord, dispraise?

Tim. A meere saciety of Commendations,
If I should pay you for't as 'tis extold,
It would vnclew me quite.

Iewel. My Lord, 'tis rated
As those which sell would giue: but you well know,
Things of like valew differing in the Owners,
Are prized by their Masters. Beleeu't deere Lord,
You mend the Iewell by the wearing it.

Tim. Well mock'd. *Enter Apermantus.*

Mer. No my good Lord, he speakes ẏ common toong
Which all men speake with him.

Tim. Looke who comes heere, will you be chid?

Iewel. Wee'l beare with your Lordship.

Mer. Hee'l spare none.

Tim. Good morrow to thee,
Gentle *Apermantus.*

Ape. Till I be gentle, ftay thou for thy good morrow. When thou art *Timons* dogge, and thefe Knaues honeft.

Tim. Why doft thou call them Knaues, thou know'ft them not?

Ape. Are they not Athenians?

Tim. Yes.

Ape. Then I repent not.

Iew. You know me, *Apemantus*?

Ape. Thou know'ft I do, I call'd thee by thy name.

Tim. Thou art proud *Apemantus*?

Ape. Of nothing fo much, as that I am not like *Timon*

Tim. Whether art going?

Ape. To knocke out an honeft Athenians braines.

Tim. That's a deed thou't dye for.

Ape. Right, if doing nothing be death by th'Law.

Tim. How lik'ft thou this picture *Apemantus*?

Ape. The beft, for the innocence.

Tim. Wrought he not well that painted it.

Ape. He wrought better that made the Painter, and yet he's but a filthy peece of worke.

Pain. Y'are a Dogge.

Ape. Thy Mothers of my generation: what's fhe, if I be a Dogge?

Tim. Wilt dine with me *Apemantus*?

Ape. No: I eate not Lords.

Tim. And thou fhould'ft, thoud'ft anger Ladies.

Ape. O they eate Lords;
So they come by great bellies.

Tim. That's a lafciuious apprehenfion.

Ape. So, thou apprehend'ft it,
Take it for thy labour.

Tim. How doft thou like this Iewell, *Apemantus*?

Ape. Not fo well as plain-dealing, which wil not caft a man a Doit.

Tim. What doft thou thinke 'tis worth?

Ape. Not worth my thinking.
How now Poet?

Poet. How now Philofopher?

Ape. Thou lyeft.

Poet. Art not one?

Ape. Yes.

Poet. Then I lye not.

Ape. Art not a Poet?

Poet. Yes.

Ape. Then thou lyeft:
Looke in thy laft worke, where thou haft fegin'd him a worthy Fellow.

Poet. That's not feign'd, he is fo.

Ape. Yes he is worthy of thee, and to pay thee for thy labour. He that loues to be flattered, is worthy o'th flatterer. Heauens, that I were a Lord.

Tim. What wouldft do then *Apemantus*?

Ape. E'ne as *Apemantus* does now, hate a Lord with my heart.

Tim. What thy felfe?

Ape. I.

Tim. Wherefore?

Ape. That I had no angry wit to be a Lord.)
Art not thou a Merchant?

Mer. I *Apemantus*.

Ape. Traffick confound thee, if the Gods will not.

Mer. If Trafficke do it, the Gods do it.

Ape. Traffickes thy God, & thy God confound thee.

Trumpet founds. Enter a Meffenger.

Tim. What Trumpets that?

Mef. 'Tis *Alcibiades*, and fome twenty Horfe
All of Companionfhip.

Tim. Pray entertaine them, giue them guide to vs.
You muft needs dine with me: go not you hence
Till I haue thankt you: when dinners done
Shew me this peece, I am ioyfull of your fights.

Enter Alcibiades with the reft.

Moft welcome Sir.

Ape. So, fo; their Aches contract, and fterue your fupple ioynts: that there fhould bee fmall loue amongeft thefe fweet Knaues, and all this Curtefie. The ftraine of mans bred out into Baboon and Monkey.

Alc. Sir, you haue fau'd my longing, and I feed
Moft hungerly on your fight.

Tim. Right welcome Sir:
Ere we depatt, wee'l fhare a bounteous time
In different pleafures.
Pray you let vs in. *Exeunt.*

Enter two Lords.

1. *Lord* What time a day is't *Apemantus*?

Ape. Time to be honeft.

1 That time ferues ftill.

Ape. The moft accurfed thou that ftill omitft it.

2 Thou art going to Lord *Timons* Feaft.

Ape. I, to fee meate fill Knaues, and Wine heat fooles.

2 Farthee well, farthee well.

Ape. Thou art a Foole to bid me farewell twice.

2 Why *Apemantus*?

Ape. Should'ft haue kept one to thy felfe, for I meane to giue thee none.

1 Hang thy felfe.

Ape. No I will do nothing at thy bidding:
Make thy requefts to thy Friend.

2 Away vnpeaceable Dogge,
Or Ile fpurne thee hence.

Ape. I will flye like a dogge, the heeles a'th'Affe.

1 Hee's oppofite to humanity.
Comes fhall we in,
And tafte Lord *Timons* bountie: he out-goes
The verie heart of kindneffe.

2 He powres it out: *Plutus* the God of Gold
Is but his Steward: no meede but he repayes
Seuen-fold aboue it felfe: No guift to him,
But breeds the giuer a returne: exceeding
All vfe of quittance.

1 The Nobleft minde he carries,
That euer gouern'd man.

2 Long may he liue in Fortunes. Shall we in?
Ile keepe you Company. *Exeunt.*

Hoboyes Playing lowd Muficke.

A great Banquet feru'd in: and then, Enter Lord Timon, the States, the Athenian Lords, Ventigius which Timon redeem'd from prifon. Then comes dropping after all Apemantus difcontentedly like himfelfe.

Ventig. Moft honoured *Timon*,
It hath pleas'd the Gods to remember my Fathers age,
And call him to long peace:
He is gone happy, and has left me rich:
Then, as in gratefull Vertue I am bound
To your free heart, I do returne thofe Talents
Doubled with thankes and feruice, from whofe helpe
I deriu'd libertie.

Tim. O by no meanes,
Honeft *Ventigius*: You miftake my loue,

I gaue

I gaue it freely euer, and ther's none
Can truely say he giues, if he receiues:
If our betters play at that game, we must not dare
To imitate them : faults that are rich are faire.

Vint. A Noble spirit.

Tim. Nay my Lords, Ceremony was but deuis'd at first
To set a glosse on faint deeds, hollow welcomes,
Recanting goodnesse, sorry ere 'tis showne:
But where there is true friendship, there needs none.
Pray sit, more welcome are ye to my Fortunes,
Then my Fortunes to me.

1. *Lord.* My Lord, we alwaies haue confest it.

Aper. Ho ho, confest it? Handg'd it? Haue you not?

Timo. O *Apermantus*, you are welcome.

Aper. No: You shall not make me welcome:
I come to haue thee thrust me out of doores.

Tim. Fie, th'art a churle, ye'haue got a humour there
Does not become a man, 'tis much too blame:
They say my Lords, *Ira furor breuis est*,
But yond man is verie angrie.
Go, let him haue a Table by himselfe:
For he does neither affect companie,
Nor is he fit for't indeed.

Aper. Let me stay at thine apperill *Timon*,
I come to obserue, I giue thee warning on't.

Tim. I take no heede of thee: Th'art an *Athenian*, therefore welcome: I my selfe would haue no power, prythee let my meate make thee silent.

Aper. I scorne thy meate, 'twould choake me: for I should nere flatter thee. Oh you Gods! What a number of men eats *Timon*, and he sees 'em not? It greeues me to see so many dip there meate in one mans blood, and all the madnesse is, he cheeres them vp too.
I wonder men dare trust themselues with men.
Me thinks they should enuite them without kniues,
Good for there meate, and safer for their liues.
There's much example for't, the fellow that sits next him, now parts bread with him, pledges the breath of him in a diuided draught: is the readiest man to kill him. 'Tas beene proued, if I were a huge man I should feare to drinke at meales, least they should spie my wind-pipes dangerous noates, great men should drinke with harnesse on their throates.

Tim. My Lord in heart: and let the health go round.

2. *Lord.* Let it flow this way my good Lord.

Aper. Flow this way? A braue fellow. He keepes his tides well, those healths will make thee and thy state looke ill, *Timon*.
Heere's that which is too weake to be a sinner,
Honest water, which nere left man i'th'mire:
This and my food are equals, there's no ods,
Feasts are to proud to giue thanks to the Gods.

Apermantus Grace.

Immortall Gods, I craue no pelfe,
I pray for no man but my selfe,
Graunt I may neuer proue so fond,
To trust man on his Oath or Bond.
Or a Harlot for her weeping,
Or a Dogge that seemes asleeping,
Or a keeper with my freedome,
Or my friends if I should need 'em.
Amen. So fall too't:
Richmen sin, and I eat root.

Much good dich thy good heart, *Apermantus*

Tim. Captaine,
Alcibiades, your hearts in the field now.

Alci. My heart is euer at your seruice, my Lord.

Tim. You had rather be at a breakefast of Enemies, then a dinner of Friends.

Alc. So they were bleeding new my Lord, there's no meat like 'em, I could wish my best friend at such a Feast.

Aper. Would all those Flatterers were thine Enemies then, that then thou might'st kill 'em: & bid me to 'em.

1. *Lord.* Might we but haue that happinesse my Lord, that you would once vse our hearts, whereby we might expresse some part of our zeales, we should thinke our selues for euer perfect.

Timon. Oh no doubt my good Friends, but the Gods themselues haue prouided that I shall haue much helpe from you: how had you beene my Friends else. Why haue you that charitable title from thousands? Did not you chiefely belong to my heart? I haue told more of you to my selfe, then you can with modestie speake in your owne behalfe. And thus farre I confirme you. Oh you Gods (thinke I,) what need we haue any Friends; if we should nere haue need of 'em? They were the most needlesse Creatures liuing; should we nere haue vse for 'em? And would most resemble sweete Instruments hung vp in Cases, that keepes there sounds to themselues. Why I haue often wisht my selfe poorer, that I might come neerer to you: we are borne to do benefits. And what better or properer can we call our owne, then the riches of our Friends? Oh what a pretious comfort 'tis, to haue so many like Brothers commanding one anothers Fortunes. Oh ioyes, e'ne made away er't can be borne: mine eies cannot hold out water me thinks, to forget their Faults. I drinke to you.

Aper. Thou weep'st to make them drinke, *Timon*.

2. *Lord.* Ioy had the like conception in our eies,
And at that instant, like a babe sprung vp.

Aper. Ho, ho; I laugh to thinke that babe a bastard.

3. *Lord.* I promise you my Lord you mou'd me much.

Aper. Much.

Sound Tucket. Enter the Maskers of Amazons, with Lutes in their hands, dauncing and playing.

Tim. What meanes that Trumpe? How now?

Enter Seruant.

Ser. Please you my Lord, there are certaine Ladies
Most desirous of admittance.

Tim. Ladies? what are their wils?

Ser. There comes with them a fore-runner my Lord, which beares that office, to signifie their pleasures.

Tim. I pray let them be admitted.

Enter Cupid with the Maske of Ladies.

Cup. Haile to thee worthy *Timon* and to all that of his Bounties taste: the fiue best Sences acknowledge thee their Patron, and come freely to gratulate thy plentious bosome.
There tast, touch all, pleas'd from thy Table rise:
They onely now come but to Feast thine eies.

Timo. They'r wecome all, let 'em haue kind admittance. Musicke make their welcome.

Luc. You see my Lord, how ample y'are belou'd.

Aper. Hoyday,
What a sweepe of vanitie comes this way.
They daunce? They are madwomen,

Like Madnesse is the glory of this life,
As this pompe shewes to a little oyle and roote.
We make our selues Fooles, to disport our selues,
And spend our Flatteries, to drinke those men,
Vpon whose Age we voyde it vp agen
With poysonous Spight and Enuy.
Who liues, that's not depraued, or depraues;
Who dyes, that beares not one spurne to their graues
Of their Friends guift:
I should feare, those that dance before me now,
Would one day stampe vpon me: 'Tas bene done,
Men shut their doores against a setting Sunne.

The Lords rise from Table, with much adoring of Timon, and to shew their loues, each single out an Amazon, and all Dance, men with women, a loftie straine or two to the Hoboyes, and cease.

Tim. You haue done our pleasures
Much grace (faire Ladies)
Set a faire fashion on our entertainment,
Which was not halfe so beautifull, and kinde:
You haue added worth vntoo't, and luster,
And entertain'd me with mine owne deuice.
I am to thanke you for't.

1 Lord. My Lord you take vs euen at the best.

Aper. Faith for the worst is filthy, and would not hold taking, I doubt me.

Tim. Ladies, there is an idle banquet attends you,
Please you to dispose your selues.

All La. Most thankfully, my Lord. *Exeunt.*

Tim. Flauius.

Fla. My Lord.

Tim. The little Casket bring me hither.

Fla. Yes, my Lord. More Iewels yet?
There is no crossing him in's humor,
Else I should tell him well, yfaith I should;
When all's spent, hee'ld be crost then, and he could:
'Tis pitty Bounty had not eyes behinde,
That man might ne're be wretched for his minde. *Exit.*

1 Lord. Where be our men?

Ser. Heere my Lord, in readinesse.

2 Lord. Our Horses.

Tim. O my Friends:
I haue one word to say to you: Looke you, my good L.
I must intreat you honour me so much,
As to aduance this Iewell, accept it, and weare it,
Kinde my Lord.

1 Lord. I am so farre already in your guifts.

All. So are we all.

Enter a Seruant.

Ser. My Lord, there are certaine Nobles of the Senate newly alighted, and come to visit you.

Tim. They are fairely welcome.

Enter Flauius.

Fla. I beseech your Honor, vouchsafe me a word, it does concerne you neere.

Tim. Neere? why then another time Ile heare thee.
I prythee let's be prouided to shew them entertainment.

Fla. I scarse know how.

Enter another Seruant.

Ser. May it please your Honor, Lord *Lucius*
(Out of his free loue) hath presented to you
Foure Milke-white Horses, trapt in Siluer.

Tim. I shall accept them fairely: let the Presents
Be worthily entertain'd.

Enter a third Seruant.

How now? What newes?

3.Ser. Please you my Lord, that honourable Gentleman Lord *Lucullus*, entreats your companie to morrow, to hunt with him, and ha's sent your Honour two brace of Grey-hounds.

Tim. Ile hunt with him,
And let them be receiu'd, not without faire Reward.

Fla. What will this come to?
He commands vs to prouide, and giue great guifts, and all out of an empty Coffer:
Nor will he know his Purse, or yeeld me this,
To shew him what a Begger his heart is,
Being of no power to make his wishes good.
His promises flye so beyond his state,
That what he speaks is all in debt, he ows for eu'ry word:
He is so kinde, that he now payes interest for't;
His Land's put to their Bookes. Well, would I were
Gently put out of Office, before I were forc'd out:
Happier is he that has no friend to feede,
Then such that do e'ne Enemies exceede.
I bleed inwardly for my Lord. *Exit*

Tim. You do your selues much wrong,
You bate too much of your owne merits.
Heere my Lord, a trifle of our Loue.

2.Lord. With more then common thankes
I will receyue it.

3.Lord. O he's the very soule of Bounty.

Tim. And now I remember my Lord, you gaue good words the other day of a Bay Courser I rod on. Tis yours because you lik'd it.

1.L. Oh, I beseech you pardon mee, my Lord, in that.

Tim. You may take my word my Lord: I know no man can iustly praise, but what he does affect. I weighe my Friends affection with mine owne: Ile tell you true, Ile call to you.

All Lor. O none so welcome.

Tim. I take all, and your seuerall visitations
So kinde to heart, 'tis not enough to giue:
Me thinkes, I could deale Kingdomes to my Friends,
And nere be wearie. *Alcibiades,*
Thou art a Soldiour, therefore sildome rich,
It comes in Charitie to thee: for all thy liuing
Is mong'st the dead: and all the Lands thou hast
Lye in a pitcht field.

Alc. I, defil'd Land, my Lord.

1.Lord. We are so vertuously bound.

Tim. And so am I to you.

2.Lord. So infinitely endeer'd.

Tim. All to you. Lights, more Lights.

1.Lord. The best of Happines, Honor, and Fortunes
Keepe with you Lord *Timon*.

Tim. Ready for his Friends. *Exeunt Lords*

Aper. What a coiles heere, seruing of beckes, and iutting out of bummes. I doubt whether their Legges be worth the summes that are giuen for 'em.
Friendships full of dregges,
Me thinkes false hearts, should neuer haue sound legges.
Thus honest Fooles lay out their wealth on Curtsies.

Tim. Now *Apermantus* (if thou wert not sullen)
I would be good to thee.

Aper. No, Ile nothing; for if I should be brib'd too, there would be none left to raile vponthee, and then thou wouldst sinne the faster. Thou giu'st so long *Timon* (I feare me) thou wilt giue away thy selfe in paper shortly. What needs these Feasts, pompes, and Vaine-glories?

Tim.

Tim. Nay, and you begin to raile on Societie once, I am ſworne not to giue regard to you. Farewell, & come with better Muſicke. *Exit*

Aper. So: Thou wilt not heare mee now, thou ſhalt not then. Ile locke thy heauen from thee:
Oh that mens eares ſhould be
To Counſell deafe, but not to Flatterie. *Exit*

Enter a Senator.

Sen. And late fiue thouſand: to *Varro* and to *Iſidore*
He owes nine thouſand, beſides my former ſumme,
Which makes it fiue and twenty. Still in motion
Of raging waſte? It cannot hold, it will not.
If I want Gold, ſteale but a beggers Dogge,
And giue it *Timon*, why the Dogge coines Gold.
If I would ſell my Horſe, and buy twenty moe
Better then he; why giue my Horſe to *Timon*.
Aske nothing, giue it him, it Foles me ſtraight
And able Horſes: No Porter at his gate,
But rather one that ſmiles, and ſtill inuites
All that paſſe by. It cannot hold, no reaſon
Can ſound his ſtate in ſafety. *Caphis* hoa,
Caphis I ſay.

Enter Caphis.

Ca. Heere ſir, what is your pleaſure.

Sen. Get on your cloake, & haſt you to Lord *Timon*,
Importune him for my Moneyes, be not ceaſt
With ſlight deniall; nor then ſilenc'd, when
Commend me to your Maſter, and the Cap
Playes in the right hand, thus: but tell him,
My Vſes cry to me; I muſt ſerue my turne
Out of mine owne, his dayes and times are paſt,
And my reliances on his fracted dates
Haue ſmit my credit. I loue, and honour him,
But muſt not breake my backe, to heale his finger.
Immediate are my needs, and my releefe
Muſt not be toſt and turn'd to me in words,
But finde ſupply immediate. Get you gone,
Put on a moſt importunate aſpect,
A viſage of demand: for I do feare
When euery Feather ſtickes in his owne wing,
Lord *Timon* will be left a naked gull,
Which flaſhes now a Phœnix, get you gone.

Ca. I go ſir.

Sen. I go ſir?
Take the Bonds along with you,
And haue the dates in. Come.

Ca. I will Sir.

Sen. Go. *Exeunt*

Enter Steward, with many billes in his hand.

Stew. No care, no ſtop, ſo ſenſeleſſe of expence,
That he will neither know how to maintaine it,
Nor ceaſe his flow of Riot. Takes no accompt
How things go from him, nor reſume no care
Of what is to continue: neuer minde,
Was to be ſo vnwiſe, to be ſo kinde.
What ſhall be done, he will not heare, till feele:
I muſt be round with him, now he comes from hunting.
Fye, fie, fie, fie.

Enter Caphis, Iſidore, and Varro.

Cap. Good euen *Varro*: what, you come for money?

Var. Is't not your buſineſſe too?

Cap. It is, and yours too, *Iſidore*?

Iſid. It is ſo.

Cap. Would we were all diſcharg'd.

Var. I feare it,

Cap. Heere comes the Lord.

Enter Timon, and his Traine.

Tim. So ſoone as dinners done, wee'l forth againe
My *Alcibiades*. With me, what is your will?

Cap. My Lord, heere is a note of certaine dues.

Tim. Dues? whence are you?

Cap. Of Athens heere, my Lord.

Tim. Go to my Steward.

Cap. Pleaſe it your Lordſhip, he hath put me off
To the ſucceſſion of new dayes this moneth:
My Maſter is awak'd by great Occaſion,
To call vpon his owne, and humbly prayes you,
That with your other Noble parts, you'l ſuite,
In giuing him his right.

Tim. Mine honeſt Friend,
I prythee but repaire to me next morning.

Cap. Nay, good my Lord.

Tim. Containe thy ſelfe, good Friend.

Var. One *Varroes* ſeruant, my good Lord.

Iſid. From *Iſidore*, he humbly prayes your ſpeedy payment.

Cap. If you did know my Lord, my Maſters wants.

Var. 'Twas due on forfeyture my Lord, ſixe weekes, and paſt.

Iſi. Your Steward puts me off my Lord, and I
Am ſent expreſſely to your Lordſhip.

Tim. Giue me breath:
I do beſeech you good my Lords keepe on,
Ile waite vpon you inſtantly. Come hither: pray you
How goes the world, that I am thus encountred
With clamorous demands of debt, broken Bonds,
And the detention of long ſince due debts
Againſt my Honor?

Stew. Pleaſe you Gentlemen,
The time is vnagreeable to this buſineſſe:
Your importunacie ceaſe, till after dinner,
That I may make his Lordſhip vnderſtand
Wherefore you are not paid.

Tim. Do ſo my Friends, ſee them well entertain'd.

Stew. Pray draw neere. *Exit.*

Enter Apemantus and Foole.

Caph. Stay, ſtay, here comes the Foole with *Apemantus*, let's ha ſome ſport with 'em.

Var. Hang him, hee'l abuſe vs.

Iſid. A plague vpon him dogge.

Var. How doſt Foole?

Ape. Doſt Dialogue with thy ſhadow?

Var. I ſpeake not to thee.

Ape. No 'tis to thy ſelfe. Come away.

Iſi. There's the Foole hangs on your backe already.

Ape. No thou ſtand'ſt ſingle, th'art not on him yet.

Cap. Where's the Foole now?

Ape. He laſt ask'd the queſtion. Poore Rogues, and Vſurers men, Bauds betweene Gold and want.

Al. What are we *Apemantus*?

Ape. Aſſes.

All. Why?

Ape. That you ask me what you are, & do not know your ſelues. Speake to 'em Foole.

Foole. How do you Gentlemen?

All. Gramercies good Foole:
How does your Miſtris?

Foole.

Foole. She's e'ne ſetting on water to ſcal'd ſuch Chickens as you are. Would we could ſee you at Corinth.

Ape. Good, Gramercy.

Enter Page.

Foole. Looke you, heere comes my Maſters Page.

Page. Why how now Captaine? what do you in this wiſe Company.
How doſt thou *Apermantus?*

Ape. Would I had a Rod in my mouth, that I might anſwer thee profitably.

Boy. Prythee *Apemantus* reade me the ſuperſcription of theſe Letters, I know not which is which.

Ape. Canſt not read?

Page. No.

Ape. There will litle Learning dye then that day thou art hang'd. This is to Lord *Timon*, this to *Alcibiades.* Go thou was't borne a Baſtard, and thou't dye a Bawd.

Page. Thou was't whelpt a Dogge, and thou ſhalt famiſh a Dogges death.
Anſwer not, I am gone. *Exit*

Ape. E'ne ſo thou out-runſt Grace,
Foole I will go with you to Lord *Timons.*

Foole. Will you leaue me there?

Ape. If *Timon* ſtay at home.
You three ſerue three Vſurers?

All. I would they ſeru'd vs.

Ape. So would I:
As good a tricke as euer Hangman ſeru'd Theefe.

Foole. Are you three Vſurers men?

All. I Foole.

Foole. I thinke no Vſurer, but ha's a Foole to his Seruant. My Miſtris is one, and I am her Foole: when men come to borrow of your Maſters, they approach ſadly, and go away merry: but they enter my Maſters houſe merrily, and go away ſadly. The reaſon of this?

Var. I could render one.

Ap. Do it then, that we may account thee a Whoremaſter, and a Knaue, which notwithſtanding thou ſhalt be no leſſe eſteemed.

Varro. What is a Whoremaſter Foole?

Foole. A Foole in good cloathes, and ſomething like thee. 'Tis a ſpirit, ſometime t'appeares like a Lord, ſomtime like a Lawyer, ſometime like a Philoſopher, with two ſtones moe then's artificiall one. Hee is verie often like a Knight; and generally, in all ſhapes that man goes vp and downe in, from foureſcore to thirteen, this ſpirit walkes in.

Var. Thou art not altogether a Foole.

Foole. Nor thou altogether a Wiſeman,
As much foolerie as I haue, ſo much wit thou lack'ſt.

Ape. That anſwer might haue become *Apemantus.*

All. Aſide, aſide, heere comes Lord *Timon.*

Enter Timon and Steward.

Ape. Come with me (Foole) come.

Foole. I do not alwayes follow Louer, elder Brother, and Woman, ſometime the Philoſopher.

Stew. Pray you walke neere,
Ile ſpeake with you anon. *Exeunt.*

Tim. You make me meruell wherefore ere this time
Had you not fully laide my ſtate before me,
That I might ſo haue rated my expence
As I had leaue of meanes.

Stew. You would not heare me:
At many leyſures I propoſe.

Tim. Go too:
Perchance ſome ſingle vantages you tooke,
When my indiſpoſition put you backe,
And that vnaptneſſe made your miniſter
Thus to excuſe your ſelfe.

Stew. O my good Lord,
At many times I brought in my accompts,
Laid them before you, you would throw them off,
And ſay you ſound them in mine honeſtie,
When for ſome trifling preſent you haue bid me
Returne ſo much, I haue ſhooke my head, and wept:
Yea 'gainſt th'Authoritie of manners, pray'd you
To hold your hand more cloſe: I did indure
Not ſildome, nor no ſlight checkes, when I haue
Prompted you in the ebbe of your eſtate,
And your great flow of debts; my lou'd Lord,
Though you heare now (too late) yet nowes a time,
The greateſt of your hauing, lackes a halfe,
To pay your preſent debts.

Tim. Let all my Land be ſold.

Stew. 'Tis all engag'd, ſome forfeyted and gone,
And what remaines will hardly ſtop the mouth
Of preſent dues; the future comes apace:
What ſhall defend the interim, and at length
How goes our reck'ning?

Tim. To Lacedemon did my Land extend.

Stew. O my good Lord, the world is but a word,
Were it all yours, to giue it in a breath,
How quickely were it gone.

Tim. You tell me true.

Stew. If you ſuſpect my Husbandry or Falſhood,
Call me before th'exacteſt Auditors,
And ſet me on the proofe. So the Gods bleſſe me,
When all our Offices haue beene oppreſt
With riotous Feeders, when our Vaults haue wept
With drunken ſpilth of Wine; when euery roome
Hath blaz'd with Lights, and braid with Minſtrelſie,
I haue retyr'd me to a waſtefull cocke,
And ſet mine eyes at flow.

Tim. Prythee no more.

Stew. Heauens, haue I ſaid, the bounty of this Lord:
How many prodigall bits haue Slaues and Pezants
This night englutted: who is not *Timons*,
What heart, head, ſword, force, meanes, but is L. *Timons*:
Great *Timon*, Noble, Worthy, Royall *Timon*:
Ah, when the meanes are gone, that buy this praiſe,
The breath is gone, whereof this praiſe is made:
Feaſt won, faſt loſt; one cloud of Winter ſhowres,
Theſe flyes are coucht.

Tim. Come ſermon me no further.
No villanous bounty yet hath paſt my heart;
Vnwiſely, not ignobly haue I giuen.
Why doſt thou weepe, canſt thou the conſcience lacke,
To thinke I ſhall lacke friends: ſecure thy heart,
If I would broach the veſſels of my loue,
And try the argument of hearts, by borrowing,
Men, and mens fortunes could I frankely vſe
As I can bid thee ſpeake.

Ste. Aſſurance bleſſe your thoughts.

Tim. And in ſome ſort theſe wants of mine are crown'd,
That I account them bleſſings. For by theſe
Shall I trie Friends. You ſhall perceiue
How you miſtake my Fortunes:
I am wealthie in my Friends.
Within there, *Flauius*, *Seruilius*?

Enter

Enter three Seruants.

Ser. My Lord, my Lord.

Tim. I will dispatch you seuerally.
You to Lord *Lucius*, to Lord *Lucullus* you, I hunted with his Honor to day; you to *Sempronius*; commend me to their loues ; and I am proud say, that my occasions haue found time to vse 'em toward a supply of mony : let the request be fifty Talents.

Flam. As you haue said, my Lord.

Stew. Lord *Lucius* and *Lucullus*? Humh.

Tim. Go you sir to the Senators ;
Of whom, euen to the States best health ; I haue
Deseru'd this Hearing : bid 'em send o'th'instant
A thousand Talents to me.

Ste, I haue beene bold
(For that I knew it the most generall way)
To them, to vse your Signet,and your Name,
But they do shake their heads, and I am heere
No richer in returne.

Tim. Is't true? Can't be?

Stew. They answer in a ioynt and corporate voice,
That now they are at fall, want Treature cannot
Do what they would, are sorrie : you are Honourable,
But yet they could haue wisht, they know not,
Something hath beene amisse ; a Noble Nature
May catch a wrench ; would all were well ; tis pitty,
And so intending other serious matters,
After distastefull lookes ; and these hard Fractions
With certaine halfe-caps,and cold mouing nods,
They froze me into Silence.

Tim. You Gods reward them :
Prythee man looke cheerely. These old Fellowes
Haue their ingratitude in them Hereditary :
Their blood is cak'd, 'tis cold, it sildome flowes,
'Tis lacke of kindely warmth, they are not kinde ;
And Nature, as it growes againe toward earth,
Is fashion'd for the iourney, dull and heauy.
Go to *Ventiddius* (prythee be not sad,
Thou art true,and honest ; Ingeniously I speake,
No blame belongs to thee :) *Ventiddius* lately
Buried his Father, by whose death hee's stepp'd
Into a great estate : When he was poore,
Imprison'd, and in scarsitie of Friends,
I cleer'd him with fiue Talents : Greet him from me,
Bid him suppose, some good necessity
Touches his Friend, which craues to be remembred
With those fiue Talents ; that had, giue't these Fellowes
To whom 'tis instant due. Neu'r speake,or thinke,
That *Timons* fortunes 'mong his Friends can sinke.

Stew. I would I could not thinke it :
That thought is Bounties Foe ;
Being free it selfe, it thinkes all others so. *Exeunt*

Flaminius waiting to speake with a Lord from his Master, enters a seruant to him.

Ser. I haue told my Lord of you, he is comming down to you.

Flam. I thanke you Sir.

Enter Lucullus.

Ser. Heere's my Lord.

Luc. One of Lord *Timons* men? A Guift I warrant. Why this hits right : I dreampt of a Siluer Bason & Ewre to night. *Flaminius*, honest *Flaminius*, you are verie respectiuely welcome sir. Fill me some Wine. And how does that Honourable, Compleate, Free-hearted Gentleman of Athens, thy very bouutifull good Lord and Mayster?

Flam. His health is well sir.

Luc. I am right glad that his health is well sir : and what hast thou there vnder thy Cloake, pretty *Flaminius*?

Flam. Faith, nothing but an empty box Sir, which in my Lords behalfe, I come to intreat your Honor to supply . who hauing great and instant occasion to vse fiftie Talents, hath sent to your Lordship to furnish him : nothing doubting your present assistance therein.

Luc. La, la, la, la : Nothing doubting sayes hee? Alas good Lord, a Noble Gentleman 'tis, if he would not keep so good a house. Many a time and often I ha din'd with him, and told him on't, and come againe to supper to him of purpose, to haue him spend lesse, and yet he wold embrace no counsell, take no warning by my comming, euery man has his fault, and honesty is his. I ha told him on't, but I could nere get him from't.

Enter Seruant with Wine.

Ser. Please your Lordship, heere is the Wine.

Luc. *Flaminius*, I haue noted thee alwayes wise. Heere's to thee.

Flam. Your Lordship speakes your pleasure.

Luc. I haue obserued thee alwayes for a towardlie prompt spirit, giue thee thy due, and one that knowes what belongs to reason; and canst vse the time wel, if the time vse thee well. Good parts in thee ; get you gone sirrah. Draw neerer honest *Flaminius*. Thy Lords a bountifull Gentleman, but thou art wise, and thou know'st well enough (although thou com'st to me) that this is no time to lend money, especially vpon bare friendshippe without securitie. Here's three *Solidares* for thee, good Boy winke at me, and say thou saw'st mee not. Fare thee well.

Flam. Is't possible the world should so much differ,
And we aliue that liued? Fly damned basenesse
To him that worships thee.

Luc. Ha? Now I see thou art a Foole, and fit for thy Master. *Exit L.*

Flam May these adde to the number ẏ may scald thee:
Let moulten Coine be thy damnation,
Thou disease of a friend, and not himselfe :
Has friendship such a faint and milkie heart,
It turnes in lesse then two nights? O you Gods!
I feele my Masters passion. This Slaue vnto his Honor,
Has my Lords meate in him :
Why should it thriue, and turne to Nutriment,
When he is turn'd to poyson?
O may Diseases onely worke vpon't :
And when he's sicke to death, let not that part of Nature
Which my Lord payd for, be of any power
To expell sicknesse, but prolong his hower. *Exit.*

Enter Lucius, with three strangers.

Luc. Who the Lord *Timon*? He is my very good friend and an Honourable Gentleman.

1 We know him for no lesse, thogh we are but strangers to him. But I can tell you one thing my Lord, and which I heare from common rumours, now Lord *Timons* happie howres are done and past, and his estate shrinkes from him.

Lucius. Fye no, doe not beleeue it : hee cannot want for money.

2 But beleeue you this my Lord, that not long agoe, one of his men was with the Lord *Lucullus*, to borrow so many Talents, nay vrg'd extreamly for't, and shewed what

what neceſſity belong'd too't, and yet was deny'de.

Luci. How?

2 I tell you, deny'de my Lord.

Luci. What a ſtrange caſe was that? Now before the Gods I am aſham'd on't. Denied that honourable man? There was verie little Honour ſhew'd in't. For my owne part, I muſt needes confeſſe, I haue receyued ſome ſmall kindneſſes from him, as Money, Plate, Iewels, and ſuch like Trifles; nothing comparing to his: yet had hee miſtooke him, and ſent to me, I ſhould ne're haue denied his Occaſion ſo many Talents.

Enter Seruilius.

Seruil. See, by good hap yonders my Lord, I haue ſwet to ſee his Honor. My Honor'd Lord.

Lucil. *Seruilius?* You are kindely met ſir. Farthewell, commend me to thy Honourable vertuous Lord, my very exquiſite Friend.

Seruil. May it pleaſe your Honour, my Lord hath ſent———

Luci. Ha? what ha's he ſent? I am ſo much endeered to that Lord; hee's euer ſending: how ſhall I thank him think'ſt thou? And what has he ſent now?

Seruil. Has onely ſent his preſent Occaſion now my Lord: requeſting your Lordſhip to ſupply his inſtant vſe with ſo many Talents.

Lucil. I know his Lordſhip is but merry with me,
He cannot want fifty fiue hundred Talents.

Seruil. But in the mean time he wants leſſe my Lord.
If his occaſion were not vertuous,
I ſhould not vrge it halfe ſo faithfully.

Luc. Doſt thou ſpeake ſeriouſly *Seruilius*?

Seruil. Vpon my ſoule 'tis true Sir.

Luci. What a wicked Beaſt was I to disfurniſh my ſelf againſt ſuch a good time, when I might ha ſhewn my ſelfe Honourable? How vnluckily it hapned, that I ſhold Purchaſe the day before for a little part, and vndo a great deale of Honour? *Seruilius*, now before the Gods I am not able to do (the more beaſt I ſay) I was ſending to vſe Lord *Timon* my ſelfe, theſe Gentlemen can witneſſe; but I would not for the wealth of Athens I had done't now. Commend me bountifully to his good Lordſhip, and I hope his Honor will conceiue the faireſt of mee, becauſe I haue no power to be kinde. And tell him this from me, I count it one of my greateſt afflictions ſay, that I cannot pleaſure ſuch an Honourable Gentleman. Good *Seruilius*, will you befriend mee ſo farre, as to vſe mine owne words to him?

Ser. Yes ſir, I ſhall. *Exit Seruil.*

Lucil. Ile looke you out a good turne *Seruilius*.
True as you ſaid, *Timon* is ſhrunke indeede,
And he that's once deny'de, will hardly ſpeede. *Exit.*

1 Do you obſerue this *Hoſtilius*?

2 I, to well.

1 Why this is the worlds ſoule,
And iuſt of the ſame peece
Is euery Flatterers ſport: who can call him his Friend
That dips in the ſame diſh? For in my knowing
Timon has bin this Lords Father,
And kept his credit with his purſe:
Supported his eſtate, nay *Timons* money
Has paid his men their wages. He ne're drinkes,
But *Timons* Siluer treads vpon his Lip,
And yet, oh ſee the monſtrouſneſſe of man,
When he lookes out in an vngratefull ſhape;
He does deny him (in reſpect of his)
What charitable men affoord to Beggers.

3 Religion grones at it.

1 For mine owne part, I neuer taſted *Timon* in my life
Nor came any of his bounties ouer me,
To marke me for his Friend. Yet I proteſt,
For his right Noble minde, illuſtrious Vertue,
And Honourable Carriage,
Had his neceſſity made vſe of me,
I would haue put my wealth into Donation,
And the beſt halfe ſhould haue return'd to him,
So much I loue his heart: But I perceiue,
Men muſt learne now with pitty to diſpence,
For Policy ſits aboue Conſcience. *Exeunt.*

Enter a third ſeruant with Sempronius, another of Timons Friends.

Semp. Muſt he needs trouble me in't? Hum.
'Boue all others?
He might haue tried Lord *Lucius*, or *Lucullus*,
And now *Ventidgius* is wealthy too,
Whom he redeem'd from priſon. All theſe
Owes their eſtates vnto him.

Ser. My Lord,
They haue all bin touch'd, and found Baſe-Mettle,
For they haue all denied him.

Semp. How? Haue they deny'de him?
Has *Ventidgius* and *Lucullus* deny'de him,
And does he ſend to me? Three? Humh?
It ſhewes but little loue, or iudgement in him.
Muſt I be his laſt Refuge? His Friends (like Phyſitians)
Thriue, giue him ouer: Muſt I take th'Cure vpon me?
Has much diſgrac'd me in't, I'me angry at him,
That might haue knowne my place. I ſee no ſenſe for't,
But his Occaſions might haue wooed me firſt:
For in my conſcience, I was the firſt man
That ere receiued guift from him.
And does he thinke ſo backwardly of me now,
That Ile requite it laſt? No:
So it may proue an Argument of Laughter
To th'reſt, and 'mong'ſt Lords be thought a Foole:
I'de rather then the worth of thrice the ſumme,
Had ſent to me firſt, but for my mindes ſake:
I'de ſuch a courage to do him good. But now returne,
And with their faint reply, this anſwer ioyne;
Who bates mine Honor, ſhall not know my Coyne. *Exit*

Ser. Excellent: Your Lordſhips a goodly Villain: the diuell knew not what he did, when hee made man Politicke; he croſſed himſelfe by't: and I cannot thinke, but in the end, the Villanies of man will ſet him cleere. How fairely this Lord ſtriues to appeare foule? Takes Vertuous Copies to be wicked: like thoſe, that vnder hotte ardent zeale, would ſet whole Realmes on fire, of ſuch a nature is his politike loue.
This was my Lords beſt hope, now all are fled
Saue onely the Gods. Now his Friends are dead,
Doores that were ne're acquainted with their Wards
Many a bounteous yeere, muſt be imploy'd
Now to guard ſure their Maſter:
And this is all a liberall courſe allowes,
Who cannot keepe his wealth, muſt keep his houſe. *Exit.*

Enter Varro's man, meeting others. All Timons Creditors to wait for his comming out. Then enter Lucius and Hortenſius.

Var. man. Well met, goodmorrow *Titus* & *Hortenſius*

Titus

Tit. The like to you kinde *Varro.*
Hort. *Lucius*, what do we meet together?
Luci. I, and I think one businesse do's command vs all.
For mine is money.
Tit. So is theirs, and ours.
Enter Philotus.
Luci. And sir *Philotus* too.
Phil. Good day at once.
Luci. Welcome good Brother.
What do you thinke the houre?
Phil. Labouring for Nine.
Luci. So much?
Phil. Is not my Lord seene yet?
Luci. Not yet.
Phil. I wonder on't, he was wont to shine at seauen.
Luci. I, but the dayes are waxt shorter with him:
You must consider, that a Prodigall course
Is like the Sunnes, but not like his recouerable, I feare:
'Tis deepest Winter in Lord *Timons* purse, that is: One may reach deepe enough, and yet finde little.
Phil. I am of your feare, for that.
Tit. Ile shew you how t'obserue a strange euent:
Your Lord sends now for Money?
Hort. Most true, he doe's.
Tit. And he weares Iewels now of *Timons* guift,
For which I waite for money.
Hort. It is against my heart.
Luci. Marke how strange it showes,
Timon in this, should pay more then he owes:
And e'ne as if your Lord should weare rich Iewels,
And send for money for 'em.
Hort. I'me weary of this Charge,
The Gods can witnesse:
I know my Lord hath spent of *Timons* wealth,
And now Ingratitude, makes it worse then stealth.
Varro. Yes, mine's three thousand Crownes:
What's yours?
Luci. Fiue thousand mine.
Varro. 'Tis much deepe, and it should seem by th'sum
Your Masters confidence was aboue mine,
Else surely his had equall'd.
Enter Flaminius.
Tit. One of Lord *Timons* men.
Luc. *Flaminius*? Sir, a word: Pray is my Lord readie to come forth?
Flam. No, indeed he is not.
Tit. We attend his Lordship: pray signifie so much.
Flam. I need not tell him that, he knowes you are too (diligent.
Enter Steward in a Cloake, muffled.
Luci. Ha: is not that his Steward muffled so?
He goes away in a Clowd: Call him, call him.
Tit. Do you heare, sir?
2.Varro. By your leaue, sir.
Stew. What do ye aske of me, my Friend.
Tit. We waite for certaine Money heere, sir.
Stew. I, if Money were as certaine as your waiting,
'Twere sure enough.
Why then preferr'd you not your summes and Billes
When your false Masters eate of my Lords meat?
Then they could smile, and fawne vpon his debts,
And take downe th'Intrest into their glutt'nous Mawes.
You do your selues but wrong, to stirre me vp,
Let me passe quietly:
Beleeue't, my Lord and I haue made an end,
I haue no more to reckon, he to spend.
Luci. I, but this answer will not serue.
Stew. If't 'twill not serue, 'tis not so base as you,
For you serue Knaues.
1.Varro. How? What does his casheer'd Worship mutter?
2.Varro. No matter what, hee's poore, and that's reuenge enough. Who can speake broader, then hee that has no house to put his head in? Such may rayle against great buildings.
Enter Seruilius.
Tit. Oh heere's *Seruilius*: now wee shall know some answere.
Seru. If I might beseech you Gentlemen, to repayre some other houre, I should deriue much from't. For tak't of my soule, my Lord leanes wondrously to discontent: His comfortable temper has forsooke him, he's much out of health, and keepes his Chamber.
Luci. Many do keepe their Chambers, are not sicke:
And if it be so farre beyond his health,
Me thinkes he should the sooner pay his debts,
And make a cleere way to the Gods.
Seruil. Good Gods.
Titus. We cannot take this for answer, sir.
Flaminius within. *Seruilius* helpe, my Lord, my Lord.

Enter Timon in a rage.
Tim. What, are my dores oppos'd against my passage?
Haue I bin euer free, and must my house
Be my retentiue Enemy? My Gaole?
The place which I haue Feasted, does it now
(Like all Mankinde) shew me an Iron heart?
Luci. Put in now *Titus.*
Tit. My Lord, heere is my Bill.
Luci. Here's mine.
1.Var. And mine, my Lord.
2.Var. And ours, my Lord.
Philo. All our Billes.
Tim. Knocke me downe with 'em, cleaue mee to the Girdle.
Luc. Alas, my Lord.
Tim. Cut my heart in summes.
Tit. Mine, fifty Talents.
Tim. Tell out my blood.
Luc. Fiue thousand Crownes, my Lord.
Tim. Fiue thousand drops payes that.
What yours? and yours?
1.Var. My Lord.
2.Var. My Lord.
Tim. Teare me, take me, and the Gods fall vpon you.
Exit Timon.
Hort. Faith I perceiue our Masters may throwe their caps at their money, these debts may well be call'd desperate ones, for a madman owes 'em. *Exeunt.*
Enter Timon.
Timon. They haue e'ene put my breath from mee the slaues. Creditors? Diuels.
Stew. My deere Lord.
Tim. What if it should be so?
Stew. My Lord.
Tim. Ile haue it so. My Steward?
Stew. Heere my Lord.
Tim. So fitly? Go, bid all my Friends againe,
Lucius, *Lucullus*, and *Sempronius*. *Vllorxa*: All,
Ile once more feast the Rascals.
Stew. O my Lord, you onely speake from your distracted soule; there's not so much left to furnish out a moderate Table.

Timon.

Tim. Be it not in thy care:
Go I charge thee, inuite them all, let in the tide
Of Knaues once more: my Cooke and Ile prouide. *Exeunt*

Enter three Senators at one doore, Alcibiades meeting them, with Attendants.

1.*Sen.* My Lord, you haue my voyce, too't,
The faults Bloody:
'Tis necessary he should dye:
Nothing imboldens sinne so much, as Mercy.
2 Most true; the Law shall bruise 'em.
Alc. Honor, health, and compassion to the Senate.
1 Now Captaine.
Alc. I am an humble Sutor to your Vertues;
For pitty is the vertue of the Law,
And none but Tyrants vse it cruelly.
It pleases time and Fortune to lye heauie
Vpon a Friend of mine, who in hot blood
Hath stept into the Law: which is past depth
To those that (without heede) do plundge intoo't.
He is a Man (setting his Fate aside) of comely Vertues,
Nor did he soyle the fact with Cowardice,
(And Honour in him, which buyes out his fault)
But with a Noble Fury, and faire spirit,
Seeing his Reputation touch'd to death,
He did oppose his Foe:
And with such sober and vnnoted passion
He did behooue his anger ere 'twas spent,
As if he had but prou'd an Argument.
1 *Sen.* You vndergo too strict a Paradox,
Striuing to make an vgly deed looke faire:
Your words haue tooke such paines, as if they labour'd
To bring Man-slaughter into forme, and set Quarrelling
Vpon the head of Valour; which indeede
Is Valour mis-begot, and came into the world,
When Sects, and Factions were newly borne.
Hee's truly Valiant, that can wisely suffer
The worst that man can breath,
And make his Wrongs, his Out-sides,
To weare them like his Rayment, carelessely,
And ne're preferre his iniuries to his heart,
To bring it into danger.
If Wrongs be euilles, and inforce vs kill,
What Folly 'tis, to hazard life for Ill.
Alci. My Lord.
1.*Sen.* You cannot make grosse sinnes looke cleare,
To reuenge is no Valour, but to beare.
Alci. My Lords, then vnder fauour, pardon me,
If I speake like a Captaine.
Why do fond men expose themselues to Battell,
And not endure all threats? Sleepe vpon't,
And let the Foes quietly cut their Throats
Without repugnancy? If there be
Such Valour in the bearing, what make wee
Abroad? Why then, Women are more valiant
That stay at home, if Bearing carry it:
And the Asse, more Captaine then the Lyon?
The fellow loaden with Irons, wiser then the Iudge?
If Wisedome be in suffering, Oh my Lords,
As you are great, be pittifully Good,
Who cannot condemne rashnesse in cold blood?
To kill, I grant, is sinnes extreamest Gust,
But in defence, by Mercy, 'tis most iust.
To be in Anger, is impietie:
But who is Man, that is not Angrie.
Weigh but the Crime with this.

2.*Sen.* You breath in vaine.
Alci. In vaine?
His seruice done at Lacedemon, and Bizantium,
Were a sufficient briber for his life.
1 What's that?
Alc. Why say my Lords ha's done faire seruice,
And slaine in fight many of your enemies:
How full of valour did he beare himselfe
In the last Conflict, and made plenteous wounds?
2 He has made too much plenty with him:
He's a sworne Riotor, he has a sinne
That often drownes him, and takes his valour prisoner.
If there were no Foes, that were enough
To ouercome him. In that Beastly furie,
He has bin knowne to commit outrages,
And cherrish Factions. 'Tis inferr'd to vs,
His dayes are foule, and his drinke dangerous.
1 He dyes.
Alci. Hard fate: he might haue dyed in warre.
My Lords, if not for any parts in him,
Though his right arme might purchase his owne time,
And be in debt to none: yet more to moue you,
Take my deserts to his, and ioyne 'em both.
And for I know, your reuerend Ages loue Security,
Ile pawne my Victories, all my Honour to you
Vpon his good returnes.
If by this Crime, he owes the Law his life,
Why let the Warre receiue't in valiant gore,
For Law is strict, and Warre is nothing more.
1 We are for Law, he dyes, vrge it no more
On height of our displeasure: Friend, or Brother,
He forfeits his owne blood, that spilles another.
Alc. Must it be so? It must not bee:
My Lords, I do beseech you know mee.
2 How?
Alc. Call me to your remembrances.
3 What.
Alc. I cannot thinke but your Age has forgot me,
It could not else be, I should proue so bace,
To sue and be deny'de such common Grace.
My wounds ake at you.
1 Do you dare our anger?
'Tis in few words, but spacious in effect:
We banish thee for euer.
Alc. Banish me?
Banish your dotage, banish vsurie,
That makes the Senate vgly.
1 If after two dayes shine, Athens containe thee,
Attend our waightier Iudgement.
And not to swell our Spirit,
He shall be executed presently. *Exeunt.*
Alc. Now the Gods keepe you old enough,
That you may liue
Onely in bone, that none may looke on you.
I'm worse then mad: I haue kept backe their Foes
While they haue told their Money, and let out
Their Coine vpon large interest. I my selfe,
Rich onely in large hurts. All those, for this?
Is this the Balsome, that the vsuring Senat
Powres into Captaines wounds? Banishment.
It comes not ill: I hate not to be banisht,
It is a cause worthy my Spleene and Furie,
That I may strike at Athens. Ile cheere vp
My discontented Troopes, and lay for hearts;
,Tis Honour with most Lands to be at ods,
Souldiers should brooke as little wrongs as Gods. *Exit.*
Enter

Enter diuers Friends at seuerall doores.

1 The good time of day to you, sir.

2 I also wish it to you: I thinke this Honorable Lord did but try vs this other day.

1 Vpon that were my thoughts tyring when wee encountred. I hope it is not so low with him as he made it seeme in the triall of his seuerall Friends.

2 It should not be, by the perswasion of his new Feasting.

1 I should thinke so. He hath sent mee an earnest inuiting, which many my neere occasions did vrge mee to put off: but he hath coniur'd mee beyond them, and I must needs appeare.

2 In like manner was I in debt to my importunat businesse, but he would not heare my excuse. I am sorrie, when he sent to borrow of mee, that my Prouision was out.

1 I am sicke of that greefe too, as I vnderstand how all things go.

2 Euery man heares so: what would hee haue borrowed of you?

1 A thousand Peeces.

2 A thousand Peeces?

1 What of you?

2 He sent to me sir——Heere he comes.

Enter Timon and Attendants.

Tim. With all my heart Gentlemen both; and how fare you?

1 Euer at the best, hearing well of your Lordship.

2 The Swallow followes not Summer more willing, then we your Lordship.

Tim. Nor more willingly leaues Winter, such Summer Birds are men. Gentlemen, our dinner will not recompence this long stay: Feast your eares with the Musicke awhile: If they will fare so harshly o'th'Trumpets sound: we shall too't presently.

1 I hope it remaines not vnkindely with your Lordship, that I return'd you an empty Messenger.

Tim. O sir, let it not trouble you.

2 My Noble Lord.

Tim. Ah my good Friend, what cheere?

The Banket brought in.

2 My most Honorable Lord, I am e'ne sick of shame, that when your Lordship this other day sent to me, I was so vnfortunate a Beggar.

Tim. Thinke not on't, sir.

2 If you had sent but two houres before.

Tim. Let it not cumber your better remembrance. Come bring in all together.

2 All couer'd Dishes.

1 Royall Cheare, I warrant you.

3 Doubt not that, if money and the season can yeild it

1 How do you? What's the newes?

3 *Alcibiades* is banish'd: heare you of it?

Both. *Alcibiades* banish'd?

3 'Tis so, be sure of it.

1 How? How?

2 I pray you vpon what?

Tim. My worthy Friends, will you draw neere?

3 Ile tell you more anon. Here's a Noble feast toward

2 This is the old man still.

3 Wilt hold? Wilt hold?

2 It do's: but time will, and so.

3 I do conceyue.

Tim. Each man to his stoole, with that spurre as hee would to the lip of his Mistris: your dyet shall bee in all places alike. Make not a Citie Feast of it, to let the meat coole, ere we can agree vpon the first place. Sit, sit.
The Gods require our Thankes.

You great Benefactors, sprinkle our Society with Thankefulnesse. For your owne guifts, make your selues prais'd: But reserue still to giue, least your Deities be despised. Lend to each man enough, that one neede not lend to another. For were your Godheads to borrow of men, men would forsake the Gods. Make the Meate be beloued, more then the Man that giues it. Let no Assembly of Twenty, be without a score of Villaines. If there sit twelue Women at the Table, let a dozen of them bee as they are. The rest of your Fees, O Gods, the Senators of Athens, together with the common legge of People, what is amisse in them, you Gods, make suteable for destruction. For these my present Friends, as they are to mee nothing, so in nothing blesse them, and to nothing are they welcome.

Vncouer Dogges, and lap.

Some speake. What do's his Lordship meane?

Some other. I know not.

Timon. May you a better Feast neuer behold
You knot of Mouth-Friends: Smoke, & lukewarm water
Is your perfection. This is *Timons* last,
Who stucke and spangled you with Flatteries,
Washes it off, and sprinkles in your faces
Your reeking villany. Liue loath'd, and long
Most smiling, smooth, detested Parasites,
Curteous Destroyers, affable Wolues, meeke Beares:
You Fooles of Fortune, Trencher-friends, Times Flyes,
Cap and knee-Slaues, vapours, and Minute Iackes.
Of Man and Beast, the infinite Maladie
Crust you quite o're. What do'st thou go?
Soft, take thy Physicke first; thou too, and thou:
Stay I will lend thee money, borrow none.
What? All in Motion? Henceforth be no Feast,
Whereat a Villaine's not a welcome Guest.
Burne house, sinke Athens, henceforth hated be
Of *Timon* Man, and all Humanity. *Exit*

Enter the Senators, with other Lords.

1 How now, my Lords?

2 Know you rhe quality of Lord *Timons* fury?

3 Push, did you see my Cap?

4 I haue lost my Gowne.

1 He's but a mad Lord, & nought but humors swaies him. He gaue me a Iewell th'other day, and now hee has beate it out of my hat.
Did you see my Iewell?

2 Did you see my Cap.

3 Heere 'tis.

4 Heere lyes my Gowne.

1 Let's make no stay.

2 Lord *Timons* mad.

3 I feel't vpon my bones.

4 One day he giues vs Diamonds, next day stones.

Exeunt the Senators.

Enter Timon.

Tim. Let me looke backe vpon thee. O thou Wall
That girdles in those Wolues, diue in the earth,
And fence not Athens. Matrons, turne incontinent,
Obedience fayle in Children: Slaues and Fooles

hh Plucke

Plucke the graue wrinkled Senate from the Bench,
And minifter in their fteeds, to generall Filthes.
Conuert o'th'Inftant greene Virginity,
Doo't in your Parents eyes. Bankrupts, hold faft
Rather then render backe; out with your Kniues,
And cut your Trufters throates. Bound Seruants, fteale,
Large-handed Robbers your graue Mafters are,
And pill by Law. Maide, to thy Mafters bed,
Thy Miftris is o'th'Brothell. Some of fixteen,
Plucke the lyn'd Crutch from thy old limping Sire,
With it, beate out his Braines. Piety, and Feare,
Religion to the Gods, Peace, Iuftice, Truth,
Domefticke awe, Night-reft, and Neighbour-hood,
Inftruction, Manners, Myfteries, and Trades,
Degrees, Obferuances, Cuftomes, and Lawes,
Decline to your confounding contraries.
And yet Confufion liue: Plagues incident to men,
Your potent and infectious Feauors, heape
On Athens ripe for ftroke. Thou cold Sciatica,
Cripple our Senators, that their limbes may halt
As lamely as their Manners. Luft, and Libertie
Creepe in the Mindes and Marrowes of our youth,
That 'gainft the ftreame of Vertue they may ftriue,
And drowne themfelues in Riot. Itches, Blaines,
Sowe all th'Athenian bofomes, and their crop
Be generall Leprofie: Breath, infect breath,
That their Society (as their Friendfhip) may
Be meerely poyfon. Nothing Ile beare from thee
But nakedneffe, thou deteftable Towne,
Take thou that too, with multiplying Bannes:
Timon will to the Woods, where he fhall finde
Th'vnkindeft Beaft, more kinder then Mankinde.
The Gods confound (heare me you good Gods all)
Th'Athenians both within and out that Wall:
And graunt as *Timon* growes, his hate may grow
To the whole race of Mankinde, high and low.
Amen. *Exit.*

Enter Steward with two or three Seruants.

1 Heare you M. Steward, where's our Mafter?
Are we vndone, caft off, nothing remaining?
Stew. Alack my Fellowes, what fhould I fay to you?
Let me be recorded by the righteous Gods,
I am as poore as you.
1 Such a Houfe broke?
So Noble a Mafter falne, all gone, and not
One Friend to take his Fortune by the arme,
And go along with him.
2 As we do turne our backes
From our Companion, throwne into his graue,
So his Familiars to his buried Fortunes
Slinke all away, leaue their falfe vowes with him
Like empty purfes pickt; and his poore felfe
A dedicated Beggar to the Ayre,
With his difeafe, of all fhunn'd pouerty,
Walkes like contempt alone. More of our Fellowes.
Enter other Seruants.
Stew. All broken Implements of a ruin'd houfe.
3 Yet do our hearts weare *Timons* Liuery,
That fee I by our Faces. we are Fellowes ftill,
Seruing alike in forrow: Leak'd is our Barke,
And we poore Mates, ftand on the dying Decke,
Hearing the Surges threat: we muft all part
Into this Sea of Ayre.
Stew. Good Fellowes all,
The lateft of my wealth Ile fhare among'ft you.
Where euer we fhall meete, for *Timons* fake,
Let's yet be Fellowes. Let's fhake our heads, and fay
As 'twere a Knell vnto our Mafters Fortunes,
We haue feene better dayes. Let each take fome:
Nay put out all your hands: Not one word more,
Thus part we rich in forrow, parting poore.
Embrace and part feuerall wayes.
Oh the fierce wretchedneffe that Glory brings vs!
Who would not wifh to be from wealth exempt,
Since Riches point to Mifery and Contempt?
Who would be fo mock'd with Glory, or to liue
But in a Dreame of Friendfhip,
To haue his pompe, and all what ftate compounds,
But onely painted like his varnifht Friends:
Poore honeft Lord, brought lowe by his owne heart,
Vndone by Goodneffe: Strange vnvfuall blood,
When mans worft finne is, He do's too much Good.
Who then dares to be halfe fo kinde agen?
For Bounty that makes Gods, do ftill marre Men.
My deereft Lord, bleft to be moft accurft,
Rich onely to be wretched; thy great Fortunes
Are made thy cheefe Afflictions. Alas (kinde Lord)
Hee's flung in Rage from this ingratefull Seate
Of monftrous Friends:
Nor ha's he with him to fupply his life,
Or that which can command it:
Ile follow and enquire him out.
Ile euer ferue his minde, with my beft will,
Whilft I haue Gold, Ile be his Steward ftill. *Exit.*

Enter Timon in the woods.

Tim. O bleffed breeding Sun, draw from the earth
Rotten humidity: below thy Sifters Orbe
Infect the ayre. Twin'd Brothers of one wombe,
Whofe procreation, refidence, and birth,
Scarfe is diuidant; touch them with feuerall fortunes,
The greater fcornes the leffer. Not Nature
(To whom all fores lay fiege) can beare great Fortune
But by contempt of Nature.
Raife me this Begger, and deny't that Lord,
The Senators fhall beare contempt Hereditary,
The Begger Natiue Honor.
It is the Paftour Lards, the Brothers fides,
The want that makes him leaue: who dares? who dares
In puritie of Manhood ftand vpright
And fay, this mans a Flatterer. If one be,
So are they all: for euerie grize of Fortune
Is fmooth'd by that below. The Learned pate
Duckes to the Golden Foole. All's obliquie:
There 'snothing leuell in our curfed Natures
But direct villanie. Therefore be abhorr'd,
All Feafts, Societies, and Throngs of men.
His femblable, yea himfelfe *Timon* difdaines,
Deftruction phang mankinde; Earth yeeld me Rootes,
Who feekes for better of thee, fawce his pallate
With thy moft operant Poyfon. What is heere?
Gold? Yellow, glittering, precious Gold?
No Gods, I am no idle Votarift,
Roots you cleere Heauens. Thus much of this will make
Blacke, white; fowle, faire; wrong, right;
Bafe, Noble; Old, young; Coward, valiant.
Ha you Gods! why this? what this, you Gods? why this
Will lugge your Priefts and Seruants from your fides:
Plucke ftout mens pillowes from below their heads.
This

This yellow Slaue,
Will knit and breake Religions, blesse th'accurst,
Make the hoare Leprosie ador'd, place Theeues,
And giue them Title, knee, and approbation
With Senators on the Bench: This is it
That makes the wappen'd Widdow wed againe;
Shee, whom the Spittle-house, and vlcerous sores,
Would cast the gorge at. This Embalmes and Spices
To'th'Aprill day againe. Come damn'd Earth,
Thou common whore of Mankinde, that puttes oddes
Among the rout of Nations, I will make thee
Do thy right Nature. *March afarre off.*
Ha? A Drumme? Th'art quicke,
But yet Ile bury thee: Thou't go (strong Theefe)
When Gowty keepers of thee cannot stand:
Nay stay thou out for earnest.

Enter Alcibiades with Drumme and Fife in warlike manner, and Phrynia and Timandra.

Alc. What art thou there? speake.
Tim. A Beast as thou art. The Canker gnaw thy hart
For shewing me againe the eyes of Man.
Alc. What is thy name? Is man so hatefull to thee,
That art thy selfe a Man?
Tim. I am *Misantropos*, and hate Mankinde.
For thy part, I do wish thou wert a dogge,
That I might loue thee something.
Alc. I know thee well:
But in thy Fortunes am vnlearn'd, and strange.
Tim. I know thee too, and more then that I know thee
I not desire to know. Follow thy Drumme,
With mans blood paint the ground Gules, Gules:
Religious Cannons, ciuill Lawes are cruell,
Then what should warre be? This fell whore of thine,
Hath in her more destruction then thy Sword,
For all her Cherubin looke.
Phrin. Thy lips rot off.
Tim. I will not kisse thee, then the rot returnes
To thine owne lippes againe.
Alc. How came the Noble *Timon* to this change?
Tim. As the Moone do's, by wanting light to giue:
But then renew I could not like the Moone,
There were no Sunnes to borrow of.
Alc. Noble *Timon*, what friendship may I do thee?
Tim. None, but to maintaine my opinion.
Alc. What is it *Timon*?
Tim. Promise me Friendship, but performe none. If thou wilt not promise, the Gods plague thee, for thou art a man: if thou do'st performe, confound thee, for thou art a man.
Alc. I haue heard in some sort of thy Miseries.
Tim. Thou saw'st them when I had prosperitie.
Alc. I see them now, then was a blessed time.
Tim. As thine is now, held with a brace of Harlots.
Timan. Is this th'Athenian Minion, whom the world
Voic'd so regardfully?
Tim. Art thou *Timandra*? *Timan.* Yes.
Tim. Be a whore still, they loue thee not that vse thee, giue them diseases, leauing with thee their Lust. Make vse of thy salt houres, season the slaues for Tubbes and Bathes, bring downe Rose-cheekt youth to the Fubfast, and the Diet.
Timan. Hang thee Monster.
Alc. Pardon him sweet *Timandra*, for his wits
Are drown'd and lost in his Calamities.
I haue but little Gold of late, braue *Timon*,
The want whereof, doth dayly make reuolt
In my penurious Band. I haue heard and greeu'd
How cursed Athens, mindelesse of thy worth,
Forgetting thy great deeds, when Neighbour states
But for thy Sword and Fortune trod vpon them.
Tim. I prythee beate thy Drum, and get thee gone.
Alc. I am thy Friend, and pitty thee deere *Timon*.
Tim. How doest thou pitty him whom yͧ dost troble,
I had rather be alone.
Alc. Why fare thee well:
Heere is some Gold for thee.
Tim. Keepe it, I cannot eate it.
Alc. When I haue laid proud Athens on a heape.
Tim. Warr'st thou 'gainst Athens.
Alc. I *Timon*, and haue cause.
Tim. The Gods confound them all in thy Conquest,
And thee after, when thou hast Conquer'd.
Alc. Why me, *Timon*?
Tim. That by killing of Villaines
Thou was't borne to conquer my Country.
Put vp thy Gold. Go on, heeres Gold, go on;
Be as a Plannetary plague, when Ioue
Will o're some high-Vic'd City, hang his poyson
In the sicke ayre: let not thy sword skip one:
Pitty not honour'd Age for his white Beard,
He is an Vsurer. Strike me the counterfet Matron,
It is her habite onely, that is honest,
Her selfe's a Bawd. Let not the Virgins cheeke
Make soft thy trenchant Sword: for those Milke pappes
That through the window Barne bore at mens eyes,
Are not within the Leafe of pitty writ,
But set them down horrible Traitors. Spare not the Babe
Whose dimpled smiles from Fooles exhaust their mercy;
Thinke it a Bastard, whom the Oracle
Hath doubtfully pronounced, the throat shall cut,
And mince it sans remorse. Sweare against Obiects,
Put Armour on thine eares, and on thine eyes,
Whose proofe, nor yels of Mothers, Maides, nor Babes,
Nor sight of Priests in holy Vestments bleeding,
Shall pierce a iot. There's Gold to pay thy Souldiers,
Make large confusion: and thy fury spent,
Confounded be thy selfe. Speake not, be gone.
Alc. Hast thou Gold yet, Ile take the Gold thou giuest me, not all thy Counsell.
Tim. Dost thou or dost thou not, Heauens curse vpon thee.
Both. Giue vs some Gold good *Timon*, hast yͧ more?
Tim. Enough to make a Whore forsweare her Trade,
And to make Whores, a Bawd. Hold vp you Sluts
Your Aprons mountant; you are not Othable,
Although I know you'l sweare, terribly sweare
Into strong shudders, and to heauenly Agues
Th'immortall Gods that heare you. Spare your Oathes:
Ile trust to your Conditions, be whores still.
And he whose pious breath seekes to conuert you,
Be strong in Whore, allure him, burne him vp,
Let your close fire predominate his smoke,
And be no turne-coats: yet may your paines six months
Be quite contrary, And Thatch
Your poore thin Roofes with burthens of the dead,
(Some that were hang'd) no matter:
Weare them, betray with them; Whore still,
Paint till a horse may myre vpon your face:
A pox of wrinkles.
Both. Well, more Gold, what then?

Beleeue't that wee'l do any thing for Gold.
Tim. Consumptions sowe
In hollow bones of man, strike their sharpe shinnes,
And marre mens spurring. Cracke the Lawyers voyce,
That he may neuer more false Title pleade,
Nor sound his Quillets shrilly: Hoare the Flamen,
That scold'st against the quality of flesh,
And not beleeues himselfe. Downe with the Nose,
Downe with it flat, take the Bridge quite away
Of him, that his particular to foresee (bald
Smels from the generall weale. Make curld'pate Ruffians
And let the vnscarr'd Braggerts of the Warre
Deriue some paine from you. Plague all,
That your Actiuity may defeate and quell
The sourse of all Erection. There's more Gold.
Do you damne others, and let this damne you,
And ditches graue you all.
Both. More counsell with more Money, bounteous *Timon.*
Tim. More whore, more Mischeefe first, I haue giuen you earnest.
Alc. Strike vp the Drum towardes Athens, farewell *Timon*: if I thriue well, Ile visit thee againe.
Tim. If I hope well, Ile neuer see thee more.
Alc. I neuer did thee harme.
Tim. Yes, thou spok'st well of me.
Alc. Call'st thou that harme?
Tim. Men dayly finde it. Get thee away,
And take thy Beagles with thee.
Alc. We but offend him, strike. *Exeunt.*
Tim. That Nature being sicke of mans vnkindnesse
Should yet be hungry: Common Mother, thou
Whose wombe vnmeasureable, and infinite brest
Teemes and feeds all: whose selfesame Mettle
Whereof thy proud Childe (arrogant man) is puft,
Engenders the blacke Toad, and Adder blew,
The gilded Newt, and eyelesse venom'd Worme,
With all th'abhorred Births below Crispe Heauen,
Whereon *Hyperions* quickning fire doth shine:
Yeeld him, who all the humane Sonnes do hate,
From foorth thy plenteous bosome, one poore roote:
Enseare thy Fertile and Conceptious wombe,
Let it no more bring out ingratefull man.
Goe great with Tygers, Dragons, Wolues, and Beares,
Teeme with new Monsters, whom thy vpward face
Hath to the Marbled Mansion all aboue
Neuer presented. O, a Root, deare thankes:
Dry vp thy Marrowes, Vines, and Plough-torne Leas,
Whereof ingratefull man with Licourish draughts
And Morsels Vnctious, greases his pure minde,
That from it all Consideration slippes ———

Enter Apemantus.

More man? Plague, plague.
Ape. I was directed hither. Men report,
Thou dost affect my Manners, and dost vse them.
Tim. 'Tis then, because thou dost not keepe a dogge
Whom I would imitate. Consumption catch thee.
Ape. This is in thee a Nature but infected,
A poore vnmanly Melancholly sprung
From change of future. Why this Spade? this place?
This Slaue-like Habit, and these lookes of Care?
Thy Flatterers yet weare Silke, drinke Wine, lye soft,
Hugge their diseas'd Perfumes, and haue forgot
That euer *Timon* was. Shame not these Woods,
By putting on the cunning of a Carper.
Be thou a Flatterer now, and seeke to thriue
By that which ha's vndone thee; hindge thy knee,
And let his very breath whom thou'lt obserue
Blow off thy Cap: praise his most vicious straine,
And call it excellent: thou wast told thus:
Thou gau'st thine eares (like Tapsters, that bad welcom)
To Knaues, and all approachers: 'Tis most iust
That thou turne Rascall, had'st thou wealth againe,
Rascals should haue't. Do not assume my likenesse.
Tim. Were I like thee, I'de throw away my selfe.
Ape. Thou hast cast away thy selfe, being like thy self
A Madman so long, now a Foole: what think'st
That the bleake ayre, thy boysterous Chamberlaine
Will put thy shirt on warme? Will these moyst Trees,
That haue out-liu'd the Eagle, page thy heeles
And skip when thou point'st out? Will the cold brooke
Candied with Ice, Cawdle thy Morning taste
To cure thy o're-nights surfet? Call the Creatures,
Whose naked Natures liue in all the spight
Of wrekefull Heauen, whose bare vnhoused Trunkes,
To the conflicting Elements expos'd
Answer meere Nature: bid them flatter thee.
O thou shalt finde.
Tim. A Foole of thee: depart.
Ape. I loue thee better now, then ere I did.
Tim. I hate thee worse.
Ape. Why?
Tim. Thou flatter'st misery.
Ape. I flatter not, but say thou art a Caytiffe.
Tim. Why do'st thou seeke me out?
Ape. To vex thee.
Tim. Alwayes a Villaines Office, or a Fooles.
Dost please thy selfe in't?
Ape. I.
Tim. What, a Knaue too?
Ape. If thou did'st put this sowre cold habit on
To castigate thy pride, 'twere well: but thou
Dost it enforcedly: Thou'dst Courtier be againe
Wert thou not Beggar: willing misery
Out-liues: incertaine pompe, is crown'd before:
The one is filling still, neuer compleat:
The other, at high wish: best state Contentlesse,
Hath a distracted and most wretched being,
Worse then the worst, Content.
Thou should'st desire to dye, being miserable.
Tim. Not by his breath, that is more miserable.
Thou art a Slaue, whom Fortunes tender arme
With fauour neuer claspt: but bred a Dogge.
Had'st thou like vs from our first swath proceeded,
The sweet degrees that this breefe world affords,
To such as may the passiue drugges of it
Freely command'st: thou would'st haue plung'd thy self
In generall Riot, melted downe thy youth
In different beds of Lust, and neuer learn'd
The Icie precepts of respect, but followed
The Sugred game before thee. But my selfe,
Who had the world as my Confectionarie,
The mouthes, the tongues, the eyes, and hearts of men,
At duty more then I could frame employment;
That numberlesse vpon me stucke, as leaues
Do on the Oake, haue with one Winters brush
Fell from their boughes, and left me open, bare,
For euery storme that blowes. I to beare this,
That neuer knew but better, is some burthen:
Thy Nature, did commence in sufferance, Time
Hath made thee hard in't. Why should'st ÿ hate Men?
They neuer flatter'd thee. What hast thou giuen?

If

If thou wilt curse; thy Father (that poore ragge)
Must be thy subiect; who in spight put stuffe
To some shee-Begger, and compounded thee
Poore Rogue, hereditary. Hence, be gone,
If thou hadst not bene borne the worst of men,
Thou hadst bene a Knaue and Flatterer.
Ape. Art thou proud yet?
Tim. I, that I am not thee.
Ape. I, that I was no Prodigall.
Tim. I, that I am one now.
Were all the wealth I haue shut vp in thee,
I'ld giue thee leaue to hang it. Get thee gone:
That the whole life of Athens were in this,
Thus would I eate it.
Ape. Heere, I will mend thy Feast.
Tim. First mend thy company, take away thy selfe.
Ape. So I shall mend mine owne, by'th'lacke of thine
Tim. 'Tis not well mended so, it is but botcht;
If not, I would it were.
Ape. What would'st thou haue to Athens?
Tim. Thee thither in a whirlewind: if thou wilt,
Tell them there I haue Gold, looke, so I haue.
Ape. Heere is no vse for Gold.
Tim. The best, and truest:
For heere it sleepes, and do's no hyred harme.
Ape. Where lyest a nights *Timon*?
Tim. Vnder that's aboue me.
Where feed'st thou a-dayes *Apemantus*?
Ape. Where my stomacke findes meate, or rather where I eate it.
Tim. Would poyson were obedient, & knew my mind
Ape. Where would'st thou send it?
Tim. To sawce thy dishes.
Ape. The middle of Humanity thou neuer knewest, but the extremitie of both ends. When thou wast in thy Gilt, and thy Perfume, they mockt thee for too much Curiositie: in thy Ragges thou know'st none, but art despis'd for the contrary. There's a medler for thee, eate it.
Tim. On what I hate, I feed not.
Ape. Do'st hate a Medler?
Tim. I, though it looke like thee.
Ape. And th'hadst hated Medlers sooner, ÿ should'st haue loued thy selfe better now. What man didd'st thou euer know vnthrift, that was beloued after his meanes?
Tim. Who without those meanes thou talk'st of, didst thou euer know belou'd?
Ape. My selfe.
Tim. I vnderstand thee: thou had'st some meanes to keepe a Dogge.
Apem. What things in the world canst thou neerest compare to thy Flatterers?
Tim. Women neerest, but men: men are the things themselues. What would'st thou do with the world *Apemantus*, if it lay in thy power?
Ape. Giue it the Beasts, to be rid of the men.
Tim. Would'st thou haue thy selfe fall in the confusion of men, and remaine a Beast with the Beasts.
Ape. I *Timon*.
Tim. A beastly Ambition, which the Goddes graunt thee t'attaine to. If thou wert the Lyon, the Fox would beguile thee: if thou wert the Lambe, the Foxe would eate thee: if thou wert the Fox, the Lion would suspect thee, when peraduenture thou wert accus'd by the Asse: If thou wert the Asse, thy dulnesse would torment thee; and still thou liu'dst but as a Breakefast to the Wolfe. If thou wert the Wolfe, thy greedinesse would afflict thee, & oft thou should'st hazard thy life for thy dinner. Wert thou the Vnicorne, pride and wrath would confound thee, and make thine owne selfe the conquest of thy fury. Wert thou a Beare, thou would'st be kill'd by the Horse: wert thou a Horse, thou would'st be seaz'd by the Leopard: wert thou a Leopard, thou wert Germane to the Lion, and the spottes of thy Kindred, were Iurors on thy life. All thy safety were remotion, and thy defence absence. What Beast could'st thou bee, that were not subiect to a Beast: and what a Beast art thou already, that seest not thy losse in transformation.
Ape. If thou could'st please me
With speaking to me, thou might'st
Haue hit vpon it heere.
The Commonwealth of Athens, is become
A Forrest of Beasts.
Tim. How ha's the Asse broke the wall, that thou art out of the Citie.
Ape. Yonder comes a Poet and a Painter:
The plague of Company light vpon thee:
I will feare to catch it, and giue way.
When I know not what else to do,
Ile see thee againe.
Tim. When there is nothing liuing but thee,
Thou shalt be welcome.
I had rather be a Beggers Dogge,
Then *Apemantus*.
Ape. Thou art the Cap
Of all the Fooles aliue.
Tim. Would thou wert cleane enough
To spit vpon.
Ape. A plague on thee,
Thou art too bad to curse.
Tim. All Villaines
That do stand by thee, are pure.
Ape. There is no Leprosie,
But what thou speak'st.
Tim. If I name thee, Ile beate thee;
But I should infect my hands.
Ape. I would my tongue
Could rot them off.
Tim. Away thou issue of a mangie dogge,
Choller does kill me,
That thou art aliue, I swoond to see thee.
Ape. Would thou would'st burst.
Tim. Away thou tedious Rogue, I am sorry I shall lose a stone by thee.
Ape. Beast.
Tim. Slaue.
Ape. Toad.
Tim. Rogue, Rogue, Rogue.
I am sicke of this false world, and will loue nought
But euen the meere necessities vpon't:
Then *Timon* presently prepare thy graue:
Lye where the light Fome of the Sea may beate
Thy graue stone dayly, make thine Epitaph,
That death in me, at others liues may laugh.
O thou sweete King-killer, and deare diuorce
Twixt naturall Sunne and fire: thou bright defiler
of *Himens* purest bed, thou valiant Mars,
Thou euer, yong, fresh, loued, and delicate wooer,
Whose blush doth thawe the consecrated Snow
That lyes on Dians lap,
Thou visible God,
That souldrest close Impossibilities,
And mak'st them kisse; that speak'st with euerie Tongue

hh 3 To

To euerie purpose : O thou touch of hearts,
Thinke thy slaue-man rebels, and by thy vertue
Set them into confounding oddes, that Beasts
May haue the world in Empire.
Ape. Would 'twere so,
But not till I am dead. Ile say th'hast Gold :
Thou wilt be throng'd too shortly.
Tim. Throng'd too?
Ape. I.
Tim. Thy backe I prythee.
Ape. Liue, and loue thy misery.
Tim. Long liue so, and so dye. I am quit.
Ape. Mo things like men,
Eate *Timon*, and abhorre then. *Exit Apeman.*

Enter the Bandetti.

1 Where should he haue this Gold? It is some poore Fragment, some slender Ort of his remainder : the meere want of Gold, and the falling from of his Friendes, droue him into this Melancholly.
2 It is nois'd
He hath a masse of Treasure.
3 Let vs make the assay vpon him, if he care not for't, he will supply vs easily : if he couetously reserue it, how shall's get it?
2 True : for he beares it not about him:
'Tis hid.
1 Is not this hee?
All. Where?
2 'Tis his description.
3 He? I know him.
All. Saue thee *Timon.*
Tim. Now Theeues.
All. Soldiers, not Theeues.
Tim. Both too, and womens Sonnes.
All. We are not Theeues, but men
That much do want.
Tim. Your greatest want is, you want much of meat :
Why should you want? Behold, the Earth hath Rootes:
Within this Mile breake forth a hundred Springs:
The Oakes beare Mast, the Briars Scarlet Heps,
The bounteous Huswife Nature, on each bush,
Layes her full Messe before you. Want? why Want?
1 We cannot liue on Grasse, on Berries, Water,
As Beasts, and Birds, and Fishes.
Ti. Nor on the Beasts themselues, the Birds & Fishes,
You must eate men. Yet thankes I must you con,
That you are Theeues profest : that you worke not
In holier shapes : For there is boundlesse Theft
In limited Professions. Rascall Theeues
Heere's Gold. Go, sucke the subtle blood o'th'Grape,
Till the high Feauor seeth your blood to froth,
And so scape hanging. Trust not the Physitian,
His Antidotes are poyson, and he slayes
Moe then you Rob : Take wealth, and liues together,
Do Villaine do, since you protest to doo't.
Like Workemen, Ile example you with Theeuery :
The Sunnes a Theefe, and with his great attraction
Robbes the vaste Sea. The Moones an arrant Theefe,
And her pale fire, she snatches from the Sunne.
The Seas a Theefe, whose liquid Surge, resolues
The Moone into Salt teares. The Earth's a Theefe,
That feeds and breeds by a composture stolne
From gen'rall excrement : each thing's a Theefe.
The Lawes, your curbe and whip, in their rough power
Ha's vncheck'd Theft. Loue not your selues, away,
Rob one another, there's more Gold, cut throates,
All that you meete are Theeues : to Athens go,
Breake open shoppes, nothing can you steale
But Theeues do loose it : steale lesse, for this I giue you,
And Gold confound you howsoere : Amen.
3 Has almost charm'd me from my Profession, by perswading me to it.
1 'Tis in the malice of mankinde, that he thus aduises vs not to haue vs thriue in our mystery.
2 Ile beleeue him as an Enemy,
And giue ouer my Trade.
1 Let vs first see peace in Athens, there is no time so miserable, but a man may be true. *Exit Theeues.*

Enter the Steward to Timon.

Stew. Oh you Gods!
Is yon'd despis'd and ruinous man my Lord?
Full of decay and fayling? Oh Monument
And wonder of good deeds, euilly bestow'd!
What an alteration of Honor has desp'rate want made?
What vilder thing vpon the earth, then Friends,
Who can bring Noblest mindes, to basest ends.
How rarely does it meete with this times guise,
When man was wisht to loue his Enemies :
Grant I may euer loue, and rather woo
Those that would mischeefe me, then those that doo.
Has caught me in his eye, I will present my honest griefe vnto him; and as my Lord, still serue him with my life.
My deerest Master.
Tim. Away : what art thou?
Stew. Haue you forgot me, Sir?
Tim. Why dost aske that? I haue forgot all men.
Then, if thou grunt'st, th'art a man.
I haue forgot thee.
Stew. An honest poore seruant of yours.
Tim. Then I know thee not :
I neuer had honest man about me, I all
I kept were Knaues, to serue in meate to Villaines.
Stew. The Gods are witnesse,
Neu'r did poore Steward weare a truer greefe
For his vndone Lord, then mine eyes for you.
Tim. What, dost thou weepe?
Come neerer, then I loue thee
Because thou art a woman, and disclaim'st
Flinty mankinde : whose eyes do neuer giue,
But thorow Lust and Laughter : pittie's sleeping :
Strange times ẏ weepe with laughing, not with weeping.
Stew. I begge of you to know me, good my Lord,
T'accept my greefe, and whil'st this poore wealth lasts,
To entertaine me as your Steward still.
Tim. Had I a Steward
So true, so iust, and now so comfortable?
It almost turnes my dangerous Nature wilde.
Let me behold thy face : Surely, this man
Was borne of woman.
Forgiue my generall, and exceptlesse rashnesse
You perpetuall sober Gods. I do proclaime
One honest man : Mistake me not, but one :
No more I pray, and hee's a Steward.
How faine would I haue hated all mankinde,
And thou redeem'st thy selfe. But all saue thee,
I fell with Curses.
Me thinkes thou art more honest now, then wise :
For, by oppressing and betraying mee,

Thou

Thou might'st haue sooner got another Seruice:
For many so arriue at second Masters,
Vpon their first Lords necke. But tell me true,
(For I must euer doubt, though ne're so sure)
Is not thy kindnesse subtle, couetous,
If not a Vsuring kindnesse, and as rich men deale Guifts,
Expecting in returne twenty for one?
Stew. No my most worthy Master, in whose brest
Doubt, and suspect (alas) are plac'd too late:
You should haue fear'd false times, when you did Feast.
Suspect still comes, where an estate is least.
That which I shew, Heauen knowes, is meerely Loue,
Dutie, and Zeale, to your vnmatched minde;
Care of your Food and Liuing, and beleeue it,
My most Honour'd Lord,
For any benefit that points to mee,
Either in hope, or present, I'de exchange
For this one wish, that you had power and wealth
To requite me, by making rich your selfe.
Tim. Looke thee, 'tis so: thou singly honest man,
Heere take: the Gods out of my miserie
Ha's sent thee Treasure. Go, liue rich and happy,
But thus condition'd: Thou shalt build from men:
Hate all, curse all, shew Charity to none,
But let the famisht flesh slide from the Bone,
Ere thou releeue the Begger. Giue to dogges
What thou denyest to men. Let Prisons swallow 'em,
Debts wither 'em to nothing, be men like blasted woods
And may Diseases licke vp their false bloods,
And so farewell, and thriue.
Stew. O let me stay, and comfort you, my Master.
Tim. If thou hat'st Curses
Stay not: flye, whil'st thou art blest and free:
Ne're see thou man, and let me ne're see thee. *Exit*

Enter Poet, and Painter.

Pain. As I tooke note of the place, it cannot be farre where he abides.
Poet. What's to be thought of him?
Does the Rumor hold for true,
That hee's so full of Gold?
Painter. Certaine.
Alcibiades reports it: *Phrinica* and *Timandylo*
Had Gold of him. He likewise enrich'd
Poore stragling Souldiers, with great quantity.
'Tis saide, he gaue vnto his Steward
A mighty summe.
Poet. Then this breaking of his,
Ha's beene but a Try for his Friends?
Painter. Nothing else:
You shall see him a Palme in Athens againe,
And flourish with the highest:
Therefore, 'tis not amisse, we tender our loues
To him, in this suppos'd distresse of his:
It will shew honestly in vs,
And is very likely, to loade our purposes
With what they trauaile for,
If it be a iust and true report, that goes
Of his hauing.
Poet. What haue you now
To present vnto him?
Painter. Nothing at this time
But my Visitation: onely I will promise him
An excellent Peece.
Poet. I must serue him so too;
Tell him of an intent that's comming toward him.
Painter. Good as the best.
Promising, is the verie Ayre o'th'Time;
It opens the eyes of Expectation.
Performance, is euer the duller for his acte,
And but in the plainer and simpler kinde of people,
The deede of Saying is quite out of vse.
To Promise, is most Courtly and fashionable;
Performance, is a kinde of Will or Testament
Which argues a great sicknesse in his iudgement
That makes it.

Enter Timon from his Caue.

Timon. Excellent Workeman,
Thou canst not paint a man so badde
As is thy selfe.
Poet. I am thinking
What I shall say I haue prouided for him:
It must be a personating of himselfe:
A Satyre against the softnesse of Prosperity,
With a Discouerie of the infinite Flatteries
That follow youth and opulencie.
Timon. Must thou needes
Stand for a Villaine in thine owne Worke?
Wilt thou whip thine owne faults in other men?
Do so, I haue Gold for thee.
Poet. Nay let's seeke him.
Then do we sinne against our owne estate,
When we may profit meete, and come too late.
Painter. True:
When the day serues before blacke-corner'd night;
Finde what thou want'st, by free and offer'd light.
Come.
Tim. Ile meete you at the turne:
What a Gods Gold, that he is worshipt
In a baser Temple, then where Swine feede?
'Tis thou that rigg'st the Barke, and plow'st the Fome,
Setlest admired reuerence in a Slaue,
To thee be worshipt, and thy Saints for aye:
Be crown'd with Plagues, that thee alone obay.
Fit I meet them.
Poet. Haile worthy *Timon*.
Pain. Our late Noble Master.
Timon. Haue I once liu'd
To see two honest men?
Poet. Sir:
Hauing often of your open Bounty tasted,
Hearing you were retyr'd, your Friends falne off,
Whose thankelesse Natures (O abhorred Spirits)
Not all the Whippes of Heauen, are large enough.
What, to you,
Whose Starre-like Noblenesse gaue life and influence
To their whole being? I am rapt, and cannot couer
The monstrous bulke of this Ingratitude
With any size of words.
Timon. Let it go,
Naked men may see't the better:
You that are honest, by being what you are,
Make them best seene, and knowne.
Pain. He, and my selfe
Haue trauail'd in the great showre of your guifts,
And sweetly felt it.
Timon. I, you are honest man.
Painter. We are hither come
To offer you our seruice.
Timon. Most honest men:

Why

Why how shall I requite you?
Can you eate Roots, and drinke cold water, no?
Both. What we can do,
Wee'l do to do you seruice.
Tim. Y'are honest men,
Y'haue heard that I haue Gold,
I am sure you haue, speake truth, y'are honest men.
Pain. So it is said my Noble Lord, but therefore
Came not my Friend, nor I.
Timon. Good honest men: Thou draw'st a counterfet
Best in all Athens, th'art indeed the best,
Thou counterfet'st most liuely.
Pain. So, so, my Lord.
Tim. E'ne so sir as I say. And for thy fiction,
Why thy Verse swels with stuffe so fine and smooth,
That thou art euen Naturall in thine Art.
But for all this (my honest Natur'd friends)
I must needs say you haue a little fault,
Marry 'tis not monstrous in you, neither wish I
You take much paines to mend.
Both. Beseech your Honour
To make it knowne to vs.
Tim. You'l take it ill.
Both. Most thankefully, my Lord.
Timon. Will you indeed?
Both. Doubt it not worthy Lord.
Tim. There's neuer a one of you but trusts a Knaue,
That mightily deceiues you.
Both. Do we, my Lord?
Tim. I, and you heare him cogge,
See him dissemble,
Know his grosse patchery, loue him, feede him,
Keepe in your bosome, yet remaine assur'd
That he's a made-vp-Villaine.
Pain. I know none such, my Lord.
Poet. Nor I.
Timon. Looke you,
I loue you well, Ile giue you Gold
Rid me these Villaines from your companies;
Hang them, or stab them, drowne them in a draught,
Confound them by some course, and come to me,
Ile giue you Gold enough.
Both. Name them my Lord, let's know them.
Tim. You that way, and you this:
But two in Company:
Each man a part, all single, and alone,
Yet an arch Villaine keepes him company:
If where thou art, two Villaines shall not be,
Come not neere him. If thou would'st not recide
But where one Villaine is, then him abandon.
Hence, packe, there's Gold, you came for Gold ye slaues:
You haue worke for me; there's payment, hence,
You are an Alcumist, make Gold of that:
Out Rascall dogges. *Exeunt*

Enter Steward, and two Senators.

Stew. It is vaine that you would speake with *Timon*;
For he is set so onely to himselfe,
That nothing but himselfe, which lookes like man,
Is friendly with him.
1. Sen. Bring vs to his Caue.
It is our part and promise to th'Athenians
To speake with *Timon*.
2. Sen. At all times alike
Men are not still the same: 'twas Time and Greefes
That fram'd him thus. Time with his fairer hand,
Offering the Fortunes of his former dayes,
The former man may make him: bring vs to him
And chanc'd it as it may.
Stew. Heere is his Caue:
Peace and content be heere. Lord *Timon*, *Timon*,
Looke out, and speake to Friends: Th'Athenians
By two of their most reuerend Senate greet thee:
Speake to them Noble *Timon*.

Enter Timon out of his Caue.

Tim. Thou Sunne that comforts burne, !
Speake and be hang'd:
For each true word, a blister, and each false
Be as a Cantherizing to the root o'th'Tongue,
Consuming it with speaking.
1 Worthy *Timon*.
Tim. Of none but such as you,
And you of *Timon*.
1 The Senators of Athens, greet thee *Timon*.
Tim. I thanke them,
And would send them backe the plague,
Could I but catch it for them.
1 O forget
What we are sorry for our selues in thee:
The Senators, with one consent of loue,
Intreate thee backe to Athens, who haue thought
On speciall Dignities, which vacant lye
For thy best vse and wearing.
2 They confesse
Toward thee, forgetfulnesse too generall grosse;
Which now the publike Body, which doth sildome
Play the re-canter, feeling in it selfe
A lacke of *Timons* ayde, hath since withall
Of it owne fall, restraining ayde to *Timon*,
And send forth vs, to make their sorrowed render,
Together, with a recompence more fruitfull
Then their offence can weigh downe by the Dramme,
I euen such heapes and summes of Loue and Wealth,
As shall to thee blot out, what wrongs were theirs,
And write in thee the figures of their loue,
Euer to read them thine.
Tim. You witch me in it;
Surprize me to the very brinke of teares;
Lend me a Fooles heart, and a womans eyes,
And Ile beweepe these comforts, worthy Senators.
1 Therefore so please thee to returne with vs,
And of our Athens, thine and ours to take
The Captainship, thou shalt be met with thankes,
Allowed with absolute power, and thy good name
Liue with Authoritie: so soone we shall driue backe
Of *Alcibiades* th'approaches wild,
Who like a Bore too sauage, doth root vp
His Countries peace.
2 And shakes his threatning Sword
Against the walles of *Athens*.
1 Therefore *Timon*.
Tim. Well sir, I will: therefore I will sir thus:
If *Alcibiades* kill my Countrymen,
Let *Alcibiades* know this of *Timon*,
That *Timon* cares not. But if he sacke faire Athens,
And take our goodly aged men by'th'Beards,
Giuing our holy Virgins to the staine
Of contumelious, beastly, mad-brain'd warre:
Then let him know, and tell him *Timon* speakes it,

In

In pitty of our aged, and our youth,
I cannot choose but tell him that I care not,
And let him tak't at worst: For their Kniues care not,
While you haue throats to answer. For my selfe,
There's not a whittle, in th'vnruly Campe,
But I do prize it at my loue, before
The reuerends Throat in Athens. So I leaue you
To the protection of the prosperous Gods,
As Theeues to Keepers.

Stew. Stay not, all's in vaine.

Tim. Why I was writing of my Epitaph,
It will be seene to morrow. My long sicknesse
Of Health, and Liuing, now begins to mend,
And nothing brings me all things. Go, liue still,
Be *Alcibiades* your plague; you his,
And last so long enough.

1 We speake in vaine.

Tim. But yet I loue my Country, and am not
One that reioyces in the common wracke,
As common bruite doth put it.

1 That's well spoke.

Tim. Commend me to my louing Countreymen.

1 These words become your lippes as they passe thorow them.

2 And enter in our eares, like great Triumphers
In their applauding gates.

Tim. Commend me to them,
And tell them, that to ease them of their greefes,
Their feares of Hostile strokes, their Aches losses,
Their pangs of Loue, with other incident throwes
That Natures fragile Vessell doth sustaine
In lifes vncertaine voyage, I will some kindnes do them,
Ile teach them to preuent wilde *Alcibiades* wrath.

1 I like this well, he will returne againe.

Tim. I haue a Tree which growes heere in my Close,
That mine owne vse inuites me to cut downe,
And shortly must I fell it. Tell my Friends,
Tell Athens, in the sequence of degree,
From high to low throughout, that who so please
To stop Affliction, let him take his haste;
Come hither ere my Tree hath felt the Axe,
And hang himselfe. I pray you do my greeting.

Stew. Trouble him no further, thus you still shall
Finde him.

Tim. Come not to me againe, but say to Athens,
Timon hath made his euerlasting Mansion
Vpon the Beached Verge of the salt Flood,
Who once a day with his embossed Froth
The turbulent Surge shall couer; thither come,
And let my graue-stone be your Oracle:
Lippes, let foure words go by, and Language end:
What is amisse, Plague and Infection mend.
Graues onely be mens workes, and Death their gaine;
Sunne, hide thy Beames, *Timon* hath done his Raigne.

Exit Timon.

1 His discontents are vnremoueably coupled to Nature.

2 Our hope in him is dead: let vs returne,
And straine what other meanes is left vnto vs
In our deere perill.

1 It requires swift foot. *Exeunt.*

Enter two other Senators, with a Messenger.

1 Thou hast painfully discouer'd: are his Files
As full as thy report?

Mes. I haue spoke the least.
Besides his expedition promises present approach.

2 We stand much hazard, if they bring not *Timon.*

Mes. I met a Currier, one mine ancient Friend,
Whom though in generall part we were oppos'd,
Yet our old loue made a particular force,
And made vs speake like Friends. This man was riding
From *Alcibiades* to *Timons* Caue,
With Letters of intreaty, which imported
His Fellowship i'th'cause against your City,
In part for his sake mou'd.

Enter the other Senators.

1 Heere come our Brothers.

3 No talke of *Timon*, nothing of him expect,
The Enemies Drumme is heard, and fearefull scouring
Doth choake the ayre with dust: In, and prepare,
Ours is the fall I feare, our Foes the Snare. *Exeunt*

Enter a Souldier in the Woods, seeking Timon.

Sol. By all description this should be the place.
Whose heere? Speake hoa. No answer? What is this?
Tymon is dead, who hath out-stretcht his span,
Some Beast reade this; There do's not liue a Man.
Dead sure, and this his Graue, what's on this Tomb,
I cannot read: the Charracter Ile take with wax,
Our Captaine hath in euery Figure skill;
An ag'd Interpreter, though yong in dayes:
Before proud Athens hee's set downe by this,
Whose fall the marke of his Ambition is. *Exit.*

Trumpets sound. Enter Alcibiades with his Powers before Athens.

Alc. Sound to this Coward, and lasciuious Towne,
Our terrible approach.

Sounds a Parly.

The Senators appeare vpon the wals.

Till now you haue gone on, and fill'd the time
With all Licentious measure, making your willes
The scope of Iustice. Till now, my selfe and such
As slept within the shadow of your power
Haue wander'd with our trauerst Armes, and breath'd
Our sufferance vainly: Now the time is flush,
When crouching Marrow in the bearer strong
Cries (of it selfe) no more: Now breathlesse wrong,
Shall sit and pant in your great Chaires of ease,
And pursie Insolence shall breake his winde
With feare and horrid flight.

1. *Sen.* Noble, and young;
When thy first greefes were but a meere conceit,
Ere thou had'st power, or we had cause of feare,
We sent to thee, to giue thy rages Balme,
To wipe out our Ingratitude, with Loues
Aboue their quantitie.

2 So did we wooe
Transformed *Timon*, to our Citties loue
By humble Message, and by promist meanes:
We were not all vnkinde, nor all deserue
The common stroke of warre.

1 These walles of ours,
Were not erected by rheir hands, from whom
You haue receyu'd your greefe: Nor are they such,
That these great Towres, Trophees, & Schools shold fall
For priuate faults in them.

2 Nor are they liuing

Who

Who were the motiues that you firſt went out,
(Shame that they wanted, cunning in exceſſe)
Hath broke their hearts. March, Noble Lord,
Into our City with thy Banners ſpred,
By decimation and a tythed death;
If thy Reuenges hunger for that Food
Which Nature loathes, take thou the deſtin'd tenth,
And by the hazard of the ſpotted dye,
Let dye the ſpotted.

1 All haue not offended:
For thoſe that were, it is not ſquare to take
On thoſe that are, Reuenge: Crimes, like Lands
Are not inherited, then deere Countryman,
Bring in thy rankes, but leaue without thy rage,
Spare thy Athenian Cradle, and thoſe Kin
Which in the bluſter of thy wrath muſt fall
With thoſe that haue offended, like a Shepheard,
Approach the Fold, and cull th'infected forth,
But kill not altogether.

2 What thou wilt,
Thou rather ſhalt inforce it with thy ſmile,
Then hew too't, with thy Sword.

1 Set but thy foot
Againſt our rampyr'd gates, and they ſhall ope:
So thou wilt ſend thy gentle heart before,
To ſay thou't enter Friendly.

2 Throw thy Gloue,
Or any Token of thine Honour elſe,
That thou wilt vſe the warres as thy redreſſe,
And not as our Confuſion: All thy Powers
Shall make their harbour in our Towne, till wee
Haue ſeal'd thy full deſire.

Alc. Then there's my Gloue,
Deſend and open your vncharged Ports,
Thoſe Enemies of *Timons*, and mine owne
Whom you your ſelues ſhall ſet out for reproofe,
Fall and no more; and to attone your feares
With my more Noble meaning, not a man
Shall paſſe his quarter, or offend the ſtreame
Of Regular Iuſtice in your Citties bounds,
But ſhall be remedied to your publique Lawes
At heauieſt anſwer.

Both. 'Tis moſt Nobly ſpoken.

Alc. Deſcend, and keepe your words.

Enter a Meſſenger.

Meſ. My Noble Generall, *Timon* is dead,
Entomb'd vpon the very hemme o'th'Sea,
And on his Graueſtone, this Inſculpture which
With wax I brought away: whoſe ſoft Impreſſion
Interprets for my poore ignorance.

Alcibiades reades the Epitaph.

Heere lies a wretched Coarſe, of wretched Soule bereft,
Seek not my name: A Plague conſume you, wicked Caitifs left:
Heere lye I Timon, who aliue, all liuing men did hate,
Paſſe by, and curſe thy fill, but paſſe and ſtay not here thy gate.

Theſe well expreſſe in thee thy latter ſpirits:
Though thou abhorrd'ſt in vs our humane griefes,
Scornd'ſt our Braines flow, and thoſe our droplets, which
From niggard Nature fall; yet Rich Conceit
Taught thee to make vaſt Neptune weepe for aye
On thy low Graue, on faults forgiuen. Dead
Is Noble *Timon*, of whoſe Memorie
Heereafter more. Bring me into your Citie,
And I will vſe the Oliue, with my Sword:
Make war breed peace; make peace ſtint war, make each
Preſcribe to other, as each others Leach.
Let our Drummes ſtrike. *Exeunt.*

FINIS.

THE ACTORS NAMES.

TYMON of Athens.
Lucius, And
Lucullus, two Flattering Lords.
Appemantus, a Churlish Philosopher.
Sempronius another flattering Lord.
Alcibiades, an Athenian Captaine.
Poet.
Painter.
Jeweller.
Merchant.
Certaine Senatours.
Certaine Maskers.
Certaine Theeues.

Flaminius, one of Tymons Seruants.
Seruilius, another.
Caphis. Varro. Philo. Titus. Lucius. Hortensis — Seuerall Seruants to Vsurers.
Ventigius. one of Tymons false Friends.
Cupid.
Sempronius.
With diuers other Seruants,
And Attendants.

THE TRAGEDIE OF IVLIVS CÆSAR.

Actus Primus. Scœna Prima.

Enter Flauius, Murellus, and certaine Commoners ouer the Stage.

Flauius.

HEnce: home you idle Creatures, get you home:
Is this a Holiday? What, know you not
(Being Mechanicall) you ought not walke
Vpon a labouring day, without the signe
Of your Profession? Speake, what Trade art thou?

Car. Why Sir, a Carpenter.

Mur. Where is thy Leather Apron, and thy Rule?
What dost thou with thy best Apparrell on?
You sir, what Trade are you?

Cobl. Truely Sir, in respect of a fine Workman, I am but as you would say, a Cobler.

Mur. But what Trade art thou? Answer me directly.

Cob. A Trade Sir, that I hope I may vse, with a safe Conscience, which is indeed Sir, a Mender of bad soules.

Fla. What Trade thou knaue? Thou naughty knaue, what Trade?

Cobl. Nay I beseech you Sir, be not out with me: yet if you be out Sir, I can mend you.

Mur. What mean'st thou by that? Mend mee, thou sawcy Fellow?

Cob. Why sir, Cobble you.

Fla. Thou art a Cobler, art thou?

Cob. Truly sir, all that I liue by, is with the Aule: I meddle with no Tradesmans matters, nor womens matters; but withal I am indeed Sir, a Surgeon to old shooes: when they are in great danger, I recouer them. As proper men as euer trod vpon Neats Leather, haue gone vpon my handy-worke.

Fla. But wherefore art not in thy Shop to day?
Why do'st thou leade these men about the streets?

Cob. Truly sir, to weare out their shooes, to get my selfe into more worke. But indeede sir, we make Holyday to see *Cæsar*, and to reioyce in his Triumph.

Mur. Wherefore reioyce?
What Conquest brings he home?
What Tributaries follow him to Rome,
To grace in Captiue bonds his Chariot Wheeles?
You Blockes, you stones, you worse then senslesse things:
O you hard hearts, you cruell men of Rome,
Knew you not *Pompey* many a time and oft?
Haue you climb'd vp to Walles and Battlements,
To Towres and Windowes? Yea, to Chimney tops,
Your Infants in your Armes, and there haue sate
The liue-long day, with patient expectation,
To see great *Pompey* passe the streets of Rome:
And when you saw his Chariot but appeare,
Haue you not made an Vniuersall shout,
That Tyber trembled vnderneath her bankes
To heare the replication of your sounds,
Made in her Concaue Shores?
And do you now put on your best attyre?
And do you now cull out a Holyday?
And do you now strew Flowers in his way,
That comes in Triumph ouer *Pompeyes* blood?
Be gone,
Runne to your houses, fall vpon your knees,
Pray to the Gods to intermit the plague
That needs must light on this Ingratitude.

Fla. Go, go, good Countrymen, and for this fault
Assemble all the poore men of your sort;
Draw them to Tyber bankes, and weepe your teares
Into the Channell, till the lowest streame
Do kisse the most exalted Shores of all.

Exeunt all the Commoners.

See where their basest mettle be not mou'd,
They vanish tongue-tyed in their guiltinesse:
Go you downe that way towards the Capitoll,
This way will I: Disrobe the Images,
If you do finde them deckt with Ceremonies.

Mur. May we do so?
You know it is the Feast of Lupercall.

Fla. It is no matter, let no Images
Be hung with *Cæsars* Trophees: Ile about,
And driue away the Vulgar from the streets;
So do you too, where you perceiue them thicke.
These growing Feathers, pluckt from *Cæsars* wing,
Will make him flye an ordinary pitch,
Who else would soare aboue the view of men,
And keepe vs all in seruile fearefulnesse. *Exeunt*

Enter Cæsar, Antony for the Course, Calphurnia, Portia, Decius, Cicero, Brutus, Cassius, Caska, a Soothsayer: after them Murellus and Flauius.

Cæs. Calphurnia.

Cask. Peace ho, *Cæsar* speakes.

Cæs. Calphurnia.

Calp. Heere my Lord.

Cæs. Stand you directly in *Antonio's* way,
When he doth run his course. *Antonio.*

Ant. *Cæsar*, my Lord.

Cæs. Forget not in your speed *Antonio*,
To touch *Calphurnia*: for our Elders say,

The Barren touched in this holy chace,
Shake off their sterrile curse.
Ant. I shall remember,
When *Cæsar* sayes, Do this; it is perform'd.
Cæs. Set on, and leaue no Ceremony out.
Sooth. *Cæsar.*
Cæs. Ha? Who calles?
Cask. Bid euery noyse be still: peace yet againe.
Cæs. Who is it in the presse, that calles on me?
I heare a Tongue shriller then all the Musicke
Cry, *Cæsar*: Speake, *Cæsar* is turn'd to heare.
Sooth. Beware the Ides of March.
Cæs. What man is that?
Br. A Sooth-sayer bids you beware the Ides of March
Cæs. Set him before me, let me see his face.
Cassi. Fellow, come from the throng, look vpon *Cæsar.*
Cæs. What sayst thou to me now? Speak once againe.
Sooth. Beware the Ides of March.
Cæs. He is a Dreamer, let vs leaue him: Passe.
Sennet. *Exeunt. Manet Brut. & Cass.*
Cassi. Will you go see the order of the course?
Brut. Not I.
Cassi. I pray you do.
Brut. I am not Gamesom: I do lacke some part
Of that quicke Spirit that is in *Antony*:
Let me not hinder *Cassius* your desires;
Ile leaue you.
Cassi. *Brutus*, I do obserue you now of late:
I haue not from your eyes, that gentlenesse
And shew of Loue, as I was wont to haue:
You beare too stubborne, and too strange a hand
Ouer your Friend, that loues you.
Bru. *Cassius*,
Be not deceiu'd: If I haue veyl'd my looke,
I turne the trouble of my Countenance
Meerely vpon my selfe. Vexed I am
Of late, with passions of some difference,
Conceptions onely proper to my selfe,
Which giue some soyle (perhaps) to my Behauiours:
But let not therefore my good Friends be greeu'd
(Among which number *Cassius* be you one)
Nor construe any further my neglect,
Then that poore *Brutus* with himselfe at warre,
Forgets the shewes of Loue to other men.
Cassi. Then *Brutus*, I haue much mistook your passion,
By meanes whereof, this Brest of mine hath buried
Thoughts of great value, worthy Cogitations.
Tell me good *Brutus*, Can you see your face?
Brutus. No *Cassius*:
For the eye sees not it selfe but by reflection,
By some other things.
Cassius. 'Tis iust,
And it is very much lamented *Brutus*,
That you haue no such Mirrors, as will turne
Your hidden worthinesse into your eye,
That you might see your shadow:
I haue heard,
Where many of the best respect in Rome,
(Except immortall *Cæsar*) speaking of *Brutus*,
And groaning vnderneath this Ages yoake,
Haue wish'd, that Noble *Brutus* had his eyes.
Bru. Into what dangers, would you
Leade me *Cassius*?
That you would haue me seeke into my selfe,
For that which is not in me?
Cas. Therefore good *Brutus*, be prepar'd to heare:
And since you know, you cannot see your selfe
So well as by Reflection; I your Glasse,
Will modestly discouer to your selfe
That of your selfe, which you yet know not of.
And be not iealous on me, gentle *Brutus*:
Were I a common Laughter, or did vse
To stale with ordinary Oathes my loue
To euery new Protester: if you know,
That I do fawne on men, and hugge them hard,
And after scandall them: Or if you know,
That I professe my selfe in Banquetting
To all the Rout, then hold me dangerous.

Flourish, and Shout.

Bru. What meanes this Showting?
I do feare, the People choose *Cæsar*
For their King.
Cassi. I, do you feare it?
Then must I thinke you would not haue it so.
Bru. I would not *Cassius*, yet I loue him well:
But wherefore do you hold me heere so long?
What is it, that you would impart to me?
If it be ought toward the generall good,
Set Honor in one eye, and Death i'th other,
And I will looke on both indifferently:
For let the Gods so speed mee, as I loue
The name of Honor, more then I feare death.
Cassi. I know that vertue to be in you *Brutus*,
As well as I do know your outward fauour.
Well, Honor is the subiect of my Story:
I cannot tell, what you and other men
Thinke of this life: But for my single selfe,
I had as liefe not be, as liue to be
In awe of such a Thing, as I my selfe.
I was borne free as *Cæsar*, so were you,
We both haue fed as well, and we can both
Endure the Winters cold, as well as hee.
For once, vpon a Rawe and Gustie day,
The troubled Tyber, chafing with her Shores,
Cæsar saide to me, Dar'st thou *Cassius* now
Leape in with me into this angry Flood,
And swim to yonder Point? Vpon the word,
Accoutred as I was, I plunged in,
And bad him follow: so indeed he did.
The Torrent roar'd, and we did buffet it
With lusty Sinewes, throwing it aside,
And stemming it with hearts of Controuersie.
But ere we could arriue the Point propos'd,
Cæsar cride, Helpe me *Cassius*, or I sinke.
I (as *Æneas*, our great Ancestor,
Did from the Flames of Troy, vpon his shoulder
The old *Anchyses* beare) so, from the waues of Tyber
Did I the tyred *Cæsar*: And this Man,
Is now become a God, and *Cassius* is
A wretched Creature, and must bend his body,
If *Cæsar* carelesly but nod on him.
He had a Feauer when he was in Spaine,
And when the Fit was on him, I did marke
How he did shake: Tis true, this God did shake,
His Coward lippes did from their colour flye,
And that same Eye, whose bend doth awe the World,
Did loose his Lustre: I did heare him grone:
I, and that Tongue of his, that bad the Romans
Marke him, and write his Speeches in their Bookes,
Alas, it cried, Giue me some drinke *Titinius*,

As

As a sicke Girle : Ye Gods, it doth amaze me,
A man of such a feeble temper should
So get the start of the Maiesticke world,
And beare the Palme alone.
Shout. Flourish.
Bru. Another generall shout?
I do beleeue, that these applauses are
For some new Honors, that are heap'd on *Cæsar*.
Cassi. Why man, he doth bestride the narrow world
Like a Colossus, and we petty men
Walke vnder his huge legges, and peepe about
To finde our selues dishonourable Graues.
Men at sometime, are Masters of their Fates.
The fault (deere *Brutus*) is not in our Starres,
But in our Selues, that we are vnderlings.
Brutus and *Cæsar*: What should be in that *Cæsar*?
Why should that name be sounded more then yours?
Write them together: Yours, is as faire a Name:
Sound them, it doth become the mouth aswell:
Weigh them, it is as heauy: Coniure with 'em,
Brutus will start a Spirit as soone as *Cæsar*.
Now in the names of all the Gods at once,
Vpon what meate doth this our *Cæsar* feede,
That he is growne so great? Age, thou art sham'd.
Rome, thou hast lost the breed of Noble Bloods.
When went there by an Age, since the great Flood,
But it was fam'd with more then with one man?
When could they say (till now) that talk'd of Rome,
That her wide Walkes incompast but one man?
Now is't Rome indeed, and Roome enough
When there is in it but one onely man.
O! you and I, haue heard our Fathers say,
There was a *Brutus* once, that would haue brook'd
Th'eternall Diuell to keepe his State in Rome,
As easily as a King.
Bru. That you do loue me, I am nothing iealous:
What you would worke me too, I haue some ayme:
How I haue thought of this, and of these times
I shall recount heereafter. For this present,
I would not so (with loue I might intreat you)
Be any further moou'd: What you haue said,
I will consider: what you haue to say
I will with patience heare, and finde a time
Both meete to heare, and answer such high things.
Till then, my Noble Friend, chew vpon this:
Brutus had rather be a Villager,
Then to repute himselfe a Sonne of Rome
Vnder these hard Conditions, as this time
Is like to lay vpon vs.
Cassi. I am glad that my weake words
Haue strucke but thus much shew of fire from *Brutus*.

Enter Cæsar and his Traine.

Bru. The Games are done,
And *Cæsar* is returning.
Cassi. As they passe by,
Plucke *Caska* by the Sleeue,
And he will (after his sowre fashion) tell you
What hath proceeded worthy note to day.
Bru. I will do so: but looke you *Cassius*,
The angry spot doth glow on *Cæsars* brow,
And all the rest, looke like a chidden Traine;
Calphurnia's Cheeke is pale, and *Cicero*
Lookes with such Ferret, and such fiery eyes]
As we haue seene him in the Capitoll
Being crost in Conference, by some Senators.
Cassi. *Caska* will tell vs what the matter is.
Cæs. *Antonio.*
Ant. *Cæsar.*
Cæs. Let me haue men about me, that are fat,
Sleeke-headed men, and such as sleepe a-nights:
Yond *Cassius* has a leane and hungry looke,
He thinkes too much: such men are dangerous.
Ant. Feare him not *Cæsar*, he's not dangerous,
He is a Noble Roman, and well giuen.
Cæs. Would he were fatter; But I feare him not:
Yet if my name were lyable to feare,
I do not know the man I should auoyd
So soone as that spare *Cassius*. He reades much,
He is a great Obseruer, and he lookes
Quite through the Deeds of men. He loues no Playes,
As thou dost *Antony*: he heares no Musicke;
Seldome he smiles, and smiles in such a sort
As if he mock'd himselfe, and scorn'd his spirit
That could be mou'd to smile at any thing.
Such men as he, be neuer at hearts ease,
Whiles they behold a greater then themselues,
And therefore are they very dangerous.
I rather tell thee what is to be fear'd,
Then what I feare: for alwayes I am *Cæsar*.
Come on my right hand, for this eare is deafe,
And tell me truely, what thou think'st of him. *Sennit.*
Exeunt Cæsar and his Traine.

Cask. You pul'd me by the cloake, would you speake with me?
Bru. I *Caska*, tell vs what hath chanc'd to day
That *Cæsar* lookes so sad.
Cask. Why you were with him, were you not?
Bru. I should not then aske *Caska* what had chanc'd.
Cask. Why there was a Crowne offer'd him; & being offer'd him, he put it by with the backe of his hand thus, and then the people fell a shouting.
Bru. What was the second noyse for?
Cask. Why for that too.
Cassi. They shouted thrice: what was the last cry for?
Cask. Why for that too.
Bru. Was the Crowne offer'd him thrice?
Cask. I marry was't, and hee put it by thrice, euerie time gentler then other; and at euery putting by, mine honest Neighbors showted.
Cassi. Who offer'd him the Crowne?
Cask. Why *Antony*.
Bru. Tell vs the manner of it, gentle *Caska*.
Caska. I can as well bee hang'd as tell the manner of it: It was meere Foolerie, I did not marke it. I sawe *Marke Antony* offer him a Crowne, yet 'twas not a Crowne neyther, 'twas one of these Coronets: and as I told you, hee put it by once: but for all that, to my thinking, he would faine haue had it. Then hee offered it to him againe: then hee put it by againe: but to my thinking, he was very loath to lay his fingers off it. And then he offered it the third time; hee put it the third time by, and still as hee refus'd it, the rabblement howted, and clapp'd their chopt hands, and threw vppe their sweatie Night-cappes, and vttered such a deale of stinking breath, because *Cæsar* refus'd the Crowne, that it had (almost) choaked *Cæsar*: for hee swoonded, and fell downe at it: And for mine owne part, I durst not laugh, for feare of opening my Lippes, and receyuing the bad Ayre.

Cassi. But soft I pray you: what, did *Cæsar* swound?

Cask. He fell downe in the Market-place, and foam'd at mouth, and was speechlesse.

Brut. 'Tis very like he hath the Falling sicknesse.

Cassi. No, *Cæsar* hath it not: but you, and I,
And honest *Caska*, we haue the Falling sicknesse.

Cask. I know not what you meane by that, but I am sure *Cæsar* fell downe. If the tag-ragge people did not clap him, and hisse him, according as he pleas'd, and displeas'd them, as they vse to doe the Players in the Theatre, I am no true man.

Brut. What said he, when he came vnto himselfe?

Cask. Marry, before he fell downe, when he perceiu'd the common Heard was glad he refus'd the Crowne, he pluckt me ope his Doublet, and offer'd them his Throat to cut: and I had beene a man of any Occupation, if I would not haue taken him at a word, I would I might goe to Hell among the Rogues, and so hee fell. When he came to himselfe againe, hee said, If hee had done, or said any thing amisse, he desir'd their Worships to thinke it was his infirmitie. Three or foure Wenches where I stood, cryed, Alasse good Soule, and forgaue him with all their hearts: But there's no heed to be taken of them; if *Cæsar* had stab'd their Mothers, they would haue done no lesse.

Brut. And after that, he came thus sad away.

Cask. I.

Cassi. Did *Cicero* say any thing?

Cask. I, he spoke Greeke.

Cassi. To what effect?

Cask. Nay, and I tell you that, Ile ne're looke you i'th' face againe. But those that vnderstood him, smil'd at one another, and shooke their heads: but for mine owne part, it was Greeke to me. I could tell you more newes too: *Murrellus* and *Flauius*, for pulling Scarffes off *Cæsars* Images, are put to silence. Fare you well. There was more Foolerie yet, if I could remember it.

Cassi. Will you suppe with me to Night, *Caska*?

Cask. No, I am promis'd forth.

Cassi. Will you Dine with me to morrow?

Cask. I, if I be aliue, and your minde hold, and your Dinner worth the eating.

Cassi. Good, I will expect you.

Cask. Doe so: farewell both. *Exit.*

Brut. What a blunt fellow is this growne to be?
He was quick Mettle, when he went to Schoole.

Cassi. So is he now, in execution
Of any bold, or Noble Enterprize,
How-euer he puts on this tardie forme:
This Rudenesse is a Sawce to his good Wit,
Which giues men stomacke to disgest his words
With better Appetite.

Brut. And so it is:
For this time I will leaue you:
To morrow, if you please to speake with me,
I will come home to you: or if you will,
Come home to me, and I will wait for you.

Cassi. I will doe so: till then, thinke of the World.
Exit Brutus.

Well *Brutus*, thou art Noble: yet I see,
Thy Honorable Mettle may be wrought
From that it is dispos'd: therefore it is meet,
That Noble mindes keepe euer with their likes:
For who so firme, that cannot be seduc'd?
Cæsar doth beare me hard, but he loues *Brutus*.
If I were *Brutus* now, and he were *Cassius*,
He should not humor me. I will this Night,
In seuerall Hands, in at his Windowes throw,
As if they came from seuerall Citizens,
Writings, all tending to the great opinion
That Rome holds of his Name: wherein obscurely
Cæsars Ambition shall be glanced at.
And after this, let *Cæsar* seat him sure,
For wee will shake him, or worse dayes endure.
Exit.

Thunder, and Lightning. Enter Caska, and Cicero.

Cic. Good euen, *Caska*: brought you *Cæsar* home?
Why are you breathlesse, and why stare you so?

Cask. Are not you mou'd, when all the sway of Earth
Shakes, like a thing vnfirme? O *Cicero*,
I haue seene Tempests, when the scolding Winds
Haue riu'd the knottie Oakes, and I haue seene
Th'ambitious Ocean swell, and rage, and foame,
To be exalted with the threatning Clouds:
But neuer till to Night, neuer till now,
Did I goe through a Tempest-dropping-fire.
Eyther there is a Ciuill strife in Heauen,
Or else the World, too sawcie with the Gods,
Incenses them to send destruction.

Cic. Why, saw you any thing more wonderfull?

Cask. A common slaue, you know him well by sight,
Held vp his left Hand, which did flame and burne
Like twentie Torches ioyn'd; and yet his Hand,
Not sensible of fire, remain'd vnscorch'd.
Besides, I ha'not since put vp my Sword,
Against the Capitoll I met a Lyon,
Who glaz'd vpon me, and went surly by,
Without annoying me. And there were drawne
Vpon a heape, a hundred gastly Women,
Transformed with their feare, who swore, they saw
Men, all in fire, walke vp and downe the streetes.
And yesterday, the Bird of Night did sit,
Euen at Noone-day, vpon the Market place,
Howting, and shreeking. When these Prodigies
Doe so conioyntly meet, let not men say,
These are their Reasons, they are Naturall:
For I beleeue, they are portentous things
Vnto the Clymate, that they point vpon.

Cic. Indeed, it is a strange-disposed time:
But men may construe things after their fashion,
Cleane from the purpose of the things themselues.
Comes *Cæsar* to the Capitoll to morrow?

Cask. He doth: for he did bid *Antonio*
Send word to you, he would be there to morrow.

Cic. Good-night then, *Caska*:
This disturbed Skie is not to walke in.

Cask. Farewell *Cicero*. *Exit Cicero.*

Enter Cassius.

Cassi. Who's there?

Cask. A Romane.

Cassi. *Caska*, by your Voyce.

Cask. Your Eare is good.
Cassius, what Night is this?

Cassi. A very pleasing Night to honest men.

Cask. Who euer knew the Heauens menace so?

Cassi. Those that haue knowne the Earth so full of faults.

For

For my part, I haue walk'd about the ſtreets,
Submitting me vnto the perillous Night;
And thus vnbraced, *Caska*, as you ſee,
Haue bar'd my Boſome to the Thunder-ſtone:
And when the croſſe blew Lightning ſeem'd to open
The Breſt of Heauen, I did preſent my ſelfe
Euen in the ayme, and very flaſh of it.

Cask. But wherefore did you ſo much tempt the Heauens?
It is the part of men, to feare and tremble,
When the moſt mightie Gods, by tokens ſend
Such dreadfull Heraulds, to aſtoniſh vs.

Caſſi. You are dull, *Caska*:
And thoſe ſparkes of Life, that ſhould be in a Roman,
You doe want, or elſe you vſe not.
You looke pale, and gaze, and put on feare,
And caſt your ſelfe in wonder,
To ſee the ſtrange impatience of the Heauens:
But if you would conſider the true cauſe,
Why all theſe Fires, why all theſe gliding Ghoſts,
Why Birds and Beaſts, from qualitie and kinde,
Why Old men, Fooles, and Children calculate,
Why all theſe things change from their Ordinance,
Their Natures, and pre-formed Faculties,
To monſtrous qualitie; why you ſhall finde,
That Heauen hath infus'd them with theſe Spirits,
To make them Inſtruments of feare, and warning,
Vnto ſome monſtrous State.
Now could I (*Caska*) name to thee a man,
Moſt like this dreadfull Night,
That Thunders, Lightens, opens Graues, and roares,
As doth the Lyon in the Capitoll:
A man no mightier then thy ſelfe, or me,
In perſonall action; yet prodigious growne,
And fearefull, as theſe ſtrange eruptions are.

Cask. 'Tis *Cæſar* that you meane:
Is it not, *Caſſius*?

Caſſi. Let it be who it is: for Romans now
Haue Thewes, and Limbes, like to their Anceſtors;
But woe the while, our Fathers mindes are dead,
And we are gouern'd with our Mothers ſpirits,
Our yoake, and ſufferance, ſhew vs Womaniſh.

Cask. Indeed, they ſay, the Senators to morrow
Meane to eſtabliſh *Cæſar* as a King:
And he ſhall weare his Crowne by Sea, and Land,
In euery place, ſaue here in Italy.

Caſſi. I know where I will weare this Dagger then;
Caſſius from Bondage will deliuer *Caſſius*:
Therein, yee Gods, you make the weake moſt ſtrong;
Therein, yee Gods, you Tyrants doe defeat.
Nor Stonie Tower, nor Walls of beaten Braſſe,
Nor ayre-leſſe Dungeon, nor ſtrong Linkes of Iron,
Can be retentiue to the ſtrength of ſpirit:
But Life being wearie of theſe worldly Barres,
Neuer lacks power to diſmiſſe it ſelfe.
If I know this, know all the World beſides,
That part of Tyrannie that I doe beare,
I can ſhake off at pleaſure. *Thunder ſtill.*

Cask. So can I:
So euery Bond-man in his owne hand beares
The power to cancell his Captiuitie.

Caſſi. And why ſhould *Cæſar* be a Tyrant then?
Poore man, I know he would not be a Wolfe,
But that he ſees the Romans are but Sheepe:
He were no Lyon, were not Romans Hindes.
Thoſe that with haſte will make a mightie fire,
Begin it with weake Strawes. What traſh is Rome?
What Rubbiſh, and what Offall? when it ſerues
For the baſe matter, to illuminate
So vile a thing as *Cæſar*. But oh Griefe,
Where haſt thou led me? I (perhaps) ſpeake this
Before a willing Bond-man: then I know
My anſwere muſt be made. But I am arm'd,
And dangers are to me indifferent.

Cask. You ſpeake to *Caska*, and to ſuch a man,
That is no flearing Tell-tale. Hold, my Hand:
Be factious for redreſſe of all theſe Griefes,
And I will ſet this foot of mine as farre,
As who goes fartheſt.

Caſſi. There's a Bargaine made.
Now know you, *Caska*, I haue mou'd already
Some certaine of the Nobleſt minded Romans
To vnder-goe, with me, an Enterprize,
Of Honorable dangerous conſequence;
And I doe know by this, they ſtay for me
In *Pompeyes* Porch: for now this fearefull Night,
There is no ſtirre, or walking in the ſtreetes;
And the Complexion of the Element
Is Fauors, like the Worke we haue in hand,
Moſt bloodie, fierie, and moſt terrible.

Enter Cinna.

Caska. Stand cloſe a while, for heere comes one in haſte.

Caſſi. 'Tis *Cinna*, I doe know him by his Gate,
He is a friend. *Cinna*, where haſte you ſo?

Cinna. To finde out you: Who's that, *Metellus Cymber*?

Caſſi. No, it is *Caska*, one incorporate
To our Attempts. Am I not ſtay'd for, *Cinna*?

Cinna. I am glad on't.
What a fearefull Night is this?
There's two or three of vs haue ſeene ſtrange ſights.

Caſſi. Am I not ſtay'd for? tell me.

Cinna. Yes, you are. O *Caſſius*,
If you could but winne the Noble *Brutus*
To our party——

Caſſi. Be you content. Good *Cinna*, take this Paper,
And looke you lay it in the Pretors Chayre,
Where *Brutus* may but finde it: and throw this
In at his Window; ſet this vp with Waxe
Vpon old *Brutus* Statue: all this done,
Repaire to *Pompeyes* Porch, where you ſhall finde vs.
Is *Decius Brutus* and *Trebonius* there?

Cinna. All, but *Metellus Cymber*, and hee's gone
To ſeeke you at your houſe. Well, I will hie,
And ſo beſtow theſe Papers as you bad me.

Caſſi. That done, repayre to *Pompeyes* Theater.
Exit Cinna.
Come *Caska*, you and I will yet, ere day,
See *Brutus* at his houſe: three parts of him
Is ours alreadie, and the man entire
Vpon the next encounter, yeelds him ours.

Cask. O, he ſits high in all the Peoples hearts:
And that which would appeare Offence in vs,
His Countenance, like richeſt Alchymie,
Will change to Vertue, and to Worthineſſe.

Caſſi. Him, and his worth, and our great need of him,
You haue right well conceited: let vs goe,
For it is after Mid-night, and ere day,
We will awake him, and be ſure of him.
Exeunt.

Actus Secundus.

Enter Brutus in his Orchard.

Brut. What *Lucius*, hoe?
I cannot, by the progreſſe of the Starres,
Giue gueſſe how neere to day.--*Lucius*, I ſay?
I would it were my fault to ſleepe ſo ſoundly.
When *Lucius*, when? awake, I ſay: what *Lucius*?

Enter Lucius.

Luc. Call'd you, my Lord?
Brut. Get me a Tapor in my Study, *Lucius*:
When it is lighted, come and call me here.
Luc. I will, my Lord. *Exit.*
Brut. It muſt be by his death: and for my part,
I know no perſonall cauſe, to ſpurne at him,
But for the generall. He would be crown'd:
How that might change his nature, there's the queſtion?
It is the bright day, that brings forth the Adder,
And that craues warie walking: Crowne him that,
And then I graunt we put a Sting in him,
That at his will he may doe danger with.
Th'abuſe of Greatneſſe, is, when it dis-ioynes
Remorſe from Power: And to ſpeake truth of *Cæſar*,
I haue not knowne, when his Affections ſway'd
More then his Reaſon. But 'tis a common proofe,
That Lowlyneſſe is young Ambitions Ladder,
Whereto the Climber vpward turnes his Face:
But when he once attaines the vpmoſt Round,
He then vnto the Ladder turnes his Backe,
Lookes in the Clouds, ſcorning the baſe degrees
By which he did aſcend: ſo *Cæſar* may;
Then leaſt he may, preuent. And ſince the Quarrell
Will beare no colour, for the thing he is,
Faſhion it thus; that what he is, augmented,
Would runne to theſe, and theſe extremities:
And therefore thinke him as a Serpents egge,
Which hatch'd, would as his kinde grow miſchieuous;
And kill him in the ſhell.

Enter Lucius.

Luc. The Taper burneth in your Cloſet, Sir:
Searching the Window for a Flint, I found
This Paper, thus ſeal'd vp, and I am ſure
It did not lye there when I went to Bed.

Giues him the Letter.

Brut. Get you to Bed againe, it is not day:
Is not to morrow (Boy) the firſt of March?
Luc. I know not, Sir.
Brut. Looke in the Calender, and bring me word.
Luc. I will, Sir. *Exit.*
Brut. The exhalations, whizzing in the ayre,
Giue ſo much light, that I may reade by them.

Opens the Letter, and reades.

Brutus thou ſleep'ſt; awake, and ſee thy ſelfe:
Shall Rome, &c. ſpeake, ſtrike, redreſſe.
Brutus, thou ſleep'ſt: awake.
Such inſtigations haue beene often dropt,
Where I haue tooke them vp:
Shall Rome, &c. Thus muſt I piece it out:
Shall Rome ſtand vnder one mans awe? What Rome?
My Anceſtors did from the ſtreetes of Rome
The *Tarquin* driue, when he was call'd a King.
Speake, ſtrike, redreſſe. Am I entreated
To ſpeake, and ſtrike? O Rome, I make thee promiſe,
If the redreſſe will follow, thou receiueſt
Thy full Petition at the hand of *Brutus*.

Enter Lucius.

Luc. Sir, March is waſted fifteene dayes.

Knocke within.

Brut. 'Tis good. Go to the Gate, ſome body knocks:
Since *Caſſius* firſt did whet me againſt *Cæſar*,
I haue not ſlept.
Betweene the acting of a dreadfull thing,
And the firſt motion, all the *Interim* is
Like a *Phantaſma*, or a hideous Dreame:
The *Genius*, and the mortall Inſtruments
Are then in councell; and the ſtate of a man,
Like to a little Kingdome, ſuffers then
The nature of an Inſurrection.

Enter Lucius.

Luc. Sir, 'tis your Brother *Caſſius* at the Doore,
Who doth deſire to ſee you.
Brut. Is he alone?
Luc. No, Sir, there are moe with him.
Brut. Doe you know them?
Luc. No, Sir, their Hats are pluckt about their Eares,
And halfe their Faces buried in their Cloakes,
That by no meanes I may diſcouer them,
By any marke of fauour.
Brut. Let 'em enter:
They are the Faction. O Conſpiracie,
Sham'ſt thou to ſhew thy dang'rous Brow by Night,
When euills are moſt free? O then, by day
Where wilt thou finde a Cauerne darke enough,
To maske thy monſtrous Viſage? Seek none Conſpiracie,
Hide it in Smiles, and Affabilitie:
For if thou path thy natiue ſemblance on,
Not *Erebus* it ſelfe were dimme enough,
To hide thee from preuention.

Enter the Conſpirators, Caſſius, Caska, Decius, Cinna, Metellus, and Trebonius.

Caſſ. I thinke we are too bold vpon your Reſt:
Good morrow *Brutus*, doe we trouble you?
Brut. I haue beene vp this howre, awake all Night:
Know I theſe men, that come along with you?
Caſſ. Yes, euery man of them; and no man here
But honors you: and euery one doth wiſh,
You had but that opinion of your ſelfe,
Which euery Noble Roman beares of you.
This is *Trebonius*.
Brut. He is welcome hither.
Caſſ. This, *Decius Brutus*.
Brut. He is welcome too.
Caſſ. This, *Caska*; this, *Cinna*; and this, *Metellus Cymber*.
Brut. They are all welcome.
What watchfull Cares doe interpoſe themſelues
Betwixt your Eyes, and Night?
Caſſ. Shall I entreat a word? *They whiſper.*
Decius. Here lyes the Eaſt: doth not the Day breake heere?
Cask. No.
Cin. O pardon, Sir, it doth; and yon grey Lines,
That fret the Clouds, are Meſſengers of Day.
Cask. You ſhall confeſſe, that you are both deceiu'd:
Heere, as I point my Sword, the Sunne ariſes,
Which is a great way growing on the South,

Weigh-

Weighing the youthfull Season of the yeare.
Some two moneths hence, vp higher toward the North
He first presents his fire, and the high East
Stands as the Capitoll, directly heere.
Bru. Giue me your hands all ouer, one by one.
Cas. And let vs sweare our Resolution.
Brut. No, not an Oath: if not the Face of men,
The sufferance of our Soules, the times Abuse;
If these be Motiues weake, breake off betimes,
And euery man hence, to his idle bed:
So let high-sighted-Tyranny range on,
Till each man drop by Lottery. But if these
(As I am sure they do) beare fire enough
To kindle Cowards, and to steele with valour
The melting Spirits of women. Then Countrymen,
What neede we any spurre, but our owne cause,
To pricke vs to redresse? What other Bond,
Then secret Romans, that haue spoke the word,
And will not palter? And what other Oath,
Then Honesty to Honesty ingag'd,
That this shall be, or we will fall for it.
Sweare Priests and Cowards, and men Cautelous
Old feeble Carrions, and such suffering Soules
That welcome wrongs: Vnto bad causes, sweare
Such Creatures as men doubt; but do not staine
The euen vertue of our Enterprize,
Nor th'insuppressiue Mettle of our Spirits,
To thinke, that or our Cause, or our Performance
Did neede an Oath. When euery drop of blood
That euery Roman beares, and Nobly beares
Is guilty of a seuerall Bastardie,
If he do breake the smallest Particle
Of any promise that hath past from him.
Cas. But what of *Cicero*? Shall we sound him?
I thinke he will stand very strong with vs.
Cask. Let vs not leaue him out.
Cyn. No, by no meanes.
Metel. O let vs haue him, for his Siluer haires
Will purchase vs a good opinion:
And buy mens voyces, to commend our deeds:
It shall be sayd, his iudgement rul'd our hands,
Our youths, and wildenesse, shall no whit appeare,
But all be buried in his Grauity.
Bru. O name him not; let vs not breake with him,
For he will neuer follow any thing
That other men begin.
Cas. Then leaue him out.
Cask. Indeed, he is not fit.
Decius. Shall no man else be toucht, but onely *Cæsar*?
Cas. *Decius* well vrg'd: I thinke it is not meet,
Marke Antony, so well belou'd of *Cæsar*,
Should out-liue *Cæsar*, we shall finde of him
A shrew'd Contriuer. And you know, his meanes
If he improue them, may well stretch so farre
As to annoy vs all: which to preuent,
Let *Antony* and *Cæsar* fall together.
Bru. Our course will seeme too bloody, *Caius Cassius*,
To cut the Head off, and then hacke the Limbes:
Like Wrath in death, and Enuy afterwards:
For *Antony*, is but a Limbe of *Cæsar*.
Let's be Sacrificers, but not Butchers *Caius*:
We all stand vp against the spirit of *Cæsar*,
And in the Spirit of men, there is no blood:
O that we then could come by *Cæsars* Spirit,
And not dismember *Cæsar*! But (alas)
Cæsar must bleed for it. And gentle Friends,
Let's kill him Boldly, but not Wrathfully:
Let's carue him, as a Dish fit for the Gods,
Not hew him as a Carkasse fit for Hounds:
And let our Hearts, as subtle Masters do,
Stirre vp their Seruants to an acte of Rage,
And after seeme to chide 'em. This shall make
Our purpose Necessary, and not Enuious.
Which so appearing to the common eyes,
We shall be call'd Purgers, not Murderers.
And for *Marke Antony*, thinke not of him:
For he can do no more then *Cæsars* Arme,
When *Cæsars* head is off.
Cas. Yet I feare him,
For in the ingrafted loue he beares to *Cæsar*.
Bru. Alas, good *Cassius*, do not thinke of him:
If he loue *Cæsar*, all that he can do
Is to himselfe; take thought, and dye for *Cæsar*,
And that were much he should: for he is giuen
To sports, to wildenesse, and much company.
Treb. There is no feare in him; let him not dye,
For he will liue, and laugh at this heereafter.
Clocke strikes.
Bru. Peace, count the Clocke.
Cas. The Clocke hath stricken three.
Treb. 'Tis time to part.
Cass But it is doubtfull yet,
Whether *Cæsar* will come forth to day, or no:
For he is Superstitious growne of late,
Quite from the maine Opinion he held once,
Of Fantasie, of Dreames, and Ceremonies:
It may be, these apparant Prodigies,
The vnaccustom'd Terror of this night,
And the perswasion of his Augurers,
May hold him from the Capitoll to day.
Decius. Neuer feare that: If he be so resolu'd,
I can ore-sway him: For he loues to heare,
That Vnicornes may be betray'd with Trees,
And Beares with Glasses, Elephants with Holes,
Lyons with Toyles, and men with Flatterers.
But, when I tell him, he hates Flatterers,
He sayes, he does; being then most flattered.
Let me worke:
For I can giue his humour the true bent;
And I will bring him to the Capitoll.
Cas. Nay, we will all of vs, be there to fetch him.
Bru. By the eight houre, is that the vttermost?
Cin. Be that the vttermost, and faile not then.
Met. *Caius Ligarius* doth beare *Cæsar* hard,
Who rated him for speaking well of *Pompey*;
I wonder none of you haue thought of him.
Bru. Now good *Metellus* go along by him:
He loues me well, and I haue giuen him Reasons,
Send him but hither, and Ile fashion him.
Cas. The morning comes vpon's:
Wee'l leaue you *Brutus*,
And Friends disperse your selues; but all remember
What you haue said, and shew your selues true Romans.
Bru. Good Gentlemen, looke fresh and merrily,
Let not our lookes put on our purposes,
But beare it as our Roman Actors do,
With vntyr'd Spirits, and formall Constancie,
And so good morrow to you euery one. *Exeunt.*
Manet Brutus.
Boy: *Lucius*: Fast asleepe? It is no matter,
Enioy the hony-heauy-Dew of Slumber:
Thou hast no Figures, nor no Fantasies,
Which

Which busie care drawes, in the braines of men;
Therefore thou sleep'st so sound.

Enter Portia.

Por. *Brutus*, my Lord.
Bru. *Portia:* What meane you? wherfore rise you now?
It is not for your health, thus to commit
Your weake condition, to the raw cold morning.
Por. Nor for yours neither. Y'haue vngently *Brutus*
Stole from my bed: and yesternight at Supper
You sodainly arose, and walk'd about,
Musing, and sighing, with your armes a-crosse:
And when I ask'd you what the matter was,
You star'd vpon me, with vngentle lookes.
I vrg'd you further, then you scratch'd your head,
And too impatiently stampt with your foote:
Yet I insisted, yet you answer'd not,
But with an angry wafter of your hand
Gaue signe for me to leaue you: So I did,
Fearing to strengthen that impatience
Which seem'd too much inkindled; and withall,
Hoping it was but an effect of Humor,
Which sometime hath his houre with euery man.
It will not let you eate, nor talke, nor sleepe;
And could it worke so much vpon your shape,
As it hath much preuayl'd on your Condition,
I should not know you *Brutus*. Deare my Lord,
Make me acquainted with your cause of greefe.
Bru. I am not well in health, and that is all.
Por. *Brutus* is wise, and were he not in health,
He would embrace the meanes to come by it.
Bru. Why so I do: good *Portia* go to bed.
Por. Is *Brutus* sicke? And is it Physicall
To walke vnbraced, and sucke vp the humours
Of the danke Morning? What, is *Brutus* sicke?
And will he steale out of his wholsome bed
To dare the vile contagion of the Night?
And tempt the Rhewmy, and vnpurged Ayre,
To adde vnto hit sicknesse? No my *Brutus*,
You haue some sicke Offence within your minde,
Which by the Right and Vertue of my place
I ought to know of: And vpon my knees,
I charme you, by my once commended Beauty,
By all your vowes of Loue, and that great Vow
Which did incorporate and make vs one,
That you vnfold to me, your selfe; your halfe
Why you are heauy: and what men to night
Haue had resort to you: for heere haue beene
Some sixe or seuen, who did hide their faces
Euen from darknesse.
Bru. Kneele not gentle *Portia*.
Por. I should not neede, if you were gentle *Brutus*.
Within tho Bond of Marriage, tell me *Brutus*,
Is it excepted, I should know no Secrets
That appertaine to you? Am I your Selfe,
But as it were in sort, or limitation?
To keepe with you at Meales, comfort your Bed,
And talke to you sometimes? Dwell I but in the Suburbs
Of your good pleasure? If it be no more,
Portia is *Brutus* Harlot, not his Wife.
Bru. You are my true and honourable Wife,
As deere to me, as are the ruddy droppes
That visit my sad heart.
Por. If this were true, then should I know this secret.
I graunt I am a Woman; but withall,
A Woman that Lord *Brutus* tooke to Wife:
I graunt I am a Woman; but withall,
A Woman well reputed: *Cato's* Daughter.
Thinke you, I am no stronger then my Sex
Being so Father'd, and so Husbanded?
Tell me your Counsels, I will not disclose 'em:
I haue made strong proofe of my Constancie,
Giuing my selfe a voluntary wound
Heere, in the Thigh: Can I beare that with patience,
And not my Husbands Secrets?
Bru. O ye Gods!
Render me worthy of this Noble Wife. *Knocke.*
Harke, harke, one knockes: *Portia* go in a while,
And by and by thy bosome shall partake
The secrets of my Heart.
All my engagements, I will construe to thee,
All the Charractery of my sad browes:
Leaue me with hast. *Exit Portia.*

Enter Lucius and Ligarius.

Lucius, who's that knockes.
Luc. Heere is a sicke man that would speak with you.
Bru. *Caius Ligarius*, that *Metellus* spake of.
Boy, stand aside. *Caius Ligarius*, how?
Cai. Vouchsafe good morrow from a feeble tongue.
Bru. O what a time haue you chose out braue *Caius*
To weare a Kerchiefe? Would you were not sicke.
Cai. I am not sicke, if *Brutus* haue in hand
Any exploit worthy the name of Honor.
Bru. Such an exploit haue I in hand *Ligarius*,
Had you a healthfull eare to heare of it.
Cai. By all the Gods that Romans bow before,
I heere discard my sicknesse. Soule of Rome,
Braue Sonne, deriu'd from Honourable Loines,
Thou like an Exorcist, hast coniur'd vp
My mortified Spirit. Now bid me runne,
And I will striue with things impossible,
Yea get the better of them. What's to do?
Bru. A peece of worke,
That will make sicke men whole.
Cai. But are not some whole, that we must make sicke?
Bru. That must we also. What it is my *Caius*,
I shall vnfold to thee, as we are going,
To whom it must be done.
Cai. Set on your foote,
And with a heart new-fir'd, I follow you,
To do I know not what: but it sufficeth
That *Brutus* leads me on. *Thunder.*
Bru. Follow me then. *Exeunt*

Thunder & Lightning.
Enter Iulius Cæsar in his Night-gowne.

Cæsar. Nor Heauen, nor Earth,
Haue beene at peace to night:
Thrice hath *Calphurnia*, in her sleepe cryed out,
Helpe, ho: They murther *Cæsar*. Who's within?

Enter a Seruant.

Ser. My Lord.
Cæs. Go bid the Priests do present Sacrifice,
And bring me their opinions of Successe.
Ser. I will my Lord. *Exit*

Enter Calphurnia.

Cal. What mean you *Cæsar*? Think you to walk forth?
You shall not stirre out of your house to day.
Cæs. *Cæsar* shall forth; the things that threaten'd me,
Ne're look'd but on my backe: When they shall see
The face of *Cæsar*, they are vanished.

Calp.

Calp. *Cæsar*, I neuer ſtood on Ceremonies,
Yet now they fright me: There is one within,
Beſides the things that we haue heard and ſeene,
Recounts moſt horrid ſights ſeene by the Watch.
A Lionneſſe hath whelped in the ſtreets,
And Graues haue yawn'd, and yeelded vp their dead;
Fierce fiery Warriours fight vpon the Clouds
In Rankes and Squadrons, and right forme of Warre
Which drizel'd blood vpon the Capitoll:
The noiſe of Battell hurtled in the Ayre:
Horſſes do neigh, and dying men did grone,
And Ghoſts did ſhrieke and ſqueale about the ſtreets.
O *Cæſar*, theſe things are beyond all vſe,
And I do feare them.

Cæſ. What can be auoyded
Whoſe end is purpos'd by the mighty Gods?
Yet *Cæſar* ſhall go forth: for theſe Predictions
Are to the world in generall, as to *Cæſar*.

Calp. When Beggers dye, there are no Comets ſeen,
The Heauens themſelues blaze forth the death of Princes

Cæſ. Cowards dye many times before their deaths,
The valiant neuer taſte of death but once:
Of all the Wonders that I yet haue heard,
It ſeemes to me moſt ſtrange that men ſhould feare,
Seeing that death, a neceſſary end
Will come, when it will come.

Enter a Seruant.

What ſay the Augurers?

Ser. They would not haue you to ſtirre forth to day.
Plucking the intrailes of an Offering forth,
They could not finde a heart within the beaſt.

Cæſ. The Gods do this in ſhame of Cowardice:
Cæſar ſhould be a Beaſt without a heart
If he ſhould ſtay at home to day for feare:
No *Cæſar* ſhall not; Danger knowes full well
That *Cæſar* is more dangerous then he.
We heare two Lyons litter'd in one day,
And I the elder and more terrible,
And *Cæſar* ſhall go foorth.

Calp. Alas my Lord,
Your wiſedome is conſum'd in confidence:
Do not go forth to day: Call it my feare,
That keepes you in the houſe, and not your owne.
Wee'l ſend *Mark Antony* to the Senate houſe,
And he ſhall ſay, you are not well to day:
Let me vpon my knee, preuaile in this.

Cæſ. *Mark Antony* ſhall ſay I am not well,
And for thy humor, I will ſtay at home.

Enter Decius.

Heere's *Decius Brutus*, he ſhall tell them ſo.

Deci. *Cæſar*, all haile: Good morrow worthy *Cæſar*,
I come to fetch you to the Senate houſe.

Cæſ. And you are come in very happy time,
To beare my greeting to the Senators,
And tell them that I will not come to day:
Cannot, is falſe: and that I dare not, falſer:
I will not come to day, tell them ſo *Decius*.

Calp. Say he is ſicke.

Cæſ. Shall *Cæſar* ſend a Lye?
Haue I in Conqueſt ſtretcht mine Arme ſo farre,
To be afear'd to tell Gray-beards the truth:
Decius, go tell them, *Cæſar* will not come.

Deci. Moſt mighty *Cæſar*, let me know ſome cauſe,
Leſt I be laught at when I tell them ſo.

Cæſ. The cauſe is in my Will, I will not come,
That is enough to ſatisfie the Senate.
But for your priuate ſatisfaction,
Becauſe I loue you, I will let you know.
Calphurnia heere my wife, ſtayes me at home:
She dreampt to night, ſhe ſaw my Statue,
Which like a Fountaine, with an hundred ſpouts
Did run pure blood: and many luſty Romans
Came ſmiling, & did bathe their hands in it:
And theſe does ſhe apply, for warnings and portents,
And euils imminent; and on her knee
Hath begg'd, that I will ſtay at home to day.

Deci. This Dreame is all amiſſe interpreted,
It was a viſion, faire and fortunate:
Your Statue ſpouting blood in many pipes,
In which ſo many ſmiling Romans bath'd,
Signifies, that from you great Rome ſhall ſucke
Reuiuing blood, and that great men ſhall preſſe
For Tinctures, Staines, Reliques, and Cogniſance.
This by *Calphurnia*'s Dreame is ſignified.

Cæſ. And this way haue you well expounded it.

Deci. I haue, when you haue heard what I can ſay:
And know it now, the Senate haue concluded
To giue this day, a Crowne to mighty *Cæſar*.
If you ſhall ſend them word you will not come,
Their mindes may change. Beſides, it were a mocke
Apt to be render'd, for ſome one to ſay,
Breake vp the Senate, till another time:
When *Cæſars* wife ſhall meete with better Dreames.
If *Cæſar* hide himſelfe, ſhall they not whiſper
Loe *Cæſar* is affraid?
Pardon me *Cæſar*, for my deere deere loue
To your proceeding, bids me tell you this:
And reaſon to my loue is liable.

Cæſ. How fooliſh do your fears ſeeme now *Calphurnia*?
I am aſhamed I did yeeld to them.
Giue me my Robe, for I will go.

Enter Brutus, Ligarius, Metellus, Caska, Trebonius, Cynna, and Publius.

And looke where *Publius* is come to fetch me.

Pub. Good morrow *Cæſar*.

Cæſ. Welcome *Publius*.
What *Brutus*, are you ſtirr'd ſo earely too?
Good morrow *Caska*: *Caius Ligarius*,
Cæſar was ne're ſo much your enemy,
As that ſame Ague which hath made you leane.
What is't a Clocke?

Bru. *Cæſar*, 'tis ſtrucken eight.

Cæſ. I thanke you for your paines and curteſie.

Enter Antony.

See, *Antony* that Reuels long a-nights
Is notwithſtanding vp. Good morrow *Antony*.

Ant. So to moſt Noble *Cæſar*

Cæſ. Bid them prepare within:
I am too blame to be thus waited for.
Now *Cynna*, now *Metellus*: what *Trebonius*,
I haue an houres talke in ſtore for you:
Remember that you call on me to day:
Be neere me, that I may remember you.

Treb. *Cæſar* I will: and ſo neere will I be,
That your beſt Friends ſhall wiſh I had beene further.

Cæſ. Good Friends go in, and taſte ſome wine with me
And we (like Friends) will ſtraight way go together.

Bru. That euery like is not the ſame, O *Cæſar*,
The heart of *Brutus* earnes to thinke vpon. *Exeunt*

Enter Artemidorus.

Cæſar, beware of Brutus, take heede of Caſsius; come not neere

neere Caska, haue an eye to Cynna, trust not Trebonius, marke well Metellus Cymber, Decius Brutus loues thee not: Thou hast wrong'd Caius Ligarius. There is but one minde in all these men, and it is bent against Cæsar: If thou beest not Immortall, looke about you: Security giues way to Conspiracie. The mighty Gods defend thee.

Thy Louer, *Artemidorus.*

Heere will I stand, till *Cæsar* passe along,
And as a Sutor will I giue him this:
My heart laments, that Vertue cannot liue
Out of the teeth of Emulation.
If thou reade this, O *Cæsar*, thou mayest liue;
If not, the Fates with Traitors do contriue. *Exit.*

Enter Portia and Lucius.

Por. I prythee Boy, run to the Senate-house,
Stay not to answer me, but get thee gone.
Why doest thou stay?

Luc. To know my errand Madam.

Por. I would haue had thee there and heere agen
Ere I can tell thee what thou should'st do there:
O Constancie, be strong vpon my side,
Set a huge Mountaine 'tweene my Heart and Tongue:
I haue a mans minde, but a womans might:
How hard it is for women to keepe counsell.
Art thou heere yet?

Luc. Madam, what should I do?
Run to the Capitoll, and nothing else?
And so returne to you, and nothing else?

Por. Yes, bring me word Boy, if thy Lord look well,
For he went sickly forth: and take good note
What *Cæsar* doth, what Sutors presse to him.
Hearke Boy, what noyse is that?

Luc. I heare none Madam.

Por. Prythee listen well:
I heard a bussling Rumor like a Fray,
And the winde brings it from the Capitoll.

Luc. Sooth Madam, I heare nothing.

Enter the Soothsayer.

Por. Come hither Fellow, which way hast thou bin?

Sooth. At mine owne house, good Lady.

Por. What is't a clocke?

Sooth. About the ninth houre Lady.

Por. Is *Cæsar* yet gone to the Capitoll?

Sooth. Madam not yet, I go to take my stand,
To see him passe on to the Capitoll.

Por. Thou hast some suite to *Cæsar*, hast thou not?

Sooth. That I haue Lady, if it will please *Cæsar*
To be so good to *Cæsar*, as to heare me:
I shall beseech him to befriend himselfe.

Por. Why know'st thou any harme's intended towards him?

Sooth. None that I know will be,
Much that I feare may chance:
Good morrow to you: heere the street is narrow:
The throng that followes *Cæsar* at the heeles,
Of Senators, of Prætors, common Sutors,
Will crowd a feeble man (almost) to death:
Ile get me to a place more voyd, and there
Speake to great *Cæsar* as he comes along. *Exit*

Por. I must go in:
Aye me! How weake a thing
The heart of woman is? O *Brutus*,
The Heauens speede thee in thine enterprize.
Sure the Boy heard me: *Brutus* hath a suite
That *Cæsar* will not grant. O, I grow faint:
Run *Lucius*, and commend me to my Lord,
Say I am merry; Come to me againe,
And bring me word what he doth say to thee. *Exeunt*

Actus Tertius.

Flourish.

Enter Cæsar, Brutus, Cassius, Caska, Decius, Metellus, Trebonius, Cynna, Antony, Lepidus, Artimedorus, Publius, and the Soothsayer.

Cæs. The Ides of March are come.

Sooth. I *Cæsar*, but not gone.

Art. Haile *Cæsar*: Read this Scedule.

Deci. *Trebonius* doth desire you to ore-read
(At your best leysure) this his humble suite.

Art. O *Cæsar*, reade mine first: for mine's a suite
That touches *Cæsar* neerer. Read it great *Cæsar*.

Cæs. What touches vs our selfe, shall be last seru'd.

Art. Delay not *Cæsar*, read it instantly.

Cæs. What, is the fellow mad?

Pub. Sirra, giue place.

Cassi. What, vrge you your Petitions in the street?
Come to the Capitoll.

Popil. I wish your enterprize to day may thriue.

Cassi. What enterprize *Popillius*?

Popil. Fare you well.

Bru. What said *Popillius Lena*?

Cassi. He wisht to day our enterprize might thriue:
I feare our purpose is discouered.

Bru. Looke how he makes to *Cæsar*: marke him.

Cassi. *Caska* be sodaine, for we feare preuention.
Brutus what shall be done? If this be knowne,
Cassius or *Cæsar* neuer shall turne backe,
For I will slay my selfe.

Bru. *Cassius* be constant:
Popillius Lena speakes not of our purposes,
For looke he smiles, and *Cæsar* doth not change.

Cassi. *Trebonius* knowes his time: for look you *Brutus*
He drawes *Mark Antony* out of the way.

Deci. Where is *Metellus Cimber*, let him go,
And presently preferre his suite to *Cæsar*.

Bru. He is addrest: presse neere, and second him.

Cin. *Caska*, you are the first that reares your hand.

Cæs. Are we all ready? What is now amisse,
That *Cæsar* and his Senate must redresse?

Metel. Most high, most mighty, and most puisant *Cæsar*
Metellus Cymber throwes before thy Seate
An humble heart.

Cæs. I must preuent thee *Cymber*:
These couchings, and these lowly courtesies
Might fire the blood of ordinary men,
And turne pre-Ordinance, and first Decree
Into the lane of Children. Be not fond,
To thinke that *Cæsar* beares such Rebell blood
That will be thaw'd from the true quality
With that which melteth Fooles, I meane sweet words,
Low-crooked-curtsies, and base Spaniell fawning:
Thy Brother by decree is banished:
If thou doest bend, and pray, and fawne for him,
I spurne thee like a Curre out of my way:
Know, *Cæsar* doth not wrong, nor without cause
Will he be satisfied.

Metel. Is there no voyce more worthy then my owne,
To

To sound more sweetly in great *Cæsars* eare,
For the repealing of my banish'd Brother?

Bru. I kisse thy hand, but not in flattery *Cæsar*:
Desiring thee, that *Publius Cymber* may
Haue an immediate freedome of repeale.

Cæs. What *Brutus*?

Cassi. Pardon *Cæsar*: *Cæsar* pardon:
As lowe as to thy foote doth *Cassius* fall,
To begge infranchisement for *Publius Cymber*.

Cæs. I could be well mou'd, if I were as you,
If I could pray to mooue, Prayers would mooue me:
But I am constant as the Northerne Starre,
Of whose true fixt, and resting quality,
There is no fellow in the Firmament.
The Skies are painted with vnnumbred sparkes,
They are all Fire, and euery one doth shine:
But, there's but one in all doth hold his place.
So, in the World; 'Tis furnish'd well with Men,
And Men are Flesh and Blood, and apprehensiue;
Yet in the number, I do know but One
That vnassayleable holds on his Ranke,
Vnshak'd of Motion: and that I am he,
Let me a little shew it, euen in this:
That I was constant *Cymber* should be banish'd,
And constant do remaine to keepe him so.

Cinna. O *Cæsar*.

Cæs. Hence: Wilt thou lift vp Olympus?

Decius. Great *Cæsar*.

Cæs. Doth not *Brutus* bootlesse kneele?

Cask. Speake hands for me.

They stab Cæsar.

Cæs. *Et Tu Brutè?*——Then fall *Cæsar*. *Dyes*

Cin. Liberty, Freedome; Tyranny is dead,
Run hence, proclaime, cry it about the Streets.

Cassi. Some to the common Pulpits, and cry out
Liberty, Freedome, and Enfranchisement.

Bru. People and Senators, be not affrighted:
Fly not, stand still: Ambitions debt is paid.

Cask. Go to the Pulpit *Brutus*.

Dec. And *Cassius* too.

Bru. Where's *Publius*?

Cin. Heere, quite confounded with this mutiny.

Met. Stand fast together, least some Friend of *Cæsars*
Should chance——

Bru. Talke not of standing. *Publius* good cheere,
There is no harme intended to your person,
Nor to no Roman else: so tell them *Publius*.

Cassi. And leaue vs *Publius*, least that the people
Rushing on vs, should do your Age some mischiefe.

Bru. Do so, and let no man abide this deede,
But we the Doers.

Enter Trebonius.

Cassi. Where is *Antony*?

Treb. Fled to his House amaz'd:
Men, Wiues, and Children, stare, cry out, and run,
As it were Doomesday.

Bru. Fates, we will know your pleasures:
That we shall dye we know, 'tis but the time
And drawing dayes out, that men stand vpon.

Cask. Why he that cuts off twenty yeares of life,
Cuts off so many yeares of fearing death.

Bru. Grant that, and then is Death a Benefit:
So are we *Cæsars* Friends, that haue abridg'd
His time of fearing death. Stoope Romans, stoope,
And let vs bathe our hands in *Cæsars* blood
Vp to the Elbowes, and besmeare our Swords:
Then walke we forth, euen to the Market place,
And wauing our red Weapons o're our heads,
Let's all cry Peace, Freedome, and Liberty.

Cassi. Stoop then, and wash. How many Ages hence
Shall this our lofty Scene be acted ouer,
In State vnborne, and Accents yet vnknowne?

Bru. How many times shall *Cæsar* bleed in sport,
That now on *Pompeyes* Basis lye along,
No worthier then the dust?

Cassi. So oft as that shall be,
So often shall the knot of vs be call'd,
The Men that gaue their Country liberty.

Dec. What, shall we forth?

Cassi. I, euery man away.
Brutus shall leade, and we will grace his heeles
With the most boldest, and best hearts of Rome.

Enter a Seruant.

Bru. Soft, who comes heere? A friend of *Antonies*.

Ser. Thus *Brutus* did my Master bid me kneele;
Thus did *Mark Antony* bid me fall downe,
And being prostrate, thus he bad me say:
Brutus is Noble, Wise, Valiant, and Honest;
Cæsar was Mighty, Bold, Royall, and Louing:
Say, I loue *Brutus*, and I honour him;
Say, I fear'd *Cæsar*, honour'd him, and lou'd him.
If *Brutus* will vouchsafe, that *Antony*
May safely come to him, and be resolu'd
How *Cæsar* hath deseru'd to lye in death,
Mark Antony, shall not loue *Cæsar* dead
So well as *Brutus* liuing; but will follow
The Fortunes and Affayres of Noble *Brutus*,
Thorough the hazards of this vntrod State,
With all true Faith. So sayes my Master *Antony*.

Bru. Thy Master is a Wise and Valiant Romane,
I neuer thought him worse:
Tell him, so please him come vnto this place
He shall be satisfied: and by my Honor
Depart vntouch'd.

Ser. Ile fetch him presently. *Exit Seruant.*

Bru. I know that we shall haue him well to Friend.

Cassi. I wish we may: But yet haue I a minde
That feares him much: and my misgiuing still
Falles shrewdly to the purpose.

Enter Antony.

Bru. But heere comes *Antony*:
Welcome *Mark Antony*.

Ant. O mighty *Cæsar*! Dost thou lye so lowe?
Are all thy Conquests, Glories, Triumphes, Spoiles,
Shrunke to this little Measure? Fare thee well.
I know not Gentlemen what you intend,
Who else must be let blood, who else is ranke:
If I my selfe, there is no houre so fit
As *Cæsars* deaths houre; nor no Instrument
Of halfe that worth, as those your Swords; made rich
With the most Noble blood of all this World.
I do beseech yee, if you beare me hard,
Now, whil'st your purpled hands do reeke and smoake,
Fulfill your pleasure. Liue a thousand yeeres,
I shall not finde my selfe so apt to dye.
No place will please me so, no meane of death,
As heere by *Cæsar*, and by you cut off,
The Choice and Master Spirits of this Age.

Bru. O *Antony*! Begge not your death of vs:
Though now we must appeare bloody and cruell,
As by our hands, and this our present Acte
You see we do: Yet see you but our hands,

And

And this, the bleeding buſineſſe they haue done:
Our hearts you ſee not, they are pittifull:
And pitty to the generall wrong of Rome,
As fire driues out fire, ſo pitty, pitty
Hath done this deed on *Cæſar*. For your part,
To you, our Swords haue leaden points *Marke Antony*:
Our Armes in ſtrength of malice, and our Hearts
Of Brothers temper, do receiue you in,
With all kinde loue, good thoughts, and reuerence.

Caſſi Your voyce ſhall be as ſtrong as any mans,
In the diſpoſing of new Dignities.

Bru. Onely be patient, till we haue appeas'd
The Multitude, beſide themſelues with feare,
And then, we will deliuer you the cauſe,
Why I, that did loue *Cæſar* when I ſtrooke him,
Haue thus proceeded.

Ant. I doubt not of your Wiſedome:
Let each man render me his bloody hand.
Firſt *Marcus Brutus* will I ſhake with you;
Next *Caius Caſſius* do I take your hand;
Now *Decius Brutus* yours; now yours *Metellus*;
Yours *Cinna*; and my valiant *Caska*, yours;
Though laſt, not leaſt in loue, yours good *Trebonius*.
Gentlemen all: Alas, what ſhall I ſay,
My credit now ſtands on ſuch ſlippery ground,
That one of two bad wayes you muſt conceit me,
Either a Coward, or a Flatterer.
That I did loue thee *Cæſar*, O 'tis true:
If then thy Spirit looke vpon vs now,
Shall it not greeue thee deerer then thy death,
To ſee thy *Antony* making his peace,
Shaking the bloody fingers of thy Foes?
Moſt Noble, in the preſence of thy Coarſe,
Had I as many eyes, as thou haſt wounds,
Weeping as faſt as they ſtreame forth thy blood,
It would become me better, then to cloſe
In tearmes of Friendſhip with thine enemies.
Pardon me *Iulius*, heere was't thou bay'd braue Hart,
Heere did'ſt thou fall, and heere thy Hunters ſtand
Sign'd in thy Spoyle, and Crimſon'd in thy Lethee.
O World! thou waſt the Forreſt to this Hart,
And this indeed, O World, the Hart of thee.
How like a Deere, ſtroken by many Princes,
Doſt thou heere lye?

Caſſi. Mark Antony.

Ant. Pardon me *Caius Caſſius*:
The Enemies of *Cæſar*, ſhall ſay this:
Then, in a Friend, it is cold Modeſtie.

Caſſi. I blame you not for praiſing *Cæſar* ſo,
But what compact meane you to haue with vs?
Will you be prick'd in number of our Friends,
Or ſhall we on, and not depend on you?

Ant. Therefore I tooke your hands, but was indeed
Sway'd from the point, by looking downe on *Cæſar*.
Friends am I with you all, and loue you all,
Vpon this hope, that you ſhall giue me Reaſons,
Why, and wherein, *Cæſar* was dangerous.

Bru. Or elſe were this a ſauage Spectacle:
Our Reaſons are ſo full of good regard,
That were you *Antony*, the Sonne of *Cæſar*,
You ſhould be ſatisfied.

Ant. That's all I ſeeke,
And am moreouer ſutor, that I may
Produce his body to the Market-place,
And in the Pulpit as becomes a Friend,
Speake in the Order of his Funerall.

Bru. You ſhall *Marke Antony*.

Caſſi. Brutus, a word with you:
You know not what you do; Do not conſent
That *Antony* ſpeake in his Funerall:
Know you how much the people may be mou'd
By that which he will vtter.

Bru. By your pardon:
I will my ſelfe into the Pulpit firſt,
And ſhew the reaſon of our *Cæſars* death.
What *Antony* ſhall ſpeake, I will proteſt
He ſpeakes by leaue, and by permiſſion:
And that we are contented *Cæſar* ſhall
Haue all true Rites, and lawfull Ceremonies,
It ſhall aduantage more, then do vs wrong.

Caſſi. I know not what may fall, I like it not.

Bru. Mark Antony, heere take you *Cæſars* body:
You ſhall not in your Funerall ſpeech blame vs,
But ſpeake all good you can deuiſe of *Cæſar*,
And ſay you doo't by our permiſſion:
Elſe ſhall you not haue any hand at all
About his Funerall. And you ſhall ſpeake
In the ſame Pulpit whereto I am going,
After my ſpeech is ended.

Ant. Be it ſo:
I do deſire no more.

Bru. Prepare the body then, and follow vs. *Exeunt.*

Manet Antony.

O pardon me, thou bleeding peece of Earth:
That I am meeke and gentle with theſe Butchers.
Thou art the Ruines of the Nobleſt man
That euer liued in the Tide of Times.
Woe to the hand that ſhed this coſtly Blood.
Ouer thy wounds, now do I Propheſie,
(Which like dumbe mouthes do ope their Ruby lips,
To begge the voyce and vtterance of my Tongue)
A Curſe ſhall light vpon the limbes of men;
Domeſticke Fury, and fierce Ciuill ſtrife,
Shall cumber all the parts of Italy:
Blood and deſtruction ſhall be ſo in vſe,
And dreadfull Obiects ſo familiar,
That Mothers ſhall but ſmile, when they behold
Their Infants quartered with the hands of Warre:
All pitty choak'd with cuſtome of fell deeds,
And *Cæſars* Spirit ranging for Reuenge,
With *Ate* by his ſide, come hot from Hell,
Shall in theſe Confines, with a Monarkes voyce,
Cry hauocke, and let ſlip the Dogges of Warre,
That this foule deede, ſhall ſmell aboue the earth
With Carrion men, groaning for Buriall.

Enter Octauio's Seruant.

You ſerue *Octauius Cæſar*, do you not?

Ser. I do *Marke Antony*.

Ant. Cæſar did write for him to come to Rome.

Ser. He did receiue his Letters, and is comming,
And bid me ſay to you by word of mouth———
O *Cæſar*!

Ant. Thy heart is bigge: get thee a-part and weepe:
Paſſion I ſee is catching from mine eyes,
Seeing thoſe Beads of ſorrow ſtand in thine,
Began to water. Is thy Maſter comming?

Ser. He lies to night within ſeuen Leagues of Rome.

Ant. Poſt backe with ſpeede,
And tell him what hath chanc'd:
Heere is a mourning Rome, a dangerous Rome,
No Rome of ſafety for *Octauius* yet,
Hie hence, and tell him ſo. Yet ſtay a-while,

Thou

Thou ſhalt not backe, till I haue borne this courſe
Into the Market place: There ſhall I try
In my Oration, how the People take
The cruell iſſue of theſe bloody men,
According to the which, thou ſhalt diſcourſe
To yong *Octauius*, of the ſtate of things.
Lend me your hand. *Exeunt*

Enter Brutus and goes into the Pulpit, and Caſſius, with the Plebeians.

Ple. We will be ſatisfied: let vs be ſatisfied.

Bru. Then follow me, and giue me Audience friends.
Caſſius go you into the other ſtreete,
And part the Numbers:
Thoſe that will heare me ſpeake, let 'em ſtay heere;
Thoſe that will follow *Caſſius*, go with him,
And publike Reaſons ſhall be rendred
Of *Cæſars* death.

1.*Ple.* I will heare *Brutus* ſpeake.

2. I will heare *Caſſius*, and compare their Reaſons,
When ſeuerally we heare them rendred.

3. The Noble *Brutus* is aſcended: Silence.

Bru. Be patient till the laſt.
Romans, Countrey-men, and Louers, heare mee for my cauſe, and be ſilent, that you may heare. Beleeue me for mine Honor, and haue reſpect to mine Honor, that you may beleeue. Cenſure me in your Wiſedom, and awake your Senſes, that you may the better Iudge. If there bee any in this Aſſembly, any deere Friend of *Cæſars*, to him I ſay, that *Brutus* loue to *Cæſar*, was no leſſe then his. If then, that Friend demand, why *Brutus* roſe againſt *Cæſar*, this is my anſwer: Not that I lou'd *Cæſar* leſſe, but that I lou'd Rome more. Had you rather *Cæſar* were liuing, and dye all Slaues; then that *Cæſar* were dead, to liue all Free-men? As *Cæſar* lou'd mee, I weepe for him; as he was Fortunate, I reioyce at it; as he was Valiant, I honour him: But, as he was Ambitious, I ſlew him. There is Teares, for his Loue: Ioy, for his Fortune: Honor, for his Valour: and Death, for his Ambition. Who is heere ſo baſe, that would be a Bondman? If any, ſpeak, for him haue I offended. Who is heere ſo rude, that would not be a Roman? If any, ſpeak, for him haue I offended. Who is heere ſo vile, that will not loue his Countrey? If any, ſpeake, for him haue I offended. I pauſe for a Reply.

All. None *Btutus*, none.

Brutus. Then none haue I offended. I haue done no more to *Cæſar*, then you ſhall do to *Brutus*. The Queſtion of his death, is inroll'd in the Capitoll: his Glory not extenuated, wherein he was worthy; nor his offences enforc'd, for which he ſuffered death.

Enter Mark Antony, with Cæſars body.

Heere comes his Body, mourn'd by *Marke Antony*, who though he had no hand in his death, ſhall receiue the benefit of his dying, a place in the Cōmonwealth, as which of you ſhall not. With this I depart, that as I ſlewe my beſt Louer for the good of Rome, I haue the ſame Dagger for my ſelfe, when it ſhall pleaſe my Country to need my death.

All. Liue *Brutus*, liue, liue.

1. Bring him with Triumph home vnto his houſe.

2. Giue him a Statue with his Anceſtors.

3. Let him be *Cæſar*.

4. *Cæſars* better parts,
Shall be Crown'd in *Brutus*.

1. Wee'l bring him to his Houſe,
With Showts and Clamors.

Bru. My Country-men.

2. Peace, ſilence, *Brutus* ſpeakes.

1. Peace ho.

Bru. Good Countrymen, let me depart alone,
And (for my ſake) ſtay heere with *Antony*:
Do grace to *Cæſars* Corpes, and grace his Speech
Tending to *Cæſars* Glories, which *Marke Antony*
(By our permiſſion) is allow'd to make.
I do intreat you, not a man depart,
Saue I alone, till *Antony* haue ſpoke. *Exit*

1 Stay ho, and let vs heare *Mark Antony*.

3 Let him go vp into the publike Chaire,
Wee'l heare him: Noble *Antony* go vp.

Ant. For *Brutus* ſake, I am beholding to you.

4 What does he ſay of *Brutus*?

3 He ſayes, for *Brutus* ſake
He findes himſelfe beholding to vs all.

4 'Twere beſt he ſpeake no harme of *Brutus* heere?

1 This *Cæſar* was a Tyrant.

3 Nay that's certaine:
We are bleſt that Rome is rid of him.

2 Peace, let vs heare what *Antony* can ſay.

Ant. You gentle Romans.

All. Peace hoe, let vs heare him.

An. Friends, Romans, Countrymen, lend me your ears:
I come to bury *Cæſar*, not to praiſe him:
The euill that men do, liues after them,
The good is oft enterred with their bones,
So let it be with *Cæſar*. The Noble *Brutus*,
Hath told you *Cæſar* was Ambitious:
If it were ſo, it was a greeuous Fault,
And greeuouſly hath *Cæſar* anſwer'd it.
Heere, vnder leaue of *Brutus*, and the reſt
(For *Brutus* is an Honourable man,
So are they all; all Honourable men)
Come I to ſpeake in *Cæſars* Funerall.
He was my Friend, faithfull, and iuſt to me;
But *Brutus* ſayes, he was Ambitious,
And *Brutus* is an Honourable man.
He hath brought many Captiues home to Rome,
Whoſe Ranſomes, did the generall Coffers fill:
Did this in *Cæſar* ſeeme Ambitious?
When that the poore haue cry'de, *Cæſar* hath wept:
Ambition ſhould be made of ſterner ſtuffe,
Yet *Brutus* ſayes, he was Ambitious:
And *Brutus* is an Honourable man.
You all did ſee, that on the *Lupercall*,
I thrice preſented him a Kingly Crowne,
Which he did thrice refuſe. Was this Ambition?
Yet *Brutus* ſayes, he was Ambitious:
And ſure he is an Honourable man.
I ſpeake not to diſprooue what *Brutus* ſpoke,
But heere I am, to ſpeake what I do know;
You all did loue him once, not without cauſe,
What cauſe with-holds you then, to mourne for him?
O Iudgement! thou are fled to brutiſh Beaſts,
And Men haue loſt their Reaſon. Beare with me,
My heart is in the Coffin there with *Cæſar*,
And I muſt pawſe, till it come backe to me.

1 Me thinkes there is much reaſon in his ſayings.

2 If thou conſider rightly of the matter,
Cæſar ha's had great wrong.

3 Ha's hee Maſters? I feare there will a worſe come in his place.

4. Mark'd ye his words? he would not take yͤ Crown,
Therefore 'tis certaine, he was not Ambitious.
1. If it be found ſo, ſome will deere abide it.
2. Poore ſoule, his eyes are red as fire with weeping.
3. There's not a Nobler man in Rome then *Antony*.
4. Now marke him, he begins againe to ſpeake.
Ant. But yeſterday, the word of *Cæſar* might
Haue ſtood againſt the World: Now lies he there,
And none ſo poore to do him reuerence.
O Maiſters! If I were diſpos'd to ſtirre
Your hearts and mindes to Mutiny and Rage,
I ſhould do *Brutus* wrong, and *Caſſius* wrong:
Who (you all know) are Honourable men.
I will not do them wrong: I rather chooſe
To wrong the dead, to wrong my ſelfe and you,
Then I will wrong ſuch Honourable men.
But heere's a Parchment, with the Seale of *Cæſar*,
I found it in his Cloſſet, 'tis his Will:
Let but the Commons heare this Teſtament:
(Which pardon me) I do not meane to reade,
And they would go and kiſſe dead *Cæſars* wounds,
And dip their Napkins in his Sacred Blood;
Yea, begge a haire of him for Memory,
And dying, mention it within their Willes,
Bequeathing it as a rich Legacie
Vnto their iſſue.
4 Wee'l heare the Will, reade it *Marke Antony*.
All. The Will, the Will; we will heare *Cæſars* Will.
Ant. Haue patience gentle Friends, I muſt not read it.
It is not meete you know how *Cæſar* lou'd you:
You are not Wood, you are not Stones, but men:
And being men, hearing the Will of *Cæſar*,
It will inflame you, it will make you mad;
'Tis good you know not that you are his Heires,
For if you ſhould, O what would come of it?
4 Read the Will, wee'l heare it *Antony*:
You ſhall reade vs the Will, *Cæſars* Will.
Ant. Will you be Patient? Will you ſtay a-while?
I haue o're-ſhot my ſelfe to tell you of it,
I feare I wrong the Honourable men,
Whoſe Daggers haue ſtabb'd *Cæſar*: I do feare it.
4 They were Traitors: Honourable men?
All. The Will, the Teſtament.
2 They were Villaines, Murderers: the Will, read the Will.
Ant. You will compell me then to read the Will:
Then make a Ring about the Corpes of *Cæſar*,
And let me ſhew you him that made the Will:
Shall I deſcend? And will you giue me leaue?
All. Come downe.
2 Deſcend.
3 You ſhall haue leaue.
4 A Ring, ſtand round.
1 Stand from the Hearſe, ſtand from the Body.
2 Roome for *Antony*, moſt Noble *Antony*.
Ant. Nay preſſe not ſo vpon me, ſtand farre off.
All. Stand backe: roome, beare backe.
Ant. If you haue teares, prepare to ſhed them now.
You all do know this Mantle, I remember
The firſt time euer *Cæſar* put it on,
'Twas on a Summers Euening in his Tent,
That day he ouercame the *Neruij*.
Looke, in this place ran *Caſſius* Dagger through:
See what a rent the enuious *Caska* made:
Through this, the wel-beloued *Brutus* ſtabb'd,
And as he pluck'd his curſed Steele away:
Marke how the blood of *Cæſar* followed it,
As ruſhing out of doores, to be reſolu'd
If *Brutus* ſo vnkindely knock'd, or no:
For *Brutus*, as you know, was *Cæſars* Angel.
Iudge, O you Gods, how deerely *Cæſar* lou'd him:
This was the moſt vnkindeſt cut of all.
For when the Noble *Cæſar* ſaw him ſtab,
Ingratitude, more ſtrong then Traitors armes,
Quite vanquiſh'd him: then burſt his Mighty heart,
And in his Mantle, muffling vp his face,
Euen at the Baſe of *Pompeyes* Statue
(Which all the while ran blood) great *Cæſar* fell.
O what a fall was there, my Countrymen?
Then I, and you, and all of vs fell downe,
Whil'ſt bloody Treaſon flouriſh'd ouer vs.
O now you weepe, and I perceiue you feele
The dint of pitty: Theſe are gracious droppes.
Kinde Soules, what weepe you, when you but behold
Our *Cæſars* Veſture wounded? Looke you heere,
Heere is Himſelfe, marr'd as you ſee with Traitors.
1. O pitteous ſpectacle!
2. O Noble *Cæſar*!
3. O wofull day!
4. O Traitors, Villaines!
1. O moſt bloody ſight!
2. We will be reueng'd: Reuenge
About, ſeeke, burne, fire, kill, ſlay,
Let not a Traitor liue.
Ant. Stay Country-men.
1. Peace there, heare the Noble *Antony*.
2. Wee'l heare him, wee'l follow him, wee'l dy with him.
Ant. Good Friends, ſweet Friends, let me not ſtirre (you vp
To ſuch a ſodaine Flood of Mutiny:
They that haue done this Deede, are honourable.
What priuate greefes they haue, alas I know not,
That made them do it: They are Wiſe, and Honourable,
And will no doubt with Reaſons anſwer you.
I come not (Friends) to ſteale away your hearts,
I am no Orator, as *Brutus* is;
But (as you know me all) a plaine blunt man
That loue my Friend, and that they know full well,
That gaue me publike leaue to ſpeake of him:
For I haue neyther writ nor words, nor worth,
Action, nor Vtterance, nor the power of Speech,
To ſtirre mens Blood. I onely ſpeake right on:
I tell you that, which you your ſelues do know,
Shew you ſweet *Cæſars* wounds, poor poor dum mouths
And bid them ſpeake for me: But were I *Brutus*,
And *Brutus Antony*, there were an *Antony*
Would ruffle vp your Spirits, and put a Tongue
In euery Wound of *Cæſar*, that ſhould moue
The ſtones of Rome, to riſe and Mutiny.
All. Wee'l Mutiny.
1 Wee'l burne the houſe of *Brutus*.
3 Away then, come, ſeeke the Conſpirators.
Ant. Yet heare me Countrymen, yet heare me ſpeake
All. Peace hoe, heare *Antony*, moſt Noble *Antony*.
Ant. Why Friends, you go to do you know not what:
Wherein hath *Cæſar* thus deſeru'd your loues?
Alas you know not, I muſt tell you then:
You haue forgot the Will I told you of.
All. Moſt true, the Will, let's ſtay and heare the Wil.
Ant. Heere is the Will, and vnder *Cæſars* Seale:
To euery Roman Citizen he giues,
To euery ſeuerall man, ſeuenty fiue Drachmaes.

2. *Ple.*

2 *Ple.* Most Noble *Cæsar*, wee'l reuenge his death.

3 *Ple.* O Royall *Cæsar*.

Ant. Heare me with patience.

All. Peace hoe

Ant. Moreouer, he hath left you all his Walkes,
His priuate Arbors, and new-planted Orchards,
On this side Tyber, he hath left them you,
And to your heyres for euer: common pleasures
To walke abroad, and recreate your selues.
Heere was a *Cæsar*: when comes such another?

1.*Ple.* Neuer, neuer: come, away, away:
Wee'l burne his body in the holy place,
And with the Brands fire the Traitors houses.
Take vp the body.

2.*Ple.* Go fetch fire.

3.*Ple.* Plucke downe Benches.

4.*Ple.* Plucke downe Formes, Windowes, any thing.

Exit Plebeians.

Ant. Now let it worke: Mischeefe thou art a-foot,
Take thou what course thou wilt.
How now Fellow?

Enter Seruant.

Ser. Sir, *Octauius* is already come to Rome.

Ant. Where is hee?

Ser. He and *Lepidus* are at *Cæsars* house.

Ant. And thither will I straight, to visit him:
He comes vpon a wish. Fortune is merry,
And in this mood will giue vs any thing.

Ser. I heard him say, *Brutus* and *Cassius*
Are rid like Madmen through the Gates of Rome.

Ant. Belike they had some notice of the people
How I had moued them. Bring me to *Octauius*. *Exeunt*

Enter Cinna the Poet, and after him the Plebeians.

Cinna. I dreamt to night, that I did feast with *Cæsar*,
And things vnluckily charge my Fantasie:
I haue no will to wander foorth of doores,
Yet something leads me foorth.

1. What is your name?

2. Whether are you going?

3. Where do you dwell?

4. Are you a married man, or a Batchellor?

2. Answer euery man directly.

1. I, and breefely.

4. I, and wisely.

3. I, and truly, you were best.

Cin. What is my name? Whether am I going? Where do I dwell? Am I a married man, or a Batchellour? Then to answer euery man, directly and breefely, wisely and truly: wisely I say, I am a Batchellor.

2 That's as much as to say, they are fooles that marrie: you'l beare me a bang for that I feare: proceede directly.

Cinna. Directly I am going to *Cæsars* Funerall.

1. As a Friend, or an Enemy?

Cinna. As a friend.

2. That matter is answered directly.

4. For your dwelling: breefely.

Cinna. Breefely, I dwell by the Capitoll.

3. Your name sir, truly.

Cinna. Truly, my name is *Cinna*.

1. Teare him to peeces, hee's a Conspirator.

Cinna. I am *Cinna* the Poet, I am *Cinna* the Poet.

4. Teare him for his bad verses, teare him for his bad Verses.

Cin. I am not *Cinna* the Conspirator.

4. It is no matter, his name's *Cinna*, plucke but his name out of his heart, and turne him going.

3. Teare him, tear him; Come Brands hoe, Firebrands: to *Brutus*, to *Cassius*, burne all. Some to *Decius* House, and some to *Caska's*; some to *Ligarius*: Away, go.

Exeunt all the Plebeians.

Actus Quartus.

Enter Antony, Octauius, and Lepidus.

Ant. These many then shall die, their names are prickt

Octa. Your Brother too must dye: consent you *Lepidus*?

Lep. I do consent.

Octa. Pricke him downe *Antony*.

Lep. Vpon condition *Publius* shall not liue,
Who is your Sisters sonne, *Marke Antony*.

Ant. He shall not liue; looke, with a spot I dam him.
But *Lepidus*, go you to *Cæsars* house:
Fetch the Will hither, and we shall determine
How to cut off some charge in Legacies.

Lep. What? shall I finde you heere?

Octa. Or heere, or at the Capitoll. *Exit Lepidus*

Ant. This is a slight vnmeritable man,
Meet to be sent on Errands: is it fit
The three-fold World diuided, he should stand,
One of the three to share it?

Octa. So you thought him,
And tooke his voyce who should be prickt to dye
In our blacke Sentence and Proscription.

Ant. *Octauius*, I haue seene more dayes then you,
And though we lay these Honours on this man,
To ease our selues of diuers sland'rous loads,
He shall but beare them, as the Asse beares Gold,
To groane and swet vnder the Businesse,
Either led or driuen, as we point the way:
And hauing brought our Treasure, where we will,
Then take we downe his Load, and turne him off
(Like to the empty Asse) to shake his eares,
And graze in Commons.

Octa. You may do your will:
But hee's a tried, and valiant Souldier.

Ant. So is my Horse *Octauius*, and for that
I do appoint him store of Prouender.
It is a Creature that I teach to fight,
To winde, to stop, to run directly on:
His corporall Motion, gouern'd by my Spirit,
And in some taste, is *Lepidus* but so:
He must be taught, and train'd, and bid go forth:
A barren spirited Fellow; one that feeds
On Obiects, Arts, and Imitations.
Which out of vse, and stal'de by other men
Begin his fashion. Do not talke of him,
But as a property: and now *Octauius*,
Listen great things. *Brutus* and *Cassius*
Are leuying Powers; We must straight make head:
Therefore let our Alliance be combin'd,
Our best Friends made, our meanes stretcht,
And let vs presently go sit in Councell,
How couert matters may be best disclos'd,
And open Perils surest answered.

Octa. Let vs do so: for we are at the stake,

And bayed about with many Enemies,
And ſome that ſmile haue in their hearts I feare
Millions of Miſcheefes. *Exeunt*

Drum. Enter Brutus, Lucillius, and the Army. Titinius and Pindarus meete them.

Bru. Stand ho.

Lucil. Giue the word ho, and Stand.

Bru. What now *Lucillius*, is *Caſſius* neere?

Lucil. He is at hand, and *Pindarus* is come
To do you ſalutation from his Maſter.

Bru. He greets me well. Your Maſter *Pindarus*
In his owne change, or by ill Officers,
Hath giuen me ſome worthy cauſe to wiſh
Things done, vndone: But if he be at hand
I ſhall be ſatisfied.

Pin. I do not doubt
But that my Noble Maſter will appeare
Such as he is, full of regard, and Honour.

Bru. He is not doubted. A word *Lucillius*
How he receiu'd you: let me be reſolu'd.

Lucil. With courteſie, and with reſpect enough,
But not with ſuch familiar inſtances,
Nor with ſuch free and friendly Conference
As he hath vs'd of old.

Bru. Thou haſt deſcrib'd
A hot Friend, cooling: Euer note *Lucillius*,
When Loue begins to ſicken and decay
It vſeth an enforced Ceremony.
There are no trickes, in plaine and ſimple Faith:
But hollow men, like Horſes hot at hand,
Make gallant ſhew, and promiſe of their Mettle:
Low March within.
But when they ſhould endure the bloody Spurre,
They fall their Creſts, and like deceitfull Iades
Sinke in the Triall. Comes his Army on?

Lucil. They meane this night in Sardis to be quarter'd:
The greater part, the Horſe in generall
Are come with *Caſſius*.

Enter Caſſius and his Powers.

Bru. Hearke, he is arriu'd:
March gently on to meete him.

Caſſi. Stand ho.

Bru. Stand ho, ſpeake the word along.
Stand.
Stand.
Stand.

Caſſi. Moſt Noble Brother, you haue done me wrong.

Bru. Iudge me you Gods; wrong I mine Enemies?
And if not ſo, how ſhould I wrong a Brother.

Caſſi. *Brutus*, this ſober forme of yours, hides wrongs,
And when you do them———

Brut. *Caſſius*, be content,
Speake your greefes ſoftly, I do know you well.
Before the eyes of both our Armies heere
(Which ſhould perceiue nothing but Loue from vs)
Let vs not wrangle. Bid them moue away:
Then in my Tent *Caſſius* enlarge your Greefes,
And I will giue you Audience.

Caſſi. *Pindarus*,
Bid our Commanders leade their Charges off
A little from this ground.

Bru. *Lucillius*, do you the like, and let no man
Come to our Tent, till we haue done our Conference.
Let *Lucius* and *Titinius* guard our doore. *Exeunt*

Manet Brutus and Caſſius.

Caſſi. That you haue wrong'd me, doth appear in this:
You haue condemn'd, and noted *Lucius Pella*
For taking Bribes heere of the Sardians;
Wherein my Letters, praying on his ſide,
Becauſe I knew the man was ſlighted off.

Bru. You wrong'd your ſelfe to write in ſuch a caſe.

Caſſi. In ſuch a time as this, it is not meet
That euery nice offence ſhould beare his Comment.

Bru. Let me tell you *Caſſius*, you your ſelfe
Are much condemn'd to haue an itching Palme,
To ſell, and Mart your Offices for Gold
To Vndeſeruers.

Caſſi. I, an itching Palme?
You know that you are *Brutus* that ſpeakes this,
Or by the Gods, this ſpeech were elſe your laſt.

Bru. The name of *Caſſius* Honors this corruption,
And Chaſticement doth therefore hide his head.

Caſſi. Chaſticement?

Bru. Remember March, the Ides of March remẽber:
Did not great *Iulius* bleede for Iuſtice ſake?
What Villaine touch'd his body, that did ſtab,
And not for Iuſtice? What? Shall one of Vs,
That ſtrucke the Formoſt man of all this World,
But for ſupporting Robbers: ſhall we now,
Contaminate our fingers, with baſe Bribes?
And ſell the mighty ſpace of our large Honors
For ſo much traſh, as may be graſped thus?
I had rather be a Dogge, and bay the Moone,
Then ſuch a Roman.

Caſſi. *Brutus*, baite not me,
Ile not indure it: you forget your ſelfe
To hedge me in. I am a Souldier, I,
Older in practice, Abler then your ſelfe
To make Conditions.

Bru. Go too: you are not *Caſſius*.

Caſſi. I am.

Bru. I ſay, you are not.

Caſſi. Vrge me no more, I ſhall forget my ſelfe:
Haue minde vpon your health: Tempt me no farther.

Bru. Away ſlight man.

Caſſi. Is't poſſible?

Bru. Heare me, for I will ſpeake.
Muſt I giue way, and roome to your raſh Choller?
Shall I be frighted, when a Madman ſtares?

Caſſi. O ye Gods, ye Gods, Muſt I endure all this?

Bru. All this? I more: Fret till your proud hart break.
Go ſhew your Slaues how Chollericke you are,
And make your Bondmen tremble. Muſt I bouge?
Muſt I obſerue you? Muſt I ſtand and crouch
Vnder your Teſtie Humour? By the Gods,
You ſhall digeſt the Venom of your Spleene
Though it do Split you. For, from this day forth,
Ile vſe you for my Mirth, yea for my Laughter
When you are Waſpiſh.

Caſſi. Is it come to this?

Bru. You ſay, you are a better Souldier:
Let it appeare ſo; make your vaunting true,
And it ſhall pleaſe me well. For mine owne part,
I ſhall be glad to learne of Noble men.

Caſſ. You wrong me euery way:
You wrong me *Brutus*:
I ſaide, an Elder Souldier, not a Better.
Did I ſay Better?

Bru. If you did, I care not.

Caſſ. When *Cæſar* liu'd, he durſt not thus haue mou'd (me.

Brut. Peace, peace, you durſt not ſo haue tempted him.

Caſſ.

Cassi. I durst not.
Bru. No.
Cassi. What? durst not tempt him?
Bru. For your life you durst not.
Cassi. Do not presume too much vpon my Loue,
I may do that I shall be sorry for.
Bru. You haue done that you should be sorry for.
There is no terror *Cassius* in your threats:
For I am Arm'd so strong in Honesty,
That they passe by me, as the idle winde,
Which I respect not. I did send to you
For certaine summes of Gold, which you deny'd me,
For I can raise no money by vile meanes:
By Heauen, I had rather Coine my Heart,
And drop my blood for Drachmaes, then to wring
From the hard hands of Peazants, their vile trash
By any indirection. I did send
To you for Gold to pay my Legions,
Which you deny'd me: was that done like *Cassius*?
Should I haue answer'd *Caius Cassius* so?
When *Marcus Brutus* growes so Couetous,
To locke such Rascall Counters from his Friends,
Be ready Gods with all your Thunder-bolts,
Dash him to peeces.
Cassi. I deny'd you not.
Bru. You did.
Cassi. I did not. He was but a Foole
That brought my answer back. *Brutus* hath riu'd my hart:
A Friend should beare his Friends infirmities;
But *Brutus* makes mine greater then they are.
Bru. I do not, till you practice them on me.
Cassi. You loue me not.
Bru. I do not like your faults.
Cassi. A friendly eye could neuer see such faults.
Bru. A Flatterers would not, though they do appeare
As huge as high Olympus.
Cassi. Come *Antony*, and yong *Octauius* come,
Reuenge your selues alone on *Cassius*,
For *Cassius* is a-weary of the World:
Hated by one he loues, brau'd by his Brother,
Check'd like a bondman, all his faults obseru'd,
Set in a Note-booke, learn'd, and con'd by roate
To cast into my Teeth. O I could weepe
My Spirit from mine eyes. There is my Dagger,
And heere my naked Breast: Within, a Heart
Deerer then *Pluto's* Mine, Richer then Gold:
If that thou bee'st a Roman, take it foorth.
I that deny'd thee Gold, will giue my Heart:
Strike as thou did'st at *Cæsar*: For I know,
When thou did'st hate him worst, ỳ loued'st him better
Then euer thou loued'st *Cassius*.
Bru. Sheath your Dagger:
Be angry when you will, it shall haue scope:
Do what you will, Dishonor, shall be Humour.
O *Cassius*, you are yoaked with a Lambe
That carries Anger, as the Flint beares fire,
Who much inforced, shewes a hastie Sparke,
And straite is cold agen.
Cassi. Hath *Cassius* liu'd
To be but Mirth and Laughter to his *Brutus*,
When greefe and blood ill temper'd, vexeth him?
Bru. When I spoke that, I was ill temper'd too.
Cassi. Do you confesse so much? Giue me your hand.
Bru. And my heart too.
Cassi. O *Brutus*!
Bru. What's the matter?
Cassi. Haue not you loue enough to beare with me,
When that rash humour which my Mother gaue me
Makes me forgetfull.
Bru. Yes *Cassius*, and from henceforth
When you are ouer-earnest with your *Brutus*,
Hee'l thinke your Mother chides, and leaue you so.

Enter a Poet.

Poet. Let me go in to see the Generals,
There is some grudge betweene 'em, 'tis not meete
They be alone.
Lucil. You shall not come to them.
Poet. Nothing but death shall stay me.
Cas. How now? What's the matter?
Poet. For shame you Generals; what do you meane?
Loue, and be Friends, as two such men should bee,
For I haue seene more yeeres I'me sure then yee.
Cas. Ha, ha, how vildely doth this Cynicke rime?
Bru. Get you hence sirra: Sawcy Fellow, hence.
Cas. Beare with him *Brutus*, 'tis his fashion.
Brut. Ile know his humor, when he knowes his time:
What should the Warres do with these Iigging Fooles?
Companion, hence.
Cas. Away, away be gone. *Exit Poet*
Bru. *Lucillius* and *Titinius* bid the Commanders
Prepare to lodge their Companies to night.
Cas. And come your selues, & bring *Messala* with you
Immediately to vs.
Bru. *Lucius*, a bowle of Wine.
Cas. I did not thinke you could haue bin so angry.
Bru. O *Cassius*, I am sicke of many greefes.
Cas. Of your Philosophy you make no vse,
If you giue place to accidentall euils.
Bru. No man beares sorrow better. *Portia* is dead.
Cas. Ha? *Portia*?
Bru. She is dead.
Cas. How scap'd I killing, when I crost you so?
O insupportable, and touching losse!
Vpon what sicknesse?
Bru. Impatient of my absence,
And greefe, that yong *Octauius* with *Mark Antony*
Haue made themselues so strong: For with her death
That tydings came. With this she fell distract,
And (her Attendants absent) swallow'd fire.
Cas. And dy'd so?
Bru. Euen so.
Cas. O ye immortall Gods!

Enter Boy with Wine, and Tapers.

Bru. Speak no more of her: Giue me a bowl of wine,
In this I bury all vnkindnesse *Cassius*. *Drinkes*
Cas. My heart is thirsty for that Noble pledge.
Fill *Lucius*, till the Wine ore-swell the Cup:
I cannot drinke too much of *Brutus* loue.

Enter Titinius and Messala.

Brutus. Come in *Titinius*:
Welcome good *Messala*:
Now sit we close about this Taper heere,
And call in question our necessities.
Cass. *Portia*, art thou gone?
Bru. No more I pray you.
Messala, I haue heere receiued Letters,
That yong *Octauius*, and *Marke Antony*
Come downe vpon vs with a mighty power,
Bending their Expedition toward *Philippi*.

Mess. My selfe haue Letters of the selfe-same Tenure.
Bru. With what Addition.
Mess. That by proscription, and billes of Outlarie,
Octauius, Antony, and *Lepidus,*
Haue put to death, an hundred Senators.
Bru. Therein our Letters do not well agree:
Mine speake of seuenty Senators, that dy'de
By their proscriptions, *Cicero* being one.
Cassi. *Cicero* one?
Messa. *Cicero* is dead, and by that order of proscription
Had you your Letters from your wife, my Lord?
Bru. No *Messala.*
Messa. Nor nothing in your Letters writ of her?
Bru. Nothing *Messala.*
Messa. That me thinkes is strange.
Bru. Why aske you?
Heare you ought of her, in yours?
Messa. No my Lord.
Bru. Now as you are a Roman tell me true.
Messa. Then like a Roman, beare the truth I tell,
For certaine she is dead, and by strange manner.
Bru. Why farewell *Portia:* We must die *Messala:*
With meditating that she must dye once,
I haue the patience to endure it now.
Messa. Euen so great men, great losses shold indure.
Cassi. I haue as much of this in Art as you,
But yet my Nature could not beare it so.
Bru. Well, to our worke aliue. What do you thinke
Of marching to *Philippi* presently.
Cassi. I do not thinke it good.
Bru. Your reason?
Cassi. This it is:
'Tis better that the Enemie seeke vs,
So shall he waste his meanes, weary his Souldiers,
Doing himselfe offence, whil'st we lying still,
Are full of rest, defence, and nimblenesse.
Bru. Good reasons must of force giue place to better:
The people 'twixt *Philippi,* and this ground
Do stand but in a forc'd affection:
For they haue grug'd vs Contribution.
The Enemy, marching along by them,
By them shall make a fuller number vp,
Come on refresht, new added, and encourag'd:
From which aduantage shall we cut him off.
If at *Philippi* we do face him there,
These people at our backe.
Cassi. Heare me good Brother.
Bru. Vnder your pardon. You must note beside,
That we haue tride the vtmost of our Friends:
Our Legions are brim full, our cause is ripe,
The Enemy encreaseth euery day,
We at the height, are readie to decline.
There is a Tide in the affayres of men,
Which taken at the Flood, leades on to Fortune:
Omitted, all the voyage of their life,
Is bound in Shallowes, and in Miseries.
On such a full Sea are we now a-float,
And we must take the current when it serues,
Or loose our Ventures.
Cassi. Then with your will go on: wee'l along
Our selues, and meet them at *Philippi.*
Bru. The deepe of night is crept vpon our talke,
And Nature must obey Necessitie,
Which we will niggard with a little rest:
There is no more to say.
Cassi. No more, good night,
Early to morrow will we rise, and hence.

Enter Lucius.

Bru. *Lucius* my Gowne: farewell good *Messala,*
Good night *Titinius:* Noble, Noble *Cassius,*
Good night, and good repose.
Cassi. O my deere Brother:
This was an ill beginning of the night:
Neuer come such diuision 'tweene our soules:
Let it not *Brutus.*

Enter Lucius with the Gowne.

Bru. Euery thing is well.
Cassi. Good night my Lord.
Bru. Good night good Brother.
Tit. Messa. Good night Lord *Brutus.*
Bru. Farwell euery one. *Exeunt.*
Giue me the Gowne. Where is thy Instrument?
Luc. Heere in the Tent.
Bru. What, thou speak'st drowsily?
Poore knaue I blame thee not, thou art ore-watch'd.
Call *Claudio,* and some other of my men,
Ile haue them sleepe on Cushions in my Tent.
Luc. *Varrus,* and *Claudio.*

Enter Varrus and Claudio.

Var. Cals my Lord?
Bru. I pray you sirs, lye in my Tent and sleepe,
It may be I shall raise you by and by
On businesse to my Brother *Cassius.*
Var. So please you, we will stand,
And watch your pleasure.
Bru. I will it not haue it so: Lye downe good sirs,
It may be I shall otherwise bethinke me.
Looke *Lucius,* heere's the booke I sought for so:
I put it in the pocket of my Gowne.
Luc. I was sure your Lordship did not giue it me.
Bru. Beare with me good Boy, I am much forgetfull.
Canst thou hold vp thy heauie eyes a-while,
And touch thy Instrument a straine or two.
Luc. I my Lord, an't please you.
Bru. It does my Boy:
I trouble thee too much, but thou art willing.
Luc. It is my duty Sir.
Brut. I should not vrge thy duty past thy might,
I know yong bloods looke for a time of rest.
Luc. I haue slept my Lord already.
Bru. It was well done, and thou shalt sleepe againe:
I will not hold thee long. If I do liue,
I will be good to thee.

Musicke, and a Song.

This is a sleepy Tune: O Murd'rous slumbler!
Layest thou thy Leaden Mace vpon my Boy,
That playes thee Musicke? Gentle knaue good night:
I will not do thee so much wrong to wake thee:
If thou do'st nod, thou break'st thy Instrument,
Ile take it from thee, and (good Boy) good night.
Let me see, let me see; is not the Leafe turn'd downe
Where I left reading? Heere it is I thinke.

Enter the Ghost of Cæsar.

How ill this Taper burnes. Ha! Who comes heere?
I thinke it is the weakenesse of mine eyes
That shapes this monstrous Apparition.
It comes vpon me: Art thou any thing?
Art thou some God, some Angell, or some Diuell,
That mak'st my blood cold, and my haire to stare?
Speake to me, what thou art.
Ghost. Thy euill Spirit *Brutus*?
Bru. Why com'st thou?

Ghost.

Ghost. To tell thee thou shalt see me at *Philippi.*
Brut. Well: then I shall see thee againe?
Ghost. I, at *Philippi.*
Brut. Why I will see thee at *Philippi* then:
Now I haue taken heart, thou vanishest.
Ill Spirit, I would hold more talke with thee.
Boy, *Lucius*, *Varrus*, *Claudio*, Sirs: Awake:
Claudio.
Luc. The strings my Lord, are false.
Bru. He thinkes he still is at his Instrument.
Lucius, awake.
Luc. My Lord.
Bru. Did'st thou dreame *Lucus*, that thou so cryedst out?
Luc. My Lord, I do not know that I did cry.
Bru. Yes that thou did'st: Did'st thou see any thing?
Luc. Nothing my Lord.
Bru. Sleepe againe *Lucius*: Sirra *Claudio*, Fellow,
Thou: Awake.
Var. My Lord.
Clau. My Lord.
Bru. Why did you so cry out sirs, in your sleepe?
Both. Did we my Lord?
Bru. I: saw you any thing?
Var. No my Lord, I saw nothing.
Clau. Nor I my Lord.
Bru. Go, and commend me to my Brother *Cassius*:
Bid him set on his Powres betimes before,
And we will follow.
Both. It shall be done my Lord. *Exeunt*

Actus Quintus.

Enter Octauius, Antony, and their Army.

Octa. Now *Antony*, our hopes are answered,
You said the Enemy would not come downe,
But keepe the Hilles and vpper Regions:
It proues not so: their battailes are at hand,
They meane to warne vs at *Philippi* heere:
Answering before we do demand of them.
Ant. Tut I am in their bosomes, and I know
Wherefore they do it: They could be content
To visit other places, and come downe
With fearefull brauery: thinking by this face
To fasten in our thoughts that they haue Courage;
But 'tis not so.

Enter a Messenger.

Mes. Prepare you Generals,
The Enemy comes on in gallant shew:
Their bloody signe of Battell is hung out,
And something to be done immediately.
Ant. *Octauius*, leade your Battaile softly on
Vpon the left hand of the euen Field.
Octa. Vpon the right hand I, keepe thou the left.
Ant. Why do you crosse me in this exigent.
Octa. I do not crosse you: but I will do so. *March.*

Drum. Enter Brutus, Cassius, & their Army.

Bru. They stand, and would haue parley.
Cassi. Stand fast *Titinius*, we must out and talke.
Octa. *Mark Antony*, shall we giue signe of Battaile?
Ant. No *Cæsar*, we will answer on their Charge.
Make forth, the Generals would haue some words.
Oct. Stirre not vntill the Signall.
Bru. Words before blowes: is it so Countrymen?
Octa. Not that we loue words better, as you do.
Bru. Good words are better then bad strokes *Octauius.*
An. In your bad strokes *Brutus*, you giue good words
Witnesse the hole you made in *Cæsars* heart,
Crying long liue, Haile *Cæsar.*
Cassi. *Antony*,
The posture of your blowes are yet vnknowne;
But for your words, they rob the *Hibla* Bees,
And leaue them Hony-lesse.
Ant. Not stinglesse too.
Bru. O yes, and soundlesse too:
For you haue stolne their buzzing *Antony*,
And very wisely threat before you sting.
Ant. Villains: you did not so, when your vile daggers
Hackt one another in the sides of *Cæsar*:
You shew'd your teethes like Apes,
And fawn'd like Hounds,
And bow'd like Bondmen, kissing *Cæsars* feete;
Whil'st damned *Caska*, like a Curre, behinde
Strooke *Cæsar* on the necke. O you Flatterers.
Cassi. Flatterers? Now *Brutus* thanke your selfe,
This tongue had not offended so to day,
If *Cassius* might haue rul'd.
Octa. Come, come, the cause. If arguing make vs swet,
The proofe of it will turne to redder drops:
Looke, I draw a Sword against Conspirators,
When thinke you that the Sword goes vp againe?
Neuer till *Cæsars* three and thirtie wounds
Be well aueng'd; or till another *Cæsar*
Haue added slaughter to the Sword of Traitors.
Brut. *Cæsar*, thou canst not dye by Traitors hands,
Vnlesse thou bring'st them with thee.
Octa. So I hope:
I was not borne to dye on *Brutus* Sword.
Bru. O if thou wer't the Noblest of thy Straine,
Yong-man, thou could'st not dye more honourable.
Cassi. A peeuish School-boy, worthles of such Honor
Ioyn'd with a Masker, and a Reueller.
Ant. Old *Cassius* still.
Octa. Come *Antony*: away:
Defiance Traitors, hurle we in your teeth.
If you dare fight to day, come to the Field;
If not, when you haue stomackes.
Exit Octauius, Antony, and Army
Cassi. Why now blow winde, swell Billow,
And swimme Barke:
The Storme is vp, and all is on the hazard.
Bru. Ho *Lucillius*, hearke, a word with you.
Lucillius and Messala stand forth.
Luc. My Lord.
Cassi *Messala.*
Messa. What sayes my Generall?
Cassi. *Messala*, this is my Birth-day: as this very day
Was *Cassius* borne. Giue me thy hand *Messala*:
Be thou my witnesse, that against my will
(As *Pompey* was) am I compell'd to set
Vpon one Battell all our Liberties.
You know, that I held *Epicurus* strong,
And his Opinion: Now I change my minde,
And partly credit things that do presage.
Comming from *Sardis*, on our former Ensigne
Two mighty Eagles fell, and there they pearch'd,
Gorging and feeding from our Soldiers hands,
Who

Who to *Philippi* heere consorted vs:
This Morning are they fled away, and gone,
And in their steeds, do Rauens, Crowes, and Kites
Fly ore our heads, and downward looke on vs
As we were sickely prey; their shadowes seeme
A Canopy most fatall, vnder which
Our Army lies, ready to giue vp the Ghost.

Messa. Beleeue not so.

Cassi. I but beleeue it partly,
For I am fresh of spirit, and resolu'd
To meete all perils, very constantly.

Bru. Euen so *Lucillius.*

Cassi. Now most Noble *Brutus*,
The Gods to day stand friendly, that we may
Louers in peace, leade on our dayes to age.
But since the affayres of men rests still incertaine,
Let's reason with the worst that may befall.
If we do lose this Battaile, then is this
The very last time we shall speake together:
What are you then determined to do?

Bru. Euen by the rule of that Philosophy,
By which I did blame *Cato*, for the death
Which he did giue himselfe, I know not how:
But I do finde it Cowardly, and vile,
For feare of what might fall, so to preuent
The time of life, arming my selfe with patience,
To stay the prouidence of some high Powers,
That gouerne vs below.

Cassi. Then, if we loose this Battaile,
You are contented to be led in Triumph
Thorow the streets of Rome.

Bru. No *Cassius*, no:
Thinke not thou Noble Romane,
That euer *Brutus* will go bound to Rome,
He beares too great a minde. But this same day
Must end that worke, the Ides of March begun.
And whether we shall meete againe, I know not:
Therefore our euerlasting farewell take:
For euer, and for euer, farewell *Cassius*,
If we do meete againe, why we shall smile;
If not, why then this parting was well made.

Cassi. For euer, and for euer, farewell *Brutus*:
If we do meete againe, wee'l smile indeede;
If not, 'tis true, this parting was well made.

Bru. Why then leade on. O that a man might know
The end of this dayes businesse, ere it come:
But it sufficeth, that the day will end,
And then the end is knowne. Come ho, away. *Exeunt.*

Alarum. Enter Brutus and Messala.

Bru. Ride, ride *Messala*, ride and giue these Billes
Vnto the Legions, on the other side.
Lowd Alarum.
Let them set on at once: for I perceiue
But cold demeanor in *Octauio*'s wing:
And sodaine push giues them the ouerthrow:
Ride, ride *Messala*, let them all come downe. *Exeunt*

Alarums. Enter Cassius and Titinius.

Cassi. O looke *Titinius*, looke, the Villaines flye:
My selfe haue to mine owne turn'd Enemy:
This Ensigne heere of mine was turning backe,
I slew the Coward, and did take it from him.

Titin. O *Cassius*, *Brutus* gaue the word too early,
Who hauing some aduantage on *Octauius*,
Tooke it too eagerly: his Soldiers fell to spoyle,
Whil'st we by *Antony* are all inclos'd.

Enter Pindarus.

Pind. Fly further off my Lord: flye further off,
Mark Antony is in your Tents my Lord:
Flye therefore Noble *Cassius*, flye farre off.

Cassi. This Hill is farre enough. Looke, look *Titinius*
Are those my Tents where I perceiue the fire?

Tit. They are, my Lord.

Cassi. *Titinius*, if thou louest me,
Mount thou my horse, and hide thy spurres in him,
Till he haue brought thee vp to yonder Troopes
And heere againe, that I may rest assur'd
Whether yond Troopes, are Friend or Enemy.

Tit. I will be heere againe, euen with a thought. *Exit.*

Cassi. Go *Pindarus*, get higher on that hill,
My sight was euer thicke: regard *Titinius*,
And tell me what thou not'st about the Field.
This day I breathed first, Time is come round,
And where I did begin, there shall I end,
My life is run his compasse. Sirra, what newes?

Pind. Aboue. O my Lord.

Cassi. What newes?

Pind. *Titinius* is enclosed round about
With Horsemen, that make to him on the Spurre,
Yet he spurres on. Now they are almost on him:
Now *Titinius*. Now some light: O he lights too.
Hee's tane. *Showt.*
And hearke, they shout for ioy.

Cassi. Come downe, behold no more:
O Coward that I am, to liue so long,
To see my best Friend tane before my face.

Enter Pindarus.

Come hither sirrah: In Parthia did I take thee Prisoner,
And then I swore thee, sauing of thy life,
That whatsoeuer I did bid thee do,
Thou should'st attempt it. Come now, keepe thine oath,
Now be a Free-man, and with this good Sword
That ran through *Cæsars* bowels, search this bosome.
Stand not to answer: Heere, take thou the Hilts,
And when my face is couer'd, as 'tis now,
Guide thou the Sword——*Cæsar*, thou art reueng'd,
Euen with the Sword that kill'd thee.

Pin. So, I am free,
Yet would not so haue beene
Durst I haue done my will. O *Cassius*,
Farre from this Country *Pindarus* shall run,
Where neuer Roman shall take note of him.

Enter Titinius and Messala.

Messa. It is but change, *Titinius*: for *Octauius*
Is ouerthrowne by Noble *Brutus* power,
As *Cassius* Legions are by *Antony*.

Titin. These tydings will well comfort *Cassius*.

Messa. Where did you leaue him.

Titin. All disconsolate,
With *Pindarus* his Bondman, on this Hill.

Messa. Is not that he that lyes vpon the ground?

Titin. He lies not like the Liuing. O my heart!

Messa. Is not that hee?

Titin. No, this was he *Messala*,
But *Cassius* is no more. O setting Sunne:
As in thy red Rayes thou doest sinke to night;

So in his red blood *Caſsius* day is ſet.
The Sunne of Rome is ſet. Our day is gone,
Clowds, Dewes, and Dangers come; our deeds are done:
Miſtruſt of my ſucceſſe hath done this deed.
Meſſa. Miſtruſt of good ſucceſſe hath done this deed.
O hatefull Error, Melancholies Childe:
Why do'ſt thou ſhew to the apt thoughts of men
The things that are not? O Error ſoone conceyu'd,
Thou neuer com'ſt vnto a happy byrth,
But kil'ſt the Mother that engendred thee.
Tit. What *Pindarus*? Where art thou *Pindarus*?
Meſſa. Seeke him *Titinius*, whilſt I go to meet
The Noble *Brutus*, thruſting this report
Into his eares; I may ſay thruſting it:
For piercing Steele, and Darts inuenomed,
Shall be as welcome to the eares of *Brutus*,
As tydings of this ſight.
Tit. Hye you *Meſſala*,
And I will ſeeke for *Pindarus* the while:
Why did'ſt thou ſend me forth braue *Caſsius*?
Did I not meet thy Friends, and did not they
Put on my Browes this wreath of Victorie,
And bid me giue it thee? Did'ſt thou not heare their
Alas, thou haſt miſconſtrued euery thing. (ſhowts?
But hold thee, take this Garland on thy Brow,
Thy *Brutus* bid me giue it thee, and I
Will do his bidding. *Brutus*, come apace,
And ſee how I regarded *Caius Caſsius*:
By your leaue Gods: This is a Romans part,
Come *Caſsius* Sword, and finde *Titinius* hart. *Dies*

Alarum. Enter Brutus, Meſſala, yong Cato, Strato, Volumnius, and Lucillius.

Bru. Where, where *Meſſala*, doth his body lye?
Meſſa. Loe yonder, and *Titinius* mourning it.
Bru. *Titinius* face is vpward.
Cato. He is ſlaine.
Bru. O *Iulius Cæſar*, thou art mighty yet,
Thy Spirit walkes abroad, and turnes our Swords
In our owne proper Entrailes. *Low Alarums.*
Cato. Braue *Titinius*,
Looke where he haue not crown'd dead *Caſsius*.
Bru. Are yet two Romans liuing ſuch as theſe?
The laſt of all the Romans, far thee well:
It is impoſſible, that euer Rome
Should breed thy fellow. Friends I owe mo teares
To this dead man, then you ſhall ſee me pay.
I ſhall finde time, *Caſsius*: I ſhall finde time.
Come therefore, and to *Tharſus* ſend his body,
His Funerals ſhall not be in our Campe,
Leaſt it diſcomfort vs. *Lucillius* come,
And come yong *Cato*, let vs to the Field,
Labio and *Flauio* ſet our Battailes on:
'Tis three a clocke, and Romans yet ere night,
We ſhall try Fortune in a ſecond fight. *Exeunt.*

Alarum. Enter Brutus, Meſſala, Cato, Lucillius, and Flauius.

Bru. Yet Country-men: O yet, hold vp your heads.
Cato. What Baſtard doth not? Who will go with me?
I will proclaime my name about the Field.
I am the Sonne of *Marcus Cato*, hoe.
A Foe to Tyrants, and my Countries Friend.
I am the Sonne of *Marcus Cato*, hoe.

Enter Souldiers, and fight.

And I am *Brutus*, *Marcus Brutus*, I,
Brutus my Countries Friend: Know me for *Brutus*.
Luc. O yong and Noble *Cato*, art thou downe?
Why now thou dyeſt, as brauely as *Titinius*,
And may'ſt be honour'd, being *Cato*'s Sonne.
Sold. Yeeld, or thou dyeſt.
Luc. Onely I yeeld to dye:
There is ſo much, that thou wilt kill me ſtraight:
Kill *Brutus*, and be honour'd in his death.
Sold. We muſt not: a Noble Priſoner.

Enter Antony.

2.*Sold.* Roome hoe: tell *Antony*, *Brutus* is tane.
1.*Sold.* Ile tell thee newes. Heere comes the Generall,
Brutus is tane, *Brutus* is tane my Lord.
Ant. Where is hee?
Luc. Safe *Antony*, *Brutus* is ſafe enough:
I dare aſſure thee, that no Enemy
Shall euer take aliue the Noble *Brutus*:
The Gods defend him from ſo great a ſhame,
When you do finde him, or aliue, or dead,
He will be found like *Brutus*, like himſelfe.
Ant. This is not *Brutus* friend, but I aſſure you,
A prize no leſſe in worth; keepe this man ſafe,
Giue him all kindneſſe. I had rather haue
Such men my Friends, then Enemies. Go on,
And ſee where *Brutus* be aliue or dead,
And bring vs word, vnto *Octauius* Tent:
How euery thing is chanc'd. *Exeunt.*

Enter Brutus, Dardanius, Clitus, Strato, and Volumnius.

Brut. Come poore remaines of friends, reſt on this Rocke.
Clit. *Statillius* ſhew'd the Torch-light, but my Lord
He came not backe: he is or tane, or ſlaine.
Brut. Sit thee downe, *Clitus*: ſlaying is the word,
It is a deed in faſhion. Hearke thee, *Clitus*.
Clit. What I, my Lord? No, not for all the World.
Brut. Peace then, no words.
Clit. Ile rather kill my ſelfe.
Brut. Hearke thee, *Dardanius*.
Dard. Shall I doe ſuch a deed?
Clit. O *Dardanius*.
Dard. O *Clitus*.
Clit. What ill requeſt did *Brutus* make to thee?
Dard. To kill him, *Clitus*: looke he meditates.
Clit. Now is that Noble Veſſell full of griefe,
That it runnes ouer euen at his eyes.
Brut. Come hither, good *Volumnius*, liſt a word.
Volum. What ſayes my Lord?
Brut. Why this, *Volumnius*:
The Ghoſt of *Cæſar* hath appear'd to me
Two ſeuerall times by Night: at Sardis, once;
And this laſt Night, here in Philippi fields:
I know my houre is come.
Volum. Not ſo, my Lord.
Brut. Nay, I am ſure it is, *Volumnius*.
Thou ſeeſt the World, *Volumnius*, how it goes,
Our Enemies haue beat vs to the Pit: *Low Alarums.*
It is more worthy, to leape in our ſelues,
Then tarry till they puſh vs. Good *Volumnius*,
Thou know'ſt, that we two went to Schoole together:
Euen for that our loue of old, I prethee
Hold thou my Sword Hilts, whileſt I runne on it.
Vol. That's not an Office for a friend, my Lord.

Alarum ſtill.

Clit. Fly,

Cly. Fly, flye my Lord, there is no tarrying heere.
Bru. Farewell to you, and you, and you *Volumnius.*
Strato, thou haſt bin all this while aſleepe:
Farewell to thee, to *Strato,* Countrymen:
My heart doth ioy, that yet in all my life,
I found no man, but he was true to me.
I ſhall haue glory by this looſing day
More then *Octauius,* and *Marke Antony,*
By this vile Conqueſt ſhall attaine vnto.
So fare you well at once, for *Brutus* tongue
Hath almoſt ended his liues Hiſtory:
Night hangs vpon mine eyes, my Bones would reſt,
That haue but labour'd, to attaine this houre.

Alarum. Cry within, Flye, flye, flye.

Cly. Fly my Lord, flye.
Bru. Hence: I will follow:
I prythee *Strato,* ſtay thou by thy Lord,
Thou art a Fellow of a good reſpect:
Thy life hath had ſome ſmatch of Honor in it,
Hold then my Sword, and turne away thy face,
While I do run vpon it. Wilt thou *Strato?*
Stra. Giue me your hand firſt. Fare you wel my Lord.
Bru. Farewell good *Strato.* ——— *Cæſar,* now be ſtill,
I kill'd not thee with halfe ſo good a will. *Dyes.*

Alarum. Retreat. Enter Antony, Octauius, Meſſala, Lucillius, and the Army.

Octa. What man is that?
Meſſa. My Maſters man. *Strato,* where is thy Maſter?
Stra. Free from the Bondage you are in *Meſſala,*
The Conquerors can but make a fire of him:
For *Brutus* onely ouercame himſelfe,
And no man elſe hath Honor by his death.
Lucil. So *Brutus* ſhould be found. I thank thee *Brutus*
That thou haſt prou'd *Lucillius* ſaying true,
Octa. All that ſeru'd *Brutus,* I will entertaine them.
Fellow, wilt thou beſtow thy time with me?
Stra. I, if *Meſſala* will preferre me to you.
Octa. Do ſo, good *Meſſala.*
Meſſa. How dyed my Maſter *Strato?*
Stra. I held the Sword, and he did run on it.
Meſſa. Octauius, then take him to follow thee,
That did the lateſt ſeruice to my Maſter.
Ant. This was the Nobleſt Roman of them all:
All the Conſpirators ſaue onely hee,
Did that they did, in enuy of great *Cæſar:*
He, onely in a generall honeſt thought,
And common good to all, made one of them.
His life was gentle, and the Elements
So mixt in him, that Nature might ſtand vp,
And ſay to all the world; This was a man.
Octa. According to his Vertue, let vs vſe him
Withall Reſpect, and Rites of Buriall.
Within my Tent his bones to night ſhall ly,
Moſt like a Souldier ordered Honourably:
So call the Field to reſt, and let's away,
To part the glories of this happy day. *Exeunt omnes.*

FINIS.

THE TRAGEDIE OF MACBETH.

Actus Primus. Scœna Prima.

Thunder and Lightning. Enter three Witches.

1. WHen ſhall we three meet againe?
In Thunder, Lightning, or in Raine?
2. When the Hurley-burley's done,
When the Battaile's loſt, and wonne.
3. That will be ere the ſet of Sunne.
1. Where the place?
2. Vpon the Heath.
3. There to meet with *Macbeth.*
1. I come, *Gray-Malkin.*
All. *Padock* calls anon: faire is foule, and foule is faire,
Houer through the fogge and filthie ayre. *Exeunt.*

Scena Secunda.

Alarum within. Enter King Malcome, Donalbaine, Lenox, with attendants, meeting a bleeding Captaine.

King. What bloody man is that? he can report,
As ſeemeth by his plight, of the Reuolt
The neweſt ſtate.
Mal. This is the Serieant,
Who like a good and hardie Souldier fought
'Gainſt my Captiuitie: Haile braue friend;
Say to the King, the knowledge of the Broyle,
As thou didſt leaue it.
Cap. Doubtfull it ſtood,
As two ſpent Swimmers, that doe cling together,
And choake their Art: The mercileſſe *Macdonwald*
(Worthie to be a Rebell, for to that
The multiplying Villanies of Nature
Doe ſwarme vpon him) from the Weſterne Iſles
Of Kernes and Gallowgroſſes is ſupply'd,
And Fortune on his damned Quarry ſmiling,
Shew'd like a Rebells Whore: but all's too weake:
For braue *Macbeth* (well hee deſerues that Name)
Diſdayning Fortune, with his brandiſht Steele,
Which ſmoak'd with bloody execution
(Like Valours Minion) caru'd out his paſſage,
Till hee fac'd the Slaue:
Which neu'r ſhooke hands, nor bad farwell to him,
Till he vnſeam'd him from the Naue toth' Chops,
And fix'd his Head vpon our Battlements.
King. O valiant Couſin, worthy Gentleman.
Cap. As whence the Sunne 'gins his reflection,
Shipwracking Stormes, and direfull Thunders:
So from that Spring, whence comfort ſeem'd to come,
Diſcomfort ſwells: Marke King of Scotland, marke,
No ſooner Iuſtice had, with Valour arm'd,
Compell'd theſe skipping Kernes to truſt their heeles,
But the Norweyan Lord, ſurueying vantage,
With furbuſht Armes, and new ſupplyes of men,
Began a freſh aſſault.
King. Diſmay'd not this our Captaines, *Macbeth* and *Banquoh*?
Cap. Yes, as Sparrowes, Eagles;
Or the Hare, the Lyon:
If I ſay ſooth, I muſt report they were
As Cannons ouer-charg'd with double Cracks,
So they doubly redoubled ſtroakes vpon the Foe:
Except they meant to bathe in reeking Wounds,
Or memorize another *Golgotha,*
I cannot tell: but I am faint,
My Gaſhes cry for helpe.
King. So well thy words become thee, as thy wounds,
They ſmack of Honor both: Goe get him Surgeons.

Enter Roſſe and Angus.

Who comes here?
Mal. The worthy *Thane* of Roſſe.
Lenox. What a haſte lookes through his eyes?
So ſhould he looke, that ſeemes to ſpeake things ſtrange.
Roſſe. God ſaue the King.
King. Whence cam'ſt thou, worthy *Thane?*
Roſſe. From Fiffe, great King,
Where the Norweyan Banners flowt the Skie,
And fanne our people cold.
Norway himſelfe, with terrible numbers,
Aſſiſted by that moſt diſloyall Traytor,
The *Thane* of Cawdor, began a diſmall Conflict,
Till that *Bellona's* Bridegroome, lapt in proofe,
Confronted him with ſelfe-compariſons,
Point againſt Point, rebellious Arme 'gainſt Arme,
Curbing his lauiſh ſpirit: and to conclude,
The Victorie fell on vs.
King. Great happineſſe.
Roſſe. That now, *Sweno,* the Norwayes King,
Craues compoſition:
Nor would we deigne him buriall of his men,
Till he diſburſed, at Saint *Colmes* ynch,
Ten thouſand Dollars, to our generall vſe.

King. No

King. No more that *Thane* of Cawdor ſhall deceiue
Our Boſome intereſt: Goe pronounce his preſent death,
And with his former Title greet *Macbeth.*

Roſſe. Ile ſee it done.

King. What he hath loſt, Noble *Macbeth* hath wonne.

Exeunt.

Scena Tertia.

Thunder. Enter the three Witches.

1. Where haſt thou beene, Siſter?

2. Killing Swine.

3. Siſter, where thou?

1. A Saylors Wife had Cheſtnuts in her Lappe,
And mouncht, & mouncht, and mouncht:
Giue me, quoth I.
Aroynt thee, Witch, the rumpe-fed Ronyon cryes.
Her Husband's to Aleppo gone, Maſter o'th' *Tiger*:
But in a Syue Ile thither ſayle,
And like a Rat without a tayle,
Ile doe, Ile doe, and Ile doe.

2. Ile giue thee a Winde.

1. Th'art kinde.

3. And I another.

1. I my ſelfe haue all the other,
And the very Ports they blow,
All the Quarters that they know,
I'th' Ship-mans Card.
Ile dreyne him drie as Hay:
Sleepe ſhall neyther Night nor Day
Hang vpon his Pent-houſe Lid:
He ſhall liue a man forbid:
Wearie Seu'nights, nine times nine,
Shall he dwindle, peake, and pine:
Though his Barke cannot be loſt,
Yet it ſhall be Tempeſt-toſt.
Looke what I haue.

2. Shew me, ſhew me.

1. Here I haue a Pilots Thumbe,
Wrackt, as homeward he did come. *Drum within.*

3. A Drumme, a Drumme:
Macbeth doth come.

All. The weyward Siſters, hand in hand,
Poſters of the Sea and Land,
Thus doe goe, about, about,
Thrice to thine, and thrice to mine,
And thrice againe, to make vp nine.
Peace, the Charme's wound vp.

Enter Macbeth and Banquo.

Macb. So foule and faire a day I haue not ſeene.

Banquo. How farre is't call'd to Soris? What are theſe,
So wither'd, and ſo wilde in their attyre,
That looke not like th'Inhabitants o'th'Earth,
And yet are on't? Liue you, or are you aught
That man may queſtion? you ſeeme to vnderſtand me,
By each at once her choppie finger laying
Vpon her skinnie Lips: you ſhould be Women,
And yet your Beards forbid me to interprete
That you are ſo.

Mac. Speake if you can: what are you?

1. All haile *Macbeth*, haile to thee *Thane* of Glamis.

2. All haile *Macbeth*, haile to thee *Thane* of Cawdor.

3. All haile *Macbeth*, that ſhalt be King hereafter.

Banq. Good Sir, why doe you ſtart, and ſeeme to feare
Things that doe ſound ſo faire? i'th' name of truth
Are ye fantaſticall, or that indeed
Which outwardly ye ſhew? My Noble Partner
You greet with preſent Grace, and great prediction
Of Noble hauing, and of Royall hope,
That he ſeemes wrapt withall: to me you ſpeake not.
If you can looke into the Seedes of Time,
And ſay, which Graine will grow, and which will not,
Speake then to me, who neyther begge, nor feare
Your fauors, nor your hate.

1. Hayle.

2. Hayle.

3. Hayle.

1. Leſſer then *Macbeth*, and greater.

2. Not ſo happy, yet much happyer.

3. Thou ſhalt get Kings, though thou be none:
So all haile *Macbeth*, and *Banquo*.

1. *Banquo*, and *Macbeth*, all haile.

Macb. Stay you imperfect Speakers, tell me more:
By *Sinells* death, I know I am *Thane* of Glamis,
But how, of Cawdor? the *Thane* of Cawdor liues
A proſperous Gentleman: And to be King,
Stands not within the proſpect of beleefe,
No more then to be Cawdor. Say from whence
You owe this ſtrange Intelligence, or why
Vpon this blaſted Heath you ſtop our way
With ſuch Prophetique greeting?
Speake, I charge you. *Witches vaniſh.*

Banq. The Earth hath bubbles, as the Water ha's,
And theſe are of them: whither are they vaniſh'd?

Macb. Into the Ayre: and what ſeem'd corporall,
Melted, as breath into the Winde.
Would they had ſtay'd.

Banq. Were ſuch things here, as we doe ſpeake about?
Or haue we eaten on the inſane Root,
That takes the Reaſon Priſoner?

Macb. Your Children ſhall be Kings.

Banq. You ſhall be King.

Macb. And *Thane* of Cawdor too: went it not ſo?

Banq. Toth' ſelfe-ſame tune, and words: who's here?

Enter Roſſe and Angus.

Roſſe. The King hath happily receiu'd, *Macbeth*,
The newes of thy ſucceſſe: and when he reades
Thy perſonall Venture in the Rebels fight,
His Wonders and his Prayſes doe contend,
Which ſhould be thine, or his: ſilenc'd with that,
In viewing o're the reſt o'th'ſelfe-ſame day,
He findes thee in the ſtout Norweyan Rankes,
Nothing afeard of what thy ſelfe didſt make
Strange Images of death, as thick as Tale
Can poſt with poſt, and euery one did beare
Thy prayſes in his Kingdomes great defence,
And powr'd them downe before him.

Ang. Wee are ſent,
To giue thee from our Royall Maſter thanks,
Onely to harrold thee into his ſight,
Not pay thee.

Roſſe. And for an earneſt of a greater Honor,
He bad me, from him, call thee *Thane* of Cawdor:

In

In which addition, haile most worthy *Thane*,
For it is thine.
Banq. What, can the Deuill speake true?
Macb. The *Thane* of Cawdor liues:
Why doe you dresse me in borrowed Robes?
Ang. Who was the *Thane*, liues yet,
But vnder heauie Iudgement beares that Life,
Which he deserues to loose.
Whether he was combin'd with those of Norway,
Or did lyne the Rebell with hidden helpe,
And vantage; or that with both he labour'd
In his Countreyes wracke, I know not:
But Treasons Capitall, confess'd, and prou'd,
Haue ouerthrowne him.
Macb. Glamys, and *Thane* of Cawdor:
The greatest is behinde. Thankes for your paines.
Doe you not hope your Children shall be Kings,
When those that gaue the *Thane* of Cawdor to me,
Promis'd no lesse to them.
Banq. That trusted home,
Might yet enkindle you vnto the Crowne,
Besides the *Thane* of Cawdor. But 'tis strange:
And oftentimes, to winne vs to our harme,
The Instruments of Darknesse tell vs Truths,
Winne vs with honest Trifles, to betray's
In deepest consequence.
Cousins, a word, I pray you.
Macb. Two Truths are told,
As happy Prologues to the swelling Act
Of the Imperiall Theame. I thanke you Gentlemen:
This supernaturall solliciting
Cannot be ill; cannot be good.
If ill? why hath it giuen me earnest of successe,
Commencing in a Truth? I am *Thane* of Cawdor.
If good? why doe I yeeld to that suggestion,
Whose horrid Image doth vnfixe my Heire,
And make my seated Heart knock at my Ribbes,
Against the vse of Nature? Present Feares
Are lesse then horrible Imaginings:
My Thought, whose Murther yet is but fantasticall,
Shakes so my single state of Man,
That Function is smother'd in surmise,
And nothing is, but what is not.
Banq. Looke how our Partner's rapt.
Macb. If Chance will haue me King,
Why Chance may Crowne me,
Without my stirre.
Banq. New Honors come vpon him
Like our strange Garments, cleaue not to their mould,
But with the aid of vse.
Macb. Come what come may,
Time, and the Houre, runs through the roughest Day.
Banq. Worthy *Macbeth*, wee stay vpon your leysure.
Macb. Giue me your fauour:
My dull Braine was wrought with things forgotten.
Kinde Gentlemen, your paines are registred,
Where euery day I turne the Leafe,
To reade them.
Let vs toward the King: thinke vpon
What hath chanc'd: and at more time,
The *Interim* hauing weigh'd it, let vs speake
Our free Hearts each to other.
Banq. Very gladly.
Macb. Till then enough:
Come friends. *Exeunt*.

Scena Quarta.

Flourish. Enter King, Lenox, Malcolme, Donalbaine, and Attendants.

King. Is execution done on *Cawdor*?
Or not those in Commission yet return'd?
Mal. My Liege, they are not yet come back.
But I haue spoke with one that saw him die:
Who did report, that very frankly hee
Confess'd his Treasons, implor'd your Highnesse Pardon,
And set forth a deepe Repentance:
Nothing in his Life became him,
Like the leauing it. Hee dy'de,
As one that had beene studied in his death,
To throw away the dearest thing he ow'd,
As 'twere a carelesse Trifle.
King. There's no Art,
To finde the Mindes construction in the Face:
He was a Gentleman, on whom I built
An absolute Trust.
Enter Macbeth, Banquo, Rosse, and Angus.
O worthyest Cousin,
The sinne of my Ingratitude euen now
Was heauie on me. Thou art so farre before,
That swiftest Wing of Recompence is slow,
To ouertake thee. Would thou hadst lesse deseru'd,
That the proportion both of thanks, and payment,
Might haue beene mine: onely I haue left to say,
More is thy due, then more then all can pay.
Macb. The seruice, and the loyaltie I owe,
In doing it, payes it selfe.
Your Highnesse part, is to receiue our Duties:
And our Duties are to your Throne, and State,
Children, and Seruants; which doe but what they should,
By doing euery thing safe toward your Loue
And Honor.
King. Welcome hither:
I haue begun to plant thee, and will labour
To make thee full of growing. Noble *Banquo*,
That hast no lesse deseru'd, nor must be knowne
No lesse to haue done so: Let me enfold thee,
And hold thee to my Heart.
Banq. There if I grow,
The Haruest is your owne.
King. My plenteous Ioyes,
Wanton in fulnesse, seeke to hide themselues
In drops of sorrow. Sonnes, Kinsmen, *Thanes*,
And you whose places are the nearest, know,
We will establish our Estate vpon
Our eldest, *Malcolme*, whom we name hereafter,
The Prince of Cumberland: which Honor must
Not vnaccompanied, inuest him onely,
But signes of Noblenesse, like Starres, shall shine
On all deseruers. From hence to Envernes,
And binde vs further to you.
Macb. The Rest is Labor, which is not vs'd for you:
Ile be my selfe the Herbenger, and make ioyfull
The hearing of my Wife, with your approach:
So humbly take my leaue.
King. My worthy *Cawdor*.
Macb. The Prince of Cumberland: that is a step,
On which I must fall downe, or else o're-leape,

mm For

For in my way it lyes. Starres hide your fires,
Let not Light ſee my black and deepe deſires:
The Eye winke at the Hand; yet let that bee,
Which the Eye feares, when it is done to ſee. *Exit.*
King. True, worthy *Banquo:* he is full ſo valiant,
And in his commendations, I am fed:
It is a Banquet to me. Let's after him,
Whoſe care is gone before, to bid vs welcome:
It is a peereleſſe Kinſman. *Flouriſh.* *Exeunt.*

Scena Quinta.

Enter Macbeths Wife alone with a Letter.

Lady. *They met me in the day of ſucceſſe: and I haue learn'd by the perfect'ſt report, they haue more in them, then mortall knowledge. When I burnt in deſire to queſtion them further, they made themſelues Ayre, into which they vaniſh'd. Whiles I ſtood rapt in the wonder of it, came Miſſiues from the King, who all-hail'd me* Thane *of Cawdor, by which Title before, theſe weyward Siſters ſaluted me, and referr'd me to the comming on of time, with haile King that ſhalt be. This haue I thought good to deliuer thee (my deareſt Partner of Greatneſſe) that thou might'ſt not looſe the dues of reioycing by being ignorant of what Greatneſſe is promis'd thee. Lay it to thy heart, and farewell.*
Glamys thou art, and Cawdor, and ſhalt be
What thou art promis'd: yet doe I feare thy Nature,
It is too full o'th' Milke of humane kindneſſe,
To catch the neereſt way. Thou would'ſt be great,
Art not without Ambition, but without
The illneſſe ſhould attend it. What thou would'ſt highly,
That would'ſt thou holily: would'ſt not play falſe,
And yet would'ſt wrongly winne.
Thould'ſt haue, great Glamys, that which cryes,
Thus thou muſt doe, if thou haue it;
And that which rather thou do'ſt feare to doe,
Then wiſheſt ſhould be vndone. High thee hither,
That I may powre my Spirits in thine Eare,
And chaſtiſe with the valour of my Tongue
All that impeides thee from the Golden Round,
Which Fate and Metaphyſicall ayde doth ſeeme
To haue thee crown'd withall. *Enter Meſſenger.*
What is your tidings?
Meſſ. The King comes here to Night.
Lady. Thou'rt mad to ſay it.
Is not thy Maſter with him? who, wer't ſo,
Would haue inform'd for preparation.
Meſſ. So pleaſe you, it is true: our *Thane* is comming:
One of my fellowes had the ſpeed of him;
Who almoſt dead for breath, had ſcarcely more
Then would make vp his Meſſage.
Lady. Giue him tending,
He brings great newes. *Exit Meſſenger.*
The Rauen himſelfe is hoarſe,
That croakes the fatall entrance of *Duncan*
Vnder my Battlements. Come you Spirits,
That tend on mortall thoughts, vnſex me here,
And fill me from the Crowne to the Toe, top-full
Of direſt Crueltie: make thick my blood,
Stop vp th'acceſſe, and paſſage to Remorſe,
That no compunctious viſitings of Nature
Shake my fell purpoſe, nor keepe peace betweene
Th'effect, and hit. Come to my Womans Breſts,
And take my Milke for Gall, you murth'ring Miniſters,
Where-euer, in your ſightleſſe ſubſtances,
You wait on Natures Miſchiefe. Come thick Night,
And pall thee in the dunneſt ſmoake of Hell,
That my keene Knife ſee not the Wound it makes,
Nor Heauen peepe through the Blanket of the darke,
To cry, hold, hold. *Enter Macbeth.*
Great Glamys, worthy Cawdor,
Greater then both, by the all-haile hereafter,
Thy Letters haue tranſported me beyond
This ignorant preſent, and I feele now
The future in the inſtant.
Macb. My deareſt Loue,
Duncan comes here to Night.
Lady. And when goes hence?
Macb. To morrow, as he purpoſes.
Lady. O neuer,
Shall Sunne that Morrow ſee.
Your Face, my *Thane,* is as a Booke, where men
May reade ſtrange matters, to beguile the time.
Looke like the time, beare welcome in your Eye,
Your Hand, your Tongue: looke like th'innocent flower,
But be the Serpent vnder't. He that's comming,
Muſt be prouided for: and you ſhall put
This Nights great Buſineſſe into my diſpatch,
Which ſhall to all our Nights, and Dayes to come,
Giue ſolely ſoueraigne ſway, and Maſterdome.
Macb. We will ſpeake further.
Lady. Onely looke vp cleare:
To alter fauor, euer is to feare:
Leaue all the reſt to me. *Exeunt.*

Scena Sexta.

Hoboyes, and Torches. Enter King, Malcolme, Donalbaine, Banquo, Lenox, Macduff, Roſſe, Angus, and Attendants.

King. This Caſtle hath a pleaſant ſeat,
The ayre nimbly and ſweetly recommends it ſelfe
Vnto our gentle ſences.
Banq. This Gueſt of Summer,
The Temple-haunting Barlet does approue,
By his loued Manſonry, that the Heauens breath
Smells wooingly here: no Iutty frieze,
Buttrice, nor Coigne of Vantage, but this Bird
Hath made his pendant Bed, and procreant Cradle,
Where they muſt breed, and haunt: I haue obſeru'd
The ayre is delicate. *Enter Lady.*
King. See, ſee, our honor'd Hoſteſſe:
The Loue that followes vs, ſometime is our trouble,
Which ſtill we thanke as Loue. Herein I teach you,
How you ſhall bid God-eyld vs for your paines,
And thanke vs for your trouble.
Lady. All our ſeruice,
In euery point twice done, and then done double,
Were poore, and ſingle Buſineſſe, to contend
Againſt thoſe Honors deepe, and broad,
Wherewith your Maieſtie loades our Houſe:
For thoſe of old, and the late Dignities,
Heap'd vp to them, we reſt your Ermites.

King. Where's

King. Where's the Thane of Cawdor?
We courſt him at the heeles, and had a purpoſe
To be his Purueyor: But he rides well,
And his great Loue (ſharpe as his Spurre) hath holp him
To his home before vs: Faire and Noble Hoſteſſe
We are your gueſt to night.
La. Your Seruants euer,
Haue theirs, themſelues, and what is theirs in compt,
To make their Audit at your Highneſſe pleaſure,
Still to returne your owne.
King. Giue me your hand:
Conduct me to mine Hoſt we loue him highly,
And ſhall continue, our Graces towards him.
By your leaue Hoſteſſe. *Exeunt*

Scena Septima.

Ho-boyes. Torches.
Enter a Sewer, and diuers Seruants with Diſhes and Seruice ouer the Stage. Then enter Macbeth.

Macb. If it were done, when 'tis done, then 'twer well,
It were done quickly: If th'Aſſaſſination
Could trammell vp the Conſequence, and catch
With his ſurceaſe, Succeſſe: that but this blow
Might be the be all, and the end all. Heere,
But heere, vpon this Banke and Schoole of time,
Wee'ld iumpe the life to come. But in theſe Caſes,
We ſtill haue iudgement heere, that we but teach
Bloody Inſtructions, which being taught, returne
To plague th'Inuenter, This euen-handed Iuſtice
Commends th'Ingredience of our poyſon'd Challice
To our owne lips. Hee's heere in double truſt;
Firſt, as I am his Kinſman, and his Subiect,
Strong both againſt the Deed: Then, as his Hoſt,
Who ſhould againſt his Murtherer ſhut the doore,
Not beare the knife my ſelfe. Beſides, this *Duncane*
Hath borne his Faculties ſo meeke; hath bin
So cleere in his great Office, that his Vertues
Will pleade like Angels, Trumpet-tongu'd againſt
The deepe damnation of his taking off:
And Pitty, like a naked New-borne-Babe,
Striding the blaſt, or Heauens Cherubin, hors'd
Vpon the ſightleſſe Curriors of the Ayre,
Shall blow the horrid deed in euery eye,
That teares ſhall drowne the winde. I haue no Spurre
To pricke the ſides of my intent, but onely
Vaulting Ambition, which ore-leapes it ſelfe,
And falles on th'other. *Enter Lady.*
How now? What Newes?
La. He has almoſt ſupt: why haue you left the chamber?
Mac. Hath he ask'd for me?
La. Know you not, he ha's?
Mac. We will proceed no further in this Buſineſſe:
He hath Honour'd me of late, and I haue bought
Golden Opinions from all ſorts of people,
Which would be worne now in their neweſt gloſſe,
Not caſt aſide ſo ſoone.
La. Was the hope drunke,
Wherein you dreſt your ſelfe? Hath it ſlept ſince?
And wakes it now to looke ſo greene, and pale,
At what it did ſo freely? From this time,
Such I account thy loue. Art thou affear'd
To be the ſame in thine owne Act, and Valour,
As thou art in deſire? Would'ſt thou haue that
Which thou eſteem'ſt the Ornament of Life,
And liue a Coward in thine owne Eſteeme?
Letting I dare not, wait vpon I would,
Like the poore Cat i'th'Addage.
Macb. Prythee peace:
I dare do all that may become a man,
Who dares no more, is none.
La. What Beaſt was't then
That made you breake this enterprize to me?
When you durſt do it, then you were a man:
And to be more then what you were, you would
Be ſo much more the man. Nor time, nor place
Did then adhere, and yet you would make both:
They haue made themſelues, and that their fitneſſe now
Do's vnmake you. I haue giuen Sucke, and know
How tender 'tis to loue the Babe that milkes me,
I would, while it was ſmyling in my Face,
Haue pluckt my Nipple from his Boneleſſe Gummes,
And daſht the Braines out, had I ſo ſworne
As you haue done to this.
Macb. If we ſhould faile?
Lady. We faile?
But ſcrew your courage to the ſticking place,
And wee'le not fayle: when *Duncan* is aſleepe,
(Whereto the rather ſhall his dayes hard Iourney
Soundly inuite him) his two Chamberlaines
Will I with Wine, and Waſſell, ſo conuince,
That Memorie, the Warder of the Braine,
Shall be a Fume, and the Receit of Reaſon
A Lymbeck onely: when in Swiniſh ſleepe,
Their drenched Natures lyes as in a Death,
What cannot you and I performe vpon
Th'vnguarded *Duncan*? What not put vpon
His ſpungie Officers? who ſhall beare the guilt
Of our great quell.
Macb. Bring forth Men-Children onely:
For thy vndaunted Mettle ſhould compoſe
Nothing but Males. Will it not be receiu'd,
When we haue mark'd with blood thoſe ſleepie two
Of his owne Chamber, and vs'd their very Daggers,
That they haue don't?
Lady. Who dares receiue it other,
As we ſhall make our Griefes and Clamor rore,
Vpon his Death?
Macb. I am ſettled, and bend vp
Each corporall Agent to this terrible Feat.
Away, and mock the time with faireſt ſhow,
Falſe Face muſt hide what the falſe Heart doth know.
Exeunt.

Actus Secundus. Scena Prima.

Enter Banquo, and Fleance, with a Torch before him.

Banq. How goes the Night, Boy?
Fleance. The Moone is downe: I haue not heard the Clock.
Banq. And ſhe goes downe at Twelue.
Fleance. I take't, 'tis later, Sir.
Banq. Hold, take my Sword:
There's Husbandry in Heauen,
Their Candles are all out: take thee that too.

A heauie Summons lyes like Lead vpon me,
And yet I would not sleepe:
Mercifull Powers, restraine in me the cursed thoughts
That Nature giues way to in repose.

Enter Macbeth, and a Seruant with a Torch.

Giue me my Sword: who's there?
Macb. A Friend.
Banq. What Sir, not yet at rest? the King's a bed.
He hath beene in vnusuall Pleasure,
And sent forth great Largesse to your Offices.
This Diamond he greetes your Wife withall,
By the name of most kind Hostesse,
And shut vp in measurelesse content.
Mac. Being vnprepar'd,
Our will became the seruant to defect,
Which else should free haue wrought.
Banq. All's well.
I dreamt last Night of the three weyward Sisters:
To you they haue shew'd some truth.
Macb. I thinke not of them:
Yet when we can entreat an houre to serue,
We would spend it in some words vpon that Businesse,
If you would graunt the time.
Banq. At your kind'st leysure.
Macb. If you shall cleaue to my consent,
When 'tis, it shall make Honor for you.
Banq. So I lose none,
In seeking to augment it, but still keepe
My Bosome franchis'd, and Allegeance cleare,
I shall be counsail'd.
Macb. Good repose the while.
Banq. Thankes Sir: the like to you. *Exit Banquo.*
Macb. Goe bid thy Mistresse, when my drinke is ready,
She strike vpon the Bell. Get thee to bed. *Exit.*
Is this a Dagger, which I see before me,
The Handle toward my Hand? Come, let me clutch thee:
I haue thee not, and yet I see thee still.
Art thou not fatall Vision, sensible
To feeling, as to sight? or art thou but
A Dagger of the Minde, a false Creation,
Proceeding from the heat-oppressed Braine?
I see thee yet, in forme as palpable,
As this which now I draw.
Thou marshall'st me the way that I was going,
And such an Instrument I was to vse.
Mine Eyes are made the fooles o'th'other Sences,
Or else worth all the rest: I see thee still;
And on thy Blade, and Dudgeon, Gouts of Blood,
Which was not so before. There's no such thing:
It is the bloody Businesse, which informes
Thus to mine Eyes. Now o're the one halfe World
Nature seemes dead, and wicked Dreames abuse
The Curtain'd sleepe: Witchcraft celebrates
Pale *Heccats* Offrings: and wither'd Murther,
Alarum'd by his Centinell, the Wolfe,
Whose howle's his Watch, thus with his stealthy pace,
With *Tarquins* rauishing sides, towards his designe
Moues like a Ghost. Thou sowre and firme-set Earth
Heare not my steps, which they may walke, for feare
Thy very stones prate of my where-about,
And take the present horror from the time,
Which now sutes with it. Whiles I threat, he liues:
Words to the heat of deedes too cold breath giues.
A Bell rings.
I goe, and it is done: the Bell inuites me.
Heare it not, *Duncan*, for it is a Knell,
That summons thee to Heauen, or to Hell. *Exit.*

Scena Secunda.

Enter Lady.

La. That which hath made thẽ drunk, hath made me bold:
What hath quench'd them, hath giuen me fire.
Hearke, peace: it was the Owle that shriek'd,
The fatall Bell-man, which giues the stern'st good-night.
He is about it, the Doores are open:
And the surfeted Groomes doe mock their charge
With Snores. I haue drugg'd their Possets,
That Death and Nature doe contend about them,
Whether they liue, or dye.
Enter Macbeth.
Macb. Who's there? what hoa?
Lady. Alack, I am afraid they haue awak'd,
And 'tis not done: th'attempt, and not the deed,
Confounds vs: hearke: I lay'd their Daggers ready,
He could not misse 'em. Had he not resembled
My Father as he slept, I had don't.
My Husband?
Macb. I haue done the deed:
Didst thou not heare a noyse?
Lady. I heard the Owle schreame, and the Crickets cry.
Did not you speake?
Macb. When?
Lady. Now.
Macb. As I descended?
Lady. I.
Macb. Hearke, who lyes i'th' second Chamber?
Lady. *Donalbaine.*
Mac. This is a sorry sight.
Lady. A foolish thought, to say a sorry sight.
Macb. There's one did laugh in's sleepe,
And one cry'd Murther, that they did wake each other:
I stood, and heard them: But they did say their Prayers,
And addrest them againe to sleepe.
Lady. There are two lodg'd together.
Macb. One cry'd God blesse vs, and Amen the other,
As they had seene me with these Hangmans hands:
Listning their feare, I could not say Amen,
When they did say God blesse vs.
Lady. Consider it not so deepely.
Mac. But wherefore could not I pronounce Amen?
I had most need of Blessing, and Amen stuck in my throat.
Lady. These deeds must not be thought
After these wayes: so, it will make vs mad.
Macb. Me thought I heard a voyce cry, Sleep no more:
Macbeth does murther Sleepe, the innocent Sleepe,
Sleepe that knits vp the rauel'd Sleeue of Care,
The death of each dayes Life, sore Labors Bath,
Balme of hurt Mindes, great Natures second Course,
Chiefe nourisher in Life's Feast.
Lady. What doe you meane?
Macb. Still it cry'd, Sleepe no more to all the House:
Glamis hath murther'd Sleepe, and therefore *Cawdor*
Shall sleepe no more: *Macbeth* shall sleepe no more.
Lady. Who was it, that thus cry'd? why worthy *Thane*,
You doe vnbend your Noble strength, to thinke
So braine-sickly of things: Goe get some Water,
And

And wash this filthie Witnesse from your Hand.
Why did you bring these Daggers from the place?
They must lye there: goe carry them, and smeare
The sleepie Groomes with blood.
Macb. Ile goe no more:
I am afraid, to thinke what I haue done:
Looke on't againe, I dare not.
Lady. Infirme of purpose:
Giue me the Daggers: the sleeping, and the dead,
Are but as Pictures: 'tis the Eye of Child-hood,
That feares a painted Deuill. If he doe bleed,
Ile guild the Faces of the Groomes withall,
For it must seeme their Guilt. *Exit.*
Knocke within.
Macb. Whence is that knocking?
How is't with me, when euery noyse appalls me?
What Hands are here? hah: they pluck out mine Eyes.
Will all great *Neptunes* Ocean wash this blood
Cleane from my Hand? no: this my Hand will rather
The multitudinous Seas incarnardine,
Making the Greene one, Red.

Enter Lady.

Lady. My Hands are of your colour: but I shame
To weare a Heart so white. *Knocke.*
I heare a knocking at the South entry:
Retyre we to our Chamber:
A little Water cleares vs of this deed.
How easie is it then? your Constancie
Hath left you vnattended. *Knocke.*
Hearke, more knocking.
Get on your Night-Gowne, least occasion call vs,
And shew vs to be Watchers: be not lost
So poorely in your thoughts.
Macb. To know my deed, *Knocke.*
'Twere best not know my selfe.
Wake *Duncan* with thy knocking:
I would thou could'st. *Exeunt.*

Scena Tertia.

Enter a Porter.
Knocking within.

Porter. Here's a knocking indeede: if a man were Porter of Hell Gate, hee should haue old turning the Key. *Knock.* Knock, Knock, Knock. Who's there i'th' name of *Belzebub?* Here's a Farmer, that hang'd himselfe on th'expectation of Plentie: Come in time, haue Napkins enow about you, here you'le sweat for't. *Knock.* Knock, knock. Who's there in th'other Deuils Name? Faith here's an Equiuocator, that could sweare in both the Scales against eyther Scale, who committed Treason enough for Gods sake, yet could not equiuocate to Heauen: oh come in, Equiuocator. *Knock.* Knock, Knock, Knock. Who's there? 'Faith here's an English Taylor come hither, for stealing out of a French Hose: Come in Taylor, here you may rost your Goose. *Knock.* Knock, Knock. Neuer at quiet: What are you? but this place is too cold for Hell. Ile Deuill-Porter it no further: I had thought to haue let in some of all Professions, that goe the Primrose way to th'euerlasting Bonfire. *Knock.* Anon, anon, I pray you remember the Porter.

Enter Macduff, and Lenox.

Macd. Was it so late, friend, ere you went to Bed, That you doe lye so late?
Port. Faith Sir, we were carowsing till the second Cock: And Drinke, Sir, is a great prouoker of three things.
Macd. What three things does Drinke especially prouoke?
Port. Marry, Sir, Nose-painting, Sleepe, and Vrine. Lecherie, Sir, it prouokes, and vnprouokes: it prouokes the desire, but it takes away the performance. Therefore much Drinke may be said to be an Equiuocator with Lecherie: it makes him, and it marres him; it sets him on, and it takes him off; it perswades him, and dis-heartens him; makes him stand too, and not stand too: in conclusion, equiuocates him in a sleepe, and giuing him the Lye, leaues him.
Macd. I beleeue, Drinke gaue thee the Lye last Night.
Port. That it did, Sir, i'the very Throat on me: but I requited him for his Lye, and (I thinke) being too strong for him, though he tooke vp my Legges sometime, yet I made a Shift to cast him.

Enter Macbeth.

Macd. Is thy Master stirring?
Our knocking ha's awak'd him: here he comes.
Lenox. Good morrow, Noble Sir.
Macb. Good morrow both.
Macd. Is the King stirring, worthy *Thane?*
Macb. Not yet.
Macd. He did command me to call timely on him,
I haue almost slipt the houre.
Ma b. Ile bring you to him.
Macd. I know this is a ioyfull trouble to you:
But yet 'tis one.
Macb. The labour we delight in, Physicks paine:
This is the Doore.
Macd. Ile make so bold to call, for 'tis my limitted seruice. *Exit Macduffe.*
Lenox. Goes the King hence to day?
Macb. He does: he did appoint so.
Lenox. The Night ha's been vnruly:
Where we lay, our Chimneys were blowne downe,
And (as they say) lamentings heard i'th'Ayre
Strange Schreemes of Death,
And Prophecying, with Accents terrible,
Of dyre Combustion, and confus'd Euents,
New hatch'd toth' wofull time.
The obscure Bird clamor'd the liue-long Night.
Some say, the Earth was feuorous,
And did shake.
Macb. 'Twas a rough Night.
Lenox. My young remembrance cannot paralell
A fellow to it.

Enter Macduff.

Macd. O horror, horror, horror,
Tongue nor Heart cannot conceiue, nor name thee.
Macb. and Lenox. What's the matter?
Macd. Confusion now hath made his Master-peece:
Most sacrilegious Murther hath broke ope
The Lords anoynted Temple, and stole thence
The Life o'th' Building.
Macb. What is't you say, the Life?
Lenox. Meane you his Maiestie?
Macd. Approch the Chamber, and destroy your sight
With a new *Gorgon.* Doe not bid me speake:

See,and then ſpeake your ſelues : awake,awake,
Exeunt Macbeth and Lenox.
Ring the Alarum Bell : Murther, and Treaſon,
Banquo,and *Donalbaine : Malcolme* awake,
Shake off this Downey ſleepe, Deaths counterfeit,
And looke on Death it ſelfe : vp, vp, and ſee
The great Doomes Image: *Malcolme, Banquo,*
As from your Graues riſe vp,and walke like Sprights,
To countenance this horror. Ring the Bell.
Bell rings. Enter Lady.
Lady. What's the Buſineſſe ?
That ſuch a hideous Trumpet calls to parley
The ſleepers of the Houſe? ſpeake,ſpeake.
Macd. O gentle Lady,
'Tis not for you to heare what I can ſpeake :
The repetition in a Womans eare,
Would murther as it fell.
Enter Banquo.
O *Banquo, Banquo,* Our Royall Maſter's murther'd.
Lady. Woe, alas :
What, in our Houſe ?
Ban. Too cruell, any where.
Deare *Duff*, I prythee contradict thy ſelfe,
And ſay, it is not ſo.

Enter Macbeth, Lenox, and Roſſe.

Macb. Had I but dy'd an houre before this chance,
I had liu'd a bleſſed time : for from this inſtant,
There's nothing ſerious in Mortalitie :
All is but Toyes : Renowne and Grace is dead,
The Wine of Life is drawne, and the meere Lees
Is left this Vault, to brag of.

Enter Malcolme and Donalbaine.

Donal. What is amiſſe ?
Macb. You are, and doe not know't :
The Spring, the Head, the Fountaine of your Blood
Is ſtopt, the very Source of it is ſtopt.
Macd. Your Royall Father's murther'd.
Mal. Oh, by whom ?
Lenox. Thoſe of his Chamber, as it ſeem'd, had don't :
Their Hands and Faces were all badg'd with blood,
So were their Daggers, which vnwip'd, we found
Vpon their Pillowes: they ſtar'd, and were diſtracted,
No mans Life was to be truſted with them.
Macb. O, yet I doe repent me of my furie,
That I did kill them.
Macd. Wherefore did you ſo ?
Macb. Who can be wiſe, amaz'd, temp'rate, & furious,
Loyall, and Neutrall, in a moment ? No man :
Th'expedition of my violent Loue
Out-run the pawſer, Reaſon. Here lay *Duncan*,
His Siluer skinne, lac'd with his Golden Blood,
And his gaſh'd Stabs, look'd like a Breach in Nature,
For Ruines waſtfull entrance : there the Murtherers,
Steep'd in the Colours of their Trade ; their Daggers
Vnmannerly breech'd with gore : who could refraine,
That had a heart to loue ; and in that heart,
Courage, to make's loue knowne ?
Lady. Helpe me hence, hoa.
Macd. Looke to the Lady.
Mal. Why doe we hold our tongues,
That moſt may clayme this argument for ours ?
Donal. What ſhould be ſpoken here,
Where our Fate hid in an augure hole,
May ruſh, and ſeize vs ? Let's away,
Our Teares are not yet brew'd.
Mal. Nor our ſtrong Sorrow
Vpon the foot of Motion.
Banq. Looke to the Lady :
And when we haue our naked Frailties hid,
That ſuffer in expoſure ; let vs meet,
And queſtion this moſt bloody piece of worke,
To know it further. Feares and ſcruples ſhake vs :
In the great Hand of God I ſtand, and thence,
Againſt the vndivulg'd pretence, I fight
Of Treaſonous Mallice.
Macd. And ſo doe I.
All. So all.
Macb. Let's briefely put on manly readineſſe,
And meet i'th'Hall together.
All. Well contented. *Exeunt.*
Malc. What will you doe ?
Let's not conſort with them :
To ſhew an vnfelt Sorrow, is an Office
Which the falſe man do's eaſie.
Ile to England.
Don. To Ireland, I :
Our ſeperated fortune ſhall keepe vs both the ſafer :
Where we are, there's Daggers in mens Smiles ;
The neere in blood, the neerer bloody.
Malc. This murtherous Shaft that's ſhot,
Hath not yet lighted: and our ſafeſt way,
Is to auoid the ayme. Therefore to Horſe,
And let vs not be daintie of leaue-taking,
But ſhift away : there's warrant in that Theft,
Which ſteales it ſelfe, when there's no mercie left.
Exeunt.

Scena Quarta.

Enter Roſſe, with an Old man.

Old man. Threeſcore and ten I can remember well,
Within the Volume of which Time, I haue ſeene
Houres dreadfull, and things ſtrange: but this ſore Night
Hath trifled former knowings.
Roſſe. Ha, good Father,
Thou ſeeſt the Heauens, as troubled with mans Act,
Threatens his bloody Stage : byth' Clock 'tis Day,
And yet darke Night ſtrangles the trauailing Lampe :
Is't Nights predominance, or the Dayes ſhame,
That Darkneſſe does the face of Earth intombe,
When liuing Light ſhould kiſſe it ?
Old man. 'Tis vnnaturall,
Euen like the deed that's done : On Tueſday laſt,
A Faulcon towring in her pride of place,
Was by a Mowſing Owle hawkt at, and kill'd.
Roſſe. And *Duncans* Horſes,
(A thing moſt ſtrange, and certaine)
Beauteous, and ſwift, the Minions of their Race,
Turn'd wilde in nature, broke their ſtalls, flong out,
Contending 'gainſt Obedience, as they would
Make Warre with Mankinde.
Old man. 'Tis ſaid, they eate each other.
Roſſe. They did ſo :

To

To th'amazement of mine eyes that look'd vpon't.

Enter Macduffe.

Heere comes the good *Macduffe*.
How goes the world Sir, now?
Macd. Why see you not?
Roff. Is't known who did this more then bloody deed?
Macd. Those that *Macbeth* hath slaine.
Roff. Alas the day,
What good could they pretend?
Macd. They were subborned,
Malcolme, and *Donalbaine* the Kings two Sonnes
Are stolne away and fled, which puts vpon them
Suspition of the deed.
Rosse. 'Gainst Nature still,
Thriftlesse Ambition, that will rauen vp
Thine owne liues meanes: Then 'tis most like,
The Soueraignty will fall vpon *Macbeth*.
Macd. He is already nam'd, and gone to Scone
To be inuested.
Rosse. Where is *Duncans* body?
Macd. Carried to Colmekill,
The Sacred Store-house of his Predecessors,
And Guardian of their Bones.
Rosse. Will you to Scone?
Macd. No Cosin, Ile to Fife.
Rosse. Well, I will thither.
Macd. Well may you see things wel done there: Adieu
Least our old Robes sit easier then our new.
Rosse. Farewell, Father.
Old M. Gods benyson go with you, and with those
That would make good of bad, and Friends of Foes.

Exeunt omnes

Actus Tertius. Scena Prima.

Enter Banquo.

Banq. Thou hast it now, King, Cawdor, Glamis, all,
As the weyard Women promis'd, and I feare
Thou playd'st most fowly for't: yet it was saide
It should not stand in thy Posterity,
But that my selfe should be the Roote, and Father
Of many Kings. If there come truth from them,
As vpon thee *Macbeth*, their Speeches shine,
Why by the verities on thee made good,
May they not be my Oracles as well,
And set me vp in hope. But hush, no more.

Senit sounded. Enter Macbeth as King, Lady Lenox, Rosse, Lords, and Attendants.

Macb. Heere's our chiefe Guest.
La. If he had beene forgotten,
It had bene as a gap in our great Feast,
And all-thing vnbecomming.
Macb. To night we hold a solemne Supper sir,
And Ile request your presence.
Banq. Let your Highnesse
Command vpon me, to the which my duties
Are with a most indissoluble tye
For euer knit.
Macb. Ride you this afternoone?
Ban. I, my good Lord.
Macb. We should haue else desir'd your good aduice
(Which still hath been both graue, and prosperous)
In this dayes Councell: but wee'le take to morrow.
Is't farre you ride?
Ban. As farre, my Lord, as will fill vp the time
'Twixt this, and Supper. Goe not my Horse the better,
I must become a borrower of the Night,
For a darke houre, or twaine.
Macb. Faile not our Feast.
Ban. My Lord, I will not.
Macb. We heare our bloody Cozens are bestow'd
In England, and in Ireland, not confessing
Their cruell Parricide, filling their hearers
With strange inuention. But of that to morrow,
When therewithall, we shall haue cause of State,
Crauing vs ioyntly. Hye you to Horse:
Adieu, till you returne at Night.
Goes *Fleance* with you?
Ban. I, my good Lord: our time does call vpon's.
Macb. I wish your Horses swift, and sure of foot:
And so I doe commend you to their backs.
Farwell. *Exit Banquo.*
Let euery man be master of his time,
Till seuen at Night, to make societie
The sweeter welcome:
We will keepe our selfe till Supper time alone:
While then, God be with you. *Exeunt Lords.*
Sirrha, a word with you: Attend those men
Our pleasure?
Seruant. They are, my Lord, without the Pallace Gate.
Macb. Bring them before vs. *Exit Seruant.*
To be thus, is nothing, but to be safely thus:
Our feares in *Banquo* sticke deepe,
And in his Royaltie of Nature reignes that
Which would be fear'd. 'Tis much he dares,
And to that dauntlesse temper of his Minde,
He hath a Wisdome, that doth guide his Valour,
To act in safetie. There is none but he,
Whose being I doe feare: and vnder him,
My *Genius* is rebuk'd, as it is said
Mark Antonies was by *Cæsar*. He chid the Sisters,
When first they put the Name of King vpon me,
And bad them speake to him. Then Prophet-like,
They hayl'd him Father to a Line of Kings.
Vpon my Head they plac'd a fruitlesse Crowne,
And put a barren Scepter in my Gripe,
Thence to be wrencht with an vnlineall Hand,
No Sonne of mine succeeding: if't be so,
For *Banquo's* Issue haue I fil'd my Minde,
For them, the gracious *Duncan* haue I murther'd,
Put Rancours in the Vessell of my Peace
Onely for them, and mine eternall Iewell
Giuen to the common Enemie of Man,
To make them Kings, the Seedes of *Banquo* Kings.
Rather then so, come Fate into the Lyst,
And champion me to th'vtterance.
Who's there?

Enter Seruant, and two Murtherers.

Now goe to the Doore, and stay there till we call.

Exit Seruant.

Was it not yesterday we spoke together?
Murth. It was, so please your Highnesse.
Macb. Well then,
Now haue you consider'd of my speeches:

Know,

Know, that it was he, in the times past,
Which held you so vnder fortune,
Which you thought had been our innocent selfe.
This I made good to you, in our last conference,
Past in probation with you:
How you were borne in hand, how crost:
The Instruments: who wrought with them:
And all things else, that might
To halfe a Soule, and to a Notion craz'd,
Say, Thus did *Banquo.*

1. Murth. You made it knowne to vs.

Macb. I did so:
And went further, which is now
Our point of second meeting.
Doe you finde your patience so predominant,
In your nature, that you can let this goe?
Are you so Gospell'd, to pray for this good man,
And for his Issue, whose heauie hand
Hath bow'd you to the Graue, and begger'd
Yours for euer?

1. Murth. We are men, my Liege.

Macb. I, in the Catalogue ye goe for men,
As Hounds, and Greyhounds, Mungrels, Spaniels, Curres,
Showghes, Water-Rugs, and Demy-Wolues are clipt
All by the Name of Dogges: the valued file
Distinguishes the swift, the slow, the subtle,
The House-keeper, the Hunter, euery one
According to the gift, which bounteous Nature
Hath in him clos'd: whereby he does receiue
Particular addition, from the Bill,
That writes them all alike: and so of men.
Now, if you haue a station in the file,
Not i'th' worst ranke of Manhood, say't,
And I will put that Businesse in your Bosomes,
Whose execution takes your Enemie off,
Grapples you to the heart; and loue of vs,
Who weare our Health but sickly in his Life,
Which in his Death were perfect.

2. Murth. I am one, my Liege,
Whom the vile Blowes and Buffets of the World
Hath so incens'd, that I am recklesse what I doe,
To spight the World.

1. Murth. And I another,
So wearie with Disasters, tugg'd with Fortune,
That I would set my Life on any Chance,
To mend it, or be rid on't.

Macb. Both of you know *Banquo* was your Enemie.

Murth. True, my Lord.

Macb. So is he mine: and in such bloody distance,
That euery minute of his being, thrusts
Against my neer'st of Life: and though I could
With bare-fac'd power sweepe him from my sight,
And bid my will auouch it; yet I must not,
For certaine friends that are both his, and mine,
Whose loues I may not drop, but wayle his fall,
Who I my selfe struck downe: and thence it is,
That I to your assistance doe make loue,
Masking the Businesse from the common Eye,
For sundry weightie Reasons.

2. Murth. We shall, my Lord,
Performe what you command vs.

1. Murth. Though our Liues--

Macb. Your Spirits shine through you.
Within this houre, at most,
I will aduise you where to plant your selues,
Acquaint you with the perfect Spy o'th' time,
The moment on't, for't must be done to Night,
And something from the Pallace: alwayes thought,
That I require a clearenesse; and with him,
To leaue no Rubs nor Botches in the Worke:
Fleans, his Sonne, that keepes him companie,
Whose absence is no lesse materiall to me,
Then is his Fathers, must embrace the fate
Of that darke houre: resolue your selues apart,
Ile come to you anon.

Murth. We are resolu'd, my Lord.

Macb. Ile call vpon you straight: abide within,
It is concluded: *Banquo*, thy Soules flight,
If it finde Heauen, must finde it out to Night. *Exeunt.*

Scena Secunda.

Enter Macbeths Lady, and a Seruant.

Lady. Is *Banquo* gone from Court?

Seruant. I, Madame, but returnes againe to Night.

Lady. Say to the King, I would attend his leysure,
For a few words.

Seruant. Madame, I will. *Exit.*

Lady. Nought's had, all's spent,
Where our desire is got without content:
'Tis safer, to be that which we destroy,
Then by destruction dwell in doubtfull ioy.

Enter Macbeth.

How now, my Lord, why doe you keepe alone?
Of sorryest Fancies your Companions making,
Vsing those Thoughts, which should indeed haue dy'd
With them they thinke on: things without all remedie
Should be without regard: what's done, is done.

Macb. We haue scorch'd the Snake, not kill'd it:
Shee'le close, and be her selfe, whilest our poore Mallice
Remaines in danger of her former Tooth.
But let the frame of things dis-ioynt,
Both the Worlds suffer,
Ere we will eate our Meale in feare, and sleepe
In the affliction of these terrible Dreames,
That shake vs Nightly: Better be with the dead,
Whom we, to gayne our peace, haue sent to peace,
Then on the torture of the Minde to lye
In restlesse extasie.
Duncane is in his Graue:
After Lifes fitfull Feuer, he sleepes well,
Treason ha's done his worst: nor Steele, nor Poyson,
Mallice domestique, forraine Leuie, nothing,
Can touch him further.

Lady. Come on:
Gentle my Lord, sleeke o're your rugged Lookes,
Be bright and Iouiall among your Guests to Night.

Macb. So shall I Loue, and so I pray be you:
Let your remembrance apply to *Banquo*,
Present him Eminence, both with Eye and Tongue:
Vnsafe the while, that wee must laue
Our Honors in these flattering streames,
And make our Faces Vizards to our Hearts,
Disguising what they are.

Lady. You must leaue this.

Macb. O, full of Scorpions is my Minde, deare Wife:
Thou know'st, that *Banquo* and his *Fleans* liues.

Lady. But

Lady. But in them, Natures Coppie's not eterne.
Macb. There's comfort yet, they are assaileable,
Then be thou iocund: ere the Bat hath flowne
His Cloyster'd flight, ere to black *Heccats* summons
The shard-borne Beetle, with his drowsie hums,
Hath rung Nights yawning Peale,
There shall be done a deed of dreadfull note.
Lady. What's to be done?
Macb. Be innocent of the knowledge, dearest Chuck,
Till thou applaud the deed: Come, seeling Night,
Skarfe vp the tender Eye of pittifull Day,
And with thy bloodie and inuisible Hand
Cancell and teare to pieces that great Bond,
Which keepes me pale. Light thickens,
And the Crow makes Wing toth' Rookie Wood:
Good things of Day begin to droope, and drowse,
Whiles Nights black Agents to their Prey's doe rowse.
Thou maruell'st at my words: but hold thee still,
Things bad begun, make strong themselues by ill:
So prythee goe with me. *Exeunt.*

Scena Tertia.

Enter three Murtherers.

1. But who did bid thee ioyne with vs?
3. *Macbeth.*
2. He needes not our mistrust, since he deliuers
Our Offices, and what we haue to doe,
To the direction iust.
1. Then stand with vs:
The West yet glimmers with some streakes of Day.
Now spurres the lated Traueller apace,
To gayne the timely Inne, end neere approches
The subiect of our Watch.
3. Hearke, I heare Horses.
Banquo within. Giue vs a Light there, hoa.
2. Then 'tis hee:
The rest, that are within the note of expectation,
Alreadie are i'th'Court.
1. His Horses goe about.
3. Almost a mile: but he does vsually,
So all men doe, from hence toth' Pallace Gate
Make it their Walke.

Enter Banquo and Fleans, with a Torch.

2. A Light, a Light.
3. 'Tis hee.
1. Stand too't.
Ban. It will be Rayne to Night.
1. Let it come downe.
Ban. O, Trecherie!
Flye good *Fleans*, flye, flye, flye,
Thou may'st reuenge. O Slaue!
3. Who did strike out the Light?
1. Was't not the way?
3. There's but one downe: the Sonne is fled.
2. We haue lost
Best halfe of our Affaire.
1. Well, let's away, and say how much is done.
Exeunt.

Scæna Quarta.

Banquet prepar'd. Enter Macbeth, Lady, Rosse, Lenox, Lords, and Attendants.

Macb. You know your owne degrees, sit downe:
At first and last, the hearty welcome.
Lords. Thankes to your Maiesty.
Macb. Our selfe will mingle with Society,
And play the humble Host:
Our Hostesse keepes her State, but in best time
We will require her welcome.
La. Pronounce it for me Sir, to all our Friends,
For my heart speakes, they are welcome.
Enter first Murtherer.
Macb. See they encounter thee with their harts thanks
Both sides are euen: heere Ile sit i'th'mid'st,
Be large in mirth, anon wee'l drinke a Measure
The Table round. There's blood vpon thy face.
Mur. 'Tis *Banquo's* then.
Macb. 'Tis better thee without, then he within.
Is he dispatch'd?
Mur. My Lord his throat is cut, that I did for him.
Mac. Thou art the best o'th'Cut-throats,
Yet hee's good that did the like for *Fleans*:
If thou did'st it, thou art the Non-pareill.
Mur. Most Royall Sir
Fleans is scap'd.
Macb. Then comes my Fit againe:
I had else beene perfect;
Whole as the Marble, founded as the Rocke,
As broad, and generall, as the casing Ayre:
But now I am cabin'd, crib'd, confin'd, bound in
To sawcy doubts, and feares. But *Banquo's* safe?
Mur. I, my good Lord: safe in a ditch he bides,
With twenty trenched gashes on his head;
The least a Death to Nature.
Macb. Thankes for that:
There the growne Serpent lyes, the worme that's fled
Hath Nature that in time will Venom breed,
No teeth for th'present. Get thee gone, to morrow
Wee'l heare our selues againe. *Exit Murderer.*
Lady. My Royall Lord,
You do not giue the Cheere, the Feast is sold
That is not often vouch'd, while 'tis a making:
'Tis giuen, with welcome: to feede were best at home:
From thence, the sawce to meate is Ceremony,
Meeting were bare without it.

Enter the Ghost of Banquo, and sits in Macbeths place.

Macb. Sweet Remembrancer:
Now good digestion waite on Appetite,
And health on both.
Lenox. May't please your Highnesse sit.
Macb. Here had we now our Countries Honor, roof'd,
Were the grac'd person of our *Banquo* present:
Who, may I rather challenge for vnkindnesse,
Then pitty for Mischance.
Rosse. His absence (Sir)
Layes blame vpon his promise. Pleas't your Highnesse
To grace vs with your Royall Company?
Macb.

Macb. The Table's full.
Lenox. Heere is a place referu'd Sir.
Macb. Where?
Lenox. Heere my good Lord.
What is't that moues your Highnesse?
Macb. Which of you haue done this?
Lords. What, my good Lord?
Macb. Thou canst not say I did it: neuer shake
Thy goary lockes at me.
Rosse. Gentlemen rise, his Highnesse is not well.
Lady. Sit worthy Friends: my Lord is often thus,
And hath beene from his youth. Pray you keepe Seat,
The fit is momentary, vpon a thought
He will againe be well. If much you note him
You shall offend him, and extend his Passion,
Feed, and regard him not. Are you a man?
Macb. I, and a bold one, that dare looke on that
Which might appall the Diuell.
La. O proper stuffe:
This is the very painting of your feare:
This is the Ayre-drawne-Dagger which you said
Led you to *Duncan.* O, these flawes and starts
(Impostors to true feare) would well become
A womans story, at a Winters fire
Authoriz'd by her Grandam: shame it selfe,
Why do you make such faces? When all's done
You looke but on a stoole.
Macb. Prythee see there:
Behold, looke, loe, how say you:
Why what care I, if thou canst nod, speake too.
If Charnell houses, and our Graues must send
Those that we bury, backe; our Monuments
Shall be the Mawes of Kytes.
La. What? quite vnmann'd in folly.
Macb. If I stand heere, I saw him.
La. Fie for shame.
Macb. Blood hath bene shed ere now, i'th'olden time
Ere humane Statute purg'd the gentle Weale:
I, and since too, Murthers haue bene perform'd
Too terrible for the eare. The times has bene,
That when the Braines were out, the man would dye,
And there an end: But now they rise againe
With twenty mortall murthers on their crownes,
And push vs from our stooles. This is more strange
Then such a murther is.
La. My worthy Lord
Your Noble Friends do lacke you.
Macb. I do forget:
Do not muse at me my most worthy Friends,
I haue a strange infirmity, which is nothing
To those that know me. Come, loue and health to all,
Then Ile sit downe: Giue me some Wine, fill full:
Enter Ghost.
I drinke to th'generall ioy o'th'whole Table,
And to our deere Friend *Banquo,* whom we misse:
Would he were heere: to all, and him we thirst,
And all to all.
Lords. Our duties, and the pledge.
Mac. Auant, & quit my sight, let the earth hide thee:
Thy bones are marrowlesse, thy blood is cold:
Thou hast no speculation in those eyes
Which thou dost glare with.
La. Thinke of this good Peeres'
But as a thing of Custome: 'Tis no other,
Onely it spoyles the pleasure of the time.
Macb. What man dare, I dare:
Approach thou like the rugged Russian Beare,
The arm'd Rhinoceros, or th'Hircan Tiger,
Take any shape but that, and my firme Nerues
Shall neuer tremble. Or be aliue againe,
And dare me to the Desart with thy Sword:
If trembling I inhabit then, protest mee
The Baby of a Girle. Hence horrible shadow,
Vnreall mock'ry hence. Why so, being gone
I am a man againe: pray you sit still.
La. You haue displac'd the mirth,
Broke the good meeting, with most admir'd disorder.
Macb. Can such things be,
And ouercome vs like a Summers Clowd,
Without our speciall wonder? You make me strange
Euen to the disposition that I owe,
When now I thinke you can behold such sights,
And keepe the naturall Rubie of your Cheekes,
When mine is blanch'd with feare.
Rosse. What sights, my Lord?
La. I pray you speake not: he growes worse & worse
Question enrages him: at once, goodnight.
Stand not vpon the order of your going,
But go at once.
Len. Good night, and better health
Attend his Maiesty.
La. A kinde goodnight to all. *Exit Lords.*
Macb. It will haue blood they say:
Blood will haue Blood:
Stones haue beene knowne to moue, & Trees to speake:
Augures, and vnderstood Relations, haue
By Maggot Pyes, & Choughes, & Rookes brought forth
The secret'st man of Blood. What is the night?
La. Almost at oddes with morning, which is which.
Macb. How say'st thou that *Macduff* denies his person
At our great bidding.
La: Did you send to him Sir?
Macb. I heare it by the way: But I will send:
There's not a one of them but in his house
I keepe a Seruant Feed. I will to morrow
(And betimes I will) to the weyard Sisters.
More shall they speake: for now I am bent to know
By the worst meanes, the worst, for mine owne good,
All causes shall giue way. I am in blood
Stept in so farre, that should I wade no more,
Returning were as tedious as go ore:
Strange things I haue in head, that will to hand,
Which must be acted, ere they may be scand.
La. You lacke the season of all Natures, sleepe.
Macb. Come, wee'l to sleepe: My strange & self-abuse
Is the initiate feare, that wants hard vse:
We are yet but yong indeed. *Exeunt.*

Scena Quinta.

Thunder. Enter the three Witches, meeting Hecat.

1. Why how now *Hecat,* you looke angerly?
Hec. Haue I not reason (Beldams) as you are?
Sawcy, and ouer-bold, how did you dare
To Trade, and Trafficke with *Macbeth,*
In Riddles, and Affaires of death;

And

And I the Mistris of your Charmes,
The close contriuer of all harmes,
Was neuer call'd to beare my part,
Or shew the glory of our Art?
And which is worse, all you haue done
Hath bene but for a wayward Sonne,
Spightfull, and wrathfull, who (as others do)
Loues for his owne ends, not for you.
But make amends now: Get you gon,
And at the pit of Acheron
Meete me i'th'Morning: thither he
Will come, to know his Destinie.
Your Vessels, and your Spels prouide,
Your Charmes, and euery thing beside;
I am for th'Ayre: This night Ile spend
Vnto a dismall, and a Fatall end.
Great businesse must be wrought ere Noone.
Vpon the Corner of the Moone
There hangs a vap'rous drop, profound,
Ile catch it ere it come to ground;
And that distill'd by Magicke slights,
Shall raise such Artificiall Sprights,
As by the strength of their illusion,
Shall draw him on to his Confusion.
He shall spurne Fate, scorne Death, and beare
His hopes 'boue Wisedome, Grace, and Feare:
And you all know, Security
Is Mortals cheefest Enemie.

Musicke, and a Song.

Hearke, I am call'd: my little Spirit see
Sits in a Foggy cloud, and stayes for me.

Sing within. Come away, come away, &c.

1 Come, let's make hast, shee'l soone be
Backe againe. *Exeunt.*

Scæna Sexta.

Enter Lenox, and another Lord.

Lenox. My former Speeches,
Haue but hit your Thoughts
Which can interpret farther: Onely I say
Things haue bin strangely borne. The gracious *Duncan*
Was pittied of *Macbeth*: marry he was dead:
And the right valiant *Banquo* walk'd too late,
Whom you may say (if't please you) *Fleans* kill'd,
For *Fleans* fled: Men must not walke too late.
Who cannot want the thought, how monstrous
It was for *Malcolme*, and for *Donalbane*
To kill their gracious Father? Damned Fact,
How it did greeue *Macbeth*? Did he not straight
In pious rage, the two delinquents teare,
That were the Slaues of drinke, and thralles of sleepe?
Was not that Nobly done? I, and wisely too:
For 'twould haue anger'd any heart aliue
To heare the men deny't. So that I say,
He ha's borne all things well, and I do thinke,
That had he *Duncans* Sonnes vnder his Key,
(As, and't please Heauen he shall not) they should finde
What 'twere to kill a Father: So should *Fleans*.
But peace; for from broad words, and cause he fayl'd
His presence at the Tyrants Feast, I heare
Macduffe liues in disgrace. Sir, can you tell
Where he bestowes himselfe?

Lord. The Sonnes of *Duncane*
(From whom this Tyrant holds the due of Birth)
Liues in the English Court, and is receyu'd
Of the most Pious *Edward*, with such grace,
That the maleuolence of Fortune, nothing
Takes from his high respect. Thither *Macduffe*
Is gone, to pray the Holy King, vpon his ayd
To wake Northumberland, and warlike *Seyward*,
That by the helpe of these (with him aboue)
To ratifie the Worke) we may againe
Giue to our Tables meate, sleepe to our Nights:
Free from our Feasts, and Banquets bloody kniues;
Do faithfull Homage, and receiue free Honors,
All which we pine for now. And this report
Hath so exasperate their King, that hee
Prepares for some attempt of Warre.

Len. Sent he to *Macduffe*?

Lord. He did: and with an absolute Sir, not I
The clowdy Messenger turnes me his backe,
And hums; as who should say, you'l rue the time
That clogges me with this Answer.

Lenox. And that well might
Aduise him to a Caution, t'hold what distance
His wisedome can prouide. Some holy Angell
Flye to the Court of England, and vnfold
His Message ere he come, that a swift blessing
May soone returne to this our suffering Country,
Vnder a hand accurs'd.

Lord. Ile send my Prayers with him. *Exeunt*

Actus Quartus. Scena Prima.

Thunder. Enter the three Witches.

1 Thrice the brinded Cat hath mew'd.
2 Thrice, and once the Hedge-Pigge whin'd.
3 Harpier cries, 'tis time, 'tis time.
1 Round about the Caldron go:
In the poysond Entrailes throw
Toad, that vnder cold stone,
Dayes and Nights, ha's thirty one:
Sweltred Venom sleeping got,
Boyle thou first i'th'charmed pot.

All. Double, double, toile and trouble;
Fire burne, and Cauldron bubble.

2 Fillet of a Fenny Snake,
In the Cauldron boyle and bake:
Eye of Newt, and Toe of Frogge,
Wooll of Bat, and Tongue of Dogge:
Adders Forke, and Blinde-wormes Sting,
Lizards legge, and Howlets wing:
For a Charme of powrefull trouble,
Like a Hell-broth, boyle and bubble.

All. Double, double, toyle and trouble,
Fire burne, and Cauldron bubble.

3 Scale of Dragon, Tooth of Wolfe,
Witches Mummey, Maw, and Gulfe
Of the rauin'd salt Sea sharke:
Roote of Hemlocke, digg'd i'th'darke:
Liuer of Blaspheming Iew,
Gall of Goate, and Slippes of Yew,
Sliuer'd in the Moones Ecclipse:

Nose

Nose of Turke, and Tartars lips:
Finger of Birth-strangled Babe,
Ditch-deliuer'd by a Drab,
Make the Grewell thicke, and slab.
Adde thereto a Tigers Chawdron,
For th'Ingredience of our Cawdron.
All. Double, double, toyle and trouble,
Fire burne, and Cauldron bubble.
2 Coole it with a Baboones blood,
Then the Charme is firme and good.

Enter Hecat, and the other three Witches.

Hec. O well done: I commend your paines,
And euery one shall share i'th'gaines:
And now about the Cauldron sing
Like Elues and Fairies in a Ring,
Inchanting all that you put in.
Musicke and a Song. Blacke Spirits, &c.
2 By the pricking of my Thumbes,
Something wicked this way comes:
Open Lockes, who euer knockes.
Enter Macbeth.
Macb. How now you secret, black, & midnight Hags?
What is't you do?
All. A deed without a name.
Macb. I coniure you, by that which you Professe,
(How ere you come to know it) answer me:
Though you vntye the Windes, and let them fight
Against the Churches: Though the yesty Waues
Confound and swallow Nauigation vp:
Though bladed Corne be lodg'd, & Trees blown downe,
Though Castles topple on their Warders heads:
Though Pallaces, and Pyramids do slope
Their heads to their Foundations: Though the treasure
Of Natures Germaine, tumble altogether,
Euen till destruction sicken: Answer me
To what I aske you.
1 Speake.
2 Demand.
3 Wee'l answer.
1 Say, if th'hadst rather heare it from our mouthes,
Or from our Masters.
Macb. Call 'em: let me see 'em.
1 Powre in Sowes blood, that hath eaten
Her nine Farrow: Greaze that's sweaten
From the Murderers Gibbet, throw
Into the Flame.
All. Come high or low:
Thy Selfe and Office deaftly show. *Thunder.*
1. Apparation, an Armed Head.
Macb. Tell me, thou vnknowne power.
1 He knowes thy thought:
Heare his speech, but say thou nought.
1 *Appar.* *Macbeth, Macbeth, Macbeth:*
Beware *Macduffe*,
Beware the Thane of Fife: dismisse me. Enough.
He Descends.
Macb. What ere thou art, for thy good caution, thanks
Thou hast harp'd my feare aright. But one word more.
1 He will not be commanded: heere's another
More potent then the first. *Thunder.*
2 Apparition, a Bloody Childe.
2 *Appar.* *Macbeth, Macbeth, Macbeth.*
Macb. Had I three eares, Il'd heare thee.
2 *Appar.* Be bloody, bold, & resolute:
Laugh to scorne
The powre of man: For none of woman borne
Shall harme *Macbeth.* *Descends.*
Mac. Then liue *Macduffe*: what need I feare of thee?
But yet Ile make assurance: double sure,
And take a Bond of Fate: thou shalt not liue,
That I may tell pale-hearted Feare, it lies;
And sleepe in spight of Thunder. *Thunder*
3 Apparation, a Childe Crowned, with a Tree in his hand.
What is this, that rises like the issue of a King,
And weares vpon his Baby-brow, the round
And top of Soueraignty?
All. Listen, but speake not too't.
3 *Appar.* Be Lyon metled, proud, and take no care:
Who chafes, who frets, or where Conspirers are:
Macbeth shall neuer vanquish'd be, vntill
Great Byrnam Wood, to high Dunsmane Hill
Shall come against him. *Descend.*
Macb. That will neuer bee:
Who can impresse the Forrest, bid the Tree
Vnfixe his earth-bound Root? Sweet boadments, good:
Rebellious dead, rise neuer till the Wood
Of Byrnan rise, and our high plac'd *Macbeth*
Shall liue the Leafe of Nature, pay his breath
To time, and mortall Custome. Yet my Hart
Throbs to know one thing: Tell me, if your Art
Can tell so much: Shall *Banquo's* issue euer
Reigne in this Kingdome?
All. Seeke to know no more.
Macb. I will be satisfied. Deny me this,
And an eternall Curse fall on you: Let me know.
Why sinkes that Caldron? & what noise is this? *Hoboyes*
1 Shew.
2 Shew.
3 Shew.
All. Shew his Eyes, and greeue his Hart,
Come like shadowes, so depart.
A shew of eight Kings, and Banquo last, with a glasse in his hand.
Macb. Thou art too like the Spirit of *Banquo*: Down:
Thy Crowne do's seare mine Eye-bals. And thy haire
Thou other Gold-bound-brow, is like the first:
A third, is like the former. Filthy Hagges,
Why do you shew me this?——A fourth? Start eyes!
What will the Line stretch out to'th'cracke of Doome?
Another yet? A seauenth? Ile see no more:
And yet the eight appeares, who beares a glasse,
Which shewes me many more: and some I see,
That two-fold Balles, and trebble Scepters carry.
Horrible sight: Now I see 'tis true,
For the Blood-bolter'd *Banquo* smiles vpon me,
And points at them for his. What? is this so?
1 I Sir, all this is so. But why
Stands *Macbeth* thus amazedly?
Come Sisters, cheere we vp his sprights,
And shew the best of our delights.
Ile Charme the Ayre to giue a sound,
While you performe your Antique round:
That this great King may kindly say,
Our duties, did his welcome pay. *Musicke.*
The Witches Dance, and vanish.
Macb. Where are they? Gone?
Let this pernitious houre,
Stand aye accursed in the Kalender.
Come in, without there. *Enter Lenox.*
Lenox. What's your Graces will.

Macb.

Macb. Saw you the Weyard Sisters?
Lenox. No my Lord.
Macb. Came they not by you?
Lenox. No indeed my Lord.
Macb. Infected be the Ayre whereon they ride,
And damn'd all those that trust them. I did heare
The gallopping of Horse. Who was't came by?
Len. 'Tis two or three my Lord, that bring you word:
Macduff is fled to England.
Macb. Fled to England?
Len. I, my good Lord.
Macb. Time, thou anticipat'st my dread exploits:
The flighty purpose neuer is o're-tooke
Vnlesse the deed go with it. From this moment,
The very firstlings of my heart shall be
The firstlings of my hand. And euen now
To Crown my thoughts with Acts: be it thoght & done:
The Castle of *Macduff*, I will surprize,
Seize vpon Fife; giue to th'edge o'th'Sword
His Wife, his Babes, and all vnfortunate Soules
That trace him in his Line. No boasting like a Foole,
This deed Ile do, before this purpose coole,
But no more sights. Where are these Gentlemen?
Come bring me where they are. *Exeunt*

Scena Secunda.

Enter Macduffes Wife, her Son, and Rosse.

Wife. What had he done, to make him fly the Land?
Rosse. You must haue patience Madam.
Wife. He had none:
His flight was madnesse: when our Actions do not,
Our feares do make vs Traitors.
Rosse. You know not
Whether it was his wisedome, or his feare.
Wife. Wisedom? to leaue his wife, to leaue his Babes,
His Mansion, and his Titles, in a place
From whence himselfe do's flye? He loues vs not,
He wants the naturall touch. For the poore Wren
(The most diminitiue of Birds) will fight,
Her yong ones in her Nest, against the Owle:
All is the Feare, and nothing is the Loue;
As little is the Wisedome, where the flight
So runnes against all reason.
Rosse. My deerest Cooz,
I pray you schoole your selfe. But for your Husband,
He is Noble, Wise, Iudicious, and best knowes
The fits o'th'Season. I dare not speake much further,
But cruell are the times, when we are Traitors
And do not know our selues: when we hold Rumor
From what we feare, yet know not what we feare,
But floate vpon a wilde and violent Sea
Each way, and moue. I take my leaue of you:
Shall not be long but Ile be heere againe:
Things at the worst will cease, or else climbe vpward,
To what they were before. My pretty Cosine,
Blessing vpon you.
Wife. Father'd he is,
And yet hee's Father-lesse.
Rosse. I am so much a Foole, should I stay longer
It would be my disgrace, and your discomfort.
I take my leaue at once. *Exit Rosse.*

Wife. Sirra, your Fathers dead,
And what will you do now? How will you liue?
Son. As Birds do Mother.
Wife. What with Wormes, and Flyes?
Son. With what I get I meane, and so do they.
Wife. Poore Bird,
Thou'dst neuer Feare the Net, nor Lime,
The Pitfall, nor the Gin.
Son. Why should I Mother?
Poore Birds they are not set for:
My Father is not dead for all your saying.
Wife. Yes, he is dead:
How wilt thou do for a Father?
Son. Nay how will you do for a Husband?
Wife. Why I can buy me twenty at any Market.
Son. Then you'l by 'em to sell againe.
Wife. Thou speak'st withall thy wit,
And yet I'faith with wit enough for thee.
Son. Was my Father a Traitor, Mother?
Wife. I, that he was.
Son. What is a Traitor?
Wife. Why one that sweares, and lyes.
Son. And be all Traitors, that do so.
Wife. Euery one that do's so, is a Traitor,
And must be hang'd.
Son. And must they all be hang'd, that swear and lye?
Wife. Euery one.
Son. Who must hang them?
Wife. Why, the honest men.
Son. Then the Liars and Swearers are Fools: for there are Lyars and Swearers enow, to beate the honest men, and hang vp them.
Wife. Now God helpe thee, poore Monkie:
But how wilt thou do for a Father?
Son. If he were dead, youl'd weepe for him: if you would not, it were a good signe, that I should quickely haue a new Father.
Wife. Poore pratler, how thou talk'st?

Enter a Messenger.

Mes. Blesse you faire Dame: I am not to you known,
Though in your state of Honor I am perfect;
I doubt some danger do's approach you neerely.
If you will take a homely mans aduice,
Be not found heere: Hence with your little ones
To fright you thus. Me thinkes I am too sauage:
To do worse to you, were fell Cruelty,
Which is too nie your person. Heauen preserue you,
I dare abide no longer. *Exit Messenger*
Wife. Whether should I flye?
I haue done no harme. But I remember now
I am in this earthly world: where to do harme
Is often laudable, to do good sometime
Accounted dangerous folly. Why then (alas)
Do I put vp that womanly defence,
To say I haue done no harme?
What are these faces?

Enter Murtherers.

Mur. Where is your Husband?
Wife. I hope in no place so vnsanctified,
Where such as thou may'st finde him.
Mur. He's a Traitor.
Son. Thou ly'st thou shagge-ear'd Villaine.
Mur. What you Egge?
Yong fry of Treachery?
Son. He ha's kill'd me Mother,
Run away I pray you. *Exit crying Murther.*

Scæna Tertia.

Enter Malcolme and Macduffe.

Mal. Let vs ſeeke out ſome deſolate ſhade, & there
Weepe our ſad boſomes empty.
Macd. Let vs rather
Hold faſt the mortall Sword : and like good men,
Beſtride our downfall Birthdome : each new Morne,
New Widdowes howle, new Orphans cry, new ſorowes
Strike heauen on the face, that it reſounds
As if it felt with Scotland, and yell'd out
Like Syllable of Dolour.
Mal. What I beleeue, Ile waile;
What know, beleeue; and what I can redreſſe,
As I ſhall finde the time to friend : I wil.
What you haue ſpoke, it may be ſo perchance.
This Tyrant, whoſe ſole name bliſters our tongues,
Was once thought honeſt : you haue lou'd him well,
He hath not touch'd you yet. I am yong, but ſomething
You may diſcerne of him through me, and wiſedome
To offer vp a weake, poore innocent Lambe
T'appeaſe an angry God.
Macd. I am not treacherous.
Malc. But *Macbeth* is.
A good and vertuous Nature may recoyle
In an Imperiall charge. But I ſhall craue your pardon :
That which you are, my thoughts cannot tranſpoſe;
Angels are bright ſtill, though the brighteſt fell.
Though all things foule, would wear the brows of grace
Yet Grace muſt ſtill looke ſo.
Macd. I haue loſt my Hopes.
Malc. Perchance euen there
Where I did finde my doubts.
Why in that rawneſſe left you Wife, and Childe?
Thoſe precious Motiues, thoſe ſtrong knots of Loue,
Without leaue-taking. I pray you,
Let not my Iealouſies, be your Diſhonors,
But mine owne Safeties : you may be rightly iuſt,
What euer I ſhall thinke.
Macd. Bleed, bleed poore Country,
Great Tyrrany, lay thou thy baſis ſure,
For goodneſſe dare not check thee : wear y^u^ thy wrongs,
The Title, is affear'd. Far thee well Lord,
I would not be the Villaine that thou think'ſt,
For the whole Space that's in the Tyrants Graſpe,
And the rich Eaſt to boot.
Mal. Be not offended :
I ſpeake not as in abſolute feare of you :
I thinke our Country ſinkes beneath the yoake,
It weepes, it bleeds, and each new day a gaſh
Is added to her wounds. I thinke withall,
There would be hands vplifted in my right:
And heere from gracious England haue I offer
Of goodly thouſands. But for all this,
When I ſhall treade vpon the Tyrants head,
Or weare it on my Sword; yet my poore Country
Shall haue more vices then it had before,
More ſuffer, and more ſundry wayes then euer,
By him that ſhall ſucceede.
Macd. What ſhould he be?
Mal. It is my ſelfe I meane : in whom I know
All the particulars of Vice ſo grafted,
That when they ſhall be open'd, blacke *Macbeth*
Will ſeeme as pure as Snow, and the poore State
Eſteeme him as a Lambe, being compar'd
With my confineleſſe harmes.
Macd. Not in the Legions
Of horrid Hell, can come a Diuell more damn'd
In euils, to top *Macbeth.*
Mal. I grant him Bloody,
Luxurious, Auaricious, Falſe, Deceitfull,
Sodaine, Malicious, ſmacking of euery ſinne
That ha's a name. But there's no bottome, none
In my Voluptuouſneſſe : Your Wiues, your Daughters,
Your Matrons, and your Maides, could not fill vp
The Ceſterne of my Luſt, and my Deſire
All continent Impediments would ore-beare
That did oppoſe my will. Better *Macbeth,*
Then ſuch an one to reigne.
Macd. Boundleſſe intemperance
In Nature is a Tyranny : It hath beene
Th'vntimely emptying of the happy Throne,
And fall of many Kings. But feare not yet
To take vpon you what is yours : you may
Conuey your pleaſures in a ſpacious plenty,
And yet ſeeme cold. The time you may ſo hoodwinke :
We haue willing Dames enough : there cannot be
That Vulture in you, to deuoure ſo many
As will to Greatneſſe dedicate themſelues,
Finding it ſo inclinde.
Mal With this, there growes
In my moſt ill-compos d Affection, ſuch
A ſtanchleſſe Auarice, that were I King,
I ſhould cut off the Nobles for their Lands,
Deſire his Iewels, and this others Houſe,
And my more-hauing, would be as a Sawce
To make me hunger more, that I ſhould forge
Quarrels vniuſt againſt the Good and Loyall,
Deſtroying them for wealth.
Macd. This Auarice
ſtickes deeper : growes with more pernicious roote
Then Summer-ſeeming Luſt : and it hath bin
The Sword of our ſlaine Kings: yet do not feare,
Scotland hath Foyſons, to fill vp your will
Of your meere Owne. All theſe are portable,
With other Graces weigh'd.
Mal. But I haue none. The King-becoming Graces,
As Iuſtice, Verity, Temp'rance, Stableneſſe,
Bounty, Perſeuerance, Mercy, Lowlineſſe,
Deuotion, Patience, Courage, Fortitude,
I haue no relliſh of them, but abound
In the diuiſion of each ſeuerall Crime,
Acting it many wayes. Nay, had I powre, I ſhould
Poure the ſweet Milke of Concord, into Hell,
Vprore the vniuerſall peace, confound
All vnity on earth.
Macd. O Scotland, Scotland.
Mal. If ſuch a one be fit to gouerne, ſpeake :
I am as I haue ſpoken.
Mac. Fit to gouern? No not to liue. O Natiõ miſerable!
With an vntitled Tyrant, bloody Sceptred,
When ſhalt thou ſee thy wholſome dayes againe?
Since that the trueſt Iſſue of thy Throne
By his owne Interdiction ſtands accuſt,
And do's blaſpheme his breed? Thy Royall Father
Was a moſt Sainted-King : the Queene that bore thee,
Oftner vpon her knees, then on her feet,
Dy'de euery day ſhe liu'd. Fare thee well,

These

These Euils thou repeat'st vpon thy selfe,
Hath banish'd me from Scotland. O my Brest,
Thy hope ends heere.

Mal. *Macduff*, this Noble passion
Childe of integrity, hath from my soule
Wip'd the blacke Scruples, reconcil'd my thoughts
To thy good Truth, and Honor. Diuellish *Macbeth*,
By many of these traines, hath sought to win me
Into his power: and modest Wisedome pluckes me
From ouer-credulous hast: but God aboue
Deale betweene thee and me; For euen now
I put my selfe to thy Direction, and
Vnspeake mine owne detraction. Heere abiure
The taints, and blames I laide vpon my selfe,
For strangers to my Nature. I am yet
Vnknowne to Woman, neuer was forsworne,
Scarsely haue coueted what was mine owne.
At no time broke my Faith, would not betray
The Deuill to his Fellow, and delight
No lesse in truth then life. My first false speaking
Was this vpon my selfe. What I am truly
Is thine, and my poore Countries to command:
Whither indeed, before they heere approach
Old *Seyward* with ten thousand warlike men
Already at a point, was setting foorth:
Now wee'l together, and the chance of goodnesse
Be like our warranted Quarrell. Why are you silent?

Macd. Such welcome, and vnwelcom things at once
'Tis hard to reconcile.

Enter a Doctor.

Mal. Well, more anon. Comes the King forth
I pray you?

Doct. I Sir: there are a crew of wretched Soules
That stay his Cure: their malady conuinces
The great assay of Art. But at his touch,
Such sanctity hath Heauen giuen his hand,
They presently amend. *Exit.*

Mal. I thanke you Doctor.

Macd. What's the Disease he meanes?

Mal. Tis call'd the Euill.
A most myraculous worke in this good King,
Which often since my heere remaine in England,
I haue seene him do: How he solicites heauen
Himselfe best knowes: but strangely visited people
All swolne and Vlcerous, pittifull to the eye,
The meere dispaire of Surgery, he cures,
Hanging a golden stampe about their neckes,
Put on with holy Prayers, and 'tis spoken
To the succeeding Royalty he leaues
The healing Benediction. With this strange vertue,
He hath a heauenly guift of Prophesie,
And sundry Blessings hang about his Throne,
That speake him full of Grace.

Enter Rosse.

Macd. See who comes heere.

Malc. My Countryman: but yet I know him nor.

Macd. My euer gentle Cozen, welcome hither.

Malc. I know him now. Good God betimes remoue
The meanes that makes vs Strangers.

Rosse. Sir, Amen.

Macd. Stands Scotland where it did?

Rosse. Alas poore Countrey,
Almost affraid to know it selfe. It cannot
Be call'd our Mother, but our Graue; where nothing
But who knowes nothing, is once seene to smile:
Where sighes, and groanes, and shrieks that rent the ayre
Are made, not mark'd: Where violent sorrow seemes
A Moderne extasie: The Deadmans knell,
Is there scarse ask'd for who, and good mens liues
Expire before the Flowers in their Caps,
Dying, or ere they sicken.

Macd. Oh Relation; too nice, and yet too true.

Malc. What's the newest griefe?

Rosse. That of an houres age, doth hisse the speaker,
Each minute teemes a new one.

Macd. How do's my Wife?

Rosse. Why well.

Macd. And all my Children?

Rosse. Well too.

Macd. The Tyrant ha's not batter'd at their peace?

Rosse. No, they were wel at peace, when I did leaue 'em

Macd. Be not a niggard of your speech: How gos't?

Rosse. When I came hither to transport the Tydings
Which I haue heauily borne, there ran a Rumour
Of many worthy Fellowes, that were out,
Which was to my beleefe witnest the rather,
For that I saw the Tyrants Power a-foot.
Now is the time of helpe: your eye in Scotland
Would create Soldiours, make our women fight,
To doffe their dire distresses.

Malc. Bee't their comfort
We are comming thither: Gracious England hath
Lent vs good *Seyward*, and ten thousand men,
An older, and a better Souldier, none
That Christendome giues out.

Rosse. Would I could answer
This comfort with the like. But I haue words
That would be howl'd out in the desert ayre,
Where hearing should not latch them.

Macd. What concerne they,
The generall cause, or is it a Fee-griefe
Due to some single brest?

Rosse. No minde that's honest
But in it shares some woe, though the maine part
Pertaines to you alone.

Macd. If it be mine
Keepe it not from me, quickly let me haue it.

Rosse. Let not your eares dispise my tongue for euer,
Which shall possesse them with the heauiest sound
That euer yet they heard.

Macd. Humh: I guesse at it.

Rosse, Your Castle is surpriz'd: your Wife, and Babes
Sauagely slaughter'd: To relate the manner
Were on the Quarry of these murther'd Deere
To adde the death of you.

Malc. Mercifull Heauen:
What man, ne're pull your hat vpon your browes:
Giue sorrow words; the griefe that do's not speake,
Whispers the o're-fraught heart, and bids it breake.

Macd. My Children too?

Ro. Wife, Children, Seruants, all that could be found.

Macd. And I must be from thence? My wife kil'd too?

Rosse. I haue said.

Malc. Be comforted.
Let's make vs Med'cines of our great Reuenge,
To cure this deadly greefe.

Macd. He ha's no Children. All my pretty ones?
Did you say All? Oh Hell-Kite! All?
What, All my pretty Chickens, and their Damme
At one fell swoope?

Malc. Dispute it like a man.

Macd. I shall do so:

But I must also feele it as a man;
I cannot but remember such things were
That were most precious to me: Did heauen looke on,
And would not take their part? Sinfull *Macduff*,
They were all strooke for thee: Naught that I am,
Not for their owne demerits, but for mine
Fell slaughter on their soules: Heauen rest them now.

Mal. Be this the Whetstone of your sword, let griefe
Conuert to anger: blunt not the heart, enrage it.

Macd. O I could play the woman with mine eyes,
And Braggart with my tongue. But gentle Heauens,
Cut short all intermission: Front to Front,
Bring thou this Fiend of Scotland, and my selfe
Within my Swords length set him, if he scape
Heauen forgiue him too.

Mal. This time goes manly:
Come go we to the King, our Power is ready,
Our lacke is nothing but our leaue. *Macbeth*
Is ripe for shaking, and the Powres aboue
Put on their Instruments: Receiue what cheere you may,
The Night is long, that neuer findes the Day. *Exeunt*

Actus Quintus. Scena Prima.

Enter a Doctor of Physicke, and a Wayting Gentlewoman.

Doct. I haue too Nights watch'd with you, but can perceiue no truth in your report. When was it shee last walk'd?

Gent. Since his Maiesty went into the Field, I haue seene her rise from her bed, throw her Night-Gown vppon her, vnlocke her Closset, take foorth paper, folde it, write vpon't, read it, afterwards Seale it, and againe returne to bed; yet all this while in a most fast sleepe.

Doct. A great perturbation in Nature, to receyue at once the benefit of sleep, and do the effects of watching. In this slumbry agitation, besides her walking, and other actuall performances, what (at any time) haue you heard her say?

Gent. That Sir, which I will not report after her.

Doct. You may to me, and 'tis most meet you should.

Gent. Neither to you, nor any one, hauing no witnesse to confirme my speech. *Enter Lady, with a Taper.*
Lo you, heere she comes: This is her very guise, and vpon my life fast asleepe: obserue her, stand close.

Doct. How came she by that light?

Gent. Why it stood by her: she ha's light by her continually, 'tis her command.

Doct. You see her eyes are open.

Gent. I but their sense are shut.

Doct. What is it she do's now?
Looke how she rubbes her hands.

Gent. It is an accustom'd action with her, to seeme thus washing her hands: I haue knowne her continue in this a quarter of an houre.

Lad. Yet heere's a spot.

Doct. Heark, she speaks, I will set downe what comes from her, to satisfie my remembrance the more strongly.

La. Out damned spot: out I say. One: Two: Why then 'tis time to doo't: Hell is murky. Fye, my Lord, fie, a Souldier, and affear'd? what need we feare? who knowes it, when none can call our powre to accompt: yet who would haue thought the olde man to haue had so much blood in him.

Doct. Do you marke that?

Lad. The Thane of Fife, had a wife: where is she now? What will these hands ne're be cleane? No more o'that my Lord, no more o'that: you marre all with this starting.

Doct. Go too, go too:
You haue knowne what you should not.

Gent. She ha's spoke what shee should not, I am sure of that: Heauen knowes what she ha's knowne.

La. Heere's the smell of the blood still: all the perfumes of Arabia will not sweeten this little hand.
Oh, oh, oh.

Doct. What a sigh is there? The hart is sorely charg'd.

Gent. I would not haue such a heart in my bosome, for the dignity of the whole body.

Doct. Well, well, well.

Gent. Pray God it be sir.

Doct. This disease is beyond my practise: yet I haue knowne those which haue walkt in their sleep, who haue dyed holily in their beds.

Lad. Wash your hands, put on your Night-Gowne, looke not so pale: I tell you yet againe *Banquo*'s buried; he cannot come out on's graue.

Doct. Euen so?

Lady. To bed, to bed: there's knocking at the gate: Come, come, come, come, giue me your hand: What's done, cannot be vndone. To bed, to bed, to bed. *Exit Lady.*

Doct. Will she go now to bed?

Gent. Directly.

Doct. Foule whisp'rings are abroad: vnnaturall deeds
Do breed vnnaturall troubles: infected mindes
To their deafe pillowes will discharge their Secrets:
More needs she the Diuine, then the Physitian:
God, God forgiue vs all. Looke after her,
Remoue from her the meanes of all annoyance,
And still keepe eyes vpon her: So goodnight,
My minde she ha's mated, and amaz'd my sight.
I thinke, but dare not speake.

Gent. Good night good Doctor. *Exeunt.*

Scena Secunda.

Drum and Colours. Enter Menteth, Cathnes, Angus, Lenox, Soldiers.

Ment. The English powre is neere, led on by *Malcolm*,
His Vnkle *Seyward*, and the good *Macduff*.
Reuenges burne in them: for their deere causes
Would to the bleeding, and the grim Alarme
Excite the mortified man.

Ang. Neere Byrnan wood
Shall we well meet them, that way are they comming.

Cath. Who knowes if *Donalbane* be with his brother?

Len. For certaine Sir, he is not: I haue a File
Of all the Gentry; there is *Seywards* Sonne,
And many vnruffe youths, that euen now
Protest their first of Manhood.

Ment. What do's the Tyrant.

Cath. Great Dunsinane he strongly Fortifies:
Some say hee's mad: Others, that lesser hate him,
Do call it valiant Fury, but for certaine

He

He cannot buckle his diſtemper'd cauſe
Within the belt of Rule.
Ang. Now do's he feele
His ſecret Murthers ſticking on his hands,
Now minutely Reuolts vpbraid his Faith-breach:
Thoſe he commands, moue onely in command,
Nothing in loue: Now do's he feele his Title
Hang looſe about him, like a Giants Robe
Vpon a dwarfiſh Theefe.
Ment. Who then ſhall blame
His peſter'd Senſes to recoyle, and ſtart,
When all that is within him, do's condemne
It ſelfe, for being there.
Cath. Well, march we on,
To giue Obedience, where 'tis truly ow'd:
Meet we the Med'cine of the ſickly Weale,
And with him poure we in our Countries purge,
Each drop of vs.
Lenox. Or ſo much as it needes,
To dew the Soueraigne Flower, and drowne the Weeds:
Make we our March towards Birnan. *Exeunt marching.*

Scæna Tertia.

Enter Macbeth, Doctor, and Attendants.

Macb. Bring me no more Reports, let them flye all:
Till Byrnane wood remoue to Dunſinane,
I cannot taint with Feare. What's the Boy *Malcolme?*
Was he not borne of woman? The Spirits that know
All mortall Conſequences, haue pronounc'd me thus:
Feare not *Macbeth*, no man that's borne of woman
Shall ere haue power vpon thee. Then fly falſe Thanes,
And mingle with the Engliſh Epicures,
The minde I ſway by, and the heart I beare,
Shall neuer ſagge with doubt, nor ſhake with feare.
Enter Seruant.
The diuell damne thee blacke, thou cream-fac'd Loone:
Where got'ſt thou that Gooſe-looke.
Ser. There is ten thouſand.
Macb. Geeſe Villaine?
Ser. Souldiers Sir.
Macb. Go pricke thy face, and ouer-red thy feare
Thou Lilly-liuer'd Boy. What Soldiers, Patch?
Death of thy Soule, thoſe Linnen cheekes of thine
Are Counſailers to feare. What Soldiers Whay-face?
Ser. The Engliſh Force, ſo pleaſe you.
Macb. Take thy face hence. *Seyton*, I am ſick at hart,
When I behold: *Seyton*, I ſay, this puſh
Will cheere me euer, or diſ-eate me now.
I haue liu'd long enough: my way of life
Is falne into the Seare, the yellow Leafe,
And that which ſhould accompany Old-Age,
As Honor, Loue, Obedience, Troopes of Friends,
I muſt not looke to haue: but in their ſteed,
Curſes, not lowd but deepe, Mouth-honor, breath
Which the poore heart would faine deny, and dare not.
Seyton?
Enter Seyton.
Sey. What's your gracious pleaſure?
Macb. What Newes more?
Sey. All is confirm'd my Lord, which was reported.
Macb. Ile fight, till from my bones, my fleſh be hackt.
Giue me my Armor.
Seyt. 'Tis not needed yet.
Macb. Ile put it on:
Send out moe Horſes, skirre the Country round,
Hang thoſe that talke of Feare. Giue me mine Armor:
How do's your Patient, Doctor?
Doct. Not ſo ſicke my Lord,
As ſhe is troubled with thicke-comming Fancies
That keepe her from her reſt.
Macb. Cure of that:
Can'ſt thou not Miniſter to a minde diſeas'd,
Plucke from the Memory a rooted Sorrow,
Raze out the written troubles of the Braine,
And with ſome ſweet Obliuious Antidote
Cleanſe the ſtufft boſome, of that perillous ſtuffe
Which weighes vpon the heart?
Doct. Therein the Patient
Muſt miniſter to himſelfe.
Macb. Throw Phyſicke to the Dogs, Ile none of it.
Come, put mine Armour on: giue me my Staffe:
Seyton, ſend out: Doctor, the Thanes flye from me:
Come ſir, diſpatch. If thou could'ſt Doctor, caſt
The Water of my Land, finde her Diſeaſe,
And purge it to a ſound and priſtiue Health,
I would applaud thee to the very Eccho,
That ſhould applaud againe. Pull't off I ſay,
What Rubarb, Cyme, or what Purgatiue drugge
Would ſcowre theſe Engliſh hence: hear'ſt ÿ of them?
Doct. I my good Lord: your Royall Preparation
Makes vs heare ſomething.
Macb. Bring it after me:
I will not be affraid of Death and Bane,
Till Birnane Forreſt come to Dunſinane.
Doct. Were I from Dunſinane away, and cleere,
Profit againe ſhould hardly draw me heere. *Exeunt*

Scena Quarta.

Drum and Colours. Enter Malcolme, Seyward, Macduffe, Seywards Sonne, Menteth, Cathnes, Angus, and Soldiers Marching.

Malc. Coſins, I hope the dayes are neere at hand
That Chambers will be ſafe.
Ment. We doubt it nothing.
Syew. What wood is this before vs?
Ment. The wood of Birnane.
Malc, Let euery Souldier hew him downe a Bough,
And bear't before him, thereby ſhall we ſhadow
The numbers of our Hoaſt, and make diſcouery
Erre in report of vs.
Sold. It ſhall be done.
Syw. We learne no other, but the confident Tyrant
Keepes ſtill in Dunſinane, and will indure
Our ſetting downe befor't.
Malc. 'Tis his maine hope:
For where there is aduantage to be giuen,
Both more and leſſe haue giuen him the Reuolt,
And none ſerue with him, but conſtrained things,
Whoſe hearts are abſent too.
Macd. Let our iuſt Cenſures
Attend the true euent, and put we on
nn 3 Induſtrious

Induſtrious Souldierſhip.

Sey. The time approaches,
That will with due deciſion make vs know
What we ſhall ſay we haue, and what we owe:
Thoughts ſpeculatiue, their vnſure hopes relate,
But certaine iſſue, ſtroakes muſt arbitrate,
Towards which, aduance the warre. *Exeunt marching*

Scena Quinta.

Enter Macbeth, Seyton, & Souldiers, with Drum and Colours.

Macb. Hang out our Banners on the outward walls,
The Cry is ſtill, they come: our Caſtles ſtrength
Will laugh a Siedge to ſcorne: Heere let them lye,
Till Famine and the Ague eate them vp:
Were they not forc'd with thoſe that ſhould be ours,
We might haue met them darefull, beard to beard,
And beate them backward home. What is that noyſe?

A Cry within of Women.

Sey. It is the cry of women, my good Lord.

Macb. I haue almoſt forgot the taſte of Feares:
The time ha's beene, my ſences would haue cool'd
To heare a Night-ſhrieke, and my Fell of haire
Would at a diſmall Treatiſe rowze, and ſtirre
As life were in't. I haue ſupt full with horrors,
Direneſſe familiar to my ſlaughterous thoughts
Cannot once ſtart me. Wherefore was that cry?

Sey. The Queene (my Lord) is dead.

Macb. She ſhould haue dy'de heereafter;
There would haue beene a time for ſuch a word:
To morrow, and to morrow, and to morrow,
Creepes in this petty pace from day to day,
To the laſt Syllable of Recorded time:
And all our yeſterdayes, haue lighted Fooles
The way to duſty death. Out, out, breefe Candle,
Life's but a walking Shadow, a poore Player,
That ſtruts and frets his houre vpon the Stage,
And then is heard no more. It is a Tale
Told by an Ideot, full of ſound and fury
Signifying nothing. *Enter a Meſſenger.*
Thou com'ſt to vſe thy Tongue: thy Story quickly.

Meſ. Gracious my Lord,
I ſhould report that which I ſay I ſaw,
But know not how to doo't.

Macb. Well, ſay ſir.

Meſ. As I did ſtand my watch vpon the Hill
I look'd toward Byrnane, and anon me thought
The Wood began to moue.

Macb. Lyar, and Slaue.

Meſ. Let me endure your wrath, if't be not ſo:
Within this three Mile may you ſee it comming.
I ſay, a mouing Groue.

Macb. If thou ſpeak'ſt falſe,
Vpon the next Tree ſhall thou hang aliue
Till Famine cling thee: If thy ſpeech be ſooth,
I care not if thou doſt for me as much.
I pull in Reſolution, and begin
To doubt th'Equiuocation of the Fiend,
That lies like truth. Feare not, till Byrnane Wood
Do come to Dunſinane, and now a Wood
Comes toward Dunſinane. Arme, Arme, and out,
If this which he auouches, do's appeare,
There is nor flying hence, nor tarrying here.
I 'ginne to be a-weary of the Sun,
And wiſh th'eſtate o'th'world were now vndon.
Ring the Alarum Bell, blow Winde, come wracke,
At leaſt wee'l dye with Harneſſe on our backe. *Exeunt*

Scena Sexta.

Drumme and Colours.
Enter Malcolme, Seyward, Macduffe, and their Army, with Boughes.

Mal. Now neere enough:
Your leauy Skreenes throw downe,
And ſhew like thoſe you are: You (worthy Vnkle)
Shall with my Coſin your right Noble Sonne
Leade our firſt Battell. Worthy *Macduffe*, and wee
Shall take vpon's what elſe remaines to do,
According to our order.

Sey. Fare you well:
Do we but finde the Tyrants power to night,
Let vs be beaten, if we cannot fight.

Macd. Make all our Trumpets ſpeak, giue thẽ all breath
Thoſe clamorous Harbingers of Blood, & Death. *Exeunt*

Alarums continued.

Scena Septima.

Enter Macbeth.

Macb. They haue tied me to a ſtake, I cannot flye,
But Beare-like I muſt fight the courſe. What's he
That was not borne of Woman? Such a one
Am I to feare, or none.

Enter young Seyward.

Y. Sey. What is thy name?

Macb. Thou'lt be affraid to heare it.

Y. Sey. No: though thou call'ſt thy ſelfe a hoter name
Then any is in hell.

Macb. My name's *Macbeth*.

Y. Sey. The diuell himſelfe could not pronounce a Title
More hatefull to mine eare.

Macb. No: nor more fearefull.

Y. Sey. Thou lyeſt abhorred Tyrant, with my Sword
Ile proue the lye thou ſpeak'ſt.

Fight, and young Seyward ſlaine.

Macb. Thou was't borne of woman;
But Swords I ſmile at, Weapons laugh to ſcorne,
Brandiſh'd by man that's of a Woman borne. *Exit.*

Alarums. Enter Macduffe.

Macd. That way the noiſe is: Tyrant ſhew thy face,
If thou beeſt ſlaine, and with no ſtroake of mine,
My Wife and Childrens Ghoſts will haunt me ſtill:
I cannot ſtrike at wretched Kernes, whoſe armes
Are hyr'd to beare their Staues; either thou *Macbeth*,
Or elſe my Sword with an vnbattered edge
I ſheath againe vndeeded. There thou ſhould'ſt be,
By this great clatter, one of greateſt note

Seemes

Seemes bruited. Let me finde him Fortune,
And more I begge not. *Exit.* *Alarums.*

Enter Malcolme and Seyward.

Sey. This way my Lord, the Caſtles gently rendred:
The Tyrants people, on both ſides do fight,
The Noble Thanes do brauely in the Warre,
The day almoſt it ſelfe profeſſes yours,
And little is to do.
Malc. We haue met with Foes
That ſtrike beſide vs.
Sey. Enter Sir, the Caſtle. *Exeunt.* *Alarum*

Enter Macbeth.

Macb. Why ſhould I play the Roman Foole, and dye
On mine owne ſword? whiles I ſee liues, the gaſhes
Do better vpon them.

Enter Macduffe.

Macd. Turne Hell-hound, turne.
Macb. Of all men elſe I haue auoyded thee:
But get thee backe, my ſoule is too much charg'd
With blood of thine already.
Macd. I haue no words,
My voice is in my Sword, thou bloodier Villaine
Then tearmes can giue thee out. *Fight: Alarum*
Macb. Thou looſeſt labour,
As eaſie may'ſt thou the intrenchant Ayre
With thy keene Sword impreſſe, as make me bleed:
Let fall thy blade on vulnerable Creſts,
I beare a charmed Life, which muſt not yeeld
To one of woman borne.
Macd. Diſpaire thy Charme,
And let the Angell whom thou ſtill haſt ſeru'd
Tell thee, *Macduffe* was from his Mothers womb
Vntimely ript.
Macb. Accurſed be that tongue that tels mee ſo;
For it hath Cow'd my better part of man:
And be theſe Iugling Fiends no more beleeu'd,
That palter with vs in a double ſence,
That keepe the word of promiſe to our eare,
And breake it to our hope. Ile not fight with thee.
Macd. Then yeeld thee Coward,
And liue to be the ſhew, and gaze o'th'time.
Wee'l haue thee, as our rarer Monſters are
Painted vpon a pole, and vnder-writ,
Heere may you ſee the Tyrant.
Macb. I will not yeeld
To kiſſe the ground before young *Malcolmes* feet,
And to be baited with the Rabbles curſe.
Though Byrnane wood be come to Dunſinane,
And thou oppos'd, being of no woman borne,
Yet I will try the laſt. Before my body,
I throw my warlike Shield: Lay on *Macduffe*,
And damn'd be him, that firſt cries hold, enough.
Exeunt fighting. *Alarums.*

Enter Fighting, and Macbeth ſlaine.

Retreat, and Flouriſh. Enter with Drumme and Colours, Malcolm, Seyward, Roſſe, Thanes, & Soldiers.

Mal. I would the Friends we miſſe, were ſafe arriu'd.
Sey. Some muſt go off: and yet by theſe I ſee,
So great a day as this is cheapely bought.
Mal. *Macduffe* is miſſing, and your Noble Sonne.
Roſſe. Your ſon my Lord, ha's paid a ſouldiers debt,
He onely liu'd but till he was a man,
The which no ſooner had his Proweſſe confirm'd
In the vnſhrinking ſtation where he fought,
But like a man he dy'de.
Sey. Then he is dead?
Roſſe. I, and brought off the field: your cauſe of ſorrow
Muſt not be meaſur'd by his worth, for then
It hath no end.
Sey. Had he his hurts before?
Roſſe. I, on the Front.
Sey. Why then, Gods Soldier be he:
Had I as many Sonnes, as I haue haires,
I would not wiſh them to a fairer death:
And ſo his Knell is knoll'd.
Mal. Hee's worth more ſorrow,
And that Ile ſpend for him.
Sey. He's worth no more,
They ſay he parted well, and paid his ſcore,
And ſo God be with him. Here comes newer comfort.

Enter Macduffe, with Macbeths head.

Macd. Haile King, for ſo thou art.
Behold where ſtands
Th'Vſurpers curſed head: the time is free:
I ſee thee compaſt with thy Kingdomes Pearle,
That ſpeake my ſalutation in their minds:
Whoſe voyces I deſire alowd with mine.
Haile King of Scotland.
All. Haile King of Scotland. *Flouriſh.*
Mal. We ſhall not ſpend a large expence of time,
Before we reckon with your ſeuerall loues,
And make vs euen with you. My Thanes and Kinſmen
Henceforth be Earles, the firſt that euer Scotland
In ſuch an Honor nam'd: What's more to do,
Which would be planted newly with the time,
As calling home our exil'd Friends abroad,
That fled the Snares of watchfull Tyranny,
Producing forth the cruell Miniſters
Of this dead Butcher, and his Fiend-like Queene;
Who (as 'tis thought) by ſelfe and violent hands,
Tooke off her life. This, and what needfull elſe
That call's vpon vs, by the Grace of Grace,
We will performe in meaſure, time, and place:
So thankes to all at once, and to each one,
Whom we inuite, to ſee vs Crown'd at Scone.
Flouriſh. *Exeunt Omnes.*

FINIS.

THE TRAGEDIE OF

HAMLET, Prince of Denmarke.

Actus Primus. Scœna Prima.

Enter Barnardo and Francisco two Centinels.

Barnardo.

WHo's there?

Fran. Nay answer me: Stand & vnfold your selfe.

Bar. Long liue the King.

Fran. *Barnardo?*

Bar. He.

Fran. You come most carefully vpon your houre.

Bar. 'Tis now strook twelue, get thee to bed *Francisco.*

Fran. For this releefe much thankes: 'Tis bitter cold,
And I am sicke at heart.

Barn. Haue you had quiet Guard?

Fran. Not a Mouse stirring.

Barn. Well, goodnight. If you do meet *Horatio* and *Marcellus*, the Riuals of my Watch, bid them make hast.

Enter Horatio and Marcellus.

Fran. I thinke I heare them. Stand: who's there?

Hor. Friends to this ground.

Mar. And Leige-men to the Dane.

Fran. Giue you good night.

Mar. O farwel honest Soldier, who hath relieu'd you?

Fra. *Barnardo* ha's my place: giue you goodnight.

Exit Fran.

Mar. Holla *Barnardo.*

Bar. Say, what is *Horatio* there?

Hor. A peece of him.

Bar. Welcome *Horatio*, welcome good *Marcellus.*

Mar. What, ha's this thing appear'd againe to night.

Bar. I haue seene nothing.

Mar. *Horatio* saies, 'tis but our Fantasie,
And will not let beleefe take hold of him
Touching this dreaded sight, twice seene of vs,
Therefore I haue intreated him along
With vs, to watch the minutes of this Night,
That if againe this Apparition come,
He may approue our eyes, and speake to it.

Hor. Tush, tush, 'twill not appeare.

Bar. Sit downe a-while,
And let vs once againe assaile your eares,
That are so fortified against our Story,
What we two Nights haue seene.

Hor. Well, sit we downe,
And let vs heare *Barnardo* speake of this.

Barn. Last night of all,
When yond same Starre that's Westward from the Pole
Had made his course t'illume that part of Heauen
Where now it burnes, *Marcellus* and my selfe,
The Bell then beating one.

Mar. Peace, breake thee off: *Enter the Ghost.*
Looke where it comes againe.

Barn. In the same figure, like the King that's dead.

Mar. Thou art a Scholler; speake to it *Horatio.*

Barn. Lookes it not like the King? Marke it *Horatio.*

Hora. Most like: It harrowes me with fear & wonder

Barn. It would be spoke too.

Mar. Question it *Horatio.*

Hor. What art thou that vsurp'st this time of night,
Together with that Faire and Warlike forme
In which the Maiesty of buried Denmarke
Did sometimes march: By Heauen I charge thee speake.

Mar. It is offended.

Barn. See, it stalkes away.

Hor. Stay: speake; speake: I Charge thee, speake.

Exit the Ghost.

Mar. 'Tis gone, and will not answer.

Barn. How now *Horatio*? You tremble & look pale:
Is not this something more then Fantasie?
What thinke you on't?

Hor. Before my God, I might not this beleeue
Without the sensible and true auouch
Of mine owne eyes.

Mar. Is it not like the King?

Hor. As thou art to thy selfe,
Such was the very Armour he had on,
When th'Ambitious Norwey combatted:
So frown'd he once, when in an angry parle
He smot the sledded Pollax on the Ice.
'Tis strange.

Mar. Thus twice before, and iust at this dead houre,
With Martiall stalke, hath he gone by our Watch.

Hor. In what particular thought to work, I know not:
But in the grosse and scope of my Opinion,
This boades some strange erruption to our State.

Mar. Good now sit downe, & tell me he that knowes
Why this same strict and most obseruant Watch,
So nightly toyles the subiect of the Land,
And why such dayly Cast of Brazon Cannon
And Forraigne Mart for Implements of warre:
Why such impresse of Ship-wrights, whose sore Taske
Do's not diuide the Sunday from the weeke,
What might be toward, that this sweaty hast
Doth make the Night ioynt-Labourer with the day:
Who is't that can informe me?

Hor. That can I,

At

At least the whisper goes so : Our last King,
Whose Image euen but now appear'd to vs,
Was (as you know) by *Fortinbras* of Norway,
(Thereto prick'd on by a most emulate Pride)
Dar'd to the Combate. In which, our Valiant *Hamlet*,
(For so this side of our knowne world esteem'd him)
Did slay this *Fortinbras* : who by a Seal'd Compact,
Well ratified by Law, and Heraldrie,
Did forfeite (with his life) all those his Lands
Which he stood seiz'd on, to the Conqueror :
Against the which, a Moity competent
Was gaged by our King : which had return'd
To the Inheritance of *Fortinbras*,
Had he bin Vanquisher, as by the same Cou'nant
And carriage of the Article designe,
His fell to *Hamlet*. Now sir, young *Fortinbras*,
Of vnimproued Mettle, hot and full,
Hath in the skirts of Norway, heere and there,
Shark'd vp a List of Landlesse Resolutes,
For Foode and Diet, to some Enterprize
That hath a stomacke in't : which is no other
(And it doth well appeare vnto our State)
But to recouer of vs by strong hand
And termes Compulsatiue, those foresaid Lands
So by his Father lost : and this (I take it)
Is the maine Motiue of our Preparations,
The Sourse of this our Watch, and the cheefe head
Of this post-hast, and Romage in the Land.

Enter Ghost againe.

But soft, behold: Loe, where it comes againe :
Ile crosse it, though it blast me. Stay Illusion :
If thou hast any sound, or vse of Voyce,
Speake to me. If there be any good thing to be done,
That may to thee do ease, and grace to me ; speak to me.
If thou art priuy to thy Countries Fate
(Which happily foreknowing may auoyd) Oh speake.
Or, if thou hast vp-hoorded in thy life
Extorted Treasure in the wombe of Earth,
(For which, they say, you Spirits oft walke in death)
Speake of it. Stay, and speake. Stop it *Marcellus*.

Mar. Shall I strike at it with my Partizan ?

Hor. Do, if it will not stand.

Barn. 'Tis heere.

Hor. 'Tis heere.

Mar. 'Tis gone. *Exit Ghost.*

We do it wrong, being so Maiesticall
To offer it the shew of Violence,
For it is as the Ayre, invulnerable,
And our vaine blowes, malicious Mockery.

Barn. It was about to speake, when the Cocke crew.

Hor. And then it started, like a guilty thing
Vpon a fearfull Summons. I haue heard,
The Cocke that is the Trumpet to the day,
Doth with his lofty and shrill-sounding Throate
Awake the God of Day : and at his warning,
Whether in Sea, or Fire, in Earth, or Ayre,
Th'extrauagant, and erring Spirit, hyes
To his Confine. And of the truth heerein,
This present Obiect made probation.

Mar. It faded on the crowing of the Cocke.
Some sayes, that euer 'gainst that Season comes
Wherein our Sauiours Birth is celebrated,
The Bird of Dawning singeth all night long :
And then (they say) no Spirit can walke abroad,
The nights are wholsome, then no Planets strike,
No Faiery talkes, nor Witch hath power to Charme :
So hallow'd, and so gracious is the time.

Hor. So haue I heard, and do in part beleeue it.
But looke, the Morne in Russet mantle clad,
Walkes o're the dew of yon high Easterne Hill,
Breake we our Watch vp, and by my aduice
Let vs impart what we haue seene to night
Vnto yong *Hamlet*. For vpon my life,
This Spirit dumbe to vs, will speake to him :
Do you consent we shall acquaint him with it,
As needfull in our Loues, fitting our Duty ?

Mar. Let do't I pray, and I this morning know
Where we shall finde him most conueniently. *Exeunt*

Scena Secunda.

Enter Claudius King of Denmarke, Gertrude the Queene, Hamlet, Polonius, Laertes, and his Sister Ophelia, Lords Attendant.

King. Though yet of *Hamlet* our deere Brothers death
The memory be greene : and that it vs befitted
To beare our hearts in greefe, and our whole Kingdome
To be contracted in one brow of woe :
Yet so farre hath Discretion fought with Nature,
That we with wisest sorrow thinke on him,
Together with remembrance of our selues.
Therefore our sometimes Sister, now our Queen,
Th'Imperiall Ioyntresse of this warlike State,
Haue we, as 'twere, with a defeated ioy,
With one Auspicious, and one Dropping eye,
With mirth in Funerall, and with Dirge in Marriage,
In equall Scale weighing Delight and Dole
Taken to Wife ; nor haue we heerein barr'd
Your better Wisedomes, which haue freely gone
With this affaire along, for all our Thankes.
Now followes, that you know young *Fortinbras*,
Holding a weake supposall of our worth ;
Or thinking by our late deere Brothers death,
Our State to be disioynt, and out of Frame,
Colleagued with the dreame of his Aduantage ;
He hath not fayl'd to pester vs with Message,
Importing the surrender of those Lands
Lost by his Father : with all Bonds of Law
To our most valiant Brother. So much for him.

Enter Voltemand and Cornelius.

Now for our selfe, and for this time of meeting
Thus much the businesse is. We haue heere writ
To Norway, Vncle of young *Fortinbras*,
Who Impotent and Bedrid, scarsely heares
Of this his Nephewes purpose, to suppresse
His further gate heerein. In that the Leuies,
The Lists, and full proportions are all made
Out of his subiect : and we heere dispatch
You good *Cornelius*, and you *Voltemand*,
For bearing of this greeting to old Norway,
Giuing to you no further personall power
To businesse with the King, more then the scope
Of these dilated Articles allow :
Farewell and let your hast commend your duty.

Volt. In that, and all things, will we shew our duty.

King. We doubt it nothing, heartily farewell.

Exit Voltemand and Cornelius.

And now *Laertes*, what's the newes with you ?

You

You told vs of ſome ſuite. What is't *Laertes*?
You cannot ſpeake of Reaſon to the Dane,
And looſe your voyce. What would'ſt thou beg *Laertes*,
That ſhall not be my Offer, not thy Asking?
The Head is not more Natiue to the Heart,
The Hand more Inſtrumentall to the Mouth,
Then is the Throne of Denmarke to thy Father.
What would'ſt thou haue *Laertes*?
Laer. Dread my Lord,
Your leaue and fauour to returne to France,
From whence, though willingly I came to Denmarke
To ſhew my duty in your Coronation,
Yet now I muſt confeſſe, that duty done,
My thoughts and wiſhes bend againe towards France,
And bow them to your gracious leaue and pardon.
King. Haue you your Fathers leaue?
What ſayes *Pollonius*?
Pol. He hath my Lord]:
I do beſeech you giue him leaue to go.
King. Take thy faire houre *Laertes*, time be thine,
And thy beſt graces ſpend it at thy will:
But now my Coſin *Hamlet*, and my Sonne?
Ham. A little more then kin, and leſſe then kinde.
King. How is it that the Clouds ſtill hang on you?
Ham. Not ſo my Lord, I am too much i'th'Sun.
Queen. Good *Hamlet* caſt thy nightly colour off,
And let thine eye looke like a Friend on Denmarke.
Do not for euer with thy veyled lids
Seeke for thy Noble Father in the duſt;
Thou know'ſt 'tis common, all that liues muſt dye,
Paſſing through Nature, to Eternity.
Ham. I Madam, it is common.
Queen. If it be;
Why ſeemes it ſo particular with thee.
Ham. Seemes Madam? Nay, it is: I know not Seemes:
'Tis not alone my Inky Cloake (good Mother)
Nor Cuſtomary ſuites of ſolemne Blacke,
Nor windy ſuſpiration of forc'd breath,
No, nor the fruitfull Riuer in the Eye,
Nor the dejected hauiour of the Viſage,
Together with all Formes, Moods, ſhewes of Griefe,
That can denote me truly. Theſe indeed Seeme,
For they are actions that a man might play:
But I haue that Within, which paſſeth ſhow;
Theſe, but the Trappings, and the Suites of woe.
King. 'Tis ſweet and commendable
In your Nature *Hamlet*,
To giue theſe mourning duties to your Father:
But you muſt know, your Father loſt a Father,
That Father loſt, loſt his, and the Suruiuer bound
In filiall Obligation, for ſome terme
To do obſequious Sorrow. But to perſeuer
In obſtinate Condolement, is a courſe
Of impious ſtubbornneſſe. 'Tis vnmanly greefe,
It ſhewes a will moſt incorrect to Heauen,
A Heart vnfortified, a Minde impatient,
An Vnderſtanding ſimple, and vnſchool'd:
For, what we know muſt be, and is as common
As any the moſt vulgar thing to ſence,
Why ſhould we in our peeuiſh Oppoſition
Take it to heart? Fye, 'tis a fault to Heauen,
A fault againſt the Dead, a fault to Nature,
To Reaſon moſt abſurd, whoſe common Theame
Is death of Fathers, and who ſtill hath cried,
From the firſt Coarſe, till he that dyed to day,
This muſt be ſo. We pray you throw to earth
This vnpreuayling woe, and thinke of vs
As of a Father; For let the world take note,
You are the moſt immediate to our Throne,
And with no leſſe Nobility of Loue,
Then that which deereſt Father beares his Sonne,
Do I impart towards you. For your intent
In going backe to Schoole in Wittenberg,
It is moſt retrograde to our deſire:
And we beſeech you, bend you to remaine
Heere in the cheere and comfort of our eye,
Our cheefeſt Courtier Coſin, and our Sonne.
Qu. Let not thy Mother loſe her Prayers *Hamlet*:
I prythee ſtay with vs, go not to Wittenberg.
Ham. I ſhall in all my beſt
Obey you Madam.
King. Why 'tis a louing, and a faire Reply,
Be as our ſelfe in Denmarke. Madam come,
This gentle and vnforc'd accord of *Hamlet*
Sits ſmiling to my heart; in grace whereof,
No iocond health that Denmarke drinkes to day,
But the great Cannon to the Clowds ſhall tell,
And the Kings Rouce, the Heauens ſhall bruite againe,
Reſpeaking earthly Thunder. Come away. *Exeunt*
Manet Hamlet.
Ham. Oh that this too too ſolid Fleſh, would melt,
Thaw, and reſolue it ſelfe into a Dew:
Or that the Euerlaſting had not fixt
His Cannon 'gainſt Selfe-ſlaughter. O God, O God!
How weary, ſtale, flat, and vnprofitable
Seemes to me all the vſes of this world?
Fie on't? Oh fie, fie, 'tis an vnweeded Garden
That growes to Seed: Things rank, and groſſe in Nature
Poſſeſſe it meerely. That it ſhould come to this:
But two months dead: Nay, not ſo much; not two,
So excellent a King, that was to this
Hiperion to a Satyre: ſo louing to my Mother,
That he might not beteene the windes of heauen
Viſit her face too roughly. Heauen and Earth
Muſt I remember: why ſhe would hang on him,
As if encreaſe of Appetite had growne
By what it fed on; and yet within a month?
Let me not thinke on't: Frailty, thy name is woman.
A little Month, or ere thoſe ſhooes were old,
With which ſhe followed my poore Fathers body
Like *Niobe*, all teares. Why ſhe, euen ſhe.
(O Heauen! A beaſt that wants diſcourſe of Reaſon
Would haue mourn'd longer) married with mine Vnkle,
My Fathers Brother: but no more like my Father,
Then I to *Hercules*. Within a Moneth?
Ere yet the ſalt of moſt vnrighteous Teares
Had left the fluſhing of her gauled eyes,
She married. O moſt wicked ſpeed, to poſt
With ſuch dexterity to Inceſtuous ſheets:
It is not, nor it cannot come to good.
But breake my heart, for I muſt hold my tongue.

Enter Horatio, Barnard, and Marcellus.

Hor. Haile to your Lordſhip.
Ham. I am glad to ſee you well:
Horatio, or I do forget my ſelfe.
Hor. The ſame my Lord,
And your poore Seruant euer.
Ham. Sir my good friend,
Ile change that name with you:
And what make you from Wittenberg *Horatio*?

Mar-

Marcellus.
Mar. My good Lord.
Ham. I am very glad to see you: good euen Sir.
But what in faith make you from *Wittemberge?*
Hor. A truant disposition, good my Lord.
Ham. I would not haue your Enemy say so;
Nor shall you doe mine eare that violence,
To make it truster of your owne report
Against your selfe. I know you are no Truant:
But what is your affaire in *Elsenour?*
Wee'l teach you to drinke deepe, ere you depart.
Hor. My Lord, I came to see your Fathers Funerall.
Ham. I pray thee doe not mock me (fellow Student)
I thinke it was to see my Mothers Wedding.
Hor. Indeed my Lord, it followed hard vpon.
Ham. Thrift, thrift *Horatio:* the Funerall Bakt-meats
Did coldly furnish forth the Marriage Tables;
Would I had met my dearest foe in heauen,
Ere I had euer seene that day *Horatio.*
My father, me thinkes I see my father.
Hor. Oh where my Lord?
Ham. In my minds eye (*Horatio*)
Hor. I saw him once; he was a goodly King.
Ham. He was a man, take him for all in all:
I shall not look vpon his like againe.
Hor. My Lord, I thinke I saw him yesternight.
Ham. Saw? Who?
Hor. My Lord, the King your Father.
Ham. The King my Father?
Hor. Season your admiration for a while
With an attent eare; till I may deliuer
Vpon the witnesse of these Gentlemen,
This maruell to you.
Ham. For Heauens loue let me heare.
Hor. Two nights together, had these Gentlemen
(*Marcellus* and *Barnardo*) on their Watch
In the dead wast and middle of the night
Beene thus encountred. A figure like your Father,
Arm'd at all points exactly, *Cap a Pe,*
Appeares before them, and with sollemne march
Goes slow and stately: By them thrice he walkt,
By their opprest and feare-surprized eyes,
Within his Truncheons length; whilst they bestil'd
Almost to Ielly with the Act of feare,
Stand dumbe and speake not to him. This to me
In dreadfull secrecie impart they did,
And I with them the third Night kept the Watch,
Whereas they had deliuer'd both in time,
Forme of the thing; each word made true and good,
The Apparition comes. I knew your Father:
These hands are not more like.
Ham. But where was this?
Mar. My Lord, vpon the platforme where we watcht.
Ham. Did you not speake to it?
Hor. My Lord, I did;
But answere made it none: yet once me thought
It lifted vp it head, and did addresse
It selfe to motion, like as it would speake:
But euen then, the Morning Cocke crew lowd;
And at the sound it shrunke in hast away,
And vanisht from our sight.
Ham. Tis very strange.
Hor. As I doe liue my honourd Lord 'tis true;
And we did thinke it writ downe in our duty
To let you know of it.
Ham. Indeed, indeed Sirs; but this troubles me.
Hold you the watch to Night?
Both. We doe my Lord.
Ham. Arm'd, say you?
Both. Arm'd, my Lord.
Ham. From top to toe?
Both. My Lord, from head to foote.
Ham. Then saw you not his face?
Hor. O yes, my Lord, he wore his Beauer vp.
Ham. What, lookt he frowningly?
Hor. A countenance more in sorrow then in anger.
Ham. Pale, or red?
Hor. Nay very pale.
Ham. And fixt his eyes vpon you?
Hor. Most constantly.
Ham. I would I had beene there.
Hor. It would haue much amaz'd you.
Ham. Very like, very like: staid it long? (dred.
Hor. While one with moderate hast might tell a hun-
All. Longer, longer.
Hor. Not when I saw't.
Ham. His Beard was grisly? no.
Hor. It was, as I haue seene it in his life,
A Sable Siluer'd. (gaine.
Ham. Ile watch to Night; perchance 'twill wake a-
Hor. I warrant you it will.
Ham. If it assume my noble Fathers person,
Ile speake to it, though Hell it selfe should gape
And bid me hold my peace. I pray you all,
If you haue hitherto conceald this sight;
Let it bee treble in your silence still:
And whatsoeuer els shall hap to night,
Giue it an vnderstanding but no tongue;
I will requite your loues; so, fare ye well:
Vpon the Platforme twixt eleuen and twelue,
Ile visit you.
All. Our duty to your Honour. *Exeunt.*
Ham. Your loue, as mine to you: farewell.
My Fathers Spirit in Armes? All is not well:
I doubt some foule play: would the Night were come;
Till then sit still my soule; foule deeds will rise,
Though all the earth orewhelm them to mens eies. *Exit.*

Scena Tertia.

Enter Laertes and Ophelia.

Laer. My necessaries are imbark't; Farewell:
And Sister, as the Winds giue Benefit,
And Conuoy is assistant; doe not sleepe,
But let me heare from you.
Ophel. Doe you doubt that?
Laer. For *Hamlet,* and the trifling of his fauours,
Hold it a fashion and a toy in Bloud;
A Violet in the youth of Primy Nature;
Froward, not permanent; sweet not lasting
The suppliance of a minute? No more.
Ophel. No more but so.
Laer. Thinke it no more:
For nature cressant does not grow alone,
In thewes and Bulke: but as his Temple waxes,
The inward seruice of the Minde and Soule
Growes wide withall. Perhaps he loues you now,
And now no soyle nor cautell doth besmerch
The vertue of his feare: but you must feare

His

His greatnesse weigh'd, his will is not his owne;
For hee himselfe is subiect to his Birth:
Hee may not, as vnuallued persons doe,
Carue for himselfe; for, on his choyce depends
The sanctity and health of the weole State.
And therefore must his choyce be circumscrib'd
Vnto the voyce and yeelding of that Body,
Whereof he is the Head. Then if he sayes he loues you,
It fits your wisedome so farre to beleeue it;
As he in his peculiar Sect and force
May giue his saying deed: which is no further,
Then the maine voyce of *Denmarke* goes withall.
Then weigh what losse your Honour may sustaine,
If with too credent eare you list his Songs;
Or lose your Heart; or your chast Treasure open
To his vnmastred importunity.
Feare it *Ophelia*, feare it my deare Sister,
And keepe within the reare of your Affection;
Out of the shot and danger of Desire.
The chariest Maid is Prodigall enough,
If she vnmaske her beauty to the Moone:
Vertue it selfe scapes not calumnious stroakes,
The Canker Galls, the Infants of the Spring
Too oft before the buttons be disclos'd,
And in the Morne and liquid dew of Youth,
Contagious blastments are most imminent.
Be wary then, best safety lies in feare;
Youth to it selfe rebels, though none else neere.

Ophe. I shall th'effect of this good Lesson keepe,
As watchmen to my heart: but good my Brother
Doe not as some vngracious Pastors doe,
Shew me the steepe and thorny way to Heauen;
Whilst like a puft and recklesse Libertine
Himselfe, the Primrose path of dalliance treads,
And reaks not his owne reade.

Laer. Oh, feare me not.

Enter Polonius.

I stay too long; but here my Father comes:
A double blessing is a double grace;
Occasion smiles vpon a second leaue.

Polon. Yet heere *Laertes*? Aboord, aboord for shame,
The winde sits in the shoulder of your saile,
And you are staid for there: my blessing with you;
And these few Precepts in thy memory,
See thou Character. Giue thy thoughts no tongue,
Nor any vnproportion'd thought his Act:
Be thou familiar; but by no meanes vulgar:
The friends thou hast, and their adoption tride,
Grapple them to thy Soule, with hoopes of Steele:
But doe not dull thy palme, with entertainment
Of each vnhatch't, vnfledg'd Comrade. Beware
Of entrance to a quarrell: but being in
Bear't that th'opposed may beware of thee.
Giue euery man thine eare; but few thy voyce:
Take each mans censure; but reserue thy iudgement:
Costly thy habit as thy purse can buy;
But not exprest in fancie; rich, not gawdie:
For the Apparell oft proclaimes the man.
And they in France of the best ranck and station,
Are of a most select and generous cheff in that.
Neither a borrower, nor a lender be;
For lone oft loses both it selfe and friend:
And borrowing duls the edge of Husbandry.
This aboue all; to thine owne selfe be true:
And it must follow, as the Night the Day,
Thou canst not then be false to any man.
Farewell: my Blessing season this in thee.

Laer. Most humbly doe I take my leaue, my Lord.

Polon. The time inuites you, goe, your seruants tend.

Laer. Farewell *Ophelia*, and remember well
What I haue said to you.

Ophe. Tis in my memory lockt,
And you your selfe shall keepe the key of it.

Laer. Farewell. *Exit Laer.*

Polon. What ist *Ophelia* he hath said to you?

Ophe. So please you, somthing touching the L. *Hamlet.*

Polon. Marry, well bethought:
Tis told me he hath very oft of late
Giuen priuate time to you; and you your selfe
Haue of your audience beene most free and bounteous.
If it be so, as so tis put on me;
And that in way of caution: I must tell you,
You doe not vnderstand your selfe so cleerely,
As it behoues my Daughter, and your Honour.
What is betweene you, giue me vp the truth?

Ophe. He hath my Lord of late, made many tenders
Of his affection to me.

Polon. Affection, puh. You speake like a greene Girle,
Vnsifted in such perillous Circumstance.
Doe you beleeue his tenders, as you call them?

Ophe. I do not know, my Lord, what I should thinke.

Polon. Marry Ile teach you; thinke your selfe a Baby,
That you haue tane his tenders for true pay,
Which are not starling. Tender your selfe more dearly;
Or not to crack the winde of the poore Phrase,
Roaming it thus, you'l tender me a foole.

Ophe. My Lord, he hath importun'd me with loue,
In honourable fashion.

Polon. I, fashion you may call it, go too, go too.

Ophe. And hath giuen countenance to his speech,
My Lord, with all the vowes of Heauen.

Polon. I, Springes to catch Woodcocks. I doe know
When the Bloud burnes, how Prodigall the Soule
Giues the tongue vowes: these blazes, Daughter,
Giuing more light then heate; extinct in both,
Euen in their promise, as it is a making;
You must not take for fire. For this time Daughter,
Be somewhat scanter of your Maiden presence;
Set your entreatments at a higher rate,
Then a command to parley. For Lord *Hamlet*,
Beleeue so much in him, that he is young,
And with a larger tether may he walke,
Then may be giuen you. In few, *Ophelia*,
Doe not beleeue his vowes; for they are Broakers,
Not of the eye, which their Inuestments show:
But meere implorators of vnholy Sutes,
Breathing like sanctified and pious bonds,
The better to beguile. This is for all:
I would not, in plaine tearmes, from this time forth,
Haue you so slander any moment leisure,
As to giue words or talke with the Lord *Hamlet*:
Looke too't, I charge you; come your wayes.

Ophe. I shall obey my Lord. *Exeunt.*

Enter Hamlet, Horatio, Marcellus.

Ham. The Ayre bites shrewdly: is it very cold?

Hor. It is a nipping and an eager ayre.

Ham. What hower now?

Hor. I thinke it lacks of twelue.

Mar. No, it is strooke.

Hor. Indeed I heard it not: then it drawes neere the (season,
Wherein the Spirit held his wont to walke.

What

What does this meane my Lord? (rouse,
Ham. The King doth wake to night, and takes his
Keepes wassels and the swaggering vpspring reeles,
And as he dreines his draughts of Renish downe,
The kettle Drum and Trumpet thus bray out
The triumph of his Pledge.
Horat. Is it a custome?
Ham. I marry ist;
And to my mind, though I am natiue heere,
And to the manner borne: It is a Custome
More honour'd in the breach, then the obseruance.
Enter Ghost.
Hor. Looke my Lord, it comes.
Ham. Angels and Ministers of Grace defend vs:
Be thou a Spirit of health, or Goblin damn'd,
Bring with thee ayres from Heauen, or blasts from Hell,
Be thy euents wicked or charitable,
Thou com'st in such a questionable shape
That I will speake to thee. Ile call thee *Hamlet*,
King, Father, Royall Dane: Oh, oh, answer me,
Let me not burst in Ignorance; but tell
Why thy Canoniz'd bones Hearsed in death,
Haue burst their cerments, why the Sepulcher
Wherein we saw thee quietly enurn'd,
Hath op'd his ponderous and Marble iawes,
To cast thee vp againe? What may this meane?
That thou dead Coarse againe in compleat steele,
Reuisits thus the glimpses of the Moone,
Making Night hidious? And we fooles of Nature,
So horridly to shake our disposition,
With thoughts beyond thee; reaches of our Soules,
Say, why is this? wherefore? what should we doe?
Ghost beckens Hamlet.
Hor. It beckons you to goe away with it,
As if it some impartment did desire
To you alone.
Mar. Looke with what courteous action
It wafts you to a more remoued ground:
But doe not goe with it.
Hor. No, by no meanes.
Ham. It will not speake: then will I follow it.
Hor. Doe not my Lord.
Ham. Why, what should be the feare?
I doe not set my life at a pins fee;
And for my Soule, what can it doe to that?
Being a thing immortall as it selfe:
It waues me forth againe; Ile follow it.
Hor. What if it tempt you toward the Floud my Lord?
Or to the dreadfull Sonnet of the Cliffe,
That beetles o're his base into the Sea,
And there assumes some other horrible forme,
Which might depriue your Soueraignty of Reason,
And draw you into madnesse thinke of it?
Ham. It wafts me still: goe on, Ile follow thee.
Mar. You shall not goe my Lord.
Ham. Hold off your hand.
Hor. Be rul'd, you shall not goe.
Ham. My fate cries out,
And makes each petty Artire in this body,
As hardy as the Nemian Lions nerue:
Still am I cal'd? Vnhand me Gentlemen:
By Heau'n, Ile make a Ghost of him that lets me:
I say away, goe on, Ile follow thee.
Exeunt Ghost & Hamlet.
Hor. He waxes desperate with imagination.
Mar. Let's follow; 'tis not fit thus to obey him.
Hor. Haue after, to what issue will this come?
Mar. Something is rotten in the State of Denmarke.
Hor. Heauen will direct it.
Mar. Nay, let's follow him. *Exeunt.*
Enter Ghost and Hamlet.
Ham: Where wilt thou lead me? speak; Ile go no fur- (ther.
Gho. Marke me.
Ham. I will.
Gho. My hower is almost come,
When I to sulphurous and tormenting Flames
Must render vp my selfe.
Ham. Alas poore Ghost.
Gho. Pitty me not, but lend thy serious hearing
To what I shall vnfold.
Ham. Speake, I am bound to heare.
Gho. So art thou to reuenge, when thou shalt heare.
Ham. What?
Gho. I am thy Fathers Spirit,
Doom'd for a certaine terme to walke the night;
And for the day confin'd to fast in Fiers,
Till the foule crimes done in my dayes of Nature
Are burnt and purg'd away? But that I am forbid
To tell the secrets of my Prison-House;
I could a Tale vnfold, whose lightest word
Would harrow vp thy soule, freeze thy young blood,
Make thy two eyes like Starres, start from their Spheres,
Thy knotty and combined locks to part,
And each particular haire to stand an end,
Like Quilles vpon the fretfull Porpentine:
But this eternall blason must not be
To eares of flesh and bloud; list *Hamlet*, oh list,
If thou didst euer thy deare Father loue.
Ham. Oh Heauen!
Gho. Reuenge his foule and most vnnaturall Murther.
Ham. Murther?
Ghost. Murther most foule, as in the best it is;
But this most foule, strange, and vnnaturall.
Ham. Hast, hast me to know it,
That with wings as swift
As meditation, or the thoughts of Loue,
May sweepe to my Reuenge.
Ghost. I finde thee apt,
And duller should'st thou be then the fat weede
That rots it selfe in ease, on Lethe Wharfe,
Would'st thou not stirre in this. Now *Hamlet* heare:
It's giuen out, that sleeping in mine Orchard,
A Serpent stung me: so the whole eare of Denmarke,
Is by a forged processe of my death
Rankly abus'd: But know thou Noble youth,
The Serpent that did sting thy Fathers life,
Now weares his Crowne.
Ham. O my Propheticke soule: mine Vncle?
Ghost. I that incestuous, that adulterate Beast
With witchcraft of his wits, hath Traitorous guifts.
Oh wicked Wit, and Gifts, that haue the power
So to seduce? Won to to this shamefull Lust
The will of my most seeming vertuous Queene:
Oh *Hamlet*, what a falling off was there,
From me, whose loue was of that dignity,
That it went hand in hand, euen with the Vow
I made to her in Marriage; and to decline
Vpon a wretch, whose Naturall gifts were poore
To those of mine. But Vertue, as it neuer wil be moued,
Though Lewdnesse court it in a shape of Heauen:
So Lust, though to a radiant Angell link'd,
Will sate it selfe in a Celestiallbed, & prey on Garbage.
Oo But

But ſoft, me thinkes I ſent the Mornings Ayre;
Briefe let me be: Sleeping within mine Orchard,
My cuſtome alwayes in the afternoone;
Vpon my ſecure hower thy Vncle ſtole
With iuyce of curſed Hebenon in a Violl,
And in the Porches of mine eares did poure
The leaperous Diſtilment; whoſe effect
Holds ſuch an enmity with bloud of Man,
That ſwift as Quick-ſiluer, it courſes through
The naturall Gates and Allies of the Body;
And with a ſodaine vigour it doth poſſet
And curd, like Aygre droppings into Milke,
The thin and wholſome blood: ſo did it mine;
And a moſt inſtant Tetter bak'd about,
Moſt Lazar-like, with vile and loathſome cruſt,
All my ſmooth Body.
Thus was I, ſleeping, by a Brothers hand,
Of Life, of Crowne, and Queene at once diſpatcht;
Cut off euen in the Bloſſomes of my Sinne,
Vnhouzzled, diſappointed, vnnaneld,
No reckoning made, but ſent to my account
With all my imperfections on my head;
Oh horrible, Oh horrible, moſt horrible:
If thou haſt nature in thee beare it not;
Let not the Royall Bed of Denmarke be
A Couch for Luxury and damned Inceſt.
But howſoeuer thou purſueſt this Act,
Taint not thy mind; nor let thy Soule contriue
Againſt thy Mother ought; leaue her to heauen,
And to thoſe Thornes that in her boſome lodge,
To pricke and ſting her. Fare thee well at once;
The Glow-worme ſhowes the Matine to be neere,
And gins to pale his vneffectuall Fire:
Adue, adue, *Hamlet*: remember me. *Exit.*

Ham. Oh all you hoſt of Heauen! Oh Earth; what els?
And ſhall I couple Hell? Oh fie: hold my heart;
And you my ſinnewes, grow not inſtant Old;
But beare me ſtiffely vp: Remember thee?
I, thou poore Ghoſt, while memory holds a ſeate
In this diſtracted Globe: Remember thee?
Yea, from the Table of my Memory,
Ile wipe away all triuiall fond Records,
All ſawes of Bookes, all formes, all preſures paſt,
That youth and obſeruation coppied there;
And thy Commandment all alone ſhall liue
Within the Booke and Volume of my Braine,
Vnmixt with baſer matter; yes, yes, by Heauen:
Oh moſt pernicious woman!
Oh Villaine, Villaine, ſmiling damned Villaine!
My Tables, my Tables; meet it is I ſet it downe,
That one may ſmile, and ſmile and be a Villaine;
At leaſt I'm ſure it may be ſo in Denmarke;
So Vnckle there you are: now to my word;
It is; Adue, Adue, Remember me: I haue ſworn't.

Hor. & Mar. within. My Lord, my Lord.

Enter Horatio and Marcellus.

Mar. Lord *Hamlet.*

Hor. Heauen ſecure him.

Mar. So be it.

Hor. Illo, ho, ho, my Lord.

Ham. Hillo, ho, ho, boy; come bird, come.

Mar. How iſt't my Noble Lord?

Hor. What newes, my Lord?

Ham. Oh wonderfull!

Hor. Good my Lord tell it.

Ham. No you'l reueale it.

Hor. Not I, my Lord, by Heauen.

Mar. Nor I, my Lord.

Ham. How ſay you then, would heart of man once (think it?
But you'l be ſecret?

Both. I, by Heau'n, my Lord.

Ham. There's nere a villaine dwelling in all Denmarke
But hee's an arrant knaue.

Hor. There needs no Ghoſt my Lord, come from the Graue, to tell vs this.

Ham. Why right, you are i'th' right;
And ſo, without more circumſtance at all,
I hold it fit that we ſhake hands, and part:
You, as your buſines and deſires ſhall point you:
For euery man ha's buſineſſe and deſire,
Such as it is: and for mine owne poore part,
Looke you, Ile goe pray.

Hor. Theſe are but wild and hurling words, my Lord.

Ham. I'm ſorry they offend you heartily:
Yes faith, heartily.

Hor. There's no offence my Lord.

Ham. Yes, by Saint *Patricke*, but there is my Lord,
And much offence too, touching this Viſion heere:
It is an honeſt Ghoſt, that let me tell you:
For your deſire to know what is betweene vs,
O'remaſter't as you may. And now good friends,
As you are Friends, Schollers and Soldiers,
Giue me one poore requeſt.

Hor. What is't my Lord? we will.

Ham. Neuer make known what you haue ſeen to night.

Both. My Lord, we will not.

Ham. Nay, but ſwear't.

Hor. Infaith my Lord, not I.

Mar. Nor I my Lord: in faith.

Ham. Vpon my ſword.

Marcell. We haue ſworne my Lord already.

Ham. Indeed, vpon my ſword, Indeed.

Gho. Sweare. *Ghoſt cries vnder the Stage.*

Ham. Ah ha boy, ſayeſt thou ſo. Art thou there truepenny? Come one you here this fellow in the ſelleredge
Conſent to ſweare.

Hor. Propoſe the Oath my Lord.

Ham. Neuer to ſpeake of this that you haue ſeene.
Sweare by my ſword.

Gho. Sweare.

Ham. *Hic & vbique?* Then wee'l ſhift for grownd,
Come hither Gentlemen,
And lay your hands againe vpon my ſword,
Neuer to ſpeake of this that you haue heard:
Sweare by my Sword.

Gho. Sweare.

Ham. Well ſaid old Mole, can'ſt worke i'th' ground ſo (faſt?
A worthy Pioner, once more remoue good friends.

Hor. Oh day and night: but this is wondrous ſtrange.

Ham. And therefore as a ſtranger giue it welcome.
There are more things in Heauen and Earth, *Horatio*,
Then are dream't of in our Philoſophy But come,
Here as before, neuer ſo helpe you mercy,
How ſtrange or odde ſo ere I beare my ſelfe;
(As I perchance heereafter ſhall thinke meet
To put an Anticke diſpoſition on:)
That you at ſuch time ſeeing me, neuer ſhall
With Armes encombred thus, or thus, head ſhake;
Or by pronouncing of ſome doubtfull Phraſe;
As well, we know, or we could and if we would,
Or if we liſt to ſpeake; or there be and if there might,
Or ſuch ambiguous giuing out to note,

That

That you know ought of me; this not to doe:
So grace and mercy at your most neede helpe you:
Sweare.
Ghost. Sweare.
Ham. Rest, rest perturbed Spirit: so Gentlemen,
With all my loue I doe commend me to you;
And what so poore a man as *Hamlet* is,
May doe t'expresse his loue and friending to you,
God willing shall not lacke: let vs goe in together,
And still your fingers on your lippes I pray,
The time is out of ioynt: Oh cursed spight,
That euer I was borne to set it right.
Nay, come let's goe together. *Exeunt.*

Actus Secundus.

Enter Polonius, and Reynoldo.

Polon. Giue him his money, and these notes *Reynoldo.*
Reynol. I will my Lord.
Polon. You shall doe maruels wisely: good *Reynoldo*,
Before you visite him you make inquiry
Of his behauiour.
Reynol. My Lord, I did intend it.
Polon. Marry, well said;
Very well said. Looke you Sir,
Enquire me first what Danskers are in Paris;
And how, and who; what meanes; and where they keepe:
What company, at what expence: and finding
By this encompassement and drift of question,
That they doe know my sonne: Come you more neerer
Then your particular demands will touch it,
Take you as 'twere some distant knowledge of him,
And thus I know his father and his friends,
And in part him. Doe you marke this *Reynoldo?*
Reynol. I, very well my Lord.
Polon. And in part him, but you may say not well;
But if't be hee I meane, hees very wilde;
Addicted so and so; and there put on him
What forgeries you please: marry, none so ranke,
As may dishonour him; take heed of that:
But Sir, such wanton, wild, and vsuall slips,
As are Companions noted and most knowne
To youth and liberty.
Reynol. As gaming my Lord.
Polon. I, or drinking, fencing, swearing,
Quarelling, drabbiug. You may goe so farre.
Reynol. My Lord that would dishonour him.
Polon. Faith no, as you may season it in the charge;
You must not put another scandall on him,
That hee is open to Incontinencie;
That's not my meaning: but breath his faults so quaintly,
That they may seeme the taints of liberty;
The flash and out-breake of a fiery minde,
A sauagenes in vnreclaim'd bloud of generall assault.
Reynol. But my good Lord.
Polon. Wherefore should you doe this?
Reynol. I my Lord, I would know that.
Polon. Marry Sir, heere's my drift,
And I belieue it is a fetch of warrant:
You laying these slight sulleyes on my Sonne,
As 'twere a thing a little soil'd i'th' working: (sound,
Marke you your party in conuerse; him you would
Hauing euer seene. In the prenominate crimes,
The youth you breath of guilty, be assur'd
He closes with you in this consequence:
Good sir, or so, or friend, or Gentleman.
According to the Phrase and the Addition,
Of man and Country.
Reynol. Very good my Lord.
Polon. And then Sir does he this?
He does: what was I about to say?
I was about to say somthing: where did I leaue?
Reynol. At closes in the consequence:
At friend, or so, and Gentleman.
Polon. At closes in the consequence, I marry,
He closes with you thus. I know the Gentleman,
I saw him yesterday, or tother day;
Or then or then, with such and such; and as you say,
There was he gaming, there o'retooke in's Rouse,
There falling out at Tennis; or perchance,
I saw him enter such a house of saile;
Videlicet, a Brothell, or so forth. See you now;
Your bait of falshood, takes this Cape of truth;
And thus doe we of wisedome and of reach
With windlesses, and with assaies of Bias,
By indirections finde directions out:
So by my former Lecture and aduice
Shall you my Sonne; you haue me, haue you not?
Reynol. My Lord I haue.
Polon. God buy you; fare you well.
Reynol. Good my Lord.
Polon. Obserue his inclination in your selfe.
Reynol. I shall my Lord.
Polon. And let him plye his Musicke.
Reynol. Well, my Lord. *Exit.*

Enter Ophelia.

Polon. Farewell:
How now *Ophelia*, what's the matter?
Ophe. Alas my Lord, I haue beene so affrighted.
Polon. With what, in the name of Heauen?
Ophe. My Lord, as I was sowing in my Chamber,
Lord *Hamlet* with his doublet all vnbrac'd,
No hat vpon his head, his stockings foul'd,
Vngartred, and downe giued to his Anckle,
Pale as his shirt, his knees knocking each other,
And with a looke so pitious in purport,
As if he had been loosed out of hell,
To speake of horrors: he comes before me.
Polon. Mad for thy Loue?
Ophe. My Lord, I doe not know: but truly I do feare it.
Polon. What said he?
Ophe. He tooke me by the wrist, and held me hard;
Then goes he to the length of all his arme;
And with his other hand thus o're his brow,
He fals to such perusall of my face,
As he would draw it. Long staid he so,
At last, a little shaking of mine Arme:
And thrice his head thus wauing vp and downe;
He rais'd a sigh, so pittious and profound,
That it did seeme to shatter all his bulke,
And end his being. That done, he lets me goe,
And with his head ouer his shoulders turn'd,
He seem'd to finde his way without his eyes,
For out adores he went without their helpe;
And to the last, bended their light on me.
Polon. Goe with me, I will goe seeke the King,
This is the very extasie of Loue,
Whose violent property foredoes it selfe,
And

And leads the will to desperate Vndertakings,
As oft as any passion vnder Heauen,
That does afflict our Natures. I am sorrie,
What haue you giuen him any hard words of late?

Ophe. No my good Lord: but as you did command,
I did repell his Letters, and deny'de
His accesse to me.

Pol. That hath made him mad.
I am sorrie that with better speed and iudgement
I had not quoted him. I feare he did but trifle,
And meant to wracke thee: but beshrew my iealousie:
It seemes it is as proper to our Age,
To cast beyond our selues in our Opinions,
As it is common for the yonger sort
To lacke discretion. Come, go we to the King,
This must be knowne, ẇ being kept close might moue
More greefe to hide, then hate to vtter loue. *Exeunt.*

Scena Secunda.

Enter King, Queene, Rosincrane, and Guildensterne Cumalijs.

King. Welcome deere *Rosincrance* and *Guildensterne.*
Moreouer, that we much did long to see you,
The neede we haue to vse you, did prouoke
Our hastie sending. Something haue you heard
Of *Hamlets* transformation: so I call it,
Since not th'exterior, nor the inward man
Resembles that it was. What it should bee
More then his Fathers death, that thus hath put him
So much from th'vnderstanding of himselfe,
I cannot deeme of. I intreat you both,
That being of so young dayes brought vp with him:
And since so Neighbour'd to his youth, and humour,
That you vouchsafe your rest heere in our Court
Some little time: so by your Companies
To draw him on to pleasures, and to gather
So much as from Occasions you may gleane,
That open'd lies within our remedie.

Qu. Good Gentlemen, he hath much talk'd of you,
And sure I am, two men there are not liuing,
To whom he more adheres. If it will please you
To shew vs so much Gentrie, and good will,
As to expend your time with vs a-while,
For the supply and profit of our Hope,
Your Visitation shall receiue such thankes
As fits a Kings remembrance.

Rosin. Both your Maiesties
Might by the Soueraigne power you haue of vs,
Put your dread pleasures, more into Command
Then to Entreatie.

Guil. We both obey,
And here giue vp our selues, in the full bent,
To lay our Seruices freely at your feete,
To be commanded.

King. Thankes *Rosincrance*, and gentle *Guildensterne.*

Qu. Thankes *Guildensterne* and gentle *Rosincrance.*
And I beseech you instantly to visit
My too much changed Sonne.
Go some of ye,
And bring the Gentlemen where *Hamlet* is.

Guil. Heauens make our presence and our practises
Pleasant and helpfull to him. *Exit.*

Queene. Amen.

Enter Polonius.

Pol. Th'Ambassadors from Norwey, my good Lord,
Are ioyfully return'd.

King. Thou still hast bin the Father of good Newes.

Pol. Haue I, my Lord? Assure you, my good Liege,
I hold my dutie, as I hold my Soule,
Both to my God, one to my gracious King:
And I do thinke, or else this braine of mine
Hunts not the traile of Policie, so sure
As I haue vs'd to do: that I haue found
The very cause of *Hamlets* Lunacie.

King. Oh speake of that, that I do long to heare.

Pol. Giue first admittance to th'Ambassadors,
My Newes shall be the Newes to that great Feast.

King. Thy selfe do grace to them, and bring them in.
He tels me my sweet Queene, that he hath found
The head and sourse of all your Sonnes distemper.

Qu. I doubt it is no other, but the maine,
His Fathers death, and our o're-hasty Marriage.

Enter Polonius, Voltumand, and Cornelius.

King. Well, we shall sift him. Welcome good Frends:
Say *Voltumand*, what from our Brother Norwey?

Volt. Most faire returne of Greetings, and Desires.
Vpon our first, he sent out to suppresse
His Nephewes Leuies, which to him appear'd
To be a preparation 'gainst the Poleak:
But better look'd into, he truly found
It was against your Highnesse, whereat greeued,]
That so his Sicknesse, Age, and Impotence
Was falsely borne in hand, sends out Arrests
On *Fortinbras*, which he (in breefe) obeyes,
Receiues rebuke from Norwey: and in fine,
Makes Vow before his Vnkle, neuer more
To giue th'assay of Armes against your Maiestie.
Whereon old Norwey, ouercome with ioy,
Giues him three thousand Crownes in Annuall Fee,
And his Commission to imploy those Soldiers
So leuied as before, against the Poleak:
With an intreaty heerein further shewne,
That it might please you to giue quiet passe
Through your Dominions, for his Enterprize,
On such regards of safety and allowance,
As therein are set downe.

King. It likes vs well:
And at our more consider'd time wee'l read,
Answer, and thinke vpon this Businesse.
Meane time we thanke you, for your well-tooke Labour.
Go to your rest, at night wee'l Feast together.
Most welcome home. *Exit Ambass.*

Pol. This businesse is very well ended.
My Liege, and Madam, to expostulate
What Maiestie should be, what Dutie is,
Why day is day; night, night; and time is time.
Were nothing but to waste Night, Day, and Time.
Therefore, since Breuitie is the Soule of Wit,
And tediousnesse, the limbes and outward flourishes,
I will be breefe. Your Noble Sonne is mad:
Mad call I it; for to define true Madnesse,
What is't, but to be nothing else but mad.
But let that go.

Qu. More matter, with lesse Art.

Pol. Madam, I sweare I vse no Art at all:
That he is mad, 'tis true: 'Tis true 'tis pittie,
And pittie it is true: A foolish figure,
But farewell it: for I will vse no Art.

Mad

Mad let vs grant him then: and now remaines
That we finde out the cause of this effect,
Or rather say, the cause of this defect;
For this effect defectiue, comes by cause,
Thus it remaines, and the remainder thus. Perpend,
I haue a daughter: haue, whil'st she is mine,
Who in her Dutie and Obedience, marke,
Hath giuen me this: now gather, and surmise.

The Letter.

To the Celestiall, and my Soules Idoll, the most beautified Ophelia.

That's an ill Phrase, a vilde Phrase, beautified is a vilde Phrase: but you shall heare these in her excellent white bosome, these.

Qu. Came this from *Hamlet* to her.

Pol. Good Madam stay awhile, I will be faithfull.

Doubt thou, the Starres are fire,
Doubt, that the Sunne doth moue:
Doubt Truth to be a Lier,
But neuer Doubt, I loue.

O deere Ophelia, I am ill at these Numbers: I haue not Art to reckon my grones; but that I loue thee best, oh most Best beleeue it. Adieu.

Thine euermore most deere Lady, whilst this Machine is to him, Hamlet.

This in Obedience hath my daughter shew'd me:
And more aboue hath his soliciting,
As they fell out by Time, by Meanes, and Place,
All giuen to mine eare.

King. But how hath she receiu'd his Loue?

Pol. What do you thinke of me?

King. As of a man, faithfull and Honourable.

Pol. I wold faine proue so. But what might you think?
When I had seene this hot loue on the wing,
As I perceiued it, I must tell you that
Before my Daughter told me, what might you
Or my deere Maiestie your Queene heere, think,
If I had playd the Deske or Table-booke,
Or giuen my heart a winking, mute and dumbe,
Or look'd vpon this Loue, with idle sight,
What might you thinke? No, I went round to worke,
And (my yong Mistris) thus I did bespeake
Lord *Hamlet* is a Prince out of thy Starre,
This must not be: and then, I Precepts gaue her,
That she should locke her selfe from his Resort,
Admit no Messengers, receiue no Tokens:
Which done, she tooke the Fruites of my Aduice,
And he repulsed. A short Tale to make,
Fell into a Sadnesse, then into a Fast,
Thence to a Watch, thence into a Weaknesse,
Thence to a Lightnesse, and by this declension
Into the Madnesse whereon now he raues,
And all we waile for.

King. Do you thinke 'tis this?

Qu. It may be very likely.

Pol. Hath there bene such a time, I'de fain know that,
That I haue possitiuely said, 'tis so,
When it prou'd otherwise?

King. Not that I know.

Pol. Take this from this; if this be otherwise,
If Circumstances leade me, I will finde
Where truth is hid, though it were hid indeede
Within the Center.

King. How may we try it further?

Pol. You know sometimes
He walkes foure houres together, heere
In the Lobby.

Qu. So he ha's indeed.

Pol. At such a time Ile loose my Daughter to him,
Be you and I behinde an Arras then,
Marke the encounter: If he loue her not,
And be not from his reason falne thereon;
Let me be no Assistant for a State,
And keepe a Farme and Carters.

King. We will try it.

Enter Hamlet reading on a Booke.

Qu. But looke where sadly the poore wretch
Comes reading.

Pol. Away I do beseech you, both away,
Ile boord him presently. *Exit King & Queen.*
Oh giue me leaue. How does my good Lord *Hamlet*?

Ham. Well, God-a-mercy.

Pol. Do you know me, my Lord?

Ham. Excellent, excellent well: y'are a Fishmonger.

Pol. Not I my Lord.

Ham. Then I would you were so honest a man.

Pol. Honest, my Lord?

Ham. I sir, to be honest as this world goes, is to bee one man pick'd out of two thousand.

Pol. That's very true, my Lord.

Ham. For if the Sun breed Magots in a dead dogge, being a good kissing Carrion——
Haue you a daughter?

Pol. I haue my Lord.

Ham. Let her not walke i'th'Sunne: Conception is a blessing, but not as your daughter may conceiue. Friend looke too't.

Pol. How say you by that? Still harping on my daughter: yet he knew me not at first; he said I was a Fishmonger: he is farre gone, farre gone: and truly in my youth, I suffred much extreamity for loue: very neere this. Ile speake to him againe. What do you read my Lord?

Ham. Words, words, words.

Pol. What is the matter, my Lord?

Ham. Betweene who?

Pol. I meane the matter you meane, my Lord.

Ham. Slanders Sir: for the Satyricall slaue saies here, that old men haue gray Beards; that their faces are wrinkled: their eyes purging thicke Amber, or Plum-Tree Gumme: and that they haue a plentifull locke of Wit, together with weake Hammes. All which Sir, though I most powerfully, and potently beleeue; yet I holde it not Honestie to haue it thus set downe: For you your selfe Sir, should be old as I am, if like a Crab you could go backward.

Pol. Though this be madnesse,
Yet there is Method in't: will you walke
Out of the ayre my Lord?

Ham. Into my Graue?

Pol. Indeed that is out o'th'Ayre:
How pregnant (sometimes) his Replies are?
A happinesse,
That often Madnesse hits on,
Which Reason and Sanitie could not
So prosperously be deliuer'd of.
I will leaue him,
And sodainely contriue the meanes of meeting
Betweene him, and my daughter.
My Honourable Lord, I will most humbly
Take my leaue of you.

Ham. You cannot Sir take from me any thing, that I will more willingly part withall, except my life, my life.

Polon. Fare you well my Lord.

Ham. Theſe tedious old fooles.

Polon. You goe to ſeeke my Lord *Hamlet*; there hee is.

Enter Roſincran and Guildenſterne.

Roſin. God ſaue you Sir.

Guild. Mine honour'd Lord?

Roſin. My moſt deare Lord?

Ham. My excellent good friends? How do'ſt thou *Guildenſterne*? Oh, *Roſincrane*; good Lads: How doe ye both?

Roſin. As the indifferent Children of the earth.

Guild. Happy, in that we are not ouer-happy: on Fortunes Cap, we are not the very Button.

Ham. Nor the Soales of her Shoo?

Roſin. Neither my Lord.

Ham. Then you liue about her waſte, or in the middle of her fauour?

Guil. Faith, her priuates, we.

Ham. In the ſecret parts of Fortune? Oh, moſt true: ſhe is a Strumpet. What's the newes?

Roſin. None my Lord; but that the World's growne honeſt.

Ham. Then is Doomeſday neere: But your newes is not true. Let me queſtion more in particular: what haue you my good friends, deſerued at the hands of Fortune, that ſhe ſends you to Priſon hither?

Guil. Priſon, my Lord?

Ham. Denmark's a Priſon.

Roſin. Then is the World one.

Ham. A goodly one, in which there are many Confines, Wards, and Dungeons; *Denmarke* being one o'th' worſt.

Roſin. We thinke not ſo my Lord.

Ham. Why then 'tis none to you; for there is nothing either good or bad, but thinking makes it ſo: to me it is a priſon.

Roſin. Why then your Ambition makes it one: 'tis too narrow for your minde.

Ham. O God, I could be bounded in a nutſhell, and count my ſelfe a King of infinite ſpace; were it not that I haue bad dreames.

Guil. Which dreames indeed are Ambition: for the very ſubſtance of the Ambitious, is meerely the ſhadow of a Dreame.

Ham. A dreame it ſelfe is but a ſhadow.

Roſin. Truely, and I hold Ambition of ſo ayry and light a quality, that it is but a ſhadowes ſhadow.

Ham. Then are our Beggers bodies; and our Monarchs and out-ſtretcht Heroes the Beggers Shadowes: ſhall wee to th' Court: for, by my fey I cannot reaſon?

Both. Wee'l wait vpon you.

Ham. No ſuch matter. I will not ſort you with the reſt of my ſeruants: for to ſpeake to you like an honeſt man: I am moſt dreadfully attended; but in the beaten way of friendſhip. What make you at *Elſonower?*

Roſin. To viſit you my Lord, no other occaſion.

Ham. Begger that I am, I am euen poore in thankes; but I thanke you: and ſure deare friends my thanks are too deare a halfepeny; were you not ſent for? Is it your owne inclining? Is it a free viſitation? Come, deale iuſtly with me: come, come; nay ſpeake.

Guil. What ſhould we ſay my Lord?

Ham. Why any thing. But to the purpoſe; you were ſent for; and there is a kinde confeſſion in your lookes; which your modeſties haue not craft enough to color, I know the good King & Queene haue ſent for you.

Roſin. To what end my Lord?

Ham. That you muſt teach me: but let mee coniure you by the rights of our fellowſhip, by the conſonancy of our youth, by the Obligation of our euer-preſerued loue, and by what more deare, a better propoſer could charge you withall; be euen and direct with me, whether you were ſent for or no.

Roſin. What ſay you?

Ham. Nay then I haue an eye of you: if you loue me hold not off.

Guil. My Lord, we were ſent for.

Ham. I will tell you why; ſo ſhall my anticipation preuent your diſcouery of your ſecricie to the King and Queene: moult no feather, I haue of late, but wherefore I know not, loſt all my mirth, forgone all cuſtome of exerciſe; and indeed, it goes ſo heauenly with my diſpoſition; that this goodly frame the Earth, ſeemes to me a ſterrill Promontory; this moſt excellent Canopy the Ayre, look you, this braue ore-hanging, this Maieſticall Roofe, fretted with golden fire: why, it appeares no other thing to mee, then a foule and peſtilent congregation of vapours. What a piece of worke is a man! how Noble in Reaſon? how infinite in faculty? in forme and mouing how expreſſe and admirable? in Action, how like an Angel? in apprehenſion, how like a God? the beauty of the world, the Parragon of Animals; and yet to me, what is this Quinteſſence of Duſt? Man delights not me; no, nor Woman neither; though by your ſmiling you ſeeme to ſay ſo.

Roſin. My Lord, there was no ſuch ſtuffe in my thoughts.

Ham. Why did you laugh, when I ſaid, Man delights not me?

Roſin. To thinke, my Lord, if you delight not in Man, what Lenton entertainment the Players ſhall receiue from you: wee coated them on the way, and hither are they comming to offer you Seruice.

Ham. He that playes the King ſhall be welcome; his Maieſty ſhall haue Tribute of mee: the aduenturous Knight ſhal vſe his Foyle and Target: the Louer ſhall not ſigh *gratis*, the humorous man ſhall end his part in peace: the Clowne ſhall make thoſe laugh whoſe lungs are tickled a'th' ſere: and the Lady ſhall ſay her minde freely; or the blanke Verſe ſhall halt for't: what Players are they?

Roſin. Euen thoſe you were wont to take delight in the Tragedians of the City.

Ham. How chances it they trauaile? their reſidence both in reputation and profit was better both wayes.

Roſin. I thinke their Inhibition comes by the meanes of the late Innouation?

Ham. Doe they hold the ſame eſtimation they did when I was in the City? Are they ſo follow'd?

Roſin. No indeed, they are not.

Ham. How comes it? doe they grow ruſty?

Roſin. Nay, their indeauour keepes in the wonted pace; But there is Sir an ayrie of Children, little Yaſes, that crye out on the top of queſtion; and are moſt tyrannically clap't for't: theſe are now the

faſhi-

faſhion, and ſo be-ratled the common Stages (ſo they call them) that many wearing Rapiers, are affraide of Gooſe-quils, and dare ſcarſe come thither.

Ham. What are they Children? Who maintains 'em? How are they eſcoted? Will they purſue the Quality no longer then they can ſing? Will they not ſay afterwards if they ſhould grow themſelues to common Players (as it is like moſt if their meanes are not better) their Writers do them wrong, to make them exclaim againſt their owne Succeſſion.

Roſin. Faith there ha's bene much to do on both ſides: and the Nation holds it no ſinne, to tarre them to Controuerſie. There was for a while, no mony bid for argument, vnleſſe the Poet and the Player went to Cuffes in the Queſtion.

Ham. Is't poſſible?

Guild. Oh there ha's beene much throwing about of Braines.

Ham, Do the Boyes carry it away?

Roſin. I that they do my Lord, *Hercules* & his load too.

Ham. It is not ſtrange: for mine Vnckle is King of Denmarke, and thoſe that would make mowes at him while my Father liued; giue twenty, forty, an hundred Ducates a peece, for his picture in Little. There is ſomething in this more then Naturall, if Philoſophie could finde it out.

Flouriſh for the Players.

Guil. There are the Players.

Ham. Gentlemen, you are welcom to *Elſonower*: your hands, come: The appurtenance of Welcome, is Faſhion and Ceremony. Let me comply with you in the Garbe, leſt my extent to the Players (which I tell you muſt ſhew fairely outward) ſhould more appeare like entertainment then yours. You are welcome: but my Vnckle Father, and Aunt Mother are deceiu'd.

Guil. In what my deere Lord?

Ham. I am but mad North, North-Weſt: when the Winde is Southerly, I know a Hawke from a Handſaw.

Enter Polonius.

Pol. Well be with you Gentlemen.

Ham. Hearke you *Guildenſterne*, and you too: at each eare a hearer: that great Baby you ſee there, is not yet out of his ſwathing clouts.

Roſin. Happily he's the ſecond time come to them: for they ſay, an old man is twice a childe.

Ham. I will Propheſie. Hee comes to tell me of the Players. Mark it, you ſay right Sir: for a Monday morning 'twas ſo indeed.

Pol. My Lord, I haue Newes to tell you.

Ham. My Lord, I haue Newes to tell you. When *Roſſius* an Actor in Rome——

Pol. The Actors are come hither my Lord.

Ham. Buzze, buzze.

Pol. Vpon mine Honor.

Ham. Then can each Actor on his Aſſe———

Polon. The beſt Actors in the world, either for Tragedie, Comedie, Hiſtorie, Paſtorall: Paſtoricall-Comicall-Hiſtoricall-Paſtorall: Tragicall-Hiſtoricall: Tragicall-Comicall-Hiſtoricall-Paſtorall: Scene indiuible, or Poem vnlimited. *Seneca* cannot be too heauy, nor *Plautus* too light, for the law of Writ, and the Liberty. Theſe are the onely men.

Ham. O *Iephta* Iudge of Iſrael, what a Treaſure had'ſt thou?

Pol. What a Treaſure had he, my Lord?

Ham. Why one faire Daughter, and no more, The which he loued paſſing well.

Pol. Still on my Daughter.

Ham. Am I not i'th'right old *Iephta*?

Polon. If you call me *Iephta* my Lord, I haue a daughter that I loue paſſing well.

Ham. Nay that followes not.

Polon. What followes then, my Lord?

Ha. Why, As by lot, God wot: and then you know, It came to paſſe, as moſt like it was: The firſt rowe of the *Pons Chanſon* will ſhew you more. For looke where my Abridgements come.

Enter foure or fiue Players.

Y'are welcome Maſters, welcome all. I am glad to ſee thee well: Welcome good Friends. O my olde Friend? Thy face is valiant ſince I ſaw thee laſt: Com'ſt thou to beard me in Denmarke? What, my yong Lady and Miſtris? Byrlady your Ladiſhip is neerer Heauen then when I ſaw you laſt, by the altitude of a Choppine. Pray God your voice like a peece of vncurrant Gold be not crack'd within the ring. Maſters, you are all welcome: wee'l e'ne to't like French Faulconers, flie at any thing we ſee: wee'l haue a Speech ſtraight. Come giue vs a taſt of your quality: come, a paſſionate ſpeech.

1. *Play.* What ſpeech, my Lord?

Ham. I heard thee ſpeak me a ſpeech once, but it was neuer Acted: or if it was, not aboue once, for the Play I remember pleas'd not the Million, 'twas *Cauiarie* to the Generall: but it was (as I receiu'd it, and others, whoſe iudgement in ſuch matters, cried in the top of mine) an excellent Play; well digeſted in the Scoenes, ſet downe with as much modeſtie, as cunning. I remember one ſaid, there was no Sallets in the lines, to make the matter ſauoury; nor no matter in the phraſe, that might indite the Author of affectation, but cal'd it an honeſt method. One cheefe Speech in it, I cheefely lou'd, 'twas *Æneas* Tale to *Dido*, and thereabout of it eſpecially, where he ſpeaks of *Priams* ſlaughter. If it liue in your memory, begin at this Line, let me ſee, let me ſee: The rugged *Pyrrhus* like th'*Hyrcanian* Beaſt. It is not ſo: it begins with *Pyrrhus*

The rugged *Pyrrhus*, he whoſe Sable Armes
Blacke as his purpoſe, did the night reſemble
When he lay couched in the Ominous Horſe,
Hath now this dread and blacke Complexion ſmear'd
With Heraldry more diſmall: Head to foote
Now is he to take Geulles, horridly Trick'd
With blood of Fathers, Mothers, Daughters, Sonnes,
Bak'd and impaſted with the parching ſtreets,
That lend a tyrannous, and damned light
To their vilde Murthers, roaſted in wrath and fire,
And thus o're-ſized with coagulate gore,
VVith eyes like Carbuncles, the helliſh *Pyrrhus*
Old Grandſire *Priam* ſeekes.

Pol. Fore God, my Lord, well ſpoken, with good accent, and good diſcretion.

1. *Player.* Anon he findes him,
Striking too ſhort at Greekes. His anticke Sword,
Rebellious to his Arme, lyes where it falles
Repugnant to command: vnequall match,
Pyrrhus at *Priam* driues, in Rage ſtrikes wide:
But with the whiffe and winde of his fell Sword,
Th'vnnerued Father fals. Then ſenſeleſſe Illium,
Seeming to feele his blow, with flaming top
Stoopes to his Bace, and with a hideous craſh
Takes priſoner *Pyrrhus* eare. For loe, his Sword
Which was declining on the Milkie head
Of Reuerend *Priam*, ſeem'd i'th'Ayre to ſticke:

So

So as a painted Tyrant *Pyrrhus* ſtood,
And like a Newtrall to his will and matter, did nothing.
But as we often ſee againſt ſome ſtorme,
A ſilence in the Heauens, the Racke ſtand ſtill,
The bold windes ſpeechleſſe, and the Orbe below
As huſh as death : Anon the dreadfull Thunder
Doth rend the Region. So after *Pyrrhus* pauſe,
A ro wſed Vengeance ſets him new a-worke,
And neuer did the Cyclops hammers fall
On Mars his Armours, forg'd for proofe Eterne,
With leſſe remorſe then *Pyrrhus* bleeding ſword
Now falles on *Priam.*
Out, out, thou Strumpet-Fortune, all you Gods,
In generall Synod take away her power :
Breake all the Spokes and Fallies from her wheele,
And boule the round Naue downe the hill of Heauen,
As low as to the Fiends.

Pol. This is too long.

Ham. It ſhall to'th Barbars, with your beard. Prythee ſay on : He's for a Iigge, or a tale of Baudry, or hee ſleepes. Say on ; come to *Hecuba.*

1.*Play.* But who, O who, had ſeen the inobled Queen.

Ham. The inobled Queene?

Pol. That's good : Inobled Queene is good.

1.*Play.* Run bare-foot vp and downe,
Threatning the flame
With Biſſon Rheume : A clout about that head,
Where late the Diadem ſtood, and for a Robe
About her lanke and all ore-teamed Loines,
A blanket in th'Alarum of feare caught vp.
Who this had ſeene, with tongue in Venome ſteep'd,
'Gainſt Fortunes State, would Treaſon haue pronounc'd?
But if the Gods themſelues did ſee her then,
When ſhe ſaw *Pyrrhus* make malicious ſport
In mincing with his Sword her Husbands limbes,
The inſtant Burſt of Clamour that ſhe made
(Vnleſſe things mortall moue them not at all)
Would haue made milche the Burning eyes of Heauen,
And paſſion in the Gods.

Pol. Looke where he ha's not turn'd his colour, and ha's teares in's eyes. Pray you no more.

Ham. 'Tis well, Ile haue thee ſpeake out the reſt, ſoone. Good my Lord, will you ſee the Players wel beſtow'd. Do ye heare, let them be well vs'd : for they are the Abſtracts and breefe Chronicles of the time. After your death, you were better haue a bad Epitaph, then their ill report while you liued.

Pol. My Lord, I will vſe them according to their deſart.

Ham. Gods bodykins man, better. Vſe euerie man after his deſart, and who ſhould ſcape whipping : vſe them after your own Honor and Dignity. The leſſe they deſerue, the more merit is in your bountie. Take them in.

Pol. Come ſirs. *Exit Polon.*

Ham. Follow him Friends:wee'l heare a play to morrow. Doſt thou heare me old Friend, can you play the murther of *Gonzago*?

Play. I my Lord.

Ham. Wee'l ha't to morrow night. You could for a need ſtudy a ſpeech of ſome doſen or ſixteene lines, which I would ſet downe, and inſert in't? Could ye not?

Play. I my Lord.

Ham. Very well. Follow that Lord, and looke you mock him not. My good Friends, Ile leaue you til night you are welcome to *Elſonower*?

Roſin. Good my Lord. *Exeunt.*

Manet Hamlet.

Ham. I ſo, God buy'ye : Now I am alone.
Oh what a Rogue and Peſant ſlaue am I?
Is it not monſtrous that this Player heere,
But in a Fixion, in a dreame of Paſſion,
Could force his ſoule ſo to his whole conceit,
That from her working, all his viſage warm'd;
Teares in his eyes, diſtraction in's Aſpect,
A broken voyce, and his whole Function ſuiting
With Formes, to his Conceit? And all for nothing?
For *Hecuba*?
What's *Hecuba* to him, or he to *Hecuba*,
That he ſhould weepe for her? What would he doe,
Had he the Motiue and the Cue for paſſion
That I haue? He would drowne the Stage with teares,
And cleaue the generall eare with horrid ſpeech :
Make mad the guilty, and apale the free,
Confound the ignorant, and amaze indeed,
The very faculty of Eyes and Eares. Yet I,
A dull and muddy-metled Raſcall, peake
Like Iohn a-dreames, vnpregnant of my cauſe,
And can ſay nothing : No, not for a King,
Vpon whoſe property, and moſt deere life,
A damn'd defeate was made. Am I a Coward?
Who calles me Villaine? breakes my pate a-croſſe?
Pluckes off my Beard, and blowes it in my face?
Tweakes me by'th'Noſe? giues me the Lye i'th'Throate,
As deepe as to the Lungs? Who does me this?
Ha? Why I ſhould take it : for it cannot be,
But I am Pigeon-Liuer'd, and lacke Gall
To make Oppreſſion bitter, or ere this,
I ſhould haue fatted all the Region Kites
With this Slaues Offall, bloudy : a Bawdy villaine,
Remorſeleſſe, Treacherous, Letcherous, kindles villaine!
Oh Vengeance!
Who? What an Aſſe am I? I ſure, this is moſt braue,
That I, the Sonne of the Deere murthered,
Prompted to my Reuenge by Heauen, and Hell,
Muſt (like a Whore) vnpacke my heart with words,
And fall a Curſing like a very Drab,
A Scullion? Fye vpon't : Foh. About my Braine.
I haue heard, that guilty Creatures ſitting at a Play,
Haue by the very cunning of the Scoene,
Bene ſtrooke ſo to the ſoule, that preſently
They haue proclaim'd their Malefactions.
For Murther, though it haue no tongue, will ſpeake
With moſt myraculous Organ. Ile haue theſe Players,
Play ſomething like the murder of my Father,
Before mine Vnkle. Ile obſerue his lookes,
Ile tent him to the quicke : If he but blench
I know my courſe. The Spirit that I haue ſeene
May be the Diuell, and the Diuel hath power
T'aſſume a pleaſing ſhape, yea and perhaps
Out of my Weakneſſe, and my Melancholly,
As he is very potent with ſuch Spirits,
Abuſes me to damne me. Ile haue grounds
More Relatiue then this : The Play's the thing,
Wherein Ile catch the Conſcience of the King. *Exit*

Enter King, Queene, Polonius, Ophelia, Roſincrance, Guildenſtern, and Lords.

King. And can you by no drift of circumſtance
Get from him why he puts on this Confuſion :
Grating ſo harſhly all his dayes of quiet

With

With turbulent and dangerous Lunacy.
Rosin. He does confeffe he feeles himfelfe diftracted,
But from what caufe he will by no meanes fpeake.
Guil. Nor do we finde him forward to be founded,
But with a crafty Madneffe keepes aloofe:
When we would bring him on to fome Confeffion
Of his true ftate.
Qu. Did he receiue you well?
Rosin. Moft like a Gentleman.
Guild. But with much forcing of his difpofition.
Rosin. Niggard of queftion, but of our demands
Moft free in his reply.
Qu. Did you affay him to any paftime?
Rosin. Madam, it fo fell out, that certaine Players
We ore-wrought on the way: of thefe we told him,
And there did feeme in him a kinde of ioy
To heare of it: They are about the Court,
And (as I thinke) they haue already order
This night to play before him.
Pol. 'Tis moft true:
And he befeech'd me to intreate your Maiefties
To heare, and fee the matter.
King. With all my heart, and it doth much content me
To heare him fo inclin'd. Good Gentlemen,
Giue him a further edge, and driue his purpofe on
To thefe delights.
Rosin. We fhall my Lord. *Exeunt.*
King. Sweet *Gertrude* leaue vs too,
For we haue clofely fent for *Hamlet* hither,
That he, as'twere by accident, may there
Affront *Ophelia.* Her Father, and my felfe (lawful efpials)
Will fo beftow our felues, that feeing vnfeene
We may of their encounter frankely iudge,
And gather by him, as he is behaued,
If't be th'affliction of his loue, or no.
That thus he fuffers for.
Qu. I fhall obey you,
And for your part *Ophelia*, I do wifh
That your good Beauties be the happy caufe
Of *Hamlets* wildeneffe: fo fhall I hope your Vertues
Will bring him to his wonted way againe,
To both your Honors.
Ophe. Madam, I wifh it may.
Pol. *Ophelia*, walke you heere. Gracious fo pleafe ye
We will beftow our felues: Reade on this booke,
That fhew of fuch an exercife may colour
Your lonelineffe. We are oft too blame in this,
'Tis too much prou'd, that with Deuotions vifage,
And pious Action, we do furge o're
The diuell himfelfe.
King. Oh 'tis true:
How fmart a lafh that fpeech doth giue my Confcience?
The Harlots Cheeke beautied with plaift'ring Art
Is not more vgly to the thing that helpes it,
Then is my deede, to my moft painted word.
Oh heauie burthen!
Pol. I heare him comming, let's withdraw my Lord.
Exeunt.

Enter Hamlet.

Ham. To be, or not to be, that is the Queftion:
Whether 'tis Nobler in the minde to fuffer
The Slings and Arrowes of outragious Fortune,
Or to take Armes againft a Sea of troubles,
And by oppofing end them: to dye, to fleepe
No more; and by a fleepe, to fay we end
The Heart-ake, and the thoufand Naturall fhockes
That Flefh is heyre too? 'Tis a confummation
Deuoutly to be wifh'd. To dye to fleepe,
To fleepe, perchance to Dreame; I, there's the rub,
For in that fleepe of death, what dreames may come,
When we haue fhuffel'd off this mortall coile,
Muft giue vs pawfe. There's the refpect
That makes Calamity of fo long life:
For who would beare the Whips and Scornes of time,
The Oppreffors wrong, the poore mans Contumely,
The pangs of difpriz'd Loue, the Lawes delay,
The infolence of Office, and the Spurnes
That patient merit of the vnworthy takes,
When he himfelfe might his *Quietus* make
With a bare Bodkin? Who would thefe Fardles beare
To grunt and fweat vnder a weary life,
But that the dread of fomething after death,
The vndifcouered Countrey, from whofe Borne
No Traueller returnes, Puzels the will,
And makes vs rather beare thofe illes we haue,
Then flye to others that we know not of.
Thus Confcience does make Cowards of vs all,
And thus the Natiue hew of Refolution
Is ficklied o're, with the pale caft of Thought,
And enterprizes of great pith and moment,
With this regard their Currants turne away,
And loofe the name of Action. Soft you now,
The faire *Ophelia*? Nimph, in thy Orizons
Be all my finnes remembred.
Ophe. Good my Lord,
How does your Honor for this many a day?
Ham. I humbly thanke you: well, well, well.
Ophe. My Lord, I haue Remembrances of yours,
That I haue longed long to re-deliuer.
I pray you now, receiue them.
Ham. No, no, I neuer gaue you ought.
Ophe. My honor'd Lord, I know right well you did,
And with them words of fo fweet breath compos'd,
As made the things more rich, then perfume left:
Take thefe againe, for to the Noble minde
Rich gifts wax poore, when giuers proue vnkinde.
There my Lord.
Ham. Ha, ha: Are you honeft?
Ophe. My Lord.
Ham. Are you faire?
Ophe. What meanes your Lordfhip?
Ham. That if you be honeft and faire, your Honefty fhould admit no difcourfe to your Beautie.
Ophe. Could Beautie my Lord, haue better Comerce then your Honeftie?
Ham. I trulie: for the power of Beautie, will fooner transforme Honeftie from what it is, to a Bawd, then the force of Honeftie can tranflate Beautie into his likeneffe. This was fometime a Paradox, but now the time giues it proofe. I did loue you once.
Ophe. Indeed my Lord, you made me beleeue fo.
Ham. You fhould not haue beleeued me. For vertue cannot fo innocculate our old ftocke, but we fhall rellifh of it. I loued you not.
Ophe. I was the more deceiued.
Ham. Get thee to a Nunnerie. Why would'ft thou be a breeder of Sinners? I am my felfe indifferent honeft, but yet I could accufe me of fuch things, that it were better my Mother had not borne me. I am very prowd, reuengefull, Ambitious, with more offences at my becke, then I haue thoughts to put them in imagination, to giue them fhape, or time to acte them in. What fhould fuch Fel-

Fellowes as I do, crawling betweene Heauen and Earth. We are arrant Knaues all, beleeue none of vs. Goe thy wayes to a Nunnery. Where's your Father?

Ophe. At home, my Lord.

Ham. Let the doores be ſhut vpon him, that he may play the Foole no way, but in's owne houſe. Farewell.

Ophe. O helpe him, you ſweet Heauens.

Ham. If thou doeſt Marry, Ile giue thee this Plague for thy Dowrie. Be thou as chaſt as Ice, as pure as Snow, thou ſhalt not eſcape Calumny. Get thee to a Nunnery. Go, Farewell. Or if thou wilt needs Marry, marry a fool: for Wiſe men know well enough, what monſters you make of them. To a Nunnery go, and quickly too. Farwell.

Ophe. O heauenly Powers, reſtore him.

Ham. I haue heard of your pratlings too wel enough. God has giuen you one pace, and you make your ſelfe another: you gidge, you amble, and you liſpe, and nickname Gods creatures, and make your Wantonneſſe, your Ignorance. Go too, Ile no more on't, it hath made me mad. I ſay, we will haue no more Marriages. Thoſe that are married already, all but one ſhall liue, the reſt ſhall keep as they are. To a Nunnery, go. *Exit Hamlet.*

Ophe. O what a Noble minde is heere o're-throwne?
The Courtiers, Soldiers, Schollers: Eye, tongue, ſword,
Th'expectanſie and Roſe of the faire State,
The glaſſe of Faſhion, and the mould of Forme,
Th'obſeru'd of all Obſeruers, quite, quite downe.
Haue I of Ladies moſt deiect and wretched,
That ſuck'd the Honie of his Muſicke Vowes:
Now ſee that Noble, and moſt Soueraigne Reaſon,
Like ſweet Bels iangled out of tune, and harſh,
That vnmatch'd Forme and Feature of blowne youth,
Blaſted with extaſie. Oh woe is me,
T'haue ſeene what I haue ſeene: ſee what I ſee.

Enter King, and Polonius.

King. Loue? His affections do not that way tend,
Nor what he ſpake, though it lack'd Forme a little,
Was not like Madneſſe. There's ſomething in his ſoule?
O're which his Melancholly ſits on brood,
And I do doubt the hatch, and the diſcloſe
Will be ſome danger, which to preuent
I haue in quicke determination
Thus ſet it downe. He ſhall with ſpeed to England
For the demand of our neglected Tribute:
Haply the Seas and Countries different
With variable Obiects, ſhall expell
This ſomething ſetled matter in his heart:
Whereon his Braines ſtill beating, puts him thus
From faſhion of himſelfe. What thinke you on't?

Pol. It ſhall do well. But yet do I beleeue
The Origin and Commencement of this greefe
Sprung from neglected loue. How now *Ophelia?*
You neede not tell vs, what Lord *Hamlet* ſaide,
We heard it all. My Lord, do as you pleaſe,
But if you hold it fit after the Play,
Let his Queene Mother all alone intreat him
To ſhew his Greefes: let her be round with him,
And Ile be plac'd ſo, pleaſe you in the eare
Of all their Conference. If ſhe finde him not,
To England ſend him: Or confine him where
Your wiſedome beſt ſhall thinke.

King. It ſhall be ſo:
Madneſſe in great Ones, muſt not vnwatch'd go.
Exeunt.

Enter Hamlet, and two or three of the Players.

Ham. Speake the Speech I pray you, as I pronounc'd it to you trippingly on the Tongue: But if you mouth it, as many of your Players do, I had as liue the Town-Cryer had ſpoke my Lines: Nor do not ſaw the Ayre too much your hand thus, but vſe all gently; for in the verie Torrent, Tempeſt, and (as I may ſay) the Whirle-winde of Paſſion, you muſt acquire and beget a Temperance that may giue it Smoothneſſe. O it offends mee to the Soule, to ſee a robuſtious Pery-wig-pated Fellow, teare a Paſſion to tatters, to verie ragges, to ſplit the eares of the Groundlings: who (for the moſt part) are capeable of nothing, but inexplicable dumbe ſhewes, & noiſe: I could haue ſuch a Fellow whipt for o're-doing Termagant: it out-*Herod's Herod.* Pray you auoid it.

Player. I warrant your Honor.

Ham. Be not too tame neyther: but let your owne Diſcretion be your Tutor. Sute the Action to the Word, the Word to the Action, with this ſpeciall obſeruance: That you ore-ſtop not the modeſtie of Nature; for any thing ſo ouer-done, is frõ the purpoſe of Playing, whoſe end both at the firſt and now, was and is, to hold as 'twer the Mirrour vp to Nature; to ſhew Vertue her owne Feature, Scorne her owne Image, and the verie Age and Bodie of the Time, his forme and preſſure. Now, this ouer-done, or come tardie off, though it make the vnskillfull laugh, cannot but make the Iudicious greeue; The cenſure of the which One, muſt in your allowance o're-way a whole Theater of Others. Oh, there bee Players that I haue ſeene Play, and heard others praiſe, and that highly (not to ſpeake it prophanely) that neyther hauing the accent of Chriſtians, nor the gate of Chriſtian, Pagan, or Norman, haue ſo ſtrutted and bellowed, that I haue thought ſome of Natures Iouerney-men had made men, and not made them well, they imitated Humanity ſo abhominably.

Play. I hope we haue reform'd that indifferently with vs, Sir.

Ham. O reforme it altogether. And let thoſe that play your Clownes, ſpeake no more then is ſet downe for them. For there be of them, that will themſelues laugh, to ſet on ſome quantitie of barren Spectators to laugh too, though in the meane time, ſome neceſſary Queſtion of the Play be then to be conſidered: that's Villanous, & ſhewes a moſt pittifull Ambition in the Foole that vſes it. Go make you readie. *Exit Players.*

Enter Polonius, Roſincrance, and Guildenſterne.

How now my Lord,
Will the King heare this peece of Worke?

Pol. And the Queene too, and that preſently.

Ham. Bid the Players make haſt. *Exit Polonius.*
Will you two helpe to haſten them?

Both. We will my Lord. *Exeunt.*

Enter Horatio.

Ham. What hoa, *Horatio?*

Hora. Heere ſweet Lord, at your Seruice.

Ham. *Horatio*, thou art eene as iuſt a man
As ere my Conuerſation coap'd withall.

Hora. O my deere Lord.

Ham. Nay, do not thinke I flatter:
For what aduancement may I hope from thee,
That no Reuennew haſt, but thy good ſpirits

To

To feed & cloath thee. Why ſhold the poor be flatter'd?
No, let the Candied tongue, like abſurd pompe,
And crooke the pregnant Hindges of the knee,
Where thrift may follow faining? Doſt thou heare,
Since my deere Soule was Miſtris of my choyſe,
And could of men diſtinguiſh, her election
Hath ſeal'd thee for her ſelfe. For thou haſt bene
As one in ſuffering all, that ſuffers nothing.
A man that Fortunes buffets, and Rewards
Hath 'tane with equall Thankes. And bleſt are thoſe,
Whoſe Blood and Iudgement are ſo well co-mingled,
That they are not a Pipe for Fortunes finger,
To ſound what ſtop ſhe pleaſe. Giue me that man,
That is not Paſſions Slaue, and I will weare him
In my hearts Core: I, in my Heart of heart,
As I do thee. Something too much of this.
There is a Play to night before the King,
One Scœne of it comes neere the Circumſtance
Which I haue told thee, of my Fathers death.
I prythee, when thou ſee'ſt that Acte a-foot,
Euen with the verie Comment of my Soule
Obſerue mine Vnkle: If his occulted guilt,
Do not it ſelfe vnkennell in one ſpeech,
It is a damned Ghoſt that we haue ſeene:
And my Imaginations are as foule
As Vulcans Stythe. Giue him needfull note,
For I mine eyes will riuet to his Face:
And after we will both our iudgements ioyne,
To cenſure of his ſeeming.

Hora. Well my Lord.
If he ſteale ought the whil'ſt this Play is Playing,
And ſcape detecting, I will pay the Theft.

Enter King, Queene, Polonius, Ophelia, Roſincrance, Guildenſterne, and other Lords attendant, with his Guard carrying Torches. Daniſh March. Sound a Flouriſh.

Ham. They are comming to the Play: I muſt be idle. Get you a place.

King. How fares our Coſin *Hamlet*?

Ham. Excellent Ifaith, of the Camelions diſh: I eate the Ayre promiſe-cramm'd, you cannot feed Capons ſo.

King. I haue nothing with this anſwer *Hamlet*, theſe words are not mine.

Ham. No, nor mine. Now my Lord, you plaid once i'th'Vniuerſity, you ſay?

Polon. That I did my Lord, and was accounted a good Actor.

Ham. And what did you enact?

Pol. I did enact *Iulius Cæſar*, I was kill'd i'th'Capitol: *Brutus* kill'd me.

Ham. It was a bruite part of him, to kill ſo Capitall a Calfe there. Be the Players ready?

Roſin. I my Lord, they ſtay vpon your patience.

Qu. Come hither my good *Hamlet*, ſit by me.

Ha. No good Mother, here's Mettle more attractiue.

Pol. Oh ho, do you marke that?

Ham. Ladie, ſhall I lye in your Lap?

Ophe. No my Lord.

Ham. I meane, my Head vpon your Lap?

Ophe. I my Lord.

Ham. Do you thinke I meant Country matters?

Ophe. I thinke nothing, my Lord.

Ham. That's a faire thought to ly between Maids legs

Ophe. What is my Lord?

Ham. Nothing.

Ophe. You are merrie, my Lord?

Ham. Who I?

Ophe. I my Lord.

Ham. Oh God, your onely Iigge-maker: what ſhould a man do, but be merrie. For looke you how cheerefully my Mother lookes, and my Father dyed within's two Houres.

Ophe. Nay, 'tis twice two moneths, my Lord.

Ham. So long? Nay then let the Diuel weare blacke, for Ile haue a ſuite of Sables. Oh Heauens! dye two moneths ago, and not forgotten yet? Then there's hope, a great mans Memorie, may out-liue his life halfe a yeare: But byrlady he muſt builde Churches then: or elſe ſhall he ſuffer not thinking on, with the Hoby-horſſe, whoſe Epitaph is, For o, For o, the Hoby-horſe is forgot.

Hoboyes play. The dumbe ſhew enters.

Enter a King and Queene, very louingly; the Queene embracing him. She kneeles, and makes ſhew of Proteſtation vnto him. He takes her vp, and declines his head vpon her neck. Layes him downe vpon a Banke of Flowers. She ſeeing him a-ſleepe, leaues him. Anon comes in a Fellow, takes off his Crowne, kiſſes it, and powres poyſon in the Kings eares, and Exits. The Queene returnes, findes the King dead, and makes paſſionate Action. The Poyſoner, with ſome two or three Mutes comes in againe, ſeeming to lament with her. The dead body is carried away: The Poyſoner Wooes the Queene with Gifts, ſhe ſeemes loath and vnwilling awhile, but in the end, accepts his loue. Exeunt

Ophe. What meanes this, my Lord?

Ham. Marry this is Miching *Malicho*, that meanes Miſcheefe.

Ophe. Belike this ſhew imports the Argument of the Play?

Ham. We ſhall know by theſe Fellowes: the Players cannot keepe counſell, they'l tell all.

Ophe. Will they tell vs what this ſhew meant?

Ham. I, or any ſhew that you'l ſhew him. Bee not you aſham'd to ſhew, hee'l not ſhame to tell you what it meanes.

Ophe. You are naught, you are naught, Ile marke the Play.

Enter Prologue.

For vs, and for our Tragedie,
Heere ſtooping to your Clemencie:
We begge your hearing Patientlie.

Ham. Is this a Prologue, or the Poeſie of a Ring?

Ophe. 'Tis briefe my Lord.

Ham. As Womans loue.

Enter King and his Queene.

King. Full thirtie times hath Phœbus Cart gon round,
Neptunes ſalt Waſh, and *Tellus* Orbed ground:
And thirtie dozen Moones with borrowed ſheene,
About the World haue times twelue thirties beene,
Since loue our hearts, and *Hymen* did our hands
Vnite comutuall, in moſt ſacred Bands.

Bap. So many iournies may the Sunne and Moone
Make vs againe count o're, ere loue be done.
But woe is me, you are ſo ſicke of late,
So farre from cheere, and from your forme ſtate,
That I diſtruſt you: yet though I diſtruſt,
Diſcomfort you (my Lord) it nothing muſt:
For womens Feare and Loue, holds quantitie,

In

In neither ought, or in extremity:
Now what my loue is, proofe hath made you know,
And as my Loue is siz'd, my Feare is so.

King. Faith I must leaue thee Loue, and shortly too:
My operant Powers my Functions leaue to do:
And thou shalt liue in this faire world behinde,
Honour'd, belou'd, and haply, one as kinde.
For Husband shalt thou——

Bap. Oh confound the rest:
Such Loue, must needs be Treason in my brest:
In second Husband, let me be accurst,
None wed the second, but who kill'd the first.

Ham. Wormwood, Wormwood.

Bapt. The instances that second Marriage moue,
Are base respects of Thrift, but none of Loue.
A second time, I kill my Husband dead,
When second Husband kisses me in Bed.

King. I do beleeue you. Think what now you speak:
But what we do determine, oft we breake:
Purpose is but the slaue to Memorie,
Of violent Birth, but poore validitie:
Which now like Fruite vnripe stickes on the Tree,
But fall vnshaken, when they mellow bee.
Most necessary 'tis, that we forget
To pay our selues, what to our selues is debt:
What to our selues in passion we propose,
The passion ending, doth the purpose lose.
The violence of other Greefe or Ioy,
Their owne ennactors with themselues destroy:
Where Ioy most Reuels, Greefe doth most lament;
Greefe ioyes, Ioy greeues on slender accident.
This world is not for aye, nor 'tis not strange
That euen our Loues should with our Fortunes change.
For 'tis a question left vs yet to proue,
Whether Loue lead Fortune, or else Fortune Loue.
The great man downe, you marke his fauourites flies,
The poore aduanc'd, makes Friends of Enemies:
And hitherto doth Loue on Fortune tend,
For who not needs, shall neuer lacke a Frend:
And who in want a hollow Friend doth try,
Directly seasons him his Enemie.
But orderly to end, where I begun,
Our Willes and Fates do so contrary run,
That our Deuices still are ouerthrowne,
Our thoughts are ours, their ends none of our owne.
So thinke thou wilt no second Husband wed.
But die thy thoughts, when thy first Lord is dead.

Bap. Nor Earth to giue me food, nor Heauen light,
Sport and repose locke from me day and night:
Each opposite that blankes the face of ioy,
Meet what I would haue well, and it destroy:
Both heere, and hence, pursue me lasting strife,
If once a Widdow, euer I be Wife.

Ham. If she should breake it now.

King. 'Tis deepely sworne:
Sweet, leaue me heere a while,
My spirits grow dull, and faine I would beguile
The tedious day with sleepe. *Sleepes*

Qu. Sleepe rocke thy Braine,
And neuer come mischance betweene vs twaine. *Exit*

Ham. Madam, how like you this Play?

Qu. The Lady protests to much me thinkes.

Ham. Oh but shee'l keepe her word.

King. Haue you heard the Argument, is there no Offence in't?

Ham. No, no, they do but iest, poyson in iest, no Offence i'th'world.

King. What do you call the Play?

Ham. The Mouse-trap: Marry how? Tropically: This Play is the Image of a murder done in *Vienna: Gonzago* is the Dukes name, his wife *Baptista*: you shall see anon: 'tis a knauish peece of worke: But what o'that? Your Maiestie, and wee that haue free soules, it touches vs not: let the gall d iade winch: our withers are vnrung.

Enter Lucianus.

This is one *Lucianus* nephew to the King.

Ophe. You are a good Chorus, my Lord.

Ham. I could interpret betweene you and your loue: if I could see the Puppets dallying.

Ophe. You are keene my Lord, you are keene.

Ham. It would cost you a groaning, to take off my edge.

Ophe. Still better and worse.

Ham. So you mistake Husbands. Begin Murderer. Pox, leaue thy damnable Faces, and begin. Come, the croaking Rauen doth bellow for Reuenge.

Lucian. Thoughts blacke, hands apt,
Drugges fit, and Time agreeing:
Confederate season, else, no Creature seeing:
Thou mixture ranke, of Midnight Weeds collected,
With Hecats Ban, thrice blasted, thrice infected,
Thy naturall Magicke, and dire propertie,
On wholsome life, vsurpe immediately.

Powres the poyson in his eares.

Ham. He poysons him i'th'Garden for's estate: His name's *Gonzago*: the Story is extant and writ in choyce Italian. You shall see anon how the Murtherer gets the loue of *Gonzago's* wife.

Ophe. The King rises.

Ham. What, frighted with false fire.

Qu. How fares my Lord?

Pol. Giue o're the Play.

King. Giue me some Light. Away.

All. Lights, Lights, Lights. *Exeunt*

Manet Hamlet & Horatio.

Ham. Why let the strucken Deere go weepe,
The Hart vngalled play:
For some must watch, while some must sleepe;
So runnes the world away.
Would not this Sir, and a Forrest of Feathers, if the rest of my Fortunes turne Turke with me; with two Prouinciall Roses on my rac'd Shooes, get me a Fellowship in a crie of Players sir.

Hor. Halfe a share.

Ham. A whole one I,
For thou dost know: Oh *Damon* deere,
This Realme dismantled was of Ioue himselfe,
And now reignes heere.
A verie verie Paiocke.

Hora. You might haue Rim'd.

Ham. Oh good *Horatio*, Ile take the Ghosts word for a thousand pound. Did'st perceiue?

Hora. Verie well my Lord.

Ham. Vpon the talke of the poysoning?

Hora. I did verie well note him.

Enter Rosincrance and Guildensterne.

Ham. Oh, ha? Come some Musick. Come ẏ Recorders:
For if the King like not the Comedie,
Why then belike he likes it not perdie.
Come some Musicke.

Guild. Good my Lord, vouchsafe me a word with you.

Ham.

Ham. Sir, a whole Hiſtory.
Guild. The King, ſir.
Ham. I ſir, what of him?
Guild. Is in his retyrement, maruellous diſtemper'd.
Ham. With drinke Sir?
Guild. No my Lord, rather with choller.
Ham. Your wiſedome ſhould ſhew it ſelfe more richer, to ſignifie this to his Doctor: for for me to put him to his Purgation, would perhaps plundge him into farre more Choller.
Guild. Good my Lord put your diſcourſe into ſome frame, and ſtart not ſo wildely from my affayre.
Ham. I am tame Sir, pronounce.
Guild. The Queene your Mother, in moſt great affliction of ſpirit, hath ſent me to you.
Ham. You are welcome.
Guild. Nay, good my Lord, this courteſie is not of the right breed. If it ſhall pleaſe you to make me a wholſome anſwer, I will doe your Mothers command'ment: if not, your pardon, and my returne ſhall bee the end of my Buſineſſe.
Ham. Sir, I cannot.
Gnild. What, my Lord?
Ham. Make you a wholſome anſwere: my wits diſeas'd. But ſir, ſuch anſwers as I can make, you ſhal command: or rather you ſay, my Mother: therfore no more but to the matter. My Mother you ſay.
Roſin. Then thus ſhe ſayes: your behauior hath ſtroke her into amazement, and admiration.
Ham. Oh wonderfull Sonne, that can ſo aſtoniſh a Mother. But is there no ſequell at the heeles of this Mothers admiration?
Roſin. She deſires to ſpeake with you in her Cloſſet, ere you go to bed.
Ham. We ſhall obey, were ſhe ten times our Mother. Haue you any further Trade with vs?
Roſin. My Lord, you once did loue me.
Ham. So I do ſtill, by theſe pickers and ſtealers.
Roſin. Good my Lord, what is your cauſe of diſtemper? You do freely barre the doore of your owne Libertie, if you deny your greefes to your Friend.
Ham. Sir I lacke Aduancement.
Roſin. How can that be, when you haue the voyce of the King himſelfe, for your Succeſſion in Denmarke?
Ham. I, but while the graſſe growes, the Prouerbe is ſomething muſty.

Enter one with a Recorder.

O the Recorder. Let me ſee, to withdraw with you, why do you go about to recouer the winde of mee, as if you would driue me into a toyle?
Guild, O my Lord, if my Dutie be too bold, my loue is too vnmannerly.
Ham. I do not well vnderſtand that. Will you play vpon this Pipe?
Guild. My Lord, I cannot.
Ham. I pray you.
Guild. Beleeue me, I cannot.
Ham. I do beſeech you.
Guild. I know no touch of it, my Lord.
Ham. 'Tis as eaſie as lying: gouerne theſe Ventiges with your finger and thumbe, giue it breath with your mouth, and it will diſcourſe moſt excellent Muſicke. Looke you, theſe are the ſtoppes.
Guild. But theſe cannot I command to any vtterance of hermony, I haue not the skill.
Ham. Why looke you now, how vnworthy a thing you make of me: you would play vpon mee; you would ſeeme to know my ſtops: you would pluck out the heart of my Myſterie; you would ſound mee from my loweſt Note, to the top of my Compaſſe: and there is much Muſicke, excellent Voice, in this little Organe, yet cannot you make it. Why do you thinke, that I am eaſier to bee plaid on, then a Pipe? Call me what Inſtrument you will, though you can fret me, you cannot play vpon me. God bleſſe you Sir.

Enter Polonius.

Polon. My Lord; the Queene would ſpeak with you, and preſently.
Ham. Do you ſee that Clowd? that's almoſt in ſhape like a Camell.
Polon, By'th'Miſſe, and it's like a Camell indeed.
Ham. Me thinkes it is like a Weazell.
Polon. It is back'd like a Weazell.
Ham. Or like a Whale?
Polon. Verie like a Whale.
Ham. Then will I come to my Mother, by and by:
They foole me to the top of my bent.
I will come by and by.
Polon. I will ſay ſo. *Exit.*
Ham. By and by, is eaſily ſaid. Leaue me Friends:
'Tis now the verie witching time of night,
When Churchyards yawne, and Hell it ſelfe breaths out
Contagion to this world. Now could I drink hot blood,
And do ſuch bitter buſineſſe as the day
Would quake to looke on. Soft now, to my Mother:
Oh Heart, looſe not thy Nature; let not euer
The Soule of *Nero,* enter this firme boſome:
Let me be cruell, not vnnaturall,
I will ſpeake Daggers to her, but vſe none:
My Tongue and Soule in this be Hypocrites.
How in my words ſomeuer ſhe be ſhent,
To giue them Seales, neuer my Soule conſent.

Enter King, Roſincrance, and Guildenſterne.

King. I like him not, nor ſtands it ſafe with vs,
To let his madneſſe range. Therefore prepare you,
I your Commiſſion will forthwith diſpatch,
And he to England ſhall along with you:
The termes of our eſtate, may not endure
Hazard ſo dangerous as doth hourely grow
Out of his Lunacies.
Guild. We will our ſelues prouide:
Moſt holie and Religious feare it is
To keepe thoſe many many bodies ſafe
That liue and feede vpon your Maieſtie.
Roſin. The ſingle
And peculiar life is bound
With all the ſtrength and Armour of the minde,
To keepe it ſelfe from noyance: but much more,
That Spirit, vpon whoſe ſpirit depends and reſts
The liues of many, the ceaſe of Maieſtie
Dies not alone; but like a Gulfe doth draw
What's neere it, with it. It is a maſſie wheele
Fixt on the Somnet of the higheſt Mount,
To whoſe huge Spoakes, ten thouſand leſſer things
Are mortiz'd and adioyn'd: which when it falles,
Each ſmall annexment, pettie conſequence
Attends the boyſtrous Ruine. Neuer alone
Did the King ſighe, but with a generall grone.
King. Arme you, I pray you to this ſpeedie Voyage;
For we will Fetters put vpon this feare,

Which now goes too free-footed.
Both. We will haſte vs. *Exeunt Gent.*

Enter Polonius.

Pol. My Lord, he's going to his Mothers Cloſſet:
Behinde the Arras Ile conuey my ſelfe
To heare the Proceſſe. Ile warrant ſhee'l tax him home,
And as you ſaid, and wiſely was it ſaid,
'Tis meete that ſome more audience then a Mother,
Since Nature makes them partiall, ſhould o're-heare
The ſpeech of vantage. Fare you well my Liege,
Ile call vpon you ere you go to bed,
And tell you what I know.
King. Thankes deere my Lord.
Oh my offence is ranke, it ſmels to heauen,
It hath the primall eldeſt curſe vpon't,
A Brothers murther. Pray can I not,
Though inclination be as ſharpe as will:
My ſtronger guilt, defeats my ſtrong intent,
And like a man to double buſineſſe bound,
I ſtand in pauſe where I ſhall firſt begin,
And both neglect; what if this curſed hand
Were thicker then it ſelfe with Brothers blood,
Is there not Raine enough in the ſweet Heauens
To waſh it white as Snow? Whereto ſerues mercy,
But to confront the viſage of Offence?
And what's in Prayer, but this two-fold force,
To be fore-ſtalled ere we come to fall,
Or pardon'd being downe? Then Ile looke vp,
My fault is paſt. But oh, what forme of Prayer
Can ſerue my turne? Forgiue me my foule Murther:
That cannot be, ſince I am ſtill poſſeſt
Of thoſe effects for which I did the Murther.
My Crowne, mine owne Ambition, and my Queene:
May one be pardon'd, and retaine th'offence?
In the corrupted currants of this world,
Offences gilded hand may ſhoue by Iuſtice,
And oft 'tis ſeene, the wicked prize it ſelfe
Buyes out the Law; but 'tis not ſo aboue,
There is no ſhuffling, there the Action lyes
In his true Nature, and we our ſelues compell'd
Euen to the teeth and forehead of our faults,
To giue in euidence. What then? What reſts?
Try what Repentance can. What can it not?
Yet what can it, when one cannot repent?
Oh wretched ſtate! Oh boſome, blacke as death!
Oh limed ſoule, that ſtrugling to be free,
Art more ingag'd: Helpe Angels, make aſſay:
Bow ſtubborne knees, and heart with ſtrings of Steele,
Be ſoft as ſinewes of the new-borne Babe,
All may be well.

Enter Hamlet.

Ham. Now might I do it pat, now he is praying,
And now Ile doo't, and ſo he goes to Heauen,
And ſo am I reueng'd: that would be ſcann'd,
A Villaine killes my Father, and for that
I his foule Sonne, do this ſame Villaine ſend
To heauen. Oh this is hyre and Sallery, not Reuenge.
He tooke my Father groſſely, full of bread,
With all his Crimes broad blowne, as freſh as May,
And how his Audit ſtands, who knowes, ſaue Heauen:
But in our circumſtance and courſe of thought
'Tis heauie with him: and am I then reueng'd,
To take him in the purging of his Soule,
When he is fit and ſeaſon'd for his paſſage? No.
Vp Sword, and know thou a more horrid hent
When he is drunke aſleepe: or in his Rage,
Or in th'inceſtuous pleaſure of his bed,
At gaming, ſwearing, or about ſome acte
That ha's no relliſh of Saluation in't,
Then trip him, that his heeles may kicke at Heauen,
And that his Soule may be as damn'd aud blacke
As Hell, whereto it goes. My Mother ſtayes,
This Phyſicke but prolongs thy ſickly dayes. *Exit.*
King. My words flye vp, my thoughts remain below,
Words without thoughts, neuer to Heauen go. *Exit.*

Enter Queene and Polonius.

Pol. He will come ſtraight:
Looke you lay home to him,
Tell him his prankes haue been too broad to beare with,
And that your Grace hath ſcree'nd, and ſtoode betweene
Much heate, and him. Ile ſilence me e'ene heere:
Pray you be round with him.
Ham. within. Mother, mother, mother.
Qu. Ile warrant you, feare me not.
Withdraw, I heare him comming.

Enter Hamlet.

Ham. Now Mother, what's the matter?
Qu. *Hamlet*, thou haſt thy Father much offended.
Ham. Mother, you haue my Father much offended.
Qu. Come, come, you anſwer with an idle tongue.
Ham. Go, go, you queſtion with an idle tongue.
Qu. Why how now *Hamlet*?
Ham. Whats the matter now?
Qu. Haue you forgot me?
Ham. No by the Rood, not ſo:
You are the Queene, your Husbands Brothers wife,
But would you were not ſo. You are my Mother.
Qu. Nay, then Ile ſet thoſe to you that can ſpeake.
Ham. Come, come, and ſit you downe, you ſhall not boudge:
You go not till I ſet you vp a glaſſe,
Where you may ſee the inmoſt part of you?
Qu. What wilt thou do? thou wilt not murther me?
Helpe, helpe, hoa.
Pol. What hoa, helpe, helpe, helpe.
Ham. How now, a Rat? dead for a Ducate, dead.
Pol. Oh I am ſlaine. *Killes Polonius.*
Qu. Oh me, what haſt thou done?
Ham. Nay I know not, is it the King?
Qu. Oh what a raſh, and bloody deed is this?
Ham. A bloody deed, almoſt as bad good Mother,
As kill a King, and marrie with his Brother.
Qu. As kill a King?
Ham. I Lady, 'twas my word.
Thou wretched, raſh, intruding foole farewell,
I tooke thee for thy Betters, take thy Fortune,
Thou find'ſt to be too buſie, is ſome danger.
Leaue wringing of your hands, peace, ſit you downe,
And let me wring your heart, for ſo I ſhall
If it be made of penetrable ſtuffe;
If damned Cuſtome haue not braz'd it ſo,
That it is proofe and bulwarke againſt Senſe.
Qu. What haue I done, that thou dar'ſt wag thy tong,
In noiſe ſo rude againſt me?
Ham. Such an Act
That blurres the grace and bluſh of Modeſtie,
Cals Vertue Hypocrite, takes off the Roſe
From the faire forehead of an innocent loue,
And makes a bliſter there. Makes marriage vowes
As falſe as Dicers Oathes. Oh ſuch a deed,

As

As from the body of Contraction pluckes
The very soule, and sweete Religion makes
A rapsidie of words. Heauens face doth glow,
Yea this solidity and compound masse,
With tristfull visage as against the doome,
Is thought-sicke at the act.

Qu. Aye me; what act, that roares so lowd, & thunders in the Index.

Ham. Looke heere vpon this Picture, and on this,
The counterfet presentment of two Brothers:
See what a grace was seated on his Brow,
Hyperions curles, the front of Ioue himselfe,
An eye like Mars, to threaten or command
A Station, like the Herald Mercurie
New lighted on a heauen-kissing hill:
A Combination, and a forme indeed,
Where euery God did seeme to set his Seale,
To giue the world assurance of a man.
This was your Husband. Looke you now what followes.
Heere is your Husband, like a Mildew'd eare
Blasting his wholsom breath. Haue you eyes?
Could you on this faire Mountaine leaue to feed,
And batten on this Moore? Ha? Haue you eyes?
You cannot call it Loue: For at your age,
The hey-day in the blood is tame, it's humble,
And waites vpon the Iudgement: and what Iudgement
Would step from this, to this? What diuell was't,
That thus hath cousend you at hoodman-blinde?
O Shame! where is thy Blush? Rebellious Hell,
If thou canst mutine in a Matrons bones,
To flaming youth, let Vertue be as waxe,
And melt in her owne fire. Proclaime no shame,
When the compulsiue Ardure giues the charge,
Since Frost it selfe, as actiuely doth burne,
As Reason panders Will.

Qu. O *Hamlet*, speake no more.
Thou turn'st mine eyes into my very soule,
And there I see such blacke and grained spots,
As will not leaue their Tinct.

Ham. Nay, but to liue
In the ranke sweat of an enseamed bed,
Stew'd in Corruption; honying and making loue
Ouer the nasty Stye.

Qu. Oh speake to me, no more,
These words like Daggers enter in mine eares.
No more sweet *Hamlet*.

Ham. A Murderer, and a Villaine:
A Slaue, that is not twentieth patt the tythe
Of your precedent Lord. A vice of Kings,
A Cutpurse of the Empire and the Rule.
That from a shelfe, the precious Diadem stole,
And put it in his Pocket.

Qu. No more.

Enter Ghost.

Ham. A King of shreds and patches.
Saue me; and houer o're me with your wings
You heauenly Guards. What would you gracious figure?

Qu. Alas he's mad.

Ham. Do you not come your tardy Sonne to chide,
That laps't in Time and Passion, lets go by
Th'important acting of your dread command? Oh say.

Ghost. Do not forget: this Visitation
Is but to whet thy almost blunted purpose.
But looke, Amazement on thy Mother sits;
O step betweene her, and her fighting Soule,
Conceit in weakest bodies, strongest workes.
Speake to her *Hamlet*.

Ham. How is it with you Lady?

Qu. Alas, how is't with you?
That you bend your eye on vacancie,
And with their corporall ayre do hold discourse.
Forth at your eyes, your spirits wildely peepe,
And as the sleeping Soldiours in th'Alarme,
Your bedded haire, like life in excrements,
Start vp, and stand an end. Oh gentle Sonne,
Vpon the heate and flame of thy distemper
Sprinkle coole patience. Whereon do you looke?

Ham. On him, on him: look you how pale he glares,
His forme and cause conioyn'd, preaching to stones,
Would make them capeable. Do not looke vpon me,
Least with this pitteous action you conuert
My sterne effects: then what I haue to do,
Will want true colour; teares perchance for blood.

Qu. To who do you speake this?

Ham. Do you see nothing there?

Qu. Nothing at all, yet all that is I see.

Ham. Nor did you nothing heare?

Qu. No, nothing but our selues.

Ham. Why look you there: looke how it steals away:
My Father in his habite, as he liued,
Looke where he goes euen now out at the Portall. *Exit.*

Qu. This is the very coynage of your Braine,
This bodilesse Creation extasie is very cunning in.

Ham. Extasie?
My Pulse as yours doth temperately keepe time,
And makes as healthfull Musicke. It is not madnesse
That I haue vttered; bring me to the Test
And I the matter will re-word: which madnesse
Would gamboll from. Mother, for loue of Grace,
Lay not a flattering Vnction to your soule,
That not your trespasse, but my madnesse speakes:
It will but skin and filme the Vlcerous place,
Whil'st ranke Corruption mining all within,
Infects vnseene. Confesse your selfe to Heauen,
Repent what's past, auoyd what is to come,
And do not spred the Compost or the Weedes,
To make them ranke. Forgiue me this my Vertue,
For in the fatnesse of this pursie times,
Vertue it selfe, of Vice must pardon begge,
Yea courb, and woe, for leaue to do him good.

Qu. Oh *Hamlet*,
Thou hast cleft my heart in twaine.

Ham. O throw away the worser part of it,
And liue the purer with the other halfe.
Good night, but go not to mine Vnkles bed,
Assume a Vertue, if you haue it not, refraine to night,
And that shall lend a kinde of easinesse
To the next abstinence. Once more goodnight,
And when you are desirous to be blest,
Ile blessing begge of you. For this same Lord,
I do repent: but heauen hath pleas'd it so,
To punish me with this, and this with me,
That I must be their Scourge and Minister.
I will bestow him, and will answer well
The death I gaue him: so againe, good night.
I must be cruell, onely to be kinde;
Thus bad begins, and worse remaines behinde.

Qu. What shall I do?

Ham. Not this by no meanes that I bid you do:
Let the blunt King tempt you againe to bed,
Pinch Wanton on your cheeke, call you his Mouse,
And let him for a paire of reechie kisses,

Or padling in your necke with his damn'd Fingers,
Make you to rauell all this matter out,
That I essentially am not in madnesse,
But made in craft. 'Twere good you let him know,
For who that's but a Queene, faire, sober, wise,
Would from a Paddocke, from a Bat, a Gibbe,
Such deere concernings hide, Who would do so,
No in despight of Sense and Secrecie,
Vnpegge the Basket on the houses top:
Let the Birds flye, and like the famous Ape
To try Conclusions in the Basket, creepe
And breake your owne necke downe.

Qu. Be thou assur'd, if words be made of breath,
And breath of life: I haue no life to breath
What thou hast saide to me.

Ham. I must to England, you know that?

Qu. Alacke I had forgot: 'Tis so concluded on.

Ham. This man shall set me packing:
Ile lugge the Guts into the Neighbor roome,
Mother goodnight. Indeede this Counsellor
Is now most still, most secret, and most graue,
Who was in life, a foolish prating Knaue.
Come sir, to draw toward an end with you.
Good night Mother.

Exit Hamlet tugging in Polonius.

Enter King.

King. There's matters in these sighes.
These profound heaues
You must translate; Tis fit we vnderstand them.
Where is your Sonne?

Qu. Ah my good Lord, what haue I seene to night?

King. What *Gertrude?* How do's *Hamlet?*

Qu. Mad as the Seas, and winde, when both contend
Which is the Mightier, in his lawlesse fit
Behinde the Arras, hearing something stirre,
He whips his Rapier out, and cries a Rat, a Rat,
And in his brainish apprehension killes
The vnseene good old man.

King. Oh heauy deed:
It had bin so with vs had we beene there:
His Liberty is full of threats to all,
To you your selfe, to vs, to euery one.
Alas, how shall this bloody deede be answered?
It will be laide to vs, whose prouidence
Should haue kept short, restrain'd, and out of haunt,
This mad yong man. But so much was our loue,
We would not vnderstand what was most fit,
But like the Owner of a foule disease,
To keepe it from diuulging, let's it feede
Euen on the pith of life. Where is he gone?

Qu. To draw apart the body he hath kild,
O're whom his very madnesse like some Oare
Among a Minerall of Mettels base
Shewes it selfe pure. He weepes for what is done.

King. Oh *Gertrude*, come away:
The Sun no sooner shall the Mountaines touch,
But we will ship him hence, and this vilde deed,
We must with all our Maiesty and Skill
Both countenance, and excuse. *Enter Ros. & Guild.*
Ho *Guildenstern*:
Friends both go ioyne you with some further ayde:
Hamlet in madnesse hath *Polonius* slaine,
And from his Mother Clossets hath he drag'd him.
Go seeke him out, speake faire, and bring the body
Into the Chappell. I pray you hast in this. *Exit Gent.*
Come *Gertrude*, wee'l call vp our wisest friends,
To let them know both what we meane to do,
And what's vntimely done. Oh come away,
My soule is full of discord and dismay. *Exeunt.*

Enter Hamlet.

Ham. Safely stowed.

Gentlemen within. Hamlet, Lord *Hamlet*.

Ham. What noise? Who cals on *Hamlet?*
Oh heere they come. *Enter Ros. and Guildensterne.*

Ro. What haue you done my Lord with the dead body?

Ham. Compounded it with dust, whereto 'tis Kinne.

Rosin. Tell vs where 'tis, that we may take it thence,
And beare it to the Chappell.

Ham. Do not beleeue it.

Rosin. Beleeue what?

Ham. That I can keepe your counsell, and not mine owne. Besides, to be demanded of a Spundge, what replication should be made by the Sonne of a King.

Rosin. Take you me for a Spundge, my Lord?

Ham. I sir, that sokes vp the Kings Countenance, his Rewards, his Authorities (but such Officers do the King best seruice in the end. He keepes them like an Ape in the corner of his iaw, first mouth'd to be last swallowed, when he needes what you haue glean'd', it is but squeezing you, and Spundge you shall be dry againe.

Rosin. I vnderstand you not my Lord.

Ham. I am glad of it: a knauish speech sleepes in a foolish eare.

Rosin. My Lord, you must tell vs where the body is, and go with vs to the King.

Ham. The body is with the King, but the King is not with the body. The King, is a thing ———

Guild. A thing my Lord?

Ham. Of nothing: bring me to him, hide Fox, and all after. *Exeunt*

Enter King.

King. I haue sent to seeke him, and to find the bodie:
How dangerous is it that this man goes loose:
Yet must not we put the strong Law on him:
Hee's loued of the distracted multitude,
Who like not in their iudgement, but their eyes:
And where 'tis so, th'Offenders scourge is weigh'd
But neerer the offence: to beare all smooth, and euen,
This sodaine sending him away, must seeme
Deliberate pause, diseases desperate growne,
By desperate appliance are releeued,
Or not at all. *Enter Rosincrane.*
How now? What hath befalne?

Rosin. Where the dead body is bestow'd my Lord,
We cannot get from him.

King. But where is he?

Rosin. Without my Lord, guarded to know your pleasure.

King. Bring him before vs.

Rosin. Hoa, *Guildensterne?* Bring in my Lord.

Enter Hamlet and Guildensterne.

King. Now *Hamlet*, where's *Polonius?*

Ham. At Supper.

King. At Supper? Where?

Ham. Not where he eats, but where he is eaten, a certaine conuocation of wormes are e'ne at him. Your worm is your onely Emperor for diet. We fat all creatures else to fat vs, and we fat our selfe for Magots. Your fat King, and your leane Begger is but variable seruice to dishes, but to one Table that's the end.

King. What dost thou meane by this?

Ham.

Ham. Nothing but to ſhew you how a King may go a Progreſſe through the guts of a Begger.

King. Where is *Polonius*.

Ham. In heauen, ſend thither to ſee. If your Meſſenger finde him not there, ſeeke him i'th other place your ſelfe: but indeed, if you finde him not this moneth, you ſhall noſe him as you go vp the ſtaires into the Lobby.

King. Go ſeeke him there.

Ham. He will ſtay till ye come.

K. Hamlet, this deed of thine, for thine eſpecial ſafety
Which we do tender, as we deerely greeue
For that which thou haſt done, muſt ſend thee hence
With fierie Quickneſſe. Therefore prepare thy ſelfe,
The Barke is readie, and the winde at helpe,
Th'Aſſociates tend, and euery thing at bent
For England.

Ham. For England?

King. I *Hamlet*.

Ham. Good.

King. So is it, if thou knew'ſt our purpoſes.

Ham. I ſee a Cherube that ſee's him: but come, for England. Farewell deere Mother.

King. Thy louing Father *Hamlet*.

Hamlet. My Mother: Father and Mother is man and wife: man & wife is one fleſh, and ſo my mother. Come, for England. *Exit*

King. Follow him at foote,
Tempt him with ſpeed aboord:
Delay it not, Ile haue him hence to night.
Away, for euery thing is Seal'd and done
That elſe leanes on th'Affaire, pray you make haſt.
And England, if my loue thou holdſt at ought,
As my great power thereof may giue thee ſenſe,
Since yet thy Cicatrice lookes raw and red
After the Daniſh Sword, and thy free awe
Payes homage to vs; thou maiſt not coldly ſet
Our Soueraigne Proceſſe, which imports at full
By Letters coniuring to that effect
The preſent death of *Hamlet*. Do it England,
For like the Hecticke in my blood he rages,
And thou muſt cure me: Till I know 'tis done,
How ere my happes, my ioyes were ne're begun. *Exit*

Enter Fortinbras with an Armie.

For. Go Captaine, from me greet the Daniſh King,
Tell him that by his licenſe, *Fortinbras*
Claimes the conueyance of a promis'd March
Ouer his Kingdome. You know the Rendeuous:
If that his Maieſty would ought with vs,
We ſhall expreſſe our dutie in his eye,
And let him know ſo.

Cap. I will doo't, my Lord.

For. Go ſafely on. *Exit.*

Enter Queene and Horatio.

Qu. I will not ſpeake with her.

Hor. She is importunate, indeed diſtract, her moode will needs be pittied.

Qu. What would ſhe haue?

Hor. She ſpeakes much of her Father; ſaies ſhe heares
There's trickes i'th'world, and hems, and beats her heart,
Spurnes enuiouſly at Strawes, ſpeakes things in doubt,
That carry but halfe ſenſe: Her ſpeech is nothing,
Yet the vnſhaped vſe of it doth moue
The hearers to Collection; they ayme at it,
And botch the words vp fit to their owne thoughts,
Which as her winkes, and nods, and geſtures yeeld them,
Indeed would make one thinke there would be thought,
Though nothing ſure, yet much vnhappily.

Qu. 'Twere good ſhe were ſpoken with,
For ſhe may ſtrew dangerous coniectures
In ill breeding minds. Let her come in.
To my ſicke ſoule (as ſinnes true Nature is)
Each toy ſeemes Prologue, to ſome great amiſſe,
So full of Artleſſe iealouſie is guilt,
It ſpill's it ſelfe, in fearing to be ſpilt.

Enter Ophelia diſtracted.

Ophe. Where is the beauteous Maieſty of Denmark.

Qu. How now *Ophelia*?

Ophe. *How ſhould I your true loue know from another one?*
By his Cockle hat and ſtaffe, and his Sandal ſhoone.

Qu. Alas ſweet Lady: what imports this Song?

Ophe. Say you? Nay pray you marke.
He is dead and gone Lady, he is dead and gone,
At his head a graſſe-greene Turfe, at his heeles a ſtone.

Enter King.

Qu Nay but *Ophelia*.

Ophe. Pray you marke.
White his Shrow'd as the Mountaine Snow.

Qu. Alas, looke heere my Lord.

Ophe. *Larded with ſweet flowers:*
Which bewept to the graue did not go,
With true-loue ſhowres.

King. How do ye, pretty Lady?

Ophe. Well, God dil'd you. They ſay the Owle was a Bakers daughter. Lord, wee know what we are, but know not what we may be. God be at your Table.

King. Conceit vpon her Father.

Ophe. Pray you let's haue no words of this: but when they aske you what it meanes, ſay you this:
To morrow is S. Valentines day, all in the morning betime,
And I a Maid at your Window, to be your Valentine.
Then vp he roſe, & don'd his clothes, & dupt the chamber dore,
Let in the Maid, that out a Maid, neuer departed more.

King. Pretty *Ophelia*.

Ophe. Indeed la? without an oath Ile make an end ont.
By gis, and by S. Charity,
Alacke, and fie for ſhame:
Yong men wil doo't, if they come too't,
By Cocke they are too blame.
Quoth ſhe before you tumbled me,
You promis'd me to Wed:
So would I ha done by yonder Sunne,
And thou hadſt not come to my bed.

King. How long hath ſhe bin this?

Ophe. I hope all will be well. We muſt bee patient, but I cannot chooſe but weepe, to thinke they ſhould lay him i'th'cold ground: My brother ſhall knowe of it, and ſo I thanke you for your good counſell. Come, my Coach: Goodnight Ladies: Goodnight ſweet Ladies: Goodnight, goodnight. *Exit.*

King. Follow her cloſe,
Giue her good watch I pray you:
Oh this is the poyſon of deepe greefe, it ſprings
All from her Fathers death. Oh *Gertrude, Gertrude*,
When ſorrowes comes, they come not ſingle ſpies,
But in Battaliaes. Firſt, her Father ſlaine,
Next your Sonne gone, and he moſt violent Author
Of his owne iuſt remoue: the people muddied,
Thicke and vnwholſome in their thoughts, and whiſpers
For good *Polonius* death; and we haue done but greenly
In hugger mugger to interre him. Poore *Ophelia*
Diuided from her ſelfe, and her faire Iudgement,

Without the which we are Pictures, or meere Beasts.
Last, and as much containing as all these,
Her Brother is in secret come from France,
Keepes on his wonder, keepes himselfe in clouds,
And wants not Buzzers to infect his eare
With pestilent Speeches of his Fathers death,
Where in necessitie of matter Beggard,
Will nothing sticke our persons to Arraigne
In eare and eare. O my deere *Gertrude*, this,
Like to a murdering Peece in many places,
Giues me superfluous death. *A Noise within.*

Enter a Messenger.

Qu. Alacke, what noyse is this?

King. Where are my *Switzers*?
Let them guard the doore. What is the matter?

Mes. Saue your selfe, my Lord.
The Ocean (ouer-peering of his List)
Eates not the Flats with more impittious haste
Then young *Laertes*, in a Riotous head,
Ore-beares your Officers, the rabble call him Lord,
And as the world were now but to begin,
Antiquity forgot, Custome not knowne,
The Ratifiers and props of euery word,
They cry choose we? *Laertes* shall be King,
Caps, hands, and tongues, applaud it to the clouds,
Laertes shall be King, *Laertes* King.

Qu. How cheerefully on the false Traile they cry,
Oh this is Counter you false Danish Dogges.

Noise within. Enter Laertes.

King. The doores are broke.

Laer. Where is the King, sirs? Stand you all without.

All. No, let's come in.

Laer. I pray you giue me leaue.

Al. We will, we will.

Laer. I thanke you: Keepe the doore.
Oh thou vilde King, giue me my Father.

Qu. Calmely good *Laertes*.

Laer. That drop of blood, that calmes
Proclaimes me Bastard:
Cries Cuckold to my Father, brands the Harlot
Euen heere betweene the chaste vnsmirched brow
Of my true Mother.

King. What is the cause *Laertes*,
That thy Rebellion lookes so Gyant-like?
Let him go *Gertrude*: Do not feare our person:
There's such Diuinity doth hedge a King,
That Treason can but peepe to what it would,
Acts little of his will. Tell me *Laertes*,
Why thou art thus Incenst? Let him go *Gertrude*.
Speake man.

Laer. Where's my Father?

King. Dead.

Qu. But not by him.

King. Let him demand his fill.

Laer. How came he dead? Ile not be Iuggel'd with.
To hell Allegeance: Vowes, to the blackest diuell.
Conscience and Grace, to the profoundest Pit.
I dare Damnation: to this point I stand,
That both the worlds I giue to negligence,
Let come what comes: onely Ile be reueng'd
Most throughly for my Father.

King. Who shall stay you?

Laer. My Will, not all the world,
And for my meanes, Ile husband them so well,
They shall go farre with little.

King. Good *Laertes*:
If you desire to know the certaintie
Of your deere Fathers death, if writ in your reuenge,
That Soop-stake you will draw both Friend and Foe,
Winner and Looser.

Laer. None but his Enemies.

King. Will you know them then.

La. To his good Friends, thus wide Ile ope my Armes:
And like the kinde Life-rend'ring Politician,
Repast them with my blood.

King. Why now you speake
Like a good Childe, and a true Gentleman.
That I am guiltlesse of your Fathers death,
And am most sensible in greefe for it,
It shall as leuell to your Iudgement pierce
As day do's to your eye.

A noise within. Let her come in.

Enter Ophelia.

Laer. How now? what noise is that?
Oh heate drie vp my Braines, teares seuen times salt,
Burne out the Sence and Vertue of mine eye.
By Heauen, thy madnesse shall be payed by waight,
Till our Scale turnes the beame. Oh Rose of May,
Deere Maid, kinde Sister, sweet *Ophelia*:
Oh Heauens, is't possible, a yong Maids wits,
Should be as mortall as an old mans life?
Nature is fine in Loue, and where 'tis fine,
It sends some precious instance of it selfe
After the thing it loues.

Ophe. They bore him bare fac'd on the Beer,
Hey non nony, nony, hey nony:
And on his graue raines many a teare,
Fare you well my Doue.

Laer. Had'st thou thy wits, and did'st perswade Reuenge, it could not moue thus.

Ophe. You must sing downe a-downe, and you call him a-downe-a. Oh, how the wheele becomes it? It is the false Steward that stole his masters daughter.

Laer. This nothings more then matter.

Ophe. There's Rosemary, that's for Remembraunce. Pray loue remember: and there is Paconcies, that's for Thoughts.

Laer. A document in madnesse, thoughts & remembrance fitted.

Ophe. There's Fennell for you, and Columbines: ther's Rew for you, and heere's some for me. Wee may call it Herbe-Grace a Sundaies: Oh you must weare your Rew with a difference. There's a Daysie, I would giue you some Violets, but they wither'd all when my Father dyed: They say, he made a good end;

For bonny sweet Robin is all my ioy.

Laer. Thought, and Affliction, Passion, Hell it selfe:
She turnes to Fauour, and to prettinesse.

Ophe. And will he not come againe,
And will he not come againe:
No, no, he is dead, go to thy Death-bed,
He neuer wil come againe.
His Beard as white as Snow,
All Flaxen was his Pole:
He is gone, he is gone, and we cast away mone,
Gramercy on his Soule.
And of all Christian Soules, I pray God.
God buy ye. *Exeunt Ophelia*

Laer. Do you see this, you Gods?

King. *Laertes*, I must common with your greefe,
Or you deny me right: go but apart,

Make

Make choice of whom your wisest Friends you will,
And they shall heare and iudge 'twixt you and me;
If by direct or by Colaterall hand
They finde vs touch'd, we will our Kingdome giue,
Our Crowne, our Life, and all that we call Ours
To you in satisfaction. But if not,
Be you content to lend your patience to vs,
And we shall ioyntly labour with your soule
To giue it due content.

Laer. Let this be so:
His meanes of death, his obscure buriall;
No Trophee, Sword, nor Hatchment o're his bones,
No Noble rite, nor formall ostentation,
Cry to be heard, as 'twere from Heauen to Earth,
That I must call in question.

King. So you shall:
And where th'offence is, let the great Axe fall.
I pray you go with me. *Exeunt*

Enter Horatio, with an Attendant.

Hora. What are they that would speake with me?

Ser. Saylors sir, they say they haue Letters for you.

Hor. Let them come in,
I do not know from what part of the world
I should be greeted, if not from Lord *Hamlet.*

Enter Saylor.

Say. God blesse you Sir.

Hor. Let him blesse thee too.

Say. Hee shall Sir, and't please him. There's a Letter for you Sir: It comes from th'Ambassadours that was bound for England, if your name be *Horatio,* as I am let to know it is.

Reads the Letter.

Horatio, *When thou shalt haue ouerlook'd this, giue these Fellowes some meanes to the King: They haue Letters for him. Ere we were two dayes old at Sea, a Pyrate of very Warlicke appointment gaue vs Chace. Finding our selues too slow of Saile, we put on a compelled Valour. In the Grapple, I boorded them: On the instant they got cleare of our Shippe, so I alone became their Prisoner. They haue dealt with mee, like Theeues of Mercy, but they knew what they did. I am to doe a good turne for them. Let the King haue the Letters I haue sent, and repaire thou to me with as much hast as thou wouldest flye death. I haue words to speake in your eare, will make thee dumbe, yet are they much too light for the bore of the Matter. These good Fellowes will bring thee where I am.* Rosincrance and Guildensterne, *bold their course for England. Of them I haue much to tell thee, Farewell.*

He that thou knowest thine,
Hamlet.

Come, I will giue you way for these your Letters,
And do't the speedier, that you may direct me
To him from whom you brought them. *Exit.*

Enter King and Laertes.

King. Now must your conscience my acquittance seal,
And you must put me in your heart for Friend,
Sith you haue heard, and with a knowing eare,
That he which hath your Noble Father slaine,
Pursued my life.

Eaer. It well appeares. But tell me,
Why you proceeded not against these feates,
So crimefull, and so Capitall in Nature,
As by your Safety, Wisedome, all things else,
You mainly were stirr'd vp?

King. O for two speciall Reasons,
Which may to you (perhaps) seeme much vnsinnowed,
And yet to me they are strong. The Queen his Mother,
Liues almost by his lookes: and for my selfe,
My Vertue or my Plague, be it either which,
She's so coniunctiue to my life and soule;
That as the Starre moues not but in his Sphere,
I could not but by her. The other Motiue,
Why to a publike count I might not go,
Is the great loue the generall gender beare him,
Who dipping all his Faults in their affection,
Would like the Spring that turneth Wood to Stone,
Conuert his Gyues to Graces. So that my Arrowes
Too slightly timbred for so loud a Winde,
Would haue reuerted to my Bow againe,
And not where I had arm'd them.

Laer. And so haue I a Noble Father lost,
A Sister driuen into desperate tearmes,
Who was (if praises may go backe againe)
Stood Challenger on mount of all the Age
For her perfections. But my reuenge will come.

King. Breake not your sleepes for that,
You must not thinke
That we are made of stuffe, so flat, and dull,
That we can let our Beard be shooke with danger,
And thinke it pastime. You shortly shall heare more,
I lou'd your Father, and we loue our Selfe,
And that I hope will teach you to imagine———

Enter a Messenger.

How now? What Newes?

Mes. Letters my Lord from *Hamlet.* This to your Maiesty: this to the Queene.

King. From *Hamlet?* Who brought them?

Mes. Saylors my Lord they say, I saw them not:
They were giuen me by *Claudio,* he receiu'd them.

King. *Laertes* you shall heare them:
Leaue vs. *Exit Messenger*

High and Mighty, you shall know I am set naked on your Kingdome. To morrow shall I begge leaue to see your Kingly Eyes. When I shall (first asking your Pardon thereunto) recount th'Occasions of my sodaine, and more strange returne.
Hamlet.

What should this meane? Are all the rest come backe?
Or is it some abuse? Or no such thing?

Laer. Know you the hand?

Kin. 'Tis *Hamlets* Character, naked and in a Postscript here he sayes alone: Can you aduise me?

Laer. I'm lost in it my Lord; but let him come,
It warmes the very sicknesse in my heart,
That I shall liue and tell him to his teeth;
Thus diddest thou.

Kin. If it be so *Laertes,* as how should it be so:
How otherwise will you be rul'd by me?

Laer. If so you'l not o'rerule me to a peace.

Kin. To thine owne peace: if he be now return'd,
As checking at his Voyage, and that he meanes
No more to vndertake it; I will worke him
To an exployt now ripe in my Deuice,
Vnder the which he shall not choose but fall;
And for his death no winde of blame shall breath,
But euen his Mother shall vncharge the practice,
And call it accident: Some two Monthes hence
Here was a Gentleman of *Normandy,*
I'ue seene my selfe, and seru'd against the French,
And they ran well on Horsebacke; but this Gallant

Had

Had witchcraft in't; he grew into his Seat,
And to ſuch wondrous doing brought his Horſe,
As had he beene encorps't and demy-Natur'd
With the braue Beaſt, ſo farre he paſt my thought,
That I in forgery of ſhapes and trickes,
Come ſhort of what he did.

Laer. A Norman was't?

Kin. A Norman.

Laer. Vpon my life *Lamound.*

Kin. The very ſame.

Laer. I know him well, he is the Brooch indeed,
And Iemme of all our Nation.

Kin. Hee mad confeſſion of you,
And gaue you ſuch a Maſterly report,
For Art and exerciſe in your defence;
And for your Rapier moſt eſpecially,
That he cryed out, t'would be a ſight indeed,
If one could match you Sir. This report of his
Did *Hamlet* ſo envenom with his Enuy,
That he could nothing doe but wiſh and begge,
Your ſodaine comming ore to play with him;
Now out of this.

Laer. Why out of this, my Lord?

Kin. Laertes was your Father deare to you?
Or are you like the painting of a ſorrow,
A face without a heart?

Laer. Why aske you this?

Kin. Not that I thinke you did not loue your Father,
But that I know Loue is begun by Time:
And that I ſee in paſſages of proofe,
Time qualifies the ſparke and fire of it:
Hamlet comes backe: what would you vndertake,
To ſhow your ſelfe your Fathers ſonne indeed,
More then in words?

Laer. To cut his throat i'th' Church.

Kin. No place indeed ſhould murder Sanctuarize;
Reuenge ſhould haue no bounds: but good *Laertes*
Will you doe this, keepe cloſe within your Chamber,
Hamlet return'd, ſhall know you are come home:
Wee'l put on thoſe ſhall praiſe your excellence,
And ſet a double varniſh on the fame
The Frenchman gaue you, bring you in fine together,
And wager on your heads, he being remiſſe,
Moſt generous, and free from all contriuing,
Will not peruſe the Foiles? So that with eaſe,
Or with a little ſhuffling, you may chooſe
A Sword vnbaited, and in a paſſe of practice,
Requit him for your Father.

Laer. I will doo't,
And for that purpoſe Ile annoint my Sword:
I bought an Vnction of a Mountebanke
So mortall, I but dipt a knife in it,
Where it drawes blood, no Cataplaſme ſo rare,
Collected from all Simples that haue Vertue
Vnder the Moone, can ſaue the thing from death,
That is but ſcratcht withall: Ile touch my point,
With this contagion, that if I gall him ſlightly,
It may be death.

Kin Let's further thinke of this,
Weigh what conuenience both of time and meanes
May fit vs to our ſhape, if this ſhould faile;
And that our drift looke through our bad performance,
'Twere better not aſſaid; therefore this Proiect
Should haue a backe or ſecond, that might hold,
If this ſhould blaſt in proofe: Soft, let me ſee
Wee'l make a ſolemne wager on your commings,
I ha't: when in your motion you are hot and dry,
As make your bowts more violent to the end,
And that he cals for drinke; Ile haue prepar'd him
A Challice for the nonce; whereon but ſipping,
If he by chance eſcape your venom'd ſtuck,
Our purpoſe may hold there; how ſweet Queene.

Enter Queene.

Queen. One woe doth tread vpon anothers heele,
So faſt they'l follow: your Siſter's drown'd *Laertes.*

Laer. Drown'd! O where?

Queen. There is a Willow growes aſlant a Brooke,
That ſhewes his hore leaues in the glaſſie ſtreame:
There with fantaſticke Garlands did ſhe come,
Of Crow-flowers, Nettles, Dayſies, and long Purples,
That liberall Shepheards giue a groſſer name;
But our cold Maids doe Dead Mens Fingers call them:
There on the pendant boughes, her Coronet weeds
Clambring to hang; an enuious ſliuer broke,
When downe the weedy Trophies, and her ſelfe,
Fell in the weeping Brooke, her cloathes ſpred wide,
And Mermaid-like, a while they bore her vp,
Which time ſhe chaunted ſnatches of old tunes,
As one incapable of her owne diſtreſſe,
Or like a creature Natiue, and indued
Vnto that Element: but long it could not be,
Till that her garments, heauy with her drinke,
Pul'd the poore wretch from her melodious buy,
To muddy death.

Laer. Alas then, is ſhe drown'd?

Queen. Drown'd, drown'd.

Laer. Too much of water haſt thou poore *Ophelia*,
And therefore I forbid my teares: but yet
It is our tricke, Nature her cuſtome holds,
Let ſhame ſay what it will; when theſe are gone
The woman will be out: Adue my Lord,
I haue a ſpeech of fire, that faine would blaze,
But that this folly doubts it. *Exit.*

Kin. Let's follow, *Gertrude:*
How much I had to doe to calme his rage?
Now feare I this will giue it ſtart againe;
Therefore let's follow. *Exeunt.*

Enter two Clownes.

Clown. Is ſhe to bee buried in Chriſtian buriall, that wilfully ſeekes her owne ſaluation?

Other. I tell thee ſhe is, and therefore make her Graue ſtraight, the Crowner hath ſate on her, and finds it Chriſtian buriall.

Clo. How can that be, vnleſſe ſhe drowned her ſelfe in her owne defence?

Other. Why 'tis found ſo.

Clo. It muſt be *Se offendendo*, it cannot bee elſe: for heere lies the point; If I drowne my ſelfe wittingly, it argues an Act: and an Act hath three branches. It is an Act to doe and to performe; argall ſhe drown'd her ſelfe wittingly.

Other. Nay but heare you Goodman Deluer.

Clown. Giue me leaue; heere lies the water; good: heere ſtands the man; good: If the man goe to this water and drowne himſele; it is will he nill he, he goes; marke you that? But if the water come to him & drowne him; hee drownes not himſelfe. Argall, hee that is not guilty of his owne death, ſhortens not his owne life.

Other. But is this law?

Clo. I marry is't, Crowners Queſt Law.

Other.

Other. Will you ha the truth on't: if this had not beene a Gentlewoman, shee should haue beene buried out of Christian Buriall.

Clo. Why there thou say'st. And the more pitty that great folke should haue countenance in this world to drowne or hang themselues, more then their euen Christian. Come, my Spade; there is no ancient Gentlemen, but Gardiners, Ditchers and Graue-makers; they hold vp *Adams* Profession.

Other. Was he a Gentleman?

Clo. He was the first that euer bore Armes.

Other. Why he had none.

Clo. What, ar't a Heathen? how dost thou vnderstand the Scripture? the Scripture sayes *Adam* dig'd; could hee digge without Armes? Ile put another question to thee; if thou answerest me not to the purpose, confesse thy selfe ———

Other. Go too.

Clo. What is he that builds stronger then either the Mason, the Shipwright, or the Carpenter?

Other. The Gallowes maker; for that Frame outliues a thousand Tenants.

Clo. I like thy wit well in good faith, the Gallowes does well; but how does it well? it does well to those that doe ill: now, thou dost ill to say the Gallowes is built stronger then the Church: Argall, the Gallowes may doe well to thee. Too't againe, Come.

Other. Who builds stronger then a Mason, a Shipwright, or a Carpenter?

Clo. I, tell me that, and vnyoake.

Other. Marry, now I can tell.

Clo. Too't.

Other. Masse, I cannot tell.

Enter Hamlet and Horatio a farre off.

Clo. Cudgell thy braines no more about it; for your dull Asse will not mend his pace with beating; and when you are ask't this question next, say a Graue-maker: the Houses that he makes, lasts till Doomesday: go, get thee to *Yaughan*, fetch me a stoupe of Liquor.

Sings.

In youth when I did loue, did loue,
me thought it was very sweete:
To contract O the time for a my behoue,
O me thought there was nothing meete.

Ham. Ha's this fellow no feeling of his businesse, that he sings at Graue-making?

Hor. Custome hath made it in him a property of easinesse.

Ham. 'Tis ee'n so; the hand of little Imployment hath the daintier sense.

Clowne sings.

But Age with his stealing steps
hath caught me in his clutch:
And hath shipped me intill the Land,
as if I had neuer beene such.

Ham. That Scull had a tongue in it, and could sing once: how the knaue iowles it to th' grownd, as if it were *Caines* Iaw-bone, that did the first murther: It might be the Pate of a Polititian which this Asse o're Offices: one that could circumuent God, might it not?

Hor. It might, my Lord.

Ham. Or of a Courtier, which could say, Good Morrow sweet Lord: how dost thou, good Lord? this might be my Lord such a one, that prais'd my Lord such a ones Horse, when he meant to begge it; might it not?

Hor. I, my Lord.

Ham. Why ee'n so: and now my Lady Wormes, Chaplesse, and knockt about the Mazard with a Sextons Spade; heere's fine Reuolution, if wee had the tricke to see't. Did these bones cost no more the breeding, but to play at Loggets with 'em? mine ake to thinke on't.

Clowne sings.

A Pickhaxe and a Spade, a Spade.
for and a shrowding-Sheete:
O a Pit of Clay for to be made,
for such a Guest is meete.

Ham. There's another: why might not that bee the Scull of of a Lawyer? where be his Quiddits now? his Quillets? his Cases? his Tenures, and his Tricks? why doe's he suffer this rude knaue now to knocke him about the Sconce with a dirty Shouell, and will not tell him of his Action of Battery? hum. This fellow might be in's time a great buyer of Land, with his Statutes, his Recognizances, his Fines, his double Vouchers, his Recoueries: Is this the fine of his Fines, and the recouery of his Recoueries, to haue his fine Pate full of fine Dirt? will his Vouchers vouch him no more of his Purchases, and double ones too, then the length and breadth of a paire of Indentures? the very Conueyances of his Lands will hardly lye in this Boxe; and must the Inheritor himselfe haue no more? ha?

Hor. Not a iot more, my Lord.

Ham. Is not Parchment made of Sheep-skinnes?

Hor. I my Lord, and of Calue-skinnes too.

Ham. They are Sheepe and Calues that seek out assurance in that. I will speake to this fellow: whose Graue's this Sir?

Clo. Mine Sir:

O a Pit of Clay for to be made,
for such a Guest is meete.

Ham. I thinke it be thine indeed: for thou liest in't.

Clo. You lye out on't Sir, and therefore it is not yours: for my part, I doe not lye in't; and yet it is mine.

Ham. Thou dost lye in't, to be in't and say 'tis thine: 'tis for the dead, not for the quicke, therefore thou lyest.

Clo. 'Tis a quicke lye Sir, 'twill away againe from me to you.

Ham. What man dost thou digge it for?

Clo. For no man Sir.

Ham. What woman then?

Clo. For none neither.

Ham. Who is to be buried in't?

Clo. One that was a woman Sir; but rest her Soule, shee's dead.

Ham. How absolute the knaue is? wee must speake by the Carde, or equiuocation will vndoe vs: by the Lord *Horatio*, these three yeares I haue taken note of it, the Age is growne so picked, that the toe of the Pesant comes so neere the heeles of our Courtier, hee galls his Kibe. How long hast thou been a Graue-maker?

Clo. Of all the dayes i'th' yeare, I came too't that day that our last King *Hamlet* o'recame *Fortinbras.*

Ham. How long is that since?

Clo. Cannot you tell that? euery foole can tell that: It was the very day, that young *Hamlet* was borne, hee that was mad, and sent into England.

Ham. I marry, why was he sent into England?

Clo. Why, because he was mad; hee shall recouer his wits there; or if he do not, it's no great matter there.

Ham.

Ham. Why?

Clo. 'Twill not be ſeene in him, there the men are as mad as he.

Ham. How came he mad?

Clo. Very ſtrangely they ſay.

Ham. How ſtrangely?

Clo. Faith e'ene with looſing his wits.

Ham. Vpon what ground?

Clo. Why heere in Denmarke: I haue bin ſixeteene heere, man and Boy thirty yeares.

Ham. How long will a man lie 'ith' earth ere he rot?

Clo. Ifaith, if he be not rotten before he die(as we haue many pocky Coarſes now adaies, that will ſcarce hold the laying in) he will laſt you ſome eight yeare, or nine yeare. A Tanner will laſt you nine year e.

Ham. Why he, more then another?'

Clo. Why ſir, his hide is ſo tan'd with his Trade, that he will keepe out water a great while. And your water, is a ſore Decayer of your horſon dead body. Heres a Scull now: this Scul, has laine in the earth three & twenty years.

Ham. Whoſe was it?

Clo. A whoreſon mad Fellowes it was;
Whoſe doe you thinke it was?

Ham. Nay, I know not.

Clo. A peſtlence on him for a mad Rogue, a pou'rd a Flaggon of Reniſh on my head once. This ſame Scull Sir, this ſame Scull ſir, was *Yoricks* Scull, the Kings Ieſter.

Ham. This?

Clo: E'ene that.

Ham. Let me ſee. Alas poore *Yorick*, I knew him *Horatio*, a fellow of infinite Ieſt; of moſt excellent fancy, he hath borne me on his backe a thouſand times: And how abhorred my Imagination is, my gorge riſes at it. Heere hung thoſe lipps, that I haue kiſt I know not how oft. VVhere be your Iibes now? Your Gambals? Your Songs? Your flaſhes of Merriment that were wont to ſet the Table on a Rore? No one now to mock your own Ieering? Quite chopfalne? Now get you to my Ladies Chamber, and tell her, let her paint an inch thicke, to this fauour ſhe muſt come. Make her laugh at that: prythee *Horatio* tell me one thing.

Hor. What's that my Lord?

Ham. Doſt thou thinke *Alexander* lookt o'this faſhion i'th' earth?

Hor. E'ene ſo.

Ham. And ſmelt ſo? Puh.

Hor. E'ene ſo, my Lord.

Ham. To what baſe vſes we may returne *Horatio*. Why may not Imagination trace the Noble duſt of *Alexander*, till he find it ſtopping a bunghole.

Hor. 'Twere to conſider: to curiouſly to conſider ſo.

Ham. No faith, not a iot. But to follow him thether with modeſtie enough, & likeliehood to lead it; as thus. *Alexander* died: *Alexander* was buried: *Alexander* returneth into duſt; the duſt is earth; of earth we make Lome, and why of that Lome (whereto he was conuerted) might they not ſtopp a Beere-barrell?
Imperiall *Cæſar*, dead and turn'd to clay,
Might ſtop a hole to keepe the winde away.
Oh, that that earth, which kept the world in awe,
Should patch a Wall, t'expell the winters flaw.
But ſoft, but ſoft, aſide; heere comes the King.

Enter King, Queene, Laertes, and a Coffin, with Lords attendant.

The Queene, the Courtiers. Who is that they follow,
And with ſuch maimed rites? This doth betoken
The Coarſe they follow, did with diſperate hand,
Fore do it owne life; 'twas ſome Eſtate.
Couch we a while, and mark.

Laer. What Cerimony elſe?

Ham. That is *Laertes*, a very Noble youth: Marke.

Laer. What Cerimony elſe?

Prieſt. Her Obſequies haue bin as farre inlarg'd.
As we haue warrantis, her death was doubtfull,
And but that great Command, o're-ſwaies the order,
She ſhould in ground vnſanctified haue lodg'd,
Till the laſt Trumpet. For charitable praier,
Shardes, Flints, and Peebles, ſhould be thro wne on her:
Yet heere ſhe is allowed her Virgin Rites,
Her Maiden ſtrewments, and the bringing home
Of Bell and Buriall.

Laer. Muſt there no more be done?

Prieſt. No more be done:
We ſhould prophane the ſeruice of the dead,
To ſing ſage *Requiem*, and ſuch reſt to her
As to peace-parted Soules.

Laer. Lay her i'th' earth,
And from her faire and vnpolluted fleſh,
May Violets ſpring. I tell thee(churliſh Prieſt)
A Miniſtring Angell ſhall my Siſter be,
When thou lieſt howling?

Ham. What, the faire *Ophelia*?

Queene. Sweets, to the ſweet farewell.
I hop'd thou ſhould'ſt haue bin my *Hamlets* wife:
I thought thy Bride-bed to haue deckt(ſweet Maid)
And not t'haue ſtrew'd thy Graue.

Laer. Oh terrible woer,
Fall ten times trebble, on that curſed head
Whoſe wicked deed, thy moſt Ingenious ſence
Depriu'd thee of. Hold off the earth a while,
Till I haue caught her once more in mine armes:
Leaps in the graue.
Now pile your duſt, vpon the quicke, and dead,
Till of this flat a Mountaine you haue made,
To o're top old *Pelion*, or the skyiſh head
Of blew *Olympus*.

Ham. What is he, whoſe griefes
Beares ſuch an Emphaſis? whoſe phraſe of Sorrow
Coniure the wandring Starres, and makes them ſtand
Like wonder-wounded hearers? This is I,
Hamlet the Dane.

Laer. The deuill take thy ſoule.

Ham. Thou prai'ſt not well:
I prythee take thy fingers from my throat;
Sir though I am not Spleenatiue, and raſh,
Yet haue I ſomething in me dangerous,
Which let thy wiſeneſſe feare. Away thy hand.

King. Pluck them aſunder.

Qu. *Hamlet, Hamlet.*

Gen. Good my Lord be quiet.

Ham. Why I will fight with him vppon this Theme.
Vntill my eielids will no longer wag.

Qu. Oh my Sonne, what Theame?

Ham. I lou'd *Ophelia*; fortie thouſand Brothers
Could not(with all there quantitie of Loue)
Make vp my ſumme. What wilt thou do for her

King. Oh he is mad *Laertes*,

Qu. For loue of God forbeare him.

Ham. Come ſhow me what thou'lt doe.
Woo't weepe? Woo't fight? Woo't teare thy ſelfe?
Woo't drinke vp *Eſile*, eate a Crocodile?

Ile

Ile doo't. Doſt thou come heere to whine;
To outface me with leaping in her Graue?
Be buried quicke with her, and ſo will I.
And if thou prate of Mountaines; let them throw
Millions of Akers on vs; till our ground
Sindging his pate againſt the burning Zone,
Make *Oſſa* like a wart. Nay, and thoul't mouth,
Ile rant as well as thou.

Kin. This is meere Madneſſe:
And thus awhile the fit will worke on him:
Anon as patient as the female Doue,
When that her golden Cuplet are diſclos'd;
His ſilence will ſit drooping.

Ham. Heare you Sir:
What is the reaſon that you vſe me thus?
I loud' you euer; but it is no matter:
Let *Hercules* himſelfe doe what he may,
The Cat will Mew, and Dogge will haue his day. *Exit.*

Kin. I pray you good *Horatio* wait vpon him,
Strengthen you patience in our laſt nights ſpeech,
Wee'l put the matter to the preſent puſh:
Good *Gertrude* ſet ſome watch ouer your Sonne,
This Graue ſhall haue a liuing Monument:
An houre of quiet ſhortly ſhall we ſee;
Till then, in patience our proceeding be. *Exeunt.*

Enter Hamlet and Horatio.

Ham. So much for this Sir; now let me ſee the other,
You doe remember all the Circumſtance.

Hor. Remember it my Lord?

Ham. Sir, in my heart there was a kinde of fighting,
That would not let me ſleepe; me thought I lay
Worſe then the mutines in the Bilboes, raſhly,
(And praiſe be raſhneſſe for it) let vs know,
Our indiſcretion ſometimes ſerues vs well,
When our deare plots do paule, and that ſhould teach vs,
There's a Diuinity that ſhapes our ends,
Rough-hew them how we will.

Hor. That is moſt certaine.

Ham. Vp from my Cabin
My ſea-gowne ſcarft about me in the darke,
Grop'd I to finde out them; had my deſire,
Finger'd their Packet, and in fine, withdrew
To mine owne roome againe, making ſo bold,
(My feares forgetting manners) to vnſeale
Their grand Commiſſion, where I found *Horatio*,
Oh royall knauery: An exact command,
Larded with many ſeuerall ſorts of reaſon;
Importing Denmarks health, and Englands too,
With hoo, ſuch Bugges and Goblins in my life;
That on the ſuperuize no leaſure bated,
No not to ſtay the grinding of the Axe,
My head ſhoud be ſtruck off.

Hor. Iſt poſſible?

Ham. Here's the Commiſſion, read it at more leyſure:
But wilt thou heare me how I did proceed?

Hor. I beſeech you.

Ham. Being thus benetted round with Villaines,
Ere I could make a Prologue to my braines,
They had begun the Play. I ſate me downe,
Deuis'd a new Commiſſion, wrote it faire,
I once did hold it as our Statiſts doe,
A baſeneſſe to write faire; and laboured much
How to forget that learning: but Sir now,
It did me Yeomans ſeruice: wilt thou know
The effects of what I wrote?

Hor. I, good my Lord.

Ham. An earneſt Coniuration from the King,
As England was his faithfull Tributary,
As loue betweene them, as the Palme ſhould flouriſh,
As Peace ſhould ſtill her wheaten Garland weare,
And ſtand a Comma 'tweene their amities,
And many ſuch like Aſſis of great charge,
That on the view and know of theſe Contents,
Without debatement further, more or leſſe,
He ſhould the bearers put to ſodaine death,
Not ſhriuing time allowed.

Hor. How was this ſeal'd?

Ham. Why, euen in that was Heauen ordinate;
I had my fathers Signet in my Purſe,
Which was the Modell of that Daniſh Seale:
Folded the Writ vp in forme of the other,
Subſcrib'd it, gau't th' impreſſion, plac't it ſafely,
The changeling neuer knowne: Now, the next day
Was our Sea Fight, and what to this was ſement,
Thou know'ſt already.

Hor. So *Guildenſterne* and *Roſincrance*, go too't.

Ham. Why man, they did make loue to this imployment
They are not neere my Conſcience; their debate
Doth by their owne inſinuation grow:
'Tis dangerous, when the baſer nature comes
Betweene the paſſe, and fell incenſed points
Of mighty oppoſites.

Hor. Why, what a King is this?

Ham. Does it not, thinkſt thee, ſtand me now vpon
He that hath kil'd my King, and whor'd my Mother,
Popt in betweene th' election and my hopes,
Throwne out his Angle for my proper life,
And with ſuch coozenage; is't not perfect conſcience,
To quit him with this arme? And is't not to be damn'd
To let this Canker of our nature come
In further euill.

Hor. It muſt be ſhortly knowne to him from England
What is the iſſue of the buſineſſe there.

Ham. It will be ſhort,
The *interim's* mine, and a mans life's no more
Then to ſay one: but I am very ſorry good *Horatio*,
That to *Laertes* I forgot my ſelfe;
For by the image of my Cauſe, I ſee
The Portraiture of his; Ile count his fauours:
But ſure the brauery of his griefe did put me
Into a Towring paſſion.

Hor. Peace, who comes heere?

Enter young Oſricke.

Oſr. Your Lordſhip is right welcome back to Denmarke.

Ham. I humbly thank you Sir, doſt know this waterflie?

Hor. No my good Lord.

Ham. Thy ſtate is the more gracious; for 'tis a vice to know him: he hath much Land, and fertile; let a Beaſt be Lord of Beaſts, and his Crib ſhall ſtand at the Kings Meſſe; 'tis a Chowgh; but as I ſaw ſpacious in the poſſeſſion of dirt.

Oſr. Sweet Lord, if your friendſhip were at leyſure, I ſhould impart a thing to you from his Maieſty.

Ham. I will receiue it with all diligence of ſpirit; put your Bonet to his right vſe, 'tis for the head.

Oſr. I thanke your Lordſhip, 'tis very hot.

Ham. No, beleeue mee 'tis very cold, the winde is Northerly.

Oſr. It is indifferent cold my Lord indeed.

Ham. Mee thinkes it is very ſoultry, and hot for my Complexion.

Oſricke.

Osr. Exceedingly, my Lord, it is very soultry, as 'twere I cannot tell how: but my Lord, his Maiesty bad me signifie to you, that he ha's laid a great wager on your head: Sir, this is the matter.

Ham. I beseech you remember.

Osr. Nay, in good faith, for mine ease in good faith: Sir, you are not ignorant of what excellence *Laertes* is at his weapon.

Ham. What's his weapon?

Osr. Rapier and dagger.

Ham. That's two of his weapons; but well.

Osr. The sir King ha's wag'd with him six Barbary Horses, against the which he impon'd as I take it, sixe French Rapiers and Poniards, with their assignes, as Girdle, Hangers or so: three of the Carriages infaith are very deare to fancy, very responsiue to the hilts, most delicate carriages, and of very liberall conceit.

Ham. What call you the Carriages?

Osr. The Carriages Sir, are the hangers.

Ham. The phrase would bee more Germaine to the matter: If we could carry Cannon by our sides; I would it might be Hangers till then; but on sixe Barbary Horses against sixe French Swords: their Assignes, and three liberall conceited Carriages, that's the French but against the Danish; why is this impon'd as you call it?

Osr. The King Sir, hath laid that in a dozen passes betweene you and him, hee shall not exceed you three hits; He hath one twelue for mine, and that would come to imediate tryall, if your Lordship would vouchsafe the Answere.

Ham. How if I answere no?

Osr. I meane my Lord, the opposition of your person in tryall.

Ham. Sir, I will walke heere in the Hall; if it please his Maiestie, 'tis the breathing time of day with me; let the Foyles bee brought, the Gentleman willing, and the King hold his purpose; I will win for him if I can: if not, Ile gaine nothing but my shame, and the odde hits.

Osr. Shall I redeliuer you ee'n so?

Ham. To this effect Sir, after what flourish your nature will.

Osr. I commend my duty to your Lordship.

Ham. Yours, yours; hee does well to commend it himselfe, there are no tongues else for's tongue.

Hor. This Lapwing runs away with the shell on his head.

Ham. He did Complie with his Dugge before hee suck't it: thus had he and mine more of the same Beauy that I know the drossie age dotes on; only got the tune of the time, and outward habite of encounter, a kinde of yesty collection, which carries them through & through the most fond and winnowed opinions; and doe but blow them to their tryalls: the Bubbles are out.

Hor. You will lose this wager, my Lord.

Ham. I doe not thinke so, since he went into France, I haue beene in continuall practice; I shall winne at the oddes: but thou wouldest not thinke how all heere about my heart: but it is no matter.

Hor. Nay, good my Lord.

Ham. It is but foolery; but it is such a kinde of gain-giuing as would perhaps trouble a woman.

Hor. If your minde dislike any thing, obey. I will forestall their repaire hither, and say you are not fit.

Ham. Not a whit, we defie Augury; there's a speciall Prouidence in the fall of a sparrow. If it be now, 'tis not to come: if it bee not to come, it will bee now: if it be not now; yet it will come; the readinesse is all, since no man ha's ought of what he leaues. What is't to leaue betimes?

Enter King, Queene, Laertes and Lords, with other Attendants with Foyles, and Gauntlets, a Table and Flagons of Wine on it.

Kin. Come *Hamlet*, come, and take this hand from me.

Ham. Giue me your pardon Sir, I'ue done you wrong,
But pardon't as you are a Gentleman.
This presence knowes,
And you must needs haue heard how I am punisht
With sore distraction? What I haue done
That might your nature honour, and exception
Roughly awake, I heere proclaime was madnesse:
Was't *Hamlet* wrong'd *Laertes*? Neuer *Hamlet*.
If *Hamlet* from himselfe be tane away:
And when he's not himselfe, do's wrong *Laertes*,
Then *Hamlet* does it not, *Hamlet* denies it:
Who does it then? His Madnesse? If't be so,
Hamlet is of the Faction that is wrong'd,
His madnesse is poore *Hamlets* Enemy.
Sir, in this Audience,
Let my disclaiming from a purpos'd euill,
Free me so farre in your most generous thoughts,
That I haue shot mine Arrow o're the house,
And hurt my Mother.

Laer. I am satisfied in Nature,
Whose motiue in this case should stirre me most
To my Reuenge. But in my termes of Honor
I stand aloofe, and will no reconcilement,
Till by some elder Masters of knowne Honor,
I haue a voyce, and president of peace
To keepe my name vngorg'd. But till that time,
I do receiue your offer'd loue like loue,
And wil not wrong it.

Ham. I do embrace it freely,
And will this Brothers wager frankely play.
Giue vs the Foyles: Come on.

Laer. Come one for me.

Ham. Ile be your foile *Laertes*, in mine ignorance,
Your Skill shall like a Starre i'th'darkest night,
Sticke fiery off indeede.

Laer. You mocke me Sir.

Ham. No by this hand.

King. Giue them the Foyles yong *Osricke*,
Cousen *Hamlet*, you know the wager.

Ham. Verie well my Lord,
Your Grace hath laide the oddes a'th'weaker side.

King. I do not feare it,
I haue seene you both:
But since he is better'd, we haue therefore oddes.

Laer. This is too heauy,
Let me see another.

Ham. This likes me well,
These Foyles haue all a length. *Prepare to play.*

Osricke. I my good Lord.

King. Set me the Stopes of wine vpon that Table:
If *Hamlet* giue the first, or second hit,
Or quit in answer of the third exchange,
Let all the Battlements their Ordinance fire,
The King shal drinke to *Hamlets* better breath,
And in the Cup an vnion shal he throw
Richer then that, which foure successiue Kings
In Denmarkes Crowne haue worne.

Giue

Giue me the Cups,
And let the Kettle to the Trumpets ſpeake,
The Trumpet to the Cannoneer without,
The Cannons to the Heauens, the Heauen to Earth,
Now the King drinkes to *Hamlet*. Come, begin,
And you the Iudges beare a wary eye.
Ham. Come on ſir.
Laer. Come on ſir. *They play.*
Ham. One.
Laer. No.
Ham. Iudgement.
Oſr. A hit, a very palpable hit.
Laer. Well: againe.
King. Stay, giue me drinke.
Hamlet, this Pearle is thine,
Here's to thy health. Giue him the cup,
Trumpets ſound, and ſhot goes off.
Ham. Ile play this bout firſt, ſet by a-while.
Come: Another hit; what ſay you?
Laer. A touch, a touch, I do confeſſe.
King. Our Sonne ſhall win.
Qu. He's fat, and ſcant of breath.
Heere's a Napkin, rub thy browes,
The Queene Carowſes to thy fortune, *Hamlet*.
Ham. Good Madam.
King. *Gertrude*, do not drinke.
Qu. I will my Lord;
I pray you pardon me.
King. It is the poyſon'd Cup, it is too late.
Ham. I dare not drinke yet Madam,
By and by.
Qu. Come, let me wipe thy face.
Laer. My Lord, Ile hit him now.
King. I do not thinke't.
Laer. And yet 'tis almoſt 'gainſt my conſcience.
Ham. Come for the third.
Laertes, you but dally,
I pray you paſſe with your beſt violence,
I am affear'd you make a wanton of me.
Laer. Say you ſo? Come on. *Play.*
Oſr. Nothing neither way.
Laer. Haue at you now.
In ſcuffling they change Rapiers.
King. Part them, they are incens'd.
Ham. Nay come, againe.
Oſr. Looke to the Queene there hoa.
Hor. They bleed on both ſides. How is't my Lord?
Oſr. How is't *Laertes*?
Laer. Why as a Woodcocke
To mine Sprindge, *Oſricke*,
I am iuſtly kill'd with mine owne Treacherie.
Ham. How does the Queene?
King. She ſounds to ſee them bleede.
Qu. No, no, the drinke, the drinke.
Oh my deere *Hamlet*, the drinke, the drinke,
I am poyſon'd.
Ham. Oh Villany! How? Let the doore be lock'd.
Treacherie, ſeeke it out.
Laer. It is heere *Hamlet*.
Hamlet, thou art ſlaine,
No Medicine in the world can do thee good.
In thee, there is not halfe an houre of life;
The Treacherous Inſtrument is in thy hand,
Vnbated and envenom'd: the foule practiſe
Hath turn'd it ſelfe on me. Loe, heere I lye,
Neuer to riſe againe: Thy Mothers poyſon'd:
I can no more, the King, the King's too blame.
Ham. The point envenom'd too,
Then venome to thy worke.
Hurts the King.
All. Treaſon, Treaſon.
King. O yet defend me Friends, I am but hurt.
Ham. Heere thou inceſtuous, murdrous,
Damned Dane,
Drinke off this Potion: Is thy Vnion heere?
Follow my Mother. *King Dyes.*
Laer. He is iuſtly ſeru'd.
It is a poyſon temp'red by himſelfe:
Exchange forgiueneſſe with me, Noble *Hamlet*;
Mine and my Fathers death come not vpon thee,
Nor thine on me. *Dyes.*
Ham. Heauen make thee free of it, I follow thee.
I am dead *Horatio*, wretched Queene adiew,
You that looke pale, and tremble at this chance,
That are but Mutes or audience to this acte:
Had I but time (as this fell Sergeant death
Is ſtrick'd in his Arreſt) oh I could tell you.
But let it be: *Horatio*, I am dead,
Thou liu'ſt, report me and my cauſes right
To the vnſatisfied.
Hor. Neuer beleeue it.
I am more an Antike Roman then a Dane:
Heere's yet ſome Liquor left.
Ham. As th'art a man, giue me the Cup.
Let go, by Heauen Ile haue't.
Oh good *Horatio*, what a wounded name,
(Things ſtanding thus vnknowne) ſhall liue behind me.
If thou did'ſt euer hold me in thy heart,
Abſent thee from felicitie awhile,
And in this harſh world draw thy breath in paine,
To tell my Storie.
March afarre off, and ſhout within.
What warlike noyſe is this?

Enter Oſricke.

Oſr. Yong *Fortinbras*, with conqueſt come frō Poland
To th'Ambaſſadors of England giues this warlike volly.
Ham. O I dye *Horatio*:
The potent poyſon quite ore-crowes my ſpirit,
I cannot liue to heare the Newes from England,
But I do propheſie th'election lights
On *Fortinbras*, he ha's my dying voyce,
So tell him with the occurrents more and leſſe,
Which haue ſolicited. The reſt is ſilence. O,o,o,o. *Dyes*
Hora. Now cracke a Noble heart:
Goodnight ſweet Prince,
And flights of Angels ſing thee to thy reſt,
Why do's the Drumme come hither?

Enter Fortinbras and Engliſh Ambaſſador, with Drumme, Colours, and Attendants.

Fortin. Where is this ſight?
Hor. What is it ye would ſee;
If ought of woe, or wonder, ceaſe your ſearch.
For. His quarry cries on hauocke. Oh proud death,
What feaſt is toward in thine eternall Cell.
That thou ſo many Princes, at a ſhoote,
So bloodily haſt ſtrooke.
Amb. The ſight is diſmall,
And our affaires from England come too late,
The eares are ſenſeleſſe that ſhould giue vs hearing,
To tell him his command'ment is fulfill'd,

That *Roſincrance* and *Guildenſterne* are dead:
Where ſhould we haue our thankes?
Hor. Not from his mouth,
Had it th'abilitie of life to thanke you:
He neuer gaue command'ment for their death.
But ſince ſo iumpe vpon this bloodie queſtion,
You from the Polake warres, and you from England
Are heere arriued. Giue order that theſe bodies
High on a ſtage be placed to the view,
And let me ſpeake to th'yet vnknowing world,
How theſe things came about. So ſhall you heare
Of carnall, bloudie, and vnnaturall acts,
Of accidentall iudgements, caſuall ſlaughters
Of death's put on by cunning, and forc'd cauſe,
And in this vpſhot, purpoſes miſtooke,
Falne on the Inuentors heads. All this can I
Truly deliuer.
For. Let vs haſt to heare it,
And call the Nobleſt to the Audience.
For me, with ſorrow, I embrace my Fortune,
I haue ſome Rites of memory in this Kingdome,
Which are ro claime, my vantage doth
Inuite me,
Hor. Of that I ſhall haue alwayes cauſe to ſpeake,
And from his mouth
Whoſe voyce will draw on more:
But let this ſame be preſently perform'd,
Euen whiles mens mindes are wilde,
Leſt more miſchance
On plots, and errors happen.
For. Let foure Captaines
Beare *Hamlet* like a Soldier to the Stage,
For he was likely, had he beene put on
To haue prou'd moſt royally:
And for his paſſage,
The Souldiours Muſicke, and the rites of Warre
Speake lowdly for him.
Take vp the body; Such a ſight as this
Becomes the Field, but heere ſhewes much amis.
Go, bid the Souldiers ſhoote.
Exeunt Marching: after the which, a Peale of Ordenance are ſhot off.

FINIS.

THE TRAGEDIE OF KING LEAR.

Actus Primus. Scœna Prima.

Enter Kent, Gloucester, and Edmond.

Kent.

I Thought the King had more affected the Duke of *Albany*, then *Cornwall*.

Glou. It did alwayes seeme so to vs: But now in the diuision of the Kingdome, it appeares not which of the Dukes hee valewes most, for qualities are so weigh'd, that curiosity in neither, can make choise of eithers moity.

Kent. Is not this your Son, my Lord?

Glou. His breeding Sir, hath bin at my charge. I haue so often blush'd to acknowledge him, that now I am braz'd too't.

Kent. I cannot conceiue you.

Glou. Sir, this yong Fellowes mother could; wherevpon she grew round womb'd, and had indeede (Sir) a Sonne for her Cradle, ere she had a husband for her bed. Do you smell a fault?

Kent. I cannot wish the fault vndone, the issue of it, being so proper.

Glou. But I haue a Sonne, Sir, by order of Law, some yeere elder then this; who, yet is no deerer in my account, though this Knaue came somthing sawcily to the world before he was sent for: yet was his Mother fayre, there was good sport at his making, and the horson must be acknowledged. Doe you know this Noble Gentleman, *Edmond*?

Edm. No, my Lord.

Glou. My Lord of Kent:
Remember him heereafter, as my Honourable Friend.

Edm. My seruices to your Lordship.

Kent. I must loue you, and sue to know you better.

Edm. Sir, I shall study deseruing.

Glou. He hath bin out nine yeares, and away he shall againe. The King is comming.

Sennet. Enter King Lear, Cornwall, Albany, Gonerill, Regan, Cordelia, and attendants.

Lear. Attend the Lords of France & Burgundy, Gloster.

Glou. I shall, my Lord. *Exit.*

Lear. Meane time we shal expresse our darker purpose.
Giue me the Map there. Know, that we haue diuided
In three our Kingdome: and 'tis our fast intent,
To shake all Cares and Businesse from our Age,
Conferring them on yonger strengths, while we
Vnburthen'd crawle toward death. Our son of *Cornwal*,
And you our no lesse louing Sonne of *Albany*,
We haue this houre a constant will to publish
Our daughters seuerall Dowers, that future strife
May be preuented now. The Princes, *France & Burgundy*,
Great Riuals in our yongest daughters loue,
Long in our Court, haue made their amorous soiourne,
And heere are to be answer'd. Tell me my daughters
(Since now we will diuest vs both of Rule,
Interest of Territory, Cares of State)
Which of you shall we say doth loue vs most,
That we, our largest bountie may extend
Where Nature doth with merit challenge. *Gonerill*,
Our eldest borne, speake first.

Gon. Sir, I loue you more then word can weild ÿ matter,
Deerer then eye-sight, space, and libertie,
Beyond what can be valewed, rich or rare,
No lesse then life, with grace, health, beauty, honor:
As much as Childe ere lou'd, or Father found.
A loue that makes breath poore, and speech vnable,
Beyond all manner of so much I loue you.

Cor. What shall *Cordelia* speake? Loue, and be silent.

Lear. Of all these bounds euen from this Line, to this,
With shadowie Forrests, and with Champains rich'd
With plenteous Riuers, and wide-skirted Meades
We make thee Lady. To thine and *Albanies* issues
Be this perpetuall. What sayes our second Daughter?
Our deerest *Regan*, wife of *Cornwall*?

Reg. I am made of that selfe-mettle as my Sister,
And prize me at her worth. In my true heart,
I finde she names my very deede of loue:
Onely she comes too short, that I professe
My selfe an enemy to all other ioyes,
Which the most precious square of sense professes,
And finde I am alone felicitate
In your deere Highnesse loue.

Cor. Then poore *Cordelia*,
And yet not so, since I am sure my loue's
More ponderous then my tongue.

Lear. To thee, and thine hereditarie euer,
Remaine this ample third of our faire Kingdome,
No lesse in space, validitie, and pleasure
Then that conferr'd on *Gonerill*. Now our Ioy,
Although our last and least; to whose yong loue,
The Vines of France, and Milke of Burgundie,
Striue to be interest. What can you say, to draw
A third, more opilent then your Sisters? speake.

Cor. Nothing my Lord.

Lear. Nothing?

Cor. Nothing.
Lear. Nothing will come of nothing, ſpeake againe.
Cor. Vnhappie that I am, I cannot heaue
My heart into my mouth: I loue your Maieſty
According to my bond, no more nor leſſe.
Lear. How, how *Cordelia?* Mend your ſpeech a little,
Leaſt you may marre your Fortunes.
Cor. Good my Lord,
You haue begot me, bred me, lou'd me.
I returne thoſe duties backe as are right fit,
Obey you, Loue you, and moſt Honour you.
Why haue my Siſters Husbands, if they ſay
They loue you all? Happily when I ſhall wed,
That Lord, whoſe hand muſt take my plight, ſhall carry
Halfe my loue with him, halfe my Care, and Dutie,
Sure I ſhall neuer marry like my Siſters.
Lear. But goes thy heart with this?
Cor. I my good Lord.
Lear. So young, and ſo vntender?
Cor. So young my Lord, and true.
Lear. Let it be ſo, thy truth then be thy dowre:
For by the ſacred radience of the Sunne,
The miſeries of *Heccat* and the night:
By all the operation of the Orbes,
From whom we do exiſt, and ceaſe to be,
Heere I diſclaime all my Paternall care,
Propinquity and property of blood,
And as a ſtranger to my heart and me,
Hold thee from this for euer. The barbarous *Scythian*,
Or he that makes his generation meſſes
To gorge his appetite, ſhall to my boſome
Be as well neighbour'd, pittied, and releeu'd,
As thou my ſometime Daughter.
Kent. Good my Liege.
Lear. Peace *Kent*,
Come not betweene the Dragon and his wrath,
I lou'd her moſt, and thought to ſet my reſt
On her kind nurſery. Hence and avoid my ſight:
So be my graue my peace, as here I giue
Her Fathers heart from her; call *France*, who ſtirres?
Call *Burgundy*, *Cornwall*, and *Albanie*,
With my two Daughters Dowres, digeſt the third,
Let pride, which ſhe cals plainneſſe, marry her:
I doe inueſt you ioyntly with my power,
Preheminence, and all the large effects
That troope with Maieſty. Our ſelfe by Monthly courſe,
With reſeruation of an hundred Knights,
By you to be ſuſtain'd, ſhall our abode
Make with you by due turne, onely we ſhall retaine
The name, and all th'addition to a King: the Sway,
Reuennew, Execution of the reſt,
Beloued Sonnes be yours, which to confirme,
This Coronet part betweene you.
Kent. Royall *Lear*,
Whom I haue euer honor'd as my King,
Lou'd as my Father, as my Maſter follow'd,
As my great Patron thought on in my praiers.
Le. The bow is bent & drawne, make from the ſhaft.
Kent. Let it fall rather, though the forke inuade
The region of my heart, be *Kent* vnmannerly,
When *Lear* is mad, what wouldeſt thou do old man?
Think'ſt thou that dutie ſhall haue dread to ſpeake,
When power to flattery bowes?
To plainneſſe honour's bound,
When Maieſty falls to folly, reſerue thy ſtate,
And in thy beſt conſideration checke
This hideous raſhneſſe, anſwere my life, my iudgement:
Thy yongeſt Daughter do's not loue thee leaſt,
Nor are thoſe empty hearted, whoſe low ſounds
Reuerbe no hollowneſſe.
Lear. *Kent*, on thy life no more.
Kent. My life I neuer held but as pawne
To wage againſt thine enemies, nere feare to looſe it,
Thy ſafety being motiue.
Lear. Out of my ſight.
Kent. See better *Lear*, and let me ſtill remaine
The true blanke of thine eie.
Kear. Now by *Apollo*,
Lent. Now by *Apollo*, King
Thou ſwear.ſt thy Gods in vaine.
Lear. O Vaſſall! Miſcreant.
Alb. *Cor.* Deare Sir forbeare.
Kent. Kill thy Phyſition, and thy fee beſtow
Vpon the foule diſeaſe, reuoke thy guift,
Or whil'ſt I can vent clamour from my throate,
Ile tell thee thou doſt euill.
Lea. Heare me recreant, on thine allegeance heare me;
That thou haſt ſought to make vs breake our vowes,
Which we durſt neuer yet; and with ſtrain'd pride,
To come betwixt our ſentences, and our power,
Which, nor our nature, nor our place can beare;
Our potencie made good, take thy reward.
Fiue dayes we do allot thee for prouiſion,
To ſhield thee from diſaſters of the world,
And on the ſixt to turne thy hated backe
Vpon our kingdome; if on the tenth day following,
Thy baniſht trunke be found in our Dominions,
The moment is thy death, away. By *Iupiter*,
This ſhall not be reuok'd,
Kent. Fare thee well King, ſith thus thou wilt appeare,
Freedome liues hence, and baniſhment is here;
The Gods to their deere ſhelter take thee Maid,
That iuſtly think'ſt, and haſt moſt rightly ſaid:
And your large ſpeeches, may your deeds approue,
That good effects may ſpring from words of loue:
Thus *Kent*, O Princes, bids you all adew,
Hee'l ſhape his old courſe, in a Country new. *Exit.*

Flouriſh. Enter Gloſter with France, and Burgundy, Attendants.

Cor. Heere's *France* and *Burgundy*, my Noble Lord.
Lear. My Lord of *Bugundie*,
We firſt addreſſe toward you, who with this King
Hath riuald for our Daughter; what in the leaſt
Will you require in preſent Dower with her,
Or ceaſe your queſt of Loue?
Bur. Moſt Royall Maieſty,
I craue no more then hath your Highneſſe offer'd,
Nor will you tender leſſe?
Lear. Right Noble *Burgundy*,
When ſhe was deare to vs, we did hold her ſo,
But now her price is fallen: Sir, there ſhe ſtands,
If ought within that little ſeeming ſubſtance,
Or all of it with our diſpleaſure piec'd,
And nothing more may fitly like your Grace,
Shee's there, and ſhe is yours.
Bur. I know no anſwer.
Lear. Will you with thoſe infirmities ſhe owes,
Vnfriended, new adopted to our hate,
Dow'rd with our curſe, and ſtranger'd with our oath,
Take her or, leaue her.

Bur. Par-

Bur. Pardon me Royall Sir,
Election makes not vp in such conditions.
Le. Then leaue her sir, for by the powre that made me,
I tell you all her wealth. For you great King,
I would not from your loue make such a stray,
To match you where I hate, therefore beseech you
T'auert your liking a more worthier way,
Then on a wretch whom Nature is asham'd
Almost t'acknowledge hers.
Fra. This is most strange,
That she whom euen but now, was your obiect,
The argument of your praise, balme of your age,
The best, the deerest, should in this trice of time
Commit a thing so monstrous, to dismantle
So many folds of fauour: sure her offence
Must be of such vnnaturall degree,
That monsters it: Or your fore-voucht affection
Fall into taint, which to beleeue of her
Must be a faith that reason without miracle
Should neuer plant in me.
Cor. I yet beseech your Maiesty.
If for I want that glib and oylie Art,
To speake and purpose not, since what I will intend,
Ile do't before I speake, that you make knowne
It is no vicious blot, murther, or foulenesse,
No vnchaste action or dishonoured step
That hath depriu'd me of your Grace and fauour,
But euen for want of that, for which I am richer,
A still soliciting eye, and such a tongue,
That I am glad I haue not, though not to haue it,
Hath lost me in your liking.
Lear. Better thou had'st'
Not beene borne, then not t haue pleas'd me better.
Fra. Is it but this? A tardinesse in nature,
Which often leaues the history vnspoke
That it intends to do: my Lord of *Burgundy*,
What say you to the Lady? Loue's not loue
When it is mingled with regards, that stands
Aloofe from th'intire point, will you haue her?
She is herselfe a Dowrie.
Bur. Royall King,
Giue but that portion which your selfe propos'd,
And here I take *Cordelia* by the hand,
Dutchesse of *Burgundie*.
Lear. Nothing, I haue sworne, I am firme.
Bur. I am sorry then you haue so lost a Father,
That you must loose a husband.
Cor. Peace be with *Burgundie*,
Since that respect and Fortunes are his loue,
I shall not be his wife.
Fra. Fairest *Cordelia*, that art most rich being poore,
Most choise forsaken, and most lou'd despis'd,
Thee and thy vertues here I seize vpon,
Be it lawfull I take vp what's cast away.
Gods, Gods! 'Tis strange, that from their cold'st neglect
My Loue should kindle to enflam'd respect.
Thy dowrelesse Daughter King, throwne to my chance,
Is Queene of vs, of ours, and our faire *France*:
Not all the Dukes of watrish *Burgundy*,
Can buy this vnpriz'd precious Maid of me.
Bid them farewell *Cordelia*, though vnkinde,
Thou loosest here a better where to finde.
Lear. Thou hast her *France*, let her be thine, for we
Haue no such Daughter, nor shall euer see
That face of hers againe, therfore be gone,
Without our Grace, our Loue, our Benizon:
Come Noble *Burgundie*. *Flourish. Exeunt.*
Fra. Bid farwell to your Sisters.
Cor. The Iewels of our Father, with wash'd eie s
Cordelia leaues you, I know you what you are,
And like a Sister am most loth to call
Your faults as they are named. Loue well our Father:
To your professed bosomes I commit him,
But yet alas, stood I within his Grace,
I would prefer him to a better place,
So farewell to you both.
Regn. Prescribe not vs our dutie.
Gon. Let your study
Be to content your Lord, who hath receiu'd you
At Fortunes almes, you haue obedience scanted,
And well are worth the want that you haue wanted.
Cor. Time shall vnfold what plighted cunning hides,
Who couers faults, at last with shame derides:
Well may you prosper.
Fra. Come my faire *Cordelia*. *Exit France and Cor.*
Gon. Sister, it is not little I haue to say,
Of what most neerely appertaines to vs both,
I thinke our Father will hence to night.
Reg. That's most certaine, and with you: next moneth (with vs.
Gon. You see how full of changes his age is, the obseruation we haue made of it hath beene little; he alwaies lou'd our Sister most, and with what poore iudgement he hath now cast her off, appeares too grossely.
Reg. 'Tis the infirmity of his age, yet he hath euer but slenderly knowne himselfe.
Gon. The best and soundest of his time hath bin but rash, then must we looke from his age, to receiue not alone the imperfections of long ingraffed condition, but therewithall the vnruly way-wardnesse, that infirme and cholericke yeares bring with them.
Reg. Such vnconstant starts are we like to haue from him, as this of *Kents* banishment.
Gon. There is further complement of leaue-taking betweene *France* and him, pray you let vs sit together, if our Father carry authority with such disposition as he beares, this last surrender of his will but offend vs.
Reg. We shall further thinke of it.
Gon. We must do something, and i'th' heate. *Exeunt.*

Scena Secunda.

Enter Bastard.

Bast. Thou Nature art my Goddesse, to thy Law
My seruices are bound, wherefore should I
Stand in the plague of custome, and permit
The curiosity of Nations, to depriue me?
For that I am some twelue, or fourteene Moonshines
Lag of a Brother? Why Bastard? Wherefore base?
When my Dimensions are as well compact,
My minde as generous, and my shape as true
As honest Madams issue? Why brand they vs
With Base? With basenes Barstadie? Base, Base?
Who in the lustie stealth of Nature, take
More composition, and fierce qualitie,
Then doth within a dull stale tyred bed
Goe to th'creating a whole tribe of Fops
Got'tweene a sleepe, and wake? Well then,
Legitimate *Edgar*, I must haue your land,
Our Fathers loue, is to the Bastard *Edmond*,
As to th'legitimate: fine word: Legitimate.

qq 3 Well

Well, my Legittimate, if this Letter ſpeed,
And my inuention thriue, *Edmond* the baſe
Shall to'th'Legitimate : I grow, I proſper :
Now Gods, ſtand vp for Baſtards.

Enter Glouceſter.

Glo. Kent baniſh'd thus? and France in choller parted?
And the King gone to night? Preſcrib'd his powre,
Confin'd to exhibition? All this done
Vpon the gad? *Edmond*, how now? What newes?

Baſt. So pleaſe your Lordſhip, none.

Glou. Why ſo earneſtly ſeeke you to put vp ẏ Letter?

Baſt. I know no newes, my Lord.

Glou. What Paper were you reading?

Baſt. Nothing my Lord.

Glou. No? what needed then that terrible diſpatch of it into your Pocket? The quality of nothing, hath not ſuch neede to hide it ſelfe. Let's ſee : come, if it bee nothing, I ſhall not neede Spectacles.

Baſt. I beſeech you Sir, pardon mee; it is a Letter from my Brother, that I haue not all ore-read; and for ſo much as I haue perus'd, I finde it not fit for your ore-looking.

Glou. Giue me the Letter, Sir.

Baſt. I ſhall offend, either to detaine, or giue it:
The Contents, as in part I vnderſtand them,
Are too blame.

Glou. Let's ſee, let's ſee.

Baſt. I hope for my Brothers iuſtification, hee wrote this but as an eſſay, or taſte of my Vertue.

Glou. reads. This policie, and reuerence of Age, makes the world bitter to the beſt of our times: keepes our Fortunes from vs, till our oldneſſe cannot relliſh them. I begin to finde an idle and fond bondage, in the oppreſſion of aged tyranny, who ſwayes not as it hath power, but as it is ſuffer'd. Come to me, that of this I may ſpeake more. If our Father would ſleepe till I wak'd him, you ſhould enioy halfe his Reuennew for euer, and liue the beloued of your Brother. Edgar.

Hum? Conſpiracy? Sleepe till I wake him, you ſhould enioy halfe his Reuennew : my Sonne *Edgar*, had hee a hand to write this? A heart and braine to breede it in? When came you to this? Who brought it?

Baſt. It was not brought mee, my Lord; there's the cunning of it. I found it throwne in at the Caſement of my Cloſſet.

Glou. You know the character to be your Brothers?

Baſt. If the matter were good my Lord, I durſt ſwear it were his : but in reſpect of that, I would faine thinke it were not.

Glou. It is his.

Baſt. It is his hand, my Lord : but I hope his heart is not in the Contents.

Glo. Has he neuer before ſounded you in this buſines?

Baſt. Neuer my Lord. But I haue heard him oft maintaine it to be fit, that Sonnes at perfect age, and Fathers declin'd, the Father ſhould bee as Ward to the Son, and the Sonne manage his Reuennew.

Glou. O Villain, villain : his very opinion in the Letter. Abhorred Villaine, vnnaturall, deteſted, brutiſh Villaine; worſe then brutiſh : Go ſirrah, ſeeke him : Ile apprehend him. Abhominable Villaine, where is he?

Baſt. I do not well know my L. If it ſhall pleaſe you to ſuſpend your indignation againſt my Brother, til you can deriue from him better teſtimony of his intent, you ſhold run a certaine courſe : where, if you violently proceed againſt him, miſtaking his purpoſe, it would make a great gap in your owne Honor, and ſhake in peeces, the heart of his obedience. I dare pawne downe my life for him, that he hath writ this to feele my affection to your Honor, & to no other pretence of danger.

Glou. Thinke you ſo?

Baſt. If your Honor iudge it meete, I will place you where you ſhall heare vs conferre of this, and by an Auricular aſſurance haue your ſatisfaction, and that without any further delay, then this very Euening.

Glou. He cannot bee ſuch a Monſter. *Edmond* ſeeke him out : winde me into him, I pray you : frame the Buſineſſe after your owne wiſedome. I would vnſtate my ſelfe, to be in a due reſolution.

Baſt. I will ſeeke him Sir, preſently : conuey the buſineſſe as I ſhall find meanes, and acquaint you withall.

Glou. Theſe late Eclipſes in the Sun and Moone portend no good to vs : though the wiſedome of Nature can reaſon it thus, and thus, yet Nature finds it ſelfe ſcourg'd by the ſequent effects. Loue cooles, friendſhip falls off, Brothers diuide. In Cities, mutinies; in Countries, diſcord; in Pallaces, Treaſon; and the Bond crack'd, 'twixt Sonne and Father. This villaine of mine comes vnder the prediction; there's Son againſt Father, the King fals from byas of Nature, there's Father againſt Childe. We haue ſeene the beſt of our time. Machinations, hollowneſſe, treacherie, and all ruinous diſorders follow vs diſquietly to our Graues. Find out this Villain *Edmond*, it ſhall loſe thee nothing, do it carefully : and the Noble & true-harted Kent baniſh'd; his offence, honeſty. 'Tis ſtrange. *Exit*

Baſt. This is the excellent foppery of the world, that when we are ſicke in fortune, often the ſurfets of our own behauiour, we make guilty of our diſaſters, the Sun, the Moone, and Starres, as if we were villaines on neceſſitie, Fooles by heauenly compulſion, Knaues, Theeues, and Treachers by Sphericall predominance. Drunkards, Lyars, and Adulterers by an inforc'd obedience of Planatary influence; and all that we are euill in, by a diuine thruſting on. An admirable euaſion of Whore-maſter-man, to lay his Goatiſh diſpoſition on the charge of a Starre, My father compounded with my mother vnder the Dragons taile, and my Natiuity was vnder *Vrſa Maior*, ſo that it followes, I am rough and Leacherous. I ſhould haue bin that I am, had the maidenleſt Starre in the Firmament twinkled on my baſtardizing.

Enter Edgar.

Pat : he comes like the Cataſtrophe of the old Comedie : my Cue is villanous Melancholly, with a ſighe like *Tom* o'Bedlam. ——— O theſe Eclipſes do portend theſe diuiſions. Fa, Sol, La, Me.

Edg. How now Brother *Edmond*, what ſerious contemplation are you in?

Baſt. I am thinking Brother of a prediction I read this other day, what ſhould follow theſe Eclipſes.

Edg. Do you buſie your ſelfe with that?

Baſt. I promiſe you, the effects he writes of, ſucceede vnhappily.
When ſaw you my Father laſt?

Edg. The night gone by.

Baſt. Spake you with him?

Edg. I, two houres together.

Baſt. Parted you in good termes? Found you no diſpleaſure in him, by word, nor countenance?

Edg. None at all,

Baſt. Bethink your ſelfe wherein you may haue offended him : and at my entreaty forbeare his preſence, vntill ſome little time hath qualified the heat of his diſpleaſure, which at this inſtant ſo rageth in him, that with the miſchiefe

chiefe of your person, it would scarsely alay.

Edg. Some Villaine hath done me wrong.

Edm. That's my feare, I pray you haue a continent forbearance till the speed of his rage goes slower: and as I say, retire with me to my lodging, from whence I will fitly bring you to heare my Lord speake: pray ye goe, there's my key: if you do stirre abroad, goe arm'd.

Edg. Arm'd, Brother?

Edm. Brother, I aduise you to the best, I am no honest man, if ther be any good meaning toward you: I haue told you what I haue seene, and heard: But faintly. Nothing like the image, and horror of it, pray you away.

Edg. Shall I heare from you anon? *Exit.*

Edm. I do serue you in this businesse:
A Credulous Father, and a Brother Noble,
Whose nature is so farre from doing harmes,
That he suspects none: on whose foolish honestie
My practises ride easie: I see the businesse.
Let me, if not by birth, haue lands by wit,
All with me's meete, that I can fashion fit. *Exit.*

Scena Tertia.

Enter Gonerill, and Steward.

Gon. Did my Father strike my Gentleman for chiding of his Foole?

Ste. I Madam.

Gon. By day and night, he wrongs me, euery howre
He flashes into one grosse crime, or other,
That sets vs all at ods: Ile not endure it;
His Knights grow riotous, and himselfe vpbraides vs
On euery trifle. When he returnes from hunting,
I will not speake with him, say I am sicke,
If you come slacke of former seruices,
You shall do well, the fault of it Ile answer.

Ste. He's comming Madam, I heare him.

Gon. Put on what weary negligence you please,
You and your Fellowes: I'de haue it come to question;
If he distaste it, let him to my Sister,
Whose mind and mine I know in that are one,
Remember what I haue said.

Ste. Well Madam.

Gon. And let his Knights haue colder lookes among you: what growes of it no matter, aduise your fellowes so, Ile write straight to my Sister to hold my course; prepare for dinner. *Exeunt.*

Scena Quarta.

Enter Kent.

Kent. If but as will I other accents borrow,
That can my speech defuse, my good intent
May carry through it selfe to that full issue
For which I raiz'd my likenesse. Now banisht *Kent*,
If thou canst serue where thou dost stand condemn'd,
So may it come, thy Master whom thou lou'st,
Shall find thee full of labours.

Hornes within. Enter Lear and Attendants.

Lear. Let me not stay a iot for dinner, go get it ready: how now, what art thou?

Kent. A man Sir.

Lear. What dost thou professe? What would'st thou with vs?

Kent. I do professe to be no lesse then I seeme; to serue him truely that will put me in trust, to loue him that is honest, to conuerse with him that is wise and saies little, to feare iudgement, to fight when I cannot choose, and to eate no fish.

Lear. What art thou?

Kent. A very honest hearted Fellow, and as poore as the King.

Lear. If thou be'st as poore for a subiect, as hee's for a King, thou art poore enough. What wouldst thou?

Kent. Seruice.

Lear. Who wouldst thou serue?

Kent. You.

Lear. Do'st thou know me fellow?

Kent. No Sir, but you haue that in your countenance, which I would faine call Master.

Lear. What's that?

Kent. Authority.

Lear. What seruices canst thou do?

Kent. I can keepe honest counsaile, ride, run, marre a curious tale in telling it, and deliuer a plaine message bluntly: that which ordinary men are fit for, I am qualified in, and the best of me, is Dilligence.

Lear. How old art thou?

Kent. Not so young Sir to loue a woman for singing, nor so old to dote on her for any thing. I haue yeares on my backe forty eight.

Lear. Follow me, thou shalt serue me, if I like thee no worse after dinner, I will not part from thee yet. Dinner ho, dinner, where's my knaue? my Foole? Go you and call my Foole hither. You you Sirrah, where's my Daughter?

Enter Steward.

Ste. So please you—— *Exit.*

Lear. What saies the Fellow there? Call the Clotpole backe: wher's my Foole? Ho, I thinke the world's asleepe, how now? Where's that Mungrell?

Knigh. He saies my Lord, your Daughters is not well.

Lear. Why came not the slaue backe to me when I call'd him?

Knigh. Sir, he answered me in the roundest manner, he would not.

Lear. He would not?

Knight. My Lord, I know not what the matter is, but to my iudgement your Highnesse is not entertain'd with that Ceremonious affection as you were wont, theres a great abatement of kindnesse appeares as well in the generall dependants, as in the Duke himselfe also, and your Daughter.

Lear. Ha? Saist thou so?

Knigh. I beseech you pardon me my Lord, if I bee mistaken, for my duty cannot be silent, when I thinke your Highnesse wrong'd.

Lear. Thou but remembrest me of mine owne Conception, I haue perceiued a most faint neglect of late, which I haue rather blamed as mine owne iealous curiositie, then as a very pretence and purpose of vnkindnesse; I will looke further intoo't: but where's my Foole? I haue not seene him this two daies.

Knight. Since my young Ladies going into *France* Sir,

Sir, the Foole hath much pined away.

Lear. No more of that, I haue noted it well, goe you and tell my Daughter, I would ſpeake with her. Goe you call hither my Foole; Oh you Sir, you, come you hither Sir, who am I Sir?

Enter Steward.

Ste. My Ladies Father.

Lear. My Ladies Father? my Lords knaue, you whorſon dog, you ſlaue, you curre.

Ste. I am none of theſe my Lord,
I beſeech your pardon.

Lear. Do you bandy lookes with me, you Raſcall?

Ste. Ile not be ſtrucken my Lord.

Kent. Nor tript neither, you baſe Foot-ball plaier.

Lear. I thanke thee fellow.
Thou ſeru'ſt me, and Ile loue thee.

Kent. Come ſir, ariſe, away, Ile teach you differences: away, away, if you will meaſure your lubbers length againe, tarry, but away, goe too, haue you wiſedome, ſo.

Lear. Now my friendly knaue I thanke thee, there's earneſt of thy ſeruice.

Enter Foole.

Foole. Let me hire him too, here's my Coxcombe.

Lear. How now my pretty knaue, how doſt thou?

Foole. Sirrah, you were beſt take my Coxcombe.

Lear. Why my Boy?

Foole. Why? for taking ones part that's out of fauour, nay, & thou canſt not ſmile as the wind ſits, thou'lt catch colde ſhortly, there take my Coxcombe; why this fellow ha's baniſh'd two on's Daughters, and did the third a bleſſing againſt his will, if thou follow him, thou muſt needs weare my Coxcombe. How now Nunckle? would I had two Coxcombes and two Daughters.

Lear. Why my Boy?

Fool. If I gaue them all my liuing, I'ld keepe my Coxcombes my ſelfe, there's mine, beg another of thy Daughters.

Lear. Take heed Sirrah, the whip.

Foole. Truth's a dog muſt to kennell, hee muſt bee whipt out, when the Lady Brach may ſtand by'th'fire and ſtinke.

Lear. A peſtilent gall to me.

Foole. Sirha, Ile teach thee a ſpeech.

Lear. Do.

Foole. Marke it Nuncle;
Haue more then thou ſhoweſt,
Speake leſſe then thou knoweſt,
Lend leſſe then thou oweſt,
Ride more then thou goeſt,
Learne more then thou troweſt,
Set leſſe then thou throweſt;
Leaue thy drinke and thy whore,
And keepe in a dore,
And thou ſhalt haue more,
Then two tens to a ſcore.

Kent. This is nothing Foole.

Foole. Then 'tis like the breath of an vnfeed Lawyer, you gaue me nothing for't, can you make no vſe of nothing Nuncle?

Lear. Why no Boy,
Nothing can be made out of nothing.

Foole. Prythee tell him, ſo much the rent of his land comes to, he will not beleeue a Foole.

Lear. A bitter Foole.

Foole. Do'ſt thou know the difference my Boy, betweene a bitter Foole, and a ſweet one.

Lear. No Lad, teach me.

Foole. Nunckle, giue me an egge, and Ile giue thee two Crownes.

Lear. What two Crownes ſhall they be?

Foole. Why after I haue cut the egge i'th'middle and eate vp the meate, the two Crownes of the egge: when thou clioueſt thy Crownes i'th'middle, and gau'ſt away both parts, thou boar'ſt thine Aſſe on thy backe o're the durt, thou had'ſt little wit in thy bald crowne, when thou gau'ſt thy golden one away; if I ſpeake like my ſelfe in this, let him be whipt that firſt findes it ſo.
Fooles had nere leſſe grace in a yeere,
For wiſemen are growne foppiſh,
And know not how their wits to weare,
Their manners are ſo apiſh.

Le. When were you wont to be ſo full of Songs ſirrah?

Foole. I haue vſed it Nunckle, ere ſince thou mad'ſt thy Daughters thy Mothers, for when thou gau'ſt them the rod, and put'ſt downe thine owne breeches, then they
For ſodaine ioy did weepe,
And I for ſorrow ſung,
That ſuch a King ſhould play bo-peepe,
And goe the Foole among.
Pry'thy Nunckle keepe a Schoolemaſter that can teach thy Foole to lie, I would faine learne to lie.

Lear. And you lie ſirrah, wee'l haue you whipt.

Foole. I maruell what kin thou and thy daughters are, they'l haue me whipt for ſpeaking true: thou'lt haue me whipt for lying, and ſometimes I am whipt for holding my peace. I had rather be any kind o'thing then a foole, and yet I would not be thee Nunckle, thou haſt pared thy wit o'both ſides, and left nothing i'th'middle; heere comes one o'the parings.

Enter Gonerill.

Lear. How now Daughter? what makes that Frontlet on? You are too much of late i'th'frowne.

Foole. Thou waſt a pretty fellow when thou hadſt no need to care for her frowning, now thou art an O without a figure, I am better then thou art now, I am a Foole, thou art nothing. Yes forſooth I will hold my tongue, ſo your face bids me, though you ſay nothing.
Mum, mum, he that keepes nor cruſt, not crum,
Weary of all, ſhall want ſome. That's a ſheal'd Peſcod.

Gon. Not only Sir this, your all-lycenc'd Foole,
But other of your inſolent retinue
Do hourely Carpe and Quarrell, breaking forth
In ranke, and (not to be endur'd) riots Sir.
I had thought by making this well knowne vnto you,
To haue found a ſafe redreſſe, but now grow fearefull
By what your ſelfe too late haue ſpoke and done,
That you protect this courſe, and put it on
By your allowance, which if you ſhould, the fault
Would not ſcape cenſure, nor the redreſſes ſleepe,
Which in the tender of a wholeſome weale,
Might in their working do you that offence,
Which elſe were ſhame, that then neceſſitie
Will call diſcreet proceeding.

Foole. For you know Nunckle, the Hedge-Sparrow fed the Cuckoo ſo long, that it's had it head bit off by it young, ſo out went the Candle, and we were left darkling.

Lear. Are you our Daughter?

Gon. I would you would make vſe of your good wiſedome
(Whereof I know you are fraught), and put away
Theſe diſpoſitions, which of late tranſport you
From what you rightly are.

Foole. May

Foole. May not an Asse know, when the Cart drawes the Horse?
Whoop Iugge I loue thee.
Lear. Do's any heere know me?
This is not *Lear*:
Do's *Lear* walke thus? Speake thus? Where are his eies?
Either his Notion weakens, his Discernings
Are Lethargied. Ha! Waking? 'Tis not so?
Who is it that can tell me who I am?
Foole. Lears shadow.
Lear. Your name, faire Gentlewoman?
Gon. This admiration Sir, is much o'th'sauour
Of other your new prankes. I do beseech you
To vnderstand my purposes aright:
As you are Old, and Reuerend, should be Wise.
Heere do you keepe a hundred Knights and Squires,
Men so disorder'd, so debosh'd, and bold,
That this our Court infected with their manners,
Shewes like a riotous Inne; Epicurisme and Lust
Makes it more like a Tauerne, or a Brothell,
Then a grac'd Pallace. The shame it selfe doth speake
For instant remedy. Be then desir'd
By her, that else will take the thing she begges,
A little to disquantity your Traine,
And the remainders that shall still depend,
To be such men as may besort your Age,
Which know themselues, and you.
Lear. Darknesse, and Diuels.
Saddle my horses: call my Traine together.
Degenerate Bastard, Ile not trouble thee;
Yet haue I left a daughter.
Gon. You strike my people, and your disorder'd rable, make Seruants of their Betters.

Enter Albany.

Lear. Woe, that too late repents:
Is it your will, speake Sir? Prepare my Horses.
Ingratitude! thou Marble-hearted Fiend,
More hideous when thou shew'st thee in a Child,
Then the Sea-monster.
Alb. Pray Sir be patient.
Lear. Detested Kite, thou lyest.
My Traine are men of choice, and rarest parts,
That all particulars of dutie know,
And in the most exact regard, support
The worships of their name. O most small fault,
How vgly did'st thou in *Cordelia* shew?
Which like an Engine, wrencht my frame of Nature
From the fixt place: drew from my heart all loue,
And added to the gall. O *Lear*, *Lear*, *Lear*!
Beate at this gate that let thy Folly in,
And thy deere Iudgement out. Go, go, my people.
Alb. My Lord, I am guiltlesse, as I am ignorant
Of what hath moued you.
Lear. It may be so, my Lord.
Heare Nature, heare deere Goddesse, heare:
Suspend thy purpose, if thou did'st intend
To make this Creature fruitfull:
Into her Wombe conuey stirrility,
Drie vp in her the Organs of increase,
And from her derogate body, neuer spring
A Babe to honor her. If she must teeme,
Create her childe of Spleene, that it may liue
And be a thwart disnatur'd torment to her.
Let it stampe wrinkles in her brow of youth,
With cadent Teares fret Channels in her cheekes,
Turne all her Mothers paines, and benefits
To laughter, and contempt: That she may feele,
How sharper then a Serpents tooth it is,
To haue a thanklesse Childe. Away, away. *Exit.*
Alb. Now Gods that we adore,
Whereof comes this?
Gon. Neuer afflict your selfe to know more of it:
But let his disposition haue that scope
As dotage giues it.

Enter Lear.

Lear. What fiftie of my Followers at a clap?
Within a fortnight?
Alb. What's the matter, Sir?
Lear. Ile tell thee:
Life and death, I am asham'd
That thou hast power to shake my manhood thus,
That these hot teares, which breake from me perforce
Should make thee worth them.
Blastes and Fogges vpon thee:
Th'vntented woundings of a Fathers curse
Pierce euerie sense about thee. Old fond eyes,
Beweepe this cause againe, Ile plucke ye out,
And cast you with the waters that you loose
To temper Clay. Ha? Let it be so.
I haue another daughter,
Who I am sure is kinde and comfortable:
When she shall heare this of thee, with her nailes
Shee'l flea thy Woluish visage. Thou shalt finde,
That Ile resume the shape which thou dost thinke
I haue cast off for euer. *Exit*
Gon. Do you marke that?
Alb. I cannot be so partiall *Gonerill*,
To the great loue I beare you.
Gon. Pray you content. What *Oswald*, hoa?
You Sir, more Knaue then Foole, after your Master.
Foole. Nunkle *Lear*, Nunkle *Lear*,
Tarry, take the Foole with thee:
A Fox, when one has caught her,
And such a Daughter,
Should sure to the Slaughter,
If my Cap would buy a Halter,
So the Foole followes after. *Exit*
Gon. This man hath had good Counsell,
A hundred Knights?
'Tis politike, and safe to let him keepe
At point a hundred Knights: yes, that on euerie dreame,
Each buz, each fancie, each complaint, dislike,
He may enguard his dotage with their powres,
And hold our liues in mercy. *Oswald*, I say.
Alb. Well, you may feare too farre.
Gon. Safer then trust too farre;
Let me still take away the harmes I feare,
Not feare still to be taken. I know his heart,
What he hath vtter'd I haue writ my Sister:
If she sustaine him, and his hundred Knights
When I haue shew'd th'vnfitnesse.

Enter Steward.

How now *Oswald*?
What haue you writ that Letter to my Sister?
Stew. I Madam.
Gon. Take you some company, and away to horse,
Informe her full of my particular feare,
And thereto adde such reasons of your owne,
As may compact it more. Get you gone,
And

And haſten your returne; no, no, my Lord,
This milky gentleneſſe, and courſe of yours
Though I condemne not, yet vnder pardon
Your are much more at task for want of wiſedome,
Then prai'sd for harmefull mildneſſe.

Alb. How farre your eies may pierce I cannot tell;
Striuing to better, oft we marre what's well.

Gon. Nay then ——

Alb. Well, well, the'uent. *Exeunt*

Scena Quinta.

Enter Lear, Kent, Gentleman, and Foole.

Lear. Go you before to *Gloſter* with theſe Letters; acquaint my Daughter no further with any thing you know, then comes from her demand out of the Letter, if your Dilligence be not ſpeedy, I ſhall be there afore you.

Kent. I will not ſleepe my Lord, till I haue deliuered your Letter. *Exit.*

Foole. If a mans braines were in's heeles, wert not in danger of kybes?

Lear. I Boy.

Foole. Then I prythee be merry, thy wit ſhall not go ſlip-ſhod.

Lear. Ha, ha, ha.

Fool. Shalt ſee thy other Daughter will vſe thee kindly, for though ſhe's as like this, as a Crabbe's like an Apple, yet I can tell what I can tell.

Lear. What can'ſt tell Boy?

Foole. She will taſte as like this as, a Crabbe do's to a Crab: thou canſt tell why ones noſe ſtands i'th'middle on's face?

Lear. No.

Foole. Why to keepe ones eyes of either ſide's noſe, that what a man cannot ſmell out, he may ſpy into.

Lear. I did her wrong.

Foole. Can'ſt tell how an Oyſter makes his ſhell?

Lear. No.

Foole. Nor I neither; but I can tell why a Snaile ha's a houſe.

Lear. Why?

Foole. Why to put's head in, not to giue it away to his daughters, and leaue his hornes without a caſe.

Lear. I will forget my Nature, ſo kind a Father? Be my Horſſes ready?

Foole. Thy Aſſes are gone about 'em; the reaſon why the ſeuen Starres are no mo then ſeuen, is a pretty reaſon.

Lear. Becauſe they are not eight.

Foole. Yes indeed, thou would'ſt make a good Foole.

Lear. To tak't againe perforce; Monſter Ingratitude!

Foole. If thou wert my Foole Nunckle, Il'd haue thee beaten for being old before thy time.

Lear. How's that?

Foole. Thou ſhouldſt not haue bin old, till thou hadſt bin wiſe.

Lear. O let me not be mad, not mad ſweet Heauen: keepe me in temper, I would not be mad. How now are the Horſes ready?

Gent. Ready my Lord.

Lear. Come Boy.

Fool. She that's a Maid now, & laughs at my departure,
Shall not be a Maid long, vnleſſe things be cut ſhorter. *Exeunt.*

Actus Secundus. Scena Prima.

Enter Baſtard, and Curan, ſeuerally.

Baſt. Saue thee *Curan.*

Cur. And your Sir, I haue bin
With your Father, and giuen him notice
That the Duke of *Cornwall*, and *Regan* his Ducheſſe
Will be here with him this night.

Baſt. How comes that?

Cur. Nay I know not, you haue heard of the newes abroad, I meane the whiſper'd ones, for they are yet but eare-kiſſing arguments.

Baſt. Not I: pray you what are they?

Cur. Haue you heard of no likely Warres toward,
'Twixt the Dukes of *Cornwall*, and *Albany*?

Baſt. Not a word.

Cur. You may do then in time,
Fare you well Sir. *Exit.*

Baſt. The Duke be here to night? The better beſt,
This weaues it ſelfe perforce into my buſineſſe,
My Father hath ſet guard to take my Brother,
And I haue one thing of a queazie queſtion
Which I muſt act, Briefeneſſe, and Fortune worke.

Enter Edgar.

Brother, a word, diſcend; Brother I ſay,
My Father watches: O Sir, fly this place,
Intelligence is giuen where you are hid;
You haue now the good aduantage of the night,
Haue you not ſpoken 'gainſt the Duke of *Cornewall*?
Hee's comming hither, now i'th' night, i'th' haſte,
And *Regan* with him, haue you nothing ſaid
Vpon his partie 'gainſt the Duke of *Albany*?
Aduiſe your ſelfe.

Edg. I am ſure on't, not a word.

Baſt. I heare my Father comming, pardon me:
In cunning, I muſt draw my Sword vpon you:
Draw, ſeeme to defend your ſelfe,
Now quit you well.
Yeeld, come before my Father, light hoa, here,
Fly Brother, Torches, Torches, ſo farewell. *Exit Edgar.*
Some blood drawne on me, would beget opinion
Of my more fierce endeauour. I haue ſeene drunkards
Do more then this in ſport; Father, Father,
Stop, ſtop, no helpe?

Enter Gloſter, and Seruants with Torches.

Glo. Now *Edmund*, where's the villaine?

Baſt. Here ſtood he in the dark, his ſharpe Sword out,
Mumbling of wicked charmes, coniuring the Moone
To ſtand auſpicious Miſtris.

Glo. But where is he?

Baſt. Looke Sir, I bleed.

Glo. Where is the villaine, *Edmund*?

Baſt. Fled this way Sir, when by no meanes he could.

Glo. Purſue him, ho: go after. By no meanes, what?

Baſt. Perſwade me to the murther of your Lordſhip,

But that I told him the reuenging Gods,
'Gainst Paricides did all the thunder bend,
Spoke with how manifold, and strong a Bond
The Child was bound to'th' Father; Sir in fine,
Seeing how lothly opposite I stood
To his vnnaturall purpose, in fell motion
With his prepared Sword, he charges home
My vnprouided body, latch'd mine arme;
And when he saw my best alarum'd spirits
Bold in the quarrels right, rouz'd to th'encounter,
Or whether gasted by the noyse I made,
Full sodainely he fled.
Glost. Let him fly farre:
Not in this Land shall he remaine vncaught
And found; dispatch, the Noble Duke my Master,
My worthy Arch and Patron comes to night,
By his authoritie I will proclaime it,
That he which finds him shall deserue our thankes,
Bringing the murderous Coward to the stake:
He that conceales him death.
Bast. When I disswaded him from his intent,
And found him pight to doe it, with curst speech
I threaten'd to discouer him; he replied,
Thou vnpossessing Bastard, dost thou thinke,
If I would stand against thee, would the reposall
Of any trust, vertue, or worth in thee
Make thy words faith'd? No, what should I denie,
(As this I would, though thou didst produce
My very Character) I'ld turne it all
To thy suggestion, plot, and damned practise:
And thou must make a dullard of the world,
If they not thought the profits of my death
Were very pregnant and potentiall spirits
To make thee seeke it. *Tucket within.*
Glo. O strange and fastned Villaine,
Would he deny his Letter, said he?
Harke, the Dukes Trumpets, I know not wher he comes;
All Ports Ile barre, the villaine shall not scape,
The Duke must grant me that: besides, his picture
I will send farre and neere, that all the kingdome
May haue due note of him, and of my land,
(Loyall and naturall Boy) Ile worke the meanes
To make thee capable.

Enter Cornewall, Regan, and Attendants.

Corn. How now my Noble friend, since I came hither
(Which I can call but now,) I haue heard strangenesse.
Reg. If it be true, all vengeance comes too short
Which can pursue th'offender; how dost my Lord?
Glo. O Madam, my old heart is crack'd, it's crack'd.
Reg. What, did my Fathers Godsonne seeke your life?
He whom my Father nam'd, your *Edgar*?
Glo. O Lady, Lady, shame would haue it hid.
Reg. Was he not companion with the riotous Knights
That tended vpon my Father?
Glo. I know not Madam, 'tis too bad, too bad.
Bast. Yes Madam, he was of that consort.
Reg. No maruaile then, though he were ill affected,
'Tis they haue put him on the old mans death,
To haue th'expence and wast of his Reuenues:
I haue this present euening from my Sister
Beene well inform'd of them, and with such cautions,
That if they come to soiourne at my house,
Ile not be there.
Cor. Nor I, assure thee *Regan*;
Edmund, I heare that you haue shewne yout Father
A Child-like Office.
Bast. It was my duty Sir.
Glo. He did bewray his practise, and receiu'd
This hurt you see, striuing to apprehend him.
Cor. Is he pursued?
Glo. I my good Lord.
Cor. If he be taken, he shall neuer more
Be fear'd of doing harme, make your owne purpose,
How in my strength you please: for you *Edmund*,
Whose vertue and obedience doth this instant
So much commend it selfe, you shall be ours,
Nature's of such deepe trust, we shall much need:
You we first seize on.
Bast. I shall serue you Sir truely, how euer else.
Glo. For him I thanke your Grace.
Cor. You know not why we came to visit you?
Reg. Thus out of season, thredding darke ey'd night,
Occasions Noble *Gloster* of some prize,
Wherein we must haue vse of your aduise.
Our Father he hath writ, so hath our Sister,
Of differences, which I best though it fit
To answere from our home: the seuerall Messengers
From hence attend dispatch, our good old Friend,
Lay comforts to your bosome, and bestow
Your needfull counsaile to our businesses,
Which craues the instant vse.
Glo. I serue you Madam,
Your Graces are right welcome. *Exeunt. Flourish.*

Scena Secunda.

Enter Kent, aad Steward seuerally.

Stew. Good dawning to thee Friend, art of this house?
Kent. I.
Stew. Where may we set our horses?
Kent. I'th'myre.
Stew. Prythee, if thou lou'st me, tell me.
Kent. I loue thee not.
Ste. Why then I care not for thee.
Kent. If I had thee in *Lipsbury* Pinfold, I would make thee care for me.
Ste. Why do'st thou vse me thus? I know thee not.
Kent. Fellow I know thee.
Ste. What do'st thou know me for?
Kent. A Knaue, a Rascall, an eater of broken meates, a base, proud, shallow, beggerly, three-suited-hundred pound, filthy woosted-stocking knaue, a Lilly-liuered, action-taking, whoreson glasse-gazing super-seruiceable finicall Rogue, one Trunke-inheriting slaue, one that would'st be a Baud in way of good seruice, and art nothing but the composition of a Knaue, Begger, Coward, Pandar, and the Sonne and Heire of a Mungrill Bitch, one whom I will beate into clamours whining, if thou deny'st the least sillable of thy addition.
Stew. Why, what a monstrous Fellow art thou, thus to raile on one, that is neither knowne of thee, nor knowes thee?
Kent. What a brazen-fac'd Varlet art thou, to deny thou knowest me? Is it two dayes since I tript vp thy heeles, and beate thee before the King? Draw you rogue, for

for though it be night, yet the Moone ſhines, Ile make a ſop oth' Moonſhine of you, you whoreſon Cullyenly Barber-monger, draw.

Stew. Away, I haue nothing to do with thee.

Kent. Draw you Raſcall, you come with Letters againſt the King, and take Vanitie the puppets part, againſt the Royaltie of her Father : draw you Rogue, or Ile ſo carbonado your ſhanks, draw you Raſcall, come your waies.

Ste. Helpe, ho, murther, helpe.

Kent. Strike you ſlaue : ſtand rogue, ſtand you neat ſlaue, ſtrike.

Stew. Helpe hoa, murther, murther.

Enter Baſtard, Cornewall, Regan, Gloſter, Seruants.

Baſt. How now, what's the matter ? Part.

Kent. With you goodman Boy, if you pleaſe, come, Ile fleſh ye, come on yong Maſter.

Glo. Weapons ? Armes ? what's the matter here ?

Cor. Keepe peace vpon your liues, he dies that ſtrikes againe, what is the matter ?

Reg. The Meſſengers from our Siſter, and the King ?

Cor. What is your difference, ſpeake ?

Stew. I am ſcarce in breath my Lord.

Kent. No Maruell, you haue ſo beſtir'd your valour, you cowardly Raſcall, nature diſclaimes in thee: a Taylor made thee.

Cor. Thou art a ſtrange fellow, a Taylor make a man?

Kent. A Taylor Sir, a Stone-cutter, or a Painter, could not haue made him ſo ill, though they had bin but two yeares oth'trade.

Cor. Speake yet, how grew your quarrell ?

Ste. This ancient Ruffian Sir, whoſe life I haue ſpar'd at ſute of his gray-beard.

Kent. Thou whoreſon Zed, thou vnneceſſary letter: my Lord, if you will giue me leaue, I will tread this vnboulted villaine into morter, and daube the wall of a Iakes with him. Spare my gray-beard, you wagtaile ?

Cor. Peace ſirrah,
You beaſtly knaue, know you no reuerence ?

Kent. Yes Sir, but anger hath a priuiledge.

Cor. Why art thou angrie ?

Kent. That ſuch a ſlaue as this ſhould weare a Sword,
Who weares no honeſty : ſuch ſmiling rogues as theſe,
Like Rats oft bite the holy cords a twaine,
Which are t'intrince, t'vnlooſe : ſmooth euery paſſion
That in the natures of their Lords rebell,
Being oile to fire, ſnow to the colder moodes,
Reuenge, affirme, and turne their Halcion beakes
With euery gall, and varry of their Maſters,
Knowing naught (like dogges) but following :
A plague vpon your Epilepticke viſage,
Smoile you my ſpeeches, as I were a Foole ?
Gooſe, if I had you vpon *Sarum* Plaine,
I'ld driue ye cackling home to *Camelot*.

Corn. What art thou mad old Fellow ?

Gloſt. How fell you out, ſay that ?

Kent. No contraries hold more antipathy,
Then I, and ſuch a knaue.

Corn. Why do'ſt thou call him Knaue ?
What is his fault ?

Kent. His countenance likes me not.

Cor. No more perchance do's mine, nor his, nor hers.

Kent. Sir, 'tis my occupation to be plaine,
I haue ſeene better faces in my time,
Then ſtands on any ſhoulder that I ſee
Before me, at this inſtant.

Corn. This is ſome Fellow,
Who hauing beene prais'd for bluntneſſe, doth affect
A ſaucy roughnes, and conſtraines the garb
Quite from his Nature. He cannot flatter he,
An honeſt mind and plaine, he muſt ſpeake truth,
And they will take it ſo, if not, hee's plaine.
Theſe kind of Knaues I know, which in this plainneſſe
Harbour more craft, and more corrupter ends,
Then twenty ſilly-ducking obſeruants,
That ſtretch their duties nicely.

Kent. Sir, in good faith, in ſincere verity,
Vnder th'allowance of your great aſpect,
Whoſe influence like the wreath of radient fire
On flicking *Phœbus* front.

Corn. What mean'ſt by this ?

Kent. To go out of my dialect, which you diſcommend ſo much; I know Sir, I am no flatterer, he that beguild you in a plaine accent, was a plaine Knaue, which for my part I will not be, though I ſhould win your diſpleaſure to entreat me too't.

Corn. What was th'offence you gaue him ?

Ste. I neuer gaue him any :
It pleas'd the King his Maſter very late
To ſtrike at me vpon his miſconſtruction,
When he compact, and flattering his diſpleaſure
Tript me behind: being downe, inſulted, rail'd,
And put vpon him ſuch a deale of Man,
That worthied him, got praiſes of the King,
For him attempting, who was ſelfe-ſubdued,
And in the fleſhment of this dead exploit,
Drew on me here againe.

Kent. None of theſe Rogues, and Cowards
But *Aiax* is there Foole.

Corn. Fetch forth the Stocks ?
You ſtubborne ancient Knaue, you reuerent Bragart,
Wee'l teach you.

Kent. Sir, I am too old to learne :
Call not your Stocks for me, I ſerue the King.
On whoſe imployment I was ſent to you,
You ſhall doe ſmall reſpects, ſhow too bold malice
Againſt the Grace, and Perſon of my Maſter,
Stocking his Meſſenger.

Corn. Fetch forth the Stocks;
As I haue life and Honour, there ſhall he ſit till Noone.

Reg. Till noone? till night my Lord, and all night too.

Kent. Why Madam, if I were your Fathers dog,
You ſhould not vſe me ſo.

Reg. Sir, being his Knaue, I will. *Stocks brought out.*

Cor. This is a Fellow of the ſelfe ſame colour,
Our Siſter ſpeakes of. Come, bring away the Stocks.

Glo. Let me beſeech your Grace, not to do ſo,
The King his Maſter, needs muſt take it ill
That he ſo ſlightly valued in his Meſſenger,
Should haue him thus reſtrained.

Cor. Ile anſwere that.

Reg. My Siſter may recieue it much more worſſe,
To haue her Gentleman abus'd, aſſaulted.

Corn. Come my Lord, away. *Exit.*

Glo. I am ſorry for thee friend, 'tis the Duke pleaſure,
Whoſe diſpoſition all the world well knowes
Will not be rub'd nor ſtopt, Ile entreat for thee.

Kent. Pray do not Sir, I haue watch'd and trauail'd hard,
Some time I ſhall ſleepe out, the reſt Ile whiſtle :
A good mans fortune may grow out at heeles:

Giue

Giue you good morrow.
Glo. The Duke's too blamein this,
'Twill be ill taken. *Exit.*
*Kent.*Good King, that must approue the common saw,
Thou out of Heauens benediction com'st
To the warme Sun.
Approach thou Beacon to this vnder Globe,
That by thy comfortable Beames I may
Peruse this Letter. Nothing almost sees miracles
But miserie. I know 'tis from *Cordelia*,
Who hath most fortunately beene inform'd
Of my obscured course. And shall finde time
From this enormous State, seeking to giue
Losses their remedies .All weary and o're-watch'd,
Take vantage heauie eyes, not to behold
This shamefnll lodging. Fortune goodnight,
Smile once more, turne thy wheele.

Enter Edgar.

Edg. I heard my selfe proclaim'd,
And by the happy hollow of a Tree,
Escap'd the hunt. No Port is free, no place
That guard, and most vnusall vigilance
Do's not attend my taking. Whiles I may scape
I will preserue myselfe: and am bethought
To take the basest, and most poorest shape
That euer penury in contempt of man,
Brought neere to beast; my face Ile grime with filth,
Blanket my loines, else all my haires in knots,
And with presented nakednesse out-face
The Windes, and persecutions of the skie;
The Country giues me proofe, and president
Of Bedlam beggers, who with roaring voices,
Strike in their num'd and mortified Armes,
Pins, Wodden-prickes, Nayles, Sprigs of Rosemarie:
And with this horrible obiect, from low Farmes,
Poore pelting Villages, Sheeps-Coates, and Milles,
Sometimes with Lunaticke bans, sometime with Praiers
Inforce their charitie: poore *Turlygod*, poore *Tom*,
That's something yet: *Edgar* I nothing am. *Exit.*

Enter Lear, Foole, and Gentleman.

Lea.'Tis strange that they should so depart from home,
And not send backe my Messengers.
Gent. As I learn'd,
The night before, there was no purpose in them
Of this remoue.
Kent. Haile to thee Noble Master.
Lear. Ha? Mak'st thou this shame ahy pastime?
Kent. No my Lord.
Foole. Hah, ha, he weares Cruell Garters Horses are tide by the heads, Dogges and Beares by'th'necke, Monkies by'th'loynes, and Men by'th' legs: when a man ouerlustie at legs, then he weares wodden nether-stocks.
Lear. What's he,
That hath so much thy place mistooke
To set thee heere?
Kent. It is both he and she,
Your Son, and Daughter.
Lear. No.
Kent. Yes.
Lear. No I say.
Kent. I say yea.
Lear. By *Iupiter* I sweare no.
Kent. By *Iuuo*, I sweare I.
Lear. They durst not do't:
They could not, would not do't: 'tis worse then murther,
To do vpon respect such violent outrage:
Resolue me with all modest haste, which way
Thou might'st deserue, or they impose this vsage,
Comming from vs.
Kent. My Lord, when at their home
I did commend your Highnesse Letters to them,
Ere I was risen from the place, that shewed
My dutie kneeling, came there a reeking Poste,
Stew'd in his haste, halfe breathlesse, painting forth
From *Gonerill* his Mistris, salutations;
Deliuer'd Letters spight of intermission,
Which presently they read; on those contents
They summon'd vp their meiney, straight tooke Horse,
Commanded me to follow, and attend
The leisure of their answer, gaue me cold lookes,
And meeting heere the other Messenger,
Whose welcome I perceiu'd had poison'd mine,
Being the very fellow which of late
Displaid so sawcily against your Highnesse,
Hauing more man then wit about me, drew;
He rais'd the house, with loud and coward cries,
Your Sonne and Daughter found this trespasse worth
The shame which heere it suffers.
Foole. Winters not gon yet, if the wil'd Geese fly that way,
Fathers that weare rags, do make their Children blind,
But Fathers that beare bags, shall see their children kind.
Fortune that arrant whore, nere turns the key toth' poore.
But for all this thou shalt haue as many Dolors for thy Daughters, as thou canst tell in a yeare.
Lear. Oh how this Mother swels vp toward my heart!
Historica passio, downe thou climing sorrow,
Thy Elements below where is this Daughter?
Kent. Wirh the Earle Sir, here within.
Lear. Follow me not, stay here. *Exit.*
Gen. Made you no more offence,
But what you speake of?
Kent. None:
How chance the the King comes with so small a number?
Foole. And thou hadst beene set i'th'Stockes for that question, thoud'st well deseru'd it.
Kent. Why Foole?
Foole. Wee'l set thee to schoole to an Ant, to teach thee ther's no labouring i'th' winter. All that follow their noses, are led by their eyes, but blinde men, and there's not a nose among twenty, but can smell him that's stinking; let go thy hold, when a greatwheele runs downe a hill, least it breake thy necke with following. But the great one that goes vpward, let him drawthee after: when a wiseman giues thee better counsell giue me mine againe, I would hause none but knaues follow it, since a Foole giues it.
That Sir, which serues and seekes for gaine,
And followes but for forme;
Will packe, when it begins to raine,
And leaue thee in the storme,
But I will tarry, the Foole will stay,
And let the wiseman flie:
The knaue turnes Foole that runnes away,
The Foole noknaue perdie.

Enter Lear, and Gloster:

Kent. Where learn'd you this Foole?
Foole. Not i'th' Stocks Foole.

Lear. Deny to speake with me?
They are sicke, they are weary,
They haue trauail'd all the night? meere fetches,
The images of reuolt and flying off.
Fetch me a better answer.
Glo. My deere Lord,
You know the fiery quality of the Duke,
How vnremoueable and fixt he is
In his owne course.
Lear. Vengeance, Plague, Death, Confusion:
Fiery? What quality? Why *Gloster*, *Gloster*,
I'ld speake with the Duke of *Cornewall*, and his wife.
Glo. Well my good Lord, I haue inform'd them so.
Lear. Inform'd them? Do'st thou vnderstand me man.
Glo. I my good Lord.
Lear. The King would speake with *Cornwall*,
The deere Father
Would with his Daughter speake, commands, tends, ser-
Are they inform'd of this? My breath and blood: (uice,
Fiery? The fiery Duke, tell the hot Duke that ——
No, but not yet, may be he is not well,
Infirmity doth still neglect all office,
Whereto our health is bound, we are not our selues,
When Nature being opprest, commands the mind
To suffer with the body; Ile forbeare,
And am fallen out with my more headier will,
To take the indispos'd and sickly fit,
For the sound man. Death on my state: wherefore
Should he sit heere? This act perswades me,
That this remotion of the Duke and her
Is practise only. Giue me my Seruant forth;
Goe tell the Duke, and's wife, Il'd speake with them:
Now, presently: bid them come forth and heare me,
Or at their Chamber doore Ile beate the Drum,
Till it crie sleepe to death.
Glo. I would haue all well betwixt you. *Exit.*
Lear. Oh me my heart! My rising heart! But downe.
Foole. Cry to it Nunckle, as the Cockney did to the Eeles, when she put 'em i'th' Paste aliue, she knapt 'em o'th' coxcombs with a sticke, and cryed downe wantons, downe; 'twas her Brother, that in pure kindnesse to his Horse buttered his Hay.

Enter Cornewall, Regan, Gloster, Seruants.

Lear. Good morrow to you both.
Corn. Haile to your Grace. *Kent here set at liberty.*
Reg. I am glad to see your Highnesse.
Lear. *Regan*, I thinke your are. I know what reason
I haue to thinke so, if thou should'st not be glad,
I would diuorce me from thy Mother Tombe,
Sepulchring an Adultresse. O are you free?
Some other time for that. Beloued *Regan*,
Thy Sisters naught: oh *Regan*, she hath tied
Sharpe-tooth'd vnkindnesse, like a vulture heere,
I can scarce speake to thee, thou'lt not beleeue
With how deprau'd a quality. Oh *Regan*.
Reg. I pray you Sir, take patience, I haue hope
You lesse know how to value her desert,
Then she to scant her dutie.
Lear. Say? How is that?
Reg. I cannot thinke my Sister in the least
Would faile her Obligation. If Sir perchance
She haue restrained the Riots of your Followres,
'Tis on such ground, and to such wholesome end,
As cleeres her from all blame.
Lear. My curses on her.
Reg. O Sir, you are old,
Nature in you stands on the very Verge
Of his confine: you should be rul'd, and led
By some discretion, that discernes your state
Better then you your selfe: therefore I pray you,
That to our Sister, you do make returne,
Say you haue wrong'd her.
Lear. Aske her forgiuenesse?
Do you but marke how this becomes the house?
Deere daughter, I confesse that I am old;
Age is vnnecessary: on my knees I begge,
That you'l vouchsafe me Rayment, Bed, and Food.
Reg. Good Sir, no more: these are vnsightly trickes:
Returne you to my Sister.
Lear. Neuer *Regan*:
She hath abated me of halfe my Traine;
Look'd blacke vpon me, strooke me with her Tongue
Most Serpent-like, vpon the very Heart.
All the stor'd Vengeances of Heauen, fall
On her ingratefull top: strike her yong bones
You taking Ayres, with Lamenesse.
Corn. Fye sir, fie.
Le. You nimble Lightnings, dart your blinding flames
Into her scornfull eyes: Infect her Beauty,
You Fen-suck'd Fogges, drawne by the powrfull Sunne,
To fall, and blister.
Reg. O the blest Gods!
So will you wish on me, when the rash moode is on.
Lear. No *Regan*, thou shalt neuer haue my curse:
Thy tender-hefted Nature shall not giue
Thee o're to harshnesse: Her eyes are fierce, but thine
Do comfort, and not burne. 'Tis not in thee
To grudge my pleasures, to cut off my Traine,
To bandy hasty words, to scant my sizes,
And in conclusion, to oppose the bolt
Against my comming in. Thou better know'st
The Offices of Nature, bond of Childhood,
Effects of Curtesie, dues of Gratitude:
Thy halfe o'th'Kingdome hast thou not forgot,
Wherein I thee endow'd.
Reg. Good Sir, to'th'purpose. *Tucket within.*
Lear. Who put my man i'th'Stockes?
Enter Steward.
Corn. What Trumpet's that?
Reg. I know't, my Sisters: this approues her Letter,
That she would soone be heere. Is your Lady come?
Lear. This is a Slaue, whose easie borrowed pride
Dwels in the fickly grace of her he followes.
Out Varlet, from my sight.
Corn. What meanes your Grace?
Enter Gonerill.
Lear. Who stockt my Seruant? *Regan*, I haue good hope
Thou did'st not know on't.
Who comes here? O Heauens!
If you do loue old men; if your sweet sway
Allow Obedience; if you your selues are old,
Make it your cause: Send downe, and take my part.
Art not asham'd to looke vpon this Beard?
O *Regan*, will you take her by the hand?
Gon. Why not by'th'hand Sir? How haue I offended?
All's not offence that indiscretion findes,
And dotage termes so.
Lear. O sides, you are too tough!
Will you yet hold?
How came my man i'th'Stockes?
Corn. I set him there, Sir: but his owne Disorders
Deseru'd

Deseru'd much lesse aduancement.
Lear. You? Did you?
Reg. I pray you Father being weake, seeme so.
If till the expiration of your Moneth
You will returne and soiourne with my Sister,
Dismissing halfe your traine, come then to me,
I am now from home, and out of that prouision
Which shall be needfull for your entertainement.
Lear. Returne to her? and fifty men dismiss'd?
No, rather I abiure all roofes, and chuse
To wage against the enmity oth'ayre,
To be a Comrade with the Wolfe, and Owle,
Necessities sharpe pinch. Returne with her?
Why the hot-bloodied *France*, that dowerlesse tooke
Our yongest borne, I could as well be brought
To knee his Throne, and Squire-like pension beg,
To keepe base life a foote; returne with her?
Perswade me rather to be slaue and sumpter
To this detested groome.
Gon. At your choice Sir.
Lear. I prythee Daughter do not make me mad,
I will not trouble thee my Child: farewell:
Wee'l no more meete, no more see one another.
But yet thou art my flesh, my blood, my Daughter,
Or rather a disease that's in my flesh,
Which I must needs call mine. Thou art a Byle,
A plague sore, or imbossed Carbuncle
In my corrupted blood. But Ile not chide thee,
Let shame come when it will, I do not call it,
I do not bid the Thunder-bearer shoote,
Nor tell tales of thee to high-iudging *Ioue*,
Mend when thou can'st, be better at thy leisure,
I can be patient, I can stay with *Regan*,
I and my hundred Knights.
Reg. Not altogether so,
I look'd not for you yet, nor am prouided
For your fit welcome, giue eare Sir to my Sister,
For those that mingle reason with your passion,
Must be content to thinke you old, and so,
But she knowes what she doe's.
Lear. Is this well spoken?
Reg. I dare auouch it Sir, what fifty Followers?
Is it not well? What should you need of more?
Yea, or so many? Sith that both charge and danger,
Speake 'gainst so great a number? How in one house
Should many people, vnder two commands
Hold amity? 'Tis hard, almost impossible.
Gon. Why might not you my Lord, receiue attendance
From those that she cals Seruants, or from mine?
Reg. Why not my Lord?
If then they chanc'd to slacke ye,
We could comptroll them; if you will come to me,
(For now I spie a danger) I entreate you
To bring but fiue and twentie, to no more
Will I giue place or notice.
Lear. I gaue you all.
Reg. And in good time you gaue it.
Lear. Made you my Guardians, my Depositaries,
But kept a reseruation to be followed
With such a number? What, must I come to you
With fiue and twenty? *Regan*, said you so?
Reg. And speak't againe my Lord, no more with me.
Lea. Those wicked Creatures yet do look wel fauor'd
When others are more wicked, not being the worst
Stands in some ranke of praise, Ile go with thee,
Thy fifty yet doth double fiue and twenty,
And thou art twice her Loue.
Gon. Heare me my Lord;
What need you fiue and twenty? Ten? Or fiue?
To follow in a house, where twice so many
Haue a command to tend you?
Reg. What need one?
Lear. O reason not the need: our basest Beggers
Are in the poorest thing superfluous,
Allow not Nature, more then Nature needs:
Mans life is cheape as Beastes. Thou art a Lady;
If onely to go warme were gorgeous,
Why Nature needs not what thou gorgeous wear'st,
Which scarcely keepes thee warme, but for true need:
You Heauens, giue me that patience, patience I need,
You see me heere (you Gods) a poore old man,
As full of griefe as age, wretched in both,
If it be you that stirres these Daughters hearts
Against their Father, foole me not so much,
To beare it tamely: touch me with Noble anger,
And let not womens weapons, water drops,
Staine my mans cheekes. No you vnnaturall Hags,
I will haue such reuenges on you both,
That all the world shall——I will do such things,
What they are yet, I know not, but they shalbe
The terrors of the earth? you thinke Ile weepe,
No, Ile not weepe, I haue full cause of weeping,
Storme and Tempest.
But this heart shal break into a hundred thousand flawes
Or ere Ile weepe; O Foole, I shall go mad. *Exeunt.*
Corn. Let vs withdraw, 'twill be a Storme.
Reg. This house is little, the old man an'ds people,
Cannot be well bestow'd.
Gon. 'Tis his owne blame hath put himselfe from rest,
And must needs taste his folly.
Reg. For his particular, Ile receiue him gladly,
But not one follower.
Gon. So am I purpos'd.
Where is my Lord of *Gloster*?
Enter Gloster.
Corn. Followed the old man forth, he is return'd.
Glo. The King is in high rage.
Corn. Whether is he going?
Glo. He cals to Horse, but will I know not whether.
Corn. 'Tis best to giue him way, he leads himselfe.
Gon. My Lord, entreate him by no meanes to stay.
Glo. Alacke the night comes on, and the high windes
Do sorely ruffle, for many Miles about
There's scarce a Bush.
Reg. O Sir, to wilfull men,
The iniuries that they themselues procure,
Must be their Schoole-Masters: shut vp your doores,
He is attended with a desperate traine,
And what they may incense him too, being apt,
To haue his eare abus'd, wisedome bids feare.
Cor. Shut vp your doores my Lord, 'tis a wil'd night,
My *Regan* counsels well: come out oth'storme. *Exeunt.*

Actus Tertius. Scena Prima.

Storme still. Enter Kent, and a Gentleman, seuerally.

Kent. Who's there besides foule weather?
Gen. One minded like the weather, most vnquietly.
rr 2 *Kent.*

Kent. I know you: Where's the King?
Gent. Contending with the fretfull Elements;
Bids the winde blow the Earth into the Sea,
Or swell the curled Waters 'boue the Maine,
That things might change, or ceafe.
Kent. But who is with him?
Gent. None but the Foole, who labours to out-iest
His heart-strooke iniuries.
Kent. Sir, I do know you,
And dare vpon the warrant of my note
Commend a deere thing to you. There is diuision
(Although as yet the face of it is couer'd
With mutuall cunning) 'twixt Albany, and Cornwall:
Who haue, as who haue not, that their great Starres
Thron'd and set high; Seruants, who seeme no lesse,
Which are to France the Spies and Speculations
Intelligent of our State. What hath bin seene,
Either in snuffes, and packings of the Dukes,
Or the hard Reine which both of them hath borne
Against the old kinde King; or something deeper,
Whereof (perchance) these are but furnishings.
Gent. I will talke further with you.
Kent. No, do not:
For confirmation that I am much more
Then my out-wall; open this Purse, and take
What it containes. If you shall see *Cordelia*,
(As feare not but you shall) shew her this Ring,
And she will tell you who that Fellow is
That yet you do not know. Fye on this Storme,
I will go seeke the King.
Gent. Giue me your hand,
Haue you no more to say?
Kent. Few words, but to effect more then all yet;
That when we haue found the King, in which your pain
That way, Ile this: He that first lights on him,
Holla the other. *Exeunt.*

Scena Secunda.

Storme still. Enter Lear, and Foole.

Lear. Blow windes, & crack your cheeks; Rage, blow
You Cataracts, and Hyrricano's spout,
Till you haue drench'd our Steeples, drown the Cockes.
You Sulph'rous and Thought-executing Fires,
Vaunt-curriors of Oake-cleauing Thunder-bolts,
Sindge my white head. And thou all-shaking Thunder,
Strike flat the thicke Rotundity o'th'world,
Cracke Natures moulds, all germaines spill at once
That makes ingratefull Man.
Foole. O Nunkle, Court holy-water in a dry house, is better then this Rain-water out o'doore. Good Nunkle, in, aske thy Daughters blessing, heere's a night pitties neither Wisemen, nor Fooles.
Lear. Rumble thy belly full: spit Fire, spowt Raine:
Nor Raine, Winde, Thunder, Fire are my Daughters;
I taxe not you, you Elements with vnkindnesse.
I neuer gaue you Kingdome, call'd you Children;
You owe me no subscription. Then let fall
Your horrible pleasure. Heere I stand your Slaue,
A poore, infirme, weake, and dispis'd old man:
But yet I call you Seruile Ministers,
That will with two pernicious Daughters ioyne
Your high-engender'd Battailes, 'gainst a head
So old, and white as this. O, ho! 'tis foule.
Foole. He that has a house to put's head in, has a good Head-peece:
The Codpiece that will house, before the head has any;
The Head, and he shall Lowse: so Beggers marry many.
The man ỳ makes his Toe, what he his Hart shold make,
Shall of a Corne cry woe, and turne his sleepe to wake.
For there was neuer yet faire woman, but shee made mouthes in a glasse.

Enter Kent.

Lear. No, I will be the patterne of all patience,
I will say nothing.
Kent. Who's there?
Foole. Marry here's Grace, and a Codpiece, that's a Wiseman, and a Foole.
Kent. Alas Sir are you here? Things that loue night,
Loue not such nights as these: The wrathfull Skies
Gallow the very wanderers of the darke
And make them keepe their Caues: Since I was man,
Such sheets of Fire, such bursts of horrid Thunder,
Such groanes of roaring Winde, and Raine, I neuer
Remember to haue heard. Mans Nature cannot carry
Th'affliction, nor the feare.
Lear. Let the great Goddes
That keepe this dreadfull pudder o're our heads,
Finde out their enemies now. Tremble thou Wretch,
That hast within thee vndivulged Crimes
Vnwhipt of Iustice. Hide thee, thou Bloudy hand;
Thou Periur'd, and thou Simular of Vertue
That art Incestuous. Caytiffe, to peeces shake
That vnder couert, and conuenient seeming
Ha's practis'd on mans life. Close pent-vp guilts,
Riue your concealing Continents, and cry
These dreadfull Summoners grace. I am a man,
More sinn'd against, then sinning.
Kent. Alacke, bare-headed?
Gracious my Lord, hard by heere is a Houell,
Some friendship will it lend you 'gainst the Tempest:
Repose you there, while I to this hard house,
(More harder then the stones whereof 'tis rais'd,
Which euen but now, demanding after you,
Deny'd me to come in) returne, and force
Their scanted curtesie.
Lear. My wits begin to turne.
Come on my boy. How dost my boy? Art cold?
I am cold my selfe. Where is this straw, my Fellow?
The Art of our Necessities is strange,
And can make vilde things precious. Come, your Houel;
Poore Foole, and Knaue, I haue one part in my heart
That's sorry yet for thee.
Foole. He that has and a little-tyne wit,
With heigh-ho, the Winde and the Raine,
Must make content with his Fortunes fit,
Though the Raine it raineth euery day.
Le. True Boy: Come bring vs to this Houell. *Exit.*
Foole. This is a braue night to coole a Curtizan:
Ile speake a Prophesie ere I go:
When Priests are more in word, then matter;
When Brewers marre their Malt with water;
When Nobles are their Taylors Tutors,
No Heretiques burn'd, but wenches Sutors;
When euery Case in Law, is right;
No Squire in debt, nor no poore Knight;
When Slanders do not liue in Tongues;
Nor Cut-purses come not to throngs;
When Vsurers tell their Gold i'th'Field,

And, Baudes, and whores, do Churches build,
Then ſhal the Realme of *Albion*, come to great confuſion:
Then comes the time, who liues to ſee't,
That going ſhalbe vs'd with feet. (time.
This prophecie *Merlin* ſhall make, for I liue before his
Exit.

Scæna Tertia.

Enter Gloſter, and Edmund.

Glo. Alacke, alacke *Edmund*, I like not this vnnaturall dealing; when I deſired their leaue that I might pity him, they tooke from me the vſe of mine owne houſe, charg'd me on paine of perpetuall diſpleaſure, neither to ſpeake of him, entreat for him, or any way ſuſtaine him.

Baſt. Moſt ſauage and vnnaturall.

Glo. Go too; ſay you nothing. There is diuiſion betweene the Dukes, and a worſſe matter then that: I haue receiued a Letter this night, 'tis dangerous to be ſpoken, I haue lock'd the Letter in my Cloſſet, theſe iniuries the King now beares, will be reuenged home; ther is part of a Power already footed, we muſt incline to the King, I will looke him, and priuily relieue him; goe you and maintaine talke with the Duke, that my charity be not of him perceiued; If he aske for me, I am ill, and gone to bed, if I die for it, (as no leſſe is threatned me) the King my old Maſter muſt be relieued. There is ſtrange things toward *Edmund*, pray you be carefull. *Exit.*

Baſt. This Curteſie forbid thee, ſhall the Duke
Inſtantly know, and of that Letter too;
This ſeemes a faire deſeruing, and muſt draw me
That which my Father looſes:no leſſe then all,
The yonger riſes, when the old doth fall. *Exit.*

Scena Quarta.

Enter Lear, Kent, and Foole.

Kent. Here is the place my Lord, good my Lord enter,
The tirrany of the open night's too rough
For Nature to endure. *Storme ſtill*

Lear. Let me alone.

Kent. Good my Lord enter heere.

Lear. Wilt breake my heart?

Kent. I had rather breake mine owne,
Good my Lord enter.

Lear. Thou think'ſt 'tis much that this contentious
Inuades vs to the skin ſo:'tis to thee, (ſtorme
But where the greater malady is fixt,
The leſſer is ſcarce felt. Thou'dſt ſhun a Beare,
But if they flight lay toward the roaring Sea,
Thou'dſt meete the Beare i'th' mouth, when the mind's
The bodies delicate: the tempeſt in my mind, free,
Doth from my ſences take all feeling elſe,
Saue what beates there, Filliall ingratitude,
Is it not as this mouth ſhould teare this hand
For lifting food too't? But I will puniſh home;
No, I will weepe no more; in ſuch a night,
To ſhut me out? Poure on, I will endure:
In ſuch a night as this? O *Regan*, *Gonerill*,
Your old kind Father, whoſe franke heart gaue all,
O that way madneſſe lies, let me ſhun that:
No more of that.

Kent. Good my Lord enter here.

Lear. Prythee go in thy ſelfe, ſeeke thine owne eaſe,
This tempeſt will not giue me leaue to ponder
On things would hurt me more, but Ile goe in,
In Boy, go firſt. You houſeleſſe pouertie, *Exit.*
Nay get thee in; Ile pray, and then Ile ſleepe.
Poore naked wretches, where ſo ere you are
That bide the pelting of this pittileſſe ſtorme,
How ſhall your Houſe-leſſe heads, and vnfed ſides,
Your lop'd, and window'd raggedneſſe defend you
From ſeaſons ſuch as theſe? O I haue tane
Too little care of this: Take Phyſicke, Pompe,
Expoſe thy ſelfe to feele what wretches feele,
That thou maiſt ſhake the ſuperflux to them,
And ſhew the Heauens more iuſt.

Enter Edgar, and Foole.

Edg. Fathom, and halfe, Fathom and halfe; poore *Tom.*

Foole. Come not in heere Nuncle, here's a ſpirit, helpe me, helpe me.

Kent. Giue me thy hand, who's there?

Foole. A ſpirite, a ſpirite, he ſayes his name's poore *Tom.*

Kent. What art thou that doſt grumble there i'th' ſtraw? Come forth.

Edg. Away, the foule Fiend followes me, through the ſharpe Hauthorne blow the windes. Humh, goe to thy bed and warme thee.

Lear. Did'ſt thou giue all to thy Daughters? And art thou come to this?

Edgar. Who giues any thing to poore *Tom*? Whom the foule fiend hath led though Fire, and through Flame, through Sword, and Whirle-Poole, o're Bog, and Quagmire, that hath laid Kniues vnder his Pillow, and Halters in his Pue, ſet Rats-bane by his Porredge, made him Proud of heart, to ride on a Bay trotting Horſe, ouer foure incht Bridges, to courſe his owne ſhadow for a Traitor. Bliſſe thy fiue Wits, *Toms* a cold. O do, de, do, de, do de, bliſſe thee from Whirle-Windes, Starre-blaſting, and taking, do poore *Tom* ſome charitie, whom the foule Fiend vexes. There could I haue him now, and there, and there ag ai ne, and there. *Storme ſtill.*

Lear. Ha's his Daughters brought him to this paſſe?
Could'ſt thou ſaue nothing? Would'ſt thou giue 'em all?

Foole. Nay, he reſeru'd a Blanket, elſe we had bin all ſham'd.

Lea. Now all the plagues that in the pendulous ayre
Hang fated o're mens faults, light on thy Daughters.

Kent. He hath no Daughters Sir.

Lear. Death Traitor, nothing could haue ſubdu'd
To ſuch a lowneſſe, but his vnkind Daughters. (Nature
Is it the faſhion, that diſcarded Fathers,
Should haue thus little mercy on their fleſh:
Iudicious puniſhment, 'twas this fleſh begot
Thoſe Pelicane Daughters.

Edg. Pillicock ſat on Pillicock hill, alow:alow, loo, loo.

Foole. This cold night will turne vs all to Fooles, and Madmen.

Edgar. Take heed o'th'foule Fiend, obey thy Parents, keepe thy words Iuſtice, ſweare not, commit not, with

with mans fworne Spoufe ; fet not thy Sweet-heart on proud array. *Tom's* a cold.

Lear. What haft thou bin?

Edg. A Seruingman? Proud in heart, and minde; that curl'd my haire, wore Gloues in my cap; feru'd the Luft of my Miftris heart, and did the acte of darkeneffe with her. Swore as many Oathes, as I fpake words, & broke them in the fweet face of Heauen. One, that flept in the contriuing of Luft, and wak'd to doe it. Wine lou'd I deerely, Dice deerely; and in Woman, out-Paramour'd the Turke. Falfe of heart, light of eare, bloody of hand; Hog in floth, Foxe in ftealth, Wolfe in greedineffe, Dog in madnes, Lyon in prey. Let not the creaking of fhooes, Nor the ruftling of Silkes, betray thy poore heart to woman. Keepe thy foote out of Brothels, thy hand out of Plackets, thy pen from Lenders Bookes, and defye the foule Fiend. Still through the Hauthorne blowes the cold winde: Sayes fuum, mun, nonny, Dolphin my Boy, Boy *Sefey*: let him trot by. *Storme ftill.*

Lear. Thou wert better in a Graue, then to anfwere with thy vncouer'd body, this extremitie of the Skies. Is man no more then this? Confider him well. Thou ow'ft the Worme no Silke; the Beaft, no Hide; the Sheepe, no Wooll; the Cat, no perfume. Ha? Here's three on's are fophifticated. Thou art the thing it felfe; vnaccommodated man, is no more but fuch a poore, bare, forked Animall as thou art. Off, off you Lendings: Come, vnbutton heere.

Enter Gloucefter, with a Torch.

Foole. Prythee Nunckle be contented, 'tis a naughtie night to fwimme in. Now a little fire in a wilde Field, were like an old Letchers heart, a fmall fpark, all the reft on's body, cold: Looke, heere comes a walking fire.

Edg. This is the foule Flibbertigibbet; hee begins at Curfew, and walkes at firft Cocke: Hee giues the Web and the Pin, fquints the eye, and makes the Hare-lippe; Mildewes the white Wheate, and hurts the poore Creature of earth.

Swithold footed thrice the old,
He met the Night-Mare, and her nine-fold;
Bid her a-light, and her troth-plight,
And aroynt thee Witch, aroynt thee.

Kent. How fares your Grace?

Lear. What's he?

Kent. Who's there? What is't you feeke?

Glou. What are you there? Your Names?

Edg. Poore Tom, that eates the fwimming Frog, the Toad, the Tod-pole, the wall-Neut, and the water: that in the furie of his heart, when the foule Fiend rages, eats Cow-dung for Sallets; fwallowes the old Rat, and the ditch-Dogge; drinkes the green Mantle of the ftanding Poole: who is whipt from Tything to Tything, and ftockt, punifh'd, and imprifon'd: who hath three Suites to his backe, fixe fhirts to his body:

Horfe to ride, and weapon to weare:
But Mice, and Rats, and fuch fmall Deare,
Haue bin Toms food, for feuen long yeare:

Beware my Follower. Peace Smulkin, peace thou Fiend.

Glou. What, hath your Grace no better company?

Edg. The Prince of Darkeneffe is a Gentleman. *Modo* he's call'd, and *Mahu.*

Glou. Our flefh and blood, my Lord, is growne fo vilde, that it doth hate what gets it.

Edg. Poore Tom's a cold.

Glou. Go in with me; my duty cannot fuffer
T'obey in all your daughters hard commands:
Though their Iniunction be to barre my doores,
And let this Tyrannous night take hold vpon you,
Yet haue I ventured to come feeke you out,
And bring you where both fire, and food is ready.

Lear. Firft let me talke with this Philofopher,
What is the caufe of Thunder?

Kent. Good my Lord take his offer,
Go into th'houfe.

Lear. Ile talke a word with this fame lerned Theban:
What is your ftudy?

Edg. How to preuent the Fiend, and to kill Vermine.

Lear. Let me aske you one word in priuate.

Kent. Importune him once more to go my Lord,
His wits begin t'vnfettle.

Glou. Canft thou blame him? *Storm ftill*
His Daughters feeke his death: Ah, that good Kent,
He faid it would be thus: poore banifh'd man:
Thou fayeft the King growes mad, Ile tell thee Friend
I am almoft mad my felfe. I had a Sonne,
Now out-law'd from my blood: he fought my life
But lately: very late: I lou'd him (Friend)
No Father his Sonne deerer: true to tell thee,
The greefe hath craz'd my wits. What a night's this?
I do befeech your grace.

Lear. O cry you mercy, Sir:
Noble Philofopher, your company.

Edg. Tom's a cold.

Glou. In fellow there, into th'Houel; keep thee warm.

Lear. Come, let's in all.

Kent. This way, my Lord.

Lear. With him;
I will keepe ftill with my Philofopher.

Kent. Good my Lord, footh him:
Let him take the Fellow.

Glou. Take him you on.

Kent. Sirra, come on: go along with vs.

Lear. Come, good Athenian.

Glou. No words, no words, hufh.

Edg. Childe *Rowland* to the darke Tower came,
His word was ftill, fie, foh, and fumme,
I fmell the blood of a Brittifh man. *Exeunt*

Scena Quinta.

Enter Cornwall, and Edmund.

Corn. I will haue my reuenge, ere I depart his houfe.

Baft. How my Lord, I may be cenfured, that Nature thus giues way to Loyaltie, fomething feares mee to thinke of.

Cornw. I now perceiue, it was not altogether your Brothers euill difpofition made him feeke his death: but a prouoking merit fet a-worke by a reprouable badneffe in himfelfe.

Baft. How malicious is my fortune, that I muft repent to be iuft? This is the Letter which hee fpoake of; which approues him an intelligent partie to the aduantages of France. O Heauens! that this Treafon were not; or not I the detector.

Corn. Go with me to the Dutcheffe.

Baft. If the matter of this Paper be certain, you haue mighty bufineffe in hand.

Corn.

Corn. True or falſe, it hath made thee Earle of Gloucester: ſeeke out where thy Father is, that hee may bee ready for our apprehenſion.

Baſt. If I finde him comforting the King, it will ſtuffe his ſuſpition more fully. I will perſeuer in my courſe of Loyalty, though the conflict be ſore betweene that, and my blood.

Corn. I will lay truſt vpon thee: and thou ſhalt finde a deere Father in my loue. *Exeunt.*

Scena Sexta.

Enter Kent, and Glouceſter.

Glou. Heere is better then the open ayre, take it thankfully: I will peece out the comfort with what addition I can: I will not be long from you. *Exit*

Kent. All the powre of his wits, haue giuen way to his impatience: the Gods reward your kindneſſe.

Enter Lear, Edgar, and Foole.

Edg. *Fraterretto* cals me, and tells me *Nero* is an Angler in the Lake of Darkneſſe: pray Innocent, and beware the foule Fiend.

Foole. Prythee Nunkle tell me, whether a madman be a Gentleman, or a Yeoman.

Lear. A King, a King.

Foole. No, he's a Yeoman, that ha's a Gentleman to his Sonne: for hee's a mad Yeoman that ſees his Sonne a Gentleman before him.

Lear. To haue a thouſand with red burning ſpits
Come hizzing in vpon 'em.

Edg. Bleſſe thy fiue wits.

Kent. O pitty: Sir, where is the patience now
That you ſo oft haue boaſted to retaine?

Edg. My teares begin to take his part ſo much,
They marre my counterfetting.

Lear. The little dogges, and all;
Trey, Blanch, and Sweet-heart: ſee, they barke at me.

Edg. Tom, will throw his head at them: Auaunt you
Curres, be thy mouth or blacke or white:
Tooth that poyſons if it bite:
Maſtiffe, Grey-hound, Mongrill, Grim,
Hound or Spaniell, Brache, or Hym:
Or Bobtaile tight, or Troudle taile,
Tom will make him weepe and waile,
For with throwing thus my head;
Dogs leapt the hatch, and all are fled.
Do, de, de, de: ſeſe: Come, march to Wakes and Fayres,
And Market Townes: poore Tom thy horne is dry,

Lear. Then let them Anatomize *Regan*: See what breeds about her heart. Is there any cauſe in Nature that make theſe hard-hearts. You ſir, I entertaine for one of my hundred; only, I do not like the faſhion of your garments. You will ſay they are Perſian; but let them bee chang'd.

Enter Gloſter.

Kent. Now good my Lord, lye heere, and reſt awhile.

Lear. Make no noiſe, make no noiſe, draw the Curtaines: ſo, ſo, wee'l go to Supper i'th'morning.

Foole. And Ile go to bed at noone.

Glou. Come hither Friend:
Where is the King my Maſter?

Kent. Here Sir, but trouble him not, his wits are gon.

Glou. Good friend, I prythee take him in thy armes;
I haue ore-heard a plot of death vpon him:
There is a Litter ready, lay him in't,
And driue toward Douer friend, where thou ſhalt meete
Both welcome, and protection. Take vp thy Maſter,
If thou ſhould'ſt dally halfe an houre, his life
With thine, and all that offer to defend him,
Stand in aſſured loſſe. Take vp, take vp,
And follow me, that will to ſome prouiſion
Giue thee quicke conduct. Come, come, away. *Exeunt*

Scena Septima.

Enter Cornwall, Regan, Gonerill, Baſtard, and Seruants.

Corn. Poſte ſpeedily to my Lord your husband, ſhew hin this Letter, the Army of France is landed: ſeeke out the Traitor Glouſter.

Reg. Hang him inſtantly.

Gon. Plucke out his eyes.

Corn. Leaue him to my diſpleaſure. *Edmond*, keepe you our Siſter company: the reuenges wee are bound to take vppon your Traitorous Father, are not fit for your beholding. Aduice the Duke where you are going, to a moſt feſtiuate preparation: we are bound to the like. Our Poſtes ſhall be ſwift, and intelligent betwixt vs. Farewell deere Siſter, farewell my Lord of Glouſter.

Enter Steward.

How now? Where's the King?

Stew. My Lord of Glouſter hath conuey'd him hence
Some fiue or ſix and thirty of his Knights
Hot Queſtriſts after him, met him at gate,
Who, with ſome other of the Lords, dependants,
Are gone with him toward Douer; where they boaſt
To haue well armed Friends.

Corn. Get horſes for your Miſtris.

Gon. Farewell ſweet Lord, and Siſter. *Exit*

Corn. *Edmund* farewell: go ſeek the Traitor Gloſter,
Pinnion him like a Theefe, bring him before vs:
Though well we may not paſſe vpon his life
Without the forme of Iuſtice: yet our power
Shall do a curt'ſie to our wrath, which men
May blame, but not comptroll.

Enter Glouceſter, and Seruants.

Who's there? the Traitor?

Reg. Ingratefull Fox, 'tis he.

Corn. Binde faſt his corky armes.

Glou. What meanes your Graces?
Good my Friends conſider you are my Gheſts:
Do me no foule play, Friends.

Corn. Binde him I ſay.

Reg. Hard, hard: O filthy Traitor.

Glou. Vnmercifull Lady, as you are, I'me none.

Corn. To this Chaire binde him,
Villaine, thou ſhalt finde.

Glou. By the kinde Gods, 'tis moſt ignobly done
To plucke me by the Beard.

Reg. So white, and ſuch a Traitor?

Glou. Naughty Ladie,
Theſe haires which thou doſt rauiſh from my chin
Will quicken and accuſe thee. I am your Hoſt,
With Robbers hands, my hoſpitable fauours

You

You ſhould not ruffle thus. What will you do?

Corn. Come Sir.

What Letters had you late from France?

Reg. Be ſimple anſwer'd, for we know the truth.

Corn. And what confederacie haue you with the Traitors, late footed in the Kingdome?

Reg. To whoſe hands
You haue ſent the Lunaticke King: Speake.

Glou. I haue a Letter gueſſingly ſet downe
Which came from one that's of a newtrall heart,
And not from one oppos'd.

Corn. Cunning.

Reg. And falſe.

Corn. Where haſt thou ſent the King?

Glou. To Douer.

Reg. Wherefore to Douer?
Was't thou not charg'd at perill.

Corn. Wherefore to Douer? Let him anſwer that.

Glou. I am tyed to'th'Stake,
And I muſt ſtand the Courſe.

Reg. Wherefore to Douer?

Glou. Becauſe I would not ſee thy cruell Nailes
Plucke out his poore old eyes: nor thy fierce Siſter,
In his Annointed fleſh, ſticke boariſh phangs.
The Sea, with ſuch a ſtorme as his bare head,
In Hell-blacke-night indur'd, would haue buoy'd vp
And quench'd the Stelled fires:
Yet poore old heart, he holpe the Heauens to raine.
If Wolues had at thy Gate howl'd that ſterne time,
Thou ſhould'ſt haue ſaid, good Porter turne the Key:
All Cruels elſe ſubſcribe: but I ſhall ſee
The winged Vengeance ouertake ſuch Children.

Corn. See't ſhalt thou neuer. Fellowes hold ỳ Chaire,
Vpon theſe eyes of thine, Ile ſet my foote.

Glou. He that will thinke to liue, till he be old,
Giue me ſome helpe.——O cruell! O you Gods.

Reg. One ſide will mocke another: Th'other too.

Corn. If you ſee vengeance.

Seru. Hold your hand, my Lord:
I haue ſeru'd you euer ſince I was a Childe:
But better ſeruice haue I neuer done you,
Then now to bid you hold.

Reg. How now, you dogge?

Ser. If you did weare a beard vpon your chin,
I'ld ſhake it on this quarrell. What do you meane?

Corn. My Villaine?

Seru. Nay then come on, and take the chance of anger.

Reg. Giue me thy Sword. A pezant ſtand vp thus?
Killes him.

Ser. Oh I am ſlaine: my Lord, you haue one eye left
To ſee ſome miſchefe on him. Oh.

Corn. Leſt it ſee more, preuent it; Out vilde gelly:
Where is thy luſter now?

Glou. All darke and comfortleſſe?
Where's my Sonne *Edmund*?
Edmund, enkindle all the ſparkes of Nature
To quit this horrid acte.

Reg. Out treacherous Villaine,
Thou call'ſt on him, that hates thee. It was he
That made the ouerture of thy Treaſons to vs:
Who is too good to pitty thee.

Glou. O my Follies! then *Edgar* was abus'd,
Kinde Gods, forgiue me that, and proſper him.

Reg. Go thruſt him out at gates, and let him ſmell
His way to Douer. *Exit with Glouſter.*
How is't my Lord? How looke you?

Corn. I haue receiu'd a hurt: Follow me Lady;
Turne out that eyeleſſe Villaine: throw this Slaue
Vpon the Dunghill: *Regan*, I bleed apace,
Vntimely comes this hurt. Giue me your arme. *Exeunt,*

Actus Quartus. Scena Prima.

Enter Edgar.

Edg. Yet better thus, and knowne to be contemn'd,
Then ſtill contemn'd and flatter'd, to be worſt:
The loweſt, and moſt deiected thing of Fortune,
Stands ſtill in eſperance, liues not in feare:
The lamentable change is from the beſt,
The worſt returnes to laughter. Welcome then,
Thou vnſubſtantiall ayre that I embrace:
The Wretch that thou haſt blowne vnto the worſt,
Owes nothing to thy blaſts.

Enter Glouſter, and an Oldman.

But who comes heere? My Father poorely led?
World, World, O world!
But that thy ſtrange mutations make vs hate thee,
Life would not yeelde to age.

Oldm. O my good Lord, I haue bene your Tenant,
And your Fathers Tenant, theſe foureſcore yeares.

Glou. Away, get thee away: good Friend be gone,
Thy comforts can do me no good at all,
Thee, they may hurt.

Oldm. You cannot ſee your way.

Glou. I haue no way, and therefore want no eyes:
I ſtumbled when I ſaw. Full oft 'tis ſeene,
Our meanes ſecure vs, and our meere defects
Proue our Commodities. Oh deere Sonne *Edgar*,
The food of thy abuſed Fathers wrath:
Might I but liue to ſee thee in my touch,
I'ld ſay I had eyes againe.

Oldm. How now? who's there?

Edg. O Gods! Who is't can ſay I am at the worſt?
I am worſe then ere I was.

Old. 'Tis poore mad Tom.

Edg. And worſe I may be yet: the worſt is not,
So long as we can ſay this is the worſt.

Oldm. Fellow, where goeſt?

Glou. Is it a Beggar-man?

Oldm. Madman, and beggar too.

Glou. He has ſome reaſon, elſe he could not beg.
I'th'laſt nights ſtorme, I ſuch a fellow ſaw;
Which made me thinke a Man, a Worme. My Sonne
Came then into my minde, and yet my minde
Was then ſcarſe Friends with him.
I haue heard more ſince:
As Flies to wanton Boyes, are we to th'Gods,
They kill vs for their ſport.

Edg. How ſhould this be?
Bad is the Trade that muſt play Foole to ſorrow,
Ang'ring it ſelfe, and others. Bleſſe thee Maſter.

Glou. Is that the naked Fellow?

Oldm. I, my Lord.

Glou. Get thee away: If for my ſake
Thou wilt ore-take vs hence a mile or twaine
I'th'way toward Douer, do it for ancient loue,
And bring ſome couering for this naked Soule,
Which Ile intreate to leade me.

Od. Alacke ſir, he is mad.

Glou.

Glou. 'Tis the times plague,
When Madmen leade the blinde:
Do as I bid thee, or rather do thy pleasure:
Aboue the rest, be gone.
Oldm. Ile bring him the best Parrell that I haue
Come on't, what will. *Exit*
Glou. Sirrah, naked fellow.
Edg. Poore Tom's a cold. I cannot daub it further.
Glou. Come hither fellow.
Edg. And yet I must:
Blesse thy sweete eyes, they bleede.
Glou. Know'st thou the way to Douer?
Edg. Both style, and gate; Horseway, and foot-path: poore Tom hath bin scarr'd out of his good wits. Blesse thee good mans sonne, from the foule Fiend.
Glou. Here take this purse, ÿ whom the heau'ns plagues
Haue humbled to all strokes: that I am wretched
Makes thee the happier: Heauens deale so still:
Let the superfluous, and Lust-dieted man,
That slaues your ordinance, that will not see
Because he do's not feele, feele your powre quickly:
So distribution should vndoo excesse,
And each man haue enough. Dost thou know Douer?
Edg. I Master.
Glou. There is a Cliffe, whose high and bending head
Lookes fearfully in the confined Deepe:
Bring me but to the very brimme of it,
And Ile repayre the misery thou do'st beare
With something rich about me: from that place,
I shall no leading neede.
Edg. Giue me thy arme;
Poore Tom shall leade thee. *Exeunt.*

Scena Secunda.

Enter Gonerill, Bastard, and Steward.

Gon. Welcome my Lord. I meruell our mild husband
Not met vs on the way. Now, where's your Master?
Stew. Madam within, but neuer man so chang'd:
I told him of the Army that was Landed:
He smil'd at it. I told him you were comming,
His answer was, the worse. Of Glosters Treachery,
And of the loyall Seruice of his Sonne
When I inform'd him, then he call'd me Sot,
And told me I had turn'd the wrong side out:
What most he should dislike, seemes pleasant to him;
What like, offensiue.
Gon. Then shall you go no further.
It is the Cowish terror of his spirit
That dares not vndertake: Hee'l not feele wrongs
Which tye him to an answer: our wishes on the way
May proue effects. Backe *Edmond* to my Brother,
Hasten his Musters, and conduct his powres.
I must change names at home, and giue the Distaffe
Into my Husbands hands. This trustie Seruant
Shall passe betweene vs: ere long you are like to heare
(If you dare venture in your owne behalfe)
A Mistresses command. Weare this; spare speech,
Decline your head. This kisse, if it durst speake
Would stretch thy Spirits vp into the ayre:
Conceiue, and fare thee well.
Bast. Yours, in the rankes of death. *Exit.*
Gon. My most deere Gloster.
Oh, the difference of man, and man,
To thee a Womans seruices are due,
My Foole vsurpes my body.
Stew. Madam, here come's my Lord.

Enter Albany.

Gon. I haue beene worth the whistle.
Alb. Oh *Gonerill*,
You are not worth the dust which the rude winde
Blowes in your face.
Gon. Milke-Liuer'd man,
That bear'st a cheeke for blowes, a head for wrongs,
Who hast not in thy browes an eye-discerning
Thine Honor, from thy suffering.
Alb. See thy selfe diuell:
Proper deformitie seemes not in the Fiend
So horrid as in woman.
Gon. Oh vaine Foole.

Enter a Messenger.

Mes. Oh my good Lord, the Duke of *Cornwals* dead,
Slaine by his Seruant, going to put out
The other eye of Glouster.
Alb. Glousters eyes.
Mes. A Seruant that he bred, thrill'd with remorse,
Oppos'd against the act: bending his Sword
To his great Master, who, threat-enrag'd
Flew on him, and among'st them fell'd him dead,
But not without that harmefull stroke, which since
Hath pluckt him after.
Alb. This shewes you are aboue
You Iustices, that these our neather crimes
So speedily can venge. But (O poore Glouster)
Lost he his other eye?
Mes. Both, both, my Lord.
This Leter Madam, craues a speedy answer:
'Tis from your Sister.
Gon. One way I like this well,
But being widdow, and my Glouster with her,
May all the building in my fancie plucke
Vpon my hatefull life. Another way
The Newes is not so tart. Ile read, and answer.
Alb. Where was his Sonne,
When they did take his eyes?
Mes. Come with my Lady hither.
Alb. He is not heere.
Mes. No my good Lord, I met him backe againe.
Alb. Knowes he the wickednesse?
Mes. I my good Lord: 'twas he inform'd against him
And quit the house on purpose, that their punishment
Might haue the freer course.
Alb. Glouster, I liue
To thanke thee for the loue thou shew'dst the King,
And to reuenge thine eyes. Come hither Friend,
Tell me what more thou know'st. *Exeunt.*

Scena Tertia.

Enter with Drum and Colours, Cordelia, Gentlemen, and Souldiours.

Cor. Alacke, 'tis he: why he was met euen now
As mad as the vext Sea, singing alowd,
Crown'd with ranke Fenitar, and furrow weeds,
With Hardokes, Hemlocke, Nettles, Cuckoo flowres,
Darnell

Darnell, and all the idle weedes that grow
In our ſuſtaining Corne. A Centery ſend forth;
Search euery Acre in the high-growne field,
And bring him to our eye. What can mans wiſedome
In the reſtoring his bereaued Senſe; he that helpes him,
Take all my outward worth.

Gent. There is meanes Madam:
Our foſter Nurſe of Nature, is repoſe,
The which he lackes: that to prouoke in him
Are many Simples operatiue, whoſe power
Will cloſe the eye of Anguiſh.

Cord. All bleſt Secrets,
All you vnpubliſh'd Vertues of the earth
Spring with my teares; be aydant, and remediate
In the Goodmans deſires: ſeeke, ſeeke for him,
Leaſt his vngouern'd rage, diſſolue the life
That wants the meanes to leade it.

Enter Meſſenger.

Meſ. Newes Madam,
The Brittiſh Powres are marching hitherward.

Cor. 'Tis knowne before. Our preparation ſtands
In expectation of them. O deere Father,
It is thy buſineſſe that I go about: Therfore great France
My mourning, and importun'd teares hath pittied:
No blowne Ambition doth our Armes incite,
But loue, deere loue, and our ag'd Fathers Rite:
Soone may I heare, and ſee him. *Exeunt.*

Scena Quarta.

Enter Regan, and Steward.

Reg. But are my Brothers Powres ſet forth?

Stew. I Madam.

Reg. Himſelfe in perſon there?

Stew. Madam with much ado:
Your Siſter is the better Souldier.

Reg. Lord *Edmund* ſpake not with your Lord at home?

Stew. No Madam.

Reg. What might import my Siſters Letter to him?

Stew. I know not, Lady.

Reg. Faith he is poaſted hence on ſerious matter:
It was great ignorance, Glouſters eyes being out
To let him liue. Where he arriues, he moues
All hearts againſt vs: *Edmund*, I thinke is gone
In pitty of his miſery, to diſpatch
His nighted life: Moreouer to deſcry
The ſtrength o'th'Enemy.

Stew. I muſt needs after him, Madam, with my Letter.

Reg. Our troopes ſet forth to morrow, ſtay with vs:
The wayes are dangerous.

Stew. I may not Madam:
My Lady charg'd my dutie in this buſines.

Reg. Why ſhould ſhe write to *Edmund*?
Might not you tranſport her purpoſes by word? Belike,
Some things, I know not what. Ile loue thee much
Let me vnſeale the Letter.

Stew. Madam, I had rather——

Reg. I know your Lady do's not loue her Husband,
I am ſure of that: and at her late being heere,
She gaue ſtrange Eliads, and moſt ſpeaking lookes
To Noble *Edmund*. I know you are of her boſome.

Stew. I, Madam?

Reg. I ſpeake in vnderſtanding: Y'are: I know't,
Therefore I do aduiſe you take this note:
My Lord is dead: *Edmond*, and I haue talk'd,
And more conuenient is he for my hand
Then for your Ladies: You may gather more:
If you do finde him, pray you giue him this;
And when your Miſtris heares thus much from you,
I pray deſire her call her wiſedome to her.
So fare you well:
If you do chance to heare of that blinde Traitor,
Preferment fals on him, that cuts him off.

Stew. Would I could meet Madam, I ſhould ſhew
What party I do follow.

Reg. Fare thee well. *Exeunt*

Scena Quinta.

Enter Glouceſter, and Edgar.

Glou. When ſhall I come to th'top of that ſame hill?

Edg. You do climbe vp it now. Look how we labor.

Glou. Me thinkes the ground is eeuen.

Edg. Horrible ſteepe.
Hearke, do you heare the Sea?

Glou. No truly.

Edg. Why then your other Senſes grow imperfect
By your eyes anguiſh.

Glou. So may it be indeed.
Me thinkes thy voyce is alter'd, and thou ſpeak'ſt
In better phraſe, and matter then thou did'ſt.

Edg. Y'are much deceiu'd: In nothing am I chang'd
But in my Garments.

Glou. Me thinkes y'are better ſpoken.

Edg. Come on Sir,
Heere's the place: ſtand ſtill: how fearefull
And dizie 'tis, to caſt ones eyes ſo low,
The Crowes and Choughes, that wing the midway ayre
Shew ſcarſe ſo groſſe as Beetles. Halfe way downe
Hangs one that gathers Sampire: dreadfull Trade:
Me thinkes he ſeemes no bigger then his head.
The Fiſhermen, that walk'd vpon the beach
Appeare like Mice: and yond tall Anchoring Barke,
Diminiſh'd to her Cocke: her Cocke, a Buoy
Almoſt too ſmall for ſight. The murmuring Surge,
That on th'vnnumbred idle Pebble chafes
Cannot be heard ſo high. Ile looke no more,
Leaſt my braine turne, and the deficient ſight
Topple downe headlong.

Glou Set me where you ſtand.

Edg. Giue me your hand:
You are now within a foote of th'extreme Verge:
For all beneath the Moone would I not leape vpright.

Glou. Let go my hand:
Heere Friend's another purſe: in it, a Iewell
Well worth a poore mans taking. Fayries, and Gods
Proſper it with thee. Go thou further off,
Bid me farewell, and let me heare thee going.

Edg. Now fare ye well, good Sir.

Glou. With all my heart.

Edg. Why I do trifle thus with his diſpaire,
Is done to cure it.

Glou. O you mighty Gods!
This world I do renounce, and in your ſights

Shake

Shake patiently my great affliction off:
If I could beare it longer, and not fall
To quarrell with your great opposelesse willes,
My snuffe, and loathed part of Nature should
Burne it selfe out. If *Edgar* liue, O blesse him:
Now Fellow, fare thee well.

Edg. Gone Sir, farewell:
And yet I know not how conceit may rob
The Treasury of life, when life it selfe
Yeelds to the Theft. Had he bin where he thought,
By this had thought bin past. Aliue, or dead?
Hoa, you Sir: Friend, heare you Sir, speake:
Thus might he passe indeed: yet he reuiues.
What are you Sir?

Glou. Away, and let me dye.

Edg. Had'st thou beene ought
But Gozemore, Feathers, Ayre,
(So many fathome downe precipitating)
Thou'dst shiuer'd like an Egge: but thou do'st breath:
Hast heauy substance, bleed'st not, speak'st, art sound,
Ten Masts at each, make not the altitude
Which thou hast perpendicularly fell,
Thy life's a Myracle. Speake yet againe.

Glou. But haue I falne, or no?

Edg. From the dread Somnet of this Chalkie Bourne
Looke vp a height, the shrill-gorg'd Larke so farre
Cannot be seene, or heard: Do but looke vp.

Glou. Alacke, I haue no eyes:
Is wretchednesse depriu'd that benefit
To end it selfe by death? 'Twas yet some comfort,
When misery could beguile the Tyranrs rage,
And frustrate his proud will.

Edg. Giue me your arme.
Vp, so: How is't? Feele you your Legges? You stand.

Glou. Too well, too well.

Edg. This is aboue all strangenesse,
Vpon the crowne o'th'Cliffe. What thing was that
Which parted from you?

Glou. A poore vnfortunate Beggar.

Edg. As I stood heere below, me thought his eyes
Were two full Moones: he had a thousand Noses,
Hornes wealk'd, and waued like the enraged Sea:
It was some Fiend: Therefore thou happy Father,
Thinke that the cleerest Gods, who make them Honors
Of mens Impossibilities, haue preserued thee.

Glou. I do remember now: henceforth Ile beare
Affliction, till it do cry out it selfe
Enough, enough, and dye. That thing you speake of,
I tooke it for a man: often'twould say
The Fiend, the Fiend, he led me to that place.

Edgar. Beare free and patient thoughts.

Enter Lear.

But who comes heere?
The safer sense will ne're accommodate
His Master thus.

Lear. No, they cannot touch me for crying. I am the King himselfe.

Edg. O thou side-piercing sight!

Lear. Nature's aboue Art, in that respect. Ther's your Presse-money. That fellow handles his bow, like a Crow-keeper: draw mee a Cloathiers yard. Looke, looke, a Mouse: peace, peace, this peece of toasted Cheese will doo't. There's my Gauntlet, Ile proue it on a Gyant. Bring vp the browne Billes. O well flowne Bird: i'th' clout, i'th'clout: Hewgh. Giue the word.

Edg. Sweet Mariorum.

Lear. Passe.

Glou. I know that voice.

Lear. Ha! *Gonerill* with a white beard? They flatter'd me like a Dogge, and told mee I had the white hayres in my Beard, ere the blacke ones were there. To say I, and no, to euery thing that I said: I, and no too, was no good Diuinity. When the raine came to wet me once, and the winde to make me chatter: when the Thunder would not peace at my bidding, there I found 'em, there I smelt 'em out. Go too, they are not men o'their words; they told me, I was euery thing: 'Tis a Lye, I am not Agu-proofe.

Glou. The tricke of that voyce, I do well remember: Is't not the King?

Lear. I, euery inch a King.
When I do stare, see how the Subiect quakes.
I pardon that mans life. What was thy cause?
Adultery? thou shalt not dye: dye for Adultery?
No, the Wren goes too't, and the small gilded Fly
Do's letcher in my sight. Let Copulation thriue:
For Glousters bastard Son was kinder to his Father,
Then my Daughters got 'tweene the lawfull sheets.
Too't Luxury pell-mell, for I lacke Souldiers.
Behold yond simpring Dame, whose face betweene her Forkes presages Snow; that minces Vertue, & do's shake the head to heare of pleasures name. The Fitchew, nor the soyled Horse goes too't with a more riotous appetite: Downe from the waste they are Centaures, though Women all aboue: but to the Girdle do the Gods inherit, beneath is all the Fiends. There's hell, there's darkenes, there is the sulphurous pit; burning, scalding, stench, consumption: Fye, fie, fie; pah, pah: Giue me an Ounce of Ciuet; good Apothecary sweeten my immagination: There's money for thee.

Glou. O let me kisse that hand.

Lear. Let me wipe it first,
It smelles of Mortality.

Glou. O ruin'd peece of Nature, this great world
Shall so weare out to naught.
Do'st thou know me?

Lear. I remember thine eyes well enough: dost thou squiny at me? No, doe thy worst blinde Cupid, Ile not loue. Reade thou this challenge, marke but the penning of it.

Glou. Were all thy Letters Sunnes, I could not see.

Edg. I would not take this from report,
It is, and my heart breakes at it.

Lear. Read.

Glou. What with the Case of eyes?

Lear. Oh ho, are you there with me? No eies in your head, nor no mony in your purse? Your eyes are in a heauy case, your purse in a light, yet you see how this world goes.

Glou. I see it feelingly.

Lear. What, art mad? A man may see how this world goes, with no eyes. Looke with thine eares: See how yond Iustice railes vpon yond simple theefe. Hearke in thine eare: Change places, and handy-dandy, which is the Iustice, which is the theefe: Thou hast seene a Farmers dogge barke at a Beggar?

Glou. I Sir.

Lear. And the Creature run from the Cur: there thou might'st behold the great image of Authoritie, a Dogg's obey'd in Office. Thou, Rascall Beadle, hold thy bloody hand: why dost thou lash that Whore? Strip thy owne backe, thou hotly lusts to vse her in that kind, for which thou whip'st her. The Vsurer hangs the Cozener. Thorough

rough tatter'd cloathes great Vices do appeare: Robes, and Furr'd gownes hide all. Place finnes with Gold, and the ftrong Lance of Iuftice, hurtleffe breakes: Arme it in ragges, a Pigmies ftraw do's pierce it. None do's offend, none, I fay none, Ile able 'em; take that of me my Friend, who haue the power to feale th'accufers lips. Get thee glaffe-eyes, and like a fcuruy Politician, feeme to fee the things thou doft not. Now, now, now, now. Pull off my Bootes: harder, harder, fo.

Edg. O matter, and impertinency mixt,
Reafon in Madneffe.

Lear. If thou wilt weepe my Fortunes, take my eyes.
I know thee well enough, thy name is Gloufter:
Thou muft be patient; we came crying h ther:
Thou know'ft, the firft time that we fmell the Ayre
We wawle, and cry. I will preach to thee: Marke.

Glou. Alacke, alacke the day.

Lear. When we are borne, we cry that we are come
To this great ftage of Fooles. This a good blocke:
It were a delicate ftratagem to fhoo
A Troope of Horfe with Felt: Ile put't in proofe,
And when I haue ftolne vpon thefe Son in Lawes,
Then kill, kill, kill, kill, kill, kill.

Enter a Gentleman.

Gent. Oh heere he is: lay hand vpon him, Sir.
Your moft deere Daughter———

Lear. No refcue? What, a Prifoner? I am euen
The Naturall Foole of Fortune. Vfe me well,
You fhall haue ranfome. Let me haue Surgeons,
I am cut to'th'Braines.

Gent. You fhall haue any thing.

Lear. No Seconds? All my felfe?
Why, this would make a man, a man of Salt
To vfe his eyes for Garden water-pots. I wil die brauely,
Like a fmugge Bridegroome. What? I will be Iouiall:
Come, come, I am a King, Mafters, know you that?

Gent. You are a Royall one, and we obey you.

Lear. Then there's life in't. Come, and you get it,
You fhall get it by running: Sa, fa, fa, fa. *Exit.*

Gent. A fight moft pittifull in the meaneft wretch,
Paft fpeaking of in a King. Thou haft a Daughter
Who redeemes Nature from the generall curfe
Which twaine haue brought her to.

Edg. Haile gentle Sir.

Gent. Sir, fpeed you: what's your will?

Edg. Do you heare ought (Sir) of a Battell toward.

Gent. Moft fure, and vulgar:
Euery one heares that, which can diftinguifh found.

Edg. But by your fauour:
How neere's the other Army?

Gent. Neere, and on fpeedy foot: the maine defcry
Stands on the hourely thought.

Edg. I thanke you Sir, that's all.

Gent. Though that the Queen on fpecial caufe is here
Her Army is mou'd on. *Exit.*

Edg. I thanke you Sir.

Glou. You euer gentle Gods, take my breath from me,
Let not my worfer Spirit tempt me againe
To dye before you pleafe.

Edg. Well pray you Father.

Glou. Now good fir, what are you?

Edg. A moft poore man, made tame to Fortunes blows
Who, by the Art of knowne, and feeling forrowes,
Am pregnant to good pitty. Giue me your hand,
Ile leade you to fome biding.

Glou. Heartie thankes:
The bountie, and the benizon of Heauen
To boot, and boot.

Enter Steward.

Stew. A proclaim'd prize: moft happie
That eyeleffe head of thine, was firft fram'd flefh
To raife my fortunes. Thou old, vnhappy Traitor,
Breefely thy felfe remember: the Sword is out
That muft deftroy thee.

Glou. Now let thy friendly hand
Put ftrength enough too't.

Stew. Wherefore, bold Pezant,
Dar'ft thou fupport a publifh'd Traitor? Hence,
Leaft that th'infection of his fortune take
Like hold on thee. Let go his arme.

Edg. Chill not let go Zir,
Without vurther 'cafion.

Stew. Let go Slaue, or thou dy'ft.

Edg. Good Gentleman goe your gate, and let poore volke paffe: and 'chud ha' bin zwaggerd out of my life, 'twould not ha'bin zo long as 'tis, by a vortnight. Nay, come not neere th'old man: keepe out che vor'ye, or ice try whither your Coftard, or my Ballow be the harder; chill be plaine with you.

Stew. Out Dunghill.

Edg. Chill picke your teeth Zir: come, no matter vor your foynes.

Stew. Slaue thou haft flaine me: Villain, take my purfe;
If euer thou wilt thriue, bury my bodie,
And giue the Letters which thou find'ft about me,
To *Edmund* Earle of Gloufter: feeke him out
Vpon the Englifh party. Oh vntimely death, death.

Edg. I know thee well. A feruiceable Villaine,
As duteous to the vices of thy Miftris,
As badneffe would defire.

Glou. What, is he dead?

Edg. Sit you downe Father: reft you.
Let's fee thefe Pockets; the Letters that he fpeakes of
May be my Friends: hee's dead; I am onely forry
He had no other Deathfman. Let vs fee:
Leaue gentle waxe, and manners: blame vs not
To know our enemies mindes, we rip their hearts,
Their Papers is more lawfull.

Reads the Letter.

LEt our reciprocall vowes be remembred. You haue manie opportunities to cut him off: if your will want not, time and place will be fruitfully offer'd. There is nothing done. If hee returne the Conqueror, then am I the Prifoner, and his bed, my Gaole, from the loathed warmth whereof, deliuer me, and fupply the place for your Labour.

Your (Wife, fo I would fay) affectionate Seruant. Generill.

Oh indinguifh'd fpace of Womans will,
A plot vpon her vertuous Husbands life,
And the exchange my Brother: heere, in the fands
Thee Ile rake vp, the pofte vnfanctified
Of murtherous Letchers: and in the mature time,
With this vngracious paper ftrike the fight
Of the death-practis'd Duke: for him 'tis well,
That of thy death, and bufineffe, I can tell.

Glou. The King is mad:
How ftiffe is my vilde fenfe
That I ftand vp, and haue ingenious feeling
Of my huge Sorrowes? Better I were diftract,
So fhould my thoughts be feuer'd from my greefes,

Drum afarre off.

And woes, by wrong imaginations loofe

The

The knowledge of themſelues.
Edg. Giue me your hand:
Farre off methinkes I heare the beaten Drumme.
Come Father, Ile beſtow you with a Friend. *Exeunt.*

Scæna Septima.

Enter Cordelia, Kent, and Gentleman.

Cor. O thou good *Kent*,
How ſhall I liue and worke
To match thy goodneſſe?
My life will be too ſhort,
And euery meaſure faile me.
Kent. To be acknowledg'd Madam is ore-pai'd,
All my reports go with the modeſt truth,
Nor more, nor clipt, but ſo.
Cor. Be better ſuited,
Theſe weedes are memories of thoſe worſer houres:
I prythee put them off.
Kent. Pardon deere Madam,
Yet to be knowne ſhortens my made intent,
My boone I make it, that you know me not,
Till time, and I, thinke meet.
Cor. Then be't ſo my good Lord:
How do's the King?
Gent. Madam ſleepes ſtill.
Cor. O you kind Gods!
Cure this great breach in his abuſed Nature,
Th'vntun'd and iarring ſenſes, O winde vp,
Of this childe-changed Father.
Gent. So pleaſe your Maieſty,
That we may wake the King, he hath ſlept long?
Cor. Be gouern'd by your knowledge, and proceede
I'th'ſway of your owne will: is he array'd?

Enter Lear in a chaire carried by Seruants

Gent. I Madam: in the heauineſſe of ſleepe,
We put freſh garments on him.
Be by good Madam when we do awake him,
I doubt of his Temperance.
Cor. O my deere Father, reſtauratian hang
Thy medicine on my lippes, and let this kiſſe
Repaire thoſe violent harmes, that my two Siſters
Haue in thy Reuerence made.
Kent. Kind and deere Princeſſe.
Cor. Had you not bin their Father, theſe white flakes
Did challenge pitty of them. Was this a face
To be oppos'd againſt the iarring windes?
Mine Enemies dogge, though he had bit me,
Should haue ſtood that night againſt my fire,
And was't thou faine (poore Father)
To houell thee with Swineand Rogues forlorne,
In ſhort, and muſty ſtraw? Alacke, alacke,
'Tis wonder that thy life and wits, at once
Had not concluded all. He wakes, ſpeake to him.
Gen. Madam do you, 'tis fitteſt.
Cor. How does my Royall Lord?
How fares your Maieſty?
Lear. You do me wrong to take me out o'th'graue,
Thou art a Soule in bliſſe, but I am bound
Vpon a wheele of fire, that mine owne teares
Do ſcal'd, like molten Lead.
Cor. Sir, do you know me?
Lear. You are a ſpirit I know, where did you dye?
Cor. Still, ſtill, farre wide.
Gen. He's ſcarſe awake,
Let him alone a while.
Lear.. Where haue I bin?
Where am I? Faire day light?
I am mightily abus'd; I ſhould eu'n dye with pitty
To ſee another thus. I know not what to ſay:
I will not ſweare theſe are my hands: let's ſee,
I feele this pin pricke, would I were aſſur'd
Of my condition.
Cor. O looke vpon me Sir,
And hold your hand in benediction o're me,
You muſt not kneele.
Lear. Pray do not mocke me:
I am a very fooliſh fond old man,
Fourescore and vpward,
Not an houre more, nor leſſe:
And to deale plainely,
I feare I am not in my perfect mind.
Me thinkes I ſhould know you, and know this man,
Yet I am doubtfull: For I am mainely ignorant
What place this is: and all the skill I haue
Remembers not theſe garments: nor I know not
Where I did lodge laſt night. Do not laugh at me,
For (as I am a man) I thinke this Lady
To be my childe *Cordelia*.
Cor. And ſo I am: I am.
Lear. Be your teares wet?
Yes faith: I pray weepe not,
If you haue poyſon for me, I will drinke it:
I know you do not loue me, for your Siſters
Haue (as I do remember) done me wrong.
You haue ſome cauſe, they haue not.
Cor. No cauſe, no cauſe.
Lear. Am I in France?
Kent. In your owne kingdome Sir.
Lear. Do not abuſe me.
Gent. Be comforted good Madam, the great rage
You ſee is kill'd in him: deſire him to go in,
Trouble him no more till further ſetling.
Cor. Wilt pleaſe your Highneſſe walke?
Lear. You muſt beare with me:
Pray you now forget, and forgiue,
I am old and fooliſh. *Exeunt*

Actus Quintus. Scena Prima.

Enter with Drumme and Colours, Edmund, Regan. Gentlemen, and Souldiers.

Baſt. Know of the Duke if his laſt purpoſe hold,
Or whether ſince he is aduis'd by ought
To change the courſe, he's full of alteration,
And ſelfereprouing, bring his conſtant pleaſure.
Reg. Our Siſters man is certainely miſcarried.
Baſt. 'Tis to be doubted Madam.
Reg. Now ſweet Lord,

ſ ſ You

You know the goodnesse I intend vpon you:
Tell me but truly, but then speake the truth,
Do you not loue my Sister?

Bast. In honour'd Loue.

Reg. But haue you neuer found my Brothers way,
To the fore-fended place?

Bast. No by mine honour, Madam.

Reg. I neuer shall endure her, deere my Lord
Be not familiar with her.

Bast. Feare not, she and the Duke her husband.

Enter with Drum and Colours, Albany, Generill, Soldiers.

Alb. Our very louing Sister, well be-met:
Sir, this I heard, the King is come to his Daughter
With others, whom the rigour of our State
Forc'd to cry out.

Regan. Why is this reasond?

Gone. Combine together 'gainst the Enemie:
For these domesticke and particurlar broiles,
Are not the question heere.

Alb. Let's then determine with th'ancient of warre
On our proceeding.

Reg. Sister you'le go with vs?

Gon. No.

Reg. 'Tis most conuenient, pray go with vs.

Gon. Oh ho, I know the Riddle, I will goe.

Exeunt both the Armies.

Enter Edgar.

Edg. If ere your Grace had speech with man so poore,
Heare me one word.

Alb. Ile ouertake you, speake.

Edg. Before you fight the Battaile, ope this Letter:
If you haue victory, let the Trumpet sound
For him that brought it: wretched though I seeme,
I can produce a Champion, that will proue
What is auouched there. If you miscarry,
Your businesse of the world hath so an end,
And machination ceases. Fortune loues you.

Alb. Stay till I haue read the Letter.

Edg. I was forbid it:
When time shall serue, let but the Herald cry,
And Ile appeare againe. *Exit.*

Alb. Why farethee well, I will o're-looke thy paper.

Enter Edmund.

Bast. The Enemy's in view, draw vp your powers,
Heere is the guesse of their true strength and Forces,
By dilligent discouerie, but your hast
Is now vrg'd on you.

Alb. We will greet the time. *Exit.*

Bast. To both these Sisters haue I sworne my loue:
Each iealous of the other, as the stung
Are of the Adder. Which of them shall I take?
Both? One? Or neither? Neither can be enioy'd
If both remaine aliue: To take the Widdow,
Exasperates, makes mad her Sister *Gonerill*,
And hardly shall I carry out my side,
Her husband being aliue. Now then, wee'l vse
His countenance for the Battaile, which being done,
Let her who would be rid of him, deuise
His speedy taking off. As for the mercie
Which he intends to *Lear* and to *Cordelia*,
The Battaile done, and they within our power,
Shall neuer see his pardon: for my state,
Stands on me to defend, not to debate. *Exit.*

Scena Secunda.

Alarum within. Enter with Drumme and Colours, Lear, Cordelia, and Souldiers, ouer the Stage, and Exeunt.

Enter Edgar, and Gloster.

Edg. Heere Father, take the shadow of this Tree
For your good hoast: pray that the right may thriue:
If euer I returne to you againe,
Ile bring you comfort.

Glo. Grace go with you Sir. *Exit.*

Alarum and Retreat within.

Enter Edgar.

Egdar. Away old man, giue me thy hand, away:
King *Lear* hath lost, he and his Daughter tane,
Giue me thy hand: Come on.

Glo. No further Sir, a man may rot euen heere.

Edg. What in ill thoughts againe?
Men must endure
Their going hence, euen as their comming hither,
Ripenesse is all come on.

Glo. And that's true too. *Exeunt.*

Scena Tertia.

Enter in conquest with Drum and Colours, Edmund, Lear, and Cordelia, as prisoners, Souldiers, Captaine.

Bast. Some Officers take them away: good guard,
Vntill their greater pleasures first be knowne
That are to censure them.

Cor. We are not the first,
Who with best meaning haue incurr'd the worst:
For thee oppressed King I am cast downe,
My selfe could else out-frowne false Fortunes frowne.
Shall we not see these Daughters, and these Sisters?

Lear. No, no, no, no: come let's away to prison,
We two alone will sing like Birds i'th'Cage:
When thou dost aske me blessing, Ile kneele downe
And aske of thee forgiuenesse: So wee'l liue,
And pray, and sing, and tell old tales, and laugh
At gilded Butterflies: and heere (poore Rogues)
Talke of Court newes, and wee'l talke with them too,
Who looses, and who wins; who's in, who's out;
And take vpon's the mystery of things,
As if we were Gods spies: And wee'l weare out
In a wall'd prison, packs and sects of great ones,
That ebbe and flow by th'Moone.

Bast. Take them away.

Lear. Vpon such sacrifices my *Cordelia*,
The Gods themselues throw Incense.
Haue I caught thee?
He that parts vs, shall bring a Brand from Heauen,
And fire vs hence, like Foxes: wipe thine eyes,
The good yeares shall deuoure them, flesh and fell,

Ere

Ere they ſhall make vs weepe?
Weele ſee e'm ſtaru'd firſt: come. *Exit.*
Baſt. Come hither Captaine, hearke.
Take thou this note, go follow them to priſon,
One ſtep I haue aduanc'd thee, if thou do'ſt
As this inſtructs thee, thou doſt make thy way
To Noble Fortunes: know thou this, that men
Are as the time is; to be tender minded
Do's not become a Sword, thy great imployment
Will not beare queſtion: either ſay thou'lt do't,
Or thriue by other meanes.
Capt. Ile do't my Lord.
Baſt. About it, and write happy, when th'haſt done,
Marke I ſay inſtantly, and carry it ſo
As I haue ſet it downe. *Exit Captaine.*

Flouriſh. Enter Albany, Generill, Regan, Soldiers.

Alb. Sir, you haue ſhew'd to day your valiant ſtraine,
And Fortune led you well: you haue the Captiues
Who were the oppoſites of this dayes ſtrife:
I do require them of you ſo to vſe them,
As we ſhall find their merites, and our ſafety
May equally determine.
Baſt. Sir, I thought it fit,
To ſend the old and miſerable King to ſome retention,
Whoſe age had Charmes in it, whoſe Title more,
To plucke the common boſome on his ſide,
And turne our impreſt Launces in our eies
Which do command them. With him I ſent the Queen:
My reaſon all the ſame, and they are ready
To morrow, or at further ſpace, t'appeare
Where you ſhall hold your Seſſion.
Alb. Sir, by your patience,
I hold you but a ſubiect of this Warre,
Not as a Brother.
Reg. That's as we liſt to grace him.
Methinkes our pleaſure might haue bin demanded
Ere you had ſpoke ſo farre. He led our Powers,
Bore the Commiſſion of my place and perſon,
The which immediacie may well ſtand vp,
And call it ſelfe your Brother.
Gon. Not ſo hot:
In his owne grace he doth exalt himſelfe,
More then in your addition.
Reg. In my rights,
By me inueſted, he compeeres the beſt.
Alb. That were the moſt, if he ſhould husband you.
Reg. Ieſters do oft proue Prophets.
Gon. Hola, hola,
That eye that told you ſo, look'd but a ſquint.
Rega. Lady I am not well, elſe I ſhould anſwere
From a full flowing ſtomack. Generall,
Take thou my Souldiers, priſoners, patrimony,
Diſpoſe of them, of me, the walls is thine:
Witneſſe the world, that I create thee heere
My Lord, and Maſter.
Gon. Meane you to enioy him?
Alb. The let alone lies not in your good will.
Baſt. Nor in thine Lord.
Alb. Halfe-blooded fellow, yes.
Reg. Let the Drum ſtrike, and proue my title thine.
Alb. Stay yet, heare reaſon: *Edmund*, I arreſt thee
On capitall Treaſon; and in thy arreſt,
This guilded Serpent: for your claime faire Siſters,
I bare it in the intereſt of my wife,
'Tis ſhe is ſub-contracted to this Lord,
And I her husband contradict your Banes.
If you will marry, make your loues to me,
My Lady is beſpoke.
Gon. An enterlude.
Alb. Thou art armed *Gloſter*,
Let the Trmpet ſound:
If none appeare to proue vpon thy perſon,
Thy heynous, manifeſt, and many Treaſons,
There is my pledge: Ile make it on thy heart
Ere I taſte bread, thou art in nothing leſſe
Then I haue heere proclaim'd thee.
Reg. Sicke, O ſicke.
Gon. If not, Ile nere truſt medicine.
Baſt. There's my exchange, what in the world hes
That names me Traitor, villain-like he lies,
Call by the Trumpet: he that dares approach;
On him, on you, who not, I will maintaine
My truth and honor firmely.

Enter a Herald.

Alb. A Herald, ho.
Truſt to thy ſingle vertue, for thy Souldiers
All leuied in my name, haue in my name
Tooke their diſcharge.
Regan. My ſickneſſe growes vpon me.
Alb. She is not well, conuey her to my Tent.
Come hither Herald, let the Trumper ſound,
And read out this. *A Tumpet ſounds.*
Herald reads.

If any man of qualitie or degree, within the liſts of the Army, will maintaine vpon Edmund, ſuppoſed Earle of Gloſter, that he is a manifold Traitor, let him appeare by the third ſound of the Trumpet: he is bold in his defence. *1 Trumpet.*
Her. Againe. *2 Trumpet.*
Her. Againe. *3 Trumpet.*
Trumpet anſwers within.

Enter Edgar armed.

Alb. Aske him his purpoſes, why he appeares
Vpon this Call o'th'Trumpet.
Her. What are you?
Your name, your quality, and why you anſwer
This preſent Summons?
Edg. Know my name is loſt
By Treaſons tooth: bare-gnawne, and Canker-bit,
Yet am I Noble as the Aduerſary
I come to cope.
Alb. Which is that Aduerſary?
Edg. What's he that ſpeakes for *Edmund* Earle of Gloſter?
Baſt. Himſelfe, what ſaiſt thou to him?
Edg. Draw thy Sword,
That if my ſpeech offend a Noble heart,
Thy arme may do thee Iuſtice, heere is mine:
Behold it is my priuiledge,
The priuiledge of mine Honours,
My oath, and my profeſſion. I proteſt,
Maugre thy ſtrength, place, youth, and eminence,
Deſpiſe thy victor-Sword, and fire new Fortune,
Thy valor, and thy heart, thou art a Traitor:
Falſe to thy Gods, thy Brother, and thy Father,
Conſpirant 'gainſt this high illuſtrious Prince,
And from th'extremeſt vpward of thy head,
To the diſcent and duſt below thy foote,

A most Toad-spotted Traitor. Say thou no,
This Sword, this arme, and my best spirits are bent
To proue vpon thy heart, whereto I speake,
Thou lyest.

Bast. In wisedome I should aske thy name,
But since thy out-side lookes so faire and Warlike,
And that thy tongue(some say) of breeding breathes,
What safe, and nicely I might well delay,
By rule of Knight-hood, I disdaine and spurne:
Backe do I tosse these Treasons to thy head,
With the hell-hated Lye, ore-whelme thy heart,
Which for they yet glance by, and scarely bruise,
This Sword of mine shall giue them instant way,
Where they shall rest for euer. Trumpets speake.

Alb. Saue him, saue him. *Alarums. Fights.*

Gon. This is practise *Gloster*,
By th'law of Warre, thou wast not bound to answer
An vnknowne opposite: thou art not vanquish'd,
But cozend, and beguild.

Alb. Shut your mouth Dame,
Or with this paper shall I stop it: hold Sir,
Thou worse then any name, reade thine owne euill:
No tearing Lady, I perceiue you know it.

Gon. Say if I do, the Lawes are mine not thine,
Who can araigne me for't? *Exit.*

Alb. Most monstrous! O, know'st thou this paper?

Bast. Aske me not what I know.

Alb. Go after her, she's desperate, gouerne her.

Bast. What you haue charg'd me with,
That haue I done,
And more, much more, the time will bring it out.
'Tis past, and so am I: But what art thou
That hast this Fortune on me? If thou'rt Noble,
I do forgiue thee.

Edg. Let's exchange charity:
I am no lesse in blood then thou art *Edmond*,
If more, the more th'hast wrong'd me.
My name is *Edgar* and thy Fathers Sonne,
The Gods are iust, and of our pleasant vices
Make instruments to plague vs:
The darke and vitious place where thee he got,
Cost him his eyes.

Bast. Th'hast spoken right, 'tis true,
The Wheele is come full circle, I am heere.

Alb. Me thought thy very gate did prophesie
A Royall Noblenesse: I must embrace thee,
Let sorrow split my heart, if euer I
Did hate thee, or thy Father.

Edg. Worthy Prince I know't.

Alb. Where haue you hid your selfe?
How haue you knowne the miseries of your Father?

Edg. By nursing them my Lord. List a breefe tale,
And when 'tis told, O that my heart would burst.
The bloody proclamation to escape
That follow'd me so neere, (O our liues sweetnesse,
That we the paine of death would hourely dye,
Rather then die at once) taught me to shift
Into a mad-mans rags, t'assume a semblance
That very Dogges disdain'd: and in this habit
Met I my Father with his bleeding Rings,
Their precious Stones new lost: became his guide,
Led him, begg'd for him, sau'd him from dispaire.
Neuer(O fault)reueal'd my selfe vnto him,
Vntill some halfe houre past when I was arm'd,
Not sure, though hoping of this good successe,
I ask'd his blessing, and from first to last
Told him our pilgrimage. But his flaw'd heart
(Alacke too weake the conflict to support)
Twixt two extremes of passion, ioy and greefe,
Burst smilingly.

Bast. This speech of yours hath mou'd me,
And shall perchance do good, but speake you on,
You looke as you had something more to say.

Alb. If there be more, more wofull, hold it in,
For I am almost ready to dissolue,
Hearing of this.

Enter a Gentleman.

Gen. Helpe, helpe: O helpe.

Edg. What kinde of helpe?

Alb. Speake man.

Edg. What meanes this bloody Knife?

Gen. 'Tis hot, it smoakes, it came euen from the heart
of——O she's dead.

Alb. Who dead? Speake man.

Gen. Your Lady Sir, your Lady; and her Sister
By her is poyson'd: she confesses it.

Bast. I was contracted to them both, all three
Now marry in an instant.

Edg. Here comes *Kent*.

Enter Kent.

Alb. Produce the bodies, be they aliue or dead;
Gonerill and Regans bodies brought out.
This iudgement of the Heauens that makes vs tremble,
Touches vs not with pitty: O, is this he?
The time will not allow the complement
Which very manners vrges.

Kent. I am come
To bid my King and Master aye good night.
Is he not here?

Alb. Great thing of vs forgot,
Speake *Edmund*, where's the King? and where's *Cordelia*?
Seest thou this obiect *Kent*?

Kent. Alacke, why thus?

Bast. Yet *Edmund* was belou'd:
The one the other poison'd for my sake,
And after slew herselfe.

Alb. Euen so: couer their faces.

Bast. I pant for life: some good I meane to do
Despight of mine owne Nature. Quickly send,
(Be briefe in it) to'th'Castle, for my Writ
Is on the life of *Lear*, and on *Cordelia*:
Nay, send in time.

Alb. Run, run, O run.

Edg. To who my Lord? Who ha's the Office?
Send thy token of repreeue.

Bast. Well thought on, take my Sword,
Giue it the Captaine.

Edg. Hast thee for thy life.

Bast. He hath Commission from thy Wife and me,
To hang *Cordelia* in the prison, and
To lay the blame vpon her owne dispaire,
That she for-did her selfe.

Alb. The Gods defend her, beare him hence awhile.

Enter Lear with Cordelia in his armes.

Lear. Howle, howle, howle: O your are men of stones,
Had I your tongues and eyes, Il'd vse them so,
That Heauens vault should crack: she's gone for euer.
I know when one is dead, and when one liues,
She's dead as earth: Lend me a Looking-glasse,

If

If that her breath will mist or staine the stone,
Why then she liues.
Kent. Is this the promis'd end?
Edg. Or image of that horror.
Alb. Fall and cease.
Lear. This feather stirs, she liues: if it be so,
It is a chance which do's redeeme all sorrowes
That euer I haue felt.
Kent. O my good Master.
Lear. Prythee away.
Edg. 'Tis Noble *Kent* your Friend.
Lear. A plague vpon you Murderors, Traitors all,
I might haue sau'd her, now she's gone for euer:
Cordelia, Cordelia, stay a little. Ha:
What is't thou saist? Her voice was euer soft,
Gentle, and low, an excellent thing in woman.
I kill'd the Slaue that was a hanging thee.
Gent. 'Tis true (my Lords) he did.
Lear. Did I not fellow?
I haue seene the day, with my good biting Faulchion
I would haue made him skip: I am old now,
And these same crosses spoile me. Who are you?
Mine eyes are not o'th'best, Ile tell you straight.
Kent. If Fortune brag of two, she lou'd and hated,
One of them we behold.
Lear. This is a dull sight, are you not *Kent*?
Kent. The same: your Seruant *Kent*,
Where is your Seruant *Caius*?
Lear. He's a good fellow, I can tell you that,
He'le strike and quickly too, he's dead and rotten.
Kent. No my good Lord, I am the very man.
Lear. Ile see that straight.
Kent. That from your first of difference and decay,
Haue follow'd your sad steps.
Lear. Your are welcome hither.
Kent. Nor no man else:
All's cheerlesse, darke, and deadly,
Your eldest Daughters haue fore-done themselues,
And desperately are dead
Lear. I so I thinke.
Alb. He knowes not what he saies, and vaine is it
That we present vs to him.

Enter a Messenger.

Edg. Very bootlesse.
Mess. *Edmund* is dead my Lord.
Alb. That's but a trifle heere:
You Lords and Noble Friends, know our intent,
What comfort to this great decay may come,
Shall be appli'd. For vs we will resigne,
During the life of this old Maiesty
To him our absolute power, you to your rights,
With boote, and such addition as your Honours
Haue more then merited. All Friends shall
Taste the wages of their vertue, and all Foes
The cup of their deseruings: O see, see.
Lear. And my poore Foole is hang'd: no, no, no life?
Why should a Dog, a Horse, a Rat haue life,
And thou no breath at all? Thou'lt come no more,
Neuer, neuer, neuer, neuer, neuer.
Pray you vndo this Button. Thanke you Sir,
Do you see this? Looke on her? Looke her lips,
Looke there, looke there. *He dies.*
Edg. He faints, my Lord, my Lord.
Kent. Breake heart, I prythee breake.
Edg. Looke vp my Lord.
Kent. Vex not his ghost, O let him passe, he hates him,
That would vpon the wracke of this tough world
Stretch him out longer.
Edg. He is gon indeed.
Kent. The wonder is, he hath endur'd so long,
He but vsurpt his life.
Alb. Beare them from hence, our present businesse
Is generall woe: Friends of my soule, you twaine,
Rule in this Realme, and the gor'd state sustaine.
Kent. I haue a iourney Sir, shortly to go,
My Master calls me, I must not say no.
Edg. The waight of this sad time we must obey,
Speake what we feele, not what we ought to say:
The oldest hath borne most, we that are yong,
Shall neuer see so much, nor liue so long.

Exeunt with a dead March.

ss 3

FINIS.

THE TRAGEDIE OF
Othello, the Moore of Venice.

Actus Primus. Scœna Prima.

Enter Rodorigo, and Iago.

Rodorigo.

Neuer tell me, I take it much vnkindly
That thou (*Iago*) who haſt had my purſe,
As if ỹ ſtrings were thine, ſhould'ſt know of this.

Ia. But you'l not heare me. If euer I did dream
Of ſuch a matter, abhorre me.

Rodo. Thou told'ſt me,
Thou did'ſt hold him in thy hate.

Iago. Deſpiſe me
If I do not. Three Great-ones of the Cittie,
(In perſonall ſuite to make me his Lieutenant)
Off-capt to him: and by the faith of man
I know my price, I am worth no worſſe a place.
But he (as louing his owne pride, and purpoſes)
Euades them, with a bumbaſt Circumſtance,
Horribly ſtufft with Epithites of warre,
Non-ſuites my Mediators. For certes, ſaies he,
I haue already choſe my Officer. And what was he?
For-ſooth, a great Arithmatician,
One *Michaell Caſſio*, a *Florentine*,
(A Fellow almoſt damn'd in a faire Wife)
That neuer ſet a Squadron in the Field,
Nor the deuiſion of a Battaile knowes
More then a Spinſter. Vnleſſe the Bookiſh Theoricke:
Wherein the Tongued Conſuls can propoſe
As Maſterly as he. Meere pratle (without practiſe)
Is all his Souldierſhip. But he (Sir) had th'election;
And I (of whom his eies had ſeene the proofe
At Rhodes, at Ciprus, and on others grounds
Chriſten'd, and Heathen) muſt be be-leed, and calm'd
By Debitor, and Creditor. This Counter-caſter,
He (in good time) muſt his Lieutenant be,
And I (bleſſe the marke) his Mooreſhips Auntient.

Rod. By heauen, I rather would haue bin his hangman.

Iago. Why, there's no remedie.
'Tis the curſſe of Seruice;
Preferment goes by Letter, and affection,
And not by old gradation, where each ſecond
Stood Heire to'th'firſt. Now Sir, be iudge your ſelfe,
Whether I in any iuſt terme am Affin'd
To loue the *Moore*?

Rod. I would not follow him then.

Iago. O Sir content you.
I follow him, to ſerue my turne vpon him.
We cannot all be Maſters, nor all Maſters
Cannot be truely follow'd. You ſhall marke
Many a dutious and knee-crooking knaue;
That (doting on his owne obſequious bondage)
Weares out his time, much like his Maſters Aſſe,
For naught but Prouender, & when he's old Caſheer'd.
Whip me ſuch honeſt knaues. Others there are
Who trym'd in Formes, and Viſages of Dutie,
Keepe yet their hearts attending on themſelues,
And throwing but ſhowes of Seruice on their Lords
Doe well thriue by them.
And when they haue lin'd their Coates
Doe themſelues Homage.
Theſe Fellowes haue ſome ſoule,
And ſuch a one do I profeſſe my ſelfe. For (Sir)
It is as ſure as you are *Rodorigo*,
Were I the Moore, I would not be *Iago*:
In following him, I follow but my ſelfe.
Heauen is my Iudge, not I for loue and dutie,
But ſeeming ſo, for my peculiar end:
For when my outward Action doth demonſtrate
The natiue act, and figure of my heart
In Complement externe, 'tis not long after
But I will weare my heart vpon my ſleeue
For Dawes to pecke at; I am not what I am.

Rod. What a fall Fortune do's the Thicks-lips owe
If he can carry't thus?

Iago. Call vp her Father:
Rowſe him, make after him, poyſon his delight,
Proclaime him in the Streets. Incenſe her kinſmen,
And though he in a fertile Clymate dwell,
Plague him with Flies: though that his Ioy be Ioy,
Yet throw ſuch chances of vexation on't,
As it may looſe ſome colour.

Rodo. Heere is her Fathers houſe, Ile call aloud.

Iago. Doe, with like timerous accent, and dire yell,
As when (by Night and Negligence) the Fire
Is ſpied in populus Citties.

Rodo. What hoa: *Brabantio*, Siginor *Brabantio*, hoa.

Iago. Awake: what hoa, *Brabantio*: Theeues, Theeues.
Looke to your houſe, your daughter, and your Bags,
Theeues, Theeues.

Bra. Aboue. What is the reaſon of this terrible
Summons? What is the matter there?

Rodo. Signior is all your Familie within?

Iago. Are your Doores lock'd?

Bra. Why? Wherefore ask you this?

Iago. Sir, y'are rob'd, for ſhame put on your Gowne,
Your

Your heart is burst, you haue lost halfe your soule
Euen now, now, very now, an old blacke Ram
Is tupping your white Ewe. Arise, arise,
Awake the snorting Cittizens with the Bell,
Or else the deuill will make a Grand-sire of you.
Arise I say.

Bra. What, haue you lost your wits?

Rod. Most reuerend Signior, do you know my voice?

Bra. Not I: what are you?

Rod. My name is *Rodorigo.*

Bra. The worsser welcome:
I haue charg'd thee not to haunt about my doores:
In honest plainenesse thou hast heard me say,
My Daughter is not for thee. And now in madnesse
(Being full of Supper, and distempring draughtes)
Vpon malitious knauerie, dost thou come
To start my quiet.

Rod. Sir, Sir, Sir.

Bra. But thou must needs be sure,
My spirits and my place haue in their power
To make this bitter to thee.

Rodo. Patience good Sir.

Bra. What tell'st thou me of Robbing?
This is Venice: my house is not a Grange.

Rodo. Most graue *Brabantio,*
In simple and pure soule, I come to you.

Ia. Sir: you are one of those that will not serue God, if the deuill bid you. Because we come to do you seruice, and you thinke we are Ruffians, you'le haue your Daughter couer'd with a Barbary horse, you'le haue your Nephewes neigh to you, you'le haue Coursers for Cozens: and Gennets for Germaines.

Bra. What prophane wretch art thou?

Ia. I am one Sir, that comes to tell you, your Daughter and the Moore, are making the Beast with two backs.

Bra. Thou art a Villaine.

Iago. You are a Senator.

Bra. This thou shalt answere. I know thee *Rodorigo.*

Rod. Sir, I will answere any thing. But I beseech you
If't be your pleasure, and most wise consent,
(As partly I find it is) that your faire Daughter,
At this odde Euen and dull watch o'th'night
Transported with no worse nor better guard,
But with a knaue of common hire, a Gundelier,
To the grosse claspes of a Lasciuious Moore:
If this be knowne to you, and your Allowance,
We then haue done you bold, and saucie wrongs.
But if you know not this, my Manners tell me,
We haue your wrong rebuke. Do not beleeue
That from the sence of all Ciuilitie,
I thus would play and trifle with your Reuerence.
Your Daughter (if you haue not giuen her leaue)
I say againe, hath made a grosse reuolt,
Tying her Dutie, Beautie, Wit, and Fortunes
In an extrauagant, and wheeling Stranger,
Of here, and euery where: straight satisfie your selfe.
If she be in her Chamber, or your house,
Let loose on me the Iustice of the State
For thus deluding you.

Bra. Strike on the Tinder, hoa:
Giue me a Taper: call vp all my people,
This Accident is not vnlike my dreame,
Beleefe of it oppresses me alreadie.
Light, I say, light. *Exit.*

Iag. Farewell: for I must leaue you.
It seemes not meete, nor wholesome to my place
To be producted, (as if I stay, I shall,)
Against the Moore. For I do know the State,
(How euer this may gall him with some checke)
Cannot with safetie cast-him. For he's embark'd
With such loud reason to the Cyprus Warres,
(Which euen now stands in Act) that for their soules
Another of his Fadome, they haue none,
To lead their Businesse. In which regard,
Though I do hate him as I do hell apines,
Yet, for necessitie of present life,
I must show out a Flag, and signe of Loue,
(Which is indeed but signe) that you shal surely find him
Lead to the Sagitary the raised Search:
And there will I be with him. So farewell. *Exit.*

Enter Brabantio, with Seruants and Torches.

Bra. It is too true an euill. Gone she is,
And what's to come of my despised time,
Is naught but bitternesse. Now *Rodorigo,*
Where didst thou see her? (Oh vnhappie Girle)
With the Moore saist thou? (Who would be a Father?)
How didst thou know 'twas she? (Oh she deceaues me
Past thought:) what said she to you? Get moe Tapers:
Raise all my Kindred. Are they married thinke you?

Rodo. Truely I thinke they are.

Bra. Oh Heauen: how got she out?
Oh treason of the blood.
Fathers, from hence trust not your Daughters minds
By what you see them act. Is there not Charmes,
By which the propertie of Youth, and Maidhood
May be abus'd? Haue you not read *Rodorigo,*
Of some such thing?

Rod. Yes Sir: I haue indeed.

Bra. Call vp my Brother: oh would you had had her.
Some one way, some another. Doe you know
Where we may apprehend her, and the Moore?

Rod. I thinke I can discouer him, if you please
To get good Guard, and go along with me.

Bra. Pray you lead on. At euery house Ile call,
(I may command at most) get Weapons (hoa)
And raise some speciall Officers of might:
On good *Rodorigo,* I will deserue your paines. *Exeunt.*

Scena Secunda.

Enter Othello, Iago, Attendants, with Torches.

Ia. Though in the trade of Warre I haue slaine men,
Yet do I hold it very stuffe o'th'conscience
To do no contriu'd Murder: I lacke Iniquitie
Sometime to do me seruice. Nine, or ten times
I had thought t'haue yerk'd him here vnder the Ribbes.

Othello. 'Tis better as it is.

Iago. Nay but he prated,
And spoke such scuruy, and prouoking termes
Against your Honor, that with the little godlinesse I haue
I did full hard forbeare him. But I pray you Sir,
Are you fast married? Be assur'd of this,
That the Magnifico is much belou'd,
And hath in his effect a voice potentiall
As double as the Dukes: He will diuorce you.
Or put vpon you, what restraint or greeuance,

The

The Law (with all his might, to enforce it on)
Will giue him Cable.
Othel. Let him do his ſpight;
My Seruices, which I haue done the Signorie
Shall out-tongue his Complaints. 'Tis yet to know,
Which when I know, that boaſting is an Honour,
I ſhall promulgate. I fetch my life and being,
From Men of Royall Seige. And my demerites
May ſpeake (vnbonnetted) to as proud a Fortune
As this that I haue reach'd. For know *Iago*,
But that I loue the gentle *Deſdemona*,
I would not my vnhouſed free condition
Put into Circumſcription, and Confine,
For the Seas worth. But looke, what Lights come yond?

Enter Caſſio, with Torches.

Iago. Thoſe are the raiſed Father, and his Friends:
You were beſt go in.
Othel. Not I: I muſt be found.
My Parts, my Title, and my perfect Soule
Shall manifeſt me rightly. Is it they?
Iago. By *Ianus*, I thinke no.
Othel. The Seruants of the Dukes?
And my Lieutenant?
The goodneſſe of the Night vpon you (Friends)
What is the Newes?
Caſſio. The Duke do's greet you (Generall)
And he requires your haſte, Poſt-haſte appearance,
Enen on the inſtant.
Othello. What is the matter, thinke you?
Caſſio. Something from Cyprus, as I may diuine:
It is a buſineſſe of ſome heate. The Gallies
Haue ſent a dozen ſequent Meſſengers
This very night, at one anothers heeles:
And many of the Conſuls, rais'd and met,
Are at the Dukes already. You haue bin hotly call'd for,
When being not at your Lodging to be found,
The Senate hath ſent about three ſeuerall Queſts,
To ſearch you out.
Othel. 'Tis well I am found by you:
I will but ſpend a word here in the houſe,
And goe with you.
Caſſio. Aunciant, what makes he heere?
Iago. Faith, he to night hath boarded a Land Carract,
If it proue lawfull prize, he's made for euer.
Caſſio. I do not vnderſtand.
Iago. He's married.
Caſſio. To who?
Iago. Marry to——Come Captaine, will you go?
Othel. Haue with you.
Caſſio. Here comes another Troope to ſeeke for you.

Enter Brabantio, Rodorigo, with Officers, and Torches.

Iago. It is *Brabantio*: Generall be aduis'd,
He comes to bad intent.
Othello. Holla, ſtand there.
Rodo. Signior, it is the Moore.
Bra. Downe with him, Theefe.
Iago. You, *Rodorigo*, come Sir, I am for you.
Othe. Keepe vp your bright Swords, for the dew will ruſt them. Good Signior, you ſhall more command with yeares, then with your Weapons.
Bra. Oh thou foule Theefe,
Where haſt thou ſtow'd my Daughter?
Damn'd as thou art, thou haſt enchaunted her
For Ile referre me to all things of ſenſe,
(If ſhe in Chaines of Magick were not bound)
Whether a Maid, ſo tender, Faire, and Happie,
So oppoſite to Marriage, that ſhe ſhun'd
The wealthy curled Deareling of our Nation,
Would euer haue (t'encurre a generall mocke)
Run from her Guardage to the ſootie boſome,
Of ſuch a thing as thou: to feare, not to delight?
Iudge me the world, if 'tis not groſſe in ſenſe,
That thou haſt practis'd on her with foule Charmes,
Abus'd her delicate Youth, with Drugs or Minerals,
That weakens Motion. Ile haue't diſputed on,
'Tis probable, and palpable to thinking;
I therefore apprehend and do attach thee,
For an abuſer of the World, a practiſer
Of Arts inhibited, and out of warrant;
Lay hold vpon him, if he do reſiſt
Subdue him, at his perill.
Othe. Hold your hands
Both you of my inclining, and the reſt.
Were it my Cue to fight, I ſhould haue knowne it
Without a Prompter. Whether will you that I goe
To anſwere this your charge?
Bra. To Priſon, till fit time
Of Law, and courſe of direct Seſſion
Call thee to anſwer.
Othe. What if do obey?
How may the Duke be therewith ſatisfi'd,
Whoſe Meſſengers are heere about my ſide,
Vpon ſome preſent buſineſſe of the State,
To bring me to him.
Officer. 'Tis true moſt worthy Signior,
The Dukes in Counſell, and your Noble ſelfe,
I am ſure is ſent for.
Bra. How? The Duke in Counſell?
In this time of the night? Bring him away;
Mine's not an idle Cauſe. The Duke himſelfe,
Or any of my Brothers of the State,
Cannot but feele this wrong, as 'twere their owne:
For if ſuch Actions may haue paſſage free,
Bond-ſlaues, and Pagans ſhall our Stateſmen be. *Exeunt*

Scæna Tertia.

Enter Duke, Senators, and Officers.

Duke. There's no compoſition in this Newes,
That giues them Credite.
1. *Sen.* Indeed, they are diſproportioned;
My Letters ſay, a Hundred and ſeuen Gallies.
Duke. And mine a Hundred fortie.
2. *Sena.* And mine two Hundred:
But though they iumpe not on a iuſt accompt,
(As in theſe Caſes where the ayme reports,
'Tis oft with difference) yet do they all confirme
A Turkiſh Fleete, and bearing vp to Cyprus.
Duke. Nay, it is poſſible enough to iudgement:
I do not ſo ſecure me in the Error,
But the maine Article I do approue
In fearefull ſenſe.
Saylor within. What hoa, what hoa, what hoa.
Enter Saylor.

Officer. A

Officer. A Messen g er from the Gallies.
Duke. Now? What's the businesse?
Sailor. The Turkish Preparation makes for Rhodes,
So was I bid report here to the State,
By Signior *Angelo*.
Duke. How say you by this change?
1. *Sen.* This cannot be
By no assay of reason. 'Tis a Pageant
To keepe vs in false gaze, when we consider
Th'importancie of Cyprus to the Turke;
And let our selues againe but vnderstand,
That as it more concernes the Turke then Rhodes,
So may he with more facile question beare it,
For that it stands not in such Warrelike brace,
But altogether lackes th'abilities
That Rhodes is dress'd in. If we make thought of this,
We must not thinke the Turke is so vnskillfull,
To leaue that latest, which concernes him first,
Neglecting an attempt of ease, and gaine
To wake, and wage a danger profitlesse.
Duke. Nay, in all confidence he's not for Rhodes.
Officer. Here is more Newes.

Enter a Messenger.

Messen. The *Ottamites*, Reueren'd, and Gracious,
Steering with due course toward the Ile of Rhodes,
Haue there inioynted them with an after Fleete.
1. *Sen.* I, so I thought: how many, as you guesse?
Mess. Of thirtie Saile: and now they do re-stem
Their backward course, bearing with frank appearance
Their purposes toward Cyprus. Signior *Montano*,
Your trustie and most Valiant Seruitour,
With his free dutie, recommends you thus,
And prayes you to beleeue him.
Duke. 'Tis certaine then for Cyprus:
Marcus Luccicos, is not he in Towne?
1. *Sen.* He's now in Florence.
Duke. Write from vs,
To him, Post, Post-haste, dispatch.
1. *Sen.* Here comes *Brabantio*, and the Valiant Moore.

Enter Brabantio, Othello, Cassio, Iago, Rodorigo, and Officers.

Duke. Valiant *Othello*, we must straight employ you,
Against the generall Enemy *Ottoman*.
I did not see you: welcome gentle Signior,
We lack't your Counsaile, and your helpe to night.
Bra. So did I yours: Good your Grace pardon me.
Neither my place, hor ought I heard of businesse
Hath rais'd me from my bed; nor doth the generall care
Take hold on me. For my perticular griefe
Is of so flood-gate, and ore-bearing Nature,
That it engluts, snd swallowes other sorrowes,
And it is still it selfe.
Duke. Why? What's the matter?
Bra. My Daughter: oh my Daughter!
Sen. Dead?
Bra. I, to me.
She is abus'd, stolne from me, and corrupted
By Spels, and Medicines, bought of Mountebanks;
For Nature, so prepostrously to erre,
(Being not deficient, blind, or lame of sense,)
Sans witch-craft could not.
Duke. Who ere he be, that in this foule proceeding
Hath thus beguil'd your Daughter of her selfe,
And you of her; the bloodie Booke of Law,
You shall your selfe read, in the bitter letter,
After your owne sense: yea, though our proper Son
Stood in your Action.
Bra. Humbly I thanke your Grace,
Here is the man; this Moore, whom now it seemes
Your speciall Mandate, for the State affaires
Hath hither brought.
All. We are veriesorry for't.
Duke. What in yonr owne part, can you say to this?
Bra. Nothing, but this is so.
Othe. Most Potent, Graue, and Reueren'd Signiors,
My very Noble, and approu'd good Masters;
That I haue tane away this old mans Daughter,
It is most true: true I haue married her;
The verie head, and front of my offending,
Hath this extent; no more. Rude am I, in my speech,
And little bless'd with the soft phrase of Peace;
For since these Armes of mine, had seuen yeares pith,
Till now, some nine Moones wasted, they haue vs'd
Their deerest action, in the Tented Field:
And little of this great world can I speake,
More then pertaines to Feats of Broiles, and Battaile,
And therefore little shall I grace my cause,
In speaking for my selfe. Yet, (by your gratious patience)
I will a round vn-varnish'd u Tale deliuer,
Of my whole course of Loue.|
What Drugges, what Charmes,
What Coniuration, and what mighty Magicke,
(For such proceeding I am charg'd withall)
I won his Daughter.
Bra. A Maiden, neuer bold:
Of Spirit so still, and quiet, that her Motion
Blush'd at her selfe, and she, in spight of Nature,
Of Yeares, of Country, Credite, euery thing
To fall in Loue, with what she fear'd to looke on;
It is a iudgement main'd, and most imperfect.
That will confesse Perfection so could erre
Against all rules of Nature, and must be driuen
To find out practises of cunning hell
Why this should be. I therefore vouch againe,
That with some Mixtures, powrefull o're the blood,
Or with some Dram, (coniur'd to this effect)
He wrought vp on her.
To vouch this, is no proofe,
Without more wider, and more ouer Test
Then these thin habits, and poore likely-hoods
Of moderne seeming, do prefer against him.
Sen. But *Othello*, speake,
Did you, by indirect, and forced courses
Subdue, and poyson this yong Maides affections?
Or came it by request, and such faire question
As soule, to soule affordeth?
Othel. I do beseech you,
Send for the Lady to the Sagitary.
And let her speake of me before her Father;
If you do finde me foule, in herreport,
The Trust, the Office, I do hold of you,
Not onely take away, but let your Sentence
Euen fall vpon my life.
Duke. Fetch *Desdemona* hither.
Othe. Aunciant, conduct them:
You best know the place.
And tell she come, as truely as to heauen,
I do confesse the vices of my blood,
So iustly to your Graue eares, Ile present

How I did thriue in this faire Ladies loue,
And she in mine.

Duke. Say it *Othello.*

Othe. Her Father lou'd me, oft inuited me:
Still question'd me the Storie of my life,
From yeare to yeare: the Battaile, Sieges, Fortune,
That I haue past.
I ran it through, euen from my boyish daies,
Toth'very moment that he bad me tell it.
Wherein I spoke of most disastrous chances:
Of mouing Accidents by Flood and Field,
Of haire-breadth scapes i'th'imminent deadly breach;
Of being taken by the Insolent Foe,
And sold to slauery. Of my redemption thence,
And portance in my Trauellours historie.
Wherein of Antars vast, and Desarts idle,
Rough Quarries, Rocks, Hills, whose head touch heauen,
It was my hint to speake. Such was my Processe,
And of the Canibals that each others eate,
The *Antropophague*, and men whose heads
Grew beneath their shoulders. These things to heare,
Would *Desdemona* seriously incline:
But still the house Affaires would draw her hence:
Which euer as she could with haste dispatch,
She'l'd come againe, and with a greedie eare
Deuoure vp my discourse. Which I obseruing,
Tooke once a pliant houre, and found good meanes
To draw from her a prayer of earnest heart,
That I would all my Pilgrimage dilate,
Whereof by parcels she had something heard,
But not instinctiuely: I did consent,
And often did beguile her of her teares,
When I did speake of some distressefull stroke
That my youth suffer'd: My Storie being done,
She gaue me for my paines a world of kisses:
She swore in faith 'twas strange: 'twas passing strange,
'Twas pittifull: 'twas wondrous pittifull.
She wish'd she had not heard it, yet she wish'd
That Heauen had made her such a man. She thank'd me,
And bad me, if I had a Friend that lou'd her,
I should but teach him how to tell my Story,
And that would wooe her. Vpon this hint I spake,
She lou'd me for the dangers I had past,
And I lou'd her, that she did pitty them.
This onely is the witch-craft I haue vs'd.
Here comes the Ladie: Let her witnesse it.

Enter Desdemona, Iago, Attendants.

Duke. I thinke this tale would win my Daughter too,
Good *Brabantio*, take vp this mangled matter at the best:
Men do their broken Weapons rather vse,
Then their bare hands.

Bra. I pray you heare her speake?
If she confesse that she was halfe the wooer,
Destruction on my head, if my bad blame
Light on the man. Come hither gentle Mistris,
Do you perceiue in all this Noble Companie,
Where most you owe obedience?

Des. My Noble Father,
I do perceiue heere a diuided dutie.
To you I am bound for life, and education:
My life and education both do learne me,
How to respect you. You are the Lord of duty,
I am hitherto your Daughter. But heere's my Husband;
And so much dutie, as my Mother shew'd
To you, preferring you before her Father:
So much I challenge, that I may professe
Due to the Moore my Lord.

Bra. God be with you: I haue done.
Please it your Grace, on to the State Affaires;
I had rather to adopt a Child, then get it.
Come hither Moore;
I here do giue thee that with all my heart,
Which but thou hast already, with all my heart
I would keepe from thee. For your sake (Iewell)
I am glad at soule, I haue no other Child,
For thy escape would teach me Tirranie
To hang clogges on them. I haue done my Lord.

Duke. Let me speake like your selfe:
And lay a Sentence,
Which as a grise, or step may helpe these Louers.
When remedies are past, the griefes are ended
By seeing the worst, which late on hopes depended.
To mourne a Mischeefe that is past and gon,
Is the next way to draw new mischiefe on.
What cannot be presern'd, when Fortune takes:
Patience, her Iniury a mock'ry makes.
The rob'd that smiles, steales something from the Thiefe,
He robs himselfe, that spends a bootelesse griefe.

Bra. So let the Turke of Cyprus vs beguile,
We loose it not so long as we can smile:
He beares the Sentence well, that nothing beares,
But the free comfort which from thence he heares.
But he beares both the Sentence, and the sorrow,
That to pay griefe, must of poore Patience borrow.
These Sentences, to Sugar, or to Gall,
Being strong on both sides, are Equiuocall.
But words are words, I neuer yet did heare:
That the bruized heart was pierc'd through the eares.
I humbly beseech you proceed to th'Affaires of State.

Duke. The Turke with a most mighty Preparation makes for Cyprus: *Othello*, the Fortitude of the place is best knowne to you. And though we haue there a Substitute of most allowed sufficiencie; yet opinion, a more soueraigne Mistris of Effects, throwes a more safer voice on you: you must therefore be content to slubber the glosse of your new Fortunes, with this more stubborne, and boystrous expedition.

Othe. The Tirant Custome, most Graue Senators,
Hath made the flinty and Steele Coach of Warre
My thrice-driuen bed of Downe. I do agnize
A Naturall and prompt Alacartie,
I finde in hardnesse: and do vndertake
This present Warres against the *Ottamites.*
Most humbly therefore bending to your State,
I craue fit disposition for my Wife,
Due reference of Place, and Exhibition,
With such Accomodation and besort
As leuels with her breeding.

Duke. Why at her Fathers?

Bra. I will not haue it so.

Othe. Nor I.

Des. Nor would I there recide,
To put my Father in impatient thoughts
By being in his eye. Most Greaious Duke,
To my vnfolding, lend your prosperous eare,
And let me finde a Charter in your voice
T'assist my simplenesse.

Duke. What would you *Desdemona*?

Des. That I loue the Moore, to liue with him,
My downe-right violence, and storme of Fortunes,

May

May trumpet to the world. My heart's ſubdu'd
Euen to the very quality of my Lord;
I ſaw *Othello's* viſage in his mind,
And to his Honours and his valiant parts,
Did I my ſoule and Fortunes conſecrate.
So that (deere Lords)if I be left behind
A Moth of Peace,and he go to the Warre,
The Rites for why I loue him,are bereft me:
And I a heauie interim ſhall ſupport
By his deere abſence. Let me go with him.
Othe. Let her haue your voice.
Vouch with me Heauen,I therefore beg it not
To pleaſe the pallate of my Appetite:
Nor to comply with heat the yong affects
In my defunct, and proper ſatisfaction.
But to be free, and bounteous to her minde:
And Heauen defend your good ſoules,that you thinke
I will your ſerious and great buſineſſe ſcant
When ſhe is with me. No,when light wing'd Toyes
Of feather'd *Cupid*,ſeele with wanton dulneſſe
My ſpeculatiue,and offic'd Inſtrument:
That my Diſports corrupt, and taint my buſineſſe:
Let Houſe-wiues make a Skillet of my Helme,
And all indigne, and baſe aduerſities,
Make head againſt my Eſtimation.
Duke. Be it as you ſhall priuately determine,
Either for her ſtay, or going: th'Affaire cries haſt:
And ſpeed muſt anſwer it.
Sen. You muſt away to night.
Othe. With all my heart.
Duke. At nine i'th'morning, here wee'l meete againe.
Othello,leaue ſome Officer behind
And he ſhall our Commiſſion bring to you:
And ſuch things elſe of qualitie and reſpect
As doth import you.
Othe. So pleaſe your Grace, my Ancient,
A man he is of honeſty and truſt:
To his conueyance I aſſigne my wife,
With what elſe needfull,your good Grace ſhall think
To be ſent after me.
Duke. Let it be ſo:
Good night to euery one. And Noble Signior,
If Vertue no delighted Beautie lacke,
Your Son-in-law is farre more Faire then Blacke.
Sen. Adieu braue Moore,vſe *Deſdemona* well.
Bra. Looke to her(Moore)if thou haſt eies to ſee:
She ha's deceiu'd her Father,and may thee. *Exit.*
Othe. My life vpon her faith. Honeſt *Iago*,
My *Deſdemona* muſt I leaue to thee:
I prythee let thy wife attend on her,
And bring them after in the beſt aduantage.
Come *Deſdemona*,I haue but an houre
Of Loue, of wordly matter, and direction
To ſpend with thee. We muſt obey the the time. *Exit.*
Rod. Iago.
Iago. What ſaiſt thou Noble heart?
Rod. What will I do, think'ſt thou?
Iago. Why go to bed and ſleepe.
Rod. I will incontinently drowne my ſelfe.
Iago. If thou do'ſt,I ſhall neuer loue thee after. Why thou ſilly Gentleman?
Rod. It is ſillyneſſe to liue, when to liue is torment: and then haue we a preſcription to dye, when death is our Phyſition.
Iago. Oh villanous: I haue look'd vpon the world for foure times ſeuen yeares,and ſince I could diſtinguiſh betwixt a Benefit,and an Iniurie: I neuer found man that knew how to loue himſelfe. Ere I would ſay, I would drowne my ſelfe for the loue of a Gynney Hen,I would change my Humanity with a Baboone.
Rod. What ſhould I do? I confeſſe it is my ſhame to be ſo fond, but it is not in my vertue to amend it.
Iago. Vertue? A figge, 'tis in our ſelues that we are thus,or thus. Our Bodies are our Gardens, to the which, our Wills are Gardiners. So that if we will plant Nettels, or ſowe Lettice: Set Hiſope, and weede vp Time: Supplie it with one gender of Hearbes,or diſtract it with many: either to haue it ſterrill with idleneſſe, or manured with Induſtry, why the power,and Corrigeable authoritie of this lies in our Wills. If the braine of our liues had not one Scale of Reaſon, to poize another of Senſualitie, the blood, and baſeneſſe of our Natures would conduct vs to moſt prepoſtrous Concluſions. But we haue Reaſon to coole our raging Motions, our carnall Stings,or vnbitted Luſts: whereof I take this, that you call Loue, to be a Sect, or Seyen.
Rod. It cannot be,
Iago. It is meerly a Luſt of the blood, and a permiſſion of the will. Come, be a man: drowne thy ſelfe? Drown Cats, and blind Puppies. I haue profeſt me thy Friend, and I confeſſe me knit to thy deſeruing, with Cables of perdurable toughneſſe. I could neuer better ſteed thee then now. Put Money in thy purſe: follow thou the Warres,defeate thy fauour, with an vſurp'd Beard. I ſay put Money in thy purſe.It cannot be long that *Deſdemona* ſhould continue her loue to the Moore. Put Money in thy purſe: nor he his to her. It was a violent Commencement in her, and thou ſhalt ſee an anſwerable Sequeſtration, put but Money in thy purſe. Theſe Moores are changeable in their wils: fill thy purſe with Money. The Food that to him now is as luſhious as Locuſts, ſhalbe to him ſhortly, as bitter as Coloquintida. She muſt change for youth: when ſhe is ſated with his body ſhe will find the errors of her choice. Therefore,put Money in thy purſe. If thou wilt needs damne thy ſelfe, do it a more delicate way then drowning. Make all the Money thou canſt: If Sanctimonie, and a fraile vow, betwixt an erring Barbarian, and ſuper-ſubtle Venetian be not too hard for my wits,and all the Tribe of hell, thou ſhalt enioy her: therefore make Money: a pox of drowning thy ſelfe, it is cleane out of the way. Seeke thou rather to be hang'd in Compaſſing thy ioy, then to be drown'd,and go without her.
Rodo. Wilt thou be faſt to my hopes, if I depend on the iſſue?
Iago. Thou art ſure of me: Go make Money: I haue told thee often, and I re-tell thee againe, and againe, I hate the Moore. My cauſe is hearted; thine hath no leſſe reaſon. Let vs be coniunctiue in our reuenge, againſt him. If thou canſt Cuckold him, thou doſt thy ſelfe a pleaſure, me a ſport. There are many Euents in the Wombe of Time, which wilbe deliuered. Trauerſe, go, prouide thy Money. We will haue more of this to morrow. Adieu.
Rod. Where ſhall we meete i'th'morning?
Iago. At my Lodging.
Rod. Ile be with thee betimes.
Iago. Go too,farewell. Do you heare *Rodorigo*?
Rod. Ile ſell all my Land. *Exit.*
Iago. Thus do I euer make my Foole,my purſe:
For I mine owne gain'd knowledge ſhould prophane
If I would tim e expend with ſuch Snpe,

But

But for my Sport,and Profit : I hate the Moore,
And it is thought abroad, that 'twixt my ſheets
She ha's done my Office. I know not if't be true,
But I, for meere ſuſpition in that kinde,
Will do, as if for Surety. He holds me well,
The better ſhall my purpoſe worke on him :
Caſſio's a proper man : Let me ſee now,
To get his Place, and to plume vp my will
In double Knauery. How? How? Let's ſee.
After ſome time, to abuſe *Othello's* eares,
That he is too familiar with his wife :
He hath a perſon, and a ſmooth diſpoſe
To be ſuſpected : fram'd to make women falſe.
The Moore is of a free,and open Nature,
That thinkes men honeſt, that but ſeeme to be ſo,
And will as tenderly be lead by'th'Noſe
As Aſſes are :
I haue't : it is engendred : Hell, and Night,
Muſt bring this monſtrous Birth, to the worlds light.

Actus Secundus. Scena Prima.

Enter Montano, and two Gentlemen.

Mon. What from the Cape, can you diſcerne at Sea?
1.*Gent.* Nothing at all, it is a high wrought Flood :
I cannot 'twixt the Heauen, and the Maine,
Deſcry a Saile.
Mon. Me thinks,the wind hath ſpoke aloud at Land,
A fuller blaſt ne're ſhooke our Battlements :
If it hath ruffiand ſo vpon the Sea,
What ribbes of Oake, when Mountaines melt on them,
Can hold the Morties. What ſhall we heare of this?
2 A Segregation of the Turkiſh Fleet :
For do but ſtand vpon the Foaming Shore,
The chidden Billow ſeemes to pelt the Clowds,
The winde-ſhak'd-Surge, with high & monſtrous Maine
Seemes to caſt water on the burning Beare,
And quench the Guards of th'euer-fixed Pole:
I neuer did like molleſtation view
On the enchafed Flood.
Mon. If that the Turkiſh Fleete
Be not enſhelter'd, and embay'd, they are drown'd,
It is impoſſible to beare it out.

Enter a Gentleman.

3 Newes Laddes : our warres are done :
The deſperate Tempeſt hath ſo bang'd the Turkes,
That their deſignement halts. A Noble ſhip of Venice,
Hath ſeene a greeuous wracke and ſufferance
On moſt part of their Fleet.
Mon. How? Is this true?
3 The Ship is heere put in: A *Verenneſſa, Michael Caſſio*
Lieutenant to the warlike Moore, *Othello*,
Is come on Shore : the Moore himſelfe at Sea,
And is in full Commiſſion heere for Cyprus.
Mon. I am glad on't :
'Tis a worthy Gouernour.
3 But this ſame *Caſſio*, though he ſpeake of comfort,
Touching the Turkiſh loſſe, yet he lookes ſadly,
And praye the Moore be ſafe ; for they were parted
With fowle and violent Tempeſt.
Mon. Pray Heauens he be :
For I haue ſeru'd him, and the man commands
Like a full Soldier. Let's to the Sea-ſide (hoa)
As well to ſee the Veſſell that's come in,
As to throw-out our eyes for braue *Othello*,
Euen till we make the Maine,and th'Eriall blew,
An indiſtinct regard.
Gent. Come, let's do ſo ;
For euery Minute is expectancie
Of more Arriuancie.

Enter Caſſio.

Caſſi. Thankes you, the valiant of the warlike Iſle,
That ſo approoue the Moore : Oh let the Heauens
Giue him defence againſt the Elements,
For I haue loſt him on a dangerous Sea.
Mon. Is he well ſhip'd?
Caſſio. His Barke is ſtoutly Timber'd,and his Pylot
Of verie expert, and approu'd Allowance ;
Therefore my hope's (not ſurfetted to death)
Stand in bold Cure.
Within. A Saile, a Saile, a Saile.
Caſſio. What noiſe?
Gent. The Towne is empty ; on the brow o'th'Sea
Stand rankes of People, and they cry, a Saile.
Caſſio. My hopes do ſhape him for the Gouernor.
Gent. They do diſcharge their Shot of Courteſie,
Our Friends, at leaſt.
Caſſio. I pray you Sir, go forth,
And giue vs truth who 'tis that is arriu'd.
Gent. I ſhall. *Exit.*
Mon. But good Lieutenant, is your Generall wiu'd?
Caſſio. Moſt fortunately : he hath atchieu'd a Maid
That paragons deſcription, and wilde Fame :
One that excels the quirkes of Blazoning pens,
And in th'eſſentiall Veſture of Creation,
Do's tyre the Ingeniuer.

Enter Gentleman.

How now? Who ha's put in?
Gent. 'Tis one *Iago*, Auncient to the Generall.
Caſſio. Ha's had moſt fauourable, and happie ſpeed :
Tempeſts themſelues, high Seas, and howling windes,
The gutter'd-Rockes,and Congregated Sands,
Traitors enſteep'd, to enclogge the guiltleſſe Keele,
As hauing ſence of Beautie, do omit
Their mortall Natures, letting go ſafely by
The Diuine *Deſdemona*.
Mon. What is ſhe?
Caſſio. She that I ſpake of :
Our great Captains Captaine,
Left in the conduct of the bold *Iago*,
Whoſe footing heere anticipates our thoughts,
A Senights ſpeed. Great Ioue, *Othello* guard,
And ſwell his Saile with thine owne powrefull breath,
That he may bleſſe this Bay with his tall Ship,
Make loues quicke pants in *Deſdemonaes* Armes,
Giue renew'd fire to our extincted Spirits.

Enter Deſdemona, Iago, Rodorigo, and Æmilia.

Oh behold,
The Riches of the Ship is come on ſhore :
You men of Cyprus, let her haue your knees.
Haile to thee Ladie : and the grace of Heauen,
Before, behinde thee, and on euery hand
Enwheele thee round.
Deſ. I thanke you, Valiant *Caſſio*,
What tydings can you tell of my Lord?

Caſſio.

Cas. He is not yet arriu'd, nor know I ought
But that he's well, and will be ſhortly heere.
Deſ. Oh, but I feare:
How loſt you company?
Caſſio. The great Contention of Sea, and Skies
Parted our fellowſhip. But hearke, a Saile.
Within. A Saile, a Saile.
Gent. They giue this greeting to the Cittadell:
This likewiſe is a Friend.
Caſſio. See for the Newes:
Good Ancient, you are welcome. Welcome Miſtris:
Let it not gaule your patience (good *Iago*)
That I extend my Manners. 'Tis my breeding,
That giues me this bold ſhew of Curteſie.
Iago. Sir, would ſhe giue you ſomuch of her lippes,
As of her tongue ſhe oft beſtowes on me,
You would haue enough.
Deſ. Alas: ſhe ha's no ſpeech.
Iago. Infaith too much:
I finde it ſtill, when I haue leaue to ſleepe.
Marry before your Ladyſhip, I grant,
She puts het tongue a little in her heart,
And chides with thinking.
Æmil. You haue little cauſe to ſay ſo.
Iago. Come on, come on: you are Pictures out of doore: Bells in your Parlours: Wilde-Cats in your Kitchens: Saints in your Iniuries: Diuels being offended: Players in your Huſwiferie, and Huſwiues in your Beds.
Deſ. Oh, fie vpon thee, Slanderer.
Iago. Nay, it is true: or elſe I am a Turke,
You riſe to play, and go to bed to worke.
Æmil. You ſhall not write my praiſe.
Iago. No, let me not.
Deſde. What would'ſt write of me, if thou ſhould'ſt praiſe me?
Iago. Oh, gentle Lady, do not put me too't,
For I am nothing, if not Criticall.
Deſ. Come on, aſſay.
There's one gone to the Harbour?
Iago. I Madam.
Deſ. I am not merry: but I do beguile
The thing I am, by ſeeming otherwiſe.
Come, how would'ſt thou praiſe me?
Iago. I am about it, but indeed my inuention comes from my pate, as Birdlyme do's from Freeze, it pluckes out Braines and all. But my Muſe labours, and thus ſhe is deliuer'd.
If ſhe be faire, and wiſe: faireneſſe, and wit,
The ones for vſe, the other vſeth it.
Deſ. Well prais'd:
How if ſhe be Blacke and Witty?
Iago. *If ſhe be blacke, and thereto haue a wit,*
She'le find a white, that ſhall her blackneſſe fit.
Deſ. Worſe, and worſe.
Æmil. How if Faire, and Fooliſh?
Iago. *She neuer yet was fooliſh that was faire,*
For euen her folly helpt her to an heire.
Deſde. Theſe are old fond Paradoxes, to make Fooles laugh i'th'Alehouſe. What miſerable praiſe haſt thou for her that's Foule, and Fooliſh.
Iago. *There's none ſo foule and fooliſh thereunto,*
But do's foule pranks, which faire, and wiſe-ones do.
Deſde. Oh heauy ignorance: thou praiſeſt the worſt beſt. But what praiſe could'ſt thou beſtow on a deſeruing woman indeed? One, that in the authorithy of her merit, did iuſtly put on the vouch of very malice it ſelfe.

Iago. *She that was euer faire, and neuer proud,*
Had Tongue at will, and yet was neuer loud:
Neuer lackt Gold, and yet went neuer gay,
Fled from her wiſh, and yet ſaid now I may.
She that being angred, her reuenge being nie,
Bad her wrong ſtay, and her diſpleaſure flie:
She that in wiſedome neuer was ſo fraile,
To change the Cods-head for the Salmons taile:
She that could thinke, and neu'r diſcloſe her mind,
See Suitors following, and not looke behind:
She was a wight, (if euer ſuch wightes were)
Deſ. To do what?
Iago. *To ſuckle Fooles, and chronicle ſmall Beere.*

Deſde. Oh moſt lame and impotent concluſion. Do not learne of him *Æmillia*, though he be thy husband. How ſay you (*Caſſio*) is he not a moſt prophane, and liberall Counſailor?
Caſſio. He ſpeakes home (Madam) you may relliſh him more in the Souldier, then in the Scholler.
Iago. He takes her by the palme: I, well ſaid, whiſper. With as little a web as this, will I enſnare as great a Fly as *Caſſio*. I ſmile vpon her, do: I will giue thee in thine owne Courtſhip. You ſay true, 'tis ſo indeed. If ſuch tricks as theſe ſtrip you out of your Lieutenantrie, it had beene better you had not kiſs'd your three fingers ſo oft, which now againe you are moſt apt to play the Sir, in. Very good: well kiſs'd, and excellent Curtſie: 'tis ſo indeed. Yet againe, your fingers to your lippes? Would they were Cluſter-pipes for your ſake.
The Moore I know his Trumpet.
Caſſio, 'Tis truely ſo.
Deſ. Let's meete him, and recieue him.
Caſſio. Loe, where he comes.

Enter Othello, and Attendants.

Oth. O, my faire Warriour.
Deſ. My deere *Othello*.
Othe. It giues me wonder great, as my content
To ſee you heere before me.
Oh my Soules Ioy:
If after euery Tempeſt, come ſuch Calmes,
May the windes blow, till they haue waken'd death:
And let the labouring Barke climbe hills of Seas
Olympus high: and duck againe as low,
As hell's from Heauen. If it were now to dye,
'Twere now to be moſt happy. For I feare,
My Soule hath her content ſo abſolute,
That not another comfort like to this,
Succeedes in vnknowne Fate.
Deſ. The Heauens forbid
But that our Loues
And Comforts ſhould encreaſe
Euen as our dayes do grow.
Othe. Amen to rhat (ſweet Powers)
I cannot ſpeake enough of this content,
It ſtoppes me heere: it is too much of ioy.
And this, and this the greateſt diſcords be
That ere our hearts ſhall make.
Iago. Oh you are well tun'd now: But Ile ſet downe the peggs that make this Muſicke, as honeſt as I am.

Othe. Come: let vs to the Caſtle.
Newes (Friends) our Warres are done:
The Turkes are drown'd.
How do's my old Acquaintance of this Iſle?
(Hony) you ſhall be well deſir'd in Cyprus,
I haue found great loue among'ſt them. Oh my Sweet,
I prattle out of faſhion, and I doate
In mine owne comforts. I prythee, good *Iago*,
Go to the Bay, and diſimbarke m y Coffers:
Bring thou the Maſter to the Cittadell,
He is a good one, and his worthyneſſe
Do's challenge much reſpect. Come *Deſdemona*,
Once more well met at Cyprus.

Exit Othello and Deſdemona.

Iago. Do thou meet me preſently at the Harbour. Come thither, if thou be'ſt Valiant, (as they ſay baſe men being in Loue, haue then a Nobilitie in their Natures, more then is natiue to them) liſt-me; the Lieutenant to night watches on the Court of Guard. Firſt, I muſt tell thee this: *Deſdemona*, is directly in loue with him.

Rod. With him? Why, 'tis not poſſible.

Iago. Lay thy finger thus: and let thy ſoule be inſtructed. Marke me with what violence ſhe firſt lou'd the Moore, but for bragging, and telling her fantaſticall lies. To loue him ſtill for prating, let not thy diſcreet heart thinke it. Her eye muſt be fed. And what delight ſhall ſhe haue to looke on the diuell? When the Blood is made dull with the Act of Sport, there ſhould be a game to enflame it, and to giue Satiety a freſh appetite. Loueline ſſe in fauour, ſimpathy in yeares, Manners, and Beauties: all which the Moore is defectiue in. Now for want of theſe requir'd Conueniences, her delicate tenderneſſe wil finde it ſelfe abus'd, begin to heaue the, gorge, diſrelliſh and abhorre the Moore, very Nature wil inſtruct her in it, and compell her to ſome ſecond choice. Now Sir, this granted (as it is a moſt pregnant and vnforc'd poſition) who ſtands ſo eminent in the degree of this Forune, as *Caſſio* do's: a knaue very voluble: no further conſcionable, then in putting on the meere forme of Ciuill, and Humaine ſeeming, for the better compaſſe of his ſalt, and moſt hidden looſe Affection? Why none, why none: A ſlipper, and ſubtle knaue, a finder of occaſion: that he's an eye can ſtampe, and counterfeit Aduantages, though true Aduantage neuer preſent it ſelfe. A diueliſh knaue: beſides, the knaue is handſome, young: and hath all thoſe requiſites in him, that folly and greene mindes looke after. A peſtilent compleat knaue, and the woman hath found him already.

Rodo. I cannot beleeue that in her, ſhe's full of moſt bleſs'd condition.

Iago. Bleſs'd figges-end. The Wine ſhe drinkes is made of grapes. If ſhee had beene bleſs'd, ſhee would neuer haue lou'd the Moore: Bleſs'd pudding. Didſt thou not ſee her paddle with the palme of his hand? Didſt not marke that?

Rod. Yes, that I did: but that was but curteſie.

Iago. Leacherie by this hand: an Index, and obſcure prologue to the Hiſtory of Luſt and foule Thoughts. They met ſo neere with their lippes, that their breathes embrac'd together. Villanous thoughts *Rodorigo*, when theſe mutabilities ſo marſhall the way, hard at hand comes the Maſter, and maine exerciſe, th'incorporate concluſion: Piſh. But Sir, be you rul'd by me. I haue brought you from Venice. Watch you to night: for the Command, Ile lay't vpon you. *Caſſio* knowes you not: Ile not be farre from you. Do you finde ſome occaſion to anger *Caſſio*, either by ſpeaking too loud, or tainting his diſcipline, or from what other courſe you pleaſe, which the time ſhall more fauorably miniſter.

Rod. Well.

Iago. Sir, he's raſh, and very ſodaine in Choller: and happely may ſtrike at you, prouoke him that he may: for euen out of that will I cauſe theſe of Cyprus to Mutiny. Whoſe qualification ſhall come into no true taſte againe, but by the diſplanting of *Caſſio*. So ſhall you haue a ſhorter iourney to your deſires, by the meanes I ſhall then haue to preferre them. And the impediment moſt profitably remoued, without the which there were no expectation of our proſperitie.

Rodo. I will do this, if you can bring it to any opportunity.

Iago. I warrant thee. Meete me by and by at the Cittadell. I muſt fetch his Neceſſaries a Shore. Farewell.

Rodo. Adieu. *Exit.*

Iago. That *Caſſio* loues her, I do well beleeu't:
That ſhe loues him, 'tis apt, and of great Credite.
The Moore (how beit that I endure him not)
Is of a conſtant, louing, Noble Nature,
And I dare thinke, he'le proue to *Deſdemona*
A moſt deere husband. Now I do loue her too,
Not out of abſolute Luſt, (though peraduenture
I ſtand accomptant for as great a ſin)
But partely led to dyet my Reuenge,
For that I do ſuſpect the luſtie Moore
Hath leap'd into my Seate. The thought whereof,
Doth (like a poyſonous Minerall) gnaw my Inwardes:
And nothing can, or ſhall content my Soule
Till I am eeuen'd with him, wife, for wiſt.
Or fayling ſo, yet that I put the Moore,
At leaſt into a Ielouzie ſo ſtrong
That iudgement cannot cure. Which thing to do,
If this poore Traſh of Venice, whom I trace
For his quicke hunting, ſtand the putting on,
Ile haue our *Michael Caſſio* on the hip,
Abuſe him to the Moore, in the right garbe
(For I feare *Caſſio* with my Night-Cape too)
Make the Moore thanke me, loue me, and reward me,
For making him egregiouſly an Aſſe,
And practiſing vpon his peace, and quiet,
Euen to madneſſe. 'Tis heere: but yet confus'd,
Knaueries plaine face, is neuer ſeene, till vs'd. *Exit.*

Scena Secunda.

Enter Othello's, Herald with a Proclamation.

Herald. It is *Othello's* pleaſure, our Noble and Valiant Generall. That vpon certaine tydings now arriu'd, importing the meere perdition of the Turkiſh Fleete: euery man put himſelfe into Triumph. Some to daunce, ſome to make Bonfires, each man, to what Sport and Reuels his addition leads him. For beſides theſe beneficiall Newes, it is the Celebration of his Nuptiall. So much was his pleaſure ſhould be proclaimed. All offices are open, & there is full libertie of Feaſting from this pre-

presenr houre of fiue, till the Bell haue told eleuen. Blesse the Isle of Cyprus, and our Noble Generall *Othello.* *Exit.*

Enter Othello, Desdemona, Cassio, and Attendants.

Othe. Good *Michael,* looke you to the guard to night.
Let's teach our selues that Honourable stop,
Not to out-sport discretion.

Cas. *Iago,* hath direction what to do.
But notwithstanding with my personall eye
Will I looke to't.

Othe. *Iago,* is most honest:
Michael, goodnight. To morrow with your earliest,
Let me haue speech with you. Come my deere Loue,
The purchase made, the fruites are to ensue,
That profit's yet to come 'tweene me, and you.
Goodnight. *Exit.*

Enter Iago.

Cas. Welcome *Iago*: we must to the Watch.

Iago. Not this houre Lieutenant: 'tis not yet ten o'th'clocke. Our Generall cast vs thus earely for the loue of his *Desdemona*: Who, let vs not therefore blame; he hath not yet made wanton the night with her: and she is sport for *Ioue.*

Cas. She's a most exquisite Lady.

Iago. And Ile warrant her, full of Game.

Cas. Indeed shes a most fresh and delicate creature.

Iago. What an eye she ha's?
Methinkes it sounds a parley to prouocation.

Cas. An inuiting eye:
And yet me thinkes right modest.

Iago. And when she speakes,
Is it not an Alarum to Loue?

Cas. She is indeed perfection.

Iago. Well: happinesse to their Sheetes. Come Lieutenant, I haue a stope of Wine, and heere without are a brace of Cyprus Gallants, that would faine haue a measure to the health of blacke *Othello.*

Cas. Not to night, good *Iago,* I haue very poore, and vnhappie Braines for drinking. I could well wish Curtesie would inuent some other Custome of entertainment.

Iago. Oh, they are our Friends: but one Cup, Ile drinke for you.

Cassio. I haue drunke but one Cup to night, and that was craftily qualified too: and behold what inouation it makes heere. I am infortunate in the infirmity, and dare not taske my weakenesse with any more.

Iago. What man? 'Tis a night of Reuels, the Gallants desire it.

Cas. Where are they?

Iago. Heere, at the doore: I pray you call them in.

Cas. Ile do't, but it dislikes me. *Exit.*

Iago. If I can fasten but one Cup vpon him
With that which he hath drunke to night alreadie,
He'l be as full of Quarrell, and offence
As my yong Mistris dogge.
Now my sicke Foole *Rodorigo,*
Whom Loue hath turn'd almost the wrong side out,
To *Desdemona* hath to night Carrows'd.
Potations, pottle-deepe; and he's to watch.
Three else of Cyprus, Noble swelling Spirites,
(That hold their Honours in a wary distance,
The very Elements of this Warrelike Isle)
Haue I to night fluster'd with flowing Cups,
And they Watch too.
Now 'mongst this Flocke of drunkards
Am I put to our *Cassio* in some Action
That may offend the Isle. But here they come.

Enter Cassio, Montano, and Gentlemen.

If Consequence do but approue my dreame,
My Boate sailes freely, both with winde and Streame.

Cas. 'Fore heauen, they haue giuen me a rowse already.

Mon. Good-faith a litle one: not past a pint, as I am a Souldier.

Iago. Some Wine hoa.
And let me the Cannakin clinke, clinke:
And let me the Cannakin clinke.
A Souldiers a man: Oh, mans life's but a span,
Why then let a Souldier drinke.
Some Wine Boyes.

Cas. 'Fore Heauen: an excellent Song.

Iago. I learn'd it in England: where indeedthey are most potent in Potting. Your Dane, your Germaine, and your swag-belly'd Hollander, (drinke hoa) are nothing to your English.

Cassio. Is your Englishmen so exquisite in his drinking?

Iago. Why, he drinkes you with facillitie, your Dane dead drunke. He sweates not to ouerthrow your Almaine. He giues your Hollander a vomit, ere the next Pottle can be fill'd.

Cas. To the health of our Generall.

Mon. I am for it Lieutenant: and Ile do you Iustice.

Iago. Oh sweet England.
King Stephen was and- a worthy Peere,
His Breeches cost him but a Crowne,
He held them Six pence all to deere,
With that he cal'd the Tailor Lowne:
He was a wight of high Renowne,
And thou art but of low degree:
'Tis Pride that pulls the Country downe,
And take thy awl'd Cloake about thee.
Some Wine hoa.

Cassio. Why this is a more exquisite Song then the other.

Iago. Will you heare't againe?

Cas. No: for I hold him to be vnworthy of his Place, that do's those things. Well: heau'ns aboue all: and there be soules must be saued, and there be soules must not be saued.

Iago. It's true, good Lieutenant.

Cas. For mine owne part, no offence to the Generall, nor any man of qualitie: I hope to be saued.

Iago. And so do I too Lieutenant.

Cassio. I: (but by your leaue) not before me. The Lieutenant is to be saued before the Ancient. Let's haue no more of this: let's to our Affaires. Forgiue vs our sinnes: Gentlemen let's looke to our businesse. Do not thinke Gentlemen, I am drunke: this is my Ancient, this is my right hand, and this is my left. I am not drunke now: I can stand well enough, and I speake well enough.

Gent. Excellent well.

Cas. Why very well then: you must not thinke then, that I am drunke. *Exit.*

Monta. To th'Platforme (Masters) come, let's set the Watch.

Iago. You see this Fellow, that is gone before,
He's a Souldier, fit to stand by *Cæsar,*
And giue direction. And do but see his vice,
'Tis to his vertue, a iust Equinox,

tt 3 The

The one as long as th'other. 'Tis pittie of him :
I feare the trust *Othello* puts him in,
On some odde time of his infirmitie
Will shake this Island.

Mont. But is he often thus?

Iago. 'Tis euermore his prologue to his sleepe,
He'le watch the Horologe a double Set,
If Drinke rocke not his Cradle.

Mont. It were well
The Generall were put in mind of it :
Perhaps he sees it not, or his good nature
Prizes the vertue that appeares in *Cassio*,
And lookes not on his euills : is not this true?

Enter Rodorigo.

Iago. How now *Rodorigo*?
I pray you after the Lieutenant, go.

Mon. And 'tis great pitty, that the Noble Moore
Should hazard such a Place, as his owne Second
With one of an ingraft Infirmitie,
It were an honest Action, to say so
To the Moore.

Iago. Not I, for this faire Island,
I do loue *Cassio* well : and would do much
To cure him of this euill, But hearke, what noise?

Enter Cassio pursuing Rodorigo.

Cas. You Rogue : you Rascall.

Mon. What's the matter Lieutenant?

Cas. A Knaue teach me my dutie? Ile beate the Knaue into a Twiggen-Bottle.

Rod. Beate me?

Cas. Dost thou prate, Rogue?

Mon. Nay, good Lieutenant :
I pray you Sir, hold your hand.

Cassio. Let me go (Sir)
Or Ile knocke you o're the Mazard.

Mon. Come, come : you're drunke.

Cassio. Drunke?

Iago. Away I say : go out and cry a Mutinie.
Nay good Lieutenant. Alas Gentlemen :
Helpe hoa. Lieutenant. Sir *Montano* :
Helpe Masters. Heere's a goodly Watch indeed.
Who's that which rings the Bell: Diablo, hoa :
The Towne will rise. Fie, fie Lieutenant,
You'le be asham'd for euer.

Enter Othello, and Attendants.

Othe. What is the matter heere?

Mon. I bleed still, I am hurt to th'death. He dies.

Othe. Hold for your liues.

Iag. Hold hoa : Lieutenant, Sir *Montano*, Gentlemen:
Haue you forgot all place of sense and dutie?
Hold. The Generall speaks to you : hold for shame.

Oth. Why how now hoa? From whence ariseth this?
Are we turn'd Turkes? and to our selues do that
Which Heauen hath forbid the *Ottamittes*.
For Christian shame, put by this barbarous Brawle :
He that stirs next, to carue for his owne rage,
Holds his soule light : He dies vpon his Motion.
Silence that dreadfull Bell, it frights the Isle,
From her propriety. What is the matter, Masters?
Honest *Iago*, that lookes dead with greeuing,
Speake : who began this? On thy loue I charge thee?

Iago. I do not know : Friends all, but now, euen now.
In Quarter, and in termes like Bride, and Groome
Deuesting them for Bed : and then, but now :
(As if some Planet had vnwitted men)
Swords out, and tilting one at others breastes,
In opposition bloody. I cannot speake
Any begining to this peeuish oddes.
And would, in Action glorious, I had lost
Those legges, that brought me to a part of it.

Othe. How comes it (*Michaell*) you are thus forgot?

Cas. I pray you pardon me, I cannot speake.

Othe. Worthy *Montano*, you were wont to be ciuill :
The grauitie, and stillnesse of your youth
The world hath noted. And your name is great
In mouthes of wisest Censure. What's the matter
That you vnlace your reputation thus,
And spend your rich opinion, for the name
Of a night-brawler? Giue me answer to it.

Mon. Worthy *Othello*, I am hurt to danger,
Your Officer *Iago*, can informe you,
While I spare speech which something now offends me.
Of all that I do know, nor know I ought
By me, that's said, or done amisse this night,
Vnlesse selfe-charitie be sometimes a vice,
And to defend our selues, it be a sinne
When violence assailes vs.

Othe. Now by Heauen,
My blood begins my safer Guides to rule,
And passion (hauing my best iudgement collied)
Assaies to leade the way. If I once stir,
Or do but lift this Arme, the best of you
Shall sinke in my rebuke. Giue me to know
How this foule Rout began : Who set it on,
And he that is approu'd in this offence,
Though he had twinn'd with me, both at a birth,
Shall loose me. What in a Towne of warre,
Yet wilde, the peoples hearts brim-full of feare,
To Manage priuate, and domesticke Quarrell?
In night, and on the Court and Guard of safetie?
'Tis monstrous : *Iago*, who began't?

Mon. If partially Affin'd, or league in office,
Thou dost deliuer more, or lesse then Truth,
Thou art no Souldier.

Iago. Touch me not so neere,
I had rather haue this tongue cut from my mouth,
Then it should do offence to *Michaell Cassio*.
Yet I perswade my selfe, to speake the truth
Shall nothing wrong him. This it is Generall :
Montano and my selfe being in speech,
There comes a Fellow, crying out for helpe,
And *Cassio* following him with determin'd Sword
To execute vpon him. Sir, this Gentleman,
Steppes in to *Cassio*, and entreats his pause:
My selfe, the crying Fellow did pursue,
Least by his clamour (as it so fell out)
The Towne might fall in fright. He, (swift of foote)
Out-ran my purpose : and I return'd then rather
For that I heard the clinke, and fall of Swords,
And *Cassio* high in oath : Which till to night
I nere might say before. When I came backe
(For this was briefe) I found them close together
At blow, and thrust, euen as againe they were
When you your selfe did part them.
More of this matter cannot I report,
But Men are Men : The best sometimes forget,
Though *Cassio* did some little wrong to him,
As men in rage strike those that wish them best,
Yet surely *Cassio*, I beleeue receiu'd
From him that fled, some strange Indignitie,
Which patience could not passe.

Othe.

Othe. I know *Iago*
Thy honeſtie, and loue doth mince this matter,
Making it light to *Caſſio*: *Caſſio*, I loue thee,
But neuer more be Officer of mine.

Enter Deſdemona attended.

Looke if my gentle Loue be not rais'd vp:
Ile make thee an example.

Deſ. What is the matter (Deere?)

Othe. All's well, Sweeting:
Come away to bed. Sir for your hurts,
My ſelfe will be your Surgeon. Lead him off:
Iago, looke with care about the Towne,
And ſilence thoſe whom this vil'd brawle diſtracted.
Come *Deſdemona*, 'tis the Soldiers life,
To haue their Balmy ſlumbers wak'd with ſtrife. *Exit.*

Iago. What are you hurt Lieutenant?

Caſ. I, paſt all Surgery.

Iago. Marry Heauen forbid.

Caſ. Reputation, Reputation, Reputation: Oh I haue loſt my Reputation. I haue loſt the immortall part of myſelfe, and what remaines is beſtiall. My Reputation, *Iago*, my Reputation.

Iago. As I am an honeſt man I had thought you had receiued ſome bodily wound; there is more ſence in that then in Reputation. Reputation is an idle, and moſt falſe impoſition; oft got without merit, and loſt without deſeruing. You haue loſt no Reputation at all, vnleſſe you repute your ſelfe ſuch a looſer. What man, there are more wayes to recouer the Generall againe. You are but now caſt in his moode, (a puniſhment more in policie, then in malice) euen ſo as one would beate his offenceleſſe dogge, to affright an Imperious Lyon. Sue to him againe, and he's yours.

Caſ. I will rather ſue to be deſpis'd, then to deceiue ſo good a Commander, with ſo ſlight, ſo drunken, and ſo indiſcreet an Officer. Drunke? And ſpeake Parrat? And ſquabble? Swagger? Sweare? And diſcourſe Fuſtian with ones owne ſhadow? Oh thou inviſible ſpirit of Wine, if thou haſt no name to be knowne by, let vs call thee Diuell.

Iago. What was he that you follow'd with your Sword? What had he done to you?

Caſ. I know not.

Iago. Is't poſſible?

Caſ. I remember a maſſe of things, but nothing diſtinctly: a Quarrell, but nothing wherefore. Oh, that men ſhould put an Enemie in their mouthes, to ſteale away their Braines? that we ſhould with ioy, pleaſance, reuell and applauſe, transforme our ſelues into Beaſts.

Iago. Why? But you are now well enough: how came you thus recouered?

Caſ. It hath pleas'd the diuell drunkenneſſe, to giue place to the diuell wrath, one vnperfectneſſe, ſhewes me another to make me frankly deſpiſe my ſelfe.

Iago. Come, you are too ſeuere a Moraller. As the Time, the Place, & the Condition of this Country ſtands I could hartily wiſh this had not befalne: but ſince it is, as it is, mend it for your owne good.

Caſ. I will aske him for my Place againe, he ſhall tell me, I am a drunkard: had I as many mouthes as *Hydra*, ſuch an anſwer would ſtop them all. To be now a ſenſible man, by and by a Foole, and preſently a Beaſt. Oh ſtrange! Euery inordinate cup is vnbleſs'd, and the Ingredient is a diuell.

Iago. Come, come: good wine, is a good familiar Creature, if it be well vs'd: exclaime no more againſt it. And good Lieutenant, I thinke, you thinke I loue you.

Caſſio. I haue well approued it, Sir. I drunke?

Iago. You, or any man liuing, may be drunke at a time man. I tell you what you ſhall do: Our General's Wife, is now the Generall. I may ſay ſo, in this reſpect, for that he hath deuoted, and giuen vp himſelfe to the Contemplation, marke: and deuotement of her parts and Graces. Confeſſe your ſelfe freely to her: Importune her helpe to put you in your place againe. She is of ſo free, ſo kinde, ſo apt, ſo bleſſed a diſpoſition, ſhe holds it a vice in her goodneſſe, not to do more then ſhe is requeſted. This broken ioynt betweene you, and her husband, entreat her to ſplinter. And my Fortunes againſt any lay worth naming, this cracke of your Loue, ſhall grow ſtonger, then it was before.

Caſſio. You aduiſe me well.

Iago. I proteſt in the ſinceritie of Loue, and honeſt kindneſſe.

Caſſio. I thinke it freely: and betimes in the morning, I will beſeech the vertuous *Deſdemona* to vndertake for me: I am deſperate of my Fortunes if they check me.

Iago. You are in the right: good night Lieutenant, I muſt to the Watch.

Caſſio. Good night, honeſt *Iago*.

Exit Caſſio.

Iago. And what's he then,
That ſaies I play the Villaine?
When this aduiſe is free I giue, and honeſt,
Proball to thinking, and indeed the courſe
To win the Moore againe.
For 'tis moſt eaſie
Th'inclyning *Deſdemona* to ſubdue
In any honeſt Suite. She's fram'd as fruitefull
As the free Elements. And then for her
To win the Moore, were to renownce his Baptiſme,
All Seales, and Simbols of redeemed ſin:
His Soule is ſo enfetter'd to her Loue,
That ſhe may make, vnmake, do what ſhe liſt,
Euen as her Appetite ſhall play the God,
With his weake Function. How am I then a Villaine,
To Counſell *Caſſio* to this paralell courſe,
Directly to his good? Diuinitie of hell,
When diuels will the blackeſt ſinnes put on,
They do ſuggeſt at firſt with heauenly ſhewes,
As I do now. For whiles this honeſt Foole
Plies *Deſdemona*, to repaire his Fortune,
And ſhe for him, pleades ſtrongly to the Moore,
Ile powre this peſtilence into his eare:
That ſhe repeales him, for her bodies Luſt'
And by how much ſhe ſtriues to do him good,
She ſhall vndo her Credite with the Moore.
So will I turne her vertue into pitch,
And out of her owne goodneſſe make the Net,
That ſhall en-maſh them all.
How now *Rodorigo*?

Enter Rodorigo.

Rodorigo. I do follow heere in the Chace, not like a Hound that hunts, but one that filles vp the Crie. My Money is almoſt ſpent; I haue bin to night exceedingly well Cudgell'd: And I thinke the iſſue will

will bee, I ſhall haue ſo much experience for my paines; And ſo, with no money at all, and a little more Wit, returne againe to Venice.

Iago. How poore are they that haue not Patience?
What wound did euer heale but by degrees?
Thou know'ſt we worke by Wit, and not by Witchcraft
And Wit depends on dilatory time:
Dos't not go well? *Caſſio* hath beaten thee,
And thou by that ſmall hurt hath caſheer'd *Caſſio:*
Though other things grow faire againſt the Sun,
Yet Fruites that bloſſome firſt, will firſt be ripe:
Content thy ſelfe, a-while. Introth 'tis Morning;
Pleaſure, and Action, make the houres ſeeme ſhort.
Retire thee, go where thou art Billited:
Away, I ſay, thou ſhalt know more heereafter:
Nay get thee gone. *Exit Rodorigo.*
Two things are to be done:
My Wife muſt moue for *Caſſio* to her Miſtris:
Ile ſet her on my ſelfe, a while, to draw the Moor apart,
And bring him iumpe, when he may *Caſſio* finde
Soliciting his wife: I, that's the way:
Dull not Deuice, by coldneſſe, and delay. *Exit.*

Actus Tertius. Scena Prima.

Enter Caſſio, Muſitians, and Clowne.

Caſſio. Maſters, play heere, I wil content your paines, Something that's briefe: and bid, goodmorrow General.

Clo. Why Maſters, haue your Inſtruments bin in Naples, that they ſpeake i'th'Noſe thus?

Muſ. How Sir? how?

Clo. Are theſe I pray you, winde Inſtruments?

Muſ. I marry are they ſir.

Clo. Oh, thereby hangs a tale.

Muſ. Whereby hangs a tale, ſir?

Clow. Marry ſir, by many a winde Inſtrument that I know. But Maſters, heere's money for you: and the Generall ſo likes your Muſick, that he deſires you for loues ſake to make no more noiſe with it.

Muſ. Well Sir, we will not.

Clo. If you haue any Muſicke that may not be heard, too't againe. But (as they ſay) to heare Muſicke, the Generall do's not greatly care.

Muſ. We haue none ſuch, ſir.

Clow. Then put vp your Pipes in your bagge, for Ile away. Go, vaniſh into ayre, away. *Exit Mu.*

Caſſio Doſt thou heare me, mine honeſt Friend?

Clo. No, I heare not your honeſt Friend:
I heare you.

Caſſio. Prythee keepe vp thy Quillets, ther's a poore peece of Gold for thee: if the Gentlewoman that attends the Generall be ſtirring, tell her, there's one *Caſſio* entreats her a little fauour of Speech. Wilt thou do this?

Clo. She is ſtirring ſir: if ſhe will ſtirre hither, I ſhall ſeeme to notifie vnto her. *Exit Clo.*

Enter Iago.

In happy time, *Iago.*

Iago. You haue not bin a-bed then?

Caſſio. Why no: the day had broke before we parted.
I haue made bold (*Iago*) to ſend in to your wife:
My ſuite to her is, that ſhe will to vertuous *Deſdemona*
Procure me ſome acceſſe.

Iago. Ile ſend her to you preſently:
And Ile deuiſe a meane to draw the Moore
Out of the way, that your conuerſe and buſineſſe
May be more free. *Exit*

Caſſio. I humbly thanke you for't. I neuer knew
A Florentine more kinde, and honeſt.

Enter Æmilia.

Æmil. Goodmorrow (good Lieutenant) I am ſorrie
For your diſpleaſure: but all will ſure be well.
The Generall and his wife are talking of it,
And ſhe ſpeakes for you ſtoutly. The Moore replies,
That he you hurt is of great Fame in Cyprus,
And great Affinitie: and that in wholſome Wiſedome
He might not but refuſe you. But he proteſts he loues you
And needs no other Suitor, but his likings
To bring you in againe.

Caſſio. Yet I beſeech you,
If you thinke fit, or that it may be done,
Giue me aduantage of ſome breefe Diſcourſe
With *Deſdemon* alone.

Æmil. Pray you come in:
I will beſtow you where you ſhall haue time
To ſpeake your boſome freely.

Caſſio. I am much bound to you.

Scœna Secunda.

Enter Othello, Iago, and Gentlemen.

Othe. Theſe Letters giue (*Iago*) to the Pylot,
And by him do my duties to the Senate:
That done, I will be walking on the Workes,
Repaire there to mee.

Iago. Well, my good Lord, Ile doo't.

Oth. This Fortification (Gentlemen) ſhall we ſee't?

Gent. Well waite vpon your Lordſhip. *Exeunt*

Scœna Tertia.

Enter Deſdemona, Caſſio, and Æmilia.

Deſ. Be thou aſſur'd (good *Caſſio*) I will do
All my abilities in thy behalfe.

Æmil. Good Madam do:
I warrant it greeues my Husband,
As if the cauſe were his.

Deſ. Oh that's an honeſt Fellow, Do not doubt *Caſſio*
But I will haue my Lord, and you againe
As friendly as you were.

Caſſio. Bounteous Madam,
What euer ſhall become of *Michael Caſſio*,
He's neuer any thing but your true Seruant.

Deſ. I know't: I thanke you: you do loue my Lord:
You haue knowne him long, and be you well aſſur'd
He ſhall in ſtrangeneſſe ſtand no farther off,
Then in a politique diſtance.

Caſſio. I, but Lady,
That policie may either laſt ſo long,
Or feede vpon ſuch nice and wateriſh diet,
Or breede it ſelfe ſo out of Circumſtances,
That I being abſent, and my place ſupply'd,
My Generall will forget my Loue, and Seruice.

Deſ. Do not doubt that: before *Æmilia* here,

I giue thee warrant of thy place. Assure thee,
If I do vow a friendship, Ile performe it
To the last Article. My Lord shall neuer rest,
Ile watch him tame, and talke him out of patience;
His Bed shall seeme a Schoole, his Boord a Shrift,
Ile intermingle euery thing he do's
With *Cassio's* suite: Therefore be merry *Cassio*,
For thy Sollicitor shall rather dye,
Then giue thy cause away.

Enter Othello, and Iago.

Æmil. Madam, heere comes my Lord.
Cassio. Madam, Ile take my leaue.
Des. Why stay, and heare me speake.
Cassio. Madam, not now: I am very ill at ease,
Vnfit for mine owne purposes.
Des. Well, do your discretion. *Exit Cassio.*
Iago. Hah? I like not that.
Othel. What dost thou say?
Iago. Nothing my Lord; or if——I know not what.
Othel. Was not that *Cassio* parted from my wife?
Iago. *Cassio* my Lord? No sure, I cannot thinke it
That he would steale away so guilty-like,
Seeing your comming.
Oth. I do beleeue 'twas he.
Des. How now my Lord?
I haue bin talking with a Suitor heere,
A man that languishes in your displeasure.
Oth. Who is't you meane?
Des. Why your Lieutenant *Cassio*: Good my Lord,
If I haue any grace, or power to moue you,
His present reconciliation take.
For if he be not one, that truly loues you,
That erres in Ignorance, and not in Cunning,
I haue no iudgement in an honest face.
I prythee call him backe.
Oth. Went he hence now?
Des. I sooth; so humbled,
That he hath left part of his greefe with mee
To suffer with him. Good Loue, call him backe.
Othel. Not now (sweet *Desdemon*) some other time.
Des. But shall't be shortly?
Oth. The sooner (Sweet) for you.
Des. Shall't be to night, at Supper?
Oth. No, not to night.
Des. To morrow Dinner then?
Oth. I shall not dine at home:
I meete the Captaines at the Cittadell.
Des. Why then to morrow night, on Tuesday morne,
On Tuesday noone, or night; on Wensday Morne.
I prythee name the time, but let it not
Exceed three dayes. Infaith hee's penitent:
And yet his Trespasse, in our common reason
(Saue that they say the warres must make example)
Out of her best, is not almost a fault
T'encurre a priuate checke. When shall he come?
Tell me *Othello*. I wonder in my Soule
What you would aske me, that I should deny,
Or stand so mam'ring on? What? *Michael Cassio*,
That came a woing wirh you? and so many a time
(When I haue spoke of you dispraisingly)
Hath tane your part, to haue so much to do
To bring him in? Trust me, I could do much.
Oth. Prythee no more: Let him come when he will:
I will deny thee nothing.
Des. Why, this is not a Boone:
'Tis as I should entreate you weare your Gloues,
Or feede on nourishing dishes, or keepe you warme,
Or sue to you, to do a peculiar profit
To your owne person. Nay, when I haue a suite
Wherein I meane to touch your Loue indeed,
It shall be full of poize, and difficult waight,
And fearefull to be granted.
Oth. I will deny thee nothing.
Whereon, I do beseech thee, grant me this,
To leaue me but a little to my selfe.
Des. Shall I deny you? No: farewell my Lord.
Oth. Farewell my *Desdemona*, Ile come to thee strait.
Des. *Æmilia* come; be as your Fancies teach you:
What ere you be, I am obedient. *Exit.*
Oth. Excellent wretch: Perdition catch my Soule
But I do loue thee: and when I loue thee not,
Chaos is come againe.
Iago. My Noble Lord.
Oth. What dost thou say, *Iago*?
Iago. Did *Michael Cassio*
When he woo'd my Lady, know of your loue?
Oth. He did, from first to last:
Why dost thou aske?
Iago. But for a satisfaction of my Thought,
No further harme.
Oth. Why of thy thought, *Iago*?
Iago. I did not thinke he had bin acquainted with hir.
Oth. O yes, and went betweene vs very oft.
Iago. Indeed?
Oth. Indeed? I indeed. Discern'st thou ought in that?
Is he not honest?
Iago. Honest, my Lord?
Oth. Honest? I, Honest.
Iago. My Lord, for ought I know.
Oth. What do'st thou thinke?
Iago. Thinke, my Lord?
Oth. Thinke, my Lord? Alas, thou ecchos't me;
As if there were some Monster in thy thought
Too hideous to be shewne. Thou dost mean somthing:
I heard thee say euen now, thou lik'st not that,
When *Cassio* left my wife. What didd'st not like?
And when I told thee, he was of my Counsaile,
Of my whole course of wooing; thou cried'st, Indeede?
And didd'st contract, and purse thy brow together,
As if thou then hadd'st shut vp in thy Braine
Some horrible Conceite. If thou do'st loue me,
Shew me thy thought.
Iago. My Lord, you know I loue you.
Oth. I thinke thou do'st:
And for I know thou'rt full of Loue, and Honestie,
And weigh'st thy words before thou giu'st them breath,
Therefore these stops of thine, fright me the more:
For such things in a false disloyall Knaue
Are trickes of Custome: but in a man that's iust,
They're close dilations, working from the heart,
That Passion cannot rule.
Iago. For *Michael Cassio*,
I dare be sworne, I thinke that he is honest.
Oth. I thinke so too.
Iago. Men should be what they seeme,
Or those that be not, would they might seeme none.
Oth. Certaine, men should be what they seeme.
Iago. Why then I thinke *Cassio's* an honest man.
Oth. Nay, yet there's more in this?
I prythee speake to me, as to thy thinkings,
As thou dost ruminate, and giue thy worst of thoughts
The

The worst of words.
Iago. Good my Lord pardon me,
Though I am bound to euery Acte of dutie,
I am not bound to that: All Slaues are free:
Vtter my Thoughts? Why say, they are vild, and falce?
As where's that Palace, whereinto foule things
Sometimes intrude not? Who ha's that breast so pure,
Wherein vncleanly Apprehensions
Keepe Leetes, and Law-dayes, and in Sessions sit
With meditations lawfull?
Oth. Thou do'st conspire against thy Friend (*Iago*)
If thou but think'st him wrong'd, and mak'st his eare
A stranger to thy Thoughts.
Iago. I do beseech you,
Though I perchance am vicious in my guesse
(As I confesse it is my Natures plague
To spy into Abuses, and of my iealousie
Shapes faults that are not) that your wisedome
From one, that so imperfectly conceits,
Would take no notice, nor build your selfe a trouble
Out of his scattering, and vnsure obseruance:
It were not for your quiet, nor your good,
Nor for my Manhood, Honesty, and Wisedome,
To let you know my thoughts.
Oth. What dost thou meane?
Iago. Good name in Man, & woman (deere my Lord)
Is the immediate Iewell of their Soules;
Who steales my purse, steales trash:
'Tis something, nothing;
'Twas mine, 'tis his, and has bin slaue to thousands:
But he that filches from me my good Name,
Robs me of that, which not enriches him,
And makes me poore indeed.
Oth. Ile know thy Thoughts.
Iago. You cannot, if my heart were in your hand,
Nor shall not, whil'st 'tis in my custodie.
Oth. Ha?
Iago. Oh, beware my Lord, of iealousie,
It is the greene-ey'd Monster, which doth mocke
The meate it feeds on. That Cuckold liues in blisse,
Who certaine of his Fate, loues not his wronger:
But oh, what damned minutes tels he ore,
Who dotes, yet doubts: Suspects, yet soundly loues?
Oth. O miserie.
Iago. Poore, and Content, is rich, and rich enough,
But Riches finelesse, is as poore as Winter,
To him that euer feares he shall be poore:
Good Heauen, the Soules of all my Tribe defend
From Iealousie.
Oth. Why? why is this?
Think'st thou, I'ld make a Life of Iealousie;
To follow still the changes of the Moone
With fresh suspitions? No: to be once in doubt,
Is to be resolu'd: Exchange me for a Goat,
When I shall turne the businesse of my Soule
To such exsufflicate, and blow'd Surmises,
Matching thy inference. 'Tis not to make me Iealious,
To say my wife is faire, feeds well, loues company,
Is free of Speech, Sings, Playes, and Dances:
Where Vertue is, these are more vertuous.
Nor from mine owne weake merites, will I draw
The smallest feare, or doubt of her reuolt,
For she had eyes, and chose me. No *Iago*,
Ile see before I doubt; when I doubt, proue;
And on the proofe, there is no more but this,
Away at once with Loue, or Iealousie.
Ia. I am glad of this: For now I shall haue reason
To shew the Loue and Duty that I beare you
With franker spirit. Therefore (as I am bound)
Receiue it from me. I speake not yet of proofe:
Looke to your wife, obserue her well with *Cassio*,
Weare your eyes, thus: not Iealious, nor Secure:
I would not haue your free, and Noble Nature,
Out of selfe-Bounty, be abus'd: Looke too't:
I know our Country disposition well:
In Venice, they do let Heauen see the prankes
They dare not shew their Husbands.
Their best Conscience,
Is not to leaue't vndone, but kept vnknowne.
Oth. Dost thou say so?
Iago. She did deceiue her Father, marrying you,
And when she seem'd to shake, and feare your lookes,
She lou'd them most.
Oth. And so she did.
Iago. Why go too then:
Shee that so young could giue out such a Seeming
To seele her Fathers eyes vp, close as Oake,
He thought 'twas Witchcraft.
But I am much too blame:
I humbly do beseech you of your pardon
For too much louing you.
Oth. I am bound to thee for euer.
Iago. I see this hath a little dash'd your Spirits:
Oth. Not a iot, not a iot.
Iago. Trust me, I feare it has:
I hope you will consider what is spoke
Comes from your Loue.
But I do see y'are moou'd:
I am to pray you, not to straine my speech
To grosser issues, nor to larger reach,
Then to Suspition.
Oth. I will not.
Iago. Should you do so (my Lord)
My speech should fall into such vilde successe,
Which my Thoughts aym'd not.
Cassio's my worthy Friend:
My Lord, I see y'are mou'd.
Oth. No, not much mou'd:
I do not thinke but *Desdemona's* honest.
Iago. Long liue she so;
And long liue you to thinke so.
Oth. And yet how Nature erring from it selfe.
Iago. I, there's the point:
As (to be bold with you)
Not to affect many proposed Matches
Of her owne Clime, Complexion, and Degree,
Whereto we see in all things, Nature tends:
Foh, one may smel in such, a will most ranke,
Foule disproportions, Thoughts vnnaturall.
But (pardon me) I do not in position
Distinctly speake of her, though I may feare
Her will, recoyling to her better iudgement,
May fal to match you with her Country formes,
And happily repent.
Oth. Farewell, farewell:
If more thou dost perceiue, let me know more:
Set on thy wife to obserue.
Leaue me *Iago*.
Iago. My Lord, I take my leaue.
Othel. Why did I marry?
This honest Creature (doubtlesse)
Sees, and knowes more, much more then he vnfolds.

Iago. My Lord, I would I might intreat your Honor
To ſcan this thing no farther : Leaue it to time,
Although 'tis fit that *Caſſio* haue his Place ;
For ſure he filles it vp with great Ability ;
Yet if you pleaſe, to him off a-while :
You ſhall by that perceiue him, and his meanes :
Note if your Lady ſtraine his Entertainment
With any ſtrong, or vehement importunitie,
Much will be ſeene in that : In the meane time,
Let me be thought too buſie in my feares,
(As worthy cauſe I haue to feare I am)
And hold her free, I do beſeech your Honor.

Oth. Feare not my gouernment.

Iago. I once more take my leaue. *Exit.*

Oth. This Fellow's of exceeding honeſty,
And knowes all Quantities with a learn'd Spirit
Of humane dealings. If I do proue her Haggard,
Though that her Ieſſes were my deere heart-ſtrings,
I'ld whiſtle her off, and let her downe the winde
To prey at Fortune. Haply, for I am blacke,
And haue not thoſe ſoft parts of Conuerſation
That Chamberers haue : Or for I am declin'd
Into the vale of yeares (yet that's not much)
Shee's gone. I am abus'd, and my releefe
Muſt be to loath her. Oh Curſe of Marriage!
That we can call theſe delicate Creatures ours,
And not their Appetites? I had rather be a Toad,
And liue vpon the vapour of a Dungeon,
Then keepe a corner in the thing I loue
For others vſes. Yet 'tis the plague to Great-ones,
Prerogatiu'd are they leſſe then the Baſe,
'Tis deſtiny vnſhunnable, like death :
Euen then, this forked plague is Fated to vs,
When we do quicken. Looke where ſhe comes :

Enter Deſdemona and Æmilia.

If ſhe be falſe, Heauen mock'd it ſelfe :
Ile not beleeue't.

Deſ. How now, my deere *Othello*?
Your dinner, and the generous Iſlanders
By you inuited, do attend your preſence.

Oth. I am too blame.

Deſ. Why do you ſpeake ſo faintly?
Are you not well?

Oth. I haue a paine vpon my Forehead, heere.

Deſ. Why that's with watching, 'twill away againe.
Let me but binde it hard, within this houre
It will be well.

Oth. Your Napkin is too little :
Let it alone : Come, Ile go in with you. *Exit.*

Deſ. I am very ſorry that you are not well.

Æmil. I am glad I haue found this Napkin :
This was her firſt remembrance from the Moore,
My wayward Husband hath a hundred times
Woo'd me to ſteale it. But ſhe ſo loues the Token,
(For he coniur'd her, ſhe ſhould euer keepe it)
That ſhe reſerues it euermore about her,
To kiſſe, and talke too. Ile haue the worke tane out,
And giu't *Iago* : what he will do with it
Heauen knowes, not I :
I nothing, but to pleaſe his Fantaſie.

Enter Iago.

Iago. How now? What do you heere alone?

Æmil. Do not you chide : I haue a thing for you.

Iago. You haue a thing for me?
It is a common thing———

Æmil. Hah?

Iago. To haue a fooliſh wife.

Æmil. Oh, is that all? What will you giue me now
For that ſame Handkerchiefe.

Iago. What Handkerchiefe?

Æmil. What Handkerchiefe?
Why that the Moore firſt gaue to *Deſdemona*,
That which ſo often you did bid me ſteale.

Iago. Haſt ſtolne it from her?

Æmil. No : but ſhe let it drop by negligence,
And to th'aduantage, I being heere, took't vp :
Looke, heere 'tis.

Iago. A good wench, giue it me.

Æmil. What will you do with't, that you haue bene ſo earneſt to haue me filch it?

Iago. Why, what is that to you?

Æmil. If it be not for ſome purpoſe of import,
Giu't me againe. Poore Lady, ſhee'l run mad
When ſhe ſhall lacke it.

Iago. Be not acknowne on't :
I haue vſe for it. Go, leaue me. *Exit Æmil.*
I will in *Caſſio's* Lodging looſe this Napkin,
And let him finde it. Trifles light as ayre,
Are to the iealious, confirmations ſtrong,
As proofes of holy Writ. This may do ſomething.
The Moore already changes with my poyſon :
Dangerous conceites, are in their Natures poyſons,
Which at the firſt are ſcarſe found to diſtaſte :
But with a little acte vpon the blood,
Burne like the Mines of Sulphure. I did ſay ſo.

Enter Othello.

Looke where he comes : Not Poppy, nor Mandragora,
Nor all the drowſie Syrrups of the world
Shall euer medicine thee to that ſweete ſleepe
Which thou owd'ſt yeſterday.

Oth. Ha, ha, falſe to mee?

Iago. Why how now Generall? No more of that.

Oth. Auant, be gone : Thou haſt ſet me on the Racke :
I ſweare 'tis better to be much abus'd,
Then but to know't a little.

Iago. How now, my Lord?

Oth. What ſenſe had I, in her ſtolne houres of Luſt?
I ſaw't not, thought it not : it harm'd not me :
I ſlept the next night well, fed well, was free, and merrie.
I found not *Caſſio's* kiſſes on her Lippes :
He that is robb'd, not wanting what is ſtolne,
Let him not know't, and he's not robb'd at all.

Iago. I am ſorry to heare this?

Oth. I had beene happy, if the generall Campe,
Pyoners and all, had taſted her ſweet Body,
So I had nothing knowne. Oh now, for euer
Farewell the Tranquill minde ; farewell Content ;
Farewell the plumed Troopes, and the bigge Warres,
That makes Ambition, Vertue! Oh farewell;
Farewell the neighing Steed, and the ſhrill Trumpe,
The Spirit-ſtirring Drum, th'Eare-piercing Fife,
The Royall Banner, and all Qualitie,
Pride, Pompe, and Circumſtance of glorious Warre :
And O you mortall Engines, whoſe rude throates
Th'immortall Ioues dread Clamours, counterfet,
Farewell : *Othello's* Occupation's gone.

Iago. Is't poſſible, my Lord?

Oth. Villaine, be ſure thou proue my Loue a Whore;
Be ſure of it : Giue me the Occular proofe,

Or

Or by the worth of mine eternall Soule,
Thou had'st bin better haue bin borne a Dog
Then answer my wak'd wrath.
Iago. Is't come to this?
Oth. Make me to see't: or (at the least) so proue it,
That the probation beare no Hindge, nor Loope,
To hang a doubt on: Or woe vpon thy life.
Iago. My Noble Lord.
Oth. If thou dost slander her, and torture me,
Neuer pray more: Abandon all remorse
On Horrors head, Horrors accumulate:
Do deeds to make Heauen weepe, all Earth amaz'd;
For nothing canst thou to damnation adde,
Greater then that.
Iago. O Grace! O Heauen forgiue me!
Are you a Man? Haue you a Soule? or Sense?
God buy you: take mine Office. Oh wretched Foole,
That lou'st to make thine Honesty, a Vice!
Oh monstrous world! Take note, take note (O World)
To be direct and honest, is not safe.
I thanke you for this profit, and from hence
Ile loue no Friend, sith Loue breeds such offence.
Oth. Nay stay: thou should'st be honest.
Iago. I should be wise; for Honestie's a Foole,
And looses that it workes for.
Oth. By the World,
I thinke my Wife be honest, and thinke she is not:
I thinke that thou art iust, and thinke thou art not:
Ile haue some proofe. My name that was as fresh
As *Dians* Visage, is now begrim'd and blacke
As mine owne face. If there be Cords, or Kniues,
Poyson, or Fire, or suffocating streames,
Ile not indure it. Would I were satisfied.
Iago. I see you are eaten vp with Passion:
I do repent me, that I put it to you.
You would be satisfied?
Oth. Would? Nay, and I will.
Iago. And may: but how? How satisfied, my Lord?
Would you the super-vision grossely gape on?
Behold her top'd?
Oth. Death, and damnation. Oh!
Iago. It were a tedious difficulty, I thinke,
To bring them to that Prospect: Damne them then,
If euer mortall eyes do see them boulster
More then their owne. What then? How then?
What shall I say? Where's Satisfaction?
It is impossible you should see this,
Were they as prime as Goates, as hot as Monkeyes,
As salt as Wolues in pride, and Fooles as grosse
As Ignorance, made drunke. But yet, I say,
If imputation, and strong circumstances,
Which leade directly to the doore of Truth,
Will giue you satisfaction, you might haue't.
Oth. Giue me a liuing reason she's disloyall.
Iago. I do not like the Office.
But sith I am entred in this cause so farre
(Prick'd too't by foolish Honesty, and Loue)
I will go on. I lay with *Cassio* lately,
And being troubled with a raging tooth,
I could not sleepe. There are a kinde of men,
So loose of Soule, that in their sleepes will mutter
Their Affayres: one of this kinde is *Cassio*:
In sleepe I heard him say, sweet *Desdemona*,
Let vs be wary, let vs hide our Loues,
And then (Sir) would he gripe, and wring my hand:
Cry, oh sweet Creature: then kisse me hard,
As if he pluckt vp kisses by the rootes,
That grew vpon my lippes, laid his Leg ore my Thigh,
And sigh, and kisse, and then cry cursed Fate,
That gaue thee to the Moore.
Oth. O monstrous! monstrous!
Iago. Nay, this was but his Dreame.
Oth. But this denoted a fore-gone conclusion,
'Tis a shrew'd doubt, though it be but a Dreame.
Iago. And this may helpe to thicken other proofes,
That do demonstrate thinly.
Oth. Ile teare her all to peeces.
Iago. Nay yet be wise; yet we see nothing done,
She may be honest yet: Tell me but this,
Haue you not sometimes seene a Handkerchiefe
Spotted with Strawberries, in your wiues hand?
Oth. I gaue her such a one: 'twas my first gift.
Iago. I know not that: but such a Handkerchiefe
(I am sure it was your wiues) did I to day
See *Cassio* wipe his Beard with.
Oth. If it be that.
Iago. If it be that, or any, it was hers.
It speakes against her with the other proofes.
Othel. O that the Slaue had forty thousand liues:
One is too poore, too weake for my reuenge.
Now do I see 'tis true. Looke heere *Iago*,
All my fond loue thus do I blow to Heauen. 'Tis gone.
Arise blacke vengeance, from the hollow hell,
Yeeld vp (O Loue) thy Crowne, and hearted Throne
To tyrannous Hate. Swell bosome with thy fraught,
For 'tis of Aspickes tongues.
Iago. Yet be content.
Oth. Oh blood, blood, blood.
Iago. Patience I say: your minde may change.
Oth. Neuer *Iago*. Like to the Ponticke Sea,
Whose Icie Current, and compulsiue course,
Neu'r keepes retyring ebbe, but keepes due on
To the Proponticke, and the Hellespont:
Euen so my bloody thoughts, with violent pace
Shall neu'r looke backe, neu'r ebbe to humble Loue,
Till that a capeable, and wide Reuenge
Swallow them vp. Now by yond Marble Heauen,
In the due reuerence of a Sacred vow,
I heere engage my words.
Iago. Do not rise yet:
Witnesse you euer-burning Lights aboue,
You Elements, that clip vs round about,
Witnesse that heere *Iago* doth giue vp
The execution of his wit, hands, heart,
To wrong'd *Othello's* Seruice. Let him command,
And to obey shall be in me remorse,
What bloody businesse euer.
Oth. I greet thy loue,
Not with vaine thanks, but with acceptance bounteous,
And will vpon the instant put thee too't.
Within these three dayes let me heare thee say,
That *Cassio's* not aliue.
Iago. My Friend is dead:
'Tis done at your Request.
But let her liue.
Oth. Damne her lewde Minx:
O damne her, damne her.
Come go with me a-part, I will withdraw
To furnish me with some swift meanes of death
For the faire Diuell.
Now art thou my Lieutenant.
Iago. I am your owne for euer. *Exeunt.*

Scena

Scæna Quarta.

Enter Desdemona, Æmilia, and Clown.

Des. Do you know Sirrah, where Lieutenant *Cassio* lyes?

Clow. I dare not say he lies any where.

Des. Why man?

Clo. He's a Soldier, and for me to say a Souldier lyes, 'tis stabbing.

Des. Go too: where lodges he?

Clo. To tell you where he lodges, is to tel you where I lye.

Des. Can any thing be made of this?

Clo. I know not where he lodges, and for mee to deuise a lodging, and say he lies heere, or he lies there, were to lye in mine owne throat.

Des. Can you enquire him out? and be edified by report?

Clo. I will Catechize the world for him, that is, make Questions, and by them answer.

Des. Seeke him, bidde him come hither: tell him, I haue moou'd my Lord on his behalfe, and hope all will be well.

Clo. To do this, is within the compasse of mans Wit, and therefore I will attempt the doing it. *Exit Clo.*

Des. Where should I loose the Handkerchiefe, *Æmilia?*

Æmil. I know not Madam.

Des. Beleeue me, I had rather haue lost my purse
Full of Cruzadoes. And but my Noble Moore
Is true of minde, and made of no such basenesse,
As iealious Creatures are, it were enough
To put him to ill-thinking.

Æmil. Is he not iealious?

Des. Who, he? I thinke the Sun where he was borne,
Drew all such humors from him.

Æmil. Looke where he comes.

Enter Othello.

Des. I will not leaue him now, till *Cassio* be
Call'd to him. How is't with you, my Lord?

Oth. Well my good Lady. Oh hardnes to dissemble!
How do you, *Desdemona?*

Des. Well, my good Lord.

Oth. Giue me your hand.
This hand is moist, my Lady.

Des. It hath felt no age, nor knowne no sorrow.

Oth. This argues fruitfulnesse, and liberall heart:
Hot, hot, and moyst This hand of yours requires
A sequester from Liberty: Fasting, and Prayer,
Much Castigation, Exercise deuout,
For heere's a yong, and sweating Diuell heere
That commonly rebels: 'Tis a good hand,
A franke one.

Des. You may (indeed) say so:
For 'twas that hand that gaue away my heart.

Oth. A liberall hand. The hearts of old, gaue hands:
But our new Heraldry is hands, not hearts.

Des. I cannot speake of this:
Come, now your promise.

Oth. What promise, Chucke?

Des. I haue sent to bid *Cassio* come speake with you.

Oth. I haue a salt and sorry Rhewme offends me:
Lend me thy Handkerchiefe.

Des. Heere my Lord.

Oth. That which I gaue you.

Des. I haue it not about me.

Oth. Not?

Des. No indeed, my Lord.

Oth. That's a fault: That Handkerchiefe
Did an Ægyptian to my Mother giue:
She was a Charmer, and could almost read
The thoughts of people. She told her, while she kept it,
'T would make her Amiable, and subdue my Father
Intirely to her loue: But if she lost it,
Or made a Guift of it, my Fathers eye
Should hold her loathed, and his Spirits should hunt
After new Fancies. She dying, gaue it me,
And bid me (when my Fate would haue me Wiu'd)
To giue it her. I did so; and take heede on't,
Make it a Darling, like your precious eye:
To loose't, or giue't away, were such perdition,
As nothing else could match.

Des, Is't possible?

Oth. 'Tis true: There's Magicke in the web of it:
A *Sybill* that had numbred in the world
The Sun to course, two hundred compasses,
In her Prophetticke furie sow'd the Worke:
The Wormes were hallowed, that did breede the Silke,
And it was dyde in Mummey, which the Skilfull
Conseru'd of Maidens hearts.

Des. Indeed? Is't true?

Oth. Most veritable, therefore looke too't well.

Des. Then would to Heauen, that I had neuer seene't?

Oth. Ha? wherefore?

Des. Why do you speake so startingly, and rash?

Oth. Is't lost? Is't gon? Speak, is't out o'th'way?

Des. Blesse vs.

Oth. Say you?

Des. It is not lost: but what and if it were?

Oth. How?

Des. I say it is not lost.

Oth. Fetcht, let me see't.

Des. Why so I can: but I will not now:
This is a tricke to put me from my suite,
Pray you let *Cassio* be receiu'd againe.

Oth. Fetch me the Handkerchiefe,
My minde mis-giues.

Des. Come, come: you'l neuer meete a more sufficient man.

Oth. The Handkerchiefe.

Des. A man that all his time
Hath founded his good Fortunes on your loue;
Shar'd dangers with you.

Oth. The Handkerchiefe.

Des. Insooth, you are too blame.

Oth. Away. *Exit Othello.*

Æmil. Is not this man iealious?

Des. I neu'r saw this before.
Sure, there's some wonder in this Handkerchikfe,
I am most vnhappy in the losse of it.

Æmil. 'Tis not a yeare or two shewes vs a man:
They are all but Stomackes, and we all but Food,
They eate vs hungerly, and when they are full
They belch vs.

Enter Iago, and Cassio.

Looke you, *Cassio* and my Husband.

Iago. There is no other way: 'tis she must doo't:
And loe the happinesse: go, and importune her.

Des.

Deſ. How now (good *Caſſio*) what's the newes with you?
Caſſio. Madam, my former ſuite. I do beſeech you,
That by your vertuous meanes, I may againe
Exiſt, and be a member of his loue,
Whom I, with all the Office of my heart
Intirely honour, I would not be delayd.
If my offence, be of ſuch mortall kinde,
That nor my Seruice paſt, nor preſent Sorrowes,
Nor purpos'd merit in futurity,
Can ranſome me into his loue againe,
But to know ſo, muſt be my benefit:
So ſhall I cloath me in a forc'd content,
And ſhut my ſelfe vp in ſome other courſe
To Fortunes Almes.
Deſ. Alas (thrice-gentle *Caſſio*)
My Aduocation is not now in Tune;
My Lord, is not my Lord; nor ſhould I know him,
Were he in Fauour, as in Humour alter'd.
So helpe me euery ſpirit ſanctified,
As I haue ſpoken for you all my beſt,
And ſtood within the blanke of his diſpleaſure
For my free ſpeech. You muſt awhile be patient:
What I can do, I will: and more I will
Then for my ſelfe, I dare. Let that ſuffice you.
Iago. Is my Lord angry?
Æmil. He went hence but now:
And certainly in ſtrange vnquietneſſe.
Iago. Can he be angry? I haue ſeene the Cannon
When it hath blowne his Rankes into the Ayre,
And like the Diuell from his very Arme
Puff't his owne Brother: And is he angry?
Something of moment then: I will go meet him,
There's matter in't indeed, if he be angry. *Exit*
Deſ. I prythee do ſo. Something ſure of State,
Either from Venice, or ſome vnhatch'd practiſe
Made demonſtrable heere in Cyprus, to him,
Hath pudled his cleare Spirit: and in ſuch caſes,
Mens Natures wrangle with inferiour things,
Though great ones are their obiect. 'Tis euen ſo.
For let our finger ake, and it endues
Our other healthfull members, euen to a ſenſe
Of paine. Nay, we muſt thinke men are not Gods,
Nor of them looke for ſuch obſeruancie
As fits the Bridall. Beſhrew me much, *Æmilia*,
I was (vnhandſome Warrior, as I am)
Arraigning his vnkindneſſe with my ſoule:
But now I finde, I had ſuborn'd the Witneſſe,
And he's Indited falſely.
Æmil. Pray heauen it bee
State matters, as you thinke, and no Conception,
Nor no Iealious Toy, concerning you.
Deſ. Alas the day, I neuer gaue him cauſe.
Æmil. But Iealious ſoules will not be anſwer'd ſo;
They are not euer iealious for the cauſe,
But iealious, for they're iealious. It is a Monſter
Begot vpon it ſelfe, borne on it ſelfe.
Deſ. Heauen keepe the Monſter from *Othello's* mind.
Æmil. Lady, Amen.
Deſ. I will go ſeeke him. *Caſſio*, walke heere about:
If I doe finde him fit, Ile moue your ſuite,
And ſeeke to effect it to my vttermoſt. *Exit*
Caſ. I humbly thanke your Ladyſhip.

Enter Bianca.

Bian. 'Saue you (Friend *Caſſio.*)
Caſſio. What make you from home?
How is't with you, my moſt faire *Bianca*?
Indeed (ſweet Loue) I was comming to your houſe.
Bian. And I was going to your Lodging, *Caſſio.*
What? keepe a weeke away? Seuen dayes, and Nights?
Eight ſcore eight houres? And Louers abſent howres
More tedious then the Diall, eight ſcore times?
Oh weary reck'ning.
Caſſio. Pardon me, *Bianca*:
I haue this while with leaden thoughts beene preſt,
But I ſhall in a more continuate time
Strike off this ſcore of abſence. Sweet *Bianca*
Take me this worke out.
Bianca. Oh *Caſſio*, whence came this?
This is ſome Token from a newer Friend,
To the felt-Abſence: now I feele a Cauſe:
Is't come to this? Well, well.
Caſſio. Go too, woman:
Throw your vilde geſſes in the Diuels teeth,
From whence you haue them. You are iealious now,
That this is from ſome Miſtris, ſome remembrance;
No, in good troth *Bianca*.
Bian. Why, who's is it?
Caſſio. I know not neither:
I found it in my Chamber,
I like the worke well; Ere it be demanded
(As like enough it will) I would haue it coppied:
Take it, and doo't, and leaue me for this time.
Bian. Leaue you? Wherefore?
Caſſio. I do attend heere on the Generall,
And thinke it no addition, nor my wiſh
To haue him ſee me woman'd.
Bian. Why, I pray you?
Caſſio. Not that I loue you not.
Bian. But that you do not loue me.
I pray you bring me on the way a little,
And ſay, if I ſhall ſee you ſoone at night?
Caſſio. 'Tis but a little way that I can bring you,
For I attend heere: But Ile ſee you ſoone.
Bian. 'Tis very good: I muſt be circumſtanc'd.
Exeunt omnes.

Actus Quartus. Scena Prima.

Enter Othello, and Iago.

Iago. Will you thinke ſo?
Oth. Thinke ſo, *Iago*?
Iago. What, to kiſſe in priuate?
Oth. An vnauthoriz'd kiſſe?
Iago. Or to be naked with her Friend in bed,
An houre, or more, not meaning any harme?
Oth. Naked in bed (*Iago*) and not meane harme?
It is hypocriſie againſt the Diuell:
They that meane vertuouſly, and yet do ſo,
The Diuell their vertue tempts, and they tempt Heauen.
Iago. If they do nothing, 'tis a Veniall ſlip:
But if I giue my wife a Handkerchiefe.
Oth. What then?
Iago. Why then 'tis hers (my Lord) and being hers,
She may (I thinke) beſtow't on any man.
Oth. She is Protectreſſe of her honor too:
May ſhe giue that?

Iago.

Iago. Her honor is an Eſſence that's not ſeene,
They haue it very oft, that haue it not.
But for the Handkerchiefe.
Othe. By heauen, I would moſt gladly haue forgot it:
Thou ſaidſt (oh, it comes ore my memorie,
As doth the Rauen o're the infectious houſe:
Boading to all) he had my Handkerchiefe.
Iago. I: what of that?
Othe. That's not ſo good now.
Iag. What if I had ſaid, I had ſeene him do you wrong?
Or heard him ſay (as Knaues be ſuch abroad,
Who hauing by their owne importunate ſuit,
Or voluntary dotage of ſome Miſtris,
Conuinced or ſupply'd them, cannot chuſe
But they muſt blab.)
Oth. Hath he ſaid any thing?
Iago. He hath (my Lord) but be you well aſſur'd,
No more then he'le vn-ſweare.
Oth. What hath he ſaid?
Iago. Why, that he did: I know not what he did.
Othe. What? What?
Iago. Lye.
Oth. With her?
Iago. With her? On her: what you will.
Othe. Lye with her? lye on her? We ſay lye on her, when they be-lye-her. Lye with her: that's fullſome: Handkerchiefe: Confeſſions: Handkerchiefe. To confeſſe, and be hang'd for his labour. Firſt, to be hang'd, and then to confeſſe: I tremble at it. Nature would not inueſt her ſelfe in ſuch ſhadowing paſſion, without ſome Inſtruction. It is not words that ſhakes me thus, (piſh) Noſes, Eares, and Lippes: is't poſſible. Confeſſe? Handkerchiefe? O diuell. *Falls in a Traunce.*
Iago. Worke on,
My Medicine workes. Thus credulous Fooles are caught,
And many worthy, and chaſt Dames euen thus,
(All guiltleſſe) meete reproach: what hoa? My Lord?
My Lord, I ſay: *Othello.*

Enter Caſſio.

How now *Caſſio*?
Caſ. What's the matter?
Iago. My Lord is falne into an Epilepſie,
This is his ſecond Fit: he had one yeſterday.
Caſ. Rub him about the Temples.
Iago. The Lethargie muſt haue his quyet courſe:
If not, he foames at mouth: and by and by
Breakes out to ſauage madneſſe. Looke, he ſtirres:
Do you withdraw your ſelfe a little while,
He will recouer ſtraight: when he is gone,
I would on great occaſion, ſpeake with you.
How is it Generall? Haue you not hurt your head?
Othe. Doſt thou mocke me?
Iago. I mocke you not, by Heauen:
Would you would beare your Fortune like a Man.
Othe. A Horned man's a Monſter, and a Beaſt.
Iago. Ther's many a Beaſt then in a populous Citty,
And many a ciuill Monſter.
Othe. Did he confeſſe it?
Iago. Good Sir, be a man:
Thinke euery bearded fellow that's but yoak'd
May draw with you. There's Millions now aliue,
That nightly lye in thoſe vnproper beds,
Which they dare ſweare peculiar. Your caſe is better.
Oh, 'tis the ſpight of hell, the Fiends Arch-mock,
To lip a wanton in a ſecure Cowch;
And to ſuppoſe her chaſt. No, let me know,
And knowing what I am, I know what ſhe ſhallbe.
Oth. Oh, thou art wiſe: 'tis certaine.
Iago. Stand you a while apart,
Confine your ſelfe but in a patient Liſt,
Whil'ſt you were heere, o're-whelmed with your griefe
(A paſſion moſt reſulting ſuch a man)
Caſſio came hither. I ſhifted him away,
And layd good ſcuſes vpon your Extaſie,
Bad him anon returne: and heere ſpeake with me,
The which he promis'd. Do but encaue your ſelfe,
And marke the Fleeres, the Gybes, and notable Scornes
That dwell in euery Region of his face.
For I will make him tell the Tale anew;
Where, how, how oft, how long ago, and when
He hath, and is againe to cope your wife.
I ſay, but marke his geſture: marry Patience,
Or I ſhall ſay y'are all in all in Spleene,
And nothing of a man.
Othe. Do'ſt thou heare, *Iago*,
I will be found moſt cunning in my Patience:
But (do'ſt thou heare) moſt bloody.
Iago. That's not amiſſe,
But yet keepe time in all: will you withdraw?
Now will I queſtion *Caſſio* of *Bianca*,
A Huſwife, that by ſelling her deſires
Buyes her ſelfe Bread, and Cloath. It is a Creature
That dotes on *Caſſio*, (as 'tis the Strumpets plague
To be-guile many, and be be-guil'd by one)
He, when he heares of her, cannot reſtraine
From the exceſſe of Laughter. Heere he comes.

Enter Caſſio.

As he ſhall ſmile, *Othello* ſhall go mad:
And his vnbookiſh Ielouſie muſt conſerue
Poore *Caſſio's* ſmiles, geſtures, and light behauiours
Quite in the wrong. How do you Lieutenant?
Caſ. The worſer, that you giue me the addition,
Whoſe want euen killes me.
Iago. Ply *Deſdemona* well, and you are ſure on't:
Now, if this Suit lay in *Bianca's* dowre,
How quickely ſhould you ſpeed?
Caſ. Alas poore Caitiffe.
Oth. Looke how he laughes already.
Iago. I neuer knew woman loue man ſo.
Caſ. Alas poore Rogue, I thinke indeed ſhe loues me.
Oth. Now he denies it faintly: and laughes it out.
Iago. Do you heare *Caſſio*?
Oth. Now he importunes him
To tell it o're: go too, well ſaid, well ſaid.
Iago. She giues it out, that you ſhall marry her.
Do you intend it?
Caſ. Ha, ha, ha.
Oth. Do ye triumph, Romaine? do you triumph?
Caſ. I marry. What? A cuſtomer; prythee beare
Some Charitie to my wit, do not thinke it
So vnwholeſome. Ha, ha, ha.
Oth. So, ſo, ſo, ſo: they laugh, that winnes.
Iago. Why the cry goes, that you marry her.
Caſ. Prythee ſay true.
Iago. I am a very Villaine elſe.
Oth. Haue you ſcoar'd me? Well.
Caſ. This is the Monkeys owne giuing out:
She is perſwaded I will marry her
Out of her owne loue & flattery, not out of my promiſe.
v v *Othe.*

Oth. *Iago* becomes me: now he begins the ftory.

Caſſio. She was heere euen now: ſhe haunts me in euery place. I was the other day talking on the Seabanke with certaine Venetians, and thither comes the Bauble, and falls me thus about my neck.

Oth. Crying oh deere *Caſſio*, as it were: his ieſture imports it.

Caſſio. So hangs, and lolls, and weepes vpon me:
So ſhakes, and pulls me. Ha, ha, ha.

Oth. Now he tells how ſhe pluckt him to my Chamber: oh, I ſee that noſe of yours, but not that dogge, I ſhall throw it to.

Caſſio. Well, I muſt leaue her companie.

Iago. Before me: looke where ſhe comes.

Enter Bianca.

Caſ. 'Tis ſuch another Fitchew: marry a perfum'd one?
What do you meane by this haunting of me?

Bian. Let the diuell, and his dam haunt you: what did you meane by that ſame Handkerchiefe, you gaue me euen now? I was a fine Foole to take it: I muſt take out the worke? A likely piece of worke, that you ſhould finde it in your Chamber, and know not who left it there. This is ſome Minxes token, & I muſt take out the worke? There, giue it your Hobbey-horſe, whereſoeuer you had it, Ile take out no worke on't.

Caſſio. How now, my ſweete *Bianca*?
How now? How now?

Othe. By Heauen, that ſhould be my Handkerchiefe.

Bian. If you'le come to ſupper to night you may, if you will not, come when you are next prepar'd for. *Exit*

Iago. After her: after her.

Caſ. I muſt, ſhee'l rayle in the ſtreets elſe.

Iago. Will you ſup there?

Caſſio. Yes, I intend ſo.

Iago. Well, I may chance to ſee you: for I would very faine ſpeake with you.

Caſ Prythee come: will you?

Iago. Go too: ſay no more.

Oth. How ſhall I murther him, *Iago*.

Iago. Did you perceiue how he laugh'd at his vice?

Oth. Oh, *Iago*.

Iago. And did you ſee the Handkerchiefe?

Oth. Was that mine?

Iago. Yours by this hand: and to ſee how he prizes the fooliſh woman your wife: ſhe gaue it him, and he hath giu'n it his whore.

Oth. I would haue him nine yeeres a killing:
A fine woman, a faire woman, a ſweete woman?

Iago. Nay, you muſt forget that.

Othello. I, let her rot and periſh, and be damn'd to night, for ſhe ſhall not liue. No, my heart is turn'd to ſtone: I ſtrike it, and it hurts my hand. Oh, the world hath not a ſweeter Creature: ſhe might lye by an Emperours ſide, and command him Taskes.

Iago. Nay, that's not your way.

Othe. Hang her, I do but ſay what ſhe is: ſo delicate with her Needle: an admirable Muſitian. Oh ſhe will ſing the Sauageneſſe out of a Beare: of ſo high and plenteous wit, and inuention?

Iago. She's the worſe for all this.

Othe. Oh, a thouſand, a thouſand times:
And then of ſo gentle a condition?

Iago. I too gentle.

Othe. Nay that's certaine:
But yet the pitty of it, *Iago*: oh *Iago*, the pitty of it *Iago*.

Iago. If you are ſo fond ouer her iniquitie: giue her pattent to offend, for if it touch not you, it comes neere no body.

Oth. I will chop her into Meſſes: Cuckold me?

Iago. Oh, 'tis foule in her.

Oth. With mine Officer?

Iago. That's fouler.

Othe. Get me ſome poyſon, *Iago*, this night. Ile not expoſtulate with her: leaſt her body and beautie vnprouide my mind againe: this night *Iago*.

Iago. Do it not with poyſon, ſtrangle her in her bed,
Euen the bed ſhe hath contaminated.

Oth. Good, good:
The Iuſtice of it pleaſes: very good.

Iago. And for *Caſſio*, let me be his vndertaker:
You ſhall heare more by midnight.

Enter Lodouico, Deſdemona, and Attendants.

Othe. Excellent good: What Trumpet is that ſame?

Iago. I warrant ſomething from Venice,
'Tis *Lodouico*, this, comes from the Duke.
See, your wife's with him.

Lodo. Saue you worthy Generall.

Othe. With all my heart Sir.

Lod. The Duke, and the Senators of Venice greet you.

Othe. I kiſſe the Inſtrument of their pleaſures.

Deſ. And what's the newes, good cozen *Lodouico*?

Iago. I am very glad to ſee you Signior:
Welcome to Cyprus.

Lod. I thanke you: how do's Lieutenant *Caſſio*?

Iago. Liues Sir,

Deſ. Cozen, there's falne betweene him, & my Lord,
An vnkind breach: but you ſhall make all well.

Othe. Are you ſure of that?

Deſ. My Lord?

Othe. This faile you not to do, as you will———

Lod. He did not call: he's buſie in the paper,
Is there deuiſion 'twixt my Lord, and *Caſſio*?

Deſ. A moſt vnhappy one: I would do much
T'attone them, for the loue I beare to *Caſſio*.

Oth. Fire, and brimeſtone.

Deſ. My Lord.

Oth. Are you wiſe?

Deſ. What is he angrie?

Lod. May be thLetter mou'd him.
For as I thinke, they do command him home,
Deputing *Caſsio* in his Gouernment.

Deſ. Truſt me, I am glad on't.

Othe. Indeed?

Deſ. My Lord?

Othe. I am glad to ſee you mad.

Deſ. Why, ſweete *Othello*?

Othe. Diuell.

Deſ. I haue not deſeru'd this.

Lod. My Lord, this would not be beleeu'd in Venice,
Though I ſhould ſweare I ſaw't. 'Tis very much,
Make her amends: ſhe weepes.

Othe. Oh diuell, diuell:
If that the Earth could teeme with womans teares,
Each drop ſhe falls, would proue a Crocodile:
Out of my ſight.

Deſ. I will not ſtay to offend you.

Lod. Truely obedient Lady:
I do beſeech your Lordſhip call her backe.

Oth.

Othe. Mistris.
Des. My Lord.
Othe. What would you with her, Sir?
Lod. Who I, my Lord?
Othe. I, you did wish, that I would make her turne:
Sir, she can turne, and turne: and yet go on
And turne againe. And she can weepe, Sir, weepe.
And she's obedient: as you say obedient.
Very obedient: proceed you in your teares.
Concerning this Sir, (oh well-painted passion)
I am commanded home: get you away:
Ile send for you anon. Sir I obey the Mandate,
And will returne to Venice. Hence, auaunt:
Cassio shall haue my Place. And Sir, to night
I do entreat, that we may sup together.
You are welcome Sir to Cyprus.
Goates, and Monkeys. *Exit.*
Lod. Is this the Noble Moore, whom our full Senate
Call all in all sufficient? Is this the Nature
Whom Passion could not shake? Whose solid vertue
The shot of Accident, nor dart of Chance
Could neither graze, nor pierce?
Iago. He is much chang'd.
Lod. Are his wits safe? Is he not light of Braine?
Iago. He's that he is: I may not breath my censure.
What he might be: if what he might, he is not,
I would to heauen he were.
Lod. What? Strike his wife?
Iago. 'Faith that was not so well: yet would I knew
That stroke would proue the worst.
Lod. Is it his vse?
Or did the Letters, worke vpon his blood,
And new create his fault?
Iago. Alas, alas:
It is not honestie in me to speake
What I haue seene, and knowne. You shall obserue him,
And his owne courses will deonte him so,
That I may saue my speech: do but go after
And marke how he continues.
Lod. I am sorry that I am deceiu'd in him. *Exeunt.*

Scena Secunda.

Enter Othello, and Æmilia.

Othe. You haue seene nothing then?
Æmil. Nor euer heard: nor euer did suspect.
Othe. Yes, you haue seene *Cassio*, and she together.
Æmi. But then I saw no harme: and then I heard,
Each syllable that breath made vp betweene them.
Othe. What? Did they neuer whisper?
Æmil. Neuer my Lord.
Othe. Nor send you out o'th'way?
Æmil. Neuer.
Othe. To fetch her Fan, her Gloues, her Mask, nor no-(thing?
Æmil. Neuer my Lord.
Othe. That's strange.
Æmil. I durst (my Lord) to wager, she is honest:
Lay downe my Soule at stake: If you thinke other,
Remoue your thought. It doth abuse your bosome:
If any wretch haue put this in your head,
Let Heauen requit it with the Serpents curse,
For if she be not honest, chaste, and true,
There's no man happy. The purest of their Wiues
Is foule as Slander.
Othe. Bid her come hither: go. *Exit Æmilia.*
She saies enough: yet she's a simple Baud
That cannot say as much. This is a subtile Whore:
A Closset Locke and Key of Villanous Secrets,
And yet she'le kneele, and pray: I haue seene her do't.

Enter Desdemona, and Æmilia.

Des. My Lord, what is your will?
Othe. Pray you Chucke come hither.
Des. What is your pleasure?
Oth. Let me see your eyes: looke in my face.
Des. What horrible Fancie's this?
Othe. Some of your Function Mistris:
Leaue Procreants alone, and shut the doore:
Cough, or cry hem; if any body come:
Your Mystery, your Mystery: May dispatch. *Exit Æmi.*
Des. Vpon my knee, what doth your speech import?
I vnderstand a Fury in your words.
Othe. Why? What art thou?
Des. Your wife my Lord: your true and loyall wife.
Othello. Come sweare it: damne thy selfe, least being like one of Heauen, the diuells themselues should feare to ceaze thee. Therefore be double damn'd: sweare thou art honest.
Des. Heauen doth truely know it.
Othe. Heauen truely knowes, that thou art false as hell.
Des. To whom my Lord?
With whom? How am I false?
Othe. Ah *Desdemon*, away, away, away.
Des. Alas the heauy day: why do you weepe?
Am I the motiue of these teares my Lord?
If happely you my Father do suspect,
An Instrument of this your calling backe,
Lay not your blame on me: if you haue lost him,
I haue lost him too.
Othe. Had it pleas'd Heauen,
To try me with Affliction, had they rain'd
All kind of Sores, and Shames on my bare-head:
Steep'd me in pouertie to the very lippes,
Giuen to Captiuitie, me, and my vtmost hopes,
I should haue found in some place of my Soule
A drop of patience. But alas, to make me
The fixed Figure for the time of Scorne,
To point his slow, and mouing finger at.
Yet could I beare that too, well, very well:
But there where I haue garnerd vp my heart,
Where either I must liue, or beare no life,
The Fountaine from the which my currant runnes,
Or else dries vp: to be discarded thence,
Or keepe it as a Cesterne, for foule Toades
To knot and gender in. Turne thy complexion there:
Patience, thou young and Rose-lip'd Cherubin,
I heere looke grim as hell.
Des. I hope my Noble Lord esteemes me honest.
Othe. Oh I, as Sommer Flyes are in the Shambles,
That quicken euen with blowing. Oh thou weed:
Who art so louely faire, and smell'st so sweete,
That the Sense akes at thee,
Would thou had'st neuer bin borne.
Des. Alas, what ignorant sin haue I committed?
Othe. Was this faire Paper? This most goodly Booke
Made to write Whore vpon? What commited,

Committed? Oh, thou publicke Commoner,
I ſhould make very Forges of my cheekes,
That would to Cynders burne vp Modeſtie,
Did I but ſpeake thy deedes. What commited?
Heauen ſtoppes the Noſe at it, and the Moone winks:
The baudy winde that kiſſes all it meetes,
Is huſh'd within the hollow Myne of Earth
And will not hear't. What commited?
Def. By Heauen you do me wrong.
Othe. Are not you a Strumpet?
Def. No, as I am a Chriſtian.
If to preſerue this veſſell for my Lord,
From any other foule vnlawfull touch
Be not to be a Strumpet, I am none.
Othe. What, not a Whore?
Def. No, as I ſhall be ſau'd.
Othe. Is't poſſible?
Def. Oh Heauen forgiue vs.
Othe. I cry you mercy then.
I tooke you for that cunning Whore of Venice,
That married with *Othello*. You Miſtris,
Enter Æmilia.
That haue the office oppoſite to Saint *Peter*,
And keepes the gate of hell. You, you: I you.
We haue done our courſe: there's money for your paines:
I pray you turne the key, and keepe our counſaile. *Exit.*
Æmil. Alas, what do's this Gentleman conceiue?
How do you Madam? how do you my good Lady?
Def. Faith, halfe a ſleepe.
Æmi. Good Madam,
What's the matter with my Lord?
Def. With who?
Æmil. Why, with my Lord, Madam?
Def. Who is thy Lord?
Æmil. He that is yours, ſweet Lady.
Def. I haue none: do not talke to me, *Æmilia*,
I cannot weepe: nor anſweres haue I none,
Bnt what ſhould go by water. Prythee to night,
Lay on my bed, my wedding ſheetes, remember,
And call thy husband hither.
Æmil. Heere's a change indeed. *Exit.*
Def. 'Tis meete I ſhould be vs'd ſo: very meete.
How haue I bin behau'd, that he might ſticke
The ſmall'ſt opinion on my leaſt miſvſe?

Enter Iago, and Æmilia.
Iago. What is your pleaſure Madam?
How is't with you?
Def. I cannot tell: thoſe that do teach yong Babes
Do it with gentle meanes, and eaſie taskes.
He might haue chid me ſo: for in good faith
I am a Child to chiding.
Iago. What is the matter Lady?
Æmil. Alas (*Iago*) my Lord hath ſo bewhor'd her,
Throwne ſuch diſpight, and heauy termes vpon her
That true hearts cannot beare it.
Def. Am I that name, *Iago*?
Iago. What name, (faire Lady?)
Def. Such as ſhe ſaid my Lord did ſay I was.
Æmil. He call'd her whore: a Begger in his drinke:
Could not haue laid ſuch termes vpon his Callet.
Iago. Why did he ſo?
Def. I do not know: I am ſure I am none ſuch.
Iago. Do not weepe, do not weepe: alas the day.
Æmil. Hath ſhe forſooke ſo many Noble Matches?
Her Father? And her Country? And her Friends?
To be call'd Whore? Would it not make one weepe?
Def. It is my wretched Fortune.
Iago. Beſhrew him for't:
How comes this Tricke vpon him?
Def. Nay, Heauen doth know.
Æmi. I will be hang'd, if ſome eternall Villaine,
Some buſie and inſinuating Rogue,
Some cogging, cozening Slaue, to get ſome Office,
Haue not deuis'd this Slander: I will be hang'd elſe.
Iago. Fie, there is no ſuch man: it is impoſſible.
Def. If any ſuch there be, Heauen pardon him.
Æmil. A halter pardon him:
And hell gnaw his bones.
Why ſhould he call her Whore?
Who keepes her companie?
What Place? What Time?
What Forme? What liklyhood?
The Moore's abus'd by ſome moſt villanous Knaue,
Some baſe notorious Knaue, ſome ſcuruy Fellow.
Oh Heauens, that ſuch companions thou'd'ſt vnfold,
And put in euery honeſt hand a whip
To laſh the Raſcalls naked through the world,
Euen from the Eaſt to th'Weſt.
Iago. Speake within doore.
Æmil. Oh fie vpon them: ſome ſuch Squire he was
That turn'd your wit, the ſeamy-ſide without,
And made you to ſuſpect me with the Moore.
Iago. You are a Foole: go too.
Def. Alas *Iago*,
What ſhall I do to win my Lord againe?
Good Friend, go to him: for by this light of Heauen,
I know not how I loſt him. Heere I kneele:
If ere my will did treſpaſſe 'gainſt his Loue,
Either in diſcourſe of thought, or actuall deed,
Or that mine Eyes, mine Eares, or any Sence
Delighted them: or any other Forme.
Or that I do not yet, and euer did,
And euer will, (though he do ſhake me off
To beggerly diuorcement) Loue him deerely,
Comfort forſweare me. Vnkindneſſe may do much,
And his vnkindneſſe may defeat my life,
But neuer taynt my Loue. I cannot ſay Whore,
It do's abhorre me now I ſpeake the word,
To do the Act, that might the addition earne,
Not the worlds Maſſe of vanitie could make me.
Iago. I pray you be content: 'tis but his humour:
The buſineſſe of the State do's him offence.
Def. If 'twere no other.
Iago. It is but ſo, I warrant,
Hearke how theſe Inſtruments ſummon to ſupper:
The Meſſengers of Venice ſtaies the meate,
Go in, and weepe not: all things ſhall be well.
Exeunt Deſdemona and Æmilia.

Enter Rodorigo.
How now *Rodorigo*?
Rod. I do not finde
That thou deal'ſt iuſtly with me.
Iago. What in the contrarie?
Rodori. Euery day thou dafts me with ſome deuiſe *Iago*, and rather, as it ſeemes to me now, keep'ſt from me all conueniencie, then ſupplieſt me with the leaſt aduantage of hope: I will indeed no longer endure it. Nor am I yet perſwaded to put vp in peace, what already I haue fooliſhly ſuffred.
Iago. Will you heare me *Rodorigo*?

Rodori. I

Rodori. I haue heard too much: and your words and Performances are no kin together.

Iago. You charge me moſt vniuſtly.

Rodo. With naught but truth: I haue waſted my ſelfe out of my meanes. The Iewels you haue had from me to deliuer *Deſdemona*, would halfe haue corrupted a Votariſt. You haue told me ſhe hath receiu'd them, and return'd me expectations and comforts of ſodaine reſpect, and acquaintance, but I finde none.

Iago. Well, go too: very well.

Rod. Very well, go too: I cannot go too, (man) nor tis not very well. Nay I think it is ſcuruy: and begin to finde my ſelfe fopt in it.

Iago. Very well.

Rodor. I tell you, 'tis not very well: I will make my ſelfe knowne to *Deſdemona*. If ſhe will returne me my Iewels, I will giue ouer my Suit, and repent my vnlawfull ſolicitation. If not, aſſure your ſelfe, I will ſeeke ſatisfaction of you.

Iago. You haue ſaid now.

Rodo. I: and ſaid nothing but what I proteſt intendment of doing.

Iago. Why, now I ſee there's mettle in thee: and euen from this inſtant do build on thee a better opinion then euer before: giue me thy hand *Rodorigo*. Thou haſt taken againſt me a moſt iuſt exception: but yet I proteſt I haue dealt moſt directly in thy Affaire.

Rod. It hath not appeer'd.

Iago. I grant indeed it hath not appeer'd: and your ſuſpition is not without wit and iudgement. But *Rodorigo*, if thou haſt that in thee indeed, which I haue greater reaſon to beleeue now then euer (I meane purpoſe, Courage, and Valour) this night ſhew it. If thou the next night following enioy not *Deſdemona*, take me from this world with Treacherie, and deuiſe Engines for my life.

Rod. Well: what is it? Is it within, reaſon and compaſſe?

Iago. Sir, there is eſpeciall Commiſſion come from Venice to depute *Caſſio* in *Othello's* place.

Rod. Is that true? Why then *Othello* and *Deſdemona* returne againe to Venice.

Iago. Oh no: he goes into Mauritania and taketh away with him the faire *Deſdemona*, vnleſſe his abode be lingred heere by ſome accident. Wherein none can be ſo determinate, as the remouing of *Caſſio*.

Rod. How do you meane remouing him?

Iago. Why, by making him vncapable of *Othello's* place: knocking out his braines.

Rod. And that you would haue me to do.

Iago. I: if you dare do your ſelfe a profit, and a right. He ſups to night with a Harlotry: and thither will I go to him. He knowes not yet of his Honourable Fortune, if you will watch his going thence (which I will faſhion to fall out betweene twelue and one) you may take him at your pleaſure. I will be neere to ſecond your Attempt, and he ſhall fall betweene vs. Come, ſtand not amaz'd at it, but go along with me: I will ſhew you ſuch a neceſſitie in his death, that you ſhall thinke your ſelfe bound to put it on him. It is now high ſupper time: and the night growes to waſt. About it.

Rod. I will heare further reaſon for this.

Iago. And you ſhalbe ſatisfi'd. *Exeunt.*

Scena Tertia.

Enter Othello, Lodouico, Deſdemona, Æmilia, and Atendants.

Lod. I do beſeech you Sir, trouble your ſelfe no further.

Oth. Oh pardon me: 'twill do me good to walke.

Lodoui. Madam, good night: I humbly thanke your Ladyſhip.

Deſ. Your Honour is moſt welcome.

Oth. Will you walke Sir? Oh *Deſdemona*.

Deſ. My Lord.

Othello. Get you to bed on th'inſtant, I will be return'd forthwith: diſmiſſe your Attendant there: look't be done. *Exit.*

Deſ. I will my Lord.

Æm. How goes it now? He lookes gentler then he did.

Deſ. He ſaies he will returne incontinent,
And hath commanded me to go to bed,
And bid me to diſmiſſe you.

Æmi. Diſmiſſe me?

Deſ. It was his bidding: therefore good *Æmilia*,
Giue me my nightly wearing, and adieu.
We muſt not now diſpleaſe him.

Æmil. I, would you had neuer ſeene him.

Deſ. So would not I: my loue doth ſo approue him,
That euen his ſtubborneſſe, his checks, his frownes,
(Prythee vn-pin me) haue grace and fauour.

Æmi. I haue laid thoſe Sheetes you bad me on the bed.

Deſ. All's one: good Father, how fooliſh are our minds?
If I do die before, prythee ſhrow'd me
In one of theſe ſame Sheetes.

Æmil. Come, come: you talke.

Deſ. My Mother had a Maid call'd *Barbarie*,
She was in loue: and he ſhe lou'd prou'd mad,
And did forſake her. She had a Song of Willough,
An old thing 'twas: but it expreſs'd her Fortune,
And ſhe dy'd ſinging it. That Song to night,
Will not go from my mind: I haue much to do,
But to go hang my head all at one ſide
And ſing it like poore *Brabarie*: prythee diſpatch.

Æmi. Shall I go fetch your Night-gowne?

Deſ. No, vn-pin me here,
This *Lodouico* is a proper man.

Æmil. A very handſome man.

Deſ. He ſpeakes well.

Æmil. I know a Lady in Venice would haue walk'd barefoot to Paleſtine for a touch of his nether lip.

Deſ. The poore Soule ſat ſinging, by a Sicamour tree.
Sing all a greene Willough:
Her hand on her boſome her head on her knee,
Sing Willough, Willough, Willough.
The freſh Streames ran by her, and murmur'd her moanes
Sing Willough, &c.
Her ſalt teares fell from her, and ſoftned the ſtones,
Sing Willough, &c. (Lay by theſe)
Willough, Willough. (Prythee high thee: he'le come anon)
Sing all a greene Willough muſt be my Garland.
Let no body blame him, his ſcorne I approue.
(Nay that's not next. Harke, who is't that knocks?

Æmil. It's the wind.

Deſ. I call'd my Loue falſe Loue: but what ſaid he then?
Sing Willough, &c.
If I court mo women, you'le couch with mo men.

So get thee gone, good night: mine eyes do itch:
Doth that boade weeping?
Æmil, 'Tis neyther heere, nor there.
Des. I haue heard it said so. O these Men, these men!
Do'st thou in conscience thinke (tell me *Æmilia*)
That there be women do abuse their husbands
In such grosse kinde?
Æmil. There be some such, no question.
Des. Would'st thou do such a deed for all the world?
Æmil. Why, would not you?
Des. No, by this Heauenly light.
Æmil. Nor I neither, by this Heauenly light:
I might doo't as well i'th'darke.
Des. Would'st thou do such a deed for al the world?
Æmil. The world's a huge thing:
It is a great price, for a small vice.
Des. Introth, I thinke thou would'st not.
Æmil. Introth I thinke I should, and vndoo't when I had done. Marry, I would not doe such a thing for a ioynt Ring, nor for measures of Lawne, nor for Gownes, Petticoats, nor Caps, nor any petty exhibition. But for all the whole world: why, who would not make her husbanda Cuckold, to make him a Monarch? I should venture Purgatory for't.
Des. Beshrew me, if I would do such a wrong
For the whole world.
Æmil. Why, the wrong is but a wrong i'th'world; and hauing the world for your labour, 'tis a wrong in your owne world, and you might quickly make it right.
Des. I do not thinke there is any such woman.
Æmil. Yes, a dozen: and as many to'th'vantage, as would store the world they plaid for.
But I do thinke it is their Husbands faults
If Wiues do fall: (Say, that they slacke their duties,
And powre our Treasures into forraigne laps;
Or else breake out in peeuish Iealousies,
Throwing restraint vpon vs: Or say they strike vs,
Or scant our former hauing in despight)
Why we haue galles: and though we haue some Grace,
Yet haue we some Reuenge. Let Husbands know,
Their wiues haue sense like them: They see, and smell,
And haue their Palats both for sweet, and sowre,
As Husbands haue. What is it that they do,
When they change vs for others? Is it Sport?
I thinke it is: and doth Affection breed it?
I thinke it doth. Is't Frailty that thus erres?
It is so too. And haue not we Affections?
Desires for Sport? and Frailty, as men haue?
Then let them vse vs well: else let them know,
The illes we do, their illes instruct vs so.
Des. Good night, good night:
Heauen me such vses send,
Not to picke bad, from bad; but by bad, mend. *Exeunt*

Actus Quintus. Scena Prima.

Enter Iago, and Rodorigo.

Iago. Heere, stand behinde this Barke,
Straight will he come:
Weare thy good Rapier bare, and put it home:
Quicke, quicke, feare nothing; Ile be at thy Elbow,
It makes vs, or it marres vs, thinke on that,
And fixe most firme thy Resolution.
Rod. Be neere at hand, I may miscarry in't.
Iago. Heere, at thy hand: Be bold, & take thy stand.
Rod. I haue no great deuotion to the deed,
And yet he hath giuen me satisfying Reasons:
'Tis but a man gone. Forth my Sword: he dies.
Iago. I haue rub'd this yong Quat almost to the sense,
And he growes angry. Now, whether he kill *Cassio*,
Or *Cassio* him, or each do kill the other,
Euery way makes my gaine. Liue *Rodorigo*,
He calles me to a restitution large
Of Gold, and Iewels, that I bob'd from him,
As Guifts to *Desdemona*.
It must not be: If *Cassio* do remaine,
He hath a dayly beauty in his life,
That makes me vgly: and besides, the Moore
May vnfold me to him: there stand I in much perill:
No, he must dye. But so, I heard him comming.

Enter Cassio.

Rod. I know his gate, 'tis he: Villaine thou dyest.
Cas. That thrust had beene mine enemy indeed,
But that my Coate is better then thou know'st:
I will make proofe of thine.
Rod. Oh, I am slaine.
Cassio. I am maym'd for euer:
Helpe hoa: Murther, murther.

Enter Othello.

Oth. The voyce of *Cassio*, *Iago* keepes his word.
Rod. O Villaine that I am.
Oth. It is euen so.
Cas. Oh helpe hoa: Light, a Surgeon.
Oth. 'Tis he: O braue *Iago*, honest, and iust,
That hast such Noble sense of thy Friends wrong,
Thou teachest me. Minion, your deere lyes dead,
And your vnblest Fate highes: Strumpet I come:
For of my heart, those Charmes thine Eyes, are blotted.
Thy Bed lust-stain'd, shall with Lusts blood bee spotted.

Exit Othello.

Enter Lodouico and Gratiano.

Cas. What hoa? no Watch? No passage?
Murther, Murther.
Gra. 'Tis some mischance, the voyce is very direfull.
Cas. Oh helpe.
Lodo. Hearke.
Rod. Oh wretched Villaine.
Lod. Two or three groane. 'Tis heauy night;
These may be counterfeits: Let's think't vnsafe
To come into the cry, without more helpe.
Rod. Nobody come: then shall I bleed to death.

Enter Iago.

Lod. Hearke.
Gra. Here's one comes in his shirt, with Light, and Weapons.
Iago. Who's there?
Who's noyse is this that cries on murther?
Lodo. We do not know.
Iago, Do not you heare a cry?
Cas. Heere, heere: for heauen sake helpe me.
Iago. What's the matter?
Gra. This is *Othello*'s Ancient, as I take it.
Lodo. The same indeede, a very valiant Fellow.
Iago. What are you heere, that cry so greeuously?
Cas. *Iago*? Oh I am spoyl'd, vndone by Villaines:
Giue me some helpe.
Iago. O mee, Lieutenant!
What Villaines haue done this?
Cas. I thinke that one of them is heereabout,

And

And cannot make away.
Iago. Oh treacherous Villaines:
What are you there? Come in, and giue ſome helpe.
Rod. O helpe me there.
Caſſio. That's one of them.
Iago. Oh murd'rous Slaue! O Villaine!
Rod. O damn'd *Iago*! O inhumane Dogge!
Iago. Kill men i'th'darke?
Where be theſe bloody Theeues?
How ſilent is this Towne? Hoa, murther, murther.
What may you be? Are you of good, or euill?
Lod. As you ſhall proue vs, praiſe vs.
Iago. Signior *Lodouico*?
Lod. He Sir.
Iago. I cry you mercy: here's *Caſſio* hurt by Villaines.
Gra. *Caſſio*?
Iago. How is't Brother?
Caſ. My Legge is cut in two.
Iago. Marry heauen forbid:
Light Gentlemen, Ile binde it with my ſhirt.

Enter Bianca.

Bian. What is the matter hoa? Who is't that cry'd?
Iago. Who is't that cry'd?
Bian. Oh my deere *Caſſio*,
My ſweet *Caſſio*: Oh *Caſſio*, *Caſſio*, *Caſſio*.
Iago. O notable Strumpet. *Caſſio*, may you ſuſpect
Who they ſhould be, that haue thus mangled you?
Caſ. No.
Gra. I am ſorry to finde you thus;
I haue beene to ſeeke you.
Iago. Lend me a Garter. So:——Oh for a Chaire
To beare him eaſily hence.
Bian. Alas he faints. Oh *Caſſio*, *Caſſio*, *Caſſio*.
Iago. Gentlemen all, I do ſuſpect this Traſh
To be a party in this Iniurie.
Patience awhile, good *Caſſio*. Come, come;
Lend me a Light: know we this face, or no?
Alas my Friend, and my deere Countryman
Rodorigo? No: Yes ſure: Yes, 'tis *Rodorigo*.
Gra. What, of Venice?
Iago. Euen he Sir: Did you know him?
Gra. Know him? I.
Iago. Signior *Gratiano*? I cry your gentle pardon:
Theſe bloody accidents muſt excuſe my Manners,
That ſo neglected you.
Gra. I am glad to ſee you.
Iago. How do you *Caſſio*? Oh, a Chaire, a Chaire.
Gra. *Rodorigo*?
Iago. He, he, 'tis he:
Oh that's well ſaid, the Chaire.
Some good man beare him carefully from hence,
Ile fetch the Generall's Surgeon. For you Miſtris,
Saue you your labour. He that lies ſlaine heere (*Caſſio*)
Was my deere friend. What malice was between you?
Caſ. None in the world: nor do I know the man?
Iago. What? looke you pale? Oh beare him o'th'Ayre.
Stay you good Gentlemen. Looke you pale, Miſtris?
Do you perceiue the gaſtneſſe of her eye?
Nay, if you ſtare, we ſhall heare more anon.
Behold her well: I pray you looke vpon her:
Do you ſee Gentlemen? Nay, guiltineſſe will ſpeake
Though tongues were out of vſe.
Æmil. Alas, what is the matter?
What is the matter, Husband?
Iago. *Caſſio* hath heere bin ſet on in the darke
By *Rodorigo*, and Fellowes that are ſcap'd:
He's almoſt ſlaine, and *Rodorigo* quite dead.
Æmil. Alas good Gentleman: alas good *Caſsio*.
Iago. This is the fruits of whoring. Prythe *Æmilia*,
Go know of *Caſſio* where he ſupt to night.
What, do you ſhake at that?
Bian. He ſupt at my houſe, but I therefore ſhake not.
Iago. O did he ſo? I charge you go with me.
Æmil. Oh fie vpon thee Strumpet.
Bian. I am no Strumpet, but of life as honeſt,
As you that thus abuſe me.
Æmil. As I? Fie vpon thee.
Iago. Kinde Gentlemen:
Let's go ſee poore *Caſſio* dreſt.
Come Miſtris, you muſt tel's another Tale.
Æmilia, run you to the Cittadell,
And tell my Lord and Lady, what hath happ'd:
Will you go on afore? This is the night
That either makes me, or foredoes me quight. *Exeunt*

Scœna Secunda.

Enter Othello, and Deſdemona in her bed.

Oth. It is the Cauſe, it is the Cauſe (my Soule)
Let me not name it to you, you chaſte Starres,
It is the Cauſe. Yet Ile not ſhed her blood,
Nor ſcarre that whiter skin of hers, then Snow,
And ſmooth as Monumentall Alablaſter:
Yet ſhe muſt dye, elſe ſhee'l betray more men:
Put out the Light, and then put out the Light:
If I quench thee, thou flaming Miniſter,
I can againe thy former light reſtore,
Should I repent me. But once put out thy Light,
Thou cunning'ſt Patterne of excelling Nature,
I know not where is that *Promethæan* heate
That can thy Light re-Lume.
When I haue pluck'd thy Roſe,
I cannot giue it vitall growth againe,
It needs muſt wither. Ile ſmell thee on the Tree.
Oh Balmy breath, that doſt almoſt perſwade
Iuſtice to breake her Sword. One more, one more:
Be thus when thou art dead, and I will kill thee,
And loue thee after. One more, and that's the laſt.
So ſweet, was ne're ſo fatall. I muſt weepe,
But they are cruell Teares: This ſorrow's heauenly,
It ſtrikes, where it doth loue. She wakes.
Deſ. Who's there? *Othello*?
Othel. I *Deſdemona*.
Deſ. Will you come to bed, my Lord?
Oth. Haue you pray'd to night, *Deſdemon*?
Deſ. I my Lord.
Oth. If you bethinke your ſelfe of any Crime
Vnreconcil'd as yet to Heauen, and Grace,
Solicite for it ſtraight.
Deſ. Alacke, my Lord,
What may you meane by that?
Oth. Well, do it, and be breefe, I will walke by:
I would not kill thy vnprepared Spirit,
No, Heauens fore-fend) I would not kill thy Soule.
Deſ. Talke you of killing?
Oth. I, I do.
Deſ. Then Heauen haue mercy on mee.

Oth.

Oth. Amen, with all my heart.
Def. If you ſay, I hope you will not kill me.
Oth. Humh.
Def. And yet I feare you : for you're fatall then
When your eyes rowle ſo.
Why I ſhould feare, I know not,
Since guiltineſſe I know not : But yet I feele I feare.
Oth. Thinke on thy ſinnes.
Def. They are Loues I beare to you.
Oth. I, and for that thou dy'ſt.
Def. That death's vnnaturall, that kils for louing.
Alas, why gnaw you ſo your nether-lip?
Some bloody paſſion ſhakes your very Frame:
Theſe are portents: but yet I hope, I hope,
They do not point on me.
Oth. Peace, and be ſtill.
Def. I will ſo : What's the matter?
Oth. That Handkerchiefe
Which I ſo lou'd, and gaue thee, thou gau'ſt to *Caſſio.*
Def. No by my Life, and Soule : ſend for the man,
And aske him.
Oth. Sweet Soule, take heed, take heed of Periury,
Thou art on thy death-bed.
Def. I, but not yet to dye.
Oth. Preſently.
Therefore confeſſe thee freely of thy ſinne:
For to deny each Article with Oath,
Cannot remoue, nor choake the ſtrong Conception
That I do grone withall. Thou art to dye.
Def. O Heauen haue mercy on me.
Oth. I ſay, Amen.
Def. And haue you mercy too. I neuer did
Offend you in my life: neuer lou'd *Caſſio,*
But with ſuch generall warrantie of Heauen,
As I might loue. I neuer gaue him Token.
Oth. By Heauen I ſaw my Handkerchiefe in's hand.
O periur'd woman, thou do'ſt ſtone my heart,
And makes me call, what I intend to do,
A Murther, which I thought a Sacrifice.
I ſaw the Handkerchiefe.
Def. He found it then:
I neuer gaue it him : Send, for him hither:
Let him confeſſe a truth.
Oth. He hath confeſt.
Def. What, my Lord?
Oth. That he hath vs'd thee.
Def. How? vnlawfully?
Oth. I.
Def. He will not ſay ſo.
Oth. No : his mouth is ſtopp'd:
Honeſt *Iago* hath 'tane order for't.
Def. Oh, my feare interprets. What is he dead?
Oth. Had all his haires bin liues, my great Reuenge
Had ſtomacke for them all.
Def. Alas, he is betray'd, and I vndone.
Oth. Out Strumpet : weep'ſt thou for him to my face?
Def. O baniſh me, my Lord, but kill me not.
Oth. Downe Strumpet.
Def. Kill me to morrow, let me liue to night.
Oth. Nay, if you ſtriue.
Def. But halfe an houre.
Oth. Being done, there is no pawſe.
Def. But while I ſay one prayer.
Oth. It is too late. *Smothers her.*
Æmilia at the doore.
Æmil. My Lord, my Lord? What hoa?
My Lord, my Lord.
Oth. What noiſe is this? Not dead? not yet quite dead?
I that am cruell, am yet mercifull,
I would not haue thee linger in thy paine?
So, ſo.
Æmil. within. What hoa? my Lord, my Lord?
Oth. Who's there?
Æmil. Oh good my Lord, I would ſpeake a word with you.
Oth. Yes : 'Tis *Æmilia* : by and by. Shee's dead.
'Tis like ſhe comes to ſpeake of *Caſſio*'s death:
The noiſe was high. Hah, no more moouing?
Still as the Graue. Shall ſhe come in? Wer't good?
I thinke ſhe ſtirres againe. No, what's beſt to do?
If ſhe come in, ſhee'l ſure ſpeake to my wife:
My wife, my wife : what wife? I haue no wife.
Oh inſupportable! Oh heauy houre!
Me thinkes, it ſhould be now a huge Eclipſe
Of Sunne, and Moone; and that th'affrighted Globe
Did yawne at Alteration.
Æmil. I do beſeech you
That I may ſpeake with you. Oh good my Lord.
Oth. I had forgot thee : oh come in *Æmilia.*
Soft, by and by, let me the Curtaines draw.
Where art thou? What's the matter with thee now?
Enter Æmilia.
Æmil. Oh my good Lord, yonders foule Murthers done.
Oth. What? now?
Æmil. But now, my Lord.
Oth. It is the very error of the Moone,
She comes more neerer Earth then ſhe was wont,
And makes men mad.
Æmil. *Caſſio*, my Lord, hath kill'd
A young Venetian, call'd *Rodorigo.*
Oth. *Rodorigo* kill'd? and *Caſſio* kill'd?
Æmil. No, *Caſſio* is not kill'd.
Oth. Not *Caſſio* kill'd? Then Murther's out of tune,
And ſweet Reuenge growes harſh.
Def. O falſely, falſely murder'd.
Æmil. Alas! what cry is that?
Oth. That? What?
Æmil. Out, and alas, that was my Ladies voice.
Helpe, helpe hoa, helpe. Oh Ladie ſpeake againe,
Sweet *Deſdemona*, oh ſweet Miſtris, ſpeake.
Def. A guiltleſſe death, I dye.
Æmil. Oh who hath done this deed?
Def. No body : I my ſelfe, farewell:
Commend me to my kinde Lord : oh farewell.
Oth. Why, how ſhould ſhe be murdred?
Æmil. Alas : who knowes?
Oth. You heare her ſay her ſelfe, it was not I.
Æmil. She ſaid ſo : I muſt needs report the truth.
Oth. She's like a Liar gone to burning hell,
'Twas I that kill'd her.
Æmil. Oh the more Angell ſhe, and you the blacker Diuell.
Oth. She turn'd to folly : and ſhe was a whore.
Æmil. Thou do'ſt bely her, and thou art a diuell.
Oth. She was falſe as water.
Æmil. Thou art raſh as fire, to ſay
That ſhe was falſe. Oh ſhe was heauenly true.
Oth. *Caſſio* did top her : Ask thy husband elſe.
O, I were damn'd beneath all depth in hell:
But that I did proceed vpon iuſt grounds
To this extremity. Thy Husband knew it all.
Æmil.

Æmil. My Husband?
Oth. Thy Husband.
Æmil. That ſhe was falſe to Wedlocke?
Oth. I, with *Caſſio*: had ſhe bin true,
If Heauen would make me ſuch another world,
Of one entyre and perfect Chryſolite,
I'ld not haue ſold her for it.
Æmil. My Husband?
Oth. I, 'twas he that told me on her firſt,
An honeſt man he is, and hates the ſlime
That ſtickes on filthy deeds.
Æmil. My Husband?
Oth. What needs this itterance, Woman?
I ſay, thy Husband.
Æmil. Oh Miſtris,
Villany hath made mockes with loue:
My Husband ſay ſhe was falſe?
Oth. He, Woman;
I ſay thy Husband: Do'ſt vnderſtand the word?
My Friend, thy Husband; honeſt, honeſt *Iago*.
Æmil. If he ſay ſo, may his pernicious Soule
Rot halfe a graine a day: he lyes to'th'heart,
She was too fond of her moſt filthy Bargaine.
Oth. Hah?
Æmil. Do thy woſt:
This deede of thine is no more worthy Heauen,
Then thou was't worthy her.
Oth. Peace, you were beſt.
Æmil. Thou haſt not halfe that powre to do me harm,
As I haue to be hurt. Oh Gull, oh dolt,
As ignorant as durt: thou haſt done a deed
(I care not for thy Sword) Ile make thee known,
Though I loſt twenty liues. Helpe, helpe, hoa, helpe:
The Moore hath kill'd my Miſtris. Murther, murther.

Enter Montano, Gratiano, and Iago.

Mon. What is the matter? How now Generall?
Æmil. Oh, are you come, *Iago*: you haue done well,
That men muſt lay their Murthers on your necke.
Gra. What is the matter?
Æmil. Diſproue this Villaine, if thou bee'ſt a man:
He ſayes, thou told'ſt him that his wife was falſe:
I know thou did'ſt not: thou'rt not ſuch a Villain.
Speake, for my heart is full.
Iago. I told him what I thought,
And told no more
Then what he found himſelfe was apt, and true.
Æmil. But did you euer tell him,
She was falſe?
Iago. I did.
Æmil. You told a Lye an odious damned Lye:
Vpon my Soule, a Lye; a wicked Lye.
Shee falſe with *Caſſio*?
Did you ſay with *Caſſio*?
Iago. With *Caſſio*, Miſtris?
Go too, charme your tongue.
Emil. I will not charme my Tongue;
I am bound to ſpeake,
My Miſtris heere lyes murthered in her bed.
All. Oh Heauens, forefend.
Emil. And your reports haue ſet the Murder on.
Othello. Nay ſtare not Maſters,
It is true indeede.
Gra. 'Tis a ſtrange Truth.
Mont. O monſtrous Acte.
Emil. Villany, villany, villany:
I thinke vpon't, I thinke: I ſmel't: O Villany:
I thought ſo then: Ile kill my ſelfe for greefe.
O villany! villany!
Iago. What, are you mad?
I charge you get you home.
Emil. Good Gentlemen, let me haue leaue to ſpeake:
'Tis proper I obey him; but not now:
Perchance *Iago*, I will ne're go home.
Oth. Oh, oh, oh.
Emil. Nay, lay thee downe, and roare:
For thou haſt kill'd the ſweeteſt innocent,
That ere did lift vp eye.
Oth. Oh ſhe was fowle!
I ſcarſe did know you Vnkle, there lies your Neece,
Whoſe breath (indeed) theſe hands haue newly ſtopp'd:
I know this acte ſhewes horrible and grim.
Gra. Poore *Deſdemon*:
I am glad thy Father's dead,
Thy Match was mortall to him: and pure greefe
Shore his old thred in twaine. Did he liue now,
This ſight would make him do a deſperate turne:
Yea, curſe his better Angell from his ſide,
And fall to Reprobance.
Oth. 'Tis pittifull: but yet *Iago* knowes
That ſhe with *Caſſio*, hath the Act of ſhame,
A thouſand times committed. *Caſſio* confeſt it,
And ſhe did gratifie his amorous workes
With that Recognizance and pledge of Loue
Which I firſt gaue her: I ſaw it in his hand:
It was a Handkerchiefe, an Antique Token
My Father gaue my Mother.
Emil. Oh Heauen! oh heauenly Powres!
Iago. Come, hold your peace.
Emil. 'Twill out, 'twill out. I peace?
No, I will ſpeake as liberall as the North;
Let Heauen, and Men, and Diuels, let them all,
All, all, crie ſhame againſt me, yet Ile ſpeake.
Iago. Be wiſe, and get you home.
Emil. I will not.
Gra. Fye, your Sword vpon a Woman.
Emil. Oh thou dull Moore,
That Handkerchiefe thou ſpeak'ſt of
I found by Fortune, and did giue my Husband:
For often, with a ſolemne earneſtneſſe,
(More then indeed belong'd to ſuch a Trifle)
He begg'd of me, to ſteale't.
Iago. Villanous Whore.
Emil. She giue it *Caſſio*? No, alas I found it,
And I did giu't my Husband.
Iago. Filth, thou lyeſt.
Emil. By Heauen I do not, I do not Gentlemen:
Oh murd'rous Coxcombe, what ſhould ſuch a Foole
Do with ſo good a wife?
Oth. Are there no ſtones in Heauen,
But what ſerues for the Thunder?
Precious Villaine.
Gra. The woman falles:
Sure he hath kill'd his Wife.
Emil. I, I: oh lay me by my Miſtris ſide.
Gra. Hee's gone, but his wife's kill'd.
Mon. 'Tis a notorious Villain: take you this weapon
Which I haue recouer'd from the Moore:
Come guard the doore without, let him not paſſe,
But kill him rather. Ile after that ſame villaine,
For 'tis a damned Slaue. *Exit.*

Oth.

Oth. I am not valiant neither:
But euery Punie whipster gets my Sword.
But why should Honor out-liue Honesty?
Let it go all.
Æmil. What did thy Song boad Lady?
Hearke, canst thou heare me? I will play the Swan,
And dye in Musicke: *Willough, Willough, Willough.*
Moore, she was chaste: She lou'd thee, cruell Moore,
So come my Soule to blisse, as I speake true:
So speaking as I thinke, alas, I dye.
Oth. I haue another weapon in this Chamber,
It was a Sword of Spaine, the Ice brookes temper:
Oh heere it is: Vnkle I must come forth.
Gra. If thou attempt it, it will cost thee deere;
Thou hast no weapon, and perforce must suffer.
Oth. Looke in vpon me then, and speake with me,
Or naked as I am I will assault thee.
Gra. What is the matter?
Othel. Behold, I haue a weapon:
A better neuer did it selfe sustaine
Vpon a Soldiers Thigh. I haue seene the day,
That with this little Arme, and this good Sword,
I haue made my way through more impediments
Then twenty times your stop. But (oh vaine boast)
Who can controll his Fate? 'Tis not so now.
Be not affraid, though you do see me weapon'd:
Heere is my iournies end, heere is my butt
And verie Sea-marke of my vtmost Saile.
Do you go backe dismaid? 'Tis a lost feare:
Man but a Rush against *Othello's* brest,
And he retires. Where should *Othello* go?
Now: how dost thou looke now? Oh ill-Starr'd wench,
Pale as thy Smocke: when we shall meete at compt,
This looke of thine will hurle my Soule from Heauen,
And Fiends will snatch at it. Cold, cold, my Girle?
Euen like thy Chastity. O cursed, cursed Slaue!
Whip me ye Diuels,
From the possession of this Heauenly sight:
Blow me about in windes, roast me in Sulphure,
Wash me in steepe-downe gulfes of Liquid fire.
Oh *Desdemon*! dead *Desdemon*: dead. Oh, oh!

Enter Lodouico, Cassio, Montano, and Iago, with Officers.

Lod. Where is this rash, and most vnfortunate man?
Oth. That's he that was *Othello*: heere I am.
Lod. Where is that Viper?
Bring the Villaine forth.
Oth. I look down towards his feet; but that's a Fable,
If that thou bee'st a Diuell, I cannot kill thee.
Lod. Wrench his Sword from him.
Iago. I bleed Sir, but not kill'd.
Othel. I am not sorry neither, Il'd haue thee liue:
For in my sense, 'tis happinesse to die.
Lod. Oh thou *Othello*, that was once so good,
Falne in the practise of a cursed Slaue,
What shall be saide to thee.
Oth. Why any thing:
An honourable Murderer, if you will:
For nought I did in hate, but all in Honour.
Lod. This wretch hath part confest his Villany:
Did you and he consent in *Cassio's* death.
Oth. I.
Cas. Deere Generall, I neuer gaue you cause.
Oth. I do beleeue it, and I aske your pardon:
Will you, I pray, demand that demy-Diuell,
Why he hath thus ensnar'd my Soule and Body.
Iag. Demand me nothing: what you know, you know:
From this time forth, I neuer will speake word.
Lod. What? not to pray?
Gra. Torments will ope your lips.
Oth. Well, thou dost best.
Lod. Sir,
You shall vnderstand what hath befalne,
(Which, as I thinke, you know not) heere is a Letter
Found in the pocket of the slaine *Rodorigo*,
And heere another, the one of them imports
The death of *Cassio*, to be vndertooke
By *Rodorigo*.
Oth. O Villaine!
Cassio. Most Heathenish, and most grosse.
Lod. Now, heere's another discontented paper
Found in his pocket too: and this it seemes
Rodorigo meant t'haue sent this damned villaine:
But that (belike) *Iago* in the interim
Came in, and satisfi'd him.
Oth. Oh thou pernitious Caitiffe;
How came you (*Cassio*) by that Handkerchiefe
That was my wiues?
Cassio. I found it in my Chamber:
And he himselfe confest it but euen now,
That there he dropt it for a speciall purpose,
Which wrought to his desire.
Othel. O Foole, foole, foole!
Cassio. There is besides, in *Rodorigo's* Letter,
How he vpbraides *Iago*, that he made him
Braue me vpon the Watch: whereon it came
That I was cast: and euen but now he spake
(After long seeming dead) *Iago* hurt him,
Iago set him on.
Lod. You must forsake this roome, and go with vs:
Your Power, and your Command is taken off,
And *Cassio* rules in Cyprus. For this Slaue,
If there be any cunning Crueltie,
That can torment him much, and hold him long,
It shall be his. You shall close Prisoner rest,
Till that the Nature of your fault be knowne
To the Venetian State. Come, bring away.
Oth. Soft you; a word or two before you goe:
I haue done the State some seruice, and they know't:
No more of that. I pray you in your Letters,
When you shall these vnluckie deeds relate,
Speake of me, as I am. Nothing extenuate,
Nor set downe ought in malice.
Then must you speake,
Of one that lou'd not wisely, but too well:
Of one, not easily Iealious, but being wrought,
Perplexed in the extreame: Of one, whose hand
(Like the base Iudean) threw a Pearle away
Richer then all his Tribe: Of one, whose subdu'd Eyes,
Albeit vn-vsed to the melting moode,
Drops teares as fast as the Arabian Trees
Their Medicinable gumme. Set you downe this:
And say besides, that in *Aleppo* once,
Where a malignant, and a Turbond-Turke
Beate a Venetian, and traduc'd the State,
I tooke by th'throat the circumcised Dogge,
And smoate him, thus.
Lod. Oh bloody period.
Gra. All that is spoke, is marr'd.
Oth. I kist thee, ere I kill'd thee: No way but this,
Killing my selfe, to dye vpon a kisse. *Dyes*

Cassio.

Cas. This did I feare, but thought he had no weapon:
For he was great of heart.
Lod. Oh Sparton Dogge:
More fell then Anguish, Hunger, or the Sea:
Looke on the Tragicke Loading of this bed:
This is thy worke:
The Obiect poysons Sight,
Let it be hid. *Gratiano*, keepe the house,
And seize vpon the Fortunes of the Moore,
For they succeede on you. To you, Lord Gouernor,
Remaines th eCensure of this hellish villaine:
The Time, the Place, the Torture, oh inforce it:
My selfe will straight aboord, and to the State,
This heauie Act, with heauie heart relate. *Exeunt.*

FINIS.

The Names of the Actors.

(:*.*:)

OThello, *the Moore.*
Brabantio, *Father to Desdemona.*
Cassio, *an Honourable Lieutenant.*
Iago, *a Villaine.*
Rodorigo, *a gull'd Gentleman.*
Duke of Venice.
Senators.
Montano, *Gouernour of Cyprus.*
Gentlemen of Cyprus.
Lodouico, *and* Gratiano, *two Noble Venetians.*
Saylors.
Clowne.

Desdemona, *Wife to Othello.*
Æmilia, *Wife to Iago.*
Bianca, *a Curtezan.*

THE TRAGEDIE OF Anthonie, and Cleopatra.

Actus Primus. Scæna Prima.

Enter Demetrius and Philo.

Philo.

NAy, but this dotage of our Generals
Ore-flowes the meaſure : thoſe his goodly eyes
That o're the Files and Muſters of the Warre,
Haue glow'd like plated Mars:
Now bend, now turne
The Office and Deuotion of their view
Vpon a Tawny Front. His Captaines heart,
Which in the ſcuffles of great Fights hath burſt
The Buckles on his breſt, reneages all temper,
And is become the Bellowes and the Fan
To coole a Gypſies Luſt.

Flouriſh. Enter Anthony, Cleopatra her Ladies, the Traine, with Eunuchs fanning her.

Looke where they come :
Take but good note, and you ſhall ſee in him
(The triple Pillar of the world) transform'd
Into a Strumpets Foole. Behold and ſee.

Cleo. If it be Loue indeed, tell me how much.

Ant. There's beggery in the loue that can be reckon'd

Cleo. Ile ſet a bourne how farre to be belou'd.

Ant. Then muſt thou needes finde out new Heauen, new Earth.

Enter a Meſſenger.

Meſ. Newes (my good Lord) from Rome.

Ant. Grates me, the ſumme.

Cleo. Nay heare them *Anthony*.
Fuluia perchance is angry : Or who knowes,
If the ſcarſe-bearded *Cæſar* haue not ſent
His powrefull Mandate to you. Do this, or this ;
Take in that Kingdome, and Infranchiſe that :
Perform't, or elſe we damne thee.

Ant. How, my Loue?

Cleo. Perchance? Nay, and moſt like :
You muſt not ſtay heere longer, your diſmiſſion
Is come from *Cæſar*, therefore heare it *Anthony*.
Where's *Fuluias* Proceſſe? (*Cæſars* I would ſay) both?
Call in the Meſſengers : As I am Egypts Queene,
Thou bluſheſt *Anthony*, and that blood of thine
Is *Cæſars* homager : elſe ſo thy cheeke payes ſhame,
When ſhrill-tongu'd *Fuluia* ſcolds. The Meſſengers.

Ant. Let Rome in Tyber melt, and the wide Arch
Of the raing'd Empire fall : Heere is my ſpace,
Kingdomes are clay : Our dungie earth alike
Feeds Beaſt as Man ; the Nobleneſſe of life
Is to do thus : when ſuch a mutuall paire,
And ſuch a twaine can doo't, in which I binde
One paine of puniſhment, the world to weete
We ſtand vp Peereleſſe.

Cleo. Excellent falſhood :
Why did he marry *Fuluia*, and not loue her?
Ile ſeeme the Foole I am not. *Anthony* will be himſelfe.

Ant. But ſtirr'd by *Cleopatra*.
Now for the loue of Loue, and her ſoft houres,
Let's not confound the time with Conference harſh;
There's not a minute of our liues ſhould ſtretch
Without ſome pleaſure now. What ſport to night?

Cleo. Heare the Ambaſſadors.

Ant. Fye wrangling Queene :
Whom euery thing becomes, to chide, to laugh,
To weepe : who euery paſſion fully ſtriues
To make it ſelfe (in Thee) faire, and admir'd.
No Meſſenger but thine, and all alone, to night
Wee'l wander through the ſtreets, and note
The qualities of people. Come my Queene,
Laſt night you did deſire it. Speake not to vs.

Exeunt with the Traine.

Dem. Is *Cæſar* with *Anthonius* priz'd ſo ſlight?

Philo. Sir ſometimes when he is not *Anthony*,
He comes too ſhort of that great Property
Which ſtill ſhould go with *Anthony*.

Dem. I am full ſorry, that hee approues the common Lyar, who thus ſpeakes of him at Rome ; but I will hope of better deeds to morrow. Reſt you happy. *Exeunt*

Enter Enobarbus, Lamprius, a Southſayer, Rannius, Lucillius, Charmian, Iras, Mardian the Eunuch, and Alexas.

Char. L. *Alexas*, ſweet *Alexas*, moſt any thing *Alexas*, almoſt moſt abſolute *Alexas*, where's the Soothſayer that you prais'd ſo to'th'Queene? Oh that I knewe this Husband, which you ſay, muſt change his Hornes with Garlands.

Alex. Soothſayer.

Sooth. Your will?

Char. Is this the Man? Is't you ſir that know things?

Sooth. In Natures infinite booke of Secrecie, a little I can read.

Alex. Shew him your hand.

Enob. Bring in the Banket quickly : Wine enough,

Cleopa

Cleopatra's health to drinke.

Char. Good sir, giue me good Fortune.

Sooth. I make not, but foresee.

Char. Pray then, foresee me one.

Sooth. You shall be yet farre fairer then you are.

Char. He meanes in flesh.

Iras. No, you shall paint when you are old.

Char. Wrinkles forbid.

Alex. Vex not his prescience, be attentiue.

Char. Hush.

Sooth. You shall be more belouing, then beloued.

Char. I had rather heate my Liuer with drinking.

Alex. Nay, heare him.

Char. Good now some excellent Fortune: Let mee be married to three Kings in a forenoone, and Widdow them all: Let me haue a Childe at fifty, to whom *Herode* of Iewry may do Homage. Finde me to marrie me with *Octauius Cæsar*, and companion me with my Mistris.

Sooth. You shall out-liue the Lady whom you serue.

Char. Oh excellent, I loue long life better then Figs.

Sooth. You haue seene and proued a fairer former fortune, then that which is to approach.

Char. Then belike my Children shall haue no names: Prythee how many Boyes and Wenches must I haue.

Sooth. If euery of your wishes had a wombe, & foretell euery wish, a Million.

Char. Out Foole, I forgiue thee for a Witch.

Alex. You thinke none but your sheets are priuie to your wishes.

Char. Nay come, tell *Iras* hers.

Alex. Wee'l know all our Fortunes.

Enob. Mine, and most of our Fortunes to night, shall be drunke to bed.

Iras. There's a Palme presages Chastity, if nothing els.

Char. E'ne as the o're-flowing Nylus presageth Famine.

Iras. Go you wilde Bedfellow, you cannot Soothsay.

Char. Nay, if an oyly Palme bee not a fruitfull Prognostication, I cannot scratch mine eare. Prythee tel her but a worky day Fortune.

Sooth. Your Fortunes are alike.

Iras. But how, but how, giue me particulars.

Sooth. I haue said.

Iras. Am I not an inch of Fortune better then she?

Char. Well, if you were but an inch of fortune better then I: where would you choose it.

Iras. Not in my Husbands nose.

Char. Our worser thoughts Heauens mend.

Alexas. Come, his Fortune, his Fortune. Oh let him mary a woman that cannot go, sweet *Isis*, I beseech thee, and let her dye too, and giue him a worse, and let worse follow worse, till the worst of all follow him laughing to his graue, fifty-fold a Cuckold. Good *Isis* heare me this Prayer, though thou denie me a matter of more waight: good *Isis* I beseech thee.

Iras. Amen, deere Goddesse, heare that prayer of the people. For, as it is a heart-breaking to see a handsome man loose-Wiu'd, so it is a deadly sorrow, to beholde a foule Knaue vncuckolded: Therefore deere *Isis* keep *decorum*, and Fortune him accordingly.

Char. Amen.

Alex. Lo now, if it lay in their hands to make mee a Cuckold, they would make themselues Whores, but they'ld doo't.

Enter Cleopatra.

Enob. Hush, heere comes *Anthony*.

Char. Not he, the Queene.

Cleo. Saue you, my Lord.

Enob. No Lady.

Cleo. Was he not heere?

Char. No Madam.

Cleo. He was dispos'd to mirth, but on the sodaine
A Romane thought hath strooke him.
Enobarbus?

Enob. Madam.

Cleo. Seeke him, and bring him hither: wher's *Alexias*?

Alex. Heere at your seruice.
My Lord approaches.

Enter Anthony, with a Messenger.

Cleo. We will not looke vpon him:
Go with vs. *Exeunt.*

Messen. Fuluia thy Wife,
First came into the Field.

Ant. Against my Brother *Lucius*?

Messen. I: but soone that Warre had end,
And the times state
Made friends of them, ioynting their force 'gainst *Cæsar*,
Whose better issue in the warre from Italy,
Vpon the first encounter draue them.

Ant. Well, what worst.

Mess. The Nature of bad newes infects the Teller.

Ant. When it concernes the Foole or Coward: On.
Things that are past, are done, with me. 'Tis thus,
Who tels me true, though in his Tale lye death,
I heare him as he flatter'd.

Mes. Labienus (this is stiffe-newes)
Hath with his Parthian Force
Extended Asia: from Euphrates his conquering
Banner shooke, from Syria to Lydia,
And to Ionia, whil'st——

Ant. Anthony thou would'st say.

Mes. Oh my Lord.

Ant. Speake to me home,
Mince not the generall tongue, name
Cleopatra as she is call'd in Rome:
Raile thou in *Fuluia's* phrase, and taunt my faults
With such full Licence, as both Truth and Malice
Haue power to vtter. Oh then we bring forth weeds,
When our quicke windes lye still, and our illes told vs
Is as our earing: fare thee well awhile.

Mes. At your Noble pleasure. *Exit Messenger.*

Enter another Messenger.

Ant. From *Scicion* how the newes? Speake there.

1. *Mes.* The man from *Scicion*,
Is there such an one?

2. *Mes.* He stayes vpon your will.

Ant. Let him appeare:
These strong Egyptian Fetters I must breake,
Or loose my selfe in dotage.

Enter another Messenger with a Letter.

What are you?

3. *Mes. Fuluia* thy wife is dead.

Ant. Where dyed she.

Mes. In *Scicion*, her length of sicknesse,
With what else more serious,
Importeth thee to know, this beares.

Antho. Forbeare me
There's a great Spirit gone, thus did I desire it:
What our contempts doth often hurle from vs,

x We

We wiſh it ours againe. The preſent pleaſure,
By reuolution lowring, does become
The oppoſite of it ſelfe: ſhe's good being gon,
The hand could plucke her backe, that ſhou'd her on.
I muſt from this enchanting Queene breake off,
Ten thouſand harmes, more then the illes I know
My idleneſſe doth hatch.

Enter Enobarbus.

How now *Enobarbus.*

Eno. What's your pleaſure, Sir?

Anth. I muſt with haſte from hence.

Eno. Why then we kill all our Women. We ſee how mortall an vnkindneſſe is to them, if they ſuffer our departure death's the word.

Ant. I muſt be gone.

Eno. Vnder a compelling an occaſion, let women die. It were pitty to caſt them away for nothing, though betweene them and a great cauſe, they ſhould be eſteemed nothing. *Cleopatra* catching but the leaſt noyſe of this, dies inſtantly: I haue ſeene her dye twenty times vppon farre poorer moment: I do think there is mettle in death, which commits ſome louing acte vpon her, ſhe hath ſuch a celerity in dying.

Ant. She is cunning paſt mans thought.

Eno. Alacke Sir no, her paſſions are made of nothing but the fineſt part of pure Loue. We cannot cal her winds and waters, ſighes and teares: They are greater ſtormes and Tempeſts then Almanackes can report. This cannot be cunning in her; if it be, ſhe makes a ſhowre of Raine as well as Ioue.

Ant. Would I had neuer ſeene her.

Eno. Oh ſir, you had then left vnſeene a wonderfull peece of worke, which not to haue beene bleſt withall, would haue diſcredited your Trauaile.

Ant. *Fuluia* is dead.

Eno. Sir.

Ant. *Fuluia* is dead.

Eno. *Fuluia?*

Ant. Dead.

Eno. Why ſir, giue the Gods a thankefull Sacrifice: when it pleaſeth their Deities to take the wife of a man from him, it ſhewes to man the Tailors of the earth: comforting therein, that when olde Robes are worne out, there are members to make new. If there were no more Women but *Fuluia*, then had you indeede a cut, and the caſe to be lamented: This greefe is crown'd with Conſolation, your old Smocke brings foorth a new Petticoate, and indeed the teares liue in an Onion, that ſhould water this ſorrow.

Ant. The buſineſſe ſhe hath broached in the State,
Cannot endure my abſence.

Eno. And the buſineſſe you haue broach'd heere cannot be without you, eſpecially that of *Cleopatra's*, which wholly depends on your abode.

Ant. No more light Anſweres:
Let our Officers
Haue notice what we purpoſe. I ſhall breake
The cauſe of our Expedience to the Queene,
And get her loue to part. For not alone
The death of *Fuluia*, with more vrgent touches
Do ſtrongly ſpeake to vs: but the Letters too
Of many our contriuing Friends in Rome,
Petition vs at home. *Sextus Pompeius*
Haue giuen the dare to *Cæſar*, and commands
The Empire of the Sea. Our ſlippery people,
Whoſe Loue is neuer link'd to the deſeruer,
Till his deſerts are paſt, begin to throw
Pompey the great, and all his Dignities
Vpon his Sonne, who high in Name and Power,
Higher then both in Blood and Life, ſtands vp
For the maine Souldier. Whoſe quality going on,
The ſides o'th'world may danger. Much is breeding,
Which like the Courſers heire, hath yet but life,
And not a Serpents poyſon. Say our pleaſure,
To ſuch whoſe places vnder vs, require
Our quicke remoue from hence.

Enob. I ſhall doo't.

Enter Cleopatra, Charmian, Alexas, and Iras.

Cleo. Where is he?

Char. I did not ſee him ſince.

Cleo. See where he is,
Whoſe with him, what he does:
I did not ſend you. If you finde him ſad,
Say I am dauncing: if in Myrth, report
That I am ſodaine ſicke. Quicke, and returne.

Char. Madam, me thinkes if you did loue him deerly,
You do not hold the method, to enforce
The like from him.

Cleo. What ſhould I do, I do not?

Ch. In each thing giue him way, croſſe him in nothing.

Cleo. Thou teacheſt like a foole: the way to loſe him.

Char. Tempt him not ſo too farre. I wiſh forbeare,
In time we hate that which we often feare.

Enter Anthony.

But heere comes *Anthony.*

Cleo. I am ſicke, and ſullen.

An. I am ſorry to giue breathing to my purpoſe.

Cleo. Helpe me away deere *Charmian*, I ſhall fall,
It cannot be thus long, the ſides of Nature
Will not ſuſtaine it.

Ant. Now my deereſt Queene.

Cleo. Pray you ſtand farther from mee.

Ant. What's the matter?

Cleo. I know by that ſame eye ther's ſome good news.
What ſayes the married woman you may goe?
Would ſhe had neuer giuen you leaue to come.
Let her not ſay 'tis I that keepe you heere,
I haue no power vpon you: Hers you are.

Ant. The Gods beſt know.

Cleo. Oh neuer was there Queene
So mightily betrayed: yet at the firſt
I ſaw the Treaſons planted.

Ant. *Cleopatra.*

Cleo. Why ſhould I thinke you can be mine, & true,
(Though you in ſwearing ſhake the Throaned Gods)
Who haue beene falſe to *Fuluia?*
Riotous madneſſe,
To be entangled with thoſe mouth-made vowes,
Which breake themſelues in ſwearing.

Ant. Moſt ſweet Queene.

Cleo. Nay pray you ſeeke no colour for your going,
But bid farewell, and goe:
When you ſued ſtaying,
Then was the time for words: No going then,
Eternity was in our Lippes, and Eyes,
Bliſſe in our browes bent: none our parts ſo poore,
But was a race of Heauen. They are ſo ſtill,
Or thou the greateſt Souldier of the world,
Art turn'd the greateſt Lyar.

Ant. How now Lady?

Cleo. I would I had thy inches, thou ſhould'ſt know
There were a heart in Egypt.
Ant. Heare me Queene:
The ſtrong neceſſity of Time, commands
Our Seruicles a-while: but my full heart
Remaines in vſe with you. Our Italy,
Shines o're with ciuill Swords; *Sextus Pompeius*
Makes his approaches to the Port of Rome,
Equality of two Domeſticke powers,
Breed ſcrupulous faction: The hated growne to ſtrength
Are newly growne to Loue: The condemn'd *Pompey*,
Rich in his Fathers Honor, creepes apace
Into the hearts of ſuch, as haue not thriued
Vpon the preſent ſtate, whoſe Numbers threaten,
And quietneſſe growne ſicke of reſt, would purge
By any deſperate change: My more particular,
And that which moſt with you ſhould ſafe my going,
Is *Fuluias* death.
Cleo. Though age from folly could not giue me freedom
It does from childiſhneſſe. Can *Fuluia* dye?
Ant. She's dead my Queene.
Looke heere, and at thy Soueraigne leyſure read
The Garboyles ſhe awak'd: at the laſt, beſt,
See when, and where ſhee died.
Cleo. O moſt falſe Loue!
Where be the Sacred Violles thou ſhould'ſt fill
With ſorrowfull water? Now I ſee, I ſee,
In *Fuluias* death, how mine receiu'd ſhall be.
Ant. Quarrell no more, but bee prepar'd to know
The purpoſes I beare: which are, or ceaſe,
As you ſhall giue th'aduice. By the fire
That quickens Nylus ſlime, I go from hence
Thy Souldier, Seruant, making Peace or Warre,
As thou affects.
Cleo. Cut my Lace, *Charmian* come,
But let it be, I am quickly ill, and well,
So *Anthony* loues.
Ant. My precious Queene forbeare,
And giue true euidence to his Loue, which ſtands
An honourable Triall.
Cleo. So *Fuluia* told me.
I prythee turne aſide, and weepe for her,
Then bid adiew to me, and ſay the teares
Belong to Egypt. Good now, play one Scene
Of excellent diſſembling, and let it looke
Like perfect Honor.
Ant. You'l heat my blood no more?
Cleo. You can do better yet: but this is meetly.
Ant. Now by Sword.
Cleo. And Target. Still he mends.
But this is not the beſt. Looke prythee *Charmian*,
How this Herculean Roman do's become
The carriage of his chafe.
Ant. Ile leaue you Lady.
Cleo. Courteous Lord, one word:
Sir, you and I muſt part, but that's not it:
Sir, you and I haue lou'd, but there's not it:
That you know well, ſomething it is I would:
Oh, my Obliuion is a very *Anthony*,
And I am all forgotten.
Ant. But that your Royalty
Holds Idleneſſe your ſubiect, I ſhould take you
For Idleneſſe it ſelfe.
Cleo. 'Tis ſweating Labour,
To beare ſuch Idleneſſe ſo neere the heart
As *Cleopatra* this. But Sir, forgiue me,
Since my becommings kill me, when they do not
Eye well to you. Your Honor calles you hence,
Therefore be deafe to my vnpittied Folly,
And all the Gods go with you. Vpon your Sword
Sit Lawrell victory, and ſmooth ſucceſſe
Be ſtrew'd before your feete.
Ant. Let vs go.
Come: Our ſeparation ſo abides and flies,
That thou reciding heere, goes yet with mee;
And I hence fleeting, heere remaine with thee.
Away. *Exeunt.*

Enter Octauius reading a Letter, Lepidus, and their Traine.

Cæſ. You may ſee *Lepidus*, and henceforth know,
It is not *Cæſars* Naturall vice, to hate
One great Competitor. From Alexandria
This is the newes: He fiſhes, drinkes, and waſtes
The Lampes of night in reuell: Is not more manlike
Then *Cleopatra*: nor the Queene of *Ptolomy*
More Womanly then he. Hardly gaue audience
Or vouchſafe to thinke he had Partners. You
Shall finde there a man, who is th'abſtracts of all faults,
That all men follow.
Lep. I muſt not thinke
There are, euils enow to darken all his goodneſſe:
His faults in him, ſeeme as the Spots of Heauen,
More fierie by nights Blackneſſe; Hereditarie,
Rather then purchaſte: what he cannot change,
Then what he chooſes.
Cæſ. You are too indulgent. Let's graunt it is not
Amiſſe to tumble on the bed of *Ptolomy*,
To giue a Kingdome for a Mirth, to ſit
And keepe the turne of Tipling with a Slaue,
To reele the ſtreets at noone, and ſtand the Buffet
With knaues that ſmels of ſweate: Say this becoms him
(As his compoſure muſt be rare indeed,
Whom theſe things cannot blemiſh) yet muſt *Anthony*
No way excuſe his foyles, when we do beare
So great waight in his lightneſſe. If he fill'd
His vacancie with his Voluptuouſneſſe,
Full ſurfets, and the drineſſe of his bones,
Call on him for't. But to confound ſuch time,
That drummes him from his ſport, and ſpeakes as lowd
As his owne State, and ours, 'tis to be chid:
As we rate Boyes, who being mature in knowledge,
Pawne their experience to their preſent pleaſure,
And ſo rebell to iudgement.

Enter a Meſſenger.

Lep. Heere's more newes.
Meſ. Thy biddings haue beene done, & euerie houre
Moſt Noble *Cæſar*, ſhalt thou haue report
How 'tis abroad. *Pompey* is ſtrong at Sea,
And it appeares, he is belou'd of thoſe
That only haue feard *Cæſar*: to the Ports
The diſcontents repaire, and mens reports
Giue him much wrong'd.
Cæſ. I ſhould haue knowne no leſſe,
It hath bin taught vs from the primall ſtate
That he which is was wiſht, vntill he were:
And the ebb'd man,
Ne're lou'd, till ne're worth loue,
Comes fear'd, by being lack'd. This common bodie,
Like to a Vagabond Flagge vpon the Streame,
Goes too, and backe, lacking the varrying tyde

To rot it ſelfe with motion.
Meſ. *Cæſar* I bring thee word,
Menacrates and *Menas* famous Pyrates
Makes the Sea ſerue them, which they eare and wound
With keeles of euery kinde. Many hot inrodes
They make in Italy, the Borders Maritime
Lacke blood to thinke on't, and fluſh youth reuolt,
No Veſſell can peepe forth : but 'tis as ſoone
Taken as ſeene : for *Pompeyes* name ſtrikes more
Then could his Warre reſiſted.
Cæſar. *Anthony,*
Leaue thy laſciuious Vaſſailes. When thou once
Was beaten from *Medena,* where thou ſlew'ſt
Hirſius, and *Pauſa* Conſuls, at thy heele
Did Famine follow, whom thou fought'ſt againſt,
(Though daintily brought vp) with patience more
Then Sauages could ſuffer. Thou did'ſt drinke
The ſtale of Horſes, and the gilded Puddle
Which Beaſts would cough at. Thy pallat thē did daine
The rougheſt Berry, on the rudeſt Hedge.
Yea, like the Stagge, when Snow the Paſture ſheets,
The barkes of Trees thou brows'd. On the Alpes,
It is reported thou did'ſt eate ſtrange fleſh,
Which ſome did dye to looke on : And all this
(It wounds thine Honor that I ſpeake it now)
Was borne ſo like a Soldiour, that thy cheeke
So much as lank'd not.
Lep. 'Tis pitty of him.
Cæſ. Let his ſhames quickely
Driue him to Rome, 'tis time we twaine
Did ſhew our ſelues i'th'Field, and to that end
Aſſemble me immediate counſell, *Pompey*
Thriues in our Idleneſſe.
Lep. To morrow *Cæſar,*
I ſhall be furniſht to informe you rightly
Both what by Sea and Land I can be able
To front this preſent time.
Cæſ. Til which encounter, it is my buſines too. Farwell.
Lep. Farwell my Lord, what you ſhal know mean time
Of ſtirres abroad, I ſhall beſeech you Sir
To let me be partaker.
Cæſar. Doubt not ſir, I knew it for my Bond. *Exeunt*

Enter Cleopatra, Charmian, Iras, & Mardian.

Cleo. *Charmian.*
Char. Madam.
Cleo. Ha, ha, giue me to drinke *Mandragoru.*
Char. Why Madam?
Cleo. That I might ſleepe out this great gap of time :
My *Anthony* is away.
Char. You thinke of him too much.
Cleo. O 'tis Treaſon.
Char. Madam, I truſt not ſo.
Cleo. Thou, Eunuch *Mardian?*
Mar. What's your Highneſſe pleaſure?
Cleo. Not now to heare thee ſing. I take no pleaſure
In ought an Eunuch ha's : Tis well for thee,
That being vnſeminar'd, thy freer thoughts
May not flye forth of Egypt. Haſt thou Affections?
Mar. Yes gracious Madam.
Cleo. Indeed?
Mar. Not in deed Madam, for I can do nothing
But what in deede is honeſt to be done :
Yet haue I fierce Affections, and thinke
What Venus did with Mars.
Cleo. Oh *Charmion* :
Where think'ſt thou he is now? Stands he, or ſits he?
Or does he walke? Or is he on his Horſe?
Oh happy horſe to beare the weight of *Anthony*!
Do brauely Horſe, for wot'ſt thou whom thou moou'ſt,
The demy *Atlas* of this Earth, the Arme
And Burganet of men. Hee's ſpeaking now,
Or murmuring, where's my Serpent of old Nyle,
(For ſo he cals me:) Now I feede my ſelfe
With moſt delicious poyſon. Thinke on me
That am with Phœbus amorous pinches blacke,
And wrinkled deepe in time. Broad-fronted *Cæſar,*
When thou was't heere aboue the ground, I was
A morſell for a Monarke : and great *Pompey*
Would ſtand and make his eyes grow in my brow,
There would he anchor his Aſpect, and dye
With looking on his life.

Enter Alexas from Cæſar.

Alex. Soueraigne of Egypt, haile.
Cleo. How much vnlike art thou *Marke Anthony*?
Yet comming from him, that great Med'cine hath
With his Tinct gilded thee.
How goes it with my braue *Marke Anthonie*?
Alex. Laſt thing he did (deere Qu ene)
He kiſt the laſt of many doubled kiſſes
This Orient Pearle. His ſpeech ſtickes in my heart.
Cleo. Mine eare muſt plucke it thence.
Alex. Good Friend, quoth he :
Say the firme Roman to great Egypt ſends
This treaſure of an Oyſter : at whoſe foote
To mend the petty preſent, I will peece
Her opulent Throne, with Kingdomes. All the Eaſt,
(Say thou) ſhall call her Miſtris. So he nodded,
And ſoberly did mount an Arme-gaunt Steede,
Who neigh'd ſo hye, that what I would haue ſpoke,
Was beaſtly dumbe by him.
Cleo. What was he ſad, or merry?
Alex. Like to the time o'th'yeare, between ẙ extremes
Of hot and cold, he was nor ſad nor merrie.
Cleo. Oh well diuided diſpoſition: Note him,
Note him good *Charmian*, 'tis the man; but note him.
He was not ſad, for he would ſhine on thoſe
That make their lookes by his. He was not merrie,
Which ſeem'd to tell them, his remembrance lay
In Egypt with his ioy, but betweene both.
Oh heauenly mingle! Bee'ſt thou ſad, or merrie,
The violence of either thee becomes,
So do's it no mans elſe. Met'ſt thou my Poſts?
Alex. I Madam, twenty ſeuerall Meſſengers.
Why do you ſend ſo thicke?
Cleo. Who's borne that day, when I forget to ſend to *Anthonie*, ſhall dye a Begger. Inke and paper *Charmian.* Welcome my good *Alexas.* Did I *Charmian*, euer loue *Cæſar* ſo?
Char. Oh that braue *Cæſar*!
Cleo. Be choak'd with ſuch another Emphaſis,
Say the braue *Anthony.*
Char. The valiant *Cæſar.*
Cleo. By *Iſis*, I will giue thee bloody teeth,
If thou with *Cæſar* Parago nagaine :
My man of men.
Char. By your moſt gracious pardon,
I ſing but after you.
Cleo. My Sallad dayes,
When I was greene in iudgement, cold in blood,
To ſay, as I ſaide then. But come, away,
Get me Inke and Paper,

Hee

he ſhall haue euery day a ſeuerall greeting, or Ile vnpeople Egypt. *Exeunt*

Enter Pompey, Menecrates, and Menas, in warlike manner.

Pom. If the great Gods be iuſt, they ſhall aſſiſt
The deeds of iuſteſt men.

Mene. Know worthy *Pompey*, that what they do delay, they not deny.

Pom. Whiles we are ſutors to their Throne, decayes the thing we ſue for.

Mene. We ignorant of our ſelues,
Begge often our owne harmes, which the wiſe Powres
Deny vs for our good: ſo finde we profit
By looſing of our Prayers.

Pom. I ſhall do well:
The people loue me, and the Sea is mine;
My powers are Creſſent, and my Auguring hope
Sayes it will come to'th'full. *Marke Anthony*
In Egypt ſits at dinner, and will make
No warres without doores. *Cæſar* gets money where
He looſes hearts: *Lepidus* flatters both,
Of both is flatter'd: but he neither loues,
Nor either cares for him.

Mene. *Cæſar* and *Lepidus* are in the field,
A mighty ſtrength they carry.

Pom. Where haue you this? 'Tis falſe.

Mene. From *Siluius*, Sir.

Pom. He dreames: I know they are in Rome together
Looking for *Anthony*: but all the charmes of Loue,
Salt *Cleopatra* ſoften thy wand lip,
Let Witchcraft ioyne with Beauty, Luſt with both,
Tye vp the Libertine in a field of Feaſts,
Keepe his Braine fuming. Epicurean Cookes,
Sharpen with cloyleſſe ſawce his Appetite,
That ſleepe and feeding may prorogue his Honour,
Euen till a Lethied dulneſſe——

Enter Varrius.

How now *Varrius*?

Var. This is moſt certaine, that I ſhall deliuer:
Marke Anthony is euery houre in Rome
Expected. Since he went from Egypt, 'tis
A ſpace for farther Trauaile.

Pom. I could haue giuen leſſe matter
A better eare. *Menas*, I did not thinke
This amorous Surfetter would haue donn'd his Helme
For ſuch a petty Warre: His Souldierſhip
Is twice the other twaine: But let vs reare
The higher our Opinion, that our ſtirring
Can from the lap of Egypts Widdow, plucke
The neere Luſt-wearied *Anthony*.

Mene. I cannot hope,
Cæſar and *Anthony* ſhall well greet together;
His Wife that's dead, did treſpaſſes to *Cæſar*,
His Brother wan'd vpon him, although I thinke
Not mou'd by *Anthony*.

Pom. I know not *Menas*,
How leſſer Enmities may giue way to greater,
Were't not that we ſtand vp againſt them all:
'Twer pregnant they ſhould ſquare between themſelues,
For they haue entertained cauſe enough
To draw their ſwords: but how the feare of vs
May Ciment their diuiſions, and binde vp
The petty difference, we yet not know:
Bee't as our Gods will haue't; it onely ſtands
Our liues vpon, to vſe our ſtrongeſt hands
Come *Menas*. *Exeunt.*

Enter Enobarbus and Lepidus.

Lep. Good *Enobarbus*, 'tis a worthy deed,
And ſhall become you well, to intreat your Captaine
To ſoft and gentle ſpeech.

Enob. I ſhall intreat him
To anſwer like himſelfe: if *Cæſar* moue him,
Let *Anthony* looke ouer *Cæſars* head,
And ſpeake as lowd as Mars. By Iupiter,
Were I the wearer of *Anthonio's* Beard,
I would not ſhaue't to day.

Lep. 'Tis not a time for priuate ſtomacking.

Eno. Euery time ſerues for the matter that is then borne in't.

Lep. But ſmall to greater matters muſt giue way.

Eno. Not if the ſmall come firſt.

Lep. Your ſpeech is paſſion: but pray you ſtirre
No Embers vp. Heere comes the Noble *Anthony*.

Enter Anthony and Ventidius.

Eno. And yonder *Cæſar*.

Enter Cæſar, Mecenas, and Agrippa.

Ant. If we compoſe well heere, to Parthia:
Hearke *Ventidius*.

Cæſar. I do not know *Mecenas*, aske *Agrippa*.

Lep. Noble Friends:
That which combin'd vs was moſt great, and let not
A leaner action rend vs. What's amiſſe,
May it be gently heard. When we debate
Our triuiall difference loud, we do commit
Murther in healing wounds. Then Noble Partners,
The rather for I earneſtly beſeech,
Touch you the ſowreſt points with ſweeteſt tearmes,
Nor curſtneſſe grow to'th'matter.

Ant. 'Tis ſpoken well:
Were we before our Armies, and to fight,
I ſhould do thus. *Flouriſh.*

Cæſ. Welcome to Rome.

Ant. Thanke you.

Cæſ. Sit.

Ant, Sit ſir.

Cæſ. Nay then.

Ant. I learne, you take things ill, which are not ſo:
Or being, concerne you not.

Cæſ. I muſt be laught at, if or for nothing, or a little, I
Should ſay my ſelfe offended, and with you
Chiefely i'th'world. More laught at, that I ſhould
Once name you derogately: when to ſound your name
It not concern'd me.

Ant. My being in Egypt *Cæſar*, what was't to you?

Cæſ. No more then my reciding heere at Rome
Might be to you in Egypt: yet if you there
Did practiſe on my State, your being in Egypt
Might be my queſtion.

Ant. How intend you, practis'd?

Cæſ. You may be pleas'd to catch at mine intent,
By what did heere befall me. Your Wife and Brother
Made warres vpon me, and their conteſtation
Was Theame for you, you were the word of warre.

Ant. You do miſtake your buſines, my Brother neuer
Did vrge me in his Act: I did inquire it,
And haue my Learning from ſome true reports
That drew their ſwords with you, did he not rather
Diſcredit my authority with yours,
And make the warres alike againſt my ſtomacke,
Hauing alike your cauſe. Of this, my Letters
Before did ſatisfie you. If you'l patch a quarrell,
As matter whole you haue to make it with,

It muſt not be with this.

Caeſ. You praiſe your ſelfe, by laying defects of iudgement to me : but you patcht vp your excuſes.

Anth. Not ſo, not ſo :
I know you could not lacke, I am certaine on't,
Very neceſſity of this thought, that I
Your Partner in the cauſe 'gainſt which he fought,
Could not with gracefull eyes attend thoſe Warres
Which fronted mine owne peace. As for my wife,
I would you had her ſpirit, in ſuch another,
The third oth'world is yours, which with a Snaffle,
You may pace eaſie, but not ſuch a wife.

Enobar. Would we had all ſuch wiues, that the men might go to Warres with the women.

Anth. So much vncurbable, her Garboiles (*Caeſar*)
Made out of her impatience : which not wanted
Shrodeneſſe of policie to : I greeuing grant,
Did you too much diſquiet, for that you muſt,
But ſay I could not helpe it.

Caeſar. I wrote to you, when rioting in Alexandria you
Did pocket vp my Letters : and with taunts
Did gibe my Miſiue out of audience.

Ant. Sir, he fell vpon me, ere admitted, then :
Three Kings I had newly feaſted, and did want
Of what I was i'th'morning : but next day
I told him of my ſelfe, which was as much
As to haue askt him pardon. Let this Fellow
Be nothing of our ſtrife : if we contend
Out of our queſtion wipe him.

Caeſar. You haue broken the Article of your oath, which you ſhall neuer haue tongue to charge me with.

Lep. Soft *Caeſar.*

Ant. No *Lepidus*, let him ſpeake,
The Honour is Sacred which he talks on now,
Suppoſing that I lackt it : but on *Caeſar*,
The Article of my oath.

Caeſar. To lend me Armes, and aide when I requir'd them, the which you both denied.

Anth. Neglected rather:
And then when poyſoned houres had bound me vp
From mine owne knowledge, as neerely as I may,
Ile play the penitent to you. But mine honeſty,
Shall not make poore my greatneſſe, nor my power
Worke without it. Truth is, that *Fuluia*,
To haue me out of Egypt, made Warres heere,
For which my ſelfe, the ignorant motiue, do
So farre aske pardon, as befits mine Honour
To ſtoope in ſuch a caſe.

Lep. 'Tis Noble ſpoken.

Mece. If it might pleaſe you, to enforce no further
The griefes betweene ye: to forget them quite,
Were to remember : that the preſent neede,
Speakes to attone you.

Lep. Worthily ſpoken *Mecenas*.

Enobar. Or if you borrow one anothers Loue for the inſtant, you may when you heare no more words of *Pompey* returne it againe : you ſhall haue time to wrangle in, when you haue nothing elſe to do.

Anth. Thou art a Souldier, onely ſpeake no more.

Enob. That trueth ſhould be ſilent, I had almoſt forgot.

Anth. You wrong this preſence, therefore ſpeake no more.

Enob. Go too then : your Conſiderate ſtone.

Caeſar. I do not much diſlike the matter, but
The manner of his ſpeech : for't cannot be,
We ſhall remaine in friendſhip, our conditions
So diffring in their acts. Yet if I knew,
What Hoope ſhould hold vs ſtaunch from edge to edge
Ath'world : I would perſue it.

Agri. Giue me leaue *Caeſar.*

Caeſar. Speake *Agrippa.*

Agri. Thou haſt a Siſter by the Mothers ſide, admir'd *Octauia*? Great *Mark Anthony* is now a widdower.

Caeſar. Say not, ſay *Agrippa*; if *Cleopater* heard you, your proofe were well deſerued of raſhneſſe.

Anth. I am not marryed *Caeſar* : let me heere *Agrippa* further ſpeake.

Agri. To hold you in perpetuall amitie,
To make you Brothers, and to knit your hearts
With an vn-ſlipping knot, take *Anthony*,
Octauia to his wife : whoſe beauty claimes
No worſe a husband then the beſt of men : whoſe
Vertue, and whoſe generall graces, ſpeake
That which none elſe can vtter. By this marriage,
All little Ielouſies which now ſeeme great,
And all great feares, which now import their dangers,
Would then be nothing. Truth's would be tales,
Where now halfe tales be truth's : her loue to both,
Would each to other, and all loues to both
Draw after her. Pardon what I haue ſpoke,
For 'tis a ſtudied not a preſent thought,
By duty ruminated.

Anth. Will *Caeſar* ſpeake?

Caeſar. Not till he heares how *Anthony* is toucht,
With what is ſpoke already.

Anth. What power is in *Agrippa*,
If I would ſay *Agrippa*, be it ſo,
To make this good?

Caeſar. The power of *Caeſar*,
And his power, vnto *Octauia*.

Anth. May I neuer
(To this good purpoſe, that ſo fairely ſhewes)
Dreame of impediment : let me haue thy hand
Further this act of Grace : and from this houre,
The heart of Brothers gouerne in our Loues,
And ſway our great Deſignes.

Caeſar. There's my hand:
A Siſter I bequeath you, whom no Brother
Did euer loue ſo deerely. Let her liue
To ioyne our kingdomes, and our hearts, and neuer
Flie off our Loues againe.

Lepi. Happily, Amen.

Ant. I did not think to draw my Sword 'gainſt *Pompey*,
For he hath laid ſtrange courteſies, and great
Of late vpon me. I muſt thanke him onely,
Leaſt my remembrance, ſuffer ill report :
At heele of that, defie him.

Lepi. Time cals vpon's,
Of vs muſt *Pompey* preſently be ſought,
Or elſe he ſeekes out vs.

Anth. Where lies he?

Caeſar. About the Mount-Meſena.

Anth. What is his ſtrength by land?

Caeſar. Great, and encreaſing :
But by Sea he is an abſolute Maſter.

Anth. So is the Fame,
Would we had ſpoke together. Haſt we for it,
Yet ere we put our ſelues in Armes, diſpatch we
The buſineſſe we haue talkt of.

Caeſar. With moſt gladneſſe,
And do inuite you to my Siſters view,

Whe-

Whether straight Ile lead you.

Anth. Let vs *Lepidus* not lacke your companie.

Lep. Noble *Anthony*, not sickenesse should detaine me.

Flourish. Exit omnes.

Manet Enobarbus, Agrippa, Mecenas.

Mec. Welcome from Ægypt Sir.

Eno. Halfe the heart of *Cæsar*, worthy *Mecenas*. My honourable Friend *Agrippa*.

Agri. Good *Enobarbus*.

Mece. We haue cause to be glad, that matters are so well disgested: you staid well by't in Egypt.

Enob. I Sir, we did sleepe day out of countenaunce: and made the night light with drinking.

Mece. Eight Wilde-Boares rosted whole at a breakfast: and but twelue persons there. Is this true?

Eno. This was but as a Flye by an Eagle: we had much more monstrous matter of Feast, which worthily deserued noting.

Mecenas. She's a most triumphant Lady, if report be square to her.

Enob. When she first met *Marke Anthony*, she purst vp his heart vpon the Riuer of Sidnis.

Agri. There she appear'd indeed: or my reporter deuis'd well for her.

Eno. I will tell you,
The Barge she sat in, like a burnisht Throne
Burnt on the water: the Poope was beaten Gold,
Purple the Sailes: and so perfumed that
The Windes were Loue-sicke.
With them the Owers were Siluer,
Which to the tune of Flutes kept stroke, and made
The water which they beate, to follow faster;
As amorous of their strokes. For her owne person,
It beggerd all discription, she did lye
In her Pauillion, cloth of Gold, of Tissue,
O're-picturing that Venus, where we see
The fancie out-worke Nature. On each side her,
Stood pretty Dimpled Boyes, like smiling Cupids,
With diuers coulour'd Fannes whose winde did seeme,
To gloue the delicate cheekes which they did coole,
And what they vndid did.

Agrip. Oh rare for *Anthony*.

Eno. Her Gentlewoman, like the Nereides,
So many Mer-maides tended her i'th'eyes,
And made their bends adornings. At the Helme.
A seeming Mer-maide steeres: The Silken Tackle,
Swell with the touches of those Flower-soft hands,
That yarely frame the office. From the Barge
A strange inuisible perfume hits the sense
Of the adiacent Wharfes. The Citty cast
Her people out vpon her: and *Anthony*
Enthron'd i'th'Market-place, did sit alone,
Whisling to'th'ayre: which but for vacancie,
Had gone to gaze on *Cleopater* too,
And made a gap in Nature.

Agri. Rare Egiptian.

Eno. Vpon her landing, *Anthony* sent to her,
Inuited her to Supper: she replyed,
It should be better, he became her guest:
Which she entreated, our Courteous *Anthony*,
Whom nere the word of no woman hard speake,
Being barber'd ten times o're, goes to the Feast;
And for his ordinary, paies his heart,
For what his eyes eate onely.

Agri. Royall Wench:
She made great *Cæsar* lay his Sword to bed,
He ploughed her, and she cropt.

Eno. I saw her once
Hop forty Paces through the publicke streete,
And hauing lost her breath, she spoke, and panted,
That she did make defect, perfection,
And breathlesse powre breath forth.

Mece. Now *Anthony*, must leaue her vtterly.

Eno. Neuer he will not:
Age cannot wither her, nor custome stale
Her infinite variety: other women cloy
The appetites they feede, but she makes hungry,
Where most she satisfies. For vildest things
Become themselues in her, that the holy Priests
Blesse her, when she is Riggish.

Mece If Beauty, Wisedome, Modesty, can sett le
The heart of *Anthony*: *Octauia* is
A blessed Lottery to him.

Agrip. Let vs go. Good *Enobarbus*, make your selfe my guest, whilst you abide heere.

Eno. Humbly Sir I thanke you. *Exeunt*

Enter Anthony, Cæsar, Octauia betweene them.

Anth. The world, and my great office, will
Sometimes deuide me from your bosome.

Octa. All which time, before the Gods my knee shall bowe my ptayers to them for you.

Anth. Goodnight Sir. My *Octauia*
Read not my blemishes in the worlds report:
I haue not kept my square, but that to come
Shall all be done byth'Rule: good night deere Lady:
Good night Sir.

Cæsar. Goodnight. *Exit.*

Enter Soothsaier.

Anth. Now sirrah: you do wish your selfe in Egypt?

Sooth. Would I had neuer come from thence, nor you thither.

Ant. If you can, your reason?

Sooth. I see it in my motion: haue it not in my tongue,
But yet hie you to Egypt againe.

Antho. Say to me, whose Fortunes shall rise higher *Cæsars* or mine?

Soot. *Cæsars*. Therefore (oh *Anthony*) stay not by his side
Thy Dæmon that thy spirit which keepes thee, is
Noble, Couragious, high vnmatchable,
Where *Cæsars* is not. But neere him, thy Angell
Becomes a feare: as being o're-powr'd, therefore
Make space enough betweene you.

Anth. Speake this no more.

Sooth. To none but thee no more but: when to thee,
If thou dost play with him at any game,
Thou art sure to loose: And of that Naturall lucke,
He beats thee 'gainst the oddes. Thy Luster thickens,
When he shines by: I say againe, thy spirit
Is all affraid to gouerne thee neere him:
But he alway 'tis Noble.

Anth. Get thee gone:
Say to *Ventigius* I would speake with him. *Exit.*
He shall to Parthia, be it Art or hap,
He hath spoken true. The very Dice obey him,
And in our sports my better cunning faints,
Vnder his chance, if we draw lots he speeds,
His Cocks do winne the Battaile, still of mine,
When it is all to naught: and his Quailes euer
Beate mine (in hoopt) at odd's. I will to Egypte:

And

And though I make this marriage for my peace,
I'th'Eaſt my pleaſure lies. Oh come *Ventigius.*

Enter Ventigius.

You muſt to Parthia, your Commiſſions ready:
Follow me, and recieue't. *Exeunt*

Enter Lepidus, Mecenas and Agrippa.

Lepidus. Trouble your ſelues no further: pray you haſten your Generals after.

Agr. Sir, *Marke Anthony,* will e'ne but kiſſe *Octauia,* and weele follow.

Lepi. Till I ſhall ſee you in your Souldiers dreſſe,
Which will become you both: Farewell.

Mece. We ſhall: as I conceiue the iourney, be at Mount before you *Lepidus.*

Lepi. Your way is ſhorter, my purpoſes do draw me much about, you'le win two dayes vpon me.

Both. Sir good ſucceſſe.

Lepi. Farewell. *Exeunt.*

Enter Cleopater, Charmian, Iras, and Alexas.

Cleo. Giue me ſome Muſicke: Muſicke, moody foode of vs that trade in Loue.

Omnes. The Muſicke, hoa.

Enter Mardian the Eunuch.

Cleo. Let it alone, let's to Billards: come *Charmian.*

Char. My arme is ſore, beſt play with *Mardian.*

Cleopa. As well a woman with an Eunuch plaide, as with a woman. Come you'le play with me Sir?

Mardi. As well as I can Madam.

Cleo. And when good will is ſhewed,
Though't come to ſhort
The Actor may pleade pardon. Ile none now,
Giue me mine Angle, weele to'th'Riuer there
My Muſicke playing farre off. I will betray
Tawny fine fiſhes, my bended hooke ſhall pierce
Their ſlimy iawes: and as I draw them vp,
Ile thinke them euery one an *Anthony,*
And ſay, ah ha; y'are caught.

Char. 'Twas merry when you wager'd on your Angling, when your diuer did hang a ſalt fiſh on his hooke which he with feruencie drew vp.

Cleo. That time? Oh times:
I laught him out of patience: and that night
I laught him into patience, and next morne,
Ere the ninth houre, I drunke him to his bed:
Then put my Tires and Mantles on him, whilſt
I wore his Sword Phillippan. Oh from Italie,

Enter a Meſſenger.

Ramme thou thy fruitefull tidings in mine eares,
That long time haue bin barren.

Meſ. Madam, Madam.

Cleo. *Anthonyo's* dead,
If thou ſay ſo Villaine, thou kil'ſt thy Miſtris:
But well and free, if thou ſo yeild him.
There is Gold, and heere
My bleweſt vaines to kiſſe: a hand that Kings
Haue lipt, and trembled kiſſing.

Meſ. Firſt Madam, he is well.

Cleo. Why there's moreGold.
But ſirrah marke, we vſe
To ſay, the dead are well: bring it to that,
The Gold I giue thee, will I melt and powr
Downe thy ill vttering throate.

Meſ. Good Madam heare me.

Cleo. Well, go too I will:
But there's no goodneſſe in thy face if *Anthony*
Be free and healthfull; ſo tart a fauour
To trumpet ſuch good tidings. If not well,
Thou ſhouldſt come like a Furie crown'd with Snakes,
Not like a formall man.

Meſ. Wilt pleaſe you heare me?

Cleo. I haue a mind to ſtrike thee ere thou ſpeak'ſt:
Yet if thou ſay *Anthony* liues, 'tis well,
Or friends with *Cæſar,* or not Captiue to him,
Ile ſet thee in a ſhower of Gold, and haile
Rich Pearles vpon thee.

Meſ. Madam, he's well.

Cleo. Well ſaid.

Meſ. And Friends with *Cæſar.*

Cleo. Th'art an honeſt man.

Meſ. *Cæſar,* and he, are greater Friends then euer.

Cleo. Make thee a Fortune from me.

Meſ. But yet Madam.

Cleo. I do not like but yet, it does alay
The good precedence, fie vpon but yet,
Bur yet is as a Iaylor to bring foorth
Some monſtrous Malefactor. Prythee Friend,
Powre out the packe of matter to mine eare,
The good and bad together: he's friends with *Cæſar,*
In ſtate of heal th thou ſaiſt, and thou ſaiſt, free.

Meſ. Free Madam, no: I made no ſuch report,
He's bound vnto *Octauia.*

Cleo. For what good turne?

Meſ. For the beſt turne i'th'bed.

Cleo. I am pale *Charmian.*

Meſ. Madam, he's married to *Octauia.*

Cleo. The moſt infectious Peſtilence vpon thee.

Strikes him downe.

Meſ. Good Madam patience.

Cleo. What ſay you? *Strikes him.*
Hence horrible Villaine, or Ile ſpurne thine eyes
Like balls before me: Ile vnhaire thy head,

She hales him vp and downe.

Thou ſhalt be whipt with Wyer, and ſtew'd in brine,
Smarting in lingring pickle.

Meſ. Gratious Madam,
I that do bring the newes, made not the match.

Cleo. Say 'tis not ſo, a Prouince I will giue thee,
And make thy Fortunes proud: the blow thou had'ſt
Shall make thy peace, for mouing me to rage,
And I will boot thee with what guift beſide
Thy modeſtie can begge.

Meſ. He's married Madam.

Cleo. Rogue, thou haſt liu'd too long. *Draw a knife.*

Meſ. Nay then Ile runne:
What meane you Madam, I haue made no fault. *Exit.*

Char. Good Madam keepe your ſelfe within your ſelfe,
The man is innocent.

Cleo. Some Innocents ſcape not the thunderbolt:
Melt Egypt into Nyle: and kindly creatures
Turne all to Serpents. Call the ſlaue againe,
Though I am mad, I will not byte him: Call?

Char. He is afeard to come.

Cleo. I will not hurt him,
Theſe hands do lacke Nobility, that they ſtrike
A meaner then my ſelfe: ſince I my ſelfe
Haue giuen my ſelfe the cauſe. Come hither Sir.

Enter the Meſſenger againe.

Though it be honeſt, it is neuer good
To bring bad newes: giue to a gratious Meſſage

An

An hoſt of tongues, but let ill tydings tell
Themſelues, when they be felt.
Meſ. I haue done my duty.
Cleo. Is he married?
I cannot hate thee worſer then I do,
If thou againe ſay yes.
Meſ. He's married Madam.
Cleo. The Gods confound thee,
Doſt thou hold there ſtill?
Meſ. Should I lye Madame?
Cleo. Oh, I would thou didſt:
So halfe my Egypt were ſubmerg'd and made
A Ceſterne for ſcal'd Snakes. Go get thee hence,
Had'ſt thou *Narciſſus* in thy face to me,
Thou would'ſt appeere moſt vgly: He is married?
Meſ. I craue your Highneſſe pardon.
Cleo. He is married?
Meſ. Take no offence, that I would not offend you,
To punniſh me for what you make me do
Seemes much vnequall, he's married to *Octauia.*
Cleo. Oh that his fault ſhould make a knaue of thee,
That art not what th'art ſure of. Get thee hence,
The Marchandize which thou haſt brought from Rome
Are all too deere for me:
Lye they vpon thy hand, and be vndone by em.
Char. Good your Highneſſe patience.
Cleo. In prayſing *Anthony*, I haue diſprais'd *Cæſar.*
Char. Many times Madam.
Cleo. I am paid for't now: lead me from hence,
I faint, oh *Iras, Charmian*: 'tis no matter.
Go to the Fellow, good *Alexas* bid him
Report the feature of *Octauia*: her yeares,
Her inclination, let him not leaue out
The colour of her haire. Bring me word quickly,
Let him for euer go, let him not *Charmian*,
Though he be painted one way like a Gorgon,
The other wayes a Mars. Bid you *Alexas*
Bring me word, how tall ſhe is: pitty me *Charmian*,
But do not ſpeake to me. Lead me to my Chamber.
Exeunt.

Flouriſh. Enter Pompey, at one doore with Drum and Trumpet: at another Cæſar, Lepidus, Anthony, Enobarbus, Mecenas, Agrippa, Menas with Souldiers Marching.

Pom. Your Hoſtages I haue, ſo haue you mine:
And we ſhall talke before we fight.
Cæſar. Moſt meete that firſt we come to words,
And therefore haue we
Our written purpoſes before vs ſent,
Which if thou haſt conſidered, let vs know,
If'twill tye vp thy diſcontented Sword,
And carry backe to Cicelie much tall youth,
That elſe muſt periſh heere.
Pom. To you all three,
The Senators alone of this great world,
Chiefe Factors for the Gods. I do not know,
Wherefore my Father ſhould reuengers want,
Hauing a Sonne and Friends, ſince *Iulius Cæſar*,
Who at Phillippi the good *Brutus* ghoſted,
There ſaw you labouring for him. What was't
That mou'd pale *Caſſius* to conſpire? And what
Made all-honor'd, honeſt, Romaine *Brutus*,
With the arm'd reſt, Courtiers of beautious freedome,
To drench the Capitoll, but that they would
Haue one man but a man, and that his it
Hath made me rigge my Nauie. At whoſe burthen,
The anger'd Ocean fomes, with which I meant
To ſcourge th'ingratitude, that deſpightfull Rome
Caſt on my Noble Father.
Cæſar. Take your time.
Ant. Thou can'ſt not feare vs *Pompey* with thy ſailes.
Weele ſpeake with thee at Sea. At land thou know'ſt
How much we do o're-count thee.
Pom. At Land indeed
Thou doſt orecount me of my Fatherrs houſe:
But ſince the Cuckoo buildes not for himſelfe,
Remaine in't as thou maiſt.
Lepi. Be pleas'd to tell vs,
(For this is from the preſent how you take)
The offers we haue ſent you.
Cæſar. There's the point.
Ant. Which do not be entreated too,
But waigh what it is worth imbrac'd
Cæſar. And what may follow to try a larger Fortune.
Pom. You haue made me offer
Of Cicelie, Sardinia: and I muſt
Rid all the Sea of Pirats. Then, to ſend
Meaſures of Wheate to Rome: this greed vpon,
To part with vnhackt edges, and beare backe
Our Targes vndinted.
Omnes. That's our offer.
Pom. Know then I came before you heere,
A man prepar'd
To take this offer. But *Marke Anthony*,
Put me to ſome impatience: though I looſe
The praiſe of it by telling. You muſt know
When *Cæſar* and your Brother were at blowes,
Your Mother came to Cicelie, and did finde
Her welcome Friendly.
Ant. I haue heard it *Pompey*,
And am well ſtudied for a liberall thanks,
Which I do owe you.
Pom. Let me haue your hand:
I did not thinke Sir, to haue met you heere,
Ant. The beds i'th'Eaſt are ſoft, and thanks to you,
That cal'd me timelier then my purpoſe hither:
For I haue gained by't.
Cæſar. Since I ſaw you laſt, ther's a change vpon you.
Pom. Well, I know not,
What counts harſh Fotune caſt's vpon my face,
But in my boſome ſhall ſhe neuer come,
To make my heart her vaſſaile.
Lep. Well met heere.
Pom. I hope ſo *Lepidus*, thus we are agreed:
I craue our compoſion may be written
And ſeal'd betweene vs,
Cæſar. That's the next to do.
Pom. Weele feaſt each other, ere we part, and lett's
Draw lots who ſhall begin.
Ant. That will I *Pompey*.
Pompey. No *Anthony* take the lot: but firſt or laſt, your fine Egyptian cookerie ſhall haue the ſame, I haue heard that *Iulius Cæſar*, grew fat with feaſting there.
Anth. You haue heard much.
Pom. I haue faire meaning Sir.
Ant. And faire words to them.
Pom. Then ſo much haue I heard,
And I haue heard *Appolodorus* carried———
Eno. No more that: he did ſo.
Pom. What I pray you?
Eno. A certaine Queene to *Cæſar* in a Matris.
Pom. I know thee now, how far'ſt thou Souldier?
Eno. Well, and well am like to do, for I perceiue
Foure

Foure Feasts are toward.

Pom. Let me shake thy hand,
I neuer hated thee: I haue seene thee fight,
When I haue enuied thy behauiour.

Enob. Sir, I neuer lou'd you much, but I ha'prais'd ye,
When you haue well deseru'd ten times as much,
As I haue said you did.

Pom. Inioy thy plainnesse,
It nothing ill becomes thee:
Aboord my Gally, I inuite you all.
Will you leade Lords?

All. Shew's the way, sir.

Pom. Come. *Exeunt.* *Manet Enob. & Menas*

Men. Thy Father *Pompey* would ne're haue made this Treaty. You, and I haue knowne sir.

Enob. At Sea, I thinke.

Men. We haue Sir.

Enob. You haue done well by water.

Men. And you by Land.

Enob. I will praise any man that will praise me, thogh it cannot be denied what I haue done by Land.

Men. Nor what I haue done by water.

Enob. Yes some-thing you can deny for your owne safety: you haue bin a great Theefe by Sea.

Men. And you by Land.

Enob. There I deny my Land seruice: but giue mee your hand *Menas*, if our eyes had authority, heere they might take two Theeues kissing.

Men. All mens faces are true, whatsomere their hands are.

Enob. But there is neuer a fayre Woman, ha's a true Face.

Men. No slander, they steale hearts.

Enob. We came hither to fight with you.

Men. For my part, I am sorry it is turn'd to a Drinking. *Pompey* doth this day laugh away his Fortune.

Enob. If he do, sure he cannot weep't backe againe.

Men. Y'haue said Sir, we look'd not for *Marke Anthony* heere, pray you, is he married to *Cleopatra*?

Enob. *Cæsars* Sister is call'd *Octauia*.

Men. True Sir, she was the wife of *Caius Marcellus*.

Enob. But she is now the wife of *Marcus Anthonius*.

Men. Pray'ye sir.

Enob. 'Tis true.

Men. Then is *Cæsar* and he, for euer knit together.

Enob. If I were bound to Diuine of this vnity, I wold not Prophesie so.

Men. I thinke the policy of that purpose, made more in the Marriage, then the loue of the parties.

Enob. I thinke so too. But you shall finde the band that seemes to tye their friendship together, will bee the very strangler of their Amity: *Octauia* is of a holy, cold, and still conuersation.

Men. Who would not haue his wife so?

Eno. Not he that himselfe is not so: which is *Marke Anthony*: he will to his Egyptian dish againe: then shall the sighes of *Octauia* blow the fire vp in *Cæsar*, and (as I said before) that which is the strength of their Amity, shall proue the immediate Author of their variance. *Anthony* will vse his affection where it is. Hee married but his occasion heere.

Men. And thus it may be. Come Sir, will you aboord? I haue a health for you.

Enob. I shall take it sir: we haue vs'd our Throats in Egypt.

Men. Come, let's away. *Exeunt.*

Musicke playes.
Enter two or three Seruants with a Banket.

1 Heere they'l be man: some o'th'their Plants are ill rooted already, the least winde i'th'world wil blow them downe.

2 *Lepidus* is high Conlord.

1 They haue made him drinke Almes drinke.

2 As they pinch one another by the disposition, hee cries out, no more; reconciles them to his entreatie, and himselfe to'th'drinke.

1 But it raises the greatet warre betweene him & his discretion.

2 Why this it is to haue a name in great mens Fellowship: I had as liue haue a Reede that will doe me no seruice, as a Partizan I could not heaue.

1 To be call'd into a huge Sphere, and not to be seene to moue in't, are the holes where eyes should bee, which pittifully disaster the cheekes.

A Sennet sounded.
Enter Cæsar, Anthony, Pompey, Lepidus, Agrippa, Mecenas, Enobarbus, Menes, with other Captaines.

Ant. Thus do they Sir: they take the flow o'th'Nyle
By certaine scales i'th'Pyramid: they know
By'th'height, the lownesse, or the meane: If dearth
Or Foizon follow. The higher Nilus swels,
The more it promises: as it ebbes, the Seedsman
Vpon the slime and Ooze scatters his graine,
And shortly comes to Haruest.

Lep. Y'haue strange Serpents there?

Anth. I *Lepidus*.

Lep. Your Serpent of Egypt, is bred now of your mud by the operation of your Sun: so is your Crocodile.

Ant. They are so.

Pom. Sit, and some Wine: A health to *Lepidus*.

Lep. I am not so well as I should be:
But Ile ne're out.

Enob. Not till you haue slept: I feare me you'l bee in till then.

Lep. Nay certainly, I haue heard the *Ptolomies* Pyramisis are very goodly things: without contradiction I haue heard that.

Menas. *Pompey*, a word.

Pomp. Say in mine eare, what is't.

Men. Forsake thy seate I do beseech thee Captaine,
And heare me speake a word.

Pom. Forbeare me till anon. *Whispers in's Eare.*
This Wine for *Lepidus*.

Lep. What manner o'thing is your Crocodile?

Ant. It is shap'd sir like it selfe, and it is as broad as it hath bredth; It is iust so high as it is, and mooues with it owne organs. It liues by that which nourisheth it, and the Elements once out of it, it Transmigrates.

Lep. What colour is it of?

Ant. Of it owne colour too.

Lep. 'Tis a strange Serpent.

Ant. 'Tis so, and the teares of it are wet.

Cæs. Will this description satisfie him?

Ant. With the Health that *Pompey* giues him, else he is a very Epicure.

Pomp. Go hang sir, hang: tell me of that? Away:
Do as I bid you. Where's this Cup I call'd for?

Men. If for the sake of Merit thou wilt heare mee,
Rise

Rise from thy stoole.
Pom. I thinke th'art mad : the matter?
Men. I haue euer held my cap off to thy Fortunes.
Pom. Thou hast seru'd me with much faith : what's else to say? Be iolly Lords.
Anth. These Quicke-sands *Lepidus*,
Keepe off, them for you sinke.
Men. Wilt thou be Lord of all the world?
Pom. What saist thou?
Men. Wilt thou be Lord of the whole world?
That's twice.
Pom. How should that be?
Men. But entertaine it, and though thou thinke me poore, I am the man will giue thee all the world.
Pom. Hast thou drunke well.
Men. No *Pompey*, I haue kept me from the cup,
Thou art if thou dar'st be, the earthly Ioue :
What ere the Ocean pales, or skie inclippes,
Is thine, if thou wilt ha't.
Pom. Shew me which way?
Men. These three World-sharers, these Competitors
Are in thy vessell. Let me cut the Cable,
And when we are put off, fall to their throates :
All there is thine.
Pom. Ah, this thou shouldst haue done,
And not haue spoke on't. In me 'tis villanie,
In thee,'t had bin good seruice : thou must know,
'Tis not my profit that does lead mine Honour :
Mine Honour it, Repent that ere thy tongue,
Hath so betraide thine acte. Being done vnknowne,
I should haue found it afterwards well done,
But must condemne it now : desist, and drinke.
Men. For this, Ile neuer follow
Thy paul'd Fortunes more,
Who seekes and will not take, when once 'tis offer'd,
Shall neuer finde it more.
Pom. This health to *Lepidus*.
Ant. Beare him ashore,
Ile pledge it for him *Pompey*.
Eno. Heere's to thee *Menas*.
Men. *Enobarbus*, welcome.
Pom. Fill till the cup be hid.
Eno. There's a strong Fellow *Menas*.
Men. Why?
Eno. A beares the third part of the world man : seest not?
Men. The third part, then he is drunk : would it were all, that it might go on wheeles.
Eno. Drinke thou : encreaſe the Reeles.
Men Come.
Pom. This is not yet an Alexandrian Feast.
Ant. It ripen's towards it : strike the Vessells hoa.
Heere's to *Cæsar*.
Cæsar. I could well forbear't, it's monstrous labour when I wash my braine, and it grow fouler.
Ant. Be a Child o'th'time.
Cæsar. Possesse it, Ile make answer : but I had rather fast from all, foure dayes, then drinke so much in one.
Enob. Ha my braue Emperour, shall we daunce now the Egyptian Backenals, and celebrate our drinke?
Pom. Let's ha't good Souldier.
Ant. Come, let's all take hands,
Till that the conquering Wine hath steep't our sense,
In soft and delicate Lethe.
Eno. All take hands :
Make battery to our eares with the loud Musicke,
The while, Ile place you, then the Boy shall sing.
The holding euery man shall beate as loud,
As his strong sides can volly.

Musicke Playes. Enobarbus places them hand in hand.

The Song.

Come thou Monarch of the Vine,
Plumpie Bacchus, with pinke eyne :
In thy Fattes our Cares be drown'd,
With thy Grapes our haires be Crown'd.
Cup vs till the world go round,
Cup vs till the world go round.

Cæsar. What would you more?
Pompey goodnight. Good Brother
Let me request you of our grauer businesse
Frownes at this leuitie. Gentle Lords let's part,
You see we haue burnt our cheekes. Strong *Enobarbe*
Is weaker then the Wine, and mine owne tongue
Spleet's what it speakes: the wilde disguise hath almost
Antickt vs all. What needs more words? goodnight.
Good *Anthony* your hand.
Pom. Ile try you on the shore.
Anth. And shall Sir, giues your hand.
Pom. Oh *Anthony*, you haue my Father house.
But what, we are Friends?
Come downe into the Boate.
Eno. Take heed you fall not *Menas* : Ile not on shore,
No to my Cabin : these Drummes,
These Trumpets, Flutes : what
Let Neptune heare, we bid aloud farewell
To these great Fellowes. Sound and be hang'd, sound out.
Sound a Flourish with Drummes.
Enor. Hoo saies a there's my Cap.
Men. Hoa, Noble Captaine, come. *Exeunt.*

Enter Ventidius as it were in trinmph, the dead body of Pacorus borne before him.

Ven. Now darting Parthya art thou stroke, and now
Pleas'd Fortune does of *Marcus Crassus* death
Make me reuenger. Beare the Kings Sonnes body,
Before our Army thy *Pacorus Orades*,
Paies this for *Marcus Crassus*.
Romaine. Noble *Ventidius*,
Whil'st yet with Parthian blood thy Sword is warme,
The Fugitiue Parthians follow. Spurre through Media,
Mesapotamia, and the shelters, whether
The routed flie. So thy grand Captaine *Anthony*
Shall set thee on triumphant Chariots, and
Put Garlands on thy head.
Ven. Oh *Sillius*, *Sillius*,
I haue done enough. A lower place note well
May make too great an act. For learne this *Sillius*,
Better to leaue vndone, then by our deed
Acquire too high a Fame, when him we serues away.
Cæsar and *Anthony*, haue euer wonne
More in their officer, then person. *Sossius*
One of my place in Syria, his Lieutenant,
For quicke accumulation of renowne,
Which he atchiu'd by'th'minute, lost his fauour.
Who does i'th'Warres more then his Captaine can,
Becomes his Captaines Captaine : and Ambition
(The Souldiers vertue) rather makes choise of losse
Then gaine, which darkens him.
I could do more to do *Anthonius* good,
But 'twould offend him. And in his offence,
Should

Should my performance perish.

Rom. Thou hast *Ventidius* that, without the which a Souldier and his Sword graunts scarce distinction : thou wilt write to *Anthony*.

Ven. Ile humbly signifie what in his name,
That magicall word of Warre we haue effected,
How with his Banners, and his well paid ranks,
The nere-yet beaten Horse of Parthia,
We haue iaded out o'th'Field.

Rom. Where is he now?

Ven. He purposeth to Athens, whither with what hast
The waight we must conuay with's, will permit:
We shall appeare before him. On there, passe along.

Exeunt.

Enter Agrippa at one doore, Enobarbus at another.

Agri. What are the Brothers parted?

Eno. They haue dispatcht with *Pompey*, he is gone,
The other three are Sealing. *Octauia* weepes
To part from Rome: *Cæsar* is sad, and *Lepidus*
Since *Pompey's* feast, as *Menas* saies, is troubled
With the Greene-Sicknesse.

Agri. 'Tis a Noble *Lepidus*.

Eno. A very fine one: oh, how he loues *Cæsar*.

Agri. Nay but how deerely he adores *Mark Anthony*.

Eno. *Cæsar*? why he's the Iupiter of men.

Ant. What's *Anthony*, the God of Iupiter?

Eno. Spake you of *Cæsar*? How, the non-pareill?

Agri. Oh *Anthony*, oh thou Arabian Bird!

Eno. Would you praise *Cæsar*, say *Cæsar* go no further.

Agr. Indeed he plied them both with excellent praises.

Eno. But he loues *Cæsar* best, yet he loues *Anthony*:
Hoo, Hearts, Tongues, Figure,
Scribes, Bards, Poets, cannot
Thinke speake, cast, write, sing, number: hoo,
His loue to *Anthony*. But as for *Cæsar*,
Kneele downe, kneele downe, and wonder.

Agri. Both he loues.

Eno. They are his Shards, and he their Beetle, so:
This is to horse: Adieu, Noble *Agrippa*.

Agri. Good Fortune worthy Souldier, and farewell.

Enter Cæsar, Anthony, Lepidus, and Octauia.

Antho. No further Sir.

Cæsar. You take from me a great part of my selfe:
Vse me well in't. Sister, proue such a wife
As my thoughts make thee, and as my farthest Band
Shall passe on thy approofe: most Noble *Anthony*,
Let not the peece of Vertue which is set
Betwixt vs, as the Cyment of our loue
To keepe it builded, be the Ramme to batter
The Fortresse of it: for better might we
Haue lou'd without this meane, if onboth parts
This be not cherisht.

Ant. Make me not offended, in your distrust.

Cæsar. I haue said.

Ant. You shall not finde,
Though you be therein curious, the lest cause
For what you seeme to feare, so the Gods keepe you,
And make the hearts of Romaines serue your ends:
We will heere part.

Cæsar. Farewell my deerest Sister, fare thee well,
The Elements be kind to thee, and make
Thy spirits all of comfort: fare thee well.

Octa. My Noble Brother.

Anth. The Aprill's in her eyes, it is Loues spring,
And these the showers to bring it on: be cheerfull.

Octa. Sir, looke well to my Husbands house: and——

Cæsar. What *Octauia*?

Octa. Ile tell you in your eare.

Ant. Her tongue will not obey her heart, nor can
Her heart informe her tougue.
The Swannes downe feather
That stands vpon the Swell at the full of Tide:
And neither way inclines.

Eno. Will *Cæsar* weepe?

Agr. He ha's a cloud in's face.

Eno. He were the worse for that were he a Horse, so is he being a man.

Agri. Why *Enobarbus*:
When *Anthony* found *Iulius Cæsar* dead,
He cried almost to roaring: And he wept,
When at Phillippi he found *Brutus* slaine.

Eno. That year indeed, he was trobled with a rheume,
What willingly he did confound, he wail'd,
Beleeu't till I weepe too.

Cæsar. No sweet *Octauia*,
You shall heare from me still: the time shall not
Out-go my thinking on you.

Ant. Come Sir, come,
Ile wrastle with you in my strength of loue,
Looke heere I haue you, thus I let you go,
And giue you to the Gods.

Cæsar. Adieu, be happy.

Lep. Let all the number of the Starres giue light
To thy faire way.

Cæsar. Farewell, farewell. *Kisses Octauia.*

Ant. Farewell. *Trumpets sound.* *Exeunt.*

Enter Cleopatra, Charmian, Iras, and Alexas.

Cleo. Where is the Fellow?

Alex. Halfe afeard to come.

Cleo. Go too, go too: Come hither Sir.

Enter the Messenger as before.

Alex. Good Maiestie: *Herod* of Iury dare not looke vpon you, but when you are well pleas'd.

Cleo. That *Herods* head, Ile haue: but how? When *Anthony* is gone, through whom I might commaund it:
Come thou neere.

Mes. Most gratious Maiestie.

Cleo. Did'st thou behold *Octauia*?

Mes. I dread Queene.

Cleo. Where?

Mes. Madam in Rome, I lookt her in the face: and saw her led betweene her Brother, and *Marke Anthony*.

Cleo. Is she as tall as me?

Mes. She is not Madam.

Cleo. Didst heare her speake?
Is she shrill tongu'd or low?

Mes. Madam, I heard her speake, she is low voic'd.

Cleo. That's not so good: he cannot like her long.

Char. Like her? Oh *Isis*: 'tis impossible.

Cleo. I thinke so *Charmian*: dull of tongue, & dwarfish
What Maiestie is in her gate, remember
If ere thou look'st on Maiestie.

Mes. She creepes: her motion, & her station are as one:
She shewes a body, rather then a life,
A Statue, then a Breather.

Cleo. Is this certaine?

Mes. Or I haue no obseruance.

Cha. Three in Egypt cannot make better note.

Cleo. He's very knowing, I do perceiu't,
There's nothing in her yet.

The

The Fellow ha's good iudgement.
Char. Excellent.
Cleo. Guesse at her yeares, I prythee.
Mess. Madam, she was a widdow.
Cleo. Widdow? *Charmian*, hearke.
Mes. And I do thinke she's thirtie.
Cle. Bear'st thou her face in mind? is't long or round?
Mess. Round, euen to faultinesse.
Cleo. For the most part too, they are foolish that are so. Her haire what colour?
Mess. Browne Madam: and her forehead
As low as she would wish it.
Cleo. There's Gold for thee,
Thou must not take my former sharpenesse ill,
I will employ thee backe againe: I finde thee
Most fit for businesse. Go, make thee ready,
Our Letters are prepar'd.
Char. A proper man.
Cleo. Indeed he is so: I repent me much
That so I harried him. Why me think's by him,
This Creature's no such thing.
Char. Nothing Madam.
Cleo. The man hath seene some Maiesty, and should know.
Char. Hath he seene Maiestie? *Isis* else defend: and seruing you so long.
Cleopa. I haue one thing more to aske him yet good *Charmian*: but 'tis no matter, thou shalt bring him to me where I will write; all may be well enough.
Char. I warrant you Madam. *Exeunt.*

Enter Anthony and Octauia.

Ant. Nay, nay *Octauia*, not onely that,
That were excusable, that and thousands more
Of semblable import, but he hath wag'd
New Warres 'gainst *Pompey*. Made his will, and read it,
To publicke eare, spoke scantly of me,
When perforce he could not
But pay me tearmes of Honour: cold and sickly
He vented then most narrow measure; lent me,
When the best hint was giuen him: he not look't,
Or did it from his teeth.
Octaui. Oh my good Lord,
Beleeue not all, or if you must beleeue,
Stomacke not all. A more vnhappie Lady,
If this deuision chance, ne're stood betweene
Praying for both parts:
The good Gods wil mocke me presently,
When I shall pray: Oh blesse my Lord, and Husband,
Vndo that prayer, by crying out as loud,
Oh blesse my Brother. Husband winne, winne Brother,
Prayes, and distroyes the prayer, no midway
'Twixt these extreames at all.
Ant. Gentle *Octauia*,
Let your best loue draw to that point which seeks
Best to preserue it: if I loose mine Honour,
I loose my selfe: better I were not yours
Then your so branchlesse. But as you requested,
Your selfe shall go between's, the meane time Lady,
Ile raise the preparation of a Warre
Shall staine your Brother, make your soonest hast,
So your desires are yours.
Oct. Thanks to my Lord,
The Ioue of power make me most weake, most weake,
You reconciler: Warres 'twixt you twaine would be,
As if the world should cleaue, and that slaine men
Should soader vp the Rift.
Anth. When it appeeres to you where this begins,
Turne your displeasure that way, for our faults
Can neuer be so equall, that your loue
Can equally moue with them. Prouide your going,
Choose your owne company, and command what cost
Your heart he's mind too. *Exeunt.*

Enter Enobarbus, and Eros.

Eno. How now Friend *Eros*?
Eros. 'Ther's strange Newes come Sir.
Eno. What man?
Ero. *Cæsar* & *Lepidus* haue made warres vpon *Pompey*.
Eno. This is old, what is the successe?
Eros. *Cæsar* hauing made vse of him in the warres 'gainst *Pompey*: presently denied him riuality, would not let him partake in the glory of the action, and not resting here, accuses him of Letters he had formerly wrote to *Pompey*. Vpon his owne appeale seizes him, so the poore third is vp, till death enlarge his Confine.
Eno. Then would thou hadst a paire of chaps no more, and throw betweene them all the food thou hast, they'le grinde the other. Where's *Anthony*?
Eros. He's walking in the garden thus, and spurnes
The rush that lies before him. Cries Foole *Lepidus*,
And threats the throate of that his Officer,
That murdred *Pompey*.
Eno. Our great Nauies rig'd.
Eros. For Italy and *Cæsar*, more *Domitius*,
My Lord desires you presently: my Newes
I might haue told heareafter.
Eno. 'Twillbe naught, but let it be: bring me to *Anthony*.
Eros. Come Sir, *Exeunt.*

Enter Agrippa, Mecenas, and Cæsar.

Cæs. Contemning Rome he ha's done all this, & more
In Alexandria: heere's the manner of't:
I'th'Market-place on a Tribunall siluer'd,
Cleopatra and himselfe in Chaires of Gold
Were publikely enthron'd: at the feet, sat
Cæsarion whom they call my Fathers Sonne,
And all the vnlawfull issue, that their Lust
Since then hath made betweene them. Vnto her,
He gaue the stablishment of Egypt, made her
Of lower Syria, Cyprus, Lydia, absolute Queene.
Mece. This in the publike eye?
Cæsar. I'th'common shew place, where they exercise,
His Sonnes hither proclaimed the King of Kings,
Great Media, Parthia, and Armenia
He gaue to *Alexander*. To *Ptolomy* he assign'd,
Syria, Silicia, and Phœnetia: she
In th'abiliments of the Goddesse *Isis*
That day appeer'd, and oft before gaue audience,
As 'tis reported so.
Mece. Let Rome be thus inform'd.
Agri. Who queazie with his insolence already,
Will their good thoughts call from him.
Cæsar. The people knowes it,
And haue now receiu'd his accusations.
Agri. Who does he accuse?
Cæsar. *Cæsar*, and that hauing in Cicilie
Sextus Pompeius spoil'd, we had not rated him
His part o'th'Isle. Then does he say, he lent me
Some shipping vnrestor'd. Lastly, he frets
That *Lepidus* of the Triumpherate, should be depos'd,
And being that, we detaine all his Reuenue.
Agri. Sir, this should be answer'd.
Cæsar. 'Tis done already, and the Messenger gone:
I haue told him *Lepidus* was growne too cruell,

That he his high Authority abus'd,
And did deserue his change: for what I haue conquer'd,
I grant him part: but then in his Armenia,
And other of his conquer'd Kingdoms, I demand the like
Mec. Hee'l neuer yeeld to that.
Cæs. Nor must not then be yeelded to in this.
Enter Octauia with her Traine.
Octa. Haile *Cæsar*, and my L. haile most deere *Cæsar*.
Cæsar. That euer I should call thee Cast-away.
Octa. You haue not call'd me so, nor haue you cause.
Cæs. Why haue you stoln vpon vs thus? you come not
Like *Cæsars* Sister, The wife of *Anthony*
Should haue an Army for an Vsher, and
The neighes of Horse to tell of her approach,
Long ere she did appeare. The trees by'th'way
Should haue borne men, and expectation fainted,
Longing for what it had not. Nay, the dust
Should haue ascended to the Roofe of Heauen,
Rais'd by your populous Troopes: But you are come
A Market-maid to Rome, and haue preuented
The ostentation of our loue; which left vnshewne,
Is often left vnlou'd: we should haue met you
By Sea, and Land, supplying euery Stage
With an augmented greeting.
Octa. Good my Lord,
To come thus was I not constrain'd, but did it
On my free-will. My Lord *Marke Anthony*,
Hearing that you prepar'd for Warre, acquainted
My greeued eare withall; whereon I begg'd
His pardon for returne.
Cæs. Which soone he granted,
Being an abstract 'tweene his Lust, and him.
Octa. Do not say so, my Lord.
Cæs. I haue eyes vpon him,
And his affaires come to me on the wind: wher is he now?
Octa. My Lord, in Athens.
Cæsar. No my most wronged Sister, *Cleopatra*
Hath nodded him to her. He hath giuen his Empire
Vp to a Whore, who now are leuying
The Kings o'th'earth for Warre. He hath assembled,
Bochus the King of Lybia, *Archilaus*
Of Cappadocia, *Philadelphos* King
Of Paphlagonia: the Thracian King *Adullas*,
King *Mauchus* of Arabia, King of Pont,
Herod of Iewry, *Mithridates* King
Of Comageat, *Polemen* and *Amintas*,
The Kings of Mede, and Licoania,
With a more larger List of Scepters.
Octa. Aye me most wretched,
That haue my heart parted betwixt two Friends,
That does afflict each other. (breaking forth
Cæs. Welcom hither: your Letters did with-holde our
Till we perceiu'd both how you were wrong led,
And we in negligent danger: cheere your heart,
Be you not troubled with the time, which driues
O're your content, these strong necessities,
But let determin'd things to destinie
Hold vnbewayl'd their way. Welcome to Rome,
Nothing more deere to me: You are abus'd
Beyond the marke of thought: and the high Gods
To do you Iustice, makes his Ministers
Of vs, and those that loue you. Best of comfort,
And euer welcom to vs. *Agrip.* Welcome Lady.
Mec. Welcome deere Madam,
Each heart in Rome does loue and pitty you,
Onely th'adulterous *Anthony*, most large
In his abhominations, turnes you off,
And giues his potent Regiment to a Trull
That noyses it against vs.
Octa. Is it so sir?
Cæs. Most certaine: Sister welcome: pray you
Be euer knowne to patience. My deer'st Sister. *Exeunt*
Enter Cleopatra, and Enobarbus.
Cleo. I will be euen with thee, doubt it not.
Eno. But why, why, why?
Cleo. Thou hast forespoke my being in these warres,
And say'st it it not fit.
Eno. Well: is it, is it.
Cleo. If not, denounc'd against vs, why should not we be there in person.
Enob. Well, I could reply: if wee should serue with Horse and Mares together, the Horse were meerly lost: the Mares would beare a Soldiour and his Horse.
Cleo. What is't you say?
Enob. Your presence needs must puzle *Anthony*,
Take from his heart, take from his Braine, from's time,
What should not then be spar'd. He is already
Traduc'd for Leuity, and 'tis said in Rome,
That *Photinus* an Eunuch, and your Maides
Mannage this warre.
Cleo. Sinke Rome, and their tongues rot
That speake against vs. A Charge we beare i'th'Warre,
And as the president of my Kingdome will
Appeare there for a man. Speake not against it,
I will not stay behinde.
Enter Anthony and Camidias.
Eno. Nay I haue done, here comes the Emperor.
Ant. Is it not strange *Camidius*,
That from Tarrentum, and Brandusium,
He could so quickly cut the Ionian Sea,
And take in Troine. You haue heard on't (Sweet?)
Cleo. Celerity is neuer more admir'd,
Then by the negligent.
Ant. A good rebuke,
Which might haue well becom'd the best of men
To taunt at slacknesse. *Camidius*, wee
Will fight with him by Sea.
Cleo. By Sea, what else?
Cam. Why will my Lord, do so?
Ant. For that he dares vs too't.
Enob. So hath my Lord, dar'd him to single fight.
Cam. I, and to wage this Battell at Pharsalia,
Where *Cæsar* fought with *Pompey*. But these offers
Which serue not for his vantage, he shakes off,
And so should you.
Enob. Your Shippes are not well mann'd,
Your Marriners are Militers, Reapers, people
Ingrost by swift Impresse. In *Cæsars* Fleete,
Are those, that often haue 'gainst *Pompey* fought,
Their shippes are yare, yours heauy: no disgrace
Shall fall you for refusing him at Sea,
Being prepar'd for Land.
Ant. By Sea, by Sea.
Eno. Most worthy Sir, you therein throw away
The absolute Soldiership you haue by Land,
Distract your Armie, which doth most consist
Of Warre-markt-footmen, leaue vnexecuted
Your owne renowned knowledge, quite forgoe
The way which promises assurance, and
Giue vp your selfe meerly to chance and hazard,
From firme Securitie.
Ant. Ile fight at Sea.

Cleo

Cleo. I haue sixty Sailes, *Cæsar* none better.
Ant. Our ouer-plus of shipping will we burne,
And with the rest full mann'd, from th'head of Action
Beate th'approaching *Cæsar*. But if we faile,
We then can doo't at Land. *Enter a Messenger.*
Thy Businesse?
Mes. The Newes is true, my Lord, he is descried,
Cæsar ha's taken Toryne.
Ant. Can he be there in person? 'Tis impossible
Strange, that his power should be. *Camidius*,
Our nineteene Legions thou shalt hold by Land,
And our twelue thousand Horse. Wee'l to our Ship,
Away my *Thetis*.

Enter a Soldiour.

How now worthy Souldier?
Soul. Oh Noble Emperor, do not fight by Sea,
Trust not to rotten plankes: Do you misdoubt
This Sword, and these my Wounds; let th'Egyptians
And the Phœnicians go a ducking: wee
Haue vs'd to conquer standing on the earth,
And fighting foot to foot.
Ant. Well, well, away. *exit Ant. Cleo. & Enob.*
Soul. By *Hercules* I thinke I am i'th'right.
Cam. Souldier thou art: but his whole action growes
Not in the power on't: so our Leaders leade,
And we are Womens men.
Soul. You keepe by Land the Legions and the Horse
whole, do you not?
Ven. *Marcus Octauius, Marcus Iusteus,*
Publicola, and *Celius*, are for Sea:
But we keepe whole by Land. This speede of *Cæsars*
Carries beyond beleefe.
Soul. While he was yet in Rome,
His power went out in such distractions,
As beguilde all Spies.
Cam. Who's his Lieutenant, heare you?
Soul. They say, one *Towrus*.
Cam. Well, I know the man.

Enter a Messenger.

Mes. The Emperor cals *Camidius*.
Cam. With Newes the times with Labour,
And throwes forth each minute, some. *exeunt*

Enter Cæsar with his Army, marching.

Cæs. *Towrus*?
Tow. My Lord.
Cæs. Strike not by Land,
Keepe whole, prouoke not Battaile
Till we haue done at Sea. Do not exceede
The Prescript of this Scroule: Our fortune lyes
Vpon this iumpe. *exit.*

Enter Anthony, and Enobarbus.

Ant. Set we our Squadrons on yond side o'th'Hill,
In eye of *Cæsars* battaile, from which place
We may the number of the Ships behold,
And so proceed accordingly. *exit.*

Camidius Marcheth with his Land Army one way ouer the stage, and Towrus the Lieutenant of Cæsar the other way: After their going in, is heard the noise of a Sea fight.
Alarum. Enter Enobarbus and Scarus.

Eno. Naught, naught, al naught, I can behold no longer:
Thantoniad, the Egyptian Admirall,
With all their sixty flye, and turne the Rudder:
To see't, mine eyes are blasted.

Enter Scarrus.

Scar. Gods, & Goddesses, all the whol synod of them!
Eno. What's thy passion.
Scar. The greater Cantle of the world, is lost
With very ignorance, we haue kist away
Kingdomes, and Prouinces.
Eno. How appeares the Fight?
Scar. On our side, like the Token'd Pestilence,
Where death is sure. Yon ribaudred Nagge of Egypt,
(Whom Leprosie o're-take) i'th'midst o'th'fight,
When vantage like a payre of Twinnes appear'd
Both as the same, or rather ours the elder;
(The Breeze vpon her) like a Cow in Inne,
Hoists Sailes, and flyes.
Eno. That I beheld:
Mine eyes did sicken at the sight, and could not
Indure a further view.
Scar. She once being looft,
The Noble ruine of her Magicke, *Anthony*,
Claps on his Sea-wing, and (like a doting Mallard)
Leauing the Fight in heighth, flyes after her:
I neuer saw an Action of such shame;
Experience, Man-hood, Honor, ne're before,
Did violate so it selfe.
Enob. Alacke, alacke.

Enter Camidius.

Cam. Our Fortune on the Sea is out of breath,
And sinkes most lamentably. Had our Generall
Bin what he knew himselfe, it had gone well:
Oh his ha's giuen example for our flight,
Most grossely by his owne.
Enob. I, are you thereabouts? Why then goodnight indeede.
Cam. Toward Peloponnesus are they fled.
Scar. 'Tis easie toot,
And there I will attend what further comes.
Camid. To *Cæsar* will I render
My Legions and my Horse, sixe Kings alreadie
Shew me the way of yeelding.
Eno. Ile yet follow
The wounded chance of *Anthony*, though my reason
Sits in the winde against me.

Enter Anthony with Attendants.

Ant. Hearke, the Land bids me tread no more vpon't,
It is asham'd to beare me. Friends, come hither,
I am so lated in the world, that I
Haue lost my way for euer. I haue a shippe,
Laden with Gold, take that, diuide it: flye,
And make your peace with *Cæsar*.
Omnes. Fly? Not wee.
Ant. I haue fled my selfe, and haue instructed cowards
To runne, and shew their shoulders. Friends be gone,
I haue my selfe resolu'd vpon a course,
Which has no neede of you. Be gone,
My Treasure's in the Harbour. Take it: Oh,
I follow'd that I blush to looke vpon,
My very haires do mutiny: for the white
Reproue the browne for rashnesse, and they them
For feare, and doting. Friends be gone, you shall
Haue Letters from me to some Friends, that will
Sweepe your way for you. Pray you looke not sad,
Nor make replyes of loathnesse, take the hint
Which my dispaire proclaimes. Let them be left
Which leaues it selfe, to the Sea-side straight way;
I will possesse you of that ship and Treasure.

Leaue me, I pray a little: pray you now,
Nay do so: for indeede I haue lost command,
Therefore I pray you, Ile see you by and by. *Sits downe*

Enter Cleopatra led by Charmian and Eros.

Eros. Nay gentle Madam, to him, comfort him.
Iras. Do most deere Queene.
Char. Do, why, what else?
Cleo. Let me sit downe: Oh *Iuno.*
Ant. No, no, no, no, no.
Eros. See you heere, Sir?
Ant. Oh fie, fie, fie.
Char. Madam.
Iras. Madam, oh good Empresse.
Eros. Sir, sir.
Ant. Yes my Lord, yes; he at Philippi kept
His sword e'ne like a dancer, while I strooke
The leane and wrinkled *Cassius*, and 'twas I
That the mad *Brutus* ended: he alone
Dealt on Lieutenantry, and no practise had
In the braue squares of Warre: yet now: no matter.
Cleo. Ah stand by.
Eros. The Queene my Lord, the Queene.
Iras. Go to him, Madam, speake to him,
Hee's vnqualited with very shame.
Cleo. Well then, sustaine me: Oh.
Eros. Most Noble Sir arise, the Queene approaches,
Her head's declin'd, and death will cease her, but
Your comfort makes the rescue.
Ant. I haue offended Reputation,
A most vnnoble sweruing.
Eros. Sir, the Queene.
Ant. Oh whether hast thou lead me Egypt, see
How I conuey my shame, out of thine eyes,
By looking backe what I haue left behinde
Stroy'd in dishonor.
Cleo. Oh my Lord, my Lord,
Forgiue my fearfull sayles, I little thought
You would haue followed.
Ant. Egypt, thou knew'st too well,
My heart was to thy Rudder tyed by'th'strings,
And thou should'st stowe me after. O're my spirit
The full supremacie thou knew'st, and that
Thy becke, might from the bidding of the Gods
Command mee.
Cleo. Oh my pardon.
Ant. Now I must
To the young man send humble Treaties, dodge
And palter in the shifts of lownes, who
With halfe the bulke o'th'world plaid as I pleas'd,
Making, and marring Fortunes. You did know
How much you were my Conqueror, and that
My Sword, made weake by my affection, would
Obey it on all cause.
Cleo. Pardon, pardon.
Ant. Fall not a teare I say, one of them rates
All that is wonne and lost: Giue me a kisse,
Euen this repayes me.
We sent our Schoolemaster, is a come backe?
Loue I am full of Lead: some Wine
Within there, and our Viands: Fortune knowes,
We scorne her most, when most she offers blowes. *Exeunt*

Enter Cæsar, Agrippa, and Dollabello, with others.

Cæs. Let him appeare that's come from *Anthony.*
Know you him.
Dolla. *Cæsar*, 'tis his Schoolemaster,
An argument that he is pluckt, when hither
He sends so poore a Pinnion of his Wing,
Which had superfluous Kings for Messengers,
Not many Moones gone by.

Enter Ambassador from Anthony.

Cæsar. Approach, and speake.
Amb. Such as I am, I come from *Anthony*:
I was of late as petty to his ends,
As is the Morne-dew on the Mertle leafe
To his grand Sea.
Cæs. Bee't so, declare thine office.
Amb. Lord of his Fortunes he salutes thee, and
Requires to liue in Egypt, which not granted
He Lessons his Requests, and to thee sues
To let him breath betweene the Heauens and Earth
A priuate man in Athens: this for him.
Next, *Cleopatra* does confesse thy Greatnesse,
Submits her to thy might, and of thee craues
The Circle of the *Ptolomies* for her heyres,
Now hazarded to thy Grace.
Cæs. For *Anthony*,
I haue no eares to his request. The Queene,
Of Audience, nor Desire shall faile, so shee
From Egypt driue her all-disgraced Friend,
Or take his life there. This if shee performe,
She shall not sue vnheard. So to them both.
Amb. Fortune pursue thee.
Cæs. Bring him through the Bands:
To try thy Eloquence, now 'tis time, dispatch,
From *Anthony* winne *Cleopatra*, promise
And in our Name, what she requires, adde more
From thine inuention, offers. Women are not
In their best Fortunes strong; but want will periure
The ne're touch'd Vestall. Try thy cunning *Thidias*,
Make thine owne Edict for thy paines, which we
Will answer as a Law.
Thid. *Cæsar*, I go.
Cæsar. Obserue how *Anthony* becomes his flaw,
And what thou think'st his very action speakes
In euery power that mooues.
Thid. *Cæsar*, I shall. *exeunt.*

Enter Cleopatra, Enobarbus, Charmian, & Iras.

Cleo. What shall we do, *Enobarbus*?
Eno. Thinke, and dye.
Cleo. Is *Anthony*, or we in fault for this?
Eno. *Anthony* onely, that would make his will
Lord of his Reason. What though you fled,
From that great face of Warre, whose seuerall ranges
Frighted each other? Why should he follow?
The itch of his Affection should not then
Haue nickt his Captain-ship, at such a point,
When halfe to halfe the world oppos'd, he being
The meered question? 'Twas a shame no lesse
Then was his losse, to course your flying Flagges,
And leaue his Nauy gazing.
Cleo. Prythee peace.

Enter the Ambassador, with Anthony.

Ant. Is that his answer? *Amb.* I my Lord.
Ant. The Queene shall then haue courtesie,
So she will yeeld vs vp.
Am. He sayes so.
Antho. Let her know't. To the Boy *Cæsar* send this grizled head, and he will fill thy wishes to the brimme, With Principalities.
Cleo. That head my Lord?

Ant.

Ant. To him againe, tell him he weares the Rose
Of youth vpon him: from which, the world should note
Something particular: His Coine, Ships, Legions,
May be a Cowards, whose Ministers would preuaile
Vnder the seruice of a Childe, as soone
As i'th'Command of *Cæsar*. I dare him therefore
To lay his gay Comparisons a-part,
And answer me declin'd, Sword against Sword,
Our selues alone: Ile write it: Follow me.
Eno. Yes like enough: hye battel'd *Cæsar* will
Vnstate his happinesse, and be Stag'd to'th'shew
Against a Sworder. I see mens Iudgements are
A parcell of their Fortunes, and things outward
Do draw the inward quality after them
To suffer all alike, that he should dreame,
Knowing all measures, the full *Cæsar* will
Answer his emptinesse; *Cæsar* thou hast subdu'de
His iudgement too.
Enter a Seruant.
Ser. A Messenger from *Cæsar*.
Cleo. What no more Ceremony? See my Women,
Against the blowne Rose may they stop their nose,
That kneel'd vnto the Buds. Admit him sir.
Eno. Mine honesty, and I, beginne to square,
The Loyalty well held to Fooles, does make
Our Faith meere folly: yet he that can endure
To follow with Allegeance a falne Lord,
Does conquer him that did his Master conquer,
And earnes a place i'th'Story.
Enter Thidias.
Cleo. *Cæsars* will.
Thid. Heare it apart.
Cleo. None but Friends: say boldly.
Thid. So haply are they Friends to *Anthony*.
Enob. He needs as many (Sir) as *Cæsar* ha's,
Or needs not vs. If *Cæsar* please, our Master
Will leape to be his Friend: For vs you know,
Whose he is, we are, and that is *Cæsars*.
Thid. So. Thus then thou most renown'd, *Cæsar* intreats,
Not to consider in what case thou stand'st
Further then he is *Cæsars*.
Cleo. Go on, right Royall.
Thid. He knowes that you embrace not *Anthony*
As you did loue, but as you feared him.
Cleo. Oh.
Thid. The scarre's vpon your Honor, therefore he
Does pitty, as constrained blemishes,
Not as deserued.
Cleo. He is a God,
And knowes what is most right. Mine Honour
Was not yeelded, but conquer'd meerely.
Eno. To be sure of that, I will aske *Anthony*.
Sir, sir, thou art so leakie
That we must leaue thee to thy sinking, for
Thy deerest quit thee. *Exit Enob.*
Thid. Shall I say to *Cæsar*,
What you require of him: for he partly begges
To be desir'd to giue. It much would please him,
That of his Fortunes you should make a staffe
To leane vpon. But it would warme his spirits
To heare from me you had left *Anthony*,
And put your selfe vnder his shrowd, the vniuersal Land-(lord.
Cleo. What's your name?
Thid. My name is *Thidias*.
Cleo. Most kinde Messenger,
Say to great *Cæsar* this in disputation,
I kisse his conqu'ring hand: Tell him, I am prompt
To lay my Crowne at's feete, and there to kneele.
Tell him, from his all-obeying breath, I heare
The doome of Egypt.
Thid. 'Tis your Noblest course:
Wisedome and Fortune combatting together,
If that the former dare but what it can,
No chance may shake it. Giue me grace to lay
My dutie on your hand.
Cleo. Your *Cæsars* Father oft,
(When he hath mus'd of taking kingdomes in)
Bestow'd his lips on that vnworthy place,
As it rain'd kisses.
Enter Anthony and Enobarbus.
Ant. Fauours? By Ioue that thunders. What art thou (Fellow?
Thid. One that but performes
The bidding of the fullest man, and worthiest
To haue command obey'd.
Eno. You will be whipt.
Ant. Approch there: ah you Kite. Now Gods & diuels
Authority melts from me of late. When I cried hoa,
Like Boyes vnto a musse, Kings would start forth,
And cry, your will. Haue you no eares?
I am *Anthony* yet. Take hence this Iack, and whip him.
Enter a Seruant.
Eno. 'Tis better playing with a Lions whelpe,
Then with an old one dying.
Ant. Moone and Starres,
Whip him: wer't twenty of the greatest Tributaries
That do acknowledge *Cæsar*, should I finde them
So sawcy with the hand of she heere, what's her name
Since she was *Cleopatra*? Whip him Fellowes,
Till like a Boy you see him crindge his face,
And whine aloud for mercy. Take him hence.
Thid. *Marke Anthony*.
Ant. Tugge him away: being whipt
Bring him againe, the Iacke of *Cæsars* shall
Beare vs an arrant to him. *Exeunt with Thidius.*
You were halfe blasted ere I knew you: Ha?
Haue I my pillow left vnprest in Rome,
Forborne the getting of a lawfull Race,
And by a Iem of women, to be abus'd
By one that lookes on Feeders?
Cleo. Good my Lord.
Ant. You haue beene a boggeler euer,
But when we in our viciousnesse grow hard
(Oh misery on't) the wise Gods seele our eyes
In our owne filth, drop our cleare iudgements, make vs
Adore our errors, laugh at's while we strut
To our confusion.
Cleo. Oh, is't come to this?
Ant. I found you as a Morsell, cold vpon
Dead *Cæsars* Trencher: Nay, you were a Fragment
Of *Gneius Pompeyes*, besides what hotter houres
Vnregistred in vulgar Fame, you haue
Luxuriously pickt out. For I am sure,
Though you can guesse what Temperance should be,
You know not what it is.
Cleo. Wherefore is this?
Ant. To let a Fellow that will take rewards,
And say, God quit you, be familiar with
My play-fellow, your hand ÿ this Kingly Seale,
And plighter of high hearts. O that I were
Vpon the hill of Basan, to out-roare
The horned Heard, for I haue sauage cause,
And to proclaime it ciuilly, were like

A halter'd necke, which do's the Hangman thanke,
For being yare about him. Is he whipt?

Enter a Seruant with Thidias.

Ser. Soundly, my Lord.

Ant. Cried he? and begg'd a Pardon?

Ser. He did aske fauour.

Ant. If that thy Father liue, let him repent
Thou was't not made his daughter, and be thou sorrie
To follow *Cæsar* in his Triumph, since
Thou hast bin whipt. For following him, henceforth
The white hand of a Lady Feauer thee,
Shake thou to looke on't. Get thee backe to *Cæsar*,
Tell him thy entertainment: looke thou say
He makes me angry with him. For he seemes
Proud and disdainfull, harping on what I am,
Not what he knew I was. He makes me angry,
And at this time most easie 'tis to doo't:
When my good Starres, that were my former guides
Haue empty left their Orbes, and shot their Fires
Into th'Abisme of hell. If he mislike,
My speech, and what is done, tell him he has
Hiparchus, my enfranched Bondman, whom
He may at pleasure whip, or hang, or torture,
As he shall like to quit me. Vrge it thou:
Hence with thy stripes, be gone. *Exit Thid.*

Cleo. Haue you done yet?

Ant. Alacke our Terrene Moone is now Eclipst,
And it portends alone the fall of *Anthony*.

Cleo. I must stay his time?

Ant. To flatter *Cæsar*, would you mingle eyes
With one that tyes his points.

Cleo. Not know me yet?

Ant. Cold-hearted toward me?

Cleo. Ah (Deere) if I be so,
From my cold heart let Heauen ingender haile,
And poyson it in the sourse, and the first stone
Drop in my necke: as it determines so
Dissolue my life, the next Cæsarian smile,
Till by degrees the memory of my wombe,
Together with my braue Egyptians all,
By the discandering of this pelleted storme,
Lye graueleffe, till the Flies and Gnats of Nyle
Haue buried them for prey.

Ant. I am satisfied:
Cæsar sets downe in Alexandria, where
I will oppose his Fate. Our force by Land,
Hath Nobly held, our seuer'd Nauie too
Haue knit againe, and Fleete, threatning most Sea-like.
Where hast thou bin my heart? Dost thou heare Lady?
If from the Field I shall returne once more
To kisse these Lips, I will appeare in Blood,
I, and my Sword, will earne our Chronicle,
There's hope in't yet.

Cleo. That's my braue Lord.

Ant. I will be trebble-sinewed, hearted, breath'd,
And fight maliciously: for when mine houres
Were nice and lucky, men did ransome liues
Of me for iests: But now, Ile set my teeth,
And send to darkenesse all that stop me. Come,
Let's haue one other gawdy night: Call to me
All my sad Captaines, fill our Bowles once more:
Let's mocke the midnight Bell.

Cleo. It is my Birth-day,
I had thought t'haue held it poore. But since my Lord
Is *Anthony* againe, I will be *Cleopatra*.

Ant. We will yet do well.

Cleo. Call all his Noble Captaines to my Lord.

Ant. Do so, wee'l speake to them,
And to night Ile force
The Wine peepe through their scarres.
Come on (my Queene)
There's sap in't yet. The next time I do fight
Ile make death loue me: for I will contend
Euen with his pestilent Sythe. *Exeunt.*

Eno. Now hee'l out-stare the Lightning, to be furious
Is to be frighted out of feare, and in that moode
The Doue will pecke the Estridge; and I see still
A diminution in our Captaines braine,
Restores his heart; when valour prayes in reason,
It eates the Sword it fights with: I will seeke
Some way to leaue him. *Exeunt.*

Enter Cæsar, Agrippa, & Mecenas with his Army, Cæsar reading a Letter.

Cæs. He calles me Boy, and chides as he had power
To beate me out of Egypt. My Messenger
He hath whipt with Rods, dares me to personal Combat.
Cæsar to *Anthony*: let the old Ruffian know,
I haue many other wayes to dye: meane time
Laugh at his Challenge.

Mece. *Cæsar* must thinke,
When one so great begins to rage, hee's hunted
Euen to falling. Giue him no breath, but now
Make boote of his distraction: Neuer anger
Made good guard for it selfe.

Cæs. Let our best heads know,
That to morrow, the last of many Battailes
We meane to fight. Within our Files there are,
Of those that seru'd *Marke Anthony* but late,
Enough to fetch him in. See it done,
And Feast the Army, we haue store to doo't,
And they haue earn'd the waste. Poore *Anthony*. *Exeunt*

Enter Anthony, Cleopatra, Enobarbus, Charmian, Iras, Alexas, with others.

Ant. He will not fight with me, *Domitian*?

Eno. No?

Ant. Why should he not?

Eno. He thinks, being twenty times of better fortune,
He is twenty men to one.

Ant. To morrow Soldier,
By Sea and Land Ile fight: or I will liue,
Or bathe my dying Honor in the blood
Shall make it liue againe. Woo't thou fight well.

Eno. Ile strike, and cry, Take all.

Ant. Well said, come on:
Call forth my Houshold Seruants, lets to night

Enter 3 or 4 Seruitors.

Be bounteous at our Meale. Giue me thy hand,
Thou hast bin rightly honest, so hast thou,
Thou, and thou, and thou: you haue seru'd me well,
And Kings haue beene your fellowes.

Cleo. What meanes this?

Eno. 'Tis one of those odde tricks which sorow shoots
Out of the minde.

Ant. And thou art honest too:
I wish I could be made so many men,
And all of you clapt vp together, in
An *Anthony*: that I might do you seruice,
So good as you haue done.

Omnes.

Omnes. The Gods forbid.
Ant. Well, my good Fellowes, wait on me to night:
Scant not my Cups, and make as much of me,
As when mine Empire was your Fellow too,
And suffer'd my command.
Cleo. What does he meane?
Eno. To make his Followers weepe.
Ant. Tend me to night;
May be, it is the period of your duty,
Haply you shall not see me more, or if,
A mangled shadow. Perchance to morrow,
You'l serue another Master. I looke on you,
As one that takes his leaue. Mine honest Friends,
I turne you not away, but like a Master
Married to your good seruice, stay till death:
Tend me to night two houres, I aske no more,
And the Gods yeeld you for't.
Eno. What meane you (Sir)
To giue them this discomfort? Looke they weepe,
And I an Asse, am Onyon-ey'd; for shame,
Transforme vs not to women.
Ant. Ho, ho, ho:
Now the Witch take me, if I meant it thus.
Grace grow where those drops fall (my hearty Friends)
You take me in too dolorous a sense,
For I spake to you for your comfort, did desire you
To burne this night with Torches: Know (my hearts)
I hope well of to morrow, and will leade you,
Where rather Ile expect victorious life,
Then death, and Honor. Let's to Supper, come,
And drowne consideration. *Exeunt.*

Enter a Company of Soldiours.

1.Sol. Brother, goodnight: to morrow is the day.
2.Sol. It will determine one way: Fare you well.
Heard you of nothing strange about the streets.
1 Nothing: what newes?
2 Belike 'tis but a Rumour, good night to you.
1 Well sir, good night.
They meete other Soldiers.
2 Souldiers, haue carefull Watch.
1 And you: Goodnight, goodnight.
They place themselues in euery corner of the Stage.
2 Heere we: and if to morrow
Our Nauie thriue, I haue an absolute hope
Our Landmen will stand vp.
1 'Tis a braue Army, and full of purpose.
Musicke of the Hoboyes is vnder the Stage.
2 Peace, what noise?
1 List list.
2 Hearke.
1 Musicke i'th'Ayre.
3 Vnder the earth.
4 It signes well, do's it not?
3 No.
1 Peace I say: What should this meane?
2 'Tis the God *Hercules*, whom *Anthony* loued,
Now leaues him.
1 Walke, let's see if other Watchmen
Do heare what we do?
2 How now Maisters? *Speak together.*
Omnes. How now? how now? do you heare this?
1 I, is't not strange?
3 Do you heare Masters? Do you heare?
1 Follow the noyse so farre as we haue quarter.
Let's see how it will giue off.
Omnes. Content: 'Tis strange. *Exeunt.*

Enter Anthony and Cleopatra, with others.

Ant. *Eros*, mine Armour *Eros*.
Cleo. Sleepe a little.
Ant. No my Chucke. *Eros*, come mine Armor *Eros*.
Enter Eros.
Come good Fellow, put thine Iron on,
If Fortune be not ours to day, it is
Because we braue her. Come.
Cleo. Nay, Ile helpe too, *Anthony*.
What's this for? Ah let be, let be, thou art
The Armourer of my heart: False, false: This, this,
Sooth-law Ile helpe: Thus it must bee.
Ant. Well, well, we shall thriue now.
Seest thou my good Fellow. Go, put on thy defences.
Eros. Briefely Sir.
Cleo. Is not this buckled well?
Ant. Rarely, rarely:
He that vnbuckles this, till we do please
To daft for our Repose, shall heare a storme.
Thou fumblest *Eros*, and my Queenes a Squire
More tight at this, then thou: Dispatch. O Loue,
That thou couldst see my Warres to day, and knew'st
The Royall Occupation, thou should'st see
A Workeman in't.
Enter an Armed Soldier.
Good morrow to thee, welcome,
Thou look'st like him that knowes a warlike Charge:
To businesse that we loue, we rise betime,
And go too't with delight.
Soul. A thousand Sir, early though't be, haue on their
Riueted trim, and at the Port expect you. *Showt.*
Trumpets Flourish.
Enter Captaines, and Souldiers.
Alex. The Morne is faire: Good morrow Generall.
All. Good morrow Generall.
Ant. 'Tis well blowne Lads.
This Morning, like the spirit of a youth
That meanes to be of note, begins betimes.
So, so: Come giue me that, this way, well-sed.
Fare thee well Dame, what ere becomes of me,
This is a Soldiers kisse: rebukeable,
And worthy shamefull checke it were, to stand
On more Mechanicke Complement, Ile leaue thee.
Now like a man of Steele, you that will fight,
Follow me close, Ile bring you too't: Adieu. *Exeunt.*
Char. Please you retyre to your Chamber?
Cleo. Lead me:
He goes forth gallantly: That he and *Cæsar* might
Determine this great Warre in single fight;
Then *Anthony*; but now. Well on. *Exeunt*

Trumpets sound. Enter Anthony, and Eros.

Eros. The Gods make this a happy day to *Anthony*.
Ant. Would thou, & those thy scars had once preuaild
To make me fight at Land.
Eros. Had'st thou done so,
The Kings that haue reuolted, and the Soldier
That has this morning left thee, would haue still
Followed thy heeles.
Ant. Whose gone this morning?
Eros. Who? one euer neere thee, call for *Enobarbus*,
Hee

He ſhall not heare thee, or from *Cæſars* Campe,
Say I am none of thine.
Ant. What ſayeſt thou?
Sold. Sir he is with *Cæſar.*
Eros. Sir, his Cheſts and Treaſure he has not with him.
Ant. Is he gone?
Sol. Moſt certaine.
Ant. Go *Eros*, ſend his Treaſure after, do it,
Detaine no iot I charge thee: write to him,
(I will ſubſcribe) gentle adieu's, and greetings;
Say, that I wiſh he neuer finde more cauſe
To change a Maſter. Oh my Fortunes haue
Corrupted honeſt men. Diſpatch *Enobarbus.* *Exit*

Flouriſh. Enter Agrippa, Cæſar, with Enobarbus, and Dollabella.

Cæſ. Go forth *Agrippa*, and begin the fight:
Our will is *Anthony* be tooke aliue:
Make it ſo knowne.
Agrip. Cæſar, I ſhall.
Cæſar. The time of vniuerſall peace is neere:
Proue this a proſp'rous day, the three nook'd world
Shall beare the Oliue freely.
Enter a Meſſenger.
Meſ. Anthony is come into the Field.
Cæſ. Go charge *Agrippa*,
Plant thoſe that haue reuolted in the Vant,
That *Anthony* may ſeeme to ſpend his Fury
Vpon himſelfe. *Exeunt.*
Enob. Alexas did reuolt, and went to *Iewry* on
Affaires of *Anthony*, there did diſſwade
Great *Herod* to incline himſelfe to *Cæſar*,
And leaue his Maſter *Anthony*. For this paines,
Cæſar hath hang'd him: *Camindius* and the reſt
That fell away, haue entertainment, but
No honourable truſt: I haue done ill,
Of which I do accuſe my ſelfe ſo ſorely,
That I will ioy no more.
Enter a Soldier of Cæſars.
Sol. Enobarbus, Anthony
Hath after thee ſent all thy Treaſure, with
His Bounty ouer-plus. The Meſſenger
Came on my guard, and at thy Tent is now
Vnloading of his Mules.
Eno. I giue it you.
Sol. Mocke not *Enobarbus*,
I tell you true: Beſt you ſaf't the bringer
Out of the hoaſt, I muſt attend mine Office,
Or would haue done't my ſelfe. Your Emperor
Continues ſtill a Ioue. *Exit*
Enob. I am alone the Villaine of the earth,
And feele I am ſo moſt. Oh *Anthony*,
Thou Mine of Bounty, how would'ſt thou haue payed
My better ſeruice, when my turpitude
Thou doſt ſo Crowne with Gold. This blowes my hart,
If ſwift thought breake it not: a ſwifter meane
Shall out-ſtrike thought, but thought will doo't. I feele
I fight againſt thee: No I will go ſeeke
Some Ditch, wherein to dye: the foul'ſt beſt fits
My latter part of life. *Exit.*
Alarum, Drummes and Trumpets.
Enter Agrippa.
Agrip Retire, we haue engag'd our ſelues too farre:
Cæſar himſelfe ha's worke, and our oppreſſion
Exceeds what weexpected. *Exit.*

Alarums.
Enter Anthony, and Scarrus wounded.

Scar. O my braue Emperor, this is fought indeed,
Had we done ſo at firſt, we had drouen them home
With clowts about their heads. *Far off.*
Ant. Thou bleed'ſt apace.
Scar. I had a wound heere that was like a T,
But now 'tis made an H.
Ant. They do retyre.
Scar. Wee'l beat 'em into Bench-holes, I haue yet
Roome for ſix ſcotches more.
Enter Eros.
Eros. They are beaten Sir, and our aduantage ſerues
For a faire victory.
Scar. Let vs ſcore their backes,
And ſnatch 'em vp, as we take Hares behinde,
'Tis ſport to maul a Runner.
Ant. I will reward thee
Once for thy ſprightly comfort, and ten-fold
For thy good valour. Come thee on.
Scar. Ile halt after. *Exeunt*

Alarum. Enter Anthony againe in a March. Scarrus, with others.

Ant. We haue beate him to his Campe: Runne one
Before, & let the Queen know of our gueſts: to morrow
Before the Sun ſhall ſee's, wee'l ſpill the blood
That ha's to day eſcap'd. I thanke you all,
For doughty handed are you, and haue fought
Not as you ſeru'd the Cauſe, but as't had beene
Each mans like mine: you haue ſhewne all *Hectors.*
Enter the Citty, clip your Wiues, your Friends,
Tell them your feats, whil'ſt they with ioyfull teares
Waſh the congealement from your wounds, and kiſſe
The Honour'd-gaſhes whole.
Enter Cleopatra.
Giue me thy hand,
To this great Faiery, Ile commend thy acts,
Make her thankes bleſſe thee. Oh thou day o'th'world,
Chaine mine arm'd necke, leape thou, Attyre and all
Through proofe of Harneſſe to my heart, and there
Ride on the pants triumphing.
Cleo. Lord of Lords,
Oh infinite Vertue, comm'ſt thou ſmiling from
The worlds great ſnare vncaught.
Ant. Mine Nightingale,
We haue beate them to their Beds.
What Gyrle, though gray
Do ſomthing mingle with our yonger brown, yet ha we
A Braine that nouriſhes our Nerues, and can
Get gole for gole of youth. Behold this man,
Commend vnto his Lippes thy fauouring hand,
Kiſſe it my Warriour: He hath fought to day,
As if a God in hate of Mankinde, had
Deſtroyed in ſuch a ſhape.
Cleo. Ile giue thee Friend
An Armour all of Gold: it was a Kings.
Ant. He has deſeru'd it, were it Carbunkled
Like holy Phœbus Carre. Giue me thy hand,
Through Alexandria make a iolly March,
Beare our hackt Targets, like the men that owe them.
Had our great Pallace the capacity
To Campe this hoaſt, we all would ſup together,
And drinke Carowſes to the next dayes Fate

Which

Which promises Royall perill, Trumpetters
With brazen dinne blast you the Citties eare,
Make mingle with our ratling Tabourines,
That heauen and earth may strike their sounds together,
Applauding our approach. *Exeunt.*

Enter a Centerie, and his Company, Enobarbus followes.

Cent. If we be not releeu'd within this houre,
We must returne to'th'Court of Guard: the night
Is shiny, and they say, we shall embattaile
By'th'second houre i'th'Morne.
1.*Watch.* This last day was a shrew'd one too's.
Enob. Oh beare me witnesse night.
2 What man is this?
1 Stand close, and list him.
Enob. Be witnesse to me (O thou blessed Moone)
When men reuolted shall vpon Record
Beare hatefull memory: poore *Enobarbus* did
Before thy face repent.
Cent. *Enobarbus*?
2 Peace: Hearke further.
Enob. Oh Soueraigne Mistris of true Melancholly,
The poysonous dampe of night dispunge vpon me,
That Life, a very Rebell to my will,
May hang no longer on me. Throw my heart
Against the flint and hardnesse of my fault,
Which being dried with greefe, will breake to powder,
And finish all foule thoughts. Oh *Anthony*,
Nobler then my reuolt is Infamous,
Forgiue me in thine owne particular,
But let the world ranke me in Register
A Master leauer, and a fugitiue:
Oh *Anthony*! Oh *Anthony*!
1 Let's speake to him.
Cent. Let's heare him, for the things he speakes
May concerne *Cæsar*.
2 Let's do so, but he sleepes.
Cent. Swoonds rather, for so bad a Prayer as his
Was neuer yet for sleepe.
1 Go we to him.
2 Awake sir, awake, speake to vs.
1 Heare you sir?
Cent. The hand of death hath raught him.
Drummes afarre off.
Hearke the Drummes demurely wake the sleepers:
Let vs beare him to'th'Court of Guard: he is of note:
Our houre is fully out.
2 Come on then, he may recouer yet. *exeunt*

Enter Anthony and Scarrus, with their Army.

Ant. Their preparation is to day by Sea,
We please them not by Land.
Scar. For both, my Lord.
Ant. I would they'ld fight i'th'Fire, or i'th'Ayre,
Wee'ld fight there too. But this it is, our Foote
Vpon the hilles adioyning to the Citty
Shall stay with vs. Order for Sea is giuen,
They haue put forth the Hauen:
Where their appointment we may best discouer,
And looke on their endeuour. *exeunt*

Enter Cæsar, and his Army.

Cæs. But being charg'd, we will be still by Land,
Which as I tak't we shall, for his best force
Is forth to Man his Gallies. To the Vales,
And hold our best aduantage. *exeunt.*

Alarum afarre off, as at a Sea-fight.
Enter Anthony, and Scarrus.

Ant. Yet they are not ioyn'd:
Where yon'd Pine does stand, I shall discouer all.
Ile bring thee word straight, how'tis like to go. *exit.*
Scar. Swallowes haue built
In *Cleopatra*'s Sailes their nests. The Auguries
Say, they know not, they cannot tell, looke grimly,
And dare not speake their knowledge. *Anthony*,
Is valiant, and deiected, and by starts
His fretted Fortunes giue him hope and feare
Of what he has, and has not.

Enter Anthony.

Ant. All is lost:
This fowle Egyptian hath betrayed me:
My Fleete hath yeelded to the Foe, and yonder
They cast their Caps vp, and Carowse together
Like Friends long lost. Triple-turn'd Whore, 'tis thou
Hast sold me to this Nouice, and my heart
Makes onely Warres on thee. Bid them all flye:
For when I am reueng'd vpon my Charme,
I haue done all. Bid them all flye, be gone.
Oh Sunne, thy vprise shall I see no more,
Fortune, and *Anthony* part heere, euen heere
Do we shake hands? All come to this? The hearts
That pannelled me at heeles, to whom I gaue
Their wishes, do dis-Candie, melt their sweets
On blossoming *Cæsar*: And this Pine is barkt,
That ouer-top'd them all. Betray'd I am.
Oh this false Soule of Egypt! this graue Charme,
Whose eye beck'd forth my Wars, & cal'd them home:
Whose Bosome was my Crownet, my chiefe end,
Like a right Gypsie, hath at fast and loose
Beguil'd me, to the very heart of losse.
What *Eros*, *Eros*?

Enter Cleopatra.

Ah, thou Spell! Auaunt.
Cleo. Why is my Lord enrag'd against his Loue?
Ant. Vanish, or I shall giue thee thy deseruing,
And blemish *Cæsars* Triumph. Let him take thee,
And hoist thee vp to the shouting Plebeians,
Follow his Chariot, like the greatest spot
Of all thy Sex. Most Monster-like be shewne
For poor'st Diminitiues, for Dolts, and let
Patient *Octauia*, plough thy visage vp
With her prepared nailes. *exit Cleopatra.*
'Tis well th'art gone,
If it be well to liue. But better 'twere
Thou fell'st into my furie, for one death
Might haue preuented many. *Eros*, hoa?
The shirt of *Nessus* is vpon me, teach me
Alcides, thou mine Ancestor, thy rage.
Let me lodge *Licas* on the hornes o'th'Moone,
And with those hands that graspt the heauiest Club,
Subdue my worthiest selfe: The Witch shall die,
To the young Roman Boy she hath sold me, and I fall
Vnder this plot: She dyes for't. *Eros* hoa? *exit.*

Enter Cleopatra, Charmian, Iras, Mardian.

Cleo. Helpe me my women: Oh hee's more mad
Then *Telamon* for his Shield, the Boare of Thessaly
Was neuer so imbost.
Char. To'th'Monument, there locke your selfe,
And send him word you are dead:

The

The Soule and Body riue not more in parting,
Then greatnesse going off.
Cleo. To'th'Monument:
Mardian, go tell him I haue slaine my selfe:
Say, that the last I spoke was *Anthony*,
And word it (prythee) pitteously. Hence *Mardian*,
And bring me how he takes my death to'th'Monument.
Exeunt.

Enter Anthony, and Eros.

Ant. *Eros*, thou yet behold'st me?
Eros. I Noble Lord.
Ant. Sometime we see a clowd that's Dragonish,
A vapour sometime, like a Beare, or Lyon,
A toward Cittadell, a pendant Rocke,
A forked Mountaine, or blew Promontorie
With Trees vpon't, that nodde vnto the world,
And mocke our eyes with Ayre.
Thou hast seene these Signes,
They are blacke Vespers Pageants.
Eros. I my Lord.
Ant. That which is now a Horse, euen with a thoght the Racke dislimes, and makes it indistinct
As water is in water.
Eros. It does my Lord.
Ant. My good Knaue *Eros*, now thy Captaine is
Euen such a body: Heere I am *Anthony*,
Yet cannot hold this visible shape (my Knaue)
I made these warres for Egypt, and the Queene,
Whose heart I thought I had, for she had mine:
Which whil'st it was mine, had annext vntoo't
A Million moe, (now lost:) shee *Eros* has
Packt Cards with *Cæsars*, and false plaid my Glory
Vnto an Enemies triumph.
Nay, weepe not gentle *Eros*, there is left vs
Our selues to end our selues.

Enter Mardian.

Oh thy vilde Lady, she has rob'd me of my Sword.
Mar. No *Anthony*,
My Mistris lou'd thee, and her Fortunes mingled
With thine intirely.
Ant. Hence sawcy Eunuch peace, she hath betraid me,
And shall dye the death.
Mar. Death of one person, can be paide but once,
And that she ha's discharg'd. What thou would'st do
Is done vnto thy hand: the last she spake
Was *Anthony*, most Noble *Anthony*:
Then in the midd'st a tearing grone did breake
The name of *Anthony*: it was diuided
Betweene her heart, and lips: she rendred life
Thy name so buried in her.
Ant. Dead then?
Mar. Dead.
Ant. Vnarme *Eros*, the long dayes taske is done,
And we must sleepe: That thou depart'st hence safe
Does pay thy labour richly: Go. *exit Mardian.*
Off, plucke off,
The seuen-fold shield of *Aiax* cannot keepe
The battery from my heart. Oh cleaue my sides.
Heart, once be stronger then thy Continent,
Cracke thy fraile Case. Apace *Eros*, apace;
No more a Soldier: bruised peeces go,
You haue bin Nobly borne. From me awhile. *exit Eros*
I will o're-take thee *Cleopatra*, and
Weepe for my pardon. So it must be, for now
All length is Torture: since the Torch is out,
Lye downe and stray no farther. Now all labour
Marres what it does: yea, very force entangles
It selfe with strength: Seale then, and all is done.
Eros? I come my Queene. *Eros?* Stay for me,
Where Soules do couch on Flowers, wee'l hand in hand,
And with our sprightly Port make the Ghostes gaze:
Dido, and her *Æneas* shall want Troopes,
And all the haunt be ours. Come *Eros*, *Eros*.

Enter Eros.

Eros. What would my Lord?
Ant. Since *Cleopatra* dyed,
I haue liu'd in such dishonour, that the Gods
Detest my basenesse. I, that with my Sword,
Quarter'd the World, and o're greene Neptunes backe
With Ships, made Cities; condemne my selfe, to lacke
The Courage of a Woman, lesse Noble minde
Then she which by her death, our *Cæsar* telles
I am Conqueror of my selfe. Thou art sworne *Eros*,
That when the exigent should come, which now
Is come indeed: When I should see behinde me
Th'ineuitable prosecution of disgrace and horror,
That on my command, thou then would'st kill me.
Doo't, the time is come: Thou strik'st not me,
'Tis *Cæsar* thou defeat'st. Put colour in thy Cheeke.
Eros. The Gods with-hold me,
Shall I do that which all the Parthian Darts,
(Though Enemy) lost ayme, and could not.
Ant. *Eros*,
Would'st thou be window'd in great Rome, and see
Thy Master thus with pleacht Armes, bending downe
His corrigible necke, his face subdu'de
To penetratiue shame; whil'st the wheel'd seate
Of Fortunate *Cæsar* drawne before him, branded
His Basenesse that ensued.
Eros. I would not see't.
Ant. Come then: for with a wound I must be cur'd.
Draw that thy honest Sword, which thou hast worne
Most vsefull for thy Country.
Eros. Oh sir, pardon me.
Ant. When I did make thee free, swor'st ỹ not then
To do this when I bad thee? Do it at once,
Or thy precedent Seruices are all
But accidents vnpurpos'd. Draw, and come.
Eros. Turne from me then that Noble countenance,
Wherein the worship of the whole world lyes.
Ant. Loe thee.
Eros. My sword is drawne.
Ant. Then let it do at once
The thing why thou hast drawne it.
Eros. My deere Master,
My Captaine, and my Emperor. Let me say
Before I strike this bloody stroke, Farwell.
Ant. 'Tis said man, and farewell.
Eros. Farewell great Chiefe. Shall I strike now?
Ant. Now *Eros*. *Killes himselfe.*
Eros. Why there then:
Thus I do escape the sorrow of *Anthonies* death.
Ant. Thrice-Nobler then my selfe,
Thou teachest me: Oh valiant *Eros*, what
I should, and thou could'st not, my Queene and *Eros*
Haue by their braue instruction got vpon me
A Noblenesse in Record. But I will bee
A Bride-groome in my death, and run intoo't
As to a Louers bed. Come then, and *Eros*,
Thy Master dies thy Scholler; to do thus
I learnt of thee. How, not dead? Not dead?
The Guard, how? Oh dispatch me.

Enter

Enter a Guard.

1.*Guard.* What's the noiſe?

Ant. I haue done my worke ill Friends:
Oh make an end of what I haue begun.

2 The Starre is falne.

1 And time is at his Period.

All. Alas, and woe.

Ant. Let him that loues me, ſtrike me dead.

1 Not I.

2 Nor I.

3 Nor any one. *exeunt*

Dercetus. Thy death and fortunes bid thy folowers fly
This ſword but ſhewne to *Cæſar* with this tydings,
Shall enter me with him.

Enter Diomedes.

Dio. Where's *Anthony*?

Decre. There *Diomed* there.

Diom. Liues he: wilt thou not anſwer man?

Ant. Art thou there *Diomed*?
Draw thy ſword, and giue mee,
Suffiſing ſtrokes for death.

Diom. Moſt abſolute Lord:
My Miſtris *Cleopatra* ſent me to thee.

Ant. When did ſhee ſend thee?

Diom. Now my Lord.

Antb. Where is ſhe?

Diom. Lockt in her Monument: ſhe had a Propheſying (feare
Of what hath come to paſſe: for when ſhe ſaw
(Which neuer ſhall be found) you did ſuſpect
She had diſpos'd with *Cæſar*, and that your rage
Would not be purg'd, ſhe ſent you word ſhe was dead:
But fearing ſince how it might worke, hath ſent
Me to proclaime the truth, and I am come
I dread, too late.

Ant. Too late good *Diomed*: call my Guard I prythee.

Dio. What hoa: the Emperors Guard,
The Guard, what hoa? Come, your Lord calles.

Enter 4. or 5. of the Guard of Anthony.

Ant. Beare me good Friends where *Cleopatra* bides,
'Tis the laſt ſeruice that I ſhall command you.

1 Woe, woe are we ſir, you may not liue to weare
All your true Followers out.

All. Moſt heauy day.

Ant. Nay good my Fellowes, do not pleaſe ſharp fate
To grace it with your ſorrowes. Bid that welcome
Which comes to puniſh vs, and we puniſh it
Seeming to beare it lightly. Take me vp,
I haue led you oft, carry me now good Friends,
And haue my thankes for all. *Exit bearing Anthony*

Enter Cleopatra, and her Maides aloft, with Charmian & Iras.

Cleo. Oh *Charmian*, I will neuer go from hence.

Char. Be comforted deere Madam.

Cleo. No, I will not:
All ſtrange and terrible euents are welcome,
But comforts we diſpiſe; our ſize of ſorrow
Proportion'd to our cauſe, muſt be as great
As that which makes it.

Enter Diomed.

How now? is he dead?

Diom. His death's vpon him, but not dead.
Looke out o'th other ſide your Monument,
His Guard haue brought him thither.

Enter Anthony, and the Guard.

Cleo. Oh Sunne,
Burne the great Sphere thou mou'ſt in, darkling ſtand
The varrying ſhore o'th'world. O *Antony, Antony, Antony*
Helpe *Charmian*, helpe *Iras* helpe: helpe Friends
Below, let's draw him hither.

Ant. Peace,
Not *Cæſars* Valour hath o'rethrowne *Anthony*,
But *Anthonie*'s hath Triumpht on it ſelfe.

Cleo. So it ſhould be,
That none but *Anthony* ſhould conquer *Anthony*,
But woe 'tis ſo.

Ant. I am dying Egypt, dying; onely
I heere importune death a-while, vntill
Of many thouſand kiſſes, the poore laſt
I lay vpon thy lippes.

Cleo. I dare not Deere,
Deere my Lord pardon: I dare not,
Leaſt I be taken: not th'Imperious ſhew
Of the full-Fortun'd *Cæſar*, euer ſhall
Be brooch'd with me, if Knife, Drugges, Serpents haue
Edge, ſting, or operation. I am ſafe:
Your Wife *Octauia*, with her modeſt eyes,
And ſtill Concluſion, ſhall acquire no Honour
Demuring vpon me: but come, come *Anthony*,
Helpe me my women, we muſt draw thee vp:
Aſſiſt good Friends.

Ant. Oh quicke, or I am gone.

Cleo. Heere's ſport indeede:
How heauy weighes my Lord?
Our ſtrength is all gone into heauineſſe,
That makes the waight. Had I great *Iuno*'s power,
The ſtrong wing'd Mercury ſhould fetch thee vp,
And ſet thee by Ioues ſide. Yet come a little,
Wiſhers were euer Fooles. Oh come, come, come,

They heaue Anthony aloft to Cleopatra.

And welcome, welcome. Dye when thou haſt liu'd,
Quicken with kiſſing: had my lippes that power,
Thus would I weare them out.

All. A heauy ſight.

Ant. I am dying Egypt, dying.
Giue me ſome Wine, and let me ſpeake a little.

Cleo. No, let me ſpeake, and let me rayle ſo hye,
That the falſe Huſwife Fortune, breake her Wheele,
Prouok'd by my offence.

Ant. One word (ſweet Queene)
Of *Cæſar* ſeeke your Honour, with your ſafety. Oh.

Cleo. They do not go together.

Ant. Gentle heare me,
None about *Cæſar* truſt, but *Proculeius*.

Cleo. My Reſolution, and my hands, Ile truſt,
None about *Cæſar*.

Ant. The miſerable change now at my end,
Lament nor ſorrow at: but pleaſe your thoughts
In feeding them with thoſe my former Fortunes
Wherein I liued. The greateſt Prince o'th'world,
The Nobleſt: and do now not baſely dye,
Not Cowardly put off my Helmet to
My Countreyman. A Roman, by a Roman
Valiantly vanquiſh'd. Now my Spirit is going,
I can no more.

Cleo. Nobleſt of men, woo't dye?
Haſt thou no care of me, ſhall I abide
In this dull world, which in thy abſence is
No better then a Stye? Oh ſee my women:
The Crowne o'th'earth doth melt. My Lord?
Oh wither'd is the Garland of the Warre,

The

The Souldiers pole is falne : young Boyes and Gyrles
Are leuell now with men : The oddes is gone,
And there is nothing left remarkeable
Beneath the viſiting Moone.
Char. Oh quietneſſe, Lady.
Iras. She's dead too, our Soueraigne.
Char. Lady.
Iras. Madam.
Char. Oh Madam, Madam, Madam.
Iras. Royall Egypt : Empreſſe.
Char. Peace, peace, *Iras*.
Cleo. No more but in a Woman, and commanded
By ſuch poore paſſion, as the Maid that Milkes,
And doe's the meaneſt chares. It were for me,
To throw my Scepter at the iniurious Gods,
To tell them that this World did equall theyrs,
Till they had ſtolne our Iewell. All's but naught :
Patience is ſottiſh, and impatience does
Become a Dogge that's mad : Then is it ſinne,
To ruſh into the ſecret houſe of death,
Ere death dare come to vs. How do you Women?
What, what good cheere? Why how now *Charmian*?
My Noble Gyrles? Ah Women, women! Looke
Our Lampe is ſpent, it's out. Good ſirs, take heart,
Wee'l bury him : And then, what's braue, what's Noble,
Let's doo't after the high Roman faſhion,
And make death proud to take vs. Come, away,
This caſe of that huge Spirit now is cold.
Ah Women, Women! Come, we haue no Friend
But Reſolution, and the breefeſt end.
Exeunt, bearing of Anthonies body.

Enter Cæſar, Agrippa, Dollabella, Menas, with his Counſell of Warre.

Cæſar. Go to him *Dollabella*, bid him yeeld,
Being ſo fruſtrate, tell him,
He mockes the pawſes that he makes.
Dol. *Cæſar*, I ſhall.
Enter Decretas with the ſword of Anthony.
Caeſ. Wherefore is that? And what art thou that dar'ſt
Appeare thus to vs?
Dec. I am call'd *Decretas*,
Marke Anthony I ſeru'd, who beſt was worthie
Beſt to be ſeru'd : whil'ſt he ſtood vp, and ſpoke
He was my Maſter, and I wore my life
To ſpend vpon his haters. If thou pleaſe
To take me to thee, as I was to him,
Ile be to *Cæſar* : if ỳ pleaſeſt not, I yeild thee vp my life.
Cæſar. What is't thou ſay'ſt?
Dec. I ſay (Oh *Cæſar*) *Anthony* is dead.
Cæſar. The breaking of ſo great a thing, ſhould make
A greater cracke. The round World
Should haue ſhooke Lyons into ciuill ſtreets,
And Cittizens to their dennes. The death of *Anthony*
Is not a ſingle doome, in the name lay
A moity of the world.
Dec. He is dead *Cæſar*,
Not by a publike miniſter of Iuſtice,
Nor by a hyred Knife, but that ſelfe-hand
Which writ his Honor in the Acts it did,
Hath with the Courage which the heart did lend it,
Splitted the heart. This is his Sword,
I robb'd his wound of it : behold it ſtain'd
With his moſt Noble blood.
Caeſ. Looke you ſad Friends,
The Gods rebuke me, but it is Tydings
To waſh the eyes of Kings.
Dol. And ſtrange it is,
That Nature muſt compell vs to lament
Our moſt perſiſted deeds.
Mec. His taints and Honours, wag'd equal with him.
Dola. A Rarer ſpirit neuer
Did ſteere humanity : but you Gods will giue vs
Some faults to make vs men. *Cæſar* is touch'd.
Mec. When ſuch a ſpacious Mirror's ſet before him,
He needes muſt ſee him ſelfe.
Cæſar. Oh *Anthony*,
I haue followed thee to this, but we do launch
Diſeaſes in our Bodies. I muſt perforce
Haue ſhewne to thee ſuch a declining day,
Or looke on thine : we could not ſtall together,
In the whole world. But yet let me lament
With teares as Soueraigne as the blood of hearts,
That thou my Brother, my Competitor,
In top of all deſigne ; my Mate in Empire,
Friend and Companion in the front of Warre,
The Arme of mine owne Body, and the Heart
Where mine his thoughts did kindle; that our Starres
Vnreconciliable, ſhould diuide our equalneſſe to this.
Heare me good Friends,
But I will tell you at ſome meeter Seaſon,
The buſineſſe of this man lookes out of him,
Wee'l heare him what he ſayes.
Enter an Ægyptian.
Whence are you?
Ægyp. A poore Egyptian yet, the Queen my miſtris
Confin'd in all, ſhe has her Monument
Of thy intents, deſires, inſtruction,
That ſhe preparedly may frame her ſelfe
To'th'way ſhee's forc'd too.
Cæſar. Bid her haue good heart,
She ſoone ſhall know of vs, by ſome of ours,
How honourable, and how kindely Wee
Determine for her. For *Cæſar* cannot leaue to be vngentle
Ægypt. So the Gods preſerue thee. *Exit.*
Caeſ. Come hither *Proculeius*. Go and ſay
We purpoſe her no ſhame : giue her what comforts
The quality of her paſſion ſhall require ;
Leaſt in her greatneſſe, by ſome mortall ſtroke
She do defeate vs. For her life in Rome,
Would be eternall in our Triumph : Go,
And with your ſpeedieſt bring vs what ſhe ſayes,
And how you finde of her.
Pro. *Cæſar* I ſhall. *Exit Proculeius.*
Caeſ. *Gallus*, go you along : where's *Dolabella*, to ſecond *Proculeius*?
All. *Dolabella.*
Caeſ. Let him alone : for I remember now
How hee's imployd : he ſhall in time be ready.
Go with me to my Tent, where you ſhall ſee
How hardly I was drawne into this Warre,
How calme and gentle I proceeded ſtill
In all my Writings. Go with me, and ſee
What I can ſhew in this. *Exeunt.*

Enter Cleopatra, Charmian, Iras, and Mardian.

Cleo. My deſolation does begin to make
A better life : Tis paltry to be *Cæſar* :
Not being Fortune, hee's but Fortunes knaue,
A miniſter of her will : and it is great
To

To do that thing that ends all other deeds,
Which shackles accedents, and bolts vp change;
Which sleepes, and neuer pallates more the dung,
The beggers Nurse, and *Cæsars.*

Enter Proculeius.

Pro. *Cæsar* sends greeting to the Queene of Egypt,
And bids thee study on what faire demands
Thou mean'st to haue him grant thee.

Cleo. What's thy name?

Pro. My name is *Proculeius.*

Cleo. *Anthony*
Did tell me of you, bad me trust you, but
I do not greatly care to be deceiu'd
That haue no vse for trusting. If your Master
Would haue a Queece his begger, you must tell him,
That Maiesty to keepe *decorum*, must
No lesse begge then a Kingdome: If he please
To giue me conquer'd Egypt for my Sonne,
He giues me so much of mine owne, as I
Will kneele to him with thankes.

Pro. Be of good cheere:
Y'are falne into a Princely hand, feare nothing,
Make your full reference freely to my Lord,
Who is so full of Grace, that it flowes ouer
On all that neede. Let me report to him
Your sweet dependacie, and you shall finde
A Conqueror that will pray in ayde for kindnesse,
Where he for grace is kneel'd too.

Cleo. Pray you tell him,
I am his Fortunes Vassall, and I send him
The Greatnesse he has got. I hourely learne
A Doctrine of Obedience, and would gladly
Looke him i'th'Face.

Pro. This Ile report (deere Lady)
Haue comfort, for I know your plight is pittied
Of him that caus'd it.

Pro. You see how easily she may be surpriz'd:
Guard her till *Cæsar* come.

Iras. Royall Queene.

Char. Oh *Cleopatra*, thou art taken Queene.

Cleo. Quicke, quicke, good hands.

Pro. Hold worthy Lady, hold:
Doe not your selfe such wrong, who are in this
Releeu'd, but not betraid.

Cleo. What of death too that rids our dogs of languish

Pro. *Cleopatra*, do not abuse my Masters bounty, by
Th'vndoing of your selfe: Let the World see
His Noblenesse well acted, which your death
Will neuer let come forth.

Cleo. Where art thou Death?
Come hither come; Come, come, and take a Queene
Worth many Babes and Beggers.

Pro. Oh temperance Lady.

Cleo. Sir, I will eate no meate, Ile not drinke sir,
If idle talke will once be necessary
Ile not sleepe neither. This mortall house Ile ruine,
Do *Cæsar* what he can. Know sir, that I
Will not waite pinnion'd at your Masters Court,
Nor once be chastic'd with the sober eye
Of dull *Octauia*. Shall they hoyst me vp,
And shew me to the showting Varlotarie
Of censuring Rome? Rather a ditch in Egypt.
Be gentle graue vnto me, rather on Nylus mudde
Lay me starke-nak'd, and let the water-Flies
Blow me into abhorring; rather make
My Countries high pyramides my Gibbet,
And hang me vp in Chaines.

Pro. You do extend
These thoughts of horror further then you shall
Finde cause in *Cæsar.*

Enter Dolabella.

Dol. *Proculeius*,
What thou hast done, thy Master *Cæsar* knowes,
And he hath sent for thee: for the Queene,
Ile take her to my Guard.

Pro. So *Dolabella*,
It shall content me best: Be gentle to her,
To *Cæsar* I will speake, what you shall please,
If you'l imploy me to him. *Exit Proculeius*

Cleo. Say, I would dye.

Dol. Most Noble Empresse, you haue heard of me.

Cleo. I cannot tell.

Dol. Assuredly you know me.

Cleo. No matter sir, what I haue heard or knowne:
You laugh when Boyes or Women tell their Dreames,
Is't not your tricke?

Dol. I vnderstand not, Madam.

Cleo. I dreampt there was an Emperor *Anthony.*
Oh such another sleepe, that I might see
But such another man.

Dol. If it might please ye.

Cleo. His face was as the Heau'ns, and therein stucke
A Sunne and Moone, which kept their course, & lighted
The little o'th'earth.

Dol. Most Soueraigne Creature.

Cleo. His legges bestrid the Ocean, his rear'd arme
Crested the world: His voyce was propertied
As all the tuned Spheres, and that to Friends:
But when he meant to quaile, and shake the Orbe,
He was as ratling Thunder. For his Bounty,
There was no winter in't. An *Anthony* it was,
That grew the more by reaping: His delights
Were Dolphin-like, they shew'd his backe aboue
The Element they liu'd in: In his Liuery
Walk'd Crownes and Crownets: Realms & Islands were
As plates dropt from his pocket.

Dol. *Cleopatra.*

Cleo. Thinke you there was, or might be such a man
As this I dreampt of?

Dol. Gentle Madam, no.

Cleo. You Lye vp to the hearing of the Gods:
But if there be, nor euer were one such
It's past the size of dreaming: Nature wants stuffe
To vie strange formes with fancie, yet t'imagine
An *Anthony* were Natures peece, 'gainst Fancie,
Condemning shadowes quite.

Dol. Heare me, good Madam:
Your losse is as your selfe, great; and you beare it
As answering to the waight, would I might neuer
Ore-take pursu'de successe: But I do feele
By the rebound of yours, a greefe that suites
My very heart at roote.

Cleo. I thanke you sir:
Know you what *Cæsar* meanes to do with me?

Dol. I am loath to tell you what, I would you knew.

Cleo. Nay pray you sir.

Dol. Though he be Honourable.

Cleo. Hee'l leade me then in Triumph.

Dol. Madam he will, I know't. *Flourish.*

Enter Proculeius, Cæsar, Gallus, Mecenas, and others of his Traine.

All. Make way there *Cæsar.*

Caes. Which is the Queene of Egypt.
Dol. It is the Emperor Madam. *Cleo. kneeles.*
Caesar. Arise, you shall not kneele:
I pray you rise, rise Egypt.
Cleo. Sir, the Gods will haue it thus,
My Master and my Lord I must obey,
Caesar. Take to you no hard thoughts,
The Record of what iniuries you did vs,
Though written in our flesh, we shall remember
As things but done by chance.
Cleo. Sole Sir o'th'World,
I cannot proiect mine owne cause so well
To make it cleare, but do confesse I haue
Bene laden with like frailties, which before
Haue often sham'd our Sex.
Caesar. Cleopatra know,
We will extenuate rather then inforce:
If you apply your selfe to our intents,
Which towards you are most gentle, you shall finde
A benefit in this change: but if you seeke
To lay on me a Cruelty, by taking
Anthonies course, you shall bereaue your selfe
Of my good purposes, and put your children
To that destruction which Ile guard them from,
If thereon you relye. Ile take my leaue.
Cleo. And may through all the world: tis yours, & we
your Scutcheons, and your signes of Conquest shall
Hang in what place you please. Here my good Lord.
Caesar. You shall aduise me in all for *Cleopatra.*
Cleo. This is the breefe: of Money, Plate, & Iewels
I am possest of, 'tis exactly valewed,
Not petty things admitted. Where's *Seleucus*?
Seleu. Heere Madam.
Cleo. This is my Treasurer, let him speake (my Lord)
Vpon his perill, that I haue reseru'd
To my selfe nothing. Speake the truth *Seleucus.*
Seleu. Madam, I had rather seele my lippes,
Then to my perill speake that which is not.
Cleo. What haue I kept backe.
Sel. Enough to purchase what you haue made known
Caesar. Nay blush not *Cleopatra*, I approue
Your Wisedome in the deede.
Cleo. See *Caesar*: Oh behold,
How pompe is followed: Mine will now be yours,
And should we shift estates, yours would be mine.
The ingratitude of this *Seleucus*, does
Euen make me wilde. Oh Slaue, of no more trust
Then loue that's hyr'd? What goest thou backe, y^t shalt
Go backe I warrant thee: but Ile catch thine eyes
Though they had wings. Slaue, Soule-lesse, Villain, Dog.
O rarely base!
Caesar. Good Queene, let vs intreat you.
Cleo. O *Caesar*, what a wounding shame is this,
That thou vouchsafing heere to visit me,
Doing the Honour of thy Lordlinesse
To one so meeke, that mine owne Seruant should
Parcell the summe of my disgraces, by
Addition of his Enuy. Say (good *Caesar*)
That I some Lady trifles haue reseru'd,
Immoment toyes, things of such Dignitie
As we greet moderne Friends withall, and say
Some Nobler token I haue kept apart
For *Liuia* and *Octauia*, to induce
Their mediation, must I be vnfolded
With one that I haue bred: The Gods! it smites me
Beneath the fall I haue. Prythee go hence,
Or I shall shew the Cynders of my spirits
Through th'Ashes of my chance: Wer't thou a man,
Thou would'st haue mercy on me.
Caesar. Forbeare *Seleucus.*
Cleo. Be it known, that we the greatest are mis-thoght
For things that others do: and when we fall,
We answer others merits, in our name
Are therefore to be pittied.
Caesar. Cleopatra,
Not what you haue reseru'd, nor what acknowledg'd
Put we i'th'Roll of Conquest: still bee't yours,
Bestow it at your pleasure, and beleeue
Caesars no Merchant, to make prize with you
Of things that Merchants sold. Therefore be cheer'd,
Make not your thoughts your prisons: No deere Queen,
For we intend so to dispose you, as
Your selfe shall giue vs counsell: Feede, and sleepe:
Our care and pitty is so much vpon you,
That we remaine your Friend, and so adieu.
Cleo. My Master, and my Lord.
Caesar. Not so: Adieu. *Flourish.*
Exeunt Caesar, and his Traine.
Cleo. He words me Gyrles, he words me,
That I should not be Noble to my selfe.
But hearke thee *Charmian.*
Iras. Finish good Lady, the bright day is done,
And we are for the darke.
Cleo. Hye thee againe,
I haue spoke already, and it is prouided,
Go put it to the haste.
Char. Madam, I will.
Enter Dolabella.
Dol. Where's the Queene?
Char. Behold sir.
Cleo. Dolabella.
Dol. Madam, as thereto sworne, by your command
(Which my loue makes Religion to obey)
I tell you this: *Caesar* through Syria
Intends his iourney, and within three dayes,
You with your Children will he send before,
Make your best vse of this. I haue perform'd
Your pleasure, and my promise.
Cleo. Dolabella, I shall remaine your debter.
Dol. I your Seruant:
Adieu good Queene, I must attend on *Caesar.* *Exit*
Cleo. Farewell, and thankes.
Now *Iras*, what think'st thou?
Thou, an Egyptian Puppet shall be shewne
In Rome aswell as I: Mechanicke Slaues
With greazie Aprons, Rules, and Hammers shall
Vplift vs to the view. In their thicke breathes,
Ranke of grosse dyet, shall we be enclowded,
And forc'd to drinke their vapour.
Iras. The Gods forbid.
Cleo. Nay, 'tis most certaine *Iras*: sawcie Lictors
Will catch at vs like Strumpets, and scald Rimers
Ballads vs out a Tune. The quicke Comedians
Extemporally will stage vs, and present
Our Alexandrian Reuels: *Anthony*
Shall be brought drunken forth, and I shall see
Some squeaking *Cleopatra* Boy my greatnesse
I'th'posture of a Whore.
Iras. O the good Gods!
Cleo. Nay that's certaine.
Iras. Ile neuer see't? for I am sure mine Nailes
Are stronger then mine eyes.

Cleo.

Cleo. Why that's the way to foole their preparation,
And to conquer their most absurd intents.
Enter Charmian.
Now *Charmian.*
Shew me my Women like a Queene: Go fetch
My best Attyres. I am againe for *Cidrus,*
To meete *Marke Anthony.* Sirra *Iras*, go
(Now Noble *Charmian*, wee'l dispatch indeede,)
And when thou hast done this chare, Ile giue thee leaue
To play till Doomesday: bring our Crowne, and all.
A noise within.
Wherefore's this noise?
Enter a Guardsman.
Gards. Heere is a rurall Fellow,
That will not be deny'de your Highnesse presence,
He brings you Figges.
Cleo. Let him come in. *Exit Guardsman.*
What poore an Instrument
May do a Noble deede: he brings me liberty:
My Resolution's plac'd, and I haue nothing
Of woman in me: Now from head to foote
I am Marble constant: now the fleeting Moone
No Planet is of mine.
Enter Guardsman, and Clowne.
Guards. This is the man.
Cleo. Auoid, and leaue him. *Exit Guardsman.*
Hast thou the pretty worme of Nylus there,
That killes and paines not?
Clow. Truly I haue him: but I would not be the partie that should desire you to touch him, for his byting is immortall: those that doe dye of it, doe seldome or neuer recouer.
Cleo. Remember'st thou any that haue dyed on't?
Clow. Very many, men and women too. I heard of one of them no longer then yesterday, a very honest woman, but something giuen to lye, as a woman should not do, but in the way of honesty, how she dyed of the byting of it, what paine she felt: Truely, she makes a verie good report o'th'worme: but he that wil beleeue all that they say, shall neuer be saued by halfe that they do: but this is most falliable, the Worme's an odde Worme.
Cleo. Get thee hence, farewell.
Clow. I wish you all ioy of the Worme.
Cleo. Farewell.
Clow. You must thinke this (looke you,) that the Worme will do his kinde.
Cleo. I, I, farewell.
Clow. Looke you, the Worme is not to bee trusted, but in the keeping of wise people: for indeede, there is no goodnesse in the Worme.
Cleo. Take thou no care, it shall be heeded.
Clow. Very good: giue it nothing I pray you, for it is not worth the feeding.
Cleo. Will it eate me?
Clow. You must not think I am so simple, but I know the diuell himselfe will not eate a woman: I know, that a woman is a dish for the Gods, if the diuell dresse her not. But truly, these same whorson diuels doe the Gods great harme in their women: for in euery tenne that they make, the diuels marre fiue.
Cleo. Well, get thee gone, farewell.
Clow. Yes forsooth: I wish you ioy o'th'worm. *Exit*
Cleo. Giue me my Robe, put on my Crowne, I haue
Immortall longings in me. Now no more
The iuyce of Egypts Grape shall moyst this lip.
Yare, yare, good *Iras*; quicke: Me thinkes I heare
Anthony call: I see him rowse himselfe
To praise my Noble Act. I heare him mock
The lucke of *Cæsar*, which the Gods giue men
To excuse their after wrath. Husband, I come:
Now to that name, my Courage proue my Title.
I am Fire, and Ayre; my other Elements
I giue to baser life. So, haue you done?
Come then, and take the last warmth of my Lippes.
Farewell kinde *Charmian, Iras*, long farewell.
Haue I the Aspicke in my lippes? Dost fall?
If thou, and Nature can so gently part,
The stroke of death is as a Louers pinch,
Which hurts, and is desir'd. Dost thou lye still?
If thus thou vanishest, thou tell'st the world,
It is not worth leaue-taking.
Char. Dissolue thicke clowd, & Raine, that I may say
The Gods themselues do weepe.
Cleo. This proues me base:
If she first meete the Curled *Anthony*,
Hee'l make demand of her, and spend that kisse
Which is my heauen to haue. Come thou mortal wretch,
With thy sharpe teeth this knot intrinsicate,
Of life at once vntye: Poore venomous Foole,
Be angry, and dispatch. Oh could'st thou speake,
That I might heare thee call great *Cæsar* Asse, vnpolicied.
Char. Oh Easterne Starre.
Cleo. Peace, peace:
Dost thou not see my Baby at my breast,
That suckes the Nurse asleepe.
Char. O breake! O breake!
Cleo. As sweet as Balme, as soft as Ayre, as gentle.
O *Anthony*! Nay I will take thee too.
What should I stay—— *Dyes.*
Char. In this wilde World? So fare thee well:
Now boast thee Death, in thy possession lyes
A Lasse vnparalell'd. Downie Windowes cloze,
And golden Phœbus, neuer be beheld
Of eyes againe so Royall: your Crownes away,
Ile mend it, and then play——
Enter the Guard rustling in, and Dolabella.
1 *Guard.* Where's the Queene?
Char. Speake softly, wake her not.
1 *Cæsar* hath sent
Char. Too slow a Messenger.
Oh come apace, dispatch, I partly feele thee.
1 Approach hoa,
All's not well: *Cæsar*'s beguild.
2 There's *Dolabella* sent from *Cæsar*: call him.
1 What worke is heere *Charmian*?
Is this well done?
Char. It is well done, and fitting for a Princesse
Descended of so many Royall Kings.
Ah Souldier. *Charmian dyes.*

Enter Dolabella.

Dol. How goes it heere?
2. *Guard.* All dead.
Dol. *Cæsar*, thy thoughts
Touch their effects in this: Thy selfe art comming
To see perform'd the dreaded Act which thou
So sought'st to hinder.

Enter Cæsar and all his Traine, marching.

All. A way there, a way for *Cæsar*.

Dol. Oh ſir, you are too ſure an Augurer:
That you did feare, is done.
Cæſar. Braueſt at the laſt,
She leuell'd at our purpoſes, and being Royall
Tooke her owne way: the manner of their deaths,
I do not ſee them bleede.
Dol. Who was laſt with them?
1.*Guard.* A ſimple Countryman, that broght hir Figs:
This was his Basket.
Cæſar. Poyſon'd then.
1.*Guard.* Oh *Cæſar:*
This *Charmian* liu'd but now, ſhe ſtood and ſpake:
I found her trimming vp the Diadem;
On her dead Miſtris tremblingly ſhe ſtood,
And on the ſodaine dropt.
Cæſar. Oh Noble weakeneſſe:
If they had ſwallow'd poyſon, 'twould appeare
By externall ſwelling: but ſhe lookes like ſleepe,
As ſhe would catch another *Anthony*
In her ſtrong toyle of Grace.
Dol. Heere on her breſt,
There is a vent of Bloud, and ſomething blowne,
The like is on her Arme.
1.*Guard.* This is an Aſpickes traile,
And theſe Figge-leaues haue ſlime vpon them, ſuch
As th'Aſpicke leaues vpon the Caues of Nyle.
Cæſar. Moſt probable
That ſo ſhe dyed: for her Phyſitian tels mee
She hath purſu'de Concluſions infinite
Of eaſie wayes to dye. Take vp her bed,
And beare her Women from the Monument,
She ſhall be buried by her *Anthony.*
No Graue vpon the earth ſhall clip in it
A payre ſo famous: high euents as theſe
Strike thoſe that make them: and their Story is
No leſſe in pitty, then his Glory which
Brought them to be lamented. Our Army ſhall
In ſolemne ſhew, attend this Funerall,
And then to Rome. Come *Dolabella*, ſee
High Order, in this great Solmemnity. *Exeunt omnes*

FINIS.

THE TRAGEDIE OF CYMBELINE.

Actus Primus. Scœna Prima.

Enter two Gentlemen.

1. *Gent.*
YOu do not meet a man but Frownes.
Our bloods no more obey the Heauens
Then our Courtiers:
Still ſeeme, as do's the Kings.
2. *Gent.* But what's the matter?
1. His daughter, and the heire of's kingdome (whom
He purpoſ'd to his wiues ſole Sonne, a Widdow
That late he married) hath referr'd her ſelfe
Vnto a poore, but worthy Gentleman. She's wedded,
Her Husband baniſh'd; ſhe impriſon'd, all
Is outward ſorrow, though I thinke the King
Be touch'd at very heart.
2 None but the King?
1 He that hath loſt her too: ſo is the Queene,
That moſt deſir'd the Match. But not a Courtier,
Although they weare their faces to the bent
Of the Kings lookes, hath a heart that is not
Glad at the thing they ſcowle at.
2 And why ſo?
1 He that hath miſs'd the Princeſſe, is a thing
Too bad, for bad report: and he that hath her,
(I meane, that married her, alacke good man,
And therefore baniſh'd) is a Creature, ſuch,
As to ſeeke through the Regions of the Earth
For one, his like; there would be ſomething failing
In him, that ſhould compare. I do not thinke,
So faire an Outward, and ſuch ſtuffe Within
Endowes a man, but hee.
2 You ſpeake him farre.
1 I do extend him (Sir) within himſelfe,
Cruſh him together, rather then vnfold
His meaſure duly.
2 What's his name, and Birth?
1 I cannot delue him to the roote: His Father
Was call'd *Sicillius*, who did ioyne his Honor
Againſt the Romanes, with *Caſſibulan*,
But had his Titles by *Tenantius*, whom
He ſeru'd with Glory, and admir'd Succeſſe:
So gain'd the Sur-addition, *Leonatus*.
And had (beſides this Gentleman in queſtion)
Two other Sonnes, who in the Warres o'th'time
Dy'de with their Swords in hand. For which, their Father
Then old, and fond of yſſue, tooke ſuch ſorrow
That he quit Being; and his gentle Lady
Bigge of this Gentleman (our Theame) deceaſt
As he was borne. The King he takes the Babe
To his protection, cals him *Poſthumus Leonatus*,
Breedes him, and makes him of his Bed-chamber,
Puts to him all the Learnings that his time
Could make him the receiuer of, which he tooke
As we do ayre, faſt as 'twas miniſtred,
And in's Spring, became a Harueſt: Liu'd in Court
(Which rare it is to do) moſt prais'd, moſt lou'd,
A ſample to the yongeſt: to th'more Mature,
A glaſſe that feated them: and to the grauer,
A Childe that guided Dotards. To his Miſtris,
(For whom he now is baniſh'd) her owne price
Proclaimes how ſhe eſteem'd him; and his Vertue
By her electiõ may be truly read, what kind of man he is.
2 I honor him, euen out of your report.
But pray you tell me, is ſhe ſole childe to'th'King?
1 His onely childe:
He had two Sonnes (if this be worth your hearing,
Marke it) the eldeſt of them, at three yeares old
I'th'ſwathing cloathes, the other from their Nurſery
Were ſtolne, and to this houre, no gheſſe in knowledge
Which way they went.
2 How long is this ago?
1 Some twenty yeares.
2 That a Kings Children ſhould be ſo conuey'd,
So ſlackely guarded, and the ſearch ſo ſlow
That could not trace them.
1 Howſoere, 'tis ſtrange,
Or that the negligence may well be laugh'd at:
Yet is it true Sir.
2 I do well beleeue you.
1 We muſt forbeare. Heere comes the Gentleman,
The Queene, and Princeſſe. *Exeunt*

Scena Secunda.

Enter the Queene, Poſthumus, and Imogen.

Qu. No, be aſſur'd you ſhall not finde me (Daughter)
After the ſlander of moſt Step-Mothers,
Euill-ey'd vnto you. You're my Priſoner, but
Your Gaoler ſhall deliuer you the keyes

That locke vp your restraint. For you *Posthumus*,
So soone as I can win th'offended King,
I will be knowne your Aduocate : marry yet
The fire of Rage is in him, and 'twere good
You lean'd vnto his Sentence, with what patience
Your wisedome may informe you.
Post. 'Please your Highnesse,
I will from hence to day.
Qu. You know the perill :
Ile fetch a turne about the Garden, pittying
The pangs of barr'd Affections, though the King
Hath charg'd you should not speake together. *Exit*
Imo. O dissembling Curtesie! How fine this Tyrant
Can tickle where she wounds? My deerest Husband,
I something feare my Fathers wrath, but nothing
(Alwayes reseru'd my holy duty) what
His rage can do on me. You must be gone,
And I shall heere abide the hourely shot
Of angry eyes : not comforted to liue,
But that there is this Iewell in the world,
That I may see againe.
Post. My Queene, my Mistris :
O Lady, weepe no more, least I giue cause
To be suspected of more tendernesse
Then doth become a man. I will remaine
The loyall'st husband, that did ere plight troth.
My residence in Rome, at one *Filorio*'s,
Who, to my Father was a Friend, to me
Knowne but by Letter; thither write (my Queene)
And with mine eyes, Ile drinke the words you send,
Though Inke be made of Gall.
Enter Queene.
Qu. Be briefe, I pray you :
If the King come, I shall incurre, I know not
How much of his displeasure : yet Ile moue him
To walke this way : I neuer do him wrong,
But he do's buy my Iniuries, to be Friends :
Payes deere for my offences.
Post. Should we be taking leaue
As long a terme as yet we haue to liue,
The loathnesse to depart, would grow : Adieu.
Imo. Nay, stay a little :
Were you but riding forth to ayre your selfe,
Such parting were too petty. Looke heere (Loue)
This Diamond was my Mothers; take it (Heart)
But keepe it till you woo another Wife,
When *Imogen* is dead.
Post. How, how? Another?
You gentle Gods, giue me but this I haue,
And seare vp my embracements from a next,
With bonds of death. Remaine, remaine thou heere,
While sense can keepe it on : And sweetest, fairest,
As I (my poore selfe) did exchange for you
To your so infinite losse; so in our trifles
I still winne of you. For my sake weare this,
It is a Manacle of Loue, Ile place it
Vpon this fayrest Prisoner.
Imo. O the Gods!
When shall we see againe?
Enter Cymbeline, and Lords.
Post. Alacke, the King.
Cym. Thou basest thing, auoyd hence, from my sight:
If after this command thou fraught the Court
With thy vnworthinesse, thou dyest. Away,
Thou'rt poyson to my blood.
Post. The Gods protect you,
And blesse the good Remainders of the Court :
I am gone. *Exit.*
Imo. There cannot be a pinch in death
More sharpe then this is.
Cym. O disloyall thing,
That should'st repayre my youth, thou heap'st
A yeares age on mee.
Imo. I beseech you Sir,
Harme not your selfe with your vexation,
I am senselesse of your Wrath; a Touch more rare
Subdues all pangs, all feares.
Cym. Past Grace? Obedience?
Imo. Past hope, and in dispaire, that way past Grace.
Cym. That might'st haue had
The sole Sonne of my Queene.
Imo. O blessed, that I might not : I chose an Eagle,
And did auoyd a Puttocke.
Cym. Thou took'st a Begger, would'st haue made my
Throne, a Seate for basenesse.
Imo. No, I rather added a lustre to it.
Cym. O thou vilde one!
Imo. Sir,
It is your fault that I haue lou'd *Posthumus* :
You bred him as my Play-fellow, and he is
A man, worth any woman : Ouer-buyes mee
Almost the summe he payes.
Cym. What? art thou mad?
Imo. Almost Sir : Heauen restore me : would I were
A Neat-heards Daughter, and my *Leonatus*
Our Neighbour-Shepheards Sonne.
Enter Queene.
Cym. Thou foolish thing;
They were againe together : you haue done
Not after our command. Away with her,
And pen her vp.
Qu. Beseech your patience : Peace
Deere Lady daughter, peace. Sweet Soueraigne,
Leaue vs to our selues, and make your self some comfort
Out of your best aduice.
Cym. Nay, let her languish
A drop of blood a day, and being aged
Dye of this Folly. *Exit.*
Enter Pisanio.
Qu. Fye, you must giue way :
Heere is your Seruant. How now Sir? What newes?
Pisa. My Lord your Sonne, drew on my Master.
Qu. Hah?
No harme I trust is done?
Pisa. There might haue beene,
But that my Master rather plaid, then fought,
And had no helpe of Anger : they were parted
By Gentlemen, at hand.
Qu. I am very glad on't.
Imo. Your Son's my Fathers friend, he takes his part
To draw vpon an Exile. O braue Sir,
I would they were in Affricke both together,
My selfe by with a Needle, that I might pricke
The goer backe. Why came you from your Master?
Pisa. On his command : he would not suffer mee
To bring him to the Hauen : left these Notes
Of what commands I should be subiect too,
When't pleas'd you to employ me.
Qu. This hath beene
Your faithfull Seruant : I dare lay mine Honour
He will remaine so.
Pisa. I humbly thanke your Highnesse.

Qu.

Qu. Pray walke a-while.

Imo. About ſome halfe houre hence,
Pray you ſpeake with me;
You ſhall (at leaſt) go ſee my Lord aboord.
For this time leaue me. *Exeunt.*

Scena Tertia.

Enter Clotten, and two Lords.

1. Sir, I would aduiſe you to ſhift a Shirt; the Violence of Action hath made you reek as a Sacrifice: where ayre comes out, ayre comes in: There's none abroad ſo wholeſome as that you vent.

Clot. If my Shirt were bloody, then to ſhift it. Haue I hurt him?

2 No faith: not ſo much as his patience.

1 Hurt him? His bodie's a paſſable Carkaſſe if he bee not hurt. It is a through-fare for Steele if it be not hurt.

2 His Steele was in debt, it went o'th'Backe-ſide the Towne.

Clot. The Villaine would not ſtand me.

2 No, but he fled forward ſtill, toward your face.

1 Stand you? you haue Land enough of your owne: But he added to your hauing, gaue you ſome ground.

2 As many Inches, as you haue Oceans (Puppies.)

Clot. I would they had not come betweene vs.

2 So would I, till you had meaſur'd how long a Foole you were vpon the ground.

Clot. And that ſhee ſhould loue this Fellow, and refuſe mee.

2 If it be a ſin to make a true election, ſhe is damn'd.

1 Sir, as I told you alwayes: her Beauty & her Braine go not together. Shee's a good ſigne, but I haue ſeene ſmall reflection of her wit.

2 She ſhines not vpon Fooles, leaſt the reflection
Should hurt her.

Clot. Come, Ile to my Chamber: would there had beene ſome hurt done.

2 I wiſh not ſo, vnleſſe it had bin the fall of an Aſſe, which is no great hurt.

Clot. You'l go with vs?

1 Ile attend your Lordſhip.

Clot. Nay come, let's go together.

2 Well my Lord. *Exeunt.*

Scena Quarta.

Enter Imogen, and Piſanio.

Imo. I would thou grew'ſt vnto the ſhores o'th'Hauen,
And queſtioned'ſt euery Saile: if he ſhould write,
And I not haue it, 'twere a Paper loſt
As offer'd mercy is: What was the laſt
That he ſpake to thee?

Piſa. It was his Queene, his Queene.

Imo. Then wau'd his Handkerchiefe?

Piſa. And kiſt it, Madam.

Imo. Senſeleſſe Linnen, happier therein then I:
And that was all?

Piſa. No Madam: for ſo long
As he could make me with his eye, or eare,
Diſtinguiſh him from others, he did keepe
The Decke, with Gloue, or Hat, or Handkerchife,
Still wauing, as the fits and ſtirres of's mind
Could beſt expreſſe how ſlow his Soule ſayl'd on,
How ſwift his Ship.

Imo. Thou ſhould'ſt haue made him,
As little as a Crow, or leſſe, ere left
To after-eye him.

Piſa. Madam, ſo I did.

Imo. I would haue broke mine eye-ſtrings;
Crack'd them, but to looke vpon him, till the diminution
Of ſpace, had pointed him ſharpe as my Needle:
Nay, followed him, till he had melted from
The ſmalneſſe of a Gnat, to ayre: and then
Haue turn'd mine eye, and wept. But good *Piſanio*,
When ſhall we heare from him.

Piſa. Be aſſur'd Madam,
With his next vantage.

Imo. I did not take my leaue of him, but had
Moſt pretty things to ſay: Ere I could tell him
How I would thinke on him at certaine houres,
Such thoughts, and ſuch: Or I could make him ſweare,
The Shees of Italy ſhould not betray
Mine Intereſt, and his Honour: or haue charg'd him
At the ſixt houre of Morne, at Noone, at Midnight,
T'encounter me with Oriſons, for then
I am in Heauen for him: Or ere I could,
Giue him that parting kiſſe, which I had ſet
Betwixt two charming words, comes in my Father,
And like the Tyrannous breathing of the North,
Shakes all our buddes from growing.

Enter a Lady.

La. The Queene (Madam)
Deſires your Highneſſe Company.

Imo. Thoſe things I bid you do, get them diſpatch'd,
I will attend the Queene.

Piſa. Madam, I ſhall. *Exeunt.*

Scena Quinta.

Enter Philario, Iachimo: a Frenchman, a Dutchman, and a Spaniard.

Iach. Beleeue it Sir, I haue ſeene him in Britaine; hee was then of a Creſſent note, expected to proue ſo woorthy, as ſince he hath beene allowed the name of. But I could then haue look'd on him, without the help of Admiration, though the Catalogue of his endowments had bin tabled by his ſide, and I to peruſe him by Items.

Phil. You ſpeake of him when he was leſſe furniſh'd, then now hee is, with that which makes him both without, and within.

French. I haue ſeene him in France: wee had very many there, could behold the Sunne, with as firme eyes as hee.

Iach. This matter of marrying his Kings Daughter, wherein he muſt be weighed rather by her valew, then his owne, words him (I doubt not) a great deale from the matter.

French. And then his baniſhment.

Iach. I, and the approbation of thoſe that weepe this lamentable diuorce vnder her colours, are wonderfully to to extend him, be it but to fortifie her iudgement, which elſe an eaſie battery might lay flat, for taking a Begger without leſſe quality. But how comes it, he is to ſoiourne with you? How creepes acquaintance?

Phil. His Father and I were Souldiers together, to whom I haue bin often bound for no leſſe then my life.

Enter Poſthumus.

Heere comes the Britaine. Let him be ſo entertained a-mong'ſt you, as ſuites with Gentlemen of your knowing, to a Stranger of his quality. I beſeech you all be better knowne to this Gentleman, whom I commend to you, as a Noble Friend of mine. How Worthy he is, I will leaue to appeare hereafter, rather then ſtory him in his owne hearing.

French. Sir, we haue knowne togither in Orleance.

Poſt. Since when, I haue bin debtor to you for courteſies, which I will be euer to pay, and yet pay ſtill.

French. Sir, you o're-rate my poore kindneſſe, I was glad I did attone my Countryman and you: it had beene pitty you ſhould haue beene put together, with ſo mortall a purpoſe, as then each bore, vpon importance of ſo ſlight and triuiall a nature.

Poſt. By your pardon Sir, I was then a young Traueller, rather ſhun'd to go euen with what I heard, then in my euery action to be guided by others experiences: but vpon my mended iudgement (if I offend to ſay it is mended) my Quarrell was not altogether ſlight.

French. Faith yes, to be put to the arbiterment of Swords, and by ſuch two, that would by all likelyhood haue confounded one the other, or haue falne both.

Iach. Can we with manners, aske what was the difference?

French. Safely, I thinke, 'twas a contention in publicke, which may (without contradiction) ſuffer the report. It was much like an argument that fell out laſt night, where each of vs fell in praiſe of our Country-Miſtreſſes. This Gentleman, at that time vouching (and vpon warrant of bloody affirmation) his to be more Faire, Vertuous, Wiſe, Chaſte, Conſtant, Qualified, and leſſe attemptible then any, the rareſt of our Ladies in Fraunce.

Iach. That Lady is not now liuing; or this Gentlemans opinion by this, worne out.

Poſt. She holds her Vertue ſtill, and I my mind.

Iach. You muſt not ſo farre preferre her, 'fore ours of Italy.

Poſth. Being ſo farre prouok'd as I was in France: I would abate her nothing, though I profeſſe my ſelfe her Adorer, not her Friend.

Iach. As faire, and as good: a kind of hand in hand compariſon, had beene ſomething too faire, and too good for any Lady in Britanie; if ſhe went before others. I haue ſeene as that Diamond of yours out-luſters many I haue beheld, I could not beleeue ſhe excelled many: but I haue not ſeene the moſt pretious Diamond that is, nor you the Lady.

Poſt. I prais'd her, as I rated her: ſo do I my Stone.

Iach. What do you eſteeme it at?

Poſt. More then the world enioyes.

Iach. Either your vnparagon'd Miſtirs is dead, or ſhe's out-priz'd by a trifle.

Poſt. You are miſtaken: the one may be ſolde or giuen, or if there were wealth enough for the purchaſes, or merite for the guift. The other is not a thing for ſale, and onely the guift of the Gods.

Iach. Which the Gods haue giuen you?

Poſt. Which by their Graces I will keepe.

Iach. You may weare her in title yours: but you know ſtrange Fowle light vpon neighbouring Ponds. Your Ring may be ſtolne too, ſo your brace of vnprizeable Eſtimations, the one is but fraile, and the other Caſuall;. A cunning Thiefe, or a (that way) accompliſh'd Courtier, would hazzard the winning both of firſt and laſt.

Poſt. Your Italy, containes none ſo accompliſh'd a Courtier to conuince the Honour of my Miſtris: if in the holding or loſſe of that, you terme her fraile, I do nothing doubt you haue ſtore of Theeues, notwithſtanding I feare not my Ring.

Phil. Let vs leaue heere, Gentlemen?

Poſt. Sir, with all my heart. This worthy Signior I thanke him, makes no ſtranger of me, we are familiar at firſt.

Iach. With fiue times ſo much conuerſation, I ſhould get ground of your faire Miſtris; make her go backe, euen to the yeilding, had I admittance, and opportunitie to friend.

Poſt. No, no.

Iach. I dare thereupon pawne the moytie of my Eſtate, to your Ring, which in my opinion o're-values it ſomething: but I make my wager rather againſt your Confidence, then her Reputation. And to barre your offence heerein to, I durſt attempt it againſt any Lady in the world.

Poſt. You are a great deale abus'd in too bold a perſwaſion, and I doubt not you ſuſtaine what y'are worthy of, by your Attempt.

Iach. What's that?

Poſth. A Repulſe though your Attempt (as you call it) deſerue more; a puniſhment too.

Phi. Gentlemen enough of this, it came in too ſodainely, let it dye as it was borne, and I pray you be better acquainted.

Iach. Would I had put my Eſtate, and my Neighbors on th'approbation of what I haue ſpoke,

Poſt. What Lady would you chuſe to aſſaile?

Iach. Yours, whom in conſtancie you thinke ſtands ſo ſafe. I will lay you ten thouſands Duckets to your Ring, that commend me to the Court where your Lady is, with no more aduantage then the opportunitie of a ſecond conference, and I will bring from thence, that Honor of hers, which you imagine ſo reſeru'd.

Poſthmus. I will wage againſt your Gold, Gold to it: My Ring I holde deere as my finger, 'tis part of it.

Iach. You are a Friend, and there in the wiſer: if you buy Ladies fleſh at a Million a Dram, you cannot preſeure it from tainting; but I ſee you haue ſome Religion in you, that you feare.

Poſthu. This is but a cuſtome in your tongue: you beare a grauer purpoſe I hope.

Iach. I am the Maſter of my ſpeeches, and would vnder-go what's ſpoken, I ſweare.

Poſthu. Will you? I ſhall but lend my Diamond till your returne: let there be Couenants drawne between's. My Miſtris exceedes in goodneſſe, the hugeneſſe of your vnworthy thinking. I dare you to this match: heere's my Ring.

Phil. I will haue it no lay.

Iach. By the Gods it is one: if I bring you no ſufficient teſtimony that I haue enioy'd the deereſt bodily part of your Miſtris: my ten thouſand Duckets are yours, ſo so is your Diamond too: if I come off, and leaue her in such honour as you haue trust in; Shee your Iewell, this your Iewell, and my Gold are yours: prouided, I haue your commendation, for my more free entertainment.

Post. I embrace these Conditions, let vs haue Articles betwixt vs: onely thus farre you shall answere, if you make your voyage vpon her, and giue me directly to vnderstand, you haue preuayl'd, I am no further your Enemy, shee is not worth our debate. If shee remaine vnseduc'd, you not making it appeare otherwise: for your ill opinion, and th'assault you haue made to her chastity, you shall answer me with your Sword.

Iach. Your hand, a Couenant: wee will haue these things set downe by lawfull Counsell, and straight away for Britaine, least the Bargaine should catch colde, and sterue: I will fetch my Gold, and haue our two Wagers recorded.

Post. Agreed.

French. Will this hold, thinke you.

Phil. Signior *Iachimo* will not from it.
Pray let vs follow 'em. *Exeunt*

Scena Sexta.

Enter Queene, Ladies, and Cornelius.

Qu. Whiles yet the dewe's on ground,
Gather those Flowers,
Make haste. Who ha's the note of them?

Lady. I Madam.

Queen. Dispatch. *Exit Ladies.*
Now Master Doctor, haue you brought those drugges?

Cor. Pleaseth your Highnes, I: here they are, Madam:
But I beseech your Grace, without offence
(My Conscience bids me aske) wherefore you haue
Commanded of me these most poysonous Compounds,
Which are the moouers of a languishing death:
But though slow, deadly.

Qu. I wonder, Doctor,
Thou ask'st me such a Question: Haue I not bene
Thy Pupill long? Hast thou not learn'd me how
To make Perfumes? Distill? Preserue? Yea so,
That our great King himselfe doth woo me oft
For my Confections? Hauing thus farre proceeded,
(Vnlesse thou think'st me diuellish) is't not meete
That I did amplifie my iudgement in
Other Conclusions? I will try the forces
Of these thy Compounds, on such Creatures as
We count not worth the hanging (but none humane)
To try the vigour of them, and apply
Allayments to their Act, and by them gather
Their seuerall vertues, and effects.

Cor. Your Highnesse
Shall from this practise, but make hard your heart:
Besides, the seeing these effects will be
Both noysome, and infectious.

Qu. O content thee.

Enter Pisanio.

Heere comes a flattering Rascall, vpon him
Will I first worke: Hee's for his Master,
And enemy to my Sonne. How now *Pisanio*?
Doctor, your seruice for this time is ended,
Take your owne way.

Cor. I do suspect you, Madam,
But you shall do no harme.

Qu. Hearke thee, a word.

Cor. I do not like her. She doth thinke she ha's
Strange ling'ring poysons: I do know her spirit,
And will not trust one of her malice, with
A drugge of such damn'd Nature. Those she ha's,
Will stupifie and dull the Sense a-while,
Which first (perchance) shee'l proue on Cats and Dogs,
Then afterward vp higher: but there is
No danger in what shew of death it makes,
More then the locking vp the Spirits a time,
To be more fresh, reuiuing. She is fool'd
With a most false effect: and I, the truer,
So to be false with her.

Qu. No further seruice, Doctor,
Vntill I send for thee.

Cor. I humbly take my leaue. *Exit.*

Qu. Weepes she still (saist thou?)
Dost thou thinke in time
She will not quench, and let instructions enter
Where Folly now possesses? Do thou worke:
When thou shalt bring me word she loues my Sonne,
Ile tell thee on the instant, thou art then
As great as is thy Master: Greater, for
His Fortunes all lye speechlesse, and his name
Is at last gaspe. Returne he cannot, nor
Continue where he is: To shift his being,
Is to exchange one misery with another,
And euery day that comes, comes to decay
A dayes worke in him. What shalt thou expect
To be depender on a thing that leanes?
Who cannot be new built, nor ha's no Friends
So much, as but to prop him? Thou tak'st vp
Thou know'st not what: But take it for thy labour,
It is a thing I made, which hath the King
Fiue times redeem'd from death. I do not know
What is more Cordiall. Nay, I prythee take it,
It is an earnest of a farther good
That I meane to thee. Tell thy Mistris how
The case stands with her: doo't, as from thy selfe;
Thinke what a chance thou changest on. but thinke
Thou hast thy Mistris still, to boote, my Sonne,
Who shall take notice of thee. Ile moue the King
To any shape of thy Preferment, such
As thou'lt desire: and then my selfe, I cheefely,
That set thee on to this desert, am bound
To loade thy merit richly. Call my women. *Exit Pisa.*
Thinke on my words. A slye, and constant knaue,
Not to be shak'd: the Agent for his Master,
And the Remembrancer of her, to hold
The hand-fast to her Lord. I haue giuen him that,
Which if he take, shall quite vnpeople her
Of Leidgers for her Sweete: and which, she after
Except she bend her humor, shall be assur'd
To taste of too.

Enter Pisanio, and Ladies.

So, so: Well done, well done:
The Violets, Cowslippes, and the Prime-Roses
Beare to my Closset: Fare thee well, *Pisanio.*
Thinke on my words. *Exit Qu. and Ladies.*

Pisa. And shall do:
But when to my good Lord, I proue vntrue,
Ile choake my selfe: there's all Ile do for you. *Exit.*

Scena

Scena Septima.

Enter Imogen alone.

Imo. A Father cruell, and a Stepdame falſe,
A Fooliſh Suitor to a Wedded-Lady,
That hath her Husband baniſh'd: O, that Husband,
My ſupreame Crowne of griefe, and thoſe repeated
Vexations of it. Had I bin Theefe-ſtolne,
As my two Brothers, happy: but moſt miſerable
Is the deſires that's glorious. Bleſſed be thoſe
How meane ſo ere, that haue their honeſt wills,
Which ſeaſons comfort. Who may this be? Fye.

Enter Piſanio, and Iachimo.

Piſa. Madam, a Noble Gentleman of Rome,
Comes from my Lord with Letters.
Iach. Change you, Madam:
The Worthy *Leonatus* is in ſafety,
And greetes your Highneſſe deerely.
Imo. Thanks good Sir,
You're kindly welcome.
Iach. All of her, that is out of doore, moſt rich:
If ſhe be furniſh'd with a mind ſo rare
She is alone th'Arabian-Bird; and I
Haue loſt the wager. Boldneſſe be my Friend:
Arme me Audacitie from head to foote,
Orlike the Parthian I ſhall flying fight,
Rather directly fly.

Imogen reads.

He is one of the Nobleſt note, to whoſe kindneſſes I am moſt infinitely tied. Reflect vpon him accordingly, as you value your truſt. Leonatus.

So farre I reade aloud.
But euen the very middle of my heart
Is warm'd by'th'reſt, and take it thankefully.
You are as welcome (worthy Sir) as I
Haue words to bid you, and ſhall finde it ſo
In all that I can do.
Iach. Thankes faireſt Lady:
What are men mad? Hath Nature giuen them eyes
To ſee this vaulted Arch, and the rich Crop
Of Sea and Land, which can diſtinguiſh 'twixt
The firie Orbes aboue, and the twinn'd Stones
Vpon the number'd Beach, and can we not
Partition make with Spectales ſo pretious
Twixt faire, and foule?
Imo. What makes your admiration?
Iach. It cannot be i'th'eye: for Apes, and Monkeys
'Twixt two ſuch She's, would chatter this way, and
Contemne with mowes the other. Nor i'th'iudgment:
For Idiots in this caſe of fauour, would
Be wiſely definit: Nor i'th'Appetite.
Sluttery to ſuch neate Excellence, oppos'd
Should make deſire vomit emptineſſe,
Not ſo allur,d to feed.
Imo. What is the matter trow?
Iach. The Cloyed will:
That ſatiate yet vnſatisfi'd deſire, that Tub
Both fill'd and running: Rauening firſt the Lambe,
Longs after for the Garbage.
Imo. What, deere Sir,
Thus rap's you? Are you well?
Iach. Thanks Madam, well: Beſeech you Sir,
Deſire my Man's abode, where I did leaue him:
He's ſtrange and peeuiſh.
Piſa. I was going Sir,
To giue him welcome. *Exit.*
Imo. Continues well my Lord?
His health beſeech you?
Iach. Well, Madam.
Imo. Is he diſpos'd to mirth? I hope he is.
Iach. Exceeding pleaſant: none a ſtranger there,
So merry, and ſo gameſome: he is call'd
The Britaine Reueller.
Imo. When he was heere
He did incline to ſadneſſe, and oft times
Not knowiug why.
Iach. I neuer ſaw him ſad.
There is a Frenchman his Companion, one
An eminent Monſieur, that it ſeemes much loues
A Gallian-Girle at home. He furnaces
The thicke ſighes from him; whiles the iolly Britaine,
(Your Lord I meane) laughes from's free lungs: cries oh,
Can my ſides hold, to think that man who knowes
By Hiſtory, Report, or his owne proofe
What woman is, yea what ſhe cannot chooſe
But muſt be: will's free houres languiſh:
For aſſured bondage?
Imo. Will my Lord ſay ſo?
Iach. I Madam, with his eyes in flood; with laughter,
It is a Recreation to be by
And heare him mocke the Frenchman:
But Heauen's know ſome men are much too blame.
Imo. Not he I hope.
Iach. Not he:
But yet Heauen's bounty towards him, might
Be vs'd more thankfully. In himſelfe 'tis much;
In you, which I account his beyond all Talents.
Whil'ſt I am bound to wonder, I am bound
To pitty too.
Imo. What do you pitty Sir?
Iach. Two Creatures heartyly.
Imo. Am I one Sir?
You looke on me: what wrack diſcerne you in me
Deſerues your pitty?
Iach. Lamentable: what
To hide me from the radiant Sun, and ſolace
I'th'Dungeon by a Snuffe.
Imo. I pray you Sir,
Deliuer with more openneſſe your anſweres
To my demands. Why do you pitty me?
Iach. That others do,
(I was about to ſay) enioy your —— but
It is an office of the Gods to venge it,
Not mine to ſpeake on't.
Imo. You do ſeeme to know
Something of me, or what concernes me; pray you
Since doubting things go ill, often hurts more
Then to be ſure they do. For Certainties
Either are paſt remedies; or timely knowing,
The remedy then borne. Diſcouer to me
What both you ſpur and ſtop.
Iach' Had I this cheeke
To bathe my lips vpon: this hand, whoſe touch,
(Whoſe euery touch) would force the Feelers ſoule
To'th'oath of loyalty. This obiect, which
Takes priſoner the wild motion of mine eye,
Fiering it onely heere, ſhould I (damn'd then)

Slauer

Slauuer with lippes as common as the ſtayres
That mount the Capitoll: Ioyne gripes, with hands
Made hard with hourely falſhood (falſhood as
With labour:) then by peeping in an eye
Baſe and illuſtrious as the ſmoakie light
That's fed with ſtinking Tallow: it were fit
That all the plagues of Hell ſhould at one time
Encounter ſuch reuolt.
Imo. My Lord, I feare
Has forgot Brittaine.
Iach. And himſelfe, not I
Inclin'd to this intelligence, pronounce
The Beggery of his change: but 'tis your Graces
That from my muteſt Conſcience, to my tongue,
Charmes this report out.
Imo. Let me heare no more.
Iach. O deereſt Soule: your Cauſe doth ſtrike my hart
With pitty, that doth make me ſicke. A Lady
So faire, and faſten'd to an Emperie
Would make the great'ſt King double, to be partner'd
With Tomboyes hyr'd, with that ſelfe exhibition
Which your owne Coffers yeeld: with diſeas'd ventures
That play with all Infirmities for Gold,
Which rottenneſſe can lend Nature. Such boyl'd ſtuffe
As well might poyſon Poyſon. Be reueng'd,
Or ſhe that bore you, was no Queene, and you
Recoyle from your great Stocke.
Imo. Reueng'd:
How ſhould I be reueng'd? If this be true,
(As I haue ſuch a Heart, that both mine eares
Muſt not in haſte abuſe) if it be true,
How ſhould I be reueng'd?
Iach. Should he make me
Liue like *Diana's* Prieſt, betwixt cold ſheets,
Whiles he is vaulting variable Rampes
In your deſpight, vpon your purſe: reuenge it.
I dedicate my ſelfe to your ſweet pleaſure,
More Noble then that runnagate to your bed,
And will continue faſt to your Affection,
Still cloſe, as ſure.
Imo. What hoa, *Piſanio?*
Iach. Let me my ſeruice tender on your lippes.
Imo. Away, I do condemne mine eares, that haue
So long attended thee. If thou wert Honourable
Thou would'ſt haue told this tale for Vertue, not
For ſuch an end thou ſeek'ſt, as baſe, as ſtrange:
Thou wrong'ſt a Gentleman, who is as farre
From thy report, as thou from Honor: and
Solicites heere a Lady, that diſdaines
Thee, and the Diuell alike. What hoa, *Piſanio?*
The King my Father ſhall be made acquainted
Of thy Aſſault: if he ſhall thinke it fit,
A ſawcy Stranger in his Court, to Mart
As in a Romiſh Stew, and to expound
His beaſtly minde to vs; he hath a Court
He little cares for, and a Daughter, who
He not reſpects at all. What hoa, *Piſanio?*
Iach. O happy *Leonatus* I may ſay,
The credit that thy Lady hath of thee
Deſerues thy truſt, and thy moſt perfect goodneſſe
Her aſſur'd credit. Bleſſed liue you long,
A Lady to the worthieſt Sir, that euer
Country call'd his; and you his Miſtris, onely
For the moſt worthieſt fit. Giue me your pardon,
I haue ſpoke this to know if your Affiance
Were deeply rooted, and ſhall make your Lord,
That which he is, new o're: And he is one
The trueſt manner'd: ſuch a holy Witch,
That he enchants Societies into him:
Halfe all men hearts are his.
Imo. You make amends.
Iach. He ſits 'mongſt men, like a defended God;
He hath a kinde of Honor ſets him off,
More then a mortall ſeeming. Be not angrie
(Moſt mighty Princeſſe) that I haue aduentur'd
To try your taking of a falſe report, which hath
Honour'd with confirmation your great Iudgement,
In the election of a Sir, ſo rare,
Which you know, cannot erre. The loue I beare him,
Made me to fan you thus, but the Gods made you
(Vnlike all others) chaffeleſſe. Pray your pardon.
Imo. All's well Sir:
Take my powre i'th'Court for yours.
Iach. My humble thankes: I had almoſt forgot
T'intreat your Grace, but in a ſmall requeſt,
And yet of moment too, for it concernes:
Your Lord, my ſelfe, and other Noble Friends
Are partners in the buſineſſe.
Imo. Pray what is't?
Iach. Some dozen Romanes of vs, and your Lord
(The beſt Feather of our wing) haue mingled ſummes
To buy a Preſent for the Emperor:
Which I (the Factor for the reſt) haue done
In France: 'tis Plate of rare deuice, and Iewels
Of rich, and exquiſite forme, their valewes great,
And I am ſomething curious, being ſtrange
To haue them in ſafe ſtowage: May it pleaſe you
To take them in protection.
Imo. Willingly:
And pawne mine Honor for their ſafety, ſince
My Lord hath intereſt in them, I will keepe them
In my Bed-chamber.
Iach. They are in a Trunke
Attended by my men: I will make bold
To ſend them to you, onely for this night:
I muſt aboord to morrow.
Imo. O no, no.
Iach. Yes I beſeech: or I ſhall ſhort my word
By length'ning my returne. From Gallia,
I croſt the Seas on purpoſe, and on promiſe
To ſee your Grace.
Imo. I thanke you for your paines:
But not away to morrow.
Iach. O I muſt Madam.
Therefore I ſhall beſeech you, if you pleaſe
To greet your Lord with writing, doo't to night,
I haue out-ſtood my time, which is materiall
To'th'tender of our Preſent.
Imo. I will write:
Send your Trunke to me, it ſhall ſafe be kept,
And truely yeelded you: you're very welcome. *Exeunt.*

Actus Secundus. Scena Prima.

Enter Clotten, and the two Lords.

Clot. Was there euer man had ſuch lucke? when I kiſt the Iacke vpon an vp-caſt, to be hit away? I had a hundred pound on't: and then a whorſon Iacke-an-Apes, muſt

must take me vp for swearing, as if I borrowed mine oathes of him, and might not spend them at my pleasure.

1. What got he by that? you haue broke his pate with your Bowle.

2. If his wit had bin like him that broke it: it would haue run all out.

Clot. When a Gentleman is dispos'd to sweare: it is not for any standers by to curtall his oathes. Ha?

2. No my Lord; nor crop the eares of them.

Clot. Whorson dog: I gaue him satisfaction? would he had bin one of my Ranke.

2. To haue smell'd like a Foole.

Clot. I am not vext more at any thing in th'earth: a pox on't. I had rather not be so Noble as I am: they dare not fight with me, because of the Queene my Mother: euery Iacke-Slaue hath his belly full of Fighting, and I must go vp and downe like a Cock, that no body can match.

2. You are Cocke and Capon too, and you crow Cock, with your combe on.

Clot. Sayest thou?

2. It is not fit you Lordship should vndertake euery Companion, that you giue offence too.

Clot. No, I know that: but it is fit I should commit offence to my inferiors.

2 I, it is fit for your Lordship onely.

Clot. Why so I say.

1. Did you heere of a Stranger that's come to Court night?

Clot. A Stranger, and I not know on't?

2. He's a strange Fellow himselfe, and knowes it not.

1. There's an Italian come, and 'tis thought one of *Leonatus* Friends.

Clot. *Leonatus*? A banisht Rascall; and he's another, whatsoeuer he be. Who told you of this Stranger?

1. One of your Lordships Pages.

Clot. Is it fit I went to looke vpon him? Is there no derogation in't?

2. You cannot derogate my Lord.

Clot. Not easily I thinke.

2. You are a Foole graunted, therefore your Issues being foolish do not derogate.

Clot. Come, Ile go see this Italian: what I haue lost to day at Bowles, Ile winne to night of him. Come: go.

2. Ile attend your Lordship. *Exit.*

That such a craftie Diuell as is his Mother
Should yeild the world this Asse: A woman, that
Beares all downe with her Braine, and this her Sonne,
Cannot take two from twenty for his heart,
Aud leaue eighteene. Alas poore Princesse,
Thou diuine *Imogen*, what thou endur'st,
Betwixt a Father by thy Step-dame gouern'd,
A Mother hourely coyning plots: A Wooer,
More hatefull then the foule expulsion is
Of thy deere Husband. Then that horrid Act
Of the diuorce, heel'd make the Heauens hold firme
The walls of thy deere Honour. Keepe vnshak'd
That Temple thy faire mind, that thou maist stand
T'enioy thy banish'd Lord: and this great Land. *Exeunt.*

Scena Secunda.

Enter Imogen, in her Bed, and a Lady.

Imo. Who's there? My woman: *Helene*?

La. Please you Madam.

Imo. What houre is it?

Lady. Almost midnight, Madam.

Imo. I haue read three houres then:
Mine eyes are weake,
Fold downe the leafe where I haue left: to bed.
Take not away the Taper, leaue it burning:
And if thou canst awake by foure o'th'clock,
I prythee call me: Sleepe hath ceiz'd me wholly.
To your protection I commend me, Gods,
From Fayries, and the Tempters of the night,
Guard me beseech yee. *Sleepes.*

Iachimo from the Trunke.

Iach. The Crickets sing, and mans ore-labor'd sense
Repaires it selfe by rest: Our *Tarquine* thus
Did softly presse the Rushes, ere he waken'd
The Chastitie he wounded. *Cytherea*,
How brauely thou becom'st thy Bed; fresh Lilly,
And whiter then the Sheetes: that I might touch,
But kisse, one kisse. Rubies vnparagon'd,
How deerely they doo't: 'Tis her breathing that
Perfumes the Chamber thus: the Flame o'th'Taper
Bowes toward her, and would vnder-peepe her lids.
To see th'inclosed Lights, now Canopied
Vnder these windowes, White and Azure lac'd
With Blew of Heauens owne tinct. But my designe.
To note the Chamber, I will write all downe,
Such, and such pictures: There the window, such
Th'adornement of her Bed; the Arras, Figures,
Why such, and such: and the Contents o'th'Story.
Ah, but some naturall notes about her Body,
Aboue ten thousand meaner Moueables
Would testifie, t'enrich mine Inuentorie.
O sleepe, thou Ape of death, lye dull vpon her,
And be her Sense but as a Monument,
Thus in a Chappell lying. Come off, come off;
As slippery as the Gordian-knot was hard.
'Tis mine, and this will witnesse outwardly,
As strongly as the Conscience do's within:
To'th'madding of her Lord. On her left brest
A mole Cinque-spotted: Like the Crimson drops
I'th'bottome of a Cowslippe. Heere's a Voucher,
Stronger then euer Law could make; this Secret
Will force him thinke I haue pick'd the lock, and t'ane
The treasure of her Honour. No more: to what end?
Why should I write this downe, that's riueted,
Screw'd to my memorie. She hath bin reading late,
The Tale of *Tereus*, heere the leaffe's turn'd downe
Where *Philomele* gaue vp. I haue enough,
To'th'Truncke againe, and shut the spring of it.
Swift, swift, you Dragons of the night, that dawning
May beare the Rauens eye: I lodge in feare,
Though this a heauenly Angell: hell is heere. *Clocke strikes*
One, two, three: time, time. *Exit.*

Scena Tertia.

Enter Clotten, and Lords.

1. Your Lordship is the most patient man in losse, the most coldest that euer turn'd vp Ace.

Clot. It would make any man cold to loose.

1. But not euery man patient after the noble temper of your Lordship; You are most hot, and furious when you winne.

Clot.

Winning will put any man into courage: if I could get this foolish *Imogen*, I should haue Gold enough: it's almost morning, is't not?

1 Day, my Lord.

Clot. I would this Musicke would come: I am aduised to giue her Musicke a mornings, they say it will penetrate. *Enter Musitians.*

Come on, tune: If you can penetrate her with your fingering, so: wee'l try with tongue too: if none will do, let her remaine: but Ile neuer giue o're. First, a very excellent good conceyted thing; after a wonderful sweet aire, with admirable rich words to it, and then let her consider.

SONG.

Hearke, hearke, the Larke at Heauens gate sings,
and Phœbus gins arise,
His Steeds to water at those Springs
on chalic'd Flowres that lyes:
And winking Mary-buds begin to ope their Golden eyes
With euery thing that pretty is, my Lady sweet arise:
Arise, arise.

So, get you gone: if this pen trate, I will consider your Musicke the better: if it do not, it is a voyce in her eares which Horse-haires, and Calues-guts, nor the voyce of vnpaued Eunuch to boot, can neuer amed.

Enter Cymbaline, and Queene.

2 Heere comes the King.

Clot. I am glad I was vp so late, for that's the reason I was vp so earely: he cannot choose but take this Seruice I haue done, fatherly. Good morrow to your Maiesty, and to my gracious Mother.

Cym. Attend you here the doore of our stern daughter Will she not forth?

Clot. I haue assayl'd her with Musickes, but she vouchsafes no notice.

Cym. The Exile of her Minion is too new,
She hath not yet forgot him, some more time
Must weare the print of his remembrance on't,
And then she's yours.

Qu. You are most bound to'th'King,
Who let's go by no vantages, that may
Preferre you to his daughter: Frame your selfe
To orderly solicity, and be friended
With aptnesse of the season: make denials
Encrease your Seruices: so seeme, as if
You were inspir'd to do those duties which
You tender to her: that you in all obey her,
Saue when command to your dismission tends,
And therein you are senselesse.

Clot. Senselesse? Not so.

Mes. So like you (Sir) Ambassadors from Rome;
The one is *Caius Lucius.*

Cym. A worthy Fellow,
Albeit he comes on angry purpose now;
But that's no fault of his: we must receyue him
According to the Honor of his Sender,
And towards himselfe, his goodnesse fore-spent on vs
We must extend our notice: Our deere Sonne,
When you haue giuen good morning to your Mistris,
Attend the Queene, and vs, we shall haue neede
T'employ you towards this Romane.
Come our Queene. *Exeunt.*

Clot. If she be vp, Ile speake with her: if not
Let her lye still, and dreame: by your leaue hoa,
I know her women are about her: what
If I do line one of their hands, 'tis Gold
Which buyes admittance (oft it doth) yea, and makes
Diana's Rangers false themselues, yeeld vp
Their Deere to'th'stand o'th'Stealer: and 'tis Gold
Which makes the True-man kill'd, and saues the Theefe:
Nay, sometime hangs both Theefe, and True-man: what
Can it not do, and vndoo? I will make
One of her women Lawyer to me, for
I yet not vnderstand the case my selfe.
By your leaue. *Knockes.*

Enter a Lady.

La. Who's there that knockes?

Clot. A Gentleman.

La. No more.

Clot. Yes, and a Gentlewomans Sonne.

La. That's more
Then some whose Taylors are as deere as yours,
Can iustly boast of: what's your Lordships pleasure?

Clot. Your Ladies person, is she ready?

La. I, to keepe her Chamber.

Clot. There is Gold for you,
Sell me your good report.

La. How, my good name? or to report of you
What I shall thinke is good. The Princesse.

Enter Imogen.

Clot. Good morrow fairest, Sister your sweet hand.

Imo. Good morrow Sir, you lay out too much paines
For purchasing but trouble: the thankes I giue,
Is telling you that I am poore of thankes,
And scarse can spare them.

Clot. Still I sweare I loue you.

Imo. If you but said so, 'twere as deepe with me:
If you sweare still, your recompence is still
That I regard it not.

Clot. This is no answer.

Imo. But that you shall not say, I yeeld being silent,
I would not speake. I pray you spare me, 'faith
I shall vnfold equall discourtesie
To your best kindnesse: one of your great knowing
Should learne (being taught) forbearance.

Clot. To leaue you in your madnesse, 'twere my sin,
I will not.

Imo. Fooles are not mad Folkes.

Clot. Do you call me Foole?

Imo. As I am mad I do:
If you'l be patient, Ile no more be mad,
That cures vs both. I am much sorry (Sir)
You put me to forget a Ladies manners
By being so verball: and learne now, for all,
That I which know my heart, do heere pronounce
By th'very truth of it, I care not for you,
And am so neere the lacke of Charitie
To accuse my selfe, I hate you: which I had rather
You felt, then make't my boast.

Clot. You sinne against
Obedience, which you owe your Father, for
The Contract you pretend with that base Wretch,
One, bred of Almes, and foster'd with cold dishes,
With scraps o'th'Court: It is no Contract, none;
And though it be allowed in meaner parties
(Yet who then he more meane) to knit their soules
(On whom there is no more dependancie
But Brats and Beggery) in selfe-figur'd knot,
Yet you are curb'd from that enlargement, by

aaa The

The conſequence o'th'Crowne, and muſt not foyle
The precious note of it; with a baſe Slaue,
AHilding for a Liuorie, a Squires Cloth,
A Pantler; not ſo eminent.
Imo. Prophane Fellow:
Wert thou the Sonne of *Iupiter*, and no more,
But what thou art beſides: thou wer't too baſe,
To be his Groome: thou wer't dignified enough
Euen to the point of Enuie. If 'twere made
Comparatiue for your Vertues, to be ſtil'd
The vnder Hangman of his Kingdome; and hated
For being prefer'd ſo well.
Clot. The South-Fog rot him.
Imo. He neuer can meete more miſchance, then come
To be but nam'd of thee. His mean'ſt Garment
That euer hath but clipt his body; is dearer
In my reſpect, then all the Heires aboue thee,
Were they all made ſuch men: How now *Piſanio*?
Enter Piſanio,
Clot. His Garments? Now the diuell.
Imo. To *Dorothy* my woman hie thee preſently.
Clot. His Garment?
Imo. I am ſprighted with a Foole,
Frighted, and angred worſe: Go bid my woman
Search for a Iewell, that too caſually
Hath left mine Arme: it was thy Maſters. Shrew me
If I would looſe it for a Reuenew,
Of any Kings in Europe. I do think,
I ſaw't this morning: Confident I am.
Laſt night 'twas on mine Arme; I kiſs'd it,
I hope it be not gone, to tell my Lord
That I kiſſe aught but he.
Piſ. 'Twill not be loſt.
Imo. I hope ſo: go and ſearch.
Clot. You haue abus'd me:
His meaneſt Garment?
Imo. I, I ſaid ſo Sir,
If you will make't an Action, call witneſſe to't.
Clot. I will enforme your Father.
Imo. Your Mother too:
She's my good Lady; and will concieue, I hope
But the worſt of me. So I leaue your Sir,
To'th'worſt of diſcontent. *Exit.*
Clot. Ile ıbereueng'd:
His mean'ſt Garment? Well. *Exit.*

Scena Quarta.

Enter Poſthumus, and Philario.
Poſt. Feare it not Sir: I would I were ſo ſure
To winne the King, as I am bold, her Honour
Will remaine her's.
Phil. What meanes do you make to him?
Poſt. Not any: but abide the change of Time,
Quake in the preſent winters ſtate, and wiſh
That warmer dayes would come: In theſe fear'd hope
I barely gratifie your loue; they faylingı
I muſt die much your debtor.
Phil. Your very goodneſſe, and your company,
Ore-payes all I can do. By this your King,
Hath heard of Great *Auguſtus*: *Caius Lucius*,
Will do's Commiſſion throughly. And I think
Hee'le grant the Tribute: ſend th'Arrerages,
Or looke vpon our Romaines, whoſe remembrance
Is yet freſh in their griefe.
Poſt. I do beleeue
(Statiſt though I am none, nor like to be)
That this will proue a Warre; and you ſhall heare
The Legion now in Gallia, ſooner landed
In our not-fearing-Britaine, then haue tydings
Of any penny Tribute paid. Our Countrymen
Are men more order'd, then when *Iulius Cæſar*
Smil'd at their lacke of skill, but found their courage
Worthy his frowning at. Their diſcipline,
(Now wing-led with their courages) will make knowne
To their Approuers, they are People, ſuch
That mend vpon the world. *Enter Iachimo.*
Phi. See *Iachimo.*
Poſt. The ſwifteſt Harts, haue poſted you by land;
And Windes of all the Corners kiſs'd your Sailes,
To make your veſſell nimble.
Phil. Welcome Sir.
Poſt. I hope the briefeneſſe of your anſwere, made
The ſpeedineſſe of your returne.
Iachi. Your Lady,
Is one of the fayreſt that I haue look'd vpon
Poſt. And therewithall the beſt, or let her beauty
Looke thorough a Caſement to allure falſe hearts,
And be falſe with them.
Iachi. Heere are Letters for you.
Poſt. Their tenure good I truſt.
Iach. 'Tis very like.
Poſt. Was *Caius Lucius* in the Britaine Court,
When you were there?
Iach. He was expected then,
But not approach'd.
Poſt. All is well yet,
Sparkles this Stone as it was wont, or is't not
Too dull for your good wearing?
Iach. If I haue loſt it,
I ſhould haue loſt the worth of it in Gold,
Ile make a iourney twice as farre, t'enioy
A ſecond night of ſuch ſweet ſhortneſſe, which
Was mine in Britaine, for the Ring is wonne.
Poſt. The Stones too hard to come by.
Iach. Not a whit,
Your Lady being ſo eaſy.
Poſt. Make note Sir
Your loſſe, your Sport: I hope you know that we
Muſt not continue Friends.
Iach. Good Sir, we muſt
If you keepe Couenant: had I not brought
The knowledge of your Miſtris home, I grant
We were to queſtion farther; but I now
Profeſſe my ſelfe the winner of her Honor,
Together with your Ring; and not the wronger
Of her, or you hauing proceeded but
By both your willes.
Poſt. If you can mak't apparant
That yon haue taſted her in Bed; my hand,
And Ring is yours. If not, the foule opinion
You had of her pure Honour; gaines, or looſes,
Your Sword, or mine, or Maſterleſſe leaue both
To who ſhall finde them.
Iach. Sir, my Circumſtances
Being ſo nere the Truth, as I will make them,
Muſt firſt induce you to beleeue; whoſe ſtrength
I will confirme with oath, which I doubt not

You'l

You'l giue me leaue to ſpare, when you ſhall finde
You neede it not.
Poſt. Proceed.
Iach. Firſt, her Bed-chamber
(Where I confeſſe I ſlept not, but profeſſe
Had that was well worth watching) it was hang'd
With Tapiſtry of Silke, and Siluer, the Story
Proud *Cleopatra*, when ſhe met her Roman,
And *Sidnus* ſwell'd aboue the Bankes, or for
The preſſe of Boates, or Pride. A peece of Worke
So brauely done, ſo rich, that it did ſtriue
In Workemanſhip, and Value, which I wonder'd
Could be ſo rarely, and exactly wrought
Since the true life on't was——
Poſt. This is true:
And this you might haue heard of heere, by me,
Or by ſome other.
Iach. More particulars
Muſt iuſtifie my knowledge.
Poſt. So they muſt,
Or doe your Honour iniury.
Iach. The Chimney
Is South the Chamber, and the Chimney-peece
Chaſte *Dian*, bathing: neuer ſaw I figures
So likely to report themſelues; the Cutter
Was as another Nature dumbe, out-went her,
Motion, and Breath left out.
Poſt. This is a thing
Which you might from Relation likewiſe reape,
Being, as it is, much ſpoke of.
Iach. The Roofe o'th'Chamber,
With golden Cherubins is fretted. Her Andirons
(I had forgot them) were two winking Cupids
Of Siluer, each on one foote ſtanding, nicely
Depending on their Brands.
Poſt. This is her Honor:
Let it be granted you haue ſeene all this (and praiſe
Be giuen to your remembrance) the deſcription
Of what is in her Chamber, nothing ſaues
The wager you haue laid.
Iach. Then if you can
Be pale, I begge but leaue to ayre this Iewell: See,
And now 'tis vp againe: it muſt be married
To that your Diamond, Ile keepe them.
Poſt. Ioue——
Once more let me behold it: Is it that
Which I left with her?
Iach. Sir (I thanke her) that
She ſtript it from her Arme: I ſee her yet:
Her pretty Action, did out-ſell her guift,
And yet enrich'd it too: ſhe gaue it me,
And ſaid, ſhe priz'd it once.
Poſt. May be, ſhe pluck'd it off
To ſend it me.
Iach. She writes ſo to you? doth ſhee?
Poſt. O no, no, no, 'tis true. Heere, take this too,
It is a Baſiliske vnto mine eye,
Killes me to looke on't: Let there be no Honor,
Where there is Beauty: Truth, where ſemblance: Loue,
Where there's another man. The Vowes of Women,
Of no more bondage be, to where they are made,
Then they are to their Vertues, which is nothing:
O, aboue meaſure falſe.
Phil. Haue patience Sir,
And take your Ring againe, 'tis not yet wonne:
It may be probable ſhe loſt it: or
Who knowes if one her women, being corrupted
Hath ſtolne it from her.
Poſt. Very true,
And ſo I hope he came by't: backe my Ring,
Render to me ſome corporall ſigne about her
More euident then this: for this was ſtolne.
Iach. By Iupiter, I had it from her Arme.
Poſt. Hearke you, he ſweares: by Iupiter he ſweares.
'Tis true, nay keepe the Ring; 'tis true: I am ſure
She would not looſe it: her Attendants are
All ſworne, and honourable: they induc'd to ſteale it?
And by a Stranger? No, he hath enioy'd her,
The Cogniſance of her incontinencie
Is this: ſhe hath bought the name of Whore, thus deerly
There, take thy hyre, and all the Fiends of Hell
Diuide themſelues betweene you.
Phil. Sir, be patient:
This is not ſtrong enough to be beleeu'd
Of one perſwaded well of.
Poſt. Neuer talke on't:
She hath bin colted by him.
Iach. If you ſeeke
For further ſatisfying, vnder her Breaſt
(Worthy her preſſing) lyes a Mole, right proud
Of that moſt delicate Lodging. By my life
I kiſt it, and it gaue me preſent hunger
To feede againe, though full. You do remember
This ſtaine vpon her?
Poſt. I, and it doth confirme
Another ſtaine, as bigge as Hell can hold,
Were there no more but it.
Iach. Will you heare more?
Poſt. Spare your Arethmaticke,
Neuer count the Turnes: Once, and a Million.
Iach. Ile be ſworne.
Poſt. No ſwearing:
If you will ſweare you haue not done't, you lye,
And I will kill thee, if thou do'ſt deny
Thou'ſt made me Cuckold.
Iach. Ile deny nothing.
Poſt. O that I had her heere, to teare her Limb-meale:
I will go there and doo't, i'th'Court, before
Her Father. Ile do ſomething. *Exit.*
Phil. Quite beſides
The gouernment of Patience. You haue wonne:
Let's follow him, and peruert the preſent wrath
He hath againſt himſelfe.
Iach. With all my heart. *Exeunt.*

Enter Poſthumus.

Poſt. Is there no way for Men to be, but Women
Muſt be halfe-workers? We are all Baſtards,
And that moſt venerable man, which I
Did call my Father, was, I know not where
When I was ſtampt. Some Coyner with his Tooles
Made me a counterfeit: yet my Mother ſeem'd
The *Dian* of that time: ſo doth my Wife
The Non-pareill of this. Oh Vengeance, Vengeance!
Me of my lawfull pleaſure ſhe reſtrain'd,
And pray'd me oft forbearance: did it with
A pudencie ſo Roſie, the ſweet view on't
Might well haue warm'd olde Saturne;
That I thought her
As Chaſte, as vn-Sunn'd Snow. Oh, all the Diuels!
This yellow *Iachimo* in an houre, was't not?

Or leſſe; at firſt? Perchance he ſpoke not, but
Like a full Acorn'd Boare, a Iarmen on,
Cry'de oh, and mounted; found no oppoſition
But what he look'd for, ſhould oppoſe, and ſhe
Should from encounter guard. Could I finde out
The Womans part in me, for there's no motion
That tends to vice in man, but I affirme
It is the Womans part: be it Lying, note it,
The womans: Flattering, hers; Deceiuing, hers:
Luſt, and ranke thoughts, hers, hers: Reuenges hers:
Ambitions, Couetings, change of Prides, Diſdaine,
Nice-longing, Slanders, Mutability;
All Faults that name, nay, that Hell knowes,
Why hers, in part, or all: but rather all For euen to Vice
They are not conſtant, but are changing ſtill;
One Vice, but of a minute old, for one
Not halfe ſo old as that. Ile write againſt them,
Deteſt them, curſe them: yet 'tis greater Skill
In a true Hate, to pray they haue their will:
The very Diuels cannot plague them better. *Exit.*

Actus Tertius. Scena Prima.

Enter in State, Cymbeline, Queene, Clotten, and Lords at one doore, and at another, Caius, Lucius, and Attendants.

Cym. Now ſay, what would *Auguſtus Cæſar* with vs?
Luc. When *Iulius Cæſar* (whoſe remembrance yet
Liues in mens eyes, and will to Eares and Tongues
Be Theame, and hearing euer) was in this Britain,
And Conquer'd it, *Caſſibulan* thine Vnkle
(Famous in *Cæſars* prayſes, no whit leſſe
Then in his Feats deſeruing it) for him,
And his Succeſſion, granted Rome a Tribute,
Yeerely three thouſand pounds; which (by thee) lately
Is left vntender'd.
Qu. And to kill the meruaile,
Shall be ſo euer.
Clot. There be many *Cæſars*,
Ere ſuch another *Iulius*: Britaine's a world
By it ſelfe, and we will nothing pay
For wearing our owne Noſes.
Qu. That opportunity
Which then they had to take from's, to reſume
We haue againe. Remember Sir, my Liege,
The Kings your Anceſtors, together with
The naturall brauery of your Iſle, which ſtands
As Neptunes Parke, ribb'd, and pal'd in
With Oakes vnskaleable, and roaring Waters,
With Sands that will not beare your Enemies Boates,
But ſucke them vp to'th'Top-maſt. A kinde of Conqueſt
Cæſar made heere, but made not heere his bragge
Of Came, and Saw, and Ouer-came: with ſhame
(The firſt that euer touch'd him) he was carried
From off our Coaſt, twice beaten: and his Shipping
(Poore ignorant Baubles) on our terrible Seas
Like Egge-ſhels mou'd vpon their Surges, crack'd
As eaſily 'gainſt our Rockes. For ioy whereof,
The fam'd *Caſſibulan*, who was once at point
(Oh giglet Fortune) to maſter *Cæſars* Sword,
Made *Luds-Towne* with reioycing-Fires bright,
And Britaines ſtrut with Courage.
Clot. Come, there's no more Tribute to be paid: our Kingdome is ſtronger then it was at that time: and (as I ſaid) there is no mo ſuch *Cæſars*, other of them may haue crook'd Noſes, but to owe ſuch ſtraite Armes, none.
Cym. Son, let your Mother end.
Clot. We haue yet many among vs, can gripe as hard as *Caſſibulan*, I doe not ſay I am one: but I haue a hand. Why Tribute? Why ſhould we pay Tribute? If *Cæſar* can hide the Sun from vs with a Blanket, or put the Moon in his pocket, we will pay him Tribute for light: elſe Sir, no more Tribute, pray you now.
Cym. You muſt know,
Till the iniurious Romans, did extort
This Tribute from vs, we were free. *Cæſars* Ambition,
Which ſwell'd ſo much, that it did almoſt ſtretch
The ſides o'th'World, againſt all colour heere,
Did put the yoake vpon's; which to ſhake off
Becomes a warlike people, whom we reckon
Our ſelues to be, we do. Say then to *Cæſar*,
Our Anceſtor was that *Mulmutius*, which
Ordain'd our Lawes, whoſe vſe the Sword of *Cæſar*
Hath too much mangled; whoſe repayre, and franchiſe,
Shall (by the power we hold) be our good deed,
Tho Rome be therfore angry. *Mulmutius* made our lawes
Who was the firſt of Britaine, which did put
His browes within a golden Crowne, and call'd
Himſelfe a King.
Luc. I am ſorry *Cymbeline*,
That I am to pronounce *Auguſtus Cæſar*
(*Cæſar*, that hath moe Kings his Seruants, then
Thy ſelfe Domeſticke Officers) thine Enemy:
Receyue it from me then. Warre, and Confuſion
In *Cæſars* name pronounce I 'gainſt thee: Looke
For fury, not to be reſiſted. Thus defide,
I thanke thee for my ſelfe.
Cym. Thou art welcome *Caius*,
Thy *Cæſar* Knighted me; my youth I ſpent
Much vnder him; of him, I gather'd Honour,
Which he, to ſeeke of me againe, perforce,
Behooues me keepe at vtterance. I am perfect,
That the Pannonians and Dalmatians, for
Their Liberties are now in Armes: a Preſident
Which not to reade, would ſhew the Britaines cold:
So *Cæſar* ſhall not finde them.
Luc. Let proofe ſpeake.
Clot. His Maieſty biddes you welcome. Make paſtime with vs, a day, or two, or longer: if you ſeek vs afterwards in other tearmes, you ſhall finde vs in our Salt-water-Girdle: if you beate vs out of it, it is yours: if you fall in the aduenture, our Crowes ſhall fare the better for you: and there's an end.
Luc. So ſir.
Cym. I know your Maſters pleaſure, and he mine:
All the Remaine, is welcome. *Exeunt.*

Scena Secunda.

Enter Piſanio reading of a Letter.

Piſ. How? of Adultery? Wherefore write you not
What Monſters her accuſe? *Leonatus*:
Oh Maſter, what a ſtrange infection

Is

Is falne into thy eare? What false Italian,
(As poysonous tongu'd, as handed) hath preuail'd
On thy too ready hearing? Disloyall? No.
She's punish'd for her Truth; and vndergoes
More Goddesse-like, then Wife-like; such Assaults
As would take in some Vertue. Oh my Master,
Thy mind to her, is now as lowe, as were
Thy Fortunes. How? That I should murther her,
Vpon the Loue, and Truth, and Vowes; which I
Haue made to thy command? I her? Her blood?
If it be so, to do good seruice, neuer
Let me be counted seruiceable. How looke I,
That I should seeme to lacke humanity,
So much as this Fact comes to? Doo't: The Letter.
That I haue sent her, by her owne command,
Shall giue thee opportunitie. Oh damn'd paper,
Blacke as the Inke that's on thee: senselesse bauble,
Art thou a Fœdarie for this Act; and look'st
So Virgin-like without? Loe here she comes.

Enter Imogen.

I am ignorant in what I am commanded.

Imo. How now *Pisanio*?

Pis. Madam, heere is a Letter from my Lord.

Imo. Who, thy Lord? That is my Lord *Leonatus*?
Oh, learn'd indeed were that Astronomer
That knew the Starres, as I his Characters,
Heel'd lay the Future open. You good Gods,
Let what is heere contain'd, rellish of Loue,
Of my Lords health, of his content: yet not
That we two are asunder, let that grieue him;
Some griefes are medcinable, that is one of them,
For it doth physicke Loue, of his content,
All but in that. Good Wax, thy leaue: blest be
You Bees that make these Lockes of counsaile. Louers,
And men in dangerous Bondes pray not alike,
Though Forfeytours you cast in prison, yet
You claspe young *Cupids* Tables: good Newes Gods.

IVstice, and your Fathers wrath (should he take me in his Dominion) could not be so cruell to me, as you: (oh the deerest of Creatures) would euen renew me with your eyes. Take notice that I am in Cambria *at* Milford-Hauen: *what your owne Loue, will out of this aduise you, follow. So he wishes you all happinesse, that remaines loyall to his Vow, and your encreasing in Loue.* Leonatus Posthumus.

Oh for a Horse with wings: Hear'st thou *Pisanio*?
He is at Milford-Hauen: Read, and tell me
How farre 'tis thither. If one of meane affaires
May plod it in a weeke, why may not I
Glide thither in a day? Then true *Pisanio*,
Who long'st like me, to see thy Lord; who long'st
(Oh let me bate) but not like me: yet long'st
But in a fainter kinde. Oh not like me:
For mine's beyond, beyond: say, and speake thicke
(Loues Counsailor should fill the bores of hearing,
To'th'smothering of the Sense) how farre it is
To this same blessed Milford. And by'th'way
Tell me how Wales was made so happy, as
T'inherite such a Hauen. But first of all,
How we may steale from hence: and for the gap
That we shall make in Time, from our hence-going,
And our returne, to excuse: but first, how get hence.
Why should excuse be borne or ere begot?
Weele talke of that heereafter. Prythee speake,
How many store of Miles may we well rid
Twixt houre, and houre?

Pis. One score 'twixt Sun, and Sun,
Madam's enough for you: and too much too.

Imo. Why, one that rode to's Excution Man,
Could neuer go so slow: I haue heard of Riding wagers,
Where Horses haue bin nimbler then the Sands
That run i'th'Clocks behalfe. But this is Foolrie,
Go, bid my Woman faigne a Sicknesse, say
She'le home to her Father; and prouide me presently
A Riding Suit: No costlier then would fit
A Franklins Huswife.

Pisa. Madam, you're best consider.

Imo. I see before me (Man) nor heere, not heere;
Nor what ensues but haue a Fog in them
That I cannot looke through. Away, I prythee,
Do as I bid thee: There's no more to say:
Accessible is none but Milford way. *Exeunt.*

Scena Tertia.

Enter Belarius, Guiderius, and Aruiragus.

Bel. A goodly day, not to keepe house with such,
Whose Roofe's as lowe as ours: Sleepe Boyes, this gate
Instructs you how t'adore the Heauens; and bowes you
To a mornings holy office. The Gates of Monarches
Are Arch'd so high, that Giants may iet through
And keepe their impious Turbonds on, without
Good morrow to the Sun. Haile thou faire Heauen,
We house i'th'Rocke, yet vse thee not so hardly
As prouder liuers do.

Guid. Haile Heauen.

Aruir. Haile Heauen.

Bela. Now for our Mountaine sport, vp to yond hill
Your legges are yong: Ile tread these Flats. Consider,
When you aboue perceiue me like a Crow,
That it is Place, which lessen's, and sets off,
And you may then reuolue what Tales, I haue told you,
Of Courts, of Princes; of the Tricks in Warre.
This Seruice, is not Seruice; so being done,
But being so allowed. To apprehend thus,
Drawes vs a profit from all things we see:
And often to our comfort, shall we finde
The sharded-Beetle, in a safer hold
Then is the full-wing'd Eagle. Oh this life,
Is Nobler, then attending for a checke:
Richer, then doing nothing for a Babe:
Prouder, then rustling in vnpayd-for Silke:
Such gaine the Cap of him, that makes him fine,
Yet keepes his Booke vncros'd: no life to ours.

Gui. Out of your proofe you speak: we poore vnfledg'd
Haue neuer wing'd from view o'th'nest; nor knowes not
What Ayre's from home. Hap'ly this life is best,
(If quiet life be best) sweeter to you
That haue a sharper knowne. Well corresponding
With your stiffe Age; but vnto vs, it is
A Cell of Ignorance: trauailing a bed,
A Prison, or a Debtor, that not dares
To stride a limit.

Arui. What should we speake of
When we are old as you? When we shall heare
The Raine and winde beate darke December? How
In this our pinching Caue, shall we discourse
The

The freezing houres away? We haue ſeene nothing:
We are beaſtly; ſubtle as the Fox for prey,
Like warlike as the Wolfe, for what we eate:
Our Valour is to chace what flyes: Our Cage
We make a Quire, as doth the priſon'd Bird,
And ſing our Bondage freely.

Bel. How you ſpeake.
Did you but know the Citties Vſuries,
And felt them knowingly: the Art o'th'Court,
As hard to leaue, as keepe: whoſe top to climbe
Is certaine falling: or ſo ſlipp'ry, that
The feare's as bad as falling. The toyle o'th'Warre,
A paine that onely ſeemes to ſeeke out danger
I'th'name of Fame, and Honor, which dyes i'th'ſearch,
And hath as oft a ſland'rous Epitaph,
As Record of faire Act. Nay, many times
Doth ill deſerue, by doing well: what's worſe
Muſt curt'ſie at the Cenſure. Oh Boyes, this Storie
The World may reade in me: My bodie's mark'd
With Roman Swords; and my report, was once
Firſt, with the beſt of Note. *Cymbeline* lou'd me,
And when a Souldier was the Theame, my name
Was not farre off: then was I as a Tree
Whoſe boughes did bend with fruit. But in one night,
A Storme, or Robbery (call it what you will)
Shooke downe my mellow hangings: nay my Leaues,
And left me bare to weather.

Gui. Vncertaine fauour.

Bel. My fault being nothing (as I haue told you oft)
But that two Villaines, whoſe falſe Oathes preuayl'd
Before my perfect Honor, ſwore to *Cymbeline*,
I was Confederate with the Romanes: ſo
Followed my Baniſhment, and this twenty yeeres,
This Rocke, and theſe Demeſnes, haue bene my World,
Where I haue liu'd at honeſt freedome, payed
More pious debts to Heauen, then in all
The fore-end of my time. But, vp to'th'Mountaines,
This is not Hunters Language; he that ſtrikes
The Veniſon firſt, ſhall be the Lord o'th'Feaſt,
To him the other two ſhall miniſter,
And we will feare no poyſon, which attends
In place of greater State:
Ile meete you in the Valleyes. *Exeunt.*
How hard it is to hide the ſparkes of Nature?
Theſe Boyes know little they are Sonnes to'th'King,
Nor *Cymbeline* dreames that they are aliue.
They thinke they are mine,
And though train'd vp thus meanely
I'th'Caue, whereon the Bowe their thoughts do hit,
The Roofes of Palaces, and Nature prompts them
In ſimple and lowe things, to Prince it, much
Beyond the tricke of others. This *Paladour*,
The heyre of *Cymbeline* and Britaine, who
The King his Father call'd *Guiderius*. Ioue,
When on my three-foot ſtoole I ſit, and tell
The warlike feats I haue done, his ſpirits flye out
Into my Story: ſay thus mine Enemy fell,
And thus I ſet my foote on's necke, euen then
The Princely blood flowes in his Cheeke, he ſweats,
Straines his yong Nerues, and puts himſelfe in poſture
That acts my words. The yonger Brother *Cadwall*,
Once *Aruiragus*, in as like a figure
Strikes life into my ſpeech, and ſhewes much more
His owne conceyuing. Hearke, the Game is rows'd,
Oh *Cymbeline*, Heauen and my Conſcience knowes
Thou didd'ſt vniuſtly baniſh me: whereon
At three, and two yeeres old, I ſtole theſe Babes,
Thinking to barre thee of Succeſſion, as
Thou refts me of my Lands. *Euriphile*,
Thou was't their Nurſe, they took thee for their mother,
And euery day do honor to her graue:
My ſelfe *Belarius*, that am *Mergan* call'd
They take for Naturall Father. The Game is vp. *Exit.*

Scena Quarta.

Enter Piſanio and Imogen.

Imo. Thou told'ſt me when we came frõ horſe, ỳ place
Was neere at hand: Ne're long'd my Mother ſo
To ſee me firſt, as I haue now. *Piſanio*, Man:
Where is *Poſthumus*? What is in thy mind
That makes thee ſtare thus? Wherefore breakes that ſigh
From th'inward of thee? One, but painted thus
Would be interpreted a thing perplex'd
Beyond ſelfe-explication. Put thy ſelfe
Into a hauiour of leſſe feare, ere wildneſſe
Vanquiſh my ſtayder Senſes. What's the matter?
Why tender'ſt thou that Paper to me, with
A looke vntender? If't be Summer Newes
Smile too't before: if Winterly, thou need'ſt
But keepe that count'nance ſtil. My Husbands hand?
That Drug-damn'd Italy, hath out-craftied him,
And hee's at ſome hard point. Speake man, thy Tongue
May take off ſome extreamitie, which to reade
Would be euen mortall to me.

Piſ. Pleaſe you reade,
And you ſhall finde me (wretched man) a thing
The moſt diſdain'd of Fortune.

Imogen reades.

THy Miſtris (Piſanio) hath plaide the Strumpet in my Bed: the Teſtimonies whereof, lyes bleeding in me. I ſpeak not out of weake Surmiſes, but from proofe as ſtrong as my greefe, and as certaine as I expect my Reuenge. That part, thou (Piſanio) muſt acte for me, if thy Faith be not tainted with the breach of hers; let thine owne hands take away her life: I ſhall giue thee opportunity at Milford Hauen. She hath my Letter for the purpoſe; where, if thou feare to ſtrike, and to make mee certaine it is done, thou art the Pander to her diſhonour, and equally to me diſloyall.

Piſ. What ſhall I need to draw my Sword, the Paper
Hath cut her throat alreadie? No, 'tis Slander,
Whoſe edge is ſharper then the Sword, whoſe tongue
Out-venomes all the Wormes of Nyle, whoſe breath
Rides on the poſting windes, and doth belye
All corners of the World. Kings, Queenes, and States,
Maides, Matrons, nay the Secrets of the Graue
This viperous ſlander enters. What cheere, Madam?

Imo. Falſe to his Bed? What is it to be falſe?
To lye in watch there, and to thinke on him?
To weepe 'twixt clock and clock? If ſleep charge Nature,
To breake it with a fearfull dreame of him,
And cry my ſelfe awake? That's falſe to's bed? Is it?

Piſa. Alas good Lady.

Imo. I falſe? Thy Conſcience witneſſe: *Iachimo*,
Thou didd'ſt accuſe him of Incontinencie,
Thou then look'dſt like a Villaine: now, me thinkes
Thy

Thy fauours good enough. Some Iay of Italy
(Whoſe mother was her painting) hath betraid him:
Poore I am ſtale, a Garment out of faſhion,
And for I am richer then to hang by th'walles,
I muſt be ript: To peeces with me: Oh!
Mens Vowes are womens Traitors. All good ſeeming
By thy reuolt (oh Husband) ſhall be thought
Put on for Villainy; not borne where't growes,
But worne a Baite for Ladies.
Piſa. Good Madam, heare me.
Imo. True honeſt men being heard, like falſe *Æneas*,
Were in his time thought falſe: and *Synons* weeping
Did ſcandall many a holy teare: tooke pitty
From moſt true wretchedneſſe. So thou, *Poſthumus*
Wilt lay the Leauen on all proper men;
Goodly, and gallant, ſhall be falſe and periur'd
From thy great faile: Come Fellow, be thou honeſt,
Do thou thy Maſters bidding. When thou ſeeſt him,
A little witneſſe my obedience. Looke
I draw the Sword my ſelfe, take it, and hit
The innocent Manſion of my Loue (my Heart:)
Feare not, 'tis empty of all things, but Greefe:
Thy Maſter is not there, who was indeede
The riches of it. Do his bidding, ſtrike,
Thou mayſt be valiant in a better cauſe;
But now thou ſeem'ſt a Coward.
Piſ. Hence vile Inſtrument,
Thou ſhalt not damne my hand.
Imo. Why, I muſt dye:
And if I do not by thy hand, thou art
No Seruant of thy Maſters. Againſt Selfe-ſlaughter,
There is a prohibition ſo Diuine,
That crauens my weake hand: Come, heere's my heart:
Something's a-foot: Soft, ſoft, wee'l no defence,
Obedient as the Scabbard. What is heere,
The Scriptures of the Loyall *Leonatus*,
All turn'd to Hereſie? Away, away
Corrupters of my Faith, you ſhall no more
Be Stomachers to my heart: thus may poore Fooles
Beleeue falſe Teachers: Though thoſe that are betraid
Do feele the Treaſon ſharpely, yet the Traitor
Stands in worſe caſe of woe. And thou *Poſthumus*,
That didd'ſt ſet vp my diſobedience 'gainſt the King
My Father, and makes me put into contempt the ſuites
Of Princely Fellowes, ſhalt heereafter finde
It is no acte of common paſſage, but
A ſtraine of Rareneſſe: and I greeue my ſelfe,
To thinke, when thou ſhalt be diſedg'd by her,
That now thou tyreſt on, how thy memory
Will then be pang'd by me. Prythee diſpatch,
The Lambe entreats the Butcher. Wher's thy knife?
Thou art too ſlow to do thy Maſters bidding
When I deſire it too.
Piſ. Oh gracious Lady:
Since I receiu'd command to do this buſineſſe,
I haue not ſlept one winke.
Imo. Doo't, and to bed then.
Piſ. Ile wake mine eye-balles firſt.
Imo. Wherefore then
Didd'ſt vndertake it? Why haſt thou abus'd
So many Miles, with a pretence? This place?
Mine Action? and thine owne? Our Horſes labour?
The Time inuiting thee? The perturb'd Court
For my being abſent? whereunto I neuer
Purpoſe returne. Why haſt thou gone ſo farre
To be vn-bent? when thou haſt 'tane thy ſtand,
Th'elected Deere before thee?
Piſ. But to win time
To looſe ſo bad employment, in the which
I haue conſider'd of a courſe: good Ladie
Heare me with patience.
Imo. Talke thy tongue weary, ſpeake:
I haue heard I am a Strumpet, and mine eare
Therein falſe ſtrooke, can take no greater wound,
Nor tent, to bottome that. But ſpeake.
Piſ. Then Madam,
I thought you would not backe againe.
Imo. Moſt like,
Bringing me heere to kill me.
Piſ. Not ſo neither:
But if I were as wiſe, as honeſt, then
My purpoſe would proue well: it cannot be,
But that my Maſter is abus'd. Some Villaine,
I, and ſingular in his Art, hath done you both
This curſed iniurie.
Imo. Some Roman Curtezan?
Piſa. No, on my life:
Ile giue but notice you are dead, and ſend him
Some bloody ſigne of it. For 'tis commanded
I ſhould do ſo: you ſhall be miſt at Court,
And that will well confirme it.
Imo. Why good Fellow,
What ſhall I do the while? Where bide? How liue?
Or in my life, what comfort, when I am
Dead to my Husband?
Piſ. If you'l backe to'th'Court.
Imo. No Court, no Father, nor no more adoe
With that harſh, noble, ſimple nothing:
That *Clotten*, whoſe Loue-ſuite hath bene to me
As fearefull as a Siege.
Piſ. If not at Court,
Then not in Britaine muſt you bide.
Imo. Where then?
Hath Britaine all the Sunne that ſhines? Day? Night?
Are they not but in Britaine? I'th'worlds Volume
Our Britaine ſeemes as of it, but not in't:
In a great Poole, a Swannes-neſt, prythee thinke
There's liuers out of Britaine.
Piſ. I am moſt glad
You thinke of other place: Th'Ambaſſador,
Lucius the Romane comes to Milford-Hauen
To morrow. Now, if you could weare a minde
Darke, as your Fortune is, and but diſguiſe
That which t'appeare it ſelfe, muſt not yet be,
But by ſelfe-danger, you ſhould tread a courſe
Pretty, and full of view: yea, happily, neere
The reſidence of *Poſthumus*; ſo nie (at leaſt)
That though his Actions were not viſible, yet
Report ſhould render him hourely to your eare,
As truely as he mooues.
Imo. Oh for ſuch meanes,
Though perill to my modeſtie, not death on't
I would aduenture.
Piſ. Well then, heere's the point:
You muſt forget to be a Woman: change
Command, into obedience. Feare, and Niceneſſe
(The Handmaides of all Women, or more truely
Woman it pretty ſelfe) into a waggiſh courage,
Ready in gybes, quicke-anſwer'd, ſawcie, and
As quarrellous as the Weazell: Nay, you muſt
Forget that rareſt Treaſure of your Cheeke,
Expoſing it (but oh the harder heart,

Alacke no remedy) to the greedy touch
Of common-kiſſing *Titan:* and forget
Your labourſome and dainty Trimmes, wherein
You made great *Iuno* angry.

Imo. Nay be breefe?
I ſee into thy end, and am almoſt
A man already.

Piſ. Firſt, make your ſelfe but like one,
Fore-thinking this. I haue already fit
('Tis in my Cloake-bagge) Doublet, Hat, Hoſe, all
That anſwer to them: Would you in their ſeruing,
(And with what imitation you can borrow
From youth of ſuch a ſeaſon) 'fore Noble *Lucius*
Preſent your ſelfe, deſire his ſeruice: tell him
Wherein you're happy; which will make him know,
If that his head haue eare in Muſicke, doubtleſſe
With ioy he will imbrace you: for hee's Honourable,
And doubling that, moſt holy. Your meanes abroad:
You haue me rich, and I will neuer faile
Beginning, nor ſupplyment.

Imo. Thou art all the comfort
The Gods will diet me with. Pry thee away,
There's more to be conſider'd: but wee'l euen
All that good time will giue vs. This attempt,
I am Souldier too, and will abide it with
A Princes Courage. Away, I prythee.

Piſ. Well Madam, we muſt take a ſhort farewell,
Leaſt being miſt, I be ſuſpected of
Your carriage from the Court. My Noble Miſtris,
Heere is a boxe, I had it from the Queene,
What's in't is precious: If you are ſicke at Sea,
Or Stomacke-qualm'd at Land, a Dramme of this
Will driue away diſtemper. To ſome ſhade,
And fit you to your Manhood: may the Gods
Direct you to the beſt.

Imo. Amen: I thanke thee. *Exeunt.*

Scena Quinta.

Enter Cymbeline, Queene, Cloten, Lucius, and Lords.

Cym. Thus farre, and ſo farewell.

Luc. Thankes, Royall Sir:
My Emperor hath wrote, I muſt from hence,
And am right ſorry, that I muſt report ye
My Maſters Enemy.

Cym. Our Subiects (Sir)
Will not endure his yoake; and for our ſelfe
To ſhew leſſe Soueraignty then they, muſt needs
Appeare vn-Kinglike.

Luc. So Sir: I deſire of you
A Conduct ouer Land, to Milford-Hauen.
Madam, all ioy befall your Grace, and you.

Cym. My Lords, you are appointed for that Office:
The due of Honor, in no point omit:
So farewell Noble *Lucius.*

Luc. Your hand, my Lord.

Clot. Receiue it friendly: but from this time forth
I weare it as your Enemy.

Luc. Sir, the Euent
Is yet to name the winner. Fare you well.

Cym. Leaue not the worthy *Lucius*, good my Lords
Till he haue croſt the Seuern. Happines. *Exit Lucius, &c*

Qu. He goes hence frowning: but it honours vs
That we haue giuen him cauſe.

Clot. 'Tis all the better,
Your valiant Britaines haue their wiſhes in it.

Cym. *Lucius* hath wrote already to the Emperor
How it goes heere. It fits vs therefore ripely
Our Chariots, and our Horſemen be in readineſſe:
The Powres that he already hath in Gallia
Will ſoone be drawne to head, from whence he moues
His warre for Britaine.

Qu. 'Tis not ſleepy buſineſſe,
But muſt be look'd too ſpeedily, and ſtrongly.

Cym. Our expectation that it would be thus
Hath made vs forward. But my gentle Queene,
Where is our Daughter? She hath not appear'd
Before the Roman, nor to vs hath tender'd
The duty of the day. She looke vs like
A thing more made of malice, then of duty,
We haue noted it. Call her before vs, for
We haue beene too ſlight in ſufferance.

Qu. Royall Sir,
Since the exile of *Poſthumus*, moſt retyr'd
Hath her life bin: the Cure whereof, my Lord,
'Tis time muſt do. Beſeech your Maieſty,
Forbeare ſharpe ſpeeches to her. Shee's a Lady
So tender of rebukes, that words are ſtrokes,
And ſtrokes death to her.

Enter a Meſſenger.

Cym. Where is ſhe Sir? How
Can her contempt be anſwer'd?

Meſ. Pleaſe you Sir,
Her Chambers are all lock'd, and there's no anſwer
That will be giuen to'th'lowd of noiſe, we make.

Qu. My Lord, when laſt I went to viſit her,
She pray'd me to excuſe her keeping cloſe,
Whereto conſtrain'd by her infirmitie,
She ſhould that dutie leaue vnpaide to you
Which dayly ſhe was bound to proffer: this
She wiſh'd me to make knowne: but our great Court
Made me too blame in memory.

Cym. Her doores lock'd?
Not ſeene of late? Grant Heauens, that which I
Feare, proue falſe. *Exit.*

Qu. Sonne, I ſay, follow the King.

Clot. That man of hers, *Piſanio*, her old Seruant
I haue not ſeene theſe two dayes. *Exit.*

Qu. Go, looke after:
Piſanio, thou that ſtand'ſt ſo for *Poſthumus*,
He hath a Drugge of mine: I pray, his abſence
Proceed by ſwallowing that. For he beleeues
It is a thing moſt precious. But for her,
Where is ſhe gone? Haply diſpaire hath ſeiz'd her:
Or wing'd with feruour of her loue, ſhe's flowne
To her deſir'd *Poſthumus*: gone ſhe is,
To death, or to diſhonor, and my end
Can make good vſe of either. Shee being downe,
I haue the placing of the Brittiſh Crowne.

Enter Cloten.

How now, my Sonne?

Clot. 'Tis certaine ſhe is fled:
Go in and cheere the King, he rages, none
Dare come about him.

Qu. All the better: may
This night fore-ſtall him of the comming day. *Exit Qu.*

Clo. I loue, and hate her: for ſhe's Faire and Royall,
And that ſhe hath all courtly parts more exquiſite

Then

Then Lady, Ladies, Woman, from euery one
The beſt ſhe hath, and ſhe of all compounded
Out-ſelles them all. I loue her therefore, but
Diſdaining me, and throwing Fauours on
The low *Poſthumus*, ſlanders ſo her iudgement,
That what's elſe rare, is choak'd: and in that point
I will conclude to hate her, nay indeede,
To be reueng'd vpon her. For, when Fooles ſhall——

Enter Piſanio.

Who is heere? What, are you packing ſirrah?
Come hither: Ah you precious Pandar, Villaine,
Where is thy Lady? In a word, or elſe
Thou art ſtraightway with the Fiends.

Piſ. Oh, good my Lord.

Clo. Where is thy Lady? Or, by Iupiter,
I will not aske againe. Cloſe Villaine,
Ile haue this Secret from thy heart, or rip
Thy heart to finde it. Is ſhe with *Poſthumus*?
From whoſe ſo many waights of baſeneſſe, cannot
A dram of worth be drawne.

Piſ. Alas, my Lord,
How can ſhe be with him? When was ſhe miſs'd?
He is in Rome.

Clot. Where is ſhe Sir? Come neerer:
No farther halting: ſatisfie me home,
What is become of her?

Piſ. Oh, my all-worthy Lord.

Clo. All-worthy Villaine,
Diſcouer where thy Miſtris is, at once,
At the next word: no more of worthy Lord:
Speake, or thy ſilence on the inſtant, is
Thy condemnation, and thy death.

Piſ. Then Sir:
This Paper is the hiſtorie of my knowledge
Touching her flight.

Clo. Let's ſee't: I will purſue her
Euen to *Auguſtus* Throne.

Piſ. Or this, or periſh.
She's farre enough, and what he learnes by this,
May proue his trauell, not her danger.

Clo. Humh.

Piſ. Ile write to my Lord ſhe's dead: Oh *Imogen*,
Safe mayſt thou wander, ſafe returne agen.

Clot. Sirra, is this Letter true?

Piſ. Sir, as I thinke.

Clot. It is *Poſthumus* hand, I know't. Sirrah, if thou would'ſt not be a Villain, but do me true ſeruice: vndergo thoſe Imployments wherin I ſhould haue cauſe to vſe thee with a ſerious induſtry, that is, what villainy ſoere I bid thee do to performe it, directly and truely, I would thinke thee an honeſt man: thou ſhould'ſt neither want my meanes for thy releefe, nor my voyce for thy preferment.

Piſ. Well, my good Lord.

Clot. Wilt thou ſerue mee? For ſince patiently and conſtantly thou haſt ſtucke to the bare Fortune of that Begger *Poſthumus*, thou canſt not in the courſe of gratitude, but be a diligent follower of mine. Wilt thou ſerue mee?

Piſ. Sir, I will.

Clo. Giue mee thy hand, heere's my purſe. Haſt any of thy late Maſters Garments in thy poſſeſſion?

Piſan. I haue (my Lord) at my Lodging, the ſame Suite he wore, when he tooke leaue of my Ladie & Miſtreſſe.

Clo. The firſt ſeruice thou doſt mee, fetch that Suite hither, let it be thy firſt ſeruice, go.

Piſ. I ſhall my Lord. *Exit.*

Clo. Meet thee at Milford-Hauen: (I forgot to aske him one thing, Ile remember't anon:) euen there, thou villaine *Poſthumus* will I kill thee. I would theſe Garments were come. She ſaide vpon a time (the bitterneſſe of it, I now belch from my heart) that ſhee held the very Garment of *Poſthumus*, in more reſpect, then my Noble and naturall perſon; together with the adornement of my Qualities. With that Suite vpon my backe wil I rauiſh her: firſt kill him, and in her eyes; there ſhall ſhe ſee my valour, which wil then be a torment to hir contempt. He on the ground, my ſpeech of inſulment ended on his dead bodie, and when my Luſt hath dined (which, as I ſay, to vex her, I will execute in the Cloathes that ſhe ſo prais'd:) to the Court Ile knock her backe, foot her home againe. She hath deſpis'd mee reioycingly, and Ile bee merry in my Reuenge.

Enter Piſanio.

Be thoſe the Garments?

Piſ. I, my Noble Lord.

Clo. How long is't ſince ſhe went to Milford-Hauen?

Piſ. She can ſcarſe be there yet.

Clo. Bring this Apparrell to my Chamber, that is the ſecond thing that I haue commanded thee. The third is, that thou wilt be a voluntarie Mute to my deſigne. Be but dutious, and true preferment ſhall tender it ſelfe to thee. My Reuenge is now at Milford, would I had wings to follow it. Come, and be true. *Exit*

Piſ. Thou bid'ſt me to my loſſe: for true to thee,
Were to proue falſe, which I will neuer bee
To him that is moſt true. To Milford go,
And finde not her, whom thou purſueſt. Flow, flow
You Heauenly bleſſings on her: This Fooles ſpeede
Be croſt with ſlowneſſe; Labour be his meede. *Exit*

Scena Sexta.

Enter Imogen alone.

Imo. I ſee a mans life is a tedious one,
I haue tyr'd my ſelfe: and for two nights together
Haue made the ground my bed. I ſhould be ſicke,
But that my reſolution helpes me: Milford,
When from the Mountaine top, *Piſanio* ſhew'd thee,
Thou was't within a kenne. Oh Ioue, I thinke
Foundations flye the wretched: ſuch I meane,
Where they ſhould be releeu'd. Two Beggers told me,
I could not miſſe my way. Will poore Folkes lye
That haue Afflictions on them, knowing 'tis
A puniſhment, or Triall? Yes; no wonder,
When Rich-ones ſcarſe tell true. To lapſe in Fulneſſe
Is ſorer, then to lye for Neede: and Falſhood
Is worſe in Kings, then Beggers. My deere Lord,
Thou art one o'th'falſe Ones: Now I thinke on thee,
My hunger's gone; but euen before, I was
At point to ſinke, for Food. But what is this?
Heere is a path too't: 'tis ſome ſauage hold:
I were beſt not call; I dare not call: yet Famine
Ere cleane it o're-throw Nature, makes it valiant.
Plentie, and Peace breeds Cowards: Hardneſſe euer
Of Hardineſſe is Mother. Hoa? who's heere?
If any thing that's ciuill, ſpeake: if ſauage,

Take,

Take, or lend. Hoa? No anſwer? Then Ile enter.
Beſt draw my Sword; and if mine Enemy
But feare the Sword like me, hee'l ſcarſely looke on't.
Such a Foe, good Heauens. *Exit.*

Scena Septima.

Enter Belarius, Guiderius, and Aruiragus.

Bel. You *Polidore* haue prou'd beſt Woodman, and
Are Maſter of the Feaſt: *Cadwall*, and I
Will play the Cooke, and Seruant, 'tis our match:
The ſweat of induſtry would dry, and dye
But for the end it workes too. Come, our ſtomackes
Will make what's homely, ſauoury: Wearineſſe
Can ſnore vpon the Flint, when reſtie Sloth
Findes the Downe-pillow hard. Now peace be heere,
Poore houſe, that keep'ſt thy ſelfe.

Gui. I am throughly weary.

Arui. I am weake with toyle, yet ſtrong in appetite.

Gui. There is cold meat i'th'Caue, we'l brouz on that
Whil'ſt what we haue kill'd, be Cook'd.

Bel. Stay, come not in:
But that it eates our victualles, I ſhould thinke
Heere were a Faiery.

Gui. What's the matter, Sir?

Bel. By Iupiter an Angell: or if not
An earthly Paragon. Behold Diuineneſſe
No elder then a Boy.

Enter Imogen.

Imo. Good maſters harme me not:
Before I enter'd heere, I call'd, and thought
To haue begg'd, or bought, what I haue took: good troth
I haue ſtolne nought, nor would not, though I had found
Gold ſtrew'd i'th'Floore. Heere's money for my Meate,
I would haue left it on the Boord, ſo ſoone
As I had made my Meale; and parted
With Pray'rs for the Prouider.

Gui. Money? Youth.

Aru. All Gold and Siluer rather turne to durt,
As 'tis no better reckon'd, but of thoſe
Who worſhip durty Gods.

Imo. I ſee you're angry:
Know, if you kill me for my fault, I ſhould
Haue dyed, had I not made it.

Bel. Whether bound?

Imo. To Milford-Hauen.

Bel. What's your name?

Imo. *Fidele* Sir: I haue a Kinſman, who
Is bound for Italy; he embark'd at Milford,
To whom being going, almoſt ſpent with hunger,
I am falne in this offence.

Bel. Prythee (faire youth)
Thinke vs no Churles: nor meaſure our good mindes
By this rude place we liue in. Well encounter'd,
'Tis almoſt night, you ſhall haue better cheere
Ere you depart; and thankes to ſtay, and eate it:
Boyes, bid him welcome.

Gui. Were you a woman, youth,
I ſhould woo hard, but be your Groome in honeſty:
I bid for you, as I do buy.

Arui. Ile make't my Comfort
He is a man, Ile loue him as my Brother:
And ſuch a welcome as I'ld giue to him
(After long abſence) ſuch is yours. Moſt welcome:
Be ſprightly, for you fall 'mongſt Friends.

Imo. 'Mongſt Friends?
If Brothers: would it had bin ſo, that they
Had bin my Fathers Sonnes, then had my prize
Bin leſſe, and ſo more equall ballaſting
To thee *Poſthumus*.

Bel. He wrings at ſome diſtreſſe.

Gui. Would I could free't.

Arui. Or I, what ere it be,
What paine it coſt, what danger: Gods!

Bel. Hearke Boyes.

Imo. Great men
That had a Court no bigger then this Caue,
That did attend themſelues, and had the vertue
Which their owne Conſcience ſeal'd them: laying by
That nothing-guift of differing Multitudes
Could not out-peere theſe twaine. Pardon me Gods,
I'ld change my ſexe to be Companion with them,
Since *Leonatus* falſe.

Bel. It ſhall be ſo:
Boyes wee'l go dreſſe our Hunt. Faire youth come in;
Diſcourſe is heauy, faſting: when we haue ſupp'd
Wee'l mannerly demand thee of thy Story,
So farre as thou wilt ſpeake it.

Gui. Pray draw neere.

Arui. The Night to'th'Owle,
And Morne to th'Larke leſſe welcome.

Imo. Thankes Sir.

Arui. I pray draw neere. *Exeunt.*

Scena Octaua.

Enter two Roman Senators, and Tribunes.

1.Sen. This is the tenor of the Emperors Writ;
That ſince the common men are now in Action
'Gainſt the Pannonians, and Dalmatians,
And that the Legions now in Gallia, are
Full weake to vndertake our Warres againſt
The falne-off Britaines, that we do incite
The Gentry to this buſineſſe. He creates
Lucius Pro-Conſull: and to you the Tribunes
For this immediate Leuy, he commands
His abſolute Commiſſion. Long liue *Cæſar*.

Tri. Is *Lucius* Generall of the Forces?

2.Sen. I.

Tri. Remaining now in Gallia?

1.Sen. With thoſe Legions
Which I haue ſpoke of, whereunto your leuie
Muſt be ſuppliant: the words of your Commiſſion
Will tye you to the numbers, and the time
Of their diſpatch.

Tri. We will diſcharge our duty. *Exeunt.*

Actus Quartus. Scena Prima.

Enter Clotten alone.

Clot. I am neere to'th'place where they ſhould meet, if *Piſanio* haue mapp'd it truely. How fit his Garments ſerue me? Why ſhould his Miſtris who was made by him that

that made the Taylor, not be fit too? The rather (ſauing reuerence of the Word) for 'tis ſaide a Womans fitneſſe comes by fits: therein I muſt play the Workman, I dare ſpeake it to my ſelfe, for it is not Vainglorie for a man, and his Glaſſe, to confer in his owne Chamber; I meane, the Lines of my body are as well drawne as his; no leſſe young, more ſtrong, not beneath him in Fortunes, beyond him in the aduantage of the time, aboue him in Birth, alike conuerſant in generall ſeruices, and more remarkeable in ſingle oppoſitions; yet this imperſeuerant Thing loues him in my deſpight. What Mortalitie is? *Poſthumus*, thy head (which now is growing vppon thy ſhoulders) ſhall within this houre be off, thy Miſtris inforced, thy Garments cut to peeces before thy face: and all this done, ſpurne her home to her Father, who may (happily) be a little angry for my ſo rough vſage: but my Mother hauing power of his teſtineſſe, ſhall turne all into my commendations. My Horſe is tyed vp ſafe, out Sword, and to a ſore purpoſe: Fortune put them into my hand: This is the very deſcription of their meeting place and the Fellow dares not deceiue me. *Exit.*

Scena Secunda.

Enter Belarius, Guiderius, Aruiragus, and Imogen from the Caue.

Bel. You are not well: Remaine heere in the Caue,
Wee'l come to you after Hunting.
Arui. Brother, ſtay heere:
Are we not Brothers?
Imo. So man and man ſhould be,
But Clay and Clay, differs in dignitie,
Whoſe duſt is both alike. I am very ſicke,
Gui. Go you to Hunting, Ile abide with him.
Imo. So ſicke I am not, yet I am not well:
But not ſo Citizen a wanton, as
To ſeeme to dye, ere ſicke: So pleaſe you, leaue me,
Sticke to your Iournall courſe: the breach of Cuſtome,
Is breach of all. I am ill, but your being by me
Cannot amend me. Society, is no comfort
To one not ſociable: I am not very ſicke,
Since I can reaſon of it: pray you truſt me heere,
Ile rob none but my ſelfe, and let me dye
Stealing ſo poorely.
Gui. I loue thee: I haue ſpoke it,
How much the quantity, the waight as much,
As I do loue my Father.
Bel. What? How? how?
Arui. If it be ſinne to ſay ſo (Sir) I yoake mee
In my good Brothers fault: I know not why
I loue this youth, and I haue heard you ſay,
Loue's reaſon's, without reaſon. The Beere at doore,
And a demand who is't ſhall dye, I'ld ſay
My Father, not this youth.
Bel. Oh noble ſtraine!
O worthineſſe of Nature, breed of Greatneſſe!
"Cowards father Cowards, & Baſe things Syre Bace;
"Nature hath Meale, and Bran; Contempt, and Grace.
I'me not their Father, yet who this ſhould bee,
Doth myracle it ſelfe, lou'd before mee.
'Tis the ninth houre o'th'Morne.
Arui. Brother, farewell.
Imo. I wiſh ye ſport.
Arui. You health.——So pleaſe you Sir.
Imo. Theſe are kinde Creatures.
Gods, what lyes I haue heard:
Our Courtiers ſay, all's ſauage, but at Court;
Experience, oh thou diſproou'ſt Report.
Th'emperious Seas breeds Monſters; for the Diſh,
Poore Tributary Riuers, as ſweet Fiſh:
I am ſicke ſtill, heart-ſicke; *Piſanio*,
Ile now taſte of thy Drugge.
Gui. I could not ſtirre him:
He ſaid he was gentle, but vnfortunate;
Diſhoneſtly afflicted, but yet honeſt.
Arui. Thus did he anſwer me: yet ſaid heereafter,
I might know more.
Bel. To'th'Field, to'th'Field:
Wee'l leaue you for this time, go in, and reſt.
Arui. Wee'l not be long away.
Bel. Pray be not ſicke,
For you muſt be our Huſwife.
Imo. Well, or ill,
I am bound to you. *Exit.*
Bel. And ſhal't be euer.
This youth, how ere diſtreſt, appeares he hath had
Good Anceſtors.
Arui. How Angell-like he ſings?
Gui. But his neate Cookerie?
Arui. He cut our Rootes in Charracters,
And ſawc'ſt our Brothes, as *Iuno* had bin ſicke,
And he her Dieter.
Arui. Nobly he yoakes
A ſmiling, with a ſigh; as if the ſighe
Was that it was, for not being ſuch a Smile:
The Smile, mocking the Sigh, that it would flye
From ſo diuine a Temple, to commix
With windes, that Saylors raile at.
Gui. I do note,
That greefe and patience rooted in them both,
Mingle their ſpurres together.
Arui. Grow patient,
And let the ſtinking-Elder (Greefe) vntwine
His periſhing roote, with the encreaſing Vine.
Bel. It is great morning. Come away: Who's there?
Enter Cloten.
Clo. I cannot finde thoſe Runnagates, that Villaine
Hath mock'd me. I am faint.
Bel. Thoſe Runnagates?
Meanes he not vs? I partly know him, 'tis
Cloten, the Sonne o'th'Queene. I feare ſome Ambuſh:
I ſaw him not theſe many yeares, and yet
I know 'tis he: We are held as Out-Lawes: Hence.
Gui. He is but one: you, and my Brother ſearch
What Companies are neere: pray you away,
Let me alone with him.
Clot. Soft, what are you
That flye me thus? Some villaine-Mountainers?
I haue heard of ſuch. What Slaue art thou?
Gui. A thing
More ſlauiſh did I ne're, then anſwering
A Slaue without a knocke.
Clot. Thou art a Robber,
A Law-breaker, a Villaine: yeeld thee Theefe.
Gui. To who? to thee? What art thou? Haue not I
An arme as bigge as thine? A heart, as bigge:
Thy words I grant are bigger: for I weare not
My Dagger in my mouth. Say what thou art:
Why

Why I ſhould yeeld to thee?
Clot. Thou Villaine baſe,
Know'ſt me not by my Cloathes?
Gui. No, nor thy Taylor, Raſcall:
Who is thy Grandfather? He made thoſe cloathes,
Which (as it ſeemes) make thee.
Clo. Thou precious Varlet,
My Taylor made them not.
Gui. Hence then, and thanke
The man that gaue them thee. Thou art ſome Foole,
I am loath to beate thee.
Clot. Thou iniurious Theefe,
Heare but my name, and tremble.
Gui. What's thy name?
Clo. Cloten, thou Villaine.
Gui. Cloten, thou double Villaine be thy name,
I cannot tremble at it, were it Toad, or Adder, Spider,
'Twould moue me ſooner.
Clot. To thy further feare,
Nay, to thy meere Confuſion, thou ſhalt know
I am Sonne to'th'Queene.
Gui. I am ſorry for't: not ſeeming
So worthy as thy Birth.
Clot. Art not afeard?
Gui. Thoſe that I reuerence, thoſe I feare: the Wiſe:
At Fooles I laugh: not feare them.
Clot. Dye the death:
When I haue ſlaine thee with my proper hand,
Ile follow thoſe that euen now fled hence:
And on the Gates of *Luds-Towne* ſet your heads:
Yeeld Ruſticke Mountaineer. *Fight and Exeunt.*
Enter Belarius and Aruiragus.
Bel. No Companie's abroad?
Arui. None in the world: you did miſtake him ſure.
Bel. I cannot tell: Long is it ſince I ſaw him,
But Time hath nothing blurr'd thoſe lines of Fauour
Which then he wore: the ſnatches in his voice,
And burſt of ſpeaking were as his: I am abſolute
'Twas very *Cloten*.
Arui. In this place we left them;
I wiſh my Brother make good time with him,
You ſay he is ſo fell.
Bel. Being ſcarſe made vp,
I meane to man; he had not apprehenſion
Of roaring terrors: For defect of iudgement
Is oft the cauſe of Feare.
Enter Guiderius.
But ſee thy Brother.
Gui. This *Cloten* was a Foole, an empty purſe,
There was no money in't: Not *Hercules*
Could haue knock'd out his Braines, for he had none:
Yet I not doing this, the Foole had borne
My head, as I do his.
Bel. What haſt thou done?
Gui. I am perfect what: cut off one *Clotens* head,
Sonne to the Queene (after his owne report)
Who call'd me Traitor, Mountaineer, and ſwore
With his owne ſingle hand heel'd take vs in,
Diſplace our heads, where (thanks the Gods) they grow
And ſet them on *Luds-Towne*.
Bel. We are all vndone.
Gui. Why, worthy Father, what haue we to looſe,
But that he ſwore to take, our Liues? the Law
Protects not vs, then why ſhould we be tender,
To let an arrogant peece of fleſh threat vs?
Play Iudge, and Executioner, all himſelfe?
For we do feare the Law. What company
Diſcouer you abroad?
Bel. No ſingle ſoule
Can we ſet eye on: but in all ſafe reaſon
He muſt haue ſome Attendants. Though his Honor
Was nothing but mutation, I, and that
From one bad thing to worſe: Not Frenzie,
Not abſolute madneſſe could ſo farre haue rau'd
To bring him heere alone: although perhaps
It may be heard at Court, that ſuch as wee
Caue heere, hunt heere, are Out-lawes, and in time
May make ſome ſtronger head, the which he hearing,
(As it is like him) might breake out, and ſweare
Heel'd fetch vs in, yet is't not probable
To come alone, either he ſo vndertaking,
Or they ſo ſuffering: then on good ground we feare,
If we do feare this Body hath a taile
More perillous then the head.
Arui. Let Ord'nance
Come as the Gods fore-ſay it: howſoere,
My Brother hath done well.
Bel. I had no minde
To hunt this day: The Boy *Fideles* ſickeneſſe
Did make my way long forth.
Gui. With his owne Sword,
Which he did waue againſt my throat, I haue tane
His head from him: Ile throw't into the Creeke
Behinde our Rocke, and let it to the Sea,
And tell the Fiſhes, hee's the Queenes Sonne, *Cloten*,
That's all I reake. *Exit.*
Bel. I feare 'twill be reueng'd:
Would (*Polidore*) thou had'ſt not done't: though valour
Becomes thee well enough.
Arui. Would I had done't:
So the Reuenge alone purſu'de me: *Polidore*
I loue thee brotherly, but enuy much
Thou haſt robb'd me of this deed: I would Reuenges
That poſſible ſtrength might meet, wold ſeek vs through
And put vs to our anſwer.
Bel. Well, 'tis done:
Wee'l hunt no more to day, nor ſeeke for danger
Where there's no profit. I prythee to our Rocke,
You and *Fidele* play the Cookes: Ile ſtay
Till haſty *Polidore* returne, and bring him
To dinner preſently.
Arui. Poore ſicke *Fidele*.
Ile willingly to him, to gaine his colour,
Il'd let a pariſh of ſuch *Clotens* blood,
And praiſe my ſelfe for charity. *Exit.*
Bel. Oh thou Goddeſſe,
Thou diuine Nature; thou thy ſelfe thou blazon'ſt
In theſe two Princely Boyes: they are as gentle
As Zephires blowing below the Violet,
Not wagging his ſweet head; and yet, as rough
(Their Royall blood enchaf'd) as the rud'ſt winde,
That by the top doth take the Mountaine Pine,
And make him ſtoope to th'Vale. 'Tis wonder
That an inuiſible inſtinct ſhould frame them
To Royalty vnlearn'd, Honor vntaught,
Ciuility not ſeene from other: valour
That wildely growes in them, but yeelds a crop
As if it had beene ſow'd: yet ſtill it's ſtrange
What *Clotens* being heere to vs portends,
Or what his death will bring vs.
Enter Guidereus.
Gui. Where's my Brother?

I

I haue sent *Clotens* Clot-pole downe the streame,
In Embassie to his Mother; his Bodie's hostage
For his returne. *Solemn Musick.*

Bel. My ingenuous Instrument,
(Hearke *Polidore*) it sounds: but what occasion
Hath *Cadwal* now to giue it motion? Hearke.

Gui. Is he at home?

Bel. He went hence euen now.

Gui. What does he meane?
Since death of my deer'st Mother
It did not speake before. All solemne things
Should answer solemne Accidents. The matter?
Triumphes for nothing, and lamenting Toyes,
Is iollity for Apes, and greefe for Boyes.
Is *Cadwall* mad?

Enter Aruiragus, with Imogen dead, bearing her in his Armes.

Bel. Looke, heere he comes,
And brings the dire occasion in his Armes,
Of what we blame him for.

Arui. The Bird is dead
That we haue made so much on. I had rather
Haue skipt from sixteene yeares of Age, to sixty:
To haue turn'd my leaping time into a Crutch,
Then haue seene this.

Gui. Oh sweetest, fayrest Lilly:
My Brother weares thee not the one halfe so well,
As when thou grew'st thy selfe.

Bel. Oh Melancholly,
Who euer yet could sound thy bottome? Finde
The Ooze, to shew what Coast thy sluggish care
Might'st easilest harbour in. Thou blessed thing,
Ioue knowes what man thou might'st haue made: but I,
Thou dyed'st a most rare Boy, of Melancholly.
How found you him?

Arui. Starke, as you see:
Thus smiling, as some Fly had tickled slumber,
Not as deaths dart being laugh'd at: his right Cheeke
Reposing on a Cushion.

Gui. Where?

Arui. O'th'floore:
His armes thus leagu'd, I thought he slept, and put
My clowted Brogues from off my feete, whose rudenesse
Answer'd my steps too lowd.

Gui. Why, he but sleepes:
If he be gone, hee'l make his Graue, a Bed:
With female Fayries will his Tombe be haunted,
And Wormes will not come to thee.

Arui. With fayrest Flowers
Whil'st Sommer lasts, and I liue heere, *Fidele*,
Ile sweeten thy sad graue: thou shalt not lacke
The Flower that's like thy face. Pale-Primrose, nor
The azur'd Hare-bell, like thy Veines: no, nor
The leafe of Eglantine, whom not to slander,
Out-sweetned not thy breath: the Raddocke would
With Charitable bill (Oh bill sore shaming
Those rich-left-heyres, that let their Fathers lye
Without a Monument) bring thee all this,
Yea, and furr'd Mosse besides. When Flowres are none
To winter-ground thy Coarse———

Gui. Prythee haue done,
And do not play in Wench-like words with that
Which is so serious. Let vs bury him,
And not protract with admiration, what
Is now due debt. To'th'graue.

Arui. Say, where shall's lay him?

Gui. By good *Euriphile*, our Mother.

Arui. Bee't so:
And let vs (*Polidore*) though now our voyces
Haue got the mannish cracke, sing him to'th'ground
As once to our Mother: vse like note, and words,
Saue that *Euriphile*, must be *Fidele*.

Gui. *Cadwall*,
I cannot sing: Ile weepe, and word it with thee;
For Notes of sorrow, out of tune, are worse
Then Priests, and Phanes that lye.

Arui. Wee'l speake it then.

Bel. Great greefes I see med'cine the lesse: For *Cloten*
Is quite forgot. He was a Queenes Sonne, Boyes,
And though he came our Enemy, remember
He was paid for that: though meane, and mighty rotting
Together haue one dust, yet Reuerence
(That Angell of the world) doth make distinction
Of place 'tweene high, and low. Our Foe was Princely,
And though you tooke his life, as being our Foe,
Yet bury him, as a Prince.

Gui. Pray you fetch him hither,
Thersites body is as good as *Aiax*,
When neyther are aliue.

Arui. If you'l go fetch him,
Wee'l say our Song the whil'st: Brother begin.

Gui. Nay *Cadwall*, we must lay his head to th'East,
My Father hath a reason for't.

Arui. 'Tis true.

Gui. Come on then, and remoue him.

Arui. So, begin.

SONG.

Guid. *Feare no more the heate o'th'Sun,*
Nor the furious Winters rages,
Thou thy worldly task hast don,
Home art gon, and tane thy wages.
Golden Lads, and Girles all must,
As Chimney-Sweepers come to dust.

Arui. *Feare no more the frowne o'th'Great,*
Thou art past the Tirants stroake,
Care no more to cloath and eate,
To thee the Reede is as the Oake:
The Scepter, Learning, Physicke must,
All follow this and come to dust.

Guid. *Feare no more the Lightning flash.*
Arui. *Nor th'all-dreaded Thunderstone.*
Gui. *Feare not Slander, Censure rash.*
Arui. *Thou hast finish'd Ioy and mone.*
Both. *All Louers young, all Louers must,*
Consigne to thee and come to dust.

Guid. *No Exorcisor harme thee,*
Arui. *Nor no witch-craft charme thee.*
Guid. *Ghost vnlaid forbeare thee.*
Arui. *Nothing ill come neere thee.*
Both. *Quiet consumation haue,*
And renowned be thy graue.

Enter Belarius with the body of Cloten.

Gui. We haue done our obsequies:
Come lay him downe.

Bel. Heere's a few Flowres, but 'bout midnight more:
The hearbes that haue on them cold dew o'th'night
Are strewings fit'st for Graues: vpon their Faces.
You were as Flowres, now wither'd: euen so
These Herbelets shall, which we vpon you strew.
Come on, away, apart vpon our knees:
The ground that gaue them first, ha's them againe:
Their pleasures here are past, so are their paine. *Exeunt.*

Imogen awakes.

Yes Sir, to Milford-Hauen, which is the way?
I thanke you: by yond bush? pray how farre thether?
'Ods pittikins: can it be sixe mile yet?
I haue gone all night: 'Faith, Ile lye downe, and sleepe.
But soft; no Bedfellow? Oh Gods, and Goddesses!
These Flowres are like the pleasures of the World;
This bloody man the care on't. I hope I dreame:
For so I thought I was a Caue-keeper,
And Cooke to honest Creatures. But 'tis not so:
'Twas but a bolt of nothing, shot at nothing,
Which the Braine makes of Fumes. Our very eyes,
Are sometimes like our Iudgements, blinde. Good faith
I tremble still with feare: but if there be
Yet left in Heauen, as small a drop of pittie
As a Wrens eye; fear'd Gods, a part of it.
The Dreame's heere still: euen when I wake it is
Without me, as within me: not imagin'd, felt.
A headlesse man? The Garments of *Posthumus*?
I know the shape of's Legge: this is his Hand:
His Foote Mercuriall: his martiall Thigh
The brawnes of *Hercules*: but his Iouiall face———
Murther in heauen? How? 'tis gone. *Pisanio,*
All Curses madded *Hecuba* gaue the Greekes,
And mine to boot, be darted on thee: thou
Conspir'd with that Irregulous diuell *Cloten,*
Hath heere cut off my Lord. To write, and read,
Be henceforth treacherous. Damn'd *Pisanio,*
Hath with his forged Letters (damn'd *Pisanio*)
From this most brauest vessell of the world
Strooke the maine top! Oh *Posthumus*, alas,
Where is thy head? where's that? Aye me! where's that?
Pisanio might haue kill'd thee at the heart,
And left this head on. How should this be, *Pisanio*?
'Tis he, and *Cloten*: Malice, and Lucre in them
Haue laid this Woe heere. Oh 'tis pregnant, pregnant!
The Drugge he gaue me, which hee said was precious
And Cordiall to me, haue I not found it
Murd'rous to'th'Senses? That confirmes it home:
This is *Pisanio*'s deede, and *Cloten*: Oh!
Giue colour to my pale cheeke with thy blood,
That we the horrider may seeme to those
Which chance to finde vs. Oh, my Lord! my Lord!

Enter Lucius, Captaines, and a Soothsayer.

Cap. To them, the Legions garrison'd in Gallia
After your will, haue crost the Sea, attending
You heere at Milford-Hauen, with your Shippes:
They are heere in readinesse.

Luc. But what from Rome?

Cap, The Senate hath stirr'd vp the Confiners,
And Gentlemen of Italy, most willing Spirits,
That promise Noble Seruice: and they come
Vnder the Conduct of bold *Iachimo,*
Syenna's Brother.

Luc. When expect you them?

Cap. With the next benefit o'th'winde.

Luc. This forwardnesse
Makes our hopes faire. Command our present numbers
Be muster'd: bid the Captaines looke too't. Now Sir,
What haue you dream'd of late of this warres purpose.

Sooth. Last night, the very Gods shew'd me a vision
(I fast, and pray'd for their Intelligence) thus:
I saw Ioues Bird, the Roman Eagle wing'd
From the spungy South, to this part of the West,
There vanish'd in the Sun-beames, which portends
(Vnlesse my sinnes abuse my Diuination)
Successe to th'Roman hoast.

Luc. Dreame often so,
And neuer false. Soft hoa, what truncke is heere?
Without his top? The ruine speakes, that sometime
It was a worthy building. How? a Page?
Or dead, or sleeping on him? But dead rather:
For Nature doth abhorre to make his bed
With the defunct, or sleepe vpon the dead.
Let's see the Boyes face.

Cap. Hee's aliue my Lord.

Luc. Hee'l then instruct vs of this body: Young one,
Informe vs of thy Fortunes, for it seemes
They craue to be demanded: who is this
Thou mak'st thy bloody Pillow? Or who was he
That (otherwise then noble Nature did)
Hath alter'd that good Picture? What's thy interest
In this sad wracke? How came't? Who is't?
What art thou?

Imo. I am nothing; or if not,
Nothing to be were better: This was my Master,
A very valiant Britaine, and a good,
That heere by Mountaineers lyes slaine: Alas,
There is no more such Masters: I may wander
From East to Occident, cry out for Seruice,
Try many, all good: serue truly: neuer
Finde such another Master.

Luc. 'Lacke, good youth:
Thou mou'st no lesse with thy complaining, then
Thy Maister in bleeding: say his name, good Friend.

Imo. *Richard du Champ*: If I do lye, and do
No harme by it, though the Gods heare, I hope
They'l pardon it. Say you Sir?

Luc. Thy name?

Imo. *Fidele* Sir.

Luc. Thou doo'st approue thy selfe the very same:
Thy Name well fits thy Faith; thy Faith, thy Name:
Wilt take thy chance with me? I will not say
Thou shalt be so well master'd, but be sure
No lesse belou'd. The Romane Emperors Letters
Sent by a Consull to me, should not sooner
Then thine owne worth preferre thee: Go with me.

Imo. Ile follow Sir. But first, and't please the Gods,
Ile hide my Master from the Flies, as deepe
As these poore Pickaxes can digge: and when
With wild wood-leaues & weeds, I ha' strew'd his graue
And on it said a Century of prayers
(Such as I can) twice o're, Ile weepe, and sighe,
And leauing so his seruice, follow you,
So please you entertaine mee.

Luc. I good youth,
And rather Father thee, then Master thee: My Friends,
The Boy hath taught vs manly duties: Let vs
Finde out the prettiest Dazied-Plot we can,
And make him with our Pikes and Partizans
A Graue: Come, Arme him: Boy hee's preferr'd
By thee, to vs, and he shall be interr'd
As Souldiers can. Be cheerefull; wipe thine eyes,
Some Falles are meanes the happier to arise. *Exeunt*

Scena Tertia.

Enter Cymbeline, Lords, and Pisanio.

Cym. Againe: and bring me word how 'tis with her,
A Feauour with the absence of her Sonne;

A

A madneſſe, of which her life's in danger : Heauens,
How deeply you at once do touch me. *Imogen,*
The great part of my comfort, gone : My Queene
Vpon a deſperate bed, and in a time
When fearefull Warres point at me : Her Sonne gone,
So needfull for this preſent ? It ſtrikes me, paſt
The hope of comfort. But for thee, Fellow,
Who needs muſt know of her departure, and
Doſt ſeeme ſo ignorant, wee'l enforce it from thee
By a ſharpe Torture.

Piſ. Sir, my life is yours,
I humbly ſet it at your will : But for my Miſtris,
I nothing know where ſhe remaines : why gone,
Nor when ſhe purpoſes returne. Beſeech your Highnes,
Hold me your loyall Seruant.

Lord. Good my Liege,
The day that ſhe was miſſing, he was heere ;
I dare be bound hee's true, and ſhall performe
All parts of his ſubiection loyally. For *Cloten,*
There wants no diligence in ſeeking him,
And will no doubt be found.

Cym. The time is troubleſome :
Wee'l ſlip you for a ſeaſon, but our iealouſie
Do's yet depend.

Lord. So pleaſe your Maieſty,
The Romaine Legions, all from Gallia drawne,
Are landed on your Coaſt, with a ſupply
Of Romaine Gentlemen, by the Senate ſent.

Cym. Now for the Counſaile of my Son and Queen,
I am amaz'd with matter.

Lord. Good my Liege,
Your preparation can affront no leſſe (ready :
Then what you heare of. Come more, for more you're
The want is, but to put thoſe Powres in motion,
That long to moue.

Cym. I thanke you : let's withdraw
And meete the Time, as it ſeekes vs. We feare not
What can from Italy annoy vs, but
We greeue at chances heere. Away. *Exeunt*

Piſa. I heard no Letter from my Maſter, ſince
I wrote him *Imogen* was ſlaine. 'Tis ſtrange :
Nor heare I from my Miſtris, who did promiſe
To yeeld me often tydings. Neither know I
What is betide to *Cloten*, but remaine
Perplext in all. The Heauens ſtill muſt worke :
Wherein I am falſe, I am honeſt : not true, to be true.
Theſe preſent warres ſhall finde I loue my Country,
Euen to the note o'th'King, or Ile fall in them :
All other doubts, by time let them be cleer'd,
Fortune brings in ſome Boats, that are not ſteer'd. *Exit.*

Scena Quarta.

Enter Belarius, Guiderius, & Aruiragus.

Gui. The noyſe is round about vs.

Bel. Let vs from it.

Arui. What pleaſure Sir, we finde in life, to locke it
From Action, and Aduenture.

Gui. Nay, what hope
Haue we in hiding vs? This way the Romaines
Muſt, or for Britaines ſlay vs or receiue vs
For barbarous and vnnaturall Reuolts
During their vſe, and ſlay vs after.

Bel. Sonnes,
Wee'l higher to the Mountaines, there ſecure v..
To the Kings party there's no going : newneſſe
Of *Clotens* death (we being not knowne, not muſter'd
Among the Bands) may driue vs to a render
Where we haue liu'd; and ſo extort from's that
Which we haue done, whoſe anſwer would be death
Drawne on with Torture.

Gui. This is (Sir) a doubt
In ſuch a time, nothing becomming you,
Nor ſatisfying vs.

Arui. It is not likely,
That when they heare their Roman horſes neigh,
Behold their quarter'd Fires ; haue both their eyes
And eares ſo cloyd importantly as now,
That they will waſte their time vpon our note,
To know from whence we are.

Bel. Oh, I am knowne
Of many in the Army : Many yeeres
(Though *Cloten* then but young) you ſee, not wore him
From my remembrance. And beſides, the King
Hath not deſeru'd my Seruice, nor your Loues,
Who finde in my Exile, the want of Breeding ;
The certainty of this heard life, aye hopeleſſe
To haue the courteſie your Cradle promis'd,
But to be ſtill hot Summers Tanlings, and
The ſhrinking Slaues of Winter.

Gui. Then be ſo,
Better to ceaſe to be. Pray Sir, to'th'Army :
I, and my Brother are not knowne ; your ſelfe
So out of thought, and thereto ſo ore-growne,
Cannot be queſtion'd.

Arui. By this Sunne that ſhines
Ile thither : What thing is't, that I neuer
Did ſee man dye, ſcarſe euer look'd on blood,
But that of Coward Hares, hot Goats, and Veniſon ?
Neuer beſtrid a Horſe ſaue one, that had
A Rider like my ſelfe, who ne're wore Rowell,
Nor Iron on his heele ? I am aſham'd
To looke vpon the holy Sunne, to haue
The benefit of his bleſt Beames, remaining
So long a poore vnknowne.

Gui. By heauens Ile go,
If you will bleſſe me Sir, and giue me leaue,
Ile take the better care : but if you will not,
The hazard therefore due fall on me, by
The hands of Romaines.

Arui. So ſay I, Amen.

Bel. No reaſon I (ſince of your liues you ſet
So ſlight a valewation) ſhould reſerue
My crack'd one to more care. Haue with you Boyes:
If in your Country warres you chance to dye,
That is my Bed too (Lads) and there Ile lye.
Lead, lead; the time ſeems long, their blood thinks ſcorn
Till it flye out, and ſhew them Princes borne. *Exeunt.*

Actus Quintus. Scena Prima.

Enter Poſthumus alone.

Poſt. Yea bloody cloth, Ile keep thee : for I am wiſht
Thou ſhould'ſt be colour'd thus. You married ones,
If each of you ſhould take this courſe, how many
Muſt murther Wiues much better then themſelues

For wrying but a little? Oh *Pisanio*,
Euery good Seruant do's not all Commands:
No Bond, but to do iust ones. Gods, if you
Should haue 'tane vengeance on my faults, I neuer
Had liu'd to put on this: so had you saued
The noble *Imogen*, to repent, and strooke
Me (wretch) more worth your Vengeance. But alacke,
You snatch some hence for little faults; that's loue
To haue them fall no more: you some permit
To second illes with illes, each elder worse,
And make them dread it, to the dooers thrift.
But *Imogen* is your owne, do your best willes,
And make me blest to obey. I am brought hither
Among th'Italian Gentry, and to fight
Against my Ladies Kingdome: 'Tis enough
That (Britaine) I haue kill'd thy Mistris: Peace,
Ile giue no wound to thee: therefore good Heauens,
Heare patiently my purpose. Ile disrobe me
Of these Italian weedes, and suite my selfe
As do's a *Britaine* Pezant: so Ile fight
Against the part I come with: so Ile dye
For thee (O *Imogen*) euen for whom my life
Is euery breath, a death: and thus, vnknowne,
Pittied, nor hated, to the face of perill.
My selfe Ile dedicate. Let me make men know
More valour in me, then my habits show.
Gods, put the strength o'th'*Leonati* in me:
To shame the guize o'th'world, I will begin,
The fashion lesse without, and more within. *Exit.*

Scena Secunda.

Enter Lucius, Iachimo, and the Romane Army at one doore: and the Britaine Army at another: Leonatus Posthumus following like a poore Souldier. They march ouer, and goe out. Then enter againe in Skirmish Iachimo and Posthumus: he vanquisheth and disarmeth Iachimo, and then leaues him.

Iac. The heauinesse and guilt within my bosome,
Takes off my manhood: I haue belyed a Lady,
The Princesse of this Country; and the ayre on't
Reuengingly enfeebles me, or could this Carle,
A very drudge of Natures, haue subdu'de me
In my profession? Knighthoods, and Honors borne
As I weare mine) are titles but of scorne.
If that thy Gentry (Britaine) go before
This Lowt, as he exceeds our Lords, the oddes
Is, that we scarse are men, and you are Goddes. *Exit.*

The Battaile continues, the Britaines fly, Cymbeline is taken: Then enter to his rescue, Bellarius, Guiderius, and Aruiragus.

Bel. Stand, stand, we haue th'aduantage of the ground,
The Lane is guarded: Nothing rowts vs, but
The villany of our feares.

Gui. Arui. Stand, stand, and fight.

Enter Posthumus, and seconds the Britaines. They Rescue Cymbeline, and Exeunt.

Then enter Lucius, Iachimo, and Imogen.

Luc. Away boy from the Troopes, and saue thy selfe:
For friends kil friends, and the disorder's such
As warre were hood-wink'd.

Iac. 'Tis their fresh supplies.

Luc. It is a day turn'd strangely: or betimes
Let's re-inforce, or fly. *Exeunt*

Scena Tertia.

Enter Posthumus, and a Britaine Lord.

Lor. Cam'st thou from where they made the stand?

Post. I did,
Though you it seemes come from the Fliers?

Lo. I did.

Post. No blame be to you Sir, for all was lost,
But that the Heauens fought: the King himselfe
Of his wings destitute, the Army broken,
And but the backes of Britaines seene; all flying
Through a strait Lane, the Enemy full-hearted,
Lolling the Tongue with slaught'ring: hauing worke
More plentifull, then Tooles to doo't: strooke downe
Some mortally, some slightly touch'd, some falling
Meerely through feare, that the strait passe was damm'd
With deadmen, hurt behinde, and Cowards liuing
To dye with length'ned shame.

Lo. Where was this Lane?

Post. Close by the battell, ditch'd, & wall'd with turph,
Which gaue aduantage to an ancient Soldiour
(An honest one I warrant) who deseru'd
So long a breeding, as his white beard came to,
In doing this for's Country. Athwart the Lane,
He, with two striplings (Lads more like to run
The Country base, then to commit such slaughter,
With faces fit for Maskes, or rather fayrer
Then those for preseruation cas'd, or shame)
Made good the passage, cryed to those that fled.
Our *Britaines* hearts dye flying, not our men,
To darknesse fleete soules that flye backwards; stand,
Or we are Romanes, and will giue you that
Like beasts, which you shun beastly, and may saue
But to looke backe in frowne: Stand, stand. These three,
Three thousand confident, in acte as many:
For three performers are the File, when all
The rest do nothing. With this word stand, stand,
Accomodated by the Place; more Charming
With their owne Noblenesse, which could haue turn'd
A Distaffe, to a Lance, guilded pale lookes;
Part shame, part spirit renew'd, that some turn'd coward
But by example (Oh a sinne in Warre,
Damn'd in the first beginners) gan to looke
The way that they did, and to grin like Lyons
Vpon the Pikes o'th'Hunters. Then beganne
A stop i'th'Chaser; a Retyre: Anon
A Rowt, confusion thicke: forthwith they flye
Chickens, the way which they stopt Eagles: Slaues
The strides the Victors made: and now our Cowards
Like Fragments in hard Voyages became
The life o'th'need: hauing found the backe doore open
Of the vnguarded hearts: heauens, how they wound,
Some slaine before some dying; some their Friends
Ore-borne i'th'former waue, ten chac'd by one,
Are now each one the slaughter-man of twenty:
Those that would dye, or ere resist, are growne
The mortall bugs o'th'Field.

Lor.

Lord. This was ſtrange chance:
A narrow Lane, an old man, and two Boyes.
Poſt. Nay, do not wonder at it: you are made
Rather to wonder at the things you heare,
Then to worke any. Will you Rime vpon't,
And vent it for a Mock'rie? Heere is one:
"*Two Boyes, an Oldman (twice a Boy) a Lane,*
"*Preſeru'd the Britaines, was the Romanes bane.*
Lord. Nay, be not angry Sir.
Poſt. Lacke, to what end?
Who dares not ſtand his Foe, Ile be his Friend:
For if hee'l do, as he is made to doo,
I know hee'l quickly flye my friendſhip too.
You haue put me into Rime.
Lord. Farewell, you're angry. *Exit.*
Poſt. Still going? This is a Lord: Oh Noble miſery
To be i'th'Field, and aske what newes of me:
To day, how many would haue giuen their Honours
To haue ſau'd their Carkaſſes? Tooke heele to doo't,
And yet dyed too. I, in mine owne woe charm'd
Could not finde death, where I did heare him groane,
Nor feele him where he ſtrooke. Being an vgly Monſter,
'Tis ſtrange he hides him in freſh Cups, ſoft Beds,
Sweet words; or hath moe miniſters then we
That draw his kniues i'th'War. Well I will finde him:
For being now a Fauourer to the Britaine,
No more a Britaine, I haue reſum'd againe
The part I came in. Fight I will no more,
But yeeld me to the verieſt Hinde, that ſhall
Once touch my ſhoulder. Great the ſlaughter is
Heere made by'th'Romane; great the Anſwer be
Britaines muſt take. For me, my Ranſome's death,
On eyther ſide I come to ſpend my breath;
Which neyther heere Ile keepe, nor beare agen,
But end it by ſome meanes for *Imogen.*

Enter two Captaines, and Soldiers.

1 Great Iupiter be prais'd, *Lucius* is taken,
'Tis thought the old man, and his ſonnes, were Angels.
2 There was a fourth man, in a ſilly habit,
That gaue th'Affront with them.
1 So 'tis reported:
But none of'em can be found. Stand, who's there?
Poſt. A Roman,
Who had not now beene drooping heere, if Seconds
Had anſwer'd him.
2 Lay hands on him: a Dogge,
A legge of Rome ſhall not returne to tell
What Crows haue peckt them here: he brags his ſeruice
As if he were of note: bring him to'th'King.

Enter Cymbeline, Belarius, Guiderius, Aruiragus, Piſanio, and Romane Captiues. The Captaines preſent Poſthumus to Cymbeline, who deliuers him ouer to a Gaoler.

Scena Quarta.

Enter Poſthumus, and Gaoler.

Gao. You ſhall not now be ſtolne,
You haue lockes vpon you:
So graze, as you finde Paſture.
2. *Gao.* I, or a ſtomacke.
Poſt. Moſt welcome bondage; for thou art a way
(I thinke) to liberty: yet am I better
Then one that's ſicke o'th'Gowt, ſince he had rather
Groane ſo in perpetuity, then be cur'd
By'th'ſure Phyſitian, Death; who is the key
T'vnbarre theſe Lockes. My Conſcience, thou art fetter'd
More then my ſhanks, & wriſts: you good Gods giue me
The penitent Inſtrument to picke that Bolt,
Then free for euer. Is't enough I am ſorry?
So Children temporall Fathers do appeaſe;
Gods are more full of mercy. Muſt I repent,
I cannot do it better then in Gyues,
Deſir'd, more then conſtrain'd, to ſatisfie
If of my Freedome 'tis the maine part, take
No ſtricter render of me, then my All.
I know you are more clement then vilde men,
Who of their broken Debtors take a third,
A ſixt, a tenth, letting them thriue againe
On their abatement; that's not my deſire.
For *Imogens* deere life, take mine, and though
'Tis not ſo deere, yet 'tis a life; you coyn'd it,
'Tweene man, and man, they waigh not euery ſtampe:
Though light, take Peeces for the figures ſake,
(You rather) mine being yours: and ſo great Powres,
If you will take this Audit, take this life,
And cancell theſe cold Bonds. Oh *Imogen,*
Ile ſpeake to thee in ſilence.

Solemne Muſicke. Enter (as in an Apparation) Sicillius Leonatus, Father to Poſthumus, an old man, attyred like a warriour, leading in his hand an ancient Matron (his wife, & Mother to Poſthumus) with Muſicke before them. Then, after other Muſicke, followes the two young Leonati (Brothers to Poſthumus) with wounds as they died in the warrs. They circle Poſthumus round as he lies ſleeping.

Sicil. No more thou Thunder-Maſter
ſhew thy ſpight, on Mortall Flies:
With Mars fall out with *Iuno* chide, that thy Adulteries
Rates, and Reuenges.
Hath my poore Boy done ought but well,
whoſe face I neuer ſaw:
I dy'de whil'ſt in the Wombe he ſtaide,
attending Natures Law.
Whoſe Father then (as men report,
thou Orphanes Father art)
Thou ſhould'ſt haue bin, and ſheelded him,
from this earth-vexing ſmart.
Moth. Lucina lent not me her ayde,
but tooke me in my Throwes,
That from me was *Poſthumus* ript,
came crying 'mong'ſt his Foes.
A thing of pitty.
Sicil. Great Nature like his Anceſtrie,
moulded the ſtuffe ſo faire:
That he d ſeru'd the praiſe o'th'World,
as great *Sicilius* heyre.
1. *Bro.* When once he was mature for man,
in Britaine where was hee
That could ſtand vp his paralell?
Or fruitfull obiect bee?
In eye of *Imogen,* that beſt could deeme
his dignitie.
Mo. With Marriage wherefore was he mockt
to be exil'd, and throwne
From *Leonati* Seate, and caſt from her,
his deereſt one:
Sweete *Imogen*?
Sic. Why did you ſuffer *Iachimo,* ſlight thing of Italy,

To taint his Nobler hart & braine, with needlesse ielousy,
And to become the geeke and scorne o'th'others vilany?
2 Bro. For this, from stiller Seats we came,
our Parents, and vs twaine,
That striking in our Countries cause,
fell brauely, and were slaine,
Our Fealty, & *Tenantius* right, with Honor to maintaine.
1 Bro. Like hardiment *Posthumus* hath
to *Cymbeline* perform'd:
Then Iupiter, ỳ King of Gods, why hast ỳ thus adiourn'd
The Graces for his Merits due, being all to dolors turn'd?
Sicil. Thy Christall window ope; looke,
looke out, no longer exercise
Vpon a valiant Race, thy harsh, and potent iniuries:
Moth. Since (Iupiter) our Son is good,
take off his miseries.
Sicil. Peepe through thy Marble Mansion, helpe,
or we poore Ghosts will cry
To'th'shining Synod of the rest, against thy Deity.
Brothers. Helpe (Iupiter) or we appeale,
and from thy iustice flye.

Iupiter descends in Thunder and Lightning, sitting vppon an Eagle: hee throwes a Thunder-bolt. The Ghostes fall on their knees.

Iupiter. No more you petty Spirits of Region low
Offend our hearing: hush. How dare you Ghostes
Accuse the Thunderer, whose Bolt (you know)
Sky-planted, batters all rebelling Coasts.
Poore shadowes of Elizium, hence, and rest
Vpon your neuer-withering bankes of Flowres.
Be not with mortall accidents opprest,
No care of yours it is, you know 'tis ours.
Whom best I loue, I crosse; to make my guift
The more delay'd, delighted. Be content,
Your low-laide Sonne, our Godhead will vplift:
His Comforts thriue, his Trials well are spent:
Our Iouiall Starre reign'd at his Birth, and in
Our Temple was he married: Rise, and fade,
He shall be Lord of Lady *Imogen*,
And happier much by his Affliction made.
This Tablet lay vpon his Brest, wherein
Our pleasure, his full Fortune, doth confine,
And so away: no farther with your dinne
Expresse Impatience, least you stirre vp mine:
Mount Eagle, to my Palace Christalline. *Ascends*
Sicil. He came in Thunder, his Celestiall breath
Was sulphurous to smell: the holy Eagle
Stoop'd, as to foote vs: his Ascension is
More sweet then our blest Fields: his Royall Bird
Prunes the immortall wing, and cloyes his Beake,
As when his God is pleas'd.
All. Thankes Iupiter.
Sic. The Marble Pauement clozes, he is enter'd
His radiant Roofe: Away, and to be blest
Let vs with care performe his great behest. *Vanish*
Post. Sleepe, thou hast bin a Grandsire, and begot
A Father to me: and thou hast created
A Mother, and two Brothers. But (oh scorne)
Gone, they went hence so soone as they were borne:
And so I am awake. Poore Wretches, that depend
On Greatnesse, Fauour; Dreame as I haue done,
Wake, and finde nothing. But (alas) I swerue:
Many Dreame not to finde, neither deserue,
And yet are steep'd in Fauours; so am I
That haue this Golden chance, and know not why:
What Fayeries haunt this ground? A Book? Oh rare one,
Be not, as is our fangled world, a Garment
Nobler then that it couers. Let thy effects
So follow, to be most vnlike our Courtiers,
As good, as promise.

Reades.

When as a Lyons whelpe, shall to himselfe vnknown, without seeking finde, and bee embrac'd by a peece of tender Ayre: And when from a stately Cedar shall be lopt branches, which being dead many yeares, shall after reuiue, bee ioynted to the old Stocke, and freshly grow, then shall Posthumus end his miseries, Britaine be fortunate, and flourish in Peace and Plentie.

'Tis still a Dreame: or else such stuffe as Madmen
Tongue, and braine not: either both, or nothing,
Or senselesse speaking, or a speaking such
As sense cannot vntye. Be what it is,
The Action of my life is like it, which Ile keepe
If but for simpathy.

Enter Gaoler.

Gao. Come Sir, are you ready for death?

Post. Ouer-roasted rather: ready long ago.

Gao. Hanging is the word, Sir, if you bee readie for that, you are well Cook'd.

Post. So if I proue a good repast to the Spectators, the dish payes the shot.

Gao. A heauy reckoning for you Sir: But the comfort is you shall be called to no more payments, fear no more Tauerne Bils, which are often the sadnesse of parting, as the procuring of mirth: you come in faint for want of meate, depart reeling with too much drinke: sorrie that you haue payed too much, and sorry that you are payed too much: Purse and Braine, both empty: the Brain the heauier, for being too light; the Purse too light, being drawne of heauinesse. Oh, of this contradiction you shall now be quit: Oh the charity of a penny Cord, it summes vp thousands in a trice: you haue no true Debitor, and Creditor but it: of what's past, is, and to come, the discharge: your necke (Sir) is Pen, Booke, and Counters; so the Acquittance followes.

Post. I am merrier to dye, then thou art to liue.

Gao. Indeed Sir, he that sleepes, feeles not the Tooth-Ache: but a man that were to sleepe your sleepe, and a Hangman to helpe him to bed, I think he would change places with his Officer: for, look you Sir, you know not which way you shall go.

Post. Yes indeed do I, fellow.

Gao. Your death has eyes in's head then: I haue not seene him so pictur'd: you must either bee directed by some that take vpon them to know, or to take vpon your selfe that which I am sure you do not know: or iump the after-enquiry on your owne perill: and how you shall speed in your iournies end, I thinke you'l neuer returne to tell one.

Post. I tell thee, Fellow, there are none want eyes, to direct them the way I am going, but such as winke, and will not vse them.

Gao. What an infinite mocke is this, that a man shold haue the best vse of eyes, to see the way of blindnesse: I am sure hanging's the way of winking.

Enter a Messenger.

Mes. Knocke off his Manacles, bring your Prisoner to the King.

Post. Thou bring'st good newes, I am call'd to bee made free.

Gao. Ile be hang'd then.

Post. Thou shalt be then freer then a Gaoler; no bolts for

for the dead.

Gao. Vnleſſe a man would marry a Gallowes, & beget yong Gibbets, I neuer ſaw one ſo prone : yet on my Conſcience, there are verier Knaues deſire to liue, for all he be a Roman ; and there be ſome of them too that dye againſt their willes; ſo ſhould I, if I were one. I would we were all of one minde, and one minde good : O there were deſolation of Gaolers and Galowſes : I ſpeake againſt my preſent profit, but my wiſh hath a preferment in't. *Exeunt.*

Scena Quinta.

Enter Cymbeline, Bellarius, Guiderius, Aruiragus, Piſanio, and Lords.

Cym. Stand by my ſide you, whom the Gods haue made
Preſeruers of my Throne: woe is my heart,
That the poore Souldier that ſo richly fought,
Whoſe ragges, ſham'd gilded Armes, whoſe naked breſt
Stept before Targes of proofe, cannot be found :
He ſhall be happy that can finde him, if
Our Grace can make him ſo.

Bel. I neuer ſaw
Such Noble fury in ſo poore a Thing ;
Such precious deeds, in one that promiſt nought
But beggery, and poore lookes.

Cym. No tydings of him?

Piſa. He hath bin ſearch'd among the dead, & liuing ;
But no trace of him.

Cym. To my greefe, I am
The heyre of his Reward, which I will adde
To you (the Liuer, Heart, and Braine of Britaine)
By whom (I grant) ſhe liues. 'Tis now the time
To aske of whence you are. Report it.

Bel. Sir,
In Cambria are we borne, and Gentlemen :
Further to boaſt, were neyther true, nor modeſt,
Vnleſſe I adde, we are honeſt.

Cym. Bow your knees :
Ariſe my Knights o'th'Battell, I create you
Companions to our perſon, and will fit you
With Dignities becomming your eſtates.

Enter Cornelius and Ladies.

There's buſineſſe in theſe faces : why ſo ſadly
Greet you our Victory? you looke like Romaines,
And not o'th'Court of Britaine.

Corn. Hayle great King,
To ſowre your happineſſe, I muſt report
The Queene is dead.

Cym. Who worſe then a Phyſitian
Would this report become? But I conſider,
By Med'cine life may be prolong'd, yet death
Will ſeize the Doctor too. How ended ſhe?

Cor. With horror, madly dying, like her life,
Which (being cruell to the world) concluded
Moſt cruell to her ſelfe. What ſhe confeſt,
I will report, ſo pleaſe you. Theſe her Women
Can trip me, if I erre, who with wet cheekes
Were preſent when ſhe finiſh'd.

Cym. Prythee ſay.

Cor. Firſt, ſhe confeſt ſhe neuer lou'd you : onely
Affected Greatneſſe got by you : not you :
Married your Royalty, was wife to your place :
Abhorr'd your perſon.

Cym. She alone knew this :
And but ſhe ſpoke it dying, I would not
Beleeue her lips in opening it. Proceed.

Corn. Your daughter, whom ſhe bore in hand to loue
With ſuch integrity, ſhe did confeſſe
Was as a Scorpion to her ſight, whoſe life
(But that her flight preuented it) ſhe had
Tane off by poyſon.

Cym. O moſt delicate Fiend!
Who is't can reade a Woman? Is there more?

Corn. More Sir, and worſe. She did confeſſe ſhe had
For you a mortall Minerall, which being tooke,
Should by the minute feede on life, and ling'ring,
By inches waſte you. In which time, ſhe purpos'd
By watching, weeping, tendance, kiſſing, to
Orecome you with her ſhew; and in time
(When ſhe had fitted you with her craft, to worke
Her Sonne into th'adoption of the Crowne :
But fayling of her end by his ſtrange abſence,
Grew ſhameleſſe deſperate, open'd (in deſpight
Of Heauen, and Men) her purpoſes : repented
The euils ſhe hatch'd, were not effected : ſo
Diſpayring, dyed.

Cym. Heard you all this, her Women?

La. We did, ſo pleaſe your Highneſſe.

Cym. Mine eyes
Were not in fault, for ſhe was beautifull :
Mine eares that heare her flattery, nor my heart,
That thought her like her ſeeming. It had beene vicious
To haue miſtruſted her : yet (Oh my Daughter)
That it was folly in me, thou mayſt ſay,
And proue it in thy feeling. Heauen mend all.

Enter Lucius, Iachimo, and other Roman priſoners, Leonatus behind, and Imogen.

Thou comm'ſt not *Caius* now for Tribute, that
The Britaines haue rac'd out, though with the loſſe
Of many a bold one : whoſe Kinſmen haue made ſuite
That their good ſoules may be appeas'd, with ſlaughter
Of you their Captiues, which our ſelfe haue granted,
So thinke of your eſtate.

Luc. Conſider Sir, the chance of Warre, the day
Was yours by accident : had it gone with vs,
We ſhould not when the blood was cool, haue threatend
Our Priſoners with the Sword. But ſince the Gods
Will haue it thus, that nothing but our liues
May be call'd ranſome, let it come : Sufficeth,
A Roman, with a Romans heart can ſuffer :
Auguſtus liues to thinke on't : and ſo much
For my peculiar care. This one thing onely
I will entreate, my Boy (a Britaine borne)
Let him be ranſom'd : Neuer Maſter had
A Page ſo kinde, ſo duteous, diligent,
So tender ouer his occaſions, true,
So feate, ſo Nurſe-like : let his vertue ioyne
With my requeſt, which Ile make bold, your Highneſſe
Cannot deny : he hath done no Britaine harme,
Though he haue ſeru'd a Roman. Saue him (Sir)
And ſpare no blood beſide.

Cym. I haue ſurely ſeene him :
His fauour is familiar to me : Boy,
Thou haſt look'd thy ſelfe into my grace,
And art mine owne. I know not why, wherefore,
To ſay, liue boy : ne're thanke thy Maſter, liue ;
And aske of *Cymbeline* what Boone thou wilt,
Fitting my bounty, and thy ſtate, Ile giue it :

Yea,

Yea, though thou do demand a Prisoner
The Noblest tane.
Imo. I humbly thanke your Highnesse.
Luc. I do not bid thee begge my life, good Lad,
And yet I know thou wilt.
Imo. No, no, alacke,
There's other worke in hand: I see a thing
Bitter to me, as death: your life, good Master,
Must shuffle for it selfe.
Luc. The Boy disdaines me,
He leaues me, scornes me: briefely dye their ioyes,
That place them on the truth of Gyrles, and Boyes.
Why stands he so perplext?
Cym. What would'st thou Boy?
I loue thee more, and more: thinke more and more
What's best to aske. Know'st him thou look'st on? speak
Wilt haue him liue? Is he thy Kin? thy Friend?
Imo. He is a Romane, no more kin to me,
Then I to your Highnesse, who being born your vassaile
Am something neerer.
Cym. Wherefore ey'st him so?
Imo. Ile tell you (Sir) in priuate, if you please
To giue me hearing.
Cym. I, with all my heart,
And lend my best attention. What's thy name?
Imo. *Fidele* Sir.
Cym. Thou'rt my good youth: my Page
Ile be thy Master: walke with me: speake freely.
Bel. Is not this Boy reuiu'd from death?
Arui. One Sand another
Not more resembles that sweet Rosie Lad:
Who dyed, and was *Fidele*: what thinke you?
Gui. The same dead thing aliue.
Bel. Peace, peace, see further: he eyes vs not, forbeare
Creatures may be alike: were't he, I am sure
He would haue spoke to vs.
Gui. But we see him dead.
Bel. Be silent: let's see further.
Pisa. It is my Mistris:
Since she is liuing, let the time run on,
To good, or bad.
Cym. Come, stand thou by our side,
Make thy demand alowd. Sir, step you forth,
Giue answer to this Boy, and do it freely,
Or by our Greatnesse, and the grace of it
(Which is our Honor) bitter torture shall
Winnow the truth from falshood. One speake to him.
Imo. My boone is, that this Gentleman may render
Of whom he had this Ring.
Post. What's that to him?
Cym. That Diamond vpon your Finger, say
How came it yours?
Iach. Thou'lt torture me to leaue vnspoken, that
Which to be spoke, wou'd torture thee.
Cym. How? me?
Iach. I am glad to be constrain'd to vtter that
Which torments me to conceale. By Villany
I got this Ring: 'twas *Leonatus* Iewell,
Whom thou did'st banish: and which more may greeue thee,
As it doth me: a Nobler Sir, ne're liu'd
'Twixt sky and ground. Wilt thou heare more my Lord?
Cym. All that belongs to this.
Iach. That Paragon, thy daughter,
For whom my heart drops blood, and my false spirits
Quaile to remember. Giue me leaue, I faint.
Cym. My Daughter? what of hir? Renew thy strength
I had rather thou should'st liue, while Nature will,
Then dye ere I heare more: striue man, and speake.
Iach. Vpon a time, vnhappy was the clocke
That strooke the houre: it was in Rome, accurst
The Mansion where: 'twas at a Feast, oh would
Our Viands had bin poyson'd (or at least
Those which I heau'd to head:) the good *Posthumus*,
(What should I say? he was too good to be
Where ill men were, and was the best of all
Among'st the rar'st of good ones) sitting sadly,
Hearing vs praise our Loues of Italy
For Beauty, that made barren the swell'd boast
Of him that best could speake: for Feature, laming
The Shrine of *Venus*, or straight-pight *Minerua*,
Postures, beyond breefe Nature. For Condition,
A shop of all the qualities, that man
Loues woman for, besides that hooke of Wiuing,
Fairenesse, which strikes the eye.
Cym. I stand on fire. Come to the matter.
Iach. All too soone I shall,
Vnlesse thou would'st greeue quickly. This *Posthumus*,
Most like a Noble Lord, in loue, and one
That had a Royall Louer, tooke his hint,
And (not dispraising whom we prais'd, therein
He was as calme as vertue) he began
His Mistris picture, which, by his tongue, being made,
And then a minde put in't, either our bragges
Were crak'd of Kitchen-Trulles, or his description
Prou'd vs vnspeaking sottes.
Cym. Nay, nay, to'th' purpose.
Iach. Your daughters Chastity, (there it beginnes)
He spake of her, as *Dian* had hot dreames,
And she alone, were cold: Whereat, I wretch
Made scruple of his praise, and wager'd with him
Peeces of Gold, 'gainst this, which then he wore
Vpon his honour'd finger) to attaine
In suite the place of's bed, and winne this Ring
By hers, and mine Adultery: he (true Knight)
No lesser of her Honour confident
Then I did truly finde her, stakes this Ring,
And would so, had it beene a Carbuncle
Of Phœbus Wheele; and might so safely, had it
Bin all the worth of's Carre. Away to Britaine
Poste I in this designe: Well may you (Sir)
Remember me at Court, where I was taught
Of your chaste Daughter, the wide difference
'Twixt Amorous, and Villanous. Being thus quench'd
Of hope, not longing; mine Italian braine,
Gan in your duller Britaine operare
Most vildely: for my vantage excellent.
And to be breefe, my practise so preuayl'd
That I return'd with simular proofe enough,
To make the Noble *Leonatus* mad,
By wounding his beleefe in her Renowne,
With Tokens thus, and thus: auerring notes
Of Chamber-hanging, Pictures, this her Bracelet
(Oh cunning how I got) nay some markes
Of secret on her person, that he could not
But thinke her bond of Chastity quite crack'd,
I hauing 'tane the forfeyt. Whereupon,
Me thinkes I see him now.
Post. I so thou do'st,
Italian Fiend. Aye me, most credulous Foole,
Egregious murtherer, Theefe, any thing
That's due to all the Villaines past, in being
To come. Oh giue me Cord, or knife, or poyson,

Some vpright Iufticer. Thou King,fend out
For Torturors ingenious : it is I
That all th'abhorred things o'th'earth amend
By being worfe then they. I am *Pofthumus*,
That kill'd thy Daughter : Villain-like, I lye,
That caus'd a leffer villaine then my felfe,
A facrilegious Theefe to doo't. The Temple
Of Vertue was fhe ; yea, and fhe her felfe.
Spit, and throw ftones, caft myre vpon me, fet
The dogges o'th'ftreet to bay me : euery villaine
Be call'd *Pofthumus Leonatus*, and
Be villany leffe then 'twas. Oh *Imogen* !
My Queene, my life, my wife : oh *Imogen*,
Imogen, *Imogen*.

Imo. Peace my Lord, heare, heare.

Poft. Shall's haue a play of this?
Thou fcornfull Page, there lye thy part.

Pif. Oh Gentlemen, helpe,
Mine and your Miftris : Oh my Lord *Pofthumus*,
You ne're kill'd *Imogen* till now : helpe, helpe,
Mine honour'd Lady.

Cym. Does the world go round ?

Pofth. How comes thefe ftaggers on mee ?

Pifa. Wake my Miftris.

Cym. If this be fo, the Gods do meane to ftrike me
To death,with mortall ioy.

Pifa. How fares my Miftris ?

Imo. Oh get thee from my fight,
Thou gau'ft me poyfon : dangerous Fellow hence,
Breath not where Princes are.

Cym. The tune of *Imogen*.

Pifa. Lady, the Gods throw ftones of fulpher on me, if
That box I gaue you, was not thought by mee
A precious thing, I had it from the Queene.

Cym. New matter ftill.

Imo. It poyfon'd me.

Corn. Oh Gods!
I left out one thing which the Queene confeft,
Which muft approue thee honeft. If *Pafanio*
Haue (faid fhe) giuen his Miftris that Confection
Which I gaue him for Cordiall, fhe is feru'd,
As I would ferue a Rat.

Cym. What's this, *Cornelius* ?

Corn. The Queene (Sir) very oft importun'd me
To temper poyfons for her, ftill pretending
The fatisfaction of her knowledge, onely
In killing Creatures vilde, as Cats and Dogges
Of no efteeme. I dreading, that her purpofe
Was of more danger, did compound for her
A certaine ftuffe, which being tane, would ceafe
The prefent powre of life, but in fhort time,
All Offices of Nature, fhould againe
Do their due Functions. Haue you tane of it ?

Imo. Moft like I did, for I was dead.

Bel. My Boyes, there was our error.

Gui. This is fure *Fidele*.

Imo. Why did you throw your wedded Lady fro you ?
Thinke that you are vpon a Rocke, and now
Throw me againe.

Poft. Hang there like fruite, my foule,
Till the Tree dye.

Cym. How now, my Flefh? my Childe ?
What, mak'ft thou me a dullard in this Act ?
Wilt thou not fpeake to me ?

Imo. Your bleffing. Sir.

Bel. Though you did loue this youth, I blame ye not,
You had a motiue for't.

Cym. My teares that fall
Proue holy-water on thee ; *Imogen*,
Thy Mothers dead.

Imo. I am forry for't, my Lord.

Cym. Oh, fhe was naught ; and long of her it was
That we meet heere fo ftrangely : but her Sonne
Is gone, we know not how, nor where.

Pifa. My Lord,
Now feare is from me, Ile fpeake troth. Lord *Cloten*
Vpon my Ladies miffing, came to me
With his Sword drawne, foam'd at the mouth, and fwore
If I difcouer'd not which way fhe was gone,
It was my inftant death. By accident,
I had a feigned Letter of my Mafters
Then in my pocket, which directed him
To feeke her on the Mountaines neere to Milford,
Where in a frenzie, in my Mafters Garments
(Which he inforc'd from me) away he poftes
With vnchafte purpofe, and with oath to violate
My Ladies honor, what became of him,
I further know not.

Gui. Let me end the Story : I flew him there.

Cym. Marry, the Gods forefend.
I would not thy good deeds, fhould from my lips
Plucke a hard fentence : Prythee valiant youth
Deny't againe.

Gui. I haue fpoke it, and I did it.

Cym. He was a Prince.

Gui. A moft inciuill one. The wrongs he did mee
Were nothing Prince-like ; for he did prouoke me
With Language that would make me fpurne the Sea,
If it could fo roare to me. I cut off's head,
And am right glad he is not ftanding heere
To tell this tale of mine.

Cym. I am forrow for thee :
By thine owne tongue thou art condemn'd, and muft
Endure our Law : Thou'rt dead.

Imo. That headleffe man I thought had bin my Lord

Cym. Binde the Offender,
And take him from our prefence.

Bel. Stay, Sir King.
This man is better then the man he flew,
As well defcended as thy felfe, and hath
More of thee merited, then a Band of *Clotens*
Had euer fcarre for. Let his Armes alone,
They were not borne for bondage.

Cym. Why old Soldier :
Wilt thou vndoo the worth thou art vnpayd for
By tafting of our wrath ? How of defcent
As good as we ?

Arui. In that he fpake too farre.

Cym. And thou fhalt dye for't.

Bel. We will dye all three,
But I will proue that two one's are as good
As I haue giuen out him. My Sonnes, I muft
For mine owne part, vnfold a dangerous fpeech,
Though haply well for you.

Arui. Your danger's ours.

Guid. And our good his.

Bel. Haue at it then, by leaue
Thou hadd'ft (great King) a Subiect, who
Was call'd *Belarius*.

Cym. What of him? He is a banifh'd Traitor.

Bel. He it is, that hath
Affum'd this age : indeed a banifh'd man,

I

I know not how, a Traitor.
Cym. Take him hence,
The whole world shall not saue him.
Bel. Not too hot;
First pay me for the Nursing of thy Sonnes,
And let it be confiscate all, so soone
As I haue receyu'd it.
Cym. Nursing of my Sonnes?
Bel. I am too blunt, and sawcy: heere's my knee:
Ere I arise, I will preferre my Sonnes,
Then spare not the old Father. Mighty Sir,
These two young Gentlemen that call me Father,
And thinke they are my Sonnes, are none of mine,
They are the yssue of your Loynes, my Liege,
And blood of your begetting.
Cym. How? my Issue.
Bel. So sure as you, your Fathers: I (old *Morgan*)
Am that *Belarius*, whom you sometime banish'd:
Your pleasure was my neere offence, my punishment
It selfe, and all my Treason that I suffer'd,
Was all the harme I did. These gentle Princes
(For such, and so they are) these twenty yeares
Haue I train'd vp; those Arts they haue, as I
Could put into them. My breeding was (Sir)
As your Highnesse knowes: Their Nurse *Euriphile*
(Whom for the Theft I wedded) stole these Children
Vpon my Banishment: I moou'd her too't,
Hauing receyu'd the punishment before
For that which I did then. Beaten for Loyaltie,
Excited me to Treason. Their deere losse,
The more of you 'twas felt, the more it shap'd
Vnto my end of stealing them. But gracious Sir,
Heere are your Sonnes againe, and I must loose
Two of the sweet'st Companions in the World.
The benediction of these couering Heauens
Fall on their heads like dew, for they are worthie
To in-lay Heauen with Starres.
Cym. Thou weep'st, and speak'st:
The Seruice that you three haue done, is more
Vnlike, then this thou tell'st. I lost my Children,
If these be they, I know not how to wish
A payre of worthier Sonnes.
Bel. Be pleas'd awhile;
This Gentleman, whom I call *Polidore*,
Most worthy Prince, as yours, is true *Guiderius*:
This Gentleman, my *Cadwall*, *Aruiragus*.
Your yonger Princely Son, he Sir, was lapt
In a most curious Mantle, wrought by th'hand
Of his Queene Mother, which for more probation
I can with ease produce.
Cym. *Guiderius* had
Vpon his necke a Mole, a sanguine Starre,
It was a marke of wonder.
Bel. This is he,
Who hath vpon him still that naturall stampe:
It was wise Natures end, in the donation
To be his euidence now.
Cym. Oh, what am I
A Mother to the byrth of three? Nere Mother
Reioyc'd deliuerance more: Blest, pray you be,
That after this strange starting from your Orbes,
You may reigne in them now: Oh *Imogen*,
Thou hast lost by this a Kingdome.
Imo. No, my Lord:
I haue got two Worlds by't. Oh my gentle Brothers,
Haue we thus met? Oh neuer say heereafter
But I am truest speaker. You call'd me Brother
When I was but your Sister: I you Brothers,
When we were so indeed.
Cym. Did you ere meete?
Arui. I my good Lord.
Gui. And at first meeting lou'd,
Continew'd so, vntill we thought he dyed.
Corn. By the Queenes Dramme she swallow'd.
Cym. O rare instinct!
When shall I heare all through? This fierce abridgment,
Hath to it Circumstantiall branches, which
Distinction should be rich in. Where? how liu'd you?
And when came you to serue our Romane Captiue?
How parted with your Brother? How first met them?
Why fled you from the Court? And whether these?
And your three motiues to the Battaile? with
I know not how much more should be demanded,
And all the other by-dependances
From chance to chance? But nor the Time, nor Place
Will serue our long Interrogatories. See,
Posthumus Anchors vpon *Imogen*;
And she (like harmlesse Lightning) throwes her eye
On him: her Brothers, Me: her Master hitting
Each obiect with a Ioy: the Counter-change
Is seuerally in all. Let's quit this ground,
And smoake the Temple with our Sacrifices.
Thou art my Brother, so wee'l hold thee euer.
Imo. You are my Father too, and did releeue me:
To see this gracious season.
Cym. All ore-ioy'd
Saue these in bonds, let them be ioyfull too,
For they shall taste our Comfort.
Imo. My good Master, I will yet do you seruice.
Luc. Happy be you.
Cym. The forlorne Souldier, that no Nobly fought
He would haue well becom'd this place, and grac'd
The thankings of a King.
Post. I am Sir
The Souldier that did company these three
In poore beseeming: 'twas a fitment for
The purpose I then follow'd. That I was he,
Speake *Iachimo*, I had you downe, and might
Haue made you finish.
Iach. I am downe againe:
But now my heauie Conscience sinkes my knee,
As then your force did. Take that life, beseech you
Which I so often owe: but your Ring first,
And heere the Bracelet of the truest Princesse
That euer swore her Faith.
Post. Kneele not to me:
The powre that I haue on you, is to spare you:
The malice towards you, to forgiue you. Liue
And deale with others better.
Cym. Nobly doom'd:
Wee'l learne our Freenesse of a Sonne-in-Law:
Pardon's the word to all.
Arui. You holpe vs Sir,
As you did meane indeed to be our Brother,
Ioy'd are we, that you are.
Post. Your Seruant Princes. Good my Lord of Rome
Call forth your South-sayer: As I slept, me thought
Great Iupiter vpon his Eagle back'd
Appear'd to me, with other sprightly shewes
Of mine owne Kindred. When I wak'd, I found
This Labell on my bosome; whose containing
Is so from sense in hardnesse, that I can

Make

Make no Collection of it. Let him shew
His skill in the construction.
Luc. *Philarmonus.*
Sooth. Heere, my good Lord.
Luc. Read, and declare the meaning.

Reades.

WHen as a Lyons whelpe, shall to himselfe vnknown, without seeking finde, and bee embrac'd by a peece of tender Ayre: And when from a stately Cedar shall be lopt branches, which being dead many yeares, shall after reuiue, bee ioynted to the old Stocke, and freshly grow, then shall Posthumus end his miseries, Britaine be fortunate, and flourish in Peace and Plentie.

Thou *Leonatus* art the Lyons Whelpe,
The fit and apt Construction of thy name
Being *Leonatus*, doth import so much:
The peece of tender Ayre, thy vertuous Daughter,
Which we call *Mollis Aer*, and *Mollis Aer*
We terme it *Mulier*; which *Mulier* I diuine
Is this most constant Wife, who euen now
Answering the Letter of the Oracle,
Vnknowne to you vnsought, were clipt about
With this most tender Aire.
Cym. This hath some seeming.
Sooth. The lofty Cedar, Royall *Cymbeline*
Personates thee: And thy lopt Branches, point
Thy two Sonnes forth: who by *Belarius* stolne
For many yeares thought dead, are now reuiu'd
To the Maiesticke Cedar ioyn'd; whose Issue
Promises Britaine, Peace and Plenty.
Cym. Well,
My Peace we will begin: And *Caius Lucius*,
Although the Victor, we submit to *Cæsar*,
And to the Romane Empire; promising
To pay our wonted Tribute, from the which
We were disswaded by our wicked Queene,
Whom heauens in Iustice both on her, and hers,
Haue laid most heauy hand.
Sooth. The fingers of the Powres aboue, do tune
The harmony of this Peace: the Vision
Which I made knowne to *Lucius* ere the stroke
Of yet this scarse-cold-Battaile, at this instant
Is full accomplish'd. For the Romaine Eagle
From South to West, on wing soaring aloft
Lessen'd her selfe, and in the Beames o'th'Sun
So vanish'd; which fore-shew'd our Princely Eagle
Th'Imperiall *Cæsar*, should againe vnite
His Fauour, with the Radiant *Cymbeline*,
Which shines heere in the West.
Cym. Laud we the Gods,
And let our crooked Smoakes climbe to their Nostrils
From our blest Altars. Publish we this Peace
To all our Subiects. Set we forward: Let
A Roman, and a Brittish Ensigne waue
Friendly together: so through *Luds-Towne* march,
And in the Temple of great Iupiter
Our Peace wee'l ratifie: Seale it with Feasts.
Set on there: Neuer was a Warre did cease
(Ere bloodie hands were wash'd) with such a Peace.
Exeunt.

FINIS.

Printed at the Charges of W. Jaggard, Ed. Blount, I. Smithweeke, and W. Aspley, 1623.

www.ingramcontent.com/pod-product-compliance
Lightning Source LLC
Chambersburg PA
CBHW020948030726
47496CB00005B/1408
* 9 7 8 3 7 4 2 8 5 8 6 6 5 *